D0363449

CATHERINE COOKSON

CATHERINE COOKSON

THE PARSON'S DAUGHTER

THE CULTURED HANDMAIDEN

THE BLACK VELVET GOWN

TED SMART

The Parson's Daughter first published in Great Britain in 1987
by William Heinemann Ltd

The Cultured Handmaiden first published in Great Britain in 1988
by William Heinemann Ltd

The Black Velvet Gown first published in Great Britain in 1984
by William Heinemann Ltd

This edition first published in Great Britain in 1990 for The Book People by
Peerage Books
an imprint of
Reed International Books Limited
Michelin House
81 Fulham Road
London SW3 6RB

ISBN 1 85052 169 7

Reprinted 1991, 1992

Printed and bound in Great Britain by
Bath Press

CONTENTS

THE PARSON'S DAUGHTER

PART ONE

Sundays

1

'To think unkindly is a sin, but to give voice to your thoughts and allow them to direct your actions is a greater sin. Who are we to condemn? Did not Christ say, He that is without sin among you, let him first cast a stone?'

Oh dear me! some people were moving restlessly in their seats. Nancy Ann looked towards the pulpit where her father seemed about to topple out of it, so far was he leaning over. He always looked too tall for the pulpit, but when he became agitated about righteousness, as he was now, he appeared about to do a somersault right into the front pew, where sat Mrs McKeowan the churchwarden's wife, and her two daughters Jancy and Eva; and next to them were Mr and Mrs Taylor from the village who had the grocery store that sold everything, and behind them were Mr and Mrs Pollock who kept the hardware and oddments shop. Then between them and Mrs Norton was an empty space reserved for Mr Norton the baker, but likely he had got drunk again last night and couldn't get up. It was known he often got drunk on a Saturday; because he hadn't to work on a Sunday not till after midnight when he made his first batch of dough for the Monday morning bread. Yet, he sometimes appeared in that seat. These were the times when he tried to go 'on the waggon' as her grandmama said; but she also said that the wheels would come off before the next Sunday, and she was usually right. Her father, though, said Mr Norton had to be given credit for trying. In her father's opinion everybody had to be given credit for trying. She loved her father.

There was nobody seated in the front seats of the gentry gallery. Hardly anybody sat there these days even when Mr Harpcore was in residence. He himself never came to church, but more servants would attend than usually did. But this morning she could count only seven: three men, three women, and a boy. Two of the women looked elderly; the other was the pretty young woman who came to church every other Sunday and sat in between them.

Her father was going on and on this morning and she knew why, although she wasn't supposed to; she had heard Peggy talking to

Jane: it was about the Winter family who had left the village to go into Gateshead and work in a factory. Of course, as Cook had said, If Jed Winter hadn't got one excuse for leaving the village he would have found another because he had known he was going to be stood off on the farm and would lose his cottage, for things were bad all round and the corn wasn't selling. It was them Americans, Cook said, who were sending the cheap stuff over here and taking the bread out of decent people's mouths. But Peggy said the real reason the Winter family had left was because Nellie had got a baby and her husband who went to sea had been gone twelve months. But what that had to do with it, she didn't know; people had babies when their husbands were away. Her grandmama had said her father had been born when her grandpa was at the war. Anyway, Mr Winter couldn't stand the disgrace of his daughter having a baby.

There was something she couldn't get straight here, because why bring Farmer Carter into it.

Her father had liked Mr Winter. He always said he was a God-fearing man, and his wife too. Nellie was their only surviving daughter. One way and another they had lost their four children. Nellie had been God-fearing too: she had come to church every Sunday, at least she had until some months ago when she had stopped all of a sudden. It was about this time her father had become agitated about Nellie.

A small clearing of the throat and a slight dig in her ribs caused her to glance to the side and at her brother James. He made a funny little twitching movement with his nose that always made her laugh, even when it came as a warning: she must have been fidgeting and not aware of it.

She was looking up towards the pulpit again from where her father was at last drawing to a close amid a rustle and coughing among the congregation not unmixed with sighs, when she felt a heel pressed on to her toecap. And this caused her to emit a stifled groan and to turn sharply, an indignant look on her face, to see her other brother Peter staring solemnly towards the altar, a look of pious intent on his handsome face. She, too, stared back at the altar; then, lifting her foot, she brought her heel sharply into the narrow-trousered shin to the side of her, and when she felt her brother jerk and cough deep in his throat, and saw her mama who was sitting to the right of him cast an enquiring glance towards him, she said to herself: I warned him. I told him what I'd do if he did it again. Now I'll have skinned toes before I get home and unblock the cap.

Why had she to wear such shoes anyway? Other girls didn't. Her mama said it was because she kicked the toes too quickly out of ordinary shoes; and only yesterday she said that such tomboyish behaviour was excusable up to eight years old but not when one was on thirteen. Her mama, she noticed, never blamed her brothers for inciting her. But of course, they weren't boys any longer and couldn't be chastised, they were young men, university men. A feeling of sadness took the place of her indignation now she realized that tomorrow they would both return to that university and life would become dull once more.

Although Peter was seven years older than her and James eight, they had always been like playmates, and the only time she could say that she was really happy was when they were at home. It had always been like that.

She understood they had been at boarding school when she was born, and when they first saw her they had fought as to who would hold her. Everything she knew and which she felt was worthwhile, they had taught her: how to climb a tree; how to stand in a loop of rope attached to a sturdy branch and swing out across the river; how to bowl at cricket and how to strike out with the bat; how to run the hills without losing your puff; how to fish, and even wrestle a bit, and fence; although they would never let her fence with anything but sticks.

She loved them, next to her father that is and equally as she loved her grandmama. Why didn't people love her grandmama? Likely it was because of her voice; and she was rude at times and didn't care what she said and how she offended people. And she offended her mama most of all. She knew that her mama considered Grandmama a trial, but she also was aware that her mama had to put up with Grandmama, because it was she who had, for years, paid for the boys' education and was now to pay for her own.

Oh my! She didn't want to go to another school. She liked the village school, at least she liked most of the children there, although, as her mama said, they were all of common folk. She didn't mind that at all, because they were all nice to her, all except the McLoughlins. Oh, they were common all right, the McLoughlins.

James and Peter used to laugh about the McLoughlins. There were thirteen of them and they lived in a little three-roomed hovel cottage, and they were all hard and healthy, and their father drank and their mother smoked a clay pipe, and they never came to church. But then, of course, they wouldn't, not this one, because they were Catholics. Catholics were queer, funny, and very common.

. . .'In the name of the Father, and of the Son, and of the Holy Ghost, Amen.' And now her father had stepped down from the pulpit, and they were standing up and singing the last hymn: 'Rock of Ages.'

There was Jancy McKeowan vying with Mr Taylor. But Jancy couldn't beat her own father, nor could Mr Taylor, for the churchwarden's voice rose above everyone else's, and when the hymn should have finished his voice still trailed on, as her grandmama said, giving god the benefit of his very own amen.

'Her grandmama wasn't at church this morning; she had a late summer cold. It had come on very suddenly because she had been all right last night. She often took quick colds, some in the spring, some in the summer, and a number in the winter.

The church was emptying now, and her father was shaking hands with each member of the congregation. Some hands he always shook more warmly than others; some people he had a word with, others he couldn't let pass him quickly enough, his handshake seeming to help them down the four steps to the gravel drive.

She was walking down the drive between her brothers. The hard cap of her right shoe was pressing on her toes. Looking straight ahead she said, 'You're horrible, Peter Hazel. Yes, you are.' And he, also looking straight ahead, answered. 'And you're a vicious little madam, Nancy Ann Hazel. Yes you are, and you'll never grow up into a refined young lady.'

'And whose fault will that be?'

Peter now looked across her to James and said, 'Don't blame me, she was born like that.'

'Oh, you!' She now took her doubled fist and dug Peter in the thigh, and as Peter said with an exaggerated groan, 'See what I mean?' James put in, 'Stop it, you two. Look who's out there.'

From beyond the lych-gate a tall young woman smiled at them, saying first, 'Good-morning, Mr James,' then 'Good-morning, Mr Peter.'

'Good-morning, Miss McKeowan.' They both inclined their heads towards the thin fair girl.

'I hear you are to return to university tomorrow.' Her voice was soft, her words precise.

'Yes. Yes' Peter nodded at her. 'We go up tomorrow.'

'Oh, I do envy you.' The well-shaped lips pursed themselves; the fair eyelids blinked; the white cotton-gloved hands joined and gently lifted the tightly laced breasts upwards. 'It must be like going into another world, a world where minds are allowed to expand, where ideas count.' She was now looking directly at James, and he, his long thinnish face a replica of his father's and red to the brim of his hat now, said stiffly, 'The minds are much the same as they are in this village, Miss McKeowan, narrow and nasty in the main. Good-day.'

The light went from the young woman's eyes. She looked from Peter to Nancy Ann and they both said, 'Good-morning, Miss McKeowan,' and, turning, hurried to catch up with James.

'That was a bit stiff.' Peter's voice was cold.

'What did you expect me to say? A world where minds count? . . . Huh! you know something? she frightens me, she does. She was walking in the lane last night just on dark. I had gone to get my coat that I'd left on the garden seat and there she was strolling past the gate, up and down, up and down.'

'Well,' Peter said on a laugh now, 'if you were so afraid of her why didn't you go in and fetch Grandmama? She would have settled her hash for her.'

'You could say you are engaged to be married. That would stop her chasing you.'

Both young men paused and looked down on their thin ungainly sister; then glancing at one another, they burst out laughing and simultaneously put their arms about her; and she, giggling, hung on to them for a moment as James said, 'You haven't only got a big head, sister Nancy Ann, you've got something in it too. Yes, of course: I'm going to become engaged to a young lady in Oxford. Spread it around, will you?'

'Yes, all right, I'll spread it around . . . for a price.'

They were again looking down on her, their faces stretched. Then, Peter, nodding towards his brother, said. 'This is a new one.'

'Yes, yes, indeed. And what is the price, sister?'

'That we have a game of cricket this afternoon.'

'Oh . . . ah!' 'Oh . . . ah!' They made their usual rejoinder together. 'Now you know that's impossible,' James said. ''Tis Sunday, 'tis banned. 'Tis banned for you on other days too – you know what Mama said – but on a Sunday . . . oh impossible.'

'No cricket, no engagement in Oxford.'

'You imp of Satan!' Peter went to catch hold of her hand, but she ran from them, whirling around like a top. At this James called to her quietly but firmly, 'Now stop acting like a child. If Mama were to see you, you know what would happen. You had all this out the other day. You've got to grow up. And you promised her . . .'

'Oh, shut up, will you. And anyway, I didn't promise Mama, I kept my mouth shut and never said a word.'

'She's right.' The brothers were walking on either side of her again, and it was now Peter, who had in the past encouraged her into many of her tomboy ways, who said, 'And James is right too; and Mama is right, too, Nancy Ann. We've all had fun together, but now . . . well, we want to see you turn into a pretty young lady, and . . . and go to balls, and have all the young men fighting to dance with you, and then you'll meet . . .'

She stopped dead in the road and stared up at her best beloved brother, but she did not utter a word: and Peter, looking down on her, thought, What am I talking about? Pretty young lady. Stooping now, he said, 'Let me have your shoe.' And he lifted her foot for him to unlace her shoe, and pulling it off, he thrust his thumb inside and pushed the stiff cap upwards; then he put it back on her foot and laced it up again. And when he straightened his back, they smiled at each other.

Turning now, they passed through a gateway and silently made their way across the field which led to the vicarage and to the cold midday meal that had been prepared last night by Peggy Knowles the cook and Jane Bradshaw her assistant, because no menial work must be done on a Sunday, only the washing of the dishes after the housemaid Hilda Fenwick had cleared the table. Such was a Sunday.

So how would anyone dare to play cricket. It had been a silly idea of hers, and she knew it.

2

The vicarage was a very cold house. It had fourteen rooms, and all were large, high-ceilinged and provided with ample windows that were so weathered and warped the pine needles blew in between the sashes in wild weather.

Although there was a mine only two miles away, coal was still expensive; except for the miners who brought it from the earth. And because the vicarage garden only ran to an acre and a half, there weren't many trees, not enough to cut down for firewood. But even if there had been an ample supply, the vicar would not have countenanced the felling of onc tree even though it be half dead.

Even in summer there were very chilly days so that for most of the time the house was like an ice-box everywhere except the kitchen, and Madam Hazel's bedroom, for, summer and winter alike, Jessica Hazel had a fire in her bedroom, and no matter how hot and uncomfortable the other members of the household might find it in attending her, she herself said, she never sweated.

Jessica was a tall woman. Her only son took after her. She had a bony frame, and it was easy to imagine she must have looked like Nancy Ann when a girl, although paintings of her in middle life showed her to be a handsome woman. She had lived with her son for the past twelve years. She had a deep affection for him, even though at times she considered he was like the man in the story who tilted at windmills. And by what the boys had told her with regard to the essence of his sermon this morning he had certainly tilted at one today.

Here he was forty-seven years old and still hadn't grown used to the ways of the world. Of course, people threw stones – there were no Christs to stop them – what did he expect from his rantings? This child sitting here, this beloved child who was very like herself both inside and out, she had more sense in her little finger than her father had in his whole body, or ever would have. She would never tilt at windmills.

And what would she herself do when, as was now being discussed downstairs, they took her away from the village school and planted her in that Dame school in Durham to be shaped, into what? A young lady? She shook her head. She couldn't see it happening; moreover, she didn't want it to happen. Not that she didn't want the child to become attractive and marry well, but what she didn't want was to be bereft of her company for most of the year. What would she do during such a period? Sit in the sitting-room at night punching her embroidery frame while her daughter-in-law cut up old clothes to make garments for the children at the orphanage, and which she never herself sewed. No, she passed over the sewing as a pastime pleasure to Peggy and Jane and Hilda in the kitchen, to be done when the evening meal was over and the evening prayers said, and the tables cleared and the dishes washed up. They could then enjoy making unwieldy trousers and coats for lesser brethren, little lesser brethren.

Why had her son become a parson? There were no such in her own family, and it went back for many generations; nor in her husband's – he and his ancestors were all fighting men. And why had he to marry a woman more pious than himself?

'Grandmama.'

'Yes, dear?'

'The boys have gone to the Manor to see Mr Mercer. Why don't they ever take me with them?'

'Well' – Jessica cleared her throat – 'they are young men. They . . . they grew up together so to speak, although Graham is a little older. I . . . I suppose they just want to talk men's talk, and that would be no place for you.'

'I . . . I don't think that's right, Grandmama.'

'That they want to talk men's talk?'

'No. I . . . I think it's because Mr Mercer doesn't like women, females . . . girls.'

'Who told you that?' Her voice was sharp.

'I heard Hilda and Jane talking.'

'And what did Hilda and Jane say?'

'Well, as far as I could gather' – she paused and nodded her head while looking into the fire that was burning her shins and making her sweat – 'it's because he was crossed in love, right at the altar . . . well, nearly, and now he doesn't go anywhere and doesn't see anybody, only . . . I suppose men, like Peter and James. Hilda said . . .'

'I don't want to hear what Hilda said, and you shouldn't go eavesdropping.'

'I don't go eavesdropping, Grandmama. They were in the kitchen and they were saying he was a good man wasted, and they laughed and said they would see what they could do.'

'They want their ears boxed, and I'll see to it.'

'Oh, Grandmama.' Nancy Ann leant forward and patted the rug that covered her grandmother's knees, saying, 'They were being funny. It sounded very funny. It made them all splutter. I like to see them laugh. I like to listen to them. They're happy. That's what Peggy once said to me, they were happy here; it was a good house to work in in spite of there not being plenty of everything, which I took her to mean that Mama watches the bills. And – ' She giggled now before she went on, 'Peggy said that her stomach took over every morning and evening when she's praying in the dining-room. In the morning it says: How are you going to spin things out the day? And at evening prayer it says, I'll make dumplings again. What doesn't fatten will fill up.'

She now watched her grandmother throw her head back and give vent to a hearty laugh that denied the croak that up till now would issue from her throat whenever anyone entered the room. And she joined in.

'Grandmama.' She had sat back in her seat and rubbed the laughter tears from her eyes with the side of her finger, and when Jessica Hazel once again said, 'Yes, my dear?' she said, 'How long does it take for a baby to be born?'

'*What!*' Jessica's face was stretched now. 'What do you mean, how long does it take?'

'Well, what I said, how long does it take? I . . . I . . .'

'Why do you ask?'

'Just because I'd like to know.'

The old lady now gently shook her head before she said, 'It all depends how long the labour is, you see, that is how long the baby takes in deciding . . . well, to . . . to come into the world.'

'No, I don't mean that kind of long. I mean . . .'

'What do you mean?'

'Well, I'm puzzled, Grandmama, as to why they should send Nellie away when she's going to have a baby and her husband at sea?'

Oh god above. Jessica looked towards the far window and her head moved in small jerks before she looked back at her grandchild and asked, abruptly now, 'Hasn't your mother talked to you?'

'About what?'

'About the question you're asking, girl.'

'No, and I wouldn't ask Mama. I . . . I couldn't. Mama doesn't talk about things like that.'

'No, she doesn't.' The head was jerking again. 'But she should, and to you. Anyway, you're only twelve years old, coming thirteen I know, and you shouldn't be asking questions about that kind of thing for . . . well, years ahead.'

'Why?'

'Don't keep asking why, either.'

'Nellie sinned, and all I want to know is how has she sinned if . . .'

Jessica sighed twice before she leant forward and, taking her grandaughter's hand, she shook it gently, saying, 'A baby takes nine months to be born. Now, if its father is not at home for those nine months then the child doesn't belong to the father . . . You understand me?'

Nancy Ann stared into the misted blue eyes. Her mind was working fast but she remained silent for almost two minutes, and then she said, 'Yes, Grandmama, I understand.'

'Well – ' Jessica straightened up, sighed again deeply, then said, 'Now that's finished. We'll talk about it no more, and you won't discuss it again with anyone, will you?'

'Oh, no!' The words were said with deep emphasis. Talk about something like that? Never! Nellie had sinned. 'Twas surprising, and she a regular churchgoer, but she had sinned. She looked towards the fire, she felt she couldn't bear the heat any more. She stood up, saying, 'I don't like Sundays, Grandmama.'

'Neither do I, my dear. Neither do I. Never have.'

'You can't do anything on Sundays, not even fish.'

'No, I suppose not. But you could take a walk, or you could go to Sunday school.'

'I don't want to go to Sunday school; I'll have to go to evening service.'

'Your mama would expect you to go to Sunday school.'

'Yes, I know, but I'm not going today because I don't want to get into trouble.'

'What do you mean?'

'Well, you know I nearly always come back messed up on a Sunday and Mama gets angry, but it's the McLoughlins, they wait for me, and I can fight them at school and on any other day, but not on a Sunday, and they always have the advantage.'

Jessica quickly turned her gaze from her granddaughter and looked towards the fire to prevent herself from now being seen to laugh, and she said, 'Go for a walk. Yes, go for a walk.'

Once outside the bedroom door, Nancy Ann ran across the landing to the top of the stairs, and there, stretching her arms out wide, she gripped the substantial rails on either side of her and, head down, she skipped two stairs at a time. But on looking up as she neared the foot of the stairs she saw her mother standing in the middle of the hall and as usual she was shaking her head from side to side.

Rebecca Hazel looked sadly at her daughter, who in no way resembled herself, either in appearance or character. She herself was of medium height, very fair, and slim; her eyes were bright blue, her skin was cream coloured, and her mouth, if not entirely rosebud shaped, was small and full lipped. Her voice had a pained sound as she said, 'Nancy Ann, that was no way to prepare yourself for Sunday school.'

'I have a headache, Mama, and . . . and I feel slight nausea.'

'Headache? You didn't appear to be in much pain as you came bounding down those stairs, child.'

'I . . . I was wanting to get into the air, Mama. I . . . I have been with Grandmama, the room was very hot.'

'Oh, yes, yes.' Now her mother nodded her head in agreement as she said, 'Indeed, yes, enough to roast an ox. And on a day like this, too. Well, I would suggest that you go and rest for a while.'

'I would rather have fresh air, Mama.'

Rebecca stared at her daughter while asking herself if there was something behind this. She was well acquainted with her daughter's ruses for getting out of Sunday school; and yet she never baulked at attending morning or evening service. She was a strange child. She troubled her. She pursed her lips, then said, 'Well, go and ask Papa to give you a suitable reading, and then you may sit in the garden quietly.'

'Thank you, Mama.' Nancy Ann had no need to ask where her father was. She turned slowly about and crossed the hall, went down a narrow passage and knocked at a stout oak door, and when she was bidden to enter she did so slowly. Closing the door behind her, she looked at the tall figure seated at his desk. But he hadn't been writing because there was no paper in front of him; nor apparently had he been reading because the space in front of him was clear. She felt a deep sense of guilt as she went slowly towards him. Somehow she didn't mind deceiving her mother, but she never liked using deception of any kind on her father.

He held out a hand towards her, saying, 'What is it, my dear?' You look peaky.'

'Grandmama's room was very hot.'

He now poked his long face towards her, and there was a twisted smile on it as he said, 'Is it ever anything else? You know, my dear, if my mother was not such a very good woman I would imagine at times that the devil himself was preparing her for the nether regions.'

She let out a high laugh, then clapped her hand tightly over her mouth. Her father, this man of God, as her gramdmama somtimes referred to him, could say such funny things. Oh, she loved him. She went to his side now and leant her head against his shoulder, and his frankness, as it always did, encouraged her own and she said, 'I don't like Sunday school, Papa.'

'I know you don't, my dear. But it is necessary, and it shows a good example.'

Still with her head pressed close to him, she murmured, 'I can't stand Miss Jancy or Miss Eva McKeowan. They yammer.'

A slight shudder under her cheek found an answering gurgle in herself and it was a few seconds before her father replied, 'They mean well. They are good women.'

'The younger one, Eva, makes eyes at James.'

'Oh, now.' He pressed her from him, and pulled his chin into the high collar on his thin neck, and, his voice reproving, he said, 'Now you mustn't say things like that.'

''Tis true, Papa. And James is scared of her.'

'Oh, that is nonsense: James is scared of nothing and no one.' There was a proud note in his voice now as he went on, 'James is a very strong character. In a way, he takes after your grandmama.' And his tone altered as he ended, 'I'm afraid I know somebody else who does, too.'

'You think I'm like Grandmama, Papa?'

'You are showing many of her characteristics.'

'What ones?'

'Which ones? Oh, we won't go into that. Anyway, I must get down to work. You know I go to Durham tomorrow to meet the Bishop and the Dean, and I've got to think about that.'

'Mama said, would you give me a suitable reading, Papa.'

'Suitable reading.' His eyes travelled over the bookshelves lining the wall in front of him, and he got to his feet, saying, 'Ah . . . Ah. Suitable reading for a Sunday.' And looking down on her, he said, 'You have your books upstairs.'

'Yes, I know, but Mama told me to ask you.'

'Dear, dear. Suitable reading.' He was walking along by the bookshelves now and touching one book after another, murmuring as he did so, 'Not suitable, not suitable.' Then picking one from the shelf, he scanned through it before replacing it, saying, 'Too old. Too old.' Then turning about, he went to another row of shelves to the right of his desk, and she watched him take out one book after another and read a line here and there. And a smile passed over his face before he returned the last book to the shelf, saying regretfully, 'Not Sunday reading. Adventures.'

'I could take Gyp for a walk, Papa.'

He nodded at her, seeming to consider for a moment, then sighed and said, 'Yes, yes, you could.' But now, once again bending his long length towards her, he added, 'But I'd go out this way.' He pointed to the half-open window. 'It's closer to the kennel.'

They looked knowingly at each other, and when he pushed the sashed window further up she bent to step through it; then quickly straightening, she reached up and put her arms around his neck and planted a quick kiss on the side of his bony chin before scrambling through the opening, then along by the side of the house, and to the dog's kennel.

At the sight of her the young labrador pranced widly and gave a howling bark, and she shushed him by gripping his mouth tightly between her hands and looking into his eyes, saying, 'Quiet, Gyp, else we'll both get wrong.' Then unlinking the chain attached to his collar, she threw the offending deterrent against the wall where the other end was fastened to an iron loop. And once again she told herself that when she was older and had more to say, she would see that Gyp wasn't attached to that thing. Animals shouldn't be tied up.

'Come on,' she whispered to him now, and wagged a warning finger at him; and seemingly taking her cue, he walked quietly beside her. But as soon as they left the vicarage grounds and entered the field that ran down to the river she grabbed up the skirt of her Sunday dress until it came just below her knees, then raced down the field, the dog bounding at her heels. And they didn't stop until they reached the bank of the river where, dropping down on to the grass, she put her arms about him, and when his lolling tongue travelled the complete length of her face, she fell back on to the ground laughing.

She looked up into the sky. It was high and clear blue. She blinked her eyes against the glare of the sun, then brought her gaze down on to the river, but it too made her blink, for there were a myraid stars dancing on the water. It was running fast here and would continue to do so all the way until it reached Durham.

It was a beautiful river; she loved walking beside it. The only thing was that such walking was checked by the Rossburn estate on her left, for just round the corner about a quarter of a mile away the boundary railings, all barbed wired, went down into the river. She always felt slightly resentful when she came up to them, telling herself it wouldn't have hurt him to let people walk along the towpath. No damage would ever have been done because it was only afternoon strollers and fishers who used the bank, at this end anyway; the children from the village had access to the river right on their doorstep.

She always thought of the owner of Rossburn House as 'He'. She had only once glimpsed him, and that seemed a long time ago. He was rarely at home as he had other houses he stayed at, so she understood. At times, Peggy and Hilda talked about the goings-on at The House, but their voices always sank to undertones and she could never follow the gist of their words; their sentences were always short and often remained unfinished. They named names. One, in particular she had heard more than once, and she connnected it with one of the women, the pretty one, who came to church every other Sunday.

But The House and its doings were of no interest to her, other than that the man who owned the place had made it impossible for her to continue her walk along the river bank.

Last year there had been a kind of rumour going around that it was questionable if the owner of The House had a right to bar the public from the towpath; it concerned ancient rights or something.

But she had heard no talk of it lately; and so, as Mr McLoughlin had shouted when he had come to the school drunk that day, she presumed, there was one law for the rich and one for the poor.

Mr McLoughlin had been angry because Mr Bolton had lathered Mike good and hard with the strap. That was after Mick McLoughlin had lit a candle in a jar and pushed it under the desk at Katie Thompson's feet and the bottom of her frilly pinny had caught alight, and she had screamed, and all the children had screamed with her. And Miss Pringle had run in from the other rooms with a wooden bucket of water that always stood at the door, and she had thrown it over Katie, and Katie had screamed worse. And there had been a terrible to-do. She herself had rather enjoyed it all, and later she had made her grandmama laugh describing how Mr McLoughlin had challenged the head teacher to a fight. And Mr Bolton had let the children out of school early and had locked himself in with Miss Pringle until the constables came and took Mr McLoughlin away.

She leant forward and hugged her knees. She'd miss the school. She had been happy there, and she liked Miss Pringle because Miss Pringle let her read aloud to the class; and she picked her for monitor, too. What would it be like at the Dame school? She hated the sound of it. Would Sundays be the same there as here? Perhaps worse. Yes, perhaps worse.

She rose to her feet now and walked slowly along the bank. Ahead of her was the fence going down into the water. Again she felt frustration. She'd often thought if it hadn't been for the barbed wire on the top she would have climbed the fence and sneaked along the bank.

Gyp was sniffing in the long grass to the side of the path and she called him, 'Here! Here, Gyp. Stay with me.'

For once, Gyp took no notice of his young mistress's voice but went on sniffing through the long grass until it gave place to a green sward and at the far side of it, sitting near the fence, were two rabbits. One second they were there, the next they were scrambling under the fence with Gyp in hot pursuit. But being unable to follow them through the small opening at the bottom of the wire, the dog ran madly backwards and forwards; and then, of a sudden, he disappeared.

It had all happened so quickly that Nancy Ann hadn't even found her breath to shout out. But she raced to where the dog had disappeared and recognized that he had got easily through a badger walk. In a moment she was on her hands and knees with the intent of trying to scramble after him; but realizing that this was impossible, she began to call, 'Gyp! Gyp! come here. Gyp! Gyp!'

But there was no sound from Gyp, not even a bark.

She stood with her hands tightly across her mouth. There were traps. Gentlemen laid traps all over their estates to catch foxes. It was illegal, so she understood, but they still did it. *He* might be one of them who defied the law. Oh, dear me! Dear me! She was now running up and down by the fence.

Suddenly she stopped and looked to where it went down into the water. In a second she had her shoes off, and she tied the laces together and slung the shoes from her neck, but she left her stockings on, telling herself that they would easily dry in the sun. Then, pulling her skirt above her knees, she stepped down into the water which immediately swirled round her calfs. Gripping the staves of the railings, she made towards the end one, and she shivered visibly as the water gradually came above her knees and soaked the bottom of her dress at the back. But she was round the end railings and now scurrying towards the bank, and having climbed up it, she knelt for a moment gasping; then again began calling softly, 'Gyp! Gyp!'

She now pulled her shoes on to her sodden feet and grimaced as she did so; then she was running along the towpath, again crying, 'Gyp! Gyp!' Once she stopped and looked to the side and into where the thick brushwood between the tall trees cleared a little, but with the thought of traps in her mind she was afraid to venture near them.

Once more she was running along the bank. Then quite suddenly she stopped dead. The trees had opened out, and there before her was a grassy sward and a kind of sandy-pebbled beach leading in to the water, and sitting on a flat slab of rock was a small boy, and by his side was Gyp. On the sight of her, the boy didn't move, but the dog turned and whined.

She approached them slowly and, looking down at the dog, she said, 'You are a naughty boy, Gyp;' then staring at the child, she said, 'You . . . you caught him?'

'What?'

'You . . . you caught my dog?'

'No. He . . . he came and sat down.' The voice was hesitant but the words were rounded: he spoke like some of the younger children in the school who were learning their letters.

'Nice dog.' The boy put out his hand and patted Gyp's head.

She stared at him. He was an odd-looking child, at least part of him was. His face was round and he had two large brown eyes, but it was his hair that gave him the odd appearance; there was something wrong with it. It was wet and there was a brown stain running from it down one side of his face.

He now surprised her by saying, 'Hello,' as if he hadn't previously spoken, and she answered, 'Hello.' Then she added, 'My name is Nancy Ann. What is yours?'

'I'm David.'

She now looked about her. He was a little boy. What was he doing here on his own? Was he from The House? Well, that was the only place he could come from. But she didn't know that *He* had a family.

Somehow she had imagined *He* wasn't married, because *He* was very old. But this child could belong to one of the servants. She said, 'Where is your mother?'

'In . . . in the kitchen . . . sometimes.' He had added the last word as an afterthought.

'What is your other name?' She watched him consider. Then when Gyp suddenly turned on to his back, the boy put out his hand and gently rubbed the dog's stomach, and he continued doing so for some time before he answered, 'My mother is called Jennie.'

'Does . . . does she know you are here?'

He looked up at her and blinked his eyelids and said, 'No, but . . . but I like to walk. It is hot up in the roof. I came down the back stairs. No one saw me.'

He spoke so clearly for such a small child, and she shook her head in bewilderment, then said, 'Your hair's wet.'

He put his hand up and ran his fingers from the crown downwards, and the sun, glinting on it, brought out the different shades. It looked almost white in parts, then brown, and white again, but the ends were all brown. She screwed up her face in inquiry when he said, 'It's the tea.' And she repeated, 'The tea?'

'Yes. Jennie washes it in tea. I don't like the tea, it's sticky.'

'And . . . and you try to wash it off?'

'Yes.' For the first time he smiled, a small tentative smile, then said, 'Do you wash your hair in tea?'

'No.' She shook her head and put her hand up towards her hair and instinctively thought: Oh, dear me. She had been walking outside without a hat and that was almost unforgivable, and on a Sunday too. She should have gone to the summer-house and got a straw bonnet.

'I would like a dog.' He continued to stroke Gyp's tummy; then thumbing over his shoulder, he said, 'There are dogs over there but they are all big and they bite. Jennie says they bite and I mustn't touch them.'

They both started now as a voice came from the wood beyond the little bay, calling in a sort of hiss, 'David! David!'

The child rose to his feet. He was dressed in a frock that reached his ankles. And now he started to run from her; but stopping, he said, 'Will you bring the dog again?'

She did not speak but nodded her head; then, grabbing Gyp by the collar, she dragged him back along the little bay and up into the shelter of the trees. She did not see the meeting between the child and the owner of the voice, but she heard a strong reprimand in the tone as it said, 'You mustn't. You mustn't. Oh! just look at you. I've told you now, I've told you.' Then the voice faded away.

She had to keep her body bent while holding tightly on to the dog's collar as she made her way back to the railings. And there she was confronted by an obstacle. If she let go of the dog he would likely make back, not for the rabbits now, but for the child, and she couldn't go through the tangle that was to the right of her and find the place to push him through. There was nothing for it, she saw, but to take him into the water with her. And she wouldn't be able to take her shoes off while holding on to him; they would just have to get wet, as the rest of her would likely be before she got round the barrier.

Gyp was nine months old and as yet had had no acquaintance with the water, but once he had been dragged into it he paddled for dear life, and his effort was much easier than Nancy Ann's, because now, with one hand holding him and the other grabbing at the railings for support, her long skirt became wet almost up to her thighs. And when eventually she dragged herself and the animal out on to the bank she let go of him and lay face downwards gasping. When the dog shook himself vigorously all over her, she made no protest.

After a few minutes she got to her feet and looked down at herself. She knew her skirt was ruined, as were her shoes because they would dry hard and she wouldn't be able to wear them because her toes were tender and skinned easily.

As she walked along the path, the dog quietly at her heels again and steam rising from both of them, she continually asked herself what she was going to do, how she was going to explain what had happened without telling lies.

It wasn't until she had crept stealthily along by the back of the buildings and tied up Gyp again, which surprisingly he didn't seem to resent this time, but went into his kennel and laid down on the sacking almost immediately, that she decided the only avenue likely to offer any help was the kitchen. She now ran back along the way she had come earlier, then entered the courtyard and in a scampering dash made for the kitchen door, and her bursting into the room caused a gasp from the three women sitting at the table. Two of them rose simultaneously to their feet, but Cook, Mrs Peggy Knowles, just looked at Nancy Ann and shook her head, and it was she who said, 'Child! what's this latest?'

'I . . . I fell into the river . . . slipped.'

'Slipped? You? She now rose and walked between her two companions and, putting out a hand, she felt the top of Nancy Ann's dress. Then looking at Jane, her assistant and maid of all work, she said, 'She fell in the river, slipped, and dry as a bone up top. Eeh! miss, what next! Your mother'll go mad.'

'She needn't know. We can dry her out.'

Cook looked at the housemaid, Hilda Fenwick, and said, 'How much time have we got?' and glancing at the clock she answered herself, 'Not an hour afore tea.' Then grabbing hold of Nancy Ann's shoulders, she commanded, 'Let's get them off. And you, Jane, put the irons on the stove; her things'll want pressin'.'

Three pairs of hands now almost tore the clothes from her, but when they came to her shoes, they looked at each other and it was Hilda who said, 'Well, nothing can be done with these. Anyway, they won't show the wet. She'll just have to put them on as they are, although it won't be much use dryin' her stockin's.'

'Here, put this round you.' Cook was bundling her into a large shawl, and as she did so she looked at Hilda, saying, 'Could you sneak a pair of bloomers and a couple of petticoats downstairs? We'll never get all these dried and ironed in that short time. Where's the mistress, do you know?'

'In the little sitting-room; the master's still in his study, at least that's where they were five minutes or so gone.'

'Well, go and see what you can do and be sharp about it.'

During all the fuss Nancy Ann hadn't opened her mouth, and it wasn't until Hilda had returned with a pair of bloomers, and a pair of stockings, a waist petticoat, and a bodice petticoat that she looked from one to the other and said, 'Thank you. Thank you very much.'

'You're an awful child, you know.' Hilda was leaning towards her, a broad grin on her face; then she added, 'But life would be very dull without you. I hate the idea of you goin' to that school. You don't like it very much yourself, do you?'

'No, Hilda, I don't . . . Hilda, why should anyone wash a child's hair in tea?'

'Wash hair in tea?'

The three women now looked from one to the other and smiled, and it was Jane who said, 'To dye it likely. My Aunt Sal used to do that. Her hair should have been white but it was a queer brown. What makes you ask that?'

'Well, truthfully' – and she nodded her head from one to the other now – 'I took Gyp out and he got under the fence into the estate . . . Rossburn's. He was chasing rabbits and I couldn't get through and I had to go into the water and round the fence, and . . . and when I found him he was with a little boy, and the little boy had been washing his hair, trying to get the tea out of it. He said somebody called Jennie washed his hair in tea.'

'You . . . you went into the estate' – Hilda's voice was full of awe – 'and saw a little boy?'

The women were looking at each other again, and it was Cook who said, 'What was he like, miss?'

'He . . . he would have been pretty, but his hair was all streaked. It was light in parts, almost . . . well fair, and then had patches of brown. The ends were all dark though, and it was long right on to his shoulders.'

The women once more exchanged glances, and it was Jane who now said almost in a whisper, 'Eeh, my! I thought he never got out only when she walked him; she had to keep him in the attic.'

'He spoke about the attic . . . or the roof.' Nancy Ann nodded at them. 'He said it was very hot up there. I think that's why he wanted to come out. He was a nice child. Who does he belong to?'

No one answered her question for a moment; then Hilda said, 'One of the staff, miss, and if I was you, miss, I wouldn't mention to the master or the mistress that you saw the boy.'

'She's not stupid.' Jane's voice broke in curtly. 'She's not gona let on that she was where she shouldn't be an' on a Sunday afternoon at that.' She turned now and looked down on Nancy Ann and added, 'She's got a head on her shoulders, haven't you, miss?'

Nancy Ann didn't give an answer to this compliment; but when she shivered Jane said, 'Look at that now. I'll bet she's in for a cold. What about a hot drink for her, Cook, eh?'

'Yes, yes, the very thing.'

Now began a scurrying around the kitchen: a pad being put on the end of the table, and an old sheet thrown over it, and the flat iron stand placed on the corner of it; then the kettle was pressed into the heart of the fire and a jar marked ginger taken down from the cupboard shelf. And all the while they talked to each other in an undertone, and the gist that Nancy Ann could catch here and there conveyed to her that Cook had been talking to the assistant cook from The House, who had told her that the master of the house was due home next week and that they had been ordered to get ready for a shooting party coming. Appartently at thc moment he was in London.

When suddenly she sneezed, Cook exclaimed, 'There you are then! This is the beginnin'.' Is that kettle boilin'?'

'Yes, Cook.'

'And have you squeezed the lemon, Hilda?'

''Tis all ready, an' I've mixed half a teaspoonful of ginger with it.'

'Oh, that's too much; it'll burn her bowels up.'

'Well, I've done it now.'

'Put more water in it then, an' thin it down.'

'Oh dear, dear.'

'There you are, miss, sip that.'

'Thank you. Thank you, Cook.'

At the first gulp of the hot liquid Nancy Ann coughed and almost choked. But Cook insisted she keep on sipping, and when the glass was half empty and she could take no more she gasped and pushed it from her, and at that moment the kitchen door opened and, to the consternation of all, her mother entered.

Rebecca Hazel came to an abrupt stop in the middle of the room and she looked from one to another of her small staff; lastly, her eyes rested on her daughter huddled in the shawl and now sneezing, and slowly she said, 'What is this?'

None of the maids answered but stood silent, eyes cast down. And then she was standing in front of Nancy Ann who, sniffing loudly, said, 'I'm sorry, Mama, I fell in the river.'

'You what?'

'I . . . I fell in the river.'

Rebecca Hazel was about to ask, How on earth did you do that, child? but she couldn't at the moment bear to hear the explanation true or false as it might be.

'Come along . . . Come!' she said, holding out her hand towards her daughter. Nancy Ann sidled from the wooden settle and when she stepped off the clippy mat that fronted the open fireplace on to the stone floor she sneezed again.

Rebecca, tugging her up the kitchen now, murmured under her breath, 'Your papa will be greatly distressed about this, greatly distressed. And on a Sunday, too. Whatever next will you get up to, child!'

Her father was sitting by the side of his bed and holding her hand, and he said, 'I am to blame. I should have insisted that you attend Sunday school. Your mother is right, quite right. I am to blame.'

'No, Papa. No, Papa.'

'Oh, yes, yes. This is what happens when we do things to please ourselves and those we love without taking into consideration there are rules to be obeyed in all things and if we break them we must stand the consequences. In this case, poor child, it is you who are suffering from the consequences. But how on earth did you manage to fall in the river? You're so surefooted; you run like a deer without tripping.'

'I . . . I went after Gyp, Papa.'

'And . . . and he swam into the river?'

She waited for a moment, her mind racing around to find an outlet that wouldn't be a lie. Then she saw herself hanging on to the dog as he paddled furiously and in a small voice she said, 'Yes, Papa, he . . . he swam in the river.'

'Well, if he swam, my dear, he wouldn't have drowned. You shouldn't have gone in after him.'

'He had never been in the river before, Papa.'

She wasn't lying.

'No, you're right; he's still little more than a puppy. How old is he now?' As he considered she said, 'Nine months, Papa.'

'Yes. yes, of course' – he smiled at her – 'nine months.' He rose from the chair, and saying, 'Be a good girl. And don't worry, I'll take the blame,' he stepped back from the bed smiling, and her throat was so full she could make no comment. Dear, dear Papa. She was overcome by guilt . . .

A short while later, when her brothers came in, she felt no such emotion. 'Well! Well!' Peter laughed down at her, and James said, 'Leave you for five minutes and this is what you get up to.' He bent above her. 'What really happened? Come on now, that pup is terrified of water. I tried to get him in myself.'

Forgetting for a moment how her head and throat ached, she said, tartly, 'If you had taken me with you it wouldn't have happened.'

'What wouldn't have happened?' Peter demanded, sitting down on the side of the bed now. 'You had a fight or something . . . the McLoughlins?'

'No, no, I didn't have a fight or something. I . . . I had an adventure.'

'Oh! Oh!' The brothers exchanged glances and pulled long faces, and James said, 'She had an adventure.'

'Oh, I love adventures,' Peter wriggled on the bed, and joined his hands under his chin; then, his voice changing, he said, 'Come on, spill it out.'

She looked from one to the other before she asked the same question of them as she had of the maids, but put in a slightly different way. 'Why should you wash your hair in tea? she said.

'What!' they both said together, 'Wash our hair in tea? What do you mean?' James added.

'Just that. Why should anybody wash a small boy's hair in tea?'

Now James pulled a chair up to the side of the bed and, his face straight, he said, 'Let's have it from the beginning.'

And so between much coughing and clearing of her throat she told them what had happened; and when she had finished she was surprised at their remaining silent, and she watched them exchange glances again, then look down at the bed quilt.

It was Peter who, getting to his feet and letting out a long drawn breath, said, 'Well, the only explanation I can give you is that the child's mother didn't like the colour of its hair. People do dye their hair with tea, you know.'

'They do?'

'Yes.'

'But it looked funny; it was all streaky and he didn't like it. Sticky, he said it was. And he had been trying to wash it off.'

'Oh, well. Mothers can do what they like with their own children. Now go on to sleep, trouble.' Peter bent and kissed her on the brow; then James did likewise; and when they reached the door they turned and waved to her, and she said, 'I wish you weren't going tomorrow.'

'So do we,' said James. Then bending forward he hissed, 'Don't forget about my engagement.'

'No, no, I won't.' She smiled and nodded at them, and when the door closed she snuggled down into the pillow and waited for her grandmama's visit . . .

But her grandmama was delaying her visit; she was sitting in her room looking at her two grandsons who were seated as far away from the fire as they could get, which wasn't all that far for the room was crowded with furniture and the backs of their chairs were tight pressed against the foot of her bed.

Peter was now saying, 'Do you think he's been kept up in the attic all these years? He must be four now.'

'All maids sleep in the attics. She's likely had to keep him up there in one room. You two were in the nursery until you were five. What's the difference?'

'A great deal, I should say,' said James. 'Nancy Ann said she heard a person scolding the child for being outside.'

'Well, of course, she would have to, because what would happen if he was running wild and Mr Bighead Dennison Harpcore came across him. That was the agreement, so I understand, that he was kept out of the way.'

'I never knew exactly what did happen,' Peter said. 'I knew there was a mighty fuss after the brother was drowned; but what took place before exactly?'

'Well, you were both at school at the time and such things were of little interest to you. You know the outline of the story: Jennie Mather was put into service there when she was ten. She came half-day to school here. She was a pretty child. She had no parents but an uncle, Tom Bristow. He drove Gibbon's cart. He was a youngish fellow, well set up. Anyway, Jennie eventually became chambermaid and when she was sixteen she came under the notice of Timothy. He was eighteen. A nice pleasant young fellow, as I remember him, very fair, but not a very strong and brewster character like his brother. Anyway, Harpcore was five years older and already making a name for himself, and not just academically. So, as I said to myself at the time, what right had he to act like an outraged father when his brother came into the open. And yet, on the other hand, it must have been like a gun at his head when Timothy, at nineteen, told him not only that he had got one of the maids into trouble but also that he wanted to marry her. The young fellow was very much in earnest. Jennie had grown into a very beautiful young girl and she had a bit of a brain to go with it apparently. She had been bright at school and had kept up her reading, and as Peggy down below would say, she didn't act common. But nevertheless, she was a chambermaid, and when people of her class give way to their masters' whims, they should know what to expect.

'Well, the story goes that Harpcore, naturally, was for sending her packing, but that young Timothy threatened to go with her. It must be said for Harpcore that he loved his brother. You see, the mother had died when Timothy was seven and Dennison had, in a way you could say, brought him up because they had been inseparable until Dennison was packed off to school. And he felt all the more responsible for his younger brother when their father died when Timothy was twelve. And so here was Timothy telling his brother, who was now master of the estate, that he intended to bring a working-class girl, a maid, into this old well-connected family. It just wouldn't be even discussed. I understand that he tried to make the boy see that his feelings were just a flash in the pan. He even consented to providing for the girl as long as Timothy had nothing more to do with her. But apparently Timothy wouldn't see it this way. Anyway – 'She paused here and said, 'Hand me that glass of lemon water off the table, James. I'm thirsty; I've never talked so much at once for years.'

James handed her the glass, and after draining it she wiped her mouth and said, 'Where was I? Oh yes. You remember the big flood? It started just as a spring tide, but then it rained for a solid week, and the wind blew and trees came down. Well, you won't recall it because you were at school, but, you know, the river along the stretch where that little monkey went today is always hazardous; even when the water's running calm, there's eddies there. Well, what possessed the young fellow to take a boat out in that weather God alone knows; but you know the rest, they found the boat a mile down the river. But they didn't find the body until four days later. They said that Dennison nearly went insane. One thing he did do was order the girl to be sent from the house. And now this is where her uncle comes in. He was a strong-minded fellow, Tom Bristow: he agitated for unions and the like for every kind of work; he spoke on platforms; he was that kind of a man. Anyway, what does he do but storm into the house, after levelling the footman, and come face to face with the half-demented Dennison. As far as I can gather and again it was hearsay, but he said as much that the child that was to be born was of that house and of his blood, and that if Dennison turned the girl out there was no place except the workhouse for her because he himself was about to emigrate to Australia, but that he wouldn't go until he saw justice done. And his justice demanded that she remain in her post and the child remain there.

'Apparently, at this, Dennison yelled to his servants to throw the man out to prevent himself from laying his hands on him. But when the butler and the second footman came into the room the fellow took up such a stance that they were awed by him, or, as the tale goes, by the ornaments he scooped up from the table in order to throw at them.

'Well, he is supposed to have given Dennison an ultimatum: either he let the girl stay in her job, or he provide her with a house and income, or he himself would give the story to the newspapers together with the information that his brother had wanted to marry the girl. And how would Dennison stand up to that scandal, he is said to have demanded.

'But Dennison couldn't have said much because nothing seems to have been passed on. I think though he must have considered that setting up the girl in a house would have been taken as acceptance of the responsibility for his brother's child; or, on the other hand, that should he turn her out it would create a scandal that the newspapers would spread countrywide, whereas if he let the girl stay and ignored her existence, the affair would not reach beyond local bounds. And . . . well, that's what he has done: Jennie was allowed to stay, but she was relegated to the kitchen; and it was understood through the household that when the child was born the master mustn't set eyes on it; and, too, that if they wanted to remain in his employ they didn't speak about the matter outside the house.'

She nodded from one to the other, then said, 'And now about the tea business. Young Timothy was very fair, as fair as Dennison is dark. His hair was almost golden, and I've heard that when the child was born it had hair on its head the colour of silver. And over the years the child seems to be growing into a replica of its father. Again, so I am told. So now you can understand the tea business, for had the child's hair been left alone and Dennison had come across him, he would have recognized him immmediately. But a brown-haired child might pass unnoticed, or be taken as belonging to one of the outside staff. That's if he takes notice of any menial the short time he's home.'

'But what's going to happen when the child grows up? Will he make a claim on him do you think? I mean on Mr Harpcore.'

'Perhaps. I don't know, that's in the future. The present is that your little sister has the knack already of creating chaos wherever she goes.' She smiled now, then added, 'I was for trying to persuade your mother – with an iron hand in the velvet glove, you know' – and she smiled, 'to forget about this Dame school business, because I shall miss the little monkey, but after this, I think a little discipline and the company of other than the village children might help to shape her future.'

'What a hope!' James rose to his feet. 'I can't see her changing. Anyway, Grandmama, you wouldn't want her to really, because she's too much like yourself, isn't she?'

'Well, is that a bad thing?' The voice was curt.

James shrugged his shoulders as if, were he to reply, it would be positively. But there was a smile on his face, and she cried at him, 'Go on, get yourself away. I'll have to go into her now and listen to the story for myself; and knowing the teller, it will undoubtedly be embroidered for my benefit, being an old lady who has to be entertained.'

As they both made grunting sounds, the bell ringing in the distance turned them towwards the door and Jessica, a tight smile on her face, said 'There's your appetizer before your meal. I've always disliked

Sundays because you're expected to pray more on a Sunday, and for less food. Enjoy your cold repast. I'm so glad I'm ill and can have warm gruel.' She laughed wickedly, and the boys laughed with her.

When they muttered something as they opened the door, she said, 'What's that you say?' And Peter, poking his head towards her, said in an undertone, 'You heard. You're a wicked woman.'

She still continued to laugh after the door had closed; then getting up smartly, she walked across the room, unlocked the drawer of her writing desk, took out a flat tin box, lifted up the lid, and extracted from the box a small meat pie and a fruit tart. Then, speading a clean handkerchief on the small table to the side of her fireside chair, she laid the pastries on it. But before sitting down again she went to the door and pushed in the bolt. It was known in the household that she always bolted the door when she was relieving herself. Returning to her seat, she made herself comfortable, stretched her feet out and rested them on the rim of the scalloped brass fender; then picking up the pie, she bit into it and munched happily.

3

If the ruling members of the household hadn't already agreed that if Nancy Ann was ever to take on the refinement of a young lady she must be sent away to the Dame school, they would certainly have come to this decision through two incidents that occurred during the following three weeks.

Nancy Ann was in bed for three days and housebound for another three days, but on the folowing Sunday she was considered well enough to attend the morning service and Sunday school in the afternoon.

Miss Eva McKeowan was winding up the proceedings of the Sunday school with, 'Now we shall sing your hymn, children, "Let Me Like An Angel Be".' Thus saying, she went to the harmonium in the corner of the room, and, turning her head to face the class, she called, 'After three . . . one, two, three.'

'Let me like an angel be,
Let me always trust in Thee.'

The voices squeaked and rose in disharmony:

'Ever present at Thy knee
Let me like an angel be.'

It was a silly hymn: Ever present at Thy knee. Nancy Ann did not raise her voice because she knew she couldn't get the tune right.

The hymn ended with Amen being sung in several different keys. Then Miss McKeowan stood up and said, 'Now you will depart quietly.'

Why did she always say, 'depart'?

Nancy Ann herself was about to depart hastily when Miss McKeowan's voice stopped her, sayhing, 'Nancy Ann, stay for a moment, will you?'

Slowly and reluctantly she walked back to where Miss McKeowan stood near her reading desk, and she waited to know what was required of her. But Miss McKeowan didn't speak until the last of the children had gone. And then smiling she looked down on Nancy Ann saying, 'I'm glad to know you are so much better, Nancy Ann.'

'Thank you.'

'I have a little present for you.' She lifted the lid of the reading desk and took out a small box, and when she opened it, it revealed what looked like a gold chain with a heart-shaped locket on the end. She now dangled it from her finger, saying, 'I . . . I would like you to have this, Nancy Ann, as a keepsake, seeing this is almost your last visit to Sunday school. A week tomorrow, I understand you go away to school, and perhaps you will be so busy next Sunday you may not attend. So I thought I would give you this today. It's a very pretty locket, isn't it?'

She now swung the chain backwards and forwards like a pendulum while Nancy Ann thought, Oh dear, dear. She wasn't fond of trinkets and she couldn't accept this one because she knew why it was being given to her: it wasn't that Miss McKeowan liked her, it was a way of finding favour in James's eyes.

Of a sudden she felt sorry for Miss McKeowan and realized, as Peter said, that she was blinded by love; and she must be, or else she would have understood James's attitude towards her, which had become rude of late. At one time he would stand and talk to her, and sometimes she had seen him laugh with her, but afterwards he would always relate what had passed between them to Peter, and they would both laugh.

'Take it. Put it on. It will show up against your blue dress.'

'I'm . . . I'm sorry, Miss Eva, but . . . but I must first ask Mama, because it looks . . . well, an expensive gift, like . . . I mean, it's very like the one James . . . James bought.'

She knew what she was saying was dreadful, yet it would be wrong to accept this gift, because this poor young woman – and now she thought of her almost in ther grandmama's words as a poor young woman – would gain nothing by its giving.

'Mr James has purchased one like it?' Miss McKeowan's voice was high, her words running up the scale as if she was going to burst into song; and there was a smile in her eyes and hovering around her mouth as she brought her head down towards Nancy Ann and said again, 'Your . . . your brother has bought one like this?'

Nancy Ann stepped slightly back from the bright hopeful look and she swallowed deeply and coughed before she brought out in a rush, 'It . . . it is a present for his fi . . . financee.' She had pronounced the word wrongly but that didn't matter, what mattered was the changed expression on the face that had now stretched itself upright and away from her. The finger no longer swung the chain holding the heart-shaped pendant, but the whole was crushed in her hand and this was held tightly against the buckle of the broad belt that spanned her narrow waist and helped to flounce her print skirt.

Now she was speaking again, her words coming through lips which didn't seem to move: 'What did you say? He has a . . . a fiancée? When? Where? Whe . . . when? Who?'

Nancy Ann took three steps backwards until the back of her knee pressed against the harmonium seat, and she stared at the agitated young woman. What she wanted to do was to go to her, take her hand away from her belt and pat it and say, ''Tis all right, 'tis all right. I was only . . . only saying that. It isn't true.' But if she were to do this she could see Miss McKeowan becoming enraged and even slapping her. She had slapped Mary Jane Norton once because she had caught her mimicking the way she walked and how she announced the hymn 'Let Me Like An Angel Be'. And she couldn't risk being slapped: having always endeavoured to join with her brothers' games, her reaction to either their teasing or roughness had been to retaliate and this had become almost a natural reaction and had been of great help to her whenever she came up against the McLoughlins.

'*Go away!*' yelled Miss McKeowan.

But she remained standing, the desire still on her to take the awful look off the young woman's face: she looked as though she were about to cry, yet was too angry to do so.

'*Get out!*'

She got out, at a run now, and when she was outside she continued running until she reached the back gate, where she bumped into Johnny.

Johnny Pratt was the vicarage handyman. He had been handy, he would tell you, for fifty years. He was now sixty-two. He drove the trap, tended the horse, saw to the kitchen garden, neglected the flower garden – he had no use for frivolities, he said. He believed in, and obeyed, the parson; not so his wife, for he considered her like the parsons' wives before her, aiming for a front seat in heaven. The old 'un, he respected, even if she had a tongue like a newly stopped razor. The lads he liked: they were fine young chaps, always civil. But this one here – he looked at Nancy Ann – he could say he more than liked her. She was a chip off the old block. He was sorry they were packing her off to a fancy school. Well, he supposed he could see their point; she was a bit of a rough 'un for a lass.

'What's wrong?' he said.

'Nothing, Johnny.'

'You're lyin', an' on a Sunday an' all. You know where you'll go for doin' that? And you've been runnin' an' all, and you know what your ma thinks about runnin' on a Sunday . . . among other things,' he added.

'Where are they?' she asked, in a whisper now.

'Well' – he pulled out a large round watch from his waistcoat pocket. It was in a case which any supposed silver had long since disappeared leaving the metal the colour of dull brass, and after studying it for a moment he said, 'Well, if things go according to Sunday plans, and I can't see them altering here, they should be in the sitting-room having their cups of tea and – ' he bent down to her, a grin on his bewhiskered face, adding now, 'and no cake, 'cos it's Sunday.' At this he nodded at her, then walked on; and she, too, walking now, went down the yard, round the side of the house and in by the garden door.

In the hall she took off her hat and coat, examined her hands to see if they were clean enough, decided they were as she hadn't been dealing with chalk, then tapping on the sitting room door, she opened it and went in and stopped what she recognized immediately was a tirade from her grandmama which had been directed towards her mama. 'There you are.' Rebecca turned a thankful glance on her daughter. 'Did you enjoy the lesson?'

'It . . . it was as usual, Mama.'

'It would be with that one taking it . . . the Eva one I suppose.'

She looked at her grandmother. 'Yes, Grandmama.'

'You would like a cup of tea?' Her mother was looking at her.

'Yes, please, Mama.'

She sat down behind the round table on which the tea-tray was set and as she did so her father smiled at her. She returned the smile, then let out a long sigh and relaxed against the back of the chair. She didn't know now what she had been frightened about. She had done James a service and Miss Eva wouldn't be silly any more, at least towards him.

She was startled out of her reverie by her grandmother's voice crying, 'Disraeli! That old woman! Instead of running round the Queen's skirts . . . Empress of India, indeed!' she sniffed – 'it would suit him better if he attended to those Turks.' And she rounded on her daughter-in-law: 'And don't tell me, Rebecca, that this is not Sunday talk, massacring Christians is a talk for any day of the week to my mind. Those Bazouks, or whatever you call them, killed thousands.'

'Oh, Mother-in-law, that is an exaggeration.'

'No exaggeration whatever, woman. You don't read your newspapers. Isn't that so, John Howard?' She addressed her son, as she always did, with his full Christian name. 'Wasn't there twelve thousand of them polished off?' And before he could answer, she again nodded on her daughter-in-law, crying, 'And it could happen here. It all started there because of a bad harvest, and it could happen here. I'm telling you.'

'Mother . . . Mother, please don't become so excited. Yes, you are right, there were Christians massacred by the Bashi – Bazouks, but it's all so far away, and . . .'

'Oh, my Lord!' Nancy Ann watched her grandmama put her cup down on the side table with such a bang that the remaining tea in the cup splashed over on to the saucer, then on to the table. She watched her mother look towards the table in dismay and yet make no move to go and wipe it. And her grandmama went on, 'So far away, you say. Don't forget, what happened yesterday in France could happen here tomorrow, and in that Germany too. And there's that stupid little man standing firm, as he calls it, on his support of Turkey while other countries are aghast at the atrocities in Bulgaria. John Howard' – she looked sternly at her son – 'did you not read the pamphlet that James brought home, that Mr Gladstone got published, showing up the Bulgarian horrors? No, I'm sure you didn't. Well, it's in the library, at least it was a week ago, if it hasn't been tidied up.' She now cast an accusing glance towards her daughter-in-law before going on, 'James, Peter, and I discussed this situation. James has a head on his shoulders; looks beyond these shores. He could do well in Parliament.'

'Oh, Mother.' John closed his eyes and, his voice weary, he went on, 'You know as well as I do that James won't think seriously along such lines. He knows . . . well' – he lowered his head – 'it's only because of your generosity that he has managed to remain at his studies so far. Please, Mother, I beg of you not to encourage him in such costly . . .'

'Encourage him! He's got a mind of his own. And don't worry, I could no more support either of them in such a career than I could fly; I couldn't even now buy us a new tr . . . ap.' Her voice trailed away, and she grabbed at her cup and gulped at the now cold tea that remained in it. And when she replaced the cup and the saucer this time, it was done quietly, and she raised her eyes and looked at her son and daugher-in-law. They were staring at her, and John, in a small quiet voice, said, 'Oh, Mother.'

'Oh, don't Mother me in that tone of voice. I've been only too pleased to do it. I thought they might as well have it now as wait till I was dead. And there's enough left to see madam there through her schooling. And then that's that, except for my quarterly pension. Now, if you don't mind, I'll away to my room before I stiffen and die here, because that fire – ' she turned her head towards the small amount of glowing coals in the large grate and, a twisted smile on her face, she ended, 'they may have stopped the human sacrifices by that king on the Gold Coast, but if they lived in this part of the world I'm sure the poor beggars would prefer the stewpot.'

And so saying and chuckling to herself, she walked smartly from the room, leaving as she usually did, consternation behind her.

Nancy Ann watched her mother go quickly over to her father and, putting a hand on his arm, say in an undertone, 'Do . . . do you think it's right, John, she has spent her all on . . . on the boys and . . .?'

'If she says so, my dear, it is right. I . . . I never guessed. I . . . I didn't know what Father left her. I thought it must be a very substantial sum because she's been so generous.' He looked into his wife's face. 'She is generous, Rebecca. Underneath all her brusqueness she is generous and warm of heart.'

Rebecca's head drooped, and in a low voice she said, 'Yes, yes I know, John; and I also know that she considers me a very stupid being.'

'No, no, my dear; it is only her manner.'

'But I am a very stupid being, John.'

'Oh, my lo . . .'

It seemed that for the first time they both became aware that their daughter was still present, and now they looked towards her and John said 'Would you leave us, Nancy Ann, please?'

Gulping in her throat, because now for some reason or other she wanted to cry, she had the urge to run to them and put her arms around them both, and hold them tightly to her; instead, she rose from the chair, saying quietly, 'Yes, Papa,' and hurried from the room.

It had been an afternoon threaded with emotion, emotion that had to be sorted out. She hurried now to her room and there, sitting on the end of the bed, she put her arms on the brass rail and leant her head against it. And in the quiet moments that followed she realized that she had never understood her mother and never loved her as much as she did at his moment. She would try, in future, to be good and always do what she was told, and never upset her.

It was four hours later, and her mother was still very upset, as was her father, and even her grandmama was asking, 'Why . . . why say such a thing?'

Nancy Ann was in the drawing-room again, and there they were, her mother and father and grandmama, as they had been in the afternoon, but the atmosphere was entirely different.

It should happen that in the vestry after conducting evening service, John had noticed that his churchwarden, Harry McKeowan, was unusually silent. After a service it was Harry's custom to give a running commentary on who had been present and who absent and the reason for the latter, and how little or much had been put on the the offertory plate. But, this evening, he had not spoken, not even to comment on the main colour of the coins on the plate, for there were very few silver pieces shining amongst them. Feeling that his warden might be in some personal trouble and needing help, he said, 'Aren't you feeling well, Harry?'

'I'm as usual, Vicar.'

'Oh, I'm glad to hear that. But is there anything else wrong?'

'No, nothing wrong as you could say.' The churchwarden had stroked his greying hair back from his temples, using the thumb pad of his plump hands. And having done this two or three times, he said, 'I've known your sons for a long time, Vicar.'

'Yes; yes, you have, all of twelve years since we came here from Gateshead.'

'And I happened to see them last Monday afore they left for the train, and wished them God-speed and a safe journey.'

'Yes, yes, you did, Harry; I was there. Now go on, tell me, what have they done that seems to have upset you?'

'Well.' The man moved his stout body as if about to rock it; then his tone changing, he said, 'Well, if not them, I would have thought you, Vicar, could have told me about Mr James's coming wedding.'

'*What? What* did you say?'

'I said . . . well, I think you heard what I said. It took the young miss to break the news to Eva. And I . . . well, I must be truthful, Vicar, it came as a bit of a shock, not only to her. Well, no, not only to her, but to us all. It's all right, it's all right, Vicar, don't trouble yourself like that.' John had moved towards the table and, gripping the edge, had leaned over it. 'I know what woman are: 'tis likely your good lady wants to surprise the village with an engagement party or some such, and so persuaded Mr James to keep quiet about it. Anyway, that's how I see it, and that's how I explained it to Eva, but nevertheless, it was a bit of a shock. Well, I'll go and finish my duties. Is there anything more you require of me, Vicar?'

It had taken an effort for John to say, 'No. No thank you, Harry.'

And now here he was confronting his daugher and asking for an explanation, and when in a tearful voice she gave it, she left him and the others quite dumbfounded. Then her father was speaking to her slowly and quietly, and as she looked at him she saw him in the pulpit again, for he was saying, 'You know what you have done? You have lied deliberately in order to hurt someone. I am sure James never meant you to say such a thing, and you, in your heart, as young as you are, must have realized this. Why? What possessed you to such wickedness?'

The lump in her throat was almost choking her. She moved her head from side to side before muttering brokenly, 'I . . . I didn't mean to hurt her. It . . . it was as I said, it . . . it was just to stop her thinking of James, and . . . and she was giving me the necklace as a sort of – ' she gulped and sniffed and wiped the tears from each cheek with her fingers before she finished, 'a sort of bribe, to get him to like her.'

'You're almost thirteen years old, Nancy Ann; you should know right from wrong by now. I'm disappointed in you. Go to your room.'

She was crying audibly now as she left the room.

When the door had closed on her they looked at each other. Then Jessica's body began to shake, and when her laughter became audible John remonstrated with her severely, saying, 'Mother!'

'Yes, yes, I know, she's put you in a fix, but it's funny when you think about it. And – ' The laughter going from her voice, she ended, 'As for that silly flighty, man-crazy girl, it's the best thing that could have happened. Because whether you've noticed it or not, John Howard, she's cow-eyed James every Sunday as far back as I can remember. And as for the older one, Jancy, if all tales are true, Farmer Boyle almost took a gun to her, because she was after his eldest and the lad was already promised and had been for three years. Now, John Howard, you take my advice and let things be as they are. If it gets round, which it will, that James is engaged, well and good. You write to him and, after laying into him, tell him to look round and put some truth into the rumour, but see that she's got a bit of money behind her. And – ' She looked at her daughter-in-law now, and a softer tone creeping into her voice, she said, 'And, Rebecca, remember, she is but a child still. But I'll say now, which I haven't up till this time, I agree with you that she needs direction of another kind from that given by her doting parents and her stupid grandmother.' She nodded her head at herself. 'Your idea of school was a good one, and there is enough to see her through until she is sixteen or seventeen. Now, go on up to her. Be firm, but not too firm: you'll only have her another week, and then life will change for all of us.'

Almost on the point of tears now, Rebecca muttered, 'Thank you, Mother-in-law,' before turning away and hurriedly leaving the room.

Jessica looked at her son. 'Why in the name of God!' she said, 'did you ever want to become a parson, because your children are always going to disappoint you, for not one of them will ever become a saint.' And all John could answer was simply, 'Oh, Mother.'

* * *

A week had passed. She had been kept in her room for the first two days with the strict order that she must not divulge to the maids why she was being punished; she was just to say she had told a lie. But today was her last Sunday at home. Yesterday, she had said goodbye to her friends in the village: Mrs Taylor, from the grocers, had given her a box of candy; Mrs Norton had given her a blue hair ribbon, and Mr Norton, who had been sober, had said he would miss her face; Mary Jane Norton gave her an embroidered needle case; Miss Linda Waters, the dressmaker, had given her a velvet band for her hair; in fact, everybody had been so kind and seemed sorry that she was going away.

There had been no mention of her attending Sunday school, or the evening service. She had attended morning service and her father had preached a sermon on lying and the different forms it could take, such as deviousness. She had never heard that word before, but somehow she knew that it applied to her and what she had said to Miss Eva McKeowan.

With a little surprise she had noted that the gentry stalls had been almost full, at least that there were lots of servants in them, but no real gentry sitting in the high front pews, even though she knew that the master of Rossburn House was home and had a lot of friends with him. Later, she had asked her mama if she could go out for a walk along by the river bank for the last time, and after some hesitation Rebecca had said, 'Yes, but put your shower coat on because I think it could rain, and if it does, come straight home. You will, won't you?' It was put in the form of a request and she had answered, 'Yes, Mama.'

And so, here she was walking by the river bank. The water was grey and choppy; the sky was low and grey; the whole world was grey. She hadn't brought Gyp with her. Although he had whined when she had passed through the back gate, she had resisted the temptation to go to him and let him have one last run with her, because she didn't want anything more to happen that would upset her mother and father.

She had gone some distance when she decided to leave the river bank and go into the copse and so call in and say goodbye to Granny Burgess.

Granny Burgess was a very old lady, but she still looked after herself: did her own housework and garden, and even made treacle toffee. She liked Granny Burgess. She was the only old person in the village and round about who, Peggy said, didn't expect you to go trudging through the snow, carrying soup to her in the winter, because she would always have her own broth pan on the hob and a ladleful for anyone who was passing.

She had no sooner reached the road than she heard the McLoughlins. She couldn't as yet see them but she recognized their raucous voices; and there was one thing she knew for certain, she mustn't meet up with them today. Apart from wearing her Sunday dress, she had on her shower coat and her second-best hat; her best, a brown straw, was being kept for the journey tomorrow.

But the McLoughins were all fast runners and before she could retrace her steps again to the gate that led down to the river bank, they had come round the corner and espied her. And now they were whooping towards her and she knew that if she turned and ran down the river bank they would come after her, and the encounter could be fraught with more danger on the river bank. So she took a deep breath and held it for a moment as she walked slowly forward.

They had stopped now and were waiting for her, shoulder to shoulder across the road. This was their usual form of mustering for an attack.

She came to a stop in front of the eldest one who was just as tall as herself but twice as broad. The other children were small made, but all were wiry. Her mind was telling her that whatever she did, or whatever they did to her, she must not retaliate: it was her last day at home and she mustn't upset her mama and papa. Oh no. So, slightly to her disgust, she heard herself saying in a placating tone, 'Will you please let me pass?'

'Will ya please let me pass?' The eldest boy was mimicking her in a broad Irish accent. 'Pass, she said, she wants to pass.' And he looked at his two brothers and two sisters lined up either side of him. The smallest girl standing at the end of the row could have been about seven years old and she was the only one who wasn't laughing.

Nancy Ann's lips began to tremble. She said a hasty little prayer as the boy stepped closer to her. He was now within an outstretched arm from her and, putting his head on one side, he said, ''Tis true then what I'm hearin' that they're packin' ya off to a fancy school to make a lady out of ya?'

When she didn't answer, he turned his head towards the others, saying, 'She's lost her tongue. She didn't last time though, did she now? She was brave last time, wasn't she now? 'cos she was at the end of the village near the blacksmith's shop. An' what did she call us then?' He nodded towards one brother, and the boy shouted, 'Scruffs.' And the other one added, 'Dirty scruffs. That's what she called us, dirty scruffs.'

He was facing her again. 'Are we dirty scruffs, Miss Vicarage? Miss Parson's Prig? 'Cos that's what you are.' His voice lost its banter now and his arm shot out and he pushed her as he added, 'A prig. A stuck up little nowt. A Protestant prig!'

'Don't do that!' All placation had gone from her voice now: her face was tight, her whole body quivering.

'Who d'you think you are tellin' me what to do?' His arm came out again and now pushed her so hard that she stumbled backwards and almost fell.

It wasn't to be borne. In a flash her doubled fist caught the boy on the side of the mouth; and the impact brought his lip sharply against his teeth and a trickle of blood ran down his chin.

In amazed silence the brothers and sisters stared at her for a moment: then came a loud chorus of, 'Get her, Mick! Let her have it, Mick!' And as quick as her own fist had contacted his chin, so he was now pummelling her, or at least trying to, for only some of his random punches were finding a target, she was warding most off with her forearms.

This tactic seemed to infuriate the lad further, because he had his own method of fighting, a few punches, then get his arms around his opponent, bring his knees up and they were on their back. But the next moment he couldn't believe what was happening to him. Encouraged by the jeers and cries of his brothers and sisters, he had been about to cluth her when he felt a searing pain in his face and he imagined that his eye had been knocked out. But that was nothing to what he experienced when her knee caught him in the stomach and his feet left the ground and the back of his head came in contact with the stony road.

The children were all screaming now, the two girls kneeling by their brother, one of them crying, 'Mick! Mick! Are you all right, Mick?' And when Mick merely groaned, she screamed, 'Killed him, she has!' Then looking towards her other two brothers, she commanded, 'Get her!'

Nancy Ann wasn't prepared for the next move. The boys weren't as big as their brother, but their impact and flailing fists bore her to the ground.

So intent had they all been on the fight that they hadn't noticed or heard the two horsemen galloping across the field beyond the ditch at the other side of the road.

When the horses jumped the ditch there was something akin to pandemonium in the road for the two boys scrambled off their victim and ran to where their sisters were dragging their brother to his feet.

'What is this, eh? What is this?' One of the riders had dismounted, but no one answered him. He looked towards the boy with the bleeding lip who was holding one hand to his stomach and the other to an eye, and the eldest girl cried, 'She hit him. That one from the vicarage, she knocked him out.'

The rider now turned sharply when a small voice from behind him said, 'Mick hit her first.'

'He did, did he?' He stared down on the child and her large blue eyes looked up at him fearlessly as she said, 'Aye, Mister, he did. But she belted him right, left, an' centre, she did at that, Mister.'

'Shut that squawkin' mouth o' yours, Marie McLoughlin. Her

bigger sister was now making for her, and the small girl, rounding on her, shouted, 'You lay a finger on me, our Cathy, an' I'll tell me da'.

While this was going on the other rider had dismounted and raised Nancy Ann into a sitting position, and when he asked, 'Are you hurt?' she answered weakly, 'I'm all right, sir.'

She wasn't all right, she was feeling battered all over. Dazedly, she looked at one of her hands. It was tightly clenched, and when slowly she opened it, it was to disclose a strand of brown hair. Quickly she flicked it from her, and the man who was holding her smiled and said, 'Spoils of war. You should have kept it as a souvenir. Come on.' And he assisted her to her feet, but finding that she was unable to stand, he put his arm around her shoulder and she leant against him. She felt dizzy. Her mind was muzzy. Then, her eyes were brought open by a raucous shout coming from somewhere behind her and the resulting consternation among the group standing a few yards in front of her.

''Tis our da comin' up from the river.'

'Oh God Almighty!'

'He'll belt the daylights outa you, our Mick.'

'He's had the daylights belted outa him.'

'You shut up, our Marie, else when I get you on the quiet, I'll skin you.'

'You and who else?'

This exchange among the McLoughlins was carried on in loud voices while they waited for their father to approach. And now here he was, doffing his cap to the two gentlemen and crying. 'What have I here, sirs? What have I here? You've knocked them down?'

'No, McLoughlin.' It was the man holding Nancy Ann who spoke. 'We haven't knocked them down. More's the pity. It was this young girl here whom your son attacked, and in defending herself, she floored him . . . Look at him.'

'In the name o' God! Tell me me eyes are not seein'. You . . . you big lout!' The man was striding towards his son now who was still holding a hand to his eye. 'Don't tell me. Aw, please God, don't tell me that you let the little chit from the vicarage knock you out. Oh, you gormless idiot, you!'

'She kneed me, Da.' The words came as a mutter.

'She kneed you? Begod! I've heard it all. She kneed you, that bit lass? Then if she did, I'd like to shake her hand, an' after that I'm gona kick your arse from here to the Crown and Anchor . . . Get!'

They got, the older girl helping her brother, the younger boys walking behind, rubbing different parts of their anatomies as they went. Only the little girl stayed. Her face unsmiling, she looked to where the gentlemen was leading the vicarage girl towards his horse and talking to her da as he did so. His voice was almost as loud as her da's, and he was saying, 'I've warned you, McLoughlin, haven't I? And now for the last time . . .'

'I'll belt him, sir, I will. I'll take it out of . . .'

'Don't change the subject, McLoughlin; you know what I'm referring to. Birds, McLoughlin, birds. I hear they've thinned out.'

'Never, sir. Never me, sir, your worship, your lordship.'

'Shut up! Shut your mouth!' The man now turned to his friend, saying, 'Here, hold her a minute till I get up.' And when he was mounted, he turned a hard glance down on the Irishman, saying, 'One more time, McLoughlin, and you go along the line. Now that's my last word, understand?'

The man remained quiet for a moment. Then touching his cap, he said, 'Good enough, sir. Good enough.'

'Give her here.' The rider bent over and caught Nancy Ann under the arms as his friend hoisted her up towards him.

There was a buzzing in Nancy Ann's ears and a strange aroma in her nose, a mixture of sweat, tobacco fumes, and leather mixed with a distinctive smell of horseflesh. Her body was being rocked and she found it soothing. She could go to sleep like this . . .

Hilda Fenwick had just changed into a clean white apron preparatory to going downstairs to serve the afternoon tea when she happened to look out of the attic window. The window was in the back of the house which was only separated from thc road by the kitchen garden, and was bordered by a low drystone wall. Behind this wall she could see the tops of two horsemen riding but there was something peculiar about one, yet something familiar. Quickly she pushed up the lower sash of the window and poked her head out. The road curved as it made its way to the front gate of the vicarage; then she exclaimed aloud, 'Eeh! dear Lord!' The next minute she was flying from the room, down the attic stairs, along a passage and on to the main landing, then down the main staircase, and as she reached the hall she shouted, 'Mistress! Mistress! Ma'am! Ma'am!' And at this she burst into the sitting-room and there startled its only occupant as she gabbled at her.

Rebecca had been sitting quietly reading but now she was on her feet, crying, 'What did you say?'

''Tis true, ma'am, two horsemen and . . . and Miss Nancy Ann lying across the front of one of them.'

Rebecca stared at her maid, wondering if the girl's mind had become deranged. Then she looked towards her husband standing by the door; and Hilda turned to him now, saying ''Tis right. They should be comin' up the drive now. She was half lyin' across the saddle.'

Almost as soon as John reached the front door Rebecca was at his side, and they stood close together at the top of the steps open-mouthed watching the two riders come slowly towards them. And there was their daughter lying limp in the saddle being supported by none other than Mr Dennison Harpcore.

Rebecca told herself, she wouldn't believe it, she wouldn't, she wouldn't: the child's things were all packed, the arrangements were made; the appointment at the school was for eleven o'clock tomorrow morning.

Nancy Ann was lifted carefully into the house and placed on the sitting-room couch. She wasn't unconscious, she hadn't fainted, but she wasn't fully aware of what was going on.

Dennison Harpcore had given an explanation of what he had seen to happen and he ended, 'She may be slightly concussed. I would get the doctor to her to be on the safe side.'

Rebecca forced herself to thank him for his services, and when he said, 'Please don't thank me; it brought a little sauce to a very unappetizing Sunday. Although I would wish that she hadn't suffered in the process. Yet I can assure you she did not suffer half as much as her opponent. She must have put up a fight to floor that boy; he's a lout of a boy, a chip off the old block.' He now turned and, glancing down on Nancy Ann, he commented, 'She looks delicate, rather fragile, yet I understand she succeeded in delivering a black eye and a belly' – he coughed – 'a stomach punch, with her knee. Of course' – he nodded now – 'your two boys, or young men as they must be, they most likely have been her tutors. Where are they now?'

It was John who answered him, saying, 'They are both at Oxford.'

'Oxford! Oh, good, good. What are they taking?'

'My eldest is reading Mathematics, the younger one, Natural Science.'

'Indeed! Indeed!'

John did not like the note of surprise in this visitor's tone; there was even a touch of condescension in his manner. He looked at the man. He hadn't seen him for two or three years. How old was he now? Nearing thirty, he imagined. He looked much older the result of the life of dissipation that he led no doubt. He also noticed that Harpcore's friend hadn't spoken a word since he came in. He was much older than Harpcore, and both his silent manner and his look were supercilious.

Mr Harpcore was bidding farewell to Rebecca, saying, that he hoped the doctor would find nothing serious wrong with her daughter, other than perhaps a few bruises and, as he had suggested, slight concussion.

John accompanied the two men to the door where, he thanked Mr Harpcore formally before making his way back across the hall to the sitting-room. But he was stopped half-way by the sight of his mother descending the stairs and asking loudly, 'What's all the narration about? There's horses on the drive, who's here?'

Without a word he waited for her to reach the bottom of the stairs;

then taking her arm, he led her into the sitting-room and, still silent, he pointed towards the couch.

After she had been given the explanation why the horses were on the drive and her granddaughter lying with eyes closed on the couch, Jessica said, 'Well, she can't go tomorrow.'

'No.' Rebecca rose from her chair and, looking at Jessica, she said, 'No, not tomorrow, Mother-in-law, but she must go.' And Jessica said, 'Yes, I agree with you entirely: blacking eyes and kneeing people in the belly, no matter who they are, has got to be stopped. Oh, yes' – she inclined her head towards her daughter-in-law – 'I agree with you.'

Yet, a few minutes later, sitting by the side of her granddaughter, both her son and daughter-in-law having left the room, he to send Johnny for the doctor, she to get Hilda to prepare the bed with a hot oven shelf, Jessica took the limp hand in hers as she muttered to herself, 'But Sundays will never be the same again.'

PART TWO

The Blossoming

1

'You are not sorry you haven't gone?'

'No, Grandmama.'

'You sure?'

'Yes, Grandmama, very sure.'

'You . . . you didn't like her very much, did you?'

'No, Grandmama, truthfully, I didn't. Did you?'

Jessica leant her grey head to one side and replied, 'No, Nancy Ann, truthfully, I didn't.' Then they both smiled.

'But you would have made a very pretty bridesmaid.'

'You think so, Grandmama?'

'Oh yes, yes.'

'I'm gawky, Peggy says.'

'Peggy!' Jessica almost spat. 'What does she know about it? You're but fourteen yet and you're developing fast. Give you another couple of years or so, and you'll be like I was at your age. And let me tell you – ' She now leant forward, a mischievous grin on her face as she whispered, 'I was something to look at in those days. You know I could have married a title.'

'You could? Then why didn't you?'

'Oh' – Jessica leant back – 'I was in love; I loved your grandfather then.'

'Didn't you love him after?'

'Don't be cheeky, miss. Yes, of course I did. I loved him till the day he died. I wonder if Miss Nicolette Hobson will be able to say the same of James.'

Nancy Ann made no reply, but if she had, her reply would have been, 'I doubt it, Grandmama.'

James had left university last year with a first class Honours Degree, and almost immediately had been offered a position to teach in a school in Bath. While at university he had made friends with a John Hobson, and for the past two years had spent weeks of his summer vacation at his home, which happened to be part of a large private school of which his father was headmaster. John Hobson had a sister. She was of the same age as James and apparently their courtship had started immediately. He had returned home in the Easter vacation of '78 to say that he was going to propose marriage to Miss Nicolette Hobson. At that time Nancy Ann recalled she had greeted this news with pleasure, for it seemed to prove that her lying had not been a lie after all. But from her first meeting with Miss Nicolette Hobson she had asked herself how James could possibly love her: she wasn't pretty, she wasn't even smart, but what she proved to them all to be, and within a very short time of entering the vicarage, was that she was a highly intelligent and knowledgeable young woman who knew her own mind and what she wanted; and it was apparent she wanted James. As her grandmama had said after their first meeting. 'She talked at him as if they were already married, and the fool of a boy seemed to like it.'

James was being married today and her mother and father had made the journey to Somerset, reluctantly, it would seem, on her mother's part, for Nancy Ann knew her mama was vexed that her daughter had not been asked to act as a bridesmaid, an honour being enjoyed by two of Nicolette's younger sisters and two cousins.

Peter was acting as James's best man, and he had said to her yesterday morning, before he left, that his heart wasn't in it, and it was a shame she wasn't coming. But she had assured him that she didn't mind in the least. And this was true. Also that somebody had to stay at home to see to Grandmama.

She now looked at the clock on the sitting-room mantelpiece. It had just struck three and Jessica, following her gaze, said, 'Yes, it will be over by now. We have lost James. Oh, yes, yes.' She nodded her head vigorously towards Nancy Ann. 'Don't let us delude ourselves. That young madam will do her best to sever the ties with this end of the country, let me tell you.' She wagged her finger at Nancy Ann, saying, 'I know women. Oh, I know women.' Then, her voice changing and her expression softening, she said, 'I only hope, my dear, I'll live to see your wedding day, and from this house. Oh yes, I pray the good God will spare me till then.'

'Oh! Grandmama, my wedding day? Me getting married? I shall never marry, I'm not . . . well, not that type.'

'Oh! When did you come to this conclusion?'

'Well, Belle . . . you know, Belle Tollington, my friend at school, she says there are types that marry and types that don't.'

'Stuff and nonsense! And I suppose she says you're not the type?'

'Well . . . well, I feel, Grandmama . . .'

'Oh, shut up! And that Belle wants a strap to her backside, that's what she wants. How old is she?'

'She's nearly fourteen, like me.'

'Well, my dear, the quicker you get a new friend the better. You will marry and you'll marry early if you're wise. Now some two years ago, I might have agreed with that Miss Belle.' She laughed now.

'Remember the day you had your fight with the McLoughlins? Well, I nearly gave you up myself on that particular Sunday. Eeh! my! The Parson's daughter giving the McLoughlin hooligan a black eye and kneeing him in the stomach. Oh, you can laugh. It's funny now. And oh' – she flapped her hand – 'I can remember when I related it to the boys Peter actually rolled on the floor. Apparently it was he who had shown you how to use your knee. Wasn't it?'

'Yes, it was, like the wrestlers do.' Nancy Ann laughed. 'But it was James who showed me how to use a straight left.'

'Anyway, you've grown out of all that. Praise be. That school has worked a small miracle on you. In that curriculum it said they turned out young ladies, and it's no lie.'

'Oh, Grandmama, huh!'

Nancy Ann's derisive 'huh' caused Jessica to say, 'What do you mean, huh?' Well, they do, don't they?'

'You should see some of them in the dormitory tearing each other's hair out, rolling about. My affray with Mick McLoughlin was child's play.'

'You don't mean that. It's another one of your tales.'

'I do, Grandmama, it's true. It nearly always happens towards the end of term. It's frustration; it builds up over the weeks. It's mostly with the girls who can't go home at all. Well, say, with one that can't go home. Her parents are abroad, or some such, and she's always talking about her home life. I've often wanted to bring Eileen Talbot home. But . . . but then I thought Mama has enough to do, and she hasn't been well.'

'No, no, you're right there. I'm worried at times about your mama. She hasn't been well, as you say, but when you ask her how she's feeling, she always says she's quite all right. But the flesh is dropping off her. I'm going to have a word with Doctor McCann shortly about her. Well now, look, the day's still bright, go out and get some air, make the best of it. Take Gyp with you; he doesn't get much exercise these days, he's getting fat, only don't go down by the river with him on your own.'

'Why not Grandmama?' She was standing by her grandmother's chair now, and Jessica, lifting her hand, slapped at the thin arm, saying, 'Why not, Grandmama? in that innocent tone of voice! Remember what happened one Sunday afternoon when you took him along there?'

'Oh, that!' She smiled now. 'I'd forgotten about that, it's so long ago.'

'Yes,' Jessica mimicked; 'oh, so long ago, all of two years in fact, a lifetime. Go on with you now, only keep to the road. And I mean that, because if anything happened I couldn't cope . . .'

'Oh! Grandmama. Really, you make me feel awful, you know; it is as if you imagine I go out looking for trouble.'

'I'm sorry, my dear, I am sorry, for you've been so good of late. Your mama and papa are really proud of you. And they are delighted with your school reports. At least they are now.' She pulled a face. 'Those they received during that first year . . . Oh dear! Do you remember? When you didn't settle in and had to be kept down. But what I mean, my dear, if I feel I'm responsible for all that happens in the house until they come back. You understand?'

'Yes, yes, of course, Grandmama. Don't worry, put your mind at ease. I'll just go towards the old toll gate; I'll not even go in the direction of the village and certainly not' – she now moved her head from side to side – anywhere near the McLoughlins.' Then laughing again, she added, 'It's funny about the McLoughlins, isn't it? I can pass them on the road now and nothing happens, in fact they give me a wide berth. Remember last Christmas when Mr McLoughlin gave me a rabbit. He had a sackful of them and he pulled one out of the top like a conjurer might out of a hat, and said, "There, missie, that's for you. You're a grand lass. You are that." '

She had dropped into the stance and accent of the Irishman and caused her grandmother to let out a bellow of a laugh, and as she dried her eyes she said, 'You know, you have a gift there, keep practising it. One day you could entertain with it.'

'I'll do that, ma'am, I will, I will. 'Tis yourself I will pleasure. I will, I'll practice it, honest to God!' Almost before the last words were out of her mouth she put her hand tightly over it; then turned and hurried from the room, closing the door behind her. But in the hall she could still hear her grandmama laughing, and as she took her coat out of the hall wardrobe she thought, Yes, I'll do what Grandmama says. I will . . . I will practice at it. It's the only accomplishment I seem to have.

She pulled on her coat, then went to take her straw hat from the shelf above, but her hand stayed on it: Why should she wear it, she hated hats. She loved the wind through her hair and there was quite a breeze blowing today. Her mother and father weren't here, there was no one to chastize her for going outside with her head uncovered, and anyway, she was just going along the road.

She went out through the side door and ran to Gyp where he was tethered as usual to the wall, and she endeavoured to silence his hysterical barking as she undid him. Then she was running through the gate and into the paddock, the dog bounding round her. In the middle of the field she stopped, slightly out of breath, and as she stood gasping while looking up into the sky there swept through her a feeling such as she had never before experienced. It came like lightning flashing, only it whirled upwards from the pit of her stomach and seemed to corkscrew out of the top of her head, lifting her from the ground. And now she was running again. Or was she dancing? The dog was barking its loudest as it raced away from her and raced back again. She came to a stop near the railings that bordered the field and as she leant over them the feeling seeped down through her and seemed to drain away through her legs.

She turned her back to the railing and became limp for a moment. She was breathing deep and slowly. She had never before felt like that: it was, she thought, as if she had only in those moments become alive. Was this what they called joy? It had come and gone so quickly, yet her mind retained the essence of it, and she told herself she would never forget this moment, this thing that had made her feel beautiful for a flashing space in the middle of the meadow.

Her hair ribbon had come loose and was dangling from the bottom of her four curls. Always when she was at home she put her hair into roller rags at night, but at school she had to plait her hair. It was long, thick and wavy and reached down below her shoulder blades; its colour was chestnut brown, and she knew it was nice. She considered it the only thing she possessed in the way of attraction, although Belle said, when she would later have to put it up she would have trouble with it because it was too coarse to fall into shape.

Gyp was foraging in the grass and she called him to her, saying now, 'Behave yourself. We're going to walk along the road. And don't forget you are now being attended by a young lady. Do you hear me?' She laughed at herself and resisted the desire to run once more, for the road was now in sight.

At the end of the field railings there was only a shallow ditch to be jumped, and then she was walking along the road, the dog trotting sedately by her side as if he really had taken his cue from her.

She was nearing a part of the road where it narrowed and turned sharply towards the old turnpike gate long since demolished, and with the keeper's cottage in ruins to the side. This often provided habitation for tramps who had stripped most of the wood away from the building to make fires. But she had promised her grandmother she didn't intend to go as far as that today, and so she was on the point of turning about when, above the noise of the wind that was swaying the trees along the edge of the wood to the left side of her, she heard the sound of a horse's hoofs. She had actually turned round in the direction of home when she swung back again to see coming towards her, and at a terrifying rate from around the corner, a high dogcart driven by a woman. The horse was almost on top of her when with a scream and one swooping action she grabbed at the dog and took him with her headlong into the ditch.

There had been rain during the night and although there was no water lying, the grass and silt at the bottom was soggy, and as she lay gasping on top of the dog she knew she wasn't hurt, nor it, but she also knew she was angry, in fact, consumed with anger blazing with it. It was as strong as the wonderful feeling that she had experienced in the field only minutes earlier.

Clawing her way out of the ditch, she stood in the roadway and looked to where the woman had pulled the horse to a standstill and when the voice, in a high-falutin tone, came to her, saying, 'Are you all right?' she screamed at her, 'Yes, of course I'm all right. You have just about run me down. You are an idiot. That's what you are.' She had moved forward and was standing now glaring up into the face that hung above hers. It was a soft-skinned, plump face, topped by a high red velvet bonnet to match the velvet suit that had a white ruffle at the neck, and the neck of the wearer was fat.

'You don't know how to drive a cart, you shouldn't be allowed on the road.'

'How dare you speak to me like that.'

'I dare, and if I'd been dead, somebody would have said to you: how dare you drive like a mad woman! And look at your poor horse.' She stepped to the side and pointed to the animal. It was in a lather. 'There should be a law forbidding people like you being in charge of an animal. And look at me!' She pointed to the streaks of mud on her light alpaca coat, and to the shoes covered with mud.

'You should not have been meandering in the middle of a road. It is a public road.'

'Yes, that's what it is, a public road for all people, not for maniacs.'

'Who are you?'

'Never mind who I am, who are you? because I intend to make a complaint against you.' Dear, dear. She closed her eyes for a moment and put out her hand and grasped the wheel of the cart. She felt dizzy. Was it going to be a repeat of he McLoughlins' business?

At this point another dogcart came round the bend and when it was brought to a stop, the man driving it called, 'You must have gone hell for leather and come over the field. That's cheating, Rene.'

Nancy Ann's dizziness ebbed, and it was she who answered the newcomer, shouting, 'Yes, she went hell for leather, and nearly killed me and the dog. You want to give her lessons in driving. Come on, Gyp!' She called to the dog, and now began to walk past the dogcart, but when she came to the horse's head she stopped and pointed to it and, looking back at the infuriated face of the lady, she said, 'Look! Poor thing, it's foaming at the mouth.' Then squaring her shoulders, she walked away, attempting to keep a beeline although her legs were trembling so much that she wanted to drop down on the grass verge and rest a while.

The man drove his cart closer to the young woman's side now, saying, 'What was all that about?' And she, her deep blue eyes blazing, replied, 'She fell into the ditch as I came round the corner. Insolent little slut! Who is she? Do you know?

'How should I know! you are here more often than me.'

'She's the parson's daughter.' The voice came from the bank bordering the wood, and there jumped down into the road a tall man carrying a gun. And the woman addressed him, saying, 'Parson's daughter? How do you know, Larry?'

Before the man could answer the man in the other dogcart put in, 'Oh, Larry knows everything and everyone.'

'Yes, yes, you could say that.' There was a coolness in the tone and it had an ominous ring. And this for the man in the other dogcart seemed to close the matter for he turned his horse about and trotted it off. But the woman continued to look at the man with the gun who was now standing close to her, and she said, 'The same one I suppose that you tell me the tale about being a miniature Amazon?'

'The very same one, although she's grown somewhat and looks promising from what view I had of her.'

'Well, parson's daughter or no, she's an uncouth little slut and wants putting in her place. I'll see Dennison as soon as I get back. He should do something, and I'll see that he does.'

The man smiled into the round furious blue eyes now and, his voice still cool, he said, 'Yes, I would do that, Mrs Poulter Myers. Yes, I would do that.'

'Oh, you!' She flounced round in the seat, jerked sharply at the reins, crying, 'Get up! there,' then turned the horse and dogcart in the narrow road, almost backing into the ditch as she did so; following which, she wielded the whip and once again sent the animal into a gallop. And the man standing in the road pursed his lips, raised his eyebrows, nodded to himself, then jumped the ditch and re-entered the wood.

'Oh, Grandmama, I'm sorry, not for what I said to her, but that somehow . . . well, I've seemed to slip back. I actually used a swear word: it was as if I'd never learnt anything at school; I . . . I could have been one of the McLoughlins. I know I was rude but . . . but I was furious. And you know, Grandmama, I . . . I could have killed Gyp, because in holding him so I fell on him.'

'You could have also broken your neck, child.'

'Yes, yes, perhaps.'

'What swear word did you use?'

'I said, hell for leather! Like Pratt says it.'

'My! My! 'Tis well your mama isn't here.' Jessica pressed her lips together and closed her eyes. Then she added, 'How are you feeling now?'

'Better, since Peggy gave me the cordial.'

'Oh, yes, her cordial, you would feel better. I'll have to have a word with Peggy about her cordial. Did she give you much of it?'

'Oh, just a drop in the bottom of the glass, and then she filled it up with hot tea.'

'Well, now, sit yourself down there quietly and be thankful you're in one piece. I wish your parents were back. You are a responsibility. Do you know that, Nancy Ann?'

'No, I'm not really, Grandmama. What I mean is, who was to know that was going to happen? There was I, walking quietly along the road, about to turn for home, when she comes round that corner. And oh, that poor horse! *That poor horse!*'

'Never mind that poor horse. It would have been poor you if you hadn't been able to jump quick enough, by the sound of it. That horse could have trampled you.'

She did not answer but she thought, Yes, yes, it could. I could have been dead or badly crippled. So, no, I'm not going to be sorry for what I said. Grandmama's right, I could have been dead. For a moment she wished she was back at school, it was much safer there. Anyway, you were protected from mad women who didn't know how to drive . . . And she was fat, wasn't she? So fat for a young woman! . . .

They'd had a lovely dinner. Jessica didn't ask from where the pheasants came: she knew that Peggy, although not even a distant relation of the McLoughlin man, considered him in kinship, because, as she said, and often, they had both come from the old country and that made them kin under the skin. Moreover, both their feet were dry and they had no intention of paddling back across . . . the water. In other words, as translated by Hilda, they both knew where they were well off.

The meal had begun with soup; then the pheasant, with potatoes and cabbage, and buttered parsnips, followed by apple pie and cream, and, of all things at a dinner, home-made biscuits, and cheese. When that was finished, what did Hilda say? 'Shall I serve your coffee in the sitting-room, ma'am?' And Jessica had answered, 'Thank you, Hilda, that would be very nice.'

They were now sitting one at each side of the fire in the sitting-room drinking their coffee. And they smiled at each other, slightly wicked smiles because they both knew that such a repast would never have come their way in the every day course of events: on Christmas Day perhaps, but on no other.

It was towards eight o'clock that Jessica noticed her granddaughter's head was leaning against the side of the winged chair and that her eyes were closed, and she sat studying her as she thought: She'll be somebody some day, that's if she can control her temper. And now she smiled to herself, then said softly, 'Nancy Ann.'

'Oh, yes, Grandmama?'

'I should go to bed if I were you.'

'Yes, yes, I will, I'm feeling a little tired and' – she patted her stomach – 'packed full. It was a lovely meal, wasn't it?'

'Yes, it was indeed, a lovely meal. We had our own wedding party. Tomorrow morning, you must go to the kitchen and thank the girls.'

'Oh, I will. Yes, I will.'

Jessica did not need to suggest that she should keep her mouth shut when her parents returned; that would have been an insult to this child.

'Are you coming up too, Grandmama?'

'No, my dear, not yet. I would like to sit here and read for a while, because for once we've got a decent fire on.' She pulled a face which Nancy Ann copied.

'Turn up the lamp wick for me.' She motioned to the table near the end of the couch, then added, 'Come on, kiss me, then off you go.'

Nancy Ann not only kissed her grandmama, but put her arms tightly around her neck and hugged her for a moment, before she hurried from the room.

Left alone, Jessica stared into the fire, and her voice just a mutter, she said, 'Dear God! Let me live to see her settled. And don't lay on her the fate of so many only daughters who sacrifice themselves to their aging parents, particularly vicarage ones.'

She did not read, but continued to sit quietly, and the pictures in the fire led her back down her life. But she told herself she would not have a day altered, except for one thing, and that concerned her son. Until the day she drew her last breath, she would never understand what had made him choose the ministry.

When the door opened suddenly and Hilda hurried up the room, she thought, She's wanting to get cleared away. Doesn't she remember that they won't be back until tomorrow night?

'Ma'am.'

'Yes, Hilda?'

'There's a gentleman called.'

'A gentleman?' Jessica pulled herself up straight in the chair. 'A gentleman, at this hour? Who?'

Hilda swallowed deeply, then bent down and whispered, ''Tis Mr Harpcore himself. He . . . he wants to speak to you.'

Jessica allowed some seconds to pass before she said, 'Well. Well show him in.'

As she watched Hilda scurrying from the room, she thought, I didn't hear the knocker; I must have dozed off. She stroked down her hair, adjusted the lace cap that she wore on special occasions, quickly picked up a book from the table and put it on her lap, then waited.

The door opened again Hilda announced in an overloud voice, 'Mr Harpcore, ma'am.'

As the man entered the room, he glanced about him for a moment, then came swiftly towards her and, extending his hand, he said, 'I'm sorry to disturb you at this late hour, Mrs Hazel, but just a short while ago I heard that one of my guests had been the cause of your granddaughter's having to . . . well, jump into a ditch to save herself from being run down. I . . . I do hope she is none the worse.'

'Take a seat, Mr Harpcore.' She pointed to the one that Nancy Ann had vacated earlier. And she watched him flick back the tails of his long coat, pull each side of his trouser leg slightly up above the knee, and seat himself half-way into the chair. Then they were looking at each other.

It was Jessica who spoke first, saying, 'This is your second visit to the vicarage, Mr Harpcore, and both on account of my granddaughter's escapades, although I don't think she can be blamed for what happened today. Yet I understand, even from herself, that she was . . . well, to put it mildly, somewhat rude.'

He now answered her smile with his own as he said, 'I . . . I wouldn't call it rudeness, more like retaliation justly deserved, which I understand left my guest at a loss for words.'

'Yes, it would do.' Jessica nodded her head now. 'I'm afraid that is her one failing, in my eyes, anyway, her very quick temper. Fortunately, it subsides as quickly as it rises, but it is something to be encountered when at its height . . . You know she has been away at school for some time past?'

'No, no, I wasn't aware of that.'

'Oh, yes, yes.' Jessica nodded proudly now, and went on. 'She is a boarder at the Dame school in Durham, and I would have said until three o'clock this afternoon that they had done a very good job on her, filing down her rough edges. Yet, when she came in mud-bespattered, I realized it was all wishful thinking on my part.'

'Oh, no, I wouldn't say that. She was provoked. And I understand, too, from one of the grooms, that the horse the lady was driving home is in a pretty rough state and will need rest for a day or two. So, I think your granddaughter was justified in anything she said, and I just wanted you to know that I'm sorry it happened, but relieved that there is no real damage done.'

'Thank you. It was most kind of you to come. I'm sorry my son and his wife are not here to greet you. You see, my eldest grandson is being married today down in Somerset.'

'Oh, really? Really? I remember the boy. He was . . .' He paused, and she put in, 'James.'

'Yes, yes, James. How old is he now?'

'Twenty-three.'

'I understood he and his brother were at Oxford. But he must be down by now.'

'Yes, yes, last year. He passed . . . with honours?' She wasn't quite sure if that was the term.

'Really? What class? A first?

That was it. She nodded now, 'Yes, he got a first, and Peter too is doing well. And if – ' she brought her head slowly forward now and repeated, 'And if there were such careers for women, I'm sure Nancy Ann would equal her brothers because she is very bright.'

'Yes, yes, I am sure she is.'

She watched him now rise slightly then settle back into the chair. For a moment she had thought he was about to take his leave. She stared at him. How old was he now? Oh – she did a quick reckoning in her head – over thirty. Oh, yes. But not all that much, perhaps thirty-two. He wasn't all that tall, about the same height as Peter. And what was Peter? Five foot seven or eight? But he was well built, rather thickish; his hair was dark brown, yet his eyes looked light, which was a strange contrast, they were greyish she supposed. He had a full-lipped mouth, and strong looking teeth. His complexion wasn't very good: it was likely the life he led with women and drink. And then there was his gambling. He was noted for that. He spent a lot of his time in London, it was said, just gambling. And also, she had heard a little while back through Peggy, who was in touch with the assistant cook up there, another one of the Irish breed, that he had a mistress and she was a married women who didn't live twenty miles away in Northumberland. Yet, looking at him, who would guess he was such a roué? He was so polite and his manner was kindly . . . warm. She could see where his attraction lay. There was something about him that stirred even her cold blood. But why, if he needed women so badly, didn't he get himself a wife? She said now. 'Are you intending to stay long, I mean in your home?'

'Just another week or so, then I'm going to Scotland for the shoot. I . . . I have a little place up there.'

Yes, she had heard about the little place he had in Scotland, almost as big as his house here, it was said. Her feelings became bitter for a moment as she thought of the fortune it must take to run those two places, not forgetting his house in London, and here was her John Howard barely able to feed them on the pittance that he received from the church. If it hadn't been for her own money these past few years they would have had short commons, and the boys, clever as they were, would never have made Oxford. As for the staff, there would have been one little runaround. Yet here was this man keeping three houses going and a mighty staff in each just for himself and his pleasures.

Her embittered thinking was interrupted by the door bursting open and there, running up the room, came the subject of their conversation. And as Jessica uttered her name in surprise, the tone holding a reprimand, Dennison Harpcore rose swiftly from his chair and looked at the girl who was now gaping open-mouthed at him.

He was seeing a slim figure in a long white nightgown partly covered by a knee-length dressing-gown of an indistinguishable colour, except to call it a muddy grey, and from her head down each side of her cheeks and on to the dressing gown there hung three long corkscrew ringlets, and what made them noticeable was that from the ears they were entwined with strips of rag. The cream coloured skin on the oval shaped face looked stretched, as indeed it was, because the eyes were wide and the jaw dropped.

Jessica had also risen to her feet and she said, 'This is Mr Harpcore. He . . . he has called about the incident this afternoon. He wondered if you were all right.' She hesitated whether to say, 'Go back to your bed, child,' or 'Come here, child,' because there she was attired in her nightie and looking at this moment less than her age. And when, having told herself that this man was old enough to be her father, she managed to say, 'Come here, child,' Nancy Ann did not obey the order, but, hugging her dressing-gown around her, said, 'I only came down to tell you – ' She did not want to finish what she had to relate, but looking from her grandmother to the visitor, she said, 'I'm all right, sir. And . . . and I'm sorry I was rude to your guest.'

He took a step to the side but not towards her as he said, 'You have no need to apologize. My guest was at fault, and through her thoughtlessness you could have been badly hurt.' Smiling now, he added, 'We seem to meet only on occasions of disaster.'

'Yes, sir.' Within the circle of the lamplight he looked to her to be very big, very broad, very dark . . . very . . . there was something else she couldn't put a name to. It wasn't frightening, yet it wasn't pleasant. Of a sudden she said, 'Good-night, sir,' then forgetting all she had learnt at school about decorum, how a young lady should enter and leave a room, especially if there was company in it, she ran out of it.

Jessica looked towards the man. He was staring towards the door and smiling. Then he turned to her and said, 'She has grown considerably sinced we last met. She seemed such a little child then.'

'She is still a child' – there was a stiffness in Jessica's tone – 'she is but fourteen.' She did not say 'coming up fifteen', as Nancy Ann herself would have said.

'Is that all? I . . . I would have thought she was older.'

'No, that is all, she is but fourteen, and has another three years at school, by which time' – her tone altered – 'I hope she will have learned to control her temper.'

'That would be a pity, I think, if she became typed. Don't you agree?'

She thought for a moment, then said, 'She is of a turn of character that I doubt will ever conform to type.'

'Well, I hope so. So many young ladies today are turned out to pattern; you can't tell one from the other. But I must not keep you, and I must add another apology for calling upon you so late in the evening.'

He held out his hand and she took it, saying, 'I've been very pleased to meet you.' Then she added on a laugh, 'Formally. I remember when I first came to live here with my son I saw you in church one Sunday morning, but only once.' She now pulled a slight face, and he lowered his eyelids, and bent his head and there was a light touch of mockery in his voice as he said, 'I'm afraid I am a great sinner.' But when she answered, 'I'm sure you are speaking the truth there,' he lifted his head sharply and laughed aloud; then bending towards her, he said softly, 'I am sure you and I would get along very nicely were we to meet frequently.' And at this she surprised him again by saying, 'I don't know about that.'

His laughter was louder now as he said, 'That last statement proves I am right.' His manner changing suddenly, he looked at her for a moment without speaking, then said, 'So few people speak the truth while looking into your face. Your friends never, even your enemies do it behind your back.'

She watched him now bow towards her, then step back from her before turning away and walking slowly from the room.

She stood where she was until she heard Hilda say, 'Good-night, sir,' and the front door close.

When she resumed her seat by the fire, she looked into the flames and asked herself why bad men were always so attractive.

2

Nancy Ann did not stay at school for another three years, she left when she was sixteen; she refused absolutely to stay on for another year, knowing that her mother was ill.

Six months previously Rebecca had collapsed. She had been coughing quite a lot of late, in fact, she'd had what she referred to as a ticklish cough for some years, but she had refused to find out the cause. Even when Doctor McCann, on John's request, had offered to give her, what he called, a run over, she had indignantly refused. And then came the day when she collapsed and Doctor McCann did examine her. For some time he'd had his suspicions that she was suffering from tuberculosis, and this was confirmed. But it wasn't the main cause of her collapse. His examination showed her heart to be in a very bad state, and he ordered immediate rest. If she did not obey his orders, he said, there would be nothing for it but to put her into a sanatorium, which brought a reaction from her of more firmness than he had imagined she possessed: Never! Never would she go into a sanatorium. Anyway, she was needed at home.

And at home she stayed: at first protesting, albeit inwardly, then gradually becoming resigned to the fact that the time she had left to her was limited.

The breakfast-room had been turned into a bedroom. It was the most pleasant room on the ground floor, as it had a French window leading out into a small conservatory, this in turn showing a stretch of lawn bordered by the low stone wall beyond which was the road.

A single bed was placed at one side of the room, but fronting the entrance to the conservatory was a couch, and it was on this that Rebecca spent most of her days. And when the weather was fine the outer door of the conservatory was opened so she could see people passing along the road, and perhaps the occasional carriage or rider. A number of villagers, especially when on their way to church on a Sunday, would pause at the wall and wave to her, and she would wave back even if she couldn't make out who they were.

Nancy Ann had her sixteenth birthday on the ninth of January, eighteen eighty; she left school at the end of the Easter term. Now it was September and she had been acting as part nurse and housekeeper for the past six months, and but for the reason of her new role she would have said she was happy to be at home. This is what she repeatedly told herself, for up to the beginning of the year she'd had the idea of following in her brother's footsteps, not, of course, going to Oxford, but going to one of the new training colleges that fitted young ladies to become teachers. Miss Craster, head of the Dame school, had encouraged her ideas along this line. But apparently it wasn't to be.

Her disappointment was somewhat modified when she had a talk with James who, on hearing of his mother's illness, had paid a quick visit to see her. He had not been accompanied by his wife and, of course, this was natural as she was now carrying his second child. But what he said to her about teaching was, 'I shouldn't worry about missing a career, for it isn't all milk and roses, it is very nerve-racking at times. Likely, I shall get used to it. I'm new to it, I admit, but . . .'

He had stopped there. She had been troubled about James. She didn't think he was as happy as he should be, and this seemed to be borne out when, on the point of leaving, he looked around the hall and said, 'I never realized how happy I was here, Nancy Ann. All my young days it seemed to be a cold house without much comfort; I didn't take into account the love that was in it. We all helped each other, didn't we? And we had fun.' Then he had smiled and said, 'Who would have thought, in those days, when you were a fighting, punching little termagent that you would blossom into . . . well, now look at you, a beautiful young lady.'

'Oh, James.' She had flapped her hand at him, saying, 'Don't tease. Beautiful young lady indeed!'

'All right, you are not a beautiful young lady.' He had put his arms around her, and they had hugged each other. And she had been on the point of tears when she said, 'I love you. We all love you. Be happy, James.'

Only this morning they had heard that James had another son, and here they were talking about the event. She was arranging some late roses in a vase on a side table to the head of her mother's couch. Her grandmama sat at the foot plying her needle on a small embroidery frame. She had just said, 'Well, they are coming thick and fast, they are wasting no time.' And when her mother had replied, 'I think it's better to have them when you are young,' she thought how strange it was that they could talk so in front of her. Her mother's illness had seemed to change everyone in the house. Her grandmama had suddenly become quite agile, and she nearing seventy. She didn't have her fire lit in her room until the evening now, and spent most of her time in this room, and even insisted on taking her turn at the nursing. And strangely, she seemed to have got her hearing permanently back for there had been times in the past when she would apparently endure periods of deafness. She smiled at herself at the thought. Then there was the changed relationship between the two women: the antagonism that had lain under the surface for years had vanished; they had become close, they talked or sat silent together. She had come into the room one day last week and was surprised to see her grandmama patting her mother's hand. They had been talking, but the conversation stopped abruptly as she entered the room, and she guessed that their topic had been herself.

Only yesterday her mother had asked her a question that had left her absolutely tongue-tied for a moment. She had said, 'Nancy Ann, do you ever think of marriage?'

When she had got over her surprise, she had said, 'Marriage, Mama? Me? No, I don't honestly think I do. Well,' she confessed now, 'once or twice I have. When I saw Elsie Ridley married last month, I suppose I wondered then if I would ever get married, but I doubt I ever will, in fact, I'm sure I never shall.

'What makes you so sure?'

'Well whom do I know, Mama? Who would want to marry me? There are Farmer Reynolds' two sons, but one's married to the sheep and the other to the cows; and they are old, well over twenty.'

She was so pleased when she saw her mother laugh. She liked to make her laugh. And when she had added, 'Of course, there's always Mick McLoughlin. Now I know he has his eye on me,' her mother had put her hand to her chest and had started to cough, spluttering, 'Oh, Nancy Ann. Nancy Ann.'

When her coughing bout was over and she had got her breath back enough to speak, she said, ''Tis very funny about that boy McLoughlin. He was the one you fought with, wasn't he, on what was to be your last Sunday at home before you went to school, remember? And there he is, your papa says he has turned out quite smart. Of course, it is since Mr Mercer took him into his service. Your father says he looks very presentable in his livery. In a way it just shows you, there's no one so lowly that cannot be risen up if given the chance.'

It was her grandmama's voice that startled her now, saying, 'Would you like to go to a ball, Nancy Ann?'

'*A ball?*' She put the last flower in the vase, then turned and looked at her grandmama, repeating, '*A ball?*'

'That's what I said, a ball; Peter is thinking of going to one in Newcastle. You can dance, can't you?'

'Oh, yes, I can dance. I have proof of that because our singing mistress once remarked to me that what music I had was in my feet . . . But would I like to go to a ball?' She considered for a moment. 'Yes and no. I've never been to a ball. Farmer Ridley's barn dance, yes, and I got my shins kicked.' Quickly now she went into mime and, assuming the posture of a stout man, she pulled an imaginary waistcoat down, then the cuffs of her coat, squared her shoulders, and, walking over to face her grandmama and with her toes turned outwards, she bent towards her and said in a deep country burr, 'How would you like to take the floor with me, missie, eh?' And as her grandmama, laughing aloud, pushed her away, she went into an imaginary dance with the farmer: one, two three, hop; one, two, three, hop, she danced into the conservatory. Her right hand held high on the imaginary shoulder, she hopped and stumbled until her grandmama's voice came at her sharply, crying, 'No more! No more!' and she stopped abruptly and ran back to her mother who was gasping for breath, her hand pressed to her side.

'Oh, Mama, I'm sorry.'

After a moment, Rebecca relaxed into her pillow, saying, 'Don't be sorry . . . child . . . because – ' she now turned her face to look at her mother-in-law, adding as she pulled at the air, 'I don't think I've laughed so much in my life as I have done these past few months.' Then patting her daughter's hand, she said, 'You have a gift, dear. You have a gift.'

'My only one sadly.' Nancy Ann now said in a low voice.

'Nonsense!' It was her grandmama's strident tones, and she turned to her and said, 'Yes, yes, of course, Grandmama, it's nonsense: I can sing like a corncrake, play the pianoforte like Beethoven, talk rapidly in French, and sparkle in company; in fact, I'm so sought after for parties and soirées that I now have to rush and see to my staff before my maid gets to work on me for my dinner tonight at the Manor.'

'Well, you could sparkle in company, miss, if you so wished. Why, with a tongue like yours, you don't let it rattle on such occasions. I'll never know.'

'Nor shall I, Grandmama. Nor shall I. Oh.' She turned and looked towards the conservatory window, crying now, 'There's The House carriage again. I wonder what he's sending you this time? Can't be strawberries, they're over, and the girls have made enough conserve to last for years. Peaches are over too, and the apples are not quite ripe. I hope it's something this time we can get out teeth into, say, half a sheep, or a sirloin of beef; I'd even accept a brace of pheasants.'

'Oh! Nancy Ann, how can you? He has been so kind.'

'Yes, he has.' She pulled a face at her mother.

And he had. He was likeable in a way and she could talk to him quite ordinarily, that is when he was on his own, but should he be accompanied by his friend, she found herself tongue-tied, as apparently did his friend: the older man hardly ever spoke, just stared at her. She knew she didn't like him.

When she reached the kitchen it was to see Peggy at the back door taking a hamper from a liveried coachman, saying, 'Thank you, Mr Appleby. Thank you indeed.' And she heard the coachman now ask, 'How is Mrs Hazel? The master would like to know.'

'Oh, about the same, no better no worse. Between you and me she could linger on for a time, or go out like the snuff of a candle.'

Nancy Ann closed her eyes and bit down on her lip. She knew that her mother was very ill and could linger on for a time, but she never thought of her going out like the snuff of a candle. Hilda, standing near the table, saw the effect Cook's words were having on her, and so, going to the door, she said, in a loud voice, 'Here's Miss Nancy Ann, Cook.'

At this, Peggy stepped back with the hamper and Nancy Ann, going to the door, looked at the coachman and said in a quite, polite, formal tone, 'Would you please convey to your master my thanks and those of my mother and father for his kindness?'

'I shall, miss. I shall.' The man touched his cap, then moved away, and she closed the door, then turned towards the table where Peggy was already lifting the food from the hamper, exclaiming as she did so, 'My! My! Now this is better than your fruit. Two brace of pheasants. And look at that! a bottle of wine, and another. What kind will they be, miss?' She handed the bottle to Nancy Ann, and Nancy Ann, looking at the label, said 'It is Burgundy.'

'And what's in this box, miss?'

'Oh, that's cheese.'

'In a box?' Hilda put in now, and Nancy Ann answered, 'It's a French cheese.'

'My! My! I wonder what it'll taste like.'

'Well, you'll never know because all you'll get is a snip,' said Hilda.

'And here's another box, two of them. I know what's in that one, sweatmeats. Eeh! My! He's not as black as he's painted, is he?'

'Shut your mouth, Jane Bradshaw.' Hilda pushed her big ungainly companion.

'Well, I'm only sayin' what . . .'

'Get over to that sink and finish those dishes.' It was Peggy who was now going for her assistant. Then she turned to Nancy Ann saying, 'We'll put them on a couple of trays and we'll take them in to your mama to see, eh? To cheer her up. She always appreciates people's kindness, does the mistress. And them bottles'll put colour into her cheeks again, eh, miss?'

'Yes, Peggy, I'm sure they will. I'll leave you to see to it.'

'Do that, miss. Do that.'

When, a few minutes later she had finished giving her mother a list of things in the hamper, it was her grandmother who said, 'He's good at bottom. You've got to say it, he's good at bottom.'

He's not as black as he's painted, and he's good at bottom. Why did everyone insinuate that he was a bad man? Well, if not bad, not quite nice. They never spoke like that about Mr Mercer. Of course they couldn't, could they, because *he was* nice. And he wasn't what you would call a recluse any more; he was getting about, in fact he had visited her mother twice and sat talking to her about the boys. He was quite old in years, three or so older than James, but he still looked young; not handsome, yet not plain, and he was kindly in a stiff kind of way. Oh yes, he was very proper; yet he had joked with her grandmama over something Peter did when he went out in a boat one day. It was when they were very young and Peter was learning to row.

He had also sent her mother flowers and fruit, but not in such lavish quantities as came from The House. Her papa liked him, he liked him very much, but what his opinion was of Mr Harpcore she didn't know because it was his rule never to judge.

And what happened the following Sunday bore out how right her papa was.

Attendance at the Sunday services over the past months had been arranged in such a way that there was always someone left at home besides Jessica, in case of need. So on alternate Sundays Nancy Ann attended either morning service, or evening service, and this applied to Peggy, Jane, and Hilda too.

On this particular Sunday morning it was Jane's turn to attend the service which began at half-past ten. What time it ended depended on how long John decided to preach. When he was feeling strongly about anything it could be an hour. But his sermon must have been short this morning, for Jane came almost at a run up the drive and into the kitchen, which caused Nancy Ann, who was leaving by the far door, to stop as she heard her cry, 'He was there! He was there!'

'Who was there?' Peggy was in the act of cutting a shoulder of lamb into thin slices, and she repeated, 'Who was there?'

'Himself, from up above . . . The House. He was there, sitting in the front pew of the specials. And there was a lady with him, and she kept fidgeting.'

'What kind of a lady?'

'A lady. She was an old 'un. She had a bonnet on and a very fancy cape with big blue silk bows at the neck. She wasn't used to church, you could see that. And there were more staff there. Oh aye. Must have been twelve or more. Couldn't see them all from where I was sittin', and I didn't get a chance to count them 'cos when I came out they were all packed into the brakes, their noses in the air as usual. But he and the lady were in the coach. Eeh! There was quite a stir among the folks. Hat liftin', cap touchin', knee bendin', an' things. You would think it was a visitation from the Lord himself.'

'Don't be blasphemous, Jane Bradshaw . . . But how was he got up?'

'Oh, smart like, plain, but smart like. He's handsome in a way, you know. I wonder what brought him to church this mornin'? Turned over a new leaf likely.'

'Shut up! Shut your mouth! There's dishes waitin' for you there in the sink. So get your things off.'

Peggy now turned to where Nancy Ann was still standing, and she called, 'D'you hear that, miss? Good news isn't it, himself at the service?'

'Yes, Peggy, yes.' She went through the door, then closed it and walked slowly across the hall, thinking as she did so of how pleased her father would be. Oh, yes, and so would her mother. She now quickened her step into the breakfast-room. Her mother was in bed this morning: she felt a little tired, she'd said, and wouldn't rise until later in the day.

'Mama.'

'Yes, my dear?'

'Guess what?'

'Well, I don't know what I have to guess at.'

'Mr Harpcore was at church this morning.'

Her mother didn't answer for a moment, and then she said, 'He was?'

'Yes. Jane came bursting with it. He must have caused a stir.' She laughed now and, turning to her grandmama who had been sitting near the window reading but now had her full attention, she said, 'Jane seemed more surprised at the sight of him than she would have been if she had seen the devil kneeling in his pew. Why does everyone think him a wicked man?'

'He is not a wicked man.' Jessica now slapped the open pages of her book. 'He is merely a man of his time. He's only doing what many of the other so-called pious individuals in the village get up to, but he does it in a bigger way, and . . .'

'Mother-in-law!' The voice came quiet, and Jessica now swivelled round in her seat and looked out into the conservatory as she said, 'I'm sorry, I'm sorry, Rebecca. But you know yourself the poison that drips from tongues soon makes a pool.'

'Yes, yes, indeed I do, Mother-in-law.' And now Rebecca put her hand out and drew her daughter towards her, saying, 'My dear, Mr Harpcore is not a bad man in that sense. He . . . well, he has led a gay life. As . . . as your grandmama has just said, he's a man of his time: he lives in a society that acts differently from ours. Yet' – the smile on her pale face widened – ''tis amazing news that you have brought. If he has started to come to church, then it shows that he is settling down. They generally do about his age. How old would he be?' She moved her head to the side and looked towards Jessica. And the old woman, turning now and facing her again, pursed her lips and said, 'Oh thirty-three to middle thirties I should say. And as you rightly comment, Rebecca, 'tis the age for settling down, among his kind anyway.' Then looking towards Nancy Ann, she said, 'I'll just trot into the kitchen and inspect the contents of that hamper that came earlier and see there's nothing halved or quartered before it reaches us.'

As the door closed on her, Rebecca moved her head slowly on the pillow, saying, 'Your grandmama would suspect the Archangel Gabriel himself.'

'She's right though, you know.' Nancy Ann now pulled a face at her mother. 'She knows people and all their funny little ways.'

'Yes, yes, she does indeed, my dear. And she was right about Mr Harpcore. There is good in everyone. Always remember that, my dear. And there's a great deal of good in him. He has shown it with his kindness; even when he was absent from the house, his gifts still came. And they've been most welcome, haven't they?'

'Oh yes, Mama, most welcome. I . . . I've never eaten so well for age . . .' She paused now and hung her head, and Rebecca taking her hand, said lightly, 'You know you are very like your grandmama, you think a lot of your stomach.'

'Well, I have four years of workhouse diet to make up for, Mama: the food at school was really awful. I'm amazed that I didn't grow fat. A number of the other girls did.'

'You have grown just nice.' Rebecca gazed at her daughter, from her hips up to the top of her shining hair, and her thoughts were a prayer as she said, Dear Lord, let me see her safely settled before I go into Your Kingdom. Guide me to know what is right. Show me that the thoughts I am harbouring, or by wishful thinking, have substance. Show me by some sign that I am not mistaken . . .

Rebecca's prayer was answered again and again during the following months. And during this time her condition remained stable; in fact, there seemed to be a slight improvement: she coughed less, there was no trace of blood in her sputum, and the condition of her heart remained stable.

PART THREE

The Leopard's Spots

1

'So that's what it's been working up to. I imagine your visits to be in the way of finding a little amusement. Perverseness on your part as usual, going from the devil to his opponent . . . You can't mean it, Dénny? She's just a chit of a girl, you could quite well be her father.

'I'm aware of that, Larry, well aware that I am old enough to be her father. But as for her being a chit of a girl, you're wrong there. She'll be seventeen, as I understand it, in January, but she appears older; and she is a beautiful and intelligent young person.'

The two men studied each other for a moment before Laurence Freeman said, 'Have you thought of how she'll fit in here? How will she manage to run this place? Don't forget I've seen the girl. I've met her. Can you visualize her giving orders to Conway who is something of a tyrant, and in age she'll be on a par with your maids in the kitchen and . . .'

'Say no more, Larry. She'll never be on a par in a way with the maids in the kitchen. She is the daughter of a clergyman, a highly intelligent man, whose own father was a colonel in the army. Her mother is from good stock, the Bennets of Northumberland. They were poorer than their proverbial church mice, but they were of the class.'

'My! My! We have gone into their heredity, haven't we?'

'Yes, you could say that, Larry. And it might prove to you now that my future action in this matter doesn't stem from a flash in the pan; I've thought deeply on it.'

'And she . . . what does she say?'

Dennison turned away and walked down the length of the long library, and he stood looking out over the lawn to where the barrier of topiary birds cut off the view; then slowly but firmly he said, 'I have yet to find out.'

'What if she doesn't accept you?'

There was a long pause before the answer came: 'Then I am back to where I am standing now.'

Again there was a pause before Larry Freeman asked, 'Have you considered the effect on one temperamental wench of all this?'

'Yes, I have; and I hope Rene will understand . . .'

'God Almighty! I never thought to hear you utter words denoting utter stupidity. Understand? Rene Myers? God! you are besotted. Others have come and gone, but she's been firmly within your horizon for a long time. Do you think she's just going to slip away and say, "I understand Denny, dear boy. You want to take a sweet little girl into your bed, so I shall return quietly to the arms of my husband." '

'Stop it! Shut up! It isn't only Rene you're thinking about. And I must say this, Larry: I can't see you liking the changed situation when I do marry. So, if you wish to find new quarters I shall understand.'

They were facing each other now over a distance and the older man's countenance had darkened. His thin lips were drawn in tight against his teeth; his eyes unblinking held a look of anger. The whole of his tall, stiff body expressed anger. And when he spoke his words came sieved through his teeth: 'Marching orders then.'

'No, not marching orders, Larry. It's up to you. We can be friends as always, but either way I'll ever be grateful for your companionship over the years.'

'I cannot believe it.'

'What can you not believe?'

'That I'm getting my marching orders.'

'If you wish to take it like that, Larry, then that is up to you. You'll always be welcome here, but there comes a time in one's life when a stocktaking is necessary, and I have reached that stage. I have no heir and no close relative except Beatrice. And the thought of dying and the estate passing to her keeps me awake at night. Imagine the house filled with dolls. She brought twenty-five with her on her last visit.'

'Her claim could be challenged. Have you ever thought of that?'

'*No*, and I don't intend to, because there's not the slightest possibility of that happening.'

'I wouldn't be too sure.'

'You would enjoy such proceedings, wouldn't you, Larry?'

'I would find it interesting, seeing you being forced to open your eyes to the fact that for the last eight years or so he's been under your nose.'

Dennison stared at the older man. He had always seen him as a cold imperturbable individual, and he had admired this part of his character since, as a young man escaping sorrow, he had, in a way, been taken under his wordly-wise wing. It was he who introduced him to his first mistress even though he himself had been inclined to shun any such intimacy. He hadn't probed into his new friend's life, he only knew he had been cashiered from the army abroad, supposedly for an affair he'd had with a superior officer's wife. Yet he had somehow felt that wasn't the whole story. He had always found him an amusing companion because he had a cunning wit. But in latter years he had detected a possessiveness that irked at times. He had never allowed himself to admit that he was an expensive companion: friend Larry, like himself, loved to gamble, and he wasn't' always lucky, and with the passage of time whatever debts he incurred had come to be automatically settled with his own.

Now, and not for the first time, doubt about the true value of this friendship was entering his mind. But he had never seen his friend look as he was now: the calm, suave poise had gone, there was on his countenance an expression that could only be termed hate.

But no, no, he wouldn't go that far. Larry could never hate him. For one thing, he owed him too much. For the past ten years he had provided him with a home and all the advantages that went with it. No, he was wrong, the expression must be one of hurt and disappointment and, in a way, he could understand that. But then he was startled by his friend's next words, deep-throated and full of bitterness: 'If you take her you lose me . . . entirely.'

Dennison found himself stretching upwards and he knew that his face had become scarlet as it always did when it evinced temper. Indignantly he cried, 'An ultimatum? My God! you're giving me an ultimatum? Well, Larry, let me tell you this, you have the answer and I don't need to voice it, do I?'

The man glared at him, then muttered thickly, 'No, you don't. And yet I can't believe it.' He drew in a deep breath and let it slowly out before he added, 'So this is the end of an episode. Well, I'm going to say one more thing, I wish you luck with your little vicarage piece, and my God, you're going to need it, because Rene will tear you both to shreds. It's a pity she's abroad because I would like to be present when the battle begins, and begin it will.' He now brought his thin lips tightly together, and sucked them inwards before swinging around and making for the door. But there he stopped and, looking back, he demanded, 'The coach, I suppose I can order it to take me to the station?'

When Dennison made no reply to this he went out, and the sturdy panelling in the room shuddered as the door clashed to.

Dennison now sat on the window seat, but he did not look out for his eyes were closed and his hand was covering them. He leant his back against the deep stone bay and his breath escaped in a long slow sigh. It was over. It had to come one way or another. Perhaps this was as good as any, perhaps better than indicating to him that he couldn't afford his companionship any longer. He had been finding it difficult enough to pay his own gaming debts, but that last five hundred had been a bit too much. And all taken for granted.

That had been the odd thing about Larry's friendship, he had never discussed money but from the start whatever he bought, or owed, had been put down to his name. It was as if he himself could draw from a spring that would never run dry, but the spring had dwindled to a mere trickle of late, aided by both his and Rene's call on his purse.

The name brought him up from his seat and he thumped one fist into the palm of his other hand; Larry had been right about Rene's reactions. There'd be hell to pay in that quarter. For some long time now, he had to confess, he had become weary of her too. He also felt that Poulter Myers was tired of being made a cuckold of. It was known that he had his own leisure occupation, set up in a house in Newcastle, but then he was discreet about it; unlike his wife who flaunted her pastimes, and he himself had been openly declared as one of them for some time now. Of course, he must own to having enjoyed the game, for that's what it was. And she had proved to be a lively companion, often acting like a bawdy eighteenth century wench in that she lacked subtlety of any kind. Yes, what Larry had said was true, there would be hell to pay in that quarter. But he had some respite, for she was with her husband on his diplomatic business across the channel: it would be a month, perhaps two before she returned; she hated the English winters especialy in these northern climes, and undoubtedly she would spend most of her time in the South of France. It would be the longest separation between them in the last three years, and from now on it would be extended. Oh, yes – he walked up the room now, shaking his head – if he could make that charming child his wife then the disassociation with Rene would have to be extended indefinitely.

Even so, doubtless he would have to explain away, in the lightest manner of course, his past connection with Mrs Rene Poulter Myers. The parson, at a stretch, might accept that he was a man of the world, now determined to settle down, but the man's wife was another matter altogether, as was his mother. Oh, yes, as was his mother.

He sighed deeply as he gnawed at his lower lip for a moment. Tomorrow he would start his offensive by paying the vicarage a visit and inviting Miss Nancy Ann Hazel and her brother Peter, whom he understood was coming home for the Christmas holidays, to the ball, which had been a yearly event used as a means of bringing friends together for a romp. But now there must be no more such romps, and he would have to think, and think carefully, about whom he should invite.

2

Dennison sat on the straight-backed chair towards the foot of Rebecca's couch. The vicar was sitting on a straight-backed chair close to the head of the couch. The couch today was placed with its back to the bed and facing the fire. The doors leading into the conservatory were tightly closed to keep out the wind that whirled through the slack panes of glass of which there were many devoid of putty, much of it having being picked out by the hungry jackdaws in the winter.

As usual, Jessica sat nearest the fire, while furthest away from it, slightly behind her father but facing the visitor, sat Nancy Ann, trying her hardest to comply with the Dame school's training of how one should act in company: not to fidget or show too much excitement, not to laugh loudly or speak out of turn. And she managed very well till now, when, on a high note, she exclaimed, 'Yes! Yes, I'd love to come to your ball. Thank you.'

'Nancy Ann, please!' Her mother's soft voice held a deep reprimand, and she brought Nancy Ann to stillness by saying, 'It is for your father to decide.'

'Of course. I'm sorry.' She bowed her head, knowing that the guest was smiling to himself, and also, from the stiffness of her father's profile, that he didn't approve of the invitation. And she had been silly, oh, so silly to make such an outburst. Now she had placed him in a position that would make it difficult for him to refuse Mr Harpcore's request. Yes, the invitation had been for Peter too. Peter would have enjoyed the ball, she knew that. He had wanted to take her to one in Newcastle, but her mother had had a turn, and so the treat had been deferred.

'I'm sorry if my proposal has caused some embarrassment.' Dennison had risen to his feet and was looking directly at the parson, who had slowly risen from his chair too, and he went on, 'As it was the festive season I thought that perhaps your son and daughter might like to come up to the house. I used the word ball, but I think I should have explained myself better by saying there will be a select gathering of my friends. We always meet the day following Boxing Day and have a little dinner and a dance. But if it doesn't meet with your approval I'll understand. May I take my leave of you, Mrs Hazel?' He bowed towards Rebecca, adding, 'I'm glad to see you looking much better than when I was last here. May I hope the improvement continues.' He now bowed towards Jessica who, unusual for her, had not spoken one word during the time he had been in the room.

Now, to the surprise of them all, it was Rebecca who said, 'Let me assure you, Mr Harpcore, your kind offer has not caused any embarrassment, and as she has so spontaneously declared, Nancy Ann would be pleased to accept your invitation, as I'm sure will Peter when he returns.' She drew in a short shuddering breath; then looking at her daughter, she said, 'Would you see Mr Harpcore out, Nancy Ann?'

'Yes, Mama.' It was a mere whisper. And now with her head raised and eyes bright, she smiled at the visitor, then followed him after he had bowed his farewells to each of the company in turn.

In the hall, Nancy Ann handed him his greatcoat and waited for him to put it on before offering him his hat. Then smiling at him, she said bluntly, 'It nearly didn't come off, did it? That's me, I should have kept quiet and let things take their drawing-room course.' She now hunched her shoulders slightly as she added, 'That was an expression of my teacher at school. It's a silly expression, isn't it?'

He wanted to put his head back and laugh, he wanted to throw out his arms and hug her to him; he wanted . . . he wanted. But what he wanted, he realized by her manner towards him, was further away than ever, for she was treating him like a kindly uncle; she had no idea in that beautiful head of hers that he was acting as a suitor. He was tempted to put things right this very minute, but he warned himself, make haste slowly, especially in this household. So, in a conspiratorial whisper, he said, 'Yes, you nearly did put your foot in it.'

Suddenly, her face became straight and her voice serious as she said, 'I've never been to a ball; I likely won't know how to behave. But then' – she shrugged her shoulders – 'Peter will be with me. He has attended a number of balls, at least, dances.'

Again he spoke quietly; 'Well, between Peter and myself,' he said, 'we will show you the ropes.'

She smiled, then held out her hand, saying, 'Goodbye, Mr Harpcore. And may I take this opportunity to thank you for all your kindness to my mother in sending such beautiful food and fruit.'

'Oh that . . . that. Nothing. Nothing.' He went quickly from her, shaking his head; but at the bottom of the steps he turned and looked at her again, then raised his hand in a little wave. And she responded in the same way.

She stood watching him walk towards the stable to get his horse, and when he reappeared, mounted, he looked pleased to see her still standing at the top of the steps. It was she who waved first; and he responded holding the horse reined in for a moment before putting it into a trot.

After closing the door she stood looking towards the stairs. She liked him, he was nice, and she was going to a ball. She was actually going to a ball . . .

As soon as Nancy Ann had left the room with the visitor, John looked at his wife with a pained look, and there was bewilderment in his tone as he said, 'Rebecca. Why?'

She stared at him for a long moment before she said, 'I . . . I have my reasons, John. I . . . I will talk about them later. And with you, too Mother-in-law. But I think you know what they are already, don't you?'

'Yes, yes, Rebecca, I think I do.' Jessica nodded at her daughter-in-law, then looked at her son and said, 'She'll be back in a minute. This matter needs mulling over; but in the meantime, John Howard, I would advise you to act as natural as you can. In fact, show her that you're pleased she can go to the ball, or dinner or dance, or whatever it is. And besides, whatever you think, remember that she's had very little pleasure in her young life and no fun, as I see it, whatever.'

'Oh, Mother, she's happy.'

'Up to a point. But what you don't realize, my son, is that your daughter's no longer a little girl, she's a budding woman.'

'Nonsense. Nonsense. She is but sixteen.'

'She is seventeen in a matter of weeks and you know it. And your bride' – she turned her head and nodded towards Rebecca – 'was not yet eighteen when you married her. It is a small thing as yet she is asking, but what she'll say when something greater is asked of her, I don't know.'

'Greater? What do you mean, greater?' Her son looked at her, his face screwed up in inquiry, and to this his mother answered, 'Rebecca will explain it later.'

Nancy Ann had prepared the couch for her father where he slept at night at the foot of his wife's bed, having flatly refused for weeks now to sleep upstairs.

She had taken up her grandmother's last drink of the day, hot milk with a sprinkling of ginger in it. She had said good night to her parents, then had gone into the kitchen and had said good night to the girls, and while doing so had imparted to them the wonderful news that she was going to a ball. And none of them gave away the fact that they already knew this. As Peggy said, Hilda had ears like a cuddy's lugs and through practice she could move from a keyhole with the lightning speed of a young colt, all of which Hilda took as praise. But they had all oohed! and aahed! and made a fuss of her.

And now she had gone upstairs to bed, and Rebecca and John were alone.

John had been very quiet all evening. Of course, he had been sitting at a side table preparing his sermon for the coming Sunday. Nevertheless, he hadn't turned occasionally and smiled at her, as was his usual habit. And now she held out a thin hand to him, saying, 'John. Come and sit near me.'

Having obeyed her, he took her hand in his own and stroked it, and he looked tenderly into her face as she said, 'Will you hear me out?'

'I've always heard you out, my dear.'

'Yes, you have, John. Yes, you have. But I am sure you will want to interrupt what I am going to say to you now.'

When he made no answer she leant back into her pillows and rested for a moment before, in a low voice, she began. 'As you know only too well John, my days are numbered. How many are left? I don't rightly know; that depends on the good God's will, but, of late, I have prayed to Him and asked Him to spare me until I see our daughter settled.' When she felt his hand move she entwined her fingers in his, then went on. 'When I go she will take over the household. Well, she has done that already, but she will think it her duty to look after Grandmama and you for the rest of your days. Our daughter, John, is a beautiful girl. She is intelligent and so full of spirit. I would hate to think that the loneliness of the future, that of an unmarried woman, would dim that spirit. I have searched in my mind of the men of our acquaintance, and who are they? Apart from Mr Mercer, they are farmers, and tradesmen, and farmers, as you know, both old and young, are notorious for using wives as upper servants. Just think of the Bradfords, the Henleys, and the Fords, their women work harder than does our washerwoman. Anyway, the young farmers seem to be paired off immediately they leave school and usually it is to a robust daughter of another farmer. Then turn to the village. Which young man would be a suitable match for her? The Taylors? The Pollocks? The Nortons? They have seven sons among them, all worthy young men, but rough cast. And what is noticeable, at least to me, not one of them has yet turned his eyes in her direction.'

'She is but a child.'

'Please John, let me finish. And I repeat what your mama said, earlier, she's on seventeen; moreover, she is old for her years. The school did very good work on her: she is equipped for life, more so than many young girls of her age. Now I come to the point. Mr Harpcore has been very kind over these past months in sending me hampers. As you know their content has leant flavour to our diet, not, believe me, John, that I ever thought our way of eating was anything but good and wholesome.' She paused now and drew two deep breaths before going on, 'Those hampers weren't really meant for me; they were a means of gaining entry, so to speak, into our home, and my illness has given him the excuse to call. No matter how kindly his thoughts were concerning me, his main intention was to see Nancy Ann. Please, don't bow your head like that, John. I know what you think of him. He is a man of the world, and not our world; he has been known to be a womanizer and a gambler, a man of high living, but, have you noticed for the past four months – no, indeed, five months – he has remained at The House? The man is changing, if he has not already changed. One thing I feel sure of with regard to his character, he is of kindly heart, and, John, sooner or later, in fact I think sooner, he is coming to ask for her hand.'

John lifted his head and looked at this woman who to him was a dear creature, one to whom at times he put the name pious; in fact, there were times when her righteousness had grated on him, for she had been adamant in adhering to the letter of the Good Book while he himself might have looked at it with a wider view. Yet, here she was willing to let her daughter marry a man like Harpcore, a roué, a man old enough to be her father. He couldn't really believe that she was the same person with whom he had spent almost thirty years. Could the approach of death alter a person so much? He would like to think that her mind had become affected; but no, her thinking was as clear as ever, yet not, to his mind, clean. Dear God, he mustn't put the term unclean to her thoughts. She was doing what she thought best for their child. And she voiced this with her next words.

'He is a man of substance. Undoubtedly he will take her into another world, but, and I am firmly convinced of this, she will eventually lead him into her world. Apart from such a marriage securing her future, it could, in a way, John' – she now moved her head slowly as she looked at her husband – 'be the means of saving a soul. Think on that, John. Think on that.'

He couldn't think on that. He gently withdrew his hand from hers and got to his feet, and he stood with his back to her when he said, 'I cannot help but say it, Rebecca: I am amazed that you should wish for this match.'

'I knew it would affect you, John, but it is my one wish before I go to see her settled. I'll . . . I'll die happy then. The boys, they can fend for themselves, but . . . but I have seen the result so often in the parishes where you have served of good women left in a lonely existence after having done their duty by their parents. I have never brought the subject up with you before, John, but it has pained me. Most women are made for marriage, I think the same applies to men. Look at poor Mr Mercer. What a waste there, not only of his own life, but that of some good woman who could have shared it by now. John, I dread that kind of fate for my Nancy Ann, our Nancy Ann. All I ask is that you think on it, and when he comes to speak to you, as he will, deal with him as you would any man who is seeking a better way of life.'

She watched him bow his head, then slowly turn down the lamp until the wick was a mere glimmer before undressing himself.

3

Rebecca gazed at her daughter wearing what had been her own wedding dress. Miss Waters from the village had finished it only this morning, and even after three fittings there were still some adjustments to be made by the little dressmaker: for with the three petticoats underneath, the skirt still didn't look really full enough, especially over the hips. There had been the letting out of tucks here, the pulling in of tucks there and, very important, the heightening of the neckline in order to cover the breastbone.

The material looked as new as it had been when the dress was first made, because, of course, it had been turned inside out and so the pattern of the silver thread showed up much more. The only new thing on the dress was the broad blue ribbon that formed the sash, the original one had been too faded. And then there were the satin slippers, a present from Peter.

But the most surprising thing Rebecca noted about her child was the fact that she no longer looked a child or a young girl, but a young woman, for the hair style had transformed her daughter.

For the first time Nancy Ann had put her hair up, at least her grandmama and Peggy had put it up for her. Her ringlets were arranged on the top of her had and a white silk flower set in the midst of them, and when she looked at her reflection in the mirror, she couldn't believe what she saw.

For some years now she had told herself that she didn't want pretty clothes, that she didn't like frilly dresses, that she wasn't made for that kind of attire, but she also knew this way of thinking was because there was no money for pretty clothes, and, too, that her mother didn't approve of frills and furbelows. Yet here she was holding her hands out of her, tears in her eyes, and saying. 'Oh!, my dear, my dear, you look so lovely, beautiful.'

'Oh, Mama, it's . . . it's your dress.'

She watched her mother shake her head slowly and look towards her husband who was standing at the foot of the bed, and she said one word, 'John,' and he nodded at her, saying, 'Yes, my dear.

Vanity of vanities, all is vanity, but you have a beautiful daugher, and so have I.'

And now with a gallant gesture he held out his hand to Nancy Ann and said, 'Your carriage is waiting, madam.' There was a smile on his face that wasn't really a smile because it was the kind of smile she had seen on his countenance for some days now. There was a sadness in it, an acquiescence to something that puzzled her. As she took her father's hand, her grandmama appeared at the door saying, 'The horses are prancing, they'll be frozen stiff if you don't come this minute.'

'Goodbye, Mama.'

'Goodbye, my dear. Enjoy yourself.'

'I will, Mama. I will.'

She went to put her arm around her grandmother, but Jessica pushed her off, saying, 'Stop it. You'll crush your ruche.' And she pointed to the frill of lace hanging between the small breasts, then added, 'Go on, get your cloak on.'

Peter was holding out her hooded cloak; and the three maids were standing to the side, their faces expressing their admiration.

The sight of the young girl, who almost looked like a bride, was too much for Jane, and she blubbered, 'Eeh! miss, I've never seen anything so beautiful. I can't believe it's you.'

'Shut your mouth, you goat!' She had received a dig in the ribs from Peggy, who now said, 'Enjoy yourself, miss.'

Nancy Ann said again, 'I will. I will.'

'That's it,' Hilda put in; 'do that, miss. 'Tis your first ball an' you'll never forget it.' Her voice had broken, and her words suggested that she was acquainted with balls and was recalling her own adventures.

Peter was the only one who had made no comment. Gently lifting the hood over the piled hair, he smiled softly at her, but as they made for the door, he turned and looked towards his father, saying quietly, 'Don't wait up, Father, everything will be all right.' And he inclined his head forward as if to emphasize his statement.

They were at the open door now; in fact, Nancy Ann was on the top step when suddenly she turned about, rushed back into the room, and, pushing her cape wide, she reached up her arms and put them around her father's neck and kissed him; then, turning as swiftly, she rejoined Peter, who now said, 'That'll do your dress a lot of good.'

The coachman was holding a lantern. He held it high with one hand, while with the other he kept the door of the carriage open. Peter helped her up the steep steps; then he followed her; the door closed on them, and the next minute they were off and seemingly thrown into total darkness when the light from the vicarage door disappeared.

When she sought Peter's hand, he squeezed it and said, 'Stop trembling. You'll enjoy it, you'll see.'

'Yes, everyone keeps saying that, and it's all very well for you, you are used to these things.'

'Oh no, I'm not, not affairs like this. A dance, yes. Believe me, I'm as nervous as you are.'

'I don't believe you. Anyway, I'm so glad you're with me; I couldn't have come on my own. Oh' – she moved closer to him – 'it's lovely to have you at home, Peter.'

'Oops! a daisy.' They were rocking from side to side as the wheels of the carriage hit a pothole, and he, assuming a lordly manner, said, 'Disgraceful, holes in the road, I shall have them filled in tomorrow.'

She giggled, then became quiet for a moment before she said, 'Wouldn't it have been nice if James had come home for Christmas. I wrote to him and said we could put the babies in a special room and I would see that there was a fire on all the time. I . . . I told him how ill Mother was. Yet, what does he do? Writes a stiff letter back saying that Nicolette has a cold. That made me angry. Nicolette is not dying.'

'Now, now. Oh, for goodness sake! Nancy Ann, don't start and weep. Remember where you're going. And listen. Listen; I'll tell you something, James and I met for a few hours before I came home. I didn't say anything to Father or Mother about this. Well, the fact is, James is not happy.'

'That doesn't surprise me.'

'No, it may not, but what might surprise you is, he is very unhappy. He doesn't think he can stand living with Nicolette much longer.'

'What!'

''Tis true. He doesn't see his own children; and her mother has practically taken over the house. As you know, they all live together in the schoolhouse. He works ten hours a day. He's in charge of the boarders. And . . . and there is something else which I can't explain, but which is making life impossible for him. You think Mama is strictly religious; well, by the sound of it, she can't hold a candle to Nicolette.'

'But . . . but why? What do you mean? Explain yourself.'

'I . . . I can't. It is a very delicate matter. I can only say that Nicolette considers marriage mainly for . . . Oh dear me!' She felt him move restlessly on the seat, then he finished off with the word, 'Procreation.'

Procreation. Something to do with babies. Dear, dear. Her eyelids blinked rapidly.

'He badly wanted to come home and see Mother. You know what he said to me? Believe it or not, he said he was sorry he had scorned Eva McKeowan, for at least there would have been love on one side and perhaps on both sides, because love cannot but beget love. Then he contradicted that by saying, "That's not right or I wouldn't be in the state I'm in now."'

'Poor James.'

'Oops! Here we go again.' They fell against each other now and laughed. Then presently Peter said, 'I'll tell you something. I may come home. Oh, I don't mean, really home, but near Durham. You see, I'm another one who isn't very happy, at least in my work. Testing ingredients for food colouring isn't exactly an exciting occupation, and Graham Mercer has put a proposal to me. You know, or perhaps you don't, that his father endowed the Halton Grammar School outside Durham, and he is one of the governors and, as you can imagine, has some say in matters concerning the school. For some years he didn't bother with outside affairs, but now he's getting back to public life and taking an interest in the school once again. Apparently they are needing a man who can teach natural philosophy and a little mathematics and geography. I could manage a little mathematics, but the geography, oh! dear me. That's like asking me to find my way around Durham blindfold. Still, I think the post could be mine if I decide on it.'

'Oh Peter, do, do. Mother would be overjoyed. She misses you both, and I think she worries about James. You know, she didn't like his choice, no more than I did. I'm so sorry he's unhappy. Oh, but' – she squeezed his hand – 'it would be lovely if you could be near.' She paused a moment, then said, 'It was so thoughtful of Mr Mercer to offer you the post. He too has been so kind of late.'

'He's a good man, and he thinks a lot of you, you know.'

'Me?'

'Yes, you. He often speaks of you. He calls you a charming little girl, but if he was to see you now, he would drop the little girl.'

'Oh, Peter.' She shook his hand up and down. 'You are always making up compliments. Whom do you take after? Not Papa or Mama, and certainly not Grandmama.'

'I'm a special specimen, a throwback. But that was no compliment; at least what I mean is, I was recounting Graham's exact words. Oops!'

They were again jolted; but following this, they sat silent and Nancy Ann would have been surprised if she could have read her brother's thoughts, because he was asking himself: How did one suggest to another man, who had always been a benevolent friend, that he should propose marriage to his young sister before someone else got in. It might have been easy had he been otherwise than highly sensitive and not embittered by one rejection already. Likely the first thing he would say would be, I'm old enough to be her father. Well, so was this other person old enough to be her father. Of a sudden, he regretted he was taking this journey; it was like leading a lamb to the slaughter. Yet, Nancy Ann was no lamb. When it came to the push she would decide for herself. Or would she be influenced by their mama's dying wish? He knew his sister was a highly impressionable girl, she was all feelings. Oh, yes, there was no doubt about that, but she was also clear-headed and intelligent. Yet would her head rule her heart when she knew her mama's wishes? He doubted it.

'Oh, look!'

The coach was bowling between the iron gates now and on to the gravel drive which was lit by lanterns hanging from the trees, and showing here and there carriages, their shafts pointing to the ground, which meant their horses had been taken into the stables; then two or three times they were pulled to the side of the drive to allow other carriages to pass on their way out, these likely to return later. Suddenly the drive widened out into a huge forecourt brilliantly lit by lights from all the windows in the house.

The carriage stopped, the door was opened by the footman, and Peter descended, then helped her down. They were walking towards the broad steps that led to a stone terrace with a pillared portico . . . and there, coming through the wide open doors towards them, was their host. His hands outstretched, he said, 'Welcome. I hope you've not had a rough ride. Everyone's complaining of the potholes and asking why I don't see to the road. I've told them that my stretch is perfectly flat, the potholes are fronting Mercer's land. Come away in.'

He was walking by her side now, and when she entered the hall she stood blinking for a moment; she had never seen any place so brilliantly lit. Her eyes lifted to the glass chandeliers that looked to her like a galaxy of stars. Her cloak was taken from her by one of the liveried servants, who seemed to be all over the place. There was the sound of music in the distance and the buzz of voices; then a woman was standing in front of her. She was tall and was wearing a high goffered cap. Her dress was of black alpaca with a small white embroidered apron at the waist, around which was a belt supporting a chatelaine of keys.

'Mrs Conway will show you to the ladies' room, my dear.' He bowed slightly towards her and indicated that she should go with the tall person.

'This way, miss.' The woman went on ahead, across the large hall, down a corridor, past numerous doors; then pushing one open she allowed Nancy Ann to go before her, then closed it after her.

Nancy Ann stood for a moment, her back to the door, wondering what was expected of her. To the right of her, placed in a row, were a number of velvet-backed chairs, each facing a small dressing-table. Two of them were occupied, and the ladies who were powdering their faces turned and looked at her. It was a long inquisitive glance. Then they turned away again and proceeded with their toilet. She noticed immediately that one dress was blue and the other green and apparently made of silk taffeta; the skirts looked enormous.

Opposite her at the far end of the room, a huge fire was burning in the basket grate. To the left of her she saw a number of doors lining this wall. Then she felt the heat go to her face as one of the doors opened and a lady edged her way out while adjusting her skirt, and she continued to adjust it while making her way towards a table on which were two ewers and two basins, and to the side of it, a towel rack, each rail holding a number of towels.

The woman, after washing her hands, stood back and looked in the long mirror to the side of the table, then turned her gaze in the direction of the door. Her eyebrows were raised, the expression on her face saying plainly, What is the matter with you standing there?

There were long mirrors on the walls at each side of the fireplace, and now, her legs feeling like jelly, Nancy Ann made her way towards the one furthest from the ladies at the dressing-tables, and there, looking at herself, she thought, It's gone plain of a sudden. She felt dowdy, out of place. She put her hand to her hair and pushed the curls here and there, all for something to do rather than with the intention of altering their position, then opened her vanity bag and took out a handkerchief and dabbed at her lips with it. And as she did so, there came to her the muttered voice of one of the ladies, saying, 'Never! Never!' And the other answering, 'Yes I tell you, yes.' There was a pause, then as Nancy Ann adjusted her sash one of the women spoke again, saying, 'That's why the Crosbies or the Grahams aren't here.'

'Nor the Taylors, nor you know who.'

'Oh, she's still away; he was sent to Holland.'

'But this, I . . . I can't believe it.'

'You can believe it.'

Nancy Ann could see in the mirror that they were both on their feet now. She also saw that they had turned and were surveying her, the while pretending to adjust their dresses.

The last words she heard one of them utter as they left the room were, 'He's got a nerve. There'll be hell to pay.' She didn't know whom they were talking about but she guessed they were pulling someone to shreds, and swearing at that, and they ladies.

The woman at the other mirror now turned around and amazed her with her next words: 'Don't worry,' she said; 'they're a couple of bitches. You'll be all right.' And at this she went out abruptly.

Nancy Ann stood with her hand held tightly against one cheek. Those ladies, they must have been in some way referring to her, but she couldn't even recall at the moment what they had said, only that it sounded spiteful. Of a sudden she wished she had ever come, she wished she was home.

The door opened and there was the tall servant again, and the woman stared at her for some seconds before she said, 'Are you ready, miss?'

'Yes. Yes, thank you.'

She was surprised at the calm sound of her own voice. And she was further surprised that she could keep her shoulders back and her head up as she walked past the woman and into the corridor. It was, she told herself, as if she were preparing herself for a row, as she used to do years ago when any of the McLoughlins approached her. But it came to her now that this wasn't just a row she was facing, but a sort of covert battle. But why? Why? She was bewildered. Was it because Mr Harpcore had shown kindness to her mother and the family? A parson's family, she knew, was considered lowly compared to those in this house.

As she entered the hall she was surprised to see Peter standing talking to the woman who had been sitting at the other mirror. He was laughing and she was wagging her finger at him. Then she saw Mr Harpcore hurrying across the floor from the far side and before he reached them, he cried, 'Don't believe a word she says, Mr Hazel. She's a wicked woman.'

'Ah, there you are.' He turned his gaze on Nancy Ann and held it for some moments; then he put his hand out towards her while at the same time looking at the overdressed middle aged woman, saying, 'Pat, this is Miss Nancy Hazel, and this – ' he now indicated the woman, saying 'is Lady Patricia Golding.'

'How do you do?' Nancy Ann inclined her head and hesitated whether to dip her knee or not. Then Dennison said, 'Well, let us join the others.'

He now put his hand on Nancy Ann's elbow and led her across the hall and into a small ante-room, and from there into a ballroom, and such was the sight before her that she hesitated in her step, and he looked at her and she turned a quick glance on him, but didn't speak.

There was a dance in progress which she recognized as the Sir Roger de Coverley, and it was causing hoots of laughter. The dancers clapped as the end partners met in the middle of the two rows, swung round and danced away again. The orchestra, she could see, was on a raised balcony at the end of the room. There were couches and velvet seats arranged against the walls. And now, she was being led along between the seats and the dancers to the top of the room.

When she was seated on a single chair Dennison indicated the one next to her for Lady Golding, but she waved it away and, pointing to the couch to the right of Nancy Ann, she said, 'I like to spread myself. You should know that. Anyway, your seats are not big enough to take me.'

He laughed as he watched her seat herself on the couch and spread her russet-coloured gown to each side of her.

Peter had taken a stand to the side of Nancy Ann's chair, and he was gazing about him in as much wonderment as she, only his was more concealed.

'You told me you liked dancing.' Dennison was bending towards her. 'What is your favourite dance?'

She smiled up into his face, saying, 'I like the waltz.'

'Then waltz we shall.' He now bowed to her, then to Lady Golding before threading his way towards the orchestra who had just finished playing. The dancers were dispersing and not a few of them cast their glances in Nancy Ann's direction. And one lady, preparing to take her seat further along the row, changed her mind and came up to them, and, addressing Lady Golding, said, 'Hello, my dear. I didn't expect to see you tonight. I understood you were going up to town to meet George.'

'Did you, Grace? Now who could have told you that? because the last thing I heard from George was that he was chasing another bug in Africa. Well, I don't know if it was a bug or a rebel chief, anyway I'll be lucky if I and the family see him before the end of March. Now who could have misinformed you to such an extent, Grace?'

'Oh, it was just . . . well, Alice happened to mention.

'Oh, Alice. Well, you should know by now, Grace, Alice doesn't know whether she's coming or going. She doesn't know if tomorrow is Pancake Tuesday or Whistle Cock Monday.' A choking sound to her side caused Lady Golding to turn and glance at Nancy Ann, whose eyes were bright and whose finger tips were pressing her lips. Then looking at the woman again, she said, 'I am sure you would like to meet Miss Hazel. Miss Hazel, Mrs Grace Blenheim.' Then waving her hand towards Peter, she added, 'Mr Peter Hazel.' And as the lady now returned Peter's bow by slightly inclining her head, Lady Golding said, 'Happy now, Grace?'

'Oh, Pat.' The embarrassed woman turned away, her taffeta rustling as if with indignation.

Dennison, standing before them once more, was about to speak to Nancy Ann when Lady Golding said, 'I had a visit from Grace.'

'Oh, Grace.' As they smiled at each other the band struck up, and Dennison, bending towards Nancy Ann, said, 'May I have the pleasure?'

She rose, took the vanity bag from her wrist and placed it on the seat behind her, then extended her arms, placing the right one tentatively on his shoulder, and the tips of the fingers of her left hand in his palm. She felt his arm go around her waist and then she was swung into the waltz.

For the past few days she had been practising with Peter, but this was different. Her feet hardly seemed to touch the floor. This wasn't just: one-two-three; she seemed to be lifted into the flow of the music. She smiled at him and he smiled back at her, and as they reached the end of the room she became aware for the first time that they had the floor to themselves. It wasn't until they had circled the room once that other couples joined in.

He was speaking to her, but she couldn't hear what he was saying, And so she said, 'What?' when she should have said, 'Pardon?'

His face came close to hers: 'You dance beautifully.'

'You do too.'

'Thank you.'

'Different from Peter.'

'Different from Peter.' He repeated on a laugh.

And now, her mouth wide, she laughed back at him, saying, 'We've been practising.' And she laughed louder now. She was no longer aware of the couples passing them or twirling round them; she was feeling happy in a most strange kind of way. This was what was meant by being at a ball, this being held in someone's arms and floating around and around and around.

When the music stopped she opened her eyes. She hadn't known she had had them closed during the last few minutes. And as he led her back to her seat she said, 'That was lovely,' then bit on her lip and, glancing at him, her voice low, muttered, 'That was the wrong thing to say, wasn't it? My time at the Dame school was wasted.'

His laughter drew eyes towards him, and when she had taken her seat, he bent over her and said, 'That was lovely, Miss Hazel.' And at this she suppressed her laughter. Then he said, 'Excuse me, I will be back shortly.' She watched him go and talk to a group of people standing in the middle of the room; then her gaze was brought from him by Lady Golding saying, 'You enjoyed that?'

'Yes, my lady. He dances, beautifully, very light.'

'Yes, yes, he dances beautifully. And by the way, so do I.' She had now turned to Peter who was sitting to her right on the couch, adding, 'I may not look it, but I am very light on my feet, so what about you asking me for the next dance, young man? Or let us say the one after that, for the next is sure to be a polka and perhaps you'll be taking your sister.'

'My sister I see every day, ma'am, she causes me no excitement . . . I should consider it an honour to partner you in the polka, ma'am.'

Her fan now came none too gently across Peter's knuckles as she murmured, 'You may have been brought up in a vicarage, young man, but you are all there. I have gathered that much. As for you, young lady – ' she turned now towards Nancy Ann and demanded, 'what do you think of this set-up?'

'You mean, the ballroom?'

'I mean, all of it: the extravaganza, the people, the servants you trip over everywhere.'

Nancy Ann stared into the heavily powdered face before she said, and unsmiling now, 'This is my first visit here. I cannot give you my opinion of the people or the servants, only that from what I have seen of it, it seems a very beautiful house.'

'Ha! Ha! Ha!' The curled dyed hair bobbed backwards and forwards. 'Couldn't have been better said. From whom did you learn diplomacy, girl? Certainly not from your father. I've heard him preach once or twice and it's a wonder his frankness didn't empty the church. How old are you really?'

Nancy Ann didn't know quite how to take this person: she wasn't her idea of a Lady, yet she had a title. Ladies, she imagined, didn't talk like her, not did they put their finger in their ear and wag it about as she was doing now.

'Well, is it a secret?'

'No, my lady, it is no secret. I shall be seventeen years old in a fortnight's time.'

'Seventeen. I was married when I was seventeen and one week. I had three children before I was twenty and that number had swollen to eight before I was thirty. What would have happened if George, that's my husband, hadn't decided to go and look for his bugs abroad, God alone knows. I wouldn't have been still light on my feet.' The fan came once again across Peter's hands startling him now, but he laughed and looked across this amazing lady, as he thought of her, towards Nancy Ann. But there was no smile on her face and Lady Golding, noticing this leant towards her and in a soft voice said, 'You think I'm a queer old bird, don't you? I'm not really. But what I will tell you is, I am a friend of Dennison's and he's a good chap at heart.' Then raising her voice slightly, she said, 'And speaking of queer birds, wait till you meet Beatrice . . . Beatrice Boswell his cousin . . . or half, whichever, with her entourage of dolls. Now there is a funny one. She's got the sniffles at present and is wrapped up to the eyes in her room, or perhaps she is having her daily bath. She has one every day, you know.' She now turned towards Peter, saying, 'A bath every day! Have you ever heard of it; it's enough to weaken a rhinoceros, that. But then she is a bit of a rhinoceros. Ah!' She bent forward and looked down the room to where a servant was standing in green, knee-breeched livery, white stockings and black shoes, and she exclaimed, 'Controller of the menagerie.' And without pause, and now slanting her eyes towards Nancy Ann, she went on, 'I'm only putting you in the picture, dear.'

In some bewilderment Nancy Ann's eyes were brought from the woman to the servant who was now saying, 'Ladies and Gentlemen, dinner is served.'

There followed a slow rising from seats; and when the master of the house approached them, he did not stand before Nancy Ann but before Lady Golding, and it was to her he offered his arm, saying at the same time to Peter. 'You'll take your sister in, Peter, will you, please?'

As he went to move away with Lady Golding on his arm, that strange lady muttered in an aside to Nancy Ann, 'Keep close.'

Nancy Ann stood up, and when Peter drew her hand through his arm she looked at him in slight apprehension, and he smiled at her and, bending his head towards her, whispered, ''Tis as good as a play, enjoy it. Come on, into battle. Remember the McLoughlins.'

It was odd he should say that when only a short while ago she had been thinking about them. So she smiled.

The tables were set in the shape of an open-ended square. The master of the house was seated at the middle place of the upper table. Lady Golding was seated immediately to his right, and next to her was Peter. The gentleman to her own right hand was apparently called Oswald, for as such he was being addressed by the lady sitting opposite to him on the inner side of the top table. There was a great deal of cross talk and chatter and every now and again, Lady Golding would lean in front of Peter and address some remark to her.

The food was of such variety that she could not eat half that was put on her plate. And by the time they came to the puddings, she politely put her hand up to wave them away, which she thought was a shame because she loved puddings.

And then there was the wine. There were four glasses before her and only one had been filled, and that was only half full now, and she wouldn't have touched it again only that Peter, nudging her slightly, said, 'Sip on it, it's very nice. It will do you no harm.' So she sipped on it until the glass was empty; and strangely it made her feel nice.

She noticed with some amazement that Peter ate everything put before him and drank all the different wines. Of course, she told herself, Peter had been out in the world; and yet he couldn't have experienced anything like this kind of life. But he had spoken of the grand dinners they sometimes had at Oxford, so perhaps this wasn't so strange to him after all.

She was feeling very hot: she wished she could get out into the air, even freezing as it was; the room was stifling and the noise and the chatter were incessant. How long had she . . . had they all been sitting here? Oh, more than an hour, nearer two. They couldn't possibly dance again immediately after such a meal . . .

They didn't dance immediately after the meal. The ladies adjourned, some to the drawing-room, some to the powder-room. It was as she rose from the table that Lady Golding said under her breath, 'Stay by me.' And so, she stayed by her and found herself once more entering the powder-room.

Inside, Lady Golding, wending her way towards the closets, took her arm and said, 'Wait there,' then pushed unceremoniously past two ladies who themselves were waiting to enter a cubicle and who showed their annoyance at such high-handed treatment, and it was a natural reaction for them to look fully at Nancy Ann.

She stared back at them for she was becoming a little tired of the covert scrutiny that had been levelled at her during the evening, thinking as her grandmother might, with the aid of the wine, Who are they anyway? Most of them certainly didn't act like her idea of gentry.

There was loud laughter coming from the direction of one of the dressing-tables and a high voice exclaimed above the buzz, 'In future, it'll be grace before meals. If Johnny had been here tonight he would have stood up and given it to us: For what we are about to receive may the devil and the vicarage take the kindmost.'

Suddenly it bcame clear to her; it was because she was from the vicarage they were looking down on her; and, too, were jealous because Mr Harpcore had danced with her. But then a strange thought came into her head, it was more of a muzzy feeling than a thought, but it centred around why her mother had raised no objection to her coming here tonight. And why Lady Golding had taken her under her wing. Whatever it was her reaction must have astonished everyone in the room: as the door of the closet opened and Lady Golding emerged, Nancy Ann turned and, looking straight at the woman by the dressing-table, brought the room to silence by exclaiming in a loud high-falutin voice that was an exact replica of the lady who had made the statement, 'In future it'll be grace before meals. If Johnny had been here tonight he would have stood up and given it to us: For what we are about to receive may the devil and the vicarage take the hindmost.' Then in her own voice cried, 'No doubt your Johnny would have done his best, but I can assure you my father would have made a better job of it and acted like a gentleman, just as my mama would, a real lady.'

And on this, she turned from the astonished faces, almost pushing Lady Golding over, who was muttering under her breath, 'Oh, my God!' and entered the closet where she stood with her eyes tightly closed for a moment. When at last she opened them it was to see two candles burning, one at each end of a narrow shelf on which there were a row of small bowls, very like the finger bowls that had been on the dining table, and on the shelf beneath, two small copper cans of water.

The closet consisted of a wooden box with a hole in the middle, the hole being surrounded by a leather pad.

She did not use it but she poured some water into a bowl, took a small finger towel from a pile placed next to the cans and, wetting the end of it, dabbed her brow with it. Then she sat down on the edge of the wooden seat and waited. She couldn't go out there and face them again. She wanted to go home. Oh, how she wished she was home.

How long she sat there she didn't know, but there were no further sounds or rustlings coming from the other cubicles now. When she heard a tap on the door and a voice say, 'Come out, child, there's no one here,' she rose slowly and pushed back the bolt. Then she blinked rapidly in an endeavour to hold back the tears as she stared into the round and concerned face of this woman whom she thought of as old, but who had actually not yet reached fifty.

'It's all right; they're all gone.' A smile now widened the powdered face. 'They've learnt their lesson I think. Anyway, you sobered Betty Connor up. She couldn't believe the sound of her own voice. How did you do that?'

Nancy Ann gulped and said, 'I'm . . . I'm quite good at mimicry.'

'You are that. You are that. Now, come along. Stop blinking those long lashes of yours. No tears. You've won your first battle. Vicarage or no vicarage they'll not misjudge you, or him in the future. If they didn't understand why he's doing it, they will now.'

'Doing what? Who?'

Lady Golding screwed up her face now, then said, 'Oh, dear me.' And she repeated, 'Oh, dear me,' before she added, 'Come along, they'll be starting the dance again.'

'Wait a moment.' Nancy Ann put her hand tentatively on the older woman's arm. 'Could you explain?'

'No, I can't. No, I can't, my dear. I've done all the explaining and meddling that I'm going to do for this evening.'

'I . . . I would like to go home, Lady Golding.'

'*You are doing no such thing.*' The voice had changed. 'You are going into the ballroom with your head as high as it was a few minutes ago, and you are going to dance, and I don't think you'll be short of partners.'

A dance wasn't in progress as she entered the ballroom: the band was tuning up and people were standing in groups talking.

Following Lady Golding, she made her way to her seat where Peter was waiting. He had been talking to a lady, one of the few who had smiled at her kindly during the first part of the evening, and it was an apprehensive look and a shaking of the head that he greeted his sister. However, the lady stretched out her hand and patted Nancy Ann's arm, saying in an undertone, 'That was the best bit of entertainment I've had in a long while. She needed that, she's been asking for it. I only wished I'd had the courage to do it myself.' Then turning to Lady Golding, she said, 'What do you think, Pat?'

'The same as you, Flo. The same as you.'

'Ah, there they go.' The band had struck up with a polka. 'And here comes the master of the house.' The lady turned and left them, smiling and nodding her head.

As Nancy Ann went to seat herself, Dennison reached her and, thrusting out his arm towards her, said, 'No, you don't. No more sitting down for you,' and without ceremony he whirled her towards the middle of the floor and they were lost amongst the other dancers.

'Did you enjoy your meal?' he asked.

'Yes, yes, it was lovely.' She looked into his face. It was flushed and his eyes were very bright, his lips looked red and he smiled all the while. He's drunk a lot of wine, she thought.

'You know something?'

'I know very little.' And that was true, she thought; there was much explanation needed as to why she was here tonight.

'I think you are wonderful . . . a wonderful dancer.'

'It is because you are so good yourself, you make me dance.'

"I would like always to make you dance, and dance, and dance.'

Someone dunched into them, and there was much laughter and excusing; then they were off again . . .

What Lady Golding had said turned out to be true: she wasn't at a loss for partners. But no one danced as smoothly as Mr Harpcore. Some held her too tightly, some she felt she herself had to guide.

And then came another interval during which there were more refreshments.

The woman whom she had imitated was quite drunk now and she was still drinking wine and talking loudly, and for the first time during the evening Nancy Ann found herself unprotected by either her host, Lady Golding, or Peter, for her last partner had paid his respects and left her settled near a door. The maids were handing round the refreshments, but all she herself wanted was some fresh air, or to get into a room that wasn't full of people, and one that hadn't a roaring fire in the grate.

Quietly, she sidled out of the door, crossed the ante-room, then made her way down a passage which she imagined would lead her into the main hall. It was a long passage, with a number of doors. One was open, and she saw that it led into a library, and she sighed with relief as she said to herself: Nobody will think of coming into a library tonight, at least none of those guests, for most of them are much the worse for wine.

There was a fire in this room too, but it was low in the grate. She walked to the far end, where there was a desk, behind which hung two enormous curtains. To one side, was a tall Chinese screen. She looked around it and saw a small chaise-longue upholstered in red velvet. As she thankfully sank on to it, she told herself she'd like to lie down on it, but she mustn't. Anyway, it was too small. She laid her head back and let out a long slow sigh. It was wonderful, to get away from the heat and the bustle, and the noise, because the music had ceased to be music for it could hardly be heard above the chatter.

How many people were here tonight, or this morning, or whatever time it was? Sixty, she would say. She had tried to count them at dinner, but the maids and waiting men had got in the way. What a lot of servants it took to run a house like this. It was another world. Oh, she could just go to sleep here.

The next second she was sitting bolt upright when she heard the door open, then close, and a recognized voice saying, 'Well, you should have explained.' Then came Mr Harpcore's voice answering, 'There's nothing to explain so far.'

'You mean, she had no inkling?'

'No, not really, Pat.'

'Oh, my God!' There was a pause; then Lady Golding's voice came again, saying, 'There have I been all night making a bloody fool of myself. I thought she must have had some inkling and I was trying to be helpful; I imagined this was a sort of breaking-in do.'

'Breaking-in do, be damned!'

'Well, what else did you mean it to be?'

'Oh, I don't know, Pat. Quite candidly, I don't know where the hell I am. I only know I can't go on in the old way.'

'You've been a long time thinking about changing.'

'No, I haven't been a long time, only there were difficulties.'

'Yes, indeed there were difficulties, and will be in the future. Does Rene know?'

'No.'

'Well, I don't envy you the scene that lies ahead of you. Anyway, you should have put me in the picture. I only came tonight because you seemed to want me here specially.'

'I did want you specially here.'

'But what for?'

'Oh.' He paused. 'Well, to give a little balance to . . .'

'Oh, Denny, what have you got yourself into! For years I've told you you should settle down. There was Angela Dearing. I thought . . . Well, what happened there?'

'Nothing; it might seem irrational, but I didn't want a wife who had been worked over by at least two of my friends.'

'Irrational! That is the word. Oh, you men! Well, we'd better be moving into the fray again. But the quicker you bring this into the open the better, I should say, because everyone seems to have an inkling of what is going on except the one concerned.'

The door opened and closed again. She put her head on one side. What could she make of that conversation? Did it concern her? No, no. Why should it? Yet, what about those women in the toilet room scoffing . . . Was he? No, no; that was impossible, absolutely impossible. But was it? She recalled her earlier instance when it had occurred to her the reason why her mother had allowed her to accept the invitation to come here. But thinking about it now, she pooh-poohed the very idea that her mother would have such a thought in her head: her mother was a good woman, a very good woman, a God-fearing woman, and she knew that no matter how nice and kind Mr

Harpcore was, he was not what you would call a good man. She guessed that her father didn't consider him a good man. So her thoughts had been nothing but wild imaginings.

. . . Oh, she was tired. She wished she was home. Had she to go back into that ballroom? It was lovely to be quiet. But would anyone be able to be quiet in this house with so much coming and going? You practically bumped into servants at every step. Of course, they were all on duty tonight; in the usual way they would be spread all over the house, she supposed. She closed her eyes and had a mental picture of the ladies in the powder-room staring at her as she mimicked the lady at the dressing-table. Tomorrow she would make them all laugh at home by taking off some of the guests. And she would make the girls in the kitchen laugh their heads off. She'd barge in and pretend she was Lady Golding: she would stick her finger in her ear, and sniff, and nip the end of her nose between her finger and thumb, and take her tongue round her teeth and push her top lip out, and she would say, 'Oh, my God! man,' in that tone of voice . . . Eeh! no, she mustn't say that, using God's name frivolously. It was blasphemy. But hadn't Lady Golding sworn? And Mr Harpcore too? When she came to think about it, most of these people present here tonight weren't far removed from the McLoughlins. No, no; they weren't. And on this last thought she leaned her head against the back of the little couch and closed her eyes.

'My God! Where can she have got to?' Peter was sweating visibly, and for the countless time he was asking the question of Dennison, and he, with a hand on his brow, turned to Lady Golding, saying, 'You are sure, Pat, that no one said anything to her to upset her?'

'No. I've told you, man. She was dancing with Gabriel Chester when I left the room, and when I went back she wasn't there.'

Dennison now turned to his valet who was standing a little way behind him and said, 'You've searched the upper rooms, Staith?'

'Yes, sir. And the men have been up in the attics.'

Dennison gritted his teeth and walked away from the group to the far end of the hall where the housekeeper, Mrs Amelia Conway, was standing, and he almost barked at her, 'You're sure her cape's in the cloakroom?'

'Yes, sir.'

'Fetch it here.'

The housekeeper was about to pass the order to the first housemaid who was standing in a group with other maids, but thought better of it, and hurried away. She returned within a minute and held the cloak out to him.

He took it from her, then walked towards Peter, saying, 'She wouldn't have gone without her cloak not in that flimsy dress; she'd get her death out there, it's below freezing.'

'Well, if she's not in the house, she must have gone out.' Lady Golding let out a deep sigh. 'She's a young girl, she would run and she's likely reached home by now. Something must have happened after I left the ballroom. That's the best explanation I can give you.' She now turned to Peter, saying, 'And I think if you're wise, young man, you'll ride back there and find out if she's done just that.'

'I can't see her doing it, not dressed as she was. However, I'll go.' Then turning to Dennison, Peter asked, 'May I take the coach, sir?'

'Of course, of course, anything, only hurry. Get Mr Hazel's coat.' He waved to the first footman now, and the man, forgetting the dignity of his position, almost sprinted across the hall. And Dennison shouted to another liveried man, 'Take Mr Hazel to the stable, the coach will be ready. Move! man.'

Without further words, Peter followed the scurrying servant out of the room. Dennison turned to where Lady Golding was sitting on a high, black-carved, hall chair, and, his voice holding concern, he said, 'You're tired.'

'Yes, I'm tired, Denny, but I'll wait until he comes back. In the meantime, though, I'll go into the drawing-room and put my feet up.'

'Yes, yes, do that.' He hurried forward and opened the door for her, then said, 'Is there anything I can get you?'

'I think I would like a hot coffee with a little brandy.'

Having given a servant this order, he saw to the couch, and when she was seated, he said, 'For it to end like this. But I'll tell you this much, Pat, if she has been upset by anyone and I find out who it is, they'll answer to me.'

He went from the room now, and as he entered the hall the grandfather clock boomed three. It was more than half an hour since the last guest had departed, but it had been around two o'clock when Peter had first asked him where his sister was. And he had replied, 'I thought she was with you. I have been looking for her.' And he had laughed and said, 'She's likely wandered upstairs and lost herself. She won't be the first one to have done that.' But after the last carriage, with the exception of Lady Golding's, had rolled away down the drive and Nancy Ann had still not appeared, then the search had begun in earnest, and with each passing moment there had grown in him the fear, not that something dreadful had happened to her, but that she had run out into the night away from him because of something she had overheard. And it came to him that once again he was to lose someone that he loved.

Since losing his brother, he had never had any real feelings of love for anyone. He'd had the experience of three mistresses, but that wasn't love. However, since he had first set eyes on that child the day he had carried her back to the vicarage, she'd had an effect upon him. But now she was no longer a child, she was a blossoming woman and he wanted her and needed her more than he imagined he would ever want or need anyone in his life again.

Tim had been taken from him through scandal; and the aftermath of that was somewhat in this house still. And now he felt the scandal of his own past life had killed this second love.

He walked slowly along the corridor and into the library. The fire was dead but he sat down on a chair to the side of it. This was his favourite room. It was in this room he had spent wondrous days with his younger brother during the holidays. Although there had been five years between them, they had talked as equals.

He had leant forward, his elbows on his knees, his hands dangling between them when he lifted his head with a jerk and peered down the long length of the room to the far corner where the Chinese screen stood. Slowly he rose to his feet. Again he heard a rustle, and then a slight cough.

He was standing now at the foot of the small couch staring wide-eyed down on the curled up sleeping figure. She was lying on her side, her knees up, one arm above her head. Her face was dim in the shadow of the screen.

There now arose in him a great gurgle of laughter that was almost hysterical. He wanted to throw his own arms wide, toss his head back and let out a bellow. It was impossible to stop his next reaction: he was on his knees by the side of the couch, his arms were about her, his cheek touching hers and his voice muttering, 'Oh, Nancy Ann. Nancy Ann.'

When her eyes opened wide and he saw the look in them he pulled himself upright, saying, 'Please, my dear, my dear, don't be afraid. We've been looking all over for you. We . . . we thought you were lost.'

Seeing the look still on her face, he withdrew further from her and, standing up and aiming to keep the emotion from his voice, he said, 'Do you know what time it is?'

She pulled herself upright while pushing her dress over her ankles; then slowly swinging her feet to the floor, she blinked up at him, saying, 'I . . . I must have fallen asleep.'

'Yes, my dear, and . . . and you've given us all a scare.'

'Why?'

'Well, no one could find you. We had searched the house from attic to cellar. Your brother has taken the coach back to the vicarage thinking you might have run out into the night. We . . . we surmised that someone must have upset you.'

She pulled herself to her feet now, saying quietly, 'Peter has gone back? Oh! my parents will be upset.'

'Don't worry.' He put his hand out and placed it on her shoulder. 'He will be back within a matter of minutes.' Suddenly he turned from her and put his hand to his head, and this action elicited from her an immediate query. Her voice full of concern, she said, 'What is it? Are you ill?'

He did not answer straightaway. When he did, it was a mutter: 'Just a reaction at finding you alive and well. Oh! my dear.' He turned to her again and now drew her from behind the screen and down the room and to the leather couch that was facing the dead fire, and he said, 'Sit down for a moment.'

She sat down, saying now, 'Oh, I am sorry I have caused an upset, but it was the heat, and . . . and I ate too much and had wine. I'm . . . I'm sorry.'

'Don't be sorry, my dear Nancy Ann.' He had hold of both her hands now. 'I'm going to ask you something and I want you to give me just a plain straight answer. Do you like me?'

She blinked rapidly before she answered, 'Yes, yes, I like you.'

'Nothing more?'

She considered for a moment, then said, 'I . . . I hardly know you, do I? except through your kindness to Mama.'

'No; that's true. But do you think you could ever come to . . . well, more than like me?'

She turned her gaze away from his, and she began to shiver inside. 'I . . . I have never thought of you in that way,' she said and slowly withdrew her hands from his.

'Well, would you consider thinking of me in that way from now on?'

She looked straight at him now, and after a moment she said softly, 'Truthfully, I don't know. And there is Mama and Papa to consider.'

'Yes, yes, of course, I understand, but would you consider it too precipitate of me if I were to speak to your father sometime soon? I . . . I don't want to rush you. We . . . we could be friends and get to know each other more.'

She looked towards the dead ashes; then softly she said, 'Am I not too young for you?'

As her face was turned from him, he could bite tight down on his lower lip; 'No, my dear, the question is, am I too old for you? Do you consider me old?'

Slowly she turned her gaze on him once more. He was a handsome man in a sort of way, but at the moment she just could not understand why he would want to marry her. Bluntly she asked, 'How old are you?'

Unsmiling, he answered, 'I am thirty-three next birthday which is close to your own.'

'Thirty-three.' She seemed to consider. It was old but not all that old. He was sixteen years older than her, almost twice her age.

'Do I appear so old to you?'

'No' – she gave him a small smile – 'not all that old.'

'I'm glad of that, Nancy Ann.' His hands came out swiftly and caught hers again and he went on, his voice low and rapid, 'I must tell you now, I love you. I feel I have loved you for a long time and I promise that if you will marry me, I'll make it my life's work to see that you are happy.'

He could sense the increased trembling within her through her hands, and he said, 'You are not afraid of me?' Please say you are not afraid of me.'

'No. Oh no, only I have never been . . . well, I mean no one has ever said they wanted to marry me, or that they' – she lowered her gaze – 'loved me. It is all very stange; and it will all have to depend on Mama and Papa and . . .'

Suddenly he left hold of her hands and, rising to his feet, he said, 'Come. I think your brother must have returned, there is a commotion in the hall.'

But before opening the library door to let her out, he caught her hand once more and, lifting it upwards, he did not kiss it but pressed it against his cheek for a moment as he stared into her flushed face. Then, taking her by the arm, he hurried her out along the corridor and into the hall, there to see, not only her brother but her father too.

'Where was she?' It was Peter, his voice loud now and demanding; then not waiting for an answer he looked at Nancy Ann and cried, 'Where have you been?'

'I . . . I fell asleep in . . . in the library behind a screen. I . . . I was so hot. Oh! Papa.' She ran to John now and put her arms around his neck, and he patted her shoulder while he looked at the man who was now saying, 'I couldn't believe my eyes. I had been in that room half a dozen times and never thought to look behind the screen. It is a small screen in the corner of the room and hides a still smaller couch, a miniature. That's why no one thought of looking behind it. I'm sorry, sir, that you have been troubled.'

John now looked at this man whom he saw was perturbed in some way, and naturally he would be, and he said, 'I am sorry too, sir, that you have been put to so much trouble. It seems a weakness of my daughter to get into scrapes that enlist your help.'

'Father is right.' Peter was nodding at Dennison now. 'She always manages to create a stir. And it was such a lovely evening; I enjoyed myself immensely, and so did she. Didn't you?' He turned to her, and she nodded at him and, leaving her father's side, she walked the few steps until she was once again standing in front of Dennison and, holding out her hand, she said, 'Good night. And thank you for the evening and everything.'

Her words seemed to please him and he smiled warmly at her. Then going towards her father, he said, 'Couldn't I offer you something hot before you make the journey back?'

'No, thank you. Her mother is naturally perturbed, so we must make all haste and return home. And I must say again, I am sorry for the disturbance my daughter has caused. It was most inconsiderate of her, not to mention very ill-mannered. Good night, sir.'

Nancy Ann had been given her cloak by a very stiff-faced housekeeper, and her father now marshalled her before him out of the door, and down the steps to where the coach stood; but Peter, before following them, held out his hand to Dennison, saying, 'If she had been just a year younger, I would have boxed her ears.'

At this, both men laughed.

As Dennison stood on the top step and watched the coach door close on Peter, his valet came out and put a cape around his shoulders, and he made a motion of thanks with his hand, then continued to stand until the coach had disappeared into the lamplit trees bordering the drive. Presently he slowly turned and went indoors, and when he realized his valet was following him up the stairs he stopped and turned, saying, 'It's all right, Staith. Get to bed, I'll see to myself.'

'Are you sure, sir?'

'Yes, yes, I am sure.'

In his room he tore off his cravat and his velvet jacket, threw off his patent leather shoes, then dropped into the easy chair that was placed to the side of a fire that was still burning brightly and, leaning back, he closed his eyes and muttered aloud, 'Oh, Nancy Ann. Nancy Ann.' And he saw again in his mind, her sleeping face when he had first laid his head against hers. That was before the look of terror had come into her eyes. Then he muttered, 'May all the gods that be, including the parson's, stand by me in this.'

PART FOUR

The Engagement

1

The fact that Dennison should attend a church service on New Year's morning suggested to the household staff there was indeed something in the wind. The thought that he might be serious about the chit from the vicarage was really unbelievable to them; yet, all the signs pointed to the fact there were changes in the air, and the top hierarchy of the butler, the housekeeper, the valet, and the first footman were greatly disturbed. It was they who ran the household; they who, for the most part of the year, gave the orders, and especially did this apply to the valet and the housekeeper. But what was significant to all the members of the household was that this was the first New Year in the last ten that the master had not welcomed in in Scotland, where, accompanied by a number of his staff and a greater number of his friends, a riotous time was wont to be had by one and all. And what had happened here last night? The master's only company had been Lady Beatrice and Lady Golding, and at one o'clock Lady Golding had been able to walk straight to her coach while Lady Beatrice had had to be helped upstairs. It was well known she couldn't carry her drink. As for the master, well they just shook their heads: he had walked steady when he had gone upstairs at two o'clock this morning. Of course, he was used to carrying his drink; it was very rarely it floored him . . .

The fact that it had been the strangest New Year his staff had ever experienced wasn't lost on Dennison, and he wondered if the man who was sitting opposite to him now and who was attempting to cover his disapproval knew to what extent he himself had altered, if only by way of changing his life style, in order to bring himself to utter the words he had just spoken: 'I hope it comes as no surprise to you, the reason for my visit this morning. I wish to ask for your daughter in marriage.'

He watched the parson rise and then tower over him for a moment as if he were God himself; he watched the plain black-buttoned coat swell; he watched him turn away and stretch out his hand and grip the mantelpiece and look down into the fire. And when the man spoke, it seemed it was with an effort he said, 'There, in a way, you are wrong, sir, for I fail to understand why a man of your position and' – there was a sound of a deep swallow before the next words came – 'way of life, should wish to chose my daughter for a wife.'

Dennison too now rose to his feet, and quietly he said, 'May I answer that by saying, she's had such an effect upon me it has caused me to alter my way of life. I am well aware that that has not been blameless, but in defence of myself I can say that I have never knowingly hurt anyone. What I mean, if I may speak plainly, sir, is that what associations I have had have been with my own class, I have never given cause for pain or scandal to anyone below my station. It could be said of me, I have been a man of my time and class. Yet now I wish to change all that: my one desire is to settle down and have a family, and I've never met a woman in my life that I've had an affection for as for your daughter. I know she is young and I'm quite willing to wait a reasonable time if I have your permission to put my suit to her.' He dare not state that he had already made evident his suit to her. 'I promise you, sir, I shall cherish her.'

It was a full minute filled with unease before John turned from the fireplace and said, 'I must not lie to you about my feelings in this matter. You would not be my choice for a proper husband for my daughter, but my wife, who has only a certain time left to her, wishes to see her settled before that time expires. That is a factor in your favour. But finally, the choice lies with Nancy Ann herself. Naturally, I have not spoken to her of marriage so I don't know where her feelings lie, or even if she has given any thought to it at all. Young girls usually have romantic ideas, but she is of a very sensible turn of mind and older than her years, so in this matter I will trust her to make her own decision. If you will excuse me, sir, I shall send her in to you.'

Left alone, Dennison now stood with his back to the fire and looked around the room. To him it was the most depressing sight, showing not one sign of comfort. The furniture was heavy and ugly, in fact all he had seen of the rest of the house was depressing. Oh, what a different life he would open up for her. He would show her London, Paris, Rome. There was so much beauty to be seen. And how her own beauty would ripen in such surroundings.

He looked towards the door, waiting for it to open, and when after some moments it didn't, he not only became impatient, but worried. He moved from the fireplace and walked to the window, and found he was looking on to a vegetable garden that appeared full of cabbages, here and there their naked stumps standing petrified with the frost. The ground at one end was hacked into mounds as if someone had just finished digging. He swung round from the window when he heard a noise outside the door. But when it didn't open he walked quickly to the fireplace again, and now literally shivered. The room was cold and he couldn't expect a fire such as this one to heat it. He drew his lips tight in between his teeth. She wasn't coming.

When the door eventually opened, it was with an effort that he stopped himself from rushing foward; instead, smiling quietly, he went towards her and held out his hand.

Nancy Ann hesitated a second or so before placing her hand in his, and he held it whilst drawing her up the room towards the fireplace. Here, he took her other hand and they looked at each other without speaking.

Strangely, her mind wasn't in a whirl. It had stopped whirling yesterday after a talk with her grandmama who had said, 'Think hard. Forget about your mother for a moment. One thing is sure, you'll never in your life again get such an offer as he is making you. It doesn't, or very rarely does, happen to young girls in your position. Mating up with another young parson is the rule, and then, generally, bread and scrape for the rest of you life, as happened to your mother. But this, of course, is compensated for where love is. You say you like him. Well, that's a good start to any marriage. And liking, like pity, is the first cousin to love. But when you next meet him give yourself an answer to the question: Could you bear him to put his arms about you and hold you close? because marriage is made up of close proximity of the body, if not of the mind.'

Could she bear him to put his arms about her? He looked strong; she supposed, handsome. His hair was thick and of a dark brown shade; his eyes were grey, his eyebrows were dark; he was clean-shaven, but there was a faint bluish hue about his chin.

She took her eyes from his face and looked down on their joined hands. His did not seem to match his body which was thick set and sturdy looking, because they were long, the fingers thin.

'Well, Nancy Ann, what is my answer?'

She looked at him, again holding his deep gaze for a moment before saying quietly, 'Yes, I will marry you.' Then almost painfully, she went on, 'But there are conditions.' His head moved, his face stretched slightly whilst waiting for her to state these. And she did: 'You will continue to attend church on a Sunday as you have been doing of late, but now you will accompany me,' she said.

He wanted to throw back his head again and roar at her condition. She was such a child. But in the next moment she disabused him of this idea by adding, 'Because your presence there has only been a lead up to this moment, hasn't it?'

'Oh, Nancy Ann.' His tone sounded as if he were offended. 'Do you think that?'

'Oh!' Her hands were tugged from his in an impatient movement and, her voice loud, she cried, 'If . . . if we are to become acquainted, better acquainted, please don't treat me as a child and underestimate my . . . my intelligence.'

He looked at her in stupefied silence. She was right. Oh, she was right. Good gracious. She had character. In this moment she put him in mind of Pat. Yet she looked so young, so . . . so . . .

'I'm sorry. Forgive me,' he said. 'And I assure you from now on I shall not underestimate your intelligence. Oh no. And yes, you are right, it was all a lead up to this moment.' There was a slight smile at the corner of his lips now. 'What is more, I'll agree to your terms: whenever we are at home I'll accompany you to church. Is that the only term?'

Now she allowed a smile to touch her lips as she answered, 'No; there are others, but all in due course.' Her smile widened. She felt a wave of relief sweeping over her: she could talk to him like this; that must augur good for the futue.

Again he caught her hands, and drawing them together now and to the front of his high-buttoned jacket, he said sofly, 'May I kiss you?' Even as he spoke the words he was thinking that it was the first time in his life he'd asked a woman if he had permission to kiss her.

When she made no reply but blinked her eyelids rapidly, he left hold of her hands, put his arms around her and gently drew her towards him, and when he put his mouth on her lips that made no response, he felt such a surge of feeling sweep over him that he warned himself: Steady. Steady. Go easy.

It was over. She had been kissed by a man on the mouth. And it had been quite a pleasant sensation. She couldn't remember being kissed on the mouth even by her mama or grandmama; the boys and her father, of course, always kissed her on the cheek.

'Nancy Ann, you have made me a very happy man, and so now I will make you a promise that I hope I shall be able to keep, and that is, I shall never willingly cause you distress.'

That was nice of him. She liked him better the more she saw of him. And she had liked his arms about her too . . . Oh, yes she had.

'I'm forgetting the most important thing,' he said, putting his hand into the pocket of his three quarter length coat. He drew out a small box; then having opened it, he presented it to her.

She looked down on the sparkling ring. It was a gold band with a half hoop of six diamonds, and not small ones. She had never been one to wear jewellery, for the simple reason that she had only the gold pendant given to her on her last birthday by her mama, and a brooch that supposedly had belonged to her grandmother's grandmother.

He had taken the ring from its case and now, holding her hand gently, he slipped it on to the third finger of her left hand. Then, raising her hand to his lips, he kissed it saying, 'It is sealed.' Then he added, 'How say you, my dear?'

She gulped in her throat before, holding her hand in front of her face, she looked at the ring and whispered, 'Yes, it is sealed.'

'Now shall we go and show it to your mama and grandmama and your brother?'

He did not mention her father, and this omission did not pass her unnoticed. Taking her hand now, he led her down the room, but at the door he drew her to a standstill, saying softly, 'We shan't experience any privacy for some time, and so may I?' Again he was requesting that he kiss her.

She said nothing but bent slightly towards him; and this time, when he placed his mouth on hers, her lips were not as tight as they had been previously. And all the more he had to quell the urge to press her tightly to him.

On opening the door into the hall, the first person he saw was Peter, who stopped and looked towards them. And Dennison, still holding Nancy Ann's arm, led her forward, saying, 'Well, my future brother-in-law, will you wish us happiness?'

Peter glanced at him for a moment; then he looked at his sister and, taking her into his arms, he hugged her in a way that Dennision envied, saying, 'I wish you all happiness, Nancy Ann. You know that.'

'Yes, Peter. Thank you.'

Then he said, 'You just missed Father. He's gone to the church.'

'Well, we'll go and see him there after we've seen Mama and Grandmama.'

She now walked hurriedly away across the hall and into her mother's room, and it would seem that both her mother and grandmother were awaiting her entry.

At a run, she made for the bed and, without a word, bent forward and kissed her mother tenderly, then held out her hand with the ring on it.

Rebecca's thin white hands held the warm tinted one as she looked down on the ring. Then lifting her gaze to the man who was now standing at the foot of the bed, she said, 'You will be good to her?' And he answered simply, 'On my life, madam.'

Nancy Ann had now turned to her grandmama, and Jessica, the tears running freely down her face, said nothing, but pulling herself up from the chair, she held her granddaughter tightly to her. Then, as was her way, she looked at Dennison, saying bluntly now, 'You don't deserve her, you know, and I hope you realize how lucky you are.'

'I do indeed. I do indeed, madam. No one realizes it more than I do.' And bending slightly towards her, he smiled as he said, 'Now I must raise the question of how long it is before I may take the liberty and have the honour of calling you Grandmama?'

'Oh.' She flapped her hand at him. 'Time enough for that; the proceedings have just begun.'

Their attention was now drawn to the woman in the bed, for she was saying softly, 'June is a lovely month for a wedding. You can nearly always rely on the weather in June, at least towards the end.'

Dennison's countenance stretched. Nancy Ann's mother's words had utterly amazed him. He had been prepared for a fight on his hands against a long engagement, with the Parson suggesting two years, even three. But he wouldn't have had that: he would have beaten him down to a year, enough time to have the house refurbished to his bride's taste and the wedding preparations put into motion. Yet, here was the mother suggesting June.

He forced the look of surprise from his face and kept his tone flat as he said, 'Yes, indeed, June is a good month,' only to be slightly dismayed when Nancy Ann put in on a surprised note, 'June? But Mama, that is not time . . .' But she stopped as she stared at the thin face lying in the hollow of the pillow, and a great sadness overwhelmed her. She knew why her mother had proposed so early a time for the wedding and she wanted to fling herself on to her breast and cry out, 'No! No! You will have much longer than that, so much longer.' But her grandmama was deciding things for her; 'Yes, I agree with you, Rebecca, June is the right month for a wedding,' she was saying, and then she turned to Dennison: 'Are you in agreement, sir?'

'Yes. Oh, yes. That is, if it's agreeable with Nancy Ann.'

And Nancy Ann returned his look, saying, 'Yes, I'm quite agreeable.'

When Rebecca let out a thin long sigh, Jessica said, 'Away with both of you now, and go and tell the girls.'

'Oh, yes' – Nancy Ann smiled – 'we must tell the girls. They won't believe it.' And she glanced at Dennison and repeated, 'They won't believe it, but we must tell them.'

In the hall, Dennison drew her gently to a stop, saying, 'The girls. Who are the girls?'

'Oh.' She pulled in the left corner of her lip as she was wont to do when secretly amused, and now she said, 'The maids. We have three, Peggy the cook, Jane her assistant, and Hilda the housemaid.'

The quirk to her lips disappeared as he said, 'Well my dear, you go and break my glad news to them, I'll have a word with Peter.' He pointed. 'I can see him in the sitting-room.'

'Very well.' She stepped back from him, then walked slowly towards the kitchen door. It was understandable, she supposed, that he wouldn't want to meet the maids; he had a house full of servants, some of whom likely he couldn't recognize . . . And she was to be mistress of them. The thought daunted her. Would she be able to go into the kitchen and chat with them? No, never; at least she supposed not, from what she had seen of them at the ball.

Peggy had been scraping the frame of a chicken, preparatory to mincing the bits and pieces to make patties for the evening meal, and those would be preceded by soup derived from the carcass; Hilda had been preparing vegetables, while Jane had been pulling up a wooden clothes-horse on which she had just hung some wet towels. But now they were all gathered round her. Peggy, wiping her greasy hands on her apron, was indeed reacting in the way Nancy Ann had forecast to Dennison: 'I'll never believe it,' she was saying, 'that you're going up there to be mistress of that place. I'll never believe it.'

'Nor me,' cried Jane. 'You're much too young for it,' which brought a sharp rebuke from Peggy, 'Shut your mouth, you!' while Hilda said, 'Miss. Miss. 'Tis like a fairy tale. I wish you all the happiness in the world.'

'And me an' all, miss, and me an' all,' Jane put in. 'Oh, yes, I wish you happiness. We all wish you happiness. Don't we, Cook?'

Her face unsmiling now, Peggy nodded, saying somewhat sadly, 'Aye, Miss Nancy Ann, that's what we all wish you, happiness, long life, a big family, and happiness.'

'Oh, aye, a big family, ten of 'em.' Jane grinned now, and Hilda pushing her, said, 'Shut up, will you!'

'I must go.'

'Is . . . is he still here?' asked Jane now, who was always quite undaunted by her superiors' rebuffs.

'Yes, yes, he's still here.' Nancy Ann smiled at her.

'When d'you expect it to happen, miss?' Hilda asked, and when Nancy Ann answered, 'June, towards the end,' they all exclaimed loudly, 'June! So soon?'

Her face straight now, Nancy Ann answered quietly, 'Yes; Mother would like it in June.'

'Oh, aye. Aye.' Peggy nodded at her.

'Well' – Nancy Ann backed from them – 'I'll be seeing you shortly.'

'Yes, miss. Yes, miss.' They nodded at her, then sent more good wishes to her as she walked up the kitchen. But once the door had closed on her, they looked at each other and Peggy said, 'June. My God! And she not yet turned seventeen and he old enough . . . Well, he's old enough to be her father.'

'And with a name like he's got.'

This time Peggy did not silence Jane, but it was Hilda who said, 'Black sheep or white, under the skin I think there's good in him, and if there is she'll bring it out.'

2

Nancy Ann did not see her intended husband the following day, but in the early evening when it was already black dark, the coach drew up at the door and the footman delivered a very large cardboard box covered in fancy paper with a letter attached to the bow of coloured tape tying the box.

Nancy Ann took the box to her mother's room, and there, in the presence of her father and mother and grandmother, she untied the tape, leaving the letter aside for the moment, and after lifting the lid and parting the layers of fine paper, she stood gaping down at the articles of fur lying there. It was her grandmother who prompted, and in no small voice, 'Well, take them out, girl! Take them out. See what they are.'

There was a sable three-quarter length cape, a matching hat, and a large muff. The hat had a crown but the back was shaped like a bonnet and fell over the collar of the cape, and from it there dangled four strips of fur; the same trimming was on the front of the muff.

When she was attired in the outfit, her mother smiled and moved her head backwards and forwards on the pillow as if in amazement. And her grandmother's eyes glowed. Only her father showed no appreciation.

Jessica, fingering the collar of the cape, said in awe, 'Sable. Pure sable. Look at it, John Howard.'

'I can see. I can see.' And John Howard looked into his daughter's face bedecked with the fur hat and framed by the round fur collar, and he knew he should be happy for her. And he wished he could be. And in this moment he told himself, he must try, he must try. Perhaps, as Rebecca had said, their daughter could be the making of the man. He had already shown a form of courage in coming to church, for he must well know that this would have held him up to ridicule by many of his friends. Yes, he must, as his dear wife said, try to see the good in the man. And so now he smiled at his daughter, saying in as light a tone as he could muster, 'Your vanity will no doubt be increased when everyone acclaims your beauty to be enhanced.'

The compliment was precise, but nevertheless it was a compliment. Forgetting her fine apparel, she flung a hand from the muff and her arms around the tall thin man; and he held her to him for a moment. Then, pressing her from him, he said, 'It'll all be crushed.'

'Fur doesn't crush, Papa.'

'No, it only goes shiny and bald.'

They all laughed now at Jessica's remark. And when she added, 'Open the letter and see who it's from, girl,' the laughter rose.

The letter was short.

My dear one,

This, my first gift to you, I hope you find suitable.

I shall call for you tomorrow about three o'clock, with the intention of taking you to The House and introducing you to the staff and the rest of your future home.

The letter ended,

The library you are well acquainted with. If it complies with your wish I shall have a certain piece of furniture removed from there and set in your boudoir.

Ever your loving and grateful Dennison.

She folded up the sheet of paper and returned it to the envelope. It was her first love letter. She had the desire to press it tightly to her, but she told herself that would be silly, for she wasn't as yet in love with him. Yet what was love? Was it this excitement which the gift had filled her with? And more so, the tone of his letter? She liked him. Oh, she did, she did . . . But tomorrow, having to meet the staff.

She looked from one to the other, saying now, 'He wishes me to go tomorrow to The House to . . . to see what is to be done and to meet the staff.' She shook her head, then added, in a small voice, 'I'll . . . I'll be scared, so afraid. I . . . I won't know how to react.'

'Don't you be so silly.' It was her grandmama speaking again. 'You will react as you always do, sensibly, with your shoulders back and your head held up.'

The door opened as Jessica finished speaking and Hilda said, 'Parson, Mr Mercer has called. He'd like a word with you.'

'Oh, yes. Yes.'

It seemed that John left the room with relief, and his greeting of Graham Mercer was hearty. He held out his hand, saying, 'This is a pleasant surprise, Graham.'

'I hope I am not disturbing you at this hour.'

'Not at all. Not at all. You could never disturb me. Come in. Come in.' He led the way into the sitting-room and immediately went to the table and turned up the wick of the lamp, then said, 'Sit down, my friend. Sit down.'

'I won't stay long. I . . . I just want to ask you a question, even while I already know the answer. Is it true that . . . that your daughter has become engaged to Harpcore?'

It was a moment before John answered him, for he was staring at the man whom he saw was agitated. And this was strange, because his manner could usually be called sedate, even more so than his own. And so it was quietly that he answered, 'Yes. Yes, that's so.'

'Why have you allowed it?'

Again he was taken aback, albeit slightly, by the forthright question, and it flummoxed him for a moment. However, before he could give an answer Graham said, 'You know what kind of a man he is: he's an inveterate gambler; besides which . . . well, there are other things, but his gambling has made him notorious. He is, I know, a member of Tangents in Newcastle, a very unsavoury club. He also goes up to town, to London, where he is a member of one which is an absolute byword. And then there are the . . .' His head dropped forward and the words now seemed to come from between his teeth as he demanded, 'Why did you do it? Why did you allow it?'

John was totally nonplussed now; yet there was a light dawning in his mind, and he said quietly, 'Sit down.' And when Graham shook his head, he appealed, 'Please.'

When they were seated opposite to each other at either side of the fireplace, it was Graham who spoke. 'I'm . . . I'm sorry, but it came as rather a shock,' he said. 'If . . . if only I had known. You see, she is so young. I considered her so young. I was a fool, a slow fool. I've always been a fool.' He raised his head and looked at John. 'Right from the beginning of my life I've been a fool.'

'Oh, no, no.' John drew himself to the edge of his chair and put out his hand, saying, 'You are no fool, Graham, but a gentleman of rare quality. My sons have always esteemed your friendship. No, never call yourself a fool.'

'Then I can say I am fated never to know happiness because I never go about things in the right way: I always walk when I should leap; I remain dumb when I should speak. As you well know I hid myself away because I couldn't face life after one disappointment.' He bowed his head, and John said, 'I'm sorry. I can say this in all truth, I am sorry that you walked instead of leaping in this instant and remained dumb when you should have spoken. Yes, indeed, I am sorry.'

A silence ensued between them for a moment; then Graham, raising his head, said, 'Is she happy?'

'How can one say? To me she is still a child, but the womenfolk would impress that she is no longer a child but a young woman. And I suppose they are right because next week she will be seventeen years old. What she really feels, I must admit I don't know.'

'She must care for him in some way.'

'There are different shades of caring, and, as we all know, this period in a young person's life is made up of values that are often questionable. It is only later when one looks back one is amazed at having escaped the consequences of such wrong thinking. My dear Graham, I can honestly say at this moment I am sad as to the future of my daughter, but I would not have felt this in any way if I could have seen her future joined to yours.'

'Thank you.' Graham rose to his feet and John did likewise, and as they looked at each other Graham said quietly, 'You will not, of course, give her any hint of this?'

'No. No, never,' John answered.

'Thank you.'

Together they walked down the room and out into the hall, there to see Nancy Ann about to go upstairs. She was carrying the fur cape, muff, and hat across her arm. Turning, she smiled widely at the visitor, and taking a few steps towards him, she said, 'Good evening, Mr Mercer.'

'Good evening, Nancy Ann.'

He was looking at the furs across her arm, and she looked down at them too, and, as if apologizing for them, she said, 'They . . . they are a present.'

'Yes, yes, a present.'

Now she looked at her father before returning her gaze on Graham Mercer and to ask quietly, 'Did Papa tell you?'

Graham slanted his eyes towards, John, then said, 'Yes, yes, your papa told me, and . . . and I wish you happiness, Nancy Ann. I shall always wish you happiness.'

She watched him turn away and pick up his hat from a side table. She too turned away and went slowly up the stairs. What was the matter? What had they been talking about? He looked sad, different. She liked Mr Mercer. The boys thought the world of him. He had wished her happiness, but it hadn't sounded right. She hoped nothing was wrong with him. She had always liked him; he was such a nice man, a good man.

She laid the furs on her bed and as she stroked the muff her thoughts left Mr Mercer. They were so beautiful. He . . . he must have gone out today and bought them for her. He was kind. She did like him; yes, she did.

It had just begun to snow when the carriage drew up at the foot of The House steps. The doors were open and two footmen stood on the terrace, and when Dennison shouted, 'Bring an umbrella,' one of them disappeared, to reappear within a few seconds with a large umbrella, which he pushed up as he ran down the steps. And as Dennison helped Nancy Ann down from the coach the footman held it over her, and she smiled at him whilst checking herself from saying, There was no need for this, I'm quite used to snow, for the man's actions immediately brought back to her all her grandmama had said earlier on this morning.

'Now I am not saying you should be stiff-necked with servants,' she had said, 'but that lot up there aren't like those three in our kitchen. They have been with you all your life: they are connected with the family, they seem part of it and you are familiar with them, too familiar at times. But now you are going into a different world, and those up there will likely all be lined up in the hall. And whatever you do, don't attempt to shake hands, or stop and speak to any individual one. And as for your countenance, keep it pleasant, but don't smile. Somebody, likely the housekeeper or the butler, will call out their names and give you their positions. Incline your head if it's necessary, but that's all. Now remember that. And if any of the upper hierarchy take a high hand with you, walk up the steps of your position and look down on them. You know what I mean?'

Oh, she knew what her grandmama meant all right, but she was going to find great difficulty in carrying out her instructions, especially the last piece of advice: she didn't like the idea of looking down on anyone; in fact, it was against her papa's teaching. Of course, he also said that God had placed each and every one of us in a certain position in life and we had to act in that position according to our capabilities. God expected nothing more of us.

She was inside the hall now, and the warmth struck her immediately, causing her to glance towards the roaring fire set in the deep stone fireplace at the end of the room. It was deep enough for suits of armour to be placed in the alcoves at each side of it.

The butler was taking her cloak and muff and woollen gloves. She knew that the woollen gloves didn't really match the fur, but they were her best ones; as was her plain grey winter coat, and only yesterday she had turned down the cuffs because her arms had grown too long for the sleeves. It was a very nice coat, made of Melton cloth, which her grandmama had bought for her two years ago. It was the nicest coat she had ever had, and she liked it, at least she had up to this moment. But now, divested of the furs, she glanced down at herself. Her whole body looked thin and long.

Having now unbuttoned her coat, she let the butler take it. She then smoothed down the front of her blue alpaca dress. She had always thought that this was pretty, but of a sudden like her coat, it, too, felt dowdy set against the colours of the menservants' livery and the carpets and drapes in this hall. Somehow she was noticing things more now than she had done on the night of the ball.

'Come, my dear.' Dennison took her by the elbow, saying in an aside to one of the menservants, 'We will have tea in the pink drawing-room. I shall then ring when I want you to assemble them.'

He led Nancy Ann across the hall, down a broad corridor, and into a room, which she saw immediately why it was so called: the drapes at the window were pink velvet with deep tasselled pelmets; the carpet, too, had once been a bright pink but was now faded in parts; as was also the upholstery of the two velvet couches and small chairs arranged here and there. But it was a lovely room, so warm and welcoming.

He drew her towards the couch that was placed opposite the fire, another large one, not so large perhaps as the one in the hall, but piled high with burning logs and coal, which she knew immediately was an extravagance because you shouldn't burn logs and coal together: coal didn't last half as long when it was mixed with wood . . . Why was she thinking like this?

He was shaking her hands, saying now, 'Don't look so far away, look at me.'

Obediently she looked at him, and now he sid, 'This is a great occasion, our first tea together. I love this time of day, don't you?' And without waiting for an answer he went on, 'No matter where I am, I always try to have a cup of tea about this time, even if – ' ne put his face so close to hers their noses almost touched and in a mere whisper he added, 'even if I've indulged in overmuch wine.'

She kept her lips tightly together to suppress a smile; then she actually laughed aloud when he added, 'I consider it a great virtue, one I should be given recognition or an award for, that I should like tea.'

He was saying, 'I love to see you laugh,' when the door opened and the butler entered, carrying a large silver tray, on which was placed a full silver tea service. A footman followed pushing a tea trolley. It had two shelves and these were laden with plates, each holding an assortment of small sandwiches or a variety of pastries.

As the servants set about arranging the small tables to each side of them and preparing to serve tea, she was slightly embarrassed that he continued talking to her as if they weren't there, saying such things, as, 'Are you prepared for a two mile walk around the house? I must confess there are parts I haven't seen for years. And we must discuss the engagement party. Yes, that is important.'

When there came the sound of a teacup being rattled in a saucer, he turned his head abruptly, saying, 'Leave them . . . leave it. We'll see to it.'

Both men bowed towards him, then hastily went from the room. Smiling at her, Dennison rose from the couch, saying, 'Men are clumsy with teacups. I am myself. Will you do the honours?'

She was quite used to serving the tea, but her hands trembled as she lifted the silver teapot. Then abruptly placing it back on its stand, she said, 'If they made' – she nodded towards the door – 'a tinkle with the cups, I'm going to make a clatter, because . . . well, I'm as nervous as a kitten. And . . . and look, there's a lemon here and milk, which do you want?'

The answer she was given was a loud laugh, almost a bellow, as he flopped back on to the couch, very like the boys would do when something amused them greatly. And it brought her from the table to stand looking down at him. He had one arm tightly around his waist and she noticed with amazement that tears of laughter were running down his cheeks. She herself couldn't really see anything at all very funny in what she had said; but then of a sudden she felt herself gripped and pulled down on to the couch, almost across his knees. And now he was holding her close and crying, 'Nancy Ann, you are delightful. You're as fresh as the wind from the sea. Oh, I love you, I love you, my dear.' And he hugged her to him tightly, kissing her face, not just her mouth, but her eyes, her cheeks, the tip of her nose, and then her lips. And when at last his face moved away from her she was gasping for breath and his voice came to her softly now, saying, 'Believe me, Nancy Ann, I love you. I love you so much I wonder just how I've lived without you for so long. Say that you will grow to love me. Come, say it.'

There was a constriction in her throat, and there was a feeling inside of her that wasn't unpleasant: she was so relieved that his caress hadn't aroused fear in her. Her voice came very small as she said, 'I . . . I think I might. I'll try.' She croaked in her throat, then coughed, and he laughed and pulled her to him again, but gently now; then playfully, almost as one of the boys might have done, but less roughly, he pushed her away, saying, 'I have lemon in my tea, woman. What do you have?'

'Milk.'

She was at the table again and she noticed that there was a silver strainer resting on each cup. Dear, dear; they were afraid of a few tea-leaves. Well!

She poured out the tea, then said, 'Do I squeeze the lemon in?'

Now he was standing beside her and pointing to a silver half-moon shaped object with two small handles attached to the middle. He picked it up, opened it out, took a half slice of lemon, placed it between the two silver half-moons; then, holding it over the tea, he pressed it, and the juice was squeezed out. Then looking sternly at her, he said, 'Miss, you have a lot to learn before I can take you into my service.'

And she answering in what she thought a similar vein, and mimicking Peggy's voice, said, 'I don't think I'll accept your service; it's too finicky, sir.' And at this he swung her round towards him, almost upsetting the cup of tea, and holding her by the shoulders, he said, 'That was said in fun, but it frightens me.'

'Oh, I'm sorry, mister, I am that, I am that.' This was said in Mrs

McLoughlin's voice, and she closed her eyes and tried to suppress a smile.

'Yes, you are a clever mime, aren't you? You've got it to a fine art. But don't you dare mimic me.'

'No, Mr Harpcore, I won't. I won't.' She was enjoying herself when he said, 'You've never called me by my name yet.'

Her eyelids were blinking as she answered, 'I know. It is Dennison.'

'I can't stand the sound of that. I'm known as Denny to most of my friends, and I would like my wife to think of me as Denny.'

His wife. The thought brought the colour flooding to her face, and she turned from him and picked up his cup of tea and handed it to him. But he waited until she had taken up hers too, and was seated, before he took his place beside her. Then reaching out and pulling the trolley towards him, he said, 'Let's look at what they've given us,' and he lifted the end of one sandwich, saying, 'Salmon;' then another, saying, 'Paté;' and another, saying now, 'I don't know what this is. But anyway, come along, let us eat, because you know, I haven't broken my fast since breakfast time. You madam, have ruined my appetite. Do you know that?' . . .

It was almost half an hour later when he rang the bell. And when the butler appeared he said, 'We shall be ready for you in five minutes, Trice.'

'Very good, sir.' The man closed the door, and Dennison turning to Nancy Ann, said, 'Well, are you ready for battle?'

'I'm . . . I'm afraid . . . really I am. There are so many of them. Why do you need so many servants?'

'Well, my dear, it is a very large establishment.'

'Are there as many in your other houses?'

'Oh, no. There are only four permanently in the London house, and, really, that's a very ordinary place. It's one of a terrace, you know, and in three storeys. The only outstanding thing about it is it has a magnificent stairway. I . . . I think there are only ten rooms apart from the basement. If I'm staying there for any length of time, I take staff from here. Now Scotland. Oh well, that's a different kettle of fish altogether: it's a nice old place, not over large but it's got quite a bit of land. But once we go up there we could stay for a few months. It all depends upon the weather and the fishing and shooting and so on . . . Don't look so concerned, my dear; you'll enjoy it all, I promise you. I'll make it my business to see that you do. Have you ever done any shooting?'

Her answer came prompt and from a straight face, 'No, and I never want to shoot. I . . . I think it's cruel.'

She watched him close his eyes and bow his head slightly. 'We must go into this question, my dear, concerning your likes and dislikes,' he said; 'all our likes and dislikes . . .' Then he asked the question, 'Do you like roast meat, roast lamb, roast pheasant, or chicken? I can see you do. Well, we'll talk about it later. What do you say?'

She could say nothing. She just wiped her mouth with a napkin, smoothed up the sides of her hair towards the rolls on the top, tugged at the waist of her dress, then smiling faintly at him, she said, 'I'm ready.'

'My dear, dear.' He leant towards her and kissed her gently on the lips; then taking her hands, he led her down the room and into the passage. But there, he relinquished his hold. And now slanting his eyes towards her, he lifted his chin. But she had no need to take the hint for she was following her grandmama's instructions: her shoulders were back, her head up, her chin, not out, but drawn slightly into her neck. But then, her brave front almost dissolved when she entered the hall and saw the long line of servants stretching from one end of it to the other.

Two men were standing apart, together with the housekeeper, and Dennison turned towards them and indicated first the shorter of the two men, saying, 'This is Staith, my man, and Trice the butler. You have met Mrs Conway, the housekeeper.'

As the three people inclined their heads one after the other towards her, she moved hers slightly in recognition of the introduction. Then addressing the housekeeper, Dennison said, 'You may take over now, Mrs Conway.'

The housekeeper stepped forward and, her manner matching her prim voice, pointed to the first man in the row, saying, 'John McTaggart, first footman.' Then moving down the line, she went on, 'Henry Robertson, second footman.' Now she came to the maids. 'First housemaid, Jane Renton. Second housemaid, Annie Fuller. Top floor maid, Pattie Anderson. Lily Sheeney, cook. Assistant cook, Sarah Brown. Vegetable maid, Mary Carter. Scullery maid, Florie Kilpatrick. First seamstress, Mary White. Second seamstress, Lily Davison. Third seamstress, Daisy Fulton. Boot-boy, Jimmy Tool.' The bowing of the heads and dipping of the knees were deeper now as she got towards the end of the line.

At the name of the boot-boy she paused. This was certainly not the child she had seen by the river all those years ago. This boy had red hair and a small pinched face.

The stiff voice of the housekeeper went on: 'Laundress, Kathie Smart. Assistant laundress, May Stout. Washer, Jane Cook.'

They had come to the end of the line but, going off at right angles, was another line of men. And now it was the butler who came slowly down the hallway and, when he reached Nancy Ann, in matching censorious tones he said as he pointed to a man in his late fifties, 'William Appleby, coachman.' Then to the next man, middle-aged this one: 'David Gillespie, groom.' Then two men in their thirties: 'Johnny Winter, stable-boy . . . Jimmy Pollock, second stable-boy.'

And now turning to her, he looked her in the face, saying, 'The gardeners and the lodge-keepers come under the farm management, miss.'

She stood still for a moment looking fully back into the face of this superior individual, whom she instinctively knew would not have used that tone to her had he been at the other end of the hall and still within hearing of his master. She was quite good at remembering faces and names. It wasn't hard to remember this man's name, Trice, because Peggy was wont to say to Jane, 'I don't want it in a minute, I want it in a trice.' And so, her voice cool and clear sounding, she said, 'Thank you, Trice,' before turning to the housekeeper and surprising her by adding, 'And you Mrs Conway, thank you also.' Then she walked back up the line of staring faces and here and there an open mouth, and when she reached Dennison, she smiled at him and to his surprise and not a little amazement, she said coolly, 'That is over, shall we now look around the house?'

After a moment's pause and a successful attempt not to smile, he said, 'Yes, my dear. Of course, of course.' And with that they both walked away and towards the pink drawing-room again; and once inside, she leant against the door and closed her eyes, and he, standing before her, said, 'You did perfectly, magnificently.'

'They don't like me.'

'What?'

'They don't like me, at least those at the top.'

'Nonsense. What makes you think that?'

'I know. I somehow listen to voices, even when I'm not aware of doing so. I can sense what is behind their tone. It's to do with the mimicking, I think.'

'Well, my dear, as clever as you are at mimicking, I think you are wrong here for they cannot help but like you. Just . . . just give them time. They've never had a mistress in this house since my mother died, and that is a long, long time ago. Come.' His voice was quiet. He held out his hand and they turned and went through the doorway again, and she began her inspection of the house that was to be her home.

3

The neighbouring gentry responded to the news of Dennison Harpcore's engagement in various ways, but all showed astonishment, except of course those who had attended the Christmas ball: 'Well, we could have told you so,' was their comment.

Generally, the reactions came from those neighbours near at hand who could not believe that the gambling, womanizing owner of the Rossburn estate should take for a wife a parson's daughter, and her just a slip of a girl. It was indecent, some said; others, that they had heard of such men marrying their housekeepers, but a parson's daughter! And the parson himself of such little account, for St George's covered a very sparse and indifferent parish. True, it had within its bounds two estates, but you couldn't say either of them patronized the church. A few of the staff might be sent from Rossburn, but Graham Mercer of the manor had never darkened the church's door for years, nor anybody else's door for that matter, until recently.

Particularly was it being asked by the wives, how a chit like that was going to manage such a household and staff. And that same question was loudly asked in The House itself immediately after the inspection of the staff. There was a meeting in Mrs Amelia Conway's sitting-room, and she demanded of the butler, 'Did you see the way she spoke to me, Edward? She was put up to it, I'm sure of that, because she looked like a scared kitten the night she came to the ball. And there she was, walking down the row as if she had been brought up among the best. My God! We're in for something.'

'Don't take on, Amelia.' The first footman interposed. 'There's ways and means of putting her in her place. And the wedding hasn't come off yet. Mr Staith here' – he nodded towards the valet – 'pointed that out to me.' It was noticeable that John McTaggart didn't call the valet by his Christian name, but gave him his title.

'And what would they be?' asked the houskeeper.

Roger Staith stroked back the thinning hair on the top of his head, and his manner precise as always, he said, 'Mrs Poulter Myers should be returning soon. Can you imagine what her reaction will be to the news? But more so, the reaction of the vicarage sprite when she comes up against the formidable Rene. And you cannot imagine that plump little lady withdrawing her claws from the master, now can you? She's already lasted longer than any of them, and for the simple reason that she wouldn't let go, not because he still wants her. You remember Miss Honor Campbell? He seemed to favour her about three years ago when he made those frequent visits to Scotland and stayed with her people. We thought that might be serious, didn't we? But the fair Rene put an end to that. I happened to be there at the kill. It was a shoot in more ways than one. Madam Rene wasn't invited, but she landed, and was all charm to Miss Campbell. Even so she managed to make it evident that she was still warming his bed at night. So' – he spread out his hands, very much as a Frenchman might do – 'I say leave it, and us await events. And what is more, a little bird perched on the wings of Appleby while he's ploughed backwards and forwards with the coach to the vicarage these past few days has told me it would seem that the vicar himself, if one is to go by his countenance, is not the happiest of men over the arrangement.'

'Then why has he allowed it?'

The valet turned and looked at the housekeeper. 'That I have yet to find out. The mother is sick unto death, they say, but there is a formidable grandmother in the background. And, from what I can gather, the parson is as poor as his own church mice and that it is his mother who has the money and has been the means of sending her two grandsons to university. So likely, she is the power behind the throne. However, we must all be patient, and we must all assume a front of acceptance, because' – he now rose to his feet – 'we all know where we are well off, don't we?'

With this, the valet left the room, and the butler and the housekeeper looked at each other. Neither of them liked the man because they knew that he assumed, and this was a word he frequently used, that he ran the household, whereas they considered that the power behind the particular throne of the master of the house was themselves, each in his or her own way.

4

The morning following the inspection Nancy Ann kept her mother and grandmother laughing as she mimicked the butler and the housekeeper, then began an imitation of herself walking down the line of servants. But in the middle of doing this she stopped and, looking towards her grandmother, she exclaimed, 'That's odd, Grandmama.'

'What is, dear?'

'That nice looking young woman that comes to church every Sunday with the other two. She wasn't there.'

'Oh, she must have been. She's one of the staff.'

'She wasn't. Now I come to think of it, I recognized one of the woman that usually accompanies her, but *she* wasn't there. I must ask him when . . .'

'No, don't do that.' Her grandmother's chin and finger were both raised.

'But why, Grandmama?'

It was her mother who answered now, saying, 'Do as your grandmama says. She is, as your grandmama explained to you some long time ago, the mother of the little boy you saw by the river that day, and he is the cause of some embarrassment and hurt to . . . to Mr Harpcore. you would be wise to leave that matter alone, dear. Anyway' – she drew in three short breaths before going on – 'tell us more about the house, and then what your arrangements are for today.'

'Oh.' Nancy Ann sat down by the side of the bed and took her mother's hand, but she looked into space as she said, 'The house. I . . . I don't know where to begin. And apparently I've only seen a portion of it. Well, there's the hall, with the biggest fireplace one could ever imagine. It's half as big as this room. Oh, yes, half as big. And it has a suit of armour standing in each alcove. You expect them to turn round and poke the fire.' She shook her mother's hand gently and laughed. 'And the walls of the hall inside are the same as outside, bare stone, but they are softened here and there with banners and tapestries.'

'Oh? Banners and tapestries?' her grandmama put in. 'But the family doesn't go all that far back. But go on, I'm sorry I stopped you.'

And she went on: 'The big drawing-room, that's mostly in blue: blue carpet, blue velvet couch and chairs, lots of little tables with knick-knacks on them. Of course – ' she now looked at her mother and nodded, 'they won't be just knick-knacks. I'll likely become better acquainted with them later. Then there is the room I told you about earlier on, the little pink drawing-room. That's pretty and cosy. Oh, what else?' She put her head back. 'There is the ballroom, and the powder-room. Oh, yes, the powder-room.' She did not go on to explain why she had emphasized the powder-room, but continued, 'There is a huge dining-room; the centre table alone seats twenty-six, so Dennison . . . Denny informed me.' She now turned towards her grandmama, explaining, 'I have to call him that, he doesn't like Dennison.'

'Well, it's a nice name . . . Denny. Yes, a very nice name.'

'Then there was a breakfast-room and further along the corridor, the library. Oh, that's a splendid room, the library.' She nodded to herself.

'What about the kitchens?'

'He . . . he didn't take me into that quarter; he said I'd be acquainted with them soon enough. I only know there's a servants' hall, and that the butler, the valet, and the housekeeper dine together, and that she has a bedroom and sitting-room of her own on the ground floor. I think most of the staff sleep in the attics, but three married ones have cottages in the grounds. Oh, there seem to be so many wings in the house. The east wing, the west wing,' she said, waving her hand from side to side, then added on a laugh, 'It's a wonder it doesn't take off.' Then more soberly now she continued: 'The bedrooms are a maze. There's a section of guest-rooms with dressing-rooms attached. I lost count; I think there must be twelve or more.' She lowered her eyes now as if in some confusion, and her voice slowed as she went on, 'I am to have a rest room, boudoir, he called it. It is to one side of the bedroom. At the other side there is a large dressing-room, then another smaller bedroom beyond, and then offices. These are on both sides of the bedrooms.' She did not go on to explain what the offices were, but it was evident to the two older women, and both nodded their heads.

More brightly now, she said, 'All the rooms were very pleasant. Well, really lovely. One of them has a balcony.' She did not say, 'It is to be our bedroom,' but went on, 'It is edged with beautiful wrought-iron railings. And the view from there is simply marvellous. I saw our chimneys.'

'You didn't!'

'Yes, I did, Grandmama. You know we are in somewhat of a hollow here, and there were our chimneys just above the outline of the trees.' She looked into space again for a moment and, more to herself than to them, she said, 'Yes, I saw our chimneys.'

'Well, go on.'

She obeyed her grandmama's command and described the billiard room, the gentlemen's smoking-room, the endless flights of stairs, and when she came to the long steep ones that led to what used to be the nurseries, she said, 'There is a rocking-horse still up there, and a great big iron fireguard around the fire. And there's a little schoolroom.' Her smile widened. 'The table is all marked where names have been cut out.' She paused here, remembering that she had begun to read them out but Dennison had pulled her away, almost roughly, saying, 'Leave that, leave that.' And then, half in apology, he had added, 'Some of those names go back fifty years; we could spend all day. Come.'

Her mother said now, 'Where are you going today?'

'Into Newcastle, mama. You'll never guess what for.'

'No, I'll never guess.' The thin lips moved into a smile.

'To choose satin material for the panels in my boudoir.'

'Satin material for the panels?'

She turned to her grandmama. 'Yes. The room isn't papered. The walls have narrow panels, wooden panels, made like long picture frames, but in between is satin. It is very faded, and torn in one or two places, so I am going to choose – ' her head now moved in a deep obesiance as she added, 'satin panels.' Then she ended soberly, 'Of all things in the world, satin panels.'

'What do you think of the house as a whole?'

She didn't look at her grandmama but bit on her lip and looked down at the hand she was holding before she said, 'It is beautiful, but . . . but much too large, and sort of . . . well – ' She seemed to search for a word, then said, 'Lonely, in a way.'

'Well, it is a house that's been used to a lot of company and I'm sure it will be again.'

She didn't answer her grandmama, but she thought: I hope not. And thinking back to the ball, she emphasized her thoughts: *Oh, I hope not.*

5

It was towards the end of January, and the arrangements for the wedding were already going ahead. A day never passed but he would go to the vicarage, always with the intent of bringing her over to The House for even a short time. Often she would say she had too much to do, or her mother wasn't well enough to be left, but nearly always Rebecca would give the final word, sayng that she had five people running round after her, in one way or another, and that surely she could spare her daughter for an hour or two.

Dennison had come to like his future mother-in-law very much. She was an ally, had been, he recognized, from the beginning; as, too, was the grandmother. Oh, yes, the grandmother was for him. But in no way had he so far penetrated the reserve of the parson.

It was eleven o'clock in the morning. Dennison was preparing for yet another journey along the road that had become so familiar to him over the past weeks. His valet had just handed him a freshly cut cigar when there came a tap on the door and the first footman entered, saying, 'Mrs Poulter Myers has called, sir.'

The cigar half-way to his lips, he looked from the footman to his valet, and for almost a full minute he remained silent. Then turning from the men, he walked to the window, saying, 'Where have you put her?'

'She went into the drawing-room, sir.'

Of course Rene wouldn't be put anywhere, she would go where she willed. 'Give me two minutes,' he said, 'then tell her I am in the library. Bring her there.'

'Yes, sir.' The man departed, and Dennison stood for a moment looking out of the window. There was a cab on the drive, a hired cab. If she had come in the family coach someone would have warned him earlier, because the coach was distinctive, having the Myers's coat of arms on the panel, Myers being a man who liked to call attention to himself and his possessions. He now turned to the valet, saying, 'If my visitor hasn't departed within the next half-hour, come and remind me that I shall not get to Durham in time for the London train. You understand?'

'Fully, sir.'

Dennison passed the man and went quickly across the landing and down the broad stairs, turned at the foot, then made his way to the library.

He had hurried in his walk and run down the stairs yet wasn't out of breath. This pleased him greatly. He felt he had returned to his twenties these past few weeks: there was new life in him; and of course, he had cut down drastically on his wine.

But he walked slowly now up the long room to the fire and stood with his back to it, and not until the door opened, admitting his late mistress, did he move from it. Then without haste he advanced towards her, saying, 'How nice to see you, Rene.'

She took his outstretched hand but made no reply; then she passed him and, going to the couch, she lowered her plump body down into it.

She had discarded her outer coat and the blue cord velvet dress she was wearing was fitted to her ample figure. The bodice was plain, the waist nipped in, then billowed out into two overskirts edged with ruching. Her hat of three different shades of mauve velvet was turned up at both sides. It was high crowned and set on the top was what resembled a flower made of feathers. The whole did nothing to add to her height. The skin of her face was what was termed warm peach. Her eyes were round and blue, shaded by curling dark lashes. Her nose was small, as was her mouth, but full lipped. Yet, when it was open as it was now in a fixed smile, it appeared wide and showed two rows of quite large white teeth.

Her eyes were like slits as she looked up at him and said, 'Well! Well! How long is it since I've seen you?'

In contrast to her plump figure her voice was thin and high. How high, he knew only too well when she got into a jealous rage., He put his head back as if he were counting, then said, 'Five weeks, six weeks.'

'You didn't count the days then?' Her lips came together and pursed themselves questioningly.

'I . . . I have been very busy.'

'And otherwise engaged?' She now seemed to pay attention to her dress as her hands arranged the sides of her skirt and pulled it away from her small feet.

'Well, yes, you could say that, Rene. I don't have to be naïve and tell you anything that you already know.'

'You didn't think about writing and telling me.' She continued to arrange her skirt.

'No; no, I didn't; I didn't want to disturb your holiday.'

'Huh!' She was looking at him now and he saw her white teeth grinding over each other, in fact he heard them. Then her mouth was open and she was smiling again, and this made him more nervous than ever.

'When did you return?' he asked.

'A week yesterday.'

The skin round his eyes crinkled, almost closing them. She had been home over a week and this was her first visit to him. Why hadn't Pat let him know? But what was he talking about? Pat was in London. But there were the Rylands and the Crombies and others. It was like a conspiracy. What was her game?

'That surprises you?'

He shrugged his shoulders while she stared at him without speaking now. The fact that she'd kept away from him for eight days not only surprised but amazed herself. Yet, she knew from what she had heard that he was absolutely infatuated with that vicarage chit; he had already introduced her to the household, and apparently was preparing her to become its mistress. Well, she felt she knew her Dennison and she could never imagine, not in this world, that little slip of a thing satisfying his needs, so many and varied. She also knew that if she caused a scene, in his autocratic way, he would say, 'Enough is enough,' as he had done to Larry, but were she to play her cards right, she could stay on the outskirts for the present and, with time, give that little snipe one hell of a life. And in taking this line she'd be killing two birds with one stone, because Arnold had become very testy since his own private affair had gone awry. As he was now always pointing out to her, he was a diplomat and there were limits even to the discretion of friends.

She said, 'You don't expect me to congratulate you, do you, Denny?'

He shook his head, amazed at her control. He knew her well enough to know that she was worked up inside; the blue of her eyes had darkened so much as to become almost black. Yet here she was, adopting a pose, a philosophical pose to the whole affair.

And so he answered quickly, 'No, I don't expect you to congratulate me, but I thank you for your understanding so far.'

'Then I am not to be thrown to the dogs?'

'Oh, Rene, Rene, what an expression.'

'That's how I feel at the moment' – she bowed her head – 'thrown off, discarded. It's . . . it's hard to take because I was always there when you needed me.'

'I . . . I know that, Rene.' He walked to the couch and sat down beside her and, taking her hand, he said, 'I shall be forever grateful for the past. You know that.'

Her head was still bent when she said, 'Then we can remain friends?'

'*Certainly. Certainly.*'

She glanced at him sideways now, and there was a small deprecating smile on her lips as she said, 'But I'll not put in an appearance very often. You will understand that?'

'Of course. of course, my dear.' He raised her hand to his lips, the while his mind shouted at him, 'Thank God. Thank God for this.'

'You won't expect me to meet her, will you, unless it is unavoidable?'

'Of course not, Rene. Of course not.'

She wriggled her buttocks towards the front of the couch, and he quickly rose and helped her to her feet. 'I'm not going to wish you happiness,' she said, adjusting her hat; 'it would be quite out of character, wouldn't it?'

He made no reply to this but smiled gently at her while shaking his head. Then his hand cupped her elbow and he led her down the room. But before reaching the door he stopped, 'You haven't had any refreshment,' he said; 'I'm lax. Can I get you something?'

'No, thank you, Denny. No, thank you. It was refreshing enough to see you once again.'

The sad note in her voice touched him and once more he said, 'Oh, Rene.'

He opened the door and to the amazement of the butler and the footman he led the visitor, not only across the hall, but also down the steps, preceded at a run now by the footman towards the hired vehicle. And here, as he helped her into the carriage, he was heard to say, 'Thank you, my dear.' And he stood bareheaded until the cabby had turned his horse about and driven it from the drive.

In the hall he passed the waiting butler, the two footmen, and his valet, their faces all aiming to remain expressionless, and as he now made for the drawing-room he said to the butler, 'Fetch me the brandy.'

He dropped heavily down on the sofa and, laying his head back, he muttered aloud, 'I can't believe it.' And he couldn't believe that he had got off so lightly. She had really done the decent thing. People when he came to think about it, were most unpredictable. He had imagined he knew her inside out and that she would have played merry hell and raised the house on him, but there, she went off like a lamb.

Quite suddenly he pulled himself up straight and bit down on his lip. That wasn't like her. Had she some scheme in her mind? No, no. He shook his head. She was genuine. Naturally, as she said, she wouldn't want to meet Nancy Ann. The only thing she wanted was to remain friends with him. And friends it would be. No further. Oh no, no further. Never, not again. Nancy Ann was his life from now on. He could swear on that. Look what she had done to him already. For two months now he had abstained. That was the longest he had gone since he was seventeen or eighteen, anyway, since very early on. And yet he could manage; just being with her was fulfilment enough, at least at the moment. But there were another four months or more to go. Oh, he'd get by. If things became too wearing he'd slip up to town; not Newcastle, no, that was too near. Anyway, he'd see. He'd get by.

He lifted the decanter that Trice had placed on a tray to his hand and poured himself out a good measure of brandy. He didn't usually drink so early in the day, but this was a special occasion, a kind of victory, but a victory that had sapped him somewhat. And – he smiled to himself as he watched his butler depart – it had surprised that lot out there too. They had expected a battle royal; likely been looking forward to it. He had no doubt but that every member of his staff had been awaiting the consequences. And now they were disappointed. Oh, yes, he knew human nature all right, as least his staff, and they were predictable. He threw off the remainder of the brandy, got to his feet, straightened his cravat, stroked his hair back, then marched from the room. He was going to his love.

6

John Howard Hazel was well aware of his own weaknesses and of his lowly standing in the hierarchy of the church, but he had always felt that he was worthy of a better living than that of St George's. The reforms introduced by Parliament thirty or forty years before were supposed to have applied to the Established Church too. For one thing, cathedral clergy had to give up certain benefices, and the money saved should have been used to raise the stipends of the poorer parsons. But it had yet to affect his stipend at St George's.

And yet there still remained the plum livings where the vicar passed his days almost in the style of the local gentry: he rode to hounds, fished, and shot with them, and, as some dissenters were wont to declare, was not always above sharing their sport of whoring. Moreover, it was questioned why single parsons should have housekeepers. They should either marry or have menservants. They were as bad as the Catholics in this way.

John was well aware that it was the leading Conservatives in towns and villages that supported the church, whereas the Liberals and radicals tended, as did the working classes, especially those in the towns, towards the chapels. He knew it was said, and rightly, there was more class-consciousness in the upper and lower churches of England than there was between the rich and the poor, and that that order of things was very prevalent in his parish, which was why his daughter's coming marriage to the Lord of the Manor, as it were, was causing such a furore.

There was much more snobbery and vying for positions in this parish than in any of the other three parishes he had held. Perhaps it was because it lay just outside the industrial mining area of Durham, on one side, and the shipbuilding and factory towns on the other. He often thought of his parish, not as an oasis, but as an island, its inhabitants barren of understanding of the frailties of human nature . . . not of each individual's own lack, but of his neighbours'. And he knew that he himself could not be counted as one apart from this company, because at present he was being tested above all others.

Why couldn't he recognize that the man who was soon to become his son-in-law was a changed individual? He had been a gambler, and yet he was giving himself very little time to gamble now. And the same applied, apparently, to his other needs, because he seemed to spend his time coming backwards and forwards to this house, if not just to see Nancy Ann, then to take her off to Durham or Newcastle in order to choose yet something more for the house of which she was to become mistress . . . Mistress of that House? He could not imagine Nancy Ann as such. And what would happen when the mistress of *this* house was taken from him? Her days were running out fast, and with Nancy Ann gone his life would indeed be grey. Only one small piece of brightness was on his horizon: Peter would be returning; but not to live at home; like James, he would be attached to the school. Yet he would be near at hand. But what would it matter which of them was at hand when he lost his dear Rebecca?

His thoughts were checked when the door was pushed open unceremoniously and Hilda, in a whisper, said, 'Lady Golding has called.'

This wasn't the first time in the last few weeks that this lady had called upon them, and he supposed he should consider it an honour. His servants expressed awe at the mention of her name as if she was a holy visitation. But there was nothing holy about this woman: she was a robust, forthright individual, and likeable, but nevertheless, she was of Harpcore's class, a close friend of his and a woman of the world, and it would be with her like that Nancy Ann would have to associate, and learn . . . What? Yes, what would she learn?

Hilda's hushed tone came again, saying, 'Miss Nancy Ann has taken her into the mistress.'

'Well, that's all right.' His voice was unduly sharp and the door closed abruptly.

It was a full ten minutes before he decided to go and greet the visitor. But when he entered the room she was apparently on the point of leaving for she was rising from her seat, saying, 'Well, I won't tire you, Mrs Hazel. I'm on my way to call on Denny. His head full of arrangements, he's obviously missing a mother and is treating me as such, and I consider it no compliment.' She smiled broadly as she turned her glance on Jessica, who, being diplomatic and tactful for once, replied, 'An elder sister perhaps, but certainly not his mother.' And at this Pat Golding smiled more broadly still and, inclining her head towards the older woman, said, 'I thank you. That remark is most kind and will buoy me up for the rest of the day.' She turned again towards the bed, 'Goodbye, Mrs Hazel. I shall call upon you soon if I may.'

'Please do, Lady Golding. You are very welcome. See Lady Golding out, Nancy Ann.'

It was all very formal, and as her ladyship came up with John she merely inclined her head towards him, saying, 'Vicar,' then passed on. In the hall she pulled her fur cape tightly up to her neck as she muttered, 'Don't you feel the cold, dear?'

'Not really; I prefer it to the heat.'

Pat put out her hand and touched Nancy Ann's cheek, saying now, 'What it is to be young. But wait till you get up there.' She pointed towards the door. 'It's like a hothouse; they have a coal mine delivered every week. And that daft creature is there again. Have you met her?'

'You mean Lady Beatrice?'

'That's who I mean.'

Nancy Ann smiled. 'Yes, I've met her and been introduced to her family.'

'Oh, did you ever know such a thing. You can understand one or two dolls to compensate for a broken romance, but how many has she brought with her this time? Conway told me she had three hampers full. But – ' She leant towards Nancy Ann now, and in a low voice said, 'She's not as daft as she makes out. Oh, no, she's wily.

She was wily before her head got muddled. I've known her since she was a girl. Do you think when she's down with her cousin she has maids waiting on her and a bath every day? No, of course not. If I could get into that room when she's taking a bath I'd be accompanied by a scrubbing brush, and use it. Believe me, Denny's a fool for putting up with her. And when you get up there, my girl, learn to put your foot down. And not only on her. There's lots of things behind the scenes in that house which want rectifying; half that lot wouldn't last five minutes under me. Well, I must away.'

At the open door she turned and, nodding at Nancy Ann, now said, 'I wish your wedding was over, my dear, I do that, I'm worn out already.' Then she smiled broadly, put out her hand again and patted Nancy Ann's arm before stepping outside and hurrying through the frosty air to her coach . . .

Lady Patricia Golding marched into Rossburn House and, almost throwing her cloak and fur stole at Robertson, she demanded, 'Where's your master?'

'He . . . he was in his study, m'lady.'

Without further ado she stalked across the hall and down the passage opposite, past the library, turned right along another short passage and, pushing open the end door, she walked in and surprised Dennison, who wasn't writing at his desk but sitting in a leather chair by the window. He had been gazing out on to the garden and thinking of the future, but now he was quickly on his feet, saying, 'My! my! Pat, you came in there like a devil in a gale of wind. What's your hurry? Sit down. Will you have a drink?'

'Yes, something hot. I've just come from your future wife's ice-box. My! how they exist in that house God alone knows. But I suppose' – she grinned – 'He sees they survive because He needs the vicar. But enough of this. I've come to tell you something and it's just this, Denny. That woman in that bed is not going to last out till June if I know anything.'

'You think not?'

'I feel sure not. And you know what that implies: your wedding will certainly be postponed then. Can't you do anything about it to bring it forward if the invitations haven't gone out yet? And there's another thing. When the mother goes you'll have more opposition from the father; that man isn't for you.'

'I'm well aware of that, Pat. But I can do nothing about bringing the wedding forward. Why, I was amazed when I knew it was to be June. If he'd had his way it could have been a village engagement going on for three or four years. No, I couldn't do anything about it.'

'Well, that's up to you . . . Get me that drink.'

He rang the bell, and when the footman appeared he ordered hot coffee and brandy. A few minutes later, as they sat, one at each side of the fire, drinking the laced coffee, Pat said, 'Have you seen anything of Rene lately?'

'Only once since she called here, all light and understanding, and that was at the Fentons last Thursday. I understood from her that she was going up to town the following day.'

'Oh, yes, she goes up to town quite a bit. And you know who she sees up there?'

'Is this a guessing game? She has many friends, as you know.'

'Well, Larry Freeman wasn't one of her closest, was he? He was jealous of her association with you and she was jealous of the power he seemingly wielded over you. But it came out just in casual conversation on one particular night. I was having a word with Jim Boyle and he happened to turn the conversation in his undiplomatic way to you and her, and what your relationship was now, which led, as usual, to his dropping bits of tittle-tattle. And in this case it was that your late friend Larry and your late mistress Rene seemingly meet in London, and not infrequently. He had seen them once dining together and at another time riding in Rotten Row. Now what do you make of that?'

'I wouldn't know unless I gave it some thought.'

'You don't need to think about that. Neither of them loves you now. No matter what kind of a front she puts on, the quieter she is, the smoother she is, the more dangerous I would sense her to be. By the way, how are your finances?'

'Oh! Pat. Pat.'

'Never mind, Oh! Pat. Pat. You can't have lost much lately because you haven't been playing, but last year by all accounts you went through a hell of an amount. Now, as I told you then and I'm telling you now, you can't keep it up.'

'I . . . I don't intend to, so don't worry.'

'Oh.' She took a gulp from her cup, then wiped her lips with the back of her thumb before saying, 'The instinct that has caused you to warm your bed in the past will soon be provided for legitimately; and how long you remain faithful, that depends. But the gaming is a different problem altogether. You're not a lucky gambler, you know, Denny.'

'I'm like everyone else, Pat, I have runs.'

'You had one winner with your horses last year. And that's an expensive business alone, but the cards can outdo it. You know I'm speaking the truth and I'm not going to apologize for taking the liberty of talking the way I'm doing; I've always done so since I first knew you, and I'm not changing now. I seem to have taken over from where your mother left off. I often used to wish I was a little younger. I would have made a damn sight better bed warmer than the one you picked.'

'Oh, my dear Pat.' He turned away, his face screwed up with suppressed laughter. 'What will you come out with next?'

'What I'll come out with next is to repeat the main cause of my visit here this morning when I should be with George in Newcastle supporting him supporting Roland who is determined to stand for the by-election in Fellburn. That son-in-law of mine hasn't got an ounce of sense in his head, yet he thinks he can beat the Tory candidate. Now that's something you should do, take up politics, get into Parliament. That would steady you up.'

'My dear Pat, I don't need any more steadying than I am at present. I've never felt steadier in my life.'

She drained the last of the coffee, then pulled herself to her feet, saying, 'Say those words to me after three years of marriage and I'll believe you're a changed man. Now I've got to go, but let me finish what I meant to say, marry that girl as soon as possible. The mother apparently wants to see her daughter settled, so that would be an excuse for bringing the wedding forward.'

'I couldn't do it, Pat.' His tone was emphatic. 'That would be utterly cruel. It would be like saying to her: you were going to die in July after having seen your daughter settled, but now you won't last that long, so I would like to bring the marriage forward, that's if you wish to see it. No, no; things must stand as they are, I must take my chance.'

'Well, all I can say is, if she dies and the wedding is postponed, as it surely will be, prepare yourself for a fight with that man, because the girl's loyalties will be torn assunder. And from the way she talks she looks upon her father as someone special, an embryo saint. Anyway, I must be off. Think about what I've said, not only about her, but about your two friends. I never liked Larry Freeman and he never liked me. I used often to think, put a couple of horns on his head and you would have a good replica of the devil and someone just as smooth.'

'Go on with you.' He pushed her gently in the back. 'You forget that he was a good companion to me for years.'

'Yes, anyone can be a good companion if they have board and lodgings free and their gambling debts and their bills paid. Oh – ' She was trotting towards the door as she said, 'I would be a friend to you myself if you would make me an allowance of two thousand a year, provide me with shooting and fishing for my married brood and grandchildren, travelling expenses, holidays abroad. Think about that an' all. I'm sure George wouldn't mind.'

'You're incorrigible. Get on your way, woman.'

In the hall the footman had helped her on with her cloak, and she flung her great fur stole over her shoulder, then saying, 'Don't see me off, you'll get your death,' she turned to depart but he laughed at her suggestion and, taking her arm, led her towards the coach, and when she was seated he leant forward and said, 'Thanks for everything, Pat. I appreciate your concern and I'll think on it.'

'You do.' She nodded at him.

He closed the door, gave a signal to the coachman, then stood for a moment watching her carriage being driven away before returning to the house and into the study again. And there, sitting down by the fire, once more he leant forward, one elbow on his knee, his closed fist supporting his chin, and as he stared into the flames he asked himself what he would do if the wedding was postponed. He had been firm with himself during the past weeks and had hoped his firmness would stand by him for the weeks ahead. They were now in the middle of April with only May to go. But what would happen if Pat were proved to be right. Well, in that case he would have to go up to town every now and again and have a few days at the club. Anyway, he would have to go up next week; there was the business of the bank to see to.

7

Dennison had been away in London since Tuesday, and now it was Saturday and the letter she had received from him this morning had asked her to be at The House around four o'clock. He had begun his short letter with 'My dearest one', and ended with 'Your loving Denny'.

She hadn't imagined she'd miss him so much. She had got used to seeing him every day even if it was for only a short time, and the thought had entered her mind that if she were never to see him again her life would become empty. She had spent most of the time in the sick room, but today her mother had insisted that Pratt drive her to The House and in good time to welcome her fiancé home.

When she stepped down from the dogcart she thanked Pratt, then walked across the gravel and up the steps to the terrace. She had learned not to knock on the door, and so, turning the big ebony handle she pushed the heavy oak door open, crossed the vestibule to the glass-fronted double doors that closed off the hall and, opening one of them, she entered. At first the hall appeared empty until, from the far corner, two surprised figures turned and stared at her. One was Robertson the second footman, the other was the pretty woman whom she saw in church on a Sunday, the one who hadn't been in the line up when she was first introduced to the staff and whom she had not encountered since. The young woman was evidently flustered: she dipped her knee, bowed her head, then scurried away, while Henry Robertson came quickly forward, saying, 'Good-afternoon, miss.'

'Good-afternoon, Robertson.' She had noticed before that of all the male staff he was the most pleasant and that his voice did not hold the stiff superior tone of the others.

'Has your master arrived yet?'

'No, miss, but – ' He glanced towards the big grandfather clock with the complicated face, whose strike boomed as loud as the church bell, and he said, 'It's a little early. Can I get you some tea, miss?'

She stood uncertain for a moment. If she had tea it would be served by the butler or one of the housemaids, and, try as she would, she could not rid herself of the feeling of awkwardness in their presence. So, smiling at the man, she said, 'No thank you. I think I shall take a walk. It's the first really fine day we've had for some time. The sun is quite warm. Should . . . should your master return before I get back, you can tell him I am walking in the direction of the farm.'

'I'll do that, miss, yes.' He hastily opened the glass door for her, then the front door, and he inclined his head in a bow as she walked past him. And as she went across the drive she told herself that if the attitude of the rest of the staff was like that of Robertson she would have no trepidation in becoming mistress of this vast establishment.

She turned the corner of the house and into the courtyard formed by the north side of the house and outbuildings along the other two sides. In going this way she wouldn't have to pass the kitchen quarters. Six horses were kept here for the carriages, the rest were in stables at the farm with their own men to look after them.

Two horses had their heads over their half-doors and she went towards one and held out her hand, and the horse rubbed its wet muzzle against her palm. She did the same with the second horse and was about to move away when, from the empty stable next door, a young man stepped, and at the sight of her, he raised his cap, then smiled, saying, 'Good-day to you, miss.'

The unmistakable Irish voice caused her to pause and she looked at the man. He was a stranger in the yard, she hadn't seen him before; what was more strange still he looked like one of the McLoughlin boys, but he was a young man, well in his twenties.

She said, 'You are new here?'

'Aye, miss, yes. Me name's Shane McLoughlin. I'm . . . I'm' – his face went into a huge grin – 'I'm one of them McLoughlins. You had notice, I understand, miss, of one or two of me brothers years gone by and put them rightly in their place.'

She blushed even as she smiled and replied, 'There were six and two threes of us in those days, I think.'

'You could hold your own, miss, you could hold your own by all accounts. You see, me bein' the eldest, I was away in service. I was with Mr McMahon, you know over in Northumberland way, but he died and the place was sold up. But I wanted to be with horses and when this job was going here and it was near me home, well, I thought, it's for me.'

At the back of her mind she knew that she shouldn't stand here allowing this servant to chat to her like this, but it was so different, so refreshing.

'How is your family?'

'Oh, they are all doin' well, miss, especially since me da died. God rest him. There were fifteen of us at the end and not one of us sorry to see him go, 'cos, you know, he'd neither work nor want. Me ma's never been so happy in her troubled life, miss, an' we all stand by her.'

She wanted to laugh out loud, really loud: there was an ache in her waist almost like a pain. She must go.

She was about to give him a last word when two men appeared from out of a door at the far end of the yard, and at the sight of her they stopped for a moment. Then one came forward. It was Gillespie the groom, and after casting a sharp glance at the Irishman, he looked at Nancy Ann, saying, 'Is everything all right, miss?'

'Oh, yes, yes. I . . . I was just having a word with' – she almost said Shane – 'McLoughlin here. I'm acquainted with his family. I'm pleased to see that he has come into Mr Harpcore's service.'

She inclined her head towards him; then looking at Shane who was now straight-faced and looking not a little apprehensive, she added, 'Give my respects to your mother when you next see her. Tell her that I am so glad she is well.'

A light spread over the man's face for a moment and, touching the forelock of his thick black hair, he said, 'I'll do that, miss, with pleasure, I will, I will. Thank you, miss.'

She now walked on, keeping her step as sedate as possible. She knew she had saved the man from at least a bullying reprimand, by claiming knowledge of his family, and she considered it a small price to pay for the enjoyment he had given her, for she had never wanted to laugh so much for a long time. Oh, when she got home she would *do him* for her mama and grandmama. She had the desire to skip and run.

The decorum and sedateness which she had been made to acquire over the past months was begging to be thrown off. And she threw it off, once she had left the precincts of the formal gardens and entered the woodland that formed a shield between the house and the river, for here, picking up her skirts, she ran along the narrow path before leaving it and winding her way between the trees. At one point she stopped and stood with her back leaning against a trunk and she looked up through the branches that were just beginning to show a spattering of green to where the white clouds were racing across the sky. And she thought, as she had often done after running when she was a child and stood puffing, Oh, that was lovely. Then she asked herself why it was that running was considered most unladylike? Men ran, then why not women? This question she had put to her grandmama some time ago and the answer she received was more puzzling still: 'It's all because of the Queen,' her grandmama had said.

She turned from the tree now and, walking slowly, she decided to have a look at the river before making for the farm. She was walking on the path again and as it was opening out on to a green bank she could see in the distance, sitting on a piece of rock near the water's edge, a boy. It was the sight of him that lifted her back years.

She was half-way across the green when he turned a startled look on her; and he jumped to his feet. Seeing he was about to run, she called to him, ''Tis a nice day, isn't it?'

The tone of her voice checked him, and when she came up to him she stood looking down into his face for a moment before she asked, 'Were you fishing?'

He shook his head, then said, 'No miss, just sittin'.'

'Well, come and sit down again.' And she held out her hand to him. But he didn't take it, yet he obeyed her as though she had given him an order and sat down on the long slab of rock. And she, seating herself some distance from him, said, 'You won't remember me, but . . . but we have met before, and at this very spot. Do you remember? It's a long time ago.'

'I remember, miss, 'cos I was kept in for a long time after.'

'Kept in?' She screwed up her face, and he nodded, adding, 'In the roof. I'm not now though; I work in the boot room with Jimmy.' He turned his glance from her and, looking at the water, he said, 'I like the river, but I can only come sometimes.'

She did not question why he could only come sometimes. He was looking at her again, and as she stared back at him all the joy of the previous half-hour slipped from her. He had a most beautiful face. The great dark brown eyes held a depth of sadness that should never have been portrayed in one so young. His hair fell to the collar of his short navy blue jacket. It was quite brown at the ends and for some way up, and then it became streaky. But from where she was sitting she could see his parting, and the hair was silvery fair for about an inch on each side of it. 'Do you often come down to the river?' she asked.

He shook his head, then said, 'When Jennie lets me.'

'Jennie?' Her voice was soft and inquiring, and he said, 'She's . . . she's Jennie. I sleep with her. She works in the kitchen.'

The sadness was deep within her now: she remembered he had called his mother Jennie before.

He rose suddenly from the slab, saying, 'I must go back, Jennie'll be vexed.'

She too rose, saying now, 'I don't suppose she will if she allowed you to come out.'

'No . . . no, she never, but the sun was out' – he looked upwards – 'an' the breeze was blowin' an' they were all in the servants hall, an' so I came.' He stooped down now and retrieved something from the back of the stone, which she could see was a slate and a pencil, and she said brightly. 'Oh, you do lessons?'

'No.' He shook his head. 'I just write.'

'You can read?'

'Yes – ' He nodded at her. 'There are lots of books in the big attic, boxes of 'em.'

'Who taught you to read and write?'

'Jennie.'

'And what have you been writing today?'

'Just words.'

She held out her hand and after a moment's hesitation, and reluctantly, he passed the slate to her. And she read in printed letters the words: Birds have wings, trees have leaves, and rabbits play, but they all die.

She raised her eyes slowly from the slate and looked at the boy. She was amazed, not so much by the words, but at the meaning behind them. Her voice soft, she asked, 'How old are you now?'

'I am nine.'

'And . . . and you have never been to the day school?'

'Day school? No.'

She'd have to do something about this. She must do something about the child. It was strange, but it was as if she had first seen him only yesterday. He had made an impression on her then and it had remained, only now it was stronger. It had become an issue. She handed the slate back to him, saying, 'You're a clever boy to be able to write words like that. Now, sit down again and write some more of those words.'

As if partly mesmerized, the child sat down once more on the stone with the slate on his knee and his head turned towards her, and she nodded at him now, saying, 'We'll be seeing each other again. Goodbye.' He made no answer, but screwed round on the stone to watch her walking away into the wood.

A great deal of the light had gone from the day. It was wrong, very wrong that a child with that intelligence wasn't having some form of education. She'd talk to her father about it and ask his advice how best to broach the subject to Denny.

She had emerged from the wood and was on the main path again leading to the farm, and the outbuildings were actually in sight when she heard hurrying footsteps behind her. Turning, she saw Dennison and such was her feeling at the moment that the sight of him swept away the darkness surrounding her thoughts and she was in the light again, so much so that she picked up her skirts and ran to meet him. She had never imagined herself doing any such thing, but she was actually doing it now, and when they met his arms went about her and he lifted her from the ground and swung her round. Then he was kissing her. Hard and long he kissed her, and when at last he released her they were both breathing heavily. Her head strained back from him and resting in the circle of his arms, she gazed into his face. And when he said, 'Oh, Nancy Ann, how many years ago is it since I last held you?'

She was gasping for breath, but, answering his mood, she said, 'It must be all of ten.'

'Oh, yes, yes, that long.' Again his lips were on hers, and she was amazed at her own response and the enjoyment she was experiencing in his embrace. And her mind was telling her that she liked him. Oh, she liked him very much. And, as if picking up her thoughts, he said, 'I'm glad I went away, because you've missed me, haven't you? Tell me you've missed me, and that you like me, even . . . even . . .' He stopped and his head slightly bent, he waited while she admitted softly, 'Yes, yes, I have missed you. And I do like you very much.'

'Oh, my dear, my dear. All right, all right' – he wagged his hand between their faces – 'I won't start again, because if I do, I won't be able to stop. Come.' He put an arm around her, then added, 'Look at me in my town clothes, I didn't even stop for a moment when they told me where you were bound for. And isn't this a beautiful day! and tell me what have you been doing with yourself.'

And to this she answered, 'Oh, you have a very good idea of what fills my days, but I, in turn, haven't the slightest notion what fills yours. You tell me what *you* have been doing with yourself.'

They were walking into the wood again and he said, 'Well now, let me think. I went to the bank as was my intention and had a long talk with the head of that establishment. "How are my affairs, sir?" I said, "because I want to buy a piece of jewellery for my future wife." But he said, "What about those in the vault. There are two tiaras, a number of necklaces and rings." But I said, "I want something new and fresh, because it is for a very new and fresh young lady."' He squeezed her waist and pulled her into his side as she muttered, 'Oh, no, please. I don't want jewellery; I'm not fond of jewellery.'

'Be quiet. You want to know what I did with my days. Well then, I went to my tailor and ordered three suits, and then to the shoemaker to have shoes made to match them, but my main shopping was to a famous store that deals in silks and satins, brocades and taffetas, cords and velvets, and I chose a selection that had to be sent on to an establishment in Newcastle where this young lady that I have in mind will oblige me by being measured for several different outfits.'

She pulled herself from his grasp, saying, 'Oh, no, Denny, no. Papa wouldn't like that.'

His face losing its look of merriment for a moment, he said, 'Your papa, my dear, will shortly have no say in your life; we shall be travelling abroad after the wedding and you will need to be suitably attired.'

'Oh, dear.' She sighed, then added, 'It is so good of you. But I am not used to lots of outfits, and . . . and . . .'

In mock astonishment he now raised his arms above his head, crying, 'I'll swear to the gods you are the only young lady alive who spurns the thought of being well attired.' They halted near a tree and he gripped her by the shoulders and, pressing her against it, he bent his face towards her, saying, 'Your education is going to be much more difficult than I imagined. After our marriage you will become a different being, you will have to.'

He was amazed at the strength of her hands that pushed him backwards; and now she was standing upright, facing him saying, 'I won't be a different being, Denny. I may be clothed differently, but I shall remain myself. I . . . I know I shall. And I don't want to be changed, I don't want to have my values and . . .'

'My dear. My dear.' He shook his head slowly from side to side. 'Don't take the matter so seriously. You're the last person on earth I want to change, that way. I . . . I think that was what first attracted me, your independent spirit, and that is the person who I want to grow to love me. But you see, my dear, you'll be expected to attend functions and to dress accordingly. As for changing you, changing my Nancy Ann? Never! And' – he now pulled a comical face – 'there's one thing I'll have to accept, and it is that my future wife was trained by her brothers in combat. Haven't I witnessed it! Those fragile looking arms' – he looked from one shoulder to the other – 'have proved the case in point. Oh, yes, a little bit further and I'd have been on my back.'

'I'm . . . I'm sorry.'

He held out his hands to her now, saying, 'Never say you are sorry to me, my dear.' His arms went about her again and he held her gently and they remained quiet, looking at each other. And then they were both startled and drew apart when there came the sound of running steps quite near, and out of the brushwood to their side scrambled the boy.

He was as astonished as they were and came to an abrupt gaping halt.

Nancy Ann opened her mouth to speak, then closed it again for she was looking at her companion's face which had suddenly flushed to a deep red. He was gazing at the boy and the boy at him, and his voice, like a loud bark, yelled, 'Get away!'

As the child sped through the trees, Dennison turned from her, his hand pulling the skin tightly across his cheek. She did not speak until perhaps a full minute later after he had turned towards her again and, his voice a mutter, had said, 'I can explain. I . . . I will sometime.'

'You have no need to; I know all about it,' she said.

His eyes widened, then narrowed, and he said, 'Oh, you do?'

'Well – ' She seemed embarrassed for a moment, then said softly, 'I know some of the circumstances, and . . . and I can understand your feelings in part, but not all.'

'Not all. What do you mean?'

'The child is not to blame.'

'Oh, please, my dear, don't take that tack. He's a reminder that I was deprived of someone I loved dearly.'

'I . . . I still think you cannot lay the blame on him, and if you were to recognize . . .'

'What!' His interruption was in almost as loud a voice as when he had shouted at the boy. 'You don't know what you're suggesting. You don't know what you're talking about. You know nothing whatever about it. One doesn't recognize the likes of him, flyblows. There's a lot you have to learn.'

When she turned abruptly from him and walked hastily away, he stood nonplussed for a moment; then he was running after her, saying, 'Nancy Ann! Nancy Ann! Please! Please!'

Once again he was holding her by the arms; but she remained stiff and unyielding, and when he bent his head and said, 'I'm sorry I spoke like that, but this is a matter that has seared me over the years. Come, let us go to the bank and sit down by the river and . . . and I will try to explain.' He took her gently by the arm, and they did not speak again until they had reached the river bank and he had sat her down on the very rock that she and the boy had sat on earlier. He did not take her hand or look at her but, placing his hands on his knees he looked down into the water and began quietly. 'It was in this very river that my brother died. Whether he drowned himself or drowned accidentally, I'll never know. But I lost him at a time when I needed him most. My mother died when Tim was seven years old. I was twelve and at boarding school. My father never got over her going, they were very devoted. He was in such a state that I didn't want to leave him and go back to school, but he insisted I did. The school, though, was just in Newcastle and so, under the circumstances, the headmaster allowed me home at weekends. Each time I saw him he seemed to have let go a little more on life. I understood that he spent most of his days on horseback, riding until both he and the animal were exhausted. Then one day he didn't return and they found him at the bottom of the small gully: the horse had thrown him and broken its leg but my father had broken his neck.'

He straightened his back now and turned to her, then continued, 'Tim was alone in the house, that big rambling place. He was missing our parents very much. It was then I made a decision. Tim had a tutor, he was a good man and learned. He knew as much or more than any of the teachers at the school, so I decided to stay at home myself and join Tim in the classroom, and in a way I became mother and father to him. He was like my shadow, we did everything together. Although there was five years between us we enjoyed the same things; the only difference between us was that he was of a more emotional nature, more temperamental, I suppose. And his ideas tended that way. He could paint well, and he was already a great reader. He wrote poetry from an early age, and kept an extensive diary that read like a book. We travelled together too. Went through France; did the usual trip through Italy, museums and palaces. But most enjoyable, was the time we spent in Scotland, riding and shooting, or just walking the hills. Mr Bennett, of course, always accompanied us. Even though I was getting older I felt that Tim should continue his studies. I myself had always harboured the desire to go to university, Oxford by choice, but at twenty-two I imagined I was too late. However, Mr Bennett had different ideas. He had a friend who was a don in the university and who, he was sure, could press my case as an older than usual student.

'Tim was nearing eighteen and, as Mr Bennett pointed out, it was really time I stopped mothering him, and let him stand on his own feet. And so arrangements were finalized for me to go up to Oxford at the start of the next academic year. It was during this period that Tim was left to himself quite a bit, and at first I didn't notice the change in him, but when I did, I thought it was because of our coming separation and that he was already preparing himself for it by distancing himself from me. Then one day – ' He now turned from her again and, taking off his hard hat, he laid it on the stone to his side, then ran his fingers across his brow before going on, 'just as today as I espied you in the wood, there I saw him with a girl in his arms. Her face was familiar, as naturally it would be, she was a housemaid. What immediately followed I won't go into. When he told me he intended to marry her I imagined he had gone mad, but he assured me he hadn't as it was a matter of honour with him that he should marry her because she was heavy with his child. I remember laughing at this stage and attempting to put my arm around his shoulder while I explained that these things were happening every day in big houses all over the country, and what would happen if the sons of the house were to think it their duty to marry all the maids that fell to them during the course of their adolescence. But he threw off my hand and declared that he intended to marry this girl, that he had proposed to her sometime earlier, and what was more, he had put his intention in writing, and what was even more still, he had been to see her only living relative, an uncle, a carter in the village, and to whom he had given his solemn promise to take care of her, as the man apparently was about to emigrate to Australia. As you can imagine, I flatly refused to countenance even the idea of such an association, and the war between us raged for days. I called Bennett in to discuss the matter. Apparently, he had known about the association but hadn't told me in case it should arouse my anger. Anyway, he had imagined it was a young man's passing fancy and was, in a way, perfectly natural, because, as he said, in our society such licence wasn't afforded the women of our class until they were married.'

At this point he sighed deeply and said in a different tone, 'My dear, don't look so shocked. You are not coy, and you are so sensible. You know, it is this part of your character, I might as well tell you, that amazes me, because your upbringing I should imagine, has been on a par with that of a nun in a convent. Of course, there's your grandmama, who must have brought a little light from the outside into your existence at an early age. You should be very grateful for her. Anyway, do . . . do you wish me to continue?'

Her throat was too dry for speech, she merely inclined her head, and so he went on, 'I gave him an ultimatum: he was to give up the idea at once, and I would see that the girl was decently taken care of, and if she didn't the child it would be adopted, otherwise he'd have to face marriage as a working man, for he would have no help from me. As I told him, he had no money of his own, for the estates and all they held were in my name. Fortunately or unfortunately, my father had not made another will from the time I was born. This threw him into a state and gave me hope, because he was in no way able to earn his living. Apart from his pastimes of painting and writing, he had no other qualifications.'

He leant towards her now but did not touch her: with his two hands flat on the rock, he looked down towards them as he said in a low voice, 'The weather was bad, the river had swollen, the wooden bridge further down was blocked with debris. I didn't know he was out. But when night came and he hadn't returned I went looking for him with the men. Dawn the following morning, the rowing boat was found capsized near the bridge. The debris had gone through and must have taken him with it. Three days later his body was recovered.' Still looking at his hands, he muttered, 'I was overwhelmed with sorrow and anger. I wanted to strangle that girl. I gave orders for her to leave the house, and these were carried out. Then, a day later, she appeared again, accompanied by this uncle of hers, who Tim had said was an intelligent man. He was also a cunning man. He demanded to see me and told me plainly that if I did not give her the shelter of my house, to which she was due, at least as a servant, then he would make the matter public and show the press the letters that my brother had written to the girl, telling of his sincerity and love for her and his desire to marry her; and that now he was gone I had thrown her out, and the only place for her would be the workhouse where her child would be born, for he himself was due to leave for abroad. But he promised, or rather threatened, that if I did not meet his demands he would put off his voyage and bring the matter to light to the public. He said he had friends who would support him in his crusade in exposing the legalized licence given to sons of the wealthy, where they could use their maids as training ground, with the result that the workhouses were packed with young girls and ba . . . illegitimate children.'

He now raised his head and looked at her, continuing, 'I knew he meant every word he said, and I am so made that I couldn't stand up to the scandal. There are times now when I regret my weakness. Well, I think you know the rest. I gave orders that the girl could stay but that she must be kept out of my sight. And those orders have been carried out. Up till recently, up till I fell in love with you, I had never spent very much time here; in fact, the very thought of that woman and child kept me away. I could, I suppose, have made arrangements for them, and offered to place her in some comfort outside, but had I done so it would have been paramount to accepting responsibility for the child and that I would or will never do, and today is the first time I have seen him.'

Her voice came soft and sad as she said, 'He's still your brother's child, Denny.'

'I . . . I'm sorry, but I don't look at him in that light, and never will. You've got to understand me in this, my dear. And I don't want the subject brought up again. It is too painful for me. I only know the loss of Tim altered my life. It altered me. I asked the question, why I should be held responsible in this matter, held to ransom as it were, made a laughing stock of, when in every county in this country, where there is sited a large establishment, the surrounding farms and cottages are bespattered with the results of their sporting sons and only too willing serving girls.'

When she rose sharply from the stone, he caught at her hands, saying, 'I . . . I speak too freely and too soon. I'm . . . I'm sorry . . . Oh, my dear. I had looked forward so much all the journey down just to see your face, and a little while ago your expression told me that you . . . you more than liked me, now it tells me that you dislike me.'

She swallowed deeply, then said, 'I . . . I don't dislike you, I . . . I'm only troubled by your way of thinking.'

He rose and, still holding her hands, he drew her stiff body to him, saying gently now, ''Tis the thinking of my class. You think as you were brought, up, I as I was brought up. We are moulded by our environment. But from now on I want, I sincerely want our environments to mingle. You believe me?'

'Yes. Yes, I believe you.'

'Well, now, can you forget the last half-hour as if it had never happened and smile at me as you did before?'

'I can't smile to order.'

'No, no; of course not. That would mean you are like the other ladies of my acquaintance, with the exception of course of Pat. You know you are very like Pat in some ways, and I like that, because I'm fond of Pat. She's a straight, honest, good friend. Well now, my dear, shall we go back to the house? because I've not eaten since I breakfasted this morning, but apart from that I am very thirsty. And later this evening, I must call on your father because the banns can be called any time now. Then there are the wedding invitations to go out. Oh, there is so much to do. You know what I thought on my journey down?'

'No, I don't.'

'I thought, wouldn't it save all this trouble if we could slip into your church one morning early and your father could marry us. And we could board the train and go off, just like that, without bags of luggage, a valet, or a maid.'

She pulled him to a stop, saying, 'It's surprising, at least it will be to you, but I don't want a maid, Denny.'

'Oh, my dear, you must have a maid.'

'No. Why should I? I've always dressed myself. I couldn't imagine someone else in the room while I was dressing. And . . . and do we need to have people travelling with us?'

He stared at her for a moment; then putting his head on one side and a quizzical smile coming to his lips, he said, 'No, you're absolutely right, we don't. In London, Johnson could see to my wants, and his wife Mary could see to yours, and up in Scotland, James McBride would be only too pleased to attend me, and there's Agnes, and Nell, who would fall over themselves to see to you. No, my dear. No, you're right.' His smile widened. 'Of course, you're right. And when we are abroad we shall see to each other.'

He now grabbed her by the arm and hurried her through the woodland. It was indeed as if the last half-hour had never happened and there was no such person as a little boy who lived in the roof of his house, and slept there with his mother and wrote on a slate: Birds have wings, trees have leaves, and rabbits play, but they all die.

8

The banns had been called for the third time. The villagers were getting used to seeing the master of Rossburn sitting in his pew and often looking down to where his future wife sat in the parson's family pew beneath and slightly to the left of the pulpit.

Most of the villagers were quite agog at the event of the coming wedding for invitations had been flowing freely among the cottages and houses. There were to be refreshments in the vicarage for both villagers and guests after the wedding, but later in the day a dinner and ball was to be held for the bridegroom's friends up at The House. This was to be left in the capable hands of Lady Golding, for the bridal pair were to leave by the three o'clock train from Newcastle for London, where they were to spend the first three days of their married life before going across the Channel to France, and from there would return to finish their month of honeymooning in Scotland.

It was now the beginning of May and all the arrangements were in full swing. The weather was fine, everyone was in good spirits, even Rebecca seemed to have a new lease of life, so much so that company didn't seem to tire her as of yore. So, on this particular evening, there were gathered in her sick room, not only the family, including Peter, but Dennison too. And he was laughing loudly with others as Nancy Ann, at the request of her grandmother, mimicked the conversation she'd had with Shane McLoughlin, starting with the first one.

'How is your family?'

Her voice now changed, her whole manner changed: she took up the pose of the young man and in his broad Irish accent she said, 'Oh, they are doing well, miss, especially since me da died. God rest him. There were fifteen of us at the end, and not one of us sorry to see him go 'cos, you know, he'd neither work nor want. Me ma's never been so happy, miss, and we all stand by her.' She paused for the laughter, and then . . .

'Oh, it's you McLoughlin. You, you are in a hurry.'

'Did I startle you, miss? It's like me ma says, a bull in a china shop can't hold a candle to me. I might have knocked you flying, an' I would have sooner kicked meself than hurt a hair of your head . . . excuse the liberty I'm takin' in saying it ma'am . . . miss. And how is yourself these days?'

'I'm very well. Thank you.'

'God be praised for that. Indeed yes. Indeed yes.'

She now touched the front of her hair as if it were a forelock and, nodding her head, stepped back two paces.

Dennison had never really witnessed her mimicking, not at this length. She had, at times, repeated a phrase and taken up a pose and, in doing so, made him laugh. But this was acting, and so natural. He was both astonished and proud. He saw a picture of her entertaining his guests as no one else could. The usual accomplishments were to tap out a tune on the piano and sing in a soprano voice. But this was entertaining. His future wife would certainly be an asset in company, and moreover a beautiful asset, especially when she grew a little older and plumped out. Her figure was beautiful now, but boyishly so. Give her a year or two and children, oh yes, children, a son, his son. He wanted a son; above all things he wanted a son.

He now looked at his future father-in-law. He had never seen him laugh before. He had hardly ever seen him smile. He looked a different being . . . even jolly. He wished he could get to know the man better. He wished he would trust him.

'Good day to you, miss. Good day to you.' She was still pulling at the front of her hair now, when all of a sudden her papa said, 'Whisht! whisht!' and she stopped abruptly, and they all looked towards the bed. Her mother's head had sunk into the pillow, her face had gone a deeper pallor. And then, to their horror, a trickle of blood began to seep from the corner of her mouth . . .'

Something near to pandemonium followed. Dennison himself rode into the village for the doctor, who at first couldn't be found as he was attending a birth at a farm some distance away. So it was almost an hour later when he arrived, and he was silent as he stood by the bed and looked on the unconscious woman.

After a slight examination he took the parson's arm and gently led him from the room, and when they were in the sitting-room, his voice sad, he said, 'She will not regain consciousness. You should be thankful for that. She's in no pain.'

At this John dropped into a chair and stared before him like a blind man. He had known this hour must come, but now it was here he felt he couldn't bear it, and he cried, 'Oh! Rebecca. Oh! Rebecca,' as Nancy Ann in the other room was crying, 'Oh! Mama. Oh! Mama.'

And in the hallway, about to take his departure, was Dennison, who was also crying, but in a different way inside. My God! for this to happen at this stage, for what did it portend? Postponement of the wedding. And for how long? How long, he didn't know, but he only knew he couldn't stand much more of this delay. His need of her in all ways was so great that at this moment he felt as desperate as the whole family did at the coming loss of the dying woman, for he felt that by her going he, too, would lose, he would lose the being that had begun to shape his life into a different pattern.

Of one thing he was fully aware, he would have a fight on his hands with the parson for, his wife gone, he would have more need to hold on to his daughter, and, using his bereavement, he would play on her feeling in every way possible, and without compassion: the Christian man would be forgiven in the tactics he would use in order that his child would never leave him, especially not to marry him, the man of whom he had never approved.

PART FIVE

The New Life

1

'Papa it is five months now since Mama went, and . . . and Dennison is becoming impatient.'

'Dennison is becoming impatient.' Her father's voice was high, every word stressing his indignation, and he repeated, 'Dennison is becoming impatient. My child, he will be lucky if I allow you to marry after another year. Have you forgotten the fitness of things? A wedding you talk of and your mother hardly left this house!'

'It is five months, Papa. I shall be eighteen very shortly . . .'

'I know what age you will be very shortly and I can tell you this, there are another three years before you are twenty-one, and I can withhold my consent.'

'You wouldn't, Papa?'

'Oh, yes, I would, my child, for you well know I have never been in favour of this marriage. If it had been someone else, and there is someone else that would take care of you and honour you and provide you with a good and wholesome life . . . if it had been he . . .?'

'What are you saying, Papa? I know of no one else who would wish to marry me.'

'Then you are blind my child, quite blind. He is the friend of your brothers and a man who has become my friend . . .'

'What! You mean Mr Mercer? Oh, Papa, you are mistaken; he has never been other than polite and courteous to me.'

'Of course he hasn't, child, because he is a gentleman in every sense of the word. But let me tell you, he was upset, very upset indeed when he knew of your engagement, and he blamed himself for being slow in approaching you. Your present fiancé had no compunction in that way. And so I say to you as I said a few minutes ago, think again, break off this engagement. Wait a little while and . . .'

'No, Papa, I shan't do any such thing, no matter how long you make us wait. I have grown fond, very fond of Dennison, and I couldn't be so cruel. He has been patient and more than kind. He has been very kind to you, and I'm amazed at your attitude towards him. And I must say this, Papa, if you don't give us your consent, then I'm afraid that Dennison might take it into his own hands and obtain what he calls a special licence. And I must tell you further, Papa, that Grandmama and Peter are not with you in this. Grandmama said six months would be decent, and it is close to that now and I hate to say this, Papa, because . . . because I love you so, but if you don't marry us then we must go elsewhere.'

He looked at her the while his mouth opened and shut but without any sound coming from it: he couldn't believe his ears. But then he had refused to recognize the change in her over the past year. She was no longer a little girl, she was no longer even a young woman. He had refused to recognize her maturity, and now face to face with it he was shocked by it. When he could, he muttered thickly, 'Leave me. Leave me.'

And so she left him, the tears raining down her face.

But the door had no sooner closed behind Nancy Ann when it was opened again and Jessica entered the room, saying immediately, 'John Howard, I'm going to tell you something. You are going the right way to lose her altogether. If you don't marry them, and soon, let me tell you, someone else will. She will go off with him and the bond between you will be severed forever. She is old enough for marriage, she knows her own mind.' She did not add that which her thoughts dictated, that her granddaughter was ready for marriage. Contact with her future husband had made her eager for it, for he was a virile man and had the magnetism of such about him.

Her voice softer and her words slower, she went on, 'John Howard, John Howard, don't lose her. You'll always regret it if you do. Marry them, because marry they will sooner or later. And what you are seeming to forget, John Howard, is that Rebecca wanted this marriage.'

He came back at her sharply now saying, 'She only wanted it because she saw him as the only one who could provide for her daughter; she didn't realize that Graham was just waiting until Nancy Ann was a little older.'

'Graham? Graham Mercer?'

'Which other Graham is there, Mother? Yes, Graham, and he loves her dearly.'

'Well then, it is a pity he was so slow. But that can never be now because, face it, John Howard, she has grown to love this man; and he adores her, be he what he may. And all right, your main feeling against him is because of his past and the women in it, but all that is behind him and he's shown it to be so over the past year. And for a man like that, it could not have been easy. Oh, no, it could not have been easy. So let us have no more of it. Marry them. It can be done quietly without any fuss. No receptions, no parties, invitations, all that has been cancelled and won't be revived, not even if you were to make them wait a year or two. But you mustn't do that, because if you do' – her voice sank low in her throat – 'we could come down to breakfast one morning and find an empty space at the table. That man is strong, he has power, he has made her love him, because she didn't at first, and she's not a character that can be lightly swayed. I know that, because she takes after me. So, am I to tell her that you will marry them, say, on her eighteenth birthday?'

She watched her son close his eyes, then turn from her and lean for support on the table. He looked an old man. He was an old man, and he but fifty-three years old, and he was a broken man because he had lost his support. She had never been very fond of her daughter-in-law until the last year or so when she seemed to have shed a little of her pious manner. But she had to admit that she had been the stay that had kept this son of hers upright, and now she feared for his future, both mental and physical, for since her going, he seemed to have lost interest even in his vocation: his sermons were without spirit, and his interest in his parishioners had diminished to a point where it was as much as he could do to attend a death-bed.

Slowly she went from the room. She was tired; age at the moment was telling on here too. She had not counted her birthdays since she had turned a blind eye on seventy. The misery in the house of late had brought home to her, the fact that there was nothing kept age at bay as much as happiness and a cheerful atmosphere around one, and that nothing made it gallop towards its end quicker than misery. Well, although she couldn't bear to think what the house would be like devoid of Nancy Ann, she was determined she at least should know happiness. And to this end she went to her, where she was sitting in her bedroom, still crying, and, putting her arms around her, she said, 'Cry, no more, but put on your cloak and hood and go over there and tell him that you can be married on your eighteenth birthday.'

2

When the parson's wife died a number of staff at The House were elated, albeit they hid their faces behind masks of mournful sympathy. What did it matter if they had to forego their own special 'do' which had promised to equal that of the wedding guests, the master was still free, and if they knew anything about the vicarage and the protocol there, there would be no wedding for a year or two at least. And what would he do in the meantime? They knew what he would do: visit London more often than he had done of late. And those in the hierarchy had reminded one another that Mrs Rene Poulter Myers had not raised a storm at being thrown off, but had played clever and remained his friend. According to Staith she had visited the London house twice and had had tea with him. She was a clever woman, Mrs Rene, they all agreed.

Then in December came the news that he was to be married in January; as Mrs Amelia Conway said bitterly, on the parson's prig's birthday. But she, together with the butler and the valet, thanked their master when, the day before his marriage, he told them they must have a wedding breakfast among themselves, all the staff to be included, and that twenty bottles of wine and spirits could be taken from the cellar.

They thanked him most profusely and wished him happiness, to which he answered, 'Thank you, but that is already mine.'

As the honeymoon was to be curtailed to a fortnight, he said he knew that everything would be in order when he returned with their mistress. It seemed to them as they said later, he stressed the last word . . .

And now the valet was in the housekeeper's room, telling the butler and Mrs Conway as well as the first footman McTaggart the details of, as he said, the shabbiest wedding he had ever attended. 'The church was like an icebox,' he said. 'And there the master and her stood before her father, and the old fellow seemed to throw the service at them. Sometimes he mumbled and sometimes he almost most barked. Her brother gave her away, and Sir George Golding was the best man, while Lady Golding attended the bride. And there was the grandmother and the three maids sitting in one pew and the churchwarden and his daughters sitting at the other side. When it was over they didn't go back into the vicarage so there wasn't a glass raised. There was some kissing and shaking hands all round, but when she came to her father, who was standing apart, she threw her arms around his neck and he held her for a moment, then pushed her away, only to grab her again and hug her as if he would never let her go. Oh – ' The valet shook his head mockingly before going on, 'It was all very touching, for as she was about to get into the carriage she turned and, taking the small bouquet she had been carrying and which was half crushed now with the encounter with her dear papa, she went up to the warden's daughter and gave it to her. Then, what do you think? she, the warden's daughter, began to cry. Oh my! Oh my! I tell you, it was all very touching. Then they were off, taking only two valises, a case and a trunk. That warden's daughter would have had as much. Well now' – he looked from one to the other – 'let's make hay while the sun shines for the harvest, from now on, is going to be very poor unless we put our heads together.'

3

The couple spent the first night of their married life at their London house where they had been warmly welcomed by the four servants, particularly by the man Johnson and his wife. The house, as Dennison had described to her, was comparatively small, the rooms not as big as those in the vicarage, but so comfortably furnished and warm as to be called homely. The dinner was not elaborate but they lingered over it. Their talk was perfunctory and after dinner they sat on a sofa before the fire to have their coffee. When this was cleared away, he drew her into his arms and held her gently, saying, 'I can't believe it. I just can't believe it.'

Nor could she believe it, for not only her mind but her whole body seemed churned with a mixture of feelings: she was sad because of her father's attitude; she was full of wonderment that she was now the wife of a rich landowner and was mistress of two estates and a town house; but above all these other feelings, she was fearful of what lay ahead in this first night of marriage. Yet, childishly, she told herself, her mama, and papa, had experienced such a night, and they were good, even holy people, so what was there to be afraid of?

She was still asking the same question when Mary Johnson bid her good night and left her alone in the bedroom, after having been told gently that she could manage in her undressing.

Her grandmama had bought her her nightdress and matching negligee. Both were of soft white lawn. The nightdress had a frilled lace collar threaded with pink satin ribbon; it had a ruched front and an extra full skirt. She had taken down her hair and, remembering her grandmama's instructions, had not plaited it but had tied it loosely with a ribbon that matched the nightdress.

She was standing looking at herself in the long cheval mirror and being surprised by her reflection when a tap came on the door and it opened. Instinctively, she wanted to scamper to the bed and seek cover beneath the bedclothes, but she remained still, looking across the room to where he stood for a moment surveying her. He was wearing a brown velvet dressing-gown with deep revers; his hair was brushed well behind his ears; his face had been newly shaved; his eyes seemed lost in their own light.

It was some seconds before he moved towards her, and then, taking her gently into his arms, he said softly, 'Smile.'

'I . . . I can't. I . . . I'm afraid.'

'Oh, my dear, never be afraid of me. Just remember, I love you. Always remember, I love you, and from this night onwards you will love me.'

Her first night of marriage proved to be a mixture of embarrassment, pain, and a strange new feeling that she had no word for, as yet, for it was beyond happiness, beyond the feeling of love her family had engendered in her. It's source was somewhere outside herself, yet deep within her being. It was elusive and couldn't be held. It was born of contact, born out of pain which was to lessen as the days of the honeymoon progressed. And they progressed in a maze of wonderment.

On the second day of their marriage during which he seemed to have grown younger, so boyish did he act, he played guide through the museums, took her to see Buckingham Palace and the Tower of London and lastly the Zoological Gardens, where at the entrance the hired cabby cried, 'Mondays sixpence, evey other day a shilling.' He was a very jolly man, the cabby, and had seemed to enjoy driving them, on and off, all day through fine drifting snow.

In the evening, after a dinner served in a restaurant, the grandeur of which, she observed, outdid the ballroom at The House, she visited her first theatre and sat in a box, but could hardly keep her attention on the stage, where scantily dressed ladies danced and men sang funny songs and made jokes, the gist of which she was unable to laugh at because she could not understand them. What interested her was the galaxy of people and the way the audience was dressed, especially those in the boxes. The upper parts of many of the ladies were almost as bare as the ladies dancing on the stage. Her own dress of blue velvet had a lace top to it which ended in a blue velvet ribbon around her throat. Dennison had chosen that she should wear it.

The following day they crossed over to France. She had prided herself that she could speak French, that was until she heard the Parisians talking, and but for answering 'merci' and 'oui' she did not attempt to converse in their tongue. But not so Dennison, for he was very much at home with the language, and with the people.

The weather was cold and stormy, but did not keep them indoors. Again he played guide, but his manner now was not so much boyish as gay. They went in a rocketing cab to Versailles, to Notre-Dame, to the Conciergerie. The second evening they attended an opera and during the interval he proudly took her arm and paraded her among the packed throng in the comparatively small foyer and was not at all annoyed when gentlemen's eyes were turned on her.

It was nearly two in the morning when they drove back to their hotel. Later, as she lay in his arms, he asked her if she had enjoyed the opera, and she answered truthfully, 'Not very much, not as much as the entertainment in London.' And at this he had rolled her backwards and forwards as he laughed, saying, 'Where has my little vicarage maiden gone?'

There had been times during their short stay in London when she was rudely jolted out of this fairy-tale existence into which she had been drawn, and jolted into life that was real and awful, such as when the cab driver had driven them along out of the way routes in the city and they had passed through narrow streets where men lurked in doorways and women had hard and weary faces; even the very young ones looked old, and most of the children were ragged and barefoot. But of course she had seen ragged and barefoot children before; not so many, though, as seemed to swarm in London. And yet those London children were chirpy individuals, more so than those nearer to home. There was, she knew, great poverty in the towns round about Newcastle, even in their own village. Her papa had once got up a clog club and had asked the parishioners to subscribe whatever they could afford to provide for the needy children of the neighbourhood. And when the subscriptions had been thin, her papa had pointed out it was because the parishioners didn't like collections of any kind, especially the farming community who objected to the tithes and anything else that meant the laying out of money without visible return.

But overall the essence of the fairy-tale remained with her until what was to be their last evening in Paris when he took her to a casino. This experience would, he said, expunge the vicarage forever.

He often joked about her vicarage upbringing, but she didn't mind in the least because, in a way, she felt he was glad she'd had such a narrow experience for it gave him the opportunity to open up a new world for her.

But the visit to the casino was to have the opposite effect on her from that intended. In the first place, she was shocked at the sight of women gambling. Ladies all, at least so it was proclaimed by their dress, and the tone of their voices, and the arrogance of their manners.

She was further amazed when Dennison was greeted warmly by an immaculately dressed gentleman who was not a patron, but who seemed to be in charge of the establishment, for he greeted him by name and was enthusiastic in his welcome. But it was noticeable to her that she wasn't introduced to this gentleman. After he had left them she whispered, 'You know him?' And he whispered back, mockery in his voice, 'Yes, my dear; it is not the first time I have been in Paris.' She remembered now her papa referring to him as a gambler. 'And don't look so frightened; there are no tigers about, they are all very nice people. Come!' He took hold of her hand. 'I shall show you my only skill.' . . .

For the next hour she watched him practising his skill: first at a roulette table. And when, after twenty minutes or so, he rose from it, she looked at him in something like horror as she said, 'You have lost the equivalent of fifty sovereigns?'

'Yes, my dear, I have lost the equivalent of fifty sovereigns. But the night is young. Please,' he pleaded with her now, 'do not look so forbidding. I cannot recognize my Nancy Ann when you look like that. What is fifty sovereigns anyway?'

He now led her to a corner of the room where four men were sitting at a table, one of them rattling dice, and as they approached it he said, 'Give me three numbers.'

'What kind of numbers? High numbers?'

'No; anything from one to six.'

She blinked, thought a moment, then said, 'Two, three, six.' It was as if she was back in the nursery finding it difficult to say twice, so she would say, two, three, six, instead of twice three are six.

'Two, three, six, it will be.'

When a man vacated a chair, Dennison took it, and there followed some quick exchanges in French between him and another man.

She could not follow the game. She could see that three times out of four the die came up with a six for Dennison. After this there was more rapid exchange. One thing she noticed was, there was no actual money on the table, only small counters not unlike those she and the boys had used to play ludo, except these were larger. She watched Dennison push all the counters lying in front of him towards the middle of the table. She saw the other men shrug their shoulders, then push their counters likewise. Now Dennison glanced up at her before taking up an ivory cup and putting the die in it. There was silence round the table. When the die again turned up three there was a murmur of, 'Trois, trois, un, deux, trois.'

He glanced at her again; then proceeded to make further throws, the continued silence accentuating the ominous rattling of the die in the cub. When, for the third time, it turned up two there were exclamations of amazement from two of the men, but the third one's face looked blank. This man was sitting opposite and he now handed Dennison a bag.

Having put the counters in the bag, Dennison guided her down the room.

At the touch of his arm, Dennison turned to the man of the blank countenace who spoke rapidly at him. When Dennison shook his head and pointed to Nancy Ann, the man shrugged his shoulders and turned away. And when Nancy Ann asked, 'What was he saying?' Dennison answered, 'He wanted to know if I had a special system, or was it a trick, and I said, no, I just had a clever wife who gave me the numbers.'

The gentleman who had greeted them when they first entered was standing by the desk at which the counters were exchanged, and, his manner still bright, he said in stilted English, 'It is your lucky night, Monsieur. You are staying long?'

'Long enough to come back and lose my gains.'

'You are a sportsman. Always a sportsman. It is a pleasure both to see you and your lady.' And as he inclined his head towards Nancy Ann, Dennison said, 'My wife, Monsieur.'

'Ah! Ah!' His mouth opened wide on the exclamation and, taking her hand, he bowed over it before raising it to his lips, then saying, 'Congratulations, and happiness, Madame, always happiness.'

She was still blushing as they passed through the doors into the cold night air. When the cab rolled up out of the darkness, he helped her inside and gave the name of a restaurant on the Champs Elysées.

'How . . . how much did you win?' she now asked in a small voice. And when he, patting the pocket of his greatcoat, answered. 'Five hundred guineas,' she actually jumped away from him along the seat, and her voice seemed to come out of the top of her head as she muttered, '*Five* hundred guineas!'

'Yes, my dear, five hundred guineas, so you can say I am only four hundred and fifty guineas to the good, or at least we are only four hundred and fifty guineas to the good, because you know, you did it.'

'I didn't. I didn't. I . . . I don't like gambling. I . . . I don't like to see you gambling.'

'Oh, my dear, it is a harmless pastime . . . when you can afford it.'

'And . . . and can you really afford to lose such sums?'

'I didn't lose, my dear, I won.'

'Do you always win?'

'No.' He leaned forward and gave her a peck on the lips, then repeated, 'No, madam, I don't always win.'

'But . . . but how did you manage to win on those numbers tonight?'

He did not answer her for a moment, but lay back against the smelly leather seat of the cab, and his voice seemed to come to her from a long distance, so soft was it as he replid, 'I don't know. I'll never know. I only remember that I thought deeply, I wished deeply. It seemed as if there was another voice saying, "I will lay a bet that I can turn the die up on the same number three times out of four." It wasn't the usual game. I realized now I was taking a big chance, yet not at that particular time. I willed it to happen and it did.' He turned quickly to her now, saying, 'I know what I'll do. Every time you accompany me to a game and I win – and I will if you are beside me – I will share the spoils. So tonight, madam, I owe you two hundred and fifty guineas.'

'*No! No!*' Her voice was emphatic. 'I could never touch money got like that. No, no; never!'

In the dim light given off by the side lamps, she watched his expression change, his voice also as he said, 'Then you are saying you will have nothing to do with my home or anything in it for, my dear, I come from a long line of gamblers. I am not as foolhardy as my ancestors who lost even the clothes from their backs. Nor will I ever make enough money or bet everything on a wager that would enable me to lose or build a house like my present home, or the lodge in Scotland, or that in London. It may further surprise you that my great-great-grandfather, one of the first chronicled in the early seventeen hundreds, was famous for running a gaming house in London. He is one of the men who lost his clothes, but he regained them agan and it was his grandson who built Rossburn towards the end of the last century. My father was a moderate gambler, but he gambled. My grandfather was more daring, for he also bought the lodge and our London house.'

He had turned from her and was looking straight ahead, and she knew that she had annoyed him, not only annoyed, but made him angry. She didn't want to make him angry, ever; he was so kind, so good to her. She . . . she loved him.

The thought, like a spur, lifted her close to him. She put an arm across him, her head on his shoulder knocking her hat askew, and, the tears in her voice, she said, 'I'm . . . I'm sorry, Denny, I am. I didn't understand. Please don't be annoyed with me.'

His arms were about her now; he was holding her tight. His voice changed, he was soothing her, saying, 'There, there. No, I'm not annoyed with you, of course not. How could I be? All I want is to make you happy.'

She raised her head from his shoulder. Her eyes blinking, her lips trembling, she said softly, 'I . . . I love you.'

He didn't move: he did not hold her tighter; he just stared into her face in the dimness, then pressed her gently from him, took his silver mounted walking stick and rapped the roof of the cab and, when it stopped, spoke in rapid French. Then, sitting back, he drew her into his arms again, saying softly, 'We are going home.' There was something in his tone that made her repeat, Home? You mean to the hotel?'

'No,' he answered, 'back to England, to London. We can stay there overnight, or longer if you wish, but . . . but we are on our way home.'

4

Nancy Ann was five months pregnant and the mound in her stomach definitely indicated this. For the first four months she had felt unwell, but over the past few weeks her feeling of well-being had returned. And tonight would be the third function she had attended in as many weeks; but she was once again complaining of the tightness of her corset.

Since returning home, she had refused to engage a personal maid, but had compromised by saying that she would have the assistance of Pattie Anderson, the top floor maid, when she felt it necessary. One of Anderson's functions, she had been told, was to attend to the needs of lady guests who were without maids. Lady Golding had already prompted her, she must never address her as Pattie, but give her her surname, as she must do with all her staff. This, at the beginning she had found awkward, having been used to Peggy, Jane, and Hilda. Now she was saying, 'It is much too tight, Anderson. I can hardly breathe.'

'You'll not get into your mauve gown else, ma'am.'

'Then I'll have to get into something else. Slacken the bottom tapes, please.'

She didn't like Anderson. She was a woman in her mid-thirties and the tallest of all the female staff. And Nancy Ann compared her manner with that of a chameleon's change of colour, for she had the habit of putting on a superior tone when they were in the room together, but should her master come in, then her voice would change to a soft persuasive note and her manner suggest that of an older wiser woman only too eager to help the young mistress over the pitfalls in the way of dress.

The pale mauve brocade dress on, the myriad of small buttons fastened, Nancy Ann sat at the dressing-table, and when the woman went to touch her hair she flicked her hand away, saying, 'Thank you. I can manage.'

'What jewellery were you thinking about wearing . . . ma'am?'

Nancy Ann had noticed the pause before the use of the title 'ma'am', not only with this woman, but with other members of the household too.

'I think I'll wear the pearls.'

'Pearls, with brocade? I would have thought, ma'am, the diamond necklace.'

She swung round on the dressing-stool and, looking straight up at the woman now, she said, 'I am wearing pearls, Anderson, and I can manage to put them on myself. Thank you. That is all.'

The woman drew herself up. There was an almost imperceivable nod of the head, then, her voice stiff, she said, 'Very good . . . ma'am,' and on that she turned and walked out.

Alone in the bedroom again, Nancy Ann leant her elbow on the dressing-table and rested her head on her hands for a moment. There was a war going on in this house. She'd felt it from the moment she had come back after the honeymoon. It was understood she would see Mrs Conway each morning and discuss with her the menu for the day, or the meal if they were entertaining company. But from the beginning the housekeeper had informed her, by a look, if not by words, that she was well capable of arranging the menus and for providing for any guests that might come.

The butler's manner to her was polite, as it would be to any guest. But there was one person on the staff that she actually disliked, and that was Dennison's man. She knew her grandmama's name for his manner would have been oily. She had even expressed her feelings about the valet to Dennison, and he had been surprised, saying in the man's defence that he was a very good valet and he had found no cause for complaint during the six years he had been with him. But he had gone on to explain to her that servants were a different breed altogether from . . . well, the class. They were brought up to be subservient, and, at times, could give the impression that they were sly. This was the word she had used about Staith. And he had ended his little sermon by saying that she mustn't expect too much of them. Each of them had his appointed work and if this was done well, that was all she need worry about; in fact, she need not worry about the house at all; she could just leave it in the capable hands of Conway and Trice.

She often longed for the proximity of the girls back in the vicarage, and to be able to go into the kitchen any time she liked and talk to them. She had only once entered the kitchen of this house, which wasn't a kitchen, but kitchens, and she knew this had caused some consternation; especially to the young woman Mather who had stood at the doorway watching her as she spoke to the boy, David.

The morning following her visit, the housekeeper had said, 'If you wish to visit the kitchen, ma'am, I will make arrangements.'

And to this Nancy Ann had cooly replied, 'It won't be necessary for I don't know when I shall be feeling so inclined. But should I do so, I think I can find my way there.'

However, she had realized during the past months that although many of the staff looked upon her still as that chit from the vicarage, they were, nevertheless, coming to realize just what liberties they could take with her. There were just two of the house staff who had shown her small kindnesses since she had become their mistress, and these were Henry Robertson, the second footman, and Jane Renton, the first housemaid. Renton was small and thin with dark merry eyes, and her countenance was not always stiff. She put Nancy Ann in mind of Hilda.

Her mind on the vicarage, her thoughts dwelt on her papa. She was worried about him, as were her grandmama and Peter. He had become very forgetful of late: only a week ago he had kept a congregation waiting; then, instead of a sermon, he had just read them the twenty-third psalm; and he had not afterwards stood at the church door to bid them good day, but had stridden away into the countryside and had not returned until late in the afternoon. The doctor was to call today, and she was anxious for the morrow to come so that she could slip over and find out what his advice was regarding her father. It was evident that there was something mentally wrong with him, yet, when he spoke, his words sounded reasonable enough. But he always had to recollect himself before he could give an answer, and that wasn't like her father.

Her toilet finished, she rose from the stool, passed the big high heavy satin-draped four-poster bed to where the open door led on to the balcony, and there she stood looking out over the gardens towards the village and the vicarage, and her thoughts weren't happy.

She turned now from the balcony railings when she heard Dennison come from his dressing-room. As he walked towards her his smile widened; and now, his hands on her shoulders, he looked down into her face, saying, 'My dear, you look delightful. Curves suit you.' Then he added softly and mishchievously, 'I must see that you are never without them.'

'Oh, Denny.' She turned her head away from him then, and, walking back into the room, she said, 'Do you know how many are expected?'

'Not all that many; I don't think their table will hold more than a dozen or so. As Pat said, it's a breaking in for Flo and Arthur. You would never think that Arthur and Pat were brother and sister; he's so retiring, can't get a word out of him at times.'

'I rather liked him.'

'Yes, I like them both.'

'Who . . . who are likely to be there?'

'Oh, the Maddisons I suppose, and the Ridleys, and of course Jim and Maggie O'Toole. There's a pair for you. To listen to them you wouldn't think there were any troubles in Ireland. They are the funniest people I know. And . . . and likely Bunny and May Braithwaite. Well, that would make fourteen all told. That would be about the lot.'

He picked up her silk coat from the back of the chair and put it round her, and as he fastened the buckle at the neck he said, 'If its a cosy do, private, after dinner you must do them a mime. George loves to see you doing a mime.'

'Do a mime, like this?' She patted her stomach.

'Why not?' His face was serious. 'That's not going to object.'

She pushed him and, laughing now, she turned away. And he was still smiling at his own joke when, some minutes later, he helped her into the landau.

The June night was warm, the air was still clear, and as they drove over the bridge at Durham towards their destination, which was on the outskirts of the town, she looked down on the river, saying, 'This is a most beautiful town, don't you think?' She was about to add, 'Look at the river, isn't it lovely!' when she remembered he wasn't fond of the river, and with cause.

He answered, 'Indeed it is, beautiful. The cathedral can hold its own against any other in the land.'

She said now thoughtfully, 'I would like to spend some time just wandering around it. My acquaintance with it is mostly what I read at school, yet Papa once spent his holiday in it.'

'Your father spent his holiday in the cathedral. How on earth did he do that? Take services?'

'No. He came down every day and either strolled about or just sat, or chatted with the Dean.' She added now, 'I'm worried about Papa. I . . . I don't know what's going to happen. I . . . I don't think he can carry on much longer, even if he wanted to.'

'Well, my dear' – he took her hand – 'I've told you, he and your grandmama must come to us. There are rooms going begging in the east and west wings.'

She looked at him, her face straight but the light in her eyes soft. He was so kind. But she couldn't say to him, 'He will never come to live in your house . . . our house.' Only last week her grandmama had said, 'I think our time here is short, but there's one thing sure, he will never accept your offer to live at The House.' And she'd had no need to add,' He would accept nothing from your husband, because his opinion of him has not changed.'

This was something she couldn't understand about her father: he had always been such a forgiving man. Often of late she had recalled that Sunday long ago when he had cried from the pulpit, 'Let him first cast a stone.' That was the day she had suggested to James that she would tell Eva McKeowan he was engaged. It was odd about Eva. In those days she had seemed such a flighty stupid young woman. But since she herself had known love she realized what Eva's feelings must have been at that time. Now she quite liked her. And apparently she wasn't the only one. But she could hardly take in the fact that Peter might be taking a fancy to her.

Peter spent every other Saturday afternoon and Sunday, which were his leave days, at the vicarage, and on a Sunday she would often see him stop and speak to Eva McKeowan. When the idea first entered her head she told herself that Eva was three years older than Peter, and surely Peter would never think about marrying a woman older than himself. But why not? Anyway, that was Peter's business.

She wished she weren't going to this party; yet she always enjoyed the company of Pat and her husband George. It had become routine over the past months for them and the Goldings to alternate in inviting each other to a card evening on Wednesday nights. The game they played was whist. She had become quite proficient at it, but always felt guilty when they played for money. The highest winning never exceeded five pounds which, except for herself, they found amusing. And if Dennison and she should win, for he always partnered her, he would ceremoniously divide the spoils when they returned home.

He had made one or two trips to London lately, and she knew that they were connected with business and that in all probability there would have been no gambling; nevertheless, his visits to Newcastle were always for that purpose alone. After one such visit he spilled seventy sovereigns into her lap, saying 'You have nothing in writing so I'm not going to give you half, merely a percentage.' On other occasions, on returning, he had either not mentioned his gaming or simply spread out his hands, smiled at her and said, 'The gods weren't with me'. . .

A short drive led up to the Rowland's residence, and to one side of the house was a large lawn dotted with flower beds among which she could see a few people strolling.

Florence and Arthur Rowland were at the door to meet them. Their one manservant took her cloak and Dennison's hat, and then they were walking towards the open doors of the drawing room, behind which she could see a number of other people, among them, Pat and George Golding.'

Pat immediately came towards them, talking rapidly as usual. 'Hasn't it been a swelter! I can't stand the heat. How are you my dear? Is it getting you down?' And without giving Nancy Ann time to say whether or not the heat was affecting her, Pat went on, 'You know everybody, so come into the garden straightaway, it's cool out there.'

As they made their way up the room, a lady came through an alcove, a gentleman on each side of her and laughing with her. But on the sight of the latest guests, the lady paused for a moment and in a high and almost childish voice that did not match her appearance she came towards them, crying, 'Oh, Denny! Hello there. And what is this latest I've just heard about you, my boy . . . Parliament?

Never! Never you!' And she dug him playfully now with her fan. 'Arnold tells me you're trying to get your foot in.'

It was evident that Dennison was both taken off his guard and embarrassed, but on a laugh he replied, 'Not my foot, I always go head first,' causing further laughter from the two gentlemen whom Nancy Ann knew to be Mr Bunny Braithwaite and Mr Edward Ridley. And it was Mr Ridley who said in a loud voice as if he were shouting from the other end of the room, 'That was an answer for you, Rene.'

Nancy Ann was looking at the woman before her. She was small of stature, being only five foot three; she was plump – a more correct description would be fat – so that the flesh flowed out of the top of her gown showing the curve of her breasts. But the skin, a light cream coloured with a blush to it, was perfect, as was that of her face. Her eyes were large and round and of a steely blue.

Nancy Ann felt a sickness riving her chest. Try as she might, she could not get the idea out of her head that, in some way, this woman menaced her life. She knew she had been a close friend of Dennison's, and once before when the woman, as now, was completely ignoring her, she had later said to him, 'That woman dislikes me intensely. She cannot forget the episode on the road with the dog,' and had then naïvely asked him, 'What kind of friend was she to you?' And she recalled it was a long moment before he answered, 'She was a friend, like any other of my neighbours.'

She watched her now thrust her hand through his arm, saying, 'Come. I have something to show you. You think you have a fine garden, but you've never seen a specimen like this.'

Dennison glanced at Nancy Ann as he left her side. His eyebrows were raised and there was a puckered smile on his face as if he was helpless in the situation.

Florence Rowland, happening now to come to her side, said, 'Would you like a cool drink, Nancy Ann?' But before she had time to reply Pat put in, 'Yes, she would, but I'll see to it, Flo. Come along, my dear, let us indulge ourselves.'

Pat now led her through an archway and into a room, to a long table on which was an assortment of coloured drinks, with two maids standing behind the table ready to serve. But Pat did not guide her towards the table, but to the further end of the room where there was a deep window-seat and, gently pulling her down, she said, 'Get that look off your face.'

Nancy Ann made no reply but swallowed deeply, and Pat went on, 'Flo did not invite them, not really. Arnold Myers is in the Diplomatic Service, the same as Arthur, and so, apparently, they occasionally meet, not only in town and abroad, but here and there. Well, Arnold had just come back from a trip and was pleased to find that Flo and

Arthur had settled near here, and when they dropped in it was natural for Flo to ask them to stay on.'

'That woman ignores me, Pat. I've told you before.'

'Oh' – Pat wagged her head – 'she ignores all women. She's a man eater. Anyway, you have no need to worry about Denny.' She patted Nancy Ann's hand as she now said, 'I've never known Denny to be in love before, and now he is wallowing in it and with one whom I imagine to be a very sensible girl, even if she was incarcerated in a vicarage all her young days.'

Nancy Ann smiled faintly as she replied, 'There was no incarceration. From what I have noticed these last few months with regard to the upbringing of young ladies, I had extreme liberty; in fact, I realize now, I ran wild for most of my young days.'

'Well, it certainly didn't do you any harm. And now, don't let that little bitch get under your skin, because, let's face it, she is a bitch. However, I must admit, not of the mongrel type: she comes from a thoroughbred stock and, like most thoroughbreds, she has been pampered and spoilt all her days. And like many of them coming under that category, her intelligence is not as bright as her pedigree.'

Pat was now laughing widely at her similes; then pushing Nancy Ann gently, she ended, 'If she was a common mongrel bitch one would know how to deal with her: you would grab her by the hair, kick her in the backside, and fling her out of the door, preferably naked. But with her special kind, you must use guile and finesse.'

She was laughing loudly now and Nancy Ann was forced to join her. As they rose to their feet she put out her hand and said, 'What would I have done in this situation, Pat, without you?'

'Followed the advice of your grandmama. Anyway, she and I think alike. I'm going to call in some day this week and see her. Now come on, let us not spoil Flo's little party, which I really did think promised to be dull until I saw Jim and Maggie O'Toole. When they start on their Irish yarns they make one forget all one's troubles. Chin up! Shoulders back, and stomach out.' And on this last quip her laughter rang through the room as she led Nancy Ann out of it without allowing her to have the promised cooling drink . . .

It could be said that the evening was a pleasant one. The conversation at the dinner table was merry, made so as Pat had foretold by the two Irish guests, with the husband and wife outdoing each other in telling tales of events that took place in their homes on the outskirts of Dublin. Rene Myers, too, seemed in very high spirits as she quipped across the table with the men opposite her, and more often than not including Dennison. Her husband, on the other hand, had little to say. He was a dour man with a long face, black hair that lay flat on his head, and he had the disconcerting habit of staring fixedly at one without speaking. It was widely known that he was in love with his wife and that he put up with her foibles because he didn't want to lose her. It was also widely known that he was a very rich man. A millionaire twice over some said.

There being no room to dance and no tables set out for cards, by eleven o'clock most of the guests had departed. The night had become cooler and the remaining company were seated in the drawing-room.

Dennison was sitting on a couch with Maggie O'Toole on one side of him and Rene Myers on the other. And every time Maggie O'Toole came out with some funny remark causing general laughter, Nancy Ann noticed that the woman, as she thought of her, lolled against Dennison, even going as far as putting her head on his shoulder.

She herself was sitting on one edge of a love seat, with George on the other side.

On another couch, Jim O'Toole sat beside Florence Rowland; and flanking Florence was Arnold Myers, with Arthur Rowland sitting perched on the end. And that was the company when Dennison, leaning forward in Nancy Ann's direction, said, 'Do us the McLoughlin fellow, dear.'

'Oh no!' Nancy Ann shook her head. But when Pat and George put in together, 'Yes, do, Nancy Ann. Come on,' and Pat, turning to Maggie O'Toole, said, 'She'll beat you at your own game.'

'Well, let's see it. Let's see it,' cried Maggie O'Toole. 'What does she do?'

'She mimics. It's amazing. Come on, do.' Pat thrust out her hand in a wagging movement as if she were lifting Nancy Ann from the chair. And when Dennison said again, softly, 'Come on, dear,' she said to herself, Why not? She had this one gift, and it was a gift because, as her grandmama said, no one in the family on either side had ever been on the stage. Anyway, it was unthinkable that they should have been, so her accomplishment must be in the nature of a gift. And she had practised it for years; even lately, in the privacy of her own room and for her own entertainment she had imitated the various members of her staff.

She got to her feet and by way of explanation she said, 'I . . . I've known the McLoughlin family since I was a small girl, and I was surprised one day when I saw the eldest son in the courtyard, and this is the conversation that followed.' She moved to stand in front of the flower-banked fireplace and, assuming a matronly dignity, her hands joined at her waist, she began, 'You are one of the McLoughlins?'

Then, when her whole expression and her manner changed with very little movement of her body and there came out of her mouth the thick Irish vowels speaking the northern dialect, there was a gust of laughter from the company, and she had to stop until it subsided. And Pat's voice admonished them, 'Be quiet now. Be quiet. Let her go on.'

And they tried to let her go on, but there were tears of laughter running down the cheeks of Maggie O'Toole and that of her husband by the time she had finished.

Amid the clapping Maggie O'Toole cried, I've never seen the likes. The Dublin Group couldn't have done any better, could they now, Jim?'

'They couldn't that. It's on the stage you should be, me girl, not stuck away in this backwater. Now if you ever want a career for yourself, I know the very . . .

'Be quiet! Jimmy.'

She was about to go on when the thin voice of Arnold Myers cut in, saying, 'Give us some other servant.'

Unsmiling, Nancy Ann looked at him now from where she was still standing before the fireplace and in a cool voice she said, 'I don't do servants. I only do Shane because, as I said, I have known his family for so long and because I am sure he would enjoy being mimicked.

'Give us the ticket collector.'

She looked at Sir George and, smiling now, she said, 'All right, the ticket collector.' Then she went on to explain.

'It happened this way. I was in Newcastle station with my papa. We were to meet the boys, my two brothers coming back from university. When my papa went to the inquiry office I went to buy some platform tickets, and in front of me was a lady and her daughter who was about nine years old. She was a very prim lady and spoke precisely, and what she was saying was – ' She now took up the stance of the lady and in a high mincing voice she said, 'One and a half returns to Jayro.' Then immediately her head seemed to sink into her shoulders, and it tilted to one side as if she were looking up under a grid and, her voice changing into the thick twang and dialect, she said' What was that, missis? Where d'ya wanna go?'

Again she changed. '*Jayro*,' she said. 'One and a half returns to '*Jayro*.'

Again she changed. 'Jayroo? 'Taint on this line, missis.'

'Don't be stupid, man.'

'Tryin' not to be, missis.'

Turning her head to the side and her mouth twisting, she said, 'Willy! Here a tick. You know where this place *Jayroo* is?'

She had lifted her elbow as if nudging another man. Then quickly she again changed her stance. Her face stretched, her eyebrows went up, and this new character, Willy, turned its head slightly and apparently looked down on a child, saying, 'Where does ya ma want to go, hinny?'

'Jarrer.' The voice came out like that of a little girl.

Then with lightning speed she was once again the long faced ma turning to his companion and saying, 'It's Jarrer, man, she's askin' for . . . Jarrer!'

'Oh, Jarrer. Well why couldn't she say that instead of talkin' like a bloomin' foreigner . . . Jayroo.'

There followed enthusiastic applause, much laughter, from all present, except, Nancy Ann was quick to notice, that woman, who had never even smiled once during her performance. She had been aware of her attitude right from the start, when she had done Shane, and the advice her papa had laughingly given to James when they were discussing how to hold an audience, whether it be a congregation or a class in a schoolroom, had come to her: 'Concentrate on the one that is about to go to sleep, or on a face that you know resents you, or, in my case, on someone who has been dragged to church unwillingly,' her papa had said. 'Get that one's attention and you needn't bother about the rest of the company.'

But tonight she had been unable to apply that advice: that woman's determination not to be amused was too strong.

She now watched her pull herself to the end of the deep couch and attempt to rise, a signal for Dennison to get to his feet and offer her his hand. And now she was looking around her, saying, 'Well, we must be going because we are leaving early in the morning for London,' and glancing at her husband while adding, 'I don't know why he's got to work when other people are on holiday. Town will be empty.'

It was Maggie O'Toole's voice that broke in now, saying, 'Well, we'll be passing through next week, Rene, for we're off to Rome; the Pope's giving a ceilidh.' And she put her head back and laughed, the others also joining in. Then she turned to Rene again, saying, 'We'll look in on you and beg a meal.'

'Do. Do.'

And now Nancy Ann felt a restriction in her throat when the woman turned back to Dennison and said, 'Are you coming up, Denny?'

'I may do. I may do,' he answered casually.

'Well, you'll drop in, won't you?'

'Thank you, yes. Thank you.'

'That's a promise. I'll expect you to honour it.'

She now turned and looked towards her husband and nodded.

There followed a chorus of goodbyes, and when Arthur Rowland said, 'I'll see you to your carriage,' she flapped her hand at him, saying, 'Don't worry, we can see ourselves out.'

'Nonsense.'

Arthur and Flo went ahead, Arnold Myers followed, but his wife seemed to linger, saying a last word here and there, and when she eventually passed Nancy Ann, who was standing a little apart, she did so as if she weren't there.

Those remaining had seated themselves again, Jim and Maggie O'Toole, Pat and George, and Dennison. And to Nancy Ann they were like a family group. And with this feeling it seemed that the devil entered into her. She wanted to hit back in some way at the woman whose attitude towards her, she felt sure, had not escaped those present tonight, and so, as if she were indeed among her own family, she did another turn. Pointing her feet slightly outwards, and seeming to pull her head down into her neck, her already prominent stomach thrust further outwards, her arms held away from her sides as if by fat, she waddled two or three steps up the room saying as she did so in an exact imitation of Rene Myer's voice, 'I'm off to London tomorrow to spread my charms over the male population, and there's enough of me to cover them and plenty to spare.'

She knew she was reacting spitefully, and she really did not expect laughter from those present, but she felt they would understand the reason for her retaliation, especially Pat and George. But they were all staring at her, wide-eyed; and yet, not at her, but beyond her. She turned her head slowly to see standing there in the doorway the person she had been mimicking. She drew in a long deep breath as she watched the woman walk slowly up the room to a side table, pick up a vanity bag, turn as slowly about and walk down the room again. But when she came to Nancy Ann's side she paused for a moment but she did not speak, yet the steely glint in her eyes spoke for her. She was passing through the doorway into the hall when Dennison's voice called, 'Rene. Rene. Wait!' And as he passed Nancy Ann almost at a run, the look he too cast on her also spoke his thoughts.

She stood shivering, her eyes closed, until she felt Pat's hand on her arm and heard her voice low, saying, 'You shouldn't have done that. Come and sit down.'

'No, no. I . . . we'd better be going.' She looked to where the O'Tooles and George were standing, and she muttered, 'I'm sorry.'

'Oh, away with you!' Maggie O'Toole was by her side now. 'Don't you be sorry for having said that. It's what we all think but haven't the nerve to say it, me dear. You've got no need to worry. You're a match for her, I can see. But I'll tell you this – ' and smiling, she leant forward close to Nancy Ann as she whispered, 'Having listened to you there, it surprises me that you come out of a vicarage.'

At this point Dennison entered the room and said to George, 'We'll be away.' That was all.

He did not look at or speak to her until five minutes later when they were seated in the landau which now had the hood up. They had been driving some distance when, from deep in his throat, he said, 'If that insult had come out of a whore's mouth I could have understood it. You have made an enemy tonight where you could have made a friend.'

She had an answer to this, but she gritted her teeth and decided to wait until they were in the privacy of their room.

Once they reached the house he did not follow her upstairs as was his rule and have a drink brought up to him, but he went into the library. And when she entered the bedroom and saw Anderson waiting for her, she threw off her cloak, saying, 'Just unbutton my dress, please, and undo the lace of the corset, I will see to the rest.' Then she added thoughtfully, 'You . . . you must be tired. Get to bed.'

'Thank you, ma'am.' And the woman did as she was bid.

Half undressed, Nancy Ann sat down on the chaise-lounge and, bending forward, she buried her face in her hands.

Finally she finished her undressing and got into her dressing-gown, but she did not go to bed, she sat waiting for his coming up. It was almost an hour later when she heard him enter his dressing-room and talk to his man, and another half an hour passed before he entered the bedroom. He stood looking at her for a moment where she sat, not the picture of dejection as he might have expected, but straight-backed and stiff-faced. He seemed to be waiting for her to make some comment, and when she didn't, he said, 'What you might not know, Nancy Ann, is that the O'Tooles, as charming as they are, are chatterboxes and gossipers, and your spiteful little charade will be around half the county by this time tomorrow night.'

She rose to her feet and, her voice controlled, she said, 'I shall ask you a question, Dennison' – she gave him his full name now – 'and for once I should like a really truthful answer. Was that woman your mistress?'

She watched the muscles of his face tighten, his cheeks darken to a red hue, before the answer came, grimly, 'Yes, she was. But let me add that it was in the past, she is in the past. I shouldn't have to explain to you that I have hardly left your side since I first proposed marriage, and that my whole way of life has altered. I don't even have the friends I once had: I have dropped them, or, as has generally happened, they have dropped me, because I wanted to fit in with your type of life. And I have imagined I had achieved what I had set out to do. What is more, if I had married a woman of the world and she had suggested what you suggested at your little charade, I would have understood it. But that you, of all people, with your upbringing, and a guest in someone else's house, should imply that another guest was nothing more than a . . .'

His teeth clamped together and he shook his head, but it was she who put in the word now: 'Whore?' she suggested.

When he stared at her, she went on, 'You implied my words could have come from the mouth of a whore, and that I was implying something other than I was. What I was alluding to was her fat and her monopoly of all the men in the company. There was no deeper meaning in my mind. It was you who put the wrong construction on it.'

'Oh, my God!' He put his hand to his brow and turned from her, muttering now, 'Your innocence is worse than your knowledge.' Then he sprang round and faced her again as she cried at him, 'Then in my innocence I hit the truth, because she *is* a whore.'

'She is no such thing. And don't you dare say she is. And don't let me hear that word come out of your mouth again. She was a good friend to me, a good companion, and she took my marriage to you in a very civilized way, and I'm ashamed of your attitude. Let me tell you something, Nancy Ann, you have a lot to learn yet about this way of life. Good night.'

Her mouth dropped open, her eyes widened as she saw him walk into the closet room and close the door. She wanted to run after him and say, 'I'm sorry. Oh, I am sorry,' but she couldn't. That woman had been his mistress: she had lain with him; she had . . . She closed her eyes tightly on the thought, which provoked the reaction: It's just as well he sleeps alone, for I could not bear his touch tonight.

5

The rift between Dennison and herself was momentarily forgotten the next afternoon when she arrived at the vicarage and into a scene of some commotion, because Peter was there, having got leave from school, as also was Mr Mercer. Peter met her in the hallway and immediately drew her into the study, saying, 'The Bishop's been. Father has to retire.'

'Well,' she sighed, 'that doesn't come as a great surprise. We've been expecting it, haven't we?'

'Yes, but the point is, they've got to leave here.'

'Yes, I understand that too.'

He looked at her closely, saying, 'Are you not feeling well?'

'Not too bright today, Peter.' And his immediate assumption was that her condition was causing her discomfort.

'Graham is in with Grandmama,' he said. 'What do you think of the idea of them going to live in the little Dower House?'

'*Mr Mercer's?*'

'I wish you wouldn't keep calling him Mr Mercer. He's Graham.'

'Well, yes, I think it's a marvellous idea.'

'Come along then and let him explain.' And now he led the way to the sitting-room where, on their entering, Graham Mercer rose from his seat beside Jessica who said, 'Oh, there you are, my dear. There you are. Come and sit down. There is a lot to talk about.'

'Good afternoon.' She inclined her head towards Graham, and he said, 'Good afternoon, Nancy Ann.'

'Has Peter told you about the Bishop and . . . and the kind offer of Graham here?'

'Yes, yes he has, but . . . but what does Papa say?'

'Nothing much,' her grandmama replied, 'except that he seems quite willing to give up the living, and equally willing to take Graham's offer of living in the Dower House.' She now turned and looked at Graham, saying, 'I cannot tell you, Graham, what this means to me because, as I've already put my cards on the table to you, had we to buy a house it could, of necessity, have been little more than a cottage, and that of the meagre kind; you see, what money I had has gone. Oh, my dear.' She turned now and thrust out her arm towards Nancy Ann whom she had seen was about to protest in some way, likely to say that Dennison would provide any monies necessary. And she went on, 'I know what you're going to say, but you already know what your father thinks, and the solution that Graham here has offered is a real godsend. There's no other word for it.' And she turned to him now, adding, 'It is a beautiful little house. We are indeed fortunate.'

He smiled from one to the other as he shook his head, saying, 'Oh, I don't know that you'll still keep your opinion once you're settled. My steward used to live there until some years ago when he gave a number of reasons why he should leave. First of all, it was too big for his wife to keep up, there being eight rooms and offices. Secondly, all the chimneys smoked. Thirdly, no matter how you wedged the upper windows, they rattled. Fourthly, the well that supplied them with water would always run dry in the summer and they had to carry the water from the river. But the main reason seemed to be that it was in a lonely spot at the extreme end of the estate, adjoining your boundary.' He now nodded towards Nancy Ann, then ended, 'And no decent road within half a mile.'

'I . . . I know the house. 'Tis very pretty, and it is most kind of you. I do appreciate it.'

''Tis nothing, 'tis nothing.' He waved his gesture away with a flick of his hand.

Nancy Ann now looked at her grandmother and asked, 'What about the girls?'

'Oh, that's been settled too. Peggy and Hilda are to come with us, and Jane – ' She now glanced towards Graham, adding, 'Graham is taking her on in the kitchen; one of the maids has left.' Then, her lips trembling, the lines of her face converging into folds under her eyes, she muttered, 'They say God provides, but . . . but He's got to have an instrument.' The tears were full in her eyes as she pulled herself upwards with Peter's help as she muttered, 'Excuse me. Excuse me, Graham.' Then Peter led her from the room . . .

Graham Mercer was now thirty years old. He was of small stature, but being extremely thin, he looked more than his five feet six inches in height. His hair was dark and thick and he wore it short, trimmed well behind his ears and away from the back of his collar. His eyes too were dark, round and heavily black-lashed, which seemed to hide their expression. One was apt to gauge what he was thinking more from his voice, which was surprisingly deep coming out of such a thin frame. His mouth was wide, the corners drooping slightly. Altogether, his features gave off the appearance of sombreness.

Nancy Ann had rarely seen him smile and she had never heard him laugh, but nevertheless, she knew he was a kind and thoughtful man, and she said so now: 'You are so kind. I . . . I don't know what to say, or how to thank you. You . . . you know that I would have gladly had my papa and grandmama with me but . . . well' – she shook her head slowly – 'perhaps you know my father's views as well as I do. I cannot understand them, they trouble me; and so I am doubly grateful for your kindness.'

He made the same impatient movement as before with his hand, saying, 'If you only knew, I am acting out of selfish motives. I am very fond of your father, and it would be good to have someone near to whom I could talk. I feel sure, once he has rest he will regain all his faculties. Of course he hasn't really lost them, his present state has been brought about through the strain of losing your mama. I'm sure of that. And of course, at the same time he lost you too, and this, in a way, was another bereavement. Oh. Oh, please!' He appealed to her now, his hand outstretched. 'I am not in the least apportioning any blame, but . . . but you know what I mean.'

'Yes, yes, Mr Mercer, of course.'

He half-turned away from her, bowed his head and shook it vigorously. Then looking at her again, he said, 'If you feel in any way indebted to me, you can repay me. It is very simple.'

'How? How can I do that?'

'By forgetting that I am Mr Mercer and remember that my name is Graham. The boys have always called me Graham. Your father, your mama, and grandmama, have always called me Graham, only you have persisted in being so formal.'

She watched him smile his rare smile, straightening out the corners of his mouth, and she smiled in return, saying, 'Very well, I will repay my debt . . . Graham.'

'Thank you, Nancy Ann.' And they bowed to each other. Then quite suddenly she sat down on the horsehair sofa and, leaning forward, she put her hand to her brow.

Instantly he was bending over her, saying, 'What is it? Are you feeling unwell?'

After a moment she looked up at him. 'Yes and no,' she said.

'Physically I am well, but . . . the past few days have proved very trying.' She didn't stick to the absolute truth and say, The past day.

'Well, now your father is settled, you need worry no more. I shall see to it personally that he is well looked after, and I shall visit him daily.'

She sighed, then said, 'Thank you. Thank you.'

For a moment he stared at her; then flipping the tails of his long coat to each side, he sat down on the edge of the sofa and, staring into her face, he said, 'Is there anything else wrong?'

Her eyelids blinked rapidly, her mouth opened twice, then closed tight, and she was about to shake her head when he said, 'Is there anything wrong at Rossburn? Something happened that has upset you?'

She turned to him again. He was younger than Dennison and, in spite of the stern look he mostly carried, he was very presentable. Her father said that this man had loved her, had wanted to marry her. If she had married him he would not have said to her, Yes, I had a mistress. He would not have sat with the woman on the sofa and let her nestle against him. If she had married this man, her papa and grandmama would have come to the Manor House and they would have lived as a family.

She shuddered. What on earth was she thinking about? She loved Dennison in spite of his past.

When the hand came tentatively on hers she went to withdraw it, then let it lie. And when he looked into her face, saying, 'Nancy Ann, if ever you feel you need a friend in any way whatever, will you remember that I am here for as long as God spares me just in order to help you.'

The hand lifted abruptly from hers and she was surprised to see him swing up from the sofa and walk hurriedly from the room. And she was more surprised at her thoughts as she lay back against the hard head of the sofa, saying to herself, Yes, yes, life would indeed have been different if I'd married him.

It was evening before she saw Dennison again. She was in the bedroom changing for dinner. This was another routine she'd had to get used to, why one had to change so many times a day and especially for dinner when they were dining alone. But, as Dennison had informed her when they first came home, it was expected of them; there was a certain standard to keep up before the servants.

There came a tap on the bedroom door, She expected Anderson to enter, and so was surprised when she saw Dennison, for he never knocked on doors. She was standing near the wardrobe and he came slowly towards her and, putting his hands on her shoulders, he looked into her face, then without a word he bent and kissed her gently on the lips.

'Are we friends again?' he asked softly.

She was weary. There was no fight in her. At the moment she didn't care what he had done in the past, she only knew she wanted his arms about her again. And when, without a word, she fell against him and was enfolded once more, and as his lips traced themselves over her face the thought came to her, in something akin to horror and amazement, that only a few hours ago she had been about to confide her unhappiness, and this reason for it, to Mr Mercer . . . Graham. Really! Perhaps this is what carrying a child did to you: it weakened your reserves, for if she had felt inclined to confide in anyone, it should have been her grandmama, certainly not another man.

When she put her arms tight around Dennison's neck and returned his kisses, it was as if in relief that she had escaped some disaster . . .

Certain members of the staff were puzzled, not to say the least, when the master and mistress exchanged pleasantries during dinner, and later walked out into the garden arm in arm, for hadn't Staith reported that the master had for the first time slept in the dressing-room bed, and had been in a vile temper this morning. And it had all become so clear after Appleby, the coachman, had passed the word in that the lady Rene had been at the do last night, and that after a quick exchange between the master and mistress when they had entered the landau they had sat in silence all the way home. And yet, here they were, back to lovey-doveying again.

Well, time would tell. They knew their master's weaknesses better than most, and they had faith in the lady Rene. But if she was going to play any cards at all, they hoped she would soon get going, because this one was pushing her nose in where it wasn't wanted. Asking for the quarterly accounts to be given to her now. That was something that would have to be looked into and manoeuvred. Oh, yes, yes, that indeed was something that would have to be manoeuvred.

6

Nancy Ann did not choose her nursery-maid until three weeks before the child was due. She had interviewed five women from an agency in Newcastle. All had been over middle age, each had told her of her long history dealing with children, the one smelling strongly of spirits had related the longest history of all.

An advertisement in the *Newcastle Journal* brought twenty-two replies, and from these she chose four. And these she interviewed in her private sitting-room, Mrs Conway ushering them in, giving preference to the eldest first.

By the time Nancy Ann had reached and dismissed the third one, telling her she would be informed of the choice later, she was somewhat in despair and wondered if she was really being too pernickety, as Mrs Conway's manner suggested. The nurse for the confinement had been engaged, recommended by the doctor, but she was to stay only a month, and so the engaging of a nursery-maid was imperative.

She sighed deeply as the door opened once more and the housekeeper ushered in a young woman, saying, 'Hetherington, ma'am.'

Nancy Ann looked at the person crossing the room towards her: she could have been Hilda from the vicarage, but not so old; she was stockily built, with two bright brown eyes and a round face; she was dressed in a long blue serge coat buttoned up to the neck, and on top of a mass of brown hair she wore a straight brimmed felt hat; she carried a plaited raffia handbag and blue woolen gloves in one hand.

'Good afternoon, missis.'

Mrs Conway cast a sharp glance at her and it said, This one will never do. Speaking before she's spoken to!

'Good afternoon. Your name is?'

'Mary Hetherington, missis.'

'Ma'am.'

The young woman turned and looked at the housekeeper; then turning quickly back, she said to Nancy Ann, 'Sorry, madam . . . ma'am.'

'Sit down, please.' As she spoke the words Nancy Ann was aware of the housekeeper's surprise and annoyance. Then the young woman was seated, her hands gripping the handbag on her lap, and Nancy Ann enquired, 'Tell me what experience you've had with children, please.'

The young woman drew in a deep breath. 'Well, it goes back a long way, ma'am, because, you see, I'm the eldest of ten, and from I can remember I helped to bring them up till me father died when I was twelve, and then I went into service in the kitchen at Captain Dalton's house. I was thirteen when Mrs Dalton's first baby was born, and' – she smiled a little – 'it was a terror, missis . . . ma'am. Well, what I mean is, it cried night and day. She couldn't feed it, and the poor thing was hungry.'

Her smile widened. 'I think it was in desperation that they let me have it, I mean, to nurse. I used to put some treacle on my thumb and it would go off to sleep. Young Master Robbie, he's now seventeen and he still loves treacle.'

A cough brought both their glances to the housekeeper. Her face was tight, but Nancy Ann, feeling more relaxed than she had done for a long time, looked at the young woman again and said, 'Go on.'

'Well, that's where it started, ma'am. When Miss Florrie came the next year, I . . . I was promoted to nursemaid, and from there it went on. There was five of them, and . . . and I brought them up. Young Mister Luke was the last one and he went to boarding-school some months go. Mrs Dalton wanted me to stay on and look after the house 'cos she now joins her husband in sailing trips . . .'

'Which part of the country are you from?'

'North Shields, ma'am.'

'North Shields? It's quite a way from here.'

'Yes, ma'am, but . . . but I wouldn't mind that; I like the country. And . . . and I like dealin' with bairns . . . children, so Mrs Dalton understands, what I mean is, me looking for another position where there are children.'

Of a sudden Nancy Ann wanted to be rid of the housekeeper. She wanted to talk to this girl, this young woman. She had never felt so much at home with anyone in the way of staff since she had left the vicarage. She turned now and smiled at Mrs Conway, saying, 'Would you see to a tray being sent up?' Then instinctively she realized that the tray would be holding one cup only and she added, 'I'm expecting the master in any moment; he'll have it here. And, Conway, I have made my choice. Will you see that the other applicants have some refreshment and their expenses paid before they take the brake back to the station. I shall make arrangements for' – she turned and glanced at the young woman – 'Miss Hetherington to be sent on later.'

The housekeeper's stature seemed to increase. Nancy Ann could almost read her thoughts as she watched her turn stiffly and march from the room.

After a moment she sighed and leant back against the couch and, looking at Mary Hetherington, she said, 'By that you will have gathered, Miss Hetherington, that you are engaged.'

'Oh, ma'am, thank you. Thank you very much. I . . . I hope I'll suit. I feel sure I will in the nursery, but . . . but this is a big place. I've never been in a big house like this afore; the captain's house is like a cottage compared with it. But I'll serve you well, ma'am.'

'I feel sure you will. By the way, what was your wage?'

'Well' – Mary put her head to one side now as if apologizing for the statement she was about to make – 'I had risen to six shillings a week, ma'am, all found, uniform an' all.'

'Six shillings a week. Well, as I see it you were in a town and had access to shops and such. On your leave time here you would have to take a conveyance back to your home, which will cost you money, so shall we say eight shillings a week to begin with, this to be paid quarterly.'

'Oh, thank you, ma'am. Thank you very much indeed.'

Why was it, Nancy Ann wondered, that she was feeling more happy and contented than she had done for months past. Was it because she realized that here in this young woman she was to have an ally? She knew instinctively though that were she to make an ally of her, the young woman would have most of the household against her. There were things she would like to change in this house, and she promised herself that some day she would. Yes, she would. But she would be given no help in doing this from its master: what had happened when she had pointed out that fifty pounds of tea had been ordered during last quarter. Fifty pounds! Thirty pounds for the quarter would have been quite sufficient. When she had pointed this out to Dennison, telling him that he was being robbed, he had smiled and taken her face between his hands and said, 'I know that, my dear prim vicarage lady. It is an understood thing in all establishments like this that the servants have their perks. Without them, I can assure you, my dear, the wheels of this house would not be so well oiled. It is little enough to pay for a contented staff. And what staff, I ask you, would put up with Beatrice and her invasion twice a year? Her daily bath? Her dolls?'

That is another thing she would love to alter: that woman, who ignored her almost as much as did the Myers woman, only in a different way, for when she arrived she would take to her bed and remain there for days, only getting up to bathe and attend to her dolls. She was supposed to be eccentric, but Nancy Ann felt strongly that this was merely a façade hiding a form of utter laziness. Oh, she'd like to do something about her an' all . . . But here was this young woman, Mary Hetherington, a human being she could talk to.

She surprised the new nursery-maid by saying, 'How did your late mistress address you?'

'She called me Mary, missis . . . ma'am.'

'Well, it is the rule in this house for the staff to be addressed by their surnames. I cannot say that I like it but with a large staff I suppose it is understandable. However, I think that in your case I would, as your last mistress did, prefer to call you Mary.'

'Oh, I'd like that, ma'am. I would, I would indeed.'

The door opened, and the first footman McTaggart and a housemaid entered, both carrying trays.

When they were set on tables to the side of the couch, the footman said, 'The master has just come into the yard, ma'am.'

'Thank you. Just leave the tea; I'll see to it.' And when they were again alone she looked at Mary Hetherington and said, 'I'm sure you would like a cup of tea.'

'Me . . . ma'am? Oh yes. Thank you very much, ma'am.'

After handing the cup to Mary, Nancy Ann, pointing to the plates of sandwiches and pastries, said, 'Do help yourself,' and Mary, now somewhat ill at ease, answered, 'Thank you very much, ma'am,' but did not take up the offer. And when a few seconds later, she was about to sip at the cup and the door opened and there entered a gentleman in riding outfit, she rose quickly, spilling the tea into the saucer as she did so.

'Ah, there you are, my dear. And . . . and don't tell me' – he pointed to Mary – 'this is your choice of nursemaid.'

'Yes, yes, it is I'm pleased to say. This is Mary . . . Mary Hetherington. Mary, this is the master.'

Mary dipped her knee now, put down the cup on the table and said simply, 'Sir.'

'Mary is from North Shields.'

'Is she now?' He turned and looked at her. 'That is some way off. Are you of a fishing family?'

'N . . . n . . . no, sir, not really: sea-going, but not fishing. My . . . my father was on cargoes.'

'Oh. Oh, cargoes. He would have gone all over the world then.'

'Yes. Yes, sir, he did.'

'Would . . . would you like a cup of tea, dear? I'll ring for another cup.'

'No, not really. I'm going to get changed; I've had a rough ride.' He put out his hand and touched her hair, then turned away, giving Mary a brief nod as he did so.

'Would you like to see the nurseries?'

'I would, ma'am.'

'Well, come along then.' She swung her legs slowly from the couch, and Mary, solicitously now, said, 'You feel able to, ma'am?'

'Oh, yes, yes; and the exercise does one good.'

A few minutes later she was leading the way up the narrow staircase at the end of the long landing, and when they reached a further landing she stopped and, drawing in a deep breath, she said, 'There should be a law passed that all stairs should be shallow.'

They were now going along a narrow corridor and when it opened out on to another landing, Nancy Ann stopped, saying, 'This is the nursery floor. But that corridor' – she pointed to her right – 'leads to a maze of other corridors and the servants' quarters. And the staircase to the right leads to yet another floor made up of attics and store rooms. One can get lost up here, but you'll soon get used to it, I hope.'

'Yes, yes, of course, ma'am.'

Nancy Ann now led the way into the rooms that had been prepared as a day nursery, a night nursery, and nursery-maid's bedroom and sitting-room; also a washroom and closet.

After the inspection and out on the landing once more, Mary Hetherington said brightly, 'It's a lovely set-up, ma'am, beautiful. Your baby will grow up happy here.'

'I hope so. Yes, I hope so.'

They were met in the main corridor by the housekeeper, who seemed to be having a hard job to contain herself. And the first thing she said under the guise of concern was, 'Ma'am, do you think that was wise, all . . . all those stairs?'

'I'm perfectly all right, Conway, thank you. And I wanted to show, Mary . . .'

The very use of the young woman's Christain name seemed almost to make the housekeeper stagger. As she said later, you could have knocked her down with a feather, for if anything could have proved to her that the mistress would never fit in to a place like this, it was this lowering herself to almost hob-nob with this new piece who came from one of the commonest parts of the area. What were things coming to!

Later that night, when they were sitting side by side in the drawing-room after dinner, Dennison told her that he'd had a few words with George before the hunt, and he had advised him to go up to London at the beginning of the following week to see Arthur, and he would introduce him to one or two men who could be influential in promoting him as the candidate for Fellburn when the seat became vacant, which promised not to be very far in the future as Bradley, the present member, was known to be in a very poor state of health. He would only be gone a few days, he said. Did she think she would be all right?

Yes, she assured him, she would be perfectly all right. And if there came into her mind a suspicion that the proposed visit might not be merely political, but have two other strings to it, first, the gaming table, secondly . . . but she would not allow her thoughts to go further.

At the moment, she was, in a way, feeling strangely sure of herself, at least with regard to the household. It was as if, in engaging Mary Hetherington, she had won the first round of a battle, for in her she knew she would have an ally, and, as her father had been wont to say, 'With one staunch friend you can face the devil.'

7

On the last day in October eighteen and eighty-two, Nancy Ann gave birth to a daughter. Dennison was disappointed at the sex of the child, but did not show it. He had cradled the baby in his arms and, after gazing at her, he had looked at those present and said, 'I have made a life.' And there was laughter from the nurse when the doctor added, caustically, 'With a little help.'

The birth had been a difficult one, the labour long and hard, and Nancy Ann lay exhausted for some days following it. And such was her condition that the usual fortnight in bed after giving birth had to be extended to three weeks . . .

The baby was two months old before it was christened, and then by the new vicar. Nancy Ann was well aware that her father was ill both mentally and physically now, yet she considered he could have made the journey to the church and christened her child, for she knew he often walked the grounds around the house by day and sometimes by night.

The christening party was attended by only close friends, so it was not all that large, perhaps amounting to thirty guests including Jessica and Peter.

Over the past months Jessica had very definitely made an impression on the staff of The House; in fact, she made it the first time she entered the place, the day the child was born. She had been driven up in the trap by Johnny Pratt. He had rung the doorbell for her, and when McTaggart inquired her business she had thrust him haughtily aside, saying 'Out of the way, man! Tell your master Mrs Howard Hazel is here,' only for McTaggart to intervene quickly and no less haughtily inform her that the master was at present upstairs with the mistress. 'Then show me the way, man,' she had demanded.

Slightly intimidated now, he had been about to designate this service to his second in command when she had interrupted with, 'You!' and pointed towards the stairs, and he had gone up them without further hesitation.

And that had been the pattern the servants had adopted towards her whenever she deigned to visit The House, and it was said in the servants' hall if it had been someone like her from the vicarage with command and dignity who had become mistress of the house, they could have understood it, but as far as they could detect there was no resemblance between the grandmother and the granddaughter, not in the slightest. And they were amazed by the dissenting voice of the second footman, Robertson, who said enigmatically, 'I wouldn't be too sure of that. I've known piebalds to turn out to be dark horses with a cuddy's kick.'

The baby flourished under the care of the nursery-maid, and if ever the master of the house couldn't find the mistress, he made straight for the nursery floor.

Nancy Ann had now fully regained her health and her figure had blossomed out. Dennison was more loving towards her than ever, if that were possible. His trips to London were few and far between, but he did frequent his club in Newcastle. This, however, she didn't mind in the least. Sometimes he would return at night and throw ten guineas on to the bed cover saying, 'There, partner, that's your share.' But she knew that whatever he had won it would be much more than twenty guineas, for he did not go in for small stakes. She had no idea of his real financial position, but once or twice lately he had spoken of selling the Scottish estate, because, as he said, getting into Parliament was an expensive business and if he got the seat he would have little time for going up there, and in consequence it would be a responsibility.

He had been visiting Fellburn of late too, getting the lay of the land, as he put it; and his verdict after his first visit had been that it would be a difficult borough to hold, being three parts heavily working class. He also had told her that as soon as there was definite news of Bradley's retirement, she must accompany him and be seen round about the town as if they were taking an interest in people and things. She had wanted to remark on the implication 'as if', but she had refrained, for she had learned that he didn't like his ideas questioned, and certainly he wouldn't have been at all pleased if she had probed his meaning . . .

It was March of 'eighty-three that she fell pregnant again, and this time she promised him a son. It was about this time, too, that she discovered a happening on the nursery floor of which she had been unaware.

It should transpire this day that she was about to go into Fellburn with Dennison and was actually in the hall when Johnny Pratt came to the door and delivered a letter.

It was from her grandmother to say that James had come and apparently for only a very short visit. Would she come across?

Dennison had said, yes of course she must stay, and he would go to Fellburn as arranged for he was to meet members of a committee there.

She was dressed for town and so she went back up to her bedroom and changed her outer things. Then, being unable to resist another look at the baby, she went up to the nursery again, and when she pushed open the door of the day room she became still, for there, sitting on a low stool with her child in his lap, was the boy.

In springing up, the lad had almost dropped the child, but Mary took the baby from him and she, turning now with the child pressed close to her, said, 'I . . . I'm sorry ma'am, but I can explain. It's my fault.'

''Tisn't her fault, 'tis mine . . . ma'am. I'm . . . I'm up there.' He thumbed towards the ceiling. 'I . . . I heard the baby crying, an' . . . an' I only come when I'm sent up to change.'

Nancy Ann stared at the boy. It was months since she had last seen him, and then she had just glimpsed him that day on her first and only visit to the kitchen. He had grown much taller and, what was noticeable, the brown streaks in his hair were just at the ends now, the rest of it was of a golden fairness. His face was thin and pale, but his eyes were dark, large and deep-socketed. He ended now on a low note, 'I wouldn't have dropped her.'

Nancy Ann's hand went to her throat: she wanted to reassure him by saying she knew he wouldn't, but the thought came to her that Dennison might have come up and found him, not only in the nursery, but holding his child. He would, then, more than likely have laid hands on him. And this she voiced now by looking at Mary and saying, 'If the master had come up . . .' But her words were checked by the boy muttering, 'I never come when he's in the house. I see from the yard when he's gone.'

She noticed that he did not use the word master, and also that the fright and fear had gone from his face, although it showed some tightness. She wondered if he was aware of his relationship and, being aware, did he understand the implications, and why he was made to work in the boot room. He had often been on her mind, more so whilst she was carrying her first child: she couldn't help but think then that when it was born there would be in this house a cousin to it, illegitimate, but nevertheless, a cousin by blood.

She said quietly, 'Go along; it will be all right.'

The boy looked from her to Mary now, then back to her again, saying, 'She won't get wrong, will she?'

'No' – Nancy Ann moved her head slowly – 'She won't get wrong. Go along.'

After hunching his shoulders almost up to his ears, the boy hurried from the room; and Nancy Ann looked at Mary, who was standing with her head bowed, still holding the child tightly to her, and she said quietly, 'You shouldn't have let this happen, you know.'

'I'm . . . I'm sorry, ma'am, but . . . but he's a lonely lad, and . . . and when I first saw him, he stood in the doorway there' – she inclined her head – 'and . . . and he said, "Can I see it?" and when he put his hand out the child griped his finger, as is usual you know, ma'am . . . babies do, and the boy looked up at me and his face . . . Well, I'd been used to children all me life, as I said, but I'd never seen a look on a boy's face like there was on his. I can't explain it. I've got no words in me to explain it, but . . . but when he asked if he could slip in at changing times if . . . if, that is, you and the master were out, I said yes. I didn't think it was all that wrong, ma'am.'

Nancy Ann went towards her and took the child from her arms and sat down on the wooden chair near the square table in the centre of the room; then looking down on her daughter, she said softly, 'I . . . I suppose you know the history of the boy?'

There was a short space of time before Mary answered. 'Well, yes, ma'am, bits and pieces, from down below. I have spoken with his mother. But not about him,' she put in quickly, 'only everyday things, She's . . . she's a nice woman. But I must say it, not treated right, ma'am.'

'What do you mean, not treated right?' Nancy Ann looked up at her.

'Well – ' Mary bit on her lip and looked first to one side and then the other before saying, 'she's not given her place, ma'am, they keep her down, the housekeeper and most of them.'

Nancy Ann wanted to say, 'Well, she's at liberty to move on to another position and take her son with her,' and she had thought this very same thought often, but she could see the woman's reason for staying: her son really belonged to this household, and likely there were hopes that, in some way, somehow and at sometime he would be recognized. Poor soul; she didn't know the futility of her dreams if she so dreamed.

At times she wondered what Dennison's reaction would be when the boy grew up into a man and, should he become so minded, try to openly state his claim to recognition. Yet, what could he hope to gain from that?

Her thoughts were interrupted by Mary's saying softly, 'I'm sorry if I vexed you, ma'am, but I'll promise not to let him hold the child again. But . . . but what will I do if he wants to see her?'

Nancy Ann rose to her feet and, handing her daughter back to Mary, said, 'Let things remain as they are, only please be careful. Do any of the staff know about his visits?'

'Oh, no, ma'am. If he hears anyone on the stairs he scurries out the far door. By the way, ma'am, have . . . have you seen where he sleeps . . . he and his mother?'

'In the servants' quarters, I suppose.'

'Oh no, ma'am; they're in the far corner of the roof beyond the boxrooms.'

'Beyond the boxrooms?'

Mary nodded.

Besides the unmarried servants' quarters up on the attic floors, there was a roof space crossed by beams that ran over most of the house. When she had first come to the house and had been alone one afternoon, she had made a tour of inspection of the warren of rooms above. She had walked for some distance under the roof and was amazed at the trunks and cases and pieces of odd furniture that was stored there. But she had never travelled the whole area.

Mary was saying now, with the liberty that was a natural part of her character and seemed in no way out of place, 'It's enough to freeze you under that roof in the winter, ma'am, and boil you in the summer. And that's where, I understand, the lad spent most of his early days, that is, afore you came, ma'am . . . I hope you don't mind me speaking like this?'

'No, Mary, not at all. I'm grateful to you.' And after a moment she touched the smiling face of her daughter and said, 'I must go now; my elder brother is paying a fleeting visit home. But I won't be all that long; I'll be back before it's time for her bath.'

'I'll hold it until you return, ma'am. She won't mind.' And she gently rocked the child backwards and forwards . . .

A few minutes later Nancy Ann made her way out of the house, across the drive, through the ornamental gardens, and on to the wood path which led to the river. But a few yards along it, she branched off and zig-zagged her way through the wood until she came to a small gate in the drystone boundary wall that separated the estates.

Graham had been kind enough to have this gate made in order to make is easier for her to visit the Dower House. In the ordinary way she would have had half an hour's walk from the house into the village, then on to the old coach road; or it would have meant getting the carriage out and keeping it waiting until she made her return. But this way, she could pop through the wood most days to visit her father and grandmama, now happily ensconced in the Dower House. She often asked herself, what would have happened to them if Graham had not made this offer, for had they gone to live in a village or a town her father's wanderings would have become a source of worry, especially to her grandmama.

The house lay about two hundred yards from the boundary, bordered on two adjacent sides by stretches of lawn, and on the other two by domestic outhouses. The comfort of the house given off by its furniture and carpets was like a palace compared with that of the vicarage. And even with its smoky chimneys, and they did indeed smoke, it was warm. And even when the well dried up in the summer the girls would laugh about this as they went to the river for the washing water. If any were more happy than the others in the house, they were Peggy and Hilda, for they had never had so much food to deal with. Every day there was a fresh supply of milk from the farm and every week butter and eggs, together with vegetables and fruit, in season. Graham's farm was small and kept solely to provide for the estate.

Nancy Ann pushed open the front door, and even before crossing the hall could hear raised voices. When she opened the sitting-room door her father and James and her grandmama looked towards her.

Rising quickly from his chair, James hurried to her; and then they were holding each other tightly. After a moment he pressed her from him, and she was amazed at the change she saw in him: his face looked haggard and drawn; his clothes looked anything but smart, in fact they looked rumpled.

Her father's voice separated them as he cried, 'I am glad my Rebecca has gone; such a family would have broken her heart: one marrying into a house of sin, another stooping to court a warden's elderly daughter, and now another running away from his responsibilities.' He glared from one to the other, then turned and shambled up the room, pulled open a French window and stalked out into the garden.

When Nancy Ann made to follow him her grandmama called, 'Stay. Stay. It's no use. You won't get him to think otherwise. He's a changed man.' Then she added, 'Sit down and listen to what James has to say. So far' – she turned and looked at the tall figure of her grandson – 'you've only been able to get out that you've left your family, and that was two days ago. Now let us have the reason.'

James lowered himself slowly down on to the couch by the side of his grandmother and held his hands out to the fire, and remained like that for sometime before he said, 'It was a mistake from the beginning, but I didn't know how much until she . . . she told me that she was to have a child. From then she slept in another room. In my ignorance, I thought it must be the habit of all women. When William was four months old she came back to me. Then the pattern was repeated. By that time I was no longer ignorant. She had told me openly that marriage was mainly for – ' he wetted his lips and turned his head further away from them as he said the word, 'procreation.'

Nancy Ann stared at him in pity. She had heard that word before from Peter. She went on now listening to his voice low and hesitant: 'But that wasn't all. Her mother took complete charge of the children. I could do nothing about it. Ours wasn't a real house; we only had apartments in her father's school house. I . . . I tried to talk to her father but he wouldn't listen. And then there was my salary. The second year, it was handed to her under the excuse that I had been wasteful, having bought a pair of boots and an overcoat, and both necessary. My children hardly know me. They refer to her or their grandparents all the time.' He turned towards them again, and, his face blanched, his teeth ground together now, he seemed to spit out the words: 'I've been made to feel like an animal, kept there for stock.'

'Oh, Jamie. Jamie.' Jessica put her arms around him, and he drooped his head on to her shoulder and hot tears sped down his face. If it had been happening to herself, Nancy Ann could not have felt more anguish. She thought of the love that was showered on her by Dennison, and of her longing to be in his arms when he was gone from her.

James pulled himself upwards and turned away from his grandmother, rubbing at his face vigorously and saying, 'I'm sorry.' And when, presently, Nancy Ann said, 'What do you intend to do, James?' he stood up and, his hands gripping the mantelpiece, he looked down into the fire, saying, quietly, 'I . . . I want to go to Canada. Henry Bolton, a friend I knew up at Oxford, he's got a little business out there. Nothing very special from what I understand, but he'd be pleased to give me some kind of a job. It would be manual, but I wouldn't mind what I did. The only thing is' – he paused – 'I haven't a penny. And yet that's not quite right. I've got fourpence. You could say I stole my railway fare; I took it from her cash box.' She noticed that he always referred to his wife as 'her' or 'she', never by name. He turned now and, gazing sorrowfully at Nancy Ann, he said, 'Could you loan me enough to get across? I'll . . . I'll repay you. I promise, Nancy Ann.'

She too was on her feet and, going to him, she put her hands on his shoulders saying, 'Oh, James, don't be silly, talking like that. Of course, I'll help you. How much do you want?'

'I . . . I don't know what the fare and all that would cost.'

'Would two or three hundred be enough?'

'*What!*' Jessica was sitting bolt upright. 'Where will you get two or three hundred without asking Dennison?'

'Grandmama' – Nancy Ann looked down into the wrinkled face – 'I've got over six hundred pounds of my own. You see' – she paused – 'Dennison always give me part of his' – she did not like to say the word but was forced to – 'winnings.'

'Oh, Lordy! Lordy!' Jessica sat back in her chair with a flop. ''Tis a good job your father isn't here at this moment, else that news would surely kill him. Although' – she nodded her head vigorously – 'it doesn't affect me. And, yes, when I do have time to think about it, I'll surely consider it a nice gesture on Dennison's part. Yes, I will. Anyway' – she looked at her grandson – 'there you are, that part's settled for you. But . . . but what will happen at the end – down in Bath? Will they follow you here and try to stop you?'

'Oh, very likely. I shouldn't wonder but her father will be on this doorstep very shortly; my absconding will be very bad for his school. You might think Father is narrow in his views but they're as wide as the ocean compared with my father-in-law's.'

Suddenly becoming practical, Nancy Ann said, 'Well now, if that's the case, you want to get away from here. And get yourself a decent suit and travelling clothes. I'll go back to Rossburn. I've got over a hundred pounds in my cash box and I shall give you a cheque for the rest. But the quicker you make a start the better, for it your father-in-law should arrive, there'll be a scene, and I don't think Papa could stand it.'

He nodded in agreement. 'Yes, you are right, Nancy Ann. And . . . and thank you. I'll pay you . . .

'Oh, be quiet! Don't be silly. I have more money than I know what to do with.' She smiled gently at him, then hurried from the room.

As she was going out of the front door she almost ran into the arms of Graham, who, before she could speak, asked, 'Were you going in search of your father? Don't worry, he's in the library. He often drops in there.'

'In your library?'

'Yes' – he smiled now – 'in my library.'

'He . . . he goes in without your knowledge?'

'Oh, I am so glad he makes use of it, and I'm pleased to have him there. At times he's very good company.'

She noticed, the 'at times'. And now she said, 'I wasn't about to look for him; I'm . . . I'm just going to run to the house. I'll be back. James has come. It's . . . it's to be a very flying visit. I'm . . . I'm sure he'd like to talk to you.'

'James here? Oh, yes, yes.' He moved to the side to let her pass, and as he hurried from him, she was aware that he remained standing on the step watching her . . .

The parting between her and James was very painful; both knew they might never see each other again. For a moment they stood entwined and with their grandmother's hands on their shoulders, they all cried.

Outside, a trap was waiting to drive James to the school to see Peter. One of Graham's men was already seated in it, and Graham himself was shaking James's hand and saying, 'I'm more than sorry to see you go like this. But keep in touch. You will, won't you?' Then nodding towards the man in the trap, he said, 'John will take you to Peter's and wait for you there, and then see you to the station.'

James was now too full of emotion to speak. He stepped up into the trap, then looked to where Nancy Ann and his grandmother were standing close together, and beyond them to Peggy and Hilda, but he did not even lift his hand in farewell, he just keep his eyes on them until he could no longer see them.

When the trap had disappeared from their sight, Jessica turned and walked slowly into the house; but Nancy Ann and Graham stood in silence looking along the short drive to where it turned into an avenue of trees.

When they entered the house it was to find that Jessica had gone to her room. In the sitting-room once more Nancy Ann looked at Graham who was seated opposite to her and said quietly, 'It's strange what is happening to our family, isn't it? We were all so close just a short while ago. What has happened to us?' Her hands made an appealing motion towards him as if he could provide the answer.

'One of you died,' he said, 'and another couldn't stand the loss; the rest grew up.'

She nodded at him. 'Yes, yes, you're right,' she said. Then sighing, she added, 'It's been a strange day. I woke up this morning feeling happy and excited. I was to go with Dennison to Fellburn. He was to meet some committee members there, you know with regard to . . . well, as Grandmama says, getting his foot into politics, and we were then going down the river in one of the steamboats. But it was all changed when I got the note about James. But that wasn't all. I happened to go up to the nursery and there I saw my daughter being held in the arms of the boy. I suppose, Graham, you know all about Dennison's brother's son, David, because that's who he is. And it pains me that Dennison will not recognize him in any way. It's odd, a really weird situation, that the boy is still in the house and, from what I gather, has been brought up among the lumber in the attic. Well, there he was, sitting holding Rebecca. He's a lovely looking boy. He must be eleven now and . . . and really speaks quite well. He's had no schooling, but his mother must have taught him to read and write, because once when I spoke to him, last year down by the river, he talked of reading books. He should be at school, Graham, a good school, but I cannot bring his name up with Dennison. He came across him once in the wood and his reaction towards the child was terrible. Can you understand it?'

It was some seconds before Graham replied, 'Yes, yes, I can understand it, strange as it may seem to you, for I know he loved his brother dearly. We all act in different ways when faced with the loss of loved ones. And I can see it would be impossible for Dennison to recognize the child. You mightn't like what I'm going to say, but I think it is to his credit that he allows him to stay there.'

When she gazed at him in silence he leaned towards her and said quietly, 'I myself have been through, you could say, a similar situation in that I . . . I lost someone I loved. I don't need to relate my story to you either, for it is common knowledge. But whereas, Dennison's loss made him take up a high wild life, because he is of an extrovert nature, I, being of the opposite, an introvert, scuttled into seclusion, because I couldn't bear what I thought of as the shame. I was a quiet young man, but when Miss Constance Beverley, a beautiful young girl, accepted my proposal, it was as if I had been endowed with the stature of a god. This is a small estate. We've never been enormously rich, though quite comfortable, but I went about as if I had become king of a country.' He looked at his hands. They were lying palm down on his thighs, the fingers spread as if he were pressing something away from him. Then he added, 'When I was deposed, the day we were to marry, it was just after Tim's tragedy, and I nearly joined him. If I'd been anything of a strong character, I would have gone abroad, or even to London and found a new bride whether I loved her or not, and brought her back and flaunted her just to show my friends how little I had been affected. But no, being me, I had to make a tragedy out of it; although I must admit I didn't think at the time I was doing any such thing, nor for some years afterwards. My house, the seven hundred acres, my books and my cello became my life.'

She hadn't known he played the cello. She wanted to remark on it, but it would have been too trivial at this moment. Instinctively, she put her hand out towards him, and when both of his covered hers, their gaze held, hers soft with pity and understanding, his full of something that she recognized but would not put a name to. What she said now sounded inane: 'There's plenty of time for you to find happiness.'

He withdrew his hands from hers and, rising slowly, he said, 'The happiness you refer to, Nancy Ann, is past for me. I'm a dull fellow and quite stupid in a way: because I'm always looking inside, I'm blind to what's happening under my nose.'

'No, no. Good gracious, no. I don't see you like that, nor does anyone else, I should say.' Her declaration sounded vehement.

'That's kind of you, Nancy Ann. And I must say one thing, I've felt much happier since your family have come here. I'm very fond of Mrs Hazel, she's such a sensible person. And . . . and if I may say so, I value your friendship, Nancy Ann. Above everything else I value that. And, as I have said before, if ever you need a friend in any way and for whatever purpose, I should be happy to be that friend.'

Her eyelids blinked. She could feel the colour hot on her cheeks, and her voice was low as she murmured, 'Yes, yes, Graham, I know, and I could not imagine a better or firmer friend.'

After an ensuing few seconds of silent embarrassment, she put in, her words tumbling over each other, 'I . . . I'd better go. I'll . . . I'll just say goodbye to Grandmama. And . . . and thank you for being so kind and understanding to James. Poor James.' She nodded at him now, then turned hastily away, forgetting that, in courtesy, she should have seen him to the door.

She ran up the stairs but did not go into her grandmama's room. There were two spare rooms on the opposite side of the landing and she went into one and closed the door. Then turning and leaning her forehead against it, she asked herself what was wrong with her; she was all wrought up inside. Well . . . well, she would be, wouldn't she? James leaving his wife and family and going off to Canada. She turned now and leant back against the door and stared across the room, and she knew that the turmoil inside her hadn't been caused so much by her brother's unconventional departure as by the conversation she'd had with a man who thought of himself as dull and of little consequence. And there arose in her mind the image of Dennison. Dennison would never consider himself dull or of little consequence: Dennison was outgoing, strong, forceful, and he knew it and impressed it on others.

She stood away from the door and felt a sense of guilt sweeping over her. It was as if she was criticizing her husband's character aloud. But that was silly – she shook her head at herself – she loved Dennison and everything about him . . . everything.

Then a thought obtruded into her mind: what had her father said? That Peter was proposing to marry Eva McKeowan? Oh no. Dennison wouldn't like that. No, he wouldn't. Did she like it? Well, now she came to think about it James would have been much happier had he married Eva. But did she like the possibility of Peter marrying her? Well, one thing was sure, it wouldn't enhance her family's standing in the eyes of the staff.

8

For the last two months of her pregnancy Nancy Ann felt definitely unwell. The baby was due towards the end of December. She hoped it would come on Christmas Day; in fact, she was now almost willing to come on Christmas Day. Hang on, her grandmama had said, and you'll get your wish.

It was the beginning of December and the weather was vile, as it had been during all of November and late October. There were days when she couldn't venture outdoors, even to go to the Dower House, and on these occasions she felt exceedingly lonely and especially so when Dennison was in London.

During the past six weeks he had made two longish visits to the city. He was negotiating the selling of the Scottish estate to help pay for election expenses. Elections, as he kept saying, were very costly businesses. When she tentatively questioned him as to what he did in the evenings, he always replied, 'What do you think, my dear? Take your choice: roulette, cards, or dice.' And she left it at this, for she realized he did not favour this kind of questioning. Nevertheles, he always seemed so glad to be back in her company; and, of late, it was simply just her company, for he had not shared her bed for some weeks now, his reason being, and which he had put plainly to her, that he would be unable to bear being near her without loving her . . .

She was in the nursery. Between them, she and Mary had bathed Rebecca and got her settled for the night. And now Mary, taking the high guard away from the fire, and pulling up an old button-backed upholstered chair, said, 'Sit yourself down, ma'am, for a moment. You look a bit drawn. Are you all right?'

'To tell the truth, Mary, I'm . . . I'm not feeling too well. I haven't for the past day or so, but I suppose this is the pattern.'

'No, no, it should't be, ma'am, not if you're feeling bad like and it not due for another three weeks. Only once did ma feel bad when she was having them, and then it came a bit early.'

Nancy Ann already knew the whole history of Mary's family, and she was going to become better acquainted with another one of them as soon as the baby was born because Mary's younger sister, Agnes, was coming to act as assistant nursery-maid. This last appointment to the staff had been made without consulting Mrs Conway and so had not warmed the relationship between them. Nancy Ann did not feel any compunction in lessening the housekeeper's authority in this way, for she knew that the woman was lining her pockets, and doubtless those of the butler and valet, through co-operation with the tradesmen. She had learned a lot about housekeeping during the months of her mother's illness; the meagreness of the amount allotted to their daily needs had made her question the price of all commodities.

'Will I make you a cup of tea, ma'am?'

'No, thank you, Mary. I'd better be getting down; it's about time for Mrs Conway's round.'

'Yes.' Mary looked at the brass-faced clock on the matelpiece and they exchanged smiles and Nancy Ann, about to rise from the chair, suddenly opened her mouth wide and gasped as the air as her two hands grabbed at the mound of her stomach.

'Oh, my goodness! No!' Mary was bending over her, saying now, 'Lie back. Take it easy. That's it. That's it. Has it gone?'

Nancy Ann let out a long shuddering breath as she said, 'Yes . . . but' – she looked up into Mary's face – 'It can't be, can it?'

'It could, ma'am, it could. What was it like? Sharp like?'

'Oh, yes, yes.'

'I . . . I think you had better get down to bed, ma'am.'

'Yes, I think so, Mary.'

As Mary helped her from the couch the door opened, and the housekeeper stood there, a look of disapproval on her face, and Mary, turning her head towards her, unceremoniously said, 'She's started.'

'What?'

'I said, madam's started.'

'Nonsense, woman. It's not . . .'

'I know it's not due, but I tell you, anyway, it's comin'. Give a hand; get the other side of Madam.'

For the moment the housekeeper was too flustered to put the upstart maid in her place, but going towards Nancy Ann, she said, 'Do you think it has, ma'am?'

'I . . . I don't know, Mrs Conway, but . . . but I shouldn't be surprised.' She had hardly got the last word out before she doubled up again and they were both supporting her.

A minute later, the housekeeper left her to go to the cord at the side of the fireplace, and she pulled on it vigorously. 'The men must help,' she said; 'those stairs are steep. She . . . she shouldn't be up here.'

Nancy Ann, straightening her body as much as she could, gasped and, looking at the housekeeper, she said, 'It's . . . it's all right. I'll manage the stairs. Just . . . just let me get down.' . . .

She got down the stairs, but just in time before another spasm attacked her; and from then on she did not know much about the evening that followed, only that her grandmama was at one side of the bed with Pat, and the doctor and Mary were at the other.

Three messages had been sent off to London: one to the house and, at Pat's suggestion, one to Dennison's club, and the third to Reilly's, the private gaming-house.

By midnight Nancy Ann was in a state of collapse. Although the excruciating pains were coming at regular intervals, the child showed no sign of emerging into life.

At half-past three in the morning, Doctor McCann consulted with Doctor Maydice whom he had called in earlier, and they decided that if they didn't want to lose both the mother and the baby something definite must be done. So by four o'clock a wooden table had been brought up into the bedroom. Nancy Ann had been lifted on to it, and dishes of hot water were standing ready. Mary, Pat, and the housekeeper stood at hand, and Jessica, in a state of collapse, had been made to rest in the adjoining room.

Chloroform had been administered to Nancy Ann, and so she made no sound as the knife was put into the top of her stomach and drawn right across it, and within a short space of time a strong-limbed-and-lunged male child was taken from her body.

* * *

It seemed eons of time later when Nancy Ann emerged through the white heat of pain into a bright light. The sun was shining; and there was a well-remembered smell in her nostrils. Slowly she turned her head on the pillow and looked at the face a few inches from hers, and she thought. What is Denny kneeling on the bedstep for? And when his voice, low and broken, came to her ears, saying, 'I will love you till the day I die. Do you hear, my love? You have given me a son, a beautiful son, and I swear to you again, I will love you till the day I die.'

When he was happy he always said nice things. He would love her till the day she died. Well, he wouldn't have to wait long – would he? – because she was ready to die at any time; such pain as she was enduring killed love and the desire for life. She turned her head away from the face and looked towards the end of the bed where she saw her mother standing, and she was reprimanding her, saying, 'Go to sleep now, go to sleep. You'll be better tomorrow. And remember, never shelve a responsibility.'

PART SIX

The Woman

1

After the birth of the child Nancy Ann lay for almost a week between life and death. Her wound would not heal and she was delirious most of the time. Then came a period when the crisis passed and for two weeks following she lay in a state of calm and showed no interest in anything, not even her son. There followed a long convalescence while she sat with her feet up on the couch fronting the fire, and all the while Dennison was never far from her side, except when he made quick sorties into Newcastle or Fellburn.

He had become very interested in the political situation, about which he talked and he talked. He laughingly said, as she couldn't yet go out into the world he was bringing it to her. And she listened patiently because she liked to hear him talk; and when he was talking to her he was near to her.

Gladstone was now Prime Minister and apparently he was making as many mistakes as had Disraeli. He was having the same old trouble with Ireland, Egypt, and now South Africa.

Once she had said to him. 'You are too Liberal to be a Tory and too Toryish to be a Liberal; you should start a party of your own.' And at that he had laughed and hugged her.

Although at times she became tired of political talk, she had to admit that she had learned a great deal during the past months by just listening to him. She also knew that Dennison himself had learned a great deal since he had first delved into politics.

From April onwards her strength increased daily. She walked in the woods, sometimes accompanied by Dennison, but more often she was alone, and at such times she went through the gate and to the Dower House. She found it strange that as soon as she passed through into Graham's estate she experienced a sense of peace.

Her daughter, now eighteen months old, was trotting about the nursery and jabbering in a language all her own. And her son was already showing elements of a strong character in that he was never still. That he was the joy of his father's life was plain to everyone in the house, for Dennison visited the nursery now almost as often as she herself. And such was that atmosphere of the nursery floor that he even joked with Mary and her young sister Agnes.

All this should have made her extremely happy, but there were two worries in her mind. Her father was fast losing all his reasoning faculties. What is more he had developed a heavy hacking cough, and she feared he might go the same way as her mama. Then there was this other thing that had taken on a deeper penetration than the anxiety about her father: she could understand Dennison leaving her bed during the latter part of her pregnancy, and also in the months following the birth of the child, but for the past month or so she had never felt better physically. The trauma of the birth, although not forgotten, was well in the background, and although Doctor McCann had told them both that for her safety's sake there should be no more children, that, she felt, should not have kept him away from her side.

Now that she had given Dennison a son and a daughter, particularly a son, he was more than content, he said, that this should be the limit of their family. What she had been too embarrassed to discuss with him but felt quite able to bring up with Pat was the question: Did this mean an end to loving? at which Pat had pushed her and laughed loudly.

Then why did he not come to her bed? Oh, he came, to lie near her for a while and hug her, but such embraces were short. Other times he lay on the top of the bed quilt and talked to her while he stroked her hair and fondled her face; then kissing her good night, he would retire to the dressing-room.

Knowing his ardent nature, it was impossible for her to imagine that he abstained from satisfying his need. Then came the question, But with whom? and always at this point there loomed up in her mind the picture of the Myers woman, the fat slug, as she sometimes termed her.

Since the night she had mimicked her, they had met three times, and on each occasion the woman had openly ignored her while making a fuss of Dennison. And this never went unnoticed by the company they happened to be in. Pat had advised her that on such occasions she should smile and talk, and on no account stick close to her husband. Leave the field apparently open, Pat had said, which would show that she had nothing to fear.

This latter advice, however, she found difficult to follow for, strangely, the very sight of the woman aroused in her the almost overwhelming desire to strike out at this lump of flowing pink flesh. And she had said so to Pat: 'I have a great desire to push her on her back and see if she can rise without assistance. I imagine her rolling from side to side.'

And there was that time last year when she was greatly perturbed when Dennison was in London. George and Pat had insisted on taking her to a house-party and there she had overheard the end of a conversation: 'She's gone up to town. Well, you couldn't expect her to stay here, could you?' Then another voice saying, 'She's determined, I'll say that for her,' had completed the conversation.

She did not have to think twice to whom they were referring, Mrs Myers was not at the party.

Dennison never mentioned the woman's name, but she herself often wanted to yell it at him, especially when he returned from London full of life and high spirits. He always brought back a gift for her: a diamond brooch, a ruby-studded bangle, an ornamental hair-clip; once, a beautiful tiara, which she never wore.

June came, and the weather turned exceedingly hot. Day after day the sun shone. Thunderstorms cleared the air for a short time but the heat persisted.

During one thunderstorm, John had roamed the grounds, and when Graham found him he was soaked to the skin. His cough was worse. The doctor was called and bronchitis was diagnosed. That was towards the middle of the month. The weather cooled, but John's condition had worsened so much that Nancy Ann was now taking her turn sitting up with him at nights; her grandmother and the girls were exhausted with their day's routine. Graham, as always, was being very good, and on alternate nights he took his place by the bedside. But last night he had insisted on staying again because her grandmother had been so concerned at the sight of Nancy Ann's white drawn face that they both said she should return home. As Graham pointed out, a couch had been brought into the bedroom and so he could rest on it if necessary. Later, on looking back at the events leading up to the explosion that took place, she recalled that Dennison seemed surprised to see her that night. He had been in the library and after a moment had come towards her, saying, 'He has gone?'

When she had assured him that her father had not died he had made a fuss of her, taken her upstairs, and seen her into bed.

Today was Sunday. It had begun hot and the heat seemed to increase with the hour. She had gone to morning service, but alone, Dennison having made his excuses: not only had he an enormous amount of work to attend to, but he was sorry he couldn't stand the new parson: he was too young, too unripe, and too pious for him altogether.

In her mind Nancy Ann agreed with him, but as she said, it wasn't the parson, it was the service that mattered. She went in the open landau, and those servants who could be relieved of their duties followed behind in the brake, but the housekeeper, the butler, the first footman, and the valet were not among them.

During the day she paid two visits to the Dower House. Her father's bronchitis had worsened somewhat and the oppressive heat was not helping him.

When she emerged from the wood into the gardens after her second visit of the day, she saw Dennison at the far end of the rockery lawn. He was lying on a lounge chair in the shade of the big oak. As she approached him she saw that he was asleep, a book and some newspapers were lying to the side of the chair and his hand was dangling above them. She smiled as she looked down on him. He looked so relaxed and always much younger in sleep. He certainly didn't look anwhere near his thirty-seven years; in fact, he prided himself on his figure for as yet he had no paunch.

She went on into the house and, after sluicing her face and hands in cold water, went up into the nursery. The children were fractious. Although Mary had all the windows open, the room was stifling.

Mary, cradling William in her arms and rocking him backwards and forwards in a way she termed giving him a shuggy, said, 'By, when this breaks, ma'am, the heavens will open. I've never known anything like it. We're not used to heat like this.'

Nancy Ann agreed with her.

At dinner, she thought that his afternoon siesta must have refreshed Dennison for he was quite gay, making her laugh about some of the men associated with the coming election and whom he had met in Fellburn. 'The next time you come with me you must study them and add them to your repertoire,' he had said.

It was a long twilight, heavy and foreboding. Earlier in the evening the wind had risen, but it had died down again. She opened the library door. Dennison was sitting at his desk at the window, dressed only in a pair of breeches, carpet slippers and a white shirt that was open down to his waist and showed the dark hair of his chest. In spite of the heat he appeared to be still in a bright mood for, rising from the desk, he bent and kissed her; then, smiling down at her, he said, 'You know, in spite of all your nursing and the heat, you are looking quite robust these days.' And she answered, 'Yes, I'm feeling quite well again.'

'That's good news. How much longer do you think your father will need nursing?'

'Just till he gets over this bad bout,' she answered.

He now turned from her and walked towards the desk, saying, 'You know, as I suggested in the first place, he should have a nurse. There's no reason why not.' He had his back to her as he ended softly, 'I miss you, you know.'

Her heart warmed to him, and she answered just as softly, 'And I miss you too.'

He turned and looked at her; then walked back to her again and kissed her on the brow now. Then, pushing her away from him, he said, 'Go on and do your ministering angel act.'

She went, but reluctantly. She had the feeling that he needed her tonight in the same way as she needed him.

She walked slowly through the gardens and the wood, but at the gate she stopped and came to a decision. She would ask Hilda if she would take her place for tonight. She could sleep on the couch and, of course, would call Peggy or her grandmama if needed. Yes, that's what she would do.

And she did this, explaining the situation to her grandmama who understood as always.

As she was returning through the gate into the grounds there was a distant rolling of thunder. The wood appeared black dark now, but through use she was able to find her way. As she emerged into the comparative light of the gardens, she saw in the distance the sky split by lightning.

A plan had formed in her mind: she would not go in by the front entrance but by the side door, make her way into her bedroom, get undressed, and surprise him when he came up. Of course, that is, if he wasn't upstairs already. This she doubted, for he rarely now came up before eleven at night.

So thinking, she skirted the large lawn and made her way along by the creeper-covered wall that bordered the back of the stable yard and outhouses to where the archway led into the yard.

She had just stepped off the grassy path on to the cobbles that paved the archway and the yard when the sound of a man swearing brought her to a halt. Her fingers went to her lips: the man was saying, 'It's a bloody shame. She should be put wise.'

Now another voice came to her from the end of the archway, harsh and low, replying, 'If you know what's good for you, Irish, you'll mind your own bloody business.'

'Don't call me Irish, I've got a name. And as for me own bloody business, somebody should take it on, because that lot in there are swines of the first water. To think they would have a hand in such a game. My God! I'm glad I am Irish at this minute, 'cos it's a rotten, stinkin' English trick that, if ever I knew of one.'

'Look' – the voice came conciliatory now – 'I'm only saying this for your own good. They're a power in there, that lot. I don't like it meself, but a man's got to eat, to keep his family, and they are damn good jobs here, you must admit, no matter who's dippin' their fingers into pies and pullin' out plums.'

'That's one thing, dippin' your fingers into pies, but this other . . . the mistress is a decent young body and why the hell can't he be satisfied with her? Or go off to London as he usually does for his whorin'? But to have that drab coming to the house when they know the coast's clear. My God! I've heard it all now. The gentry are rotten, that's me opinion, rotten to the core. Anyway, how would they know she wouldn't be in the house the night?'

'Oh, are you blind, man? Didn't the plump lady ride past the main gate yesterday, and didn't she stop and have a word with Benton or his missis. They're both in it. And the mighty man Staith would have got word down to them that the coast wasn't clear. Now there's a rat if ever there was one. I've only ever seen another like him, and that was the master's so-called friend, a Mr Freeman. He was afore your time, but a real snake in the grass he was. Couldn't stand the master getting married, and up and offed it. But Staith is the leader of the big four and what they say goes, right through the whole system, and down to the farm at that. Old Taylor's getting on, and he has to keep his nose clean, but young Billy I understand's got a mind of his own, as has Frank. They don't toe the line.'

'But d'you mean to say that fat piece is comin' here the night?'

'It seems like it. She came last night right enough. Half-way through the grounds. She left her horse at the east lodge. There's nobody in there now, you know, but there's a stable at the back.'

'God Almighty! D'you know, I've got a smell in me nose that stinks. Appleby must be in this up to his neck.'

'Oh, aye, Appleby is. He passed on the message to her coachman. And it could quite easily be your Jim that could be drivin' her; he's second there now, isn't he?'

'I'd break his bloody neck if I thought Jim was in on this. That's swearin' to God.'

Nancy Ann was now leaning against the wall, her hand pressed tight across her mouth, her eyes staring wide into the darkness, and her whole being was yelling, *No! No! No!* He wouldn't! He wouldn't do that. Oh no! And they all knowing. Oh, dear God!

'You know somethin'? I always had a sneakin' likin' for the master, although I know he didn't leave her to go up to London just to take the air, or to do his bettin', or gamblin'. Anyway, he could have done that in Newcastle, 'cos there's big money floatin' around there, so I understand. Anyway, in spite of that, I always judged him to be a man with a bit of honour in him. But to bring that fat whore into his bed and his missis not a few strides away from him. Oh, my God and His Holy Mother! that to me is a sin beyond sins. I'll tell you one thing, I'm gettin' out of here shortly. This racket's too strong for me; it turns me stomach.'

'Don't be such a bloody fool. It's got nothin' to do with you. We live our lives and they live theirs. Let them sort it out. And you can sort lots of things out when you've got money. Aye, and lots of things can be forgiven you if you've got money. Money is power, lad.'

'Power, be damned! You can keep it. I'd rather be back in the old country grubbin' taties, rotten at that, but even they smell sweeter than the stink that's in me nose at this minute. What's more, and this really maddens me, all that lot when they'll be laughin' up their sleeves at the young mistress.'

'Well, that's her own fault, I suppose: she can't carry them, she hasn't got the presence. Well, you couldn't expect it, being brought up in a vicarage as she was; a bit prim, she is, priggish. Well, that's what they call her in there, Parson's Prig.'

'She's no prig; she's a decent kindly young soul.'

'Well, I can say this, she's got one follower in you, Irish. All right! All right! Shane. But, enough of this; we're goin' to have our hands full the night with those animals, 'cost just listen, that thunder's comin' closer. The big fella an' young Prince will kick hell out of their stalls if there's any more of it . . .

How long she had remained standing by the wall she didn't know, but she found herself walking back through the garden towards the wood, and in the darkness she groped towards a tree and, putting her arms around it and leaning her forehead against the bark, she moaned aloud as the tears thrust up from her being and flooded her face. She was overwhelmed as if the waters of a dam had burst over her head and she were drowning, dying, while still conscious of the agony of the process . . .

At some time she must have slipped down the tree to the ground. Her back was against the trunk, her legs tucked under her, her arms about her waist. She was no longer crying, nor was there present in her that dreadful feeling of humiliation, but what was in her was a white flame of anger. It was a new emotion, and was burning her up inside. It wasn't debilitating. On the contrary, it had a strength all its own, a separate mind of its own, and it was telling her what to do. Step by step it presented her with a plan, and on the blackness of the night about her she saw it unfolding, right up to the time when he would present her with an explanation.

When a flash of lightning lit up the woodland around her, she did not jump to her feet, telling herself that it was most dangerous to be under trees in a storm, and when the burst of thunder startled her, that's all it did. She did not run for shelter from the storm that it heralded; the storm inside her was far more frightening, for it was demanding retribution: she wanted to rend something, someone; she wanted to throw things, break things, claw, fight. She was no longer her father's daughter. 'Let him without sin cast the first stone'. Well, she was without sin in that way and there was righteousness in the stone that she was about to cast.

As she got to her feet, she thought of her father. He was the only one who had been right: he had known the nature of the man who had sought her hand; he had seen through the hypocrisy of his changed character, as had, no doubt, the staff of that house, which was why they had never accepted her as mistress, laughing at her behind her back. The Parson's Prig. Well, she would show them what a Parson's Prig could do. And for the first time in her life she blasphemed: by God! yes, she would this night.

There came another flash of lightning, then a deep roll of thunder. Still she didn't move from under the tree, but asked herself how long it was since she had heard the voices of those two men. An hour? Oh yes, it must be.

Slowly now she groped her way among the trees. Once she stopped when she heard a rustling in the undergrowth some distance away, and she asked herself what would happen were she to come face to face with someone, a poacher. And such was her strength at this moment that she told herself he would certainly get a bigger shock than she would. It was as she neared the wall again that she heard the chimes of the stable clock. They told her it was eleven o'clock. Away from the wood the night seemed light, yet the sky was low and black.

As if already following her plan, she passed the archway and walked to where the wall ended and a high hedge began. The path beside it led to the middens, but there was a gap some distance along it, wide enough to take the flat cart that carried the drums and buckets of household refuse of all kinds to the tip.

She passed through the gap and into the yard. At the far end of the buildings was a doorway that led to what was called the maids' passage, and when it opened to her touch, it appeared to be all the confirming proof that she needed, for it was the first footman's duty to go round the house and see that all doors were bolted. Apparently this had been the practice since, a few years previously, robbers had simply walked into the house and helped themselves to a quantity of silver.

She had no fear of meeting any of the staff: those who weren't in bed would, no doubt, be ensconced discreetly in the housekeeper's room. She had no difficulty in mounting the stairs going up from the passage for they were lit by the glow of a night candle on the landing above. From here another flight of stairs led to the attics, whilst a door opened on to the gallery. This too she found was softly lit here and there by candles, which was the not the rule.

How dare they! How dare they! All prepared to light my lady in and out. She'd 'my lady' her. And him. By God! she would. A small voice from some depth in her that had the echo of her mother said, 'Oh, Nancy Ann. Nancy Ann.' And she made an actual physical movement with her hand as if flinging it aside. She was past niceties of thought or action; she felt she had really come of age.

There were three ways into the bedroom: through the main door, through his dressing-room, and through hers. He had likely turned the key in the main door. But why should he, for that was hardly ever used except by herself and him, the staff customarily using one of the dressing-room approaches.

She had crossed the gallery and was in the corridor now; the thick piled carpet hushed her footsteps. She stopped at his dressing-room door, and as she did so a streak of lightning flashed past the long window at the end, lighting the space as if in daylight. This was followed immediately by a crash of thunder that brought her shoulders up to her ears. But before its vibrations had trailed away, she had turned the handle of the dressing-room door, was inside and had closed the door. Strange, there was no light here, but from under the door leading to the bedroom there was a beam showing.

As her hand gently sought the handle of the door she heard her husband's voice saying, 'Rene. Rene;' then the woman's tone, soft and laughter filled, saying, 'Denny. Denny. What I've braved for you.'

She did not thrust open the door but turned the handle gently; then she stepped into the room that was lit by the two pink glass shaded lamps, and there, lying on the high bed on top of the covers, stark naked, lay her husband and the woman. For a moment the sight seemed to blind her. All she could see was the pink flesh which appeared to encompass the bed, and the long fair hair spread over the pillows.

There was a moment of utter silence: then Dennison was sitting bolt upright, crying, '*Nancy Ann! My God!* No! No! Listen! Nancy Ann.'

Slowly she walked towards the foot of the bed, and there, over the chaise-longue, she saw the clothes, dress, corset, petticoat, fancy bloomers, stockings, all in a jumble, and by the side of them his dressing-gown, with his small clothes on top. Her mind registered this, for he always changed into his night things in his dressing-room.

As if it was part of the plan she glanced towards the doors leading on to the balcony. They were wide open. Almost as quick as the lightning that further lit the room her arms spread out and within seconds they were full of the clothes; then dashing now through the open doors, she flung them over the balcony, but did not stay to see some of them fall to the ground and others come to rest on the cherry tree whose branches extended to within a few feet of the house wall.

Dennison was on his feet now, yelling, but his words were unintelligible to her. She saw him run into the dressing-room then she looked at the woman on the bed. There had been a triumphant smile on her face when she had first looked at her lying there by the side of her husband; now that was gone and she was tugging at the quilt in order to cover herself. But the quilt was tucked into the bottom of the bed and, being unable to loosen it, she swung her fat legs over the side of the high bed. As she did so her upper body came forward, bringing her hair over her shoulders. When Nancy Ann grabbed it, the woman let out a high squeal; and then they were grappling like any fishwives. But Mrs Rene Myers had never sparred with brothers, nor had she fought with the McLoughlins, and when one of her soft breats was suddenly punched she squealed again, but had no time for anything more before she was swung round and a shoe contacted her buttocks and sent her sprawling onto the balcony where her soft body coming in contact with the iron railings wrenched from her a high-pitched scream. The next instant Nancy Ann had banged the doors closed and turned the key. And she was running to the window at the other end of the room when Dennison rushed out of the dressing-room, a towel round his middle, seemingly having been unable to find any of his clothes; even if there had been a light in the dressing-room, he wouldn't have even known in which drawer his handkerchiefs were kept, so well had he been taken care of all his life.

As her hand raised and flung the key into the night, he yelled at her, '*Have you gone mad, woman? Have you gone mad?*'

She made no answer whatsoever. She was aware that he had tucked the towel into itself in order to form a hold and when his hands now came out as if to grip her shoulders the fury in her reached its peak and almost simultaneously, just as she had seen the McLoughlins do when fighting, and not infrequently men coming out of the inn on a Saturday in the summer, she doubled her fist and levelled it at his face, at the same time lifting her knee into his stomach.

Neither of these blows had the force behind them as they would have had had they been delivered by a man, but nevertheless they staggered him and brought him bent double and wrenched a groan from his lips which was drowned by the screams coming from the balcony, added to now by the commotion in the corridor.

It needed only the gesture of her wiping her hands to say that the episode was over, for now she turned from the mêlée in the room, and as she opened the door into the corridor and looked into the horrified faces of the butler, the housekeeper, the valet, she spoke for the first time. Her voice sounded dead calm even to herself. 'The storm's breaking,' she said. Then as she went to move away, she turned to the valet and added, 'The keys to the bedroom and the dressing-room doors don't fit that of the balcony doors; I'm afraid you'll have to break it down.'

They said nothing. They could not have been more astounded if, before their eyes, she had turned into the devil himself.

She was slightly surprised to see Mary on the nursery floor landing, fully dressed, and to be greeted with, 'Oh, ma'am. Ma'am.' and then, as if giving an explanation why she wasn't in bed, saying, 'They were uneasy. It's the storm. They were so hot. I didn't wake Agnes, she sleeps through anything.'

Nancy Ann went into the day nursery and here the rain was now hitting the roof so hard that she had to almost shout to make herself heard. 'There are some boxes and hampers in the store cupboard,' she said. 'Will you bring them, Mary?'

'Sit down, ma'am. Yes, yes, I'll bring them, but sit down. Would you like a cup of tea?'

'Yes, thank you, Mary. But bring the boxes first, please.

Mary made three journeys to the store cupboard, and when the floor was littered with soft travelling bags and boxes, Nancy Ann said, 'We'll pack all the childrens' body clothes first, and then the bedding.'

'But ma'am.' Mary stood hovering over her, her face crumpled with inquiry, and Nancy Ann, looking up at her, said, 'I'm taking the children to my father's . . . the Dower House. Did you hear the commotion downstairs?'

'I . . . I felt something was afoot, ma'am.' Then she pointed to the window. 'I could see from the store room window the lights in the yard, and I made out in the rain a carriage there. Are you going by carriage, ma'am?'

'No, Mary, that carriage won't be for me or the children. We . . . we shall wait till dawn, when I'll get you to go down to the yard and seek out McLoughlin. What time exactly do the men rise?'

'Oh' – Mary hesitated for a moment – 'some of them are in the yard at half-past five, ma'am.'

'Well, I'm sure McLoughlin will be one of them. Try to take him to the side, then tell him I would like his assistance, and bring him up the back way. Will you do that?'

'Anything. Anything, ma'am. But, oh, 'tis sorry I am to the heart that . . . that you are troubled like this.'

Nancy Ann lay back in the chair and let a long drawn breath out before she said, ''Tis sorry I am too, Mary, to the heart, that I find myself like this. There's an old saying, We live and learn, but I have been very slow to learn. I did not listen to people wiser than myself. But then, it is all experience, and if we learn anything, we never make the same mistake twice.'

No, well, it would be an impossibility, wouldn't it, to make her mistake twice, to again marry a man like Dennison? It *would be* the act of a fool. Yet, hadn't she already been a fool? No, no, she hadn't. She denied her accusation. She had been, or had tried to be a trusting wife. She had tried, oh yes, she had tried, not to imagine how he spent part of his time when in London, or even in Newcastle. Well, she need wonder no more.

It was strange, but all the anger had gone from her. There was a coldness in her, an empty coldness, as if her whole being was a room without furniture or decoration of any kind. She could look back at the events of the last hour and picture each movement she had made from the time she saw the naked bodies on the bed, and it was like looking at an album. Turning the pages, she felt her fist digging into the soft flesh of the woman's breast, then the feel of her hair as she entwined her fingers in it, and the strength that came into her arm and foot as she swung her on to the balcony. Then over a page, she saw the clenched fist going into Dennison's face and her knee into his stomach. Years ago, the boys would have inwardly applauded her antics while outwardly expressing disapproval. Yet, in the rough play she'd had with them, or while defending herself against the McLoughlins, only once before had she used her knee. From whom had she inherited such traits? Her grandmama? Yes, she could see her grandmama acting in the same way, given the same provocation.

'Thank you.' She took the cup of tea from Mary, then said, 'Once we get the bags packed you must go to bed. I will sit here.'

'Oh no, ma'am, no. If you sit up, I sit up. I'll take that chair an' you put your feet up on the couch there.' She pointed to the old horsehair couch that was set under the window.

Nancy Ann made no protest at this because of a sudden it seemed that all her strength was draining out of her. She did not feel the need to cry, but a great need to sleep, to shut out life and dream that she was back in the vicarage where the pennies had to be counted and the food was always plain, but where the days were filled with happiness, and she had never come across the man called Dennison Harpcore.

Shane McLoughlin stood in the nursery looking at the cases and bundles on the floor. He then raised his eyes to where the young mistress stood, and, as he was to say to his mother when he visited her on his next leave day, he had never seen a change in anybody come about so quickly, for although her face was as white as death she seemed to have grown in stature, so straight did she hold herself. And her manner, too, was no longer that of the smiling young woman but was firm and in command of herself and her intentions.

After she had finished speaking, he touched his forelock and said, 'Yes, ma'am, don't worry about this lot. You go ahead and I will see they get to the gate – I'll take the flat cart – and from there I'll carry them to the house. Don't worry yourself, ma'am. And ma'am' – he looked into her face – 'I take this liberty of speaking as someone who has known of you for many years, and to who you've shown kindness since I came into this service. And I'll say this, ma'am, I'm your servant any day in the week.'

'Thank you. Thank you, Shane.'

At the mention of his Christian name, his eyelids blinked rapidly, and he jerked his chin and moved aside to let her pass.

She now went into the night nursery and, taking the baby from Agnes's arms, she went out, followed by Mary who was now carrying Rebecca.

Their advent into the yard and their crossing of it did not go unnoticed, but none of the male staff approached them, simply stared wide-eyed at the mistress of the house followed by her nursery-maids, one carrying a child, the other two cases.

The morning was bright, the air was fresh, the garden was giving off varied scents, but Nancy Ann neither saw the beauty nor smelt its fragrance; her future ahead appeared like a battlefield, for she knew she would have to fight for the custody of her children, but fight she would.

Her entry into the Dower House at the early hour brought her grandmother from sleep, and Peggy also. Hilda was already awake and busying herself in the sick room.

In the sitting-room, Jessica immediately dropped on to a chair and stared at her granddaughter as she gave her an outline of what had transpired, and for once she could find nothing to say. And after Nancy Ann had finished, she continued to gaze at her, and when she did speak, it was in an unbelieving mutter: 'You threw her out on to the balcony in the storm stark naked? And . . . and you struck Dennison?'

'Yes; I did both these things.'

'You actually used your knee and fist on him?'

'Yes, I did.'

'Huh! Huhl If the whole thing wasn't so tragic, child, I would laugh my head off and pat you on the back, for in your place I would have reacted in exactly the same way.'

The words of understanding, even of approval of her actions, was almost too much. She flung herself down on the carpet and buried her head in her grandmother's lap. And Jessica, stroking her hair, bent over her, muttering to herself now, 'I never thought that of him, no, no. No matter what his vices, I always gave him credit for gentlemanly instincts. But that . . . that was coarse, and blatant, and degrading.' She lifted Nancy Ann's head and was surprised to see that her cheeks were dry. She asked softly, 'Have you done any thinking beyond this moment?'

'Yes, yes, Grandmama, I've done a lot of thinking, in fact, I've thought all night. I'm divorcing him.'

'Oh, child, your father would never . . . Oh, then' – she sighed – 'what does John Howard know or care what happens now? But perhaps he, Dennison, won't let you.'

'He'll not be able to stop me. Which judge, in a court of law, could pass over an incident like that and not call it reason for divorce? There are those in the house who would deny that they knew anything about the matter. There are also those who would stand by me, a few. And anyway, those who did not witness her entry or departure from the house will have been given evidence of her having been there from some of her garments still hanging from the highest branches of the cherry tree; I noticed her blue silk under-drawers and a matching waist petticoat. They'll be awkward to get at, even with a ladder, and until they are down they'll be in full view of anyone coming up the drive.'

'Oh, Nancy Ann. I do wish it was possible to laugh. But my dear' – her tone changed – 'you look so deadly pale and tired. You haven't slept.'

'No, not at all.'

'Well, you know what you are going to do. My bed is still warm, you are going into it and have a couple of hours' rest. Now, no more talk, just do what you're told. The girls and Mary will see to the children. You have a treasure in that young woman.'

Nancy Ann did not need any further persuasion to go to her grandmama's room, and, after undressing, she put on one of her grandmama's nightdresses. But as she was about to get into bed, she paused and did what she hadn't done for almost three years, since Dennison had laughed at her when she knelt down by the bed to say her night prayers. From that time she had said them just before going to sleep. But this morning, her face buried in her hands, she found that, although she was kneeling in a suppliant attitude, she could not pray, especially could she not say 'Our Father . . . forgive us our trespasses as we forgive them that trespass against us'. So she rose from her knees, got into bed and, turning on her side, she buried her face in the pillow. But still she did not cry. And it came to her that last night in the wood she had cried all she was ever going to cry again.

When she awoke she lay quietly for some time with her eyes closed, imagining that she had really dreamed all that had happened last night. But when it was borne in upon her that it was no dream but stark reality, she opened her eyes and looked round the room. It was almost a replica of her grandmama's room at the vicarage, cluttered, but homely.

The door opened and her grandmama came in and she stood by the bed and said, 'There now, you've had a nice long rest.'

'What time is it?'

'Just on noon. Coming up twelve o'clock.'

'That late?'

As she made to rise, Jessica put her hand on her shoulder, saying, 'There's no hurry, everything is arranged. Mary and Agnes have the children on the lawn and Rebecca is running around yelling her head off, as usual. By! she has a pair of lungs on her, that one. But you have a visitor . . . No, no, it isn't him, it's Graham. He's been here this hour past; he's been playing with the children. He seemed to know all about it before I opened my mouth. Funny, how things get about. They'll likely try to hush this up over there, but it's too late already. It appears that one of Graham's gardeners was courting a kitchen maid up at The House and was paying a late visit. He was about to make his way back, apparently using your pathway, when he heard the screams between the clashes of thunder, and he ran towards them, which brought him out on the lower lawn below the balcony. And there, in a flash of lightning, he sees, what he told Graham's butler, a spectacle that you would only expect to see in a madhouse. Graham didn't go into details, he didn't need to. But he's concerned for you. Anyway, don't hurry, just take it easy. Get yourself washed and dressed, then we'll see about arranging rooms. And, my dear' – she put her hand on Nancy Ann's shoulder – 'you've got to be prepared for the other visitor.'

Nancy Ann made no reply, but the thought of the coming meeting sent a tremor through her . . .

Strangely, she felt shy of meeting Graham. She was aware of the high regard in which he held her, and she wondered if he would associate the Nancy Ann she had been with the one she had become, this brawling person who had used her fists and knees like some drunken washerwoman.

As she went down the stairs, she was asking herself if she were ashamed of what she had done, and the answer came back even before the thought had ended: *No, no, she wasn't. Not a bit. Not one bit.*

'My dear.' Graham was holding her hands. 'I'm sorry, so sorry. I mean that, I really am.'

'These things happen, Graham. They were bound to happen to someone like me, silly, gullible.'

'*You were never silly nor gullible.*'

She had withdrawn her hands from his and was leading the way into the sitting room, and there he went on, 'I cannot believe it of him. I must admit I was never very fond of him, but I imagined you were happy with him and that was enough for me. Or let us say' – his voice trailed off into a mutter, and then he said quietly, 'He'll never let you keep the children, especially his son, and, things being what they are, I'm afraid the law will be on his side.'

'Not after I explain my case.'

He now walked away from her to the far end of the room and looked out of the window. Then turning, he said, 'This will ruin him, you know, especially when he's aiming to get into Parliament.' He smiled sadly, saying, 'The moral code men demand of those who are in the public eye is really laughable: their lives must appear beyond reproach. That the majority of them lead double lives is overlooked. The surface one must be righteous in the eyes of the people, yet the so-righteous ones can make no secret of their incompatibility. The lack of tolerance of our dear Queen and our Prime Minister are two good examples, don't you think? Both righteous people, yet cannot stand the sight of each other.'

She looked at him. She hadn't known that, about the Queen and Mr Gladstone. But there he was, this kind, good, and faithful friend, speaking up for a man that he didn't really like, and whose place he would have filled if he hadn't been so slow, to use his own words. She was finding it strange that she could let her thoughts flow free like this. No longer did she admonish herself: I mustn't think like that, I am a married woman. It is a sin to think such things as another man being in love with you . . . Where had the girl gone who had thought like that? She didn't know, except that she had died last night.

He returned to her now, saying, 'If there's anything you want, anything at all I can do, you must tell me. One thing I fear, you are going to be hard pressed for room here.'

'No, no. It will be all right once I can arrange things. And I'm so grateful that I have this house to come to. What I would have done otherwise I don't know. I shall always be grateful to you, Graham.'

She thought that he was about to say something, but instead he gulped in his throat, jerked his chin out of his soft collar, then turned from her, saying, 'You know where I am if you need me.' And then he was gone.

As she stood looking down the room, she recalled what he had said about the law being on Dennison's side with regard to the children, and the thought turned her sharply around and she hurried through the French window and on to the lawn where Rebecca came running on her stubby legs to meet her, crying, 'Mama! Mama! A bunny! Bunny!' She pointed.

'Yes, darling, yes, a bunny.' But there was no rabbit in sight. Lifting the child up, she called to Agnes: 'Bring William in, Agnes. And, Mary, will you come along a moment?'

A few minutes later, in the makeshift nursery, she gave Mary an explanation for her order, saying, 'Keep them indoors until – ' She paused, dithering between using the master, my husband, their father, or Mr Harpcore; when she could use none of these terms, she added lamely, 'Just keep them in until later, Mary. You . . . you understand?'

Mary understood.

She next went into her father's bedroom, and her grandmother turned from bending anxiously over the bed and said abruptly, 'We'd better call the doctor, he's had a turn for the worse. Send Johnny straightaway.'

Nancy Ann left the room hastily and she had reached the hall when she saw Hilda opening the front door, and there stood Dennison.

She looked away from him and to Hilda, saying now, 'Would you tell Johnny to go for the doctor as quickly as possible?'

'Yes, miss . . . ma'am.'

She now turned about and walked quickly into the sitting-room, conscious that he was close behind her, and once more she was standing where she had been a few minutes earlier. But now her heart was racing, her throat was dry, her eyes were wide and unblinking. She noted without surprise that there was a slight discolouring on his cheekbone. She also noted that only his chin and lips had been shaved, the dark stubble having been left no doubt to diminish the evidence of her blow.

He was the first to speak. 'What is the meaning of this,' he said, 'taking the children?'

When she did not answer, he said. 'You will bring them back to the house at once. That is an order.'

When she still did not speak he cried louder now, 'You heard what I said?'

And now she answered him in like voice: 'Yes, I heard what you said. And now you hear what I say. I will not take my children back to your house, nor will I enter it again, and if you had any common sense you would not be standing there putting on the act of an aggrieved party. Even the mentally lowest of your band of spies would have more sense than to take up that attitude.'

'How dare you!'

'Oh I dare, I dare, and will dare more than that before this business is ended.'

He gazed at her, his lips slightly apart, his eyes narrowed, because he could not link the figure standing before him with his sweet young wife, with his pliable young wife; a transition had taken place. Here stood a woman, a woman who felt she had been grievously wronged. But if only she would listen. His voice low, and with a plea in it, he said, 'Nancy Ann, will you listen to me? There is an explanation.'

'Oh, please' – she shook her head slowly from side to side – 'I beg you, don't lower my estimation of you any further. I find you naked in bed with your whore . . .'

'Nancy Ann!' His voice was a bawl. But she continued and repeated her words, 'I say with your whore. Your clothes are lying together on the couch, and not for the first time, as you've admitted. And you expect me to believe there is an explanation, when your underlings had made the way clear for her, even to putting candlelights on the stairway and the gallery.'

His face stretched and his voice came rapidly: 'I tell you I knew nothing of this. She came unawares.'

'And I suppose she undressed unawares, and got into your bed unawares, and she lay by your side unawares. Don't, I beg of you, go on any further.'

He turned from her and sat down heavily on a chair and, leaning his elbow on his knee, he dropped his head on to his hand, and like that he muttered, 'It looked bad, I know, but if you would only listen. In any case, I beg of you, come back to the house, bring the children. I . . . I miss you. I need you.'

She was quite unmoved by his plea, and her voice was low and cool as she said, 'I've already told you, I have no intention of ever coming back to your house. I am going to divorce you.'

Her words did not cause him to spring up from the chair, but his hands slowly left his face, he straightened his back and he looked at her, and there was even a suspicion of a smile on his face as he said, 'Don't be silly.'

'I am going to divorce you, Dennison.' The very fact that she had given him his full name now brought him to his feet and, his face darkening, he said, 'You can't do that.'

'I can. You must admit I have a very good case: that woman was your mistress before we were married; and since, she has laughed up her sleeve at me over the past years, insulted me; then she dares to come into my home, into my bed. That is enough, I should imagine, to win my case.'

'Win your case!' He was bawling again. 'Well, the lady in question could bring a case against you for damages to her person.'

'She is a slut, and she got the deserts of a slut.'

'Then, in a way, last night, there was a pair of you, for your actions were not those of any lady or vicarage miss, more like those of a fishwife, a drunken one at that. You in turn, should be ashamed of yourself.'

'It may surprise you that I am not in the least ashamed of myself. My only regret now is that I didn't go further and let you join your slut on the balcony. Your staff then could have witnessed the result of their preparations.'

'Oh, God Almighty!' He now began to pace the room, his hand to his head. Then stopping abruptly, he cried, 'I don't know what's come over you, woman. I expected retaliation, of course I did, but not this. And this divorce business, you can't do it, you mustn't do it.'

'I can do it, and I will do it.'

She watched his head move forward, his shoulders rise. His whole attitude spelt of incredulity. And now he muttered, 'But the election, it . . . it would ruin me.'

'You should have thought of that and put your political life before that of your private desires.'

His whole body moved from side to side as if he were struggling against fetters. Suddenly, it stopped. For a moment he stared at her; then his face became convulsed and, an arm outstretched and its fingers stabbing at her, he cried, 'You'll never get the children! You will never get my son! No court of law would give you custody because every man worth his salt has his mistress, and those trying the case could have too. You, my prim little vicarage maiden, don't know of the times you live in. I took you as an amusing child out of that stifling atmosphere and I imagined I could teach you how to live a full life, which, in part, meant meeting the traumas of life, particularly marriage, with dignity. But I recognize now, you never had dignity. You never will. Now, here's my last word on the subject:

I'm going to London for a few days. You know where to reach me. By the time I return I expect you to have changed your plans and returned to the house. Good-day to you.'

She sank down on the sofa. She was trembling from head to foot; she could not even keep her teeth from chattering; it was more as if she were being affected by a great chill. Presently, the cold turned to a numbness; and the sensation frightened her, as it was to do until later in the day when the doctor called and said he was afraid that John had now contracted pneumonia and was a very sick man.

Such was the hurrying and scurrying now that her own troubles were pushed into the background, at least by others in the house. In her own mind, however, they remained very much to the fore.

It was on the third day, when John's condition became somewhat stationary, that Nancy Ann went into Durham, there to see her father's solicitor; and when she returned, there was a visitor awaiting her, and immediately she put her arms around her, crying, 'Oh! Pat, Pat. I'm so pleased you are back.'

Sitting on the sofa side by side, their hands gripped, Pat said, 'I shouldn't be here. We returned from Holland to London where George had business he wanted to tie up, then we were off to France. But there, yesterday morning, we had hardly got indoors when I had a visit from Denny. I couldn't believe it. I just couldn't believe what he had to tell me. My dear, you have got to go back to the house, and quickly.'

'Oh, no, Pat, no. I'm never going back there. In fact, I've just been into Durham and seen a solicitor and told him what I intend to do. I'm divorcing him, Pat.'

'*Oh, no, by God! girl, you're not, not if I can help it.* You didn't listen to him and what happened. And, now, *be quiet!*' She shook Nancy Ann's arm none too gently. 'That bitch of a woman had been working up to this ever since the day you married; in fact, ever since the day she realized that he had an interest in you. I saw it as a danger signal when she offered him friendship after he had become engaged to you. The only person she could ever be friendly with would be the devil, and then she has enough wiles to trick him. Now, I'm telling you, this is what she's been waiting for, just this situation. And her cronies over there, who should be kicked out of the place, have made it possible for her to carry it out. At this time of the year she would usually be abroad, exposing her fat to the sun and bragging about it never changing colour. But no, she's sitting there, tight. And let me tell you, girl, that Dennison loves you as he's never loved anybody in his life. He wants you, girl. He needs you. You've been a bulwark to him, you've changed his life. But if you throw him out of your life, he's a man and if he's going to be blamed for cohabiting with her, then that's just what he will do, he'll take up the idea that if he's blamed for it he might as well earn it. And she'll have won. Nancy Ann' – Pat shook her arm – '*she will have won.* She's had men in her life since she gained puberty, but he became an obsession with her. He still is. Now look, don't turn your face away like that. And listen to me, listen closely. You wouldn't hear his side of the story as to how it happened. Well, he told it to me detail for detail, and I'm giving it to you now. It was like this. It was a hot thundery night. He had been working late on his papers. That's another thing, this Parliamentary business was the best thing next to yourself that ever happened to him. It could have been a steadying influence and you mustn't ruin it, you mustn't. Anyway, as I say, he had been working late. He was very hot and tired, and, this is the point, he was missing you, even if he hadn't been in your bed for sometime. And that, by the way, was through the doctor's suggestion: he told him it would be dangerous if you had any more children. Oh, yes, yes, I know, and he knows' – she flapped her hand – 'there are ways and means. But he was being considerate, over considerate, he realizes now. Well, anyway, let me come to the point. He went upstairs, and the heat was so oppressive that he decided not to go straight to bed, but to sit on the balcony for a time. So he dismissed Staith. Then after a while he undressed, not in the dressing-room, but in the bedroom, and threw himself on top of the bed. And that storm brewing didn't prevent him from dropping into an exhausted sleep. The next thing he knew was, he thought you had come back and he put his arm around you, and then, to use his own words when he saw who was lying there, "God, I couldn't believe it. I thought I must be dreaming." Whatever madam's intention was in coming to the house in the first place, the end must surely have been what she saw presented from the bed, and she must have undressed there and then. Anyway, he remonstrated with her quietly and gently, because you must remember, Nancy Ann, and face up to the fact that that woman was once his mistress. But that was before he knew you, and he swears to God and he swore to me that he has never touched her since, although I know myself she followed him to London. I was in a London house once when she called and we all had tea together. Anyway, you can imagine he didn't go into exact detail over what followed; I could only gather as well as assume that she must have become very persuasive, to say the least, and except for kicking her out of bed, the only thing he could do was . . . well, to be counter-persuasive. And he was doing just that when, as if, again to use his own words, his conscience had conjured you up and placed you at the foot of the bed, because he was never so shocked in his life as when he saw you standing there, and for a moment he became paralysed until he saw you grabbing up all the clothes and rushing towards the balcony. He said there was no light in the dressing-room and he couldn't put his hand on anything but a towel, and there was the thunder and lightning punctuated by the screaming of Rene. When he rushed back into the room, there you were throwing the key of the balcony doors out of the window. And the next bit . . . well really! my dear' – she smiled now – 'if this business hadn't been so serious, I would have laughed my head off, to think that the little vicarage piece could use her fists and knee on her lord and master. You didn't exactly give him a black eye, but it was a beautiful blue one. The outline of it was still there when I saw him. But the knee, I thought I'd heard everything then. Katie Lynshaw. You know Katie Lynshaw who lives over Jesmond way. You met her at the Tollys. Well, she's not the size of twopennorth of copper, but she almost brained Harry with the chamberpot. She cracked it over the side of his head, and was left holding the handle. The poor fellow was never the same afterwards . . . well, you know he died last year. I'm not surprised. But to use the knee' – she tut-tutted, she was smiling now, 'it was most unladylike.'

'I've never been ladylike, Pat.' There was no smile on Nancy Ann's face.

'Don't be ridiculous. You were the most ladylike individual I ever came across, at least on the surface. But we're getting from the point.' Her voice took on a sober note again. 'You've got to believe what I've told you. He had no hand in this. He wasn't to blame. And there would have been nothing more to it that night, I can tell you that. He was so upset and so sincere. I know when a man is speaking the truth and I'd put my life on bail that every word he said was just as it happened. And what is more he's no fool; he knew that she couldn't have got in there without assistance, and he dismissed Staith straightaway.'

Nancy Ann's eyes opened slightly and she said, 'He did?'

'Yes, he did. And when he comes back he's going to sort out the others, too. Of course, he'll have to stand the racket when he does return, and you will too, because this escapade will keep the county laughing for some time. Those who are abroad will regret not having been here; but the story will be renewed and extended in the telling for some time to come. And if it wasn't for Arnold Myers's career I would like to bet that Rene would have had you up in court, because from what I can gather, her middle . . . huh! . . . her middle was badly bruised and she had to keep to her bed for a couple of days; she even called in the doctor. Well, flesh like hers can't be banged against iron railings without leaving some mark.' She now put her hand out and grapped Nancy Ann's knee, saying, 'You are a mixture, my girl, aren't you?'

'Yes, perhaps I am a mixture, but . . . but I'm no longer a girl. At this moment I have the feeling that I will never grow older, I feel I know all about life, its façades and its under-currents, and I detest it all.'

Pat sighed deeply, then smiled faintly as she said, 'In the mood you're in it would be useless to try to contradict you or dare to say you still have a lot to learn. But there, I've said it. The sun, the moon, and the stars are a mystery, but to my mind they are nothing to the mystery of human nature; its agonies, its ecstasies, why one is driven to strive for something, then regrets attaining it; why one loves the most unlikely partner – now that is a mystery to me – and why one can hate one or other of one's parents. We are admonished to love our father and our mother, but I can tell you this and I have never voiced it before, Nancy Ann, I hated my mother. She is now eighty-three years old, lively and lording it over her third husband down in Dorset, but I retain memories of her in my early days, humiliating my father who was a quiet, unobtrusive man and who, I know, was glad to die. I was nineteen years old when he died, and I told her that day that I hated her and I don't retract one word. But I ask again, why did they marry in the first place? What is the attraction between two people? Which brings me back to you. What attracted Dennison to you? Yet the answer seems simple and plain: you were so different from all the women he knew, without guile, straighforward, so young, untouched. You could say that was the attraction, but there was something deeper in this case, I feel sure. And I say again, Nancy Ann, he loves you, he needs you. Do this one big thing, give him another chance. Go back to his house, rule it as you should have done from the beginning and I'm sure now you are capable of doing just that. You have the power in your hands either to make him or break him and, knowing a little about you, if you break him, you'll have him on your conscience to the day you die, even if you were to marry again to that nice Graham Mercer, honourable gentleman that he is. Oh' – she flapped her hand once more – 'don't be abashed and don't look like that, I'm no fool, and certainly Dennison is no fool, and he knows in what regard Graham holds you and why he has been so kind to the family.'

'*Oh! Pat, don't say such things.*'

'Oh, dear, dear, dear; I thought we had reached womanhood just a moment ago. So you know as well as I do what I say is true. But even if you were to marry him you wouldn't know a moment's happiness because your first love would be forever there, and the fact would grow on you that this business that has separated you was none of his doing.' She now heaved herself up from the couch, saying, 'I'll away now. I've said enough, more than enough, but know this, Nancy Ann, I'm your friend, I'm your true friend. At a pinch I'm old enough to be your grandmama. I'm one already and I have the nerve to say at a pinch. Vanity, vanity, all is vanity . . . By the way, what is her opinion of all this?'

Nancy Ann considered for a moment before saying quietly, 'She hasn't given me her opinion; she hasn't said a word one way or the other.'

'That's a good sign. She's a wise woman. Look, I'm returning to London tomorrow; what message may I take?'

Nancy Ann turned away saying, and still quietly, 'It's done. I told you I've been to the solicitor.'

'Oh, don't be so stupid, woman; they won't have ordered the clerk to write a letter yet.' She now came towards Nancy Ann and, putting her arms about her, she said, 'Let me tell him he may come back and talk and . . . all right, you can make your own terms. Quite candidly, he would agree to anything as long as you return. Swallow your pride, my dear, we all have to.' And her voice became low as she ended, 'We all have to do it sooner or later in this life. Being women, our power lies in doing just that.' She lowered her head for a moment; then jerking up her chin, she said, 'I'm away. Get out of the house; take a walk and think seriously of what I've said. Bye-bye, my dear.'

She bent forward and kissed Nancy Ann on the cheek before turning and walking out with the gait that spoke of authority in itself.

Nancy Ann went to the window and watched the carriage rolling away. Her mind was in a turmoil, for she believed what Pat had told her was indeed the truth of the matter, yet she couldn't go back to that house and face that hostile staff. You can make your own terms. The words were to the forefront of her mind. Oh, if she could make her own terms, she knew what she would do over there.

But to live with Dennison again.

Yet what would life be like living without him? Pat had been right. Oh, what was she to do? What was she to do?

She started as the door was thrust open and Jessica called, 'Come! Come quickly!'

A moment later she was standing beside her father's bed. He was propped high up on his pillows. His eyes, deep in their sockets, gazed at her for a moment before he murmured, 'Look after your grandmother now. Bring the children up in God. Stand up against . . . Promise . . .'

Again, she was startled when Jessica, thrusting her to the side, took up her son's waving hand, saying, 'There you are, my dear. There you are. Rest now. Rest.'

'Nan . . . cy Ann.'

'She will be all right. Don't you worry.'

'Promise. He . . .'

'I promise, yes, I promise to see to the children.'

The mother and son stared at each other for some seconds. Then John Howard Hazel closed his eyes and his head drooped to the side, and Jessica made a small sound in her throat. Then she turned and looked at Nancy Ann and, tears streaming down her face, she said, 'Well, 'tis over.'

'No, no! Not like that, not so . . .'

'Yes, my dear, like that, as quick as that. Once death calls it doesn't linger, and it's just as well.'

Jessica turned from Nancy Ann and looked down on her son's parchment-skin face again; then slowly she drew the sheet up over his head, and from his half-sitting position it looked as if he were playfully hiding behind it. She turned and, taking Nancy Ann's arm, she said, 'Come; Peggy and Hilda will see to things.'

Nancy Ann allowed herself one backward glance before she was led from the room. When her mother had died they had knelt in prayer around the bed; it seemed wrong somehow that they were walking out like this. And . . . and he had wanted to say something more to her when her grandmama had pulled her away from his side.

'Oh, Papa. Papa.' Slowly, and hard now, she began to cry. They had not seen eye to eye for a long time, but at the end she should have given him some word, some reassurance that she knew he had been right all the time.

Yet had he been right? Oh, what would happen next? She was tired. If it wasn't for the children she could wish she was lying with him now.

It was forty-eight hours later. The house had become one where death lay: the blinds were drawn shutting out the bright sunlight; people had come to the door, leaving words of condolence, some having used their sympathy as a means of penetrating the manor grounds.

Peter had been given leave to be here yesterday, and was coming again tomorrow. But it was Graham who had seen to the arrangements, even to asking Nancy Ann if she had informed her husband, and when she said no, he himself had sent off a wire to the address she gave him.

It was the end of the day; a lamp had been lit to brighten the gloom, and as Nancy Ann looked at her grandmother sitting straight-backed in a chair in which she could have reclined, she was made to wonder yet again at the calmness she had shown over the last two days, for had she not lost her only son? Then she was further surprised by her reply to a statement she herself made voicing something that had been worrying her. 'You know, Grandmama,' she said, 'I feel Papa wanted to say something more to me before he went.' She did not say, 'before you pulled me aside.' And Jessica answered, 'Yes, I know he did, my dear, and I prevented him. And why? Because I do not believe in deathbed promises, and I knew that my dear boy wanted to extract a promise from you, and you being made as you are would likely have suffered for it for the rest of your life.'

'What . . . what promise could I have made that would have caused me to suffer, Grandmama?'

Jessica's voice was quiet now as she said, 'He wanted you to promise to bring the children up in a God-fearing way and to look after me, but what he meant was that you should stay here.'

Their glances held for some seconds before Nancy Ann said, 'Would that have been a bad thing?'

'Yes; yes, it would in more ways than one. I must say this to you now: no matter what has happened, and what did happen wasn't his fault. I, too, had a talk with Pat. The point is this, your place is back in that house, by his side to help him, because what you must realize, Nancy Ann, he is not a parson like your father was, he is not a man of God, he is a man of the world and, let's do some plain talking, he had two vices, women and gambling. Well now, I believe him and I believe Pat, that since he married you he has been faithful. Of course, there again, that might be only up to a point, but it is a fact that he has not taken a mistress. And now, having said that, this is where I come in. I love my grandchildren . . . when I see them from time to time. You see, you must understand that for years I've lived in a house without children and that, until your father became strange in his mind, there has been a sense of peace and quiet around me. And you might find what I'm saying may sound hard, even callous, but I can no longer put up with the constant, and that is the word, constant chatter and busyness that children create in a house. And it is their right to chatter and be busy-busy, and those who look after them to be busy-busy, too. But I am past being able to live in such an atmosphere, that is not to say that I feel I am nearing my end, but what I will say is that my patience is not what it used to be. Oh, please, my dear, don't look like that. Don't bow your head. We have been honest with each other all our years together, let us continue in that way. Peter said to me yesterday that I must go and live with them when he married. My dear, can you see me living with Miss Eva McKeowan, as nice and as affable as she has turned out to be? He said I should likely be lonely here. But how could I be lonely with you and children a walk away? And there is Graham. Who could want a better friend than Graham? And what's more, Peggy and Hilda have become very imporant to me. They are servants, I know, but one ceases to think of them as such, more like caring friends. I say all this to you to put your mind at rest concerning me, because I know, like Peter, and like my dear John Howard, you will think it is wrong that I should be on my own. But, my dear, I am going to say something to you that I've never said to anyone in my life before, and that is, there has been a longing in me for years to be on my own. Even when my dear husband was alive, and I loved him, yes, I loved him dearly, there were times when I just longed for him to go out, go away on a journey so I could have the house to myself and be on my own. We are all very complex creatures, dear. We never know what is really going on in each other's head, as I don't know what is in yours as this moment, except perhaps that you are thinking that you have discovered I am cold-blooded, nay, even cruel.'

'Oh, no, no, Grandmama, never that. And . . . and I understand, I do, I really do. But at the same time, I must tell you that . . . that I am deeply hurt. Oh, not at what you have said, but about the cause that brought me and the children here.'

'I can understand that, dear. Oh yes, I can understand that fully. But there's one way to deal with it. Treat it as a lesson and it will give you strength to face whatever happens in the future, because your life has just begun, and there could be other trials ahead of you.'

Other trials ahead of her. Nancy Ann thought of these words over the next two days for she knew that one of these trials was imminent.

Because of her grandmother's frankness about the children she had told Mary to keep them outside as much as possible when the weather was fine. So it was towards five o'clock the day before the funeral that the first of the trials took place. Mary and Agnes were giving the children a little picnic under the beech tree at the bottom of the lawn, and Nancy Ann had joined them and they were all sitting on the grass. It was as Mary was saying to Rebecca, 'No, my dear, another piece of bread and butter and then you may have your cake,' that the child's eyes sprang wide and she bounded up, crying, 'Papa! Papa!'

Nancy Ann did not turn as the child ran past her. Outwardly her body stiffened, while inside it was as if all her muscles had become fluid. Slowly, she rose to her feet and turned to see him standing some distance away along the path that led to the gate. The child was in his arms, her arms tight about his neck, her voice prattling unintelligibly.

He was standing now in front of her, and she noticed immediately that his face looked grey and that he wasn't dressed as sprucely as usual. His voice was low and level as he said, 'I came as soon as I heard. I've just got in.'

She could find no words and was saved from embarrassment by the child saying, 'Tea, Papa?'

'Yes, yes, that would be nice, a cup of tea.'

It was Mary who came forward, saying naturally, 'Come along, my dear, your papa would like a cup of tea.'

She took the child from his arms; then turning to her sister, she said, 'Go and tell Cook that the master's here and would like tea.'

At this, Nancy Ann turned away from them, and he followed her, and the protests of the children followed them.

In the dim light of the sitting-room she placed herself some distance away from him after indicating that he should be seated. And when he said, 'It was very sudden?' she spoke for the first time, saying, 'Not really. He was very ill.'

'When is the funeral?'

'Tomorrow.'

'All arrangements have been made?'

'Yes.'

He did not ask who had seen to them. But now, bowing his head, he joined his hands between his knees and looked down on them as his stretched fingers interplayed with each other as if intent on pulling them apart. Then he asked quietly, 'Have you seen Pat?'

'Yes. Yes, I have seen Pat.'

'Did she give you my explanation?' He was still not looking at her.

'Yes.'

'And you believe it?'

When she did not answer immediately he raised his head quickly, saying, 'It is the truth, absolutely. I swear on it. You must believe me, my dear.'

What happened next happened so quickly that it gave her no time to escape from his touch, for he sprang from the chair and dropped down by her side on the couch and was gripping her hands. His face close to hers, his eyes pleading, as was his voice, he said, 'Come back, Nancy Ann. Please. Please. I need you. Dear, dear God, how I need you, I'm lost without you. I'll . . . I'll do anything you ask. Make . . . make your own terms, only come back to me.'

Her lips were trembling, her eyes were moist as she looked at him; part of her was urging her to throw herself into his arms, the other, the new born part that had emerged over the last week, was telling her there would never again be another opportunity like this.

Withdrawing her hands from his and easing herself along the couch, she rose to her feet, turned her back on him and walked to the fireplace; and there she stood for a while before she said quickly, 'Very well, but only, as you said, on my own terms.'

She knew he had risen to his feet and that he was standing some way behind her, and was waiting. Swinging round now, she said, 'If I'm to go back into that house, I shall only go back as its mistress.'

'You have always been its mistress.'

'No, no, I have not.' She only just prevented herself from putting her hands up to her lips because she knew she had shouted and in the presence of death laid out in the adjoining room. And she went on, more quietly now, 'Of your large staff, no more than two or three have given me my place, and surely the events of the past week have shown you how little they consider me. Well, I want a clean sweep. If I am to be a real mistress in that house I don't want to live among spies and traitors. I shall want to reorganize the whole staff.'

His voice, too, came quietly to her, saying, 'Very well, my dear, you do that. If that is all.'

'That isn't all. There is something that has worried me since I have been in that house. You are not going to like this, but I must say it, it is the boy. He is a bright intelligent boy, he should be sent away to school.'

Even in the dimness of the room she saw his face darken and his jaws clench, and after a moment he said, 'You ask too much, Nancy Ann. You know my feelings in that way. I . . . I could never bring myself to see to the boy's education. It would be a concession, an acknowledgement that I have fought against.'

She broke in now, saying, 'Would you object to someone else educating him?'

He paused for a moment as if thinking, then said sharply, 'Not Mercer. I wouldn't have that.'

'Nor would I. I hadn't thought in that direction.'

He knew in what direction she was thinking, and again she saw the muscles in his cheekbones tighten, but he said nothing, only half turned from her, muttering now, 'Is that the sum total of your demands?'

'No.' Even the syllable trembled as it passed her lips. Now he was facing her again, staring at her, waiting, and when, her head down, she said, 'Our life together cannot . . . cannot be the same.'

There was a long pause that went into a full minute before he said, 'You mean you will not come back as my wife?'

When she made no answer he asked quietly, 'For how long do you intend such a situation to continue?'

'I don't know.'

Again there was a pause; and then, his words seeming to come from deep in his throat, he said, 'You know me, Nancy Ann, I would find that situation impossible were it to be . . . be permanent. Let us be frank when we have got this far. I want a wife. I need a wife. I need you.'

Why at this moment should she see the face of James and hear his voice saying, 'Procreation; that was all I was needed for'? And then came Peter and a wisp of the conversation on the night they were driving to the ball, and his words, 'That is no marriage'.

Her voice was small now it came, saying, 'You'll have to give me time.'

'How much time? I gave you too much time after William was born. That's where I made the mistake.'

When she turned and again looked into the empty grate, he said, 'I shall stay for your father's funeral, after which I shall return to London. The house is being redecorated; I . . . I am thinking about selling that too. Anyway, in the meantime I am staying with Pat and George. They have made arrangements to tour through Northern

France and have left it open for me to join them if I so wish. I shall do so, and in that case I will be away for three weeks. When I come back we will talk again. Will that suit you?'

She forced herself to say, 'Yes, thank you.'

'Then I will take my leave of you until tomorrow. What time is the funeral?'

'Eleven o'clock.'

'I shall be there.'

As he turned from her she said, 'Dennison.' And at this he swung round to her, waiting.

'May I ask you to inform the staff that I will now be in sole charge of the house and the yard staff?'

She saw his face stretch slightly, and he repeated, 'The yard staff?'

'Yes, the yard staff.'

'Very well.' His head moved slowly. 'I will do as you wish. When will you return?'

'The day after tomorrow.'

'I will inform them.'

Almost with military precision now, he turned and marched from the room. And she, going to the sofa again, sat down and leant her head on the corner of it while her hands gripped the back, and so mixed were her emotions that she couldn't tell whether she was happy at the turn of events or desperately sad.

2

The funeral of John Howard Hazell was well attended. Most of the men from the village joined the cortège outside the gates of the Manor House. And the new parson, the Reverend Michael Nesbit, spoke very kindly of his predecessor.

Those villagers who came back to the Dower House were given refreshments in the barn; the few carriage people who returned were received in the house. Dennison was not among them. But Pat and George, and her sister Florence and her husband did return. But within three hours of John Howard Hazel being laid in the ground the house was back to normal, except it lacked his presence.

And now Graham, who had stayed after all had gone, was bidding Nancy Ann goodbye. He did not offer any word of condolence; in fact, his words throughout the week had been few, although she had seen him every day. And she herself gave him no word of thanks, but she took his hand in between hers while her tear-filled eyes spoke for her.

They had reached the door when he said, 'You are going back then?' He did not look at her as he spoke and he had to wait for an answer: 'Yes, yes, I am going back.'

Now he did look at her while saying, 'You could do nothing else. He could, as I've said before, have claimed the children even if you had got a divorce.'

She was surprised that he could speak like this, and she was asking herself how he should know about the divorce, but then she remembered that he too was a friend of George and Pat, although he never went visiting there.

Without waiting for her to make any comment, he went on, 'Don't worry about your grandmama; she is not afraid to be on her own. But then, she won't be entirely. When are you leaving?'

She had to wet her lips before she said, 'Tomorrow.'

'Oh.' He was walking away from her when he turned his head slightly and said, 'If you want any help, just let me know.'

She watched him disappear along the path and she did not check herself as she thought, Why are there so many different kinds of love?

She did not move back to the house the following day, for the weather changed and it poured with rain. But the morning after, the sun was bright and warm and at mid-morning she sent Mary and Agnes across with the children. Agnes was to stay in the nursery to see to them and Mary was to return, bringing McLoughlin with her to carry back the things he had brought over in the first place.

This morning Jessica appeared to be her old brusque self, saying, as she watched the gangling Irishman shouldering the cases and bundles like a pack horse, 'He's a McLoughlin all right.' Then as Mary picked up the last soft bag and went out the door Nancy Ann kissed the old woman and felt herself being hugged in arms that were still strong. She returned the embrace, then hurriedly followed Mary.

It was as they entered the path through the trees that Mary, slowing her pace, said, 'Ma'am, I've heard something that I think you should know.'

'Yes?'

'Well, McLoughlin, he . . . he told me something that he . . . he thinks you should know.'

'Yes?'

'Well. Well, Jennie . . . Well, really, it wasn't her at first, it was young David. Well, as usual the boy was where he shouldn't have been; he prowls around, ma'am, and worries Jennie to death. But anyway, he saw them, the housekeeper and her sister, in one of the empty rooms upstairs and, as he described it to Jennie, Mrs Conway was putting silver things and little framed pictures like cameos into a cloth bag. And then they went down the back way. It isn't the first time, ma'am, I understand. You see, they, by what McLoughlin said, they . . . well, they didn't expect you back, so some of them must have been helping themselves, Jennie told McLoughlin, and he thought you had better know, ma'am.'

'Thank you, Mary. At least it would appear that I have one loyal servant in the house.'

'Oh, you have more than that, ma'am. But . . . but, you know, folks are frightened for their jobs, and those in a position at the top of a household like yours . . . well, ma'am, well, you know what I mean.'

'Yes, Mary, I know what you mean. But there's going to be a great change in my household.' She noticed that she said, 'my' household, and for the first time it was to be her household, and she ended, 'It will start this very day.'

The change in the staff's attitude was very apparent when McTaggart came down the steps and relieved her of her bag. And at the top of the steps there was Trice waiting, and slightly behind was Mrs Conway.

It was evident to her that they had definitely been informed who was now in charge of the house and them. She passed them without moving a muscle of her face. She did not, as she usually had done, thank the footman for his assistance, but at the foot of the stairs she turned to Mrs Conway, saying, 'I would like you, and you Trice and McTaggart, to await me in my office immediately. Also call Appleby and Gillespie, and have the rest of the staff assemble in the hall.'

The tone was one that neither Mrs Conway nor the others had ever heard her use and the woman even dipped her knee and replied smarmingly, 'Yes, ma'am.'

In her sitting-room she sat down heavily in a gold-framed Louis chair, and the long drawn breath she let escape seemed to deflate her body. Up to this moment she had felt strong in her determination to clear the household of those she now considered her enemies, and she still meant to get rid of them, but, nevertheless, she was finding it a strain to keep up this new pose. What was more, she was alone as never before: there was no Dennison to lay her head against; nor was there a grandmama to give her earthy advice and spur her on; nor yet, Graham, to tell her he was behind her waiting to be used. No, here she was, in this huge establishment, about to rule it. But there was something she must do before she went downstairs and confronted those people.

She pulled herself up from the chair and, going to the wall, she rang the nursery bell. Within a few minutes Mary appeared in the room, and she said to her, 'Will you fetch the boy up, Mary, please? Do it as unobtrusively as you can. Come up the back way. If he should be in the boot room, the best way to come would be to approach it from the yard and take him quietly out that way again.'

'Leave it to me, ma'am. I'll do that.'

She now went into the closet room and cooled her face and hands with water from the ewer. Then seated at the small dressing-table, she gazed at her reflection and asked herself if she looked the same as she had done ten days ago, and the answer was, no, the bright sparkle had gone. There was no colour in her cheeks, the light in her eyes showed a pain in their depth. No, she was not the girl she had been ten days ago. She was no longer a girl. That period of her life was over.

When she heard the door opening in the other room she went back, and there was the boy. Mary had her hand on his shoulder pressing him forward, and when she was seated and he stood before her, she said, 'Hello, David.'

And he answered, 'Hello, ma'am.'

'Would you like to tell me, David, what you saw the housekeeper doing, and which room she and her friend were in?'

He blinked his eyes, then glanced up at Mary. She nodded at him, and then he said, 'Will they get wrong?'

To this she answered truthfully, 'Not more than they deserve if they have been doing wrong. What kind of things were they putting in the case? Can you describe them? Were they little pictures like this?' She reached out and took a miniature from the table standing to her side which showed a hand-painting of Rebecca at six months old. Dennison had commissioned it. And now the boy nodded and said, 'Yes, that size. Some were bigger.'

'And what else were they putting in the case?'

His eyelids blinked again before he said, 'Just bits, ma'am, bits of silver like are on the breakfast trays.'

'How did you manage to see them doing this, David?'

'Oh.' His head wagged, then he muttered, 'I was looking around, 'cos you and the master were gone and . . . and I was in the bedroom in the far wing . . . and I heard somebody coming and I hid behind one like that.' He pointed now to her dressing-table and went on, 'And I could see through the space atween the glass and the top what they were doin'.'

'Did you tell anybody about what you saw?'

'Yes. Yes, I told . . . I told our Jennie.'

'And what did she say?'

'She was vexed.' He smiled now, a slow smile that lit up his face and seemed to spread to the bright gold of his hair that had no brown streaks in it now, as he added, 'She's pleased you're back, ma'am, and so am I, an' the cook an' all. She says . . .'

He had stopped abruptly and hung his head, and Nancy Ann, smiling gently at him, said, 'I'm pleased to hear that, David. Now go back with Mary and if you should be asked why I wanted to see you, just say I wanted to know if you had been a good boy. Will you remember that, David?'

'Yes, ma'am. Oh, yes, ma'am.'

She now turned to Mary, saying, 'After you have taken him downstairs, go straight to my office and await me there.'

She let a full fifteen minutes elapse before she left her sitting room. From the gallery she could see the whole staff assembled and the sight of them en masse brought that quivering feeling to her stomach. But, her head held high and her gaze directed straight ahead, she slowly descended the stairs, passed the end of the two ranks they had formed, went through the arch, along the passage and into her office. There, Mary pulled out the chair for her and she sat down at her desk. Then after a moment, looking up at the kindly face of the young woman who had become closer to her than even her grandmother or Pat, she said on a sigh, 'I hate doing this, Mary, but it's got to be done.'

'Yes, ma'am, an' you're quite right. The captain used to say, you know where I worked afore, whenever he had to face anything that was disagreeable, and such times were when he had to stop the mistress overspending, he would say, "Clear the decks ready for action!"'

'Oh, Mary.' She pressed her lips together, closed her eyes and shook her head for a moment; then she said, 'Well, here we go, clear the decks ready for action. Go and tell Trice, McTaggart, and Mrs Conway to come in.'

It seemed that Mary almost skipped from the room to carry out this duty, and a few minutes later the three people who had considered themselves to be heads of the house under the valet, walked quietly into the room and stood before the desk.

Nancy Ann had a pen in her hand. She was writing names on a sheet of paper and she finished the last one with a flourish before looking up at them and saying without any lead up, 'Your wages are paid by the quarter: there are three weeks to go, you will be paid in full. But you will now all pack your bags and leave this house within the next hour.'

They were so stunned that not one of them said a word, but simultaneously their lower jaws had dropped. She had never seen the butler's mouth open so wide for he always seemed to talk through his teeth. But it was he who spoke first, saying, 'But, ma'am, you can't do this, we were engaged by . . .'

'To my knowledge the master has told you that I am now in sole charge. I am dismissing you all. But there is one more thing. Unless you want to find yourselves in court, the articles you have stolen must be returned within the next two days or else the police will be informed. Particularly you, Mrs Conway, you had better tell your relative to return the bag of miniatures et cetera you filled for her just recently, or you might find yourself in a dire situation.'

For a moment she thought the woman was going to faint. She saw the colour drain from her sallow face leaving it grey and her throat expand as if she was aiming to draw breath into her body.

She now looked at the butler. His countenance looked evil, but she faced him, saying, 'You have all, for years, lined your pockets at the master's expense. You have done deals with every tradesman who has called here. This I have proved from the order books. And so I need have no worry that I am turning you out destitute. Nor shall I worry that you will all find it difficult to obtain good employment; it would be impossible for me to foist any of you onto another family . . . That is all I've got to say.'

Not one of them moved, until the footman, McTaggart, muttered, 'No reference?'

'No reference.'

'We could make you prove what you say.'

'Oh, I can prove what I say, and witnesses would come forward.' They seemed about to glance at each other but changed their minds; instead they glared at her with such ferocity that she wouldn't have been surprised if one of them had lifted his hand to strike her.

Mary was holding the door open for them and they turned on her baneful glances as they passed.

After closing the door, Mary came back to the desk and looked at Nancy Ann sitting now with her head leaning against the back of the tall leather chair, and she said, 'You did splendid, ma'am. The main battle's over. Who's next?'

'Anderson.'

When the top floor maid was ushered into the room she did not show any sign of the civil insolence that had dictated her earlier manner when dealing with the mistress of the house, but she stood before the desk and said meekly, 'Yes, ma'am?'

Nancy Ann did not beat about the bush here, she said immediately, 'You are being dismissed, Anderson. You'll have your money in advance. It will be ready for you by the time you have your bag packed.'

'Ma'am.' The woman's voice trembled. 'What . . . what have I done?'

'You needn't ask what you have done, Anderson, you know what you have done. Apart from everything else, your manner has been offensive at times. But that is by the way. I won't embarrass you further by describing your disloyalty; you know only too well how far that went.'

She now looked at Mary, saying, 'Send in Appleby and Gillespie.'

The woman did not take the hint that she had been dismissed but still stood, and then she said, 'A reference, ma'am?'

'I cannot give you a reference, Anderson. If it had just been your manner to me then I might have reconsidered, but you were in league with those who were above you and planned my destruction and unhappiness.'

She felt a tinge of regret as she saw the woman almost stumble out of the room, yet she forced herself to remember how she had been treated by this servant.

When the coachman and groom entered the room their faces were stiff and, as Mary might have put it, in their turn, looked ready for battle. But the wind was taken out of their sails immediately by Nancy Ann saying, 'You two men were the means of bringing a person to this house unknown to the master of it. You showed no loyalty to your master and certainly none to me. Well now, you are both at liberty to find employment with the person who engaged you. You are dismissed as from now. You will have your wages in advance. That is all.'

'But, my God! it isn't.' It was Appleby speaking. 'I've worked for the master twenty years, he wouldn't have . . .'

She silenced him by lifting her hand, and, her voice raised high now, she said, 'He would have. He dismissed his valet for the same offence and has given me permission to dismiss you.'

William Appleby was a small thin man with a wiry body. Now he seemed to swell as he leant across the table towards her and he almost barked at her, 'You won't reign long. Parson's Prig they call you and Parson's Prig you are. His whore was worth a dozen of you and she'll be in your place afore the end, God willin'.'

Both the groom and Mary had now to hold the man and thrust him out of the door, and after Mary had banged the door shut she leant against it and looked to where Nancy Ann was sitting with her hand pressed tight across her mouth. Then she went to her and, patting her shoulder, she said, 'There now. There now. Don't upset yourself, ma'am. He was bound to go on like that. He's had it easy for years, that one. They say he used to valet the master at odd times afore Staith came on the scene; and he was also hand in glove with Trice, especially where the wine cellar was concerned. You're well rid of that one, ma'am. Is that the lot you want rid of, ma'am?'

Nancy Ann shuddered. The man's words were ringing in her ears. 'And she'll be in your place afore the end.' After a moment she said, 'Yes, Mary. Now . . . now I want you to go and bring Robertson here. No; wait. First of all I must talk with you. Sit down.' She pointed to a chair, then looked at the young woman, her hands joined in her lap, and she said, 'Do you think Agnes would be capable of controlling the nursery if she had someone there to help her?'

Mary's eyes crinkled at the corners for a moment. 'Oh, yes,' she said; 'she's capable enough, ma'am. Like me, she had training with our squad, the lot of them, as I said. But . . . but . . .?'

Nancy Ann leant over the desk towards her, saying, 'Do you think you could take the position of housekeper? I'm sure you could, but do you think so? And would you like it?'

'*Me?*' Mary was now thumping her chest with her thumb. 'Housekeeper, here?'

'Well – ' Nancy Ann allowed herself to smile a small smile while saying, 'I have no other house.'

'Oh, but, ma'am, 'tis a big job and responsibilities. And would they accept me?'

'Oh, they'll accept you or they'll go.' There was a definite note of authority in Nancy Ann's voice now, and she straightened herself up as she said further, 'When I speak to the rest of them they will be given their choice. But we're having no more Judases here if I can help it. Well, what do you say? There is nothing, as I see it, to the position except ordering the victuals and supervizing the staff, and I'm sure you can do that. Anyone who can control children like you is capable of giving an order and seeing that it is obeyed. Then there is the salary. It would be almost doubled.'

'Oh, it doesn't matter about that, but I'm not going to be a hypocrite and say it wouldn't be welcome, especially at home. But, as for help in the nursery' – Mary smiled widely now – 'I have another sister, Alice, ready to be placed out.'

'Oh, that would be excellent. So shall we say that's settled?'

'Oh, Ma'am.' Now Mary put her flat hands on the desk and, bending over towards Nancy Ann, she said, 'I bless the day I came under your care, I do that, ma'am.' There was a break in her voice, and Nancy Ann, deeply touched, said, 'It was a good day for me too, Mary. Now go and call in Robertson, please.'

Mary walked towards the door but stood there a minute fumbling with her handkerchief; then, with a slight sniff, she went out.

When Henry Robertson came into the office Nancy Ann wanted to say immediately to him, 'Don't look so perturbed, it's all right.' He was standing now before the desk, a man of medium height with reddish hair which seemed to clash with the nut brown of his uniform. This man had always been civil towards her and helpful if he could. She spoke again without preamble: 'Do you think you can carry out the duties of butler, Robertson?'

There was a second's pause and a stiffening of the shoulders and a pulling in of the chin before the man replied, 'I could, ma'am, I could, and serve you with loyalty.'

'Thank you, Robertson.' And now she asked, 'Do we need two footmen?'

'No, ma'am, not really, one would be ample.'

'I will see one is engaged for you. Thank you, Robertson.'

'Thank you, ma'am, and it's obliged I am to you. Thank you.' He turned smartly and marched out.

When the door had closed on him Mary said, 'One loyal soldier, or sailor,' she smiled, then added, 'Ma'am.'

'Well, let's have the other loyal one, Mary, McLoughlin.'

'Oh yes, ma'am, but he's already enlisted on your side.' . . .

When Shane McLoughlin stood at the other side of the desk, she said to him. 'You will have already heard that Appleby and Gillespie have been dismissed.'

His voice was low when he replied, 'I have, ma'am.'

'Would you like the position of coachman?'

She saw the broad chest expand, and on a breath that he slowly let out, he said, 'I would that, ma'am. I would that.'

'It might entail other duties. As my husband has not now got a valet, you might be called upon to stand in and assist him, such as at those times when he goes away on a shoot.'

She now saw the man hesitate, and then he said, 'Valet the master, ma'am? Oh, I doubt if I'd be any good at that. I'm fumble-fisted. A horse now, I could handle, but to dress somebody . . . well.'

'You would not be expected to dress the master, only lay out his clothes and things like that. It's something that you can soon learn. Mary there would help you.'

At this, Mary looked at her wide-eyed. But when McLoughlin turned towards her, she said to him blithely, ''Twill be all right. You'll soon get into the way.'

'Well, if you think so, I'd be only too pleased.'

Now he turned and looked at Nancy Ann, saying in a characteristic Irish way that placed all human beings on a level, 'You'll not regret this day, ma'am; and you can tell the master so. I'll likely make a mess of everything at first, inside that is, not outside. No, no; those stables'll be run as they've never been run afore, and the carriage horses will be a credit, I promise you that. But upstairs. Well, once I get the hang of it, the master will never have been better served. You can tell him that from me. As for yourself, ma'am, I'm your servant from this day on. An' I have been since I came into the place. But what you've done for me the day has made me sign me cross at the bottom of a document.' . . .

He was in full spate and would have gone on had not Mary, looking at Nancy Ann, prompted, 'There's Winter and Pollock, ma'am. Are you makin' one or t'other of them a groom?'

'Oh, yes, Winter and Pollock. Whom do you suggest, McLoughlin?'

It seemed that now Shane was considering, and then he said, 'Winter's the first stable lad. He's a good fellow is Winter, though he's not as old as Pollock, and Pollock's been here, so I understand, some longer time. He's forty if he's a day, but he's not as bright up top as Johnny. I would say, raise the first stable boy, ma'am.'

'Then it is Winter. Well, when you go out, you can tell him to come and see me. But that will leave you short of a stable boy.'

Almost before she had finished speaking he put in, 'I can soon rectify that, ma'am with one of our lot, I mean me younger brother, Benny by name and bright up top. He's very good with dogs, training them that is. He'll fall into the ways of the horses. Can I tell him, ma'am? He's already helping out a bit in the yard.'

'Yes, do. He may come and see me tomorrow.'

''Tis settled then, ma'am, 'tis settled.' He jerked his head twice at her, a grin on his face from ear to ear; and then he said, 'Will that be all at present, ma'am?'

As the door closed on him both Mary and Nancy Ann looked at each other, and Nancy Ann knew that Mary was about to give vent to one of her body-shaking laughs, and she wagged her finger at her; but the admonition was directed towards herself, too, for she knew full well that if she gave vent to laughter it might become hysterical and end in a torrent of tears. And so she turned her attention to the list on the table.

'Do you know anything objectionable about any of the others?' she asked.

Mary thought for a moment, then said, 'No, ma'am, except that, to keep their jobs, as I said, they've had to run with the hare and hunt with the hounds. No, I think you will find all the rest all right, ma'am. But there's Benton the lodge-keeper and his wife. They keep to themselves. And yet they were in with the other lot. But they and the gardeners and the farmhands come under Mr Taylor the Ground Manager.'

Nancy Ann was considering again; and then she said, 'The cottages. Those of Trice and Appleby are already furnished; they will have only their personal belongings to take with them. But there might be some quantity of these, so you can inform them they may stay on till the end of the week, until they find some other place to live. Appleby's cottage can then be taken over by McLoughlin and his brother. As for the other one, it was a very nice cottage, Trice's wasn't it?'

'Very nice indeed, ma'am, being for married quarters.'

'Well, I have ideas about who will occupy that one.' She now rose from her chair, saying as if to herself, 'Let us get it over.'

When she entered the hall it was to be confronted by what appeared to be a sea of troubled eyes. As she remarked later to Mary, it was as if they were expecting the devil.

She began immediately. Standing with her hands joined at her waist, her head held well back on her shoulders, she said, 'You are all aware by now what has taken place. If any one of you wishes to leave my service you can report to me in my office tomorrow morning. That is all. Oh . . . just one thing.' She had half turned from them. Now she was looking down the hallway to where, at the far end, was a green-baized door which opened into the corridor leading to the kitchen and the staff quarters. And near this door stood Jennie Mather, and she said, 'I would like to see you in my office for a moment, please.'

Jennie Mather looked about her, then took one step forward and, pointing to herself, she said, 'Me, ma'am?'

'Yes. Yes, you.' And on this Nancy Ann turned away and went back into her office; and Jennie Mather slowly followed her.

Jennie Mather was now a woman nearing thirty. She had been a beautiful young girl. There were still traces of the beauty on her face because sorrow and humiliation do not alter the bone formation, merely the skin and the look in the eyes. Her skin was pale, colourless; her eyes were large and of a deep-sea blue, but they held no light, there was a dull subdued look in them.

She was doubtless surprised when her mistress said to her, 'Please, sit down.'

Before Nancy Ann could continue, Mary interrupted quietly, 'You won't be requiring me any more, ma'am, for the time being?' It was a very tactful question, and Nancy Ann, looking at her, said, 'No, thank you, Mary. That will be all for the present. I will be up in the nursery shortly.'

'Very good, ma'am.'

Left alone, the older woman looked at her mistress whom she considered a young girl, her slim body almost lost in the great leather chair. That was until she spoke; and what she said caused her whole expression to change, her eyes to widen, her lips to move one against the other as if they were speaking silent works, and the colour to flood her pale skin, for this young mistress was saying to her: 'I've wanted to speak about this matter for a long time, Jennie.' She did not say 'Mather' but 'Jennie', then went on. 'I think that you have been treated badly in this house. If I'd had my way when I first came here, I would have had your son recognized in some way. But it wasn't to be. That is, up till now. Your boy is highly intelligent. It's a credit to you that he can read and write. Some weeks ago I was looking at the books that I suppose he had been reading up in the attic and I marvelled at his advancement. But that is only one side of education. In the ordinary way he would already have been at a boarding school for some years now, so I intend the wrong to be rectified, at least in that way. Would you agree to this?'

Jennie Mather couldn't speak. She had been sitting upright in the straight-backed chair, now she was slumped, her head was bowed on her chest. And as Nancy Ann watched the tears rain down the young woman's face, she had great difficulty in restraining her own. And she said softly, 'Please, please, don't upset yourself. Come. Come now. Let us talk about this. We both have his welfare at heart.'

It was some minutes before Jennie could say, 'Oh, ma'am, I never thought to live to see the day when I should hear someone speak for us . . . because, I have been made to suffer.' Her voice now broke again and, her head drooping forward once more, she shook it from side to side as she muttered, 'Oh, God, how I have been made to suffer.'

'There, there. Please don't distress yourself. Come; dry your eyes, and answer me this. Why, when you have been humiliated so, did you stay? You could have taken your boy and gone surely?'

Again it was some time before Jennie answered, and then she asked simply, 'Where ma'am? Where could I have gone? I had only one living relative, an uncle, and he in Australia. I had no money except my wage and that a pittance, because my son had to be paid for out of it.'

'What!'

'Yes, ma'am. I had to pay for his keep until he was able to work in the boot room.'

'Who ordered that?'

'The housekeeper, ma'am.'

It was on the point of Nancy Ann's tongue now to say, Dear God! But, as if her tongue was loosened, Jennie Mather began to talk. Looking across the table, the tears still raining down her face, she said, 'It was either the workhouse or the attic. And it wasn't even an attic, it was right under the roof. And I couldn't bear the thought of the workhouse at that time, because I used to think I'd be in for fourteen years before I could leave. You see they don't allow you to leave until your child can work for himself. Little did I know then that I would do almost fourteen years of hard labour here. It couldn't have been worse there, it couldn't. Yet I must admit, ma'am, I hoped against hope that the master would relent. I thought that once he saw my son who looked the spit of his father, who was his own brother, he would forgive and accept the boy. I would have been quite willing to leave, to go away altogether as long as my son was recognized in some way. But no, he hates the sight of him. And my only wonder is, feeling as he does, he has allowed us to stay. It is only because we have hidden away as it were. But now . . . but now, ma'am, you were saying you would send him to school, a proper school. Oh, at this moment, I feel there is a God after all.'

'Well now, listen to me. I would rather it weren't known that I shall be paying for the boy's education. It will have nothing to do with the master, and I couldn't see how this could be hidden until a moment ago when you said that your only living relative was an uncle in Australia. Does he write . . . correspond with you?'

'Yes, ma'am, now and again I get a letter. He moved around when he first went out, but for some years now he's been settled in a place called Kalgoorlie. He and another man have set up a grocery business. And in his last letter he talked about buying some land. He even said that when David was old enough he would send for him.'

'Well, that has solved the problem, at least my problem. You can say that your uncle has sent you the money with which to educate your son. How about that?'

'Oh, ma'am, I'll do anything you say.'

'And it can be known to the rest of the staff that the reason why I called you in is to offer you the cottage, Trice's cottage, and your previous work back.'

'*Trice's cottage!* And my . . .' There was a look of wonderment in the young woman's face now, for it was well known that Trice's cottage was better than the other four on the estate having, besides the loft, a sitting-room and a kitchen. But then this wonderment turned to dismay as she said, 'But the master, if he were to see me.'

'Oh, I've thought about that. But I doubt if he'd recognize you now. Anyway, he is out most of the time and you could arrange your work accordingly . . . Oh, now! now!' Nancy Ann rose from her seat, saying, 'You mustn't cry any more. We will talk again tomorrow when we'll discuss which school will be suitable for David. Then you must go into Newcastle and make arrangements. I shall give you a letter of recommendation.'

Jennie had risen to her feet. She could not speak now, but what she did do was bend her knee deeply, then stumble towards the door.

Her entry into the kitchen interrupted a buzz of conversation among the entire kitchen staff, and it was the cook who said 'My God! girl, not you an' all?'

'No.' Jennie shook her head before saying thickly, 'Me and David are to have a cottage, Trice's.'

There was a complete silence for a moment; then Cook said, 'Oh, well. But not afore time I'd say. I'm glad for you, Jennie, I am that. And I'm glad a day of reckoning has come in this house; it has been long awaited. 'Tis meself that says it, although I've had to close me eyes and shut me mouth this many a long year.'

As Jennie passed the group standing between the long wooden kitchen table and the great fireplace with the big black ovens to the side, she said in an offhand way, 'And I'm to go upstairs again into my old job.' Then, without waiting for any response, she went quickly out of the kitchen, along a corridor, and into the cold meat store, where previous to being called into the hall she had been slicing bacon for the next morning's breakfast, and boning breasts of lamb ready for rolling. However, she did not immediately begin her work again, but, her teeth clenched tightly, she looked around this room where, summer and winter for years now as part of her duty, she'd had the thankless job of standing in this cold cell preparing meats. Even on the hottest day it could make you shiver. Now all that was over. Dear God! She moved slowly round to a butcher's block and, resting her buttocks against it, she bent her body forward and covered her face with her hands . . .

* * *

There followed a busy day. Much coming and going inside and outside the house. But there were to be two more incidents before this chapter of her life would close.

It happened in the late evening. She'd had her supper served on a tray in her sitting-room, after which she went upstairs and paid her last visit to the nursery to see the children already tucked up in their cots and fast asleep. Agnes was tidying the nursery and she reported that William had been a little fractious 'Cutting his teeth, ma'am, he is,' she said, her manner giving the impression she knew all about the cutting of front teeth – which she did – but more so, did it point out that she was capable of carrying out the duties of her new position.

Nancy Ann had looked down on her daughter's round pink face. She was growing fast and already her features were beginning to resemble her own, whereas the chubby baby showed marked traces of his father in the nose and lips.

She bade Agnes good-night. Then at the foot of the stairs she passed Mary, and she said to her, 'It's a lovely night. I'm going for a stroll as far as the river.'

'That'll be nice, ma'am. The air's cool now; 'twill make you sleep.'

When she reached the drive she did not go straight across the sunken garden and make for the river, but she turned to her left and made her way round the side of the house and through the yard. The men were still busy moving in and out of the stables and the tack-room. When they saw her, they stopped and raised their caps to her. And she smiled at them. One whom she hadn't seen before came out of the barn carrying a bale of hay which, on seeing her, he almost let slide from his shoulder. But, standing still, he managed to grip it with one hand while touching his forelock with the other, and in an unmistakable Irish voice, he said, 'Evenin' to you, ma'am.'

This was definitely another McLoughlin. And without her enquiring he answered a question when he added, 'I'm Benny, ma'am. Shane's me brother. I'm new.'

She had stopped. And it was in this moment more than any other that she longed for Dennison to be by her side, for, had he been, once they gained the privacy of the gardens, she would have taken on the voice and the manner of the young fellow, saying, 'Evenin' to you, ma'am. I'm Benny, ma'am. Shane's me brother.' And he would have laughed, then shaken his head and put his arm about her shoulders and hugged her to him, saying, 'You are a clever little puss, aren't you.' He often used this term after she had mimicked someone: a clever little puss. But would she ever again feel like mimicking anyone? Now she came to think of it, she had not done an imitation since the night she had taken off that woman.

The sun had set, the long twilight had begun. She emerged from the wood and on to the green sward that bordered the river here, and there she saw the boy, sitting on the very stone where she had espied him all those years ago. And as if he had sensed her presence, because he couldn't have heard her footsteps, he turned his head quickly, then rose to his feet. But he did not move towards her.

When she reached him, she said, 'Good evening, David.'

'Good evening, ma'am.'

She noticed that he had a pencil in his hand and that he had been writing. Some loose pages were lying on the flat rock to his side. She now watched him rub the pencil up and down between his fingers.

'It is a beautiful evening, isn't it?'

In answer to her remark, he said, 'Am I really to go to school, ma'am?'

'Yes. Yes, David, you are really to go to school.'

She was quite unprepared for what happened next, for the boy now flung his arms about her and laid his head on her breast and, his voice rising to almost a falsetto note, he cried, 'I love you. I do, I do. I love you.'

After taking a gasping breath, her arms went about him, and she placed one hand on his hair and stroked it. And when, in almost a gabble, he went on, 'I'll always love you. I'll love you till I die. I love you better than anyone in the world,' she pressed him from her and, holding his face between her hands and seeing that his eyes were wet, which almost brought the tears to her own, she said, 'I . . . I am very honoured that you should like me, David, but . . . but you must not say anything like that again, except to your mother. You must love your mother.'

'I do. I do. I love Jennie.'

She stopped him here by saying, 'You should call her Mother, not Jennie.'

'I . . . I think of her as Jennie, because I've always called her Jennie, because everybody calls her Jennie. And . . . and yes, I love her, but not like I love you.'

'Now David.' There was a stern note in her voice. 'You are grateful to me because I . . . I am the means of sending you to school.'

'Oh, no, no, ma'am, it isn't just that. I've always loved you.'

She closed her eyes and bit her lip. Here was a situation for which she wasn't prepared. She drew him down on to the rock seat and, taking his hand, she said, 'Now promise me something, David.'

'I'll promise you anything, ma'am, anything.'

'Well, promise me that you will not say – ' She paused. How was she to put this? Then she went on slowly, 'You will not repeat or express your feelings again because, you know, they will change.' When he shook his head, she shook his hand, saying, 'Oh yes they will. How old are you now?'

'I'm . . . I'm twelve, ma'am.'

'Yes, you are twelve, and you are a very sensible boy, and so let us now change the subject. Tell me, what would you like to be when you grow up?'

Without hesitation he said, 'I'm going to write stories, ma'am, like those up in the attic.'

'That is good. So you are going to be a writer.' She glanced down at the sheets of paper lying to her side on the rock, and she added, 'Do you write much?'

'Oh, yes, ma'am, when I can at night, or in my free time. I write poetry, ma'am. I wrote that one last year.' He pointed down to the papers. 'But I have altered it, made it better.' He picked up the piece of paper and handed it to her, and she smiled before she read what was written on it.

Softly, softly, the dove coos to me,
Softly, softly, from the branch of a big oak tree.
Would I had wings I'd fly to it there,
Then together we'd gently take to the air
And soar on the wind to the end of the sky.
O dove of grey breast, why can't I fly?

My feet touch the ground,
But my heart's in the sky
And it sighs as it asks for the reason why
You, my dove, can travel the earth
While only my mind can know its worth.
Softly, softly, dove coo to me
From your throne on the branch of the big oak tree.

After she had finished reading she sat staring into his face, and she told herself that he hadn't written those words he had copied them from some book upstairs. Then she realized she was looking at a boy who was twelve years old and who had spent most of his time, apart from his work, on his own, solitary, up in that space under the roof where were stored all kinds of things, most being boxes of books and stacks of papers. She had seen these herself. She had even read the first edition of *The Newcastle Chronicle* or the *General Weekly Advertiser*, as it was called in 1764. It was dated March 24th, and she remembered being very amused at the advertisements in it, especially the one for Mr Bank's Ball at the Assembly Rooms, tickets to be had from his dwelling house in the *Flesh* market. She also remembered shuddering at the advertisement for Mr Moles' fighting cock pit in the Bigg Market, and offering a prize of £50; another prize was a dark brown horse. Oh yes, there was all kinds of reading stored in the attics, so why shouldn't he have imbibed enough knowledge to be able to write like this? Yet at twelve years old she was sure that neither of her brothers would have even thought like this. As for herself, who was supposed to be bright where her reading was concerned, she wouldn't have been able to compose a similar piece of poetry. Constructively it had its faults, the metre was not quite right, but the essence was that of a thinker. Oh, what a shame it was that this boy had missed so much good schooling. Yet would he have learned anything more than that which he had taught himself with the help of his mother? Yes; yes, he would have had a wider knowledge. But all that was now going to be rectified.

'Do you like it, ma'am?'

'I . . . I think it is a very fine poem, and you will undoubtedly be a writer some day. But you must make up your mind to learn all you can about . . . well all kinds of things.'

The boy was staring at her, but it was some seconds before he said, 'Why does the master hate me?'

She was completely nonplussed by the question and she made to rise from the rock, but his penetrating gaze still on her forced her to remain looking back at him. And now with almost a stammer she said, 'He . . . he . . . the master doesn't hate you.'

'He does, ma'am. He is my uncle, so the men say.'

Oh, dear. Oh, dear.

'I know all about it, ma'am. I know my father was drowned in this river.' He turned his head and nodded towards the water. 'This is why I like to come down here; I feel I am near him. There are many pictures of him in the attics. He was beautiful. I look like him.' There was no suggestion of pride in the words for he went on, 'That's why they tried to dye my hair with tea. I hated it here until you came, ma'am. I was going to run away many times. I'm glad I didn't . . . but why does he hate me so . . . the master?'

'He . . . he doesn't hate you, David. It is just because he is sad. He lost his brother, you see.'

The boy now screwed round on the shelf of rock and, leaning forward, he rested his forearms on his knees as he said, ''Tisn't that. No, 'tisn't that.'

As she looked at his bent head and the position in which he was sitting, it came to her like a revelation and not a pleasant one, that although the boy looked like his father, his manner, his slight arrogance even at this age, and the position he was sitting in now, all spoke plainly that his nature was derived from the man who actually did hate him, for except for his fairness he was now as Dennison must have been at his age.

She rose hastily to her feet, saying, 'I must be going, David. We . . . we will talk again once the matter of the school is settled.'

He was standing now and looking at her, and he made a small movement with his head but did not speak. And as she walked away she knew he was watching her, and she felt as she might have done had a mature man been in his place.

* * *

The meeting with the boy last night had disturbed her, for she could see that his strength of character would in the future, in some way, create trouble.

It was half-past ten in the morning and she was sitting in the drawing-room drinking a cup of chocolate when there was a knock at the door and Robertson entered, saying hurriedly, 'Lady Beatrice has arrived, ma'am.'

Nancy Ann only just prevented herself from saying aloud the words that were running through her mind, Oh, no; not her. But she got up and went hastily through the door Robertson was holding open for her, and there, already entering the hall, was Lady Beatrice Boswell, who, ignoring for the moment Nancy Ann and looking at Robertson, said, 'Pay the cab, man.'

Robertson looked at his mistress and made a small movement with his hand as if to say that he hadn't any money, and Nancy Ann turned to where Mary was standing at the bottom of the stairs and said, 'Take some money from my cash box, Mary, and pay the cabman.'

The cabbie was now coming through the hall door laden down with packages, and as he began to drop them one after the other with a thud, Lady Beatrice cried, 'Be careful! man. Be careful!'

The man sighed and turned away, saying to Robertson as he did so, 'That's only half of it.'

Still ignoring Nancy Ann, Lady Beatrice looked at Robertson and demanded, 'Where is Trice?' And the man, glancing from Nancy Ann to the newcomer, muttered, 'He is no longer in service here, ma'am.'

'*What!* Oh, well, take these upstairs to my rooms.'

As the man hesitated, Nancy Ann said quietly, 'Leave them where they are, Robertson.' And now looking fully at Lady Beatrice, she said, 'Will you kindly come this way?' She motioned towards the drawing-room, and to this Lady Beatrice replied, 'I'll see you later when I am refreshed.'

'You will see me *now*, Lady Beatrice.'

The tone stretched the painted face, the eyes widened, the mouth fell into a polite gape. She glanced from the butler to Mary who had re-entered the hall, then to a maid who was descending the stairs, and now letting out a long and seemingly placatory breath, she stalked haughtily past Nancy Ann and into the drawing-room.

Slowly, Nancy Ann closed the door behind her. Then passing the indignant figure, she seated herself on a single chair and, her hands joined in her lap, she looked at the woman. She had not seen her for over a year because her last entry into the house had been during the week the baby was born. And on that visit she stayed only a short time because the household was in uproar. Previously her visits had often been of a month's duration; but even then she had generally kept to her bed, the while demanding the servants be at her beck and call. And so she herself had seen very little of her. Dennison always laughed about her. He was sorry for her, he said, because she had to live with her cousin, the Honourable Delia Ferguson, whom he jokingly described as being a horse minus two legs and a tail.

'I wish to say to you, Lady Beatrice, that you cannot stay here.'

'*Wh . . . at!*' The word was drawn out; the painted cheeks that looked as if they had been tinted with enamel moved into deep creases. Then the voice demanded, 'Where is Dennison?' And she looked around as if she expected him to appear from behind the furniture.

'Dennison is in London. I am now in complete charge of the house and the staff, which has lately become depleted. I have retained enough for the comfortable running of the house, but this does not provide for a guest to have servants at her beck and call fourteen hours of the day.'

'This is outrageous. How dare you! You know who I am? I'm related to your husband, much closer to him that you are. Dennison would never countenance this.'

'For your information, Lady Beatrice, Dennison has given me a free hand. For the future I may arrange my staff and invite whom I like into my house.'

'Your house? Your house? Oh, I've heard about you and the fracas you caused. I stayed overnight in Newcastle at the Barringtons. It's a scandal. Do you know your actions were scandalous? Not those of a lady, even if you were provoked. Oh, I know all about it.'

Now Nancy Ann rose to her feet and, forcing herself to remain calm, she said, 'Then if you know all about it, you will have gauged that I'm of a character capable of removing obstacles I find in my way. Now, Lady Beatrice, I have much to do. You may remain until tomorrow morning or even longer, say a week, if you will conform to the rules of the house. Breakfast is served in the small dining-room at nine o'clock, dinner at two, afternoon tea at five, and supper at seven. You will have no one to maid you . . . I don't. If you wish for a bath you can take it in one of the ground-floor closets so the maids won't have so far to carry the water. If you agree with these arrangements then, as I said, you may stay for a week. But I'd be obliged if, in any case, you did not unload your dolls.'

The woman's face had altered yet again. For a moment Nancy Ann thought it was going to crumple into tears, but then, she couldn't imagine this person giving way to tears; she was such a dominant, selfish, arrogant individual. There was only one other person she disliked more. She watched her turn about now and walk down the room. Her carriage was no longer upright. It appeared to Nancy Ann that she had lost inches. It could have been that she had taken off her brown leather buttoned boots and was in slippers, or removed the old-fashioned high silk and flower-bedecked bonnet. The attitude of the woman now brought another of Mary's nautical sayings to mind: The wind had certainly been taken out of her sails, and that, she reckoned, was a very good thing, which would mean she would soon leave. Just the thought of having her in the household for weeks on end brought tenseness to her whole body.

After a moment she followed the lady into the hall where there were at least twelve packages and boxes still remaining. Most of the boxes looked light, being made of cardboard, but amongst them were three soft travelling bags, their contents bulging the sides.

Robertson was standing looking down on the array and she said to him, 'Take the dressing-case up but the remainder of the bags in the store-room, please.'

She was somewhat surprised when Lady Beatrice did not show herself at dinner, nor yet at tea, nor yet at supper. And becoming a little apprehensive, she sent Mary up to find out if she was all right. A few minutes later Mary came down and, standing before her, she shook her head from side to side, saying, 'She's all right, ma'am, but – ' And she paused so long that Nancy Ann prompted, 'But what, Mary?'

'Well, ma'am, if I may say so, if I hadn't seen the lady that came in this morning I would not have . . . well, linked her up with the one that is sittin' upstairs now.'

'Why not?'

'She's . . . well, she's like an old woman; there's no spriteliness about her. I asked her if she would like to come down for a meal and she thanked me civilly and said she wasn't hungry.'

'Were her things unpacked?'

'Not that I could see, ma'am. She was sitting by the window looking out. And . . . and . . .'

'Yes?'

'Well, she had washed her face. You know, it . . . it was no longer painted, and it was just as if she had wiped off the other person that came in this morning. It was a kind of a shock, ma'am. She's old. Well, what I mean is, I would have taken her to be in her forties when I've seen her afore, but she always had her war paint on so to speak, and her manner was . . . well, not pleasant, as you know, ma'am. But there's a different woman upstairs tonight. If . . . if I hadn't seen it for meself I wouldn't have believed it.'

'Could . . . could she be acting? I mean, playing for sympathy?'

'No, no, ma'am. I came on her unawares like. I tapped on the door, and then went in because she hadn't bid me enter and I thought she might have been out, gone for a walk in the grounds or something. But there she was, sitting by the window like a lost soul.'

Nancy Ann thought for a while, then said, 'Get Cook to make a tray up with something light and send it up to her, will you, Mary?'

'Yes; yes, I'll do that, ma'am.'

Nancy Ann wondered if she should pay the guest a visit, then decided, No, she must not show any softening in that direction, for Mary, even with her keen insight into human nature, might have been taken in . . .

It was turned ten o'clock. She was already undressed for bed and was sitting in her dressing-gown at the open balcony door. The night was cool, the moon was rising, and as she looked into the night she was again overwhelmed by the feeling of aloneness. She had no desire to go to bed because every time she lay on that bed she could see the two figures lying side by side; yet even so, she was wishing he was here at this moment.

When the tap came on the door, she thought it might be Mary and said, 'Come in.' She was slow to turn about, but then she found herself stationary, twisted in her chair, for there, within the circle of the lamplight, stood Lady Beatrice. And it really did seem that only the name remained, for this person was far removed from the lady with the grand arrogant manners she had encountered this morning. Slowly, she rose from the chair as the woman, stepping towards her, said, 'May I talk to you?'

'Yes. Yes, if you wish.' Nancy Ann pointed to the chaise-longue, and then she watched the woman turn and look down on the couch as if she was hesitant to sit. When she did sit down, she placed her joined hands between her knees and rocked herself backwards and forwards two or three times before she said, 'I'm . . . I'm not the same, am I? This person you are seeing now, I'm not the same.'

'No, you are not the same.' Nancy Ann had seated herself on the chair some little distance from the couch. 'No, I am not the same.' Lady Beatrice shook her head again, then said, 'But this is me, this is the real me. Will you listen?'

'Yes, yes. If you wish I will listen.'

'You know why I come here and stay in bed for days on end for weeks on end?'

'No. No, I don't.'

'I . . . I come to have a rest, to be waited on, like my mother was waited on. Has Dennison told you about me.'

'Very little, only that you had a broken romance.'

'Ha-ha!' Now she put her head back and the 'ha-ha!' she emitted this time was much louder. 'Dennison is kind. He's always been kind to me, right from the beginning, and tolerant. Of course, it cost him nothing and made him laugh at times. And of course he knows what Delia's like, Delia Ferguson, the Honourable Delia Ferguson.' She stressed the last three words. 'I've lived with her for twenty-six years. Shall I start at the beginning?'

'If . . . if you wish.'

'You are sure you don't know the facts already?'

'Only what I've already told you, Dennison said you had a broken romance.'

Lady Beatrice did not repeat the 'ha-ha!' but she put a hand up to her brow and with her middle two fingers, she rubbed the furrows that were now evident there backwards and forwards as if trying to erase them.

'My mother was a very extravagant lady,' she said. 'She and my father travelled a lot. When they returned she always brought me dolls, sometimes six, one from each country they would have visited. I never went to school; I had a governess and a nurse. By the time I was twelve I had at least forty dolls, ranging from the size of my finger' – she held up the first finger of her right hand – 'to a cloth one that was four foot long and is so made that it can double up into a small parcel. When my mother was at home there were balls and parties. I was never allowed downstairs to enjoy them, but was promised that when I was sixteen I would be brought out. But my mother died before I was sixteen, two months before my birthday. After her death my father went travelling. He was away a year. When he came back I was carrying a child.'

Nancy Ann now watched her blink her eyelids rapidly, then turn her head and look round the room. It was in much the same manner as she had used in the drawing-room when she asked where Dennison was. Then, in a low voice, and her head bent forward, she continued, 'My only recreation was riding. My governess and nurse didn't bother with me much, they were engrossed in their friendship. Anyway, they thought I was grown up. My daily companion was the groom. He was married to one of the housemaids. He was thirty years of age. He was very presentable, but above all he was kind, too kind. I fell in love with him, and he promised to leave his housemaid and we would run away together. He did run away, but not with me. But he didn't run far enough, only to a village a few miles away. My father went looking for him with a gun; but it was supposed he didn't find him, that he had run further away this time.' She paused again, gasped at the air, then said, 'My baby was born and it lived a month, and I went out of my mind. My father put me into an asylum. It wasn't a really bad place. Apparently he had to pay quite a deal of money for my care and they were kind to me. When at last I was well, I didn't want to leave; it had become a form of shell, I felt secure. Then my father died and I had to go home. And what did I find? That nothing was mine except the furniture; the house and land was mortgaged. But the sale of the estate wasn't enough to meet the creditors, so some of the furniture had to be sold. But still there was quite a bit left and some good silver and china. So, my dear cousin Delia came forward with the offer of storing it for me. Her horse was large and rambling. Like her parents, she hadn't bothered very much about the interior, her main concern was the yard and the horses. So

I went to reside with Delia. I had no money, nothing personal except my dolls and my clothes. And over the twenty-five years I have been with her I have been forced, as Cook would say, to earn me keep, because Delia has a sparse staff. There is a cook and scullery maid, and one housemaid. I earn my keep, so to speak, by doing the needlework; I'm very good with my needle. I . . . I also clean the silver, my silver which Delia now considers her own, having kept me all these years, as she pointed out. The furniture, too, she considers part payment for my existence. Are . . . are you beginning to see?'

Nancy Ann could find no words to express her feelings at this moment. She was so astonished, so bewildered by this story that she felt from one moment to the next that she couldn't believe it. Yet, she had only to look at this person before her to know that every word she was saying was the truth, and that it was being painfully dragged from her.

'When Dennison came to my father's funeral he said, "You must come and stay with me," so I grabbed at the opportunity. And when I saw the number of servants lazing about the place, and there were more years ago than recently, I took the opportunity to make the best of them because I found that my mental trauma had left me, in some way, physically weak, and the demands that Delia made on me exhausted me, because as time went on I became little better than a housemaid . . . I am still little better than a housemaid. I've had a dream all these years of someone dying and leaving me their empty house, and I pictured myself bringing vans to the door and directing my furniture and plate and china into those vans, because my possessions filled two full vans when I arrived there, and I would derive pleasure from seeing Delia's house denuded. But of late that picture has faded, and all I have to look forward to is my sojourn in those two rooms upstairs and hot baths, and my family around me. Yes' – she made two deep obeisances – 'my dolls are my family. I love them. I talk to them. Because of them I am classed as an eccentric, but that troubles me no more. Now . . . well, you have stripped off my disguise. There will be one person, however, pleased about this and that is Delia herself, because when I take my jaunts, as she calls them, to Dennison's she loses a maid, a personal one now because she suffers with her back and it has to be rubbed. So when I return she will be happy knowing that my route of escape is now closed. Well, I've said what it has taken me all day to gather courage to say, and I might as well finish by adding, I scorned Dennison's choice when he married you, while at the same time knowing that if he kept up his association in other quarters my visits would have been cut drastically short long before now.'

She rose to her feet, drawing on two sharp breaths before she continued, 'You seemed so young, and you appeared typically vicarage bred. But this morning I saw you as no longer young, and realized that Dennison had seen what I and likely others had been blind to, that you possess strength of character, for which I admire and envy you at the same time. Well now, I will leave you. I'm sorry I've intruded. I'm also sorry I played the high-born lady with you. I've been a stupid woman not being capable of differentiating. I will leave in the morning. Good-night.'

Nancy Ann was incapable of speech until the figure reached the door and was about to open it, when she said, 'Wait a moment, please!' She went hastily towards the older woman and there was no hesitation when she extended her hand and said, 'You're not the only one who has been blind; I too have been quite as blind in my own way. Come and sit down.' She drew her back to the couch and now, sitting side by side, their hands still clasped, she said, 'I shall be pleased if you will stay for as long as you intended. The only thing is, as I said, I have cut down on the staff. As you have said yourself, it was wasteful. And I would be grateful if you will take your meals with me downstairs.'

She watched the face that looked as old as her grandmother's crumple into a mass of small lines. The eyes were lost in puffed flesh, the trembling lips looked colourless, the flesh under the chin hung in a loose round sack. She had never noticed this before, because when she had seen her, the strings of her bonnet, definitely drawn tight, had ended in a bow there. And now she said softly, 'Please, please, don't distress yourself.' Then, again to her surprise, for the second time in twenty-four hours a head was laid against her breast. But unlike the tears of the boy, this crying had the appearance of a river in spate, for the emotion shook them both, and as she held the bony frame tightly to her and muttered soothing words, a section of her mind was telling her indeed that she was now a woman, being a confidante of both young and old. Yet another section was longing that she herself could lay her head upon another breast and feel strong arms about her, and hear a voice murmur, 'My Nancy Ann.'

When at last Lady Beatrice's tears were dried and Nancy Ann had led her to the door and along the corridor to her own room and bade her good-night and told her to worry no more, that they would talk more on the morrow, she had already made up her mind that on the morrow, too, she would write to her husband and tell him what had transpired during the week he had been away, without, of course, mentioning the boy, and she would indicate between the lines that she would be pleased to see him return.

PART SEVEN

The Pattern of Life

1

It was Rebecca's fifth birthday. The sun was shining for the first time in a week. The rain that had been pouring down for days and had flooded fields and roads, had ceased two days ago. The water had drained from the land and only the streams and rivers were running high.

Everything was planned for the afternoon party. Ten children altogether were invited from the families of the Maddisons, the Ridleys, and the Cartwrights, together with their nurses. And, among them, were seven of Pat's grandchildren. The children's parents were to come later to join a dinner party.

A happy feeling of excitement pervaded the house; not an unusual feeling nowadays, for it could be said that the house had been happy for two or more years now. The master rarely journeyed to London since the town house had been sold. But that didn't mean he had given up his gambling, as the household well knew; on two nights a week at least he would go to his club in Newcastle. At other times he visited the O'Tooles without taking his wife there. They were the evenings when the men got together. Only three months ago he had not returned until three o'clock in the morning from one of the 'O'Toole sessions', as he called them. And he had woken her, kissed her, then scattered a great handful of sovereigns around her on the bed, saying, 'Five per cent of a thousand.'

She could not believe that he had won a thousand pounds in an evening, and among friends, and for the first time since their honeymoon he had talked about gambling. Some evenings a thousand was pin money, he had told her; on a Newcastle night some men could lose five or ten thousand.

When she had enquired where any man could have so much money to be able to lose that amount, he had laughed at her and said, 'Some of the richest men in the country live in the three counties of Durham, Northumberland and Westmorland, not mentioning Yorkshire. Why! only take the Tyne. Look at the shipyard owned by the Palmers. Look at the glass works. Although they might have changed hands over the years, the Cooksons made a fortune out of them. Then there are the chemical works, the foundries, all owned by local men. And the offshoots from these, it's unbelievable: Candle factories, blacking factories, nails, bolts and screws factories. You think hard of any commodity, and this area produces it. What's more, some of the owners hardly leave the district. They take their wives abroad once a year but can't wait to get back in case someone might be duping them. And yet there are other factories and businesses round about that never see their owners, men who consider this part of the country too dirty to stick their noses in, at least their wives do.'

But when she had said, 'If there is so much money why don't they distribute more to the workers who are now on strike in the mines?' he had chucked her under the chin and laughed as he replied, 'Miners and such are only happy when they are opposing something. They get better wages now than they have ever had in their lives and still they are not satisfied. It is the malaise of the working class, to grab.'

She remembered thinking later that night, or early in the morning, when he lay breathing heavily by her side: this was why he had lost the election eighteen months ago, he lacked sympathy for the poorer classes.

Since she was very young she had mixed with the poor of the village. Most were lacking in higher education, but in craftsmanship many of them were artists, like the blacksmith, and Mr Kell the shoemaker. His shoes lasted people for years. Her father had always said they were works of art. Then down in the hamlet there was Mr and Mrs Cooper. He was a marvellous tailor. Huntsmen often went to him to have the leather in their breeches renewed or to order a new pair rather than go to the breeches maker in Newcastle. His wife knitted stockings that you couldn't buy at the hosiers in any town, for they seemed to last a lifetime.

In a way she had detected a pride in all these people, but Dennison seemed blind to this side of the workers. Yet, had he not for years overpaid his staff and allowed them to pamper themselves. He was a strange mixture was her Dennison. She had ceased trying to understand his deeper motives. And she had told herself she mustn't worry about them any more, because the house was at peace. Everyone seemed to be happy.

Over in the Dower House, her grandmama was more spritely than she had seen her in years. She had taken to walking and visiting Graham, which seemed to please him. She herself had kept out of Graham's way as much as possible. And she would not allow herself to dwell on why she did so; she would just not allow her mind to ask questions concerning him.

Then there was Peter. He had married his Eva a year ago and they now had a little house in Durham outside the school, and both appeared extremely happy. But their marriage had caused an irritation, at least to Dennison, for it seemed to have given Mr Harry

McKeowan the idea he was now connected with the House, was of the family, and given the slightest excuse, he made it his business to call, sometimes accompanied by his wife.

She herself often worried about James. She had had only four letters from him since he'd gone to Canada. In the last two he had mentioned he had a companion. He did not say whether man or woman, but she guessed it was a woman, and she didn't feel at all shocked.

The letters had all come from Toronto. Apparently he was teaching in a school there, and from what she could gather it was in a comparatively poor quarter of the town.

In her replies to him she never told him that she'd had two visits from his father-in-law Mr Hobson, demanding to know his whereabouts. The first time she had lied and said she had not heard from him. The second time she had said she had no intention of telling him where her brother was.

She was never to forget that second visit, because Dennison had been present, and after he had told Mr Hobson that his visits would not be welcome here again, he had further shocked him, and herself a little too, by saying, 'What have you decided to do with your daughter? Put her in a convent, or send her out to stud when necessary?' The man had looked as if he was about to explode, but had then left their presence without further words. And he could hardly have reached the hall door when Dennison threw himself on to the couch, his head back and let out a great bellow of laugh, crying, 'I enjoyed that. I bet nobody's ever hit the mark before with that fellow.'. . .

She was in the bedroom finishing dressing: she was winding a silk scarf around her hair because they were going out for a walk in the grounds. It was a daily routine when the weather was fine, and whenever Dennison was accompanying them the children were apt to run wild, and he with them, especially with his son for he simply adored the boy. She always enjoyed watching them; but she rarely joined in the romps, she who had loved romping.

This morning, she was feeling a little tired. Yesterday had been a busy day. In answer to an urgent call, Beatrice had returned to her cousin's: apparently Miss Delia Ferguson had taken a bad fall from a horse and hurt her leg; she would be obliged if Beatrice would come home as soon as possible.

Beatrice had pointed out those words to Nancy Ann, saying 'Note, obliged if I would return home. Well, what can I do? But I hate to leave here, and you.'

Strangely, it would seem, Nancy Ann had answered, 'And I shall hate to see you go, Beatrice. We all shall.' But it was really true: Beatrice's visits were welcomed now by the whole household; the children loved her, the staff respected her. This Lady Beatrice was no longer a painted lady who had to be waited on hand and foot, but one who would go into the kitchen and chat with the cook and discuss recipes, one who arranged flowers, one who did exquisite needlework. Even her dolls were accepted and spoken of as people by such a thoughtful person as Jennie: Lady Jane was the tall clouty one, Miss Priscilla was a pretty china-faced one, Sambo was the little black boy, the larger black doll was Mrs Sambo, and so on.

Jennie had become very fond of Lady Beatrice. And Nancy Ann knew she did special things for her on the side. Jennie, too, had become a different person.

Whether or not Dennison had recognized her, Nancy Ann did not know: he never remarked on her, but then he very rarely saw her; she had learned the art of disappearing when he was about. Jennie's life had changed in more ways than one in the last two years. Happenings had taken place that had not only altered her life, but had freed Nancy Ann from providing for David's schooling. The boy had been in the Newcastle House school only three months when Jennie received a letter from her uncle enclosing a bank note for fifty pounds. The grocery business was apparently doing so well that he and his partner had invested in pieces of land, supposedly a good thing to do out there.

But apart from the money, the main point of the letter was about David. As soon as he had built a decent house, the uncle said, David could go out and join him.

Jennie had shown some concern when telling Nancy Ann of her breaking the good news to David. Apparently he had been emphatic in stating that he didn't want to go to Australia, that he would never go to Australia.

Jennie couldn't understand his attitude, but Nancy Ann, herself, had a glimmering of it. The boy was so full of affection and, because of the circumstances, he had had very little open love from Jennie, although there was no doubt about her feeling for him, and so he sought it from other quarters. His continued visits to the nursery were confined nowadays to the times when he was on holiday and knew that the coast was clear, which meant when the master was out. He was particularly fond of Rebecca, and she adored him and would prattle on about him.

It had been a worry to Nancy Ann at first, and then a bit of a mystery that her daughter didn't mention the boy's name to her father. But this was cleared up when Mary told her that Agnes had explained to Rebecca if she once mentioned David's name to her father he would stop David coming up to the nursery, because, after all, he belonged to the kitchen quarters. And apparently this had been enough to make even such a young child use discretion. It was all part of a game, Mary said.

Last night, Pat and George had been here for their weekly supper and card session, and their visit had lasted longer than usual, in fact, until nearly one o'clock in the morning. George and Dennison had become involved in the state of the country. George, though retired, still endeavoured to keep up with the times. His views, however, did not coincide with those of Dennison, and some wrangling had taken place.

She recalled there was some heated talk over a man called Alexander MacDonald who was in Parliament and who supported the working classes but who apparently seemed to lean towards the Conservatives for, he had said, they had done more for the working classes in five years than the Liberals had done in fifty.

This was from George. Then Dennison had put in that it was the Liberals who had made parents responsible for their children's attendance at the board schools, and when Pat had laughed at him, saying, 'Don't be daft, Denny, working-class parents don't want their broods to waste a full day at school, it'll cut down their earning time,' neither of the men had welcomed the interruption.

As Nancy Ann tied the knot of the silk scarf under her chin, she recalled the heated exchanges of the early morning, and she wondered why women were never taken seriously. The height of a woman's intellect, in Dennison's mind she knew, was the playing of an instrument, singing, being good with her needle, a confident hostess, a devoted mother . . . and, of course, a pleasing wife. Well, for herself, she couldn't sing, and her efforts on the piano were mediocre; she questioned herself as being a competent hostess for, try as she might, she found she couldn't appear overjoyed at greeting people she didn't like, and unfortunately Dennison had a number of friends in this category; she could, however, give herself points on being a loving mother, and also congratulate herself on being an entertainer when in the company of those she classed as friends. Yet, these days, Dennison rarely asked her to show off her prowess. As for being a pleasing wife . . . Her innate modesty forbade her to take this further.

The thin voices of the children carried to her from the hall which meant they must be yelling at the tops of their voices. She went out of the room smiling and when she reached the top of the stairs she looked down on to the two shining faces and demanded in mock sternness, 'Who is that who is making all that noise?'

'Come on, Mama, Papa is waiting. We are going down to the river.'

When she reached the bottom of the stairs, she held her hands out and both the children tugged at them, William more strongly than Rebecca, although he appeared to be a head shorter.

Rebecca was growing into a beautiful child: her skin was a warm peach tint; her eyes were large and appeared to lie flat on the skin at the top of her cheeks; her mouth was well shaped, but the evenness of her teeth was marred by an overlapping tooth at each side of the upper jaw, both of which became evident when she laughed.

Her brother was not what one would call a pretty child: his face was a compressed replica of his father's; his body was sturdy and seemed unsuited to the petticoats, dress, and short coat in which he was attired. Although he was fourteen months younger than Rebecca his appearance and boisterous vitality made him appear quite as old, if not older than her in many ways.

They were pulling her towards the door when Mary came quickly to her side, saying, 'Could I have a word with you, ma'am?'

Such was Mary's tone that Nancy Ann, releasing her hold on the children, tapped them towards the porch door, saying, 'Go to Papa. I'll be there in a moment.'

She turned, asking now, 'What is it, Mary?'

'I thought, I'd better tell you, ma'am, David has arrived.'

'But he's only been back at school two weeks. Why?'

'I don't know, ma'am, only Jennie told me just a moment ago. She seemed agitated. She seemed to know the reason but she didn't stop to tell me. I think she wanted to get back to him.'

'Well – ' Nancy Ann looked perplexed for a moment, then said, 'Tell Jennie to . . . to keep him out of the way.'

'Oh, she'll do that, ma'am, if possible, but you know he's been stubborn of late.'

'Yes, yes, I'm well aware of that, Mary. Anyway, see what you can do.' And she turned from Mary and went slowly out through the hall doors and into the porch. But there she stood for a moment. Yes, indeed, the boy had become stubborn of late, in fact he had ceased to be a boy. He was nearing sixteen, but an onlooker could be forgiven for thinking that he was a youth of eighteen. He was of striking appearance, being tall for his age and so very fair. As her own son took after his father, so did the boy take after his father, whose portraits had been banished to the attics years ago. She remembered seeing four of them lined up against a row of boxes. They had definitely been placed there so they could be viewed.

Over the past years the boy had not made evident his feeling for her in any way, but he had openly expressed a deep affection for Rebecca. It was understandable to her that he did not bother so much with William, no doubt seeing him as the son of his father.

There had been glowing reports of the boy's progress from the school, especially in French and Latin. The headmaster's report stated that he took naturally to languages; mathematics was not his strong point, nevertheless, he persevered with this subject and the results were quite good. The report went on to state that there was every possibility of his reaching university entrance standards.

But why had he come today?

'Mama!'

She answered the call and went out. Rebecca was at the bottom of the steps and she pointed to where Dennison, with William by the hand, was running him across the sunken garden. Then she gripped her mother's hand and endeavoured to make her run after them, shouting all the time, 'Papa! Papa!'

Her high-trebled voice stopped Dennison and he turned around, laughing, then swung the boy up into his arms and held him above his head, shaking him the while.

Now Rebecca had left loose of Nancy Ann's hands and was climbing to Dennison's side, crying, 'Lift me! Papa. Lift me!'

He dropped the boy to the ground; then, putting his hand to his back and stumbling a few steps, he said, 'Oh, you're too big and I'm a very old man,' at which both the children started to laugh and tugged him forward.

By the time they had left the garden and reached the woodland she was walking by Dennison's side and the children were scampering ahead, chasing each other around the boles of the trees.

Nancy Ann smiled as she watched them, saying, 'The weather has kept them in the house so long the air seems to have intoxicated them.' Then she shouted, 'Be careful! Rebecca. Don't be so rough; you will pull his arms out.'

'That'll take some doing. He's as sturdy as a little bull. He'll have a fine figure as he grows.' There was pride in Dennison's words and there was pride in his face. Quickly now, he took her arm and pulled her close, saying, 'You know, Nancy Ann, I've never been so contented in my life before as I have been of late.'

They had reached the edge of the wood, but the river being high, the grassy area sloping to the little bay was mostly under water. The children were running round them both and he cried at them, 'Now! now! that's enough. Calm down.' And as they sped away, he said to her, 'I was about to say, "Thank you, Mrs Harpcore, for giving me such a son . . . and a daughter, and making life worth living". . .'

What happened next Dennison described some long time later as: The devil had heard what he said, had opened the gates of hell and dragged him in, for Rebecca's voice came to them on a high scream, yelling, 'William! William! No! Leave it! Leave it!'

They both turned sharply and looked to where the children were. William was standing on a piece of rock that normally formed a seat. The water was lapping over it. He was bending forward as if trying to pick up something, while Rebecca was standing to the side above the rock. They could see a long black piece of wood in the water, one end of it jutting against the rock, and it was this that the child was trying to pull in. Then a higher scream rent the air as he toppled forward on to the piece of wood, and his impact on it caused it to swing around and into the fast-moving water.

Dennison, leaping down the bank, reached the river's edge and plunged unheeding into the river, his arms outstretched to grab the plank of wood to which his son was now clinging and screaming. Although the river here was running fast the surface was not turbulent and the boy's head and shoulders were well above it with his arms tight round the plank. Twice, Dennison's hand was within grasping distance of the child, but each time the river whirled him away.

The water had been up to Dennison's waist and then up to his chest, when all of a sudden, he himself gave a cry and disappeared for a moment under the fast-running water, to reappear, thrashing wildly. And it was only Nancy Ann's hands gripping his hair that saved him, too, from being swept down the river.

Her reaction to follow him had been as instantaneous as his: that he was unable to swim and she herself could manage only a few strokes had not been considered. Now she was dragging Dennison to the bank, but no sooner had he reached it and had stumbled to his feet than he turned about and, sweeping the wet hair from his face, he peered down the river to see his son now well into the thick of the current, still clinging to the plank.

Now he was running swiftly, with Nancy Ann stumbling behind him and Rebecca behind her still screaming at the top of her voice.

It was at this moment, further down the river, that Jennie was standing arguing with her son. She had just been saying to him, 'They are out walking. What are you asking for: trouble? What's the matter with you, boy?' And he had answered sullenly, 'It's her birthday. I . . . I wanted to give her something.' And to this Jennie had hissed at him, 'You must be mad. You would know that he would be here and there would be a party on.' And in answer he had thumbed behind him to where some thirty yards away stood the bridge that formed part of the estate's boundary at this end. And he said, 'He's not likely to come this far, he never does. And he couldn't get through the wood.' Now his thumb jerked at the right of him and up the bank where the woodland looked dense with undergrowth; and he finished, 'He wouldn't go through there, would he, and soil his pretty clothes?' The last words were said in disdain. And it was at that moment they both heard the scream which caused them to glance at each other, and when it came again, he muttered, 'That's Rebecca.'

'She must be playing a chasing game likely.'

When the scream came once more he said, 'That's no chasing scream.'

They both hurried to the water's edge and looked towards the slight bend of the river. Almost immediately they saw the figures racing along the bank, all yelling, and then their eyes were directed to the middle of the river.

'Oh, my God!' Jennie exclaimed. 'It's . . . it's the child. It's the child.' She now glanced backwards towards the bridge, crying, 'He'll be swept through there, it's free.'

She looked at her son. He seemed frozen. Then she watched him tear off his elastic-sided boots, then his short coat and muffler, and his mouth opened into a gape as he dashed from her and plunged into the river. Her eyes never left him as he swam strongly against the now turbulent water. The cries on the bank had ceased, even Rebecca's screams, for their attention was on the strongly swimming boy, who himself was being swept down stream but not as fast as the oncoming plank of wood. They had all reached Jennie's side now and like a combined body they seemed to hold their breath as they watched David's arm come out of the water to grap the end of the plank. Then there was a concerted gasp of dismay as the wood, being caught in the turbulence caused by the water converging towards the arch of the wooden bridge which was half blocked by a square structure, swung round, but on a high hysterical note Rebecca's shrill tones voiced their relief as she cried, 'He's got him? David's got him.'

Now they were all again running towards the bridge, and it must have entered David's mind, as it did that of Nancy Ann and Dennison, that he mustn't allow himself to be swept through the archway, for, beyond, the river widened considerably and ran for a good way between steep wooded banks.

David's face was near that of the child's. Its eyes were closed, and when he gripped the top of its coat, meaning to drag it from the plank, the child slipped easily from it as if it had not been gripping the plank, merely lying over it.

Now David was striking out with one arm, and with his other was aiming to hold the child's head above the water. He could see they were within yards of the archway, the water had turned into deep churning frothy waves. He saw the structure ahead. It was some kind of a coop; he could just make out the wire netting, and because of its height and the rise of the river it had become caught in the arch of the bridge.

It was looming over him now, like a house. He gasped and spluttered as the water entered his gullet, and he and the child would have been swept round the structure and through the archway, but with one great effort he brought his arm over his head and his fingers clutched the wire netting, but even as they did so the force of the water swept his body towards the gap. If he could have used his other arm he could have clawed his way quite easily to safety, but within its grasp he held the child.

His face now was pressed against the netting, but when he felt the hands on him he forced his head back and looked into the eyes of his mother. She too was clinging to the wire netting, and with her free hand she was aiming to pull him and his burden backwards, but without success.

Then another face appeared close to his. For a second he stared into its eyes; then the weight of the child was suddenly taken from his grip. His arm was stiff, but he lifted it and dug his fingers into the wire netting. Then, as one body, they were all moving slowly backwards. He could now feel the ground beneath his feet, but the water was still swirling strongly round him.

He didn't remember reaching the bank, for quite suddenly he felt sick and everything went black. When he came to, he was on his face and spewing out water. And when he turned his head to the side he saw that the child, too, was lying on its face and its father was pressing its back while his wife was holding its head up from the ground.

His mother was kneeling by him. She looked strange: her hair was hanging down her shoulders in flat strips and there were some bits of twigs sticking out of the side of it. In a cracked voice, she asked, 'You . . . you all right?'

He didn't answer but pulled himself upwards to hear the man bawling, 'Fetch a doctor!' and the voice of one of the three men standing near him answering, 'Yes, sir. Yes, sir,' before turning on his heel and running to do the bidding.

'Lift him up and bend him over.' Nancy Ann's voice was just a whisper, but Dennison obeyed it. He lifted the limp figure of his son and bent him forward from the waist, but when no water came from his mouth and the head and shoulders just drooped forward, he almost thrust him on to the ground again, face downwards, and began to pound his back.

After a few minutes, when the child showed no signs of reviving, Nancy Ann's voice, still small, said, 'Hot water. Get him into a bath of hot water.' She now turned her face up to one of the men: 'Tell them in the kitchen to get ready a bath of hot water,' she said.

The man scampered away, and Dennison raised his head and looked at Nancy Ann who was shivering, and he went to say something but, swiftly changing his mind and bouncing to his feet, he bent again and picked up the child in his arms. And now he was running with Nancy Ann by his side, her hand on the small dangling legs sticking out from the wet dress.

The third gardener too was running; only Jennie and David walked, he supporting his mother now, for she was in a paroxysm of coughing.

The party was met in the middle of the wood by most of the male staff from the yard, but they said nothing, they just followed the master and mistress through the gardens to the kitchens.

The bemused kitched staff, obeying orders, had a tin bath before the fire, and Florrie Kilpatrick was in the process of scooping hot water from the boiler to the side of the fireplace into it while Mary Carter added scoop for scoop of cold water from a bucket.

There were some rough towels lying to the side of the bath and Dennison laid the boy on these. And Mary, her face twisted with anxiety, thrust Nancy Ann unceremoniously aside, tore off the child's clothes, then lifted him into the bath. But it was Dennison's hands that rubbed him while the steam rose, not only from the bath, but from his and Nancy Ann's drenched bodies.

Mary was now supporting the lolling head and her own head was deeply bowed over the child's as she watched her master's hands massaging the child's heart, but to no avail.

Time passed. Once Dennison cried for more hot water, and some time passed again before, of a sudden, he sat back on his heels and, his teeth clenched and his lips wide apart, he made a sound like the distant cry of an animal in pain. It was echoed by a moan that ran through all those present in the kitchen.

Mary lifted the child from the water and laid it on a towel and gently folded the ends over it. Then she turned to where Nancy Ann, who was still on her knees, looked as if she was going to topple sideways. She helped her upwards. Dennison too rose, but with the child in his arms now. And those in the room parted and made way for him as, with his son hugged to him and head bowed over him, he stumbled from the room, with Mary supporting Nancy Ann following him . . .

Outside the kitchen door a crowd had gathered: the yard men, the workers from the farm, the four gardeners, and the lodge people. Standing on the outskirts of them was David. He had changed from his wet long trousers into a pair of breeches, and he was now also wearing a striped shirt. He looked no different from the rest of the men, but that he was different was made apparent when one of them said quietly, 'It's like a curse. His brother, and now his son, both in the same river. Both male heirs. Like a curse on him.'

When David turned slowly away and walked from the yard, the men's eyes followed him and the man who had been speaking ended, 'Aye, like a curse.'

It was at this moment that the doctor rode into the yard. But he had come too late. It had even been too late when the child's father had grabbed him from the boy who was his nephew, legal or not.

The child was laid out on Dennison's bed in the dressing-room, and for nine hours after he sat beside him, without eating or drinking or saying a word.

To Nancy Ann, during this time, the loss of her child was becoming unbearable. And her own inward screams of protest were almost audibly added to those of Rebecca who had become quite hysterical, so much so, that the doctor had to be called again to put her to sleep with a dose of laudanum. But as the hours of the day wore into night, her concern for her daughter and her sorrow for her dead son was diverted to an anxiety over Dennison, an anxiety which at one stage became threaded with resentment and anger. And she wanted to cry at him, 'I have lost a son too. Put your arms around me. Comfort me. I can't bear this.' But she found no response in him.

At what time of the night she fell asleep on the couch in the bedroom, she didn't know, but when she woke and went to straighten herself, her whole body was cramped because of the way she had slumped into the end of the couch.

She stumbled into the dressing-room, but to her surprise she found that Dennison was no longer there. She looked at the clock. It was quarter to six. She stood for a time staring down on her son who looked peacefully asleep, and as she cupped his face with her hands she asked herself why her body wasn't being rent asunder with tears. But there seemed to be nothing in her but a great lonely void, a dry lonely void, no sap of life anywhere in it.

On the landing she met Jennie, and for the first time she thought of the boy and she put her hand out to her, but found herself unable to express any words of gratitude for what David had done.

Slowly she went down the stairs and into the library. Dennison wasn't there; nor did she find him in any other part of the house downstairs. But meeting Robertson, she asked, 'Have you seen the master.' and he answered, 'Not since he went out first thing, ma'am, just on light. I . . . I think he took his horse.'

When she returned upstairs she knelt by her bed and dropped her head on to it. But she did not pray, she couldn't. He hadn't shared his despair, not by seeking comfort from her or comforting her, nor had he spoken one word to her or touched her hand. It was as if, in some strange way, he was holding her responsible for their son's death.

And Dennison did not speak to anyone during the following three days. There was a constant coming and going in the house but he would see no one, not even Pat and George. Pat consoled Nancy Ann by saying, 'It is understandable. He has lost his only son, and he was quite crazy about the child. Yes, it is understandable. But don't worry, this phase will pass. You will be all he wants or needs during this time.'

She did not enlighten Pat that her husband didn't seem to need her as she needed him; that, in fact, he needed no one.

When Rebecca had run to him, crying, 'Papa! Papa!' he had thrust her aside, turned his back on her and walked away, leaving the child to have another of her screaming fits. It was strange, but the only person who seemed to have any control over these was the boy. He did not cosset her or pet her, but, to her amazement, she witnessed his tactics of harshness. And she was for preventing him when he shook her daughter by the shoulders, saying, 'No more of that now, or else I walk out of here and you won't see me again, ever. And I mean it this time.' At this her daughter's screams had subsided to sobs and sniffles and she had laid her head against the boy's shoulder as the boy had once laid his head against hers. It was strange, strange. But she was thankful that at least someone could quieten her daughter's spasms of hysteria.

Peter came, and, of course, Eva came with him. That was another strange thing: Peter never visited without his wife. He seemed to need her by him all the time. And, in a way, she envied their relationship. Eva, she had to admit, was a nice person and seemed to have grown younger since her marriage. This must be what happiness did for one. Yes, she envied her.

Her grandmama came and took charge of the house. She seemed to be able to rise to any occasion. Lady Beatrice arrived only a few hours before the funeral, having come as soon as she heard the tragic news. Then there were those who left their cards of sympathy; and of these, those who came in were received by Jessica or Beatrice. Graham had come on the day of the disaster, but had not been since.

The funeral was to take place at eleven o'clock on this Friday morning. She was already dressed in deep black. She was sitting looking out of the window, her coat, hat, and long veil laid out on the couch ready for her to don. She stared into the distance, not thinking so much about the burial of her son at this moment as of the effect his death had had on her husband. At times she felt he must have lost his mind, for he had not spoken half a dozen words to her since the tragedy. In fact, he had avoided her. And if his manner continued like this she dreaded to look into the future. She wanted to cry, how she wanted to cry, but it seemed as if a wall of sand had built up between her heart and her eyes.

When she heard the dressing-room door open she turned her head. Dennison walked slowly up the room towards her. He did not look at her as he drew a chair up at the other side of the window, but just as she had been doing only a moment before so he now looked out into the grey day. She waited for him to speak, stilling her tongue and forbidding her hand to go out towards him. His neglect of her over the past few days had created in her a feeling of humiliation and deep hurt to add to the grief of her loss.

He was still looking out of the window when he said, 'Try to understand the reason for what I am about to say.'

She waited, while he still kept his gaze concentrated on the window. But when his voice came low, the words that it spoke chilled her with foreboding, for he said, 'I . . . I have made arrangements to go away for a time.' What he said next was blotted out by the scream in her head almost as loud as any made by her daughter over the past few days, and through it she was yelling, You can't! You won't! You can't be so callous. Oh no. No. What am I to do? I can suffer your silence, but not your absence. Don't do this to me, please.

She had lost some of his words, but when she heard him say, 'The Fergusons have been kind enough to invite me,' her mind yelled again: The Fergusons, at the lodge in Scotland. He sold it to the Fergusons. He's never been there since. He . . . he must have been in correspondence with them right . . . right from the . . . She could not even let her thoughts go on and say, 'The day my darling boy died.'

'This house,' he was saying now, 'and everything around will . . . will drive me mad. You . . . you can't understand. I see him everywhere, running . . . running, jumping, always running and jumping.'

He had said, 'You can't understand.' He was now looking at her: his grey eyes appeared colourless, his skin seemed as if it had been drawn tight over the bones of his face and looked like dull parchment. She could see that he was suffering, but so was she. Oh, so was she. She heard her voice, sounding to her own ears like that of a little girl, saying, 'Don't leave me. Please, please, Denny, don't go. Not right away. Later perhaps, we . . . we could all go.'

When he shook his head vigorously and got to his feet, she stared up at him, then watched him walk from her half-way down the room before he stopped, saying, 'Try to understand, Nancy Ann. I'm on the verge of despair. I'm at breaking point. Don't you understand I have lost my son, my only son? I will never have another.'

When she heard the scream she couldn't believe it was from her own throat, and the words just spewed out of her as she cried, 'What you seem to forget is that he was my son too. I bore him and, as I understand, at peril of my own life. You are so made you imagine that you are the only one that's suffering. There is your daughter upstairs, the shock could affect her for the rest of her life. *Your* son. *Your* son. Always *your* son. He was *my* son too. And there were days, yes, even weeks when you never saw him; you were too busy at your gaming table and other pursuits.' And she closed her mouth on the last words: the thought that always strove to the surface of her mind concerning his London visits and which she would not give place to was aired now.

He had turned and was looking at her, but he did not say, 'What are you suggesting?' he said, 'Please lower your voice; the household will hear you.'

'Does that matter? They all know that you have hardly spoken to me; and that when you haven't been sitting in vigil, you have slept alone. These are things that do not escape the household which you seem so anxious should not hear me raise my voice in protest at your treatment, and this treatment from one who is supposed to love me.

"I shall love you till the day I die," you once said; no, not once, but many times.'

She watched him draw in a deep breath: his waistcoat expanded, his cravat was pressed out; then they slowly sank back into place and, as if on a sigh, he said, 'I do love you, Nancy Ann. But that is from another part of me. It is no use trying to explain the conflict of emotions that is tearing me at the moment, I only know that I must get away from these surroundings.'

'And me?'

He bowed his head, shaking it slowly now. 'Try to understand, Nancy Ann, try to understand the turmoil I am in. You, most of all, are connected with what I have lost. At the moment, I haven't the power or the words to explain, or even to sort out my feelings.' He now looked at her fully for the first time, saying, 'Talk to your grandmama. She's a wise woman. She will no doubt help you to understand my motive. Anyway – ' He looked downwards now, pulled out from his waistcoat pocket a gold watch that was attached to a gold chain lying across his chest, then, his voice a mere mutter, he ended, 'The time is almost on us. I . . . will see you downstairs.' And with that he turned from her, and she clasped her hands, one on top of the other, tightly over her mouth. She had been unable to take in the tragedy of the loss of her child for days, it still wasn't believable. But this scene just enacted was certainly unbelievable. This man, who had been so full of love for her five days ago, this man who the night previous to the awful day had knelt in this very room, his arms about her, his head buried in her breast, and in between repeating and repeating her name had told her she was the most beautiful thing that had ever happened to him in his life, and that she was now more desirable than on the day he first married her, this was the same man who was leaving her to bear her loss alone. The loss that should have brought them even closer together had opened a great chasm between them, and she was falling into it, down, down down . . . Oh my God, no. She said it as a prayer, joined her hands, looked upwards now and appealed, Help me through this day.

Mary watched the cortège from the nursery window. The black-plumed prancing horses, the black carriages, the black-clothed people were all smudged together because her face was aflood with tears. He had been her baby too. She had been the first to handle him, to wash him. And although, during these last two years since she had been made housekeeper, she hadn't spent as much time up here, nevertheless, she considered this her domain rather than the housekeeper's confortable apartments.

The cry of, 'I want my mama,' turned her head to where Agnes was cradling Rebecca in her arms, and Agnes said, 'It's starting again. She's trembling like a leaf. Has he gone . . . David, this mornin'?'

'I don't know; Jennie's still in bed. She was feverish last night. That river nearly did for her an' all. Anyway, I'll go and see if he's still around and bring him up.' Then turning from the window, she said, 'Oh dear God. Dear God. What a day! And how she's going to survive this, an' the master the way he is, I don't know.' . . .

It was ten minutes later when she returned, the boy with her. He was dressed in a navy-blue suit. The tight trousers came down to the well-polished boots. His coat was double-breasted. It had no revers, but the starched white linen collar he wore stood up stiffly beyond the rim of the jacket, almost giving the appearance of a parson's insignia. Although he appeared older than his years, he still looked a schoolboy, except when he spoke; then his voice sounded that of a man.

He walked straight across the nursery to Agnes who was holding Rebecca's shuddering body to her. The tears were running down the child's face and she was gabbling. Gently, David put his hands on her shoulders and pulled the dazed child on to her feet, then dropping on to his hunkers before her, he said, 'What's this?'

She went to lean against him, her sobs shaking her body, but almost roughly now, he gripped her shoulders and held her up straight, saying, 'Now, no more of that! Do you hear? No more of that! because if there's another whimper out of you, I'm off. Do you hear? And for good this time mind, and I mean it.'

The child blinked her eyes. Her head was bobbing, her body shaking, and she muttered, 'Davey. Davey. I want my mama. I want William.'

'Now we've been through all this, haven't we?' His voice was quiet and steady, and he was about to go on when Agnes, her own voice trembling now with weariness and agitation, said, 'I've told her till I'm tired, Master William's gone to heaven; she won't see him again. I've told her till I'm blue in the face.'

'Shut up!'

'How dare . . .! Who are you to . . .?'

Mary had moved forward now saying harshly, 'That's enough of that kind of talk.' And the boy twisted round and looked up at her, saying, 'Then tell her to talk sense.'

'David, you've gone too far this time. You've . . .'

'I haven't gone far enough.'

He turned now from the two astonished faces and, looking at the small girl again and his voice changing, he said, 'You remember Snuff . . . you know, the puppy?'

When she nodded tearfully, he said, 'Well, you know what happened to Snuff? Prince didn't mean to kick him, Snuff ran under his feet. And what happened to Snuff?'

The small lips trembled, the eyelids blinked, the voice whimpered, 'He died.'

'Yes, he died. And what did we do? Where did we put him?'

'In . . . in a box, on . . . on a blanket.'

'Yes, in a box on a blanket, to keep him nice and warm. And we buried him, didn't we, in a nice grassy part in the wood, didn't we?'

'Yes, yes, in a nice grassy part, yes.'

'Well now, when William died and they put him in a box . . .'

'Get up out of that!' Mary's hand was on his shoulder, and he swung round and glared at her, saying, 'Leave me alone, I'm telling you. Leave me alone.' And the look in his eye caused her to step back from him.

He turned his attention to the child again, saying, 'As I said, William died and they put him in a box and he's nice and warm, and when you stop crying and having tantrums we'll go and see him, like we used to do with Snuff, you remember?'

'Yes, yes, Davey, but . . . but when will he go to heaven?'

He stopped for a moment and glanced, first to the right of him, then to the left where the two faces were glaring down on him. Then looking at Rebecca again, he said, 'Well now, that depends upon you. When you stop crying and stop having tantrums, because he'll never get to heaven if you keep crying; your crying upsets everybody, you know, your mama' – he didn't add papa – 'your great-grandmama, and . . . oh . . . oh, everybody.' He shook his head slowly, then went on. 'Now, if you promise me you'll stop crying and be a good girl, I'll come back next weekend and I'll take you to see that William's lying nice and warm, all covered with flowers. Now, is that a promise?'

She sniffed and sniffed and at each sniff Agnes bent over her and wiped her nose; then the child muttered, 'Promise.'

'And you'll be a good girl?'

'Yes, Davey. You . . . you won't go away though, will you? You won't go?'

'I'll not go very far. Look, put up your hand.' She put up her hand. 'And the other one.' She put up the other one. 'Now, count me seven on your fingers.' She counted seven on her fingers. He took the first finger of her left hand and wagged it, saying, 'I'll be back on that day. Now, you count all those days until I come back. All right? No more screaming.'

She shuddered and paused, then said, 'No more screaming.'

'And you'll be a good girl?'

'I'll be a good girl.'

'Well, on that promise you deserve a shuggy. Come on in and get on Neddy.' He straightened himself, then pulled her upwards and walked with her into the day nursery. And there, lifting her on to the rocking-horse, he rocked her backwards and forwards.

After a time he sat her on a low chair before an equally low table, put some paper and coloured pencils in her hand, and said, 'I'm going now, but mind, I want to see all the numbers up to twenty and all the letters of the alphabet down there when I come back.'

'But . . . but I can only write up to 'F', Davey.'

'Yes, I know you can. But I want to see that you've written all the other ones down, and that means that you've got to work hard.'

He bent down now, his face on a level with hers and looked into her eyes. They were deep dark brown. Her hair was a shining brown with red lights in it. Her skin was like flowing milk. He touched her cheek with his finger as he said softly, 'Be a good girl for me.' Then of a sudden, her arms came up and went round his neck, and she was clinging to him. But she did not cry or make any sound, and he held her pressed to him for a moment, before pushing her gently back into the chair.

Mary and Agnes were standing at the door. When he passed between them they turned and also walked back to the middle of the room, and there, swinging round, he addressed himself to Agnes, saying, 'Drop all this stuff about William being in heaven.' But before Agnes could retort Mary put in, 'Now you look here, young man, I think you've gone far enough in this quarter of the house. Who do you think you are, anyway?'

It was a silly question to ask and she knew it immediately. And when he came back, saying those same words, 'That's a silly question to ask, isn't it?' she spluttered, 'You're . . . you're getting above yourself.'

'No, not above myself, Mary, not yet anyway. But I'll still say to Agnes,' and now he nodded to the younger woman, 'stop pumping the heaven stuff into her. Just think. It's so stupid anyway. Ask yourself a simple question. How can everybody get up there? Do you know what air consists of?' He shook his head. 'No, you don't. It's a fairy tale, this heaven business. Anyway, I've got some news for you . . . I'm rich.'

'What?'

'You heard what I said, Mary, I'm rich.'

The two sisters exchanged glances, then Mary fixed her gaze on the face before her, which was already a handsome face and topped by the mass of fair hair. It could have been representative of the haloed angel in the stained glass window of the village church. The eyes, though, certainly weren't those of any angel, except perhaps when he was talking to the child. But generally they gave off a cold hard stare that had been nurtured on a bed of bitterness, animosity, and shame, the shame that lay deep in all born such as he. She said quietly, 'What d'you mean by rich?'

'*Rich . . . rich.* You've no doubt heard, haven't you, of the uncle who created a place for my mother in this household, by blackmail as far as I can understand? Well, we'd been hearing a lot from him of late, and his idea was for me to go out to Australia, where he was doing well, he and another man. But now he's dead, and the other man, an honest man apparently, has sent us his fortune, together with the deeds of three pieces of land.'

The sisters turned and looked at each other in amazement, and it was Agnes who said, 'You're not just making this up?'

He almost barked at her, saying, 'I never make things up. I'm what you would call a realist, if you know what that means, a realist; I see things as they are. I've been made to, haven't I? right from along there.' He thrust his hand out towards the door indicating the attics and the space under the roof, and he repeated, 'Yes, right from along there. I don't imagine things. I never had the chance. My only mirror was the polish that I put on boots. *Boots*, *boots*, *boots*, leggings, shoes, gaiters and boots . . . *boots* . . . *his boots*.'

They both looked at him almost with fear in their eyes. This was no boy, this was a man, and there was something familiar about him. He stood before them, tall, exceedingly fair, yet dark. His words made him appear dark, and menacing.

Mary, aiming to bring things down to a normal natural level, wagged her head as she said, 'So you are rich, but what d'you mean by rich? Fifty pounds? A hundred?'

'Thousands.' His voice was quiet. 'Five thousand four hundred pounds. There was much more but the solicitor here and a solicitor over there took their share. But that is what is in the bank, five thousand four hundred pounds.

Mary was disbelieving. 'Out of a grocery shop? A share in a grocery shop, five thousand four hundred, or more?' She curled her lip.

'No, not completely out of a grocery shop. Your calculation is good, Mary. Apparently the thing to do out there is to buy or lease land. He had done that, five pieces of it, and just before he died he sold two, and the others could turn out to be valuable. Mr Barrow, his partner, has told me that if I wish I can sell the land to him, or keep it, or come out there and take up where my uncle left off.'

There was silence in the room. They stared at each other: a triangle, triumph at one vertex, amazement and disbelief at the other two. Yet, no sooner had he turned away and walked out than the disbelief vanished as they looked at each other. And it was Agnes who said, 'God Almighty! What'll happen now? What'll he do?'

'God knows, him being who he is.'

'D'you know something, Mary?'

'What Agnes?'

Agnes swallowed deeply, moistened her lips, then said, 'Who d'you think he . . . well, he appeared like, standing there talkin', even him being the colour he is? Who d'you think?'

'Well, yes, you're right. I thought that an' all. He might have the colour of his father, but his father's brother's in him right up to the look in his eyes. It was as if it was the master himself talking.' They nodded at each other.

'Eeh! What's going to happen next in this house? Eeh! this house.' Agnes shook her head, and Mary answered, 'God alone knows.'

2

The close friends and sympathizers had all left. For Nancy Ann it had been a day like an eternity. She was in the evening of it, but she knew it would never end, because there could be no finality to the emotions that were tearing her into shreds. She saw them spreading down the years all radiating from their centre, a deep burning place just below her ribs: the sand wall that had prevented her crying had spread and formed a desert. She was aware in a half-ashamed fashion that the overriding emotion in that centre did not emanate from sorrow for her dead son. It was there. Oh yes, it was there. And it was the foundation for the other emotions, for it had bred them. Yet, emanating from the core was the most frightening emotion, an emotion that was new to her and terrifying in its intensity, for, apart from everything else, her Christian religion had forbidden hate. She had disliked, and strongly, but hated never. Although she'd had no previous acquaintance with it, she certainly recognized it when it flashed into her being an hour ago as her husband stood before her, dressed for his journey, saying, 'I shall write to you.' She hadn't heard herself asking how long he intended to be away, for there was a great whirling in her head; yet, she heard his answer: 'A few weeks. I . . . I may stay for the shoot.'

Nor did she hear herself say, 'What will people say, leaving me like this?' because she imagined the question had been only in her mind and she hadn't voiced it. But he had answered it. 'Our friends understand,' he had said; 'Pat and George and the others will visit you regularly. I have spoken to them. Try to understand my feelings, dear.' And he had bent towards her but she had shrunk from him as he placed his lips on her cheek. And a dreadful thought sprang into her mind, but she throttled it before it escaped her lips, for it would have said, 'Have you made arrangements to meet up with your past mistress?' For she had the picture of the woman making her way towards him in the churchyard, where he stood apart with two gentlemen and George. She saw her take his hand and he nod his head as she spoke. Then they were joined by Larry Freeman. They shook hands, and she had noticed that Dennison put his other hand out and clasped that of his one-time friend. Then the Myers woman had patted the lapel of Dennison's coat before she turned from him to be accompanied by the man Freeman to her carriage.

It was as Dennison walked away from her that the hate consumed her. And if, in that terrifying moment, it had become tangible it would have felled him to the ground. And when the door closed on him she had felt the desire to scream as her daughter had screamed.

Then, as if a hand had been laid gently on her shoulder and turned her about, she found herself walking to the couch on which she sat slowly down, and her mind became filled with the presence of her father, and, as if he were sitting by her side, she said, 'You were right. Oh, you were right. You could always read inside a man. You used to say that gambling was bred of greed, and licentiousness of selfishness, and that selfish people dug their own graves, and when they lay in them no one mourned their loss and no sincere tear softened the clay.'

Yet, she asked herself, how she could have loved someone these past six years without coming to know his selfishness. It was true she could recollect countless incidents that should have pointed to his self-centredness, but, loving him as she did, she had accepted them as part of his strong character. Anyway, weren't we all selfish in different ways?

But this, this desertion, this thrusting her aside at the moment when she needed him most.. . . Never again in her life would she know such suffering; her whole being and spirit were devastated. She was in such trauma it was almost too much to bear; it was as if she had lost not only her son but her husband, too, in one fell blow.

She did not witness his departure, but when her grandmama came and, putting her arms around her, said, 'He won't stay away long, my dear. He is in torture at the moment, try to understand. Yet I know how you feel,' then she knew he had gone.

Dry-eyed and white-faced she looked at Jessica and asked, 'Would my father have left my mother? Would your husband have left you at such a time?'

And after a moment's silence, Jessica's answer was, 'All men are different; it's how they are brought up, the environment: some expect little from life and are glad to pay for that little; it all depends on where the Lord placed you when you were born.'

Beatrice, in a way, was more understanding, for she had flounced into the room and, nodding first at Jessica and then at Nancy Ann, she had cried in a high-pitched voice, 'I wouldn't have believed it of him. Callousness, that's what it is, callousness. All men are callous. I'm . . . I'm sorry for you, Nancy Ann. I am. I am. Now I'm going to bed before I say any more, I'm going to bed. Good-night, Jessica. Good-night, Nancy Ann.' . . .

The house was quiet. Rebecca was asleep in the nursery, her grandmama and Lady Beatrice were in their rooms. The household, too, was quiet; except for Robertson and Mary, the staff had retired.

Mary had just left the room. She had tried to persuade her to eat, but eating was something, she felt, that she would never want to do again. She couldn't force the food down her gullet, liquid yes, but no solid food. Mary had sat by her and held her hand and, supposedly to divert her thoughts, she had told her the strange news about David and Jennie and the money coming from Australia. But Nancy Ann had made no comment on it, merely nodded her head to signify that she had heard. But as Mary was about to leave, carrying the tray, she had said to her, 'Go to bed, Mary.' And Mary had turned and said, 'Not until I see you there, ma'am,' then she had gone out.

As she sat, her gaze fixed mostly on her hands lying in her lap, she kept telling herself, I must go upstairs; I cannot keep her waiting. Yet she didn't move. She didn't want to go upstairs. She didn't want to lie in that bed alone, yet she didn't long for his presence, she felt she would never long for his presence again, either in bed or out of it.

She lay back and stared into the flames and in them she saw her son. He was waiting at the top of the nursery stairs, hanging over the gate that had been placed there for his safety since the day he had tumbled half-way down them. His arms were about her neck and he was crying, 'Mama. Mama. Good morning, Mama. Good morning, Mama.' She could see Rebecca, too, in the background, but just as a shadow. Her son was to the fore, his face close to hers demanding, 'Going for ride. Papa taking us for ride.' Then, 'Come play with Neddy. Watch me gallop.'

She watched him gallop high up on the rocking-horse, high up among the flames of the fire. Suddenly she closed her eyes to shut out the sight because the picture in the flames had changed from the nursery to the cemetery.

She opened her eyes when there was a tap on the door and Roberston entered, saying, 'Mr Mercer, ma'am. He asks if it is too late for you to see him.'

'No, no. Show him in.'

Graham came slowly up the room towards her. She had not stood up to meet him; Graham was Graham and there was no need for ceremony. She had seen little of him this past week. In fact, not since . . . that day. Dennison and he had nothing in common and so he had never been a regular visitor.

He sat down on the couch at an arm's length from her, and he looked at her, and she at him, and neither of them spoke for a full minute. Then he said, 'Forgive me for intruding at this late hour, and . . . and I didn't really expect to see you, I thought you might have retired.' He did not add that it was only ten minutes ago that he heard from one of his men that his counterpart had driven her husband to the station to begin his journey to Scotland, and that he couldn't believe it. But he said, 'I . . . I won't stay; I just wanted you . . . well, to know how deeply I feel for you at this moment.'

She had laid her head against the back of the couch. Her face was turned towards him; her mind was saying, He would never have left you at a time like this; he would have put his arms around you and comforted you and said, 'We'll have another son. Don't worry, my love, we'll have another son.' Those were more or less the words she had spoken to her husband: 'I . . . I could give you another son,' but he had wiped the idea away with one violent movement of his hand as he cried at her, 'You couldn't, unless I was prepared to sacrifice your life for him. You know as well as I do what happened the last time. The next would be fatal. Don't talk such rubbish. I've had one son. I'll never have another.' And with his next words he had then seemed to disown both her and his daughter: 'You had your daughter. I had my son,' he said. 'Now I have lost him I have nothing. I cannot expect you to understand; only a man knows what it is to lose a son, a legitimate son, the essence of his very being.'

A strange thing was happening somewhere inside, in that big knot below her ribs. It was disintegrating. She had the most odd feeling that pieces of herself were flying off in all directions, and as they left their base, they melted. And their melting caused a flood of emotion to rise inside her. It pushed out her ribs, it widened her throat. Then, such was its eagerness to spurt from her mouth, that it blocked its own outlet, and she gasped and moaned: she was choking. Then an agonized cry escaped her, and with it all her melted emotions swept through every duct they could find: her eyes, her nose, her mouth, even her ears seemed to be an outlet. She was drowning in her emotions, yet she was being held firmly and a voice was repeating, 'There, there, my dear. That's it, cry, cry. There, there, my love. Don't worry. Don't worry. That's it, cry. Oh, yes, cry.'

She clung to the voice. She pressed it close to her, yet she could not stop her crying. And now she began to wail. She wailed for the loss of her son. She wailed for the loss of her husband. She wailed for her father whose words she had not heeded. She wailed for her mother who, she knew now, and had known for some time, had pressed her against her own instincts into security, the security that had led her to this agony. Her wailing reached the hall and brought Mary and Robertson into the drawing-room to stand, mute for a moment, to see their mistress being held in the arms of Mr Mercer, while clinging tightly to him.

Graham turned his head in the direction of the servants and cried at them one word, 'Bromide!'

'Bromide,' Mary repeated; then turning, she flew from the room and up the stairs and to the medicine cupboard. And from the top shelf she took a bottle of laudanum, then ran downstairs again. Mr Mercer was still holding her mistress, and she was still clinging to him.

It took all Robertson's and Mary's efforts to disengage her hold on Graham. And when at last she was lying slumped in the corner of the couch and still crying, still wailing, Graham, turning to Robertson, said, 'I think you had better fetch the doctor.'. . .

It was almost an hour and a half later when the doctor came into the house. He had been away on another call and his never even temper was at its lowest point. 'What now? What now?' he said, as he entered the room. He was well aware of the tragedy that had come upon this family, but in his line of work there was very rarely a day passed he didn't come face to face with tragedy. Yet when he looked upon the mother of the child that had been buried this day, his innate kindness and professionalism overcame his irritability, and, sitting down beside Nancy Ann, he took her hand and while patting it said, 'Now, now, my dear. Now, now. Come along, we must stop this crying, or it will only make you ill. And you know, you have a daughter to see to. By the way – ' He turned his head upwards and looked to where Graham was standing, and through a puzzled frown he asked him, 'Where's he, the husband?' And Graham answered bitterly, 'He's gone on a shooting trip, I understand.'

The two men exchanged glances for a moment and then the doctor said bluntly, 'Then all I can say is, I hope his gun backfires,' and rising to his feet, he addressed a shocked Mary and an equally shocked Robertson with a command: 'Well now, let's get her upstairs to bed. She'll need to be carried. You, Mr Mercer, will kindly, I'm sure, give a helping hand.'

'I'll manage her myself,' Graham said. 'It will be easier.' And bending, he put one arm under her knees and the other under her armpits, and with Mary supporting her head, he carried the woman he loved, the girl he had loved and whom he had lost because he was too considerate to plead his cause.

Consideration, he had learnt, was a vice not a virtue. Yet, if her husband had been considerate he himself would not now have been holding his beloved in his arms for the one and only time.

3

When does the fall of any house begin? Not necessarily when the rot is discovered, for then it can be too late: the timbers may have been attacked, eaten away with worm; the bricks beginning to crumble; the foundations starting to sink into bog, with walls taking on crazy angles. The whole place becomes so rotten that nothing can save it.

That is the deterioration of a house.

But what if it's the owner who has disintegrated? Where did the rot start in him? With the loss of his son? Or, before that, the loss of his brother? Or, going back further still, did it begin with the fantasy created in him by his father that he was someone special? That God had seen fit to place him in a position of wealth which spelt power? That he was bred specifically to be a member of that society that believes itself privileged because privilege had been the right of its ancestors, right back to the time when they were thieves and vagabonds, traitors and sycophants, their loyalty given only where it would show good return?

Coming down the line from that, could the descendant then be blamed for his traits? Not if he was a good loser; not if he was the kind of real sporting fellow who would bet on a fly crawling up a window. Not if he was Dennison Moorland Harpcore, and not if the said Dennison Moorland Harpcore had still a well from which to draw. There was no disgrace in owing money to a bank, but there was deep disgrace in being unable to settle your gambling debts, and the disgrace at the moment was weighing heavily not only on Dennison Harpcore, but also on his whole household.

Many things had happened in the years since the day of the child's funeral.

Dennison's stay in Scotland had lasted five weeks. And following on from the day of his return Nancy Ann had known that another phase of life had begun. He had remained at home for four days, during which time he showed no desire to see his daughter. On one occasion when Rebecca, seeing him, had flown to him and grabbed his hand, he had patted her on the head; and when the child cried, 'Oh, Papa, I'm glad you are home,' he had pressed her aside, saying, 'Be a good girl now,' and left her standing mute with tears in her eyes. To Nancy Ann herself, his manner was coolly polite. When he had asked after her health she had answered, 'I have been rather unwell.' And he had replied, 'That's to be understood'; then had added, 'We have both been rather unwell, and are likely to be for some time.'

During his short stay he did not seek her bed, for which she was thankful; nor did he sleep in the dressing-room, but had ordered his things to be moved to a guest suite. This action had created deep humiliation in her: although she did not desire any bodily contact with him, the fact that he was moving himself from the proximity of her emphasized in some tortured way that he was blaming her for the loss of their son. And yet, she asked herself again and again, how could that be? If it hadn't been for her timely rescue of himself, he, too, might have been drowned.

How near she was to the reason for his behaviour she wasn't to know till some years later.

Looking back on that year, Nancy Ann saw it as a nightmare in which she had become a young girl again, telling herself she couldn't go on, that she wasn't able to cope with these changed circumstances and begging her grandmama to let her take Rebecca and stay with her, and then being upset by Jessica's blunt refusal: the emphasis on it being that she was a wife and mother, that life was full of ups and downs. A tragedy had been experienced. This would pass; time was the healer.

But time did not prove to be the healer. When Dennison was at home he spent most of his time in the library. What he read she did not know; she wondered if he was once again aiming for a place in Parliament, even though his first attempt had ended in an ignominious defeat. Such was the wall he had put up between them that she could not have penetrated it even if she had so wished. She rarely saw him after he left the dinner table, at which his efforts at conversation would almost drive her to yell at him, 'Your small talk is not fooling the servants. They know the position. They know everything. Why bother? You are only fooling yourself.' But she never raised her voice; she would answer him politely. However, she made a point of never opening the conversation or asking a question.

Pat had said, 'Patience. I know Denny; this phase will pass.' She said that in the first year. She didn't say it so often in the second. And there were times now when she called that she never mentioned his name.

It was towards the end of the second year that a number of things happened. Jennie died. David, at seventeen, left school and went to Australia, from where she had since received four letters. He was working hard and he was making money; life was rough and men from all over the world were flooding the country. In his first letter to her he had spoken of Mr Barrow, that he had been greatly surprised on meeting him, expecting a very old man, but he was only middle-aged . . . He seemed to get on well with this Mr Barrow, as his uncle had evidently done, too. The fourth letter she had received some months ago, and in it he had spoken of coming back for a holiday. He had not said coming home.

It was during the third year that she had to ask Dennison to meet the tradesmen's bills, for some were pressing. It was after that he sold the hunters that were kept at the farm and, seemingly in consequence, his drinking became heavier.

Then at one period last year he had come to her somewhat shamefacedly and asked her if she had any loose cash as he had run out and he wanted to get up to London to see his banker. She had given him all that was in her cash box, nine pounds ten shillings. That time he had been in London a week and when he returned he seemed greatly agitated. It was then he asked her if she would loan him one or two pieces of her jewellery, and she had replied, 'They are yours.'

As she did not often wear jewellery and had no great fancy for it, it was all kept in the safe which was situated behind a picture in the library. On that occasion he showed her the pieces he was taking, a diamond and ruby studded tiara, three rings, and two brooches. At that moment she had been sorry for him, for he had stood with his head bowed, muttering, 'You shall have them back. I promise you, you'll have them back.' She wanted to cry, 'I don't want them, it's you I want back,' only a second later, to ask herself: Did she? Did she want this man back? This man who had killed all love within her, for nothing could wipe out his neglect which, over the past years, had amounted to cruelty.

Now had come the spring of 'ninety-two, and she felt strongly that an end to her present existence was looming near. Things could not go on as they had been. He was having to sell the farm and five hundred acres of land. Last week she had forced herself to confront him and say that some of the tradesmen had stopped delivering. At the same time she had reminded him that next month the staff wages were due. But it was during this evening that a happening would take place which would lead to final severance.

He had been in the library for some hours. He didn't go there to work any more, but to drink.

She was crossing the hall on her way to say good-night to Rebecca when she saw Robertson coming from the direction of the servants' quarters. He was carrying a tray on which was a decanter, and just as she put her foot on the bottom stair, he stopped and said, 'Ma'am, may I have a word with you?'

'Yes, Robertson, of course.'

The man looked down at the decanter as he said, 'I'm sorry, ma'am, but I have decanted the last bottle of whisky. I . . . I put the order in some weeks ago but they haven't as yet sent it.'

She swallowed deeply and gripped the bottom of the bannister tightly before saying, 'What about the wine and the older stock?'

'There are only half a dozen bottles of wine left, ma'am.'

'But the vintage?'

The man was still looking down at the decanter, and it was a moment or so before he said, 'The master has been taking them with him to . . . to town, ma'am.'

She turned her gaze from him and looked up the stairs. The humiliations. To what depths had her husband sunk when he had to sell, or bribe, with the contents of the cellar. She very rarely went down into the wine cellar, but she remembered it as she had first seen it, stacked from floor to ceiling, rows and rows of bottles, one particular section with the cobwebs of years on them. Dennison had proudly pointed out to her that some of these bottles had been laid down in his father's youth. Swiftly now she turned about and, putting out her hand, she said, 'I will take the tray.'

The man held on to the salver, looking her in the face now and saying, 'Are you sure, ma'am?'

'Yes, yes, Robertson, I'm sure.'

At this he relinquished his hold and watched her walk across the hall, her gait wavering as if she too had been drinking.

Without knocking at the library door she went straight in. He was sitting to the side of the fire in a deep chair, his legs sprawled out. On a small table to his side was another decanter and glass. He had not turned his head, and when she reached his side he said, 'Put it there.' It was only when she said, her voice grim, 'This, so I have been informed, is the last of your cellar,' that he lumbered round in his seat and blinked at her, then said, 'That's nonsense, nonsense. Get out! Go to bed!'

'I shall not go to bed.' She walked round to the front of the chair and faced him, and there, her face tight, her hands clenched at her waist, she cried at him, 'You are a disgrace to your house, your name, me, everything.'

He thrust himself back in the chair and peered at her. His whole face was bloated, his skin blotched; his neck was thick and his paunch bulged. There was very little left of the man he had been five years ago, and the picture he presented caused her lip to curl as she said, 'You are disgusting.'

Her words acted on him like an injection, for so quickly did he pull himself up from the chair that she jumped back in some fright. And now he was yelling at the top of his voice, 'Disgusting, am I? Disgusting. And who's to blame for that? Eh? Have you asked yourself who's to blame for that? Disgusting, you say. I would have believed it if you had said I was a fool, yes, a fool, to have ever married you. Do you know that? I haven't had a day's luck since I married you. They told me it was a mistake. But would I listen? No.

No. Parson's Prig they nicknamed you, and by God they were right, for you've brought the vicarage with you. And from the day you entered the door of this house – ' he now took his hand and wiped the saliva from his mouth before spluttering, 'my luck went down. I could lose before, but I could win twice as much, and things might have levelled out. Aye. Aye, they might have. But you had to go and strip Rene, and I, like the bloody fool I was, threw her off. But she's got her own back. By God! she has. Because, you know what, my little lady? 'Tis her man that has stripped me, with the assistance of my dear friend Larry. Oh, yes. Oh, yes. Funny that, funny.' He paused, as if thinking now, before he went on, muttering, 'Bloody underhand game somewhere. Can't put a finger on it. All honourable. Huh! All honourable play. Skilful, not cheating. Oh, no, not cheating, just skilful. But it's cheating.' His voice had suddenly risen to a scream, and now he was pointing at her. 'They are bloody well cheating me. Do you hear? They've cheated me out of everything, and all through you. If I'd only had the sense to make it up in town everything would have been all right. But I was thinking of you, you, my little prig, and told myself, whoever warmed my bed it mustn't be her . . . thinking of you. I must have been mad. And she went mad. Aye, aye, she did, in a different way.' He had turned and flung his hand out towards the decanter, and he stared at it for a moment before looking back at her again, and, his voice lower now and each word coming as if sieved through his teeth, he growled, 'And you humiliated me. I could have saved my son, but you had to put your pious little hands out and stop me.'

When her face stretched in amazement he nodded at her, then went on, 'I couldn't swim, but a dog thrown in the water will paddle, and I just needed one more arm's stretch and I would have had him. But no, my wife had to humiliate me, save me from drowning. God! How I hated you that day. You look amazed, and so right you are to look amazed. You will say, I could never have saved him, but in my heart I know I could. I am strong. It only needed another split second and I could have conquered that bloody river. But no . . .'

'You shan't, you shan't put the blame on me. You . . . you sank, you went under. You were threshing like a mad dog. You could never have saved him. You just told yourself that to ease your conscience, because since your brother drowned in the river you have been afraid of it. Yes, you have.'

As his hand came up to strike her she sprang back and watched his doubled fist hover in the air. Then he screamed at her, 'Get out of my sight before I do you an injury.'

And she got out of his sight, stumbling, as if she herself was drunk.

Robertson and Mary met her in the hall. They had made no pretence they were there by accident, and Mary helped her up the stairs to her room. And there she had given way and cried in Mary's arms, and asked of the woman who had become her friend, 'What's to be done? Where's it going to end?' And Mary had said, 'God knows, ma'am, but it must have an end soon. You can't go on like this. You'll kill yourself.'. . .

Two further incidents took place before the end actually came. The first occurred on a pleasant evening when she had taken Rebecca for a walk. She no longer walked by the river bank; the paths from the garden were overgrown. The usual daily walk was to the Dower House to visit Jessica or, if the day was bright and dry and she wanted exercise, she would walk to the village. But she hadn't taken that road for some time now, because she could not face the tradesmen to whom money was owing. So, if they went out of the main gates, she would walk along the coach road in the opposite direction. And this is what she was doing this evening.

She was holding Rebecca's hand and her daughter startled her by saying, 'You know something, Mama?'

'No,' she had answered. 'What is the something that I should know?'

'I was just going to say, wouldn't it be lovely if we could live with Great-Grandmama.'

She had remained silent for a moment; then she had said, 'Yes, my dear, it would be lovely if we could live with her.'

She did not treat her daughter as a child: Rebecca at ten might still look a child of ten, a beautiful child, but her mind and disposition seemed at times almost adult.

The day her brother had drowned had changed her too. She'd had intermittent screaming fits for a year afterwards, but when they stopped, so stopped her childish games. She had in a way, become a sedate little girl. She had stopped running to her father when she saw him. She had not laughed much, except with David, and when he had gone to Australia, she had cried for days afterwards.

Her daughter was saying now, 'It is always bright there, Mama. Great-Grandmama is always cheery.'

'Yes, yes, she is, my dear, she is always cheery. She's a wonderful woman.'

'You know what she said to me yesterday?'

'No; what did she say?'

'She said that when I was sixteen I would be married and live happy ever after.'

Nancy Ann came to a dead stop and looked down on her daughter. She could not believe that her grandmama had said that, but she must have, for her daughter didn't lie, nor was she given to making up fairy-tales.

'Grandmama said that to you?'

'Yes, yes, she did.'

'What a strange thing to say.'

'Not really, Mama, because I had been asking her about Great-Grandpapa, and if she had a happy life, and was that why she was happy now?'

'Oh. Oh, I see.' They were walking on again when she saw, coming round the curve of the road, a carriage approaching. As the vehicle came nearer she could see there were two people seated in it. Then, to her consternation she recognized one of them, the fat face under the high hat, the voluptuous body. She also recognized instantly that the woman had espied her, for she was now leaning over the side of the carriage, her mouth wide open, one hand waving.

When the carriage came abreast of Nancy Ann, the woman cried at her, 'You know nothing yet. There's more to come. I promised you. By God! I promised you.'

The carriage passed on but the fat body twisted round and was still hanging over the side, her words loud but unintelligible now.

Nancy Ann was shaking from head to foot. There was a high grass bank behind her, and she leant against it. The last time she had looked on that woman's face she had been aware of the beauty of the skin and that it hadn't been painted. But the face that had just thrown hate at her was like a mask, with deep pink cheeks, red lips, and darkened eyes. And there was proof that she was on the same escape route as Dennison for she was drunk.

'What is it, Mama? Who is that lady? Are you all right, Mama?'

Nancy Ann pulled herself up from the bank and stepped on to the road again and, looking down into her daughter's concerned face, she said, 'It's all right. Let us go home.'

'But the lady, who is she?'

'Oh, she is a person who lives some distance away and she . . . she is ill.'

'Ill?' The girl frowned. 'Like Nelly Sand in the village?'

'No, no, not that kind of ill. She . . . she is just unwell. Come. Come, my dear.' And she began to hurry now back towards the house, each step seeming to beat out the woman's words: There is more to come . . .

The second happening brought surprise and pleasure . . . at first. She was in her office going over yet again the accounts and the bills. She was worrying about not only the staff's wages and how they were to be met, but also the fact that she would have to dismiss some of them, either the first or second housemaid, either the vegetable maid or the scullery maid, and, too, one of the laundresses. They were already down to one seamstress. When two had left to go to America with their parents she had not replaced them. There were now only two gardeners, and three of the men from the farm had been dismissed since the horses had gone. She was telling herself that when he returned from town and whether he was drunk or sober, she would insist that he find some means of paying the staff when her thoughts were interrupted by the excited voice of her daughter, crying, 'Mama! Mama!' and before the office door had opened she was on her feet and moving towards it.

'What is it? What is it?' She held Rebecca by her shoulders and looked into the beaming face.

'It's . . . it's David. He's come by cab. I . . . I saw him from the window. Come. Come.' She was pulling her mother forward; but there was really no need, for Nancy Ann too was hurrying.

At the open door she looked on to the drive where a man was handing boxes and packages to Robertson, who, laden down but smiling, carried them up the steps. She watched the cabby raise his hat to his passenger, and then there he was, striding towards them, a tall handsome man, no vestige of the youth or boy left.

She put her hand firmly on Rebecca's shoulder to stop her running forward, and under her breath she said, 'Wait. Wait.'

Then hc was standing in front of them, looking from one to the other, and her being was filled with a mixture of emotions that was impossible to sort out, at least at the moment. And she could restrain Rebecca no longer, for her daughter now had her arms tight about his waist and was looking up at him, saying over and over again, 'Oh, Davey, Davey. Oh, Davey, Davey.'

'Well, let me in. Am I permitted?' Even his voice had changed. It was deep, so pleasant sounding, and he had said, 'Let me in.' It was the first time he had entered this house by the front door. He had made no attempt to go round the back. Evidently he had told the cabby to stop on the drive. Thank God Dennison was away. Did David know he was away? How could he? He had just arrived. Or had he?

She motioned with her hand towards the door, asking the question now, 'When did you arrive?'

'Oh' – he was walking into the hall now, his arm around Rebecca's shoulders – 'six days ago. No . . . no, a week.'

'A week?' she repeated questioningly. And he turned fully and looked at her, saying, 'Yes, a week. I've been doing business in Newcastle. But yesterday I booked into an hotel in Durham, and . . . and here I am.' He turned from her and looked round the hall, his head back. But when Robertson's voice came, saying, 'Can I take your coat, Dav . . . Mr David?'

The two men exchanged glances for a moment. Then smiling, David said, 'Yes, Henry, you can take my coat.'

The fact that Robertson had addressed him as if he were the young master of the house was not lost on Nancy Ann. And again she thought, Thank God Dennison is not here, for she realized she was being confronted by someone who would not be confined to the kitchen quarters ever again. But where should she receive him? In the drawing-room of course.

As she attempted to speak casually, saying, 'Well, come along in, and let me hear all your news,' he turned from her and going to where the parcels and boxes stood on the floor, he picked up two of the largest and, handing them to Robertson, said, 'Pass them around, will you, please? There's a number inside; they've all got names on. Are all the old ones still here?'

The man hesitated, glanced at Nancy Ann, then said, 'One or two have left.'

'Oh well, you'll have to raffle those. And these two' – he pointed down to two small packages – 'these are for Mary and Agnes. Where are they?'

It was Rebecca who answered, saying, 'It's Mary's time off. I think she has gone to the village. Agnes is upstairs. Shall I take them up?'

'Yes, you can. But first of all, this one's for you. Take that too. Can you manage it? Or perhaps Henry will take it up for you. Open it upstairs, then let me see how they look.'

She went to take the parcel but, first, reaching up, she threw her arms around his neck and, pulling his head down to her, she kissed him; then, grabbing the long box, she ran from him. Robertson followed her, and he followed Nancy Ann into the drawing-room.

Inside the room he put his hand behind him to close the door, then stood in that position for a full minute while he looked round the room. She was already standing at the fireplace when he moved slowly towards her, saying, 'This is the first time I've seen this room. Splendid, isn't it?'

'It's a nice room. Sit down.' She pointed to a seat, an armchair, while she sat down at the end of the couch. And when he stared at her without speaking, she said, 'If you've been back a week, why didn't you call in before?'

'As I said, I had business to do and, you may as well know, I have been here before, at least as far as the lodge. But – ' His face lost its pleasant look and now he said stiffly, 'Your lord and master was at home and I was determined that this time I wasn't going to crawl in through the kitchen.'

'Oh, David.'

'Why do you say, "Oh David" like that? Do you wish me always to keep to the kitchen quarters? In London I have a suite of rooms. In Newcastle I have a suite of rooms. In Durham I have booked into something similar. But here I have to crawl through the back door. No more. No more.' He looked hard at her for a moment then said, 'I'm a comparatively rich man – do you know that? – and hope to be richer.'

'I'm glad for you.'

'Are you?'

'Yes, of course.'

'Knowing how things stand with him and that he's on the verge of bankruptcy, you can honestly say the tables have turned, and you're glad for . . ..?'

'Who said he was on the verge of bankruptcy?'

'Who said? It's a well-known fact. If you don't know it, you must be the last person not to.'

When she bowed her head, he went on, 'I can't say I'm sorry, except that I wish you weren't involved in it, that it wasn't going to have repercussions on you. But his state of affairs is like salve on the sores that he inflicted on me. Can you understand that?'

Yes, she could understand it. But she couldn't tell him so; she had to defend Dennison in some small way, so she said, 'You can't blame him entirely for what happened to you. It was your father's doing in the first place.'

'By all accounts my father would have been willing to marry Jennie, my mother. That was something, too, that was painful to discover. I knew from the beginning that I was different because I hadn't a mother and father like other people. I was tied up in the corner of that roof; I wasn't allowed out; I mustn't go in the yard when the master was about; the master mustn't set eyes on me or on Jennie. And who was Jennie? Jennie was the woman who slept with me. Jennie was the woman who cried herself to sleep night after night and who took me in her arms and hugged me to give herself comfort. But where were my mother and father? I got the answer to this when I was seven. One of the maids told me. For a long time after that I didn't like Jennie. She was my mother and she hadn't told me that she was my mother. But even then it hadn't dawned on me that we were kept in that state because he ordained it. And you tell me he wasn't to blame.'

She bowed her head now, saying softly, 'I'm sorry. I . . . I blame myself. I should have done more.'

'No, no.' He put his hand out towards her. 'Anyway, you saved my life. Before we had a penny you sent me to school. I don't know what would have happened to me if you hadn't taken that brave step, because at that stage I was ready to do something desperate, even setting fire to this house.' He poked his head towards her now and smiled, a wide smile, showing a mouthful of even white teeth. 'Yes, yes' – he nodded at her – 'I had considered it. And I was situated in the best place to do it, wasn't I? Up in the roof among all that junk and debris of years. But it would have been such a pity if I had, because I wouldn't be sitting here now.'

When he paused and kept his eyes fixed on her, she said, 'How long do you intend to stay?'

'Oh, a week or so, perhaps a month. I must get back because things are moving so fast out there they could run away with me. And to think that I am where I am this day because my uncle was persuaded to buy three pieces of land, arid stretches of nothing.

Fools' land, they called it. Some of the sages laughed and said it would only show profit when the rains came, and, as everyone knew, water was rarer than gold, and still is in that part of the world. Oh, if a man could dig a well and find water, he'd be a millionaire overnight. Then shortly after my uncle died, in eighteen eighty-seven and eighty-eight gold was discovered. Oh, not in one of his patches, but not so far away. And from then the fever started. And now they're rushing in like lemmings, but not to death, to life. It's sad to think though that where one man will strike it rich a hundred might go on digging until their beards grow down to their pants.'

'Has gold been found on your land?'

'A little, on a bit I sold, but they expect more. Of course until recently, a man didn't actually buy the land, he leased it. But it's the same thing, because when the ore runs out it's not worth the ownership.'

'What do they call the place again?'

'Kalgoorlie. It's situated in the western part.'

'What is it like to live there? Have you nice houses?'

He laughed at this. 'Not what you would call nice.' He stretched the word. 'But they'll come. You wouldn't think much of it as a town if you were to see it: beer halls, dance halls, Chinese washhouses. But civilization is definitely making an inroad. We have our preachers . . . oh, of all denominations, and they're going to build a big hospital there which will take care of the whole district, a certain religious order called Saint John of God. Oh' – he made a face now – 'we will soon be civilized. Our only real need is water, but that'll come. Nothing can deter an Australian once he has set his mind on it. I've learned that much. They're rough, tough, coarse individuals, but get on the right side of them and you couldn't wish for better men; get on the wrong side of them, though, and God help you. But then, you look around and you ask who are the real Australians, for there's Irish, Scots, Germans, Swedes, French, Chinese. Oh yes, Chinese. And, of course, our breed, and among our lot you'll find the most experienced tricksters and swindlers.'

When he stopped talking he continued to stare at her, and after a while she said, 'You seem to enjoy the life.'

'I do. Yes, I do. It's free; there's no restriction. That's the best part of it for me.' The bitterness had come back into his voice, and he asked again, 'Can you understand that? Being able to walk where I like, and now do as I like. Money is power. Before I had any I recognized that truth and determined, in some way, to get it. Through writing, I thought. And I still might: I'm half-way through a book on my particular small section of that vast country. Who knows but that some day it, too, may bring me fortune, and perhaps fame?'

She looked away from him towards the fire. She didn't know if she liked this new David, this cocksure man. Yet, he wasn't new: the facets of his character showing now had been there years ago, and were but replicas of his despised uncle, but with strength attached to them and an honesty that likely had been part of his own father's character, a young man who would have gladly married beneath him for love.

She was startled when he jumped up from the chair, saying, 'What's the matter with me! Your present is still in the hall.'

She watched him stride down the room, pull open the door and disappear for a moment; then he was walking back towards her, an oblong parcel in his hand. And bending over her, he placed it on her knees, saying, 'I hope you like it.'

Slowly, she undid the wrapping to disclose a fancy striped-coloured box done up with ribbon. When she undid this and lifted the lid she stared down at the brilliant rose and blue patterned garment lying there. When she took it out she had to raise her arms well up in front of her, but even then the bottom of it fell in folds on the carpet. But now she stood up and held the garment to the side.

'Well, do you like it?'

'It's . . . it's beautiful. I . . . I've never seen anything like it. Is it a dressing-gown?'

'No, it is what is called a kimono, a Japanese kimono. All the work on it is hand-done. I bought the silk and an old Chinese woman did the work. It took her many months.'

The garment had a high collar, and now her fingers touched what looked at first like a buckle attached to it. Then she saw it was a brooch, and she turned her gaze on him and said, 'This . . . this is a brooch?'

'Yes, it is a brooch.'

She unpinned it, then let the garment drop across one arm while she examined the brooch where it lay in the palm of her hand.

It was of an intricate design in filigree bands of gold, and on them were two ruby-studded hearts. 'Oh! David.' She looked up at him. 'I couldn't accept . . .'

'*Don't*' – he jerked his head to the side – 'don't for goodness sake be coy, not you. The question is, do you like it?'

Her lips trembled; she felt her teeth chattering against each other. She had to steady her whole body before she could say, 'Yes, yes, of course I like it. Who wouldn't?'

'Well then, that's done.'

She had to sit down. As she sank on to the couch she knew he was about to take a seat beside her. But she was saved from whatever this might lead to when the door burst open and Rebecca stood there poised.

The girl was wearing a white fur hat and a matching necklet and muff. Then, on a gurgling laugh, she flew up the room and once more flung her arms about David, crying, 'Oh, they're beautiful! Beautiful,

David. Thank you so much. You are kind. Oh, I am glad to see you back. You'll stay? You're going to stay? Oh, Mama' – she turned her head towards Nancy Ann – 'do make him stay.'

'Rebecca, now, now, behave yourself and let David alone for a moment. Where is Mary?'

Rebecca now swung round and pirouetted with her hands held out before her and tucked into her muff, and she almost sang, 'She's in the kitchen. They're all in the kitchen, and everybody is very excited. It's like Christmas, only better.' She turned again to David and was once more about to embrace him when Nancy Ann said sternly, 'Now, now, no more; let David sit down. And behave yourself. You're not a little girl any more. And she's acting like one, isn't she, David?'

He said nothing to this but he put out his hand and gently touched Rebecca's cheek. The gesture caused her to remain still while she stared at him. And then, he said softly, 'She's going to be a beautiful woman like her mother.'

'Will I? Will I be beautiful like Mama?'

'Yes, yes, you will.' The question had been quiet and the answer was equally quiet. Then they both looked at Nancy Ann folding up the kimono and seemingly unaware of what they had been saying. But her voice, too, was quiet as she said, 'Go and ask Mary to bring us tea, will you, dear?'

'Yes, yes, Mama.'

'But first of all, go upstairs and put those beautiful furs away. You don't want to soil them, do you?'

'No, Mama.' Sedately now the girl walked from the room.

Left alone, there was silence between them, except for the rustling of the tissue paper that she placed over the garment before putting the striped lid on the box again. She had pinned the brooch back on to the neck of the garment and, after a while, she raised her head and looked towards him. But he wasn't looking at her now, his gaze was directed towards the fire. And it stayed so for an embarrassingly long time, for neither of them spoke until, his voice hardly audible now, he said, 'You know what I'd like to do?'

'No, David. I've . . . I've no idea.'

'Well, I'd like to take you into Newcastle to a theatre. I'd like to sit beside you in a box and see you laugh at the antics of those on the stage. Then after that, I'd like to take you to supper in a discreet restaurant. There we'd have a table to ourselves and we'd drink wine and have a good meal. And then – ' His voice stopped.

Her lips were trembling again, her teeth chattering and, like the percussions given off from a drum, the vibration was passing through her whole body and a voice was saying to her, Oh, no, no, don't be ridiculous, when he turned and looked at her and said, 'But I can't, can I? Because you are married, and because I'm David, the garret creature, as Staith once called me.'

She looked down at her joined hands as she said, 'I'm sorry you should feel like that, and I'm sorry it was necessary for you to keep to the kitchen quarters, but . . . but then you lived in the cottage for . . .'

'For how long? And that came too late. My home, as you know, wasn't even the garret, it was a corner under the roof. You know, when I think of it now I want to lash out, break something.' He looked around, before adding quietly but bitterly, 'But most of all I want to break him.'

'Please, please.' She went to rise, then changed her mind. 'Please don't say things like that. He . . . he allowed you and your mother to stay and, knowing him as I do, that was a big concession. It may not appear so to you.'

'Oh, don't talk to me like that, my dear.' He had called her 'my dear', not ma'am any more. 'He was forced into that by my uncle. Although just a common working man, he was an intelligent one, and if my mother had been thrown out he would have blazoned it in the main papers of the day. And you say your husband allowed us to stay. But how did he allow it? It was all right, I understand, if I could be strapped in the basket, but once I began to toddle around and cry, that was another thing. I was put on a lead. Did you know that? Like an animal. A circle was cleared on the floor and, like an ox, I could walk or crawl round it. And should I cry, then I was administered drops of laudanum. I look back now and think it was very strange that I should, at the age of three, have learned not to cry, because even then, something in me rebelled at my mind being dulled. And at an early age, too, I learned cunning. I could undo the buckle and the straps and wander round the attics. It was in one of them that I first saw the picture of my father. But I only saw him as a man with golden hair, while mine was streaked with tea.

He paused here, and his look and voice altering, he said, 'During one of the days I escaped I made my way down to the river and I sat on a stone and a dog came and sat beside me; then a fairy came out of the wood looking for it. That day is as clear in my mind as this moment.'

Her eyelids were blinking. She was near to tears, but she told herself she must not allow them to flow, because once she allowed the water gate to open, God knows what would happen, especially with this man sitting there looking at her the way Graham looked at her, and as Dennison once had. She forced herself to smile and say lightly, 'I never thought of myself as a fairy, and I'm sure my parents didn't. I know I was a source of worry to my mother because I was such a tomboy. I had two good tutors.' Her voice trailed away and they were left staring at each other. And she was searching in her mind for something to say to break the deadlock and alter that look in his eyes when the door burst open and Mary stood there, and in a hoarse whisper she said, 'The master . . . the master's just come into the yard.'

Then she was gone again, banging the door behind her.

They were both on their feet and she was gasping now, 'Oh, David, David, please, please come out this way, and go to the . . . and go to . . . I mean, please . . .'

'Why should I? We've got to meet sometime.'

'David – ' She was standing in front of him, her hands joined tightly together, imploring him now, 'He . . . he's a sick man. He . . . he's half demented with worry. And, please, I beg of you.'

When he still didn't move, she put her hands out and gripped the lapels of his coat and, her voice a mere hissing whisper now, she said, 'If you love me, do what I ask. Please go.' There was a pause while their gaze held fast; then she had hold of his hand, drawing him up the room and through the far door which led into the dining-room. Still holding his hand, she pulled him across it and through another door and into a passage, and there was the green-baized door that led to the kitchen quarters.

She grabbed the handle to open the door, but he stopped her, saying gently, 'I know the way, my dear,' and taking her hand, he lifted it to his mouth and pressed the palm against his lips. Then quite slowly, he opened the door, went through, and closed it after him.

Now she leant her back against it and, lifting her eyes to the ceiling, once again she asked of something beyond it how it was possible to love two men at the same time, and she wasn't including Dennison in her thoughts now.

4

She had warned Rebecca not to mention David's visit to her father, even knowing the while that this would be unlikely for Dennison rarely held any conversation with his daughter even when he was sober, and feeling, too, that her daughter had grown a little afraid of this distant man. Nevertheless, she warned her; however, she never expected that it would be Dennison himself who would mention David's name and through white fury.

It was more than three weeks since David arrived in England and he hadn't paid another visit to the house. Rebecca was constantly asking after him and only yesterday she'd had to reprimand her strongly and remind her that David was a man who had his own life to live and was no longer a member of the household. And her daughter had silenced her for a moment when she had said tearfully, 'I like David, Mama. I love him. And . . . and anyway, he's my cousin.'

'Who . . . who told you that?'

'He did. And anyway, Mary explained it a long time ago. His father was drowned in the river like William. His father was my uncle, so he is my cousin, and . . . and I've always known that Jennie was his mother.'

The next question she could have asked her daughter was: Did you know that Jennie wasn't married to your uncle and so, therefore, legally he is no relation to you? He is what you call illegitimate. Oh, that word, that beastly stigma. She had always thought it was unfair that a signature on a paper could scar so many lives. There were two children she remembered at the village school with her who bore the stigma and at times were taunted by others.

She wished from the bottom of her heart that David would return to Australia and without calling on them again.

She had noticed for days there was a strong atmosphere in the house: it was as if the staff knew something that she didn't know. She questioned Mary, saying, 'Is anything afoot, Mary?' And Mary looked at her full in the face and said, 'Not that I know of, yet I feel the same as you, ma'am. But I can't put my finger on anything. I feel that Robertson knows something, but what, he doesn't say, although I've quizzed him.'

For the past week Dennison had been at home and he had been sober, but this was of necessity because there were only a few bottles of light wine left in the cellar. Yesterday he had come knocking on her bedroom door, and she had been surprised it was he who entered after she had called 'Come in.'

'I must talk to you, Nancy Ann,' he had said; and he seemed very much his old self. 'Sit down.' He had pointed to a chair near the window, and she had sat down. But he had remained standing, looking out over the balcony, and she could only see part of his profile. He had begun by saying, 'I don't have to tell you things are in a bad way. You know I'm selling the farm and five hundred acres?'

She made no reply, and after a moment he went on, 'Well, it went through today, but it's not going to make all that difference, the bank has swallowed up the lot. And I . . . I had better tell you that unless I can raise twenty thousand within the next few days, they'll . . . they'll foreclose.' He swung round now and looked down on her and, his teeth grinding against each other, he said, 'Did you hear what I said? They'll foreclose. More than that, they'll confiscate everything, every stick in the house. Do you understand?'

'Yes, I understand,' she had said. 'And now, I'll ask you a question, Dennison. Who are you blaming for this misfortune?'

She noticed his stomach and his chest swell before he ground out, 'All right, all right. I've been mad, foolish, but I haven't been played straight with; there's been some dirty business. Myers is at the bottom of it. Yes, yes, my one-time mistress's husband. She said she would get even, and by God! she has, with the help of my one-time friend. I tell you, I've been cheated, drugged and cheated.'

'Drugged?' Her face was screwed up and she repeated, 'Drugged?'

'Yes, my dear, drugged. These things happen. Your drink is doped; you gamble stupidly, wildly, sure that you are going to make a fortune. It happened more than once. I should have known, twigged something, but I wouldn't believe it. I wouldn't have risked five thousand at a time, even ten thousand once, if I had been in my ordinary senses. Oh yes, you can look shocked, but these things happen. And now . . . oh my God!' He turned from her and put his hands to his head, grinding out the words, 'I won't be able to stand it. I can't.'

She looked at him, pity filling her as she watched him turn from the window and drop on to a chair and, resting his elbows on his knees, hold his head in his hands and say, 'When the end comes, as it's bound to, you'll go and stay with your grandmama. She'll be pleased to have you, as will your friend Graham. He'll see you never starve.'

She was on her feet, crying now in indignation, 'How dare you!' And to this he raised a weary face, saying, 'Oh, don't be silly, woman. I know how the man feels about you, even before we married. He was just too late stepping in, that's all. Had he had the courage to ask for you, your father would have welcomed him with open arms, whereas he loathed me from the day we first met. I represented the devil to him. Perhaps he was right.' His voice sank on a weary note. 'Anyway' – he now rose to his feet – 'I've told you how things stand.' And as he turned towards the door, she said quietly, 'Dennison. I'm . . . I'm sorry. Believe me, I'm . . . I'm heart sorry. May I ask if you've sought help from any of your friends?'

He turned fully towards her now, his expression one of utter weariness as he said, 'Yes, my dear, I've applied to my friends. Those who would have helped me, such as Pat and George, are just managing to keep their own heads above water. Those of my so-called friends whose heads are well above the water have suddenly decided to take early holidays abroad.'

He now went to the door, but stopped there and looked down towards his hand gripping the knob and, quietly, he said, 'I'm sorry for my treatment of you over the past few years.'

'Dennison.'

He turned towards her.

'What . . . what will you do?'

'I don't know. I haven't got that far. I don't know how I'm going to take this, I really don't.'

'Dennison.' She ran to him now and gripped his hand. 'There is one person who would help you. Go to Graham. He would, he would help you, I know he would.'

He looked at her sadly for a moment before he said, 'He has already offered a sum of ten thousand pounds. I thanked him, but refused, because it would just be like throwing money down a well, and, apart from taking advantage of a man whom I have never called friend, whom I've never even liked, I would have no hope of repaying him. The twenty thousand the bank needs is just the beginning. What would we live on? I have no money to pay the staff, nor the mountain of bills. I'll say this, Graham Mercer is a good man; I wish I'd had the sense to make friends with such as he years ago.'

She took her hand from his and watched him open the door and go out. She watched him walk along the landing on to the balcony. She saw him pause and look first one way then the other, before going down the stairs. She then went back into the bedroom and, sitting down on the couch, she buried her face in her hands, and, racked now with pity, she cried for him.

The farm had been sold through an agent. Dennison hadn't met the buyer, a man from abroad, by the name of Mather. Apparently he didn't want to farm the land, he wanted only the house but had been quite willing to take the five hundred acres which he was prepared to let off as agricultural land. Taylor and his wife were ready for retirement anyway. They had found a little place in Low Fell. Their sons, Billy and Frank, had found jobs on other farms and had taken the last of the stock to market before leaving three days ago.

The house was more than a farmhouse; it had once been the manor house before his present home had been built . . . His present home! He had said he didn't know how he was going to stand the break-up, and it was true. What could he do with his life? He had been trained for nothing but living like a gentleman.

The thought did enter his head that when the whole business was over he would take up Mercer's offer of ten thousand and perhaps he could start again somewhere. But then, his step quickening, he muttered aloud, 'No, no. By God! no. Not from him,' for it would be like accepting a fee for leaving his wife in his charge. He did not know how Nancy Ann felt about the man but he certainly knew how the man felt about her, he knew that Mercer desired her for the same reason as he had done all those years ago.

If only she had been the kind of wife who could have countenanced an affair on the side, even lightly, he knew he wouldn't have been in the position he was at this moment, for then he would have taken Rene again. Especially that time when she had openly offered herself to him in town and he had refused her, none too tactfully either. He knew he had been a fool, for, as Rene had pointed out, he was in any case dispensing his favours here and there, and so why not include her among them.

He could date the complete change in his luck from that meeting. She had been scorned and her rejection had likely become evident to Poulter Myers. The man had always hated him because his wife had made no secret of her feelings. So whether it had been openly planned or merely suggested, his downfall had been her aim. It had, however, been brought about by cheating, but in such a way that no one could lay a finger on them. He should have suspected something that night he had woken up in Freeman's rooms and found he owed him five thousand and Myers seven. They had all been very clever. They had let him win more than half of that back the next night. And so the pattern had gone on: one step forward and two steps backward.

He stopped on a rise and there, away down in the valley, lay the village. He could make out the chimneys and distinctly the spire of the small church, and bitterly he thought it was that House of God that had been his curse, not his gambling, his drinking, or his whoring. No, none of these, but because from out of the vicarage had come a little girl full of spirit and freshness and naïve purity which had attracted him from the first time he laid eyes on her. And the attraction had grown into a desire, a craving that could not be assuaged except by having her. And he'd had her, and with what result? She had been his ruin. Knowingly or unknowingly, she had been his ruin.

He entered the farmyard. There was no bustle here today: the line of horse boxes had no bobbing heads sticking over the half doors; there was no sound of cattle from the byres; Minnie Taylor wasn't waddling her fat body towards him, her face one big smile; her husband wasn't there to doff his cap; there was no shepherd, no cowman; there were no stable hands. The yard was swept clean, the ivy-covered house looked lonely. There were no curtains fluttering from the window, but – his eyes narrowed – the kitchen door was open. He walked towards it; then, pushing it wide, he stepped into the stone-flagged kitchen with its only remaining piece of furniture, a trestle-table, and standing to the side of it was a tall, fair man.

They surveyed each other for a full minute while Dennison's heart leapt within his body. Here was his long lost brother, only taller and broader. The face was as he remembered it; yet, not quite. The eyes looking at him had not the soft quality of Tim's: these eyes were dark and brooding and sending towards him something that his own answered.

His voice was a growl as he said, 'What do you want here? You're trespassing. Get out!'

'It is you who are trespassing, sir.' The lips were drawn back from the teeth. For the moment David's face took on the ferocious look of a wild-cat; then the words were hissed through his teeth. 'This is my property, as from yesterday. Now, Mr Harpcore, sir, I have pleasure in telling you to get out, off *my* property.'

My God! My God! No, not him! So he was the Mather that had bought the place. He recalled the name from dim memory: the servant girl's name had been Mather. He had paid nine thousand for it. Where had he got the money? Yes, yes, he remembered now rumours that he wouldn't listen to, conversation that broke off in the middle. The boy that had been brought up in his service had gone to Australia and had made his fortune. He had an uncle out there . . . yes, the uncle, that man who had confronted him, blackmailed him.

He appealed to something outside himself now, crying, *Oh, no, no, not this*, not this too. I can't stand this. And because he couldn't stand it he flung himself round and out of the door, across the yard and on to the path that led its twisting way back to the house. And he didn't stop until he was in sight of it, when he seemed to stagger towards a tree, against which he leant back, and gasping as if he had been running hard. His head was bowed and so deep did he feel his humiliation that he imagined it was touching the ground . . .

When he reached the house Robertson, meeting him in the hall, thought for a moment that he was drunk, though knowing he couldn't be. And his master's sobriety was confirmed when he said, 'Tell your mistress I wish to see her in the library.'

A few moments later Nancy Ann entered the room, and immediately he rounded on her, crying, 'Did you know of this?'

Thinking, what now, she instinctively shook her head before she said, 'Know what? What are you talking about?'

'The farm.'

'The farm? No. Only that you said the matter was closed yesterday.'

'*And who to? Who to?*' His voice was almost a scream now.

'I don't know who has bought it.'

'You mean to stand there and tell me you don't know?'

She stiffened and, her own voice also ringing now, she cried, 'Yes, I do. I don't know who has bought the farm.'

'Then it will be news to you that your protégé, your fair-haired boy is now the owner of it.'

She put her hand up to her mouth and muttered through her fingers, 'No, no.'

'But yes, yes. Just one more humiliation for me to suffer. Do you know I would rather have burnt the place down.'

She stood quietly now, her hands joined at her waist, staring at him, and then she said, 'Would you? Would you have rather burnt the place down than your nephew have bought it?'

'*Don't, woman.* Don't aggravate me at this time, because I can't stand any more. He is no nephew of mine.'

'He saved your son, or at least attempted to and risked his own life.'

She watched his cheek bones push out against his mottled skin, and, his words low now, and even appearing as a plea, he said again, 'Don't woman, don't.'

'I will. I will. Someone has to say it. You've let that boy be an obsession with you all your life, whereas he could have been a comfort to you.'

The crash of his fist as it hit the sofa table and bounced oddments on the floor caused her to jump back and clutch her throat. Then they were staring at each other across the space in silence.

She could stand no more. She turned and ran from the room and almost into the arms of Robertson who, halting her with his attentive touch on her arm, said, 'Ma'am, there are two men' – he did not say gentlemen – 'waiting in the hall. They . . . they wish to see the master.' His voice was low, and there was meaning in his words which she did not comprehend at the moment, and she muttered, 'Then tell him, tell him,' before she rushed along the corridor and into the hall passing two waiting men whose sombre appearance caused her to pause momentarily before running on upstairs and into her room.

Robertson delivered his message, held open the door for his master to pass him, then followed him into the hall. He stood to the side and watched one of the men hand his master a paper. He saw him scan it, then look at the men before turning his gaze towards the stairs; then, like a man in a daze, his glance swept the hall, and there was a pause while he wetted his lips, cleared his throat, before he said, 'Show these gentlemen into . . . into the kitchen. Give them the assistance that they need.'

'Yes, sir.' Robertson stepped forward now and beckoned the men to follow him, leaving Dennison alone and standing quietly staring down at the floor. Slowly he walked across the hall and along the corridor again to the far end and into a room. After a while he emerged, took his hat and coat from the hallstand and paused for a moment before a mirror, then went out.

The bums were in. The staff had been expecting them for days, but nevertheless it caused great consternation. Most of them had already arranged their future life and service. Robertson was to take over Mister David's new home. He had impressed upon the staff that the 'Mister' was, from now on, compulsory for all of them. Cook was to take up her place in the smaller kitchen accompanied by Sarah Brown. Jane Renton was leaving to get married. But Annie Fuller, the second housemaid, was to be housemaid at the farm. Jimmy Tool the workhouse boy, now a young man and courting, was to be given the place as stable lad under Shane McLoughlin, and set up house in two of the rooms above the stables. Shane and his brother were to have the other two. It had all been worked out during the past three weeks. The remainder of the staff had applied for and had found positions elsewhere. This wasn't including Mary or Agnes, for it was understood that wherever the mistress went they would accompany her. And as they all knew, she was for the Manor, for . . . well, where else would she go?

As Mister David had said he had no intention of living in the farmhouse permanently for his business was in Australia, why then, they had asked each other, had he bought it? It was rumoured there had been numbers of people after it, real farmers, but he had outbid them. Was it to spite the master?

Aye, very likely, very likely. It was also rumoured that he had enough money to buy The House, too, if he liked. But that surely would have finished the master. It would be bad enough when he got to know who the new owner of the farm was, because they knew only too well he would never recognize him. Altogether a queer business, they said.

And that's what Shane McLoughlin said to David when he made a point of running across the grounds to the farm to tell him the latest news. Standing before David in the farmyard, he said, 'I just thought I'd tell you. The end has come, the bums arrived a while ago. 'Tis a queer business that The House should end like this.'

It was no surprise to David that the bums were in. He remained silent until Shane, looking hard at him said, 'Could you do anything, Davey?' when he answered with a question, 'What would you expect me to do?'

'Nothin'. If justice was to be observed, nothin', 'cos, God himself knows you've had a rotten deal right from the start through him. But . . . but it's her I'm thinkin' about, the mistress. God only knows what she's had to put up with since the child went. He's been like a maniac at times. Yet, I've got to say this word for him, as masters go you couldn't have found much better.'

'As long as you kept your place, eh?'

'Aye, yes, well, I suppose so, as long as I kept me place, as long as we all kept our places. But that's in the scheme of things.'

'Damn the scheme of things! And you know, inside you, you say the same.'

'Perhaps. Aye, you may be right, but looking at you I ask meself, and I say this to your face, Davey, if you had been born into that house would you have acted any differently. It's the way things are.

Money an' position set the standards, they pattern a man's life. Anyway, I thought I'd come and tell you . . .'

'And ask me to go back there and offer to bail him out, is that the idea?'

'Aye, perhaps. Aye, somethin' of the sort.'

'Well, we've met up already this morning, and for your information, Shane, I'll tell you that he ordered me out of the house. I was an intruder trespassing.'

'No.' The word was soft and low.

'Yes, yes. Anyway, there's one thing he and I share and in equal measure, and that's hate. I've always hated the sight of him, and it's never lessened; nor has it in his case, although I don't think he's set eyes on me for years, not since the encounter in the wood when I was a boy; or, for that matter, given me a thought. But he must have seen my father in me in that kitchen there' – he thumbed back over his shoulder – 'for by God! wasn't he startled. That was some satisfaction anyway. No, Shane, I appreciate your motive, but to go back there and have my offer thrown in my face, as it would be, I couldn't attempt it.'

'No, perhaps you're right. It was just a thought.' Shane grinned. 'It's the Irish in me. Me ma used to bring tears to me eyes telling' me of the folks being turned out of their cabins by the agents of them English landlords.' He stressed the words, then added soberly, 'Now it's the landlord's turn an' I'm not cheering . . . When are you proposin' to leave?'

'I've booked my passage for the nineteenth, that's eleven days time. I hope you'll be all settled in by then.'

'Aye. An' you can rely on me. I'll see things are kept shipshape: you'll find everythin' as you expect it even if you arrive on the hop.' He smiled, then added, 'I'll say it, Davey, your buyin' this place has been a godsend to us all, for we'd have been scattered to the four winds, an' most of us have worked together for years, an' you get used to people, like a family, so we're all grateful.'

'How's your mother these days?'

'Oh, pretty fit considerin'. As long as she has her pipe and her porter she'll go on for many a long year. It's funny about families. You know, Davey, a nephew turned up from nowhere the other day. She had forgotten she had him. It was her youngest brother's son, and he had his son with him, a thirteen-year-old lad, and you know something Davey?' Shane now poked his head forward. 'Believe it or not, her nephew is an accountant. Did you hear that? An accountant connected with our family, and he's sendin' his son to a private school. We fell about laughin' after he'd gone. The McLoughlins are surely comin' up. An' you know what his name is, his surname? Flannagan. The McLoughlins an' the Flannagans. Talk about little Ireland.'

David found himself laughing for the first time in days. He had always liked Shane. Shane had been his friend since he had first come into the yard. The others in the stables had just been men, but Shane had been different. He put out his hand to grip Shane's and, still laughing, said, 'Long live the McLoughlins and the Flannagans.'

'Amen to that. Amen to that, Davey.' They nodded at each other. Then, seemingly embarrassed at his emotion, Shane rubbed his hands together as if chaffing corn and said, 'Well, you'll be going straight back to Durham, I suppose.'

'Not yet a while. I brought a hamper over with me, I've got a lunch in there. I'll walk around a bit . . . *around my land.*'

Shane said nothing, but after lowering his head and biting on his lip, he turned away muttering an unintelligible word of farewell.

And David did survey his land. All afternoon he walked through the fields, jumped drystone walls, passed through gates, all known ground to him, until he came to the river. And there, standing on the bank, he stared at the arch of the bridge, the water flowing calmly through it today. He should hate this river. It had taken his father; it had taken his cousin; and, in a way, it had taken his mother, for she had never recovered from the cold she had developed through plunging into the icy water on that fatal day. She had died of consumption, but she had never had consumption until after she had rushed into the river to save him. And it was a fact he had faced a long time ago: she had saved him, for he couldn't have held on much longer, when he too, with the child, would have swept to his death.

He turned and walked along the stretch of the river bank that was now his, until he came to where the brush had been cleared and where the white posts with wire attached denoted the limit of his property. He walked up by the side of this fence which now ran through a belt of trees beyond which the pasture land would start. It was pleasant walking for there was a wind blowing that tangled the branches and caused a singing in the tops of the trees.

He was about to emerge from the woodland and into the light of the open field when he glanced sideways to where, beyond the overgrown pathway, was a mass of brushwood that hid the boles of a number of trees. And he saw what he imagined at first to be a boot sticking out, an old boot.

He had moved forward two or three steps when he stood stock still, turned his head slowly and looked again in the direction of the boot. It wasn't an old boot, the light on it from this angle showed it to be a polished boot.

No, no. The words were deep but quiet in his head.

He didn't move. Again came the words, 'No! no!' Loud now, yelling. Still he didn't move. Something was telling him to walk on and ignore the boot. Something else was saying, Go and look, it mightn't be. Yet, he knew it was. Even before he bent stiffly under the wire and crossed the path and parted the undergrowth, he knew what to expect.

The body was lying on its side. The face was bloody; the hand lying across the breast was bloody. The pistol was lying against his side. 'Oh my God! Oh, God Almighty!' As he stared down on to the shattered form, there swept over him a feeling of aloneness such as he had never experienced in his life before, and he had had plenty of experience of aloneness. But this was so intense, so devastating, for there at his feet lay his one and only relative in this world. He had hated him with a deep abiding hate; but he had been a live thing, something, in a way, part of himself, or he part of it. The same blood running in their veins; no class or legality had been able to wipe out that fact. Oh, God, why hadn't he gone and offered to help.

No, no. That would only have precipitated this just as likely his acquiring the ownership of the farm had done. He turned away and staggered now on to the path, and held his hand to his brow for a moment. Then he was running up the overgrown path, and not stopping until he reached the yard. And there he shouted, 'Shane! Shane! Pollock!'

It was Shane who came from the stables, and David gripped him by the shoulders, crying, 'Get a door! Fetch a door, he's . . . he's dead.' He jerked his head to the side. 'Shot. In the wood.'

'Jesus, Mary and Joseph. No! No!'

'Yes. You'll need another hand. Fetch Robertson quick.'. . .

Before long the three servants were staring down on their master while David stood to one side, now unable to look. Then when they went to place the door near the body it was Pollock who said, ''Tis suicide. D'you think we should touch him? The police should be called.'

Shane looked across at the young fellow in silence for a moment; then, turning to David, he said, 'He's right. Pollock's right. I don't think we should touch anything.' And to David, Shane's words seemed to imply: You found him and it was well known you didn't get on. Pollock's right, although he doesn't know how right.

Shane turned to the groom, saying, 'Go on now, as fast as you can. You might find the constable in the village, he's roundabout there at this time. If not, ride on to Chester-le-Street. But put a move on.'

After Pollock had left, Robertson said quietly, 'Who's to break it to the mistress?' Then both he and Shane looked at David.

But David did not say anything, and Shane said, 'Robertson and me will stay here, if you would, sir.' Not Davey any more, not Mr David even, but sir.

Slowly David turned away and, his step dragging, he made for The House . . .

He was standing before her and, his voice trembling, he muttered, 'There's been an accident. He's in . . . in the wood . . . No, it's no use going.' He put out his hand towards her but didn't touch her, but when he saw the colour drain from her face and heard her whimper, 'Oh, Dennison. Dennison,' he pulled a chair forward and she sank into it and sat staring ahead for a moment; then she asked a question, seemingly of herself when she said, 'Why? Oh, why?'

It was almost two hours later when they brought the body back to The House. David was holding one end of the door on which they had laid it, and his hand was within inches of the mangled head. How strange, he thought, that it was only in death he had become close to his kinsman.

Nor, probably, was the strangeness of the situation lost upon those who waited in the hall.

5

'Suicide while the balance of his mind was disturbed.' Such was the verdict. 'The body had been found by Mr David Mather who had only recently purchased part of the estate.'

That was what the newspapers said. But the villagers and those in the county houses for miles around were now aware of who this Mr Mather was, and the knowledge provoked many to think: Wasn't it a strange coincidence that almost the same day he takes on part of the estate the man whom legally he could have called uncle had taken his own life. And wasn't it more strange still that it should be this young man who had come into a fortune and who, in a way, had come back to flaunt it, should have found the body. Very strange. However, it had been verified as suicide, and that was that. And anyway, some of the wise ones said, what else could Harpcore have done? He wasn't a man who could have earned his own living. And what was more, he was too high-handed and proud to go begging. No, it was indeed the best thing that could have happened. But what about her, his wife?. . .

The fact that Harpcore's suicide meant he would be buried in unconsecrated ground could not have deterred many from attending the burial, for people were there in their hordes: many had come in coaches and cabs, others had walked to the cemetery, the majority out of curiosity.

Nancy Ann had left The House and, with Rebecca and Mary, had taken up abode with her grandmother. There wasn't enough room to take Agnes, but Graham, in his constant kindness, had found a position for her in his overstaffed house, so that she could be near her sister until they could both make up their minds what they wanted to do: Rebecca now had no need of a nursemaid; nor had Nancy Ann of a housekeeper; but she was very definitely at the time in need of a companion and friend. And Mary was both to her. Also, she could in a way, handle Rebecca better than she herself could, as she'd had the early rearing of her.

Rebecca had been attending a private day school in Durham. But on being informed that she must now go to the village school, she had shown some pique, in fact, temper, which was surprising, for, generally, she had been a most obedient child. Mary put it down to what she called, the recent narration, but Nancy Ann saw another source for the change in her daughter's character, and she could date the change from David's arrival. More than once she'd had to check her for the way she spoke to him and for making demands on him. Only yesterday she had asked him if he would take her back to Australia. And he had smiled as he answered her, saying, 'Ask me that question in another five years time.' And at this she had flounced away.

Today was the last day of the sale in The House. Nancy Ann was sitting with her hands resting idly in the lap of her black gown. Jessica sat opposite to her. She was cracking her knuckles: she would put her right hand into a loose fist, push each finger on the left into the tunnel, then grip it and pull. The fingers did not crack every time as they once had done. She would break her bones, she used to say to amuse the boys and her when they were young. Later, she had discovered that her grandmama would often crack her knuckles when she was worried: and apparently she was worried now, for she said, 'Do you think the money from the sale will cover all his debts?'

'No, not anywhere near, Grandmama. The House itself will have to be sold. The sale of that will take place after all the goods have gone.'

'You say that David has stocked the farmhouse up with all the best pieces?'

'Yes, so Graham tells me.'

'Well, I'm glad of that, although I don't think the farm is the kind of setting for French furniture, and there was a lot of that there, wasn't there?'

'Yes, Grandmama.'

'They are dealing with the things outside today, I suppose?'

'Yes, Grandmama.'

'And The House will come up after?'

'Yes, Grandmama.' Oh she wished, she wished she would stop talking about it. Her head was going round and round. She felt ill. Since they had brought Dennison into The House and she had looked down on his shattered face, she had been haunted by the thought that the words he had levelled at her were true that nothing had gone right for him since he had married her and that, in a way, she was to blame for what had overtaken him.

She was feeling very tired. She had the great desire to lie down and sleep: if she could sleep long enough she would wake to find that at least the past five years were forgotten and that she could now start another life. But always the question would yell at her, Who with? Who with? In the small hours of this morning she had lain staring ahead in the comparatively small room upstairs and asking herself if she were on the verge of going mad. Her husband had just died a dreadful death; there was a mountain of business to be seen to, debts from every quarter to be cleared; and yet, she would keep asking herself, with whom would she begin her new life? Yes, she must be on the verge of going mad.

Her grandmama was saying, 'I think I'll go and rest for a little while, dear,' and so she got quickly to her feet in order to help her up, and when, her arm about her grandmama, they reached the sitting-room door, the old woman smiled at her wanly, saying, 'I'm all right, dear. I'm all right. I can manage. I've been managing on my own for a long time now, you must remember. When I need help, there's always the girls.'

It was as if she was being dismissed. She dropped her hand from her grandmama's shoulder and watched her walk steadily across the small hall, then grip the bannister and slowly, one by one, pull herself up the stairs and then for some distance edge her way past the boxes containing their personal belongings now stacked against the landing wall.

There's always the girls. Her presence, and that of Rebecca and Mary, were going to disturb her grandmama. She had lived comparatively on her own for years now and she was happy that way . . . Who shall I start a new life with?

Dear God! There it was again. She must get outside and walk, breathe deeply, try to flood her mind with sanity.

She took a light coat and a straw hat from the wardrobe in the hall, and she donned the coat and pulled on the hat as she hurried outside. She had the desire to run as she had done when a girl, but now it wasn't towards home or in joyful skipping along the river bank, but away, away from everything, everyone.

After walking some distance she wasn't surprised to find herself by the river and quite near the stone where she had first seen David sitting. She wasn't afraid of the river. It had taken her child; and for this she had herself accepted part of the blame; she should have been more watchful of him, knowing how high spirited he was. No, she didn't blame the river, but she did blame God for allowing these things to happen. Her father had instilled into her that God was kind and merciful; everything He did had a purpose behind it, even good came out of evil, you only had to wait long enough. Well, she had known quite a lot of evil of late, but where would the good come out of it?. . . It all depended on whom she would begin her life with.

Oh, dear, dear God. She dropped down on to the stone and bowed her head deeply on to her chest. Please, she prayed now, stop me from thinking this way. Give me peace. Oh, please, give me peace. Oh, please, bring peace into my soul. I don't want to marry anyone. I don't. I don't. This twisted feeling of love inside me is not natural. I am ill. Make me better in my mind. Please, please, God, make me better in my mind. Oh, Papa, speak for me.

How long she sat on the stone she didn't know. An hour? Perhaps more. But when at last she got to her feet, she felt strangely calm. It was as if, in this instance at least, her prayer had been answered. She now turned and walked up through the tangled path, having to push the brambles back here and there, and she was nearing the end of it when she saw the figure hurrying towards her, and her heart jerked in her breast.

She stopped, and he stopped an arm's length from her, and quietly he said, 'Well, it's all done.'

'What? What did The House bring?' Her voice sounded calm.

'It didn't go. Nobody would rise to the price. They were all out for bargains in every way. But the auctioneer saw that they got very few. You will do well out of the sale.'

'The creditors will.'

'Yes, yes, I suppose that's what I mean. I could have bought The House, you know. Yes, I could. But what would I do with it? Burn it down? Yes, I'd like to do that, burn it down. It's an unhappy house. Always has been, and not only in his time, from what I've gathered lately; the supposedly ideal marriage between his parents was a sham too. You're well out of it.'

She began to walk on, and he, suiting his step to hers, walked by her side, his hands behind his back. And, looking ahead, he said, 'Well, the farm is all ready for you.'

'What!' She jerked her head towards him.

'The farmhouse. Most of your stuff is there and all the furniture that it would take, from the drawing-room and dining-room to kitchen ware.'

She stopped, and they faced each other again, and she said, 'Do you think I would go and live there? Is that why you've done this?'

'Yes, I think you will go and live there, and that's why I've done this.'

'Then' – she shook her head slowly – 'you're suffering under a delusion. I couldn't possibly go and live in that house. You know that.'

'How do I know that?' His face looked grim. 'What's to stop you going to live there? I'll be gone next week. I've outstayed my visit by a month just so that I could see you settled there.'

'Oh, David.' Her voice was low now and sad. 'You must have known, under the circumstances, I couldn't have accepted such an offer from you. I'm already in debt to so many people.'

'But you don't want to be in debt to me? If you look at it that way, I'll sign the place over to you tomorrow.'

She closed her eyes and put her hand tightly across them now, muttering, 'Stop it! Stop it!'

Her hand was pulled roughly away from her face and his came close to hers and in a hoarse whisper he said, 'A few weeks ago you said words to me, "If you love me, do what I ask. Please go." You said that, didn't you, because you knew I loved you? I've always loved you. Now I'm asking you something. Do you love me?'

She gave a shudder and pulled herself from his grasp and, stepping back from him, she stared at him, her mouth opening and shutting like a fish's before she could stammer, 'I . . . I am eight years or more older than you, I . . . I've looked upon you as I might a s . . . son.'

'Don't talk rot.' He flashed his hand between them now, his little finger tweeking her nose in the process, causing her head to jerk back. 'That was when you were a girl and I was a boy. I've thought of nobody but you for years. Do you know something? Women chase me. Yes, they chase me. Mothers with marriageable daughters hound me. Even the short time I've been in Durham I've had visitors, even a county lady or two. Can you believe that? Money talks; it can even cover bastardy. But every woman I look at, every girl I see, has your face, your manner, your voice, everything about you. But I know there is somebody else in the running. I've known that for a long time. He's a good man and I like him, but not for you. When I think of him having you I could hate him as much as I hated him that's gone. Do you love Mercer?'

She felt she was going to cry and was forbidding herself to do so. She wanted to sink to the ground. She wanted to rest. The tired feeling was on her again. She heard her voice saying limply, 'I don't love anyone at the moment. No one. You . . . you forget, my husband has just died . . .'

'Oh, don't be a hypocrite. What feelings you had for him died years ago, and Mercer stepped in. And he is sure to ask you to marry him, love or no love. What will you say? Tell me, tell me truthfully, what will you say?'

She opened her eyes wide as if to get him into focus. He looked beautiful. His hair was the colour of the sun. He was the most handsome man she had seen in years, or had ever seen, and he was young. Youth emanated from him. What was he? Twenty? Twenty-one? And she? Nearly twenty-nine. Soon she would be in her thirties and it would be a tired thirties, because oh, she was so tired, so tired of everything. But he, he would still be vibrating with youth. There would be no peace for her when near him; his very youth and energy would make demands on her that she wouldn't be able to meet. Whereas Graham, Graham with his tenderness, his consideration; Graham with his love that had been tried over the years; Graham had to have something for his loyalty, something for his kindness. And besides gratitude, she really did love him. Yes, she loved Graham.

Simply now, she answered, 'I shall say yes to him, David. He has earned my love and respect for years now. But I will say this to you. Yes, I do love you, but in a different way. And if you really love me you would not want to marry me, for marriage with you would bring me no peace. The gap in our ages is too wide; our outlooks are so different. And everything that has happened over the years has already created a gulf that neither of us can really step over.'

She watched his face tighten; she watched his whole body stiffen; and she pleaded now, 'Please, don't be bitter. And for all your thoughtfulness with regard to the farmhouse, I'll never forget your kindness. What . . . what will you do with it now?'

It was some time before he answered her. The tan of his face had paled, his eyes had darkened, they looked almost black; he wetted his lips a number of times before he said, 'What will I do with it?' His voice rose higher. 'Leave it as it is. I'll come back every now and again. Who knows, I might even settle here in my old age. And, on one of my visits, should The House still be empty, I might buy it and wait for Guy Fawkes night and have one big splendid bonfire.'

She turned her head to the side and drew her lips tight between her teeth before she murmured, 'Oh, David,' and he repeated scornfully, 'Oh, David.' But then he demanded, 'And what would you say if, in five years time when she's sixteen, I decide to marry your daughter? She'll be willing enough; she's had an affection for me since she was a tot. And you heard what she said yesterday, she wants to come back with me to Australia. So, my dear *old lady*, what would you say to that?'

'Goodbye, David.' She half turned away, and he cried at her, 'I mean it. I mean that, mind.'

She took no heed but walked on; and then she found herself dragged round with his arms about her and his mouth on hers, and she was being kissed as even Dennison in the height of his passion had never kissed her. When it was over she staggered back from him, her mouth open, dragging in air to prevent herself from choking. Then, gripping the front of her skirt, she pulled it up and ran now as swiftly as when she was a young girl along the path and away from him. And she didn't stop until she reached the gate leading into Graham's estate. Once through it, she still ran until she was well within the shadow of the trees, and there she sank down by a broad bole and, leaning her head against it, she gave vent to a paroxysm of weeping.

And it was here, sometime later, that Graham came across her and, having gently lifted her up, he led her as gently back to the house, thinking that she had been overcome by all the turmoil and worry of the past days.

6

She'd had no word from David since he had returned to Australia, but the newspapers were prophesying a gold rush in the place where he lived, Kalgoorlie.

Life, she was finding, was not easy. The Dower House, as her grandmama said, housed so many people now that they were falling over each other. Rebecca, too, was proving more of a problem every day. She had taken into her head to pay uninvited visits to the farmhouse, and often Mary would have to go in search of her and would find her installed as if she owned the place. Apparently, too, she had got into the habit of giving orders to the staff, and when these weren't obeyed she would get into a tantrum and say she would write and tell David.

This information Mary tactfully gave to Nancy Ann because, as she said, something had to be done and she wasn't in a position to take the matter into her own hands.

When Nancy Ann forbad Rebecca to go to the farmhouse on her own, the girl retorted, 'David said I could. He said I had to keep an eye on it.'

'David said nothing of the sort. You're lying.'

And to this, Rebecca had come back, 'He indicated as much, because he said we were going to live there. After Papa died he said we were going to live there.'

Very likely he had. But what she said to her daughter was, 'Well, we're not living there and you're not to go unless accompanied by Mary or myself.'

'But you don't go there,' the girl had replied.

That was true; she didn't go there.

For weeks now she'd had the urge to get away, not only from this house, but from the confines of both estates, out in the open, as she put it. To this end, she had taken to walking to the village; she could do this now for the tradesmen's bills had been met, at least in most part. But even this outlet had been checked recently on a suggestion from Shane McLoughlin. Shane had actually made it his business to come to the house this day and to ask if he could speak to her. And he had begun, 'I'm sure you'll pardon me, ma'am, but it's about your little walk to the village. There's . . . well, there's been one or two incidents lately, quite unpleasant, and I would be careful if I were you for the time bein'.'

'What kind of incidents, Shane?' she had asked.

'Oh.' He had seemed reluctant to explain the nature of the incidents but said, 'Well, not pleasant things. And unless you have somebody with you, Mr Mercer or one of the stable lads, well, I don't think it would be wise, not for the present anyway, to do any jauntin'.'

She was puzzled. She had not heard of any incidents happening on the road between here and the village. And only last week she had been in the grocer's-cum-post office-cum-general stores, and Miss Waters the dressmaker was present and if there was any gossip going she was the one to spread it around: tragedies large and small were meat and drink to Miss Waters.

However, she had thanked Shane and said she would be careful.

But there came the day that Rebecca did not return from school at her appointed time. There were two roads to the school. One along the main coach road and through the village, and the other by a lane that branched off the coach road and ended at a field gate over which you had to climb because it had been padlocked for years, ever since some cattle had escaped through it and along the path and on to the coach road, and there caused havoc when meeting the horse-drawn post van head on, resulting in a dead cow, an injured horse, a post van on its side in a ditch, the driver with a broken leg.

So on this early evening of a day that had been very hot and was still warm and soft, she did not bother to put a dust jacket over her grey spotted voile dress, with the black waistband proclaiming she was still in mourning, but pulled on a light straw hat and made her way through the bottom of the garden, so avoiding coming within sight of the Manor House, and through a small wicket gate and on to the coach road. It was only a five minutes' walk to where the path that afforded the short cut branched off from the roadway, and she was within a few yards of it when she saw the landau approaching. But she took no notice – carriages were frequent sights on this road – but after she had turned into the side road and then heard the landau being driven from the main road into it, she did take notice.

What did a landau want on this narrow strip of road? It was a dead end, and the only place for it to turn would be near the gate, and it would have a hard job to do it there.

She stepped on to the grass sward at the side of the path and, as she did so, turned to look back, and experienced a feeling of fright like that which a child might at being faced with something goulish. And within seconds the fright turned into actual fear, for the landau had stopped, and there was a woman glaring at her; and still glaring, she thrust open the door of the landau and tottered down the step and towards her. One of the coachmen had alighted and was saying, 'Careful, madam. Careful.'

'I'll be careful, Hawkins, I'll be careful. Look at her, the white-livered bitch.'

The woman's drunken breath was wafting over her now and she pushed her hands out to ward her off, saying, 'Get out of my way. Let me pass.'

'Oh, aye. I'll let you pass, my pious prig, after I've dealt with you. You finished him, didn't you? You killed him. If you had just let a bit of him go, he'd be alive today. But no, you had to have him all, you mealy-mouthed vicarage bitch, you. You once stripped me, didn't you? Well, now it's my turn. Yes, 'tis. Oh yes, 'tis . . . my turn!'

Before she knew what was happening the fat body had hurled itself upon her and they were both borne to the ground. And now she was back in her young days, fighting with the McLoughlins but with a difference, for now she was trying to save her clothes from being torn from her back. Then she screamed as her hair seemed to leave her scalp.

There was a chorus of voices: the woman crying, 'Hold her legs, Hawkins. Hold her legs!' and another voice yelling, 'You do and I'll bash your face in.'

A knee came in her stomach and for a moment everything went black.

When she came to herself it was to the sound of tearing and she knew there was air on her flesh. When a fist landed in her eye she cried aloud and groaned, and she heard herself pleading, 'Please. Please.' There was no resistance in her arms now. Then the weight of the knee on her stomach was lifted from her and a voice yelled, 'Leave her be, you dirty drunken scab!'

And another voice cried, 'Get up on the box unless you want to lose your job.' And then the woman's voice, screaming, 'Yes, do as Hawkins says, or you will lose your job.'

'I've lost it, missis. You've sickened me belly for a long time now but this is the finish. I'd rather work for a whorehouse madam, than touch your bread again. You're a drunken slut, that's what you are.' And the man spat in her direction.

'Hit him! Hit him, Hawkins!' the fat woman demanded and, swaying, clambered her way back to the landau.

But all Hawkins did was to put his hands on her fat buttocks and heave her up to her seat, then bang the door shut and mount the box and drive towards the gate.

Jim McLoughlin stood looking down at the almost bare body of the young vicarage lass, as he still thought of their Shane's mistress; her clothes were lying in ribbons around her. Quickly he gathered them up and placed them over her middle. And when a few minutes later, the landau passed them again he made a sign with his hand to his late mistress that caused her to turn in the seat and yell some obscenity back at him.

Returning to Nancy Ann, he raised her head, saying, 'Are you all right, madam? Are you all right?' But receiving no reply, he stood up and looked around him. If she could have walked he could have helped her, but he had no hope of carrying her. He knew he must get help. But how could he leave her like this?

Bending down, he rearranged the torn clothes about her middle and legs. Then, taking off his short jacket, he covered her naked breasts and shoulders with it. Looking up, then down the roadway, he wondered what he should do. His first thought was to get his brother; but that would mean going to the farmhouse and twice the distance from the Manor.

With one last look down on the still figure that appeared now like a bundle of rags, he sprinted back up the side road and on to the coach road, and the half mile along it to the lodge gates of the Manor. The small side gate was open, and he ran through and, receiving no response to his battering on the lodge door, he continued his dash up the drive and into the yard, yelling as he did so. 'I want help! Help!' This time and almost simultaneously, three men appeared, two from the stables and one from the house, and one of the men from the stables was his brother Mick.

Graham had been about to set out to pay his daily visit to the Dower House. But now he hurried to the man, calling, 'What is it? What is it?

'Miss . . . madam, she . . . she was attacked.'

'Attacked? What do you mean attacked? Who?'

'Madam, Mrs Harpcore, along the road, the fat one that I work for. She stopped the landau; been on the lookout for her for days. She stripped her. I've left her lying . . . Come on!'

'My God!' Graham was running now, but Mick called after him, 'Better bring a cover or somethin', sir, a shawl, a blanket.'

At this, the other man dashed into a room next to the stables and came out carrying a couple of blankets. Then the four of them were running down the drive . . .

Nancy Ann hadn't moved. Nothing mattered. She wasn't unconscious, but she knew that she was going into a deep sleep and that was good; she would get away, get away from everything.

She heard a voice saying, 'Oh, my dear, my dear. Someone will pay for this. Oh, yes, they'll pay for this. That dirty creature, that madwoman.'

Then there were voices above her as if in discussion, and the sound of feet running away. And now there was that Irish voice, one of the McLoughlins. She would know that voice anywhere, and he was talking to Graham, saying, 'I couldn't stand it. She's been out lookin' for her for weeks now. But I thought she would just have her say and that would be that, and it would satisfy her. She's never been sober for God knows how long; the cure last year was no cure. She'll end up in an asylum, that one.'

'She'll end up in jail if I have anything to do with it.'

She had never heard that tone in Graham's voice, before. She wished they would stop talking, she just wanted to go to sleep.

And then, when they lifted her quite gently, the rocking of the carriage gave her her wish and she knew nothing for a long time after . . . A countless time.

7

They had not carried Nancy Ann to the Dower House, for Graham had ordered her to be taken to the Manor. And there, she had lain for a week oblivious of where she was or what was going on.

Graham, determined in his way to bring the perpetrator of the outrage to justice, had informed the police. And this must have hastened the visit from Mr Poulter Myers himself, apologizing profoundly and saying that his wife had been admitted to a clinic for a cure.

So rumours abounded again. Wasn't it strange, people said, that the ill-luck of The House had seemed to follow her.

Mary and Rebecca, too, had taken up their abode in the Manor, and a new kind of life and routine had begun. Graham gave Rebecca a pony, much to her delight, and after a time she rode to school on it, and through it made friends with some of the children from whom she had kept aloof and they from her.

Mary was happy to be working in a big house once more. Admittedly it wasn't half as big as Rossburn, but it was more beautiful, more confortable, and had an atmosphere of warmth about it.

It was a full four weeks before Nancy Ann showed signs of really being fully aware of her surroundings. And when the realization came that she was being cared for in Graham's house, she did not protest, but continued to lie day after day on a chaise-longue at the window of the bedroom looking out on the gardens below, for it seemed that at last her mind was at peace. She could look back on the events of the past five years and feel no bitterness, no pain. The emotion she retained for Dennison was pity, and even when the recent past came up and her thoughts touched on David, they were calm. She saw his love as that of an impressionable young man for an older woman, and the feeling she had had for him as having been bred of his admiration for her, a form of vanity.

But that was all in the past now. Even the attack by that dreadful woman she saw as something that had to take place for the woman to expunge the hate she felt for her. And now there was only Graham, dear, dear Graham, kind and loving Graham. If only she had married Graham in the first place. If only. If only . . .

Three weeks later Graham accompanied her and Mary to Harrogate and saw her settled into a comfortable hotel, and on each of the following four week-ends he visited them; then on the fifth week-end, when he had arrived to accompany her back home, she said to him, 'I must return to the Dower House, Graham.'

They were sitting on the couch in her private sitting-room, and quite firmly he answered, 'You are not returning to the Dower House. There's not enough room for you all there, and what's more' – he smiled – 'I must tell you, your grandmama is much happier to have the house to herself.'

She was already aware of this, but she insisted quietly, 'It . . . it wouldn't be right for me to stay on, I mean, to impose any longer.'

'Don't talk nonsense, Nancy Ann.' He turned to her now and, gripping her hands, repeated, 'Don't talk nonsense. You are never going back to the Dower House. We are going to be married, aren't we? And I'm not going to apologize in a mealy-mouthed way by saying I am speaking too soon after your bereavement.' He jerked himself nearer to her and held her hands tightly against his breast, and his deep brown eyes alight with the suppressed emotion of years, he said thickly, 'You know I love you and have done for years. At times it's been torment, seeing you so unhappy and being unable to do anything about it. But now I may, and I can. You . . . you do care for me a little, don't you?'

'Oh, Graham, Graham, yes, I care for you, very deeply.' And she could say this in all truth.

When he put his arms about her and kissed her for the first time, she had a flashing memory of another kiss when the breath had been taken from her body, but it was only a flashing memory. And then she was responding to his embrace and in doing so she knew she was setting the seal on a life of peace and security, tenderness and caring. And what more could anyone wish for in this life?

Three months later she was married. The wedding was a quiet affair, only personal friends and the staff attended. She was not married this time in the village church, but at Saint Saviour's in the next parish. Thirty people were at the reception. And when later, they all crowded round the coach that was to take them to the station, the last person she kissed and with deep affection was not Pat, nor her grandmama, but Mary, and she whispered, 'Look after her, won't you?' And Mary, tears in her eyes, said, 'Don't you worry, my dear. I'll see to her.'

It was when all the guests had gone and Agnes and Mary were in the main bedroom tidying up that Agnes stopped and, looking out of the window, said, ''Tis just as well. She'll be happy in a way. The other wouldn't have worked out.'

'What did you say?'

Mary pushed a drawer in, straightened her back, then said again, 'What did you say, our Agnes?'

Agnes turned from the window and answered, 'With Davey. It wouldn't have worked out.'

'What d'you mean, with Davey?'

'Oh, you know what I mean; don't play innocent, it's your Agnes you're lookin' at. You know for a fact there was something there, more than something. What d'you think he bought the farm for? You know very well he expected her to go and live there.'

Mary sighed now and said, 'You know more than is good for you. But I'm tellin' you, our Agnes' – she turned now and wagged her finger at her sister – 'don't you breathe a word of what you're thinking outside this room.'

'I'm not daft altogether.'

'No, not altogether, just a bit.'

They grinned at each other, then laughed. Then it was Mary who said, 'But you're right, it would never have worked out. I was worried to death at one time wondering what he would get up to. Anyway, that's been nipped well and good in the bud. What she wants after what she's gone through is a peaceful life, not a mad romantic fling like he would have offered her.'

'You're right. Oh, yes, you're right. But . . . but he has turned into a handsome fellow, hasn't he? My! just to look at him did something to your guts. An' wouldn't I have just loved a mad romantic fling with some like man.'

'*Our Agnes!*'

At this Agnes turned from the window again and exclaimed in an equally loud voice, '*Our Mary!*' Then having the final word, she added, 'What d'you think will happen when he comes back?'

'What can happen? Nothing. It's all signed and sealed, she's a married woman again.'

8

Nancy Ann had been married about eighteen months when word came that David had returned.

It had been a peaceful time, a happy time. Graham was a loving and tender husband. The feeling she'd had for him had deepened from day to day, and his love and care encased her. She felt secure and happy as she had never done in her life before. Even in those early days before she married her happiness was deep inside her; it was a peaceful happiness, like floating on a calm sea. But a sea doesn't remain calm forever and now and again there had been a ripple caused by Rebecca.

Rebecca was jealous of the attention her mother paid to her new husband; in fact, she did not really like Graham, and this dislike was made evident in spurts of peevishness and temper. She had grown rapidly during the past two years; she was now twelve but could easily be taken for a girl of fourteen or more. She was mad on riding but objected to being accompanied by any of Graham's men, even by Mick who had taught her to ride. Whenever she could make her way unobserved from the house or yard, she went over to the farmhouse on foot or on horseback, for over the past six months there had been an added attraction there in Shane's nephew. Dennis Flannagan had become very attached to his uncle and spent most of his time with him during his holidays and odd week-ends. He was a boy of fifteen with dark hair, deep brown eyes, a laughing mouth like his uncle's, and a sturdy athletic body. He, too, had a passion for riding.

In her childish way Rebecca had also taken a dislike to Shane and Robertson, because Shane had forbidden his nephew to accompany her into the farmhouse and Robertson had strongly endorsed this order. In fact, Robertson, at times, had told her that it was inconvenient for her to be in the house as she got in the way of the maids.

On this particular day when she pushed the front door open and walked in, she was brought to a halt and an open-mouthed gape when she saw the man coming down the shallow staircase. It was

David. Yet it wasn't David. This man looked larger, his skin was deeply tanned, and his hair looked almost white, so light it was. Then, when he reached the bottom of the stairs and said, 'Hello, there,' she answered, 'Hello. Then . . . then you've come back?' She did not fly to him and throw her arms about him as she had been wont to do, and when he said, 'Well, if this isn't me, I'm haunting the house,' she asked, 'When . . . when did you come?'

'Last night.'

'Oh, how lovely to see you.' Now she did spring towards him and throw her arms about him; but then immediately felt nonplussed when, his hand patting her head, he said, 'Well now, well now, I thought I was being greeted by a young lady, not a little girl any more.'

Something in his voice made her loosen her hold on him, and she stepped back and gazed up into his face. And the thought that entered her mind was, He's different, different from the last time. And she was on the point of saying, What have you brought me? when she realized he had said she was no longer a child. And that was true; as her great-grandmama was always saying to her, she was at an age when she must mind her manners. And so she said, 'How long are you here for this time?'

He moved from her across the small hall and towards the sitting-room as he said, 'That depends. I have a little business to do.'

Tentatively now, she followed him. There was something strange about him. She felt slightly afraid of him, and that was silly. David was hers. He had always been hers. She hurried now to his side and said, 'You know that Mama is married and we're living at the Manor House?'

He did not answer her until he reached the middle of the room and there, turning and looking down on her, he said, 'Yes, I am aware that your mama is married and that you are living in the Manor House.'

His voice was stiff, and then he smiled and his teeth looked very white in his tanned face as he said, 'Marriages are in the air. I, too, am to be married shortly.'

'What!'

'What! Young ladies don't say, What! You heard what I said: I, too, am to be married shortly.'

'Married?'

'Yes, that's what I said, married.'

She blinked at him; then in a small voice she said, 'Is . . . is she from Australia?'

'No, no.' He shook his head, still smiling, 'She's an English lady.'

An English lady. She did not say the words aloud. But the term made her feel very small, a little girl again.

There was a tap on the door and it opened and Robertson stood there, saying, 'The cab has arrived, sir.'

As David turned and said, 'Thank you. I'll be there in a moment,' it came to her that Robertson had been their servant, and this man standing in front of her giving orders had been a servant, although in an odd way he was a relation. For some strange reason she felt a desire to cry. Then she looked to where he was halting Robertson's departure by saying, 'Henry, I'm expecting two ladies for dinner tonight: A Mrs Dawson Maitland and her daughter. If I'm not back in time, make them comfortable. There will also be a Mr Benedict; but he'll likely return with me. Ask cook to put on something good.'

'I'll do that, sir. Yes, I'll do that.'

'Well now – ' He turned towards her, saying, 'I must be off; I've a great deal of business to get through.'

Her voice was merely a whisper as she said, 'Are you going to live here?'

'Here?' He pointed his finger towards the floor, then said, 'Well yes, partly I suppose, but I'll still have to spend some time in Kalgoorlie, although my fiancée doesn't care much for Kalgoorlie, what little she has seen of it.' He now looked around the room, saying, 'Yes, yes, we'll settle here for a time until I find a nice little estate, or a large one.' He pursed his lips now. 'It all depends on what takes my fancy. Well, now, I really must be off. Give my regards to your mother. I hope she is well.'

'Yes, she is very well.' Then she did not know what made her stress the last words for, looking up at him, her face straight, she added, '*Very well.*'

'That is good to hear.'

They were in the hall now and Robertson was helping him into his coat. Then they were in the yard and there was the cab with the cabbie standing holding the door open. She did not walk with him to the cab but stood in the middle of the yard. And as he was about to step into the vehicle, he turned and looked at her, and smiled. Then the door closed on him, the cabbie got on the box and drove away.

She stood where she was, feeling dazed. When she turned round towards the house the front door was closed, and she took it as a sort of symbol and she said to herself, 'I'll never go in there again. Never. Never. Never.'

She was running straight along the path towards the house that had once been her home, which now stood like a ghost house, empty, alone, deserted. She dashed into the yard, where the grass was growing up between the stone slabs, then through the archway, and through the overgrown gardens to the gate that led to home. And for the first time she thought of Mr Mercer's house as home. And it was him she ran into at the top of the lawn as she sped from the trees.

And when he caught her and looked down and into her streaming face, he said, 'What is it, my dear? What is it?'

'Oh. Oh, Mr Mercer.' She always gave him his title. She now leant her head against him and he put his arms about her and said, 'There, there. What has happened? Tell me.'

'I . . . I want Mama. Where is she? Where is Mama?'

'I've just left her; she's in the conservatory. Go along, you'll likely find her still there.'

She disengaged herself from him and nodded at him, then was running again.

Nancy Ann was watering plants when she found herself almost toppled over as Rebecca threw herself into her arms, causing the small watering can to drop to the ground.

'What is it? What is it, my dear? What's happened?'

'Oh, Mama. Mama.'

'Come. Come.' Nancy Ann led her to a white wrought iron seat at the end of the conservatory and, pressing her down, she said, 'Tell me, what's upset you? Come along, now, stop that crying.' And she stroked Rebecca's hair from her face the while thinking, It's that boy. They've had a tiff. She's likely found him riding with someone else. Dear, dear.

'He's back. He's come back . . . David.'

Nancy Ann's body stiffened and became cold for a moment, but her voice sounded calm as she said, 'Well, he was bound to come at some time, that's his home now.'

'But . . . but he's changed, different. He . . . he's not nice, Mama.'

'Not nice? What do you mean, not nice?'

The girl shook her head and she just stopped herself from saying something awful, which would have been, He was like Papa, Mama; instead, she said, 'He looks different. He was nasty to me.'

'Nasty? Now, now; explain yourself.'

'Oh.' Rebecca pressed her head against her mother's breast and muttered through her tears, 'He was just nasty. He's going to be married, and they are coming to dinner tonight, a lady and her daughter. He gave the order to Robertson before he went off. He . . . he was going in to Newcastle. I don't like him any more. I don't. I don't. I don't.'

Nancy Ann's hand became still on her daughter's hair. He was going to be married. Well, wasn't that the best thing? Yes, yes of course. But how would she react when he broke the news to her? Especially if he used the high-handed manner he had obviously taken with Rebecca. He had once said he would come back and marry Rebecca. Well, that was one thing she had to be thankful for. It had remained a secret dread in her that he would do just that. He was capable of it.

The door opened and Graham came in, saying, 'What is the trouble?'

She pressed Rebecca from her and, her manner taking on a lightness, she said, 'David is back, and apparently he is a much changed individual, by what Rebecca tells me. And also, he's going to be married, she says.'

'Oh. Oh.' He pulled a long mouth, and gave her a sly smile as if he understood the situation. Then he looked to where Rebecca had turned herself towards the corner of the seat, her head resting on the end of it, and thinking to throw oil on to the troubled waters of a young passion, he said, 'Well, he is an oldish man, isn't he, and it's about time he married. How old is he, my dear?'

Before Nancy Ann could force herself to answer in the same vein as her husband's playful mood, Rebecca swung round, crying, 'He is not old. He is no older to me than you are to Mama.'

'Yes, yes. Well, you're right there, my dear.' His voice took on a soothing note. And now addressing Nancy Ann, he said, 'I was thinking this morning about Harrogate again, and that now the school holiday had begun, I thought it would be nice if you two could go for a jaunt. It's such a refreshing place, Harrogate, and there's so much to do. Well, what about it?'

Nancy Ann grabbed eagerly at the suggestion, saying, 'Oh, I should love that. And I think it's time Rebecca had some new clothes, more fashionable ones.'

She turned to her daughter now, saying, 'You're growing out of your present dresses at such a rate that . . . that you will soon be showing your knees.' She laughed a forced laugh, which was cut off by her daughter jumping up from the seat and crying, 'I don't want to go to Harrogate. I won't be able to ride.'

'Of course you will. Of course you will.'

'No, I won't, Mama. And now the holidays are here I want to ride. I want to ride every day. I don't want to go to Harrogate. I don't. I don't.'

'Now stop that! And stop it immediately. Whether you like it or not, we are going to Harrogate. That's all that has to be said.'

With that, Nancy Ann turned from her daughter, while giving Graham a silent signal to follow her, and she didn't speak until they were both in the privacy of the bedroom. And then, turning to him, she said, 'We'll . . . we'll go tomorrow.'

'As soon as that?'

'Oh, I'm sorry. It . . . it isn't that I want to leave you, or here, you know that.'

She was within the circle of his arms when he replied quietly, 'I know that, my dear, I know that. And I know the reason you are going, why you want to get her away. She's been much too fond of that gentleman for years. He was a nice enough boy when he was a boy, and as a youngster I liked him, but I can't say that I'm fond of the man, at least, of the man I saw a couple of years ago. There was an arrogance about him that annoyed me, to say the least. And he was very fond of you, too, you know.' He moved his head slowly up and down. 'Rather possessive of you. I noticed that too. He acted as if you belonged to him. It was as if the blood tie was between you and him, and not Harpcore.' Whenever he mentioned Dennison, he always referred to him as Harpcore. And he ended, 'Somehow, it isn't as if his wealth has altered his character very much at all. As I see it, he felt he belonged to that house and acted likewise. Anyway' – he tossed his head now – 'I'm due for a holiday too, aren't I? We'll all go to Harrogate.' Then, his voice becoming sober, he added, 'You know, it's only since you came into my life, really into my life, that I could think of leaving this place for more than a few days at a time, because it was the only life I had. But now, I have a wonderful, wonderful life, with a wonderful, wonderful, wonderful, wife.'

When his lips fell on her, she returned his kiss, thinking, Yes, so have I, so have I. And I must cherish it. Yes, I must cherish it and appreciate it. But the quicker they got to Harrogate the better, for when they returned, *he* would be gone.

The visit to Harrogate turned out to be a success, particularly in Rebecca's case. She rode in the morning, grumbling at first because it was only for an hour; but accepted this when the afternoons turned out to be exciting with shopping, then tea at the Spa, or in a fashionable restaurant, and then on three evenings a week they attended either the theatre or a concert.

With regard to the shopping, Nancy Ann received a very generous dress allowance from Graham, and so she indulged her daughter, if not herself, in the dress departments. Graham had been with them for the first fortnight, but not relishing hotel life, he returned home, and for the next three weeks visited them at the week-end.

They were due to leave on the Saturday, and he arrived on the Friday night. After their first warm greeting Nancy Ann realized that he was disturbed. They were alone together when tentatively, she said, 'Is something wrong, dear? Something worrying you?'

'Yes, you could say something is wrong and is worrying me,' he answered her, 'but only with regard to how it will affect you. It . . . it concerns the house.'

'Rossburn, you mean?'

'Yes.'

'What about it?'

'Well' – he took her hand and drew her down on to the window seat of the bedroom – 'what I can gather from Brundle, who's gathered it from Mick who heard it from his brother Shane, Mather had bought the house some time ago. No wonder we couldn't understand its not being sold.' There was a slight note of annoyance in his voice now as he went on, 'Apparently, he was comparatively rich before the gold rush in the Kalgoorlie district, but now, as far as I can understand, he's a millionaire twice over, and he spends money like water. But it's always the way with the newly rich, they have no values.'

He was indeed annoyed. Her voice had a soothing note in it as she said, 'Well, perhaps, he intends to put it to some good use.'

'Good use? My dear, he is having it pulled down.'

'What?'

He nodded at her. 'Just what I said, pulled down. I couldn't believe it. In fact, I went straight away. Apparently his *lordship* had departed back to Australia sometime previously, together with his fiancée, I'm told. But he had engaged a contractor to level the whole place. I spoke to the man himself. The tiles were already off. It was a sorry sight. I felt . . . well, really, my dear, I just don't know how I felt. If it had been my own place I couldn't have felt worse at that moment. The man himself said it was a da . . . shame, and went on to list all the ways in which it could have been used, some of which, of course, because the house is so near to us, would have been unwelcome. Yet, I had to agree with him. But no, it has to be levelled. He may sell, this is what the man said to me, he may sell what he can, such as panelling, doors, and the paintings from the drawing-room ceiling, if he can get them down whole. There's one thing he was firmly instructed he had to keep and place in the farm barn, likely for shipment to Australia. And do you know what that is?'

She made a small motion with her head, while all the time inside she was saying, Oh, David. Oh, David.

'A sloping beam from the far end of the roof, a truss, the man called it. He said it's about twelve feet long. One end rests on the wall and forms part of the eaves; the beam slopes up to a height of about four feet at the apex of the room. The man said it has carvings on it roughly hacked out here and there and drawings in coloured crayons. It's something, he said, one would see in a nursery, like the scribblings of a child. But this is at the extreme end of a roof, not in the attics proper.'

Oh, David. David.

'Can you understand it?'

Yes, yes, she could understand it. Oh, she could understand it all right. That corner had been his home for so long. Very likely his harness had been attached to that beam. Oh, she could understand it all right.

'You are upset. I knew you would be.'

'No, no. In a way, Graham, I can understand his action.'

'You can? Well, I certainly can't.' He rose from the seat and walked towards the middle of the room. 'It is sheer wanton destruction. The exterior might have been stylized, but it was a splendid house, beautifully built. And that drawing-room was magnificent. I think it's a sacrilege.'

'He . . . he suffered in that house, Graham.'

He turned on her almost roughly now and exclaimed loudly, 'Suffered? He was damn lucky under the circumstances to be allowed to stay there. No matter what my opinion of Harpcore was, I admired him for taking on the responsibility of that boy.'

She too was on her feet. 'He took no responsibility, Graham. You . . . you don't know anything about it and his life there. He . . . he was treated like an animal. It wasn't natural; he hadn't any liberty at all. That beam he wants is the one he was tied to. He wouldn't have been treated so in an asylum.'

'Oh, my dear, my dear.' He was holding her by the shoulders now, repeating, 'My dear, my dear, don't upset yourself so. I . . . I didn't look at it that way. Forgive me. Forgive me.'

She found she had to take in some deep breaths to stop the tears from starting, but as she stared at her husband's kindly and concerned countenance, she thought, They are all of a pattern underneath, these men who have been bred to think of themselves as landed gentry. Their opinions on most things might be diverse, but when it came to class and the division between the servant and the master, there they stood firmly together.

He was talking rapidly, soothingly now. 'I know you have always been concerned for the boy and I wasn't aware that he had been . . .' he seemed to search for a word; he couldn't say humiliated as his mind suggested, but added, 'treated so roughly. Anyway, you have got to be prepared, my dear, to see merely a piece of land where once your home stood.'

A slight shudder passed through her. 'It was never my home, Graham,' she said. 'It was as much my prison during the last five years I lived there as it had been David's from the day he was born. And . . . and don't worry' – she gently touched his cheek – 'don't be so concerned for me, please. But I know one thing: he had to do this to try to expunge his feelings and the memories of his treatment, although I'm sure they will be with him until the day he dies. You know yourself, Graham, that those early years of environment remain with you always. I can't forget how happy my childhood days were in the vicarage. You, I am sure, have wonderful memories of your early days too.'

She did not probe, nor ever had probed into the years preceding his being jilted; and so she went on, 'You can see, at least I can, how those years under the roof must have affected that boy, and the man he is now cannot forget them.'

'You were very fond of him, weren't you? I . . . I mean as a boy.'

It was some seconds before she answered, 'Yes, I was very fond of him.' Then she forced herself to utter the next words to allay any suspicion that he might be harbouring in his mind. 'He . . . he looked upon me, in a way, as his mother. More so, after I was the means of sending him to school. But there' – she smiled – 'one thing I must tell you, and that is, I can't wait to get home. In fact, I've been very impatient for the past week or more for your coming.'

'Oh, my dear, dear Nancy Ann. How it does my heart good to hear you say that, because at times I wonder if you are happy.'

'Oh, never doubt that I am, I am. Life now is like heaven . . . the vicarage transported.'

At this they both laughed and clung to each other, and as he kissed her, she thought, And that is true. Then, as if she were indeed transported back to those days in the vicarage when she would ask herself funny questions, especially in church, she wondered now if angels in heaven were as happy as they were supposed to be.

9

After arriving home she had made up her mind not to go and view the destruction of The House, nor to enter the grounds again.

Life reassumed its normal pattern and sometimes she found herself slightly bored, because the household ran on such well-oiled wheels. They had visitors, but not a great many. Pat and George called in at least once a week and often stayed for a meal. But she and Graham rarely made a return visit. Graham did not take to visiting. He preferred their evenings by the fire when she did her embroidery or played the piano and he looked through his collection of stamps or read, or when he tried to instruct her in the intricacies of chess . . . there was no playing cards in this house.

Each day she walked through the grounds to the Dower House, where Jessica was still in amazingly good health, but the closeness between them seemed to have dwindled of late. Nancy Ann put this down to ageing for her grandmama must now be nearing eighty, although she would never state her true age.

At times, Nancy Ann was made to wonder what she would have done without the companionship of Mary. And one morning, on her way back to the Manor House, she was startled when she thought that she might lose her, at least be forced to have only her divided attention.

It was an early October day. The air was brisk; there was a light wind blowing; it was a day for walking. So she left the main drive connecting the houses and cut down by a pathway that would take her through the wood and into the Manor gardens, and it was where it left the wood and entered the formal gardens that she saw the man standing by the tall hedge. For a moment she thought he was a gardener taking a breather to have a smoke of his pipe. But when the figure turned towards her, she saw that it was Shane McLoughlin, and there was surprise on her face as she walked towards him. And he, looking a shade embarrassed, greeted her with, 'I'm sorry, ma'am. I hope I didn't disturb you. I mean . . .'

'No, no, not at all, Shane. Is . . . is anything the matter?'

He looked down at the ground for a moment, saying now, 'Nothin' that you would call serious, ma'am, but . . . well, it's . . . it's Miss Hetherington.'

She repeated the name to herself and with some consternation, which gathered force when he said, 'I've . . . I've asked her to come into the open, but . . . but she won't, ma'am. She doesn't like to disturb things, and . . . and I'm not gettin' any younger. And neither is she, as I tell her.'

No, she wasn't; Mary was over forty. And how old was Shane? He must be over thirty-five. Again the older woman and the younger man.

'I wanted to do the honourable thing, ma'am, an' come an' put it to you, but she wouldn't let me. I've never been underhand, as I hope you realize, ma'am. Straightforward, that's what I am, and I hate this hole-and-corner business. Of course, as I know an' she knows, no matter how I do up the rooms above the stables, they won't be anything like the quarters she's got here, because she's in such a well-set-up position. But we've got a life to live, as you yourself only too well know, ma'am, an' this business has been goin' on for the last three years and I'm gettin' tired of it. I was goin' to give her . . . well, a sort of ultimatum this mornin'. She knows that, and that's why she hasn't turned up.'

She felt slightly sick. Oh, Mary, Mary. What would she do without her? But she wouldn't have to do without her altogether, for Shane was saying now. 'I've told her, it would just be a sort of change of quarters; she could come back here every day. And then she's put up another obstacle, saying that her sister, your Mary, you know, ma'am, mightn't like it.'

Nancy Ann felt her face spreading: she wanted to burst out laughing; she wanted to take his hand and say, 'Yes, by all means, Shane, you and Agnes must marry. I'll see to it.' What she said was, 'You're talking about Agnes?'

'Yes, yes, of course, ma'am. Oh.' His face stretched and then he put his head back and laughed aloud, before saying, 'You thought it was your Mary? Oh, ma'am, I like Mary, she's a fine woman, but . . . but a bit long in the tooth. Not that she wouldn't make a fine wife for any man. No, no' – he shook his head – ''tis Agnes.'

'Don't you worry.' She actually did put her hand out and pat his sleeve as she said, 'I'll make her see sense.'

'Oh, thank you, ma'am, thank you.' Then pausing for a moment, he stared at her, and his voice was much lower now as he asked, 'How are you, ma'am?'

'Me, Shane? Oh, I'm . . . I'm very well, thank you. Very well.'

'You . . . you are bound to be a bit upset.' He jerked his head in the direction of the house. ''Twas a mad thing to do. I said that to him, but there was no gainsaying him. But in a way, I could understand it, ma'am. Yes, I could understand it.' He was looking straight into her face as he went on quietly, 'He's not a happy man, ma'am. He was never a happy child, I know that, but all his money hasn't compensated him as one would think it should. Now wouldn't you, wouldn't you now think so? 'Cos he's a millionaire twice over, they say. An' between you and me, ma'am, I can't see his marriage makin' him any happier.'

'No? What makes you say that, Shane?'

'Well, ma'am, to my mind she's not the right type, not for a man like him, because he's the double of the old master if . . . Oh, ma'am, I'm sorry.'

'It's all right, Shane. It's all right.' She reassured him by patting the air between them and adding, 'I've thought the same.'

'Have you ma'am? Well, 'tis truly there, although he won't touch drink or go near a playing-card. Oh – ' he shook his head and closed his eyes, saying, 'I'm talkin' me head off as usual, but, as I said, I don't think his afancied young woman is his type, too dollified. Now if it was her mother. Oh, you could tell, ma'am' – he was nodding at her now – 'who was the pusher there. From what I understand it was her who pushed them both to Australia to visit him. That was after they had met for the first time in a friend's house in France. Melbourne or some place she made for, then had to travel all those miles to Kalgoorlie.' Now he was grinning widely. 'From scraps that I heard of the dinner talk that came out of the dining-room, the young lady didn't take to Kalgoorlie at all. But that's where he proposed to build a house, so he told me. He wanted to take me across there with him. He did, ma'am, he did. And who knows, I might have taken him at his word if it hadn't been for Agnes.' His mood changed again, his voice dropped as he said, 'I felt sorry for him, ma'am. God knows he wasn't very happy in The House, but he was a damn sight . . . excuse me, he was a lot happier than he is now.'

He was looking into her face, so straight that her gaze dropped from his. And she said, 'I'm sorry to hear that, Shane.'

'I knew you'd be, ma'am, for money isn't everything.'

'No, indeed, Shane, money isn't everything. Anyway' – she glanced at him again, smiling now – 'I will go and tell Agnes that someone is waiting in the shrubbery and that she's got to stop this nonsense and name the day. And I can assure you, Shane' – she bent slightly towards him – 'we'll see that she's well set up, that you are both well set up.'

'Oh, thank you, thank you, ma'am. You know, I've said to me ma, time and time again, it was the best thing that ever happened to us when you knocked our Mick out. It was a kind of introduction to the family, and if it was possible for every one of us to be in your service, we'd feel honoured, ma'am, we would that. You'll be pleased to know an' all, ma'am, I'm sure, that Jim's in good service again.'

Touched by the commendation, she answered, 'Oh, yes, indeed I am. And I, too, have benefited from that introduction, Shane. In many ways you have been more than a servant. You have acted as a friend and for that I am grateful, and always shall be. Now I must go and tell Agnes what she must do . . . or else.'

They were both smiling as she moved away. But she was no sooner out of his sight than she paused for a moment and, her head drooping, she said to herself, 'He's not a happy man . . . Oh, David. David.' She walked swiftly now, not daring to ask herself, Was she a happy woman?

10

There was much talk in the newspapers about the unrest among certain sections of women folk, and not in the working class, let it be said, but among ladies, who considered their so-called sisters were being victimized: those who worked in the attics of millinery shops fourteen hours a day and slept where they worked; those who worked in damp cellars; and those who worked in the mills, many of them children, part-timers as they were called, and all for a pittance.

The century was coming to a close. There were great things afoot. It was even stated that before long every household would have an indoor closet. Of course that was taking things too far. How could it be possible, even the most moderate ones said, for every house to have an indoor closet. It was like saying that all houses would have this new lighting called electricity, and that gas would be done away with; and even more so, a telephone communication.

It was acknowledged everywhere that things were moving forward for the better, much thanks due to the glorious Old Lady up there in London.

But all the change, all the advancement, all the stirring headlines in the newspapers of wars and victories . . . and defeats caused no impression on those in the estate of the Manor House, for the period of the last four years had brought its own particular wars and defeats, particularly to the woman who was now the sole owner of the estate.

Nancy Ann could not believe that Graham had gone from her, nor that her daughter had gone from her, both dead to her, though in different ways. At times she felt there must be a curse on her, else why should her daughter have behaved as she had done, knowing that her stepfather was dying. Well, she may not have been sure that his death was imminent, but she had assuredly known that he was seriously ill.

Just a week after her sixteenth birthday Rebecca had come to her and said, 'I'm not going back to school, Mama. I . . . I want to marry Dennis Flanagan.'

She remembered gazing at her daughter open-mouthed, and that before she could make any reply Rebecca was saying, 'You weren't much older when you married Father.'

And when she had spoken she had said the wrong thing: 'Oh, that may be so, but . . . but you're still at school. And anyway, I don't think Mr Mercer would countenance any such entanglement,' for Rebecca had screamed at her, 'I don't care what Mr Mercer says or doesn't say. He's nothing to me. I've . . . I've never liked him. And I'm going to marry Dennis no matter what he or anybody else says. I . . . I thought I was doing the right thing by telling you.'

At this Nancy Ann had hissed at her daughter, 'Don't you raise your voice to me like that! And remember, whether you like my husband or not, he's been a very good father to you for years now, and he is, at this moment, rather ill. So mind your manners. You're ungrateful, spoilt and ungrateful. And have you thought what life would be like married to this boy?'

'He's not a boy, he's twenty. And he has a position, or will have shortly. And his people have no objection.'

'No, of course, they wouldn't, but I have.'

'Why have you?'

'First of all, because you are much too young, the word is immature. In all ways you are immature. And secondly, I know nothing about the man except that I have seen him at odd times.'

'Well, Mama, I can tell you, I have seen him more than at odd times, at every possible time. If you hadn't been so taken up with yourself and him' – she had jerked her head upwards indicating the bedroom – 'then you might have noticed what I was doing. As for being immature, if it comes to the point, I'm an old woman compared to what you were like at my age, so I've been told, because Uncle Peter said you were a scatterbrain and a tomboy up till you were married.'

She knew that Peter would not have said this in a derogatory way, and lamely she said so: 'Your uncle was joking. Anyway, I am not concerned with what I was like at sixteen or seventeen, but what you're like now. And I'm telling you I won't countenance your marrying anyone at all for at least another year, if not longer. And what you can do, madam, is send that young man to me and I will talk to him and tell him exactly what I have said now. If he can prove himself able to keep you, and I can imagine it will be two or three years before he's out of his time, then we'll talk about your marrying. That is all I have to say on the subject.'

Later she wondered if she had said too much on the subject. She put it to Mary, saying, 'What am I going to do with her?' And Mary shook her head as she said, ''Tis a pity the master's laid up. He could go and see this fellow. But I tell you what I can do, I'll tell our Agnes to have a word with Shane, and he might be able to talk sense into him.'

And so it was left at that. And six days passed, during which Graham became much worse. He had sickness and diarrhoea, and the doctor, at first, frightened her to death by suggesting it might be cholera. Yet there had been no cases of cholera reported for some long time now. Later he had diagnosed his condition as gastric enteritis. Then it seemed that overnight he developed pneumonia.

Nancy Ann had never felt fearful of his condition until, sitting to the side of the bed, wiping his brow with a cold cloth, he lifted up his hand and caught hers. And through gasping breath, he said, 'Thank you, my dear, for the happy years you have given me.'

'Oh, Graham, Graham. It's going to be all right. You're going to get well. It will pass.'

His only answer was gently to press her fingers to his cheek. Then, after a while, he said, 'Everything's in order.'

On this, she lifted her agonized gaze to Mary at the other side of the bed and the fear in her own eyes was reflected in Mary's. And Mary couldn't, at this moment, beckon her from the room to tell her something that was worrying her, in fact, more than worrying her, astounding her. For when Brundle had come to tell her that Miss Rebecca's pony had been brought back to the yard by the carter and that she had given him this letter to be delivered to the house – it was addressed to her mother – she had dashed upstairs to the girl's room, opened the wardrobe door and seen that quite a number of her clothes were missing, as also was the jewellery box from the dressing-table. She had rushed downstairs into the bedroom, but realized she could not, at the moment, upset her dear friend and mistress with the news that her daughter had run away.

Some time later, following the doctor's visit and the installation of a nurse, Nancy Ann was persuaded by Mary to take a short rest from the sickroom. She saw to it that she had a glass of port before she told her the news. And then, sitting opposite to her, she held her hands as she said, 'Now what I'm going to tell you is going to come as a shock. But your main concern at the moment is with the master; you can do nothing about this. I took it upon myself earlier on to send for Mr Peter. I saw him and told him what was afoot, and he went straight over to Shane, and the last I heard is that they've both gone to this young fellow's house.'

'What are you saying, Mary?' she had said. And Mary answered, 'Well, it's plain, isn't it, ma'am? She's gone off with this young fellow. And look' – she put her hand into her apron pocket – 'here's a letter she sent with the carrier who brought her pony back some time ago.'

With trembling fingers Nancy Ann had opened the letter. Characteristically it had no beginning, it just said,

> 'By the time you get this, Mama, I shall be married. You would never have given your consent, and even if you had, you would have made us wait, and we couldn't. You needn't worry about me, I'll be all right. I love Dennis and he will look after me.'

The brief note was signed, 'Rebecca.'

She remembered thinking, Those few terse lines for sixteen years of love, tenderness, and caring. She also remembered Mary's surprise when she said calmly, 'I'm sorry Peter and Shane have had the trouble of going to his home. She is gone, Mary, and at this moment, I can say to you, it doesn't matter if I never see her again. Somehow, she's the last link in a bad chain. All I'm concerned with at the moment is that my husband survives.'

She knew that Mary thought her attitude somewhat strange, for it wasn't generally in her nature to show indifference or hardness. And so she had said to her, 'It isn't like me to say that, is it, Mary? But that is honestly how I feel at the moment. For the last few years I've known a certain peace, and now, if it's about to be snatched from me I don't know what I'll do.'

Mary had risen and put her arms about her and held her head against her breast, saying, 'He'll pull through. He's of a good constitution. Never give up. Come on now, try to eat something.'

As she shook her head against the mention of food, she thought in an odd way that most people, out of kindness, advise you to eat when you are in trouble. It seemed a panacea for all ills.

She remembered also that as she returned upstairs to the bedroom, she had begun to pray as she had done years ago, making a bargain with God: telling Him that if He would spare her husband's life she would never again miss her daily prayers or a Sunday Service, and she would thrust all unworthy thoughts out of her mind forever. She did not elaborate on the type of thoughts that she would no longer think.

God did not answer her prayers. Fourteen hours later Graham Mercer died. And, from his going there was opened in her a chasm of loneliness that outdid all the combined feelings of aloneness she had experienced before.

11

They were in the little sitting-room above the stables. The two armchairs were close together opposite the small blazing fire. Shane and Agnes had been married for three years now and Agnes was heavy with her first child. Their hands were joined across the arms of the chairs and they were sitting in silence, staring into the flames.

It was Shane who broke the silence, saying, 'Well, he's got to come back sometime. It's three years now since he showed his face, and then it was only for a couple of days. He was here and gone again. He was supposed to come again before he left England, but he didn't. As they said at the table the night' – he jerked his head backwards indicating the farmhouse – 'if Henry hadn't come across that heading in that newspaper last week, we would have all gone on surmising he was married. Well, we did when he was last here, didn't we? Henry remembers the night asking him if the mistress would be coming back with him. That was when he promised to look in again afore leaving the country. And he remembers him looking at him hard and saying, "No, she won't be coming back with me." As Henry said then, he thought something wasn't right. But he didn't think that he hadn't been married at all. Anyway, there it was, the headlines with his photo: Bachelor millionaire, shareholder in shipping company, and he was once a youth in the North. And so on. And if it's right what you think, and what Mary thinks, and what Cook thinks, and Henry thinks, and meself have known for a fact for this long time, something should be done about it. What d'you say?'

'I say like you, something should be done about it, but what?'

'You could write, write him a letter.'

'Me write him a letter!' She heaved her swollen body further up in the chair. 'Why not you? I mean, he doesn't know I'm here; he doesn't know you're married. Or let Henry write, it's his place.'

'Oh, you know what Henry is like with a pen, nearly as good as meself . . . Hope this finds you as it leaves me at present. That's about as far as both of us can go. Now you have a good hand.'

'Not to write a letter, telling him . . . well, what you want me to tell him.'

'You can put it atween the lines.'

'Our Mary is the one that could do it, but she won't. 'Twould be no use me askin' her, 'cos she wouldn't know how the mistress would take it.'

'Well, perhaps not. But I bet she wouldn't put a foot out to stop you if she knew you were doin' it.'

'No, perhaps not. but I wouldn't know how to start.'

'I'll show you.'

He got up swiftly and went to the chiffonier that was standing in the corner of the room, pulled open one of the doors, lifted out a box. Then, placing it on the table, he lifted the lid, took out a bottle of ink, a steel-nibbed pen and some loose sheets of paper and a packet of envelopes, and looking towards her, he said, 'There, imagine you're writin' to your mother, and givin' her all the news. Only head it differently.'

Slowly she pulled herself up while shaking her head and smiling at him. Then, seated at the table, she dipped the pen in the ink, bit on her lip, stared down on the paper, and began in a round childish hand:

Dear David,

You will never guess who this is. I am writing from one of the rooms above the stables. I'm Agnes, and me and Shane got married sometime back. And I thought I would like you to know that we are very happy and I am expecting a baby in six weeks time. I wish it was later cos I would like it to have been born at Christmas. But there, these things happen don't they?'

She paused and looked across at Shane, and when he said, 'Read what you've done,' she answered firmly, 'No, you'll just wait. If you want me to do it, you'll just wait. 'Cos I've got to think.'

We have been expecting to see you back this long while, cos many things have happened. You won't know that Miss Rebecca ran off and got married when she had just passed her sixteenth birthday. And of course it upset madam, because she was very worried at the time as Mr Mercer was very ill and died shortly afterwards. Miss Rebecca, or Mrs Flannagan, as she now is, cos she married Shane's nephew who he says he's not proud of and has stopped liking because of the awful thing he did, running off with Miss Rebecca. And Miss Rebecca never came to Mr Mercer's funeral, and she's only been here once since to see her mother. And from what our Mary says she wasn't a bit nice, quite cocky like. But then she was always a bit cocky. You will likely remember when she was a child. Things are much the same here from day to day, except our Mary is worried about the mistress, cos she's got so thin and never goes out. Lady Pat calls sometimes, but even she can't get her out. Mary's gona try and get her to Harrogate for the winter.

Everything in the farmhouse is all right. It is kept lovely and clean. But they all say they would like to see you. We read in the papers lately that you have got a ship now. That must be very nice for you. We all remember you fondly and hope you are very well. We are all well here, even Mrs Hazel. She never seems to ail anything and her a good age.

I am, yours respectfully,
Agnes.

When she read the letter over to Shane, he kept nodding his head, until he came to the part where she had said he owned a ship. And he stopped her there and said, 'He's only part of a company. He doesn't own a ship.'

'Well,' she answered, 'he can put it down to my ignorance. I could have written a better letter if I'd given meself time to think. But then I wouldn't likely have got it all in. Anyway, there it is.' She pushed it across to him. 'It goes, or it doesn't. It's up to you.'

'Well, if it's up to me, it goes.'

And the letter went.

October was a windy blustery month. November was wet. It was the first week in December when Nancy Ann said to Mary, 'All right, all right, have it your way. I'll go to Harrogate . . . we'll go to Harrogate. Although what I'll do sitting in an hotel all day, I don't know.'

'You won't sit in an hotel all day. You'll get out and about, like you can't here. You've got to walk or drive miles to get to the town here. There you're on the main thoroughfare.'

'Yes, and don't I know it at night; it takes me ages to get used to the noise.'

'Oh, you'll soon get used to the noise. And we'll go to the concerts and the theatre and there'll be Christmas festivities in the hotel . . .'

'Mary. Mary. It is only a matter of months since I was made a widow.'

'It is close on a year, ma'am. And you've lived like a hermit all that time. It can't go on. We . . . we are all worried about you. The flesh has dropped off you; just look at yourself. You haven't got a dress that fits you. Anyway, there'll be nobody in Harrogate to criticize if they see you attending a concert, and you'll be in company.'

Nancy Ann turned her head away, shaking it the while as she said, 'Oh, Mary, Mary. I thought you knew me better than that. I don't want company. That's the last thing I want at this moment, is company.'

'Excuse me for contradicting you, ma'am.' Mary's voice was prim now, that of a servant. 'It is company you want at this time. You keep up this attitude, ma'am, and you'll go into decline, like lots of ladies afore you. And I'm not the only one concerned about you. Lady Pat is very concerned, and so is Sir George, and others an' all, Mr Peter and his wife. And then there's all the staff. Oh, yes, all your staff, ma'am, so I think it is only fair that you consider them. An' don't forget Lady Beatrice, she's forever writing, she's so concerned and only wishes she could be with you but has to look after that cousin of hers with her broken back. There's only one good thing about that, it's she who can do the bossing now.'

Nancy Ann looked at Mary and smiled wanly. What would she have done without this woman? Gone mad likely. Yes, gone mad. For there was a time after Graham's death when she felt so desolate that she thought she was losing her mind. During that time she couldn't bear company at all. Peter had come over two or three times a week bringing Eva with him. And Eva had held her hand and spoken words, as she thought, of comfort, but which had almost made her want to scream, when her thoughts would return to Rebecca and her screaming fits, causing her to realize how easy it would be to let go.

But now she realized, as Mary said, she must make an effort, and perhaps in making the effort this feeling of guilt that was with her constantly would fade. Because at times her feeling of desolation wasn't so much that she had lost Graham, though his loss was genuine, but that she hadn't loved him enough when he was alive. Oh, she had been loving, but that wasn't love. Of one thing she was certain, the emptiness within her would prevail until the day she died.

She'd had visits from the vicar who had talked to her of the love of God and told her that she must not worry because her husband, who was a very good man, was now in heaven. On each visit his theme was always the same, and the very last time he was there she had been prompted to say, 'But what of my other husband? Where is he? the man who was buried in unconsecrated ground. Would you say that he was in hell?' His answer had been so garbled that at the end of the visit she was none the wiser for asking.

She had never been to church since the day they buried Graham. At times she accused herself of being childish in this matter, paying God out as it were for not answering her prayer . . .

It had been snowing on and off for two days now and the roads in parts were impassble. And she smiled as she said to Mary, 'Well, there's one thing, you won't be able to get me to Harrogate within the next day or so, I should think.' And to this Mary answered lightly, 'Oh, we'll get to the station somehow.'

'Go and get your supper,' she said, dismissing Mary with a light wave of her hand. As seemed fitting, when they were at home, Mary ate with the rest of the staff in the servants' quarters which, as in Rossburn, had its own hierarchy, but when in Harrogate they ate together.

She had finished her meal some time ago. She very rarely ate in the dining-room but had her main meals served in the small drawing-room where she was now sitting. It was a very comfortable room, beamed and half-panelled, with a large open stone fireplace, holding a basket of logs which gave off a fierce heat. She sat in the corner of the deep brown velvet couch, staring towards it.

The room was situated at the far end of the house and no sounds from the hall or kitchen quarters penetrated to it. Outside, too, was the deadening silence snow brings. The world . . . her world was quiet. There was no crackle, even from the logs, for they were all settled into a scarlet mush. She, too, was quiet inside; she was thinking over what Mary had said, and she was agreeing with her in her mind. The sojourn in Harrogate would be a move for the better, for she knew no matter how great the depth of loneliness was inside her she couldn't go on in this forced isolation much longer.

She wondered at times, if she'd had Rebecca for company would she have felt different. Perhaps her daughter's presence would have forced her before now to have made some effort. But she hadn't Rebecca; all she had of Rebecca was a feeling of sadness, tinged with bitterness. And sometimes these emotions were eclipsed by bewilderment that a daughter of hers could have acted in such a callous way. Yet, at such times she would remind herself that Rebecca wasn't her daughter only, she was Dennison's too.

Then there was James. She rarely heard from him now, but she gauged he was living with a woman, and reading between the lines of his last letter, she'd had children to him. And he couldn't have married her, for that would have made him a bigamist.

She felt no sense of shock knowing that her brother, son of a parson, was sinning grievously. What was sin anyway? Mostly the outcome of circumstances, at least in cases like James. But Dennison's sins, were they the outcome of circumstances? Her mind became still, waiting, but there was no answer forthcoming to that question.

So sitting, her mind probing, she did not hear the commotion on the drive; she did not hear the talk and bustle in the hall; she heard nothing till Mary thrust open the door and hurried up the room, saying, 'You . . . you have a visitor.'

Nancy Ann pulled herself up into a sitting position on the couch, saying, 'Lady Pat in this weather?'

'No, no.' Mary's face was bright. 'No, not Lady Pat. Someone . . . someone else.'

Nancy Ann stared up at her quite bemused. Then she thought, It's Rebecca. I must . . . I must be loving towards her. Something has happened; perhaps she has come home. I must make her welcome.

The thought became choked in her mind as she pulled herself up from the couch and looked down the room to where a tall bronzed-skinned man was standing. He had a handkerchief to his face and was wiping the snow from his eyebrows. She saw the snow was still clinging to the laceholes of his high-topped boots. He was wearing a thick tweed jacket and she saw him unbutton the top two buttons and look at Mary as she hurried back down the room and passed him, nodding at him all the while. And then the door closed and he was moving towards her. When he stopped, she stared at him. This was David, yet not David. It was four years since they had met. Then he had been a handsome young man. He was still handsome, but . . . but in a different way. His skin was brown, his hair looked bleached and it was long, reaching almost to his shoulders, and the sides were trimmed down to his cheekbones. He looked bigger, broader, not fatter, but older, so much older. What was he, twenty-six? He could be thirty-six . . . forty.

'Hello.'

She couldn't answer him. She swallowed deeply. Then as if she were greeting a guest, she pointed to the couch and with an effort said, 'Won't . . . won't you sit down?'

'No, no.' He shook his head. 'I don't want to sit down. I've been sitting for hours, for days. It's a long way from Australia.'

'Have you come straight from Australia?'

'Yes, as straight as one can travel when coming from that country.'

He was being facetious. Why had he come?

He was saying now, 'But you sit down. I disturbed you. Are you not well?'

She sat down slowly, and looked up at him as she answered, 'I am well enough.'

'You have got very thin.'

She made herself answer lightly, 'That is fashionable these days.' Then she asked politely, 'Is . . . is your wife with you?'

'Which one?'

Dear God! She drooped her head and closed her eyes. He was in one of these moods, was he? She remembered them only too well. He was fencing, but why? Why was he here? To torment her?

'That was silly of me. That's what you're thinking, isn't it? Just like him to be facetious, you're saying. I can read your thoughts still, you know.' He was smiling down on her now. And then quite suddenly he dropped on to the couch within a bent arm's length from her. And his nearness brought sweat oozing out of every pore in her body. She felt faint and his voice seemed to come to her from a distance as he said, 'Everyone asks me if I have my wife with me, and that is my stock answer, because up till now, unfortunately, I haven't had a wife.'

His voice was clearer now.

'What!' she said. 'You didn't marry?'

'No. I didn't marry.'

'But everyone thought . . .'

'Yes, everyone thought and I let them think. I nearly did marry. Oh yes.' His eyebrows moved upwards and his wide lips went into a pout. 'But the young lady in question was horrified when she knew that I meant to spend part of my life, and expected her to spend it with me, in Kalgoorlie. Now her mother wouldn't have minded, she was a sensible woman and knew that money could buy most things, and she had trained her daughter to think the same, but her daughter couldn't see any of the things she wanted to buy in Kalgoorlie. Then there was another thing: the society was a little rough for her delicate mind. Her mother offered to take her place, but I declined as gracefully as possible. It cost me, but it was worth it in the end.'

She had turned her head away from him and was staring stiffly towards the fireplace when, his voice changing, he said, 'I'm being objectionable. It's the only way I can cover my feelings at the moment. Look at me, Nancy Ann.'

She did not obey him, she couldn't, and when his hand came on hers, she shivered. And now he was speaking quietly, saying, 'I didn't know you had lost your husband until quite recently. A kind friend sent me a letter. I wasn't in Kalgoorlie when it arrived. But as soon as I got back and read it I left immediately. I can't say I'm sorry he died. I am no hypocrite, whatever else. I can only say that at this moment I'm so churned up inside I really don't know quite where I am. I cannot believe yet that I'm sitting here holding your hand, and that there is nothing in the wide world separating us any more. Look at me, Nancy Ann. Please look at me.'

She looked at him. Although her whole body was sweating her mouth was dry and her eyes were burning. She too couldn't believe that he was sitting there and there was nothing separating them any more. No, no, she couldn't believe it. She was dreaming and she would wake up and turn her head into the pillow and cry for a life that could never be.

'If you love me, do as I ask.' His voice came soft to her. 'You once said that to me, remember? Now I say that to you, if you love me, Nancy Ann, look at me and at least say, David, I am glad to see you.'

The dryness was going out of her eyes, the moisture was filling them. She turned her head slowly towards him, her lids blinking and, her voice a mere croak, she said, 'David, I am glad to see you.'

'Just glad?'

She gulped now before she could utter the words, 'More than glad.'

When the tears welled from her eyes, his arms went about her and they both fell into the corner of the couch. And his mouth on hers now, he kissed her as he had done once before until the breath seemed to leave her body. But it didn't matter, nothing mattered, nothing would ever matter again; she was in his arms, at last, at last, at last. Now he was kissing her face, her hair, her neck, gasping out words, 'We'll never be separated again, never, never, never. Do you hear, never, never.' He laughed now and his voice low, he said, 'Can I sleep here tonight?' And her voice low and matching his mood, she replied, 'No, sir, you may not sleep here tonight. You have a house of your own.'

'Oh, my, yes.' Still within the circle of his arms, he pulled her upwards and they leant against the back of the couch, their faces so close that they breathed each other's breath. And he said softly, 'This time next week we shall be married.'

As she went to pull away sharply from him, he held her tight, saying, 'Now then, now then. What is it?'

'Oh, no, David, not so soon. I . . . well, it's only.'

'It's only almost a year since he died, and I wouldn't care if it was two months. We are to be married next week by special licence. My secretary is making arrangements.'

'Your what?' She screwed up her face.

'My secretary. Don't look so surprised. Wherever I go, business follows me, and I have to have a secretary. You'll like him. I call him Willie. He's an Australian and talks like a London Cockney. But he's very efficient, marvellous at making arrangements.'

She made small movements with her head and he laughed now, saying, 'Don't look so surprised; there's lots of things you'll have to get used to when we're travelling.'

'Travel . . .?'

'Yes, I said travelling. We'll spend our honeymoon in France. Yes.' He now rubbed his nose against hers, so close was he that she couldn't make out his features, only the depth and dark light in his eyes. 'I said, honeymoon, Nancy Ann.' Gently now, his lips touched hers before his head moved away from her again and back into focus. 'And we'll spend some time in Italy, any place where it's warm. Then it will be Australia, here we come. You must see Kalgoorlie. All the fervour, all the dirt, all the heroism, all the good, the bad, and the indifferent. The place has grown in the last few years since the rush, but I'll always remember it as I first saw it. You know, Nancy Ann, my love, I did not gain my education here, although you gave me the chance. No, it started when I got to Kalgoorlie, and for the first time

I understood the word greed, and another word, stupidity. This was attached to supposedly normal men working like slaves; then when they made a find, little or much, losing it again through drink or gambling. If they had gambled when they were stone sober there might have been hope for them, but the sharks were too clever and too many. And men who, the previous night, would have had enough to set them up modestly for life, found themselves the next morning sober, but standing up with only the clothes on their back and one dollar in their pocket.' His voice had turned serious now, the smile had left his face, as he ended, 'Joe Barrow was, and still is, a good, what you would call, God-fearing churchman. He's as honest as the day's long. But I hadn't been over there a week when he took me the rounds through the dives and showed me what would happen if I let myself be led to drink, gambling . . . *or women.*'

Taking note of the quirk, to his lips, she now asked, 'Did you resist all temptation?'

The quirk widened. He looked to the side, then said, 'Not all, madam, not all.'

When her gaze suddenly turned from his, he brought her face almost roughly towards him again with the palm of his hand against her cheek and, his mood taking a lightning change, he said thickly, 'Remember, Nancy Ann, you have been married twice.'

There was a tight feeling in her chest. He was right of course, he was right. She had been married twice. But the thought of him with other women. Don't be stupid, woman, don't be stupid. The voice seemed to be shouting at her. He's a man and has been for a long time, and so attractive women must have swarmed about him. And remember how upset you were by the name of Parson's Prig. You were never priggish, so don't start now. Accept the miracle that has happened. As he said, you've been married twice and the fact must have been agony to him.

She smiled at him as she asked, within an assumed prim manner, 'Are the Australian ladies pretty?'

She saw him now bow his head and press his lips tightly together before he answered, 'Oh, so pretty, madam, beautiful, voluptuous' – made a curving movement with his hand – 'you have no idea.' Then his voice breaking into a laugh, he said, 'There was hardly an Australian among them, my dear. From every gutter in the world they came. No, I can honestly say that those ladies didn't attract me. But now' – he wagged his finger at her – 'the French mademoiselles. Oh, la-la. And the Italians. Oh, very warm, the Italians.' His fingers twirled. Then on a sound that was half a shout, he pulled her roughly towards him, saying, 'Why are we playing this game? The past is past for both of us. There is only the future and I can see it stretching down the years. We have a lot of time to make up for, you and I, Nancy Ann.'

He now turned his head away from her for a moment and looked upwards towards the ceiling, and then to the fireplace. 'I could live here,' he said; 'I like this house, it would hold no ghosts for me, not like the other place. And I thought Peter might like the farmhouse. What do you say? From what I know of boarding schools there's no comfort for either master or pupil. That would be a good arrangement, wouldn't it?'

She stared at him in amazement, saying now, 'You have it all planned out.'

'Yes, yes, I've had a lot of time to think on the journey here. Yes, my dear, my beloved, I've got it all planned out. And this time it's going to work just as I planned.'

Then again his mood changed and, his voice dropping so low she could scarcely hear the words, he muttered, 'Hold me, dear. Hold me.' And when she put her arms about him, he closed his eyes and said, 'Tightly.' And she held him tightly to her. Then, as if she was listening to the voice of the child she had first seen sitting on the stone by the river, he said, 'Never let me go. Promise you'll never let me go. Promise you'll stay with me always, no matter what happens.'

His head buried in her shoulder, the tears were streaming down her face and her voice too was a mutter as she answered, 'I'll never let you go, my David. Never. Never. You'll always be mine, as you have been from the beginning.'

Neither of them saw Mary open the door and hold it wide to allow Brundle to push in the trolley of food. But what greeted her gaze caused her to push the trolley backwards and pull the door softly closed. And she smiled at Brundle, 'We'll have to wait a bit.'

'But the broth'll be cold.'

'I don't think they'll mind.' Mary's smile widened. Then instinctively, they pushed their hands out towards each other's shoulders, and Mary said something that Brundle couldn't understand, for what she said was, 'God bless our Agnes and Shane.'

THE CULTURED HANDMAIDEN

PART ONE

1

'Listen, and listen carefully, because you'll remember what I'm saying till the day you die, and it's this: chastity is the most expensive commodity in the whole world. The longer you keep it, the more you pay for it. The expense will shrivel you up. Some women are born virgins because the male in them has tipped the scales; others, like you, who aim to become one of the Brides of Christ, whose bloody harem must be chock-a-block by now, are nothing but runaways, runaways from life . . . The essence of it . . . And what's the essence of it? Why, that dreadful word, sex. You're afraid of it, so you sublimate it in locking yourselves up; submitting to obedience, tyrannical obedience, and humiliating practices: spreadeagled on floors . . . face down of course . . . kissing feet . . . God! to think of it . . . I wonder if He does, does He turn a little sick to see what rights man has inflicted on woman, and all in His name? . . . Go. Yes, go; hurry, your spouse is waiting for you. One last word: remember He's promised there's no giving or taking in marriage on the other side. So you are going to lose out all along the line . . . What did you say?'

'I said, I'll pray for you.'

'Go to hell.'

'I've been there; I'm going the other way.'

Jinny Brownlow's hand holding the prompting script dropped to her side, and she was about to lean for support against a piece of scenery, when its very decided inclination warned her that it would be dangerous inasmuch as her action could bring it and a number of pieces behind it tumbling about her, and that would indeed be the finale to a disastrous week.

She watched the comany of eight players now taking their bows amid the dismal clapping. The curtain dropped, and there was no second lift: the clapping had ceased and there was only the sound of scuffling feet and the scraping of chairs as the last of the small audience scrambled for the exit.

She turned and joined the players now as they made their way to the so-called dressing-rooms provided by the Fellburn Social Hall, and her eyes sought out Ray Collard, but he was away ahead of the others. He hadn't looked at her as he passed her. There was something wrong. She had guessed at it for some time now, but mostly during this week while he had been playing the lead in this disastrous play. Even the notice in the *Fellburn Gazette* on Wednesday referring to the bad taste of the final speech . . . almost blasphemous, it had said . . . had failed to bring in the atheists, the agnostics, or the merely doubters. The critic had gone on to say, that if the play had been trying to prove that all good women lived in misery and that there was nothing worth having in life but sex it had failed, for the hero had wanted to marry the girl, he hadn't said, 'What about it? Let's shack up.'

Saying, 'Excuse me,' she pushed past Jess Winters who, always the comedienne, laughed as she said, 'Now why should I excuse you, Jinny, you've done nothing for me, only got me over those two bad patches the night. I'm supposed to be funny; the only light relief in that damned indigestible tirade . . .'

The rest of her words faded away; and again Jinny excused herself as she went to pass Hal Campbell, the actor-manager, the man who kept the whole thing going and the one who usually had the final word with regard to which four plays the Fellburn Players would put on each year. But he wasn't to blame for this last one. Philip Watson, the producer, had plumped for it on the surmise that it was time the people at this end of Fellburn were made to think.

Well apparently they had thought . . . and thought it best to stay away, after the first night.

Hal Campbell now put his hand on her arm and drew her to a momentary stop, saying, 'See what you can do with Ray. He says he's not coming to the party. Anything wrong?'

'Not that I know of.'

He pulled a face and let her go. She knew he didn't believe her. Well, what did she know, anyway? The only thing she knew, and with certainty, was that she was a fool. But then she couldn't help being her particular kind of fool.

She caught up with Ray Collard at the end of the passage. He was going for the producer. 'Well, you got your bloody way, didn't you? During the three years I've been with this dud outfit there's never been a flop like it.'

'Perhaps it wasn't the fault of the play so much as of the acting: some people can put it over and some can't . . .'

'*Ray*!' Her voice surprisingly was almost a yell.

Collard lowered his arm; then turning to her, he barked, 'Get your coat! I'm leaving now.'

He opened a door to the side of him and went in, then banged it closed behind him. And Philip Watson, looking at Jinny, said, 'Do as your boss tells you. He said, get your coat. Well, why aren't you running?'

She stared at him. She had never liked him, yet he had always been very nice to her. In a way, she supposed, he had tried to make up to her. She was about to turn from him when in a different tone of voice he said, 'If you take my advice, Jinny, you won't get your coat, you'll come to the party with the rest of us. I'm . . . I'm only speaking for your own good.'

She paused, and looked hard at him over her shoulder before moving away. Whenever there was something unpleasant to impart, people always said they were only speaking for your own good.

She made her way down the passage to the so-called ladies' dressing-room, and there, ignoring the prattle, all concerning the madness of putting on such a play in this town, she took up her coat, woolly hat, and scarf and went out without anyone having commented on her presence, for after all she wasn't considered to be an actress, so-called: she was good for prompting or accompanying a singer at the piano, but, as had been pointed out to her more than once, not in a very professional style. In fact, her lack of an accompanist's talent had often caused the performer to give anything but of his or her best.

When they did a musical show there was always a post-mortem by the leading lady and soprano Gladys Philips, the wife of the tenor, Peter Philips. It was odd, Jinny thought, that singers never blamed their voices for anything that went wrong with their performances: it was the acoustics, or the draught whizzing along the passages at each side of the stage, or they didn't feel at their best, but more often than not it was the accompanist who had put them off.

Ray Collard was in the car waiting for her, and she was hardly seated before he started it up. He gave her no explanation for the rush, nor did she ask for any. She knew what was coming and she didn't want to hear it, for in a way she was to blame . . . No! she chided herself; she wouldn't use that word blame in connection with this matter. No, she wouldn't.

No word was exchanged between them as the car sped along Bog's End waterfront where the headlights picked up the name *Henderson & Garbrook, Engineers*, in huge letters along the top of a blank wall. Then they showed up the gates and another long wall dotted with windows. The third from the end of the bottom row was her window, at least the typing pool's window by which, for the past year, she had sat most days, except when called upon to fill in for a secretary on holiday, or someone who had fallen sick in one of the offices.

It crossed her mind that she wouldn't miss the pool if she left. A week ago she had put in for another post and she had the qualifications for it: she was good at shorthand, although it must have got a little rusty over the past months through lack of use, but her French wasn't at all bad. This she had kept up through radio programmes and reading, but never once in Henderson's had she been given the opportunity of using it. In fact, Miss Cadwell, the head of the pool, for some reason seemed set to retard the progress of anyone with a knowledge of French. Neither she herself nor Noreen Power, whose

French was also good, had ever been given the chance to go to the top floor.

But what did French matter, what did work matter, what did anything matter but what Ray wanted to say to her?

The car had stopped in a street of tall narrow terraced houses. And now Jinny thrust open the car door, crossed the pavement, passed through a little iron gate, went down the area steps, put her key in the lock, then entered her home, the three room, kitchen-cum-bathroom flat, and she switched on the lights to reveal a comfortable looking but cold room. She lit the gas-fire; then turned towards her escort.

Collard was standing with his hands by his sides staring at her. The look on his face was aggressive. Then without any preliminary chat he barked at her, 'You've brought this on yourself. Do you hear? You've brought this on yourself.'

She didn't ask what she had brought on herself, but she waited for him to go on.

'I told you weeks ago, I was nearly round the bend and I couldn't wait. It would have been the simplest thing in the world for you to . . . to . . .' He jerked his head to the side, then shot out his arm and, his finger pointing not a foot from her face, he added, 'All this bloody week I've been speaking the last lines of that blasted play to you. Do you hear me? I've been speaking them to you not to that silly bitch Wainwright, but to you. And I'm telling you this now, you'll end up like that character. Not in a convent, no, you're not made for that, but in this stinking little basement room with a couple of cats.'

Still she didn't speak, she just continued to stare at him. Stinking little basement room, he had said. It might be a basement, but it had some better pieces of furniture in it than ever he would see in his life. What had he been offering her, anyway? Two rooms and a kitchen above his shop. And what was the shop? A single house window with the words: *Raymond Collard, Painter & Decorator*. He was a one man business. But he meant to expand. Oh yes, that was his aim he said, to expand. That was why he had joined the Players and the Fellburn Bog's End Working Men's Club. He couldn't get into anything like the Rotary, but, as he said, the more things you joined the more connections you made, and already he had got two jobs from among the amateur actors. And another thing, he had already decided what pieces of furniture she was going to sell, and what she would take to the rooms above the shop. But he was talking again.

'Emily has more sense and understanding than you'll ever have, and you've looked down your nose on her, haven't you?'

So it was Emily. Of course it was Emily. Why was she still kidding herself? She had known it all along, so why had she closed her eyes to it all?

Just over a year ago when her mother died, she had been forced to leave the house to which her father had brought her mother on the day they were married, the house in which she herself was born and had been brought up in an atmosphere of love and gaiety. That was the word, gaiety; the feeling that emanated from both her parents had been one of pure happiness: her father managed a small antiques shop and her mother had been a music teacher. There was never an overabundance of money but that lack had never seemed to trouble them. She supposed it was the example of their married life that had set the pattern deep within her of how she wanted her own life to be formed. She was nineteen when her father died and within a year her mother had followed him. They were both comparatively young, in their late forties, but it appeared that her mother had been unable to bear to be separated from her husband, for as the doctor had said, there had been nothing physically wrong with her, she had just pined.

They hadn't owned the six-roomed house they had lived in. The controlled rent was still only nine pounds a week, and she could have managed very nicely, but she had been harassed into leaving it: she couldn't stand up to the pressure of the landlord, and he had offered her this basement in replacement. But as this was in a good class quarter of the town, the rent was fourteen pounds a week. What was more, she had to sign a three years lease to get it. But she considered herself fortunate in almost immediately getting someone to share it, a state registered nurse called Emily Houselea, whose work was obtained mainly through an agency, and since she preferred night work the arrangements suited them both and they only saw each other for any length of time on alternate Saturdays and Sundays.

It was some weeks ago that Jinny had smelt the cigarette smoke, and as neither she nor Emily smoked she had concluded Emily must have had her boy friend in. But why hadn't she mentioned him? In the course of the time they had been living together, Emily had had a number of boy friends. They came and went and she had joked about them. But she'd never referred to this last one.

When she now purposely looked towards one of the doors leading from the sitting-room his voice came at her almost in a growl, saying, 'She's gone. She's taken her things. It was better that way. And look' – his voice softened now – 'I didn't want it this way, you know I didn't. And what's more, she's eight years older than me, and so nothing would have come of it. I would have still waited, but she's fallen. I think she's done it on purpose, but that's neither here nor there. And I'll say again, you brought it on yourself.'

What was the matter with her? What was this strange feeling inside? She had never experienced anything like it before; never had she had any occasion to feel aggressive; but she was experiencing now the greatest desire to hit him. No, not just to hit him, but to tear at him, to scratch his face, to break things on him. She didn't want to talk this out, she wanted to act it out violently.

And then he said, 'I'm sorry, Jinny. Oh, for God's sake! why don't you say something? Retaliate, woman. That's another thing about you, you're like a wooden dolly; people hit you and you come back for more. Those two Philipses always at you about your playing, why haven't you turned on them before now and told them to go to hell? Or better still, told the great Hal Campbell to pay for a proper pianist if he wasn't satisfied with what you were doing. But no, you just took it. And from the rest of them an' all, running here and there at their bidding like a bloody cultured handmaiden. Yes, that's a good description of you, a cultured handmaiden. So agreeable, so polite, so damned eager to please, you let people wipe their boots on you. I'll tell you again, Jinny, you'll end up here' – he stubbed his finger towards the floor now – 'unless you learn to be hard to get.'

She would . . . she would . . . she would go for him.

She felt her head snap back on her shoulders and she heard somebody laughing, but she couldn't at the moment believe it was she herself who was making that sound, nor that she was now yelling at him, 'Well, it didn't work on you, did it? Being hard to get it, it didn't work on you. Get out! Get out before I do something. Go on! Go on!'

He was at the door, his back towards her, and he stood there in silence for a moment before slowly turning and looking at her again and, his voice low now, he said, 'I'm sorry, Jinny. Honestly I am. I'd do anything to alter things at this minute, but I can't. And the irony of it is, she's not keen to marry me, just live with me. But I'll marry her when the bairn comes, because after all it's only fair to it. Goodbye, Jinny.'

As she watched the door close after him she repeated to herself, 'I'll marry her when the bairn comes, it's only fair to it.' Strange the ideas of some people, these sparks of morality that oozed through. Why couldn't he marry her before the bairn came? No; she saw his reasoning: she might have a miscarriage, the baby might be born dead; he would have tied himself up when he needn't have done and be left with no solace for having done the right thing by this child, the decent thing.

Slowly she unwound the scarf from around her neck, pulled off her woollen hat, then her coat, and went into her bedroom and hung them in the wardrobe. The room was icy cold and without their warm comfort she shivered visibly.

Back in the sitting-room she drew a pouffe up towards the fire and, crouching on it, she crossed her forearms tight against her waist and sat string into the glowing red vertical bars. Cultured handmaiden. She supposed it was as good a description of her as any. It was a failing of hers wanting to please people. Ever since she had lost her parents and her home there had been in her this thing which was like a craving to belong, to be part of a family once again. She had been an only child but her family seemed to have encompassed the world. There were just the three of them, they had needed no one else. There had been one discordant note in their lives: Nell Dudley, her mother's cousin. Nell, she had always been given to understand, was kind of common, and being her mother's cousin, she found this strange because her mother was genteel, refined. But cousin Nell had a nice husband who was a solicitor. Her mother often said she could never understand how Nell had got him, and she was very lucky for he had provided her with a nice terraced house and a garden on the outskirts of Shields.

On one of her duty visits to Cousin Nell's that lady had said in the voice of a prophet: 'It can't go on: you and your mam and dad are living in a fool's paradise up there. 'Tisn't natural, all sweetness, and light, and wanting nobody else. There'll be a bust up one of these days. Just you mark my words, an' prepare yourself for it, girl.'

Even at her mother's funeral Cousin Nell's censoring didn't stop: she had been really too good to live, she said. And then she had turned the statement from one of approbation into a comment that almost held disdain when she finished, 'You've got to have guts to face up to people and this life,' only for her tone to change again when she said kindly, 'You know where we are if you ever need us, lass.'

But she had made up her mind on that particular day that no matter how badly off she was for company, she wouldn't seek it in Cousin Nell's house. Before long, however, she found out it was as her cousin had said, you had to gave guts to face up to people and this life, and at times she felt she was a little short on them.

She thought back over the events of the past year. She had been working at Henderson's only a month when she came under the notice of Mr Pillon. One rainy night he stopped her and asked her if she would like a lift home, and she had gladly accepted it. Another time he asked her to join him for a drink before going home. The third time she had accepted his invitation he had turned the car into a quiet land and set about what he considered to be the real business of the night and payment for his entertainment. She had almost pushed him through the car door. And when she had made to leave, he had grabbed at her and said, 'Come off it. You know what it's all about, else why did you come?'

She hadn't experienced any rage on that particular occasion only fear and humiliation, and a cold on the Sunday as a result of having become drenched walking home in a downpour.

But on the Monday morning her humiliation had been increased a thousandfold when Betty Morris said to her, 'I saw you out with Pillon on Friday. You want to watch your step there, else you'll have his wife after you.'

She had never for a moment dreamed he was married; he hadn't acted like a married man. But what did a married man act like? She was an idiot, a fool. But she was learning.

It was through Betty Morris, too, that she had joined the Fellburn Players, and there had met Ray Collard. His acting in school plays and scout pantomimes had given him a taste for the stage, and most members of the company said he was talented.

She dropped her head until her chin lay deep on her chest. She wanted to cry. She could see the days stretching ahead, five days a week at the office: the click, click, click of the typewriters, interspersed by Miss Caldwell's grating commands; then the clatter and chatter and gossip in the canteen, the white-collar workers at one end, the floor men at the other. Mr Henderson's idea that they ate under the same roof but at different ends. His idea of doing away with class distinctions had caused more trouble than enough. As someone said, they had never known a strike there, but forced fraternization had nearly brought one on.

He was a devil of a man was Mr Henderson. She hadn't glimpsed him more than a dozen times. They said he was in the works before anybody else in the morning and he left late. Not so his partner Mr Garbrook. He showed up about once a quarter on board days.

At five o'clock, not a minute before at Henderson's, there was a rush for the gates and the car parks or the buses. Her mode of transport was the bus. Sometimes she was lucky in getting into the first one, more often it would be the second or even the third. Then back to these rooms and a scrap meal; perhaps a word with Emily if she wasn't out. Then if there was a play in preparation, two nights a week she would go to rehearsals. One night a week she kept for the pictures; on the others she stayed at home listening to the radio – she hadn't television – or she brushed up her French. Sundays were the worst days, especially so should it be wet.

But all this had been before Ray Collard had asked her out. She liked him from the beginning, primarily because he hadn't pushed her. They had been out three times before he attempted to kiss her, and although his love-making had become more intense as time went on, he had never attempted, as she put it to herself, to eat her up.

When he asked her to marry him she had gladly accepted. Oh, and so gratefully . . . Why had she been so grateful? for he was no great shakes. In no way was he any great shakes, in looks, or position, or personality. When she got to know him better, she began to realize he was more than a bit of a know-all, he was an egotist. Yet, she had still loved him, or at least had a feeling for him. But once they were engaged, his attitude had changed. It was as if he had taken out a licence for intercourse: he seemed to expect it as his due. What were they waiting for? They were engaged. They were going to be married, weren't they? And why was she acting so old fashioned? She was twenty-one, wasn't she, and this was nineteen seventy-eight; Victoria was only remembered in the antique shops. And what was marriage anyway, only a bit of paper.

When she attempted to straighten her back, she found it a painful process. She had sat so long in the one position she'd got cramp in her neck. Slowly she turned her head from side to side, and the very action recalled the numbers of times she had done that in desperation as she had fought him off. It was during one such battle that Emily Houselea had returned unexpectedly. That must be four months ago, and it was the last time she'd had to struggle with him.

As she rose to her feet she asked herself if she had known all along what was going on. Had she asked herself, even wondered, why he had stopped plaguing her and was barely civil to her? And there had been no more talk whether they should live here until the lease ran out or live above the shop and relet this flat as furnished accommodation.

She must have known, so why hadn't she done something?

'Why?'

The answer was all around her: the quietness, the silence that could be heard, broken only by the hissing of the gas-fire. Of a sudden she ran to the door and turned the key in the lock; then still running, she went into the bedroom and, dressed as she was, she flung herself on to the bed and, burying her face into the pillow, she cried, 'Mam! Mam! I can't bear it. I won't be able to stand the loneliness. Help me not to do anything silly. Oh, God, God help me not to do anything silly.' . . . The author had been right in the final speech in that play: chastity was the most expensive commodity in the whole world.

2

Her eyes felt stiff, her face was swollen with the bouts of crying that had gone on intermittently all yesterday. This morning she had put on extra make-up, but it didn't hide from Noreen Power the fact that there was something amiss. 'What's up?' she said tactfully. 'Heading for a cold?'

'Yes, I think so.'

'Well, don't expect any sympathy from the Cad. Look at her through there.' She made an almost imperceptible nod towards the screened off glass-fronted office at the end of the room. 'There's someone on the phone giving it to her, unless I'm mistaken.'

The office door opened and the supervisor stalked down the row of eight desks. She kept her eyes directed towards the last one and when she reached it she looked down on the typist, saying, 'Miss Power, you are to go up to Mr Henderson's office. Miss Honeysett has been taken ill and is in hospital. How is your French?'

Noreen Power opened her mouth to speak, then glanced towards Jinny before looking back at Miss Cadwell and answering, 'It's . . . it's all right I . . . I suppose, speaking it, that is. But . . . but not writing it.'

'There shouldn't be any suppose about it, you're *supposed* to be proficient in French, Miss Power, so please go up at once and give Mr Henderson the benefit of your proficiency.'

'Yes, Miss Cadwell.'

As Jane Cadwell turned about and made back towards her office, Noreen Power gathered up a clean pad from her drawer, quickly attempted to sharpen a pencil, broke the point, then started again, before glancing across at Jinny and muttering under her breath, 'She . . . she should have sent you.'

Forgetting her own particular misery for the moment, Jinny whispered back, 'You'll be all right. I hear his bark's work than his bite.'

'I've heard otherwise.' This muttered remark came from Miss Ann Cartnell in the desk in front of Jinny, and she, turning to Noreen again, said, 'Don't worry. Take it slowly.'

'God! That's advice to give, take Old Thunderbolt slowly. Huh! You won't have time; he'll eat you.'

As Jinny continued with her work she supposed that there would be an Ann Cartnell type wherever girls worked together. Perhaps they were lucky they had only one out of eight of them here.

With regard to herself, she was well aware that Miss Cadwell had never liked her. Why, she didn't know; she only knew that the feeling was mutual. But Miss Cadwell had power, she could make things easy or otherwise, and she had certainly made it otherwise in her case.

It was quarter-past ten exactly when the telephone rang in Miss Cadwell's office and almost simultaneously the outer door opened and Noreen came hurrying back into the room, her head down and the tears streaming from her eyes.

All the typewriters stopped at once, and Jinny, rising from her seat, went towards her, saying, 'What is it? What's happened?'

'He . . . he threw . . . he threw a pad at me and . . . and swore something . . . something awful.'

They were all looking towards Miss Cadwell's office. She had the phone held away from her face which had turned scarlet. They watched her slowly place the instrument on its stand as if it were so fragile it might break, and she stared at it for a moment before opening her door and coming into the office proper. And her eyes now fixing on Jinny, she said, 'Miss Brownlow, go upstairs at once to Mr Henderson's office and see if you can do a better job than Miss Power.'

All eyes were on Jinny, until Miss Cadwell cried, 'Why, may I ask, have you stopped working? You have before now, I suppose, seen a girl making a fool of herself. Inefficiency!' She was glaring at Noreen now and, her voice almost cracking, she ended, 'Get back to your desk and see if you can accomplish the ABC of typing there . . . in English. *English*!'

Miss Cadwell was nothing if not emphatic.

As Jinny left the room she said to herself, imitating Miss Cadwell's voice, English! English! then aloud, 'She can't even speak it.'

As she stepped out of the lift into the carpeted hall of the top floor, young Paul the lift boy pointed to a door almost opposite and in an undertone said, 'I'd put your armour on, miss, if I was you, he's in fine fettle the day, been bawlin' since early on.'

She smiled faintly at him and she had the urge to say, 'I couldn't care less.' And at this moment she couldn't, for she was at war with men, all men.

Yesterday she had sat by herself the whole day and between her bouts of crying had thought things out. And she had come to the conclusion that she hadn't met a decent man since her father had died; and that men today wanted one thing only: they had one aim in life. The approaches to it might be different, but the end product was the same in all cases, to strip you of your clothes . . . No! not even to wait for that.

It was at this point there came to her mind a phrase of her grandmother's to fit her feelings. It was a common phrase, something that her mother wouldn't have used: it was, 'she'd had her bellyful'. But immediately she contradicted the saying because in her case it was the wrong metaphor . . . She was becoming coarse; she must watch it. Her mother would never . . . Oh damn! That was another thing she must watch, becoming pi.

Well, here she was going to see another of them, and if he threw a pad at her she'd throw it back at him. Yes, she would. All right, she'd lose her job, but the way she was feeling at this moment she didn't give a damn. There she was at it again. She mustn't start swearing; there was no need for it. Her father had always said that if you couldn't express what you meant without swearing it only went to prove you were mentally inadequate.

'Come in!' The shout brought her through the door and almost to the middle of the room, and she looked at the man sitting behind the desk. She had never seen him full face before; the glimpse of him she'd had, had been fleeting. He looked tall sitting there, but he must have short legs because she knew he was only of medium height. His hair at one time must have been of a nondescript sandy colour, bits of it were sticking up straight from the crown of his head, but around the sides it was a grizzly grey. His eyes were a sharp blue, his skin looked rough, and not so much wrinkled as marked with deep lines. The top of his shirt was undone and his tie, although still knotted, was hanging a good way down his chest.

'Well!' He stared at her, and she continued to stare at him. 'Well, girl, what are you here for?'

'That's what I'm waiting to find out, sir.'

'Oh, you are, are you?' His eyes narrowed as he glared at her in complete silence for a full minute before he said, 'What's up with you? You've got a chip on your shoulder.'

'Well, if I have it's been placed there since I came in, sir.'

Why on earth had she said that? It was as if she was with her father and they were chaffing each other. She had been very good at repartee when she was at home. Her father had once paid her a compliment: he said that she was witty, not humorous, but witty, Apparently there was a difference.

'Huh!' he pulled his chin into his chest and sat back in his chair now as he said, 'Well, miss, if your French is as sharp as your tongue we'll get along well together. I suppose you know that's why you're here?'

'Oui, monsieur.'

'Oh, that doesn't wash any clothes with me, lass. Any damn fool can say, Oui, monsieur. There, even me. The last one that was in said, Oui, monsieur, and her French wasn't as good as my English, and that's saying something, for the accent anyway. Now get your book and sit yourself down; then later, after you've taken down what I say you'll translate it.'

She sat down, thinking as she did so, He's a hog of a man. There were only hogs among men, Emily had said . . . Oh . . . Emily. Why had she to think about her now? Get on with it.

'What have I just said?'

She raised her eyes as she replied, 'You have just said, "Dear Monsieur Fonier, With regard to your order of two thousand steel rods, which was agreed between you and my son on the 24th October, 1978, I have pleasure . . ." That is as far as you got, sir.'

'I didn't say that, did I?'

'You said words to that effect, sir.'

'I said, "About that order." '

'I thought, "With regard to," sounded better.'

'Oh, you did, did you? Did you know Miss Honeysett?'

'No, sir; I never met her. Not to speak to, but I've seen her.'

'She would have done it like that. How old are you?'

'I was twenty-one last September.'

'Ah! You look older.'

She said nothing.

'Where did you learn your French?'

'From my parents mostly. My paternal grandmother was French; she spoke very little English. My father spoke the language well.'

'How long have you been workin' here?'

'Over a year, sir.'

'Over a year!' He screwed himself forward to the edge of his seat now, his forearm on the desk. 'Why the hell hasn't she sent you up here afore, that Cadwell woman? Have you been stuck in the pool all that time?'

'No; at times I've been directed to other offices.'

She watched him turn his head to the side as if he was thinking. Then looking at her again, he said, 'Old Aggie . . . I mean Miss Honeysett has been off for weeks at a time over this last year. Why weren't you sent up then?'

'You had Miss Bellamy, sir. She . . . she left to get married.'

'Oh, aye, yes, Miss Bellamy. Huh! Miss Bellamy. Bloody lot of good she was; she couldn't spell . . . And don't look like that. You're goin' to hear a lot of words that aren't in the dictionary if you're goin' to work for me. Well, now, let's get on with it. Where were you up to?'

She repeated again what she had written; then continued taking down his dictation. He said nothing while she was typing the letter, but when she had finished he said immediately, 'Let's have a look at it.'

She rose and went towards his desk and handed him the sheet of paper. After staring at it for some seconds, he turned his hard blue eyes up to her and said with a grin on his face, 'You know, I can't read a blasted word of it, and I don't know if you've made any mistakes. Have you?'

That sounded like a demand, and so she said, 'Yes, I put a full stop there' – she pointed – 'it would have read better with a semicolon.'

'Huh. Semicolon. Huh! Long time since I've even heard that word. You know something, lass?' He narrowed his eyes at her. 'I think you'll do. You know why? You've still got that chip on your shoulder, and as long as it's there you'll be alert, on the qui vive, so to speak. Well now, let's get on with it. There's a pile there and I don't suppose you'll have them finished by five o'clock or half-past. Are you a stickler for time?'

'Not particularly.'

'What do you mean by that? Married?'

She drew in a long breath before she said, 'No, sir, I'm not married.'

'Well, in a way that's a pity because somebody will come along and snap you up. They do that in this place, you know. The only one

I could rely on was old Aggie. Nobody came and snatched her up.' The corner of his lip twisted into a smile, then he added, 'But she was a good old stick. She knew her job. But when she comes back I'll see that you don't return to the swimming pool.' He grinned widely now at his own joke and she was forced to give a faint smile in return and add, 'Thank you, sir' . . .

At lunch-time the girls from the pool were waiting for her. How had she got on? Wasn't he terrible? What was the work like? Did she think she could stick it? They said he had his secretary's desk in his office and not in the adjoining office so he could see what she was up to.

She had got on very well. The work was just ordinary business letters. And yes, she could stick it . . .

It was twenty minutes past five when she finished the last letter. He was still sitting behind the desk and when she said, 'Will that be all, sir?' he looked up at her and said, 'Yes, lass, that'll be all for the day. It'll be the same routine the morrow an' the day after that. Do you think you'll be able to stick it?'

'I don't see why not.'

'What's your first name?'

'Jinny.'

'Jinny, not Jenny?'

'No, Jinny, with an "I".'

'Well, I like that . . . Jinny. Got a good North Country sound. There's nothing fancy about that, not like your voice an' manner.'

She felt her face blushing.

'Do you live with your parents?'

'My parents are dead. I live alone.'

'That's a pity. Nobody should live alone, least not at your age. Now if I'd been younger I would have seen to it . . . Oh! Oh!' He lifted his hand. 'Get that look off your face, lass. And while we're on, if we're gona work together, an' it looks like it 'cos old Aggie is going to be in that hospital for some weeks yet, we should know where we stand, eh? Now me, I'm in me fifties but I'm not past it: I can still admire a pretty face, an' I like something nice to look at from across that desk now and again when I have time to look up. But don't get any ideas into your head about the secretary an' the boss. Oh! Oh!' Again he lifted his hand, 'Pull the curtain down on that colour of yours, and I'll put me case to you. Perhaps you've heard it already, but I'll say it plain. I'm a very happily married man with six of a family. The one you've been writing about today, Glen, he's the eldest. He's going to be married next month, and who but a bloody fool would want to be married in December and in white an' all. But that's her of course, not him.' He laughed now.

As he was speaking the phone rang and she put out her hand and picked it up and a voice said, 'Mrs Henderson speaking. Has Mr Henderson gone yet?'

The phone was grabbed from her hand and he yelled into it, 'Hello, pet. No, I haven't gone yet. I'll be another half-hour. I'm just saying goodbye to me secretary.' He turned his head and winked at her. 'She's a young 'un. Old Aggie's in for an operation on that bloody stomach of hers. I've been at her for years to see to it. Yes, I know we're having company, love, and I wish we weren't. I'm tired; I'm gettin' old.'

He listened for a moment, then pulled a face. His lips tight together, his eyes wide, he nodded up at Jinny. Then his voice dropping, he said, 'Be with you soon, dear. 'Bye.'

As he replaced the receiver, he looked again at Jinny and said, 'Wonderful woman. If you stay long enough you'll likely meet her some day, but it won't be here, 'cos she'll never come near the office. She's never been in it since the day we married. A kind of principle of hers. Wonderful woman. And a looker. Aye. Wait till you see her.' And then his voice rose. 'An' you'll likely say like the rest of the bloody dimwits, what in the name of God did she see in him!' He was digging his thumb into his chest now. 'Well, she saw somebody who was goin' places, and is still goin'. Go on, get yourself away lass; you've had enough for one day. Given you something to think about, eh?'

She had reached the door when he shouted, 'Is that chip still on your shoulder?'

She turned to him now and looked at him for a few seconds before she said, 'Yes. Yes, it's still there. But it isn't as heavy as it was this morning.' It was again as if she were chaffing with her father.

It had been a long day, an exciting day, but a tiring one. How tiring she hadn't realized until she reached home. She was about to cook herself a poached egg, and had just dropped it into the boiling water when she suddenly closed her eyes tightly and sat down. It was for a moment as if all the strength had drained out of her. She sat with her forearms on the small kitchen table, her head bent over them. It seemed a long, long time since this morning; so much had happened, yet all that had really happened was that she had been sent into another office to work. But what an office. And what a man. She had never encountered anyone like him. Would she like to continue working for him? She paused before her mind gave her the answer. Yes, she would. He was rough. She had never met anyone as rough. Coarse would be a better description of him. Yet there was an honesty about him. She couldn't imagine anyone ever getting the better of him. But having said that, she knew it would be a very tiring job working for him. There was no let-up where he was. He was either telling you something or demanding something of you. She imagined that he very rarely asked anything of anyone. She could understand how he had terrified Noreen.

Why hadn't he terrified her too? Likely because she had been in a temper when she first went in to him. If she hadn't been it was more than surmise that she would have come out as quickly as Noreen had done. No, she wouldn't; she would have stood her ground, yet without standing up to him. But feeling as she had done, she had stood up to him, and he had seemed to like it.

Well, it had certainly taken her mind off the business of Saturday night and Mr Ray Collard. Her nose twitched slightly as if at a bad smell . . . and there was a smell in the kitchen. She rose hastily and went to the stove. The water had boiled dry and the egg was sticking to the bottom of the pan.

Ah well, she wasn't hungry. She'd have a bath and an early night . . .

An hour later she was sitting in her dressing-gown before the gas-fire munching slowly at an apple when she heard the doorbell ring. She didn't get up immediately and go towards it, but stared at it for a number of seconds . . . She hadn't heard anyone come down the area steps; and now that Emily had gone, and Ray with her, she knew of no one who was likely to call on her.

When the bell rang again, she went towards the door and to her question, 'Who's there?' the voice answered, 'It's me . . . Hal.'

Hal? Mr Campbell? Quickly now she glanced back and around the room; then pulled her dressing-gown cord tight about her waist before she opened the door.

'Do you mind? I . . . I saw your light on as I was passing.'

'No. No, not at all. Come in.'

When she closed the door behind him she looked at his hair, and then at his shoulders, saying with some surprise, 'It's snowing!'

'Yes; it's just started, just a bit of sleet.'

'Come to the fire. I was just about to make some coffee. Would you like one?'

'Yes. Yes, thank you; I would.'

'That seat's the most comfortable.' She pointed to the wicker chair with the padded seat and back.

'Thank you. Do you mind if I take off my coat?'

She paused before she said, 'No. No, not at all.'

In the kitchen as she put some milk into a pan, then switched on the kettle, she was asking herself why he had come. As far as she knew they hadn't even thought about another play. And anyway, they only did four a year and the next rehearsals shouldn't start until February.

His voice came to her now as if he were calling from a distance: 'I told you a lie.'

She went to the kitchen door and looked across the room at him. 'You what?'

'I told a lie.'

Her face stretched in enquiry, and he smiled as he now said, 'I wasn't just passing; I made it my business to call. I was rather worried about you.'

'Oh.' She looked downwards for a moment; then, 'That was kind of you,' she said before turning and walking back to the stove.

'I . . . I wanted to tell you some time ago' – his voice came to her – 'but I thought it was none of my business, that perhaps it was only a flash in the pan and he would see sense . . . He's a fool.'

Not until she had made the coffee, put the two cups on a tray, and had taken it into the sitting-room did she speak, and then she asked, 'Did they all know?'

'No, I wouldn't say all of them. But some of them did. They wanted to tell you about . . . well . . .'

As she handed him the cup of coffee she said, 'I suppose they considered me an idiot not to have guessed something was up . . . so let her find out for herself, they said; one has to live and learn. I can actually hear Gladys Philips saying it.'

He was staring at her; then his eyes narrowed and he peered at her for a moment before saying, 'Odd, but you seem different.'

'In what way different?'

He smiled gently. 'I can't put my finger on it at present,' he said.

She sipped at the coffee, then laid her cup and saucer down on the side table before she spoke again. 'Perhaps I can help you by simply repeating what Ray said to me on Saturday night. He said I was a handmaiden. He did me the honour of putting cultured before it . . . a cultured handmaiden. If he had used ordinary terms he would have said I was a bloody fool' – there she was swearing again – 'making myself cheap. Not, I may add, in the way he wanted me to, but that I was so anxious to please everybody I did all the dirty work during the rehearsals without complaining, and was too gullible to realize that I was being put upon . . .'

'No. No.'

'Oh yes, yes. And he was right. I was so anxious to make friends that for two evenings a week I became a doormat. But you see, they were the only company I knew. And when Ray Collard took notice of me right away my gratitude can be explained by the usual phrase, it knew no bounds.'

'You surprise me.'

'In what way?'

'That you acted as you say you did while thinking as you do.'

'Oh, I can afford to be honest now because, you see, I've grown up. The Fellburn Players has provided me with a kind of Open

University course, a short course admittedly, but one that has certainly paid off.'

'You sound very bitter; it isn't like you.'

Slowly now she bowed her head and looked towards the fire; and after a moment she said, 'I'm . . . I'm not really bitter; I'm angry because I've been such a fool. When people are nice to me I feel so indebted to them I can't do enough for them. It stems, I suppose, from having had loving parents.'

'Jinny.' He was leaning towards her now, his elbows on his knees. 'I'm going to tell you something. I understand every word that you've said, I mean the feeling behind it, because I've experienced the same emotion stemming from the same needs, wanting to be liked, wanting to be loved, wanting to be one of a family. It's still with me. I suppose you've heard I've been divorced?'

She nodded at him, saying, 'Yes, yes, I've heard that.' She did not add that she'd heard he would have been divorced twice only his first wife died before the proceedings could go through.

'I've been married twice, and both times have been failures. Yet I shouldn't say that because I got what I wanted from them, and that's a family . . . Do you want to hear about it?'

'It's a private matter . . .'

'No, no. Most of my life is public property now. Anyway, it started like yours, having a loving mother. I can't remember my father, but my mother was everything to me. When she died, I was as empty as you described yourself. And then I met Peggy. She was twenty-four, I was twenty-five, and she had two small children, a boy and a girl; the boy was eight and the girl seven. She had been married very young, and I must say it, she was still very young, almost childish. But there was my ready-made family. We were married just over two years when – ' He paused, looked to the side and said, 'when she died. It was a bit of a struggle looking after the children but I wouldn't part with them. They were all the family I had. But . . . well, in my job as an estate agent, I sometimes had to go out at night, and so I applied for a housekeeper. And I got one.' He laughed now. It was a gentle, deriding laugh. 'Her name was Dora Morton. She had a sixteen-year-old son called Michael. Well . . . two years later we were married, and then two years after that she walked out. She did ask Michael if he wanted to go with her, and surprisingly he said no. That was two . . . no, more, nearly three years ago now. And well . . . now I can say I have almost brought up a family: Michael has passed his finals in accountancy; he's a very bright fellow. And Rosie, at fifteen, is a sweet girl; and Arthur . . . oh, Arthur' – He laughed gently now – 'he still remains a bit of a problem. Chips on both shoulders.'

She was smiling now as she said, 'I know how he feels. But it was very good of you to take them all on.'

'Oh, I enjoyed it . . . well, in parts . . . But anyway, how would you like to meet them next weekend?'

'Oh, thank you; I'd like that. Yes, I would.' She nodded at him.

'Good. So we'll leave it at that. Say Sunday for dinner? But now I must be off . . .'

After she had seen him to the door and said goodbye she returned to the fireplace and stood looking down at the glare. Things weren't turning out too badly, were they? But then she immediately gave herself the answer, she had a week of nights to get through. But still – she made a face at herself – there were the days, new kind of days ahead, and they certainly wouldn't be lacking in interest as long as she was on the top floor; in fact, if they were anything like her initiation today she'd be too tired to bother about what she was going to do with her evenings in the future, she'd be only too glad to get to bed and sleep.

Of a sudden there came a change in her feelings: she couldn't say she felt happy, but she felt brighter and eager for the morning; which was a change anyway, she told herself.

3

Naturally she wasn't as yet acquainted with all her boss's moods, but as soon as she entered the office the following Friday morning she knew she was about to be introduced to a new one.

'Are you goin' to be one of them clock watchers?' he greeted her, turning his head and looking at the wall clock. 'Nine o'clock on the dot. I was down on the shop floor turned eight this mornin'.'

She stared at him, lost for words. But only for a moment; and then she said, 'Well, of course; it's your business, sir; you have a special interest in it.'

'Now, look here, young lady, don't you come that with me! I'm not havin' any bloody cheek from a youngster.'

'And you won't get any, sir, if you don't bully. My bus gets in the yard at five to nine. If I get an earlier one from my district I would be here at twenty minutes past eight, and not having a vested int – '

She stopped even before he checked her. She was going too far. She didn't know how she'd had the nerve.

'That's enough!' She watched his lower jaw moving from side to side; his hard blue eyes were flashing their anger straight at her.

His hand was already gripping the coarse hair hanging over his brow and he was making to turn away as she said, 'I'm sorry.'

He stopped and looked at her again; then after a moment he said, 'I suppose you're going to add, you don't know what came over you.'

'No, I wasn't.'

'Huh!' Again he made to turn away. But then his tone slightly more moderate, he said, 'Well, it's all experience, I suppose. Get your things off and get on with it.'

She got on with it for the next half-hour. The phone had rung a number of times, and she had answered it. When it rang again she recognized the voice as that of Mr Arthur Pillon. She listened to him speaking for a moment; then covering the mouthpiece, she looked across at Mr Henderson, saying, 'It's the assistant works manager, sir. He says there's a deputation; they wish to see you.'

'Deputation? Which deputation? Where from?'

'The rod sheds, and the transport, I think.'

'Huh! Union or canteen trouble again. Well, I'm in right fettle for them. Tell him to send them up.'

She gave the message, then put the phone down, and she had started to type again when he said, 'What class do you reckon you're in?'

'What class? What do you mean, sir? Social class?'

'Aye, I mean just that, social class.'

'Well, I'm . . . I'm a working girl, but I should say . . . well . . .' She hesitated before ending, 'Lower middle class.'

'Oh, you would, would you?'

'Yes, I would, just because you asked; but I really haven't given it much thought, in fact, none at all.'

'Well, that's something in your favour anyway. So you reckon you're in the middle class, the bottom end like?'

'For the sake of argument, sir, we are all working class.'

'Oh! Traces of the socialist in you then. But it's my guess that's only on the surface, an' that's only for argument. With your refined twang and your manner I think you're right to place yourself in the middle lot.'

'My parents placed me where I am, I had no say in the matter.'

'Eeh, we're getting deeper now, lass, aren't we? That's what folks generally say when they're rejecting religion.'

He was in a mood. Something had evidently upset him.

Within a few minutes she knew what it was. After a knocking on the door and he having bawled, 'Come in!' there entered two workmen. Their chins were out, their necks stiff, and she recognized they were in much the same mood as he was.

His greeting was overlaid with heavy sarcasm: 'Oh, good morning, Mr Newland. And you, Mr Trowell. And what can I do for you the day? Wait. Don't tell me. You have come to tell me that you are underworked and overpaid, that you have been given better conditions of work here than anywhere else on the Tyne, but that, being bloody fools, you don't appreciate it. And you're here now to say that you're going to turn over a new leaf. Isn't that why you've come?' He looked from one to the other, and it was the taller of the two men, Jack Newland, who said, 'We're quite used to your approach, Mr Henderson. Being sarcastic won't help. You know why we're here; it's about the canteen.'

'Oh, the canteen. The canteen.' He now turned his head and nodded towards Jinny, saying, 'Now you go to the canteen, don't you? And wouldn't you say it's a fine canteen, as good as any high-class café you'd get in Newcastle?'

She made no reply; nor apparently did he expect any, for, turning back to the men and, his tone changing, he said, 'Now look here, Jack Newland, and you Peter Trowell. I had that canteen built to supply refreshments for all, and I repeat for all the workers in this factory.'

'Aye, we know you did, Mr Henderson.' Peter Trowell's neck was no longer stiff and his head was moving from side to side as he went on, 'But you see, it's like this. We want a place of our own. It would be quite easy to put a partition up, sort of. In any case, the white-collar lot stick to one end and us at the other. You never see them sit at the same table. It was better the way it was afore.'

'Officers, sergeants, and men, like.'

'Aye, if you say so, Mr Henderson, like that.'

'And where do you two come in, being shop stewards? The sergeants' mess?'

'Well, no. It was Jack Newland speaking now. 'We . . . we . . . we mix.'

'Oh, but that isn't right.' Mr Henderson now shook his head. 'In the army, the sergeants' mess is . . . What's the word?' He turned his head from side to side; then looking at Jinny, he said, 'Can you give me a word that'll fit this?'

After a moment's hesitation she said, 'Sacrosanct.'

'Oh aye. Yes, now, she's said it, sacrosanct. That means, if I know anything, keep out.'

'Well, it isn't that with us.'

'Don't tell me that, Newland' – his voice had changed to a deep growl, all light sarcasm gone now – 'because you've had the makings of an upstart right from the first. Now when I started this business thirty years ago, you came in straight from school and you didn't know B from a bull's foot, but afore many years were gone you soon found out that you had pretensions, but of course you had nowt up top to carry them out. It's the sheep down on the shop floor who've put you where you are the day: follow me leader. If the other fellows who get on with their jobs and use common sense took the trouble to fill the meetings you would be out on your arse, let me tell you.'

'I object to your manner, Mr Henderson.'

'You can damn well object to anything you like. You've objected afore to it, and it won't be the last time I suppose. Who's put you up to this anyway, about dividing the canteen? Some of your red friends?'

'I object . . .'

'Shut your mouth, and don't spout any more of your objections to me . . . What were you going to say, Peter?' He now looked at Trowell.

The man's voice was quiet and his tone reasonable as he said, 'Well, Mr Henderson, I was just gona say I don't think the white-collar lot . . . I don't think the clerks and such want to mix. I mean, they would prefer a dinin' place on their own. In fact, some of them have said so.'

'Aye, I can believe you, Peter, that some of them would say so, but I'm astounded that you lot say it because it gives them the idea that you don't consider yourself fit company to eat alongside them. I still think of meself as a working man; I go and eat downstairs, don't I? Sometimes at one table, sometimes at another.'

'Well, you can do that, you're in that position, Mr Henderson.'

'I do it' – he now leant across the table towards the man – 'not because of my position but because I think I'm bloody well as good as anybody down there, white-collar, high topper and tails, the lot, and I haven't thought that just the day or yesterday, I thought it when I was workin' on the shop floor, and humpin' those rods from the sheds to the lorries in Carter's over in Sunderland. And there the bloody manager wouldn't give me the time of day or the smoke that went up the chimney. That's what spurred me on and got me where I am the day. And yes, I know what you all say, marrying a woman with money was a damn good help. It was an' all. I was lucky, wasn't I? But the thing is I was determined then and I'm as determined now to break down bloody narrow-minded barriers. There's only one barrier that I recognize an' that's intelligence, 'cos if I had my way I would divide the intelligent lot from the numskulls. Aye, I would.' As he finished speaking he kept his eyes on Jack Newland, and this big man, red in the face, muttered, 'It's no good talkin' to you, Mr Henderson, is it? If you won't listen to our demands we could go to Mr Garbrook.'

'You can go to hell, if you like. And let me tell you, Newland' – he laughed now – 'you'll get better joy out of hell than you'll get out of me partner, because I can tell you exactly what he'll say. He'll look at you and he'll smile and he'll say, "Yes, Jack" – oh, he'll always call you by your Christian name – "Yes, yes, Jack", he'll say; "I understand you perfectly, and I'll have a talk with Bob about this." That's what you'll get from Mr Garbrook, word for word. But go on, try your welcome. And now both of you' – his voice dropped – 'get yourselves downstairs to your respective departments, and then at dinner-time, be brave, aye, be brave, go into the canteen, to the far end, and sit down next to, say, Mr Pillon, or Mr Waitland, or . . . Oh aye, go and sit next to Mr Waitland, from along the corridor here. Then there's Mr Meane from the drawing-office. Now he's a nice fellow. They're all nice fellows. Forget you feel inferior, put yourselves to the test. That'll be all . . . gentlemen.'

The two men stared down at him for a matter of seconds before both turned away and without a word left the room.

There was silence for perhaps one whole minute; and then his fist came down on the desk so hard that the heavy paperweight slid almost to the edge of the polished wood surrounding the blotting pad, and through clenched teeth he exclaimed, 'Bloody numskulls!'

She kept on typing. He was a dreadful man, really; yet, strangely, she agreed with what he had said. But it was the way he said it. The only thing was that she hadn't seen him in the canteen when she herself had been there. But there must have been times when he had been, or else he wouldn't have said it. She knew that on Fridays he had a tray sent up with sandwiches and coffee.

He startled her now by yelling, 'Enjoy your first lesson in shop floor diplomacy?'

After hesitating just a moment she said quietly, 'Well, it was enlightening in its lack of the latter.'

'What! . . . What did you say?'

'I . . . I think you heard what I said, sir.'

'Aye, I did. You meant that diplomacy was the last thing it had in it?'

'Yes, sir.'

'By!' He was looking down on the papers on his pad. 'You don't only find them on the shop floor, they seep up into the bloody offices. But you're right when you say you're from the bottom of the middle. By, aye, I'd confirm that any day.'

After glaring at her for a moment longer, he attacked the papers on his desk, and she continued with her typing.

However, the atmosphere changed absolutely at eleven o'clock, when the door burst open and a young man came in. He was of medium height, dark complexion, with bright brown eyes. And he stood for a moment in the doorway, then banged the door closed behind him before coming to the desk and, leaning over it, saying, 'Well, hello there. I'm back.'

'I haven't lost me eyesight yet. Does your mother know?'

'Of course, she knows.'

'Aye, of course she would. You've been home first then?'

'Again, of course I have.'

'You should have come straight here from the plane; I want to know about things.'

'You'll get to know soon enough.'

The young man turned and looked to where Jinny was continuing to type, and he said, 'What's happened to Aggie?'

'She's in hospital, where she should have been this long while. We've got a new one here; and I can tell you straightaway she's a . . . cheeky piece. Her name's Jinny.'

Still Jinny didn't look up; but she heard the muttered reply, 'Oh yes?'

Glen Henderson now took off his coat and sat down at the side of the desk. There was no resemblance between him and his father, either in looks, manner, or speech, yet they had one strong bond, they were both very much alive. And this came over in their cross-talk. Jinny could hear only snatches of it above the rattle of the typewriter keys, but when the letter was finished she heard Mr Henderson saying, 'Good. That's good. Better than we'd ever hoped for.'

'It wasn't easy. Don't think that. Six competitors. One gets the idea out there that every country in the world is turning out steel now. You've got to realize that the profit margin on this order is thin. Well, it had to be to beat the others.'

'But it's a new contract; that's what we want, new contracts.'

'They want delivery on date stated.'

'Well, don't we always deliver on the date stated? That's what's made us, laddie, delivery on the date stated. Hell or high water – that's the motto – we'll deliver.'

'What's this I hear about strike?'

'They won't strike. It'll come to nothing. They're not bloody fools altogether, cutting off their noses to spite their faces. There'd be a close down like nothing that's ever happened afore in this industry if they did. A pity some of them couldn't be sent over to Japan and Germany. That would open their eyes and make them realize that we're not the only people in the world who are turning out steel; and that there's such a thing as competition, cut-throat competition; and that if we can't get the orders they can't have the work . . . There's something happened to men, these days. Something. Something.'

Glen laughed now as he said, 'By what you've told me, pumped into me about bygone conditions, it didn't happen soon enough.'

'Aye, but there's moderation in all things. And there's such a thing as greed. The motto the day seems to be, You've got it and I want it, but I'm not bloody well going to work for it . . . Anyway, you going back home for dinner?'

'Yes. And Mother says you are to come back with me.'

'Eeh! I can't do that, man.'

'Of course, you can. The place is not going to fall down because you've left it for an hour.'

'Now look here, me lad.'

'I am looking.'

Glen had turned to Jinny and he asked, 'What does he do at dinner-times anyway, Jennie?'

'I wouldn't know, I haven't been here long enough.'

'And that's right' – his father nodded at him now – 'she wouldn't know. And by the way, her name's Jinny not Jennie, Jinny, common like. And, as she says, she hasn't been here long enough. But the time she has been here she's given me some stick. I can tell you that.'

'I'm glad to hear it.'

Glen smiled across at Jinny, and she answered his smile.

'And you know something else?' Mr Henderson was now looking at his son. 'She's middle class; from the lower end, she says.'

'Oh, that's interesting.' Glen pursed his lips as he nodded towards Jinny now. 'It's good to know where we stand.'

'It was the position your father put me into. As I told him, I hadn't give it any thought up till then.'

'You see' – Bob Henderson was nodding at his son – 'she's got an answer for everything, this one. And in that polite voice of hers.'

'Well, I'm glad to know you've met your match at last, because poor Aggie had a time of it.'

'She didn't. Old Aggie could hold her own.'

'Yes, when you weren't reducing her to tears.'

'Nonsense. When Aggie cried it was because I was kind to her.'

'Speaks for itself.' Glen picked up his coat and hat and said, 'Listen. Don't forget' – he looked at his watch – 'leave here on the dot.'

'We'll see.'

'Goodbye, Jinny.'

'Goodbye, sir.'

The office to themselves again, Bob Henderson looked at Jinny and with an air of pride he said, 'What did you think of him?'

'I don't know him. And anyway . . .'

'Oh my God! lass.' He now leaned his elbow on the desk and rested his head on his hand and closed his eyes as he continued to say slowly, 'Don't add, it isn't my place to say.'

'I had no intention of doing so.'

He lifted his head again. 'Well, what were you going to say?'

'If I had been going to say anything sir, I would have said that I would imagine he is the exact opposite from yourself.'

'Oh, you would, would you?'

'Yes, since you ask.'

'And what makes you think that?'

'Well, for one thing he doesn't bellow; and for another . . .' She stopped. No, she just couldn't say, he doesn't have to stress his position; that would be going too far. Rising to her feet, she said, 'These letters are ready for you to sign.'

'You finish what you were going to say.'

'I have no intention of finishing what I was going to say.'

'Because it was something nasty, something against me?'

'Perhaps.'

'Eeh! Oh, you know you are a cheeky bugger.'

She swallowed deeply. She should walk out. She should be running back to the pool crying, like Noreen had done.

He surprised her now by bursting out laughing and saying, 'Lass, I think you and me'll fit in nicely. Low middle class and lower working class, eh?'

What a strange man. He had a very endearing side to him.

The lights had been on in the office all afternoon; it had been raining heavily.

'Is it still coming down?'

She went to the darkened window, saying, 'I think it's turned to snow. It's so early, only November.'

'Aye, well it's likely working up to a white Christmas. Then it'll change its mind again. I like a white Christmas . . . How do you get home?'

'Oh.' She paused. 'By bus.'

'Aye, that's what you said afore. You haven't got your own car yet then? Most of them have. My God, when you think of it. My dream of transport in me young days was having a bike; now they take a car for granted. They don't know they're born. Oh' – he flapped his hand at her as he went towards the wash room – 'I know that saying's got whiskers, but it's true, nothing more true. And the more they get the more they want. People are greedy. You know that?' Before closing the door he turned round and looked at her.

She stood now gazing down at her hands resting on the desk and thinking yet again he was the strangest man she had ever come across. But she liked him, and she would find working for someone else very tame after him. Most people in the building seemed to be scared of him, yet she knew that were she working in any of the other offices she wouldn't dream of answering her particular boss back. Yet she could do it with him. It was a most peculiar situation.

She was placing the cover over her typewriter when he came into the office again, saying, 'Get your coat on, I'll give you a lift home. With the weather like this they'll be rushing like Gadarene swine for the buses the night.'

The Gadarene swine. That was a quote from the Bible. He was a funny man . . .

A few minutes later they got out of the lift and were going across the main hall together towards a porter who opened the door ready for their exit, saying as he did so, 'Good-night, sir. Nasty weather.'

Mr Henderson gave him no reply, not even a thank you. But as he settled himself in the car – she'd had to go round and let herself in the other side – he said, not without a note of glee in his voice, 'That'll set the tongues waggin', 'cos nobody ever saw me come downstairs with Aggie Honeysett. You're honoured. You know that? You're honoured.'

'Well, I would think the honour is questionable if its only merit is to set tongues wagging.'

As he swung the car out of the main gate he chuckled as he said, 'You get a kick out of coming back with things like that at me, don't you? All precise and nicely parcelled up. A cross atween a schoolmistress and a news-reader.'

Really! A cross between . . . Really! But she knew he was right, she did get a kick out of answering him back, and in that precise fashion as he had said, which wasn't a bit like how she thought. She was amazed at herself. If the Fellburn Players could hear her at times talking to this man they wouldn't believe it was the same person who had skittered, and that was the right word because she had skittered here and there at their bidding, tripping over herself to please them. What a fool they must have thought her, inane, characterless, and all because she wanted to be with people, please them. Well, that part of herself was finished, she'd never be like that again.

'What do you do with yourself over the weekend?' he said. And she replied truthfully: 'Read and tidy up mostly. But this Sunday I've been invited out to dinner.'

A short while later when the car stopped and he leant over her to open the door, he said, 'Don't sit mopin' alone there the night. Get yourself out to the pictures or some place. Leave your tidyin' up. Go for a drink . . . Well, no, that isn't such good advice, not on your own. But it's a long time till Sunday, till you go to that dinner.'

On the pavement, she bent down before he closed the door and said quietly, 'I'll be all right. Thank you, Mr Henderson. Have a nice weekend. See you Monday.' And she banged the door closed, and saw him through the rain-splattered window jerk his head at her in farewell before driving off.

Underneath all that bombast he was a kind man, thoughtful; she felt that he was concerned for her being on her own. It was nice to feel that someone was concerned for you.

It was like stepping into an icebox when she opened the door of the flat. It seemed colder inside than out. And so she didn't take off her outdoor things until the fire had been lit for some time, and she had a tray set for her tea.

It was as she sat with her knees almost touching the glowing bar, drinking her second cup of tea, that there swept over her the most odd feeling. It seemed to erupt from deep within her. It brought her to her feet, her hand, outstretched, gripping the mantelpiece, her chest heaving as if she were gasping for breath, and when the tears spurted from her eyes she dropped her head on to her hands while asking herself, 'What's wrong with me?' Yet at the same time being aware of what was wrong: Mr Henderson's kindness and concern had highlighted this evening, and tomorrow, and stretched it into an eternity.

Hal Campbell called for her at eleven o'clock on Sunday morning. The streets were wet after the night of rain, but the sun was shining. He drove the car through town, past the park, and up Brampton Hill, and as they passed some tall iron gates that gave on to a long drive he inclined his head towards them and said, 'That's where your boss lives.'

'Really?' She leant forward, but the car was already past the gates and all she saw was a high laurel hedge.

'And his son who's getting married shortly has bought the one at the top. It's not so big, but he must have paid a pretty penny for it.'

'Your firm didn't sell it then?'

'No; worse luck.' He laughed. 'But we've got charge of three houses on the Hill. They're all in flats. I think there must be only five private ones left altogether. This used to be the swell end of Fellburn at one time. I suppose it still is even in the flats, because they cost a pretty penny.'

At the top of the Hill the road passed between agricultural fields before coming to a modern estate. When he drove through this she said, 'You live a long way out?'

'Not all that far. It's just about a mile further on. We were very lucky. We came across this, I mean my mother and I, when houses were dirt cheap, at the beginning of the sixties. The only trouble is the garden, it's too big. I have a man come in twice a week, but he doesn't seem to get through much. They don't when you're not standing over them. It's the same inside: Mrs Grayson leaves a lot to be desired where cleanliness is concerned. I spend most of my weekend cleaning up and cooking. I hope the meat isn't burnt.' He cast a quick smile at her. 'I left Rosie in charge, and with orders not to switch the television on. I doubt if I'll be obeyed.'

They were well past the modern estate and on a country road now, and as he swung the car into a narrow lane he lifted his hand from the wheel and pointed, saying, 'See there? That's it.'

She looked over a field to where, rising from a clump of trees, she could see the upper storey of a house. After a moment she said, 'It looks big.'

'Oh, it isn't all that big; but there's ten rooms altogether. That includes the attics. It was in a pretty rough state when we took it. I've had a lot done to it.'

'It seems right out in the country.'

'Well, we are between two farms. We're lucky, I suppose. For how long one never knows these days. Farming land was sacrosanct at one time, but now, if it's a freehold farm and hasn't any conservation tags laid down on it, it only needs a developer to come along and you have a new town.'

He turned the car now between two open white gates, and there, at the end of the short drive, stood his house. She was amazed at the sight of it; it was like a little mansion. It was built of natural stone. The front door which looked black and solid was flanked on each side by three tall windows, with replicas above them but on a smaller scale. And above these were attic windows.

He helped her out of the car. Then pushing open the front door, he held out his hand and guided her over the step and into the hall, calling as he did so, 'Where's everybody?'

As if at a signal three people appeared. The first she noted was a young girl who looked to be sixteen or seventeen. But this must be Rosie, the fifteen-year-old. She was standing in the kitchen doorway.

The stairs, she noted, led up from the side of the hall, and next to them was a half door with a head peering round. It was that of a slightly built boy. This must be the brother. His face was thin, with a pinched look. But in the doorway to the extreme left of her there stood a young man. He was tall, as tall as Hal. His hair was brown, and his face rather long. She scanned the three faces in turn; then Hal Campbell, helping her off with her coat, said, 'This is Miss Brownlow, otherwise known as Jinny, and' – he nodded – first to the girl – 'that's Rosie'; then to the boy, 'And that's Arthur'; and lastly he inclined his head towards the far door, saying, 'And Adonis there is Michael.'

Michael Morton was the first to move towards her. 'Hello,' he said. And she answered, 'Hello.'

Then the girl came, and standing some distance from her, she nodded her head slightly, and Jinny said, 'Hello.'

'Come on out of that!' It was Hal calling to the boy now; and he came from the doorway, but did not speak. He just looked at Jinny, and she at him. Then the awkward silence was broken by Michael saying to her, 'Come into the sitting-room.'

'That's right. All of you get yourselves in there, while I see to the dinner.'

The young man now led the way into the sitting-room which Jinny noticed immediately was very well furnished: a comfortable chesterfield suite, besides a sofa table, and two china cabinets each holding a colourful array of figures. There was a fire burning in an open grate set back in a stone fireplace, and the room, like the hall, was covered in a deep red carpet.

Jinny sat in one corner of the couch, and the young man in the other; the girl curled up on the rug before the fire, but the boy remained standing with one shoulder leaning against the corner of the stone fireplace. His head turned slightly, he continued to survey Jinny with a penetrating stare, of which she was conscious all the time she was answering Michael Morton's questions.

She worked at Henderson's, didn't she?

Yes.

Did she like it?

Yes, she liked it very much. Particularly lately since she had been working for the boss.

He said he had heard about old Henderson; he was a bit of a devil, wasn't he?

She wasn't finding him so.

How long had she been there?

Over a year.

Had she always lived in Fellburn?

Yes, she was born here.

He understood she was an orphan.

Before she had time to answer this the boy spoke for the first time: derisively, he said, 'Little Orphan Annie came to our house to stay, to chase the chickens from the porch and sweep the crumbs away.'

'That's enough of that, Arthur. Now watch it.' Michael Morton turned and looked at Jinny again, saying, 'I'm sorry to say that my stepbrother is uncouth and ignorant, but there is one excuse for him, he is young, so there's some hope that he may develop into a normal human being before long. At times I have my doubts though.' He smiled at her now.

'Oh, you fancy pants!' The boy now pulled himself from the support of the fireplace and went hurrying from the room, and the girl, getting to her knees and leaning forward to push a log further on to the fire, spoke for the first time, too, saying, 'Don't take any notice of him. I bet he'll be all over you the next time you come. He likes to show off.'

She turned and smiled at Jinny, and Jinny smiled back at her, thinking, Well, the boy's rudeness had broken the ice, if nothing else, and it had been very thick to begin with.

'Would you like a drink?'

'Yes, I would please. A sherry.'

'May I have a drop, Michael?'

'All right then, but get it down you before Big Pop sees you, else I'll be for it.'

As she sipped at her sherry Jinny wondered why no one was going to the kitchen to help Hal with the dinner; then as if her thoughts had been picked up by Michael, he said to Rosie, 'Did you set the table?'

'Yes. Of course, I did. And I've done the vegetables too. I can if I like, you know.'

'Yes, I know, but you don't always like, do you?'

'Well, I don't see why I should when there's Mrs Grayson all the week and Big Pop dashing around at weekends. There's no need for me.'

'Well, I think there might be need for you now, miss. So go in the kitchen and see what you can do. Go on now!'

'You're worse than him. You know that?'

Jinny watched the girl rise slowly from her knees; then when she was standing she made a face at Michael before saying, 'Behave yourself or I'll tell Pop.'

'Get out!' he said, making a pretence of rising; only to sink back into the couch, saying, 'She'd embarrass a New York detective. Girls of her age are dreadful: no veneer, life oozing out of every pore.'

'Why a New York detective?'

'Oh.' He jerked his chin upwards now as he laughed. 'It's the television, I suppose; they seem tougher than the English ones, unflappable . . . Have you known Hal long?'

She was slightly surprised at the question; she had somehow thought that Hal Campbell had put them all in the picture as to why she was here today, the recipient of his compassion for the lonely.

'A little over a year. Let's say the time it's taken to do four plays.'

'You've been with the Players for a year?' There was a note of surprise in his voice now.'

'Yes.'

'What do you think of them?'

'What do you mean, what do I think of them? Their individual characters, or their acting abilities?'

He now slanted his gaze at her as if he was slightly puzzled by her reply; then he said, 'A bit of both.'

'Well, there are some and some; but they all have one thing in common, they think they can act.' Now why had she said that? It sounded bitchy.

His peal of laughter brought her head towards the door expecting any minute one or other of the family to come in to see what the joke was about. But it remained closed. And as she looked back at him again he said, 'You certainly hit the nail on the head there. How some of that lot dare get up on a stage and expose themselves, and that's the word, expose, I just don't know.'

'I don't think Mr Campbell holds that opinion, else he wouldn't have gone on with them.'

He was looking at her now, his face quite straight, and the question he put to her caused her own face to become stiff, for he said, 'How long have you been going out with him?'

Her voice reflected her expression as she said, 'I have never gone out with him. He was kind enough to ask me to dinner today because he knew I had suffered a disappointment and was on my own.

He made no reply other than to raise his eyebrows; then looked down towards his feet, and made a number of small movements with his head as if in disbelief, before saying quietly, 'We live and learn;' then turned his head and stared at her in silence until she became embarrassed and searched for something to say.

'You're an accountant, I understand.'

'Yes, you're right; I am an accountant. Just lately fully fledged. Our offices are not far from Henderson's works. We are Ford and Branham's.'

'Oh. It's quite a way to travel each day.' Her immediate thought was, What a stupid thing to say? What was five miles in a car? But he answered, 'Yes, I've thought so, too, for some time now, but from February next I'll be living in the town. Setting up house there.' He pursed his lips.

'Are you going to be married?'

He lowered his head for a moment while keeping his eyes on her, saying now, 'I'm not going to shock you by saying this, females are unshockable these days: no, I'm not going to be married, but we're setting up together, my girl friend and I.'

She did not say, 'Oh,' she just looked at him.

And now his head jerked upwards in what she was already recognizing to be a characteristic gesture, and he laughed softly as he said, 'You are shocked. Good Lord! You are shocked.'

She could find nothing immediately to say to this, but she asked herself why testy replies just skipped off her tongue when she was with Mr Henderson, but now in the presence of this young man she seemed to be back in the Social Hall, chary about opening her mouth in case she displeased some one . . . But those days were past; she wasn't afraid of displeasing this fellow or anyone else, and so now she heard herself saying coolly, 'You're mistaken; I wasn't shocked; I was only thinking it was so unoriginal. Everybody is shacking up with everybody else. It's like musical chairs, and one day there'll only be one person left on the chair. The music will have stopped but there'll be no more partners on either side. He'd be the winner, but of what?'

She saw immediately that she had annoyed him, yet his voice had an airy sound as he said, 'A female philosopher as ever was: public library graduation.'

When she made to rise from the couch he sprang to his feet and, standing in front of her, he said, 'I'm sorry. It's very bad of me. I'm acting worse than Arthur. Please . . . please overlook it.' And he smiled now gently. 'Let's imagine you've just come in.'

It was at this point that the door opened and Hal entered, saying, 'Well, it's ready, if anyone feels inclined to eat. Have you had a drink? Has he been looking after you?' He came over to her and put his hand on her shoulder. It was a possessive gesture, but she didn't shrink from it, and he went on, 'Has he been entertaining you? He's a cynic, you know, out to break all the rules of society. But come on, let's eat.' And he took her elbow and led her from the room, across the hall, and through a door into the dining-room. The boy and girl were already there, and the food was on the table, the vegetables in covered dishes, and at the top of the table a joint of sirloin on a side dish.

The dinner was excellent but didn't seem to be anything out of the common to them, even the wine glasses set for the young people as well. They had a glass each but were offered no more, while her glass and Michael's and Hal's were refilled.

Following the main course, they had a plum crumble. Plums out of their own garden she was informed; they had enough fruit of different kinds in deep freeze to last them all winter.

When the meal was over she asked if she could help with the washing up, and she was surprised that the offer was accepted when there were the other three who could have helped, but here she was in the kitchen drying the dishes, and liking it.

She was beginning to feel more at ease. She had learned that she needn't waste any sympathy on Hal for having to do the cooking for on his own admission he loved cooking. He had asked her if she could cook, and she'd replied she could cook a roast dinner, but then had been quick to add not of the quality that he had presented today. However, one thing she could do in the cooking line was make cakes. Her mother had been an expert cake-maker.

What kind of cakes could she make? Rosie asked.

Oh, fruit loaves, sponges, Swedish wedding-cakes.

What were Swedish wedding-cakes? The enquiry came from all quarters, and she replied, 'Oh, they are not our idea of wedding-cakes, they are simply like apple tarts, made in a deep tin, with cinnamon pastry.

What was cinnamon pastry?

Should she show them?

So she cooked a Swedish wedding-cake, and later they had it for tea; and the meal turned out to be quite merry.

Following this Hal asked her if she would play the piano, and as if she were at a Players rehearsal she consented immediately. It was when Hal, Michael, and Rosie were standing round her singing one of Jim Reeves's old favourites 'I love You Because', which was a favourite of hers too, that Arthur, who hadn't joined in but was sitting near the fire, suddenly shouted, 'I'm going out.'

His voice had been so loud that Jinny stopped playing and the voices of the singers trailed off, but Hal Campbell didn't turn round to his stepson. What he did was to take up a piece of music from the piano, place it in front of Jinny and say, 'You're not. Not tonight.'

'I am.'

'Then you'll have to walk. You're not taking that bike out tonight; it's pouring with rain.'

'I can manage it. You know I can.'

'Not in the dark.' He still hadn't turned towards the boy.

'You can go to hell; I'm going out.'

Almost before the boy started to make for the door Hal Campbell swung round, rushed at him, caught him by the shoulders and pushed him from the room.

The door was left open and the boy's protesting cries came to them. Quickly now, Michael walked to the door and closed it. Then returning to the middle of the room, he was about to speak when Rosie, throwing herself on to the hearthrug and into her usual position, said, 'He spoils everything. He always spoils everything.'

'He doesn't.'

Jinny looked from one to the other and was surprised at the tone of Michael Morton's voice.

'You always take his part.'

'I take the part of those in the right.'

Well, well. So he thought the young, uncouth, bad-mannered youth was in the right. And Hal, the patient – and he certainly was patient – stepfather was in the wrong. But why? There was something below the surface here. Well, it was none of her business, but somehow it had spoilt the day.

There was the sound of a door banging overhead; then as if somebody was kicking against it. The next sound that came to them was definitely recognizable as somebody stamping on the floor. And at this, Rosie scrambled to her feet, gave Michael a hard stare, and then almost ran from the room. Michael sat down heavily and turned to Jinny with an apologetic shrug of his shoulders.

'I'm sorry about this, but if you are going to be a visitor here you might as well be initiated into the pattern right away: The stepfather dominating the stepson; the stepson doesn't like it. A lot to be said on both sides. But mostly on the stepfather's you think?'

She didn't answer for a moment, and he scrutinized her through lowered lids before she said, 'Yes, you're right. To the outsider, which I am, he appears like a handful.'

'Yes, he would do. Anyway, come and sit down, because you won't be seeing your host again for a quarter of an hour at least; he likes time to cool down before putting in an appearance;' which remark she thought suggested that the bouts were not infrequent.

She was once more seated at the other end of the couch from him, and he said, 'I'm not usually here on Saturday or Sunday evenings;

or very few evenings for that matter, but my girl friend, Cath, is away for the weekend, and at the moment I am not very popular with her people, particularly her mother who has a fixation about marriage.'

He waited for her to make some reply to this, but when she didn't he said, 'Are you set on marriage?'

She gulped in her throat before she answered, 'Well, let me say I'm not set on shacking up, as the term is, with anyone.'

'Your answer doesn't surprise me.'

'Why is that?'

'Because it's the usual one. No nice girl such as you are is going to admit that she would like to follow her instincts and inclinations.'

She felt the colour sweeping over her face, and she had the urge to jump up from the couch and stalk out of the room. But then, with that action she felt she would have acknowledged him to be right. He was making her angry, even causing her to feel as she had done the night she was confronted with Ray Collard. It was as if some secret part of her was being attacked and a new force was being created in her with which to defend it, because up till lately there had never been an occasion in her life which had aroused such anger in her.

Michael leant towards her, apologizing again, saying, 'I've rattled you. Believe me, I didn't mean to. It wasn't my intention. You know' – he laughed softly – 'perhaps it's as well we are not likely to meet very often after this because we'd always be arguing. That's if you'd deign to answer me. Perhaps you'd just sit looking at me as you are now as if you were wishing me far enough. Ah' – his voice dropped – 'here's the saviour of all mankind.'

She turned her head quickly and looked towards the door to where Hal Campbell was entering the room, and she noticed immediately that his face looked strained. Yet his voice sounded ordinary as he said, 'Family dispute. Show me the family that doesn't have one and I'll say it's no real family.'

He sat in a chair to the side of the fireplace, and now looking at her but inclining his head towards Michael, he said, 'Has he been behaving himself? He's an agitator, you know, a natural stirrer. If he hasn't got a cause he creates one. Isn't that so, Michael?'

Jinny now looked at the two men who were exchanging glances, and she recognized the feeling of animosity between them, and this came over in Michael's reply as he said, 'Yes, you're right. I'm always for the underdog wherever I may find him.'

So much for the happy home. Yet it seemed to be Hal Campbell's one aim in life to create such an atmosphere; he seemed to go out of his way to do everything for all of them. But then, she was only thinking of the material things, such as their bodily welfare through his cooking, and providing a comfortable home; for apparently there were other things needed for harmony, and in a way, Michael was accusing him of missing out on them, whatever they were. One of them was likely his being too harsh with the boy. Yet, taking a father's place, he would have to show some authority; and, as she had already remarked, that boy was a handful. For a moment she wished she were home, home being the lonely flat. Yet, she wanted company. There was something in her that craved companionship.

That one member of the family was loyal to the head of the house was shown when Rosie re-entered the room, for, sitting down on the hearthrug, she leant her head against her stepfather's knee and he, putting his hand on her hair, began to stroke it. And they sat like that while the talk wavered in a desultory manner from one topic to another.

At nine o'clock Jinny thought she had better be making her way home, for she had to prepare for work tomorrow morning. It was at this point that Michael, standing with his back to the fire, looked at Hal, saying, 'You've had two drinks tonight. You're against drinking and driving, shall I see Jinny back, because I've got no scruples along that line, feeling that I can keep my head.'

For a moment Jinny saw the dark look spread over Hal's face that she had witnessed earlier when he had run the boy from the room, but his voice did not betray his feelings as he replied, 'Oh, I think I can manage on this occasion. You don't mind if we hit a lamppost or two, do you, Jinny?'

'No, not at all.' She forced herself to smile, not because she felt any nervousness at being driven by Hal but because she wanted to convey in some small way whose company she preferred.

When a short while later she stood in the hall saying goodbye to Rosie, the girl smiled widely at her as she said, 'Will you come again?' And Jinny answered, 'Yes. Yes, I'd like to.'

She then turned to where Michael Morton was standing some little way back from them, and she inclined her head towards him, saying, 'Good-night.'

And he answered in the same vein: his head bowing a little deeper than hers, he said, 'Good-night . . .'

They had driven some distance towards the town before Hal Campbell remarked, 'I don't think it's been a very nice day for you.'

'Oh, yes it has. I've thoroughly enjoyed it.'

He kept his eyes on the dark road as he said, 'That do with Arthur, then Michael showing his worst side, couldn't have left you with a very good impression of my family.'

'Well, let's say my initiation started at the deep end, and can now only get better.'

'Well, that's one way of looking at it.' He gave a short laugh. Then presently he said, 'I'm sorry I had to leave you to hold your own with Michael.'

'Oh, I think I managed.'

'Yes, somehow I think you would now. You know, you're a bit of a surprise, Jinny.'

'In what way?'

'Well, the Jinny I knew in the Players was . . . a sort of kindly mouse, scampering hither and thither at everybody's bidding, giving the impression you'd be frightened to say boo!'

'Yes.' Her voice held a sad note now as she replied, 'I suppose that's how I did appear. As I said the other night, I was starving for company. I suppose I still am.'

'Well, in your case that trouble shouldn't be difficult to erase. If you put your mind to it I think you could get any kind of company you chose. I . . . and the family will just be a stop gap.'

'No . . . No. I'll never forget how kind you've been to me. If you never invited me back again I'll always be grateful for today, and for the other evening.'

'That's nice to know anyway. Are you going any place for Christmas? I mean to a relative?'

'No. Not that I know of yet. My only relative is a cousin who lives in Shields, and I have to be pretty desperate before I visit her.'

'Would you like to come and spend it with us? I can't promise that the Christmas spirit will prevail all the time, but there'll be breaks. Of course, it's a few weeks ahead yet, but it'll sort of give you a focal point for the holidays.'

She didn't answer for a moment; then she said, 'You know you are very kind, Hal . . . I keep on thinking of you as Mr Campbell, but from now on I'll think of you as Hal. And yes, I would love to come and spend Christmas with you all, and feel so at home that perhaps I could join in with the domestic disputes.' They laughed together. But presently, after he had stopped the car and had got out and opened her side door for her and they were standing in the dimly lit street facing each other, she wondered for a moment what his next words would be. Likely, could he come in for a moment? Or would he take her down the area steps to the door and put his arms around her, expecting to extract payment for the holiday? Or would he just kiss her here?

He did none of these things, but, putting his hand out, he touched her cheek, saying gently, 'Good-night, Jinny. It's been nice having you. If I'm past this way one evening in the week I'll look in, but if not I'll pick you up next Sunday again. All right?'

'Yes, all right, Hal. And thank you, thank you again. Good-night.'

'Good-night, Jinny.'

He was nice. Oh, he was nice. And so different. She liked him. She liked him very much.

4

'Would you like to come to the weddin'?'

'To the wedding?'

'Aye, that's what I said: would you like to come to the weddin'?'

'But . . . but it's next week and I don't think I have suitable clothes. And what's more, Mrs Henderson . . .'

'Don't worry about Mrs Henderson. If you had been Old Aggie you would have been asked. As for suitable clothes, if the weather keeps like this the appropriate gear'll be flannel underwear and a blanket coat . . . Anyway, would you like to come?'

'I should love to, Mr Henderson. And thank you very much.'

'Well, be at St Matthew's around twelve next Wednesday. That's a week the day. Eeh, my! how time flies. I'll miss our Glen, you know, breezin' in an' out, although he'll only be up the road. But it won't be the same. We'll just be left with Lucy. And then as far as I can gather now from her mother she'll not be long afore she's off an' all, and not just to the top of the road from what I'm told, but New Zealand. Not if I can help it though. Things happen under me nose and I can't see them.' He nodded at Jinny, saying, 'She's been spoilt rotten.'

'And who is responsible for that?'

'Cheeky. Cheeky.' He jerked his chin towards her. 'Well, she was the last, and you always tend to make a fuss when you come to the end of the road, so to speak. Anyway, it'll be nice havin' me wife to meself, for short periods at any rate because they all keep descending on us like locusts. You know something?' He closed the folder of papers on his desk and, putting his hands on top of it, he patted it before saying, 'It's a funny thing but after the second one was born, that was Florrie, or Florence as she demands to be called, I got a bit jealous of the attention Alicia gave to the bairns. Funny that. I couldn't understand meself being jealous of me own bairns. I could make as much fuss of them as I liked but if she gave all her time to them when I was kicking around, I used to get peeved. Can you believe it?'

'Oh yes.' She nodded at him. 'It's a known fact that men's eyes, and not only their eyes, but their hands too, are inclined to stray after the second child.'

He swung round in his swivel chair towards her desk, and now his face stretched and his eyes widened as he said mockingly, 'Now is that a fact?'

'You're laughing at me.'

'Well, what do you expect me to do? Say, eeh! aren't you clever? Did you go to university and take psychology or some such? Well, let me put you right about that one. If a man's eyes . . . and hands, as you put it, start straying after his wife has a second bairn, both his eyes and his hands would have started strayin' long afore that. Tommy-rot! . . . Tommy-rot.' He swung round again, then said briskly, 'Now back to business; enough personal nattering. You know' – he cast his glance at her once more – 'I never had this with Old Aggie; she knew her place. If I had, as I did just a while ago, mentioned flannel underwear to her she would have flushed scarlet and said, "Oh, Mr Henderson!"' And he accompanied his last words by putting his hands to his chest and pushing up an imaginary bust. Then ended, 'And she would have stomped out. But she was of an age when women knew their place.'

She had to suppress her laughter. How was it, she asked herself, that she could feel so much at home with this man, that work had become a pleasure under him. She had been working in this office now a month and three days, and her whole life and outlook seemed to have changed. And she felt he was responsible for it, not Hal. Although Hal was so kind, so good, she could never be bright, even gay in his presence like she could in this man's. But during the last two days there had come on her a dread for she had heard that Miss Honeysett was out of hospital and convalescing. What would she do if she had to go back to the pool? She'd be unable to stand it. Miss Cadwell's attitude towards her had been petty before, but she could see her becoming even sadistic if she once more had to work under her control.

'Jinny.'

'Yes, sir.'

'Get me wife on the phone, will you? And ask her if she'll meet me outside around half-past four.' He poked his head towards her now, saying, 'There's a piece of jewellery in Bentley's that I would like her to see. I was talking about it to her last night. She thinks it's for the bride, but it isn't, it's for her. But don't go and tell her that. Just say what I told you: can she meet me outside?'

She picked up the phone and got through to the house.

A male voice answered and she said, 'Mr Henderson would like to speak to Mrs Henderson, please.'

'Then tell Mr Henderson that Mrs Henderson is out. Better still, put Mr Henderson on the line, Jinny.'

'Yes, Mr Henderson.'

'By the way – ' The voice on the other end dropped on the next question, 'How's His Nibs?'

She stopped herself just in time from saying, 'His Nibs is as usual,' because His Nibs was looking at her. What she said was, 'Yes, the weather is stormy as usual. But the sun has peeped through once or twice today.'

When a burst of laughter came over the phone she pressed her lips together, widened her eyes, and tried not to look towards her employer. But she saw his hand going out to his phone, and now she heard his voice as if from two different levels yelling, 'You get your mother for me, smarty-pants, and pronto. And stop wasting my secretary's time. I'm not paying her in order that she may sharpen her wits on you, or anyone else. Now, where's your mother?'

As she put her extension down she heard Mr Glen Henderson say, 'She's out, Dad. Can I be of any use?'

'Where is she?'

Covertly she watched her boss looking into the mouth piece, and then he demanded, 'What's she doing up there?'

But after a moment he said, 'No, you can't. And no, I'm not telling you what I wanted her for. I'll see you later.'

He banged the phone down and sat muttering to himself for a moment before he said, 'Get me the Longman's file. And tell Mr Waitland I want him. And Bill Meane from the drawing office.'

She had picked up her phone again and had got through to Mr Waitland's office when Mr Henderson barked at her, 'Put it down!' He was standing now, pulling his waistcoat into place and straightening his tie. 'Give me me coat,' he said; 'and get your coat and hat on.'

'Me?'

'Yes, you; there's nobody else here,' he said, turning and looking round the room.

'Where am I to go?'

'Oh, you want to know where you're to go now? Well, you're going with me to a jeweller's shop . . . I'm sorry.' He hung his head now, rubbed his hand over his chin that had been clean-shaven this morning but was now showing a slight stubble and said, 'Here I go again, apologizing to you. I've done more apologizing to you, lass, since you came on this floor than I've ever done in me life. Look, would you like to come with me to a jeweller's and pick a piece of jewellery for me wife?'

'Yes, Mr Henderson. I would enjoy that very much indeed.'

'Thank you. Thank you, Miss Brownlow. So what you waitin' for? Get our coats.'

With a feeling of bubbling excitement inside her she got their coats. Then she glanced at the clock as she left the office. It was a quarter to four. She doubted if he had ever before left his office at this time.

In the hall, the doorman looked at them in surprise, and he said, 'You want your car, Mr Henderson?'

'Well, Sam, I wasn't thinking about walkin' the day.'

'Well, if you give me your keys I'll fetch it for you to the door.'

'It's almost at the door, Sam.'

'Well, Mr Henderson, not quite the day. Mr Waitland moved it. He got the spare keys from the office because his secretary, Miss Phillips, couldn't get in and it was pouring.'

'*He what!*' The two words resounded around the mosaic floored hall, and people crossing it turned their heads, but they didn't look at all surprised.

'The bugger moved my car? Wait till I see him! Nobody . . . Nobody – ' he was stubbing his index finger towards the doorman's chest, and he repeated, '*Nobody*, Sam, moves my car! You should know that by now.'

'Yes, sir. Yes, Mr Henderson, sir. But he expected to be down and away before . . . Well, you see you're early.'

'Early be damned! If I never came downstairs for three weeks I'd still expect my car to be in the same place. It's been there for years. At least all the cars I've had have been on that spot. My godfathers! just you wait till I get me tongue round him the morrow. Come on!'

He almost pushed Jinny through the door.

His car was beyond the shelter of the awning. It was running with water and by the time they got into it they were both slightly damp. But Jinny had the great desire to let rip a loud, loud laugh. There was never a dull moment where this man was. And here she was on a working day being taken to a jeweller's shop to buy a present for his wife.

His driving was erratic, and she found this not a little frightening. He talked all the time. His conversations peppered as usual with damns, bloodies, and buggers which were as natural as God bless you to him. She had the sneaking feeling that he prided himself on not being like other factory owners. But whatever business he had been in she knew he'd have remained an individualist.

It was apparent he was known to the jeweller, and was greeted with something near to obsequiousness; also that her own presence was viewed with not a little surprise.

'It's the pendant you were interested in when you were last here, Mr Henderson?'

'Aye, yes, that's what I said. Still got it, I suppose?'

'Oh, yes, we've still got it . . . Was the future bride pleased with her gift?'

'I don't know, she hasn't got it yet.'

'Oh.' The man turned away and went to a glass cabinet, from which he took down a velvet plaque and on which reposed a gold chain supporting a medallion in the shape of a bow rimmed with two rows of stones.

Placing it on the counter, his hand moved over it as if performing some rite as he said, 'It's a beautiful piece, isn't it?'

'Aye, and it's a beautiful price an' all.'

'One gets what one pays for.'

'Aye, an' I've heard that an' all afore the day. Well' – he turned to Jinny – 'what d'you think of it?' And she, dragging her eyes from the pendant, looked at him and smiled. 'It's beautiful; more so, it's exquisite.'

'That's the right word.' The jeweller was looking at her. 'It is made for a young neck.'

'What do you mean, made for a young neck? What you gettin' at? The bloody thing's for the wife, this is me secretary.'

The words seemed to knock the jeweller back from the counter. His face paled slightly and his hand now wavered in front of it as it had done over the pendant a few minutes earlier as he muttered, 'I'm sorry. Indeed, indeed, I'm sorry. It . . . it was a mistake.'

'I'd say it was a mistake. I'm bloody embarrassed, and for Miss Brownlow.'

'I . . . I apologize.' The poor man was looking appealingly at Jinny now; and she smiled at him, saying, 'It's perfectly all right. It's understandable. It certainly isn't your fault.' She now glanced at her employer, and she knew it was on the point of his tongue to reply, 'And whose bloody fault is it, then?'

But something in her look seemed to reveal to him the situation that he himself had created. And now his tone somewhat subdued, he said, 'My wife couldn't come; I wanted a bit of advice, female advice, because I haven't got two thousand three hundred quid to chuck about every day.'

Jinny almost gasped audibly. Two thousand three hundred pounds! Granted the thing was beautiful, but she had seen imitations somewhat similar for twenty pounds in a shop in Northumberland Street in Newcastle.

'Wrap it up.'

The jeweller wrapped it up; then took Mr Henderson's cheque with grateful thanks, and he himself ushered them to the door.

Once in the car and settled behind the wheel, he did not immediately start up the engine, but looking at her, he said with a wry grin, 'Ever been taken for a mistress afore?'

'No; that was the first time.'

He continued to stare at her, the smile widening now as he said, 'You said that as if you hoped it won't be the last.'

'There you are mistaken, because I have no desire in that direction.'

'Good for you, lass. Stick out for the ring.'

As he started the car, he said, 'I could do with a cup of tea, what about you?'

She hesitated for some seconds before saying, 'A cup of tea is always acceptable, but . . .'

'Aye, but.' He turned into the main thoroughfare. 'Go on. What were you goin' to say?'

'Nothing.'

'That's something new . . . Can you risk goin' in Germaine's Tea-Rooms with me? But I'd better warn you, you'll get your name up if you're seen.'

'I'll risk it.'

'Good. Then we'll go to Germaine's. A bit since I've been there. It used to be a favourite place of Alicia's when the bairns were small. It's a bit posh, but they didn't mind bairns. And the teas'll take some beatin'. The . . . the restaurant'll take some beatin' an' all, 'cos it's under good management. He's a Frenchman. Why do Frenchmen go down better with women than us blokes? He's kept the same staff for years. One waitress has been there now on thirty years, and I'm sure it's just 'cos she fell in love with him at the beginning.' He jerked his head towards her and laughed out loud. 'Not many lasses fall for English bosses. Oh aye!' He was nodding now towards the windscreen. 'They marry them, but it's their position and money and their big houses that are the main attraction; and gettin' one over on the others in the company. Oh, I know what I'm talkin' about.' His head again jerked towards her. 'It's happened in our place. Bloody fools. Ah well, here we are. It's stopped raining, thank God. The car park's at the side, and we can go in by the side door.'

A few minutes later he pushed open the swing doors that led into the lower end of the restaurant. This end was made up mostly of glass and one could look out on to a pleasant stretch of lawn bordered by rockeries and trees. And looking towards it, he stopped dead as he exclaimed under his breath, 'My God! What a situation! I can't believe it.' He turned and looked at her; then back to the three people sitting at the corner table to the left of them and who were looking directly towards them.

Putting his hand out, he caught hold of her arm and led her towards the table, saying in the loudest of voices, 'Caught in the act. Here I am presenting the evidence.'

She found herself standing looking down on the faces of two women – his son had risen – and when he said, 'This is Jinny,' and added, 'Jinny, let me present to you the other woman in the case, me wife,' his hand went out towards an extremely smart woman who looked to be in her forties. She was plainly dressed, but with plainness that expressed exclusiveness. Her face was unlined except for some laughter lines at the corners of her eyes, which were almond shaped.

Jinny wished at this moment she could sink through the ground, at the same time thinking, She's beautiful. And so unlike him. It was like Beauty and the Beast. No, no. She couldn't liken him to a beast, he was too good, too nice. It was just his rough manner that caused her to make the comparison because he wasn't bad to look at. But still, he looked much older than her.

'How do you do? Come and sit down. We've just this minute ordered tea.'

Jinny had no need to answer for her boss was now saying, 'And this piece here is me future daughter-in-law, as if I haven't got enough females to contend with.'

'Hello.'

Still Jinny could make no reply. But she took the seat which Glen Henderson was holding out for her. There was a grin on his face that indicated it could spread into laughter at any moment.

'What you doin' here?' Bob Henderson was looking at his wife.

'Now don't you think, Mr Henderson' – her eyes were twinkling as she looked from one to the other – 'that that's the question I should be asking? Glen' – she turned to her son – 'when have you known your father leave the office before five o'clock in the evening? I'm asking you, because, as you know, I never go near the works.'

Looking solemnly back at his mother, Glen said, 'I've never known it happen before, Mother. As I've told Yvonne here' – he inclined his head towards his fiancée – 'if it wasn't that he's curious to know how we'd manage without him he'd take up his quarters there.'

'Aw! you lot. It would serve you right if I was goin' off the rails. I'm not appreciated. But mind, I can tell you this, if I was thinkin' about it it wouldn't be anybody like her' – he thumbed now towards Jinny – 'because she's too much like you.' His look now was directed towards his son as he ended, 'Has an answer to everything and can't mind her own business.'

'I don't think I'd want a better recommendation for my husband's secretary.' Mrs Henderson was now looking at Jinny, whose face was scarlet. 'Poor Miss Honeysett allowed herself to be trampled on. I tried to tell her it was the wrong way to tackle him. I once told her to either stand up to him or ignore him.' She now leaned towards Jinny, and her voice becoming lower, she added, 'She was slightly shocked. She couldn't understand my attitude.'

'Nor can many people.' Mr Henderson was looking at his wife, a deep warm glow in his eyes now. 'A lot of people are sorry for me.'

'Name one.' Glen Henderson now turned to his fiancée and said, 'Even you thought he was someone from the backwoods when you first met him.'

'I did not. I did not, Papa Bob. Believe me. What I said was you were different from the Englishmen I had met, more outstanding.'

The girl was French and, like most French people speaking English, she had an attractive accent. She wasn't very pretty to look at; a better word that could explain her was, she supposed, petite. She was small, and in a way dressed much like Mrs Henderson. Both their suits were dark, a touch of white showing at the neck. In the young lady's case it was a small frill attached to the dress of the suit. She was wearing a tiny hat to match, which was more of an accessory than a covering for her hair, which was dark, almost as dark as her fiancé's. For a fleeting moment she thought that they could be brother and sister except for their height and build.

The young girl turned towards Jinny now, saying, 'You find him a nice man under the skin, do you?'

When Jinny now looked at her employer and laughed, he said, 'Well, go on an' tell her.'

And with a twinkle in her own eyes now, Jinny looked back at the girl and said, 'Unfortunately, I haven't penetrated very far into the skin as yet.'

The ensuing chorus of laughter and chattering remarks was interrupted by Bob Henderson saying, 'Your time'll be short, miss.' And at this the girl turned to Jinny again, saying, 'I shouldn't worry about that threat. You can come over to the French office. I understand your French is very good, Glen says.'

'Perhaps it's as well my accent doesn't come over in the written word; it's . . . it's rather provincial, I'm afraid.'

'What matters that? Mine is too – You have been to France?'

'Some years ago, and then only for a short time. My grandmother was French, from the north . . .'

'When you're finished jabbering about your ancestors I'll thank you all to give me a little of your attention. And I'll tell you why I left the office so early. And it isn't the first time, laddie' – he nodded now towards his son – 'that I've done a bunk in the afternoon, if you only knew. But if you remember rightly I phoned me home to ask if I could speak to me wife, didn't I?'

'You did, sir.' Glen nodded solemnly across the table towards him.

'And you informed me that she was out.'

'Right again, sir.'

'Well, just by the way, a kind of insertion like, I'll put a question in here, and it is, how do you manage to be along of these two now if she was out and you were in?'

'Well, sir, I had arranged to meet them, precisely here at a certain time.'

'Oh! Well, missis' – he now turned and looked at his wife – 'you'll grant that I tried to get you first afore I decided to trail her' – again his thumb was stabbing towards Jinny – 'along of me.'

'Yes, dear. I take your point.'

'Well, remember last week when we were in Bentley's spending money like water?'

'Yes, I do, dear. And we were spending money like water, just as you say. And it was such a nice experience.'

'Shut up! And listen. I saw you looking at a pendant, an' I heard you asking the price of it on the side . . . so.' He put his hand into his inner pocket and, pulling out the case, he pushed it towards her.

There was silence at the table for a moment; and then his wife said, 'Oh, Robert. Robert. Oh, my dear.'

'Well, don't waste so much time on slavering. Open it and see if it looks the same here as it did in the shop.'

Immediately she opened the case she bit tight down on her lip.

'It's outrageous,' she said. 'The price was outrageous.' Her eyes were shining bright. She once more bit her lip; then, rising quickly from her chair, she stepped behind him and put her arms around his neck and, bending her face to his, she kissed him on the lips.

'Eeh! Did you ever see anything like that! What'll the people think?' He was looking about him at the two or three tables that were occupied. But he still kept hold of her hand; and now looking up at her, his gaze soft on her and the tone of his voice one that Jinny had not heard before, he said, 'Presents can't pay for what we've had together, lass, and we'll go on having together, eh?'

As she nodded at him he gulped audibly; then his voice returning to its normal timbre, he commanded, 'Well, go on, sit yourself down and don't make an exhibition of yourself.'

She sat down, and, taking the pendant from its case, she held it in the palm of her hand, and looking first at her future daughter-in-law and then at Jinny, she said, 'Isn't it ridiculous, getting a gift like this in a public tea-room! He should have presented it to me when I was in my negligée.'

'Don't give them mucky ideas, they know enough already. And look, me tongue's hanging out. I came in for a cup of tea. At least, we did, didn't we?' He poked his head towards Jinny.

At this moment she was overcome with a new and strange emotion, as strange as had been her first experience of raw anger, for she knew she was in the presence of an association that was rare: the love that these two had for each other encased them like a halo. If she could have followed her inclinations she would have laid her head and her arms on the table and cried.

And Glen Henderson who happened to look her way must have sensed something of what she was feeling, for now he brought the conversation around to his coming wedding by saying abruptly, while nodding towards his parents, 'If you two can forget your maudlin passion for a few minutes and pay attention to an event that has to happen next week we'd be much obliged, shouldn't we, Yvonne?'

'Yes, we should be much obliged.' The young girl seemed to have taken her cue from Glen; and she went on, 'Today I had a letter from an aunt in Bordeaux; at least it came from my mother. We had never been touched with her for a long time, my aunt I mean.' She now turned to Jinny and in an aside she said, 'My English *is* very provincial, yes?'

'Yes, I'd say, Birmingham accent, I think,' Glen said.

'Nonsense!' his mother put in now; 'it's a lovely accent. Go on, Yvonne.'

And so Yvonne went on to explain how the aunt would like to come to the wedding, and that her mother wasn't very happy about it.

'Then write back and tell her we're full up, both houses.'

'Don't be silly, Father. They can stay at an hotel.'

The conversation ranged back and forth, and eventually they all rose from the table. And in the foyer of the restaurant Mr Henderson said, 'I'm going to run Jinny home. Are you going on straight ahead?' He looked at his son. 'Or are you going to follow us?'

'We'll follow you, 'cos we don't trust you.' Glen turned his head and grinned at Jinny. And she smiled back at him.

As they made towards the exit, Mr Henderson looked from one to the other, saying, 'By the way, I've asked her to the weddin'. Jinny, I mean. She'll be no bother. And you, Yvonne, the last thing you do afore leaving is to throw your bouquet at her because it's time she was married. I don't know what the fellows are thinking about. Go in with you.' He herded them all towards the door now, and as the two men went to get the cars Mrs Henderson turned to Jinny, saying quietly, 'There's no better meaning man in the world than my husband, Miss Brownlow, but he can be the most tactless person in the whole of that same world. And he likes arranging other people's lives. At the same time he can't manage his own.' She now pulled a little face, and Jinny, warming to her, said, 'Oh, please don't worry on my account; I've never been so happy working for anyone. He does me good.'

'His manner has never frightened you then?'

'No. Never. I can honestly say that. I'm afraid I've got into the habit of answering him back.'

Mrs Henderson now looked at Yvonne and shook her head as she remarked, 'His last secretary, Old Aggie as he called her, was scared stiff of him. She liked him; in fact she was very fond of him, but she couldn't stand up to him. It's just as well she's retiring.'

There was no time for Jinny to make any comment on this, even if she had decided to, for the cars drew up at the kerb. But as she took her seat beside her employer, she thought, He's known this, yet hasn't told me, keeping me on tenderhooks. The Devil . . .

Ten minutes later, as he leaned over to open the door for her to leave, he kept his hand on the handle for a moment while looking at her, and he said, 'Thanks for your company, lass. It's been a good day. I've enjoyed it.'

'Thank you, Mr Henderson. I, too, have enjoyed it, most of all meeting your wife.'

'Aye, well.' He pushed the door open. 'You can see there's no chance for you, can't you?'

She had the handle of the door in her hand ready to close it, but she bent down and said, 'You know something?'

'No, what is it?'

'I wouldn't have you if . . . if there was.'

She thought she heard his last words which sounded like, 'Eeh! you cheeky bitch.' Then she was standing on the pavement answering the waving hands from the other car.

Oh, they were nice. A wonderful family. And wasn't she lucky! She had fallen on her feet.

The street was ill-lit, the pavement was greasy, she was going downstairs into a cold, cheerless basement flat, yet she was feeling strangely happy. A week today she would be at a wedding. A posh wedding. But before that she'd be seeing Hal. Oh, yes, she'd be seeing Hal. And she'd be with him most of Sunday. Saturday was still a day to be filled up. She usually stretched it out by the cleaning of the flat. But on this Saturday she'd go out looking for a wedding present. It would have to be something not too expensive, but nice, good quality.

The world was suddenly a beautiful place. Had she ever felt shy? Lost and lonely? Yes, she had, but she'd never feel that way again. No, never.

Never is forever,
Never never ends.
Be careful what you tack it to,
It's a word that can sever
Lovers and friends.

Now why should she think that? Where had she read that? Just because she had said she would never be lonely again. Yes, now she remembered. Her grandfather had been in the habit of spouting rhymes and sayings, and that was one of them. She hadn't thought of it for years. But why should she recall it to mind now? Funny, how one's thoughts had the habit of jumping out of the blue and putting a damper on you. Of late she had been inclined to be pessimistic. She'd have to get out of that way of thinking. Yes, she would, because the future promised to be bright.

5

Hal Campbell endeared himself further to Jinny on the Sunday afternoon when in the sitting-room she told him that she had been invited to Glen Henderson's wedding, and how she had walked the town all yesterday looking for a present, but had failed to find one at her price. After Michael's suggestion, 'Take a bottle of plonk; it's always acceptable,' and Rosie's derisive reply, 'Don't be silly, they swim in champagne at weddings like that,' Hal had got up and walked to one of the china cabinets, and opening the door, he had stood looking at the shelves before his hand went to a small figurine. Lifting it out, he turned towards her where she was sitting in a chair to the side of the fireplace, a seat she had chosen in preference to the couch and the close proximity of Michael, which she was finding disturbing, and he said, 'Perhaps this will fit the bill, small but good. It's a piece of Worcester.'

She rose and went to him; but she did not take the figurine from his hands, she just stared at it. It was about four inches high and depicted a lady sitting on a chair, one arm extended over the back, the other holding a red parasol. Her bonnet was yellow, the skirt of her gown white lace and arrayed in four tiers. The bodice of the gown was mauve, as were her shoes. The figure was based on a white and gold platform.

As she heard herself muttering, 'I . . . I couldn't accept that,' Michael's voice came at her, saying, 'Never look a gift horse in the mouth. Take it and gallop.'

'Could you temper your remarks to the occasion for once, Michael?' Hal's voice was cool. And Michael retorted, 'I thought I was very appropriate. You don't often go around giving your prize pieces away.'

'I've always liked her; she's dainty.' Jinny looked at Rosie who was now standing by her side; then away from her to Arthur who was saying, 'I saw one in a shop window recently, not as big as her, and it was ninety-six pounds.'

It was rarely he commented on anything, but his manner of late had seemed to undergo a slight change for the better towards her. Looking at him, Hal said, 'Well, this certainly didn't cost me anything like that.'

'I . . . I couldn't take it, Hal; I mean . . . unless I bought it.'

'Well, all right, if you want to buy it, if it would make you any happier, fifteen pounds.'

'That's ridiculous.'

'Too much?' He was smiling widely at her.

'I can go to twenty-five.'

'Fifteen or nothing.'

She held out her hands and took the figure from him, and gazed at it. 'Did you mean that? It's beautiful. I won't want to give it away.'

'Well, don't.'

'Oh, yes. I must. And thank you. Thank you very much.' She looked up into his face. It was just as she had imagined it last night before going to sleep, warm, kindly . . . handsome. Her mother used to say that blue eyes could never look warm, but his did. He had brought a sort of niceness into her life. After the episode of Ray Collard, it was wonderful to meet a man who could take you out and not expect payment. Last week he had kissed her for the first time. It had been a gentle kiss, and she had closed her eyes at the feel of it. And more than once during the past week she had asked herself what type of women had they been that they could walk out on such a man as him. But the first one had died, hadn't she? How could such a nice man make the same mistake for a second time? Likely just because he was nice.

'I've got the right box for it. I'll parcel it up for you.'

As he went from the room she sat down again, and as she did so Michael rose to his feet, saying, 'Well, here's someone off to see his true love. And – 'he took a step towards her and, bending down, said softly, 'don't look so damned grateful. It could be a sprat to catch a mackerel: our dear Bella, Mrs Grayson, has left, so I shouldn't be surprised if you find yourself here on a Saturday helping him to clean through.

'Mrs Grayson's left?'

'That's what I said.'

'Oh well' – she forced herself to smile at him – 'it would be no hardship to come on a Saturday and help, except your room, and I'm sure you do that yourself. And anyway, after you've inveigled your girl friend into giving a hand during your spare evening in the week I'm sure there won't be that much left to see to at the weekend.'

He straightened up now and laughed down on her as he said, 'You know, there's more than one of you. I was wondering whom you reminded me of lately. And then I got it on the television the other night in *Butterflies*. You look like Wendy Craig. But that's only on the outside for you're not a bit like her underneath, are you?'

'Nobody could be as dippy as she is.' Once again Arthur had got their attention. 'She can't cook; and she goes out and sees another fellow every day. And her husband never finds out. There wouldn't be anybody as dumb as him, even if they tried. Week after week he comes home to meals that you wouldn't give to the dog, and nobody's let on to him about her mooning about with this other bloke, with the chauffeur trailing after them in the car while her red, white and blue banger sticks out like a sore thumb wherever she parks it.'

They were all laughing now, except Arthur, and when Jinny said to him, 'I like *Butterflies*; I think she's marvellous,' he retorted, 'Oh well, you would because you are a little bit dippy underneath. You must be to . . .' He now shook his head. And when he didn't finish what he was about to say, she put in, 'When I fall for such programmes?'

He made no answer, nor did Michael, but he, saying, 'Be seeing you,' went out of the room.

The door had hardly closed on Michael when Rosie asked her, 'Would you really come and help on a Saturday?'

'If needed, yes. Why not?'

'But you're a secretary; you're not used to housework.'

'I do my own flat, and before my mother died I used to help with the housework.'

Rosie now looked towards the fire, saying, 'I never thought secretaries would sort of . . . well, take to jobs like that. Mary Randall at school whose mother is a nurse, she says that nurses don't like housework either. She wants to be a secretary . . . Mary does. She's good at French . . . Would you look at my homework?'

'Yes, of course. Go and get it,' she said, nodding towards Rosie who scrambled up from the hearthrug and ran from the room. And now she was left alone with Arthur, and she found this an embarrassing situation for the boy sat staring at her for some while before, jerking himself up from his chair, he went to the fireplace and reached out to the log basket, saying as he picked up a log, 'Do you like Hal?'

She paused and smiled gently at his bowed head as she answered, 'Yes, of course I like Hal, or I wouldn't be here.'

'I . . . I don't mean just liking. Do you more than like him?'

'Now what do you expect me to say to that? What I should say is that it is an impertinent question and mind your own business.'

'But you're not going to.' He slanted his eyes towards her.

'No, I'm not going to.'

His hand went out again and he picked up another log, and as he pressed it into the grate he said, 'Michael likes you.'

Her eyes widened slightly, the smile went from her face and she said, 'I . . . I don't know exactly what you mean by that because Michael hasn't shown me a very good side of himself since I started coming here.'

'That's because he likes you.'

'Don't be silly.'

'I'm not silly.' The words were like a harsh bark. He had swung round on his knees and was within an arm's length of her, and he almost glared up into her face as he said, 'You're soft, and you'll be chewed up. Michael says you will, and you will. And he'd be a better bet for you than Hal. So there, I'm telling you.' And on this he pulled himself to his feet and stomped out.

She was shivering. The warmth had gone from the room; the pleasantness had gone from the day. She should be thinking that that boy is vicious, but her mind was telling her that his attitude was one of concern; he wasn't resenting her being here. And she knew this; in fact she had been thinking of late that they might get on quite well together once they started talking. But now he had set her mind asking why, why he should take this attitude against his step-father. Perhaps he was retaliating against restraint, the slightest discipline. And in a quiet way Hal was a disciplinarian. He was used to directing, ordering. In his ordinary life he was still manipulating players. But that boy's statement that Michael liked her and that he'd be a better bet than Hal, what exactly did it mean? Hal was a lovely person; there was no one kinder than Hal, and not only to her, but his kindness spread in all directions. Three nights a week he visited old people; that was when there was no play in preparation of course. She sat now staring at the fire, and into her mind came a word which she rejected immediately. Oh no, he couldn't be a homosexual. He didn't look like that; you couldn't pin the word 'gay' on to him in any way, and as far as she knew he hadn't any special men friends. But then she saw him only at week-ends. No, he wasn't a homosexual. Then what was it? There was something. But it couldn't be anything of great importance.

Then her face stretched slightly. Perhaps that was it, perhaps Arthur was jealous: he didn't want Hal to marry again. This often happened. The boy wouldn't mind her marrying Michael, for then in a way both she and Michael would be out of his hair, so to speak, and he'd have Hal to himself. Yes, yes, this could account for his aggressiveness. It was a cover-up for his feelings for Hal; he was afraid of losing him, his second father.

She sat back in the chair and closed her eyes and smiled to herself. It's a wonder she hadn't seen it before. The source of emotions such as those shown by Arthur were not always evident. If they were they could be solved directly. She would in a way, a very, very tentative way, make him aware that she didn't want to deprive him of Hal's love.

The room was warm again; the day was pleasant; the future bright; she was going to a wedding on Wednesday, and she had a beautiful present to give to the bride. And that was thanks to Hal. So much of her happy feeling now was thanks to Hal.

6

She had never imagined a wedding like it; she had never envisaged a spread like it; and even her dreams hadn't conjured up a house like it.

The bride and bridegroom were almost ready to go. They were standing amidst a chattering throng in the hall. The bride had changed from a cream brocade, white fur-trimmed wedding-gown to a travelling suit. She was looking so happy at this moment that there returned to Jinny's breast the small pain that she had felt when she saw her walking up the aisle to meet her waiting bridegroom. She thought now as she has thought then, Such a ceremony, such a day, such evident happiness was worth waiting for . . . worth fighting for.

She watched Glen Henderson now zig-zag his way through the crowd, and she was somewhat surprised when she saw him raise his hand and signal to her to move towards the corner of the room that was temporarily clear.

When, excusing herself, she pressed past people, and met up with him, he said immediately, 'Jinny, about the bouquet.'

'Bouquet?'

'Yes. Yvonne's wedding bouquet. You know, Father told Yvonne to throw it to you. Well, she was a bit worried. You see, she had already told her aunt that she would throw it to her cousin Jeanette.' He now pulled a face, then went on, hurriedly, 'Jeanette's kicking thirty-three, and her mother's despairing. You understand?'

'Oh, yes.' She was laughing now. 'I have thought no more of it; I thought it was a joke.'

'Oh, Father didn't. He's set on getting you married off, thinks you're wasting time.' He pursed his lips now and added, 'For once I'm in agreement with him. And look, Jinny.' He leant slightly towards her. 'Take care of him, will you? What I mean is, try to lighten things there and get him out of the office early. Mother . . . well, the house is getting more empty every day, and Mother misses him. Oh, she doesn't say so, but she does. She misses all of us, but mostly she misses him. So do your best, won't you?'

'Certainly. Yes, yes, I will.'

'Thanks, Jinny.'

As he went to turn away he added, 'He thinks a lot of you, you know. After Miss . . . after Old Aggie, you're like a breath of fresh air to him. And you can hold your own with him. By! that's something. Oh, look; they're yelling for me now. Goodbye. Goodbye, Jinny.'

'Goodbye, Mr Henderson.'

Over his shoulder he shouted now, 'Glen!'

As he disappeared into the throng she laughingly repeated to herself, 'Glen.'

Weren't they a lovely family! Wasn't she lucky to be working for them?

Everybody was surging towards the double doors; the car was drawn up just outside the porch. She couldn't see what was happening outside; she could only hear the laughter, the shouts, the goodbyes, and then the sound like that made by tin cans being dragged over the paved drive.

A few minutes later they were all back in the hall and making their way to the drawing-room, and Mr Henderson in no small voice was saying, 'It's bloody childish, sticking pans and things on the back of a wedding car.'

Jinny now saw Mrs Henderson laughing as she took her husband's arm. 'Let's all take it easy,' she called, 'at least for the next half-hour. Wander where you will until the music starts.' She turned to someone at her side and as if in answer to a request she said, 'Oh, the library's been cleared.' Then added, 'Would you like to go up and see the babies? The girls will be going up there.'

Jinny was standing on the outside of the throng when Mrs Henderson, stopping quite near her, said in an undertone to her husband, 'Don't worry. John's at the bottom of the drive; he's going to see to taking them off.'

'Oh, aye. Well, it's a good job he can do something right for once.' Then looking towards Jinny, he said, 'What you standing there for, lass, with all these men about? Why hasn't somebody got you in a corner?'

Alicia Henderson now closed her eyes whilst still continuing to smile as she said, 'It's a good job you know him, Miss Brownlow.'

'O . . . oh! Away with surnames; her name's Jinny. You never called Old Aggie Miss Honeysett.'

'And I never called her Old Aggie either. Look, I've got to go and see to things. Now behave yourself; be polite. Oh, I know. Miss . . . Jinny' – her smile broadened now – 'will you see to him? If you think he is going to make use of one of his northern phrases, press none too gently on the side of his shoe. He has a very tender corn on his right little toe.'

She went off laughing, and Mr Henderson, looking at Jinny, said, 'She meant it an' all. But if you mean to carry it out you'll have to keep on the right side of me, won't you?' He grinned at her.

'I can do that while at the same time following instructions.'

'And I wouldn't put it past you either . . . What do you think of the wedding?'

His tone had altered, and hers did too as she answered, 'I . . . I haven't got words to express what I think about it. The ceremony, the wedding feast, and it was a feast, beautiful; and . . . and your home.' She spread out her arms. 'I never imagined it being like this.'

'Too good for me you think? Too uppish?'

'No, I don't think that.'

'No, you wouldn't. But it's no credit to me. All I did at the end of twenty-five years' work was supply the money. It wasn't her money this time, it was mine. I was able to give her the kind of home she'd been used to, buy it meself. But I only bought the bricks and mortar, the taste comes from her. What do you think of her?'

They were walking now down a side corridor towards a glass door that led into one end of a long L-shaped conservatory and she didn't speak until she was standing looking out of the window into the dark garden that was partly illuminated from the lights in the house, and she said, 'I've never met anyone like her. I . . . I think she's remarkable, and' – she turned her head – 'and so right for you.'

'You think that, lass?'

'Yes, I do indeed. I'm not just saying it; I really think that. And also, you for her.'

'Eeh, now!' He rubbed his foot on the stone slab of the floor and looked down towards it as he said, 'I can't go with you there. I'm a rough lot. I could have learnt, smoothed meself out a bit, but I've prided meself on havin' got where I was through being what I was. She took me like I was, so there I stayed. You know something?' He looked into her face now, 'When we first got married, prophets from all quarters said we were doomed. It wouldn't last. Chalk and cheese. Oh, chalk and cheese was a poor description. Gold dust and carts would be more like the mixture they attributed to us. They waited day in, day out; week in, week out; some, year in, year out, for the break. And you know something?' He grinned devilishly at her. 'It almost broke some of their hearts when they found out they were wrong. Like Chris Waitland, him in there' – he inclined his head backwards – 'hanging on to Garbrook. He went to university, and as I once told him it dulled the only bright part of his intellect. And that's why he couldn't understnd Alicia falling for me. And there's something else he can't understand, why with his type of education he isn't in my seat. Anyway, he's only on the board because he's Garbrook's wife's second cousin. That reminds me. Talking about him, I heard a rumour. Oh' – he nodded at her – 'I've got wires running here and there through these works. Top floor, middle floor, and bottom. Well, I heard that he'd been enquiring privately like if there was any chance of me retiring afore me time. And so I sent a message along the wire that yes, I just might, but me son was prepared to take me place. I bet that gave him sleepless nights. Oh, lass, I'm tired.' He sat down now on an ornamental iron chair. Then pulling his trousers away from his thighs, he said, 'My! won't I be glad to get out of these togs. The crutch is so bloody tight it's choking me.'

As Jinny spluttered into her hand and his laughter joined hers a young man entered the conservatory, saying, 'Oh, there you are, Father. I just wanted to say I'm going.'

'Why?' Mr Henderson now turned his head and glanced in Jinny's direction and in his usual manner, he stated, 'This is my other son, John. He's kept himself in the background else you'd have met him afore now.'

The young man who was of medium height and fair and not unlike his father except that his face had a tight, drawn look inclined his head towards her, saying, 'How do you do?'

She answered in the same vein; then looked from father to son as Mr Henderson said, 'Not going to stay for the dance, then?'

'No.' The answer was brief.

'Your mother would like it.'

'I would have liked to, too, Father, but I've left my partner outside.'

'Aw, to hell! You know what I feel about these things. I can't understand you, lad. There's nothin' to stop either of you. Why are you doing it?'

'For the simple reason that we want to.'

'You've never been shown a bad example here.'

'No; that's perfectly true. But this house isn't the only example we've got to go on. And perhaps neither of us is very sure of the other. That might be the reason. But anyway' – his voice was lowered – 'it's a private matter.'

'Oh, if you're worried about her' – Mr Henderson indicated Jinny with a motion of his thumb – 'there's nothing that she doesn't know, she's me secretary.'

The young man stared hard at his father before saying, 'I'm going now.'

'All right, you go; but when you're tired of your freedom the door's open.'

As his son marched out of the conservatory Mr Henderson got to his feet and, looking down at Jinny, said, 'Stubborn young bugger. Living with a lass, he is. Only one of my lot to go off the rails. Walked out when he was twenty-one . . . Like I said to him, why did he wait? If he was in such a bloody hurry to get down to it he should have left when he was eighteen; the law was on his side. The bloody law's on the side of everything that's rotten these days. Pornography's as common as God Bless You now . . . Do you go along with loose livin'? And don't go and tell me it isn't loose livin'. Oh aye, men go off the rails, I know, and it was only the rich at one time who could afford their mistresses. But at one time an' all the majority of men seemed to have respect for a woman. They've got none now. If any of them even have the common courtesy to stand up and give a woman a bus seat they expect to nip her backside in payment. And I'm tellin' you this' – he wagged his finger in her face now – 'I don't consider meself old-fashioned. I'm as advanced as the next man when we get down to rock bottom, and rock bottom is sex. But in my young time if you had a boy friend or a girl friend it meant just that, it didn't mean that a lass was lowering herself to the level of a whore. And as regards that lot, they've got to suffer the name, it's a kind of profession, but an ordinary lass in college the day can flit from one man to another like a bitch in season. Oh, one mustn't defame the animal world; they're clean compared to some of them.'

He now stood back from her, put his hand up to his cheek, held his head to one side, and as he gave a small wry smile he said, 'You know, lass, next to Alicia you're the only one I can let off steam to, for I'd have them falling around me feet in faints. Our Florrie, the one that looks like me you know, with the three youngsters, up from Devon, when she hears me at it she practically swoons. Aye, she does. You'd think she had been brought up in a convent, and she's been used to me language since the day she poured some scalding soup over our John's head. He was on two at the time, and she was coming up five. He nearly died from shock. You can see the scar round his ear yet.' He turned from her now, adding sadly, 'Wish somebody would pour something over him now and bring him to his senses. Eeh! I do that. Well, come on, lass; we'll get our name up for sitting here talkin' . . . Do you like dancing?'

'Yes. Yes, I like it very much.'

'Well, get your fill of it. Go on with you, get your fill of it.' He pushed her from him and towards the conservatory door and almost into the arms of Mr Garbrook who, looking past her shoulder towards his partner, said, 'There you are. I've been looking for you. What you up to? Oh, your secretary. Talking business again, eh? Must put a stop to this.'

Jinny passed him, having to walk sidewards to do so. He was a big man, with broad shoulders and a protruding stomach. His face was red, and his voice was hearty. She had met him a number of times before; she hadn't liked him. He was a man who didn't improve on acquaintance. She was glad that he spent most of his time at the metal box factory.

There were several of the staff here. Mr Meane, head of the drawing-office. He was a pleasant man; always had a word for you. Not so Mr Waitland . . . Mr Waitland, his wife and daughter had all ignored her. In a way she could see their point: why should she be invited when neither Mr Garbrook's nor his own secretary had received an invitation? Still, what did it matter; she was going to dance . . . That's if anyone asked her.

Jinny was asked. She hardly left the floor during the next four hours, except to take refreshments. And when at last the band packed up and the guests left one by one, most of the men unsteady on their feet, she was left alone with the family, nine in all. And under Mr Henderson's insistence and that of his wife, she joined them in a room on the first floor, which was the only place in the house apparently that hadn't been invaded by the guests, and which, she learned, was Mrs Henderson's own private sitting-room.

There was a great deal of cross-talk between the daughters Florence, Nellie, and Monica and their husbands, all trying to guess the hotel at which the bridal couple would be staying in Paris. Mr and Mrs Henderson sat together on the couch, and Lucy, no care now for her peach bridesmaid's dress, sat curled up close to her mother's side.

The scene presented such a family picture that Jinny felt she was looking through a window on to it and was not part of it. And as if Alicia Henderson had caught her feeling, she said, 'It's turned two in the morning, and there's no sense in you going home now, Jinny. There are plenty of spare rooms. Lucy here will show you and get you settled.'

'Oh, but . . .'

'Now shut up and do what you're told. Her word goes here.' Bob Henderson was shouting again. 'And I'm too bloomin' tired to argue with you. In fact we're all bloomin' tired. So, come on, let's break up. There'll be plenty of time for more talk the morrow night, and the night after that.'

'Oh, there won't, not for me. We're off tomorrow, you know, Father.'

This was Florence, the one who lived in Devon. And now Nellie's husband, a plump, fair man, put in, 'I've got a business to see to, Father-in-law. We must be off tomorrow too. We haven't secretaries to do our work, have we, Harry?' He was now looking at Monica's husband, who looked little more than a young boy and who now caused a laugh by declaring, 'For my part, I don't care if I never go back to Manchester.'

The company broke up with good-nights all round; and Jinny, about to leave the room, looked towards her benefactors and said quietly, 'Thank you for a most wonderful day . . . and night.'

Alicia Henderson said nothing, she just smiled; but in his usual manner Bob Henderson, in a pleasant growl, answered, 'Go on. Stop your soft-soaping and get to bed.'

In the bedroom Lucy waved her hand casually as she said, 'I think you'll find everything you want;' then pausing on her way to the door, she turned and, looking at Jinny with her head held slightly to the side, she asked, 'Don't you mind the way Father speaks to you?'

'No.' Jinny's smile was broad now. 'Not in the least.'

'Some people do. They think he's coarse, awful.'

Her smile slowly faded as she looked at the young girl, and she wondered if she too considered her father coarse, awful.

'I think your father's a wonderful man, exceptional.'

'Oh yes' – the fair young head was bobbing now – 'he is in a way, I suppose. There's one thing sure, he always stands alone in company.' And after a pause she added, 'Huh! You never know what he's coming out with.'

'It's mostly sense . . . common sense.'

'Oh, I can see you and Mother will get on famously together. She thinks he's related to Socrates.' She laughed now, shrugged her shoulders, then said, shortly, 'Good-night. Sleep well.'

'Good-night . . .'

She had thought she would drop off to sleep as soon as her head touched the pillow, but for a long time she lay wide-eyed looking around this beautiful room, illuminated now only by the light of the bedside lamp. Her thoughts ranged over the whole day and the whole family until they rested on Lucy, the youngest and the one who, on her father's admission, had been spoilt silly. And she was spoilt, because she didn't appreciate what she had, not only this beautiful home, but also her male parent. But then she wasn't the only one; there was the son John, who was living with his girl friend.

It was as she was drifting into sleep the thought wavered in her mind that possessions such as the things this beautiful house held and luxuries like the bathroom going off this guest bedroom with its separate shower and bidet, and even having servants in the house in this day and age when nobody wanted to be a servant, all these things put together couldn't compete against a personal want, a personal need, such as the one which must have possessed the son John to leave his home, nor yet erase the condemnation of her father that was in Lucy. If she herself had the choice of having this house and all it possessed or Hal, not in his very comfortable home but living in the basement flat, she knew without hesitation which she would choose. And so what it all boiled down to was the need for love, the need to care and to be cared for; yes, that's all it boiled down to. She went to sleep happy.

7

'Now are you telling me the truth? You've really got some place to go over Christmas?'

'Yes, I really have. I'm spending Christmas Day and Boxing Day at Mr Campbell's house.'

'Why *Mister* Campbell? Hasn't he got a Christian name? And he's the fellow you're going with, isn't he?'

'Yes, he's got a Christian name, it's Hal.' She gave a slight shrug of her shoulders. 'And yes, I suppose you could say he's the fellow I'm going with.'

'You don't seem very certain.'

And he was right, she wasn't very certain: there wasn't a firm name she could put to the relationship that existed between her and Hal. He hadn't as yet asked her out for a meal or suggested going to the pictures or the theatre. When she had told him she was going to the theatre in Newcastle he had said, 'Good. You'll enjoy that.' But he hadn't suggested going with her. Yet he was most affectionate whenever he left her at home. But she questioned her thinking here: what did she mean by most affectionate?

'Take that look off your face, I know I poke me nose in where it isn't wanted, but it's just that Alicia said to tell you that if you're at a loose end you've got to come up. And ten days takes some filling in. Why the devil there should be a ten-day break at Christmas God alone knows. There never used to be. The time's not far ahead when they'll be working ten days a quarter; and that'll be their lot. And then they'll find something to go on strike for out of that. Aye, but I suppose I shouldn't grumble as far as strikes are concerned, we're pretty fortunate with our lot; although I don't know how long it will last for there's trouble brewing ahead in the steel business. They're shutting down plants, and that's going to cause a hell of an uproar, if I know anything. And it's no use us saying why worry 'cos we don't make it, we just transport it and turn it into odds and ends, because even an idiot knows that you can't make bricks without straw.'

'There's breeze blocks.'

'Don't you be funny, miss. Anyway, have we wound up everything as far as we can go?'

'Yes, I think so.'

'The Radley concern all tied up? Of course; I've just signed them.

I must be slipping.' He leaned back in the chair now and closed his eyes; then put his thumb and first finger on his lids and pressed them as he said, 'I'm tired. It's been one hell of a year one way and another. I'll be glad of the rest. Yet, I was saying only last week to Alicia that I wasn't looking forward to Christmas and an almost empty house: no bairns running about mad, all the lasses having decided to spend Christmas in their own homes this year. Well, I suppose you can't blame them. Then no John and no Glen, just the pair of us left, because Lucy will be running hither and thither like a scalded cat. Speaking of Glen, we had a card from them this morning. They've reached Barbados. Did you know I have a house out there?'

'No, I didn't . . . In Barbados?'

'Aye, in Barbados. It's amazing the number of relatives you've got when you've got a house in Barbados. It's never empty. It's not a big affair, mind; half a dozen rooms. Eeh! . . . I say that offhandedly, don't I, Jinny? Just half a dozen rooms. And there were eight of us in two rooms for years. And I'm the only one left. Odd that, isn't it? I've often thought what I could have done for me parents and me five brothers and sisters now: put them all on easy street. I lost me dad, two brothers and a sister in the last six months of the war. Life's funny . . . Why do you get me talking like this?'

'It's better than talking to yourself, I suppose. And listening's part of the job.'

''Tisn't part of the job. And neither is my nattering part of the job . . . Sure you won't come along for Christmas?'

She paused on her way to the cloakroom and quietly she asked, 'Could I accept for New Year's Eve?'

'Aye, you could, if not afore, and be very welcome. And here.' He opened the desk and took out an envelope and held it out to her, saying, 'A Merry Christmas. And don't open it till you get home. I don't want any more arguments the night. With some folks I know I wouldn't have any, but with you I'm not sure. Anyway, Happy Christmas, Jinny.'

'And the same to you, sir. And may I say thank you for my job.'

He raised his eyebrows, pursed his lips, then said, 'Aye, you may because you're very lucky to be working for me.'

'That's a matter of opinion because you're known as an awful man.'

They looked at each other, and then laughed loudly, but when a minute later, in the cloakroom, she stood with her back to the door and looked down at the opened envelope in her hand disclosing five ten pound notes, she bit on her lip to suppress the moisture that was gathering in her eyes. It was as he had said, in fun or not, she was indeed lucky to be working for such a man. She had the feeling at this moment that there hadn't been a time when she hadn't worked for him, when she hadn't known him. His daughter Lucy came to mind, and she envied her her father.

8

Christmas Day itself had been wonderful; not one incident had marred the harmony; even Arthur had appeared happy. How much this was due to Hal's generosity in buying him a new motor-cycle helmet, gloves, and leather boots, Jinny questioned. Not a hundred pounds would have covered that bill. And there had been no innuendos from Michael. Again Jinny wondered if the silk shirt and matching tie might not have something to do with his pleasantness. As for Rosie, among other things the sheepskin coat and gloves had been received with whoops of joy. For herself she had been delighted with the crocodile handbag and small matching dressing-case. But his generosity made her own presents to them all appear very insignificant.

Hal had picked her up early on the Christmas Eve morning. They had gone shopping together, and in the afternoon she had helped prepare the turkey for the next day, and then busied herself generally about the house.

After the present giving on Christmas morning she had again helped Hal in the kitchen, which they had to themselves as Arthur had gone out on his bike and Michael visiting, he hadn't said where. Rosie, as usual, was curled up before the fire reading one of the books she had been given.

It was during this time in the kitchen together as Jinny stood at the sink preparing the vegetables, that Hal came behind her and put his arm about her and kissed her on the back of the neck, saying, 'You know, you are a beautiful being, Jinny. There's something about you that gets hold of one.' He now turned her towards him and, taking his fingers, drew them down her cheek, across her chin, and up the other side of her face, and his voice just a mere whisper, he said, 'It's wonderful to have you here.'

Her lids blinked rapidly as she answered as softly, 'It's wonderful to be here.'

Again his fingers moved round her face, and again his voice low, he said, 'You . . . you know how I feel about a family; well, you make this part of my life complete, like . . . like no one else has. And . . . and I feel you understand.'

Their faces were close now and as she looked into his eyes she wanted to say 'What should I understand? Is there something I don't know?' But her mind came back at her, crying, Be content. Make haste slowly. Leave it to him. A man who has divorced two wives is going to be chary about taking a third. Make haste slowly.

When he kissed her his lips rested gently on hers; and now, her hands still red from the vegetable water, she put them round him, and in spite of herself she held him close for a moment. Whether he pressed himself gently away from her before the sound of the sitting-room door being opened came to them or just as it was actually being opened she didn't know, but he was back at the table and she had turned to the sink again when Rosie entered the room . . .

Only one little jarring note marred the day. It was in the evening when, sitting on the couch next to Hal, he for the first time put his arm about her shoulders and drew her to his side. And it was this gesture of his that caused the concentration that had been on Arthur's face as he endeavoured to demonstrate a magic trick to change suddenly to an expression she could only name as resentment. And when the trick misfired, he threw down the cards and sat for a time in sulky silence.

On Boxing Day, all was merry and bright again because it was snowing. In the afternoon they all went out into the garden and had a snowball fight. She had Michael, Hal had Rosie and Arthur. It was as Michael stooped down to scoop up more snow that he said, in an aside. 'There's a dance on tomorrow night in the Assembly Rooms. How about it?'

She threw the snowball she already had in her hand, then stooped to gather up more snow and said, 'Has your girlfriend deserted you?'

He now turned his back on a snowball that Arthur had aimed at him and as he did so he muttered, 'I suppose you could say so.'

'Is that why we've been honoured with your company?' She was forced to duck her head to evade a snowball coming at her, and this brought them facing each other, as he replied, 'Not really. I wanted to be home. And then of course, we had a guest.' He lifted his arm now and threw a snowball before he finished, 'And that doesn't happen often here.'

The last remark made her recall her observations of yesterday: there had been no visitors of any kind over the holidays; the only person who had knocked at the door was the postman. Rosie had often talked of her school friends, but she hadn't seen even one on any of her visits. As for Arthur's, his friends seemed to be of the motor-cycle fraternity who met in a café in the middle of the town, and, knowing Hal, that type certainly wouldn't have been welcome under any circumstances. And she hadn't yet met Michael's girl friend. By the sound of it she wouldn't in the future either.

Michael made her uneasy. It wasn't that she didn't like him;

actually he improved on acquaintance, and he was attractive . . . and intelligent. She had found that she liked listening to him, but with a wariness because most of their conversation ended in exchanges dealing with personalities.

She said now, 'How about Hal? What would he think if I went to a dance with you?'

There was a pause while more snowballs were exchanged and shouts and cross talk. And then he answered her, saying, 'I don't suppose he'd mind as long as I brought you back here to be one of the fixtures.'

She threw the snowball with increased force, saying angrily, 'I don't suppose you consider yourself as being disloyal to him or insulting to me? Let me tell you, I don't consider myself one of the fixtures of this house. Nor do I think for a moment that he does either.'

Pressing a snowball tightly between his palms now, he said, 'You're a strange mixture. As I see you, you're one third super-secretary, business woman. That's the top end of you. In the middle, you're what's known around these parts as a nice lass, a canny lass; but the last part is most important as I see it, for it's that bit of you that'll direct you in spite of yourself because you're a product of your nice parents, and today that's a handicap.'

As she stood stiffly, watching him stooping, Hal's voice came to her shouting, 'Come on! You're losing; we're thirty-three to your thirty.' And Michael, after yelling, 'So you should be with one extra battalion,' said to her in a much lower tone, 'Aren't you going to ask me what name I put to the third part of you?'

She clapped her chilled hands together; then said, 'I'm not interested in your trisection of my character; I know myself, and that's all that matters.'

She wasn't prepared for his turning on her now and hissing, 'Well, if you do, all I can say is you are a bloody fool; and I take back my assessment of your character as far as it has gone because you must be inane, or insane, to want nothing more from life but what is offered here.'

On this, he did not throw the snowball towards their opponents but turned about and pelted it towards his feet as he started towards the house.

The angry gesture was not lost on Hal. Leaving Arthur and Rosie, who had now begun to pelt at each other, he came towards Jinny, saying, 'What was all that about?'

'Nothing. Nothing.'

'What was he saying to you?'

He turned and looked towards the house now before, looking at her again, saying, 'You mustn't take much notice of what Michael says; he's very emotional, easily upset about trifling things.'

Well, if she were assessing Michael's character she would certainly not say he was easily upset about trifling things. Nor did she think he was emotional; his conversation was too caustic to tend that way.

'What did he say?' Hal asked again.

She paused a moment. She couldn't say. 'He suggests that you only want me here to use me in some way. At least that's the impression I get. Is there any truth in it?' Instead, she said, 'He asked me if I would like to go to a dance. He said you wouldn't mind. I . . . I thought you might.'

His blue eyes were bright with the cold. Then his lids covered them for the moment as he looked downwards before raising them again to her and saying, 'In a way, he was right. If it would made you happy to go to the dance with him I . . . I wouldn't have minded, as long as you came back here.'

Her mouth was slightly agape; her eyes were wide: he had, almost word for word, repeated Michael's statement. And he had not changed it at the important point which would have changed here to me; he had not said, 'As long as you come back to me;' it was, as Michael had said, to here . . . his house.

The gaiety of Christmas faded away. She felt cold all through, perplexed and strangely sad.

9

It had been snowing for days and the roads beyond the town were almost impassable. Last night, Hal had brought her home. She had wanted to leave on the day after Boxing Day; but, except for Michael, they had all pressed her to stay; even Arthur had joined his voice to those of Hal and Rosie, which was somewhat surprising. And so she had stayed until yesterday.

The flat was dark and cold, and smelt musty, and looked dismal after the large airy rooms in Hal's house. He had remarked on it immediately, saying, 'This is awful. You'll freeze here. And the bed will be damp. Come on back. I'll get you in tomorrow in time to meet Mr Henderson.' But she had assured him that the bed would be all right, that she had an electric blanket on it, and once the fire had got going and the curtains were drawn and the lights put on, it would take on a different atmosphere altogether.

The fact that he was leaving her with evident reluctance brought her some little comfort, and when he took her in his arms and kissed her, she hugged him, and he stroked her hair as he said, 'My place is not going to be the same without you. It isn't often, you know, Jinny, that one meets someone like you, warm and understanding, making no demands. Women as a rule are very demanding, at least that's how I've found them, but you, you're so different.' He lifted her face up to his and, his voice thick with feeling now, he said, 'You're so wonderful, Jinny. You know that? I'm amazed that you've bothered with someone like me; a man who has had two wives is always suspect, especially when he's been divorced. Most women want to know why you were divorced, what happened, who was to blame, and, you know, there's never the one person to blame in such a case, it's usually fifty-fifty. Granted, sometimes sixty-forty.'

Even as he talked her mind was teeming with questions that could not be asked. One of the main things now was where she stood with him. True, she had only really known him for two months, but their association had seemed to have made no progress since the first time he had kissed her . . . Well, what did she expect? What did she mean by progress? The end that Ray Collard envisaged? Did she expect that? No, no. Then what was she grumbling about? What was niggling at her? She didn't know.

She was ready and waiting when Mr Henderson called on the Sunday morning at eleven o'clock; and when she opened the door to him and he stepped into the room, now unsoftened by the glow of the fire, he stood looking about him for a moment.

'Lass, you must freeze down here,' he said.

'Oh,' she replied lightly, 'when the fire's on it gets very warm.'

'But it's so bloody dark, lass.' He looked towards the window that was shadowed by the outer basement wall.

'Well, it's a basement flat, and I was lucky to get it.'

'Eeh, my!' He walked across the room now and pushed open the kitchen door; then turning to her, he said, 'You deserve something better than this, I'll say.'

'What do you propose? Setting me up in a flat?' She laughed as she made the statement at the same time thinking, Fancy daring to say such a think like that to him.

Coming towards her now, he said flatly, 'No, I don't. You know me better than that. But I think you should put yourself into a better one. At least somewhere on ground level.'

'For the time I'm in it, it serves its purpose.'

'Haven't you any ambition?'

'Oh, yes, yes.' She picked up her woollen gloves and weekend bag now as she said, 'I've got my eyes set on a millionaire.'

'Aye, well, and why not? Most models seem to aim for them. That's what you should have been, you know. With no bust and no backside you'd have made a good model.'

'Thank you. Shall we go?'

'Aye, we'd better. Be warmer outside . . .'

They had hardly entered the house before he was describing her flat to Alicia. 'Like a bloody mausoleum, it is. You want to go and see it.'

'Do you think, dear, there'll ever be a time when you'll learn to mind your own business? Come along, Jinny. Sit down. Lucy's out; we've got the place to ourselves. It's going to be a very quiet time, you know; there'll be one or two dropping in for the first-footing, but that's all. I hope you won't find it dull.'

'Oh, Mrs Henderson.' Jinny laughed quietly before adding; 'Dull? Apart from everything else, I don't know who could be dull when your husband is about.' She inclined her head now to where Bob Henderson was going into the hall calling, 'Dorry! Dorry! What about that coffee?'

Alicia Henderson pouted her lips slightly as she said, 'You've got something there. But he can be a trial at times.' The smile slipping from her face now, she said, quietly, 'People respond to him in two ways: either they love him or they hate him.'

'Oh, I couldn't imagine anyone really hating him.'

'You'd be surprised, my dear. Oh, you'd be surprised. A self-made man is a target for enemies. And strangely, the majority come from his own people; not his relations in this case because he's lost them, but from so-called friends. As he is apt to say, you would expect an enemy to shoot at you and you could survive, but when the bullet comes from a friend no operation can ever get it out. Anyway, that's enough of that. Come, tell me about yourself. We've never had a talk together.'

And so Jinny told her all there was to tell, until she came up to the Fellburn Players. Then her telling became rather stilted, and when Alicia prompted, saying, 'Have you got a boy friend?' she answered, rather hesitantly, 'I . . . I have a friend, but boy friend has a very wide connotation these days, and he's not a boy friend in that sense, if you know what I mean.'

'Oh, yes, I know what you mean, dear.'

'I met him through the Players and he has three adopted children. Well, they're his stepchildren from his previous wives.'

As she watched Alicia's eyebrows give the slightest movement upwards, she said, 'His first wife died and he divorced his second. His first wife had been married before, and she had two children; his second wife also had been married' – she gave an embarrassed laugh now – 'she had a teenage son. He is now . . . well, about twenty-three. The other two are still teenagers. They were the friends I stayed with over Christmas, just a mile or two on from here.'

Following a silence between them, Alicia asked quietly, 'Are you thinking of getting married?'

What answer could she give to that? Yes, she was thinking of getting married; but it took two people to think of marriage. And so she answered, half in truth, 'I think about it. But that's as far as it goes.'

Mr Henderson re-entered the room at this moment, followed by a middle-aged woman carrying a tray. She was wearing a light blue woollen dress. When she placed the tray bearing the coffee jug, and cups and saucers, on a table to Alicia's hand, she asked in a broad north-country voice, 'D'you want the brandy, ma'am?'

But before Alicia could speak Bob Henderson put in, 'Aye, we do. But I'll get it meself, 'cos you'd have half the bottle empty afore it reached her.'

'Eeh! Mr Henderson, you get worse.'

'That's impossible, Dorry,' said Alicia, shaking her head; and Dorry answered, with a broad smile on her homely face, 'Yes, ma'am, I think it is . . .'

Jinny had never before had brandy in her coffee; she found she liked it. She liked the lunch, too, that followed; she liked the dinner that night; in fact she liked everything about this house and the people in it. Mr Henderson had cornered her during the afternoon and taken her into his office, which was bigger than the one on the top floor at the works, and as well equipped, which surprised her, as did the fact that he'd had it set up like this four years ago after a heart attack, when for a time he worked from the house.

Sitting in the big leather chair behind the desk, he said to her, 'Eeh! I'll be glad to get back to work, won't you?'

And when she replied immediately, 'Not me,' he said, 'So much for enterprise.'

She then asked him why he didn't work more from the house, as it would be easier for him, cut out the travelling, most of it, and he answered, 'What! And let that lot have the run of the place? I know what happened afore when I was off. Chris Waitland likes me as much as I like poison. He'd not only jump into me boots, but pull me socks off as well. You see, I was against his being on the board in the first place. But, as I've told you afore, he's a relation of Dick Garbrook. I think the word is nepotism isn't it, Jinny?'

'Yes, the word is nepotism,' she said.

'I've always tried to keep the company on an even keel; but I'm not so sure I can do that much longer, 'cos the whole country's gone mad; strikes everywhere. And now if the bloody transport drivers come out we'll be in a pickle because half our business is transport. It's no good making things, and even gettin' orders for them, if you can't deliver them, is it? I wish our Glen was back. He can sniff out things . . . Glen. I never thought he'd take to this business like he's done. Now, John . . . Oh aye, I thought our John was made for it, seeing he looks like me.' He grinned at her. Then his expression and his tone tinged with sadness, he added, 'Cuts me to the bone the way our John carries on. He was at university an' all you know when he packed things up. That's where he met this hot head of a lass. And what's he doing now? Helping with backward bairns. Eeh, my God! to think of it. And with his brains. Because he was smarter than Glen; smarter than any of them. Although our Florrie's got quite a bit up top, but Nellie and Monica are just two lasses. And our Lucy. Oh, our Lucy. As I said afore, she's spoilt rotten. I've got to admit that all Lucy thinks about is Lucy.'

He paused for a while; then looking hard at her he said, 'You know, behind that soft look of yours you've got a head on your shoulders. You could have been one of mine, you know. I thought that the first day you came into the office. And after a week or so I knew I was right, 'cos you've got the hang of the business; you know how to deal with people, like you dealt with that French representative. I'd have been all at sea.'

He got up from the desk and, more briskly now, said, 'Well, there'll be some afternoon tea goin' on somewhere; let's go and find it. And by the way, I'm doubling your wages, from the morrow.'

'Oh no.'

'Good God! Somebody doesn't want a raise. Look, it isn't my idea, and it's not goin' on the books either, else there'll be hell to pay; it's Alicia's idea, 'cos she knows you're right and in the right place, and you should get the right money. But as things stand, were I to put you up by threepence a week I'd have a deputation on the doorstep. You know that yourself. As Alicia says there's nothing to stop me doing a private deal. And you'll get it in offer to get yourself out of that dungeon you live in. Go on, and shut your mouth; you look like a fish.'

Later that evening, when she had tried to express her thanks to the elegant woman, Alicia Henderson had said, 'It is nothing, my dear. You are good for him, and you have lightened his work. And not only are you good for him business-wise but also because you are a match for him verbally, although it amazes me that you are able to do this, because you have that delicate, refined appearance . . .'

At this point Jinny had laughed aloud, saying, 'Oh, Mrs Henderson, delicate, I certainly am not. I never ail anything. As for being refined, oh dear, the only claim I can lay to that is . . . well, I don't go along with the modern thinkers. I suppose it's because of the way I was brought up. But I think there's a lack of morality in all ways today, so much so that what was wrong once is accepted as right now, and if you can't see it that way you are . . . well, out.'

As Alicia Henderson stared at her in silence she closed her eyes and lowered her head for she remembered that this woman's son, perhaps her favourite son, was one of those people who accepted the morality of today, not only accepted it but had acted upon it to the extent that he had broken away from her and his father.

Lifting her head again, she said, 'I'm sorry. I shouldn't have expressed myself like that.'

'I understand perfectly, my dear, and I admire you for it.'

'Oh, there's nothing to admire, really; I sometimes feel a fool and an idiot to take the stand. You see, I was engaged to be married, and it was broken off because I couldn't see eye to eye that way.'

'Yes, yes, I see. I'm sorry. But you have your present boy friend?'

'Yes. Yes, I have.'

She took the conversation no further for she had the idea that whereas she herself didn't hold with . . . shacking up, Mrs Henderson was not very enthusiastic about men who had twice been divorced . . .

They had numerous friends in, and during the evening she was introduced to so many people that she couldn't remember their names. And then the phone was constantly ringing, and Alicia, answering it, would look across the room and cry to her husband, 'Oh this is Florence and the children', or 'Nellie', or 'Monica', and he would go across and take the phone from her and shout into it nearly always the same thing: 'Happy New Year. But you should be here, you know.'

Then when Glen phoned there was great excitement. And his father yelled at him, 'It's about time you were back. Three weeks is enough for anybody.' Then, 'Yvonne! you get him back here; I'm sick of lookin' after your house. It's freezing here an' the pipes have burst; it's runnin' with water.' And Alicia would pull the phone from her husband and cry into it, 'Don't take any notice, Yvonne. Everything's all right. Beautiful. It's waiting for your coming . . .'

Yet, there were only three of them standing together when the New Year was brought in on the television.

'A Happy New Year, me love.'

'And to you, my dear.'

Watching them embrace and their tenderness towards each other brought a lump to Jinny's throat. That was how her mother and father used to act, holding each other, looking into each other's eyes in silent seconds that spoke of an eternity of loving.

And then Mr Henderson put his arms about her and kissed her with a smacking kiss on the lips. Then Alicia kissed her, saying, 'A Happy New Year, Jinny. A very Happy New Year.'

'Aye, and that goes for me an' all. A very Happy New Year, lass. Oh' – he turned – 'and here's Dorry. Happy New Year, Dorry. Come in. Come in, love . . . And Cissie and Eddie.' The man and woman behind Dorry came into the room, saying, 'A Happy New Year, sir. Happy New Year, ma'am.'

As exchanges were being made Bob Henderson said, 'I thought you had the family over in the cottage.'

'We have, sir, but we've never missed calling in on a New Year in the last twenty years and we don't want to break it. Just wanted to wish you again a very happy new year, and may they go on.'

Cissie Gallon was the cook and Eddie the gardener, and Dorry, she understood, had been with them for twenty-five years. And who wouldn't want to stay with people like these.

After the three had gone the phone began to ring. Then from half-past twelve onwards there were various people kicking the snow from their shoes before coming in and calling, 'Happy New Year, Bob! Happy New Year, Alicia!'

It had all been wonderful. She couldn't remember ever spending a New Year like it. At half-past two when the last caller had just gone and Alicia, looking at her husband, said, 'It's bed. You've had more than enough of everything for one night, including food and drink,' there came another ring on the bell.

'Oh, God above! This can go on till dawn. I wonder who it is this time. I thought we'd seen the lot. No! sit where you are, I'll go . . . I tell, you, I'll go!' He pushed his wife back into her chair and went out of the drawing room, across the hall and to the front door. When he opened it his eyes narrowed at the sight of the figure standing there silhouetted against the snow; and then in a whisper he said, 'John.'

'Yes, Father. Happy New Year.'

'Come in. Come in, lad. Happy New Year.' His voice was still low. And now he caught his son's hand in both of his and shook it vigorously before turning to close the door. His hand going out again, he put it gently on his son's arm, saying, 'By! She'll be glad to see you. Aye, she will that. A Happy New Year indeed! Come on. Come on.' And as if his son were a stranger to the house he led him towards the drawing-room door; then thrusting this open and his voice assuming its usual loud timbre, he called, 'Look who's here!'

Alicia Henderson was already standing in the middle of the room as if awaiting a guest, and she didn't move towards her son; it was he who walked towards her, saying, 'Happy New Year, Mother.'

'Oh, John!' For a moment they were enfolded in each other's arms; but only for a moment for, gripping his hands, she said, 'You're frozen. Come and sit down. Here, give me your coat. Oh, you are cold. Where have you been? Did you walk?'

'No, no. But you can't keep the heat on in a stationary car.'

'Stationary car? You mean you have been sitting out there?'

'Well, it was like Newcastle Central; I thought I'd wait until the last train left.'

'Silly bugger.'

Jinny watched Alicia close her eyes, but there was a smile on her face as she did so.

'Have you had anything to eat?'

John Henderson looked at his mother, and then at his father, and he said, 'Not since half-past ten last night. Candidly, I'm starving.'

When his parents exchanged glances, Jinny thought it was as if they had both been given a gift, and under the circumstances perhaps they looked upon the fact that their son wanted to eat with them as a gift indeed.

'I'll go and get you something.'

'Has Dorry gone to bed?'

'Oh, ages ago.'

'Well, don't bother.'

'Don't be silly.' As Alicia went to leave them, Bob Henderson said, 'I'll come and give you a hand with the tray.' It was as if at this moment, at least, he was finding it an embarrassment to be with his son unless his wife was there too. But before he made to follow her, he turned and said, whilst pointing to Jinny, 'She's not a figment of your imagination; you've never wished her a Happy New Year.'

John Henderson had been standing with his back to the fire, and he now came forward to where Jinny was seated in a wing chair. Bending towards her, he said, formally, 'A Happy New Year.'

'And to you.'

Then going back to the fire, he took up his position again with his back to it. Looking round the room, he said, 'The first time in my life I've seen this place so empty on a New Year's morning. Of course, I didn't see it at all last year, but I knew that they were all here.'

He brought his gaze to rest on her, and he looked at her without speaking for a moment; then he said, 'It was good of you to have stayed with them.'

'Oh; it was very good of them to ask me. It's been wonderful.'

'Wonderful? They're an elderly couple. Well' – he shrugged his shoulders now – 'Mother isn't. Mother never acts her age. Let's say they're settled middle-aged. Wouldn't you rather be at one of the mad New Year's do's?'

'No, not at all. And I'm surprised that you think they are old, even, as you say, settled middle-aged. Neither of them appears like that to me.'

'Well, that's nice for them.' He shifted his stance now and rested his elbow against the high mantelshelf as he said, 'I suppose Lucy's out gallivanting?'

'She's at a dance.'

'Yes, she would be.'

He sounded disgruntled, and somewhat sad. She didn't find his remarks detrimental to his people; she felt sorry for him. Why, she didn't really know. He had chosen to lead his own life, yet, here he was, drawn back to his people. He was of a different temperament altogether from Glen, more thoughtful, more introspective, she imagined.

His next question surprised her because it came sharp and more in the form of a demand: 'How old are you?' he said.

'I'm twenty-one.'

'You sound older, but you look younger.'

'Compliments come in all shapes and sizes; I'll have to have time to work that one out.'

'It was merely a statement.'

'Yes, I should imagine it would be, but statements usually have to be looked into.'

'He now turned fully towards her for the first time and smiled as he said, 'I can see how you get along with Father; you're quick on the draw. He admires anyone who can stand up to him verbally.'

'Couldn't you?'

'Yes. Yes, I could, but there can only be one winner in a verbal battle, and I should imagine your success with him lies in the fact that you realized that from the beginning: he's got to be right. Still' – again he shrugged – 'it's New Year's Day, forgive and forget. If only one could. Oh, here!' – he turned – 'let me take that,' he said, hurrying down the room to where his father was carrying a laden tray. And his very action conveyed to Jinny what he had said earlier: he looked upon his father as an elderly man. And she found that strange because there was one thing certain, no matter what Mr Henderson's age was he acted young, vigorously, and he certainly talked in the same way. Oh yes, indeed.

About ten minutes later she made her excuses and, after bidding them all good-night, she left them alone together. And she was to remember long after this that her last waking thought before dropping into luxurious slumber was that she hoped something would happen to bring Mr Henderson and his John together again. And it did; but at what a price.

PART TWO

1

The weather had been and still was the worst most people could remember. There seemed to be no let up. This, coupled with the state of the country, made Bob Henderson's language more colourful as the days went on. But on this particular Friday in February he sat with his fists doubled on the desk, and in between them lay a sheaf of letters ready for his signature. Glaring at Jinny, he said, 'What's the bloody good of signing them? If they won't bury their own dead now they're not going to move our stuff! Eeh! That I've lived to see the day when the dead are lying stinking in the mortuaries, and north-country fellows who pride themselves as honest to God men letting them lie there. It's unbelievable. And if they get what they're asking for what'll happen. The bloody prices'll go up, and they'll be no better off. Silly buggers can't see it. And all the school bairns roaming the streets 'cos the schools are closed; and the car workers out again. And now 'tis unbelievable, but even the civil servants are at it. I've always scorned the bloody lot, sitting on their backsides all day. No wonder the fellows on the floor get edgy. I've got a representative lot downstairs, haven't I, on both counts. It'll be all out next' – he nodded at her – 'you'll see, once the steel blokes get the smell in their noses they'll be like hound dogs. We're a private firm: it can't happen to us, we say. But nothing's private, nobody's private, everybody depends on somebody else. Why can't the silly buggers understand this?'

Jinny watched him take up his pen and jab his signature at the bottom of the letters. Then when he had finished she gathered them up and said quietly, 'Don't forget you've got to be downstairs by quarter-past five. Mr Glen's picking you up. And then you're to go and meet Mrs . . .'

'Aye, I know, Jinny. I'm not in me dotage yet. And don't say that surprises you, because I'm not in the mood either for backchat.' He paused as he looked at her now, and then said quietly, 'I'm worried. It's bad enough the strikes and us not being able to deliver things on time, but I'm not happy about Garbrook an' the container company. No, I'm not. Not enough attention paid to work there. If the waistband gets slack, then the skirt drops off. That's what me mother used to say. And it's right you know; there's got to be a firm hold in the middle to keep the rest in place so to speak. And if that lot goes broke we'll have to carry the can.'

'Are you not empowered to alter the management there?'

'No, I can't go over Dick's head. He's a managing director like meself. *No*. What am I sayin'? He's not like meself. I don't take a month's holiday three times a year.'

'Perhaps it's a pity you don't.'

'Now don't start talkin' bloody rot, girl. I thought you had more sense than to come out with palaver like that. You know the state of affairs on the floor as well as I do now, and when the cat's away the mice'll play. It's just human nature. By! there's a lot of truth in these old sayings.'

'Yes, there is.' Her voice too was loud now. 'My father used very often to quote one. And it went like this: Everybody can be done without, and if they don't realize this death will come as a shock to them.'

'Did he now? Did your father say that?'

'Yes, he did.'

'Oh aye? And you're not putting a tooth in it in telling me that I could be done without.'

'If you die tomorrow you'd have to be done without.'

'Thank you for telling me.'

'I'm sure I'm not telling you anything that Mrs Henderson hasn't told you a thousand times before.'

'Now what I should answer to that, Jinny, is, aye, and I'll take it from her but I don't see why I should take it from you. But there, I know you mean well. But, lass, you've got a long way to go yet. And being a woman, you'll never understand that being loved by a marvellous woman isn't enough in a man's life: it's the threads that hold it together, but it isn't the whole of it, it's work in the long run that matters to a man. Aye, work. Have you ever wondered why I had that verse framed up there? I'm no man for poetry, never was. I leave that to those who think they know better than others, numskulls half of them, never done a day's work in their lives. But when I came across that bit it spoke my thoughts, and I had it framed. I don't know who wrote it. But look, take it down and bring it here.'

Jinny crossed the room to where, above a filing cabinet in a small frame and under glass, was a sheet of quarto paper and on it a verse headed *The Workers*. She had read it a number of times, and wondered why it was the only form of picture in the office. Taking it down, she returned with it to the desk and handed it to him. And he stared at it for some time before handing it back to her, and saying, 'Read it to me. Go on, read it to me. I've never heard anybody read it aloud; I've only heard it in me own head. Go on.'

She paused for a moment, then began to read:

'Without work the days are long
And the nights are longer

And the weeks stand still in frustrating ease
Which slide into months of boredom,
And the year is gone without appease.

And in the days that are long
And the nights that are longer
Respect shrinks to a wizened core,
For work is the oil of man's existence,
The only resistance against the endless death
Of enforced ease.'

'What does it say to you?'

'It simply speaks your thoughts.'

'Aye, well, that's one way of putting it. And that last line: the only resistance against the endless death of enforced ease. You know, I think hell must be a place where there's nothing to do, nothing to come to grips with.'

'You could be right.'

'I could be?' He stretched his face at her. 'I know I am.'

She looked down on him now and, a slow smile spreading over her face, she said, 'It would be funny, wouldn't it, if you were made to endure the endless death of enforced ease for your sins? That would be poetic justice, don't you think?'

It was only to be a matter of days before she was asking herself, why in the name of God had she come out with a remark like that? Why did one say such things? Did some creator of destinies pick up your thoughts and, using them as a blueprint, build them into life?

He was saying, 'You cheeky bitch, you! Put it back on the wall. You know' – he turned his head now and looked at her where she was hanging the framed poem above the cabinet again, and he went on, 'They made a mistake when they were giving out faces in your case because underneath that ladylike exterior of yours you're a hard nut. The fellow who gets you is going to have my sympathy. If he doesn't hold his own he'll be a doormat.'

'Definitely.'

'Aw! away with you. Get those letters off and let's get downstairs.'

'No; I won't be coming yet, there are one or two things I want to clear up.'

'But how are you going to get home in this? There are hardly any buses running.'

'I'm being met.'

'Oh. Then why didn't you say so? Who is it? Still the same bloke? You're mad, you know. If a man can't make a success of two goes he's going to have a hard job on the third try. You're worth something more than that. My God, if you belonged to me I'd send him off with a flea in his ear.'

Tolerantly now, she said, 'No doubt. No doubt,' as she made her way to the cloakroom. She returned with his outdoor things. Having helped him into his coat, she handed him his scarf and his gloves, and as she did so she had the almost irresistible desire to lean forward and kiss him, just on the cheek. The thought brought the colour flushing to her face, and he, noticing it and thinking it to have been caused by his last remark, said, 'Don't take it as an affront, the things I say. It's because I'm concerned for you. And Alicia is an' all. I'll tell you something now.' He leant towards her, his rough red face close to hers. 'She's planned to take you out to Barbados with us in the autumn.'

'Oh.' She shook her head. Then on a whisper, she said, 'Oh, Mr Henderson.' Her eyelids blinked, she swallowed deep in her throat; and he, now tucking his scarf inside his coat, said, 'Oh, don't start slobbering; you haven't got there yet. And who knows, you might go and marry that fellow.' He stepped back from her and, as he pulled on his gloves, he surveyed her through his narrowed eyes and, his voice low, he said, 'I'm getting out of range.' Then he added, 'Are you living with him?'

Before answering, she drew in a deep breath, 'No, I'm not living with him,' she said. 'And I have no intention of doing so.'

'I'm . . . I'm – ' His head was bobbing now, and he said again, 'I'm – ' before pursing his lips and finishing, 'glad to hear it. Very glad to hear it. Well, good-night, lass. And stop lookin' daggers at me. Good-night.'

He had reached the door before she said, 'Good-night, Mr Henderson.'

She rested an elbow on her desk and, gripping her chin within the palm of her hand, she muttered aloud, 'And I have no intention of doing so.'

Then what was going to be the end of it between her and Hal, for he certainly hadn't mentioned marriage, not even an engagement? And his love-making was mild in the extreme, even, she had to admit to herself, creating in her a feeling of frustration. Although she had denied that she would ever live with Hal, nevertheless she wondered what her answer would be if the proposition were put to her. If it meant that or losing him, what would she do? After all, what was marriage but a man muttering a few words over you, and afterwards being supplied with a piece of paper to prove you had gone through some sort of ceremony and that everything from then on would be all right: you could go to bed as many times as you liked with the man because you were what was called married; you had entered another state, a smug state.

She lifted her head from her hand. Yes, she supposed it could be called smug; nevertheless, that was the state she wanted to be in. But she also wanted to be loved. Oh, how she wanted to be loved. Well, it was up to her; she was a free agent.

But was it up to her where Hal was concerned? Love after marriage or love before, neither the one way nor the other had come into their conversation. And not once by the extra pressure of his lips or his arms had he suggested that he had need of her.

And so what was she going to do, feeling as she did about him? But how did she feel about him? Did she love him? Yes. Yes, she loved him. But how did she know it was really love? Whom had she loved before? Ray Collard? She had thought she loved him. The calf feelings she had experienced at school, the love she'd had for her father and mother, all these feelings came under the heading of love. Was the feeling she had for Hal so different?

Oh, yes, yes, it was, because more frequently now she had imagined what it would be like if he actually made love to her . . . Of course after they were married.

Damn! She had sprung up from the desk, and, her hands now gripping the edge of it, she was on the point of adding, Blast it! Blast everything! when the nice refined girl that was still dominant in her make-up chastised her, saying, 'Stop it. This is what comes of working with Mr Henderson.'

And now she was attacked by another section of her mind. Don't start finding fault with Mr Henderson, it said; you'll never find another boss like him as long as you live, nor a kinder person. Get the business finished and get out . . .

It was nearly a half-hour later when Sam opened the door for her, saying, 'I think we must have entered the ice age, miss. In all my sixty years I've never experienced anything like it, not to go on day after day like this. Go careful now; it's like glass.'

She went carefully across the now almost empty car park, and there at the gate a car was waiting. But it wasn't Hal's. Before she reached it, Michael had got out and, holding the door open for her, he said immediately, 'Don't ask questions, just get in. I'm frozen.'

Once seated inside, she said, 'What's the matter?' and to this he answered, 'Nothing serious. Only his car got stuck in a drift. It's likely to be there for days. He took the side road. He must have been mad. Do you want to go home first or straight there?'

'I would like to call in at the flat, if you have the time.'

'All the time in the evening.'

She glanced at him. He was bent over the wheel, peering ahead as he said, 'I'm at your service from now on, I'm a bachelor again. She walked out on me, left a note last Monday. Our trial trip was short and sweet . . . Then, on reflection, not so sweet. She's taken up with a dustman.'

He nodded a number of times before enlarging on this: 'I'm not joking; she actually has. A tough guy. Muscles like a rhino's.' His head was still nodding, his eyes narrowed. 'I should hate all dustmen from now on, shouldn't I, but I don't. I knew it wasn't going to work out.'

'Careful!' She put out her hand towards the windscreen. 'Didn't you see that car?'

'Yes, I saw that car, but he didn't seem to see me. Don't worry, I'm a very careful driver. I love my skin and don't want it damaged. Here we are!' He looked out of the side window. 'Nobody's bothered to clean these pavements. Good lord! it's nearly up to the railings.'

'Well, I think nearly everybody in the street goes to work.'

After she had unlocked the door and switched on the light, he followed her into the room. But he didn't speak for some time, he just stood looking around him. Then, unlike Mr Henderson's, his remarks were complimentary. 'Could be quite comfortable,' he said. 'Better than the one we had. I've got to get rid of it now. I'd signed the lease for a year. Some hopes I had, hadn't I? But Hal will see to that.'

'I won't light the fire,' she said; 'I only want to pick up my case and a few things.'

'I wish you would.'

'What?' She turned to him from the bedroom door.

'Light the fire, and we could sit here and talk.'

'Don't be silly.'

'I'm not being silly, Jinny.' His bantering tone had changed. 'I'm serious, and . . . and I want to talk to you.'

'Well, we can talk in the car on our way.'

'No, we couldn't talk in the car. There are things I've got to say to you, things I must say to you.'

'What if I don't want to hear them?'

'You're not silly.'

'Perhaps I am.'

She went into the bedroom now, and a few minutes later she returned with her case, saying briskly, 'Let's go.'

As he came towards her she watched his face darken, and when he said, 'You may be sorry you didn't listen. In any case, what I intended to say was not what you expected me to say, namely, that I have fallen for you . . . because that's what's in your mind, isn't it?'

For the second time in less than an hour her face became scarlet, because that was exactly what she had thought he had been about to say. And she was unprepared to be disgusted at his disloyalty to Hal. But now she could not bring herself to ask, 'What is it then you want to say to me?' And so she walked past him and towards the door. But here she paused, and to save her own face, she turned and confronted him, saying now, 'You have an opinion of yourself, haven't you, while your opinion of my intelligence is almost nil.'

His expression was almost as angry as her own as he replied,

'You're quite right there, perfectly right: you're dim, stupid, you haven't got the sense you were born with.'

He marched past her and up the area steps, and as she locked the door she found herself gasping as if she had been ploughing through a heavy snowdrift.

The journey seemed interminable because they never exchanged a word. When they reached the house, Hal was waiting for them at the opened door. After taking her hands in his he kissed her, then looked to where Michael was making straight for the stairs, and in a low voice said, 'What's the matter with him?'

Hers equally low, she answered, 'We . . . We've had a slight argument.'

'Oh. There's nothing like a family for providing grounds for slight arguments. Come on, get your things off; the tea's all set. I've got some muffins, all hot and buttery. I had all the groceries in the car when I went into that drift. What a job it was to lug them back here.'

It was Hal who talked during most of the meal; Michael's quietness could have been put down to his broken romance, yet Jinny knew that Hal was aware of something beyond this. But it only seemed to make him talk the more. His questions to Arthur about school received laconic answers. Only with Rosie had he any cross-talk.

It was after the meal was finished and the washing up done that he called from the kitchen doorway to Michael who was making his way into the sitting-room: 'I've got to slip out for a while. May I take your car again? One of my old people isn't too good. This weather's getting a lot of them down.'

Michael turned and looked back at Hal, but did not immediately answer; but when he did his voice was bright and high, over high, as he replied, 'Of course, Hal, take the car. I can understand your need to see to the old people. Most commendable of you.'

When Hal returned to the kitchen again Jinny could see that all his teatime joviality had gone from him. The expression on his face was one she hadn't seen before: it recalled to her the day he had run Arthur from the room. Yet his look now did not wholly indicate anger, but had in it a kind of surprised wariness.

For a moment he didn't speak; then looking at her, he said, 'I've got to go. You understand?'

'Yes, yes.' She nodded at him. 'But it's an awful night and, the roads the way they are, would they be expecting you?'

'*What*?' It was as if his thinking had been far away. Then he said slowly, 'Yes, they'll be expecting me. People get very lonely. Well, you know all about that, don't you, Jinny?'

Yes, she knew all about that. Yet, that niggling part of her mind was telling her there was something here that she didn't know all about. And Michael could and would perhaps have explained it if she had only listened to him. But she didn't listen to him, and she didn't wholly believe him when he said he hadn't intended to tell her that he had fallen for her. If the attitude he adopted with her was the same as that he used with all women then he must have raised quite a few high hopes. Even she had asked herself: if she hadn't felt the way she did about Hal would she have responded to Michael? But she had given herself no answer; life was complicated enough without creating further obstacles.

Hal's kiss of goodbye at the front door was a perfunctory one, similar to one he might have bestowed on Rosie, and as he pulled up his collar in the act of turning away from her, he muttered, 'Don't wait up, I . . . I might be late, or get stuck. You never know. Anyway, don't wait up.'

After she had closed the door on him and was crossing the hall towards the stairs, intending to go to her room, Michael appeared at the sitting-room door.

He didn't speak, but he raised his eyebrows and pursed his lips, and his expression appeared like one large question mark that was saying, 'Well?'

Just for a moment, she half turned as if to go towards him and demand an explanation of the innuendoes he was always dropping. But what would she find out? Not that Hal was a homosexual. No, she couldn't believe that. Not that he had another woman. Hadn't he told her how afraid he was of marriage? But with this thought her mind hit her like a blow, astonishing her by bringing with it Mr Henderson's favourite word, bloody. Don't be a bloody fool, it said. Is a man going to keep away from women because he's expressed an opinion against a third marriage?

She mounted the stairs. No, no. There was no other woman. She was sure of that. He wasn't like that. If he wanted a woman that way, his love-making would have been different; by now he would have shown himself in a different light altogether. You couldn't hide those kind of feelings of passion for long . . . Then what was it?

In her room, she sat on the foot of the bed. The room was warm, as was the whole house. Everything here was made for comfort; perhaps not in the grand style of Mr Henderson's house, but nevertheless, everything that one needed was here. She had thought more than once that Hal's mother must have been an ideal home-maker. Since that night in the flat when he had talked about the loss of his mother he had never mentioned her. There were four photographs of her in his room: in one she was cradling him in her arms when he was a baby; the other three were of her alone, one full length, the other two head and shoulders. She had looked a big woman, rather handsome, but her features were bony; her eyes were large, like Hal's, but more heavily lidded.

Her whole attitude now was denying the warmth of the room, for she sat with her hands under her oxters, her arms crossed, and she rocked herself gently as a child rocks itself in a cot when in need of comfort. And that's what she needed at this moment, comfort. She wanted someone she could talk to, explain her feelings to. She thought of Alicia Henderson. Yes, she could talk to Mrs Henderson. She could even talk to Mr Henderson. Yes, that was strange. If either of them had been here at this moment she would have said to them, 'I feel like walking out but I'm frightened. I'm frightened of being on my own again. No place to go at the week-ends. I should have it out with him but what could I say?' And they would have said, 'You must come to us.'

Could she have then gone on to say to them, 'I want more than companionship from him, I want love, real love, like you two have, married love?' Could she have said that to them? Perhaps. Yes, perhaps she could; they were special people.

She rose from the bed and, going to her case, she took out a woollen cardigan, and as she put it on her chin jerked upwards as she came to a resolution: she wasn't going to be made a fool of for a second time. At the first opportunity she would ask him point blank if there was any one else.

2

The opportunity didn't arise over the weekend for her to bring things into the open, for Hal had caught a cold, and on the Saturday and Sunday he remained in bed. When approached even to ask how he was feeling he showed yet another new side. However, his particular peevishness she put down to the fact that most men thought they were going to die when they caught a cold; at least, she had been given to understand that. Even her mother had said it.

On the Monday morning she left for work on foot for the drifts were so high that now Michael couldn't get his car out and on to the side road. But the buses were running and although the main road was not half a mile away, it took Michael and her almost half an hour to reach it. And during the journey they even laughed together, when she had to pull him out of a drift and, the snow having gone down the top of his Wellington boots, he did a kind of St Vitus dance in an effort to get it out.

They were lucky enough to get a bus and before he got off, some way before her stop, he was smiling broadly as he said, 'You know,

Jinny, I've enjoyed this journey better than any I've made for a long time.'

She had turned towards him, while she smiled too, saying now, 'Well, I hope you enjoy it going back tonight.'

'I might turn up at your place looking for shelter.'

'You'll find a closed door.'

'Never.'

He waved to her from the pavement, and she lifted her hand in reply.

It was five-past nine when she walked through the cleared path in the car park. Only about a third of the usual cars were scattered here and there, and Mr Henderson's wasn't parked under the awning.

As she approached the glass door Sam opened it for her, and she said to him, 'It doesn't get any better, does it? There'll be a few empty seats here today, I've no doubt.'

The doorman stared at her; and as she went to move away from him and across the hall his voice stopped her. 'Miss!'

'Yes, Sam?'

'Where are you going?'

'Where am I going?' She moved back to him and looked into his face. 'I'm going to work.' And she gave a small laugh. Then when he didn't speak she said, 'What's the matter? What is it?'

'Don't you know, miss?' His voice was a mere whisper.

It was some seconds before she managed to say, 'Know what?' And when he still didn't answer, she repeated, 'Know what?'

'About the accident on Friday night.'

'Accident to . . . Mr Henderson? *Oh no! No!*' She put her hands tightly across her mouth. 'What . . . what happened? Is he . . .?'

'Have you been away for the weekend? Didn't you hear it on the wireless?'

'Hear what? Yes, yes, I've been away . . . But hear what?'

'Well, it's going to be a shock, lass. It has been to everybody. A lorry ran right through them. The two women, the two wives . . . went instantly, so it's said. They were in the back seat. But Mr Henderson and Glen . . . they were smashed up badly, so I hear. Very little chance.'

'*Oh my God!*'

'Sit down, miss. Sit down.' He led her towards a chair which stood near a rubber plant, and when she was seated he said, 'Stay there; I'll get you a drink of water.'

She sat staring before her, unable to take it in, yet already devastated by the news, part of her mind screaming at her: 'Not those two. Not those two! Not Mrs Henderson and that nice girl. No. No. God wouldn't do things like that.' You read about it in the papers. It happened to other people, people you didn't know, people who hadn't been kind to you, people about whom you could say, Isn't it awful?

but without feeling this terrible sense of loss which was creating in her a pain the like of which she had never before experienced. She had been so distressed when her father died, and had never thought to experience again the sense of aloneness she'd had after she buried her mother. But those feelings now appeared like rippling waves compared to the deluge of compassion and sense of loss that was enveloping her now.

'Here. Drink this.'

She sipped at the water; then looking at Sam she said, 'Where . . . where's Mr Henderson?'

'As far as I know, miss, they're both in the Royal Victoria over in Newcastle.'

There seemed to be a long pause before she said, 'Are there any taxis running, Sam?'

'I could try for you, miss.'

'Please.'

She sat still on the chair, oblivious of the door opening and shutting and of people crossing the hall towards the lift. Some looked in her direction, but no one came up to her, until Sam returned, saying, 'There'll be one here in five minutes, miss.'

When she rose to go towards the door, he took her arm, and as he did so he said, 'By! if anything happens to Mr Henderson this place'll know it. I'm telling you.'

If anything happened to Mr Henderson . . . if anything happened to Mr Henderson. Not only this place, but she would know it. Her life would be changed completely. That man had come to mean so much to her. She hadn't realized before just how she looked forward to coming in to work. His brusque, very often rude remarks seemed to stimulate her; nothing he said ever offended her. Yet it would have done coming from another man. She felt she understood him, perhaps in a way that Mrs Henderson hadn't done. Oh! that sounded awful. Like the prattle of the "other woman". But she wasn't meaning it in that way; she was meaning the business side of him, how he treated people, and why so roughly, as at times he did. There was nothing mean or small about him.

And now he was near death by the sound of it. But people exaggerated. Yet would he want to live now that his wife had gone, because he had adored her? Oh yes, if any man had adored a woman he had. And she in turn had reciprocated his feelings, and looked up to him. Yes, that was the strange part about it, a well-bred woman had looked up to him, because likely there were qualities in him that only a wife would know of.

A few minutes later Sam took her arm and led her to the taxi, saying, 'You'll be coming back, won't you, miss? I'll be glad to hear the latest news.'

The taxi was held up three times during the journey, and it was slow going all the way. It was almost a half-hour later when she entered the hospital.

From the desk she was directed towards the ward. There she was met by a staff nurse who said, 'I'm afraid you'll not be able to see them.'

'Are . . . are they very bad?'

In answer the nurse said, 'Are you a relative?'

'No, I am Mr . . . Henderson senior's secretary.'

'Oh. I am afraid only the family are being allowed in so far. The young Mr Henderson is in a coma, and Mr Henderson himself is not aware of very much.' She paused now as Jinny turned her head quickly and looked along the corridor to see John Henderson coming towards them.

At first he did not notice her, but, speaking to the nurse, he said, 'What time will the doctor be in?'

'About ten, I should say, if not before.'

'Thank you.' He turned to Jinny, and when he looked at her but did not speak, she said, 'I've . . . I've just found out. I've been away for the weekend. I . . . I can't believe it.'

When he walked away she went with him, and, her voice almost a low gabble, she said, 'I don't know what to say. It's so dreadful. I . . . I just can't believe it . . . that . . . that your mother is . . . is really . . .' She stopped.

They had entered the waiting-room and when he sank into a chair she took one opposite him; and she watched him lean forward, then drop his forearms on to his knees, and clasp his hands tightly together. His head was bent towards them as he said, 'Yes, she is really dead.' His head was moving in time with his words, giving each one emphasis. Then casting his glance towards her, he said, 'How he's going to take it if he comes round God alone knows. I hope he doesn't come round.'

'Oh, don't say that.'

He sat up straight now, his back tight against the chair, and staring at her, his eyes and face hard, he said, 'Why not? What is there left for him? He cared for her like no man should allow himself to care for a woman. It was of such deep intensity that it hurt one to watch it in action. I've witnessed it since I was a child. The both of them cared for us as the family, in a way I suppose you could say they loved us, but they adored each other; it was painful . . .'

Under other circumstances she would have replied to this, 'How selfish can you get? You should have been glad that they loved each other so much.' But she realized that this son, the only one of the family, as Mr Henderson had said, that had gone wrong, was suffering intensely, likely feeling guilt for walking out on them. Yet perhaps he had been drawn by a love as strong as theirs. She didn't know, she was only guessing. But there was one thing sure, this haggard young man was not the same person she had met on New Year's morning. That one had had a large chip on his shoulder – she could recognize chips – but this one who seemed to have aged ten years in the past few weeks was wide open, rent apart by pain as it were.

'Is there anything I can do?' she said softly. 'I . . . I mean business-wise.'

'I wouldn't really know; but Mr Waitland would likely tell you, he's taken charge for the time being.'

'Are . . . are all the family here?'

'Yes. And Yvonne's too.' He closed his eyes now as he said, 'That was terrible, having to tell them. Their only daughter. I hope Glen dies too. Why should he be asked to suffer that loss because he and Yvonne were going to be like Father and Mother. Glen patterned himself on Father. He always denied it, but he did. And he saw his marriage being like theirs. He once said they were the most ideal couple in the world.'

'I think they were too.'

He looked at her now as he said quietly, 'Everything in life has got to be paid for; you should never let yourself care like that. From such heights, there's only one road, and that's down; you can't stay on top of the mountain forever.'

Again at another time his cynicism would have evoked a tart reply from her, but now she could only look at him and think that whoever he had been living with certainly hadn't made him happy, and she doubted if he had made the girl happy either. His life must have been a battleground governed by his thinking.

She now asked softly, 'What . . . what is the extent of the injuries?'

'With Glen it's his head. They are going to operate on him later today.' She watched him swallow twice before going on, when he said, 'Father's back's broken; at least that's as far as they know. And he hasn't regained full consciousness yet. There's . . .'

He was about to go on when he looked towards the entrance to the waiting-room, and she followed his glance and saw the eldest daughter Florence coming towards them.

They both rose and Florence gave her a perfunctory nod before looking at her brother and saying, 'I have to go now; my train leaves at half-past ten. I'll be back on Wednesday. Ronnie'll come with me then. Granny Brook will stay on and see to the children. I . . . I don't want to go' – she shook her head – 'but there's nothing one can do at the moment. You'll phone me if there's the slightest change, won't you?'

'Yes, yes, I'll do that.'

As John took his sister's arm to escort her away, Florence said stiffly, 'Goodbye, Miss Brownlow,' and Jinny inclined her head as she answered, 'Goodbye, Mrs Brook.'

Of the three daughters, she liked Florence the least. Florence had her father's colouring but none of his disposition; nor yet did she possess any of her mother's charm, as far as she could see. If there was a snob in the family then it was Mrs Brook.

Alone in the waiting-room, she knew she was about to cry, and she put her hand tightly across her mouth, telling herself she must get outside or she would break down.

As she made her way along the corridor she saw John Henderson coming back towards her, but now he was accompanied by Mr Garbrook. When they were almost abreast of her he inclined his head towards her but said nothing, and they went on.

A few minutes later she was standing in the street like someone dazed, looking first one way, then the other. It was no use hoping she could get a taxi back; she would have to catch a bus.

After some searching she caught a bus that would take her as far as Gateshead. From there it was comparatively easy to get transport to Fellburn . . .

When Sam once again opened the door for her she was feeling on the point of exhaustion, and she gasped as she answered his question: 'How did you find them?'

When she told him he said, 'God help them,' then added, 'No one here can believe it. The place is in a hubbub.'

He opened the lift door for her, and when she stepped out on to the top floor she found the impression of hubbub was for the first time made evident. There were six doors on this landing, and four of them were open. There was a coming and going from one room to another. She went towards what she termed her office, and as she stood in the doorway her mouth opened into a gape. Her typewriter and the table were gone; but not very far. She could see it at an angle in the adjoining room. There was another filing cabinet next to hers. Mr Waitland was standing behind the desk; his secretary, Miss Phillips, was standing in front of it, and she had a number of files in her arms.

Becoming aware of her presence they both turned and looked at her.

She moved into the room, but didn't speak, she merely looked about her, until Mr Waitland, his voice seeming to demand the reason for her presence there, said, 'Well?'

'What is happening?'

The coolness of her own question surprised her.

'What do you think is happening, miss? You are aware, I suppose, that Mr Henderson is in hospital, but what you are not apparently aware of, because' – he now looked at his watch – 'you happen to be just a couple of hours late, is that I am taking his place until . . . well, such time as he will return.'

'I . . . I know Mr Henderson's business, I could . . .'

'I, too, know Mr Henderson's business, miss.' The miss was

stretched somewhat. 'I think I have been familiar with this business a little longer than you, ten years longer, I should say, as has my secretary.' He nodded towards the tall woman who was surveying Jinny with a look that could only be described as triumphant; it was as if she had won a long and hard battle.

The animosity of both the man and the woman hit her as if with physical blows; yet in a way she knew these weren't directed at her, but at Mr Henderson. Mr Henderson had never trusted this man, and, being himself, he must have made it evident.

Miss Phillips now said, 'You are expected in the pool.'

My God! the typing pool. Oh no, no, not that again.

She only just managed to prevent herself from protesting as she said now as calmly as she could, 'I will collect my things.'

'They are on the table there.' The secretary was pointing to a small table to the side of the room, above which had hung Mr Henderson's parable as he called the poem. But now it was no longer hanging there.

Swiftly she turned about and, pointing to the wall, said, 'The poem. Where is it?'

Mr Waitland looked at his secretary and she looked at him. 'It's been put away,' she said.

'Then you had better get it out from where you've put it; I've just come from the hospital and seen him, he would like it.'

Again Mr Waitland and his secretary looked at each other – her tone had more than surprised them – but after a moment he inclined his head towards her and she went into what was now presumably her office, and after a moment returned holding the offending 'picture' between finger and thumb, as if she were about to drop it into a waste-paper basket.

Jinny took it from her, and as she did so she held the woman's eye for some seconds, her look conveying her thoughts. Turning away, she gathered up her notebooks and pencils from the desk; then paused and looked from one side to the other before saying, 'There were two French books; I would like them please.'

Miss Phillips nipped at her lower lip, as she muttered, 'I . . . I must have overlooked them. They are likely in the cupboard.'

When she returned with the books, she did not hand them to Jinny, but threw them down on to the desk, and as Jinny picked them up she glanced sideways at the woman, saying, 'There are quite good French night classes at the Technical College. Of course, it's much easier if your English is good.'

She walked out with the satisfaction of seeing the woman's face turn scarlet.

In the lift once more, she thought, I'm going to be sick. Oh, I am going to be sick.

When she entered the typing pool it was as if everybody had been awaiting her arrival. There they were, all the old faces: Noreen Power, Ann Cartnell, Betty Morris, Nancy Wells, Flo Blake . . . and Miss Cadwell. Miss Cadwell was in her little glass office at the end of the room. She had been seated, but had now risen. And Jinny watched her move slowly towards the door and pause a moment before entering the office proper.

There was an empty desk behind Nancy Wells, and she dropped her books and papers, also her handbag, on to it. She was pulling off her woolly hat as Miss Cadwell came to her side.

Miss Cadwell was smiling. Jinny had never really seen her smile before, and had she witnessed it when she had first come into the office it would have filled her with apprehension, to say the least. But now it left her cold because she was no longer afraid of Miss Cadwell. At this moment she was afraid of nobody. The deep sorrow she was experiencing was almost overshadowed by anger, anger at the evident pleasure, almost joy, that was emanating from Mr Henderson's office. Talk about jumping into dead men's shoes. Mr Waitland wasn't even waiting for that.

'So we have the pleasure of your company again, Miss Brownlow.'

'I'm glad you see it like that, Miss Cadwell. That being so, doubtless we can work amicably together for the time being.'

The tone of her voice and the audacity of the words seemed to stun the occupants of the room, and Jane Cadwell too. But in her case only for a moment, for, rearing, she almost yelled, 'Don't you dare take that attitude with me, miss! Who do you think you are anyway?'

'I am Mr Henderson's secretary. Mr Henderson is not here at the moment, but he is likely to return, at which time I shall again move up to the top floor.'

'You think . . . you hope. Oh, the nerve of you!' Miss Cadwell now looked about her, turning her head from side to side to take in the staring faces; and she repeated, 'The nerve of her!' Then her eyes sending out shafts of venom, she said, 'You . . . you should be ashamed to show your face. But now that his wife's dead you hope to make it legal, I suppose. Your type will do anything for money and position. And with a man like that, old enough to be your grandfather, and coarse-mouthed into the bargain. Nobody would stay up there, only you, because you knew what you wanted, jewellery. Supposed to be buying it for his wife. You've been the talk of the works. And now you dare come in here . . .'

'Shut up! Shut up, this minute!'

Miss Cadwell not only shut up, but she took two paces backwards up the aisle between the desks, and Jinny, stepping towards her, her body leaning forward, her face aflame, cried, 'You dirty-minded old bitch, you! There was never anything like you suggest. And Mr Henderson's a gentleman. You filthy, frustrated hag!' And with the last word, her hand came out with such force across Jane Cadwell's face that the woman cried out and staggered back. But when she was hit on the other side she fell sideways over the desk.

And now there was pandemonium. Jinny was only aware that Betty Morris was tugging at her arm, pulling her backwards, and that the other girls were helping to support Miss Cadwell. And now Miss Cadwell, the tears streaming down her face, which she was holding between both hands, screamed, 'This'll be the end of you. I'll have you in court for this.'

Jinny, after grabbing her things from her desk, turned and, pushing Betty Morris aside, took three steps up the aisle again towards the woman; and she answered her, but she did not scream or yell, for her voice was now deep and each word carried weight as she said, 'You do that. I'll be waiting for you doing it. And you'll have to take all the money you've scraped up for years to meet my slander charge, and that against Mr Henderson. There are five witnesses here; they heard every word you said, and I didn't hit you before you said them, I hit you after. Think of it, Miss Cadwell. Put your charge in as soon as ever you like, you dirty old woman, you. And that goes for the rest of you who thought along her lines.' And on this she turned and marched from the room.

Once more in the front hall and sinking on to a seat, she was approached by Sam. 'What's up, lass?' he said. 'You look like death.'

The tears oozing from her eyes now, she answered, 'They've already taken over Mr Henderson's office . . . Mr Waitland and his secretary . . . and I went down to the typing pool, Sam, and – ' She squeezed her eyes tightly and swallowed before she said, 'They are saying . . . Miss Cadwell said that I've been having an affair with Mr Henderson, and that he bought me jewellery. And Sam, it isn't true, not a word of it.'

'No. No, lass. I never believed it either.'

Her eyes widened now. 'So they have been saying *that*?' The last word ended on a high note, and he nodded and said, 'Aye. Yes. Somebody that works in . . . the jeweller's has a cousin in the offices up here. Mr Henderson was supposed to be buying you a necklace and pretending it was for his wife when his wife walks in and there was a bit of a polite shindy.'

'It wasn't like that at all. Mrs Henderson was never near the jeweller's that day. Oh, Sam.' Her voice broke, and she ended, 'People are awful. People are awful.'

'Aye. Aye, lass, they are. As you go on in life you'll find people are awful. But there's good 'uns an' all, and Mr Henderson was a good 'un. And I pray God that things aren't as bad as they say they are with him and that he'll come back, because between you and me, Garbrook isn't much good. As for Waitland, well, he'll be as welcome on the shop floor as a dose of poison. Look, can I get you another taxi?'

'Yes. Yes, please, Sam.'

When she was alone she asked herself where she would go in the taxi? Back to the flat? No, no; she couldn't be alone. And it was so cold there. She wanted warmth, because she was cold to the very, very core of her. She wanted the warmth of a kindly voice, of tender arms. She would go to Hal's office. And he would take her home, and she could stay with them for a time, for she would go mad if she were left on her own . . .

When Sam came back, he said, 'You're lucky again, lass; there's one coming. He's dropping off somebody just along the road and he should be here in a few minutes. He bent towards her now, adding, 'I'll miss you an' all, because you won't be coming back.'

'No, I won't be coming back Sam, not . . . not unless Mr Henderson comes back.' She now looked up at him, her eyes blinking the moisture away, and her lips tried to move into a smile as she said, 'You know what I did up there, Sam?'

'No, miss. What did you do?' He spoke to her as if she were a young child, softly, coaxingly.

'I hit Miss Cadwell. I slapped her face. Not once, but twice. Both sides . . . Huh. Huh!'

'You what, miss? *You* . . . you hit Miss Cadwell? Never!'

'I did, Sam. I lashed out at her when she said that about me and Mr Henderson.'

She watched his shoulders shaking; she watched him nip on his prim grey moustache; she watched him close his eyes and rub his hand across them; then in a voice that wasn't steady he said, 'I can't believe it. You're so ladylike, gentle looking. You don't look as if you'd say boo to a goose.'

'I'm not ladylike, and I can say more than boo to a goose. I . . . I'm so shocked, no, outraged is a better word, that I would have gone on pummelling her if they hadn't pulled me off.'

'You know something, miss?'

'No, Sam?'

'That's the best bit of cheery news I've heard in a long while, for I've been on that door, you know' – he thumbed towards the end of the hall – 'these ten years or more, and that woman hasn't bidden me good-morning once, not a word. You can open the door for her when she comes in, you can open the door for her when she goes out, the only sign of recognition that you're there at all is she turns her eyes on you . . . Come on.' He chuckled as he took her arm. 'The car should be here any minute now.'

As he opened the door for her he looked at her and said, 'You know, you haven't been here all that long, but you've been the subject of more talk than anybody I know of. And this latest . . . why, wait till that reaches the shop floor. I bet some of the lads'll be after you, seeing that you've struck a blow against the white collar lot. It won't matter to them in what cause it was, just that you've done it. Here you are, lass. Here's your car. One last word. I pray to God that you'll be back some day along of Mr Henderson.'

'Thank you, Sam. Thank you very much.' She took his hand and shook it; then got into the taxi and was driven away . . .

Hal was surprised to see her, and she was surprised to see his office. She had seen it from the outside, but had never been in it. There were two girls in the outer office, both young, under twenty, she would say. The place was well-furnished, well-carpeted, and the walls held sporting prints. It had the same overall well-kept feeling as his house.

When she asked one of the girls if she could see Mr Campbell, she was in turn asked what her business was.

And to this she said, 'Just tell Mr Campbell that Miss Brownlow would like to see him.'

Within a minute Hal was out of his office and taking her into his room. He wasn't all that surprised to see her, for apparently he had already heard the news of the Henderson accident. And yes, yes, of course, he said, she must go home to his place. And stay there as long as she liked. She knew she could, didn't she? She hadn't any need to ask. Give him five minutes and he'd take her there.

During the five minutes that turned into fifteen she listened to him phoning, making arrangements with clients. And lastly he spoke to a Mrs Taylor, saying it was difficult to get out to the house at the moment but if she came at ten o'clock the following morning they would discuss the situation.

Having put the phone down he looked at her and said, 'I advertised for a housekeeper; we just can't go on the way we are. It's all right at the weekends when you and I are there. But Rosie comes back from school and has to let herself in, and it's rather lonely out there, and I get a bit worried at times. Then there's the meal to get ready at nights. And so I thought it the best thing to do.'

The bus took them as far as the side road again, and from there they had to plough their way to the house as she'd had to plough her way away from it just a few hours earlier.

Once inside, she again almost collapsed on to the settee. Solicitous as always, he took off her boots and brought an electric fire on to the rug to warm her feet; then he chafed her hands, after which he gave her a not too small glass of brandy.

It was when she had recovered herself somewhat that she told him in detail the happenings of the morning, and like Sam he gaped at her about the incidents with Miss Cadwell. But he didn't laugh as Sam had done, nor did he even seem amused. She couldn't quite make out his reaction, except, as she put it to herself, he seemed very surprised that she was capable of doing such a thing, for he said, 'Oh, Jinny. You actually hit her?'

'I told you. Yes, I hit her. Well, after what she said.'

'Well, you should have expected people to talk.'

'Why? Mr Henderson's in his fifties, he's a grandfather.'

'Don't be so naïve about such things, Jinny. Men of that age go for young girls, they prefer them, as some young men prefer older women. It's nothing to be ashamed of.'

'But Mr Henderson was not like that. You've never met him or even heard him. He swore practically every third word. And he was so in love with his wife that, as his son said just this morning, it was somehow painful to witness.'

'Painful to witness?'

'Yes. He was trying to explain the intensity of the love between his mother and father. Well, I think it must have aroused a kind of jealousy in him; they must have been so taken up with each other. And she was a lovely woman, and a beautiful woman, really beautiful. I felt dowdy beside her, the way she dressed, the way she looked, the way she talked. And . . . and he was just the opposite. Well, it proved to me that opposites attract.'

'Yes, I suppose so. But knowing there was no truth in the rumour, why did you let it disturb you to the point of hitting the woman? There'll be trouble about it, I suppose.'

'Oh, I fully expect so. But just let her take any action and I'll have her up for slander.'

He sat back on his hunkers and slanted his eyes towards her as he said, 'This isn't the Jinny I know. 'Tisn't like you a bit.'

'Perhaps you don't know me at all, Hal. I'm unfortunate in having an exterior that, as Arthur says, looks like Wendy Craig, a bit up in the air. But I'm not like that inside. Oh, I know I made myself cheap with the Players, acting dogsbody to everybody, because I suppose there is a part of me that wants to please and will put up with most things rather than that I should be alone. I'm still a bit like that, but beyond that there is another me, and somehow it's developed in the companionship of Mr Henderson; I've sort of come into my own being . . . Oh I don't know how to express it. And anyway, I'm feeling too upset to talk about myself now; I just can't get over the tragedy. I'm devastated. You know, they were all so nice to me, it was like another family. I . . . I felt I had two families, yours and theirs.'

'Well, you've still got this family, and for as long as ever you want it. You know that, don't you, dear?' He was holding both her hands now. 'I . . . I love to have you here. And the others do too . . .Now I'll have to get back. Will you be all right on your own?'

'Oh yes.'

'I'll give Michael a ring. If he's got free time, he'll likely come home.'

'Oh no! No, I'd rather be on my own. I've got to think. I'll have a lot of thinking to do because I shall have to get a new job. And it's just struck me that I'd need a reference, and I'd certainly not get it from Mr Waitland, or Mr Garbrook, not after this business. I'm going to be in a bit of a quandary.'

'Well, don't worry, something will turn up. With your experience you won't have much trouble. I know that. And there are other things to do besides office work. Be a courier, you could. You could be anything. Anyway, in the meantime take it easy and rest.'

'Thank you, Hal. You are so kind.'

'Who could help but be kind to you?' He bent and kissed her. 'You're a very special person, you know, Jinny. If only . . . Oh' – he shook his head – 'I've got to go; we'll talk tonight. Bye-bye.' He smiled now and patted her cheek, then went out.

She sat where he had left her for almost an hour. She wanted to cry again, but found she couldn't. She had the impression that part of her life had been cut off, as if she had lost a limb. She felt she would never be the same again, she would never see the world again from the same viewpoint as she had done yesterday. The loss she was experiencing now far exceeded any in her life before: the loss of her parents, though not trivial, seemed a minor affair. She admitted without even a touch of guilt that her feelings for them must have been on a different plane, their loss having engendered only an apprenticeship to grief, because now she was really experiencing grief. But nowhere in her grief was she mourning for the loss of her job. No, it was for the loss of people, for Alicia Henderson and for Yvonne. She hadn't met Yvonne often but when she had they were, as Yvonne had once said, *sympathique*. Perhaps her understanding of the language had gone a long way towards this feeling; but not all the way because it was also as two young girls they had responded to each other.

And there was Glen. Glen of the sharp wits, the sharp tongue which, unlike that of his father, was not punctuated with swear words, and so in a way lost a little of its colour. It was odd how she had become used to swear words. Her parents had never sworn. Nor had she liked to hear people swearing. But Mr Robert Henderson was a special man . . . had been a very special man. What would he be now with a broken spine? Oh dear God. If only she could see him. Do something: hold his hand and say 'Broken spine or no broken spine – do you hear? – you're coming through, you're coming through.' For that's what he would have said to her had she been in a like situation. 'Bugger it!' he would have said. 'What's a broken back? You've still got your tongue, your eyes, your hearing.' And he would have counted all the faculties she had left.

Oh, Mr Henderson . . . Oh, Mr Henderson . . . Oh, Bob Henderson. Oh, Bob Henderson. Get better. Please, please get better.

She was crying now and gasping for air. She stood up and began to walk around the room, her hands to her head, and all the while muttering like a nun saying her novena, 'Bob Henderson. Bob Henderson, get better. Do you hear?' until, stopping abruptly, she cried at herself, 'Give over. Stop it! You're becoming hysterical.'

Yes, she was, she was becoming hysterical. She would go to the kitchen. She would do something. Work. That was it. Use her hands. Bake. Make a meal for them coming in. Yes, yes. Anything. Anything to take her mind off this tragedy . . . But her mind would never be off . . . 'Go on, get get yourself into the kitchen. No, no, don't sit down. No, go on into the kitchen.' She was talking aloud and she obeyed her last command and went into the kitchen.

The tears still raining down her face, she began to prepare a meal.

They were all very grateful for the meal, hot shepherd's pie with apple tart to follow; and they were all nice to her.

It was Michael who towards the middle of the evening looked at Hal and remarked, 'You said you were interviewing a woman for housekeeper tomorrow, didn't you?' And Hal said, 'Yes; yes, I did.'

'Well, why bother, at least for a time? Jinny's not, as she just said, going to fall into a job straightaway without a reference. She'll have to wait and see if Mr Henderson recovers. She could get one from the son, but she can't ask for anything like that yet awhile. And so, in the meantime, her remedy is to keep busy, isn't it?' He looked at Jinny; and after a moment she said, 'Yes, I suppose so.'

'Well, then. We've got a housekeeper.'

'Would you like that?' Hal was looking at her.

'Yes. Yes, I would, for a time, and be grateful for it.'

'And you wouldn't have to go out in the mornings.' Rosie grinned at her, and she smiled weakly back at her, saying, 'You're right there. That would be an advantage I'd have over all of you.'

'And if you give me the key I'll drop into your flat and see that it's all right. I've got to pass that way.'

She was sure Michael meant this as a kind offer; yet she would be reluctant to give him her key. But she said, 'Thank you. I'll be grateful.'

And she was grateful to all of them, for they all seemed to be pleased that she was staying; even Arthur. Yes, even Arthur.

And so she became a housekeeper.

It was Michael who drove her to the crematorium on the Thursday. In the chapel, a number of chairs had been left empty for the family, the rest were already full, and there was a crowd standing outside. She joined this, and later watched two hearses arrive, followed by a line of cars. She watched the families file into the chapel; she listened to the muted tones of the organ; she watched women here and there wiping their eyes; she watched men, their heads bowed deeply, stand in reverence; and she wondered why she alone among all these mourners wasn't feeling any emotion whatever. It was as if this wasn't the funeral, that Alicia and Yvonne weren't in boxes in there soon to be reduced to ashes; she wanted to say to someone, 'They can't be dead. That's not them in there.' You couldn't kill a woman with a lovely spirit like that, a woman whose life was made up of love, and such love that it joyfully enslaved people. You couldn't kill someone like that. She was bound to be somewhere.

Was there such a place as heaven? No. That was ridiculous. But spiritualists claimed to be in touch with people on the other side, and spiritual healers healed through doctors who had died and chose people whom they could work through, so she understood. And they did heal. They had a neighbour once who had been cured of something by a spiritual healer in the town. Perhaps, Alicia and Yvonne were with them . . .

What was the matter with her? For days now she had at times felt that she was becoming odd, or sickening for something, for her mind would jump from one thing to another and present her with the most weird thoughts, as it was doing now.

She started somewhat when Michael came to her side, saying, 'Must you wait?' He had only a short while before refused to come into the crematorium, saying he couldn't stand funerals; he had made a joke about it, saying he hated standing up when the principals in the play were lying down. But here he was, and she caught hold of his arm, saying, 'Stay with me, will you, Michael? Stay with me.'

'Yes, of course. Of course.' He took her hand and pulled it through his arm, and held it close to his side. And his voice low, he said, 'You shouldn't have come. They are the most depressing things at the best of times. And there's no best of times about a funeral. To my mind they should be strictly private, just the family, no more . . . You're shivering. Come on. Come on home.'

'No. No. Wait until they come out.'

'But why?'

'I . . . I just want to see them again . . . well, all together.'

Some time later she saw them; but not all together. They were dispersed among a large number of people, all offering condolences. The three girls passed close to her without seeing her. But John saw her, and cast a glance in her direction, but didn't speak.

She had been to the hospital twice this week to make enquiries. Each time she was told that there wasn't any improvement in either

Mr Henderson or his son. And also that only the family were allowed to visit.

'Let's go,' she muttered, and as they turned away her mind said, 'It's over.' It was as if she had said goodbye to Mr Henderson, and to Glen too. She felt that a phase of her life had ended, and with it had gone forever the subservient self, the cultured handmaiden as Ray Collard had dubbed her, because never again would she meet people like the Hendersons; and the world as she viewed it now would be full of Mr Waitlands and Miss Cadwells.

She didn't ask herself at this moment in what category she placed Hal and his family, because deep down in her she knew there was something here she had to straighten out, for she had no intention of ever being any man's dogsbody or handmaiden. However she felt that with Hal she was on the border of it, and so the sooner there was some plain speaking the better.

3

After the fourth visit to the hospital she had the impression that someone in the family had left orders that she wasn't to be admitted to Mr Henderson's room.

'Nobody but the family are allowed in,' the nurse said. 'It's doctor's orders. They are both still in a very bad way. Young Mr Henderson hasn't come out of the coma yet, and they're to operate on him again.'

As the nurse continued to stare at her she wanted to ask, 'Did Mrs Brook leave orders that I wasn't to be admitted?' but she refrained, for whichever answer she got wouldn't make any difference, she wouldn't be allowed in.

After that visit she did not go back to the hospital again, but phoned the house. Generally it was Dorry who answered the phone, and the report was always, 'Very little change.'

Once, Florence's voice came over the wire, saying, 'Father and Glen are being sent to other hospitals. Glen is to have further treatment. That's as much as I can tell you, Miss Brownlow.'

She felt she was being dismissed, and she couldn't understand why, unless the gossip had reached the family and they thought there was something in it. Yet they knowing their parents, how could they imagine such a thing. But people also being what they were, they could. Oh yes, they could . . .

After the third week acting as housekeeper she was finding life boring. She was alone most of the day. The only consolation was that she hadn't to go out into the atrocious weather because there seemed to be no end to it.

She had seen one advantage in taking on the post: she had imagined she would have more time with Hal and that they would come to some understanding. But Hal had taken not only to visiting his old people during three weekday evenings, but the last fortnight he had gone out on Sunday too. And on the second occasion they'd had what she could call their first quarrel, although the anger had been mostly on her side.

She had offered to accompany him, and to this he had said, 'It's bad enough one of us having to brave the weather.' But she had immediately come back at him, 'I've never been out for almost a week; I feel housebound. And I've had to brave worse storms than this to get to work.'

His response had been to turn and walk from her, and she had put out her hand and grabbed his arm, saying, 'Look, Hal. What am I supposed to be?'

'What do you mean?'

'You know what I mean. I think we should do some talking around that particular question, what I am supposed to be.'

At this his face had assumed the stiff mask which he adopted when anything didn't please him, and he said, 'Don't become intense, Jinny. It doesn't suit you. And remember, we are both free agents.'

She supposed she was acting like a nagging wife. No, she wasn't, she came back at herself; she just wanted this thing talked out, that's all. There was something going on and she couldn't get to the bottom of it.

It was later in the day she decided that she must get out, if it was only for a walk down the lane.

She made her way through the kitchen into the utility room and was about to open the door that led into the garage where the wellingtons were kept when she heard Arthur's voice coming from behind the door, saying, 'I thought when he brought her here and let her stay he . . . he'd marry her. He's a twister, and I'm going to tell her.'

'You'll do no such thing. Let her find out herself.'

'She'll never find out. She'll just go on and on being a cat's-paw. I didn't like her at first, but she's all right, and it's a bloody shame.'

'Now look here, Arthur, you keep your mouth shut, at least for the present. She's in need of company at the moment. She'll have to find out sooner or later that he has no intention of marrying her. He's got the best of both worlds, and he thinks it can go on. Being so crafty, you can't imagine him being such a fool.'

'You like her, why don't you tell her?'

'She wouldn't take it from me. She's got to find out for herself.'

'But how can she? I only spotted it by chance. Who would have thought about him going there? Daisy's Parlour: Hair Stylist.'

'You've been following him then?'

'Aye. Yes. The old people was a cover-up; they always have been.'

'Not entirely. He's always done that work. Apparently he and his mother . . .'

'Oh, his mother.'

'Yes, you can say that again, Oh, his mother. But anyway, you promise me you won't let on.'

'But she'll go on thinking . . .'

'She won't go on thinking. I tell you she won't. I can see a storm rising. She's asking questions herself all the time; in fact, she's been asking him questions. But naturally, he's evaded them. So it won't go on. But don't you do anything about it, because you've got to live here, at least for another year or two. And you were talking of going to university, weren't you? Well, you get on the wrong side of him and you'll be out on your neck. And you'll end up one end of a conveyor belt on a factory floor.'

'I won't though.'

'You will if you have to go out now and fend for yourself.'

'You've still got your flat, you haven't let it. I could go there.'

'Oh, no, you couldn't. I have other ideas for my flat, so get that out of your head. Now come on, and just think before you open your mouth. Play him at his own game. Act as if everything was normal.'

'Normal? Did you say normal?'

Jinny sprang back from the door, ran quietly through the kitchen, across the hall and up the stairs into her room. Standing in the middle of it, her fists doubled against her lips, she bit on the flesh of her first finger. What could it mean, Daisy's Parlour, Hair Stylist?

Don't be stupid.

She had never heard of Daisy's Parlour. There were four hairdressers in the centre of town, but none of that name . . . Bog's End? Yes, there was likely such a hairdresser down there.

One thing at last was clear now. There was a woman in it somewhere . . .

Why a woman?

No. She shook her head as she again answered her thought, No; I . . . I can't see him as a homosexual. He wouldn't have married twice in that case. Once, yes, but not twice. No, it's a woman. But what kind of a woman?

Wasn't she herself a woman?

Yes, but had he ever treated her as a woman? Had he ever become passionate? Had his hands ever attempted to stray? Had there been a look in his eyes that told her he wanted more than kisses? The answer was no.

Well, her sojourn here was going to end abruptly. She knew that. But before she went she would get the answer to why she held no appeal for him. Marriage apart, he hadn't even wanted to seduce her. At least Ray Collard's attentions had proved to her that she was female and desirable; he hadn't left her feeling as if she was a neuter . . .

The weather on the Monday was really atrocious. The radio gave out that the whole North was cut off, with even twenty foot drifts in some parts. Earlier on Hal had phoned to say that both Rosie's and Arthur's schools were closed for the day. Both he and Michael had made their way out together hoping to get transport on the main road if the gritting machines had got this far.

She had ascertained in the phone book that there was a hairdresser trading under the name 'Daisy's Parlour', and that it was in Bog's End. Bog's End ran along by the waterfront. At one time there had been a thriving shipyard there, but it had been closed down these five years or more. Nobody who was of any account in Fellburn had lived in Bog's End. Now a small West Indian quarter had grown up, as also had a Pakistani quarter, and it was said that the lower white quarter caused more trouble than either of these two factions.

She was full of unrest all morning, and after giving Rosie and Arthur a light lunch, she dressed herself for the weather and, going to the sitting-room door, she said, 'I don't know what time I'll be back. Be good.'

They were both surprised and Rosie, who had been sitting on the rug reading, called, 'Where are you going?' And to this she replied, 'Into the town.'

But Arthur, leaving his spread of homework on the table, got up quickly, saying as he moved towards her, 'What are you going out for?'

She looked at him closely for a moment; then turned without speaking and went towards the front door. And when he followed her and asked again, anxiously now, 'What are you going out for, Jinny? You'll never get down the road.' She answered, 'I'll get down the road, Arthur. I'm . . . I'm going to have my hair done.'

She watched his mouth fall into a slight gape, and a feeling of tenderness coming over her, she put out her hand and touched his cheek, saying, 'Stick it out. Work at your A levels. It'll pay off in the end.'

She was half-way down the path when his voice came to her, calling, 'Jinny! Jinny!' And when she turned he called, 'Don't go. Please don't go.'

'I've got to, Arthur. You know I have, I've got to. As Michael said, I've got to find out for myself. But don't worry. Be a good lad.'

She thought the last admonition sounded faintly like one from Mr Henderson. If only things were as they had once been, she could walk out of here now and go straight to the Hendersons' house. And if that had been possible she might not have bothered to probe. But things would never be as they were. Her world was rocking, not only backwards and forwards, but from side to side. It was like being in one of those tubs at the fairground: they knocked you all over the place before they ran down a slope and dived into the water. Well she had been shaken about these last weeks. And she was on top of the slope now. In a very short time she would be in the water.

When she mounted the bus, she asked the driver, 'Do you go as far as Bog's End?'

'To the very end, miss,' he said.

'Anywhere near Chambers' Row?'

'Oh yes. We pass the end of it. You're in luck,' he said.

Twenty minutes later as she went to step off the bus he pointed across the road, saying, 'There it is, Chambers' Row. Sort of cul-de-sac. Couple of shops and a warehouse. Old part of the town. Oldest part of the town, that is. All right?'

'Yes, thank you.' She crossed the road and entered the narrow street. The first shop was a second-hand clothes shop; then followed two narrow houses, and these were separated from the hairdresser's shop by an alleyway.

She stood for a moment looking in the window. It wasn't at all prepossessing. In the front stood one or two cardboard adverts showing hair styles; then half-way up the window, in a recess, was a rod from which hung lace curtains. The shop, strangely enough, was single-storeyed. And next to it was what appeared to be two garages. These formed the end of the street, and running at right angles to them and down the other side were warehouses. There was no sign of a habitable house attached to the shop as far as she could see. But then she hadn't been up the alleyway.

Slowly now she turned and went up the alleyway. She passed a window through which she could just see into the hairdressing salon; then she saw the house. It was set back but attached to the end of the shop. It was in the style of a bungalow, and looked to have been recently painted. The yard was open to the alleyway, and on each side of the gateway and along the wall facing the side of the house were flower-tubs. She looked at these. She felt she had seen them before. They were painted green, and although the tops were snow-covered she could see that they held plants of some form. They were the same as Hal had arranged as borders to the patio of his house. She felt the urge to knock on the door, but resisted. What would or could she say? Did she look like somebody selling things? She had only a small handbag with her.

She went back to the street. And now she stood staring at the price list hanging to the side of the window. The next minute she had pushed open the door and had entered the square room with a counter just large enough to hold a till. There were four wash-basins along one side of the room and four standing driers interspersed with chairs along the other side. At the far end of the room a passage led off somewhere.

There were two customers sitting in front of wash-basins: one was obviously in the middle stage of having a perm, the other was having her hair washed. The assistant attending to the perm looked towards Jinny; then kept her gaze on her for some seconds before leaving her customer and coming to the small desk, enquiring, 'Yes?'

'I . . . I haven't made a . . . What I mean to say is, do you think I could have a trim?'

The girl looked her up and down; then looked towards her companion who made a small movement of her head, and the girl said, 'Well, I suppose so. But you should book, you know.'

The voice was thick with the north-country twang, and when Jinny said, 'I'm . . . I'm sorry, but . . . but I was just passing, and it's getting a bit long. I don't want much off.'

'Well, sit down there.' The girl pointed to a chair further along the room. It was opposite a basin with a mirror above it, and to the side was the window she had noticed from the alleyway.

She took off her hat and woolly scarf and sat down. And the girl looked at her through the mirror as she approached, saying, 'I might have to leave you in the middle of it, 'cos I've got a perm goin'. See?'

'That's all right.'

'What d'you want doin'?'

She wondered what would take the longest: the trim would be over in minutes and she would have no time to ask questions, and so she said, 'I don't mind if it's just a trim, but if you have time and could layer it a bit.'

'Well, if you've got a mind to have it done in bits.'

'I . . . I have plenty of time.'

As the girl started clipping she said, 'You've got nice hair. You're not from round here, are you?'

'No, I'm just passing through. Terrible weather.'

'Aye, it's awful.'

'I said I'm just passing through, but I've been in Fellburn before; yet I never knew there was a hairdresser here. Is it your establishment?'

'Mine? Oh no. It's Mrs Smith's. She's the owner.'

Jinny now turned her head and looked towards the other girl, and the indication wasn't lost on the assistant because she laughed as she said, 'Oh no, she's not Mrs Smith.'

A minute or so later, when the older assistant left her customer and came down the room and took a bottle from a shelf, the girl who was doing Jinny's hair left her for a moment and went towards the shelf as if she was going to pick up something, and the whispered words came to Jinny on a laugh: 'She wanted to know if you were Mrs Smith.'

'Oh aye?' Then followed a joined laugh; then the words: 'They're on their way. I saw them comin' across the road. He's changed his time, hasn't he? Couldn't wait.'

They parted now, and as the girl began to snip again at Jinny's hair, the window to the side darkened and there, as plain as if she was looking at him in the sitting-room at the house, was Hal, and to his side she caught the fleeting glimpse of a woman, a big woman. But an old woman.

She caught the assistant looking at her through the mirror and when she asked 'Did I hurt you?' she said, 'No. Only I've got a very tender sc . . . scalp.' And she stammered on the word scalp.

When a few minutes later the girl said, 'I won't be a tick' and left her to attend to her perm customer, Jinny looked to the side to where she could see the passage and a small board that stuck out from the wall and on which was plainly painted the word *Ladies*.

What was the meaning of it? If that was the woman he came to see it could be for no bad motive. How old would she be? She'd had only a fleeting glimpse of her, and the impression that she'd got was that she was big and fat. But that was likely the fur coat she was wearing. No, her face had been fat . . . and old. What did she mean by old? When you were in your teens everyone in their thirties appeared old, so what did she mean by old? Mrs Henderson had been forty-seven. Had she considered her old? No. No. Well, how old did she consider *that* woman was? In her late fifties? Oh, she didn't know . . . But what was it? Why all the secrecy if he was only visiting an old woman? But this was no ordinary old woman; she had a business. And the way she had walked past the window hadn't indicated age. Nor had her laugh. Yes, she had laughed. And Hal had laughed.

When her hair was finished she'd go round and knock at the door. And what would she say? I've been spying on you. Could she say that? But there must be something to find out, or else Michael wouldn't have gone for Arthur like he did yesterday.

First of all she must go to the lavatory; her stomach was turning over so much she felt she could be sick.

When she paid her bill and tipped the girl well, she said 'There's a toilet there?'

'Yes. Just where it says.' The girl pointed.

And on this Jinny went down the short corridor. But she paused outside the lavatory door, for there, at the end of the corridor, was another notice across the top of the door, and this said: *Private*.

She was shaking from head to foot as she stood in the lavatory, telling herself that if she went and knocked on the door he would have time to come up with some excuse, but if she barged in . . . But dare she? Yes, she dared, because wasn't he supposed to be in

Durham today? That's what he had told her before he left. But again, she must also remind herself that he'd said they were free agents.

Free agents be damned! He had used her. For months now he had used her. And he had pretended to be in love with her. Even though his love-making left a lot to be desired, he had pretended to be in love with her, and told her countless times how he needed her and how he loved to come back to the house, knowing that she'd be there. And at first she had loved him all the more for what she had imagined to be his consideration.

Quietly she returned to the corridor. The two girls were busy with their customers. It took three steps for her to reach the door marked *Private* and to open it. And then she was through and standing in a kitchen.

It was surprisingly modern, with all the latest gadgets. She put out a hand and supported herself against the formica topped table and drew in two long shuddering breaths before she quietly opened the further door and found herself standing in a small hall, from which the front door and three other doors led off. The door to her right was half open and showed what she took to be a sitting-room. There was no sound coming from there. But from the far door she heard the murmur of voices and the distinctive sound of a giggle. This was followed by a laugh. It was Hal's laugh. Sometimes for no reason whatsoever, he would laugh like that, when he was in the kitchen baking or when he was sitting on the couch, one arm around Rosie, the other around her. Perhaps they would be looking at the television, when he would suddenly laugh, and there would have been nothing on the screen to have evoked laughter; and she would look at him and smile, and he would squeeze her tightly to him.

Slowly she moved towards the far door. Before opening it she knew it would be a bedroom, and she knew in a way what she would witness. Yet when, with a sudden jerk, she pushed the door open she stood, her eyes stretched wide, her mouth agape and her whole body stiff, and the two figures on the bed looking back at her with similar expressions.

She saw that the woman who looked like a mountain of wobbling flesh had bright metallic red hair, her breasts and stomach were enormous, and her thighs like those she had seen bursting out of bloomers on coarse seaside postcards; her whole body seemed to spread over the bed. And there was Hal, the gentle, thoughtful, charming Hal, naked as the day he was born.

She saw his mouth frame her name. She saw him reach to the foot of the bed and grab at a bedcover lying there; she saw the great mountain of flesh sit up and yell in a voice as coarse as her body, 'What the hell you doin' here?' before the rage in her burst.

To the side of her was a dressing table, and the first thing her hand caught up was an open box of talcum powder. She threw it, and as it spread over both of them they choked and jumped from the bed. The next thing she gripped was a scent spray. When she saw it make contact with the top of his head she wanted to shout. She watched him, one hand held against his bleeding brow, endeavouring to restrain the woman from advancing towards her, her flesh billowing like waves, as she yelled, 'Who is she? The bugger's mad.'

'Get out, Jinny! Get out. Stop it, for God's sake!'

But she couldn't stop it, she wanted more things to throw, and there was nothing left on the dressing-table. Suddenly, however, she was caught by the arms and turned about and dragged sideways, one of the assistants pulling, the other pushing her back into the shop and towards the door. And there it was the elder one who gasped, 'Are you his wife then?'

She stared back at the girl but couldn't speak. And then as if he had dropped out of the heavens there was Michael running down the street towards her.

The shop assistant kept hold of her arms until he came up to them, and when he said, 'Come on. Come on, Jinny,' she said to him, 'Who is she anyway? She's gone berserk.'

'And not before time,' he answered. Then he led Jinny along the street to where a taxi was standing. She hadn't spoken, nor did she wonder how he had come to be there at that precise moment. But she sat in the back of the cab staring in front of her.

When the taxi stopped outside her flat Michael paid the driver; then taking her handbag, which luckily was still in the crook of her arm, he took out the key. And they went down the area steps.

Once in the flat, Jinny sat down. She did not take off her things, but she watched him light the gas fire; she heard him put the kettle on and do all the things that are supposed to bring one comfort, such as make tea. And when eventually he handed her the cup, and she didn't raise her hand to take it, he said, 'Come on. Come on. Snap out of it! It isn't the end of the world. Remember, I tried to tell you ages ago, but you wouldn't listen. And it isn't his fault; he just likes older women. That's why his two marriages went astray. He should have married his mother. She was the trouble. Some men should never leave the breast. It isn't their fault; it's the women, the mothers. Don't blame him too much. But it's a pity he had to pick such types. He's in conflict all the time: he wants youth, he wants a family, but he can't help himself the other way. Come on now. Drink this tea.'

She had to force her hand to take the cup from him. It was as if she was dragging her limbs up out of a bottomless sea of misery. Her body had certainly hit the water. But having done so, it had sunk and, just as in a nightmare, she seemed to be swimming for her life, but in a well. Water was supposed to be cleansing, but she told herself she would never feel clean again in her lifetime. Worse still, she was back to where she had been, lonely, ineffectual.

As if Michael was reading her thoughts, he said, 'You're looking upon this as the end of the world, seeing yourself all messed up as if you were to blame. You feel you're dirty and you'll never scrape it off, for the simple reason that you've let him near you, touch you. You wouldn't be feeling so bad if he had wanted more. But no, he didn't. He used you as he used my mother, and Arthur's and Rosie's. It was my mother who told me about his peccadilloes. He did try with her though, because she wasn't all that young. But she was still not old enough to be a cuddly mother.'

'Shut up!'

She hadn't intended to speak; she had wanted to remain in the well, walled in by silence; but if you had hearing there was no such thing as silence.

But he came back at her now, saying, 'You're sorry for yourself. How do you think I felt when my mother walked out? At that time when I was eighteen I couldn't really see why it mattered. Let him have his entertainment on the side, I thought. But then I wasn't a woman. But Arthur's and Rosie's mother had it worse; she was going to divorce him on the conjugal rights bit.'

'Michael'

'Yes, Jinny?'

'Will you stop talking about it, please?'

'If you say so, but it's much better to get it off your chest. Do you want to see him?'

'*No! Never again!*' She was on her feet now. 'And he won't want to see me. I've split his head open; at least I hope I have.'

'Jinny! *You what?*' He looked amazed.

'The scent bottle caught him on the brow. I hope it went deep.'

'You threw things?'

'Yes, I threw things. Everything that was on the dressing-table: talcum powder, the lot; I smothered them.'

She now began to walk up and down the room, and he shook his head as he watched her; then said slowly, 'You know, Jinny, you're a bit of an enigma. This is the second attack in the matter of weeks. No one would believe it.'

She stopped and, putting her arms around her waist, she hugged herself as she thought, He's naming my retaliation as attacks, and a voice inside her head almost in a whimper now said, I . . . I wouldn't attack anybody. But you did. There was Miss Cadwell; and now today. But she came back at the whimper, crying, It was justified. In both cases it was justified.

Of a sudden she felt weak and faint. She sat down on the couch again, and now she looked up at him and said quietly, 'Would you bring my things, Michael? I've packed my case.'

'You intended to leave him before you went there?'

'Yes. Yes, I did. I . . . I heard you and Arthur talking yesterday.'

'Oh, I had guessed that already from what Arthur told me. He phoned me just after you left. That's why I was on hand. He's a good kid, Arthur, underneath; and he's very fond of you, you know. He'll miss you. So will Rosie. And so shall I . . . Do you want your things tonight?'

'Would it be too much to ask to get them now?'

'No, no. I've nothing else to do. It's a good job I'm in charge of my own little department. If I can get a bus along there now, I should be back around teatime. Will you be all right?'

'Yes, I'll be all right. And . . . Michael. Thank you. Thank you for being so kind.'

'That's what I want to be; I had hoped to be kind to you all this time. But what did I achieve? Nothing, except make you hate my guts at times.'

She didn't smile at him, for what he had said was true.

It was almost eight o'clock when he returned. When she opened the door to him and he dropped her case at her feet she thought that he too was about to fall beside it, and she put out her arms to steady him, saying, 'You shouldn't have come tonight. Not . . . not so late. I . . . I could have waited.'

He was gasping as he replied, 'It was the last part of the journey. The bus got no further than the market square. I'd had a taxi, but he dropped me with my things off at my flat, and I thought the bus would make it along here, but it didn't.'

Looking at her large case, she said, 'How on earth did you manage your things, too, down the road?'

'Arthur helped me. Have you got a drink? Anything stronger than coffee?'

'No, I'm sorry.'

'A black coffee'll do then.' He sank into a chair before the fire and, closing his eyes, said, 'What a night! Storm outside and storm in.' He turned his head towards the kitchen now, saying, 'We nearly came to blows. He blames me for the exposure. And by jingo! You must have thrown that scent bottle with some force. You know, he's had to have his brow stitched. He said his lady friend, or his mother friend, whatever you like to call her, was for putting the police on to you. I said he should have let her; it would have made a good story for the *News Of The World.* You know, this afternoon I was defending him to you; but that was this afternoon. His whining explanation sickened me. I couldn't believe he would find so many ways of excusing his actions. He wanted to put it over as simply a by-product, that his real life was at home with us all.'

He paused for a while; and then he said, 'Jinny!'

And after a moment when she appeared at the sitting-room door, he turned his head towards her, saying, 'He was emphatic that he'd explained everything to you right from the beginning of the whole situation.'

'*What!*' Her head was poked forward as she came towards him. 'He said what?'

'He said the first time he came here' – he now thumbed towards the floor – 'he was sorry for you over the broken affair you'd had with one of the Players. He said he explained things to you that night.'

'Oh, the liar! Do you for a moment think that I would have gone to that house, that I would have . . .? Oh!' She thrust her head back on her shoulders and rocked it from side to side. Then looking at him again, she said, 'The only thing he told me that night was that he missed his mother and how he loved young people about him, loved the family, and that you were his family. You didn't believe him, did you?'

'No, I didn't, and I told him so, and in no polite language either. Anyway, that's the end. And – ' He looked at her, then he finished, 'The beginning I hope.'

She turned quickly away from him now, and went back into the kitchen where she made the coffee. And when she brought it into the room and handed him the cup, he said, 'Thanks, Jinny;' then tapping the sofa, he said, 'Come and sit down here. Not over there, come and sit here.'

She sat on the couch, but not close to him, and for the space of a full minute there was silence between them. Then, his voice low, he said, 'You know how I feel about you, Jinny, have done from the very first I may tell you now, but we sparked off each other like a match against brimstone. On my part, it was because I was so mad at you for I thought you were being purposely blind. Then I realized you were too nice to think anything bad of him . . . Well, anyway, now we are both adrift, and . . .'

'Michael, please don't.'

'All right. I won't go any further tonight. Only I'll say this, we could make a go of it, we two, and I can assure you you would be fulfilled because . . . because I'm in love with you.'

Oh my God! You would be fulfilled. Why didn't he say, Come and kip in with me. And there wasn't any doubt but that she would be fulfilled.

'I'm sorry, Jinny; I shouldn't have started it. I'll go now.' He drained his coffee cup; then getting to his feet, he put on his coat without speaking further. But now, bending, he took her hands and pulled her up from the couch and, looking into her face, he said, 'I can make you happy, Jinny. I can. I know I can.'

'Are you asking me to be your girl friend, Michael?'

She watched his teeth drag at his lower lip for a moment; then his right shoulder moving upwards in the characteristic gesture, he said,

'Putting it boldly like that, yes, I suppose that's what I'm saying. But I'm also saying that I love you, and I can make you happy. And I can make you love me. You don't dislike me, do you?'

'No, I don't dislike you, Michael.'

'Then that's a start. Liking's always a good start.'

She wanted to say, 'You've found that this has proved a good basis on other occasions?' But no; all she wanted now was to get him out of the flat, and never to set eyes on him again; or, for that matter, anyone connected with Hal Campbell.

'Good-night, Jinny. I'll look in tomorrow dinner time. All right?'

'All right.'

As he leant forward to kiss her she drew back, and he smiled wryly as he said, 'That was a silly move; I'll improve. Make haste slowly, as the saying goes. Good-night, dear.'

'Good-night, Michael.'

After closing the door on him she stood with her back to it, her hand covering her eyes, and she whispered to herself, 'Goodbye, Michael.'

She now walked over to the fire, her mind racing. She had to get away from here. She'd go to the agent tomorrow morning and see if he would sublet the flat on a monthly basis, for there was over a year of the lease still to run. But would she be able to get another flat? It would have to be a furnished one, and they charged the earth. She had £250 in the bank; but that wouldn't last her very long these days. She'd have to get a job. But in the meantime where could she stay?

Her cousin Nell? Oh, she had always said she'd be the last person she'd go to. But there was nobody else she could think of. Anyway, it would only be for a few days, until she knew what she was going to do. Perhaps she could get work in Shields on Peter's recommendation. And then she wouldn't need a reference. Well, she could only ask them. It was her last resort. There was a phone in the hall upstairs; she would do it now . . .

When she heard Nell's voice on the phone, she said, 'It's me, Nell, Jinny.'

'Who?'

'Jinny. Jinny Brownlow.'

'Jinny? . . . Oh, Jinny. Well, fancy hearing from you. Where are you?'

'I am still in Fellburn.'

'Are you all right?'

'Yes, and . . . and no. I was wondering if I could impose upon you for a few days.'

This request was greeted by silence; then Nell's voice, the tone of which had changed now, said, 'Are you in trouble, Jinny?'

'No, Nell; not the kind of trouble that you mean.'

'Oh.' The voice was much lighter now.

'I will explain if I could come just for a couple of days.'

'Well, you're welcome. We've never seen you for ages, but again I say you're welcome. When are you coming?'

'Tomorrow. Tomorrow morning.'

'All right, lass; yes. Will you be able to get through the snow?'

'Yes, I'll manage. And thank you, thank you very much, Nell . . . How is Peter?'

'Oh, still being Peter, still bullying poor thieves in the court. You know Peter.'

Jinny smiled and nodded towards the phone as much as to say, 'Yes, I know Peter.' Her poor father used to call him The Lord Chancellor. He was a small dark man who appeared quiet, until he got into court; and there, her father used to say, he was a holy terror and one of these days he'd make a mistake and find the judge guilty.

She thanked Nell again, said goodbye, and put down the phone. Then going back to the flat, she packed another suitcase, wrapped a few good ornaments and the silver that she had collected, and placed them in another case and some cardboard boxes, and labelled them ready for storage.

It was close on midnight when she finished the packing. Then she went to bed. But it was some time before she fell asleep. And her last conscious thought was, Wouldn't it after all be easier to go along with Michael's offer, because he was a nice enough fellow, and sooner or later, nature being what it was, she would find herself succumbing to its demands, because marriage had gone out of fashion and shacking up was in . . .

When the alarm went, she couldn't believe she had been asleep. It was half-past six, and the bed was warm, and she had no desire to get up; she felt heavy and miserable, and whereas last night she'd felt too angry to cry, now she felt she wanted to howl.

As she stepped out of bed and into the ice-cold room, she asked herself, Why not just stay put and fight Michael off? Then there returned to her the thoughts that had drifted with her into sleep, and these seemed to add a spur to her movements.

Getting into her dressing-gown, she hurried into the sitting-room, lit the fire, then filled the kettle and while she waited for it to boil she went through the cupboards, sorting out the crockery. Her mother's best dinner service and tea service, together with some good glass, she put away in a cupboard that had a lock on it.

By half-past eight she was all ready to go. When she phoned for a taxi and asked if it could be there by nine o'clock, they said they would do their best. It didn't arrive until a quarter to ten. But then the taxi driver was very helpful. He carried up the labelled boxes; then ran her to a Pickford's depository where she left them in store. When they returned to the flat she looked down on her three cases. She wondered how she was going to manage them on the train, and she realized she wouldn't be able to on her own for the large one was as much as a man could lift. The taxi driver was proving it as he went out of the door. And she halted him for a moment, saying, 'I know I said I wanted to go to the station, but do you think it would be possible for you to run me right into Shields?'

'I don't see why not, miss,' he said. 'Which part?'

'The top of Sunderland Road, The Heath.'

'Oh, I know Shields well. I used to deliver papers round that quarter when I was a nipper. The only thing that will stop us getting there is the road.' He laughed now; then added, 'But it's a good one; straight through. An' the gritters will have been busy . . . Nothing easier.'

Before closing the flat door she looked back into the room. She had never been happy here, and she would never live here again. Once the lease was up she'd collect her furniture, if not before, because she might be lucky and get a flat in Shields. Which reminded her: she would get the taxi driver to stop at the agent's so she could make arrangements with regard to the business of subletting.

As she reached the top of the area steps the sun suddenly burst through the clouds, and the taxi driver, gazing skywards, exclaimed, 'Well! just look at that. Happy days are here again.'

As he took his seat behind the wheel he leant his head back and said, 'I think you can put up with most things if the sun's shinin'; puts a sort of different complexion on life. Don't you think, miss?'

'Yes; yes,' she answered; 'I suppose that's one way of looking at it,' while thinking it would take more than the sun to put a different complexion on her life. And as the taxi stopped and started its way through Fellburn, she thought, Not only will I never go back to the flat, but I'll never come back to this place. Nothing good has ever happened to me here.

Her father had died here; her mother had died; her first real romance had died; then Alicia Henderson and Yvonne Henderson had died; and Mr Henderson could be dead now for all she knew, and his son with him; and lastly all the romantic feeling she had garnered and stored over the years with regard to love and men had certainly died yesterday. No; never again would she come back here; this part of her life was finished. In fact, when she got herself straight she would leave the North altogether; there were bound to be better places in which to live. There could hardly be any place worse, what with the fact that you daren't go out into the streets by yourself at night, and the old people being murdered by youngsters, and these hooligans rampaging through the city. And this didn't take into account the strikes and the moonlighters and the work dodgers. Then there were so many bitches among women, such as Miss Cadwell, and Mr Waitland's secretary, and some of the girls in the pool; not counting those middle-aged women in the Players who were fighting off age with their claws out.

Why hadn't she noticed all this before? One thing was certain: there wasn't one person in the world for whom she had a kind word at this moment. And certainly not the taxi driver, who, again putting his head back in his shoulders, regaled her with; 'I hope it clears up afore next Saturday, me daughter's getting married. The eldest of six. One off and five to go. It's gona be a church do, an' I said to her this mornin' afore I came out, "You pray to God that He doesn't bring the parson out on strike, else that'll put the kibosh on it."'

A church do. Likely the only time the girl would have been in church since she was christened; and more likely she was five month's pregnant . . .

Oh my God! How she wished she could stop thinking like this. And oh no, she mustn't cry, she mustn't, not in front of this man.

There was silence in the taxi for a few minutes, and then the driver who had been watching her through the mirror said, 'You all right, miss?' And when she didn't answer but put her hand to her throat, he said, 'Anything I've said upset you? I . . . I keep chattering like this, you see. Betty used to say that I was like a gramophone, I kept on an' on. But I'm apt to do it when I'm worried. You see, miss, as I said, me daughter's gettin' married, but' – he paused – 'but her mother's in hospital and . . . and I don't think she'll come out again. Talking, chattering, yammering seems to be the only way to keep me mind off it.'

She blinked her eyes, swallowed deeply, and said, 'Oh, I'm sorry; very sorry. And no, no, it's nothing you've said. And please go on telling me about your wife and your daughter. Please.'

But after this the man didn't have much to say, his talking becoming at best spasmodic, and when he finally carried her luggage into the hall of the tall terraced house, she thanked him warmly and hoped that his wife would get well. But once the door was closed she immediately fell into her cousin's outheld arms and cried unashamedly. And after some moments when Nell Dudley said, 'Come and sit down, lass, and tell me what it is. What's happened?' all she could say was, 'A nice man, the taxi driver. His daughter's going to be married on Saturday, and his wife is dying of cancer in hospital.'

4

For almost six weeks now she had been living with Nell and Peter Dudley. She knew that they were pleased to have her, and she was equally pleased to be with them, except for one thing, one snag: they seemed determined to get her married off. They had the man. He was Peter's partner, name of George Mayborough, and he had a very nice house, almost twice as big as this one, and this one was no small terraced house, but had ten rooms if you included the attics, and a forty foot long back garden that sported a fountain. But George Mayborough's house was near Sunderland, in an acre of land, and with a view of the sea. His wife had been dead for two years, but he was prepared to let someone take her place, so long as, or so it seemed, this person was prepared to live with the furniture his late wife had chosen and arranged, and with the decor.

Jinny was cynically amused by George Mayborough. Twice she had been to dinner at his house, and on the second occasion he had given her a personally conducted tour around every room, with a running commentary on when he'd had that particular wardrobe put in, and when he'd had the en-suite attached to the second guest room. Moreover, he gave her the price of everything that he had bought for years past, all the time comparing his distant purchases with what they would cost today.

George Mayborough was forty-three years old. He was tall and stolidly built, and the stolidness had penetrated his character: he was referred to by Peter Dudley as, 'Good old George, a most reliable type, none better. They don't make them like that today. The kind of man you'd be lucky to have in a tight corner. And a man most women would give their eye-teeth to call husband.'

Her relationship with both Nell and Peter Dudley was such that now she could laugh at their friend George, and as a rejoinder to the last recommendation she had said, 'Peter, I want my eye-teeth,' causing Nell, in her hearty way, to slap her on the back and say, 'That's what I mean. I said to Peter last night you'd be good for him; you've always got an answer. He's everything that Peter says he is, but he wants stirring up.'

'Oh Nell,' Jinny had said, 'do you want rid of me so much?'
And Nell had come back at her, not in a jocular way, but in a serious

voice: 'We want you to be happy, lass, to see you settled, after what you've told us you've gone through.'

Jinny had indeed been able to tell them from the start all that had happened to her since her mother had died, leading right up to the reason why she was staying with them now. And Nell had voiced Jinny's own thoughts when she said, 'Life being what it is there'll come a time when you mightn't have any strength left to hold out against the licensed rapers.' And then she had laughed at herself, ending, 'That's a good description of them isn't it? Licensed rapers. I'll take a copyright out on it.'

More and more, Jinny was finding that Nell was nice; she was a comfort. And she was made to wonder why she hadn't taken up their acquaintance before now. But then she recalled what her mother had thought, that Nell was just a wee bit common, and very lucky to have married a solicitor; while Nell herself had confessed she had not only stood in awe of her mother but was more than a little jealous because she had a daughter, whereas she herself was unable to have children.

Apart from being very comfortably housed, well fed, and enjoying the good company of Nell during the day, Jinny was becoming a little bored, and was looking forward to the week after next when she would enter Peter's firm as secretary to the third partner. The present girl was emigrating to Australia with her family and, as Peter said, she couldn't have been doing it at a better time. It all fitted in.

But on this Friday evening in early April, the romance that was being manoeuvred by Nell and Peter Dudley with the sole purpose of Jinny's welfare at heart was not only nipped in the bud but the whole branch wrenched from the tree. And this incident was followed the very next morning by a letter that was to alter the course of Jinny's life, yet again, for good or ill, whichever way you looked at it.

Being Friday night, Peter went as usual to his bridge club, and Nell, which had at first surprised her, had three friends in to make up a foursome at home. Jinny didn't like bridge. Canasta yes; chess, yes; but not bridge. So, during past Friday evenings, she had looked on, made the coffee, and whenever the rubbers finished early, she had, as Nell put it, knocked out a few tunes on the piano for them, making a nice finish to the evening. Tonight Nell was a little taken aback when Peter returned before her friends had left. Most Friday evenings he didn't get back till elevenish, and here he was just turned ten. She knew immediately that something had displeased him, and the door had hardly closed on her friends before she heard what it was: 'George,' he said.

'What's wrong with George?'

'Everything to my mind at this minute.' He now looked towards Jinny and added, 'You were right not to lay much stock on him. I wouldn't have believed it.'

'Believe what? Come clean,' said Nell. 'State your case' – she laughed – 'present your witness.' And glancing at Jinny, she ended, 'And I can assure you, milord, that anything old George has done won't be enough to send him down.'

'I don't know so much.'

The expression on Nell's face changed; her humorous approach disappeared as she said, 'That so?'

'Yes.'

'What's he done?'

'Made us look damn fools, that's what he's done. And led her up the garden path.'

'Oh no!' – Jinny was looking towards Peter, and shaking her head – 'no, whatever he's done, Peter, it isn't concerned with leading me up the garden path. He's never done that. As Nell might say' – she glanced towards Nell – 'he never got any further than the gate.'

'Out with it. What's happened? I've never seen you like this, not concerning George, anyway.'

'It just shows you; you never know anybody. In this business you think you've learned to know human nature inside out. You've come up through a school that deals with nothing else but emotions, emotions expressed on the face: the tightening of the jaw muscles; the flicker of the eyelid; how a man's mouth is set; what a woman does with her hands when she's talking. It's all there in the book. And I thought I could read George Mayborough from the title page to the end. But there's one thing I forgot . . . Yes, there was one thing I forgot, there's always a cover to a book: paper or hard back, there's a cover and by God, his is a hard back. Do you know what he told me tonight?'

'No; I'm waiting patiently. And stop smoking; that's the fourth one you've lit since you came in. Your pension won't be all that big.'

'Well – ' Peter stubbed out his cigarette. Then looking towards Jinny, he said, 'He got me to the side and started talking about Lola, his late wife, you know, and how he missed her. And I said, of course, yes he would. I went along with him all the way. Even when he prattled on about the wonderful woman she was . . .'

'She was no wonderful woman, she was a bitch.'

'I know that, you know that, and he knows that, and because of that I thought he would be out to marry some one different.' He cast a glance towards Jinny. 'But he turned the tables, saying that he didn't think he could ever put any woman in her place, Lola's place. Eeh! when you think of it. So he had vowed he would never marry again. But – ' and now he wagged his finger at his wife as he went on, 'wait for it. He decided instead to take a girl friend. Aha! Our George, our placid, God-fearing, church-on-Sunday George decided to take a girl friend. He's got her ensconced in a house in Sunderland, conveniently near yet not too near. He even described her. She's in her twenties. Like Jinny here.' He nodded at Jinny now, saying, 'Like you.'

'The dirty old bugger.'

It was too much. The sound of the exclamation, so much like Mr Henderson, and the outraged look on Nell's face caused Jinny to turn her head into the corner of the couch and laugh until the tears rolled down her face. Strangely, she was finding she could laugh these days, and she'd put it down to Nell's lively company.

Almost immediately Nell's laughter joined hers, but not Peter's. He, going to the sideboard, poured himself out a stiff whisky and, throwing it off almost at one gulp, he turned on them, saying now, 'It's all right, you can laugh, but he's been our lifelong friend and I've got to work with him. He's made a fool of us; he must have known what we were after. Of course he did, else he wouldn't have spilled the beans tonight. But why didn't he spill them before? Well, that's me and him finished.'

'Oh, Peter.' Jinny wiped her eyes. 'Don't blame him, because it would never have come off, not . . . not on my part. I couldn't imagine living day in day out with a man like Ge . . . orge.' She drew the name out. 'I should have become fossilized, or gone mad looking at Lola's décor. And I knew he had no intention of changing it because it had cost . . . What had it cost?' She glanced laughingly towards Nell, but she was looking away from both of them, her head bobbing slightly and she exclaimed, 'Sunderland! I'll find out who it is, and when I do I'll play him up. I'll frighten the wits out of dear George, the nasty old swine.'

Jinny bit on her lip as she thought as a man might think, for her mind said one word, 'Women!' The kind, loving Nell would in her own way blackmail George for not falling in with her plans . . .

Half an hour later, as she lay in bed staring into the darkness, she repeated Peter's words: 'She's in her twenties, like you.' Had that girl succumbed suddenly, or had she started earlier, perhaps before she left school? She turned restlessly. Was she a fool?

The letter came with the eight o'clock post. It was from the agents in Fellburn. Inside was a single sheet of paper and another envelope, stamped and addressed to the flat. She read the single sheet first and was half-way through it when she exclaimed, 'Oh no! No!'

'What is it?' Nell turned from handing the dirty breakfast dishes to Mrs Bailey her daily help, adding, 'Something wrong?'

'I'll say. I . . . I can't believe it. Peter.' She handed the letter to Peter, but looking at Nell, she said, 'They've cleared the flat, everything. The agent says that couple must have done it shortly after they went in. They hadn't paid the second month's rent in advance, and when for the second time he had gone there and found the curtains still drawn, he forced the back door open. And' – she pointed to the letter – 'he says the place is utterly stripped. They only left the curtains. They even took . . . They've broken into the cupboard where the china was too. Everything.'

'Dear God! What will they do next? And your mother had some nice pieces.'

Peter looked up from the letter and in a businesslike way he said, 'Well, it's happening all the time. I've got a case on now. The people came back from their holidays and found even the chandeliers and the wall lights gone. Are you insured?'

'Well, I have a small insurance that I've kept up on the furniture. It's a continuation of what Mother used to pay. She took it out mostly to cover the bureau. It's got Verni Martin paintings on it. And there's a matching cabinet. They're the only antiques. But there was so much.' She shook her head. 'I simply can't believe it.'

'Oh, there are frightful people about.' Nell nodded at her. 'Some of them would take your eyes out and come back for the sockets. I once left a sweeping brush outside the back door. I couldn't have been gone for a couple of minutes, but me broom was gone. And there wasn't a soul to be seen.'

'Leave it to me. I'll contact the agents and the insurance company. Did you keep an inventory of your furniture?'

'No.' She shook her head. 'But I could name practically everything that was in the flat.' She now turned her attention to the envelope that had accompanied the letter, and the gasp she gave as she read it could be described as one of delight and, turning to Nell and Peter, she waved the letter at them, saying, 'It's . . . it's from Mr Henderson, the son John. He's got his father home, and he, Mr Henderson senior, he wants to see me . . . He's asked to see me. So . . . so he mustn't be too bad. Oh my!' She was looking at the letter again. 'It must have been lying there for nearly a fortnight, it was written last month. Oh, I'll have to go.' She was looking from one to the other. 'It will be wonderful to see him again . . . alive. I never thought I would.'

'How old is he?'

'Who?'

'Mr Henderson, the one that was your boss.'

'Oh, in his fifties.'

'And the son?'

Jinny just prevented herself from biting on her lip and lowered her head as she made herself answer flatly, 'In his twenties – ' adding, 'He lives away from home in a flat and has a girl friend.' And on this she turned from them, saying, 'I'll look up the times of trains.'

'You needn't bother about trains, we'll take you up.'

'Oh, I can't put you to that . . .'

'Don't be silly!' Nell waved her hand. 'I feel like a run out. It's

April anyway, and spring's in me blood. And I'd like to see how the other half live, the top half, in this grand house you've described.'

'You'll be disappointed,' she said; 'they don't live as well as you do. And I'm warning you' – she looked at Peter – 'you'll likely be shocked at his language.'

Peter Dudley didn't swear. The nearest to a swear word she had heard him use was damn, and then he apologized. But he didn't seem to object to his wife using colourful language, and it was Nell who now said, 'Sounds someone after me own heart. Well, let's get ready. It could be an interesting day.'

As Jinny ran up the stairs she called back, 'And the happiest day I've known in a long time, for he must be better if he's asked to see me.'

PART THREE

1

'Woman! If you straighten that quilt just once more I swear I'll get onto me legs and kick your backside out of that door.'

'Now, now, Mr Henderson.'

'And don't now, now, me, miss. I'm not a bairn at the breast.'

'Really! In all my. . .'

'Yes, I know. In all your long service you've never come across anybody like me. So you should think yourself privileged, damned lucky I'd say.'

The nurse drew in a deep breath, and so expanded her already full bust still further as she looked down upon her charge, her prostrate charge, with an expression that was utterly devoid of any sympathetic feeling. And she told herself she couldn't stand much more of this man, this thankless, rude, ignorant type who had such a high opinion of himself that he could not be made to understand that he was not the only one in the world who had had an accident which had left him almost powerless. And not for the first time during the past fortnight she had been looking after him did she wish that his paralysis had affected his speech also. She was being paid good money, but all the money in the world couldn't make up for this type of abuse. She would speak to Dr Turner about him when next he came.

She was about to leave the room when the door was opened and Florence entered, and the look on the face of the nurse told Florence that her father was at it again, as she called it.

Approaching the bed, she smiled down at her father, saying lightly, 'And how are we this morning?'

'We are not feelin' very well this mornin', Florence. And we are not in the mood to take kindly to bein' turned over, powdered, and having our backside smacked. And while we are on it, I haven't reached royal rank yet and so we'll drop the "we" and return to "Father", shall we?'

As the nurse had done, so Florence drew in a long breath, then let it out slowly as she said, 'She's only trying to do her best for you; she's carrying out her duty.'

'Aye; she might be, but she's a stranger to me and I have three married daughters, women who know all there is to know about a man's body, and I would have thought they could have arranged it atween them to take a turn to see to me now and again. I don't expect it of Lucy, she's still a lass.'

'Father . . . we've been through all this. I have three children to see to. But even so, if you would be reasonable and see it our way, then I could see it your way, and yes, yes, I could attend to you.'

'And the payment, Florence, is that I've got to take Ronnie into the business, is it?'

'He's very good, Father.'

'Shut up, girl! Your Ronnie's very good at nothing. He wouldn't be able to keep down the little job he has now if it wasn't for his own old man. Greengrocery's his line. And what in the name of God could he do in a factory like ours? You imagine him sitting in an office all day dictating little notes to a typist. No, Florence, never! You tell him that from me. If it was a business man you wanted you should not have married him, one of four brothers all in the fruit game. I know what's in your mind, our Florrie. Oh aye, I do.' He moved his head on the pillow, and he lifted his right arm slowly from the eiderdown towards his neck, and when his hand fell on to it he lay gasping for a moment before he could go on, 'When his old man goes the split won't be all that big; but if he was ensconced here and expecting me not to be long for the top he'd . . .'

'Oh, how dare you say such things to me!'

'I can because I know they're true, lass, and because everything's changed, everything. I'm bein' treated as if I was an idiot. I may have lost the use of me body, but not of me mind. And there's another thing: nobody has spoken a word about your mother since it happened. She need never have existed.'

'That's because nobody wants to hurt you. And I'm telling you too, you'll get no one to stay with you in the end: Lucy's scared stiff of you; and by the look of Nurse Lasting, she's already packing her bags. Something else while I'm on, because if you're strong enough to give it you're strong enough to take it: you won't hold our John for long. You think he's back here for good, don't you? But I know John, and at the first opportunity he'll be off. I'm surprised that he's stuck it this long. You never got on, and you never will. And I'm . . . I'm going now, and I'll say this, Father: there might come a time when you'll be glad of Ronnie's services, because there's no hope of your getting Nellie and Bill from Jersey. As for our Monica, she can't look after her own children; she has to have a nursemaid for them, and two helps in the house. So I can see her attending to you. By! yes, I can. Well, I'm going; and if you want me there's always the phone.'

When the door was shut none too gently behind his daughter, Bob Henderson closed his eyes and, the words coming slow and deep, he muttered aloud, 'Oh my God. My God.' He looked up towards the panelled ceiling. 'Why has it come to this? Why? Tell me, why?'

What had he done in his life that this should have happened to him? Aye, he had been rough of tongue, but that was all. He had put out a helping hand where it was needed most, unknownst to many; he had slaved sixteen hours a day for years to build up a business: at first Garbrook had provided the money and he had done the work, but their positions had levelled out when Alicia's father had died and left her a tidy sum, the whole of which she put into the business. But now the world had fallen about his ears. Nobody would tell him anything: he didn't know what was happening, except what he heard on the television, and what he heard was happening to steel was anything but good news because trouble in steel works meant trouble for people like them manufacturing engineers. You couldn't manufacture if you hadn't the basic materials. And even then you couldn't distribute if you didn't get the market. And there was no one in that firm now who could get markets like their Glen. Oh, Glen. Glen. If only he could change places with him. If Glen's body had been crippled and his mind left he would have managed. But Glen's body was whole, his brain wasn't. He wondered what news John would bring back today.

His head moved on the pillow, and he looked about the room. It had always seemed a beautiful room, because Alicia had made it so, but now it was like a cage.

His breathing became rapid. If only somebody would come in, just to say a word to him, stop his racing inside his chest. Why could he feel he was alive inside yet couldn't move his limbs? Why? Why? Oh God, he'd go mad. If he could only get his hands on those damned tablets, he'd put an end to it. He would. Yes, he would.

The nurse came back into the room. He wanted to say to her, 'I'm sorry if I upset you,' but he couldn't because he wasn't really sorry he had upset her; he didn't like the woman. But anyway, she was somebody who was moving about, and he watched her make several trips into the bathroom. When she finally came to the bed, she looked down at him unsmiling as she asked, 'Would you like tea or coffee?' and he answered, 'Coffee please, and black.'

She had hardly been left the room a moment when the door was opened again and Dorry entered.

Going swiftly to the bed, she said, 'You've got some visitors . . . I mean one, one visitor.'

'Aye? Aye well, who is it?'

Dorry's smile widened. 'It's the one you were asking for, your secretary, Miss Brownlow.'

'No! No! Oh! Where is she? Fetch her up. Oh Dorry, fetch her up.'

His head was raised from the pillow when she entered the room, and she went straight towards him and, taking the hand that was raised from the eiderdown, she gripped it tightly as she looked down on him; and her throat was so full she found it impossible to speak for a moment.

It was he who spoke first. 'Oh, lass,' he said; 'am I glad to see you! Where've you been? Why didn't you come afore? I sent for you to the flat. And got John to write. Where've you been?'

'Oh, it's a long story. I'll . . . I'll tell you later. I only got the letter this morning.'

'Just this mornin'?' He swallowed deeply and wetted his lips; then said, 'Aw, sit down, lass. Get a chair and come and sit down.'

She loosed her hand from his and brought a chair to the bed, and when she sat down she took hold of his hand again as she said, 'Oh, it's good to see you, so good.'

'Lass. Lass. I'm nearly bubblin'.' His throat was full, and he blinked his eyelids but could not prevent the moisture from seeping down on to his cheeks. And his voice was husky as he said, 'Did you ever know anything like it? Whole lives, two of them, blown like the wind into eternity. Laughing their heads off one minute, mangled the next. We never knew what hit us. Oh, lass, lass. I'm sorry.' He turned his head away from her, and she, taking a handkerchief from her pocket, reached over and wiped his face. And when he looked at her again she could scarcely see him for tears streaming down her own cheeks. After a moment she said, 'How . . . how is Glen?'

It was some seconds before he answered. 'In a bad way, lass. He got it in the back of the head. He's in a special unit in Newcastle. He went through another operation on Thursday. John's down now seeing how things have gone. But he should be home soon. Tell me, what are you doing now? You're not back there? I soon found that out. So what are you doing?'

'Nothing at present. I'm due to start a new job on Monday week. I'm . . . staying with my cousin, and have been for some weeks. That's why I didn't get your letter, and didn't know you wanted to see me. I tried often at the hospital . . . But you were too ill then.'

'You say you're not yet in a job? . . . Jinny' – there was a light pressure on her fingers – 'would you come back? I mean, there's lots of things you could do. I want to know what's goin' on, and oh, Jinny, I need somebody to talk to. Nobody mentions . . . Alicia, and that bloody nurse gets on my wick. And I've had a row with our Florrie. Nothing's gone right. Huh!' He moved his head again as he looked at her, saying, 'That's putting it mildly. The house has exploded; the world has exploded; the only thing of any worth that has happened is that our John's come home. And the payment's been very high, lass: two dead, a mind taken away from a brilliant young fellow, and a man left useless.'

'What do you mean, useless? You've still got your tongue. And that' – she smiled faintly at him – 'from what I remember of you, and from what I've just picked up from a conversation in the hall, is still at its top worst. Lots of men have been paralysed and continued to make their mark. History tells me that the President of the United

States, Roosevelt, helped to run a war . . . and women, from a wheelchair.'

'Aye, you've said it, lass, from a wheelchair. But let's face it, I'm gone from the neck down, Jinny.'

She stared at him in silence now; then moved her lips one over the other before she said, 'You can move this hand.'

'Just.'

'Have you tried to move the other one?'

'Oh, lass' – he closed his eyes – 'they progged an' pulled an' probed an' pushed every single pore of me. That's how much they've tried. Anyway, what about it, Jinny? Will you?'

She put her head on one side and her smile was wide as she said, 'Come back and be bullied to death by you? Have to put up with your swearing, your cursing, your never saying thank you? Not – ' She leant towards him now, her face almost touching his as she ended, 'In the words of Eliza Doolittle, not bloody likely.' But then, her mouth wide, she said, 'My pay cheque starts from now, and it's double for weekend work. Don't forget that.'

'Aw Jinny. Jinny. Aw, lass.' His eyelashes were wet. 'You don't know how good it is to . . . to see you again . . . Aw.'

'And you. And you. Mr Henderson.' Her voice was cracking and she swallowed and added crisply, 'But now I'll have to go downstairs: my cousin and her husband are there; they brought me from Shields. They've been very good to me. I can tell you something, they won't like it, me letting them down. Peter, that's my cousin's husband, has got me this job in his office. He's a solicitor. The pay would have been good, the hours short. I must be daft, taking you on.' She smiled softly at him now. 'Could I bring them up to see you?'

'Aye. Do that, lass. I'll explain to them my need is greater than theirs. Go on; bring them up.'

Less than a half-hour later when Jinny stood on the drive saying goodbye to Peter and Nell, it was Nell who shook her head as she said, 'I don't know, Jinny. I don't know. He's helpless. That kind of man can sap you. Between bullying and coaxing, your life isn't going to be your own. I'm . . . I'm sorry for him as much as you are, but, the situation he's in, he'll hang on to you like an anchor. And it'll take more than pity and sympathy to put up with it; you'll want the stamina of a horse.'

'Be quiet, Nell. Be quiet.' Peter pushed her gently in the arm. 'The man's got a nurse; he's got a son and daughter at home. That so, Jinny?'

'Yes, Peter. And look, don't worry.' She turned to Nell. 'I'm going to be all right. In fact, I'm going to enjoy looking after him. We got on so well together. And what's more, Nell, I'm . . . well, to put it plainly, I'm going to be needed.'

'Well, we need you, lass. We'll miss you. Won't we, Peter? We'll miss her.'

'That's nice of you, nice of both of you. And I can't thank you enough for what you've done for me. And what you're going to do' – she put her hand out towards Peter – 'about the flat and the insurance and that. And bringing my things over here . . . it's very good of you. And on Saturday too, and I know you like your golf.'

'Well, that's one good thing you've done.' Nell was nodding towards her now. 'I won't be a golf widow this afternoon. But did you see his face when you said you'd have to go back for the things? It dropped a mile. I could see him thinking that once you left the house you wouldn't come back. An' I'm telling you, Jinny, if you take my advice you'll put your foot down and have stated hours. And another thing, and this is diplomacy, you make friends with the kitchen lot, else they can lead you . . .'

'Nell' – Peter had his court voice on now – 'will you kindly get into the car; but before you do will you please shut up.'

'I know what I'm talking about, Peter Dudley. I don't have to study law to know people. I tell you again she's going to have her work cut out . . .'

'Get in.'

After he had got his wife seated, Peter turned to Jinny, saying, 'Take no notice. Do what you have to do for as long as you like. But always remember, when you want to come back home, the door's open.'

'Thank you, Peter. Thank you. I'll remember.'

Nell, winding down the window, now had the last word. As the car was about to move off, she said, 'And to think this time yesterday I was hearing your wedding bells.'

It was as she closed the door behind her and saw Dorry disappearing with the tray into a passage to the right of her that she recalled Nell's advice with regard to the staff. And she knew that a household such as this would be run very like an office, and she'd had experience of the tensions in an office, hadn't she just, and so she followed Dorry into what was for her a new quarter of the house. She went along the passage, and passed a door opening into the dining-room. There was no one in there that she could see. And she went on to a further door, and guessing that the kitchen lay beyond, she knocked on it. It was a moment or so before it was opened, and Dorry, looking at her, said enquiringly, 'Yes, miss? You're wanting something?'

'Just . . . just a word. But is Mrs Gallon in?'

'Oh yes. Aye, Cook's here. Come in.'

Jinny went into the room, a very modern kitchen, she could see at once. It held a double Aga, besides electric wall ovens. The cook was at the table, and she turned and awaited her coming.

Jinny began hesitantly, 'I . . . I thought I'd better come and tell you, I'm taking up my duties with Mr Henderson again. I say' – she shrugged her shoulders – 'my duties. I don't know really what they'll consist of as yet. But he has asked me to stay, and as Miss Lucy is not in I . . . I wonder if you could tell me where I'm likely to be put.' She smiled from one to the other. And they both smiled back at her; but it was the cook who answered. 'Oh well,' she said, 'Dorry here'll show you a room. And if I may say so, I think it's a good thing he's takin' an interest in something because, between you and me, miss, if he didn't have a change soon I think he'd go off his head. He's had Miss Lucy scared at times. And its taken Mr John all his time to manage him. As for Nurse Lasting – ' Cook now turned and looked at Dorry, and they pulled faces at each other. And it was Dorry who went on, 'Between you and me, miss, I don't think she's gonna stick it out. An' mind, to be honest, I can't blame her, 'cos he does get rough at times. We understand him, see, and I suppose you do an' all, workin' along of him in the office, but strangers, well . . . they consider it a bit thick what he comes out with.' Again the two elderly women laughed, and Jinny now said, 'Perhaps he'd be better with a male nurse.'

'Eeh! now. Isn't that odd?' Dorry stuck her thumb into cook's arm, saying, 'Didn't I say that only last night, now didn't I? I said, what the boss wants is a man up there, and a hefty one at that. Mr John does his best, but he's got him practically worn out. Now isn't that funny? I said the very same thing.' She was now nodding at Jinny, and she added, 'If this one leaves, Nurse Lasting I mean, you want to put it to the boss, you do.'

'It's a thought.'

'Aye, it is a thought.' Cook bobbed her head now. And they all smiled at each other. They were conspirators.

It was a good start. Nell had been right, on this point anyway.

'Come on, miss, and I'll get you settled. Are your things here?'

'No. My cousin and her husband have gone to fetch them.'

'Oh well, in the meantime I'll show you your room.' And Dorry turned to the cook, saying, 'The one opposite, eh?'

'Well, I don't know.' Cook put her head on one side and looked at Jinny. 'It all depends, because you see, that's the one, isn't it, with the intercom telephone in? And you don't want him to get you up in the middle of the night, do you, 'cos you know, he's very demanding. And if you've been on your feet all day you want your rest. We all know that.'

'Oh that'll be all right. I won't mind.'

'Well, come on, miss, we'll see.' And they went out, Dorry still talking. 'Miss Lucy had that room for a time, but she changed it and went into the one that you were in over Christmas. And then when Mr John came home permanently we had to do a move round, 'cos the girls have always had their rooms kept ready for them, and after the accident and when three of them were here together and all the children, oh my! And the French families. We had ten bedrooms going with Mr Glen's house up the road. Eeh! I just can't believe what's happened to him.'

They were going up the stairs now. 'The changes this place has seen.' She turned her head and looked down at Jinny as she whispered, 'It used to be a happy house, gay like. Always somebody laughin' or jokin', or him . . . the boss, callin' out . . . Well, you had a taste, didn't you, at New Year? But of course, it was quiet then. Yet it was nice. Wasn't it nice?'

'Yes, it was very nice,' Jinny said softly; 'very nice indeed. In fact, it was the best New Year I can remember for a long time.'

They crossed the broad landing and went down another corridor where, Dorry's voice now dropping to a mutter, she said, 'They were very fond of you, miss, very fond. I know that.'

Jinny said nothing but followed her into the bedroom. It wasn't unlike the room she had slept in before, only much larger, and with a double bed.

'Will this do, miss?'

'Beautifully. Beautifully.'

'I can't say I'll unpack for you, can I?' Dorry poked her head forward, then giggled. Then going quickly to the window she put her head close to a pane and after a moment said, 'It's Miss Lucy. She's back. Will I tell her you're here?'

'If you please, Dorry.'

Left alone, she sat in the chair by the side of the bed, thinking: I should have gone down. But it was only a matter of minutes later when there came a tap on the door and it was pushed open and Lucy entered.

Jinny had risen and was already standing in the middle of the room but the sight of the girl checked the greeting she was about to make. This wasn't the Lucy she remembered from Glen's wedding: she had lost her plumpness, and the slightly petulant look had gone from her face and was replaced by a wide-eyed, worried expression. Altogether she looked older.

She spoke immediately, her words almost tumbling over each other. 'Hello,' she said. 'Dorry's just told me. You've come to stay. Oh, I am glad. If he could get his mind on some work it might help. Oh, I am glad. Have you brought your things?'

'No. My cousin has gone back home for them; I've been staying with them in Shields.'

'Oh, that must be why he didn't hear from you. You're the only one that seems to know about the business. Mr Waitland's called, and Mr Garbrook too, but he got so upset after. Oh, it's been awful.' She now dropped down on to the side of the bed, and began to loosen the button of the smart suit she was wearing, and when she had undone them she let out a long slow breath as if the coat had been tight, which it wasn't. And now Jinny watched the girl's lips tremble and the eyelids blink rapidly before tears began to run down her cheeks.

Quickly Jinny sat down beside her and put her arm around her shoulder, and immediately Lucy turned and buried her face in Jinny's neck while muttering through choking gasps, 'It's been awful. It doesn't seem to get better. I miss Mummy. Oh, I miss Mummy. And I've had to do everything in the house. I mean bills and things. And he barks at me, Father, he barks at me every time I go in. I can do nothing to please him.' She lifted her head and began to dry her eyes, saying, 'You would have thought with me losing Mummy that he would have understood and been kind, wouldn't you, wouldn't you now?'

Here was the spoilt child talking. The tragedy had aged her outwardly but apparently hadn't affected her character, for she wasn't giving much thought to the loss her father had sustained, nor yet her brother. And now she went on, 'I . . . I was going to be married. I was. Yes, I was.' Her head was bobbing. 'Father wouldn't have it because it meant my going to New Zealand. Reg has been offered this post, and if he doesn't go by November he'll lose it. I could have got round Father. I feel sure I would have, and then this had to happen. And now I . . . I feel tied for life because none of the girls will come back. Florence wanted to; but then Father wouldn't take Ronnie into the firm. He can't stand Ronnie. But she's the only one who could come and take over. And so, there I was left with everything to do. Oh – ' She now caught hold of Jinny's hands and, shaking them, she said, 'Oh, I am glad you're going to stay.'

Jinny smiled quietly. The girl was glad she was going to stay, not because of any personal liking but because she saw her as a means to an end. She would have said there wasn't a selfish bone in Alicia Henderson's body, nor yet in her husband's, but from someone along the line their youngest daughter had picked up the threads of selfishness. Perhaps they themselves were to blame for spoiling her: the youngest of the family was often treated like an only child. Yet, she herself had been an only child; and she didn't consider her parents had spoiled her. They had been loving, very loving, but, as she remembered, firm, especially about morals. Oh, yes, especially about morals. Perhaps too firm in that way for the present day. One's character and actions should be moulded to the times in which one lived, and if she hadn't been brought up as she was . . .

Oh, here she was, doing it again. Well, from now on she'd have something to think about other than what she was missing because she was being silly enough to adhere to certain standards that every day the television, wireless and newspapers informed her were out of date.

'Everything will work out all right, you'll see.' They were standing now.

'You think so?'

It was like an appeal from a child, and Jinny paused before answering, 'Yes, I'm sure, for you it will be anyway. As for your father, well, we'll have to see. And . . . and what about Glen?'

'Oh, he's in a dreadful state. John should be back anytime. He goes in almost every day to see him. It's his brain.' The tears once more coming into her eyes, she turned away, muttering, 'You can't believe it, can you? You just can't believe it.' Then at the door she turned and said, 'We have a midday dinner. It's easier for Cissie Gallon. I used to come up and sit with Father while Nurse had hers, but now perhaps . . . well . . .'

'Yes, I'll see to him. Don't worry, I'll see to him.'

'Thank you. I'm . . . I'm glad you're here.'

'I'm very pleased to be here. I hope I'll be of some use.'

'Oh' – Lucy now jerked her chin upwards – 'if you can talk work you will. You can be sure of that.' Then as she made to go out she screwed up her eyes tightly and bent her head down as her father's voice came bawling from the room opposite, 'When I'm ready for it, not afore!'

Jinny saw through the open door the nurse coming out from the bedroom opposite. The woman's face was scarlet, and she addressed Lucy now as if speaking to the mistress of the house, saying, 'That's it! I give notice. I'm leaving. I don't have to put up with such talk.' She now reached behind her and closed the door with a bang. Then looking at Lucy again, she went on, 'You must get a replacement because he must be seen to. I'll stay till Monday, not a minute longer. Understand? And at this she turned and marched down the corridor, leaving Jinny and Lucy looking at each other.

And Jinny, seeing that the girl's face was about to crumple again, put out her hand and said, 'Don't worry. We'll manage somehow. Go on downstairs; I'll see to him.'

Lucy almost scampered away, like a child who had evaded a spanking, and Jinny was left looking at the door opposite. She did not immediately go across to it, for she was thinking again of Nell and what she had prophesied, and she knew now that whatever it was she had thought she was taking on she hadn't included nursing in it. But then she told herself, that wouldn't come about for there was John; he would see to that side of it until they got a nurse . . . a male nurse. Yes, that's what was wanted, a male nurse. But would he stand for it? Well, they would have to see.

She now approached the door, opened it and went in; and she saw immediately that he was still seething about whatever had upset him, and before she could approach the bed his voice came at her: 'Thought you had changed your mind. You've been some time coming back. And that woman's a bloody fool. If you tell somebody you don't want to be treated like a child and they're not deaf, dumb or daft, then they should take note, shouldn't they? We had a session about it first thing this morning. You would think she would have learnt. But oh no, not her. In she comes, forgiveness written all over her, and starts again. "Oops-a-daisy!" she says. "Shall we do the back now, eh? Eh?" And the tone of her voice like that you'd use to a bairn in nappies. Jinny' – his voice suddenly dropped and he screwed up his eyes – 'I'm nearly at the end of me tether. It's true, lass, I'm nearly at the end of me tether.'

'Well, we'll have to see what we can do about it, won't we?'

She sat down on the edge of the bed and took the limp hand in hers. 'But I'll tell you one thing: it's no good wasting what energy you've got left bawling at people. If you ever want to get back into the swim again, I mean work, you've got to conserve what strength you've got left.'

'What do you mean, get back into the swim again, work? How the hell can I get back into the swim again?'

'Oh' – she drew her chin in – 'you don't mean you have no intention to talking or getting back to it? If that's the case, then you've got me here on false pretences. What am I here for? Because, let me tell you I'm no nurse, I'm merely a secretary. I'm not going to start rubbing your back for you or carrying out other – ' she swallowed before she forced herself to bring out, 'disagreeable duties. I'm here to get you back to work. Nothing more, nothing less.'

His eyes were staring up at her now, and he said quietly, 'You're a cheeky bitch. You know that? You always were.' Then his head moving slowly on the pillow, he said, 'Oh, Jinny; I'm glad you're back.'

'Well, I'm back, but only on conditions. And let's get them straight.' She was nodding at him now. 'First, you have a nurse. Whether male or female, you have a nurse. And I think a male nurse would be preferable.'

After a moment of glaring at her, he growled. 'Aye, well, perhaps you're right there.'

'The secondly, we'll all have our hours on duty: John, Lucy, me, and the nurse.'

'Oh God in heaven!'

'No, not Him, just the four of us.'

It was a facetious statement, but that, she knew, was the way he liked things, at least when there was no big work issue at stake. And his answer was in his usual vein: 'Now stop trying to be so bloody clever. You're so sharp you'll cut yourself on your tongue one of these days. An' look, lass, let me put things straight to you. I'm at home, in me own house. I don't want a hospital routine; I played hell until I got out of hospital.' He paused and turned his head away from her and looked to the other side of the room as he went on, 'I have the idea that once I got home things would be different. I thought they'd all rally round me. And it's funny, the only one who's stood by me is our John, and he's the one I've taken it out of most all his life, 'cos we never got on, you know.' He was looking at her again. 'Funny that, isn't it? We couldn't hit it off. Our ideas were like chalk and cheese. He was supposed to despise money: far left, so to speak, he was for a time. They all go like that, these fellows who get the chance of a better education. They bite the hand that's worked to put them there. They despise the means that's keeping them there. Share and share alike is their motto. Wealth should be shared, they say. And when you ask them who is going to pay the bills, they come out with some high-falutin jargon. Yet they're not above saying that can't live on their grants. Oh, that used to madden me, the times they said that. If anybody got to university in my day he got there on his brains; and not by sittin' on his backside or goin' on holiday during what they call the vac, you worked. And I know what I'm talking about. There's Meane in the drawing-office; he came up that way. Navvied during the holidays, he did. He told me.'

As she listened to him talking she thought, he could soon get back into his stride. If only he had the use of his hands.

His chattering suddenly stopped and he returned to her demands. 'Now, you have a point there, Jinny, about a male nurse. There was a fellow in the hospital, Mason his name was, everybody called him Willie, Willie Mason. He was as strong as a bull. And kind with it. I said to him in fun one day, 'I'll set you on.' And he laughed back at me and said, 'All right, but for time and a half.' I wonder now. I wonder. I'd give him time and a half, Jinny. If I remember rightly an' all, he's single. Now I think you've got something there' – he nodded at her – 'because it won't only be me that needs some attention; our Glen, as far as I can understand, is in a pretty bad state. And we'll be having him home soon. John promised me that he would see to it and ask about it the day. He's had three operations . . . Poor lad. I'm longing to see him.' He pressed his lips tight together and moved his head slightly. 'He was a wonderful son, one to be proud of, an' he was going places. He was already well-known abroad, and highly respected. Why, Jinny? Why?'

The look on his face caused her to put out her hand and smooth his hair back from his brow as she said softly, 'I can't tell you. There's no answer to it. I've asked the same question again and again, even about the petty things that have happened in my own life. But when this happened to you all . . . well I was stunned by it, because, you see, to me you were all so wonderful. Alicia, Glen,

Yvonne, and . . .' she nodded her head slowly now – 'and you. I . . . I was away that weekend with' – she pursed her lips – 'my one-time friend.'

Taking no notice of his raised eyebrows, she went on, 'I went to the hospital, but I couldn't see you. Then I returned to the office.' She hesitated, wondering if she should tell him what had transpired, and decided to do so. It would stir his interest, and perhaps give him a laugh. And so she went on, 'As you have since gathered. I suppose you know that Mr Waitland has taken over your . . . our office? Well, he politely, or impolitely, sent me packing down to the typing pool.'

'He did?'

'Yes, he did.'

'I heard a different version. But go on.'

'Well, you can imagine how I felt returning there, and to be met by Miss Cadwell, who was in her element as she told me in no small voice what was in store for me. Well, that was all right as far as it went, until she attacked my character and accused me of – ' Her head moved from one side to the other before she ended, 'having an illicit affair.'

'You having an illicit affair? Who with, in the name of God?'

'You, of course.'

'*Me?*' His face stretched. 'My God! *me*? Well, I haven't heard this afore. Is that why you slapped her?'

'That is why I slapped her, and on both sides of the face.'

'Good for you. And so we had an illicit affair?'

'Yes, we had. And you bought me expensive jewellery, and your wife caught you at it, came to the jeweller's shop and caught you . . . us at it.'

'Never!' His voice was low now. 'Eeh!' He shook his head. 'If only Alicia had been here to listen to this. Lass' – his fingers moved slowly over hers – 'as much as I like you, if you had the royal insignia on you, or if you had been a multi-millionaire and as beautiful and young as you are, you couldn't have moved Alicia one jot in my affections.'

'I know that.'

'Eeh, the minds of people. They must have been thinking that all along.'

'Yes. Yes.'

'My God! It's a good job I didn't know. But then, if I had I'd have played them up, and Alicia would have gone along with me. Aye, she would. Oh, Jinny . . . Jinny, I miss her. The days are empty. At times I think I am goin' to go mad because life's like eternity stretching away with just me head to see it. Can you understand that, just me head to experience eternity?' He swallowed deeply. Then his voice rising, he said, 'I had to fight that bloody nurse to have her picture left there. She said it wasn't good for me when she found me talking to it one day.'

His voice dropping again, he said. 'She's very close to me you know, Jinny; she doesn't seem really to be gone. It's a strange thing: I can talk to you now about this, but I couldn't to anybody else. Night-time, I can see her standing as clear as if she was alive; but you know, it's as if she were asking me to let her go. Can you understand that, Jinny? It's just as if she were saying, "Leave go, Bob. Leave go."'

When she didn't answer, he said, 'No, you wouldn't understand; I cannot understand it meself. But it helps just to talk about it.'

Jinny looked across the bed to the large photograph of Alicia standing on a side table and felt a little cold shiver pass through her, and the thought came to her that perhaps the nurse was right, he was living with the dead. And the dead were, in some way, telling him that they were where no one could really reach them or hold them, and that if they didn't of their own accord release them, time would. But the interval could be painful.

She wished she could have expressed her feelings, in words that would not have been painful to him, for he was in need of comfort at the moment, and was finding it only in the mirage his brain conjured up in the night.

Changing the subject abruptly now, he said, 'Have they got you settled in?'

'Yes. I'm just across the corridor.'

'Oh, good. Good. Well, go on now downstairs and have something to eat. It's near dinner-time. One last word about our arrangements.' He stressed the last word. 'Call me Bob, will you?'

'Oh.' She stood up. 'I'm going to find that difficult.'

'Why?'

'Just because I'd rather call you Mr Henderson.'

'Look. We're at home now, not in the office. Bob it is. That's an order.'

'Right, Mr Henderson.' She turned on her heel, and walked from the room, closing the door quietly behind her. She heard his voice muttering something, but she couldn't catch the words.

Before going down the stairs, she went into her room and stood with her back to the door as she muttered aloud. 'Poor soul. Poor soul. How's he going to stick it, being made as he is? How's he going to stick it?'

The rest of the day passed somewhat uneventfully; only one thing became more certain, Nurse Lasting, becoming aware that Jinny was to be a permanent member of the household, emphasized her decision that she was leaving, replacement or no replacement.

It was now ten o'clock at night. Bob was asleep, but only after a fight over the taking of his pill for he had wanted to keep awake until after John should return with news of Glen. His mind would be at rest for the next four hours or so: he hardly ever slept, he said, after two in the morning. The nurse had retired to her room; Dorry and Cissie had gone off duty; and Lucy, after saying good-night to her father at nine o'clock, had slipped out of the house, saying she wouldn't be long. She hadn't said where she was going, she really had no need. The man, Reg Talbot, Jinny had learned from Bob, was twelve years Lucy's senior, and, being divorced, was no suitable partner for his daughter. Jinny could have put in cynically from her own experience, that nine-tenths of men seemed to be either divorced or living on the side with someone, and so a young girl's chance of meeting up with an unattached man these days was on a par with a man meeting a girl who hadn't had it off with someone. Even while thinking this way she chastised herself for the crudeness of her approach to the situation; but then told herself it was the present-day approach, so what? And although she still might be a cultured handmaiden, and her new position seemed to merit that very title, she was no longer a gullible cultured handmaiden, nor yet would she ever again break her neck to please people in order to retain their company.

Anyway, Lucy had definitely gone to meet this man, and she was just asking herself if she should wait for her coming in when she heard the sound of a car on the gravel drive.

She rose from the chair by the fire as the door opened; then her face stretched slightly as she saw it wasn't Lucy who had entered but John. And for a moment he looked as surprised as she did. Then coming forward, he said, 'Well! Well! So you got here after all?'

'Yes, about a fortnight late. I didn't get your letter until this morning.'

'This morning?' He raised his eyebrows; then ran his fingers round the inside of his collar before adding. 'And you're here, all set to stay?'

'Yes, that seems to be the position.'

'Well! Well!' he said again; then went towards the fire, adding now, 'Sit down. Sit down.' Then dropping into a chair himself, he closed his eyes as he said, 'Lord I'm tired.'

'Your . . . your father expected you earlier. Can I get you anything? Dorry and Cook have gone to bed. But I know where things are. At least I could find them. I could make you a coffee.'

'That would be nice. Thank you.'

She hurried from the room and into the kitchen, and quickly found what was needed; and while she stood waiting for the water to boil she said to herself, How does it happen that he's so unlike his father in temperament, manner, and everything. But at this point she checked herself: How did she know what he was really like? Except for that meeting on New Year's morning she knew nothing about him, only what his father had told her. And from that she gathered that he was a stubborn individual, if not an egotistical one . . . Had he been pleased to see her just now? He had looked surprised. Yet it was he who had written to her. Well, she would have to see how they got on.

A few minutes later she was handing him a cup of coffee; then sat down opposite him again and waited for him to speak.

He had drunk half the coffee before he said, 'Is Lucy in bed?'

She did not immediately answer. But then, her voice expressionless, she said, 'She went out for a short while.'

'What time?'

'Well, it was . . . Again she paused. 'I think it was just before nine.'

He finished the coffee and set the cup down on the table before speaking again. 'I needn't ask you where she's gone because you wouldn't know,' he said; 'but you'd be doing her a favour if you don't mention to Father her leaving the house at that time.'

'Well, it won't be necessary for me to mention her at all.'

'Oh, if you intend to stay here you'll be expected to answer all kinds of questions about everything and everyone. Particularly about the works. Has he started on that yet?'

'We talked a little about it this afternoon.'

She watched him close his eyes again, then run his fingers through his hair. It was sandy hair, of a wiry texture, the kind that wouldn't take kindly to grooming. It was shortish yet for the most part covered his ears. She thought his eyes could be hazel, with a fleck in them. When he opened them wide and stretched his facc as if to relax his muscles, she saw that they were grey.

'He's bent on my going into the business. He seems to forget that's what our disagreement was about in the first place . . . among other things, I suppose. But I've never felt cut out for that kind of business. Glen was his man. Glen was always his man, in all ways . . . Glen. Glen.'

When he shook his head slowly, she said, 'How did you find your brother?'

'It's hard to describe. It's hard to imagine someone as vital as him who seemed to be all brain, alert, on the spot – as Father used to say, on the spot all the time, that's Glen – and now like a child . . . well, a boy, a young boy.'

'Oh no!'

He nodded at her. 'Yes. Yes. They operated on him again on Wednesday, and they hope that this time it will quell the aggressiveness in him: they didn't call it the last vestige of real life. It's terrible to see him. He clung on to me just like a child . . . That's why I'm late.' He rose now and walked towards the fire, and leaning his forearm on the mantelpiece, he looked down into the fire as he said, 'I think they should have left him as he was.' He turned his head towards her. 'You see, neither can he remember anything of the accident, nor, if this operation should be what they call successful, will he ever recall Yvonne. After the first do he went berserk when some undamaged fragment of his mind touched on her. It was just as if he was experiencing the split second before the end, because he was screaming for her. I sometimes think it would have been better if his body had been paralysed and his mind had been left like Father's; he would eventually have been able to cope.' He turned his face towards the fire again, and his voice was low as he ended, 'Between them, I think I'll go round the bend myself before long.'

She broke the ensuing long silence by saying. 'Will . . . will he ever be able to come home?'

He sighed and turned his back to the fire, and looking down on her he nodded his head as he said, 'If Father got his way he'd be here tomorrow. I've tried to tell him that there's no Glen left. But he won't be convinced. He imagines time will bring him round to what he was, or a semblance of it. I sometimes feel like bawling at him, "What Glen was has been mashed to pulp. There's no Glen left." Oh – ' Again he strethced his face; then for the first time a slight smile came to his lips as he said, 'You've had it all day, and now you're getting it far into the night. Does it give you a picture of what you've let yourself in for?'

She smiled back at him as she answered quietly, 'Just about.' Then getting to her feet, she said. 'I'm here to help. And with regard to the work, I . . . I really think that if he could join in some way, be in touch with them at the works, it would help, take his mind off other things. The pity of it is, he's so handicapped: if he could only move his hands . . .'

'He could if he liked.'

Her face actually screwed up as she peered at him, and she repeated, 'He could if he liked? What do you mean?'

'Just what I say.'

'But he's totally paralysed, except for his head and the feeble use he has of his left arm.'

They were standing looking eye to eye now; they were, she noticed, of the same height, and his voice came flat and slow as he said, 'He's only really paralysed from the legs down. He'll never move those again. But he could have the use of the whole top part of his body, if he put his mind to it. He has what they call a lumbar fracture. This has caused paraplegia, true paraplegia. The rest of him is affected by hysterical paraplegia.'

'Hysterical paraplegia?' She mouthed the two words, and he nodded at her.

'When he was told this was the case he nearly gave himself a heart attack. His mind wasn't affected, he said; him to imagine he was paralysed when he wasn't. Well' – he nodded at her now – 'as long as he tells himself that he'll remain as he is. I've had two tries at getting through to him, but not again.'

She just checked herself from saying, 'He must be made not to try and move.' Yet for a man like that to be told that he was suffering from anything appertaining to hysteria would clamp down on any attempt at trying to move; should he succeed it would go to prove there was a weakness in him, a mental weakness. And she felt she understood him enough to know that he couldn't face up to that. His was an outsize ego; he was a big man in his own eyes; a car crash wasn't going to deprive him of that conception, not right away, at any rate.

'Dr Turner is bringing a specialist to see him next week. We'll have to take it from there. By the way – ' His voice softened a note as he now added, 'You look as tired as I feel. I'm sorry I've kept you up. Where have they put you?'

'In the room opposite.'

'Oh.' He pursed his lips and jerked his chin upwards as he said, 'That wasn't a good move. You'll be getting calls in the night, there's an intercom there. He's awake now in the early hours. I moved from there; I just had to. He's got to learn some kind of discipline and recognize that people can't be up all day on their feet and all night too.'

As she looked into the face before her she saw the lines of deep strain on it. He had, she surmised, been pressured almost beyond his strength these last months. Doubtless, his private life had been disrupted too; his present way of living wouldn't leave much time for his girl friend.

She wondered what type of girl he had chosen. She must have been sufficiently attractive to make him leave home, leave this house and what had, under his mother's control, been a life of easy going luxury. He wasn't an unattractive man, and in happier moments and his face without strain, she could imagine that he would appear quite good-looking in an austere kind of way. She said, 'Will you be waiting up for Lucy?'

'I certainly shall,' he answered.

'Good-night.'

'Good-night,' he said. No names were exchanged.

Before entering her own room she quietly opened the opposite door and through the dull pink glow from the bedside lamp she could see the head turned on the pillow; the eyes were closed, and from the look of him he could have been dead, all dead. Yet he was alive. She wouldn't have believed it.

Minutes later as she was undressing for bed, she visualized what he would be able to do with the use of his body: he could get about in a wheelchair; he could get into a car; he could go back to the office.

He could go back to the office.

2

'If he's able to walk about the hospital floor he's able to walk about this house.'

'John thinks . . .'

'Never mind what John thinks; I'm sick of listening to what John thinks. Jinny' – Bob lifted his hand slowly towards her – 'I want to see my lad. It's been months. They've had three goes at him. The way I see it, if he's not any better now he's never going to be any better. As John reports, he can walk and he can talk . . .'

'Yes, but it's how he can talk.' She was nodding towards him now. 'John's only trying to . . . well, to prevent you from being further hurt because . . .'

'Aye, go on.'

'Well, you'd better have it.' Her voice was cold. 'Only the truth will get through to you and it's this: you'll never see Glen again as he was. His mind has reverted . . . back, gone back . . .'

They stared at each other now for a while; then he said, 'Reverted to what? Gone back to what?'

'Well, from what I can gather, he's gone back to his childhood; he doesn't remember anything about the accident. Well, he did the once, and then he became aggressive.'

'Aggressive, you say? And now reverted to a lad?'

When he closed his eyes she said, softly, 'He's had no aggressive turns since the last operation, and they don't think they will recur.'

He was looking at her again. 'All right,' he said quietly, 'he's a lad once more; what's to stop him acting like a lad in his own home? And if he needs any looking after, there's Willie. Willie has a job to fill up his time with me. An' there's you: you have a job to fill your time with me; yet, if you would do what I ask you might be doing something towards earning your keep.'

'Oh, really!' For the first time since coming into the house she lost her temper with him; and she almost barked at him now, 'Let me tell you that just being with you is paying dearly for my keep, and I consider myself vastly underpaid. But I can alter that tomorrow. No, today, this very morning. There's another vacancy in Peter's office. Nell is begging me to go back there. She was only on about it on Friday when she was here . . .'

'Oh, to hell with Nell! And all the bloody lot of you, you especially.

If you don't know what I mean now when I open me mouth and let me frustration out you never will. Go on, get out!'

She turned from him and went quickly from the room, and she almost ran into John. Closing the door behind her, she stood looking at him in silence as she gnawed on her lip; and he, jerking his head towards the door, said quietly, 'He's hit you where it hurts at last, has he? You've amazed me you've stood it so long without retaliating.'

'I'm amazed myself.' Her voice certainly wasn't quiet as she went on, 'I think I'm mad. Yes, I am mad, because I seem to spend my left putting up with thankless people. Well I'm not too old to change that.' She almost thrust him aside, then marched across the landing and down the stairs. And John stood looking after her for a moment before opening the bedroom door and going in.

When he reached the side of the bed he stared at his father: 'You've done it this time, you know,' he said. 'The mood's she's in she could up and go.'

'Let her.'

'Let her, you say?' John's eyebrows moved upwards. 'You would know it if she did. Who do you think's been running this place? Not Lucy; I can tell you that. And Dorry and Cissie do what they're told. They always have done. As good as they are there's no initiative there. What was it all about anyway?'

'If you want to know, it was about you baulking me with regard to Glen.'

'Oh.' John turned from the bed, saying now, 'Well, I'll go tomorrow, and if the doctors say it's all right I'll bring him back with me.'

'You will?' Bob's voice was quiet now, and John, turning to him again, said tersely, 'Yes, I will. But I want you to prepare yourself, because your Glen is no more.' Leaning towards his father now and his voice dropping low, he said, 'He was your pride and joy, wasn't he . . . Glen? Wasn't he . . . Glen? There was nobody like Glen. He had it all up top, and in the right places. But now, Father, you've got to face the fact that Glen has nothing left up top, except memories of a young boy, about twelve I'd say. And why he's reverted to that age nobody can tell. But he talks of school and passing exams, and he writes poetry, little rhymes. Do you remember: Do you remember that stage? No, I don't suppose you do, because you would have thought it silly, so he wouldn't have told you that he went through the arty stage, as I did, only mine lasted much longer and it got your back up. He knew that, so that's why he didn't let you into that part of his life. But now, he'll present you with it from the minute he shambles in the door and you look on him.'

'There's a cruel streak in you, you know, John.'

'Well, I know where I get it from. It didn't come from my mother. Now I'll have to take meself and my cruel streak downstairs and see what I can do with Jinny, because, frankly, I've never seen her look like she did a minute ago. There's more to her than meets the eye, you know, Father.'

'You can't tell me anything about Jinny.'

'No?'

'No. She came on to my horizon with a chip on her shoulder as big as a plank, and she's spoken to me as nobody else has dared do. You can't tell me there's another side to Jinny.'

'Well, that being so, the other side is very much in evidence at the present time. The only thing I'm surprised about is she's lasted so long without rebelling.'

'You make me out to be a bloody tyrant. You always have done.'

'Well, to use an old phrase of yours, I speak as I find.' And on this he turned and walked from the room.

On the landing he stood looking down towards the carpet. How unfair life could be where love was concerned. For as long as he could remember he had longed for the love of that irascible man lying in that room. He could recall waiting for him to come home at nights just to see if for once he would look at him like he did at Glen. But he never did. If he put his hand on his shoulder he could rest assured that his other arm would be hugging Glen to him. And he himself had loved Glen too; and Glen had been understanding of the situation. There were times when they had talked, when his elder brother had tried to persuade him that their father was as fond of the one as of the other. Glen could see his need, his father never.

He found Jinny in the office. She was sitting behind the desk, sorting out some bills, and she didn't lift her head when he entered the room.

Pulling up a chair on the opposite side of the desk, he sat down, then said quietly, 'I'm the representative from the firm of Meek, Meek & Meek, ma'am; I'm their conciliatory agent. My client in question is in a poor state at the moment. Such is his unusual state of mind that he cursed only twice during a five minutes conversation.'

'Oh, shut up!' Jinny's lips moved one over the other in an effort not to smile. She clipped a number of bills together, pulled open a drawer in the desk, threw the bills in before pulling another small pile towards her.

'Jinny.' John's voice was without jest now. 'He's in a bit of a state, so I told him I'd bring Glen back tomorrow, that's if they'll allow it.'

She lifted her eyes to his as she asked, 'Does he know what to expect?'

'I've told him bluntly, but I didn't tell him that what he's feeling now will be nothing to what he'll go through after a couple of days of Glen. I've been with him for only a few hours at a time, and it's wearing. He chatters, never stops. It's so pitiable. You want to cry, and at the same time land out and box his ears as you would do a boy that kept rattling on senselessly. Yet, I shouldn't say senselessly because what he talks about makes sense to him and could have to any young boy in the late sixties. But then of course, he's not going to be the only one that's to be affected. There's you. It'll be Willie's job to look after him, and he's used to all kinds of cases, but you'll be in contact with him too for most of the day.'

He stopped speaking and looked at her, and she returned his glance but paused before saying, 'Well, as I said a little while ago, I can walk out, that's my position, but you, you can't, not any more. And if . . . Well, Glen has already got on your nerves after a couple of hours of him, what's going to happen when he's here twenty-four hours of the day?' She now leant her elbows on the desk and, joining her hands, lowered her chin on them as she now added, 'I was thinking the other day, there's no reason why with Willie and me being here, and Lucy, that you can't have a little private life, like you used to.'

His expression didn't alter. He rarely smiled, which she thought was a pity because he looked most attractive when he smiled. He was a sad person, was John, which his caustic tongue, very like his father's but without the colouring words, did not hide. Over the past months she had come to know him fairly well, and she knew that the more she saw of him the more she liked him, because in a way she recognized something in him that she identified with. It was a sense of loneliness. Undoubtedly, the reasons for such a feeling were difficult for each of them, but it was there.

Her own expression altered to one of mild surprise as he, as if imitating her stance, put his elbows on the table and rested his head on his hands and drooped it slightly to the side before saying, 'Are you suggesting that I should be happier if I spent my nights in sin?'

She let out a long breath, pursed her lips, then said, 'Yes, I suppose I am. Yes, I suppose that is just what I am advocating that you should do. You have a flat, and you have a girl friend . . .'

'What makes you think I have a flat and a girl friend?'

'Well, haven't you? You had. You left home to pursue this course, so I understand.'

'That was not the sole reason I left home, there were many, and the main one is lying upstairs. But to return to the girl friend and the flat. What makes you assume that I have a girl friend at the flat?'

She shook her elbows from the table and rested her hand on the blotter, and her lips parted, then closed and parted again before she said, 'Well, I just . . . assumed, as you say, that . . . that when you went out . . . Oh, what does it matter?'

She tossed her head.

'It matters. *It matters* to me, *Miss Brownlow*, what you think, for, in a way, I have to live with you. Just in a way, of course.' His face stretched now, and he nipped at his lower lip, his expression indicating laughter. But she didn't respond, she didn't feel like laughing. There was still some annoyance left in her, and she was tired. For the first time she had admitted to herself, what Nell had for some time been stressing on her weekly Sunday visits, she was tired, deeply tired, and it was showing.

As if he was picking up her thoughts, he said, 'I'm sorry. It's the wrong time for the funnies. You are tired, and no wonder. And thank you for your concern. I mean, for me and my . . . private life. But I can tell you now that I haven't a flat, and I haven't a girl friend. And what is more, I hadn't had a flat and I hadn't had a girl friend for a long time before my New Year visit.'

As her eyes widened he nodded at her and said, 'I was in digs with a Mrs Burrows in Bog's End; in fact that's where my flat was; I couldn't afford this end of the town.' A small grin spread over his face; then he went on, 'I must tell you this, Jinny, and please don't be annoyed, but Mrs Burrows had a daughter who was a hairdresser.' As he watched the colour flood over her face he said, quickly, 'Now I asked you not to be annoyed. Betty, that's the daugher, came back one night and told us what had happened. Her employer, Mrs Smith, apparently knew all about you, even if you didn't know about her. She knew you had worked at Henderson and Garbrook. Your dear friend, Mr Campbell, had put her in the picture, just to allay her jealousy I suppose. Well, whatever it was, I put two and two together. And as you might have gathered, I don't laugh much – well, there's nothing much to laugh at in this life – but I laughed until I cried. What with you having a bash at Miss Cadwell, then going for that swine of a pervert and this trollop, well, I thought: Never believe your eyes, John; there goes a fighter.'

'Oh, be quiet!' She got up and walked towards the window, one cheek of her face cupped in the palm of her hand. And now on the verge of tears, she said, 'I'm no fighter. I . . . I never want to fight, or argue, or . . . But well, I'd had so much of it, I could stand no more. And the circumstances were such . . .'

'Jinny – ' His arm was around her shoulders, and he turned her about to face him, saying, 'Don't apologize for being a fighter. Be glad you are. You should offer up a prayer that there's some part of you that resists. If I could only do that, strike out physically. But what did I do? I turned and ran; like a hotheaded teenager I ran away from home. And what did I do next? Being spiteful, I did what I knew would hurt him most, I shacked up with a girl instead of in the first place standing up to him and telling him what I thought, what I felt. And now here I am, still without the courage to tell him what I feel, because now it's too late. He would think it pity or at best compassion; he would never take it as love.'

She had the urge to let the tears flow, not for herself now but for him; she had the urge to put out her arms and hold him, as she sometimes held his father, yet differently. Oh, yes, differently. She drew back from him. 'It's never too late to tell someone of that kind of love,' she said.

'Just that kind of love?'

She was walking from him now towards the desk, and she turned and said, 'Yes, just that kind of love. The other kind just asks for trouble.'

'You seem to have made up your mind firmly on that score.'

'I have. Oh yes, I have.' She was now seated behind the desk, and he stood looking down on her bent head for some seconds before he said, quietly, 'Well, I'd better be off now. I'm to go to the factory once again and get a report from Waitland. It'll be the same as before, and Father knows it. They're telling him nothing.'

'I can tell you one thing. Those reports are faked; they make no mention of the order we were negotiating in January . . . Perhaps they've lost it. I shouldn't be a bit surprised. Then there was the business in Hamburg. No mention of that either. It did mention a new contract in Belgium, but that's all; just a contract with a firm. And he's worried about the looks of things in the steel industry. There could be trouble there. They're closing down right, left and centre.'

'Well, there's nothing we can do about that; I feel just like an errand boy.'

'There *is* something that could be done.'

'What?' He had turned from the desk but was looking at her once more, and she answered, 'Well, you could get information on how things are really going from someone in the offices, or from a worker on the floor. You could walk round and have a word with them, and ask them to come up and see your father.'

He shook his head slowly as he said, 'Espionage.'

'Yes, if you like to call it that.' Her voice was flat. 'There's Mr Meane. He's in the drawing-office. And also the head clerk, Mr Bury. They're friends, Mr Meane and him. They would know how the land lay, at least contract-wise, I should think. Then there's the shop floor.' She smiled now. 'Jack Newland and Peter Trowell; and there's a Jimmy Moford. They are the spokesmen down there. Always looking for trouble, but any one of them would know the temper of the floor and what's going on. You could have a natter with them and say your father would like to see them. Yes, that's an idea. Any one of them. Oh, particularly Jack Newland would feel he was getting somewhere if he came here. And you'd get more out of them than you'll ever get out of Mr Waitland or Mr Garbrook, or Pillon . . . Arthur Pillon, who dubs himself assistant works manager.' She grinned now. 'He runs with the hare and hunts with the hounds, and he'll likely tag on to you if he sees you around the shops. Get rid of him if you can.'

He was looking at her now and was actually smiling broadly as he said, 'There's more than even two sides to you, Jinny, I think. You should be in the diplomatic service. I can understand that it wasn't only your backchat that made you a necessity to Father.'

'Your father would never be so stupid as to pay anyone for backchat. He just had to go down to the floor to get plenty of that. I was his secretary, and an efficient one.'

'Huh! You should add, although I say it myself.'

'I have no need to; I know my own value, what there is of it.'

'Well, as a secretary, you're rotting away here, aren't you?'

She sighed now as she said, 'It looks like it. But things never stay still for long. Who knows but I'll be back in harness some day soon.'

The smile left his face. 'Don't say that,' he said flatly; 'you're needed here, not only by him.' And he held her gaze for a moment before turning abruptly and marching from the room.

She stared for some time towards the door before rising and going to the window; and then she stood looking out on to the side garden where the roses were blooming in profusion. Then like a shot ringing down from the mountain top, there passed through her head the words, 'No! No! Not again.'

If she was to be a handmaiden she would be paid for it as she was in this house. But then she'd be handmaiden again to no man, unless . . . unless? What was she thinking about? Now don't let her start kidding herself; there would be no wedding bells connected with John Henderson, for in conversations they'd had over the past months he had firmly expressed his antipathy to marriage. He had made no bones about it, which was why she had thought he still had his flat and was seeing his girl friend occasionally.

He had said she was needed by more than one. Well, his need was going to bring him cold comfort for she had played ministering angel for the last time. By God! yes, she had.

She too now marched from the room, and as if she were closing the door on an opponent she banged it behind her.

3

It was around two o'clock in the morning when the intercom bell dragged her from deep sleep. And groping, she put her hand out and said, 'Yes?'

'Jinny.'

'Yes?' She hitched herself up in the bed, then endeavoured to rub the sleep from her eyes.

'I'm . . . I'm sorry to disturb you, I just wanted a word. Don't bother getting up. I'm . . . I'm just . . . well, het up a bit. It's because of the morrow. You see, I've been thinking of what our John said, and I wonder if I'm doing right. Yet I've got to see him. I've got an awful feeling on me that if I don't see him soon I won't see him at all. Oh, I'm sorry if I woke you, Jinny.'

She had thrown the bedclothes back and was sitting on the side of the bed now and she bent over and called into the phone, 'I'll be with you in a minute.'

'Oh no, I don't want you . . .' she put the receiver down, then pressed her eyeballs with her fingers and thumbs, and let out a long slow breath before getting up and taking her dressing-gown from the back of the chair.

When she opened his door she saw his head raised from the pillow, and he said in a whisper, 'I . . . I didn't want to disturb you. You shouldn't have come. I just wanted a word.'

'It's all right. It's all right.' She pulled a chair towards the bed and, reaching out, she took his hand, and as she did so he muttered, 'Oh, Jinny. Jinny. And there's another thing: I want to say I'm sorry for yesterday. I wouldn't have blamed you if you had walked out; but God, I don't know what I would have done without you.'

'Now don't try to soft soap me, not at this hour in the morning. I'm liable to melt and succumb to your advances.'

'Oh, Jinny.' There was a wavering laugh in his voice; and as he bit on his lip, whether to stem his laughter or tears she didn't know, she added, 'And as Nell would say, that'll get you into the *Gazette*.

'The *Gazette*'

It was a question and she said, 'Yes, you know the *Gazette*, the *Shields Daily Gazette*.'

'Oh aye, the newspaper. I must be going dim . . . No, no, I'm not. You know that's something, Jinny' – he turned his head towards her now – 'the times I've wished it was my head that had got it, and Glen his body, because I've lived most of my life but his was only beginning, and if he had his mind it wouldn't have mattered so much about his body, not now he's lost Yvonne.'

'Well, it didn't turn out like that, and so you have to accept things as they are. But I must say this, I feel as John does, if you were to make an effort . . .'

'No, lass, no. What's the point? Don't start on that tack again, not the night, or the morning, whatever time it is. By!' – he smiled at her now – 'you look bonny in this light.'

'Thank you very much.' She had assumed a hurt tone. 'That means to say that the pink shade is very kind to me. What a pity it's got to be daylight.'

'Eeh, by! your tongue. I've never known another like it. Oh yes, I have.' He moved his head slowly. 'Alicia could come back like lightning an' all, but in a different way. She wasn't a Geordie, you see.'

'I'm not a Geordie either.'

'Oh yes, you are.'

'Oh no, I'm not. I don't talk the twang; I speak as I write, plain English.'

'Eeh my! Proud of it, aren't you? Well, don't let any Geordie hear you bragging like that else your number'll be up.'

A silence ensued until he said, 'I'm all right now, lass. I think I might get off.'

'Well, go on then.'

'You go on back to bed. And thanks.'

'I'll stay here for a while. I can put my feet up on this other chair. And here's a rug. I'll stay until you do go off, so be quick about it.'

As she settled herself he turned his face towards her, saying softly now, 'I've wondered lately if you get any satisfaction out of playing the ministering angel, you certainly can't get any pleasure.'

She did not look at him, but pulled the rug up under her chin as she said, 'I'm no ministering angel; I'm what you call a cultured handmaiden.'

'A what?'

'You heard, a cultured handmaiden.'

'Where did you get that from? Who called you that?'

'Oh, it's a long story. I'll tell you some day, or some night when you can't get to sleep. But not tonight. Go on, I'm tired. Good-night.'

'Good-night, Jinny. And . . . God bless you.' The words were faint but audible to her.

She closed her eyes thinking of the form in which God's blessing fell on cultured handmaidens. Down the ages they had been given different names: dutiful daughters, mother's help, lady companions, all cultured handmaidens.

She woke with a crick in her neck and Willie bending over her, saying, 'Here, drink this.'

Slowly, she pulled herself up in the chair and, blinking, she took the cup from him; and she watched him turn and look towards the bed where Bob was still sleeping soundly. And when he put his head down to her and said, 'You're a fool, you know; he'll keep you at this,' she asked, 'What time is it?'

'Just seven o'clock. Get yourself up and go to bed for a few hours. And I'm telling you' – his voice was lower still – 'he'll play on you. I've had experience. Even the best of them, like him, they suck you dry. You haven't got to let it happen. Come on, get yourself up.'

His large thick hands came out now and hoisted her to her feet as she muttered, 'Look! You'll spill the tea.'

'Better if you don't drink it. Go on. Get some kip.'

She liked Willie. He was a practical man, down to earth, and he was kind and attentive to his patient, yet although she was aware that he was talking sense she knew that if Bob wanted her company in the middle of the night she'd be hard put not to answer his call . . .

She went to bed and slept till nine o'clock. Then after having a bath she picked up the morning routine. It was broken about eleven o'clock by a phone call from Mrs Florence Brook, and as usual, when it was Jinny's voice which came over to her, Florence's reply was a very telling 'Oh,' which could be interpreted as, 'You're still there then?'

'How's Father?'

'He is about the same.'

'I would like to speak to John.'

'I'm afraid he's in . . . at the hospital. He's bringing Glen home today.'

'What!'

'I said he was bringing Glen home.'

'And who's idea was that?'

'Apparently your father's. He wants to see him.'

'My God! Do you know what our Glen is like now?'

'No, I'm afraid I don't.'

'John said he would never allow him to come back.'

There was a pause before Jinny replied, 'Your father is still head of the house.'

'I'm well aware of that, madam! . . . miss.'

'I was only meaning to infer . . .'

'I know what you were meaning to infer. Has he got the male nurse still there?'

'Yes, Willie is still here.'

'Then may I ask what your duties are?'

'My duties, Mrs Brook, are exactly what yours would be if you were running this household.'

There was a telling silence on the phone now; then Florence's voice came, the words stubbing over the wires, 'You've taken too much on yourself. Do you know that? You were a secretary, and there's no secretarial work to be done now. As for running the house, Dorry can see to that. She and Cissie have done so for years . . . And you're forgetting that Lucy's there; she's quite capable of running the house.'

'I don't think your mother would have agreed with you.'

'*My* . . .'

At this point the phone went dead, and Jinny, putting it back on its rest, stood for a moment with her head bent and her teeth nipping at her lower lip. It was certainly a good job that Mr Henderson had no room for his son-in-law in any capacity or her own life here would have been made impossible. As for Lucy being able to run the house, Lucy was hardly ever in it, but when she was she made a point of spending most of the time with her father. It was a diplomatic cover, for then he rarely asked questions about what she did with the rest of her time.

A short while later, standing by Bob's bed, she said, 'Mrs Brook phoned.'

'Aye. And what had she to say?'

'She wanted to know how you were and to speak to John.'

'And you told her where John was?'

'Yes.'

'And what he was doing?'

'Yes.'

'And what was her reaction?'

'Not favourable.'

'Well, that's nothing new. I've never known our Florence to be in favour of anything except what pleased herself. She was the odd man out to me, always was, our Florrie. I don't know who she took after. Certainly not Alicia. And I can't see anything of her in me . . . Can you?'

She paused a moment before nodding her head and saying, 'A little: if she can't get her own way she plays up.'

'Well, I'll be damned. You know, at times you're no comfort at all. Anyway, did she play up this morning?'

'A little.'

'What about?'

'She thought my presence here was unnecessary.'

'Begod! she did. And of course, you took that meekly.'

'No, I didn't.'

'No, I thought you wouldn't. I should like to have heard you . . . What time is it now?' He turned his head towards the clock.

'Gone twelve.'

'They should be here soon.'

'Yes, they should.'

'Jinny.'

'Yes?'

'I'm all het up inside.'

'Well, all I can say is you asked for it.' But as she spoke she lifted his hand and squeezed it gently as she went on, 'Just remember you're not going to see the old Glen, so you'll have to brace yourself.'

'Aye. Aye, but I'm always havin' to brace meself. Just to go on breathing I'm havin' to brace meself.'

She could find no words with which to answer him for a moment; then she said. 'We all seem to be looking on the black side. Let's wait until we see him. And then we might be agreeably surprised, eh?'

'The answer to that, lass, is we can't do anything else. But as for being agreeably surprised . . . Oh dear! Oh dear!' He moved his head slowly on the pillow, and she let his hand drop and went out of the room.

It was a quarter to one when John and Glen arrived. When Jinny looked at the man standing just inside the front door she wanted to put her hand over her mouth and press an agonized sound back into her being because this was Glen, his body, his face, everything about him was Glen Henderson, everything, that is, except the eyes. And it was the eyes that made the difference to the man. They were bright, yet vacant; and their glance was darting here and there as if in search of something while his head remained still. And when they came to rest on her, he opened his mouth and spoke. And what he said was, 'I'll not sit again; I didn't pass.'

'Do you remember Jinny?' John spoke quietly.

'Yes; of course I remember Jinny. What's the matter with you? Of course I remember Jinny.' There was laughter in the tone. 'I'm hungry. I want my tea . . . What about the bike?'

'We'll see about that later.'

'But he's had it for about a week now. Anyway, I should have a new one.' His eyes stopped flickering; and his gaze coming to rest steadily on Jinny, and his tone changing, he said quietly, 'Could I have a drink, nurse?'

She swallowed deeply before saying, 'Yes, yes, of course. Come along.' And she put out her hand and touched his arm, and as she guided him into the drawing-room she said, 'What would you like, a cold drink or tea?'

'Orange squash.'

In the drawing-room the man now stood looking about him. His eyelids blinked and at one point they screwed up so tightly that there seemed to be nothing left but the sockets, and when he opened them again he turned his head slowly as if he were trying to recall something. Quietly he sat down on the couch, his hands resting on his knees, very like a young boy who was visiting and on his best behaviour.

When Dorry brought him a glass of orange juice, she bent towards him and said, 'Hello, Mr Glen.'

'Hello,' he replied politely.

'You remember Dorry?' John's voice was quiet and persuasive. But his brother turned on him almost angrily, saying, 'Of course, I remember Dorry. What d'you keep on for?' Then looking at Jinny, he said, 'And Nurse Jinny. And Nurse Pratt. And Piggy Eyes.'

'Piggy Eyes.'

John bent his head towards him, and Glen nodded at him, saying,

'She's on duty at night. We call her Piggy Eyes because she screws up her face when she looks at us.' He now smiled widely and spread his gaze from one to the other. And Jinny again wanted to press the pain down but this time to stop the moan that could have preceded a bout of weeping.

John was right. This boy . . . this man should never have been brought home. If he'd had a mother to see him, then that might have been different. But he had only a father lying upstairs who was expecting to see his son, different but not so different. Oh no, not this different. Well, there was one thing sure, this house would never be the same again. Here was a handful, and it was going to take, not only John's and Willie's whole time, but also her own in a way, for already he had selected her as a nurse.

It was fifteen minutes later when they took him upstairs. John went in first, his hand behind him drawing Glen forward, and she followed. She had not wanted to be present at this meeting, but Glen had insisted, saying, 'Nurse always comes with me.'

Willie was standing by the head of the bed, and he moved aside, and Bob looked at his elder son. And his elder son looked on him. And neither of them spoke. It was John whose voice came out as a croak, saying, 'We had a good journey, Father. Glen . . . Glen enjoyed it.'

'You got a cold?'

Jinny was gripping the front of her dress as she looked at Bob and waited for the answer to his son's question. The pain seemed to be rising like sweat from his face. It was red. His lips were tight together, while his eyes were wide. The question gave no clue to whether Glen recognized the man lying there as his father, and it was John again who spoke to him, saying, 'Your . . . your father hasn't been well.'

Now Glen did turn a mildly enquiring look on John. It was as if the word had penetrated through some thick mist in his mind. But he didn't repeat it or ask for an explanation, he just turned his gaze once more on Bob. Then for the second time since coming into the house he said, 'I'm hungry.'

'In that case we shall have to find you something to eat, won't we?' With practised ease Willie had taken the situation in hand; and coming to Glen's side, he said, 'Come on downstairs and tell me what you like best. Come on.'

Glen turned immediately from the bed, saying, 'Not fish and chips. And not sausages; I like meat.'

'Steak or roast meat?'

'Oh either.' He laughed now, and the sound was more strange because it was a man's laugh; the only thing that was recognizable about him to his father and his brother was his laugh.

Like bosom friends they went from the room, Willie with his arm around Glen's shoulder. And when the door closed on them Bob's mouth went into a large gasp. His limp hand fluttered over the eiderdown, and John, looking down on him, muttered, 'I warned you.'

'God damn you, yes you warned me. All right. All right. But he's your brother, and this is his home.'

'Well, Father, you reminding me that he is my brother, let me remind you that he is your son. But you won't have the job of looking after him. He's got to be watched; he wanders. I might as well tell you they weren't for letting him come home. And it's only for a trial period.'

'Trial period, be damned! You'd have him put away, locked up some place?'

'It isn't like that, he's not locked up in some place. It's a hospital, where he's given excellent care. And strangely, he was happy there. Don't you understand? He's lost years; he's back in his boyhood. And not only that: it isn't the boyhood that you and I remember; apparently it's only a boyhood which he alone was cognizant of, a kind of subconscious place. We all have it. From what the doctor says he goes in and out of this place. And it's just as well that he doesn't now remember exactly what happened. Like he did after the first operation. Willie's going to have more than his hands full.'

'Then we'll get somebody to help him.'

'But what about Jinny here? John now threw out his arm towards where she was standing silently at the foot of the bed. 'He's taken her for a nurse. There were two nurses on the ward at times, and he used to follow them about.'

'Well, she's got nothing else to do but to see to him.'

When Bob turned his eyes on her and waited for her reply, she answered, 'Yes, I could see to the boy in him, but not to the man. And what would happen if his mind should leave the boy and return to the man?'

'My God! What am I surrounded with? Bloody psychiatrists? If only I could use my . . .'

'If only you could use your common sense, which you would have us believe you've still got plenty of, you could, even at this point, possibly solve the problem.'

As she marched from the room, leaving John and his father staring at her, she paused for a moment outside her own door before going in. Once inside, she stood and pushed her hand up through her hair. What had made her say that? Only seconds before she was hoping that John would go gently with him, yet she knew what she had said was right. That man who had been Glen, the jolly go-ahead Glen, and who had now turned into an overgrown, great outsized boy, filled her with a dread that touched on real fear, at the same time arousing her deepest pity.

Going to the window, she sat down on the chair, and for the first time she thought, I wish I was far away from here. Somehow things had become complicated.

She could pack up this minute and go to Nell's. There was nothing to stop her . . . Nothing to stop her? Only him lying across there, with his tongue so alive it could whip pieces out of you, while at the same time his eyes were telling you he was so lost that if you let go of his hand he would sink.

'Huh!' she said to herself as her mind touched on Nell again. Nell had never been happy about her being here, but on the sight of Glen, without even hearing him speak, she would likely say, 'Come on, get yourself out of here, lass, afore something happens. Paralysed men are one thing, but mad'uns are another.' And that was the name she would put to Glen. That was the name anybody would put to Glen.

4

'I'm hungry.'

'But you've just had your lunch, Glen.'

'No; my tea.'

'No; your lunch. Tea won't be ready for . . . well, three hours.'

'I'm hungry.'

'There are some sweets in your room; go and get them.'

'Will you play cards?'

'I can't play just now; I'm busy writing letters. See . . . I'm at my typewriter.'

'I can write letters; I write poetry.'

'Do you?'

'Yes, I do.'

'You'll have to show me some.'

'No, I won't do that. I never show anybody.'

She looked up at the man standing to the side of her and she told herself yet again, as she had done over the past two weeks, not to feel repulsed by him; he couldn't help his state, he was still Glen. Yet he wasn't Glen, he was a weird . . . man-cum-boy, and it wasn't only she who found she couldn't bear his presence for long. The pity of it was, the very sight of him agonized his father. Bob knew that he had made a mistake in bringing his son home, but being the man he was he wouldn't own up to the mistake.

'I'm going out on my bike.'

'Very well.' She nodded at him. He was always going out on his bike. But strangely he never made any attempt to go out through the front door, not even into the garden unless someone was with him. And what was more strange, yet on thinking back to the source of his troubles perhaps not so strange, he was showing evidence of being afraid of the car. When John offered yesterday to take him for a ride he had turned from him, and in a kind of shambling run had made for the kitchen. And when John followed him he stood by the kitchen table and picked up a wooden spoon and started to beat a tattoo on the side of an earthenware bowl which Cissie had just half filled with flour. And then he had smacked the wooden spoon into the middle of the flour, sending a spray over the table and partly over himself and John. At this, John had become angry and said, 'Enough of that now!' and had led him protesting from the room.

She often thought that were Glen to become aggressive John would have little chance against him, because he was at least three stones heavier and inches taller.

John and Willie had worked out a system whereby they relieved each other in looking after Glen, and although the strain wasn't as yet showing on Willie, it certainly was on John, and he had said to her only last night, 'I don't know how much longer I can stick this. He shouldn't be here, he should be back in hospital.'

John had told her at the beginning that he didn't want her involved with Glen in any way. But he hadn't taken Glen into account. Glen had seen to it that she was involved because whenever possible he followed her about, and over the last three days had formed a new pattern. Whenever he could he would now take hold of her arm and say 'You coming for a walk, Jin?' or 'I'm hungry,' or 'Play cards, nurse.'

At the present moment, she didn't want to rise from the chair because she knew he would again take hold of her arm; but nevertheless, she wanted him out of the room.

She was about to reach for the intercom button that would put her through to John's room, even though she knew he was off duty so to speak, when Glen spoke. And for a moment there was no trace of the boy in his voice. 'You ringing for Willie?' he said.

'No. No.'

'You are.'

'No, I wasn't. Not for Willie.'

'Oh.'

Her finger was wavering over the button when the door opened and Willie himself appeared; and he said, 'Oh, there you are, then,' Glen looked down on Jinny and said angrily now, 'Knew you were ringing for Willie. Knew you were.'

'I didn't ring, Glen. Look, I haven't pressed the button. I didn't ring for you, Willie, did I?'

'No, no; I just happened to pop in. You coming for a walk?'

'No.'

'Aw, come on. I'm dying for a breath of fresh air, man. And I've got a couple of Mars bars in me pocket.'

The expression on Glen's face altered, and without further ado he walked towards the door, and Willie nodded towards Jinny and raised his eyebrows before closing the door behind him.

She sat back in the chair and let out a long slow breath. It was no use; she'd just have to speak to Bob. She gathered up the letters from the desk, and then went upstairs to Bob's room.

When she had first seen Bob lying in his bed she had thought that he could never look worse except if he were to die. But over the past weeks she had seen that he could look worse and still live. His features were drawn, his cheeks hollow and there was no longer any disgruntled remark from him; he seemed to have given up the battle.

She stood by the bed, saying now, 'I've done these letters, a personal one to Bill Meane and another to Mr Bury. I've just said you would like to see them. Shall I read them?'

'There's no point.'

She made no comment, but said, 'John of course told you he'd had a few words with Jack Newland and Peter Trowell from the shop floor, and indicated that you'd be pleased to see them to have a natter sometime.'

'A lot of damn good that'll do, won't it?'

'Well, we'll only have to wait and see, won't we?'

He turned his head and looked at her; but he did not speak. And she said, 'I've got to bring this up, whether you are vexed or pleased. It's Glen.'

'What about him?'

'I'm . . . well, to tell you the truth, I'm slightly afraid of him.'

'What have you got to be afraid of? He's turned into a lad, the man's gone, so what have you got to be afraid of?'

'I don't really know, but the only thing I do know is that I am afraid. His manner is changing; he follows me around.'

'Is that so terrible.'

'Yes, it is to me.' Her voice had risen. 'And I've got to tell you, I . . . I can't stand it. This is the third week, and it's getting on my nerves. John and Willie do their best.'

'That's what they're paid for, both of them.'

'You can never pay John for what he's doing, so don't say a thing like that.'

'Oh, you're on his side now. I didn't think you two hit if off.'

'It isn't a case of hitting it off, it's a case of giving credit where it's due. And if you want to know anything, I think he's had about as much as he can stand too.'

'So what's the answer.'

'It's . . . it's up to you; Glen should go back to hospital.'

'Be damned if he will! This is his home; I'm his father; if I don't have him who will? You're telling me he should end his days in a loony house. Well now, miss, if you can't put up with him there's always a way out.'

She stared down at him, and he turned her stare while his lips moved one over the other as if he was sucking something from them.

Slowly she said, 'Yes, there's always a way out, and I shall take it tomorrow.' And on this she turned from him. And his voice didn't stop her as it once would have done when it came to her, saying, 'Jinny! Jinny.'

The tears almost spurted from her eyes as she closed the door behind her, and when through the mist she saw John approaching from the end of the corridor, she ran the few steps across the landing and into her own room. But she had no sooner closed the door than it was opened again, and John, going to her and taking her by the shoulders, looked down on her bent head as he asked, 'What is it? What's happened?'

She was unable to speak because her throat was blocked, and he said urgently, 'Jinny! Jinny! What is it? Tell me. What has he said to you?'

She was going to choke; she let out a long shuddering sob, and when he put his arms about her and held her close her body shook them both with the force of her weeping.

It was a good minute later when she pulled herself from his embrace and searched blindly around for something on which to dry her face. When he brought his handkerchief out and wiped her cheeks with it, she took it from him and, turning away, went and sat down in a chair by the side of the bed. And he followed her. Sitting on the edge of the bed, he leaned towards her, saying, 'What happened? Tell me. Was it about Glen?'

She nodded. Then between gasps, she said, 'I'm . . . I'm afraid of him. He's . . . he's always wanting to – ' She could hardly bring herself to say the words, 'touch me. And I said to your father that I can't stand it any longer and that he should be sent back to hospital. And' – she gulped deep in her throat – 'he told me, if I couldn't put up with it the door was open. And so . . . and so, I told him I'm going tomorrow.'

'By God! you're not.'

She lifted her head and her eyes blinked rapidly and her mouth opened and shut a number of times before she was able to say, 'Yes, I . . . I am. I . . . I feel . . . I fear something could happen. I don't know what, but, John, I can't help it. I'm afraid of him. And Lucy is too. She told me so. That's why she's gone to stay with Monica.'

'He'll go back to hospital; I'll see to that.'

'Please! No!' She put her hand out and laid it on his. 'No. Your father wants him here. As he said, he couldn't bear to think of him . . . well, in a sort of asylum.'

'That's where he will have to go in the end; and Father's got to face up to it. It's terrible, I know. Not for Glen. Oh no, not for Glen, because he's gone back to a place in his mind where nothing can touch him, only his physical needs, such as food. He's put on nearly a stone since he came home. I've told Dorry and Cissie not to give him anything to eat between meals, but as they say, what can they do when he just goes to the fridge and takes it. Look, Jinny.'

He now put one hand on her shoulder and the other under her chin and lifted her face up as he said softly, 'Let me try with Father. Give it a day or two, and I'll see that Glen doesn't come near you; I'll tell Willie not to let him out of his sight. But you must know this: you must know it in your own mind that whatever Father says he's going to miss you like mad if you go; in fact, I don't know what he'll do without you. You know' – he smiled at her now, one of his rare smiles – 'it's odd, if I hadn't known he was so devoted to Mother I would have imagined he was having an affair with you. Oh . . . oh, don't look like that. It would have been the most natural thing in the world . . . if you had been willing. And now I don't know how he looks upon you; not as a daughter, he's got four of them, and they do nothing for him mentally; in fact, Florence irritates him to the point of fury at times; and one couldn't classify you in the role of mother figure, could one?'

She didn't give him an answer to this, but what she said was, 'Some one once said of me that I acted like a cultured handmaiden, and, looking back over the last eighteen months, I . . . I can see that I have fitted that role, with emphasis on the handmaiden.'

'Cultured handmaiden? Who on earth said that to you? That's the last category I'd put you in, because a handmaiden implies submissiveness, and no one could say that Miss Jinny Brownlow was of the submissive type. Now could they?'

'It's all how the other person views you. As for how your father sees me; I was a good secretary; I can't lay claim to any other ability; and why he liked me around was because I wasn't afraid of his caustic tongue and rough manner. I thnk he still views me as part of the fitments of the office and his last contact with the works. I can still talk business with him, at least I could up to . . . well, up to Glen's arrival. But since then he seems to have lost interest. I'm sorry' – she shook her head – 'but even if you can control Glen's movements, which I'm afraid you're going to find difficult because if he decides to use force I don't think even Willie could handle him. Anyway, the way things are . . . have turned out, it's better that I go, because . . .'

'Jinny. Jinny' – he hitched himself closer to her – 'I . . . I find it difficult to ask favours of anyone, but I'm going to ask this of you now: hang on till the end of the week. If you still feel the same then, all right, leave on Saturday with your cousin. But give me a few days. And it isn't only because . . . well – ' He turned his head to the side and brought his teeth together before adding, 'We . . . we didn't hit it off at first, did we? But that was my fault. I . . . I might as well tell you, I too would miss you if you left.' Again he turned his head away from her as he said, 'A house isn't a house without a woman in it.'

'Oh, if that's all that a house needs, then you can bring Lucy back.'

'Oh, I didn't mean it like that. Why do you always take me up wrong? As for Lucy, I'm afraid Lucy's not coming back. I was on to Monica last night and by what she says Reg Talbot's been over there and it wouldn't surprise me if they get married on the quiet and she goes off with him. In fact, she's so besotted with him, Monica says she wouldn't be surprised if she side-stepped the ceremony. But that wouldn't make anyone faint, not these days, would it?' There was a slight upward twist to the corner of his mouth now.

And she answered stiffly, 'No; it wouldn't. Yet, I suppose there are still a few that would like a ceremony to authorize the union.'

'Oh, good Lord!' He hitched himself away from her now, and, his chin dropping almost to his chest, laughed as he said, 'You're amazing. You know that, Jinny? You're amazing. That sounded like a piece out of a Victorian novel.' Now his head was lifted, and the smile had gone from his face as he asked her, 'Do you think that a piece of paper and a few words said over you by a man makes all that difference to the act? That it solemnizes it, blesses it, whether you enjoy it or not? And if you don't enjoy it, because of that piece of paper you've got to stick it out for life, submit for life, as women had to do at one time. But now they're doing without the paper, and if they don't like it, or if he doesn't, one or other can get up and leave. Isn't that a cleaner way?'

She was on her feet now looking down at him; her face was set and her lips scarcely moved as she said, 'Your purpose in following me in here was to find out why I was upset. Well, now you know; but I cannot see the connection between that purpose and the topic you have just raised. And I don't wish to carry on with the discussion.'

He rose from the bed and his face was as stiff as hers and his voice was almost a growl as he said, 'You know what you're made of, Miss Brownlow? You're made of the material from which they used to cut out spinsters. It's written on your face, it's in the way you walk, it's in your defensive repartee; all of it real material of a frustrated woman.'

He had reached the door before she turned and cried after him, 'Well, this spinster is leaving in the morning; or perhaps tonight.'

The handle of the open door still in his hand, he turned and said, 'Good. Good,' then banged the door closed.

* * *

She had got her suitcases from the store room and packed her belongings before she took up the phone to contact Nell. When there was no reply to her ring, she stood nipping on her thumb nail before replacing the receiver. It was Tuesday, and Tuesday was the ritual tea with Mrs Collins . . . Mamie, Nell's lifelong friend. And on a Tuesday Peter usually stayed late at the office; that's if he hadn't a meeting of the Rotarians or the Masons, or some such. If she'd had a key to the house she would have ordered a taxi here and now. They had given her one before the end of the first week there, but when she came here she naturally left it behind, thinking she would never need it again.

Odd that . . . Odd. Why should she have imagined she was here for life? And what kind of a life had it represented to her other than doing a few letters and keeping a paralysed man amused by answering him back in his own vein, a vein that very often had irritated her because you could get too much of anything, good, bad, or indifferent? And familiarity, although it did not breed contempt in this case, had often bred weariness.

It had been different when they were in the office together: backchat often stemmed from a focal point, maybe comments upon letters, reactions to visits from the shop floor, irritations stemming from his partner's ideas, or the power fight that went on in the three offices along the top corridor, but in the main from Mr Waitland's office.

She would have to stay until tomorrow morning, but she was determined not to leave this room till then. It wouldn't hurt her to go without a meal for the next few hours; as for a drink, she always kept some bottles of orange juice in the bathroom cupboard. That would suffice.

She went to the window and stood looking out on the sprawling town down below, with Bog's End and the Mill Bank standing out clearly in the afternoon sunshine . . . The bus had gone along the Mill Bank that day she had . . .

Her mind shrank from the scene she had witnessed in the room behind the hairdresser's shop, yet it followed the road leading out of the town and to Hal's house.

Her thoughts now scampered away, and she started when a knock came on the door, but she did not call, 'Come in,' but asked, 'Who is it?'

'It's me, Dorry, miss.'

She went and opened the door, and Dorry said, 'There's a gentleman downstairs asking for you.'

'A gentleman, asking for me? Who . . . who is it? Did he give his name?'

'No. I suppose I should have asked, but he just said could he see

Miss Brownlow. And he looked all right, not common or anything. So I asked him in. He's waiting in the hall.'

Jinny continued to look at Dorry. It wouldn't be Peter; Dorry knew Peter . . . Was it? No, no; Hal wouldn't dare come here, he wouldn't dare. Yet she had just been thinking about him.

'Is he old . . . I mean middle-aged, or . . . or?'

'No, he's young, miss.'

'Young?' Her mind was blank. She couldn't think who it could be. She said, I'll be down in a minute.'

It wasn't until she was descending the stairs that she thought, Michael. Of course, Michael. It could only be Michael. Why hadn't she thought of him straight away?

He was standing near the tall window looking on to the drive and he hadn't heard her descend the thickly carpeted stairs.

'Hello, Michael.' There was a welcome in her voice.

He swung round but didn't move towards her and it was some seconds before he replied, 'Hello, Jinny. Long time no see.'

She was about to say, 'Will you come into the drawing room?' when John appeared from the passage to the left of the stairs, and he stood staring from one to the other.

Looking at him straight faced, Jinny said, 'Will it be all right to take Mr Morton into the drawing-room?' and he looked for a moment a replica of his father and, also like his father, as if he was about to come out with a mouthful of abuse. But he said in stilted theatrical tones, 'Yes, you are at liberty to take . . . Mr Morton into the drawing-room.'

In the room and the door closed behind them, Michael, turning to her, said, 'Who's he?'

'He's Mr Henderson's son John.'

'Pleasant individual.'

'I'm not excusing him but I can say he's not himself today.'

When she indicated he should take a seat on the couch he nodded and, impulsively putting out his hand, he said, 'So this is where you've been hiding?'

'I haven't been hiding.'

His face straight now, he asked, 'Why did you do it, go off like that?'

'I should think that was obvious, I couldn't stand any more . . .'

'Any more what?'

'Oh, don't be silly, Michael.'

'All right, I won't be silly, but I'll tell you, I've spent almost a month looking for you. That damned house agent was as close as a clam. Then I had to go to London. I suppose you could say it was promotion: I was drafted there to do a job. I've been back three weeks and . . . well' – he pursed his lips – 'I thought I'd got rid of you from under my skin, but when I returned I found I hadn't, so I started again, blindly. Then just by chance an oldish fellow came into the office only yesterday with his son who wanted advice about tax. We got on talking. The father was a nice old fellow. It came out he worked at Hendersons. The doorman, he said. And yes, he knew a Miss Jinny Brownlow. Oh, yes, he did; he remembered her very well.' Michael nodded his head at Jinny now as he went on, 'Had he any idea where she was now? Oh, yes, she was looking after the boss – and he would always think of Mr Henderson as the boss – in his house on Brampton Hill.' Michael now spread his free hand wide as he ended, 'So here I am.'

'It's nice to see you, Michael.'

'Do you mean that?'

'Yes, yes, I do.' And she did. She had always liked Michael, and she knew she had been rather attracted to him from the first and, if he had put in an appearance when she was living with Nell, who knew but things might have grown between them. As it was now, well that was impossible. How many times could your affections be assailed by this thing called love. But then she hadn't loved Michael. Had she loved Hal Campbell? No, she hadn't loved Hal Campbell. Had she loved Ray Collard? No, she hadn't loved Ray Collard. Had she loved George Mayborough? Somewhere inside of her a laugh rippled. No, she certainly hadn't loved George Mayborough. Did she love . . .? A door banged shut, and a voice, sounding raucous to her ears, said, 'Enough of that. No more humiliations.' Then a question came, sharp, piercing: What about the man upstairs? She loved him, didn't she? Oh yes, she could own up to that love, she loved him; or she had loved him, but it was a love without desire, a passionless love; yet nevertheless a love. But no more, no more of love of any kind . . . 'What did you say?'

'I said, you weren't listening to what I was saying.'

'What were you saying.'

'I am saying I am a changed man with regard to views on matrimony. Please, please,' he said, gripping her hand tightly when she went to pull it away from him; 'I'm in earnest, Jinny, very much in earnest. This is the first time this kind of thing has ever hit me. I swore it wouldn't, I might as well tell you. I'd seen so much of marriages going wrong. Well you know all about that, don't you? But there are marriages that can go right; and Jinny, I'd make ours go right. Believe me, I would. Will you?' He lifted her hand to his breast and with his other hand on her shoulder was drawing her towards him when they both stiffened at the sound of the door being thrust open and their heads both turned to look down the room to where John was standing in the doorway, his face looking blank, his eyes mere slits as if he was peering at them over a distance; but his voice sounded quite calm as he said, 'I . . . I wondered if you would like some tea?'

'No, thank you.' Jinny had disengaged from Michael's hold and had risen to her feet.

'It's . . . it's all ready. Dorry's got a tray set.'

'No thank you. We won't bother. Mr Morton is just going.'

John let his eyes rest on Michael for some seconds before he said, 'Very well,' then turned away, closing the door quietly after him.

Looking back at Jinny and sighing, he said, 'May I continue where I left off?'

'No, Michael, please.'

'You don't dislike me?'

'Oh, no, no. I never have.' She smiled gently at him.

'Well then, that could be a beginning.'

'No, because it would stay there. I'm . . . I'm not in love with you.'

'There's a difference between being in love and loving. They say if you like somebody, that's the best beginning.'

'Well, I like you, Michael, but I know the other is impossible.'

'Why?' His face was straight now. 'Somebody else on the horizon, or let's say closer inland?'

'No . . . no one.'

'What about him?' He nodded towards the closed door. 'If ever I've seen jealousy, there it was.'

'That wasn't jealousy, that was – ' She swallowed deeply before adding, 'temper.'

'You're sure?'

Her pausing before answering caused him to say, 'You're not sure, are you?'

'I'm so sure that I'm leaving here tomorrow.'

'You are?' His face stretched. 'Why?'

'A difference of opinion on various matters.'

'Where are you going.'

There was no reason why she shouldn't tell him, because she considered it would be silly if he started another search for her. And anyway, should he call here they would tell him where she was. So she said, 'I have a cousin in Shields.'

'And you say you're going there tomorrow? Can . . . can I run you in?'

Yes, yes, he could. That would save the bother of getting a taxi or of Peter coming to fetch her, for when she phoned Nell and Peter later tonight Peter would be sure to insist. And so she said, 'That would be kind of you.'

'What time?'

'What time would suit you?'

'Any time, I'm my own boss.' He pulled a face at her. 'Promotion since London. So, say ten o'clock?'

'That'll be fine. Thank you.' She now moved from him towards the door, but before she reached it he had caught her arm and, looking into her face, said, 'I'm making a habit of rescuing you, so I'm going to take it as a good sign.'

She shook her head slowly now, saying, 'Please, Michael, don't. I . . . I must be honest with you, there . . . there is someone else.'

'Oh!' He rubbed his fingers across his chin. 'Well, where is he now, when you need him?'

'He doesn't know I need him.'

'It's like that, is it? Married?'

'No, he's not married.'

'Then there's something funny somewhere. Oh' – his head nodded now – 'he's not the marrying kind, and you don't go for that lark, do you? Well' – he smiled faintly at her now – 'I've offered to make an honest woman of you and I wouldn't mind playing second fiddle because there's always the chance that something will happen to the leader of the orchestra.'

'Oh, Michael.' She found herself laughing and she put her hand out and laid it on his as she said, 'You are nice.' Then swiftly and before he could take hold of her arms as he was about to do, she pulled open the door and led the way into the hall. And when they were on the outside step and he looked upwards as he said, 'It's a fine house this. Will you be sorry to leave it?' she answered simply, 'Yes.'

'Well, till tomorrow at ten.'

'Thank you, I'll be ready. Goodbye.'

'Goodbye, Jinny.'

As she closed the door on him a shiver ran through her entire body: she didn't know whether it was the cold wind or the fact that through Michael's unexpected visit she had surprised herself into admitting something she had refused to recognize for weeks now. As she made for the stairs she saw John descending and about to follow him, Glen, accompanied by Willie.

'Nurse! Nurse! I want . . .' Glen's request was drowned by Willie saying, 'Now, now; nurse is busy. Steady on, Steady on.'

And as if to protect her, John ran down towards her and taking her by the arm, led her back into the drawing-room. But Glen's protests came to them. His voice hardly that of a boy, he was yelling, 'Why can't I? Why can't I? Nurse likes playing cards. Leave me alone.'

At the sound of a scuffle, Jinny put her hand, fingers spread wide, on the top of her head and brought it forward as if in doing so she would shut out all sound; and she didn't raise it until John's voice, coming at her quietly, said, 'You were right. One of you would have to go.' Then his tone changed slightly as he added, 'It seemed fortunate that your friend should arrive at an opportune time. Is . . . is he an old friend?'

'You could say that.'

'I suppose he's pleased you're leaving?'

'Yes, you could say that too.'

'He's a good-looking fellow.'

'I think so.'

'Why hasn't he called on you before?'

She turned away from him and put her hand on the door handle as she said, 'He didn't know where I was, he's been looking for me.'

'And now he's found you, what happens next?'

She seemed to detect a slight note of amusement in his voice, even though his expression belied his tone, and her whole body stretched until she appeared to be looking down at him before she said, 'What happens next will likely be a wedding.' And on this she pulled the door open, but had to push past him because he did not move out of her way, and as she mounted the stairs she was aware that he was watching her from where he still stood within the doorway.

She stood in the middle of her room, her eyes closed, her arms around her waist as if hugging herself against the cold, and she muttered aloud, 'Oh dear God.' And it wasn't because of anything he had said, but because at the moment she'd imagined she detected amusement in his voice she'd had a great urge to take her hand and slap his face. It was a similar feeling to that which had welled up in her when she had hit Miss Cadwell, and again when she had witnessed Hal Campbell in bed with that elderly blowzy woman. What was the matter with her? She never used to be like this. She could look back on herself right until she had lost her parents as being a gentle naïve creature, she could even put the term genteel to herself, but since she had begun to mix with people and to search for companionship – she skipped the word love – there was being revealed in her character a facet that she imagined to be the antithesis of her real self. Aggressiveness, she would have said, was not in her nature; but, given the circumstances, there it was. Yet why should she wish to strike at John of all people? Granted he had a caustic tongue, but that wasn't why she was mad at him. No.

She went towards the bed, sat down on the foot of it and, putting her arms on the rails, she rested her head on them. Let her face it, she knew why she wanted to hit him. Come clean. Come clean. She knew he was in love with her, but she also knew that he would never ask her to marry him. Live with him, oh yes. He had need of her, she knew this, as much as his father had, but the need wasn't strong enough to force him to take on the responsibility of a wife. Michael had changed, he was offering her security . . . and respectability. That was the word, respectability.

She straightened up and muttered the word aloud, 'Respectability.' It was so damned old-fashioned, people laughed at it. Why couldn't she do the same? What was really wrong with her? Was there part of her that had been bred for a convent? No, no. Her urges were such that they could not be sublimated. Then why was she sticking out for a wedding ring? A piece of paper?

Oh, God, she didn't know; all she knew was that chastity was the most expensive commodity, and that there must come a time when your nerves refused to pay the high price demanded of it, and the terrifying truth was that she knew she was nearing that time.

It was about seven when she finally got through to an 'I told you so' Nell to explain what had happened and that Michael would be bringing her over to Shields in the morning. And she had hardly put down the phone when Dorry brought a meal up on a tray and, after placing it on the table, she turned and looked at Jinny for a moment before she said, 'I'm sorry, an' Cissie is the same. We've just said, we don't know what himself will do, 'cos you seemed to be the only one that could raise his spirits. But I understand how you feel about Mr Glen. He gets on our nerves. We've had to move half the food to the big freezer in the stable. He took a whole two pound veal and ham pie yesterday. Cissie tried to take it off him, but he's as strong as a horse, and, as she said herself, she was frightened.' Her voice dropped now. 'It's as we said to Willie, we don't think he's really well enough for the house. And Willie says, Mr John's very much of the same opinion, but himself says he stays, and so he stays. I don't know what the end of it's going to be. Come on and eat this meal, miss. Oh, we are going to miss you. As Cissie says, you fitted in like an old glove. And you're young at that. But as Cissie says, you've got common sense and your head's older than your age.'

If she could have laughed, she would have laughed: her head was older than her age. Oh, if only that were true. She said quietly, 'I'll be sorry to go, Dorry, and I'll miss you both. It's . . . it's been like home, especially in the kitchen.'

'Did you have a good home, miss? I know you've had a good upbringing, being educated like, but it isn't them that could educate their children that give them the happiest homes. Oh, no, not by a long chalk.'

'I had a very happy home, Dorry. I was very fortunate. I know that now. You don't appreciate it at the time though, do you? As for education, it was pretty ordinary. School till sixteen, then on to a secretarial course.'

'Oh.' Dorry's face stretched. 'You've never been then to a university? Not like Miss Florence and Miss Nellie? Miss Monica never went, nor Lucy.'

'No; no university.'

'Now that surprises me. And Cissie'll be surprised an' all, because you have that kind of air, you know like people who have been to university, sort of sure of themselves.'

Now Jinny did smile. They were funny these two, Dorry and Cissie: they were still in the Thirties when, her father had said, one paid homage to anyone who had been to a college or university, because it meant something in those days.

Changing the subject now, Dorry said, 'Mr John's in a tear. He's like a bear with a sore skull. Him and Willie have been talking but they can't come up with any solution. Well, they can't, can they? Oh dear me, nothing'll ever be the same again in this house. Anyway, dear, get your supper. Your soup will be clay cold by now although it's covered up.'

'Thanks, Dorry, and thank Cissie. But I'll see you both in the morning. Good-night.'

'Good-night, miss. Good-night.'

She drank the soup and ate a little of the cold meat and salad; and afterwards, she tried to settle down and read, but when she found she couldn't concentrate, she wrote a letter. It was to Bob, simply thanking him for his kindness to her and wishing things could have turned out differently. The letter was in place of visiting him, because she knew she couldn't bear to see his face and the accusation in his eyes. His look would suggest not only that she was leaving the sinking ship but also that she, who was a good swimmer, was refusing to put her hand out to a drowning man.

At half-past nine she book a bath; and the last thing she did before getting into bed was to take three aspirins. She had never as yet taken a sleeping pill, but she told herself that if she had had one handy she would have taken it. But the aspirins might ease her rising headache and steady her nerves.

As she lay wide-eyed, she heard John come along the corridor and go into his father's room. She knew it was him by his cough which was more in the nature of a clearing of his throat. It had become a habit of late.

She had heard Willie leave sometime earlier after he had finally settled Bob for the night. She'd heard nothing of Glen, not even his voice from the distance. Often he talked so loudly he could be heard all over the house, but twice during the past week he'd had a quiet period when he hadn't spoken for hours. One evening as he sat playing cards he had made no comment on the game, which was very unusual, but Willie had explained this. It was part of a pattern, he'd said, and the aftermath could mean Glen would be more volatile than before; or there might even be a glimpse of his real self; or lastly, and he hoped this wouldn't happen, he could become very aggressive. And he had repeated that he hoped the latter wouldn't happen because Glen, at the weight he'd be now, would be a tough guy to handle.

After some time she heard John's cough again; he had come out of his father's room. A silence followed. The house had settled down for the night, her last night in it. How long she lay awake she didn't know. The last she remembered was telling herself that it was going to be a long, long night. And then she was dreaming. Strangely, she always knew when she was dreaming. If there was any happening in her dream that was frightening she would say to herself, 'Wake up, it's only a dream.' In this particular dream someone had switched on the bedside lamp, and this had frightened her, but she had said to herself, 'Don't be afraid, it's only a dream. Wake up.' She was deep in the dream but a voice was pulling her upwards, calling her name. She recognized the name yet it wasn't hers. When at last she forced her eyes open, her mouth sprang open too and all sleep left her as she stared up into the face staring down at her. It was smiling and it had a soft light in its eyes, and it was the soft light that prevented her from screaming. But she hitched herself up on her elbows and, her voice a grating whisper, she said, 'go . . . go back to bed, Glen. That's a good fellow.'

His response to this was not to give her an answer but to put his hand on to her cheek and stroke it.

'Now, now, Glen, you . . . you shouldn't be here, you should be a . . .' She was about to say asleep, but the word caught in her throat when his other hand with just one sweep threw the bedclothes aside. Now she did cry out: 'Go away! Stop i . . .!' The 'it' was strangled by his hand across her mouth.

Staring up into his face, she saw that his expression had changed: his eyeballs were moving from side to side and his lids were flicking up and down over them. Using both her hands now, she went to push them against his face to press him away, but he caught her wrists in a grip that was like a vice, then with a heave he was lying beside her and muttering a name over and over, 'Yvonne. Yvonne. Yvonne.'

Because he was on his side now his hold was more awkward and when his hand momentarily eased from her mouth she let out a strangled cry before bringing her teeth sharply down on to the flesh of his second finger.

His hand jerked from her mouth and brought a resounding blow on to the side of her face, and now she screamed both from pain and from terror. The next minute he was crying, 'Sorry. Sorry. Sorry. Yvonne. Sorry. It's me. It's me. Glen your Glen. Yvonne. Yvonne. Yvonne, your Glen.'

She was about to scream again when with a twist of his body he rolled on top of her, and in doing so he freed her hands and when they tore at his hair he seemed to go really berserk, for his hands, now clawing at her body, rent the night-dress from her.

As she struggled to escape his grasping fingers and the weight of his body she knew she was going to pass out, and she was no longer aware that she was screaming, calling on the three men in the house:

'Bob! John! Willie!' Then when his hands tore at her breasts, his nails penetrating the flesh, she let out one great agonized scream that smothered Willie's name.

It was at that instant Willie and John burst into the room almost simultaneously, and when the weight was dragged from her she lay heaving, gasping and sobbing, and unconscious that she was naked or that there were thin streaks of blood running down from her breasts on to her forearms. She took no notice whatever of the scuffling going on to the side of the bed or of Willie yelling, 'I can hold him. It's in a box in the medicine cabinet in my bedroom, a brown box. It's on the front of the shelf. Be quick! Be quick!'

John scattered from the room. Within a minute he was back with a hypodermic syringe, and not until Willie had shot the needle into Glen's hip did they both become aware of the voice yelling across the corridor. But neither of them took any notice. Rising now, they went to the bed, and it was John who quickly pulled the bedclothes up over her, then gently placed his hands on each side of her face and turned it towards him. But he said no word, nor did she. She had stopped crying, only now and again a small moan escaped her.

'I'll phone the hospital right away,' Willie said. 'We'll have to leave him here though until they come; we could never manage him downstairs, he's a dead weight.'

As he went towards the door Bob's voice could be heard clearly now coming from the bedroom, yelling, 'Here! Here! Come here!'

Willie turned and looked at John and asked simply, 'What about it?'

And John answered, 'It's out of his hands; he'll have realized that by now.'

'I'll phone from his room; and for the doctor too. That'll make it final.' And with that Willie hurried across the corridor, opened the bedroom door, then stopped dead. His mouth open, his eyes wide, he stared at his patient; then jerking his head to the side, he shouted, 'John! John! Come here. Come here.'

John went at a run, to see his father sitting upright in the bed, his body well to the edge of it as if he had been attempting to get out.

'My God!'

He moved slowly towards the bed, and his father, his voice trembling, said, 'What's he done to her?'

'Tried to rape her I should say and battered her in the process. But after all, what does it matter? It's got you sitting up. Something which common sense could have done before,' he said; then turned about and hurried back to Jinny's room.

Bob now looked at Willie, saying, 'Is she badly hurt?'

'I . . . I don't really know, except there was blood on her breasts and she looks as if she's collapsed. John saw to her. One thing I do know, boss, is that with his strength and the urge that was on him, he could have done her in quite easily, because there's nothing of her.'

'Where's he now?'

'On the floor.' Willie jerked his head back. 'I've put him out.'

'Have you . . . have you phoned the hospital?'

'I'm going to do that now. I thought I'd do it from here.'

'You're blaming me, aren't you?'

'No, no, I'm not blaming you. He's your son; I've got an idea how you feel about him. There's nobody to blame really, it's just one great pity. But these things happen and I think what you've got to face up to is, unless they come up with a miracle in brain surgery he's going to remain pretty much as he is.'

'Help me straighten up.'

When Bob was lying back in his pillows, he said, 'I'm going to ask you now, where were you? She had been yelling for some time. I heard her from the beginning.'

'We were both downstairs wondering what we could do to prevent her going. Funny, but I'd been waiting all day for something to happen; Mr Glen had been too quiet. I'd given him a double dose of tablets, but like many such cases they become wily, they put the tablets in their mouth, swallow the water, then when your back's turned they spit them out from under their tongue. He has done that once or twice before, but tonight I stood and watched him take them, *tonight*, at least I thought so, but you can never be up to them when their minds are like that. He had known what he was going to do; he also knew a sleeping tablet would prevent him from doing it. He had taken a fancy to her from the beginning you see; she must in some way have reminded him of his wife, because he's still a man . . .'

Across the landing John was thinking the same thing: his brother was still a man, but with the beast added.

He was bathing her face with a cold sponge. Her eye was beginning to swell and her cheek was already puffed out. As yet not one word had passed between them. Her eyes were closed and her breath was coming in shuddering gasps. It wasn't until the sound of a snort came from the far side of the bed that she showed any sign of life, for her body shuddered and her eyes opened and she gasped at the air; and for the first time he spoke. Softly he said, 'It's all right, Jinny. It's all right.'

She looked at him now and her lips moved as if mouthing words, but no sound came, and again he said, 'It's all right. It's all right, my dear. He's going. They're coming for him. It's all over. It should never have happened, but it's all over now.'

When she closed her eyes again and the tears pressed through her lashes, he put his arm under her head and, his voice low, he said, 'Oh, Jinny. Jinny. Oh, my dear, don't. I . . . I blame myself for it happening. And so will Willie. But we were downstairs trying to work out ways and means to keep you. We had decided to contact the doctor first thing in the morning and Willie was going to tell him of the change that he was detecting in Glen and that he thought he was in need of qualified attention, but it was how we could stop you leaving before anything further could be done about him, because I couldn't bear the thought of you leaving. Oh, Jinny. Jinny. All right, don't get agitated. Look, I'll get Willie to go and wake Dorry. She must sleep like a log. And you could have your cousin here tomorrow; she'll see to you. Everything's going to be all right.' He knew he was gabbling on but he couldn't stop.

When he made to move away she suddenly caught at his hand as at the same time another snort came from the other side of the bed, and he said gently, 'He's under sedation. He won't wake up for some long time. They . . . they are coming to fetch him.' Then raising his voice, he called to Willie, and when Willie appeared at the doorway he said, 'Go and fetch Dorry, will you? . . . Have you got in contact with the hospital?'

'They'll be here within half an hour.'

'And the doctor?'

'As soon as he can.' . . .

It was almost an hour later when Glen was lifted on to a stretcher and taken downstairs, and it was a half-hour later still when the doctor came. He'd been out on an urgent call and only just got the message.

John was waiting for him in the hall when he came downstairs. He hadn't spent more than ten minutes in Jinny's room, and when John asked the question with one word, 'Well?' the doctor replied, 'She wouldn't permit me to examine her. She's in a highly nervous state, which is only natural. I've given her a sedative.'

'So you don't know if . . .?'

'No, I don't know if; only she can answer that question. The only thing that I can say at this stage is I would imagine if there's any result of his action, it wouldn't be welcome, because the process must have been more than painful. He has ripped the skin from her breasts in four places. In an ordinary way you could call them scratches, but these are more like gores. And tomorrow her eye will be black and blue and the rest of her face a bruised yellow. No, I don't think the result, if there should be any, of tonight's affair would be welcome. Let's pray your intervention was in time. And also that your father will admit he can be wrong at times, greatly wrong. I was against Glen's return from the first. I have seen this type of case before and you never know from one day to the next how they are going to react. Well, we know how this one reacted, but it remains to be seen how she reacts to it. Yes, it remains to be seen.'

5

'Oh, my God, lass, what did he do to you?' Nell bent over her and with gentle fingers she touched Jinny's cheek where the black and blue of her bruised eye faded into puffed yellowness. 'He should be brought up, he should be. Or more so, those responsible for bringing him into the house should be. Now you're getting out of here as quick as we can carry you. Just look at her, Peter. Did you ever see anything like it?'

'Leave her alone, Nell; she's distressed and you're not making it any better.'

'What are you talking about, man? She's getting out of here.'

'All right, all right.' Peter's voice was low. 'She'll come if she wants to. Leave it to her.' He was thinking of a short conversation he'd had with the son of the house just before he came downstairs. The young fellow had taken him aside and, his voice urgent, he had said, 'Please do something for me . . . for us. Don't persuade her to leave. Everything's all right now. My . . . my brother shall never come back and my father needs her. We will see to her. We will look after her.'

His answer had been much as it was a moment ago, 'Well, that'll be her decision. I don't think we'll have much say in it. If she wants to come, we'll only be too glad to have her, and she knows that.'

'Nell' – Jinny found it painful to open her lips, her mouth seemed to have slipped to one side – 'I'm . . . I'm all right. I just want to . . . rest. I'll . . . I'll come down later and . . . and stay for a time. Don't . . . don't worry, I'm all right.'

'You're not all right. And it's like men's point of view to look on the bright side, like that Willie saying if it hadn't happened his boss would likely have lain there till he died. He didn't look upon it that you could have been battered to death in order that his boss could be shocked into sitting up.'

"Wh . . . what?'

'Be quiet, Nell, will you?' Peter was bending over Jinny now, saying, 'We'll be going, dear; you . . . you need to rest. We'll look in again this afternoon.'

'Peter.'

'Yes, my dear?'

'What . . . what about Bob?'

Peter glanced towards his wife and made a small impatient

movement with his head at her before looking at Jinny again, saying, 'Well, it appears that Mr Henderson heard you calling and . . . well, he made an effort and apparently it broke the paralysis, which wasn't real paralysis, that's in the upper part of his body, and now he's . . . well, all right except for his legs.'

Jinny closed her eyes. Dear God. Dear God. Was it possible? Yes, yes, it was possible. The doctors had said it was hysteria, but no one and seemingly nothing could get that through into his head. But her cries of help and his immediate recognition of their meaning had got through to him, overcoming his hysteria. Now he must face the irrevocable fact that his son's mind was damaged to such an extent that in part he was mad.

The sedative the doctor had given her last night had worn thin and she was still screaming in her mind and his weight was still on her body and his bare flesh still searing her. There was no part of her that his hands hadn't clutched at, and she was still seeing his face, but strangely, not as it appeared last night, wild, distorted, the eyes blazing as they flickered like flashing lights, but she was seeing him as he had looked on his wedding day and at those times when he had bounced into the office, bursting with confidence and satisfaction after completing another order. Yet even so his face looked different: she was seeing it without the smile on it, without the happiness Yvonne had been bringing to him, and as she had never really seen it, sad, unsmiling, the eyes seeming to beg something of her. There was penetrating her still fear-filled thoughts the idea that he was here in the room: some part of him was here begging her forgiveness, telling her that that which was perpetrated last night was not him, asking for her understanding.

She heard Peter's voice as if coming from a distance saying, 'She's gone to sleep,' and Nell answering, 'They've got her sedated, now, but just wait until she really comes to herself; she'll not stay here, you'll see.'

It was some moments before she became fully aware that they had left the room.

When she opened her eyes, Dorry was sitting by her bedside and after a moment she said to her, 'Would . . . would you tell John I . . . I would like to see him, please?'

'Aye, miss. Yes, I'll tell him. He's . . . he's just across the passage.'

She closed her eyes again and it seemed only the next minute she heard his voice saying, 'What is it, Jinny?'

'Oh, John.'

'Yes my dear, what is it?'

'Don't . . . don't ask Nell to stay; I'll be all right. I just want to sleep, but don't ask her to stay.'

'If that's what you wish.' He didn't say that Nell and her husband had already left and although he had said he would ask her to stay, he hadn't done so because from the moment she had entered the house he had realized her excitable nature wouldn't do Jinny any good and, too, that her main intention was to remove Jinny as quickly as possible. He left inordinately pleased that Jinny should make this request of him. It seemed to prove to him that she was to stay where she was.

He put his hand out now and gently stroked her hair back from her forehead. She was beautiful. A black eye, a swollen discoloured cheek, she was still beautiful. What was he going to do about her? She'd never understand him. She would understand his father, she seemed on the same wavelength with him, but with himself the wires always got crossed. Perhaps it was his fault; he was always on his guard, afraid to show his feelings. He had shown them once and what had happened? He had been made a monkey of. By God, yes. What would have happened if he had married her, the beguiling Janice, the great free-thinker? Eighteen months they had lived together; then of a sudden she had talked of marriage, not only talked but asked, what about it? And he'd decided he was less for it than ever; he was discovering facets of her character that annoyed him. Yet, he told himself, this was bound to happen, for after all it was like a marriage. But then she had brought up the idea of a special licence. It was the rush that made him pause; and he spoke to Nick Hobson about it. Nick had been married for the past year to the girl he had previously lived with. It was the fear of illegitimacy on the coming child that had made her press for marriage. Anyway, it was Nick who had said, 'Don't do it, boy, not in this case, she's just using you. You've been hoodwinked long enough. The reason for her haste is that she's going to be named by the wife of one of the professors who's suing for a divorce. He was on her horizon long before you appeared, and has been there ever since more or less. She's got four years' start on you. And there's been at least three other members of the staff before.'

He could recall the white rage that burned him up as he waited for her coming home when she would follow the same procedure: breeze in, throw off her coat, switch on the record player, then flop into the couch, and he'd bring her a drink; then, depending on her mood, she would lay back and recite a few lines from Shakespeare, some modern jingle, or, as she did on that last night, the rhyme that she always resorted to when she was uncertain of his mood:

'Pussy-cat, pussy-cat, where have you been?
I've been to London to see the Queen.
Pussy-cat, pussy-cat, what did you there?
I spied John Henderson under a chair.
Pussy-cat, Pussy-cat, did he mew?
No, the last I saw of him he up and flew.

'Well, out with it, Johnny boy,' she had said. 'Why greet a hard-working girl with a look like that?'

He remembered he'd had the strongest urge to get her by the neck and choke her, in fact, to react almost as Glen had done last night on poor Jinny here. But the more sane part of him at that moment must have recongized how easy it would be to kill someone and he had warned himself to get out. And so he'd answered her: 'I'm adopting the last line and flying.'

A barrage of terse questions and answers followed, and at the end she had stood screaming at him as he went towards the door after having said, 'I removed my belongings this afternoon.'

'You are what you always were, a weak-kneed milksop. Now run back to your mammy and your daddy and ask them to show you how to keep a woman, because you haven't even reached the kindergarten stage in that school . . . boy.'

He had stayed with Nick that night and found a place the next day, and for almost a week afterwards he had been sick every night, actually sick, bringing up the food he had forced down himself during the day, and as his stomach emptied he saw himself shrinking until he felt there was nothing left of his manhood.

Looking back, it was hard to believe that he had loved Janice, but the truth was he had. She was bright, intelligent, and four years his senior. She was at first everything he needed in a woman. But then he had known very little about women and so his knowledge of them stemmed mostly from her. The period of living alone had only increased the devastating feeling against his parents for having thrown him off; and this he now knew to be ridiculous. And yet the fact wasn't ridiculous that his father had always preferred Glen. That his mother's affection was weighed in his direction didn't seem to make up for the indifference towards him shown by his father: too arty-crafty was the term he used about him, and later made it obvious that he would never be any good in business, not like Glen would be.

But all that seemed to be in another world for the tables had turned completely. He might be still arty-crafty, but he knew that his father needed him now more than he had ever needed Glen, and he knew that he himself needed this girl here more than he ever imagined he could need anyone in his life again. The thought of her leaving the house had been agony to him, even the fact that they hardly ever seemed to say a civil word to each other and that she didn't really like him, hadn't prevented him from willing her to stay.

But after she got over the shock, what if she still decided to leave. She could have left today, though, with her cousin and she had refused, hadn't she? Yet that might have been because she was feeling too ill to make the move . . . Oh, why in the name of God couldn't he think positively for once. That was his trouble. Outwardly he gave off the impression of assertiveness, while inwardly he courted defeat even before the battle had begun.

Propped up on his pillows, Bob looked at Willie and said, 'How long would it take to get one of those wheelchairs?'

'Oh, not so long, a few weeks. You'd have to have it specially adjusted.'

'Hell! man, I wasn't talking about weeks; I was talking about hours. Isn't it possible to borrow one from the hospital? The corridors seemed lined with the blasted things when I was there.'

'I could try, but I can't promise anything.'

'Well, try. Get on the phone.'

Willie smiled at Bob now before he said, 'Where do you intend to go in it? Back to work?'

'Aye, yes, that's an idea.'

At this moment the bedroom door opened and when John entered his father cried at him, 'This big lout here has just given me an idea. I've asked him to get me a wheelchair.'

'A wheelchair? But . . .'

'Never mind any buts. That's what I want, a wheelchair, and I want it today or tomorrow at the latest.'

'So, you want a whelchair.' John came and stood by the side of the bed. 'And you want it today or tomorrow at the latest.' Then turning to Willie, he said, 'Well, what about it, Willie, is that possible?'

'Well, you know what they say, John, anything is possible to them that have faith.' And they laughed at each other.

'Not so much of the light banter,' Bob barked; 'I haven't finished what I'd started to say. He's just suggested' – he jerked his head in Willie's direction – 'that if I get a wheelchair I can take up work again, and by God, that's what I'll do. Aye, that's what I'll do. But I want that wheelchair first.' And in a lowered voice, he said, 'I want to get into it and go across the passage. And when she sees me, it might . . . well, take some of the sting out of it. What do you think?'

'You could be right.' John nodded at him; then looking at Willie, he said, 'Leave it to me. I'll see what I can do.'

And he turned about and went out again.

Bob seemed to have to drag his gaze from the door before turning to Willie and saying, 'There's a changed lad if ever I saw one. Well, he's no longer a lad, he's a man. And it certainly wasn't brought about by his going off on his own, the big "I am" setting up house with a woman. No, he was still the lad then. It didn't happen until the accident. That seemed to change him; well, changed us all, didn't it? And it must be still changing us, because two days gone I was asking meself what's the use of going on. And I can tell you something, Willie, if those pills had been handy I wouldn't be here to tell the tale now. Oh, you can open your eyes, but that's honest to God truth. I was as low as that. And then having to face up to the fact that you were all right about Glen. Oh God! Glen. Glen. I daren't think about him . . . But in spite of all that, here I am grabbing at life with half a new body. And, you know, it's a wonderful feeling. Do you know that, Willie? It's a wonderful feeling.'

'Yes, I know it's a wonderful feeling, and it'll continue to be a wonderful feeling if you go steady. You know what doctor said: no high jinks; take it slowly at first, your body's got to adjust. So come on, more exercises. Come on now, up with those arms.'

Bob had jerked his head now, saying, 'Oh well, everything's got to be paid for. Do you know, I say that again and again, every day of me life, everything's got to be paid for.'

Taking hold of Bob's wrist in one hand and his elbow in the other, Willie said, 'And there's another saying that's a companion to it: You only get what you pay for; bargains are mostly second-hand.'

She was sitting up in bed. Her head was clear. She had asked the doctor not to give her any more sedatives because for the past three days she felt she had been in a kind of limbo where she knew yet didn't know what was going on around her, where the faces were familiar yet distorted, where at times she imagined she heard a man's voice talking to her and fingers stroking her hair. And once had had felt she was being kissed, right on the lips. It had been a soft kiss and she'd told herself to open her eyes to see who it was. But she had been too tired – she only knew she liked the kiss and wished it would go on.

But now, in her clear-thinking state, she was finding no room for pity for the man who, if he hadn't been caught in time, could have killed her. The compassion she had felt earlier had dissolved in the drugged mist, for the fact was there had been murder in his eyes: his pent-up passion against fate that had robbed him of his wife and his senses had broken through and had to be recompensed.

But the question was, what was she going to do now? Was she going to stay here? Or was she going to Nell's? Somehow she didn't want to go to Nell's, any more than she had done yesterday, or the day before, or the day before that, because Nell's conversation for weeks ahead would be a reiteration of the whole situation, and although she knew it wasn't possible ever to forget it, the thought of hearing it over and over again would, she knew, become unbearable and would, in the end, cause her to leave the pleasant homely house and the caring couple. And that would hurt them both more than if she were to say to them she had decided to stay on here.

But did she now want to stay on here? Because the future would not be even anything like it was before Glen came on the scene. Bob, restored to partial mobility, wouldn't be as easy to handle as the paralysed man. That was sure. And then there was John.

If they could have been good companions it would have helped matters, but they acted like fighting cocks towards each other. Why, after all, she asked herself now, should this too have happened to her? Hadn't she been through enough without having to fight another sex battle?

No, she didn't want to stay. But how was she going to leave? What excuse would she give? And where would she go?

Yes, where would she go? If not to Nell's, where?

She was fully dressed and sitting by the window. Occasionally she turned her gaze towards the door hoping that someone would come in, denying that her wish centred upon John because she felt that through another abrasive exchange she would be forced to come to a decision.

Her head jerked round as she heard a slight commotion in the corridor outside. There was the sound of voices and she thought she must be mistaken when she recognized Bob's. Then unceremoniously her door was thrust open, and there he was half-way across the threshold in a wheelchair.

She was on her feet now staring at him. He looked different, almost like he used to do. His wiry hair was licked back, his face was clean-shaven, but what was most astounding, he was fully dressed in a grey suit, blue shirt and matching tie.

'It's a case of that Mohammed not coming to the mountain and the mountain having to get up and push itself to the stubborn stiff-necked Mohammed, eh?'

He was pushing at the wheels now while John pressed him forward from behind, and when he reached the side of the window he stopped.

'Well, what do you think?'

Her neck muscles were tight, her throat for a moment was so blocked she couldn't get words past it. She looked from him to John who was staring at her, his expression enigmatic as usual, then from him to where Willie was standing in the doorway smiling. And Willie nodded at her, pursed his lips, then closed the door.

'Well, if you've got nothing to say to me, sit down.'

She sat down; and now he went on, 'I thought you'd be over the moon to see this new man that I've become. I'm back where I was, or soon will be. Heigh-ho for Henderson and Garbrook's. Wait till we get on that top floor and go into that office. Can you imagine Waitland's face? I've had Jack Newland here and Peter Trowell and also Bill Meane and Bury, and from what I can gather the quicker we get back there, lass, the better. And here's news for you. His nibs there' – he nodded towards John – 'is going to come in. What do you think of that? That's an achievement, isn't it? Bury's going to coach him regarding the basics. You know, getting orders like.'

For the first time since coming into the room his quick fire talk halted, but only for a second. Then he went on, 'He's got a head on his shoulders, although I say it meself.' He glanced again at his son. 'And there's charm somewhere there, though it might take a pick and shovel to get at it. But he'll have to use it when he gets abroad, and the quicker he does that the better, because there's trouble brewing in the steel business if I know owt from what I hear. They talk of nothin' else on the bloody television these days. Oh' – he drew in a long breath – 'I can't wait, lass. I can't wait.'

Of a sudden there was silence in the room, with Bob, his fingers now working against each other, staring at her while John looked towards his feet; that was until his father said, 'Would . . . would you get me a hanky, lad? I've . . . I've forgotten one.'

Without hesitation John left the room; and they were alone together.

Putting his hands on the wheels of the chair, he brought it close to her side and with not the space of a forearm between their faces he stared at her. Then his hand went out and gently touched her cheek and in a voice unrecognizable from what it was a minute earlier he said, 'Lass, I'll never forgive meself, never as long as I live. When I think of it I could . . . aye, I'll say it, I could cut me own throat, because what happened was all my fault. I knew from the moment I saw him he wasn't right and never would be. I'm not going to say, Do you understand that I felt he was mine and this was his home, because that would be to ask you to understand that I was as mad as him. It was just sheer bloody cussedness on my part. I wanted to prove everybody wrong, particularly John, because somehow John had taken his place in me mind, and I didn't want that. I'd always put Glen first, 'cos Glen was like me inside, he was a go-getter, a pusher. He knew what he wanted and he went after it. Lass' – he now caught hold of her hand in his – 'can you ever forgive me? I've gone through hell. Even though you were the means of giving me back me body I know I'd rather have stayed like that for the rest of me life than have it bought at the price of what you went through. And all that talk just gone about the factory and one thing and another, 'twas all palaver. At least, it will be if you can't find it in your heart to forgive me, because you know, somehow I couldn't take it on again without you. Doesn't that seem strange? No, I don't suppose it does to you. But you see I did take it on, I did run that place, I did do everything without Alicia's help. I had her love, but that was here in this house sort of. Now I know for a certainty I couldn't go back into that place and work as I did if you weren't there to support me. You've come to mean a lot to me, Jinny, and at times I've treated you rough. But I did think you understood that part of me. About the other though . . . well, there's no excuse. I never thought I would say I wanted to kill me own son for what he had done to you, but I think if I could have got at him that night I would have. Aw, lass, lass, please don't cry.' He put his hand and cupped her cheek, and when her chin dropped on to her chest he asked in a whisper, 'One thing more, I'm . . . I'm terrified to ask it but it's got to come, are you all right? You know what I mean.'

It was some seconds before she could raise her head, and now she nodded as she wiped her face slowly with a handkerchief.

'You're sure?'

For the first time she spoke, 'Yes, I'm sure.'

'Thanks be to God.' It was the most fervent prayer he had ever said in his life, and it seemed to leave him almost exhausted. His hands lay limp on his lifeless thighs, his shoulders hunched and his head fell forward, and the sight touched her as nothing else would have; and now it was she who put her hand out and touched his, and when he raised his eyes to hers she said softly, 'When do we start work?'

It was some seconds before he spoke. The lines at the corners of his eyes crinkled into folds, his lips quivered for a moment, and then he said brokenly, 'You will? You're game?'

'I'm game.'

'Aw, lass.' He let out a long slow breath. 'It'll be a new life for me. You can't imagine. And' – his eyebrows moved upwards now and his eyes widened – 'for our John an' all. What do you think of that, him consenting to come in? Well, when I'm making me confession I might as well add that I misjudged that lad. And that's another thing.' He poked his head towards her now. 'He hates to be called a lad. We must be careful, mustn't we? By the way, another question. Do you like him?'

Again her throat was tight, but she forced her tone to be nonchalant as she replied, 'There's nothing to dislike about him.'

'Well, that's a neither here nor there answer. Anyway' – he turned his head – 'where's he got with that damned hanky. John!' he bawled and within seconds the door was opened and John entered; and the handkerchief he held out his father put straight into his pocket where the corner of another one was in evidence. Then looking up at John, he said, 'We're away, son: Henderson and son and private secretary are invading those works as soon as that damned doctor gives me the go-ahead. And that, if I know anything, will be next week.'

Standing now behind his father's wheelchair, John looked at Jinny, and she at him, and they smiled tolerantly at each other.

6

It was some weeks later before the doctor gave his permission for Bob to make his assault on the factory.

Following Bob's strict orders, neither Mr Christopher Waitland nor anyone at the works, apart from those he'd seen at the house, had been informed of the extent of his recovery. So it was on a biting cold day towards the end of October that his wheelchair was pushed up the ramp of the estate car and he, with Jinny, was driven by John to the works.

John had previously compared the width of the chair with that of the lift, and he knew that the lift would take the chair with a foot to spare.

It was half-past ten in the morning when they arrived. As Bob had said, he wanted to be sure that Chris Waitland would be at his desk for, being able to play lord and master, he would likely be choosing his own time to arrive, and so, following Garbrook's pattern, it could be ten or thereabouts.

When Sam opened the glass door for the man in the wheelchair and his two companions, he stood gaping. Then, his voice like a small squeak coming out of a large balloon, he said, 'Mr Henderson?'

'In the flesh, Sam, in the flesh.'

'Eeh God!'

'No, no, not God, Sam, just me, as ever was.'

'I can't believe it. Eeh! I can't believe it. Oh man, I'm pleased to see you, Mr Henderson. But I thought . . .'

'Aye, so did a lot of other people, Sam, so did a lot of other people. Still, don't you go near that telephone and ring upstairs now. Do you hear me?'

'No, not if you don't want me to, Mr Henderson.'

'I don't want you to, Sam. Give me ten minutes to get up to the top floor and into me office and then you can pass it round.'

'I'll do that, Mr Henderson, I'll do that. Eeh, I am glad to see you. You an' all, miss. Eeh! it's like new life comin' back into the place.'

'And this is me son, one of your new bosses.' Bob jerked his head back towards John, and Sam said, 'Well, if he's a chip off the old block, he'll do me, Mr Henderson. But . . . but we've met afore, haven't we, sir?'

'Yes, we have, Sam.'

Sam now led the way across the hall to the lift, exclaiming as he did so, 'Eeh! by lad. Eeh! by lad.'

When the lift opened two men and a young girl emerged, and all three paused and looked at the man in the wheelchair before walking on; and then, as if of one mind, they stopped dead and turned and looked towards the lift doors which were now closing. 'Good as a play, isn't it?' Bob said. His voice was low, and John replied, 'Yes. First act coming up. I only hope all the company are in their places. What do you say?' He turned and looked at Jinny, and she said, 'You know what I'm waiting for?'

Both men looked at her now. 'To get on that phone and speak to Miss Caldwell.' Her voice now assumed a superior air as she said, 'This is Miss Brownlow speaking from Mr Henderson's office. Would you please send up a secretary? One who has good knowledge of French. I would like this attended to immediately.' They were still chuckling when the lift stopped at the top floor, and when John pushed his father's chair on to the thick pile carpet, Bob held up his hand for a moment, and he sat looking about him at this place he had built. He had given special attention to how this floor should be laid out, and the size of each office.

He now took in a long slow breath, straightened his tie, slicked back his hair; then nodding his head, they went forward. According to the plan, Jinny tapped on the main office door, then opened it, went in and stood aside, and John pushed the chair over the threshold into the room and almost caused the collapse of the two people in it.

Christopher Waitland was sitting behind his desk. There had been a smile on his face as if he had been exchanging a joke with his secretary who was standing to the side of the desk, her body leaning over it and towards him. Now, as if one, they became transfixed, every feature of their faces appeared stretched to twice its capacity, and they didn't move until Bob said, 'Well, aren't you pleased to see me?'

Christopher Waitland slowly rose from his chair; then he put his hand out as if to push his secretary away and she stepped aside, allowing him to pass her and come to the front of the desk, and when at last he spoke his words sounded like a challenge. 'What's this?' he said.

'What does it look like, Chris? I'm back.'

'You . . . you can't be. I mean, you can't do this, not like this, all of a sudden.'

'All of a sudden? What are you talking about? I've been gone eight months. You should have known I'd turn up sometime.'

'I . . . I understood . . . I thought.'

'I know what you understood and what you thought. You thought I was flat on me back for life, didn't you? And you were settled here. Well, I'm sorry to tell you, Chris, you're not. I've got me harness on again, and so would you mind removing yourself into your old office? And I'd be obliged if you would do it as quickly as I understood you left it to come in here.'

'This is not right. It . . . I mean, I should have had notice. What I mean is . . .'

'I know what you mean.' Bob's voice was flat now. 'You mean you should have had good notice to try to straighten things out afore I appeared on the scene. Well, by all accounts, and I've had accounts – ' He nodded at the purple-faced man now and went on, 'Oh, yes, I've been kept informed: you've made a pretty poor go of being my replacement.'

'Now look here, I've done all I could . . . well, you only have to read the papers and you'll know the predicament steel is in.'

'You're talking about the Steel Corporation. We are not the Steel Corporation, Chris, we are a private engineering firm, we just make the stuff up and push it around and as far as I can gather you haven't been pushing it very hard, have you?'

'That isn't fair; things are in a bad way. I've got two men out.'

'Yes, I know you've got two men out. And one of them is your nephew, Broadway, who was in the clerk's office. Got a quick promotion. Nepotism it's called, isn't it? Nepotism. Well, as far as I can gather, up to now he's lost the Belgian orders and he's even lost Swinburne's. Now Swinburne's are on the doorstep, so to speak, only two hundred miles away, and they've dealt with us for fifteen years. Aw, bloody hell! don't you tell me what you've done and what you haven't done. Get yourself out of here.'

'You can't do this. I'll see Mr Garbrook, he it was who put me here.'

'Well, he might have, but Garbrook is not running this factory. And let me tell you something in case you don't know, I own seventy-five per cent of the shares here and fifty-one per cent at the container concern. Now you work that out and tell me who's in charge and who can say you go here or you stay. Now, an ultimatum: I give you half an hour to get your gear out and back to where you were, or you might find yourself joining your nephew in the dole queue. Oh, I forgot, they don't have any queues these days, they have their cheques sent to them. Well, that should be nice for both of you.'

Chris Waitland now came and stood in front of the chair and, staring down at Bob, he said, 'You forget that I'm on the board and, big shareholder or not, it will cost you dear to get rid of me.'

'Aye, I'd thought of that and not just today or yesterday, Chris. Well, get going, and we'll see about it.'

All this while John had stood with his eyes cast towards the carpet. That he was deeply embarrassed by the scene in which a man was being made to look small Jinny could see. Yet it didn't affect her that way. No, for she was remembering the morning this man had turfed her out of the office, and because of it, as she told herself now, this bit of retaliation was sweet. All right, she was holding a grudge, being spiteful if you like, but what was good to give shouldn't be bad to take.

She turned now and looked at the secretary Miss Phillips. Miss Phillips looked almost to be on the point of fainting. She had both hands to her throat and her flat breast was doing its best to heave. When her boss spoke to her, saying. 'Go and inform Rodgers and Carter,' she repeated in an almost childlike voice, 'Inform Rodgers and . . .?'

But her last words were cut off by Chris Waitland yelling, 'Yes! Tell them to come and move the things, woman.' Then looking at Bob as if for a moment he was having to restrain himself from striking him, he brought his teeth together and ground them audibly before marching from the room, followed by his bewildered secretary.

Bob and Jinny smiled at each other, but John turned away and went towards the window, and as he stood looking out his father said to him, 'You didn't enjoy that, did you, lad?'

'No, I didn't.' John swung round. 'I know he's too big for his boots and that he wanted taking down a peg, but I think your hand was too heavy, and although I was for you doing it like this, I didn't realize what it was going to mean.'

'Oh, John' – Bob sighed now – 'you're new to this game. That fellow just gone is a toady. I've put up with him for years because of his connection with Garbrook, but he's a mean man in all ways. He's got a small mind. I'm not a bit disturbed at what I've done. Neither are you, Jinny, are you?' He looked up at Jinny, and she, looking at John, held his eyes for a moment before she said, 'No, I'm not. You see, you weren't here the morning they sent me scudding like the merest schoolgirl down to the pool where I wiped the floor with Miss Cadwell. I didn't mind that, but when she accused me of having an affair with my boss' – she now cast a smiling glance down at Bob – 'well, that was just too much, that was the moment when I hit her. But now I'm only waiting to get on that phone and hit her in a different way. All right, I'm spiteful, but I've never enjoyed anything so much for a long, long time. And as your father says, Mr Waitland is a mean man.'

'She's right, John, so save your pity.' Then looking back at Jinny, he said, 'I wonder what they'll say now about us, scandalwise, eh? We'd better give them something to think about, lass, eh? Put it about that we've shacked up, eh? That's the term, isn't it, shacked up? What about it then, eh?'

She was going towards the inner room and she turned her head and looked in his direction as she said, 'I've never been in favour of shacking up and I'm not going to start now.'

'Oh, it's marriage you're after, is it? Well, we'll have to see about it, won't we?'

He was laughing, until he looked at his son, and then the laughter slid slowly from his face as he saw that his bit of fun had touched a sore spot. Well! Well! . . . Well! Well!

The door opened now to admit Miss Phillips who had evidently regained her composure, which was proclaimed by the stiffness of her body and face as, none too quietly, she cleared the desk drawers.

And all the while John stood at the broad window looking down into the side yard where men were loading lorries with steel plates and rods; but his mind wasn't on the business, it was on what had been said a few minutes ago. Although he knew his father was joking, it had nevertheless startled him.

He turned now to see his father heaving himself from the wheelchair on to the revolving leather chair behind his desk. And there he sat with his hands on it, looking straight ahead into the room. And John watched his face become suffused with an expression of infinite sadness which his voice expressed as he said, 'The last time I sat here, John, I was pulsing with life, almost as much as our Glen. But look at us now, him with no reason left and me with no legs. And Alicia and Yvonne, where are they now? I'd have the answer if I could believe in either heaven or hell.'

As Bob's head began to sink on to his chest, John said, 'It's over. You're here, you're back. Look upon it as a challenge, as I've got to do.'

'Aye.' His father lifted his head to the side now and glanced up at him and repeated, 'Aye, but you are whole, lad.'

'I've never been whole.' The words held a deep ring of bitterness that surprised both Bob and Jinny. But then, in his mercurial way, John turned to Jinny, his voice light now, saying, 'Well, have you forgotten your purpose in life?'

'My purpose in . . .?' She screwed up her eyes for a moment, then smiled as she said, 'Oh. Miss Cadwell?'

'Yes, Miss Cadwell. I'm dying to hear the exchange.'

'I'll do it from the other room.'

'No, you won't.' Bob put his hand out and pushed the phone along the desk. 'You'll do it from here. I wouldn't miss this for anything.'

Now that she was on the point of getting her own back, Jinny hesitated, for a fleeting picture she saw herself as Miss Cadwell when she should reach her late forties, when her only pleasure in life might be in showing her authority over others. But then the image was thrust aside by the thought that she would never grow to be like that. Miss Cadwell must have been born bitchy. Moreover, she'd had it in for her since she had first entered the firm and without reason. That was the crucial point, without reason.

She picked up the phone, and when the voice at the other end spoke, she said, 'Typing pool, please.'

It was some seconds before the voice said, 'Yes? Miss Cadwell speaking.'

Jinny let a few seconds more elapse; then the voice came again, higher now: 'Miss Cadwell here.'

'Oh. Miss Cadwell, this is Miss Brownlow speaking from Mr Henderson's office.' Did she hear a gasp? 'We are in residence again.' Yes, she did hear a gasp; there was no mistaking it this time. 'Please send up a typist. I would prefer Miss Power. Is she available?'

When there was no response whatever to this question she said, 'I asked you, Miss Cadwell, if Miss Power is still available.' There was a choking sound at the other end of the phone; then the voice, like a hoarse whisper, said, 'Miss Power is with Mr Brignall.'

'Then put someone in her place and send Miss Power up at once.'

'I don't think I . . . I can do . . .'

'Oh, what a pity! The work is important. Perhaps you wouldn't mind filling in yourself.'

When the phone was banged down Jinny drew her head back, then slowly put down her receiver.

Bob was smiling widely at her, but not John. He was looking at her in a scrutinizing way which caught her attention, and when he said, 'Feel better?' she said slowly, 'No. I should do, but I . . . I feel . . .' She could not add the word, cheap, yet this feeling was for the moment overlaid by a wave of resentment brought about by the look on his face which was distinctly conveying her own impression of herself, and before she could check her tongue she cried at him, 'Oh, don't look so smug! I know it was taking advantage, and you wanted me to do it, just to test me, didn't you? Well now, you have your answer; I can be as bitchy as the rest, and more so.'

'Here, here. What's this?' She did not answer Bob but, turning quickly, she went into the outer office and closed the door.

Leaning back in his chair, Bob looked at his son, who was taking his overcoat from the stand in the corner of the room, and said, 'Why is it, lad, you get people on the raw? Now, she would have been less than human if she didn't get back on that dried old stick. And don't forget why she did it. That woman had taken her character away, coupled her name with mine, set her up as a loose piece and' – his voice dropped almost to a whisper as he ended – 'I guess she's been fighting a battle for years against such a title. Why the hell she hasn't been picked up – no; that's the wrong word in this case, married is the word – before now beats me. There must be a lot of blind buggers kicking around. Yet that Michael bloke isn't blind and he's a presentable sort, too, but too young for her, although he could give her a couple of years. But it's someone older, steadier, somebody who's going to make her use that mind of hers, 'cos, let me tell you, she's got it up top where business acumen is concerned.' There was a short silence before he ended, 'It makes you think. Aye, it does, it makes you think.'

He watched his son turn and look towards him. There again was that odd look in his eye. 'You off now?' he said flatly. 'I thought we'd have a bite together at dinner-time.'

'I don't feel like lunch. I'm going down to the floor.'

'Ay; well, yes, you'll need all the information you can pick up within the next week or so. Anyway, don't worry about seeing me back, I'll get in touch with Willie and tell him to come down around three because by that time I think I'll have had enough for one day. Excitement has its price an' all.'

'Yes. Yes it has, so don't overdo it. I'll see you this evening if not before. Take care.'

'Aye. Aye, I will. The boss'll see to that.' He motioned towards the closed door, and John looked towards it, before going out. The Boss he had called her: no, no. He was letting his imagination and, yes, his jealousy run wild.

As he made for the lift, its doors opened and Noreen Power came out. She stopped, uncertainly, and when she stammered, 'M . . . Miss Brownlow sent for me,' his only reply was to point to the door next to the main office, and she said, 'Oh yes, there. Thank you.'

After tapping on the door of the outer office and being told to enter, Noreen was confronted by a smiling Jinny, and immediately she cried, 'Eeh! I'm glad to see you back, Jinny. Eeh! I am. And you wouldn't believe what's going on downstairs. It's like you had dropped a bomb down there. She couldn't believe it . . . Miss Cadwell. We thought she was going to pass out; she has the jitters, she really has. What do you want me to do? I'm not too good at French; you know I'm not.'

'There's nothing very much as yet, Noreen,' Jinny said quietly now. 'I just want you to sort out these letters, you know like you do downstairs, filing the firms together in their date order and transferring the salient points of each on to the index cards. Then when you're finished they can all be sent into Mr Waitland's office. They're mostly bills and orders and such, covering the last six months.'

'Yes, I'll do that, Jinny. I'd . . . I'd like to work up here. He's still a terror though, isn't he?' She jerked her head backwards. Then pulling a small face, she smiled, adding, 'I shouldn't say that, should I? Not to you, anyway, because then you've always been able to manage him. Do you mind if I ask if it's right what they're saying?'

There was a pause before Jinny said stiffly, 'And what are they saying?'

'Oh, just that you're going to marry him.'

7

'We're back, Dorry.'

Jinny had entered the hall, and as Dorry came hurrying towards her she added with an attempt at lightness, 'I hope Cissie is preparing a dinner fit for a conquering hero.'

But Dorry made no reply; she looked past Jinny to the drawing-room. And when Jinny followed her gaze she saw Florence standing in the doorway, and even over the distance the hostility was evident.

'Why wasn't I informed that my father had recovered?' Florence demanded as she moved towards Jinny.

It was almost in the same vein that Jinny replied, 'You had better ask him that, Mrs Brook.' And turning now, she waited as Willie pushed the chair up the ramp and over the threshold and into the hall.

As soon as Bob saw his daughter he greeted her: 'Well, hello there, stranger. What brings you to Fellburn in this weather? I thought you and your lot were still away on that pricey-sounding world cruise or whatever.'

'We flew back from Venice yesterday and stayed at one of the Heathrow hotels overnight, but as we were right by the airport I thought I'd take a quick flight up here to surprise you and find out what was going on. Why wasn't I . . . I informed of . . . of your recovery?'

'Well now, Florence, you've hardly been all that accessible of late, have you? Anyway, it's a long story and at the moment I'm rather tired and I think I'll have me bite to eat upstairs. By the way, Willie – ' He turned his head and looked back and up into Willie's face, saying, 'It was a good idea of John's, don't you think, about a lift in that corner?'

'Yes, boss, a very good idea.'

'I'll get some estimates and we'll get to work on it. Make a note of that, Jinny, estimates for lift . . . pronto.' Then looking at his daughter again, he said in an off-hand manner, 'You come alone?'

'Yes, I came alone. Ronnie went straight home with the children.'

'How long do you mean to stay?'

'Would you like me to go on to Devonshire tonight?' Her tone was icy.

'Now, now, Florence, I was just thinking that . . . well, you'd be here on your own during the day because I'm a working man once again. And you must be wanting to see how things are down there after being away so long.'

He watched her suck at her lips before she asked, 'Where is John?'

'When I last saw him he was learning the business on the shop floor, finding out how to lift a three hundredweight steel rod without breaking his fingernails.' As he gave a small laugh at his own weak joke and indicated by a movement of his head that he wanted Willie to lift him from the chair, Florence said, 'And our Glen?'

'Get me upstairs, Willie,' Bob said quietly. And when the big fellow lifted him up and laid him partly over his shoulder as he would have done a child, before mounting the stairs, Jinny turned away because that was a sight she couldn't bear to watch; such dependence deprived the man not only of his bombast but also, in a way, of all dignity.

It was a full minute before Jinny turned towards the stairs again, and as she did so Florence almost thrust herself in front of her, saying, 'As you seem to have taken on yourself the running of the house, will you tell me what has happened to Glen?'

Jinny drew in her chin and pressed her head back as if to remove herself further from the face that was confronting her before she said, 'He's back in hospital under strict surveillance.'

'What! What do you mean? Who's doing this?'

'Your brother, Mrs Brook, attacked me. He wasn't accountable for his actions, but nevertheless he attacked me.'

'Glen? Glen attacked you? Glen wouldn't hurt a fly.'

'The Glen you knew mightn't have hurt a fly, but the Glen he has become would; he would even have gone as far as to kill me if he hadn't been stopped in time.'

They stared at each other in hostility for almost a full minute; then Florence, her full lips pressing one against the other, almost spat out the words, 'I suppose you'll tell me now that it was a bedroom scene.'

'Yes, it was just that.'

'Then all I can say, miss, is that you encouraged him. Deranged or otherwise, you must have encouraged him. You're that type. You've worked on my father; it's evident to us all. It wouldn't surprise me what you get up to next, but I'll put a spoke in your wheel, I'll get the family together.'

Jinny put out her hand and slowly pressed the woman aside as she said, 'Do that, Mrs Brook, do that;' then with shaking legs she mounted the stairs and when she entered her room she dropped down on the bed fully dressed as she was and lay as one exhausted. It had certainly been a day, a day and a half. She had been shocked by Noreen Power's remark, and then this, going to get the family together to prevent her . . . from doing what? Marrying their father.

Slowly she sat up on the bed and, staring ahead, she nodded as if at the reflection of herself as she said, 'Well then, why not give credence to the lie; nobody else wanted her. Oh yes, there was Michael. He was persistent, but she had no real feeling for Michael, and the one for whom she had any real feeling only wanted her on the cheap. But Bob. What feelings had she for her boss? Oh, she liked him; her feelings for him were deep. Was it love? Well, she had learned of late there were all kinds of love, and in spite of his disability Bob Henderson was still a man. Oh yes, very much so. She had been handmaiden to him for some time now and he would always need a handmaiden. Well, let her be practical. Oh God, yes, let her be practical for once. If she was she could become mistress of this house, and what was more she would be a rich woman with her finger deep in the pie of Henderson and Garbrook.

The decision almost made, she rose from the bed, but it was as she unbuttoned her coat a voice said, 'And you'll have a stepson and you'll have to work with him, and there will be times when you'll see him day after day. What price then the compensation for being the handmaiden?

It was early evening when Bob said, 'I think I'll go to bed, Willie. It's been a day and a half.'

'It has that, sir, and you've done splendidly. My! you set that place alight this morning. I went into the canteen; you should have heard them. You'd think there'd been a revolution and the president was back.'

'Really?'

'Oh, yes, yes, sir. I'm afraid Mr Waitland wasn't very popular in himself. As for the new systems he was devising, well I think a strike would have been the end result. Apparently, he wasn't approachable. As I heard one fellow put it, one mouthful from you solved more problems than all the typewritten notices coming down from the top floor.'

'Well, that's nice to know. It's always nice to know you're wanted, Willie. And by the way, you'll still be wanted. I've been thinking about it, this business of you and me, how you're going to fill your time in when I'm at the office, so I thought that after you'd got me dusted and powdered and to the office in the mornings, what about you running a first-aid room at the works? They run off to the infirmary with scratches. There's a first-aid box with bits and pieces. But seriously, some of those fellows get nasty gashes in their hands from the rods, so how about you working out a few hours a day there, either morning or afternoon or spread around, taking your free time in between, then every other night seeing me home. John'll take over when you're off duty like, that's if he's not abroad. Which means the sooner we get that lift installed the better, and Jinny on to driving lessons. Anyway, how does the idea strike you?'

'Strikes me very well, sir. Just leave it to me and Mr John; we'll fix it up between us.'

'Aw, well, that's settled. Now get these bloody pants off me.' He laughed as he added now, 'I've been so used to a bare pelt for months that I feel all trussed up in . . .'

The door being thrust open cut off his words as Florence entered, and now her father bawled at her, 'What the hell do you mean coming in like that! Can't you see I'm practically naked? Here, give me that cover.' He grabbed at the quilt that was lying over the foot of the bed and put it over his bare limp legs; then he glared at Florence where she stood in the middle of the room glaring back at him, and now he bawled, 'Answer me! What do you bloody well mean, stalking in like that? Even when your mother was alive you never did anything like . . .'

'When my mother was alive things were different.'

He paused before he nodded, and, his voice quieter now, he said, 'Aye. Yes, of course when your mother was alive things were different.'

'But her place has been taken downstairs; in fact, all over the house, as far as I can gather.'

'What are you getting at?'

'That one, your so-called secretary, she was sitting in Mother's place at the dining table.'

Bob lowered his head, closed his eyes, drew his lower lip tight between his teeth, then muttered, 'Girl, your mother is dead. I've had to batter that into my brain for months now, she won't come back. Things have altered. As for Jinny taking her seat downstairs, she wasn't to know where your mother always sat.'

'She knew all right. She's taken command.'

'Aye, well, let me tell you, if that's the case I'm glad of it, because there's been nobody else come forward, rushed like to look after me or the house.'

'I offered . . . we offered.'

'Aye, on your own terms, that I promote that lump of a husband of yours from a fruit shop into my factory. Not on the bottom floor. Oh no, but the top one. Well, I wasn't having it, not for any price. So I've been damned glad of Jinny, and always will be. She's got more brains in her little finger, let me tell you, than you or your three sisters put together can account for, although I say it as shouldn't . . .'

'Oh yes, yes, I'm sure she has. Oh, yes, I know that. We four are dim. We haven't got enough sense to be wily, crafty, cunning . . .'

Bob's arm was extended to its length, its index finger stabbing out towards her, when the door opened again and John entered. His face looking almost as angry as his sister's and ignoring his father, he addressed her straightaway, saying, 'One of these days somebody's going to belt you right across the mouth.'

'Well, it certainly won't be you . . . or her.'

'Don't you be too sure. If I'd been her I'd have knocked you on your back.'

'What's this? What's this now?'

John turned and, looking at his father, he said, 'She went for Jinny as if she was some low slut you had brought in from the streets; in fact, she almost said as much.'

'I did nothing of the kind. I merely told her to get out of my mother's chair, that she wasn't mistress of this house . . . not yet anyway.' She now glanced at her father, and the room became still for a moment, no one speaking, for his head was wagging slowly now, and, his words keeping in time with his nodding, he said, 'So you said she wasn't mistress of the house?'

This elicited no response from Florence, and he went on, 'Well, now, Florence, you've opened up a question that's been in me mind for some time. I've always believed in paying people the right wage for the right labour, and Jinny's laboured well for me for months now, and at times she's kept me from losing me reason, and I've wondered how I could repay her. This morning when I was in the office, it came to me that I could put her on the board. Aye, I thought, that's what I'll do, eventually I'll put her on the board. But I knew that wasn't enough, I knew I wanted to do something more, not only in the way of repaying her but of satisfying meself, some want in me.'

'You wouldn't! You wouldn't!' The words were spurted from Florence's lips in a spray of saliva. 'You . . . you wouldn't dare put her in mother's place.'

'Don't you say to me, lass, what I would dare to or what I wouldn't dare to. I've always gone on me own bloody way and I'll do it in this. Only one thing you're right about: I wouldn't put her in your mother's place; nobody can fill your mother's place. I know that, and Jinny knows that; but, as I said, I've to realize the dead are dead, an' if I've got to go on living I've got to have some kind of companionship. I'm made that way. Man or woman.' He now flashed an angry glance at John; and he held the look as he saw that his son's face looked distorted, it was as if he had witnessed something utterly abhorrent; his eyes were mere slits, seemingly lost in their sockets; his lips had squared away from his teeth; and his cheeks that the winter climate always reddened were now devoid of colour. His face looked grey and, of a sudden, old. He was about to say, 'And what's the matter with you? Don't you approve?' but he told himself that would be hitting below the belt. Of course he wouldn't approve. What he wanted to say in this moment was, 'Don't look at me like that, lad. Please don't look at me like that. You don't understand me. I doubt if you ever will.' But his thoughts were interrupted by Florence's crying. 'I'm going home and I'll never enter these doors again as long as she's here.'

'Well, that's entirely up to you, lass,' he called after her as she hurried towards the door, 'but I'd better warn you: if it lies with me, she's going to be here for a long, long time. An' tell that to your Ronnie. But I don't suppose it will make any difference to him, because he would bow his knee to a trollop if he thought he could get his foot in here.'

When the door banged he hunched his shoulders against the shudder for a moment and, looking at Willie who had been standing well back in the room, he said, 'Leave us for a minute, will you, Willie?'

When the door had closed on Willie, Bob did not immediately speak, nor did he look at John, but, his hands making nervous movements, he smoothed the quilt that was covering his legs before he said, 'Now it's your turn to spit it out, else you'll burst. You look like thunder. You don't hold with the idea, do you?'

'*You can't do it.*'

Strangely enough Bob did not bawl his reply to this: his voice was slow and level as he said, 'I can, lad, I can. It's up to her.' He watched John's adam's apple bouncing in his throat before he could bring out, 'She'll take you out of pity.'

'Oh, aye. Well, that could be, but there's worse things than pity. They say it's akin to love, an' she's very easy to love. And apparently I'm not the only one who thinks that way.' He paused a moment before he added, 'There's a big handsome Romeo. I hear from Willie he called again the other day. She happened to be out. He's tenacious. I'll have to look slippy, won't I? But lad, come and sit down, I want to have a talk with you.'

'The hell you do. You've said enough.'

As Bob watched his son stalk out of the room he bowed his head to his chest and gritted his teeth; then he rubbed his hand firmly round his face and pressed his fingers against his eyeballs before straightening his shoulders and reaching out and pressing the bell to the side of him.

When Willie opened the door, he was stayed from entering by Bob saying, 'Tell Jinny I'd like a word with her, will you?'

'Now? You wouldn't like me to help you to bed first?'

'No. I'd like to see her now.'

It was almost five minutes later when she entered the room. Her face looked white and drawn. She held herself stiffly. Another time he would have greeted her with, 'Hello, what's up with you? On your high horse?' But tonight he simply beckoned her forward with a lift of his hand, then said quietly, 'Pull up a chair.'

She did as he bade her, and when she placed the chair opposite to him he said, 'Bring it round the side here, I want to hold your hand.'

These words were accompanied with a little wry smile, but they did not affect her expression, and when she sat down by his side and he had taken her hand in both of his, he said, 'No beating about the bush. I know the gist of what happened downstairs. Now I'm going to put a question to you, it's one of these "if" questions, without . . . well, how can I put it, real meaning, sort of pushed in between something else, if you follow. Is parenthesis the right word? Or is it hypothetical. I don't know. But you see' – he squeezed her hand – 'I know some big words an' all. That surprises you, doesn't it?' Still she didn't respond to his mood, and so he went on, 'Well, the question I want to push in, which isn't really a question mind, is this. *If . . . if* I was to ask you to marry me, would you do it? Mind, I'm not asking you, I'm just putting it to you, would you do it?'

'Stop playing games.'

'Aw, now look . . . look Jinny, I'm . . . I'm not playing games. All right, all right, I put it that way, and I repeat, I'm not really asking you, I'm just saying *if*.'

She swallowed deeply then said, 'The "*if*" has come about because of your daughter?'

'No, no, not really. It's been in me mind some time now. Well, not exactly that, but . . . Aw, how can I put it? Look, just for me own satisfaction, answer me straight, if I asked you, or if I was to ask you, what would your answer be?'

She looked into the round eyes, that in this moment were looking so much like John's had a short while ago when Mrs Brook had slated her in such a fashion and so unexpectedly that she had found no words with which to combat her accusations. No rage had risen in her to help her defend herself; on the contrary, the effect of the woman's slating remarks had left her feeling weak as if she had been physically attacked. And then John had put his arms about her. He hadn't uttered a word but had pressed her close to him and brought her face to rest against his. That embrace had lasted perhaps for a minute, and then he had released her and hurried from the room.

She heard herself say, 'I couldn't give you an answer straightaway. I would have to say, I would like to think about it.'

'Do you like me?'

'Yes, I like you. You know I do.'

'Do you more than like me?'

'I like you very much.'

She watched him wet his lips before he said, 'I'm still a man, Jinny. You made me into one again. I could love you a damned sight better than any younger fellow would, I know that; and cause you less heartache, too. Yet, I don't know about that, because where there's any kind of love between a man and a woman there's bound to be jealousy. It makes me sick when I hear partners saying, oh, I'm not jealous of my husband . . . or wife, I trust him. Well, my answer to that is, to put it boldly as is my wont, they're bloody liars, or, on the other hand, they don't know what love is. So I don't suppose I'd be any better than the young 'uns in that way, especially with a lass like you. And then there would be the fear. There's always the fear of losing the loved one, that's if you really love. You get jealous if he or she pays a little attention to somebody else, or as a couple of silly bitches of my acquaintance are always doing, praise up other fellows to their men. Do you know something, Jinny? You're a sensible lass but I don't think you've reached the stage where you understand men, because, you know, we never grow out of our childhood. To put it crudely, we're at the breast so to speak all our lives, for we need comfort, we need reassurance, and when we go looking for a wife, we've got the potential mother in our eye all the time. Alicia knew this. Oh yes, Alicia knew this. That's why we had such a happy life together. I'll never stop loving Alicia, Jinny. There's part of me cut off like a deep freeze, and she's in there, and always will be, but there's another part of me that's got to go on living, as I just said to that numskull of a daughter of mine, and I want companionship. But . . . but don't pull your hand away. Listen. I'm not asking you to be any old man's darling; in fact, let me come clean, I'm not asking you to marry me at all. I don't want to marry you . . . Aw, bugger me eyes! that's a lie.' He jerked his head to one side; then turning to her again, a small grin on his face now, he said, 'A man wouldn't be in his right senses if he didn't want you. But Jinny, there's something I want more than a wife. You might think this strange, but I want a son. I had two sons and I've lost one.' His voice broke slightly now. 'So I've got one son left. And I'm telling you something that I wouldn't tell him. I love him, I love him dearly, and I always have, but I haven't been able to convince him of that. He always thought it was Glen and nobody else. And in a way perhaps he was right, because Alicia seemed to favour him and I didn't like Alicia favouring anybody else but me. There it is again, you see, it's the jealousy of your own son. He's a pigheaded, stubborn, obstinate . . . Aw, God above! I could go on, but this much I know, Jinny.' He now patted her hand and leant towards her, and his voice dropped to a mere whisper as he said, 'If I was to have you, I'd lose him, because he wants you. And I know that he wants you more than anything else he's ever wanted in his life. That episode he had . . .'

'Wait. Wait, Bob.' She tugged her hand from his. 'Yes, yes, I know he wants me, but only for bed, and I'm putting that plainly too.'

'Aw, no, lass, no.' He pulled back from her, his voice rising now. 'You've got him all wrong.'

'Oh, no, I haven't. He said as much.'

'He has?'

'Well, when we've talked, it's nearly always ended up in heated words because his covert opinion implied he was against marriage and what went with it, except . . .' She paused and jerked her head to the side, refusing to add, 'the bed.'

There was silence between them for a moment, and then, his voice low once more, he said, 'You're wrong, Jinny. He was as near doing murder, an' he might have done if I hadn't been his father, not ten minutes gone, because I indicated that I was going to marry you. If I ever wanted proof that he had fallen, and it was hurting, I had it then. Do you like him?'

'I don't know.'

'Well, do you love him?'

She stared straight into his face as she answered quietly now, 'I think perhaps I do, yet I'm not sure. Someone said, to love without liking foreshadows the divorce before the wedding.'

'Oh, there's always somebody saying something, lass, and coining clever phrases, an' they are generally bitter disillusioned individuals. Look, Jinny.' He again leant towards her and took her hand. 'If you have him, I'll have both of you. If you don't, then in a way I'll lose both of you, because he'll think we'll hitch up sometime together and he'll go off. And I couldn't stand that, Jinny, not to lose two sons. I've got four girls but quite candidly, lass, they don't mean much to me, never did. It was the lads I was for from the beginning. You see, a son is something different, he's the male part of you. You won't understand that, but a man would because a son's the one that's going to carry your name on down the generations like. Tell me something, lass, if he was to ask you to marry him, would you? Now come on, straight.'

'Yes.'

There it was, she had committed herself. Yes, if he asked her to marry him she would. But would he ask her to marry him? Yes, perhaps sometime. But days or weeks could go by before he would bring himself to it, for he would determine he wasn't going to jump in to do his father one in the eye.

There now arose in her a lightness. It was like slow laughter. It took the stiffness out of her limbs and softened the look on her face; it even brought a little colour back on her cheeks, and he was quick to notice this, and he said, 'Well, well, you're smiling. What's funny?'

'Nothing. Nothing.' Then rising to her feet, she leant towards him. Softly she placed her lips on his, and as she did so she felt his body jerk and she expected his arms to come about her, but he remained still, stiffly still. When she withdrew her face from his she kept it still leaning forward towards him. Their eyes held, each reflecting inner depth, desire and unimaginable imaginings. For a split second the gates of their inner minds were flung back and they stood as it were with arms outstretched holding them wide and viewing each other across a gulf that was too dangerous for them to jump.

When she straightened up and turned away neither of them uttered a word, and a moment later she was in her own room and once again sitting on the side of the bed. And now slow tears were running down her face. The feeling of lightness had vanished; there was on her now, a sadness, and it was a revealing sadness, like a lesson being learnt through pain. It was telling her that there were levels of love that went beyond the body, that transgressed the desire to express yourself through a man, that surmounted the imagined joy of suckling a child. By such love she was learning one desired only to give, in fact, simply to be a handmaiden. That was the feeling the man across the corridor had aroused in her a moment ago . . . a great overwhelming desire to give. And if there hadn't been John, she would have joyfully put it into practice. But there was John and in her need of him there was no vestige of the handmaiden. Her need here, she reckoned, came under the heading of love, but a love that was as yet wholly physical.

She dried her face and rose from the bed and as she did she heard the strident tones of Florence Brook coming from the landing saying, 'Three cars in the garage and I have to take a taxi. Take that case downstairs, Dorry. It'll be the last time you'll do anything for me in this house.'

Her voice was determinedly loud enough to carry to her father's bedroom, but there came no answering shout from that quarter. A moment later the front door was banged, and when there was the distant sound of a car starting up Jinny let out a long slow breath. Then after combing her hair back, and powdering her nose, she went out and down the stairs. In the hall, seeing Willie coming from the dining-room carrying a tray on which there was a decanter and a glass, she asked quietly, 'Where's John?'

And he answered as quietly 'He went out in a tear. He took the Jaguar and the roads are icing.' Then bending towards her, his voice even lower now, he said, 'I'm speaking out of turn, but we've worked together for quite a bit, so perhaps I can say to you, on the one hand you'll be a fool if you don't take the chance that's hovering, but on the other, you want something different out of life. He's a fine man, the boss, nobody better, but he's had his run, so to speak, whereas John . . . well, you could do a lot for him. I should imagine, emotionally, he's been knocked from dog to devil, and not just lately either. Big boy Glen, I understand, was the apple of the old man's eye. You see, Jinny, I understand this situation because I was an also ran, although my case went in the opposite direction: I was the oldest of six brothers and had to leave school to help me mother bring them up, because me father was too busy in the pubs, and then when they were all up, there was nobody like our Harry, Jimmy, Dan, Peter and Mike. Where did Willie come in?' He stretched his long face still further. 'Oh, Willie was the old maid of the family. Oh, Willie didn't want to marry. I was thirty-four, you know Jinny, before I went for me nurse's training. So in a way I understand John's situation. Do you know what I mean? When you've got to take a back seat, people forget that you're there.'

She put her hand gently on his arm. Saying, 'Nobody could forget you're there, Willie, but . . . but I get the gist. Anyway, I might as well tell you, I'm not going to be Mrs Henderson senior, and I might as well also confess to you, Willie, that in a certain kind of way I'm sorry it's to be like that.'

'Aye, I can understand that an' all. But go on now, get yourself a drink and wait for the younger version to come back and see if you can smooth the bristles, because they were standing up like a porcupine's when he left.

He laughed now as he mounted the stairs, and she went into the dining-room and poured herself out a sherry, then took it into the drawing-room and sat sipping at it.

It wasn't until the glass was empty that she looked at the clock and saw that it said half-past eight. At nine o'clock she began to think of the Jaguar on the slippery roads.

At half-past nine she went upstairs to say good-night to Bob. He was sitting straight up in bed as if waiting for her and he said immediately, 'Not very much movement downstairs. Is our John out?'

'Yes.'

'Since when?'

'Oh, earlier on in the evening. I don't know really what time he left.'

'Bloody fool. If I didn't know I would have said he had gone out to get drunk, but he doesn't drink . . . It's frosty, isn't it?'

'No' – she shook her head – 'not very. It's cold, but the roads are dry,' she lied convincingly.

He now thumped the eiderdown with the flat of his hands, saying, 'Is anything ever going right again in this bloody house? Which car has he taken?'

'Oh, I don't know.'

'Well, I'm not taking that' – he pointed to a glass and a sleeping pill – 'until I know he's in and in one piece. Talking of peace, you're a disturber of the peace, Jinny. Do you know that? You are, you are. You upset men, you always will.'

'Oh, please, don't start on that line.'

'No, no. I'm sorry, but I'm worried. Look, go on downstairs. Wait for him and . . . and put things right, will you?'

She smiled softly at him now as she said, 'All right, I'll put things right. He'll hardly get in the door before I'll put things right. Satisfied?'

'Aye, go on. Then both of you come up here, no matter what time it is, mind. Come up here, because I'll be awake.'

'All right. But I would doze in the meantime if I were you.'

'Ah, go on with you.'

She continued to smile as she left the room, but once on the landing her expression changed to one of almost annoyance. She was a disturber of the peace. At bottom, men were all alike. They didn't see themselves as disturbers of the peace. Where had that fool of a fellow got to?

She stood now in the hall looking towards the front door; then she went and opened it. The outside light was on and it showed up the bare drive with the frost glistening on the gravel like sprayed stardust. She looked up into the sky. There was a moon shining somewhere. After a moment she shivered, then came in and closed the door.

Dorry was passing through the hall and she said, 'Is there anything more you want, miss?'

'No thanks, Dorry.'

'I've left a tray ready for Mr John in the dining-room: cold stuff, but there's a flask of soup. He likes soup and he didn't have much dinner. Well, I'll be off to me bed. Will you put the lights off, miss?'

'Yes, I'll see to them, Dorry. Good-night.'

'Good-night, miss.'

Jinny was entering the drawing-room and Dorry was near the kitchen door when she turned and called, 'Miss.'

She looked towards Dorry who said, 'I wouldn't take any notice of Miss Florence, miss. She was always argumentative, spoilt she was, the least likeable of the lot, jealous nature. I wouldn't take any notice.'

'Thank you, Dorry. I won't.'

Dorry was nice, comforting. She had the urgent desire to follow her into the kitchen and talk to her and feel her motherly warmth, feel the comfort of her pat on the arm. She had a habit of doing this: 'You all right, miss?' Pat, pat. 'Come and have your breakfast, miss.' Pat, pat.

She wanted someone to be on her side, not a man, a woman. There were times when you needed a woman, and she had a feeling now that she wanted to fly to Nell. Nell would have been a comfort . . . but with qualifications because Nell would have wanted to slaughter Florence and anyone else who had said a wrong word against her.

As she sat down before the fire, annoyance rose in her again as she asked herself why she should be having this worry. What had she ever done to deserve it? All she had ever aimed to do in her life was to please people. Oh, that was a mistake. She had found that out some time ago. Yet she still went on doing it, pleasing people. And now here she was, stuck in this house with two men who waged war on her emotions. She was tired of it all, she was really.

Oh, stop it.

She got to her feet and began to pace the room. That's all she needed now was to cultivate self pity when, before her, whatever road she took, was a life of service. Yes, no matter how she looked at it, it stretched before her, a life of service . . . to father and son. So, before it was too late she'd better ask herself if she was up to it. In a way she knew where she stood with the father: he came out with things, he was straightforward. But the son: torrid silences, black looks, sarcastic remarks, throwing opinions at her that he knew to be in absolute opposition to her principles, and revelling in it . . . But he had been so gentle as he held her in his arms. She stopped her pacing. Where was he? Where on earth had he got to? She looked at the clock. It said quarter to eleven.

She was sitting by the fire again when the door opened. She swung round, only to see Willie standing there.

'No sign of him yet?'

She shook her head.

'Oh, he'll turn up, never fear. Look, I'll go up to my room. If you need me, just give me a knock.'

'Thank you, Willie . . . Good-night.'

'Good-night.'

'Willie.'

'Yes?' He turned from the door.

'What . . . what if he doesn't come home at all?'

'Well' – he nipped at his lower lip – 'give him till twelve o'clock. If he's not in then, come and knock me up. We'll have to do something about it then. He hasn't got that flat, has he?'

'No, not for a long time.'

'He's driving round somewhere then, I expect, getting the sweat out of him. He'll be cool when he comes in, never fear.' He grinned at her, then nodded and went out.

She built the fire up, pushed the couch nearer to the hearth rug, then propped the cushions in the corner of it and settled herself against them. She was tired. She'd had a long day; and the excitement of the morning had been enough for anyone without the drama of this evening, and it certainly had been drama. Nobody would believe it. She shook her head at herself. If you read it in a book you wouldn't believe it.

She resisted the urge to drop off. She looked at the clock. It was half-past eleven. When she next looked it said a quarter to twelve. She had dropped off, but something had woken her.

She got hastily to her feet and went into the hall. The house was quiet. There was no sound either inside or outside it, but something had disturbed her. She looked apprehensively around, then slowly made her way towards the front door. She turned the key in both locks but left the chain on, and when she pulled the door open for the few inches the chain allowed she could see, through the outside light, the bonnet of the car in the middle of the drive.

Quickly now, she undid the chain and pulled the door open, then stood looking towards the car. The lights were full on. Had he come in the back way and not switched them off? She looked behind her. There was still no sound of anyone moving about. Slowly now she walked out on to the porch, then on to the drive and out of the glare of the lights. Then she could see him, slumped in the passenger seat.

She pulled open the door. 'John! John! What is it?'

There was no answer.

As she climbed into the driving seat the smell of spirits wafted over her: and when his head lolled back he groaned deeply, she drew away from him and sat back and surveyed him for what might have been a full minute before she said aloud, 'Our John doesn't drink. Come on!' She was yelling at him now. 'Come on! John. Come out of this.'

'Wh . . . at?'

She got out from behind the wheel, went round to the other door and made an effort now to drag him from the seat, but he fell sideways from her. She stood shivering on the drive glaring down at him. Then turning and running into the house, she went up the stairs as quietly as possible. Tapping on Willie's door, she opened it and through the darkness she whispered, 'Willie.'

'Yes?' His voice came muffled. 'Oh, is that you, Jinny? What is it?'

'He's back.' Her voice was a hiss. 'And he's blind drunk. I can't get him out of the car.'

'John blind drunk?' The bedside light switched on now to show him sitting straight up in bed blinking at her.

'Yes; but don't say he doesn't drink. Come on, help me.' She turned from him. As she went to run on tiptoe down the corridor there came a bellow from Bob's room: 'You, Jinny!'

She stopped for a moment and closed her eyes while lowering her head. Then running back up the corridor, she pushed open his bedroom door, and as she did so he demanded, 'What is it? Something happened to our John?'

'Yes, something's happened to your John.'

'Well, lass, what is it? For God's sake!'

'Your John doesn't drink, does he? Well, your John is drunk, not only drunk, the word is paralytic.'

'Never! He's never liked the stuff.'

'Well, everybody's got to start sometime. I'll be back shortly.' On this she turned and closed the door none too gently after her.

Willie was already at the bottom of the stairs and, looking at her in her thin wool house dress, he said, 'Get a coat on before you come out there.'

She now ran into the cloakroom and picked up the first overcoat she came to, which was one of Bob's; then dragging it on, she followed Willie out to the car.

'God! He is sozzled. Well, I never! Come on, up with you!'

'Lea . . . me.'

'I know, leave you alone. We'll leave you alone when we get you inside. We're freezing. Come on, out!' And putting his arms under John's now, Willie heaved him from the seat and on to his feet, and between them they got him through the front door, through the hall and into the drawing-room, and there they dumped him on to the couch.

'Well, well.' Willie stood panting as they looked down on the almost unrecognizable figure of his boss's son, and slowly he began to chuckle as he again said, 'Well, well. I've seen some sozzled, but he's really pickled. How in the name of God did he get the car home without being stopped by the police?' He looked at Jinny now, but she continued to look down on John. His coat was hunched up above his shoulders, his face looked red and swollen, and his fair hair, pushed up at the back by the cushion, seemed to be standing on end. She bit her lip to prevent herself from laughing, because really she didn't feel like laughing. She had been worried sick over the past hours thinking he might have done something silly . . . And he had; he was showing the evidence of it.

Another mumbled word brought Willie bending down and gripping John's shoulders, he heaved him into a more restful position as he said, 'Aye, lad, you'll get another when the cows come home.' He turned his head towards Jinny again, saying now, 'Did you hear him? That's likely what he's been doing all night, standing leaning against some bar saying, "Another" . . . then, "Another". I wonder how many it took to get him like this. Eeh' – he shook his head – 'but I'm amazed that he could drive that car. It's a miracle he's not in clink with a breathalyser on him.'

'Take . . . take ya . . . hands . . . off . . . me.' As John now muttered the fuddled words he tried to rise from the couch, and Willie, pushing him back, said, 'There's nobody got their hands on you. Lie down and go to sleep.'

'Are you going to leave him here?'

Before Willie could answer John tried to rouse himself again, saying, 'Jinny. Jinny. Where's Jinny?'

She made no reply, but moved behind the head of the couch and watched him flop back on to the cushions again, muttering now, 'He's rotten, rotten. He knew. He knew, Willie. Aye, he knew.'

'What did he know?'

'What . . . did . . . he know? Who? Father . . . he's rotten, rotten. Crafty. Rotten.'

'He knew what?'

'You mind . . . your owns . . . business . . . Willie. You like her an' all . . . Oh yes. You like her an' all. Bloody . . . bloody male harem 's what she's got. But we're all . . . eunuchs to her.'

At this point the smile slid from Jinny's face and she turned away, only to stop, caught by the drunken muttering of his next sentence.

'He knew I was gonna ask her . . . marry me. He . . . he knew it. If I could have . . . if I could have got her to stop arguin', fightin'.' His voice trailed away and he fell back into the cushions, and Willie said softly, 'He's off for the night, I should say. But I wouldn't like to have his head when he wakes up. I'll get a rug to put over him.'

When he left the room Jinny went and stood by the side of the couch, and, putting her hand out, she lifted the tangled hair from John's brow. It was the first time she had touched his hair, but it had aroused no emotion in her such as she was feeling at this moment, for there wasn't a tinge of compassion in this feeling; its main ingredient was irritation, for she wanted to grip handfuls of his hair and shake him as she cried, 'You're an idiot! That's what you are, a stiff-necked idiot. You could have prevented all this, that scene with your father. I've been torn to shreds between the lot of you. Oh!' She thrust a quiff of his hair impatiently to one side, then turned away.

She was nearing the door when Willie entered, carrying a travelling rug, and she said, 'I'm off to bed, Willie. I feel I've had more than enough for one night.'

'Yes, I think you have, Jinny.'

Her lips pressed together now, she said, 'I hope when he wakes up he feels he's got six heads and they're all aching.'

Willie laughed softly now as his hand flapped towards her. 'You don't mean a word of it. He's a good lad. I've said it before. He may not be as tall or as smooth as your other friend that calls, but he's got more in him of the right stuff. I'd bet on that.'

'Well, he's got a champion in you anyway. Good-night, Willie.' She heard him chuckle as he went up the room.

When she reached the landing, there was the voice waiting for her. 'That you, Jinny? Jinny?'

She pushed open the door but kept her hand on the knob, and before he had a chance to speak she said, 'As I told you, he's drunk, paralytic, mortalious, all the words that you yourself would use to describe his state, and that's all I'm going to say about him. I'm tired and my temper is anything but sweet at this moment. Good-night.'

As she pulled the door closed he yelled, 'Good-night. Good-night, Jinny.' And she detected laughter in his voice.

Although she felt very tired, she didn't expect to sleep, for as soon as she lay down her mind presented her with varying attitudes she should adopt when she next came face to face with that stupid individual downstairs, snorting his drink away.

Which of the attitudes she had decided to adopt she never knew. She was only aware that she had been asleep. When she woke up feeling cold, half the bedclothes were on the floor, which pointed to the fact that she must have tossed and turned.

Tucking the quilt around her and preparing to snuggle down again, her mind suddenly cleared and picked up the train of thought that had been snapped by sleep, and at this she put her hand out and lifted up the illuminated bedside clock and she was surprised to see through her blinking lids that it said twenty minutes to seven.

She lay still for a moment staring into the darkness. Then throwing the bedclothes off her, she grabbed up her dressing gown from a chair and very softly she opened the bedroom door and on tiptoe went along the corridor and down the stairs.

When she reached the hall she heard movements coming from the direction of the kitchen. Likely Dorry was up, although seven o'clock was her usual time for rising.

When she gently pushed the drawing-room door ajar, she stood still for a moment, her expression becoming alert. She blinked the last of her sleep from her eyes and went towards the couch. The rug was still there, rumpled at the bottom of it, but there was no body. She looked towards the fire. It had been made up.

Well, well. He had likely woken up during the night and gone upstairs.

She turned quickly as someone pushed the drawing-room door open; then her mouth fell into a slight gape as John entered carrying a tray. He was in his shirt-sleeves and it looked as if he had just had a bath or a shower, for his hair was wet and plastered down. He showed no surprise at seeing her, nor did he speak to her, but placed the tray on the table and poured himself out a cup of black coffee. Then going towards the fireplace, he sat down in the leather chair and took a long drink of the seemingly scalding liquid. And as she stood watching him, she again found irritation rising in her. 'Don't speak,' she prompted herself. 'Just see how long he can keep it up.'

She was on the point of giving in and saying, 'Well!' which single word would express all she felt at this moment, when, looking up at her, he said, 'All right. All right. I was drunk. Haven't you ever seen anyone drunk before?'

'Why? Why did you do it?' Her inquiry was quiet.

'Why?' He raised his eyebrows at her; then quickly put his hand to his head and screwed up his face for a moment before saying, 'I . . . I was celebrating a number of things: a new way of life that begins today, meeting up with my old girl-friend. By the way, what happened to her? I know she drove me back. That's the last thing I can remember. Janice is a good sort at bottom. I was, if I remember rightly, for shacking . . . Oh.' He screwed up his face again, and now shut his eyes and held his brow as he went on, 'You don't approve of that term. Well, let me say, taking her as my girl-friend. But she had a current one if I remember, a little fellow. I felt big beside him. A good feeling that, to feel bigger than your successor. He must have followed us.' He opened his eyes and looked at her and said, 'You didn't see her?'

When she didn't reply he said, 'Pity; you would have liked her.

She's very broad-minded, she would have understood all your actions, all your motives. She always reasons things out. Most of all, she would have understood. Oh, she would have applauded you being my mother, my stepmother, because she says everything that happens to me I've brought on myself. I'm one of those . . .'

'Stop being sorry for yourself.'

She jumped back a full step as the cup and saucer went flying into the fireplace and splintered into countless pieces, and for a moment she couldn't recognize the man who was confronting her.

'Don't you tell me I'm sorry for myself. You come into this house and you cause havoc. You beguiled my father even before my mother died, because your name was never off his tongue then. You get those other two fellows trailing after you and, not satisfied with egging them on, you become disgusted when one of them prefers an older woman. You're the type that ingratiates yourself into men's lives, then when it comes to the crunch you act the innocent maiden. You want marriage, but will you have anything to offer a man when you get your piece of paper? You know what I could do at this moment? I could throttle you.'

When his hands shot out and gripped her by the shoulders she knew a moment of paralysing fear. Then his arms were about her, and he was holding her to him. His face pressed painfully hard against hers and his body was shaking as if with ague.

He had insulted her. Yes, she supposed he had insulted her. He had said some terrible things to her. But it didn't matter. It only went to prove one thing; even that moment of fear he had aroused in her was proof of his feeling for her. That's all she wanted to know.

'Jinny . . . Oh Jinny. Jinny. I'm sorry.'

When she put one arm about him and with the other gently stroked his damp hair, he became still. After a moment, when he raised his head and they looked at each other she said softly and hesitantly, 'Do you believe in long engagements?'

When she saw the shadow cross his face she added quickly, 'We could be married by special licence.'

He took his hand from around her shoulders and brought it once again to his head, and his eyes narrowed but he didn't speak. And she went on, 'You . . . you told me last night you were going to ask me to marry you and I accepted.'

'What? You . . . What do you mean?'

'Just what I said. You said you intended to ask me to marry you. I . . . I have a witness. Willie was there.'

His face was stretching now. He wetted his lips, then, his voice thick, he muttered the word, 'Father.'

'Oh' – she pursed her lips – 'he sort of let me down.' She smiled now. 'He told me he had no intention of ever asking me to marry him. I think he was killing two birds with one stone, letting his daughter see that he was still his own master and trying to bring his son up to scratch with regard to how he felt about . . . the secretary.'

'Oh, Jinny. I can't believe it . . . He's right, it's true. I've fought you every step of the way and fallen deeper with each step. How . . . how do you feel about me, really?'

'I can't tell you how I feel about you, John. I only know I want you, and want you to want me. Oh yes, I want you to want me.' She now smiled at him wryly as she added, 'At the same time I can tell you that you madden me, and I want to throw things at you . . .'

He tugged her to him now as he said, 'That's a good sign.' Then, his voice taking on a sober note, he said, 'What do you think the reception will be like upstairs?' He jerked his head backwards.

'Well, we had better go and see, hadn't we? But wait. I want to tell you something. It's just this. He . . . he *would* have asked me to marry him but for one thing, he was afraid of losing you. You see, he weighed up the result and found it wasn't worth it, because no matter what you think, he loves you dearly; in fact, whether you believe it or not, you are his main interest in life. And it isn't only because he's lost Glen. Apparently he's always felt this way about you, but he was jealous of your mother's love for you. He'll never tell you this; that's why I'm doing it now. And it isn't surmise on my part, it's exactly as it came from his mouth. So no matter what his attitude is in the future, just remember that above everything and all, he loves you and . . . needs you.'

She watched him now turn to the side and rub his hand tightly across his mouth. Then his other hand reaching out, he gripped hers. And so he stood for a moment perfectly still and in that time she knew that the bitterness and resentment that had replaced his love for his father had gone from him, and from now on they would come together as never before. At the same time she understood there would be the clash of similar personalities, there would be eruptions from time to time causing minor wars, not only in the business but in the household, and she'd have to cope with them. She might be married, but as she saw it, she would, in this household, have to continue being the handmaiden, and definitely not cultured. No, definitely not, but, nevertheless, the handmaiden running between them both, while at the same time trying to ignore outside comments which she could hear now; 'Well, she was determined to get one of them, wasn't she? An affair with the old 'un, now marrying his son, and all to get a finger into the business. Never trust the quiet ones.'

And then there would be Florence. Oh! Florence. And what would the others say?

But what did it matter? What did anything matter? She had John, and she had never felt like this about anyone before. If this wasn't love, real love, then she would settle for it, because she knew it was all she wanted.

When he suddenly thrust his arm around her waist, they ran from the room like children and up the stairs, and paused only at the main bedroom door, and there, their faces falling together, their lips gently touched before John, thrusting out his hand, opened the door.

THE BLACK VELVET GOWN

PART ONE

The Journey

1

The pit shaft would have been in their backyard if the pit rows had had a combined backyard, but they stood one behind the other, separated only by the ash-middens and the new innovation, the wooden-box privies.

The rows had dainty names: Primrose, Cowslip, and Dog Daisy. There were twenty-five cottages to each of the first two rows and thirty-three to the third row, Dog Daisy. The residents in Dog Daisy considered themselves lucky because from their single window in the downstairs room and their similar but smaller one in the upstairs they could view the fells, and on a clear day see the top of the mast of a ship going down the river.

The pit community was like one large family, yet, like a family, separated through marriage. So did the inhabitants of each row combine to gather together and preserve their own interests; until a time of calamity hit them, when, just as would a family at a funeral, so all three rows would group as one.

They were all well aware, even as tiny children, from where calamity sprang. It came out of that hole in the ground: it came out through water or fire, and it didn't even provide some men with the dignity of a funeral, not under the open sky anyway; it buried them, certainly, under mausoleums of stone.

But the latest calamity to strike the rows hadn't come from the mine. It was a strange new calamity, like a fever, but worse. It emptied the stomach both ways and brought water from the pores like tears from the eyes, and had a strange name, they called it cholera.

The scourge had passed now, but there were four men, two women, and three children less in the rows.

Seth Millican had been the first to go; and the one, they whispered, who had brought the disease to the rows. And all because he must visit that man in Gateshead who had taught him his letters.

Pride went before a fall, they said when he had died. He had been an overproud man, had Seth Millican, and not because of the work he could do with his hands and because he set the pace down below at the coal-face, but because he could write his name and read the Bible. But his pride had stretched too far when he refused to let his eldest son and daughter go down below, and the boy ten and the lass nine. No, it had to be working in the fields for them, under God's sky. And he hadn't been shamed into doing it, even after Parson Rainton had told him that God allotted man a certain free time to enjoy the sun and light according to the station in life to which he had been appointed. And it was known far and wide what answer Seth Millican had given to Parson Rainton 'To hell with that idea,' he had said. And it was also said that the parson hadn't cursed him in words but in his look, and his look had borne fruit. And it was also said that Seth Millican would now be sorting his ideas out in hell.

Then there was Seth Millican's wife Maria, known as Riah. She had come as an intrusion into the row, for she was the daughter of a fishwife from Shields. And, as everybody knew, such a marriage wasn't a good thing: those who sailed over the land and those who crawled under it could never meet.

But Seth Millican and Maria Rishton had met, and married when he was twenty-six and she but sixteen, and in the ten years since they had reared four of the eight children she had given birth to. Such was her stamina.

Unlike many women in the row, Riah still carried herself straight. Her stomach wasn't flabby; her hair still retained its bright auburn shade; her eyes still flashed; and her tongue, it was said, could clip clouts, so sharp was it. And it had sharpened since her man had died, especially when directed towards Bill Norsecott.

Others had turned their eyes on her, but the one who seemed unable to turn them away was Bill Norsecott. And it was this man who was under discussion now in the Millicans' two-roomed earth-floored habitation that was called a house

Riah stood to the side of the table, one hand on the edge of it, the other spanning her hip. Her head was up and back and held slightly to the side as she looked at her brother-in-law and said, 'I've told you, Ted, if Norsecott was the last man on God's earth I wouldn't let him touch the mud trail on me skirt. What you're proposin' in order to provide meself with a roof is for me to take him and his nine bairns on. Ted – ' Her face screwed up until the eyes were lost in their large sockets, and now the lips spread away from her teeth as she finished, 'Man, there's no room in that pigsty for them lot never mind me and my four. Fifteen of us in that hovel! Oh' – she now shook her head slowly from side to side – 'I thought you had a little more respect for me, Ted Millican, than to propose that.'

Ted Millican, so unlike his deceased brother in all ways in that he was small in stature and of a poor intelligence, muttered now, 'It's either that or the road, Riah. If Seth had died in the pit there might have been a chance of them transferring you down to The Mouldings, but even those have gone to the new men coming in. He didn't die in the pit though, and so there's no chance they'll let you stay here. Brannigan's coming along any time now to tell you to get. That's why I mentioned Bill, in fact.' He stumbled on now, 'Well, it's like this, I . . . I had a word with him and he's willing to take you and . . .'

Before he could draw breath for the next word, she almost screamed at him, 'Willing to take me! Bill Norsecott, that snotty-nosed, dirty, drunken numskull willing to take me. Go on, get out, Ted. Get out afore I lose me temper altogether . . . But wait, let me tell you this: I'm not goin' to wait to be put out. I'm going', an' back to me people. And if I have nothing else there, I'll have fresh air, for I can tell you now, I've hated every day I've been on the doorstep of this pit, with the mountains of slag getting nearer an' the middens and the folks an' all. Aye, an' the folks an' all, who had the nerve to look down on my Seth because he wanted to make somethin' of himself and his family. If it hadn't been for the respect I had for him and the kind of man he was, I'd have up and went in the first months of me marriage. And one last thing I'll say to you before you go, Ted. I notice that you and Mary Ellen haven't offered us shelter. There's only two of you and your two lads, and one of them's courting and will soon be gone.'

She watched her brother-in-law now hang his head before he said, 'Tisn't that I didn't think of it, Riah, 'tisn't that, but you know Mary Ellen. You and her has never seen eye to eye, and, put under the same roof, there would be hell to pay.'

Riah's attitude changing now, she sighed, then said quietly, 'Yes, I know that, Ted. And I feel if it had been left to you things would have been different. But don't worry about us. I'm capable of seeing to me own. I always have and I always will.'

The man stood at the open door now and looked into the roadway where the April showers coming over into early May had left puddles in which tiny children splashed their bare feet and cried joyfully in their play, being as yet unconscious of the dark days ahead. 'When are you goin'?' he said.

'The morrow, early.'

He turned his head as he asked, 'What about your bits and pieces? Mary Ellen . . .' He checked himself, then said, 'I'd store your bed and things.'

There was a cynical note in her voice as she replied, 'Yes, I know you would, and Mary Ellen too, but I've thought about me bits and pieces over the last few days. It took money and hard grime to get them and I don't want to give them up, so Arthur Meddle and Kate are going to take them into their place for me. They've hardly anything upstairs except the shaky-down, so they'll be glad to make use of them for a time. And Kate's a clean and careful woman.'

His head still turned towards her, he said, 'You haven't been idle then?'

'No, Ted, I've never been idle in me life, whether it was workin' with me hands or me head.'

'You're a strange lass, Riah. I've never met anyone with as much gumption. If I don't see you again, because I go down at two o'clock an' you'll be away afore noon when I rise, I wish you luck. In all you do, I wish you luck, Riah.'

'Thanks, Ted.'

She waited until he had taken so many steps from the doorway, and then she went to it and closed it. And now standing with her back to it, she pressed her hands flat against its rough wood, and, her even white teeth coming down sharply on her lower lip, she made a small sound; it was the echo of a groan deep within her. Gumption, he had said she had. She could go back to where she had come from, she had said. If they had nothing else, they would have fresh air, she had said. Her gumption, at this moment, she knew was threaded with fear and she knew exactly the welcome that awaited her when she went back from where she had come; and as for having fresh air, if nothing else, the fresh air she remembered from those far times reeked with the stink of fish.

She brought herself from the door and went towards the fire, and taking up a bucket of small coal that stood on the hearth, she flung its contents on to the back of the grate. As she did so a cloud of dust went up the chimney, but the rest wafted its way over her face. She puffed at it for a moment; then taking a cloth from the brass rod that ran under the wooden mantelpiece, she went to the table and began to wipe it down.

Of a sudden she stopped and, pulling from underneath it a wooden stool, she sat down and, leaning her elbows on the table, she rested her head in her hands. She wanted to pray but she could find no words; and anyway, Seth had always said, God helps those who helps themselves. He used to laugh when he said it because he called it a contradiction: as he said, if you didn't help yourself, then nothing happened and you blamed it on God. She had often wondered what he had talked about with the Methodist man in Gateshead who appeared to be a good Christian, because at bottom Seth hadn't much time for God and His Doings; even the Bible, he said, was just stories thought up and written by men.

She had learned a lot from Seth. He had taught her to use her mind, and he had taught her to read and write, as he had them all. She had been proud of the fact that she was mother to the only children in the three rows who could write their names. This alone had set them all apart. Seth could have taught lots of men in the rows to read and write, but they were afraid in case the pit keeker split on them to the manager, because reading was frowned upon, and, as some of the older men had pointed out forcibly to Seth, it got you nowhere except into trouble with those that provided your livelihood. And after all they had them to consider: you didn't turn round and bite the hand that fed you.

Only two men in the rows had braved the wrath of the owners and the management and sat in of a night with Seth: Arthur Meddle and Jack Troughton. But they'd had to pay for it. They, like Seth, had been put on to poor seams down below, seams that gave more rock than coal and where a twelve hour shift barely brought in three shillings.

Oh, education had to be paid for and paid for dearly. But what filled the head didn't fill the belly, and Seth had always been aware of this. That's why he had prepared for a rainy day. For ten years he had prepared for that rainy day, saving only coppers some weeks, a shilling others. In the first month of their marriage he had told her of his scheme to save, because he didn't always want to work in a mine, and he envisaged buying a little cottage of their own and a piece of land. And she knew that in the first year he had saved one pound fifteen shillings. But strangely, from that time onwards he had never told her how much he put away each week. He was paid once a fortnight and some pay days he had put as little on the table as a single sovereign. He had been sparse in his dealings with a number of things. After the second year of marriage he had never said he loved her, but she took it for granted that he did; nor had he been gentle with her without expecting to be satisfied in return.

He had first seen her when she was fifteen, when, late on a free Saturday afternoon, he had walked along the Shields quay. She had been standing amid a group of fishwives. Her head was bare and she wasn't wearing the usual thick blue flannel voluminous skirt with its white apron in front, nor the cross-over body shawl, but she was in a blouse dress, the top layer of the skirt taken back and pinned under her buttocks, and she had a yellow patterned neckerchief over her shoulders. The skirt came just below her calves, and she had clogs on her feet. He said it was her eyes that he noticed first. He said he spotted the intelligence in them when they first looked at him.

From that day he had come to the quay on a Sunday and any free Saturday night he had; and on his sixth visit he spoke to her. 'Hello,' he said. 'Hello,' she said.

'You are a fisherman's daughter?' he said.

'Yes,' she said.

'You don't look like one,' he said.

'Oh, what did you expect me to look like? Cod, salmon or smoked fresh herring?'

He hadn't laughed but said, 'You know what I mean.' And that had caused her to be silent.

It was on that day that her mother said, 'Who was that pit lout you were talking to?' And she had asked, 'How do you know he's a pit lout?' And her mother's answer had been, 'You can tell, the coal's got into his veins. There's blue marks on his brow. Have nothing to do with him,' she had warned her. 'There's plenty of fisher lads for your choosing. If you feel ripe the sooner you look among them the better.'

Odd; she had never liked her mother; but she had loved her father. He had put out to sea one day with her two brothers when she was ten years old and they were never seen again. Three boats were lost that day, two from North Shields and one from the South side.

She'd also had a strong dislike for the smell of fish, and she wondered why that was because she had been reared on it. She had been forced to eat so much fish that her stomach had revolted; cod in particular made her retch. At times when this happened her mother would say she took after her grandfather for it was known that he was a landsman and finicky, besides which he was a square-head Swede, and had hair so fair that it was as rare among their own men as a woman's bare backside.

Her first-born, David, took after the square-head, for he too had hair and skin that stood out markedly from the children about the doors; and, working in the fields as he did, his hair became even more bleached by the sun, and, unlike that of many of his age down the mine, was not matted with coal-dust or running with head-lice.

That was another thing that Seth had been particular about: everybody had to wash all over on a Friday night, summer and winter alike. He himself washed his upper parts every day and his water couldn't be used again. But on a Friday night he saw that the children one after another went into the tin bath, and she herself followed them; then he, last of all, washed himself straight down.

She had come to like the ritual on the Friday nights. It added to the feeling that her family were different. The only time the routine was broken was when Seth lay on the plank bed in the corner of the room waiting for the hearse to come and take him away. He had died only that morning; but he was to have the honour of being ridden to his grave in a hearse. That honour wasn't awarded to the poor very often unless there was a great whip round to pay for an undertaker. But in the case of the cholera the authorities transported all the bodies to the graveyard in a hearse.

She sighed deeply now, then rose to her feet. It was on half-past six; the children would be in from the fields shortly. Johnny, seven, and Maggie, six, had been stone picking on Bateman's farm for the past two weeks. It was hard work for bairns from eight in the morning till six at night. And then there was the mile walk there, and back. But sixpence a week was sixpence a week and not to be sneezed at. David who was working near Gateshead Fell, brick carrying for the men who were putting up houses, was getting three shillings a week.

And Biddy who was a year younger was working in Mrs Bateman's kitchen for a full one and six a week and her food. Five and sixpence from four of them was nothing to what they could have earned down the mine. But she had been with Seth all the way in being determined that none of her bairns should go below if she could help it.

But now they would all lose their jobs because there wasn't a house to be let within miles, and no farm mistress would take her on with the addition of four youngsters. She had even made a suggestion to Mrs Bateman, and the farmer's wife had laughed at her, saying, 'If I had a pigsty, missis, I could let it for rent. Anyway, what use could I put four of them to? Things are bad; we can hardly sell our stuff in the market at times. And it's your lot that causes it, with their strikes. Strikes. My word! I know what I would do with them; gaol them; shoot them.'

She hadn't answered the woman, for what answer could she give to gaol them, shoot them?

But as regards rent: that was a point nobody but herself knew about, for she could pay the rent on any cottage, and all because of Seth's little hoard . . . But what was she talking about, terming it little? Eighteen pounds, fifteen shillings was a small fortune. It was odd when she came to think about it. Seth had known he was dying, yet he never mentioned the money or where it was hidden. She had known for a long time it was behind one of the bricks in the fireplace. But most of them were loose, and she had never attempted to pry because, being sharp-eyed and sharp-witted like he was, he would have known, and that would have caused a difference between them, and she had never wanted that.

Although during the past years the warm feeling she had for him had dwindled and its place had been taken by respect, they still lived a peaceful and comparatively happy life; at least so she had told herself, especially when she'd had to clamp down on the inner feeling and unrest that rampaged about the stomach at times, those times when a little gentleness, a touch of the hand on her hair, or her cheek, or his arm thrown over her in the night would have sufficed to soothe the unrest within her. But he wasn't a man like that, so life had gone on from day to day.

Bridget was the first to come home. She was known as Biddy. She was tall for her nine years and was of the same colouring as her mother. Her hair might have had a brighter sheen, but her eyes were the same brown, and her height promised that she would grow taller than her mother. All her movements spoke of liveliness, the way she lifted her feet, the turn of her head, her lips that opened to laugh easily and often at something she herself had said, because she was of a quick wit. 'Hello, Ma,' she said.

'Hello, hinny,' said Riah.

'She let me keep the slippers. But then they wouldn't hold much water, would they?' She now stuck her fingers through the holes in the house slippers. 'I nearly said, "Thank you very much, missis, you can pass them on to the next one," but I thought I'd better not.'

'I should think better not. You shouldn't be cheeky.'

'I'm tired, Ma.' The brightness went out of the child's voice for a moment, and her mother said to her, 'Well, sit yourself down then. There's some broth ready.'

The girl sat down on a cracket near the fire; then turning her head to her mother, she said. 'She was like the prophet from the Bible, Ma. She spoke of nothing else but doom because we are leavin'. I don't think she wanted to lose me.'

'No, she wouldn't, because you can work as good as anyone twice your age. Of course, she wouldn't.'

'You know what she said, Ma?'

'No. What did she say?' Riah was putting some wooden bowls on the table.

'She said we were all too big for our boots, and you would find your mistake out she said, bein' able to write your name wouldn't peel any taties . . . She can't write, Ma. None of them can, not even the master; he counts up the cans of milk with straws in a jar.' Her face now broke into a broad smile and she bent forward, her arms hugging her waist, as she said. 'You know what I did the day, Ma?'

'No. What did you do?'

'Well, when she sent me over to get the milk, I stuck in six more straws.'

It was a long time since Riah had laughed, but she turned and leant her buttocks against the side of the table and, like her daughter, she also leant forward and with her arms around her waist, too, she laughed until the tears came into her eyes. Then not knowing whether she was laughing or crying, she went swiftly to her daughter and sat down beside her on another cracket, and, taking her hands, gripped them tightly as she said, 'We'll be all right. We'll be all right. As long as we can laugh we'll be all right. Oh dear me!' She shook her head. 'What a fuss there'll be when she tries to find the other six pails of milk.'

'I thought of that, Ma.' Biddy's face was wet. 'And I could see the missis skittering around blaming everybody for drinking them; and then it might dawn on them that the cows couldn't give all that much extra in one day, and then they would start to think.'

Riah now nodded her head and bit on her lip, 'Yes, and who would they think about?' she said.

As they were laughing the door opened, and when the boy came into the room and dropped his bait tin and cap on to the table his mother rose and, looking at him, said one word, 'Well?'

He answered quietly. 'He didn't mind. He said I was a fool, 'cos there's another twenty to step into me shoes.'

'They wouldn't work like you.'

'Yes, they would.' He moved his head slowly. 'When you're hungry you'll work twice as hard, and most of them are hungry.'

She turned away as if ashamed of depriving him of his work. But quickly she was confronting him again, her voice harsh as she said. 'We've got to get out of here. There's no other way. Anyway, you said yourself you would be glad to get away because it was killing work.'

'I know. I know.' He nodded at her now, his tone soothing. 'But I'm just afraid I won't get another job, for I wouldn't be able to fish, 'cos you know I can hardly stand going over in the ferry let alone go out to sea.'

'Nobody'll expect you to fish; there'll be plenty of other work in Shields. There's chemical works there, and there's Cookson's glass works, blacking factories and nail making places. When I was a young lass the place was alive with factories and there'll be many more now. Then of course there's the boat building. Oh, there'll be heaps to choose from, more than around here. This place is a dead end.'

'But where'll we live?'

She paused and half turned from him before she said. 'Well, we'll stay at your granny's for a time, and then we'll get a house.'

'Me granny doesn't like us.'

Riah turned and looked at her daughter now and drew in a deep breath before saying to her, 'That's as may be, but when people are in a fix she's all right that way; I mean, she'll help. Anyway, it'll just be for a day or two till I can look round. And as your dad always said, education's starting there, people are looking ahead. There's Sunday Schools an' things.'

'We can beat anybody from Sunday Schools.' Biddy now glanced at her brother as she added, 'We could beat them at Sunday School, couldn't we Davey?'

The boy didn't answer; he was looking at his mother. 'Have we any money to carry on with?' he asked her.

'Yes' – she nodded – 'we have money to carry on with.' She hadn't told them what she had found in the bag behind the loose bricks, the fourteenth one she had taken out of the fire breast, because she was of the opinion that no matter how much children were told to hold their tongues, they let things slip out, particularly if they thought they were rich, and eighteen pounds fifteen shillings would have spelt a great fortune to them at this moment.

The boy waited, his eyes narrowed towards her as if he was expecting her to go on, but she turned towards the fire and opening the door of the round oven she took out an earthenware dish which she carried to the table and there ladled out two bowlsful of soup, saying as she did so, and at the same time jerking her head towards the bucket at the end of room, 'Wash your hands. And then after your meal you'd better go down to the burn and starting bringing up the water for the bath.'

''Tisn't Friday.' Biddy was now seated at the table, spoon in hand and half-way to her mouth, and her mother answered, 'No, it isn't Friday, and I doubt if there'll be any more Fridays for a long time. We'll have to see how it goes.'

'Will we have to wash in the river at Shields?' There was a twinkle in Biddy's eye and her mother slapped her face gently with the back of her hand, saying, 'You'll have to put up with worse things than that afore you're much older, girl.'

Presently she looked towards the narrow window and said, 'The others are late. They are likely waiting for Paddy's cart,' Davey said as he sat down at the table. 'He sometimes gives them a lift.'

Presently, speaking as if to herself, Biddy said. 'They get tired, especially Maggie. Her back aches. It isn't right . . . 'tisn't . . .'

'Now don't you start on that, girl; there's nobody knows better than me that it isn't right. But what would you have, her go down the pit?'

'Aw, Ma.'

'Never mind, aw Ma. Get on with your dinner. That tongue of yours is too sharp by far.'

As she finished speaking the door opened and the two younger children came in. Johnny, aged seven, was a replica of his father, dark haired, dark eyed, slightly built, whereas the girl was a different colour from any of the others. Her hair was brown, her eyes green and her skin, even under the dust and dirt, showed up in patches to be deeply cream tinted. It was the boy who spoke first. His voice was bright like his sister Biddy's, and he said, 'I told him, Ma. He didn't like it, but he said there were others to fill our place.'

Riah made no reply to this but said, 'Clean yourselves,' and nodded towards the pail before going to the oven once more and taking out the dish.

Not until the children were all seated did she herself sit at the table. Although Davey and Biddy soon emptied their bowls, they wouldn't ask for more until all had finished, and they both watched their mother spooning the soup slowly into her mouth and noticing the difficulty at times she seemed to have in swallowing it. They weren't given bread with their soup; this would come as a sort of extra after it with pig's fat or dripping.

Riah knew they were waiting patiently for her to finish. The two younger ones too had golloped up their meal and were now scraping round their bowls. She wanted to talk to them but she couldn't find the words. She wanted to say to them, You'll never know life more hard from this day on. But that would be throwing reflections back on their father as if he hadn't given them all he could. True, he had worked for them and had saved and fed and clothed them better than the majority of those in the rows; but it wasn't best as she saw it, her best saw a cleaner, brighter side of life. Not less hard working. No. She was prepared to work all the days of her life as she had done since she was four years old – her mother had seen to that – but she wanted something different for the result of her labour and the labours of her children. Oh yes, particularly she wanted something different for them, and at this moment she wanted to say to them, I'm going to see that you get it. But she felt too full and it was almost with a feeling of horror she knew she was about to cry. And not one of her children had ever witnessed her crying; what crying she had done in her life had been in the dead of night when those about her were in deep sleep and dulled with the labour of the day, or mazed with ale or gin. She had only experienced the latter up till she was sixteen, for if Seth had ever touched strong drink there wouldn't have been anything in the bag behind the brick in the mantelshelf. But nevertheless she had often cried in the deep of the night during the last ten years. Sometimes she had wondered what she was crying for: something missing? something she had lost? something that she wanted? She didn't know, she only knew it was a relief to cry. But never, never had she cried in front of her children. They looked upon her as someone strong with no weakness.

She got up hastily from the table, saying, 'Take a slice of bread each,' and pointed to the cupboard as she walked past it and on to the steep ladder that led to the attic room above. And there, she held her hand tightly over her mouth, saying to herself, 'No. Not now, not now. For God's sake, woman, not now.' And at this she began tearing clothes from the old chest and putting them into bundles.

2

The children were standing outside, each dressed as if for a winter expedition, for they were wearing all the clothes they possessed, it being easier for them to be carried that way; besides, they each had to hump two bundles, one holding a piece of bedding, a blanket or a patch quilt, the other, in addition to mug, plate and spoon, odd items of kitchen utensils.

Riah stood in the bare room and looked about her for a moment and her last unspoken words to herself were, May I never have to live in your like again. Then she stooped and with an effort lifted up a large roll of bedding in one hand and a canvas bag in the other, the contents of which jingled together as she moved out through the doorway. She had asked herself two or three times since last night why she was determined to take such things as a kettle and pans and she could give herself no answer, only that she didn't mind the Meddles using her furniture, but cooking utensils were a different thing.

The sun was shining, the road was dry. They had to pass down the whole length of the row to gain the coach road where they hoped to pick up the carrier cart. But their departure seemed to have been awaited and there was hardly a doorway that wasn't open and a woman standing in it and often her man by her side, his bait tin in his hand, ready to go on his shift but staying long enough to see the Millicans take to the road and feeling not a little satisfaction in the sight, for hadn't they foretold this: Millican had always been above himself. Any man who wasted his time on reading and writing was a fool. What good did it do you? Got you thrown out into the gutter in most cases. It was a wonder that Millican had lasted so long. He wouldn't have done if he hadn't been considered one of the best workers on the face and a man who set the pace. And this opinion itself was enough to make his fellow-men turn against him.

Well, there they went, was the opinion of most; but not of all, for now and again a voice would say, 'Good luck, lass,' and Riah would turn to the speaker and say, 'Ta, Thanks.'

Then at the bottom of the road she came face to face with Bill Norsecott. He had come round the corner of the row and when he saw her had stopped dead almost blocking her path, and he muttered through his coal-grimed lips. 'Might be bloody well glad of an offer afore you're finished, Mrs Millican . . . ma'am.'

'That might be so, Mr Norsecott' – her chin was up – 'but you can take it firmly that I'd be hard put afore even thinking about taking an offer from you. Rock bottom I'd be, and I'm far from that. Good-day to you.'

'And to hell with you.'

The children were moving on, but Davey stopped and turned towards the man, and Riah had to nudge him forward with her knee, saying, 'Go on. Go on.'

At the coach road they all dropped their bundles down on to the grass verge and the younger children were for sitting down beside them, but Riah said harshly, 'Don't do that. Them's your Sunday clothes, on top, remember.'

And so they all stood silently now looking along the dusty road that curved downhill to a hamlet in the dip, and the silence was broken by Biddy saying, 'I would have died if we had gone into the Norsecott's house.' And to this Riah said tartly, 'Be quiet. Save your breath to cool your porridge.' Which censure Biddy took, as usual, to mean she was talking too much. But she repeated to herself and emphatically, 'I would. I would. Dirty, snotty-nosed lot.'

They had to wait a half-hour for the cart, and just as they espied it in the distance coming over the hill, the men from the pit, their ten hour shift at an end, passed them in straggling groups. Most of them looked towards them; few had anything to say. But Arthur Meddle and two other men from Primrose Row stopped, and Arthur said. 'Ready for the road, lass?' And Riah answered, 'Yes, Arthur. Ready for the road.'

The two men almost simultaneously now said, 'Good luck, lass.' And one went on to add, 'Nobody could blame you for makin' the choice. By God, no. Nobody could blame you. We wish you well. More than us do an' all; we all wish you well.'

'Thank you.' The cart drew up in front of them and Arthur Meddle said. 'I won't give any of you a hoist, lass, seein' me being so mucky and you all dressed up nicely. You look a credit, you do that, you look a credit. Goodbye then. Goodbye.'

Paddy McCabe, the carter, looked at Riah with a grin on his face, saying. 'You've filled me up. This lot's going to cost you, lass.'

'I can pay. I can pay.'

'Oh, I know you can. I wasn't meanin' nowt. Would you like to sit up front along o' me? They're all settled in the back there, snug.' He jerked his head to where the children were sitting amidst the bundles, their hands already gripping the sides of the cart, and she said, 'Thank you. I'd be obliged.'

And so they set off on the six miles to Shields. But before they had travelled half the distance they were joined by another five customers, so causing the children to have to sit on the bundles, which brought their bodies well up above the sides of the cart, and as the road was potholed, this made for dangerous travel and brought from them cries of 'Eeh!' and 'Oh!' which made the elders in the cart laugh.

By the time they reached Shields market, their stomachs were well shaken up. But they all felt merry and it showed in their faces as once more they lifted their bundles then said, 'Goodbye,' to Paddy McCabe and his cart. And Paddy wished them, 'Good luck;' at the same time adding words that filled Riah with apprehension, for he said. 'Shouldn't surprise me, missis, to see you takin' the journey back some day, an' not too long ahead, for things is bad around here, especially where you said you were going. Fish is goin' rotten in piles along there, they say.'

She said nothing to this but marched off, pushing the children before her, while she herself rocked from side to side with the weight of the awkward bundles she was carrying.

They went down the cobbled slope to the quay, where tall sailing boats were lined as close as herrings in a crate. Then leaving the quay, she led the way now between a morass of rotting boats, rusted anchors and chains piled in places four foot high. Then some distance along they mounted a bank and found themselves walking between whitewashed cottages. And presently she saw the end of Low Street where she had been born and had played for a little while and worked for a longer while and had hoped, as she had also done on leaving the pit village today, that she would never set eyes on it again. But she had, although at long intervals.

It was three years since she was last here. Seth had brought them down one bright Sunday in the summer of twenty-nine. Their reception on that day had not been cold, yet it had not been effusive. The visit had gone off as well as it had because within a few minutes of being in the house she had slipped a shilling into her mother's hand. It had made all the difference. What would her mother say now if she told her that she had eighteen pounds dangling in a bag between her breasts? Oh, she'd surely be all over her. But she wasn't going to know about that money. That was for setting them up in a new home. As long as she stayed with her mother, she would work for their keep. At least this was what she had imagined until she reached the door, and the first person to greet her was her mother.

Dilly Riston was fifty years old. Her back was stooped with rheumatics, her fingers were misshapen with the same complaint. As she would tell you, what could you expect? because she had handled cold fish from she was three years old. She looked like a woman well into her sixties, except that her eyes were clear and glinted with hard knowledge of life. It was she who spoke first: 'In the name of God!' she said. 'What are you doin' here?' Then her eyes scanned the four small figures standing behind Riah, and she added, 'The lot of yous.'

'Seth died of the cholera. They wouldn't let us stay. I'm going to look for a house.' Her tone softened now, it had a plea in it: 'I . . . I thought you might put us up for a few days.'

'Put you up? God in heaven! you don't know what you're askin'. Put you up? You could never be put up here. Come in and see for yourself.' She stood aside, and Riah hesitated before dropping her burdens down on to the shingled road; then slowly she squeezed past her mother and entered the room that had once been so familiar to her. And there she saw three small children, two sitting on a mat before a low fire and one very young one in a basket to the side of it. A young woman was standing near the table that was set underneath the small square window. She had been chopping on a board, but her hands stopped at their work and she now stared at Riah. And Riah blinked her eyes for a moment because she could hardly recognize her elder sister. It was all of five years since she had seen her, when her husband Henry Fuller had got himself a job in Jarrow village; his work was that of a boat-builder. She'd had three children then round about Johnny's and Maggie's age, but here were another three, one a recent delivery by the looks of it. She said quietly, 'Hello, Ada.'

It was some seconds before Ada answered, 'Hello.' Then, as if about to greet Riah she walked towards her, saying. 'What's brought you?' but when Dilly repeated, 'Seth died of the cholera,' she seemed to rear back from her sister.

'Tis all right,' Riah said quickly: 'it was some weeks gone, it's all over.'

'Tis never over, the cholera.'

'And look at this lot.' It was her mother's voice now and she was pointing out into the road as she addressed her elder daughter. 'She's brought the four of them.' And now shuffling towards Riah, she said, 'Where d'you intend to put them up?'

'I've just told you, haven't I? I thought you might . . .'

'Now look here, don't take that tone with me: not in the door a second but playing the high and mighty. Well, you can see how we're fixed. Besides those three' – she pointed – 'there's another three on the beach, raking up, and Henry besides.'

Not out of real concern for Henry but simply for something to say to quieten the atmosphere, Riah looked at Ada and said, 'Is he out of work?'

Ada didn't get a chance to answer because her mother yelled, 'Out of work! Is anybody in work here? Where you been? Haven't you heard of the strike at the Hilda pit? Been on weeks now. They are bloody maniacs. Didn't know when they were well off. Wanting to start unions, and them getting four shillings for a seven hour stint; then goin' and rioting and smashing up the pit. Where've you been? Oh, but I suppose your pit was working, so you shut your eyes and close your ears. You've had it easy, madam, you don't know you're born. This place is dead. The town is dead. They started burying it after Waterloo, and now they've nearly filled it in. Out of work? she says.' She tossed her head. 'The fishing's dead, but that's all we've got to live on, fish, fish, fish. If I'm forced to eat another mouthful of salmon I'll spew.'

'What about the factories?' Riah said and as she spoke she looked out through the open door to the children now grouped about it. She made no signal for them to come in, but she saw young Maggie jump at the sound of her mother's strident voice yelling, 'Factories, you say. They're sleepin' out to pick up a job in them. Anyway, when fishing's been your life, who wants to go standin' in a factory, blackin', bricks, pottery, glass, what have you? 'Tisn't for fishermen. We'll have a repeat of the big strike with our lot an' all, you mark my words, because it isn't only the fishermen, it's the deep sea 'uns as well. There'll be a repeat, you'll see, and they'll bring in the dragoons again and the cavalry. My God Almighty. I've seen it all, but never as bad as this.' Her voice had lessened for a moment, but now it resumed its almost screeching tone as she cried, 'And now you land with four of them! You must be mad. And from what I hear the pits inland are crying out for bairns. You mightn't have a man to go down but he looks big enough. And the lass an' all.' She had pointed from Davey to Biddy.

Now it was Riah's voice that almost seemed to raise the low roof of the cottage as she cried. 'I've told you afore, Ma, an' I'll tell you again, none of mine are going down below. And they won't starve either, I'll see to that. I'll get work, I've got a pair of hands on me.'

'Don't be so bloody soft, girl; we've all got pairs of hands, even mine.' She held up her twisted fingers. 'I could still gut, if it was any use guttin'. Look you.' She advanced on Riah, and now her fingers forming into a fist, she punched at her daughter's arm, saying. 'You don't know you're born. You never have. I don't know where in the name of God you come from, but from the minute you could open your mouth I knew it wasn't from my side. And although you've passed the colouring on to that one' – she pointed to Davey – 'you've got the Swede inside of you. He was a skunk and he skunked off and left me mother of six of us, and every now and again his mark comes up either inside or out. So now let me put it plain to you, miss or missis, there's no work hereabouts; and there's no habitation either because the bloody sea captains are buyin' up the property and letting' 'em out at rents only the foreigners can pay. And there's plenty of them kickin' about.'

The mother and daughter glared at each other for a moment; then Riah, with a catch in her voice, said, 'Well, thank you for your welcome, Ma,' and, turning, made towards the door, pushing the children aside and pointing towards their bundles to indicate that they pick them up.

Ada followed them out of the cottage, and standing near her sister, she whispered, 'She's right, Riah, she's right, there's no work. But . . . but where are you goin'?'

'I don't know. But don't worry; I'll find a place.'

'Have you got any money?'

'Enough to get by on.'

'Well, look' – Ada pulled her to a stop – 'there's Mrs Carr, she's at the very far end of the street. They're not fishers, they're river men, one's on the keels, the rest do the trips to London Town and often they're gone for a week or more. When the house is clear she takes lodgers. Go along there and see if she'll take you. If not, I don't know what you're going to do.'

Neither did Riah. But she patted Ada's arm, saying, 'Thanks, lass. I'll find something. And let me say, I'm sorry you're landed in this plight with me ma.'

'There was nothing else for it. It was last year they went on strike for a better deal and now they're a thousand times worse off than ever they were afore. I'm weary, Riah, utterly weary. She gets you down.'

'I know that, Ada. I'm sorry.'

'Well, go on. Let me know.'

'I will.' As Riah turned away, Ada, casting her eyes over the burdened children, said, 'You've got a nice little crew, healthy lookin'.'

Riah smiled at her and nodded and once more ushered her crew before her, and they went on down the long street to the end.

Mrs Carr turned out to be a young old woman. Riah guessed she must be as old as her mother, but was as spritely as someone half her age.

'Oh,' said said. 'Well now, four bairns and you. Well now. Well now. 'Twill be the floor for two of you, I'm afraid, 'cos our Harold will be back in the night after his keeling. But himself and Bob and Mickie started the London trip last night. God keep them safe and quiet the waters. Come in. Come in.'

The little room was clean and packed with relics of the sea and foreign voyages. Cheap bric-a-brac were nailed to the walls side by side with ships' brasses, and in one corner there actually hung, from close to the low ceiling, an anchor, its iron burnished like a piece of brass.

'Now sit yourselves down if you can.' She pointed to the children, then to a form that ran at an angle to the fireplace. 'Throw your bundles in the corner. And you, missis, take this seat. It's himself's; he's not here so you can sit in it, but he'd kick the backside out of anybody that went near it if he was about the house.'

Thankfully Riah sat down and her whole body slumped in weariness as she looked at the vibrant old woman, and when this business-like lady said, ''Tis sixpence a night I charge with a bowl of broth afore sleep and one to set you on the road; and the bairns we'll say half price. What about it?'

Riah merely inclined her head in acceptance while she thought, My, this is the business to be in. She must have acquired a small fortune over the years. By! should she stay here a week, that would take all of ten and sixpence, besides buying their food. And the rapid totalling in her head told her she wouldn't see anything of a pound at the end of it. She also told herself that she must look sharp and find work, not only for herself but for them all.

The old lady now said, 'What's brought you here, may I ask?'

And so Riah told her, and as she did so, she watched the wrinkled face stretch until the lined lips formed an elongated, 'Oh,' before they emitted the word, 'Riston. Oh, Dilly Riston's a bitter pill. Always was, always will be. Oh' – she pointed now – 'I remember you. Yes I do. I remember you as a youngster, although I never had anything to do with anyone along that end. Fighting, drinking, bashin' lot. But I'll say this for them, they're the crowd to have behind you when you're in a tight jam, and there was some tight jams here last year.

Oh aye. Oh aye. Our men made a stand. Three pounds, that's all they got for a trip to London and back, and when they asked for four, God Almighty! all hell was let loose. By lass, you should have been here then. Do you know, a warship was sent here. That didn't help; skull and hair flew. You should have seen it. Two blokes, blacklegs, signed on for less than the four pounds, and God, they nearly lynched them. Eeh! the things that go on in this town, nobody would believe. As our Hal said, he's a joker you know, but he said, "Why shanghai the blokes for the navy to go across the sea and fight wars when there are ready-made ones here?"'

She turned her attention on to the children now who were sitting wide-eyed staring at her, and she said, 'You hungry, bairns?' And it was Biddy who answered for them, saying, 'Yes, please, missis, we're all hungry.' She glanced at her mother now but Riah didn't chastise her. And the old woman said, 'Well, it's many a day since I lodged bairns so I'll give you a treat. I'll make some griddle, eh? Take off your coats and things. And look' – she turned to Riah – 'that's your room' – she pointed – 'there's two beds in there, one of them's for our Hal.'

'You mean . . . he'll be sleepin' – ?'

'Aw, missis, Hal wouldn't interfere with you. But . . . but if you feel so nickety-pickety about it, he'll go up in the roof for the night. He's been up there afore.' She motioned with her head to a hatch set in the low ceiling, then added, 'You can't straighten up but as I've said to him, when you're asleep you lie flat.'

'Thank you.'

'You're welcome, missis, you're welcome.'

In the room, Riah pushed the door closed for a moment and looked about her. There was scarcely room to move between the beds and they had to stack their bundles one on top of the other in the corner. The patched covers on the beds looked rumpled and she doubted if the bedding would be clean underneath. But anyway, it was a shelter.

The children had all dropped on to the edge of the bed. They sat in a row all tired and dismal looking, and she, lowering herself down on to a wooden structure opposite, held out her hands to them saying, 'I know you're tired but I want you to change your things: get into your working clothes. We'll go out and look around; there's a lot of daylight left.'

'Ma.'

'Yes, Davey?'

'I wouldn't like to live here long.'

'We'll have to take what we can get for the time being, we can't pick and choose. It's not worse than what we've left.'

'It's the smell.'

'Well, you had that an' all back there.'

'It was different somehow.'

'Yes, Ma, it was different,' Biddy put in now. And Johnny, as if taking his cue from his brother and sister, piped up, 'I'm going to be sick.'

'You're not going to be sick. Now stop it, all of you.' She looked from one to the other. 'We're going out, and we're going to try and find work. And as soon as I get a job, even if you get nothing, I'll get a house and we'll settle down to a new life. It's going to be all right, you'll see. Now get up and get yourselves changed.'

As they obeyed her, she thought: a new life of drudgery. It had been that for the last ten years, but then she had had a man behind her. A man was necessary. Without a man your life was like a ship without a captain: there was mutiny on all sides, and within you too, deep within you.

She looked down on the two low wooden-base beds . . . The old woman had taken it for granted that her son would sleep in this room tonight with her. Of course the children would be here, but that wouldn't matter to some men. Her thoughts swung back, but as if reluctantly now, and she almost muttered them aloud, 'The family needs a man to steer it.' But before the words had time to evaporate she was attacking them, 'You going soft, Maria Millican, out of your mind? You've had one man and that's enough for you. Get about it. Get outside and see what's doing.'

For a week she saw what was doing, and that was mostly nothing. She herself was offered three jobs during that period but they were all in bars, and her presence wasn't required until seven o'clock at night; and she had recalled enough of the river front to know what happens to a woman, if not in the bars, then when she tried to leave and walk along the apparently deserted streets close to midnight.

Biddy could have been set on in the blacking factory, but when Riah saw the conditions under which the children worked, the sight of them running around like little black imps, and when she caught here and there the gist of their conversation, she said, 'You're not going in there.' And to this Biddy said in protest, 'Ma, it's three shillings a week.' And Riah answered, 'I wouldn't care if it was thirty-three.'

At the beginning of the second week Davey got work. It was on the waterfront, but he was paid in fish.

Then there was the matter of a house. In the lower end they were asking two shillings a week for a rat-infested room. If the house had two or more rooms it was used as a lodging house with four to six sleepers in a room. Some of the beds were used both by day and by night. Further into the town, where the respectable quarter began, they were asking as much as four shillings a week for two rooms downstairs, and four and six for an upper apartment because this had a let into the roof. Still, houses were hard to come by here, and twice she was refused one because she hadn't a man to support her: as the agent said, he understood their plight, but once in it was getting them out again if she couldn't pay the rent. When she assured him she could, and for weeks ahead, he wanted to know how she intended to do this, as she had admitted she and the children were not in work. She was wise enough not to tell him of her little store, because she couldn't trust anyone, and especially not this agent, who looked a mean man.

They were now into June and the day was hot when, footsore, she led Biddy, Johnny, and Maggie back to the house. And there Mrs Carr greeted them with a friendliness that had been absent during the last few days. 'You look hot,' she said. 'I've just got a bucket of water from the tap.' She pointed to a bucket standing near the table. 'Help yourselves. And I've got a bit of news that could be of help.'

Uninvited Riah sat down on a cracket and said, 'Yes?'

'Well, I was in the market this mornin' an' who should I run across but Steve Procket. He was with our Arthur at the pit way out beyond Gateshead. Well, what do you think? He's left the pit and gone back to his old job in Jarrow as a chips.'

'Chips?'

'Aye, chips. Shipbuilding you know. Chips.'

'Oh!'

'Well, I said to him, how was our Arthur, 'cos it's months since I've seen hilt or hair of him, and what d'you think he told me?' She waited a moment, but when Riah remained silent, she went on, 'Winnie's in a bad way, that's his wife . . . our Arthur's. A weakling she's been for years; couldn't carry bairns, you know. Well, Arthur got a woman to see to things, but she only stayed three days as it's back of beyond, lonely as hell. It was the pit keeker's cottage, a good one, but way out, he said; that's why he couldn't stand it either. If you wanted a drink you had to take the cart into the town an' shank it back at night. Anyway, the long and short of it is, our Arthur needs somebody there, an' so when he told me that I thought of you. There's four good rooms in the house, but what's more there's outbuildings and a barn almost twice the size of the house running alongside. Would you like to give it a try?'

Riah stared at the old woman; then she looked at the children, her eyes resting on Biddy, and Biddy said, 'It'll be in the country, Ma.'

Yes, it would be in the country. She was tired and weary to her inmost bone with walking and worrying, and Biddy's words, 'It'll be in the country, Ma,' brought a picture before her mind of a rural scene. She saw the cottage and the outhouses, she saw the children racing down the field to the river, she saw herself, white apron on, her blue striped blouse open at the neck, her hair combed back from her forehead and she was looking up into the sky and smiling.

Mrs Carr's voice blotted out the picture saying, 'Well, there it is. I thought it would give you a chance.'

She was on her feet now, her voice rapid: 'Oh, it will, Mrs Carr, thank you. Yes, thank you. Where did you say it was?'

'Fuller's Moor, beyond Fellburn. Rowan Cottage.'

'Oh, yes, I know that way, at least yon side of Fellburn. We'll start first thing in the morning. Oh, thank you, Mrs Carr. Thank you.'

'You're welcome. I'm sure he'll be glad to see you.'

The brightness going from her face and voice now, she said, 'What if he's already got somebody?'

'I doubt it. Steve only came back two weeks ago. Anyway, that's a risk you'll have to take, but I'm sure it'll be all right. And even if he has somebody, he'd put you up in the barn until you got settled. He's a kind lad is our Arthur. And it's in the country an' the bairns'll love it.' She looked at the children. 'They've never taken to the quayside, have they? Your lad doesn't like the smell of fish. Funny that; I can't stand the sight of grass, not big clumps anyway. We're all made different. Thanks be to God for it, I say.'

Riah nodded to her, then went quickly towards the other room. And there she looked at her family who had preceded her. They were sitting in a tight tow on the bed, their faces bright, and Biddy as usual was the spokesman. 'Eeh! Ma, the country,' she said. 'Should I run and tell our Davey?'

'Yes, do that, hinny.'

Biddy was at the door and was about to open it when she turned and, looking at her mother, she said, 'Shouldn't wonder but he'll tip the fish all back into the river when I tell him.'

'Go on with you.' Riah was laughing as her daughter ran out, pulling the door behind her. She often said, 'Thank God for Biddy.' She knew she was the brightest of the four, and being so she should have loved her more than the rest and she felt guilty when she knew that she didn't. But there was one she loved the best, and that was her son David. He might not have the wit of Biddy, but for her there was a light that shone out of him. She only had to look at him and her throat became tight with emotion that went beyond maternal love.

3

It was half past ten when they left the cart to the south of Gateshead Fell. She didn't know the part at all, but Mrs Carr had said that Fuller's Moor was nothing but a good walk from the top end of Gateshead Fell.

When she stopped a couple of workmen and asked the way, the men looked at each other, and one of them said, 'Fuller's Moor? By, you're a tidy step from there, missis.'

'How far?' she asked.

'Oh!' The men again exchanged glances; then the other man spoke, saying. 'Well, go straight on and you'll come to The Stag. Now turn off down there, and I should say . . . Oh' – he shook his head – 'it's a good four miles from there.'

Four miles could be nothing to her or perhaps Davey or Biddy, but the two youngsters tired easily. 'Is there a carrier that way?' she asked.

The men seemed to think about it. 'Aye, when I come to think of it,' one said. 'There's one leaves round here eight in the mornin' and goes by there in a roundabout way to Chester-le-Street and Durham, an' comes back 'bout four in the afternoon.' Then he added, 'But that won't be much help to you, missis. Still' – he smiled – 'it's a fine day, doesn't look like rain, in fact we've never had any for two weeks now so the roads should be nice and hard.'

She thanked them and was about to turn away when she asked, 'Are there any villages on the way?'

'Well, no, not what you call villages,' one of the men said. 'Hamlets, two, Brookdip and Rowdip, a few houses and a blacksmith's in Rowdip.'

'Well, you ain't got no horse, so you won't need that.' This caused both men to laugh and the children to titter but it found no answering mirth in herself. She nodded at them, thanked them again and went on . . .

It was near noon when they reached The Stag Inn and Johnny and Maggie were already trailing their feet.

Once they left the main road there was one thing that Riah noticed and Biddy exclaimed on, 'It's bonny country, Ma, isn't it?'

'Yes,' she said as she looked from one side to the other of the bridle-path on which they were walking, and it seened to her that the gently rising ground dotted here and there with belts of woodland must go on forever.

'My toes are hurting, Ma. They're skinned.'

She took off Johnny's boot. Sure enough the middle joints of two of his toes were red raw. 'Oh,' she said softly, 'you should have mentioned them afore. How long have they been like this?'

'Some way, Ma.'

She clicked her tongue. 'Sit down, all of you and we'll have something to eat.'

'Ma' – Davey was pointing – 'there's a beck down there.'

'A beck?' They were all on their feet again and standing near Davey looking down to where a narrow stream could be seen through some low shrubland.

'Oh, come on!' Riah sounded like a child herself, and she picked Johnny up in her arms and, calling to the others, 'Bring the stuff,' she scrambled down through the bushes to where the land levelled out into a green sward alongside the stream.

Riah was to remember the next hour for a long, long time. It seemed like a foretaste of heaven. They made a fire and they fried bacon, and as it sizzled its aroma was like perfume to their nostrils, and Davey, with unusual humour, said dryly, 'If only we had thought to bring some fish along, Ma, we could have fried them an' all,' whereupon they all fell against each other with their laughing.

After the meal, like the children she, too, took off her boots and stockings and plodged in the stream. They sprayed water on her and she sprayed water on them, and later, when she had to call a halt and they had to gather up their things again, Biddy, looking about her, said quietly, 'Wouldn't it be nice, Ma, if we could stay here forever?' And she answered, 'Well, we will be just further along the road.' . . .

They were all walking very slowly as they made their way up the slight incline out of the hamlet of Brookdip. There were five buildings in the dip; one was the church and the biggest house, which was next to it, looked like the vicarage. Who inhabited the other three she didn't stop to enquire. Two miles back in the hamlet of Rowdip there had been about twelve houses altogether but they were scattered, two being farmhouses, and one a smaller manor.

The few people they had encountered on the road, all had looked at them with interest but no one had stopped and questioned them. It was, Riah thought, perhaps not an unusual sight to see a woman and four children hugging bundles along the highway. And that could be true, and folks didn't want to become involved with people in her situation.

They'd had two further stops since they'd played by the stream, but they hadn't been so merry, not merry at all, for now Maggie's heels were skinned and Biddy had stopped talking, which was a sure sign that she was very tired, and to Davey's face had returned that apprehensive look which told her that he was worrying about something.

They had come to a small kind of crossroads and didn't know which way to go when they saw a man driving a flat cart coming towards them. As he approached nearer, Riah noticed that he sat high above the horse. It was the way his seat was placed: the cart looked like a converted brake, but there were no seats in the back, just sacks of something. He pulled up the horse and looked down at them, and she was the first to speak. She said, 'Could you tell me, please, the way to Rowan Cottage?'

He didn't answer immediately but looked from her to the four children, then over her head and down the road from which they had come as if he expected someone else to appear; then still not speaking, he turned round and pointed along the road by which he had come, saying abruptly, 'Half a mile back.'

'Thank you.' She stared at him a moment longer. He was a brusque man, not friendly. Again she said, 'Thank you.' Then she walked away, and the children followed. She had gone some distance when Biddy muttered, 'He hasn't gone on, Ma, he's sitting looking at us.'

'Take no need.'

The half-mile turned out to be a long half-mile before they saw the cottage, but the sight of it seemed to make them forget their sore feet. When they reached the gate, they all stood huddled together leaning over it, looking towards the side of the house.

The front door faced a yard. It was a fine big yard, and opposite were the outhouses that Mrs Carr had described. Riah was smiling inside. There was plenty of room; she would settle here and gladly, oh yes. She thrust open the gate and, her step quickening, she marched across the yard and to the front door and she knocked upon it. When there was no answer she turned and looked at the children, saying, 'He's likely at work and his wife in bed poorly,' and she nodded at them.

It was Davey who, standing behind the others, turned his head towards the window. Taking two steps to the side, he stood in front of it; then with his face close to the pane, he cried, '*Ma!*' His voice was high. '*'Tis empty, empty.*'

She almost jumped to his side and stared through the window. They were looking into a room. On the far wall was a fireplace with dead ashes in the grate. Now she moved quickly to the other side of the door and, looking into another room, saw that that too was empty. She turned and leant her back against the wall and muttered thickly, 'My God. There's nobody here.' She stared down at Davey.

'I don't want to go back, Ma.' She turned her eyes now on to Maggie whose face was crumpled up on the verge of tears, and, pulling herself from the wall, she took in a deep breath, squared her shoulders and said, 'Well, we're not going back, not the night anyway. Let's go and see what's in the stables.'

They found the two stables dirty, the floor covered with horse muck and dank straw. The barn wasn't much better, but at its end was a narrow platform and on it were two broken bales of straw. She looked up and could see the sky where the tiles were off the barn roof. Fortunately, the straw was at the other end.

'We'll sleep up there the night,' she said. 'Come the morning I'll think of something.'

But what was she going to think of in the morning? Return to Shields? Never. Never in this world. As terrible as the thought of the workhouse was she would rather take them there, yet at the same time knowing that she never would as long as she had money in her pocket. That was the only bright spot on the horizon at the moment, she had money in her pocket, or literally between her breasts. She started to bustle now, urging them, 'Put the packages up there' – she pointed – 'to the dry end of the platform. We'll make a fire in the yard. We've still got some milk left and there's bound to be a well.' . . .

It was about half an hour later when she was boiling up the water that the children had brought from a rill that ran at the bottom of the field adjoining the cottage – there was no well – that she heard the words. 'Whoa! there,' and turned her head sharply towards the gate. She had been so preoccupied with what she was doing that the cart seemed to have dropped there out of thin air.

She stood up, rubbing her hands down the sides of her skirt, and looked to where the man who had directed them a little earlier sat staring towards them; but by his side now was an old woman. It was she who beckoned her forward; and when she reached the gate, the woman said, 'You arrived then?'

Riah blinked, then muttered, 'Aye, yes.'

'Where's your man?'

'My man?'

'Aye, that's what I said. You're not daft or stupid, are you? Your man, who's for the mine.'

'I . . . I think you've made a mistake.'

The two people on the cart exchanged glances. Then the old woman, her voice not so sharp now, said, 'You're not with your man? Then why are you here at the cottage?'

'I . . . I understood I was coming to look after Mr Carr's wife who's ill. His mother sent me.'

The two pairs of eyes were staring into hers. Then the old woman gave a shrill laugh as she said. 'Well, did you ever. Well I've got to tell you, missis, that Winnie Carr's been dead and buried this past week, so she's beyond your help. An' I should guess, too, you're more in need of it than she is at the moment.'

'But Mr Carr?'

Again the two on the cart exchanged glances, and once more it was the old woman who spoke, 'Oh, he had a piece in to look after his wife, but like the others afore her, the place got on her nerves. Townsfolk can't stand looking at the sky, there's too much of it.' She again laughed her shrill laugh, then ended, 'He had taken to her so when she made back for the town he went with her, and a man called McAllister is being set on at the mine and bringing his family out here the morrow. Six of them I understand. That's so, Tol?' She turned to the man at her side, and he inclined his head towards her. 'Where you from?'

She paused a moment thinking, Where was she from? Shields? Fellburn? Beyond Gateshead? She said, 'From South Shields, lately.'

'You've come all that way the day?'

'Yes.' She saw the man turn his head away and look towards his horse. The old woman moved her head to the side and said, 'I see you're bedding down here for the night.'

'Yes.'

'Well, there's no harm in that. But come the morrow, it would be wise to be on your way early, 'cos I understand they're an Irish lot that are comin' in, and perhaps you know what they're like, scum of the earth an' fighters . . . You're a widow then, are you?' She looked at the four children who were standing further back in the yard.

'Yes.'

'And you're lookin' for a housekeeper's job?'

'Well, yes.' She was going to add, or a house, when the old woman put in, 'You'll be hard set to find one with a tribe of four at your heels. Yet your two eldest could be in work.'

Before either of them could speak again the man said softly, 'Fanny, time's gettin' on.' And she answered, 'Aye, yes, all right, Tol. 'Tis kind of you it is; sorry I've kept you. Goodbye missis, and good luck.' She nodded at her and the man said, 'Gee-up! there,' and the cart moved forward leaving Riah standing looking after them.

She wanted to cry. Stop it. Stop it. It was no time for crying. Oh my God! What was it a time for? Praying, aye; but then she wasn't much good at praying. Planning was what she must do, and the immediate plan was to get them to bed; although it was still day-light they were all dog-tired. But she must get them up at sunrise the morrow morning and they must be on their way before that family came in. She wanted no rows, no barraging, because Davey, she admitted to herself, wasn't a boy to seek a fight, he was a peaceful lad, thoughtful. Now if he'd had Biddy's nature, he would go in with fists flailing to anyone twice his size, she was sure of that.

It was Biddy who, sometime later when they were crossing the yard to bring the last of the pans in and to stamp out the fire, said, 'We'll have to make it back the morrow then, Ma?'

'Yes, hinny.'

'Where do you think we'll settle, Ma?'

She stopped by the edge of the fire and she looked across it and over the gate into the thicket at yon side of the road, and her mind at this moment seemed as closed against thought as the low shrub woodland did against entry.

'I don't know, lass,' she said. 'I don't know, and that's God's truth.'

Breaking the short silence that had ensued, Biddy said softly, 'Something will turn up, Ma. Something always does. It'll have to, 'cos we've got to be settled somewhere, haven't we?'

Riah looked down at her daughter and said, 'Yes, we've got to settle somewhere.' Then her mind squeezed out the question, But where? Where?

She received the answer the following morning.

The sun was well up before she roused the children; and when they struggled down from the platform they were still bleary-eyed and tired from the previous day's tramping.

She had a fire going in the yard and she cooked the last of the fat bacon and dipped the remaining pieces of bread in the fat. Then she put a can of water on the fire, and when it was boiling they washed the greasy breakfast down with mugs of it. The meal over, she sent them down to the rill to sluice their faces and hands; then she herself followed them and did the same. Afterwards she combed their hair, then saw to her own.

They were ready, the bundles in their hands, the yard left as they had found it, when the cart appeared at the gate again, and they all stared towards it as if it was an apparition, for there sat the man and the old woman as they had done last evening, except now they were facing the other way. It was the old woman who called to her again, saying, 'Here a minute!'

Riah did not look at the children as she said to them, 'Stay where you are,' before she walked forward. And now she was looking up at the old woman who surprised her by saying, 'Can you cook?'

She hesitated before, her chin jerking slightly, she said, 'I've been doing it for years.'

'Aye, frying-pan stuff likely. But can you make a good dinner?'

Her voice slightly terse, she said, 'I've been told I've made many a one.'

'Well, tastes differ an' that remains to be seen, but it's like this. I might be able to get you a place. I'm not promising', mind, I'll have to talk to him, that's if I can get a word in and he doesn't shout me down every time I raise the subject. But look. Stay put for the next hour or so an' if the news is to your good, Tol here' – she turned and inclined her head towards the man – 'he'll come back and pick you up.' She now looked fully at her companion and, to Riah's ears, her tone seeming to soften considerably, she added, 'You will do that, Tol, won't you?' and he replied, 'I'll do it, but I can't promise you to be back straight on the hour.'

'Well, as they don't seem to be going any place in particular I don't suppose she'll mind waitin' a couple.'

She was looking down at Riah again and she said, 'Is that so?' And Riah said, 'What are you proposing?'

The old woman now bristled and she repeated the word as if it was foreign to her, 'Pro . . . posin', she says.' She was looking over her shoulder towards the man again and thumbing back towards Riah. 'Proposin'. I'm only tryin' to get you set up in a good place, that's if he'll take the youngsters. Proposin'! Carry on, Tol.' She lifted her hand in an imperious movement now as if she was ordering a servant, and the cart moved off. But as it did so, the man turned his head and looked behind the old woman, and although his expression hadn't altered the movement of his head conveyed to Riah a message which could have been, Take no notice, she means well.

She stood where she was and watched the cart until it disappeared from view at the end of the long narrow lane; then she turned into the yard again.

'What is it, Ma? What did she want?'

She looked at Biddy. 'I don't know,' she said, 'but it seems as if there might be a job in the offing. What it is . . . well, you know as much about it as I do. She's a queer old lady.'

'The man seemed nice.'

She looked at Davey, and nodded at him, saying, 'Yes, he did, when he could get a word in, although he didn't seem inclined for much talk. Well, we can sit down again. I'll tell you what, leave your bundles inside the barn door and go on down to the stream and have a bit plodge.'

'I don't want to. I'd rather stay here, Ma,' said Biddy.

'Me an' all.' Davey came to her side. The two younger ones said nothing but they, too, came closer to her and held on to her skirt. She looked down on them lovingly; then she said, softly, 'I'll tell you what you can do. You two get into your Sunday frocks' – she indicated the girls – 'and Davey, you can put on your good trousers, an' I'll see to Johnny, because if we've got to go and see whoever this is what wants a cook or some such, we should look tidy.'

'What about you, Ma? You look lovely in your blue blouse. Will you put it on?'

'Oh.' She hesitated as she looked down on Biddy. Her blue blouse was special. Seth had bought her the material as a surprise present.

He had thrown the parcel on to the table one Saturday night and there was this length of blue cotton with a tiny pink flower here and there as a pattern. She had spent hours making the blouse and she hadn't worn it more than half a dozen times since. She had thought of it as a garment for occasions and there hadn't been many occasions in her life that warranted its wearing. But now, here might be an occasion, and she smiled broadly as she said, 'Aye, I'll put it on.'

Excitement ran high now as they all went into the barn to change their clothes, then they were ready and stood at the gate waiting . . .

They waited and they waited, the minutes dragging.

'How long is it now, Ma?' said Johnny.

'Oh,' she considered, 'well over an hour, I would say.'

'If he doesn't come at all, will we have to change back?' Biddy smoothed down her short coat with both hands and reluctantly Riah answered, 'Yes, I'm afraid so.'

Her reply seemed to cause the children to go limp, for now Johnny and Maggie leant against the bars of the gate, only to be brought upright by Riah saying firmly, 'Stand straight, the gate's green with mould, you'll mark yourselves.'

As she finished speaking Davey let out a cry that almost verged on a shout: 'He's coming, Ma!' Then he clapped his hand over his mouth and ran towards her. And once again they were standing all close together.

And that was the picture of them that Tol Briston held in his mind for a long time: the woman with the auburn hair topped by a black straw hat, her deep brown eyes holding an anxious greeting, her wide mouth partly open, her whole expression seeming to hold a plea for good news; and the children now differently dressed, all clean and tidy, their faces bright, but the two elder ones reflecting something of their mother's look.

After pulling the horse to a stop, he smiled, a slow smile that warmed his thin face, and there came a twinkling light into his dark eyes, and his lips were showing a set of short big white teeth. His chin, like his nose, jutted out from his face and might tend to suggest a rigidness of character, but at this moment his expression could have been termed merry, and his tone definitely held a jolly note as he said, 'Up with you, the lot of yous.'

Grabbing up the bundles, the children made for the back of the cart. But Riah didn't move. Looking up at Tol, she said, 'Is it settled?'

'Oh' – the smile slid from his face – 'that I can't tell; it will lie between you and Mr Miller. Fanny's got you an interview, that's all I can say. But having got that far, it's like a pistol to his head; she could walk out.'

Riah couldn't quite follow his meaning, but she turned to where her bundles had lain, only to see that Davey had them already on the back of the cart, and when she made to follow him, Tol Briston said, 'You could be seated here if you so like.' He edged a little along the wooden seat, and when, after a moment's hesitation, she put her foot on the hub of the wheel, he thrust out his hand and she clasped it; then perched high beside him and looking straight ahead, she began the journey that was to set the seal on her life.

The entry to Moor House was through two unimposing iron gates, both of them thrust back with their bottom bars bedded firmly in weeds and dead grass. The drive was short, not more than fifty yards, and it curved to an open area that was almost as long as the drive itself; but unlike the roughness of the drive, this was paved with large stone slabs, most of them, like the gates, cemented with grass. The house took up about half the width of the forecourt and the word that came into Riah's mind at the sight of it was higgledy-piggledy, because it looked as if a large cottage had been stuck either side of a three storey medium-sized house. Beyond the forecourt was a yard bordered on two sides by what looked like a stable and a barn.

Tol had brought the cart to a stop opposite the front door and there, almost filling it, stood the old woman. The children were slow to get out of the cart until her voice came at them in a hiss, saying, 'Well, come on! Put a move on, you all.' And when they had done her bidding she looked them over and said, 'Oh, you're tidy. That's good.' Her gaze now on Riah, she surveyed her from her black straw hat down to her black boots; then she said, 'Come on in the lot of yous.' And with that she almost pulled them one after the other over the low step and into a hallway. But before she closed the door she leant forward and called quietly towards the cart, 'Thanks, Tol. See you later then.'

Now she was crossing the hall, saying in a whisper, 'Come this way.'

The first impression that Riah got of Moor House was that it needed a good clean up: there was no shine on the hall floor surrounding the carpet, and the pieces of furniture dotting the walls showed plain evidence of dust.

The old woman, who Riah noticed now was limping badly, pushed open the door at the end of the hall, saying, 'Go in there and sit yourselves down until I get him.'

Pressing the children before her, Riah entered a long room. Although this, too, showed it could do with a good clean, it was evidently used, for a big couch whose upholstery had once been yellow and now was a dirty faded grey in parts showed tumbled cushions at its head, and between the two tall windows stood a desk littered with papers and books, looking as if someone had thrown them on it from a distance, so mixed up were they.

Silently she stopped the children sitting on the couch and directed them to a long backless upholstered seat set at right angles to the fireplace which showed a pile of ashes in which were buried half-burnt logs.

Seating herself on the edge of a chair opposite the children, she smoothed her skirt over her knees, opened the two buttons of her three-quarter length serge coat in order that her bright blue blouse should be in evidence and show her proposed employer that she was neat and tidy. Finally, she tucked her hair swiftly behind her ears, felt that her hat was absolutely straight on her head, then joined her hands on her lap and waited.

A minute was a long time to wait when four pairs of eyes were staring questioningly at you. But when five minutes passed and the children began to move restlessly on the seat, she unclasped her hands and with a raised finger cautioned them to silence; then her hand became transfixed by the sound of a voice coming from the far end of the room. For the first time she noticed that there was a door in the side wall and the voice was coming from there. It was somewhat muffled, yet the words were still clear: 'No, Fanny. *No.* 'Tis blackmail. That's all it is, blackmail. I've told you, *no*.'

'An' I've told you, Mr Miller, an' for the last time, I can't make the journeys no more. If it wasn't for Tol I wouldn't be here now. And he's riskin' somethin', cartin' me mornin' and night. If them up at The Heights get wind of it, he could be for the push. An' look at me leg, it's as big as me body. Now, you either take her an' her tribe on or you're left alone to fend for yourself, 'cos nobody in their right senses'll come here an' look after this place for what you have to offer them.'

'Is that my fault, Fanny? Is it? Is it?'

'Yes, it is. In a way, yes it is, 'cos come quarter time you've enough money for books, beer, and baccy.'

'Oh, leave me my breath. What else have I to live for?'

'Oh, Mr Miller, don't make me say it again.'

The man's voice now fell to almost a mutter as he said, 'And don't make me say it again, Fanny. What good am I in the outside world? I've tried it, haven't I?'

'I can't understand you, I can't, Mr Miller.'

'Well, that's a pity, Fanny. That's a pity. I thought you were the only one who could. But about this woman. You say she's got four children? My God! And you think I'll take on a woman with four children? For fifteen years I tried to knock sense into the . . .'

'Oh, shut up, will you? Shut up. I've heard your whinin' until I'm sick of it. Now, you're seein' this woman or I walk out, not this evenin' after I've made your meal, but now, along of her an' her tribe. Now I say to you, you've got no other option. No, you haven't, Mr Miller. No, you haven't.'

There followed a long silence during which the children, wide-eyed and open-mouthed, stared at Riah while she, her head turned slightly, kept her eyes fixed on the door at the far end of the room. Then the voices began again.

'What are they?'

'They're two lads and two lasses.'

'How old?'

'Well, I think the boy seems about twelve and the youngest, I should say, five or six. The two lads you could set clearin' on outside. They've likely been used to work. As for the lasses, well, this house could do with a couple of lasses to help muck it out.'

'What's she like?'

'Pleasant, youngish, capable looking.'

There followed another silence; and then the man's voice, which held a deep plea in it now, said 'Oh, Fanny, you don't know what you're asking. You really don't know what you're asking me to do.'

'Don't be silly, Mr Miller. Go on . . . go on, have a look at them.'

The few minutes seemed a long time before the door opened and a man entered the room.

The four children turned their heads towards him, and it was to them he looked first, not at Riah. When he did look at her he was about two yards from her. She had risen to her feet and they surveyed each other like combatants before a battle. She saw that he was a man in his mid-forties, perhaps nearing fifty, she would say. He had a round face and fair hair with a slight bald patch on the top of his head. He was of medium height and, although not fat, was inclined to thickness. After having listened to his voice, she had expected a tall, very imposing figure; the man before her appeared like a gentle creature, rather shy. In fact, she couldn't remember ever seeing anyone quite like him at all. She hadn't come across many gentry with whom to compare him, but she would have said he belonged to that class.

When he said hesitantly, 'You . . . you're wanting a position?' she answered. 'Yes, sir.'

'You . . . you are a widow?'

'Yes, sir.'

'Your children, can they work?' He turned now and his eyes rested on Davey, and she said, 'Yes. Yes, sir. My son David, he's comin' up eleven and he's been workin' in the fields for the past three years. And Bridget' – she inclined her head – 'she's very good at housework. She is coming up ten. She too has been working for the past three years.' What made her utter the next words she never knew, but she said, 'An' they're both learned; they can read and write, sir.'

His head came quickly round to her as he said, 'Indeed. Indeed . . . What was your husband?'

'He was a miner, sir.'

His eyebrows moved slightly upwards. 'A miner? A coal miner?'

'Yes, sir.'

'And your children . . . can read and write? Did they go to school?'

'No, sir. My husband taught them.'

His eyebrows moved further upwards and he said, 'Your husband taught them? And he was a miner? And he could read and write? May I ask who taught him?'

'A Methodist man in Gateshead, sir.'

'Oh. Oh. What is your name?'

'Mrs Millican, sir. Maria Millican.'

'Well, Mrs Millican, I must be plain with you. I'm a man of very poor means. And I couldn't afford to engage you and your children at the wage you would likely require. Mrs Briggs has four shillings a week and her food. You, I am sure, would not consider that enough for your services and those of your family.'

Four shillings for the lot of them. It was nothing, but at the present moment if he had suggested that she worked for their board and lodgings only she would have accepted. She said quickly, 'I would be pleased to accept your offer, sir.'

'You would?' He half turned from her, one shoulder moving as if with the twitch; then, looking at her again, he said, 'It is nothing.'

'I'll . . . I'll be grateful for it at the present, sir, and we would do our best to serve you well.'

She was surprised to see him sit down in a chair and, resting his elbow on the table, lean his head on his hand; then, after a moment during which they all stood staring at him, he rose and, without first looking at them, he turned from them, saying, 'See Fanny; she'll tell you what to do.' And he walked up the room again and through the door, and as it closed on him the other door opened and the old woman hobbled in, her face bright, her lips pursed and her hands beckoning them towards her.

When they reached her all in a bunch, she said, ' 'Tis done then. Come.' And with that she led them back into the hall, through a heavy oak door into a stone passage, through another door and into the kitchen.

Riah took in three things immediately about the kitchen: it was very big; it was cluttered and dirty; the barred fire of the iron cooking stove had a hob attached to its top bar.

'Sit yourselves down' – Fanny pointed to the table – 'and I'll make you a drink. Would you like tea?'

'Tea?' Riah muttered the word and Fanny said, 'Aye, tea, real tea. He gets it in Newcastle but it comes from China. It's the one luxury in this house. But I'm not partial to it meself; too scenty like.' And then she went on, 'Well now, you're all set, and it's up to you.'

'Where will we sleep?'

As Riah slapped Biddy's arm gently for asking the question Fanny nodded at her and in a broad toothless smile she said, 'Practical one you are, aren't you? Well then, I'll answer you. There's a hayloft outside. But better than that, along at the low end' – she motioned with her head to a door leading off by the side of a dresser – 'there's half a dozen rooms along there that haven't been slept in for many a long year. But they are like Paddy's market, full up with this, that an' the other. Anyway, it'll be one of your first jobs to clear one of them and get settled for the night. But first I'll make you a drop of tea and then I'll take you round. It's a hoppity-hoppity house; you've got to get used to goin' up a step an' down a step that you didn't know was there. That's what's worn me legs out over the past ten years. I never meant to take this on, you know.' She was nodding at Riah now as she poured some boiling water into a cream china teapot which was stained brown around the lid. 'You see, me old man was gardener here for years, an' his father afore him. That was when there was only the house standing, this middle one, an' it was of no size as these houses go, just ten main rooms. But there was about thirty acres of land then, but now it's down to three. The odd bits on the sides were built by Mr Miller's father when he was young. I always says that the builder must have been drunk at the time, but my old man said it was to get the levels of the ground as it slopes away at the side like. Anyway, now they amount to twenty-five rooms altogether, an' that's not countin' larders and cellars an' the like. An' how many does he use . . . Mr Miller? Two mostly; one if he got his own way, 'cos he lives in the library room most of his time an' sleeps in it more often than not on the couch. He'll be found dead in there one of these days, I tell him. Eeh, by!' She now poured a small amount of milk into six cups she had brought from a cupboard; then as she filled them with the black tea she added, 'I never thought I'd bring it off, not really, 'cos he's agen people: never sees anybody but Parson Weeks and Miss Hobson from The Heights, or when he goes once a quarter into Newcastle to pick up his allowance. And more often than not those times he can hardly walk back from the coach road. But then on quarter days Tol keeps a look out for the coach and generally picks him up from it. I don't know what we'd do without Tol. He keeps us stocked up with wood and he drops the milk in most mornings except when the weather's very bad an' he can't get through.'

'Tol . . . it's a funny name.'

Riah looked warningly at Biddy, but again the old woman smiled as she said, 'Aye, I suppose it is.'

'What's his second name?'

'Briston, Tol Briston . . . Is there anything more you'd like to know, miss, or would you like to wait and ask him?' She was laughing down on Biddy now, and Biddy lowered her head as her mother said, 'I'm sorry she speaks out of turn.'

'Oh, I wouldn't give you tuppence for any bairn that didn't speak out of turn. Anyway, you'll all likely see a bit of Tol if you see nobody else here, for as I've said visitors are few an' far between here now, not like it once was. Anyway, Tol's the nearest neighbour. His cottage is in Fuller's Dip and the cottage is called The Dip.' She bent towards Biddy again, saying, 'That's a funny name an' all, isn't it, for a cottage, The Dip? Don't ask me how it came by it 'cos I couldn't tell you. Nor could my old man, and he was born in the hamlet. He used to say it was a natural name 'cos the cottage was in a hollow: an' it was Tol's father's, an' his afore him. All forest men. The grandfather bought an' built on a bit of freehold land with stones from an old stone ruin and timber from an old ship, lugged from the river . . . Would you like some more tea?'

All the children spoke at once, saying, 'Yes, please,' which caused Fanny to nod down at Riah, saying, 'Well they have manners anyway.'

'I like to think they were brought up proper.'

A few minutes later Fanny said, 'Well now, finish your drink and let's away for an inspection trip.' And on this they immediately rose from the table and stood waiting while they looked at her as she put a hand to one side of her face and muttered as if to herself, 'Now where shall I start?' Then turning fully to Riah, she said, 'I've got no need to point out that this is the kitchen an' here you'll find all the things necessary for cooking except perhaps the stuff to cook with. Meals are pretty sparse 'cos I've had to stretch his shillin's. But there's one thing there's plenty of, an' that's fruit. The orchard's all overrun, but it's there for the pickin', goin' rotten most of it.' Her eyes scanned the children now as she said, 'You can eat to your heart's content an' be up all night with the gripes.' And with this she turned away laughing as she added, 'Come on; we'll start this way.'

She now led them through the door to the side of the dresser and they found themselves tightly packed in another stone passage from which led three doors. She pushed them open one after the other, saying, 'Coalhouse, pantry an' meat store,' adding, 'That hasn't seen a carcass for years. An' lastly, wine cellar. As you can see' – she moved to one side to let them glimpse in – 'the racks are full of bottles. Unfortunately, they're all empty. But there was a time, my old man's father used to tell me, when there was as many as five hundred bottles on those shelves. But them days are gone.'

She now opened another door, giving them a warning as she did so: 'Mind, there's a step down.'

When they had all stepped down, Riah saw that they were in another small hall with stairs leading up from the middle as in the main hall.

Fanny now pushed open another four doors leading off the hall and saying as she did so, 'This was old Mrs Miller's sitting-room. In fact, this was her end of the house, 'cos she kept to herself, I understand, the last years of her life. You see, I wasn't here then. It was Lizzie Watson who was the previous housekeeper. I've always lived in the hamlet. Still do. I like me own fireside. That's what annoys him' – she jerked her head backwards – 'I wouldn't live in. Ten hours a day's enough for anybody, especially when there's nobody to open your mouth to. 'Cos there's days when you'd fancy he'd gone dumb . . . Well, that was his mother's room. Never seen a duster for months I can tell you. Well, I can't get round to it, can I?'

As Riah shook her head she thought, Never seen a duster for months? Years would be nearer the truth. What a pity the moths had gone into the upholstery; it must have been such a nice suite at one time.

They followed the old woman into the next room which was a small dining-room; then to a music-room where a spinnet stood in the corner. It had a fretwork front and the silk behind it had dropped away here and there. As Riah followed their guide up the stairs to the four rooms above and saw that their condition was much the same as those down below she kept repeating to herself: What a shame. What a shame.

When they were once more back in the kitchen Fanny led them through the door opposite to that next to the dresser and into a set of rooms much the same as those they had left. And when again they returned to the kitchen there was only the main house to go through. And now Fanny faced them, saying, 'Well you've seen the hall and the drawing-room and now I'll show you the dining-room, but he hardly ever eats there. He mostly eats off a tray in his library room, except when the parson comes. Then I used to knock up a meal for them and they sat down to it properly. There's one thing we'd better not do and that's go near his library room. You can see that later on, but' – she lifted her hand and wagged a finger at Riah – 'don't, on the peril of your life, try to straighten up anythin' in there. You'll think on first sight that a great wind had been through it, but he seems to know where everything is. Anyway, I'll take you up above and show you his bedroom. There's another four up there, but they've never been used for years. And the attic above. Oh God alive! the attic. I shouldn't be surprised if some of the old clothes don't come walking down the stairs one of these days, so alive will they be. I've only been up there a couple of times. That was when I first came and I hinted at him that a lot of the stuff could be cut down for frocks and things for needy people in the village, and one of them was meself, 'cos some of the material was fine, the women's things. And there was men's toggery made up of fine worsted and serges. But you know, he nearly went down me throat. It's the only time he's ever gone for me. He told me those things were to be left alone and kindly not bring up the subject again. Oh, he played the master that day all right. Other times he talks like a lost lad. And if I say, what shall I do about this, that, and the other, he'll say, do what you think best, Fanny. You do what you think best. But about those clothes, oh my! So don't think, lass, when you go up there that you will be able to cut anything up for the bairns 'cos that's one thing he's firm on. Why? Don't ask me, I don't know. My man used to say it was just a quirk 'cos he had lived alone so long and the clothes were kind of memories he was hanging on to.'

'Has he always lived alone here?'

'No, just for the last fifteen year. Well, not that long. He came back fifteen years gone and it's ten years ago now since his father died. And Lizzie Watson, as I said, was the housekeeper and she went shortly after. And that's how I came in. It was my man who asked me to help out. Just for a week or two, he said; then it went into years. He was always going to leave, my man was, because he was seventy-six and bent double with gardening, and he left all right when he dropped down dead near the rose patch, three years gone. Oh aye, he left all right. And I was left here on me own with young Mr Miller, 'cos that's what he was called when his father was alive and they never got on, his father an' him. Different as chalk from cheese. Used to ride every day, his father did; drunk as a noodle most times; an' gambled like somebody who had lost his brains. That's where the money went. But young Mr Miller was a different kettle of fish. Books seemed to be his weakness. Of course it's brandy now an' all, but in those days it was just books, 'cos he went to this college in Oxford. And then he went teaching. Then something happened. I don't know what, but one day he lands home and decided to stay. And that was funny 'cos when he were at the school in Oxford, he rarely came home for the holidays. His mother used to go there an' stay with him. They were fond of each other. They must have been, 'cos when he came home that time for good they used to wander about the moors and lanes together. I've seen them meself, hand in hand as if he was a young lad or like a couple courtin'. Perhaps it was to make up to her, kind of, for Lizzie Wat . . . son.' Her voice tailed away as she glanced quickly at the children. 'Well, there you are. Let's get out and see the garden, or what was a garden, an' then I'll show you the kitchen ropes. And that'll be that.'

Tol Briston stood in the kitchen looking across the table to where Riah was expertly dissecting a rabbit. She had split it down the middle with a copper and was now snipping off the limbs, and he watched her hands for a few moments before saying, 'You're settled in then?'

She lifted her eyes to him and then smiled as she said, 'Yes, thanks be to God. I really can't believe it because this time yesterday I was at the bottom of despair.'

His eyes were again concentrated on her hands as he said, 'It isn't much of a job, as jobs go, I mean what he offers, but you won't find him any trouble. You'll be your own boss, so to speak, as long as you keep the children of his way. That's the main thing.'

'Oh, I will. I will.' She nodded at him. 'Mrs Briggs has told me.'

He lifted his eyes to her face now as he said, 'I'll . . . I'll drop your milk in by every day an' a load of wood once a month. He . . . he doesn't buy much coal. But I meself, I find I like a wood fire better than a coal one. But you bein' from a mining village, I . . . I suppose you're used to coal.'

'Yes. Yes, I've been used to coal. But . . . but I'll manage with wood all right. Oh yes, I'll manage, never fear.' Her smile was wide, her eyes were bright.

'That's good then,' he said.

He watched her now salt each piece of rabbit before dropping it into a brown earthenware dish, and when she put the lid on the dish he said, 'You'll miss an onion and a turnip and such for it.'

'What?' She brought her head up quickly towards him, then nodded: 'Oh, yes, yes. But Davey is going to get a patch ready, and come next spring we should have vegetables.'

'You feel settled then?'

Her hands became still on the table and she stared at him as she said, her voice a little above a whisper, 'I hope so. Oh, I hope so.'

A slow smile spread over his face, and he nodded his head twice before saying, 'That's good. It's good when one feels settled. And . . . and if you want any help any time just ask.'

'I will. Thank you very much.'

'Seeing we're your nearest neighbours, you . . . you must meet me sister.'

'Your . . . your sister?'

'Yes, I live with me sister.'

'I would like that.'

The door opened at the far end of the kitchen and Fanny entered. She was dressed for the road, and her voice was quiet and held a note of sadness as she said, 'I never thought he'd be so touched at me goin'. He's given me that . . . Look.' She held out her hand. 'Isn't it beautiful? 'Tis a brooch. 'Twas his mother's.' There were tears in her eyes now and she swallowed deeply before repeating, 'Never thought he's be so touched. An' to give me that. Why, 'tis worth somethin'. Look, Tol.'

He picked up the brooch that was made up of three ivy leaves, their stems twisted, and in the centre of each leaf was a small stone. He looked at her a long time before he said. 'I think it's gold, Fanny. And the stones, they could be good ones. You'll have to guard that.'

'I will, I will, Tol. I will. An' to think he's given it to me when he could have sold it for good money likely. But gold or no, good stones or no, I'll not sell it.'

'Oh, no, no, don't sell it. You mustn't do that.' There was a shocked note in Tol's voice.

The old woman shook her head, then turned to Riah, saying, 'Well, I'm off, lass. It's all yours now, but Tol here will tell me how you go on. An' afore the bad weather sets in he might drop me over for a day to visit you.'

'I'd like that.' Riah came round the table and took Fanny's hand, saying, 'I'll . . . I'll never be able to thank you for what you've done for me and my family. If . . . if I owned anythin' as precious as that brooch at this minute I'd give it to you. Such is my gratitude to you.'

''Twas nothin'. 'Twas nothin'. If I've done you a good turn, you've done me one an' all. And don't forget what I told you about the rabbit.' Her tone had changed now to its usual matter of factness, and, pointing to the oven, she said. 'Put in in the bottom an' leave it for the night; it'll be as tender as a day old chick the morning: and let him have it round about twelve o'clock. And don't forget what I told you about the suet pudding. He likes it crusty on top, the harder the better, and plenty of dripping in the gravy. Well, I showed you.'

'Yes, thank you very much.'

She made for the door now that Tol was holding open for her; yet seemed reluctant to go, she turned again and, looking at Riah, she said, 'And don't forget, six o'clock for his cheese and bread, and the fruit cut up in a dish, and the molasses on it, not sugar mind, the molasses. An' keep the bairns out of his way.'

'I'll remember.'

There was a tightness in Riah's throat: she could sense the feelings of the old woman who, in spite of her desire to be free of the burden of work and the travelling at her age, was reluctant to leave, perhaps not the house, but its master.

She stood alone in the yard and watched the cart being driven from it and on to the gravel, then down the drive. When it was out of sight she still remained standing. And when she eventually turned about she did not go immediately towards the kitchen door, but her eyes went from the one building to the other that hemmed in the yard on two sides; then she looked along the length of the back part of the house. Like the front, it too looked higgledy-piggledy, yet there rose in her the most odd desire, and she only just stopped herself from throwing out her arms in a wide gesture of embrace as, her thoughts tumbling over one another, she spoke to it, saying, 'I'll take care of you. I'll bring you back to what you were. I'll make you shine, and him comfortable. Oh, yes, I'll make him comfortable. And the work here will be like giving each of the bairns a trade.' And she almost skipped towards the kitchen door now and inside began preparing her new master's evening meal . . ..

It was half an hour later when, balancing the tray against her waist with one hand, she tapped on the library door. She did it softly at first; then when she received no command to enter she knocked more firmly, and when this brought a kind of smothered grunt, she opened the door and entered the room.

She saw that he was sitting before another cluttered desk, one forearm resting on it, his body leaning over it, and he continued to write while she stood wavering as to where she should place the tray.

He did not alter his position or raise his head, but his hand, still holding the pen, jerked outwards and pointed to the corner of the table as he said, 'Put it there.'

Slowly, she placed the tray on the top of a bundle of papers and books; but seeing that its position was uneven and that the bowl of fruit might slide, she tentatively put her hand under the tray with the intention of moving the papers when his voice came at her, saying, 'Don't touch those; just leave it.'

She did as she was bid, but could not help but put her hand out to arrest the progress of the sliding bowl, and this caused him to sigh. Quickly now, he put down the pen, leant back in his chair, then still without looking at her he said, 'Are you settled in?'

'Yes, yes, thank you, sir.'

'Fanny has told you everything?'

'Yes, yes, sir.'

'Good.'

Once he began to write, she turned and made for the door; and she had just opened it when he said, 'I . . . I hope you understand I don't want to be troubled by your children.'

There was a space of a second before she said, 'I understand, sir. You won't be troubled.'

Again he said, 'Good.' And she went out and closed the door. But there she stood for a moment and drew in a sharp breath before hurrying across the hall, through the kitchen and the door that led into the east wing of the house, where she had set Biddy and Maggie the task of dusting and cleaning two of the bedrooms which entailed putting the mattresses out to air in the sun and brushing the threadbare carpets.

When she came upon them, they were both sitting on the edge of a bed, and to begin with she laughingly said, 'I've caught you then, have I, dodging the column?'

'Eeh, I'm tired, Ma.' She looked at her six-year-old daughter. Then putting her hand on the child's dark brown hair she stroked it back from the sweating brow, saying, 'Yes, I bet you are, hinny, but' – she looked about her – 'I can see you've done a good job. I suppose you've done all the work while Biddy there's been sitting watching you.' At this they all laughed softly together, and Biddy said seriously, 'Ma. I wonder how long it is since this house had a clean out? It'll take ages to get all the muck out of this carpet.' She stamped her foot on it. 'And look, there's cobwebs hanging in the corners. We couldn't reach them. You'll have to have a brush, a long brush to get at them.'

'All in good time.' Riah pushed them apart and sat down between them; then putting her arms about them, she looked first at one and then at the other as she said, 'Do you think you're going to like it here?'

'Oh, aye, Ma.' Biddy nodded her head while young Maggie just smiled.

'Well now.' Riah's face became serious, as was her voice as she spoke slowly but distinctly, saying, 'All right then. And I think so too. But there's one thing that you must remember, both of you. Now listen. You've got to keep out of the master's way. Whenever you see him coming, scoot! It seems that he can't stand bairns. So remember.' She stopped and, again looking from one to the other, she asked, 'What have to got to remember?'

'To keep out of his way.'

Riah now turned her glance from Biddy to Maggie, and the little girl said, 'To keep out of the master's way, Ma.'

'Will you do that?'

They both nodded, and with this she said, 'Well, come on. You can finish for the day. It's been a day and half, hasn't it? And you Biddy, go to the garden and tell the boys to come in. But tell them to do it quietly. And you can tell them what I've just told you. Everything depends upon them keeping out of the master's way.'

'I'll tell them, Ma.'

When Biddy made to run from her, Riah thrust out her hand and grabbed the collar of her dress, saying, 'And don't scamper. Learn to walk.'

When Biddy walked away but not without first sighing, Maggie, looking up at her mother, said. 'Will we never be able to scamper again, Ma?' And Riah, pressing the child to her side, laughed down on her as she answered, 'Yes, of course you will. Every now and again we'll go out into the fields and we'll all scamper and have a bit carry-on. What about that, eh?'

And as she walked her youngest daughter from the room she thought, Yes, they'll have to scamper; and I'll have to arrange a time when they can be free and play a bit, because all bairns should play a bit.

4

It was the week before Christmas. For days now the ground had been frozen hard and the boys couldn't do anything outside. This morning, they were over in the stables, lime-washing the walls. They had been there for the past three hours and Riah was about to take them a drink of hot broth. She had on her old coat and a woollen head shawl, and now she tucked a tin bowl into each of her pockets, picked up the lidded can and, opening the kitchen door, she went out. The sharpness of the air caught at her breath, and she was glad when she entered the stable for in comparison it felt warm. The two boys turned from their task and Johnny said, 'Ma, I'm near froze.'

'You should wear your mittens,' she said, and the boy replied, 'They get all messed up and sticky.'

'Well, that's your look out. Come and have this drop of broth.'

After laying down his brush, Davey came and stood by the manger where his mother had laid the bowls, and he smiled at her and asked, 'How does it look?' She turned to the wall. 'Good,' she said. 'Good. And it smells fresh.'

'But not the fresh smell of horses. An' you know what, Ma?'

'No. What?' Riah watched her son take a drink of the hot broth before he answered: 'I wish the master had a horse an' trap; anyway, just a horse. It would be lovely if he had a horse.'

'That's a hope; he can barely manage to feed us, never mind a horse.'

'Funny that, I think, Ma, a gentleman an' no money.'

'Well, he's got some, as I've told you, but its very little, and it takes him all his time to eke it out.'

Davey laughed now and he poked his face towards her, saying, 'He didn't eke it out yesterday, did he, Ma?'

She pulled a prim face at him, trying to suppress her smile as she said, 'No, perhaps not. Anyway, come on, finish your broth, I've got to get back. I've got work to do, I can't play about.'

'Oh, Ma.' Johnny looked up at her, his dark eyes twinkling as he said, 'I'd rather play about in the house.'

She cuffed his ear gently, saying, 'Yes, I know you would, you lazy lump.' And although she looked tenderly down on her younger son she knew that there was some truth in her last words, for if Johnny could get out of working he would. He still wanted to play as if he was a bairn, but he'd had his eighth birthday last month. Yet wasn't he still a bairn? Weren't they all bairns? Except perhaps Davey. She let her eyes linger on her son. He was dressed in his oldest clothes, the cap was covering his fair hair and there was dirt on his cheeks, but nothing could hide his beauty, nor dull the brightness of his blue eyes. He was so good to look on, and during the last months he seemed to have put on inches. His body was slim and straight, and at times the sight of him pained her and she couldn't imagine he had come out of her and Seth. She was on her way out when Johnny's words stopped her, for in a loud whisper he called to her, 'I saw the master this morning, Ma.'

Swinging round, her expression dark, she demanded, 'Now I've told you. Where were you?'

It was Davey who answered, saying, 'It's all right, Ma, it's all right. We were crossing the yard and nosey here turned towards the house' – he pushed his brother – 'and he said he saw the master watchin' us from the drawing-room window as we cleaned the steps.'

'Did you see him?'

'No. I told nosey here to keep on with his work and not turn round.'

She took a step towards Johnny as she said, 'You're sure you saw him at the drawing-room window that early on?'

'Aye, Ma. And he wasn't dressed like, not for the day, he had his robe on.'

She stared at the boys for a moment; then muttering, 'Well, well,' she turned about and went hurrying out across the yard and into the kitchen again. And there she slowly took off her head shawl and coat, thinking as she did so, It must have been around nine, and hardly light enough for him to see anything.

She was smiling to herself as she now poured herself out some broth: he must be looking at the children on the sly; and on top of what happened yesterday.

It was only the second trip he had made to the city since she had come into the house, and it was, she knew, to visit his solicitor and collect his allowance. His return had brought a number of surprises because, whereas the first time he had returned Tol had had to help him down from the cart and into the house, this time he had got down himself, and after thanking Tol he had turned about and walked to the front door. Not that he had returned sober, he'd had a small load on that had affected his walking slightly, but nevertheless he hadn't been drunk. And he was hardly in the house when he had rung the bell for her. It was the drawing-room bell, and he had been sitting before the fire, his hands extended to the flames, when she entered the room. But he hadn't turned to her until she stood to the side of the fireplace and said, 'You rang, sir?' And then it was some seconds before he said, 'I did, I did, Maria, I did ring for you. It is very cold out today.'

'Yes, sir, it is very cold,' she had replied.

'Newcastle is packed with people. I was glad to get home.'

'I'm . . . I'm sure you were, sir,' she said.

'The shops in the city are very gay, Maria.'

'Are they, sir?'

'Yes, yes indeed, they are.' He still wasn't looking at her. He still had his hands extended to the fire. Then he went on, 'They made me wish I was a rich man, or a highwayman.' Now he slanted his gaze towards her and for the first time in their acquaintance she saw that there was a twinkle in his eye, and she returned it with a smile, saying, 'I don't think you'd make a very good highwayman, sir.'

'No, perhaps not.' He straightened up now and, resting his hands on his knees, he ended, 'I don't think I'd make a very good anything. In fact I know it. I'm proof of it, aren't I?' He turned his gaze fully towards her now, and she looked at him but didn't answer. Men got maudlin when they had drink in them; he would never have talked like this if he had been sober; in fact, it was the longest conversation they'd ever had. The first time she had seen him on his return from Newcastle he had tried to do a dance in the hall, but he hadn't spoken to her, and the next morning he had gone down to the river and plunged in. He had often gone into the river earlier on, and even on the hottest days the water was inclined to be cold, as she herself knew for when she had taken the bairns down she sat on the bank and dangled her feet in the water.

Then he had surprised her by handing her two sovereigns, saying brusquely, 'Take these. They are to get extra for the table and such during the holidays. Spend it sparingly because there's no more where that came from.' And with a slight touch of humour he added, 'You'd better hold it tight in your fist because I might ask for it back tomorrow, you never know, because by then the spirit will have evaporated and I shall be back to normal. But . . . but as I am not yet normal – ' He turned about and grabbed at a long coloured paper bag that was lying on the couch to his hand and, thrusting it towards her, he said, 'For your brood. Only mind' – he now wagged his finger at her – 'don't take it as a breakthrough; I don't want to see them. Keep them out of my way. You understand?'

'Yes, sir.' Her voice was soft. 'And thank you. Thank you most kindly for remembering them.'

He was on his feet when he almost barked at her, 'I didn't remember them, I . . . I was just thinking back.' And turning, he staggered up the room and out of the far door leaving her still standing holding the two sovereigns in one hand and a fancy coloured bag in the other. There were tears in her eyes when she reached the kitchen.

The children had been seated round the table doing their nightly half hour of reading, which she insisted upon, and she stood looking at them for a while before she opened the bag. Then one after the other she drew out four long multi-coloured twists of candy sugar, and the children's astonishment came as one large gasp, and slowly she handed one twist to each of them, saying, 'The master bought them for you in Newcastle.'

As usual it was Biddy who was the first to speak. 'He never did,' she said. And her mother, looking at her, smiled as she said in a strained voice, 'He did.'

The four children had stared at the twisted columns in awe, but when Johnny bit deep into his, his mother cried at him, 'Now don't think you're going to go through that all at once. Break it in three and make it last. Look at the length of them! I've never seen such long ones afore, nor any as bonny.'

'Ma, will this mean we can go and thank him?' Biddy said, only to shrink back in her chair immediately as her mother almost pounced on her, crying low, 'No, it doesn't, madam! You make a move in that direction and I'll skin you alive. Do you hear? Things are just the same: he doesn't want to see you; he's not going to be pestered.

But undaunted by her mother's attituded, Biddy muttered, 'Pestered? We keep miles from him. I did a bunk into the bushes the other day when I saw him coming down the drive.'

'Well, keep on doing bunks, and don't you dare go near him. I'm warning you.' Then her voice softening, Riah looked from one to the other of her children and said, 'You like being here, don't you?' And immediately Johnny and Maggie nodded their heads. But Davey and Biddy said nothing which caused her to bark at Biddy, 'Well!'

'We don't see many people, only Tol.'

'She's right, Ma.' – Davey's face was solemn – 'we don't, we don't see many people.'

She sat slowly down at the head of the table, her two hands on it, one still doubled, and, her voice slow, she said, 'We've got a roof over our heads; we are well fed; plain, but well fed; you've got beds like you've never had in your life afore; you're healthy. What more can you want?'

Their answer came into her mind: A bit of jollification, a bit of fun, young people to mix with; a fair now and again. Seth used to take them to the fair at holiday times, but there were no holidays kept here. She understood how they were feeling.

Slowly she unfolded her fist and slid the back of her hand towards the centre of the table showing them the two sovereigns and, her voice still slow but quiet, she said, 'He gave me these, so we could have a bit of jollification at Christmas. We'll all go into Fellburn, perhaps into Gateshead Fell an' all, and' – she ended – 'we'll buy up the town.' And as she watched their faces brighten and their bodies become animated, she thought, I'll have to ask him for a full day off.

Sometimes Riah felt that she had known Tol Briston all her life. He had become a friend, a friend in a million as she put it to herself. Nothing was too much trouble for him. He would bring messages from the villages, or even do an errand in the town when he had to go in there to help the other outside men from The Heights bring in fodder. He delivered the milk and wood as if it was part of his duty. He had also brought Fanny over twice during the past month, and that had been a treat for both of them, and listening to the old woman she had learned a lot more about her master and his early days in the house. Of course, she realized the old woman's knowledge had come second-hand through her husband, but nevertheless it rang true. And the more she heard the more she realized how her solitary master had loved his mother. But what Fanny didn't know and so couldn't tell her was what had brought this man home and made him into a recluse, because something must have happened to bring a highly learned and presentable man, as he must at one time have been and still could be if he smartened himself up, back to this house to hide away, as it seemed, from human companionship. A broken love affair, most likely. But would that make him detest children?

Anyway, tomorrow was Christmas Eve, and here they were all going into Gateshead Fell to buy Christmas fare.

She'd had her work cut out these past three days to keep her brood from screaming and yelling at the prospect. She had made them keep their voices down but she coudn't stop them from running. Wherever they went they wanted to run. And now here they were, all being piled into the cart, muffled up in their Sunday clothes and the woolly hats and scarves she and Biddy had knitted during the winter evenings.

She felt happy as she had never felt in her life as Tol finally helped her up into her seat; then taking his place at her side, he cried, 'Gee-up! there.'

They had left the yard and were crossing the drive when Biddy tugged at the back of her coat, and she turned and looked down at her daughter who whispered, 'The master, he's at the landing window.'

She experienced a quick inclination to turn her head and look towards the house, but she kept her gaze on Biddy as she said, 'Keep your eyes down and behave yourself.' Then when she turned round, Tol, his gaze fixed ahead, said, 'He must be coming round.'

'Oh, I don't think so. He never comes near them.'

'Oh, time's young yet, time's young yet. An' there's one thing, you've made a change in him: I saw him walking the other day and he was quite spruced up, shaven and a coat on that for once looked as if he hadn't slept in it.'

She laughed gently now as she said, 'I see to his clothes on the quiet, press them and starch his cravats and such.'

'You've been a blessin' to him. Fanny did her best, God knows, but at her best that wasn't much even on her good days. She was never given to housework an' such, was Fanny. Her own cottage is like Paddy's market, but she's happy in it, and content, and that's the main thing. Some people can be too clean.'

'You think so?' Her voice had risen at the end of the words into a question because she felt he was censoring her. Then he said, 'Yes, in a way, when it brings no comfort. Now your kind of cleanness brings comfort, but there are some that would prevent a cinder falling from the fire if it were possible because it would alter the arrangement of the coal.'

She laughed to herself as she thought: So that's it, it's his sister.

She had met Annie Briston only four times altogether. She was a woman in her mid-thirties, but she looked much older. She had a pleasant face and voice and, being Tol's sister, Riah had thought she would take to her straightaway, but somehow she hadn't.

When she herself was in Fanny's company, so free was her own chatter that she often smiled to herself, thinking, People won't have far to look to know where Biddy comes from. But with Annie Briston, she found herself being merely polite, correctly polite. During their first two meetings the woman had acted quite friendly, but on the latter two there had been a change in her attitude. She had talked a lot about Tol. Told how she had left good service to come home and take care of him after their mother had died eight years ago. Yesterday, in their last meeting, she had given her two clouty dolls as Christmas surprises for the girls and a wooden cradle which had been made by Tol for Maggie's doll. She had also remarked, as if in passing, how she would miss Tol when he got married and went to live in Rowdip.

Her first reaction to this news had been one of surprise. But then she had asked herself, why should she be surprised? It was a wonder that a presentable man, such as Tol, had gone so long without a wife, and she hoped the one he had chosen would be worthy of him, for he was a good man. She herself would miss him, and not only for his fetching and carrying.

She said now, 'Before I forget, I must wish you good luck for the future.'

He tugged on the right-hand rein, guiding the horse round a bend in the road, then said, 'Careful, careful,' before casting a glance at her and saying, 'What have you got to wish me good luck for in the future?'

'Well, your . . . your wedding.'

'Weddin'?' He pulled sharply on the reins again; then swivelled his body towards her, saying, 'What weddin'?'

'Oh!' She knew her colour had risen, and now she muttered, 'Well, perhaps I misunderstood her, your sister. She gave me the impression you were going to be married, and . . . and might move away.'

He was staring at her and she at him, but he didn't speak, at least not until he was once more looking ahead, when he said, his voice almost a growl, 'I'm not gettin' married.'

'I'm sorry. I must have made a mistake.'

'You made no mistake.' His tone was flat. 'When I think of gettin' married I'll tell you.'

'Oh, there's no need.' She felt annoyed both with his sister and at the attitude he was taking towards her now, and she added, 'It has nothing to do with me. I only spoke out of politeness.'

'Yes, I know you did.' His tone had altered again. 'But Annie had no right to give you that impression.'

She was still feeling annoyance as she answered, 'Well, I should imagine it isn't something that a body would say if they hadn't something to go on.'

She has nothing to go on, except that I sometimes visit this family in Rowdip. Betty is the daughter, but she's just coming up nineteen. I've taken her to the fair and the races, things like that. There's not much fun down in Rowdip. And her parents are elderly. But her mother and my mother were friends for years and I've known Betty since she was a baby. Talkin' of getting married, I should have been a married man for many years now. I was courtin' a girl when my mother died. It was then Annie came home for the funeral and decided to stay. I couldn't do anything about it, that was her home. Well, my future wife didn't see eye to eye with Annie, I mean living in the same house – three rooms and a scullery are not big enough to hold two women – and so she gave me her answer to it all by finding a better man.'

'I'm sorry.'

'Oh, as things have turned out, I'm not. It's odd' – his voice was light now – 'queer in a way, how things work themselves out and how your mind accepts the changes, how little things of no account at the time become of vast importance. My dad used to say, all encounters lead to big battles, and he was right. You can apply that to anything.'

Now changing the subject abruptly he lifted his whip and pointed, saying, 'Look at that sky. I haven't travelled at all, but I doubt if there's any place in the world where you'll find skies like here. The fire in that sun, you would think, should warm the earth, yet the sky is so vast and the horizons so long, so deep, that its flame is a mere candlelight by the time it touches us.'

Her head was turned fully towards him and she said softly, 'That was lovely.'

'What was?' He glanced at her.

'What you said.'

His head swung round fully towards her. 'What I said? You mean about the sun an' that?'

'Yes, it's like something I read in a book.'

Again his eyes were fixed ahead and it was some time before he spoke; and then, his voice low, he said. 'Aye, they tell me that you can read. And not only you, but the bairns an' all. That's amazing. And here's me a fully grown man, an' I can't write me own name. Yet me head's full of words an' thoughts that colour me thinkin'.'

She was bending towards him now, her voice low. 'I'll learn you, Tol,' she said. 'I never thought about putting it to you, but I'll learn you.'

'Oh, it would never do. It would never work. What use would it be to me now?' he muttered.

'Good gracious!' she said, a note of indignation in her voice. 'You're young; you . . . you could have forty years to go, and think of all you could learn in forty years through reading. Why, even in the last few months when I've had time to meself at night I've improved. I could write a letter now as good as Biddy. I'm sure I could.'

'Biddy can write a letter?'

'Yes, oh yes. Biddy's clever. I think she's going to be the only clever one among them. They can all read and write, an' they know their numbers, but Biddy thinks, she tries to work things out.' Her voice had been low, and he turned towards her now, his own voice as low and a smile on his face as he said, 'I think she's a bit special, is Biddy. She'll go places.'

She sat back, and when she spoke it was as if she was asking a question of someone who wasn't there: 'Where?' she said. 'Where? What chance has she here, but to sweep and clean all her life?'

As if Biddy had heard her name mentioned her head came between them now from where she was standing in the cart and, her voice high, she said, 'You know something, Ma? You know what I'm gona buy when I get into Gateshead Fell?'

'No, I don't know what you're going to buy. What?'

'A bundle of pipe cleaners.'

'A bundle of pipe cleaners? Whatever for?'

'To give as a present to the master.'

'Don't be silly, child, the master doesn't smoke.'

'I know that, but he should. It'll soothe him like it used to do me da, and when he sees them it'll put the idea into his head.'

She now looked from one to the other as her mother and Tol exchanged glances before bursting out laughing. And when she, also laughing, now sat down in the cart, Davey, shaking his head at her, said, 'You know, at times I think you're up the pole, our Biddy.' And in answer she nodded at him brightly, saying, 'Yes, I know. But from up there you can see more of what's going on.'

Now they were all laughing. Biddy knew that the two younger ones didn't know what they were laughing about, but she knew: they were all laughing because they were joyful. Everybody was joyful. It was Christmas; they were going into Gateshead Fell; they had money to spend and their ma looked beautiful; so everything was joyful, so joyful, like bells ringing all the time on a Sunday morning. Joyful.

5

Today was Christmas Day and tomorrow, Boxing Day, she'd be twenty-seven years old. And she'd been aware of Christmases since she was four years old, but she had never known a one like this, full of excitement, yet peaceful. Yesterday, Christmas Eve, they'd had three callers, counting Tol, that was. The other two had been Parson Weeks and a stranger, a correctly dressed woman who looked like a lady, but turned out to be only a lady's maid. Of course, that was still something. She was from the big house called The Heights that lay a good mile beyond the village, which, she now knew from Tol, was owned and lived in by the Gullmington family.

Miss Hobson, she had also learned, was lady's maid to the present master's mother, a grand person well into her seventies. She also learned that Miss Hobson's first post had been in this very house, and not as a lady's maid but as a trainee parlour-maid when she was fourteen. She was twenty-six years old when she went as head parlour-maid to The Heights, and she had remained as such for fifteen years until Madam Gullmington, having lost her maid, chose her to fill the vacancy. But at least once a year she made it her business to come and see Mr Percival, for as she said, she had seen him a few minutes after he was born, and had always retained a soft spot for him.

Riah had wanted to put questions to her regarding her master. But Miss Hobson was so prim and her manner so correct that Riah felt in a way she was in the presence of one of the gentry themselves, and she was wise enough to know that one didn't put questions to the gentry.

Of her own accord she had set a tray, using the best cups from the cabinet in the dining-room, and she had warmed the pot before mashing the tea, and when she took it into the drawing-room where

Mr Miller was sitting talking to his visitor, she knew that he was surprised at her gesture, but not annoyed. She knew that Miss Hobson, too, was surprised, likely because she had set the tray correctly, but she wouldn't have been able to do so if she hadn't found in the back of the dresser drawer the book called *Household Management*. It covered almost everything that was required in the running of a large establishment, from making blacking for the horses' hooves and the ingredients that went into their mash, to attending to the mistress's wants before retirement. There were a number of pages at the back of the book full of do's and don'ts, and one of the don'ts was: Never make the mistake of offering a visitor pastries or cakes with a cup of tea if they should call before three o'clock in the afternoon. It went on to state that it should be noted that the best tea service did not carry plates, merely cups and saucers. Furthermore, should you be required to offer your guests any sweetmeats, see that they were of a delicate and light quality. A footnote to this statement reminded the reader that it was only the common people who made a meal of sandwiches, buns and pastry.

In parts she had found the book very amusing; in fact, it had become like a joke book, especially when Biddy read it aloud to them, which she often did for her reading exercise, and she accompanied her reading with mimicry, causing them all to laugh so loudly Riah had often to quieten them, while her own face was wet with tears of laughter.

One thing had disappointed her about Miss Hobson's visit: the lady's maid had made no reference to the change she saw in the house, and she must have noticed that it was different.

Then Parson Weeks had come. He was a very dominant man was Parson Weeks, and he had stayed over an hour, and had spent it in the library with the master. And when he was about to take his leave he had spoken to her, saying, 'Will I be seeing you all at church tomorrow morning?' And after a moment's hesitation she had said, 'I should like to send the children, sir, but I'm afraid I wouldn't be able to attend myself.'

'Well, send the children,' he had said.

Again she had hesitated before saying, 'Well, if the weather holds and it doesn't snow, sir.'

'Oh, the weather will hold,' he replied airily; 'and the walk will do them good. You send them, ma'am. You send them.'

'Yes, sir.'

'And every Sunday after. Do you hear?'

'Yes, sir.'

Percival Miller had been standing near during this conversation, but he had said nothing, just stood apart, his hands behind his back, his head bowed slightly, his gaze directed towards his shoes. Riah glanced at him before turning away. It was as if he were affected by even the mention of the children . . .

But here it was, Christmas morning. The children had gone to church and they hadn't to walk the mile or so there and the mile back because Tol, like the good friend that he was, had come and taken them. She had a fire blazing in the drawing-room and one in the dining-room, and in this room she had set the table in style, as she put it, even putting a trail of holly on the stiffly starched white cloth. It was a round dining table and she had covered the whole of it, not just the end as she usually did on a Sunday which was the only time he used the dining-room; the rest of the week he had his meals served on a tray in the library. She often wondered at what time he left that room at night and went to bed. Some nights he didn't leave it for she would find the bed hadn't been slept in. These were the mornings when she'd come downstairs again with his tray of tea and find him asleep on the couch with books strewn by the side of it. That's all he seemed to live for, books. She felt sorry for him, deeply sorry. She wished she could do something for him to lift him out of this despondency that he seemed to be in. And she knew the full meaning of that word because it came in *Pilgrim's Progress* and Seth had read that to them.

She had placed two glasses on the table, one for wine and one for water, and in front of them she had put the bottle of wine that was their Christmas surprise to him. But she wondered if he would remark on it.

She looked around the room. Everything was ready. The meal was waiting to be served. She knew he had just come back from his walk. He had taken to going for a brisk walk these past few weeks, sometimes being out for half a day at a time.

There was a large hall mirror at the end of the dining-room and she stood in front of it for a moment and smoothed back her hair from her brow. She did not wear a cap; she hadn't one, and he hadn't insisted on it. But today she was wearing her Sunday frock and over it a large white apron. As she smoothed the apron down over her hips she told herself she would do; then she hurried out of the room and made her way to the kitchen, there to be greeted by the children. They had already taken off their outdoor things and they crowded round her, all talking at once.

She silenced them, saying, 'One at a time! One at a time! Now what was it like?' She looked at Davey and he said, 'It was very nice, Ma, and the singing was nice.'

'And the church was decorated,' said Biddy. ! 'And oh, Ma, it was lovely. And there was a shelter, like a stable with straw and donkeys, and, oh Ma – ' Biddy's lips began to temble and Maggie put in now, 'There was a cradle like mine, Ma, like Tol made me, only mine was better.'

'Ma – ' It was Davey speaking, and his voice seemed to silence the others and he looked at her for a moment before he went on, 'We saw him.'

'The master?'

'Aye, close up. He . . . he was walking along the road, and Tol stopped the cart and spoke to him.'

'What did he say?'

'Tol? Oh, he talked about the weather an' if it was going to snow.'

'What did the master say?'

'Oh, he agreed with Tol, an' he said it could happen any time.'

'Ma – ' Riah turned her attention to Biddy again, and Biddy said, 'He looked at us.'

'He did?'

'Aye, one after the other. It was funny the way he looked at us, like . . .'

'Like what?'

'Oh, I don't know. Not nasty, not as if he didn't like us. I don't know how he looked. Anyway, it was just for a minute, and then he walked off.' Riah stared at the children for a moment, then said, 'Well, go on now, go in the other room, and don't make a lot of noise. The fire's on, the table's set, and I'll be in with your dinner in a few minutes.'

'Oh! pork' – Johnny was hopping from one leg to the other – 'an' roast taties.'

'Go on greedy guts!' She pushed him and the others towards the door, then busied herself getting the meat out of the oven.

She had just completed setting the large tray with three vegetable dishes and the gravy tureen and a meat dish, on which lay slices of pork trimmed with the choice of roast rabbit separated by his favourite baked dumplings, when one of the ten brass bells arranged above the kitchen door tinkled. Almost staggering under the weight of the tray, she left the kitchen.

Outside the dining-room door she placed the tray down on a side table, pushed open the door, then entered the room.

He was sitting by the fire and he did not speak as she arranged the dishes on the table, but he watched her. When she was finished and had turned and looked at him, saying, 'I hope you enjoy your meal, sir,' he continued to stare at her for a moment; then turning his gaze back to the table, he said, 'The wine. That was thoughtful of you, Maria, but you should not have wasted the housekeeping money on such.'

Her chin moved slightly as she said, 'I didn't use the housekeeping money, sir; it is my . . . our present to you for your kindness to us.'

She watched his eyes widen as he rose from the chair to go to the table; and there, sitting down, he lifted up the bottle and looked at it, saying softly, 'It is a good wine. May I ask what you paid for it?'

She hesitated for a moment before she said, 'One and ninepence, sir.'

When he replaced the bottle on the table his hand remained on it and he repeated, 'One and ninepence. Almost half of what I give you for your week's wages. You are very kind, and . . . and I thank you. Maria, What is more' – he now looked fully at her – 'my thanks are also overdue for the way you have kept the house. It hasn't been like this for many, many years; you have brought comfort back into it.'

The colour, she knew, was rushing over her face and she stammered slightly as she said, 'I . . . I . . . I'm glad you find it so, sir.'

'I do. I do.'

When a silence fell between them she looked at the table and said hastily, 'Your dinner will be getting cold. Will I . . . serve it out for you?' And he answered, 'No. No, thank you; I . . . I can see to it. Thank you very much.' It was a note of dismissal and she was about to turn away when he said softly, 'You have a fine looking family, Maria.'

Her colour deepened still further as she smiled widely at him. 'Thank you, sir,' she said. 'I'm glad you find them so.'

He was reaching out to fork a piece of rabbit as he spoke again, saying, 'Why is your elder boy so fair, and the others dark?'

'He takes after his grandfather, sir, who came from Sweden.'

'Oh. Oh, is that the reason? He's a fine looking boy. They are fine looking children.'

She said again, 'Thank you, sir.' And when he said no more she turned hastily about and left the room. But in the hall she joined her hands and pressed them tightly against the nape of her neck. He was going to recognize the children, soon they'd be able to move about freely. Whatever thing he had against children as a whole was disappearing; she could feel it. Oh, what a lovely Christmas this was. And it wasn't near ended, because this afternoon, Tol had promised to drop in and have tea with the children . . . Tol. She closed her eyes for a moment and a slow smile spread over her face, only to be wiped off quickly and for her whole body to jerk as an inner voice cried, None of that now! None of that! And Seth hardly cold; and Tol a younger man; and you with four bairns. Have sense, woman, have sense. Don't spoil things.

As if answering the voice, she said, 'No, no; I mustn't spoil things. I'll take what is offered and be thankful.' And on this she started hurriedly towards the kitchen.

6

The winter had been long and hard. Yet, on looking back, it had passed quickly; she'd had so much to do. Every room in the house had been cleaned from floor to ceiling. Where it was possible she had washed curtains and bedspreads. She had also carefully darned worn fabrics, using a box of coloured silks she had found in a drawer in Mrs Miller's room. The lady had evidently spent a lot of her time doing tapestry for there was much evidence of it in chair-back covers and seats.

At night, when she went to bed, very often too tired to sleep, she would lie awake going over and over the activities of the day, especially of those days or evenings when Tol had come for his lesson. He was progressing nicely and could now not only write his own name and address, but could spell over fifty words of two syllables. His progress hadn't been due so much to herself, and to his own adaptability, but to Biddy, who had now read right through the Bible, and not only that, but was able to memorize and quote passages. So bright did she appear at times that Riah thought she was getting a bit above herself and so had to check her in small voice, at such times as when she read pieces from the Newcastle weekly paper that Tol picked up for the master, and which Mr Miller usually threw in the wastepaper basket the day after arrival.

Since Christmas the master had seemed more relaxed. Sometimes he would talk to her when she took in his meals, asking her questions about her early life.

Yesterday she had asked leave to go into Gateshead Fell, saying she wanted to do a little shopping for the children. She didn't state the exact nature of the shopping, which was to go to the second-hand stall, the equivalent to Paddy's market in the city, and there pick up some old clothes that she could cut down for trousers for the boys and dresses for the girls, for now their clothes were getting very threadbare.

So here she was, making the journey alone, for she knew if she had brought the girls with her they would hold her up wanting to see this an' that in the market.

She had to walk the mile to the coach road and from there she took the cart into the town.

Once in the market she too had the desire to wander around the stalls; but this she curbed and made straight for the clothes pile. There was an assortment of garments on a trestle table, but the kind she was looking for were thrown here and there on the ground, which fortunately was dry. She wasn't the only one on the same errand and at one stage she had a gentleman's tail-coat almost wrenched from her hands. But as she had already seen it transformed into a pair of knickerbockers for Davey, who was growing so fast that the two pairs he possessed were not only thin in the seat but now well above his knees, she hung on to it fiercely.

When she finally left the stall her two canvas bags held two cotton dresses, a voluminous serge skirt which would eventually provide her with a dress, two men's corduroy coats, both lined and padded which was an asset, and the swallowtail-coat.

Before leaving the market she treated herself to a plate of hot peas, and afterwards, after waiting an hour and half by the side of the road, she mounted the cart for home. She felt so pleased with her purchases and her day's outing that somewhere inside herself she was humming.

She hadn't told Tol where she was going so he hadn't made an effort to meet her. She had of late made as few requests of him as possible. If he did anything for them it must be, as she thought, off his own bat. In fact, at times of late she had been a little reserved with him, not laughing as freely as she used to do, and she knew he was puzzled by it. But, as she told herself, it was her only safeguard, even though it was a poor one.

Although she had shared the clothing between her two bags she was finding them heavy and when she reached the old toll gate that was no longer in use, having been transferred to the main coach road, she sat down on a low dry stone wall, behind which was a bank of trees bordering a woodland walk. This was the beginning of the Gullmingtons' estate and the woodlands that came under Tol's care.

There was also a grassy drive on this side of the wall, and this was bordered on its other side by another wood, and half a mile along this drive lay Tol's cottage where the two woods spread out to make what was known as Fuller's Dip.

Riah now narrowed her eyes to take in the distant figure walking down the drive in the shadow of the trees. It was still some distance away when she recognized Annie Briston. The coming meeting didn't fill her with any pleasure for she knew that, unfortunately, Annie had come to resent her; and she wasn't unaware of the reason. But up till now they had continued to be civil to each other.

Annie Briston was of medium height. She was of a delicate appearance and one would have imagined her voice would have complemented her features, but, unfortunately, it was in sharp contrast, its tone mostly ranging between peevishness and a stridency which indicated temper; and it was the latter that came over in her first approach to Riah, as she said, 'Well, you seem loaded up. Been out begging again?'

It would appear that Riah had been pushed from the wall, so quickly did she jump to her feet; and now her voice almost matching that of Annie Briston she said, 'What do you mean, Miss Briston, out begging again? I've never begged in me life.'

'Well, I must be misinformed, because from what I hear you begged hard enough from Old Fanny Briggs.'

Riah stared at her. This was an open attack, no subtlety. It was as if they had met every day and were continuing a row of some sort. So she spoke plainly now, saying, 'What are you getting at, Miss Briston? Why are you taking this attitude towards me?'

'You know well enough why I'm taking this attitude. You've caused nothing but trouble since you settled yourself into Moor House.'

Trouble? What trouble had she caused up at the house? She never saw anyone to fight with except the master and Tol, and the parson, and that one visit from the lady's maid from The Heights. What was she meaning, causing trouble? She repeated her last thoughts, saying. 'What do you mean, causing trouble?'

'You know what I mean all right. You've got our Tol not knowing whether he's coming or going. Running back and forward like an errand boy with your wood and your milk and lifting your bairns to church, twice on a Sunday now. Then learning him to read and write. Who do you think you are anyway?'

Riah, drawing herself up and assuming a dignity she was far from feeling at the moment because she felt that she wanted to take her hand and slap this woman's face for her, said, 'Your brother has always delivered the milk an' the wood. As for taking the children to church and Sunday school, he did it at the parson's bidding. The only thing me and my family have done for him is teach him his letters.'

'Yes, and disturb his peace thereby.'

'How can that disturb peace, woman?'

'Becuase it's putting ideas into his head. He's no longer just satisfied being a forester, and he's wastin' time, his master's time, and it'll be found out. What's more there's things to do around the cottage. But whereas at one time he used to be outside mendin', now he's sittin', his nose stuck in bairns' books. It's pathetic like, he's making himself a laughing stock.'

'Do you want to know something, Miss Briston?' Riah didn't wait for an answer but went on, 'I think the only laughing-stock in your household is you. What I'm just finding out must be already well known, that you're an embittered old spinster an' that you're afraid of losing your bread support, because then you would have to go out and work for yourself like many a one better than you has had to do.'

For a moment it would appear that Annie Briston was lost for words; then, her mouth puckering, and almost spluttering, she cried, 'Oh, you! You'll come to a bad end. I've seen your like afore. You'll come to a bad end. You mark my words.'

'And you'll try to see I do, won't you? But let me tell you something, miss, I'll be here when you're gone. Yes, I will. I'll be here when you're gone.'

'Oooh!' It was a long-drawn-out sound, and they glared at each other as if it would take very little to make them spring. Then Annie Briston flounced around and walked back up the way she had come, and Riah sat down on the wall again because she was trembling. Oh, that woman! She was jealous, madly jealous. Well, there was one thing sure, whatever came of her association with Tol – and at times, and more often now, she was longing for it to ripen – she would never be able to share his house with that piece in it. Oh no. He'd have to make a choice. And what could he do? His hands were tied. Something like this would have to happen to spoil the day, wouldn't it? Life never went smoothly for long. Out here in the wilds you would have thought it would be impossible to come across an adversary like Annie Briston. There were so few people in this neighbourhood, yet one of them had to be a bitch of a woman like her, because that's what she was, a bitch.

The last word had not died in her mind when she gave a cry and sprang from the wall as a voice behind her said, 'I'm sorry to disturb you, but this is the lowest part and I usually get over here.'

She turned and in amazement saw her master making his way in between the branches of the two trees, and when he reached the wall she watched him vault it with an agility she would not have given him credit for. And when he was standing looking at her he said. 'I arrived almost at the same time as your late companion did.' She saw his shoulders lift, and the shrug told her that he had witnessed her meeting with Annie Briston and heard every word of it. But he made no further reference to it; instead, he looked down at the bundles placed against the wall and asked, 'What have we here? You certainly have done some shopping.' As he went to lift one up, she said, 'No, I'll carry them, sir.'

'You carry one and I the other. Come.' He walked away and she followed, a step behind him.

Presently he turned to her and asked, 'What have you been buying?'

'Clothes . . . I got some articles second-hand to remake for the children; their . . . their things are getting rather threadbare.'

He stopped and stared at her for a moment before he said, 'Paddy's market stuff?'

She was surprised that he knew about Paddy's market, but she was quick to deny the association, saying, 'No, no, not like that, sir; they are from a proper clothes stall in the market.'

'But worn stuff, second-hand . . . dirty.'

Her head moved from side to side before she answered, 'I mean to wash them before I alter them.'

They were walking on again and had travelled some distance before he spoke again, 'You don't know who's been wearing these things,' he said; 'they could belong to anybody . . . scum.'

In defence she now answered, 'They are gentlemen's clothing and ladies', padded and lined and of good material.'

Again they walked on in silence, and it wasn't until the gates of the house came in view that he said, 'So I understand you've been teaching Tol to read and write?'

'Yes, sir; but only in the evenings when my work is done.' She didn't want him to think she was using any of his time.

'Of course. Of course.' He was nodding at her now. 'Why couldn't he have asked me to teach him?'

'I don't think it would have entered his head, sir. Anyway, it was me that proffered.'

'Did you know I used to be a teacher?'

'No, sir?' There was a note of surprise in her voice, and he glanced at her slowly with a smile on his face now, as he said, 'Oh yes; I was a teacher, for many years, but I had a fancy name, I was a tutor, and my pupils were young men in the university.'

She remained silent.

They had almost reached the front of the house where he would enter by the front door leaving her to go round to the kitchen door, when he stopped once again and, looking at her squarely, he spoke, and his words actually made her drop her bag to the ground: 'I shall take it upon myself to instruct your children,' he said; 'it is not enough that they should be able to read and write. If at their age they have got this far, then it is only fair that their knowledge be extended. I shall take them for two hours each morning. See they come to the library at nine.' And on this he turned from her, his departure being as abrupt as his voice, and went in the front entrance.

It was a good half-minute before she lifted the two bags and then almost scurried towards the kitchen, bursting to tell her news to Biddy. Why only to Biddy? she asked herself. And the answer she got was, Biddy would likely be the only one of the four to welcome this, as she saw it, utterly fantastic change of front in the master.

It was dark when a knock came on the kitchen door, and when Maggie opened it she cried, 'It's Tol! It's Tol, Ma.' Tol had made himself a favourite with the children, and they now crowded round him, all talking at once, until Davey, dashing to the settle, took up the large swallow-tail coat and, putting it on, strutted round the table, causing roars of laughter.

'Was that what you went in for?' Tol looked from the bundle of old clothes lying to the side of the fireplace to Riah, and she answered softly, 'Yes. It's the only way I can keep them decent. But after I've unpicked them I'll wash them before making them up again.' He nodded at her; then turned to Biddy, saying now, 'What's that you say?'

'I said, what do you think, the master's going to make us go to school.'

'School? Where? There's none hereabouts.'

'Oh, it's a long way; we'll have to take the coach.'

Tol glanced down at Johnny who now doubled up at his own joke. But then Davey, taking off the coat, said flatly, 'He's going to do us here, two hours every morning. How will I get the garden done? There's so much to do outside.'

'That a fact?' Tol was asking the question of Riah now, and she nodded as she said, 'Yes, a surprising fact, the last in the world I expected to hear. But it's marvellous, don't you think? I mean' – she looked around her brood and her face softened – 'to get the chance of being educated by a man like him, because he's very learned.'

'Aye' – Tol nodded at her – 'there's no doubt about that. I should imagine that's half of his trouble.'

'Trouble?'

'Well, I mean, just shutting himself up in the room there. You can get too much of a good thing, anything.' He now turned half from her, saying under his breath, 'can you step outside a minute?' And she, looking from him first to Davey and then to Biddy, said to them, 'Get on with the unpicking. And mind, do it carefully, don't tear the stuff.' Then taking a shawl from the back of the door, she put it around her shoulders and followed Tol into the yard.

She had closed the kitchen door behind her and now stood blinking in the light from his lantern which he had left at the door, and before he could speak, she said, 'I know what you're going to say.'

'Aye, well then, it doesn't need any lead up to. I'm . . . I'm sorry, but . . . but that's our Annie, she causes more trouble than enough. Always has done, I think, since the day she was born. But . . . but what I want to say to you, Riah, is, not to take any notice of her. She's always been like that, always wanting to rule the roost. To tell you the truth, I don't know what to do about her. Our Mary would take her off me hands for a time but there's her man Robbie, and he can't stand the sight of her.'

'You have another sister?' There was a note of surprise in her voice and he said, 'Oh, yes, she's Annie's twin, Mary, and she's as different as chalk from cheese. There was eight years between them and me and I suppose' – he gave a short laugh – 'because I came late in me mother's life, she left me upbringing to the pair of them. Mary was always kind and gentle, but Annie, she had to boss the show or know the reason why. I used to give her most of her own way just to keep the peace; not any more though. But what I wanted to say to you was, I'm sorry if she upset you.'

'Well' – she laughed softly now – 'if she upset me, I certainly upset her.'

'Aye, by all accounts you did that.' He too chuckled, then said, 'I suppose she told you I was neglecting me duties and the house?'

'Something to that effect.'

'It isn't the first time I've heard that and for different reasons. Anyway – ' He stepped closer to her and looked down on her and, his voice coming deeper from his throat, he said, 'I wouldn't like anything to spoil what's atween us, Riah.'

The gulp she gave in her throat was audible and the desire just to fall against him and feel the closeness of him was almost overpowering. And when, his voice still low, he said, 'The way I'm placed I cannot say what I want to do, but I think you know what's in me mind,' her body trembled with the thought, Let him kiss me, just once, just this once.

But then what would happen? What would come of it? With his sister lording it in the cottage, there would be no hope for them setting up a home there. And don't let her forget she had four bairns to bring up and, what was more, she was living like a lady in this house, practically her own boss, more content and happy than she'd ever been in her life before. So no, no kissing. Don't light up your pipe near a haystack in the height of summer.

She was surprised at the matter of fact tone she was able to assume as she said, 'It's all right, Tol. I understand. Just let things go on as they are. But I'll . . . I'll tell you this, I'm . . . I'm grateful for your friendship.'

When he took her hand in both of his, in spite of herself, she nearly allowed the haystack to ignite; but at that moment the door behind was pulled open and Davey said hastily, 'The drawing-room bell's ringing, Ma.'

'All right. All right.' And she pushed him back into the room before saying to Tol, 'I'll have to go. But don't worry. It's all right; everything will pan out.'

'Aye, aye. Good night, Riah.'

'Good night, Tol.'

In the kitchen, she said, 'How many times?'

'Just the once, Ma.'

She now hurried up the room, through the passage and into the hall, meaning to make her way straight to the drawing-room. But there he was, standing at the foot of the stairs holding a lamp in his hand, and without any preamble he said to her, 'Bring the other lamp,' and pointed to the pink globe lamp standing on a table to the side of the front door. Mystified, she picked up the lamp and followed him up the stairs.

For a moment she imagined he was making for his bedroom, but he passed all the doors on the landing and went to the very end of it, then round the corner into a narrow passage and began to mount the attic stairs.

She hadn't been in the attics more than three times in the months she had been here because, adding to what Fanny had told her, her master had said formally at the beginning of her service, 'I don't wish you to disturb anything in the attics.' So when she had come up here all she had glimpsed were a number of cedar trunks at one end and, standing down the middle where the roof was highest, two long wardrobes, each with four sections, and their ornamental tops were stacked against the attic walls. She knew that both held an assortment of clothes: the first one was a gentleman's wardrobe, the second one a lady's. And her glimpses into both of them had shown that all the garments were arranged neatly on hangers and that each hanger also carried a bag of scented herbs. And she had said to herself, so much for Fanny saying everything was moth-eaten.

When he put his lamp down on one of the trunks she did the same, then stood waiting while he slowly walked to the wardrobe that was at the far end of the attic. Opening the door to the first compartment, he pulled out the top tray, revealing a number of silk shirts. Lifting one up by the collar, he shook it out, then handed it to her, saying. 'Would you be able to make shirts out of these for the boys?'

Holding the beautiful soft material in both her hands now, her words spluttered over it as she muttered, 'But 'tis silk, sir. Much too good. It's not . . . practical like.'

'They have a change of clothes on a Sunday, haven't they?'

'Yes, sir.'

'Then, make them Sunday shirts. You'll find something for week-days in that trunk there.' He pointed to one of the trunks. And now he opened another compartment. Taking down a suit, the trousers of which were clipped to the bottom rail of the hanger, he said, 'That's a rough tweed; that should make them workaday clothes. And this one' – the next one he picked was a fine blue gaberdine – 'could match the silk shirt for Sunday.'

'But, sir.'

He stopped on the point of opening another door and repeated, 'But sir, what?' His voice had an edge to it as if what he was doing was against the grain.

In pulling open the next wardrobe door to disclose a row of dresses, his voice softening, he said, 'These belonged to my mother. She wasn't a woman for frills and furbelows. Her day dresses were inclined to be plain and her evening dresses the same, with one exception.' He now put his hand to the end of the rail and took from it a long black velvet gown. The neck was square, the sleeves were short. The bodice was gusseted into the waist, from which the skirt fell in three tiers. The only ornament on it was a faded pink silk rose hanging by its stem from a vent at the waistline. As he held it up there emanated from it a perfume as faded as the rose yet, at the same time, pungent.

'It was my mother's favourite,' he said. 'Although she had many other evening gowns she always returned to this; but she only wore it on special occasions. She had beautiful skin; it enhanced it.'

'It's lovely,' Riah said softly.

'Yes, I think so too.' He turned to her now, the dress still held in his hand. 'I often come up here and look at it. It recalls many memories.'

He hung the dress back in the corner of the wardrobe; then, pushing the other garments here and there, he brought down two at once, saying, 'These were her morning dresses. They're print, aren't they?' He held one out for her to feel, and she said, 'Yes, sir; and lovely print if I may say so.'

'You may say so.'

She stiffened slightly as she thought, That's the second time he's mimed me. And it isn't that I'm talkin' cheap; many people say words like, If I may say so.

'Well then, take these' – he pushed the dresses into her arms – 'and the suits and the shirts and get to work on them. But before you do that, throw that dirty rubbish out that you bought today. God knows who had them on last.'

Throw them out? She certainly wouldn't do any such thing. She'd wash them and unpick them and when she'd time to sew them, he wouldn't recognize them on the children. Anyway, she needed clothes herself. She would get a skirt, a couple of petticoats and the blouse out of them. Throw them out indeed!

'Did you hear what I said?' He had picked up both lamps now, and she turned her head over the bundle of clothes that lay across her arms and, looking at him, she said slowly, 'Yes, sir. I heard what you said.'

'Good.'

She was going to move down the room but stopped as she searched for words with which to thank him and which he wouldn't mime or mimic, and what she said was, 'I'm grateful for your kindness, sir.'

'You're welcome. Being able to help in this way, I shall not now feel under such an obligation to you.'

'Oh.' Her precise manner fled and she turned squarely to him, where he was standing, his face illuminated from the lamps, and in the second that she stared at him she was made aware once more of the great loneliness that lay, not only in his eyes, but in the drooping of his mouth and the slackness of his shoulders. There was no spring in him. The only thing in him that had any urgency was his voice. And she said rapidly, 'Oh, sir, you needn't be beholden to me; the boot's on the other foot. What would have happened to us if you hadn't taken us in that night, God alone knows. And my children have never been so happy, nor so healthy, nor, may I add, so well housed in their lives. Oh, sir, the boot's on the other foot.'

Well, she felt he had plenty with which to come back at her from that little speech. However, he didn't come back at her, not in the way she expected, but with words that surprised her, for he said, 'You're a good woman, Riah. I almost said a good girl, because sometimes you don't look or act much older than your daughter.'

'Oh. Oh . . . oh, sir.'

'Oh, sir.'

There he was, mimicking her again. This was a new line he was taking. She would have to laugh at it. And this is what she did. Then she turned from him and walked the length of the attic and down the narrow stairs; and he followed her, holding the lamps high.

When they reached the hall she turned to him and smiled but said nothing more; then hurried towards the kitchen to display her new-found treasures to the children, recalling, as she did so, his face as she had seen it in the light of the two lamps, and she thought, If only he didn't look so sad. I wish I could do something for him to lighten his days.

But perhaps when he got to teaching the children it would make a difference. Yes, yes, perhaps it would.

7

It was past high summer; the ground was hard, the grass was yellowing. Riah had now been in Mr Miller's service for fifteen months, and it was difficult now to remember that she had ever lived anywhere else. This shining house seemed to be her own. And it was shining. For Biddy and Maggie took as much pride in it as she did. But once it had been bottomed there was less work to do in it, and for some weeks now Biddy had been out helping the boys picking fruit, clearing brushland ready for more planting in the autumn. No one would recognize the garden from what it had been when they first came here. The drive was grass free, the hedges bordering parts of the garden were clipped, that is all except the great yew hedge that had, at one time, divided the kitchen garden from that which was laid out in beds and walks and whose top had been cut into the shape of birds. There was little the boys could do about this hedge other than clip it as far as a short ladder would reach.

Except for a piece of land that had once been a games lawn and which was now more like a hayfield, the whole garden was in order, and the credit for its rejuvenation could not be given alone to Davey and Johnny, for Tol had, at the beginning, done a lot of the rough work, and she herself and the girls, too, had gone out of an evening and helped. This was after Davey had complained that he would never get through his work if he had to knock off for two hours of book learning in the morning.

Davey wasn't at all taken with book learning, not like the other three, and Riah was sorry about this for the master seemed to have taken a special interest in Davey and seemed bent on his learning. She had wished more than once of late that Davey and Biddy could have changed places, at least in their minds, because Biddy's wits were needle sharp and her mind like a sponge for soaking up things, whereas Davey seemed to have great difficulty in remembering his lessons. And sometimes she didn't wonder at it, especially those about gods and goddesses; they would bemuse anybody. But the master insisted that these were part of the lessons, besides history and geography.

And of all the things on God's earth to make them learn was this Latin. For what good was a Latin language going to be to her bairns? And what was more, not only did the master insist on the two hours in the morning but they had to do an hour in the evening after their day's work was done. He had even come into the kitchen once or twice with the idea, she imagined, of catching them out.

She supposed she should be grateful for all this attention her children were getting from such an educated man. She was. Oh she was. And if they had all taken it alike, she would have had no question in her own mind about it. But in some way it seemed to be souring Davey. He got sulky at times and he went for Biddy. Not that Biddy couldn't hold her own with him, or two or three like him, but he had never done it before. She supposed it was because he realized that she could take in things that were an absolute puzzle to him.

She was making it her business to sit with Davey at night and try to help him, and therefore she knew she herself was learning. Not that she could see it was going to do her any good.

But these were things, she told herself, that she could control: they were all in a day's work, part of bringing up a family; in a very odd way, she had to admit, but nevertheless, bringing them up, and in a style she had never imagined possible. But there was this other thing in her life, this private thing, this thing that was a want in her, a hot urge which she knew there was little hope of alleviating because Tol had surprised her one night by making it clear to her that he was in a forked stick and he could see no possible way of getting out. So therefore he couldn't, as it were, speak his mind to her. His sister, it seemed, had taken on a kind of illness that put her to bed at times, and at such times she wasn't capable to looking after either him or the house. So he had his hands full, and that was why, he said, he couldn't slip round as often as he might. Did she understand?

Yes, she had said, she understood, while at the same time feeling sick.

He still brought the milk and the wood, but he did not always take the children on the cart to Church on Sunday. And naturally he no longer came at night to learn his letters and his tables.

She had, as it were, had it out with herself that she must stop thinking in his direction, for even if he had spoken what could have come of it? If the bell hadn't rung from the drawing-room that night and they had come together just with a kiss where would it have gone from there? She knew where it would have gone. Anyway, it hadn't happened, and it was just as well, because what you never had you never missed . . . Oh! that was a damn silly saying. Look at the things she hadn't had in her life and yet was aware of missing them: a decent house of her own; decent clothes for the bairns . . . and herself; food, just a little out of the ordinary, a taste of the fancy meats she had seen in the shops in Gateshead Fell; a long ride on a coach to a distant town, past Newcastle, away, away somewhere, perhaps London where the King lived . . . What you never had you never missed! How did these sayings originate?

She was standing at the stone sink under the kitchen window. There were two jars of flowers on the kitchen window-sill and lace curtains to the side. She had got these from the store cupboard and cut them down. She like prettying places up. The whole house was pretty. The sad thing about it, nobody saw it but themselves and the parson. Fanny had told her there used to be a lot of callers at one time but that he had been rude to them, and so now he was left to himself. It was odd: to look at him you wouldn't think he was that kind of a man, a man who would be rude to people; but he had only to open his mouth at times and his words cut like a cleaving knife. She had heard them used on Davey. He bawled at him in the library at times. Yet she knew he was very fond of him. Oh yes, she had sensed that from the very beginning.

She lifted her head now from where she was peeling apples for a pie, and her hands became still and the apple peeling snapped before she had reached the end. She always tried to take off the peeling whole; it gave her a feeling of satisfaction somehow. But her gaze had become focused on where the master and Davey were entering the yard. The master had his hand on Davey's shoulder. It was such a nice picture that it brought a lump to her throat and she leant her head further towards the pane to watch their progress. They had stopped now opposite the stable door and the master had his two hands on Davey's shoulders and he was bending down towards the boy's bent head. He seemed to be talking to him earnestly. Then she watched the master take his hands from her son's shoulders and ruffle his hair before pushing him gently towards the stable.

She swallowed deeply as she thought, What a pity he's not married and has children of his own. He'd been different altogether since he had taken up with the children. He was made for children. Poor man. What age was he now? Nearing fifty, she would say; she didn't know for sure. What a pity some of the spinsters who were sitting in their drawing-rooms wasting their time in needlework or at best in visiting and at parties hadn't come along here and forced his hand in some way or another.

She finished peeling the apples, put them into the pastry cases ready waiting, dribbled some honey over the top of them, covered this with more pastry and trimmed the top with cut out pastry leaves, after which, she brushed the tarts with milk and put them in the oven. This done, she washed her hands; then went out of the kitchen, across the yard and into the barn.

The barn was used mostly for stacking wood and it had a chopping block at one end of it, and on this Davey was slowly splitting small logs. When he saw her approaching he stuck the batchet in the log and said, 'Is it time to knock off, Ma?'

'It's nearing six. You can go and tell the others in a minute. By the way, what was the master talking to you about?'

He turned from her now but he didn't answer her, just kicked against the chopping block with the toe of his boot; and so, going to him, she turned him about, saying, 'What was it?'

'Oh' – he tossed his head impatiently – 'about learning. Wanted to know what I want to be later on.'

'Yes?' She looked at him. 'And what did you say to that?'

'I . . . I told him I wanted to drive a coach.'

He raised his head now and, a puzzled expression on his face, he said, 'He got angry, Ma. He said, couldn't I think any further than that? Well Ma, what further is there? Ma – ' he put out his hand towards her now and she caught it and gently soothed it between her own as he appealed to her, saying, 'I can't take in all this. And what good is it anyway? I'm not like our Biddy. She likes it. But . . . but Ma, I just can't understand half of what he's saying to me about them myths an' that Latin. What do I want with Latin, Ma? I can read and write and I can count up as well as the next, better than most, you know I can. But I can't remember all those names in the Illyard thing he keeps yapping on about. Our Biddy says they are just fairy stories. Well, that's for lasses, Ma. What do I want with fairy stories or the like?'

'They're not fairy stories, Davey' – her voice was soft and gentle –

'they're a kind of history. At least that's how I see it, ancient. It came about afore Jesus, afore the Bible like.'

'I thought nothing came about afore the Bible, Ma, and the Garden of Eden.'

She closed her eyes now, saying, 'Oh Davey, don't get me as bamboozled as yourself. Look, leave what you're doing; go and fetch the others. Your tea'll be ready by the time you get back. See that they wash well under the pump first.' She now leant towards him and smiled as she ended, 'I'm as bamboozled as you are, I've got to admit, about the things he wants to learn us. Anyway, we'll put our heads together after tea and see what we can make out of the day's lesson, eh?'

He didn't smile back at her and say, 'Right Ma;' instead, he turned from her and went out of the barn, leaving her standing gazing after him and thinking again, Oh, if only Biddy and him could change places. God has a funny way of dealing out brains.

They were all seated round the table when a knock came on the kitchen door; and when Biddy opened it, she cried, 'Oh! Hello, Tol.' Then turning her head, she called, ''Tis Tol, Ma.'

Riah got to her feet and, her voice polite sounding, she said, 'Hello there, Tol.' And he answered, 'Hello, there. You all busy?' And he looked from one to the other.

'Doing our lessons.' It was Biddy coming to the fore again. 'Do you want to sit in, Tol? I'm on Latin; but t'others are still learning their English.' She laughed at her brothers and sister.

'Latin?' He screwed up his face at Biddy; then looked at Riah, and she nodded at him, saying, 'Yes, it's Latin now.'

'Good God! He's gona make a scholar out of her.'

'Here, take a seat, Tol.' Riah had pulled a chair to the end of the table where he could sit between Davey and Biddy. And she asked now, 'Have you eaten?' And he said, 'At dinner-time; yes, I had a bite.'

'Haven't you been home?'

'No; I'm just on me way. But' – he looked up at her – 'I put Annie on the coach this morning for me sister Mary's. She's lost her man, you know. Annie thought she'd better go an' stay with her for a few days.'

'Oh, yes, yes. So . . . so you're looking after yourself; and I bet you've had very little the day. Could you do with some cold mutton and apple pie?'

'Could I do with some cold mutton and apple pie!' He was looking round at the children now, and they were all laughing, Davey included. 'Did you hear what your mother said? Could I do with some cold mutton and apple pie? What would you say?' And together they all shouted, 'Aye!' then added, 'He could do with some cold mutton and apple pie, Ma.'

Amid much laughter she set down a plate of neck chops before him and to the side a shive of bread and butter. As he ate the children all watched him, and after chewing a couple of mouthfuls, he put down his knife and fork and gulped as he said, 'Get on with your lessons, 'cos if you don't I'll feel that I'm in a menagerie an' you've come to see me eat.'

'I don't want to get on with me lessons.'

Tol turned to Davey. 'You don't?' he said.

'No.'

'He hates lessons.'

Tol turned his attention to Biddy now, saying, 'And you don't?'

'No, I don't. It's like a holiday from work every mornin'. Do you want to hear me talk Latin?'

Tol glanced up now at Riah where she was standing with her hand on Davey's shoulder, and he grinned widely at her before looking at Biddy again and saying, 'Yes, yes, I'd like to hear you talk Latin; not that I'll understand a word of it.'

'I could learn you . . . No, the master says nobody can learn anybody, they can teach you an' it's you who learns. Do you understand?'

'Yes, Miss Schoolma'am. Yes, I understand.' There was more laughter now as Tol nodded his head in jack-in-the-box fashion, as a simpleton might.

'Well, listen . . . now listen, this is Latin, Tol. Am . . . mo . . . me . . . am matrem.'

'Well, well!' Tol showed exaggerated astonishment as he gazed at the beaming face of Biddy, who now said, 'It means, I love my mother.' And her eyes flashed up to Riah whose lips were pressed tight together to suppress her laughter.

'Do you want to hear some more?'

'I can't wait.'

'Oh, you!' She tossed her head, recognizing Tol's sarcasm, but she went on, 'Add . . . erbem – ayo utt . . . parnem . . . aymam.' She gulped as she finished, then stated triumphantly, 'That means, I am going to the city to buy some bread.'

'*You ain't!*'

'Don't make fun, Tol. The master said nobody can be learned unless they know Latin.'

'And the master says you don't pronounce it properly.'

Anger showing in her face, Biddy turned towards Davey, and she pursed her lips for a moment before she retorted, 'Well, that's better than not being able to pronounce anything at all, not even English.'

'Now, now, now! Get on with your work, madam, and not so much of that cheek. Davey will pronounce his words all in good time.'

'What have you got to learn tonight?' said Tol, trying to throw oil on the troubled waters flowing across the table. But it was Johnny who answered now, saying, with a wide grin, 'A story from an ee-pick.'

'Oh, and what might it be about?'

'Oh.' Johnny shook his head, then slanted his eyes towards Biddy as he said, 'Oh, funny names, about men fightin' and turnin' boats into rocks an' things.'

And now Biddy, preening herself with her knowledge, supplied the details in her own way, saying, 'It's this, U . . . lissees,' only to be stopped by Davey saying, 'You've got it wrong. That's how you said it this mornin' an' he said it was wrong.'

'Who's he? The bull's uncle?' Riah's tone held a deep reprimand as she looked down on her beloved son, and Davey, his chin jerking, said, 'The master.' Then returning to his protest, he looked up at his mother, saying, 'Well he did. He said she pronounced the names all wrong.'

'I like that!' put in Biddy. 'But anyway, I remember them, an' the stories. An' that's something you don't, thick skull.'

'Enough! Enough! either tell Tol the story or get yourself up and away to bed.'

Biddy nipped on her bottom lip before she turned to Tol, saying, 'Well, this man had been tramping a long time round about in wars and things and he comes across a friend, and they have a meal and the friend puts him in a boat and sends him off home with presents. But the sailors know there's something afoot and they put him on an island when he's asleep. But when they got home they were met by U . . . lisses's enemy called Neptune who ruled the sea, and he was mad at what they had done and he hit their vessel with his pronged fork and turned it into a rock.'

'It's a daft story.' The quiet comment came from Maggie and caused everybody to explode again, including the teller and Davey. And Tol, patting the dark brown head of the little girl, said, 'And I think I'm with you there, Maggie. It does sound a bit daft to me. But then, 'tis but a tale, and you learn words through it, so I suppose it's of some good after all.'

Maggie again caused a renewal of laughter when, looking up at Tol, she said, 'I like Baa! Baa! black sheep, better.' And at this Biddy and Johnny started to chime;

Baa! Baa! black sheep
Have you any wool?
Yes, sir. Yes, sir,
Three bags full:
One for the Master,
And one for the Maid,

And one for Maggie Millican
Who lives up the lane.

The two younger children now threw themselves about with laughter; and Riah, looking at her son whose face was straight, wondered for a moment why, if he didn't take to the hard bits of learning, he couldn't enjoy the simple bits. In a way she was getting worried about Davey.

She said briskly, 'Now come on, all of you's, away to bed with you. And no noise, mind, no carry on.'

One after the other they kissed her and said good night to Tol before gathering up their books and scrambling from the room.

The kitchen to themselves, there was silence between them, and Riah was aware of the embarrassment on both sides. And when Tol stood up and made ready to go, she said, 'You've got to get back then?'

'Aye, there's odd and ends to do, but it's nice calling in.' He looked at her, asking now, 'How are you getting on?'

'Oh, as usual. Me days are full, I keep busy, and the master's very kindly given me some of his parents' clothes to cut down for the children.'

'My, my! I should say you're honoured there, because Fanny was often after pieces from the attic, but he warned her off and in no small voice, so she tells me.'

'I think the company of the children has changed him.'

'Definitely. Definitely. I came across him going through the woods the other day, and he walked along of me and talked amiably. He seems a different man, lighter in himself. Yes, there's no doubt about it, the bairns have made a difference to him, and he to them, because you've got to admit, it isn't every day working-class bairns are educated. Now, is it?'

'No, you're right there, Tol. I'm grateful. Oh, yes, I'm grateful. Except – ' She now rubbed one palm against the other before she continued, 'I'm . . . I'm a bit worried about Davey. He doesn't take to the lessons like the others, and what's more, he's got this thing about horses, working with horses. He's disappointed there's not a horse here. But I've told him the master can't afford one. And he angered him the day, so he says, when he told him he wanted to drive a coach.'

'Is that what he wants to do?'

'It seems so.'

'Well, his education would be wasted if that's as far as he wants to go. And I can see Mr Miller's point of view. At the same time I understand Davey's, because all I wanted to do when I was a lad was to go to sea. But,' he said smiling at her now, 'from what I hear of the life sailors have, it's a good job I didn't have me wish.'

She nodded. 'You're right there,' she said; 'I've seen a bit of it when the ships docked in the Tyne. It's a brutal life, and it breaks some. You don't get that kind of cruelty in the woods.'

'Oh – ' he turned his head to the side and nodded slowly as he commented, 'the woods have their own cruelty, animal to animal. 'Tis amazing what you see. Even trees in winter suddenly decide to snap a branch and you're lucky if you get away alive. Then there's man's cruelty.' His face became stiff now. 'The master's thinking of trapping the wood.'

'You mean mantraps?' Her voice was a whisper.

'Aye, just that. I can't keep me eyes on a thousand acres, and I must admit I close me eyes when the locals are just after the rabbits. But when it comes to the birds, well, I've warned them on the quiet, and that's all I can do.'

'I think that's cruel, traps of any kind for animals, but when it's for men . . . eeh!' She now whipped a towel from the brass rod and, going to the table, she rubbed it vigorously, muttering as she did so: 'There's so much cruelty. I heard tell through the paper of two men being hung for sheep stealing.'

'Well, it's a serious offence that; they know what to expect when they go in for it.'

'Yes, but hung. I could understand in a way them gibbeting that Mr Joblin for murdering the mine manager, but for stealing sheep they could have been transported.'

'If it was meself, I'd plump for hanging.'

When she looked at him he was smiling, and she stopped her rubbing and sighed; then folding the cloth into a square, she said, 'When are you expecting your sister back?'

'I'm not sure, a week, perhaps a fortnight. The only thing I'm sure of is that she'll be back.'

She looked up at him. His eyes were waiting for her, and he added, 'Life's not easy. It seems that few people can do what they wish.'

As she stared back at him, the words came into her mouth, but stuck there, for how could she say, 'You've got a week, perhaps a fortnight to do what you wish. Why don't you speak? Why don't you come round here now and take me in your arms? It would be some sort of compensation to both of us.' But she couldn't say that, the risk would be too great. She guessed though that he knew what she wished, it must be written all over her face. Yet he wouldn't take the risk either, for he, like herself, knew that their arms had only to entwine, and that would be that, for they were both starved of the same thing. And she was also aware that the ensuing result was in both their minds, perhaps more so in hers, because what if she was to have another bairn? And she fell easily. Oh yes, she fell easily.

'I'd better be on me way now, Riah.'

'Yes, yes.'

'Is there anything you want doing, outside I mean?'

'No. No, thank you. The boys are managin' fine.'

'Yes, it's amazing the difference they've made in that garden, them bits of lads. Well, I'll be off then.' He still stood, and she said, 'Yes. Good night then.'

'Good night, Riah.'

He picked up his cap from the knob of the chair and went towards the door, and there he turned, and again he said, 'Good night, Riah.' And she answered once more, 'Good night, Tol.'

Going to the fireplace, she put the towel back on the rod, then turned its ends into a corkscrew as she muttered bitterly, 'Why has he to come?' And after a moment she released her hold on the towel and watched it unscrew itself, and with it the tenseness went out of her body; then leaning her head against the wooden mantel, she muttered, 'That's that. That's final. He'll never have a better chance and he didn't take it. So that's final. I'll think no more of him.'

The four children were seated at the table in the library, the two boys at one side, the two girls at the other. Percival Miller sat at the top end and, holding his hand to his head, he said, 'Your accents are atrocious. Do you know that? Atrocious.'

They gazed at him in silence, until Johnny caused a diversion. Aiming to be a peacemaker, he said, 'Do you want us to read from me book?'

'Oh, my God!' The master now gave Johnny his full attention. 'By "us", I suppose you mean "me", boy? And tell me, where was your tongue when you said, uss?'

Johnny looked for help across to Biddy, and Biddy, hoping to be unobserved, sat back in her chair and under cover of rubbing her nose with her forefinger, pointed to her mouth; and Johnny, quick to take her advice, said brightly, 'In me mouth, sir.'

Which part of your mouth? And perhaps your sister will help you to answer this too. When you said, uss, where was your tongue?'

Johnny remained silent, his round bright eyes staring at the man who appeared like God to him; and after a moment, Percival Miller slowly turned his gaze on Biddy, saying, 'Well, you've done your excavation, and where, tell me, was your tongue when you said, uss?'

Her head gave him an almost imperceivable wag as she said, 'Sticking to me bottom teeth, sir.'

'Yes, exactly. Sticking to your bottom teeth and pushing your jaw out. All of you say, uss.'

So they all said, 'Uss,' their faces showing different forms of contortion and so causing the word to emerge in different ways. After the fifth attempt their pronunciations still varied widely, and it was Biddy as usual who came in for censure and caused another diversion, because after she had been asked to pronounce the word by herself, he bawled at her, 'It is not "arse", you happen to be sitting on that.'

An explosion of laughter brought the other three bodies wagging; even Davey had his head bent over the table and his hand pressed tightly across his mouth; and more surprising still, their master had a deep twinkle in his eye, as he said, 'Your exaggeration of "us" will, I have no doubt in the years to come, cause more comment than the raw pronunciation of these, your brothers and sister. You are well set, madam, to becoming a Mrs Malaprop, I think. We must go into that later.' Now his voice rose and with it his hand and he brought his ruler down on the table close to the fingers of Maggie's left hand, while her right one jerked away from her face as he cried, 'Leave your nose alone, girl! Doesn't your mother give you a handkerchief? That is a disgusting habit of yours.'

As the tears spurted to the child's eyes, he continued, 'None of that now. None of that.' Then after a moment of staring at her bowed head, he said, 'Anyway, your primitiveness has given me a further lead. Tomorrow you will learn what Lord Chesterfield thinks of people who pick their noses. Now to return to fundamentals. Johnny and Maggie, you will do these sums,' and he passed them a piece of paper. 'You may make use of the abacus. And you two' – nodding to Biddy and Davey – 'you will render me speechless with admiration while listening to your reading.'

And so it went on for the next hour, until it was time for them to get back to their work, when he dismissed Johnny and the two girls; but to Davey he said, 'I want to talk to you. Stay where you are.'

When they were alone together, he did not immediately begin to talk but, leaning back in his chair, his hands covering the large knobs on the arms, he stared at the boy, whose eyes were cast down and head was slightly bent forward.

The sun from a mullioned window had turned the boy's hair almost to silver and Percival Miller gazed on it for some minutes before he said softly, 'You are not a dullard, David, so why don't you try harder at your lessons?'

Davey raised his head and his eyes were still cast down as he said, 'They . . . they don't interest me, sir. I . . . I mean I don't seem inclined that way.'

'What way are you inclined?' Percival Miller was now sitting on the edge of his seat, his forearms on the table, his hands joined tightly together, and he entreated the boy, 'Tell me. Tell me.'

Davey now turned his gaze fully and frankly on his master as he said, 'I've told you, sir, I . . . I just want to be with horses, drive horses, or something like that.'

Their faces were only a few inches from each other.

It was some seconds before Davey blinked and, as if coming out of a trance, he drew his head back on his shoulders and straightened up; and as he did so, his master caught his hand and said, 'If I promised to buy you a horse . . . well, say a pony, will you promise to pay attention to your work, and . . . ?'

'You'd get me a pony, sir? Really?' The boy's face became alight. 'For me own? Really mine?'

'Yes, yes, really yours.'

'Oh! sir. Yes, yes, I'll try. Oh, yes I will, I'll try. I'll pay attention. An' . . . an' – ' His mouth opened and closed twice before he brought out, 'There's the remains of an old trap beyond the summer-house, sir. A dog cart it was, sir. I could fix it, I'm sure I could. I could fix it. Yes, sir.' He was nodding his head now, his face showing his joy. 'Yes, sir, I'll try. Oh, yes, I'll try.'

They were both standing now and Percival Miller still retained the boy's hand; and now he laid his other hand on top of it and said, 'That is a promise?'

'Yes, sir. I promise. Oh, thank you, sir. Thank you, thank you very much.' And Davey withdrew his hand from the warm grasp and backed three steps away before turning and, almost at a run, left the library.

Bursting into the kitchen, he startled Riah by shouting, 'Ma! Ma! What do you think?'

She dried her hands of blood from a hare that she was cutting up, and her face too was bright as she looked at her son and said, 'I don't know. Tell me. Tell me.'

'The master, he's . . . he's gona get me a horse . . . a pony. He's promised. That's if I stick into me lessons. An' I will, Ma. I will. But just think – an' it's going to be mine, not his; he said it'll be mine – a pony, Ma.'

She pulled a chair towards him and sat down, and she said quietly, 'He really said that?'

'Yes, yes, he did.'

Her face became serious as she put her hand up and gripped the boy's arm, saying. 'Well, I hope you appreciate the sacrifice he'll be making, because, you know, he's got very little money. And you know what happens on quarter day with his books and baccy and beer.'

'Yes, Ma, I know.' And Davey's face lost some of its brightness as he said, 'Do you think he'll have to go without all those?'

'Yes, I can't see any other way he can do it. And you know, if it wasn't for what you grow in the garden and the fruit, and the eggs we're getting from the hens now, and such like we would not live as we do. He's hard put to pay me the four shillings a week that he does, so Davey' – she gripped both his arms now – 'you'll have to do as you promised and stick in because that'll please him more than enough. All he thinks about is learnin'.'

'I will, Ma. I will.'

'Go on then, get on with your work.' And after the boy ran out of the kitchen she stood and watched him flying across the yard as if he had wings to his feet, and she felt troubled, for deep within her she knew that her son, unlike her eldest daughter, hadn't it in him to pay more attention to learning than he was already doing. Davey was one of those who would always work better with his hands than with his brain. And she returned to chopping up the hare, thinking it was a great pity the master was so set on education that he could think of nothing else.

8

The man seemed to be a changed being. Yesterday he had actually played ball with the children in the yard there. She couldn't believe her eyes. And then for the past week he had been coming into the kitchen to talk to her. He had sat in the chair and their conversation had ranged over all things. He treated her as an equal. Yesterday, they had even discussed how strange it was, this thing called coincidence. Had it been a coincidence that she had arrived at Rowan Cottage, hoping to look after another man's wife? Had it been coincidence that Tol and Fanny had come across her? Had it been coincidence that she had come here with her four children? Didn't she think life was planned? And when she had agreed with him, saying 'Yes, God has strange ways of working,' only then had he contradicted her and very sharply, saying, that God had nothing to do with it. There was a power, yes, that shaped their lives but it had nothing to do with a God who was supposed to be a person sitting up there in the clouds on a throne.

He had gone on and on about this, and she had become a little shocked, but had made herself remember that he wasn't as other men. Being learned like he was, he was bound to think differently. And that he did think differently, she had been made aware before this, because she had heard him arguing with Parson Weeks. But Parson Weeks, although dominant when it came to church-going, was a tolerant man. Likely, because he enjoyed his ale.

And then last evening, when the children were all standing round the pump getting the grime off themselves, he had come through the kitchen and stood at the door watching them. And when he had muttered, 'Beautiful. Beautiful,' she had felt so sad for him. Here was a man who, behind all his odd ways, was starved of a family. He would have made a wonderful father. In that moment she had felt drawn to him. She had wanted to put her arms about him and bring his head to her breast, as a mother might . . . or perhaps not as a mother might. And this had jerked her mind back to Tol.

She had seen Tol twice during the last week and his manner hadn't changed; in fact, she thought, if anything, it had become a little cool. He hadn't stayed to chat with her, and in a way she had been thankful for this. So, she had made up her mind about Tol, and she faced the fact that if he had cared for her enough, he would have made it known when he had the opportunity. He liked her. Oh yes, she knew that, but liking and loving were two different things . . .

It was later that evening when the children had gone to bed and she was clearing up for the night and preparing for the following morning by setting the table for breakfast, that the kitchen door opened and her master appeared. He began with an apology. Standing a few feet from her, he asked, 'Am I intruding?'

'Not at all, sir. Not at all. Would you like to sit down?' She felt he wanted to talk, but he refused the offer of the seat and walked to the fire and, looking down into it, he said, 'I think we understand each other, Riah, don't we?' And after a moment's hesitation she said softly, 'Yes, sir.'

'You're an intelligent woman. Even from your background you must know the ways of the world and that what appears right to some people is vastly wrong to others.'

Again she said softly, 'Yes, sir.'

Another silence followed before he turned to her and said, 'Well then, come along upstairs, I want to give you something.'

After a moment's hesitation she followed him as he led the way up into the attic once again. And when he opened the wardrobe door and took down the black velvet gown her mouth fell into a gape, for now, holding it with both hands, he put it up in front of her, saying, 'As I told you, this was my mother's favourite gown, and I love it because I loved her. In some ways you remind me of her, you're the same build and' – he paused – 'you have the same kind heart, an understanding of human nature and its strange twists, turns and foibles . . . There take it, it is yours.'

As he let loose of the garment, it fell over her joined hands, and the softness and the weight of it seemed to flow through her, and when he said, 'Go down and put it on. Then come into the drawing-room; and we shall drink to this occasion,' she was unable to utter a word, and it was he who took the lamp and led the way down the stairs . . .

In her bedroom, she sat on the edge of the bed and looked at the gown now lying across the foot of it. Her heart was thumping against her ribs as if she was a young girl about to go to her first man. As she chastised herself saying, 'Well, you knew what was coming; and face it, woman, you need him as much as he needs you.' Then her eyes travelled to the door and across the corridor to the children's rooms.

What would they think? Well, they needn't know. Oh, Biddy with that uncanny way of hers would be bound to sense something. She was like a weathercock, that one, where emotions were concerned. Well, what did it matter? In a way, their livelihood as well as her own depended on her pleasing this man, and it would be no hardship. No, it wouldn't.

She rose abruptly to her feet and, stripping off her workaday clothes, she sponged her face and hands, telling herself that she needn't worry about being clean as, fortunately, she'd had a wash down last night. But when the time came for her to step into the gown she held it up in front of her and as if it were embodying its previous owner, she said, 'I'll be as kind to your son as you were.'

The gown, she found, was a little tight under the arms and around the waist, but, nevertheless, she managed to fasten the myriad hooks that went down each side of the gown from the oxter to the hips. She found this kind of fastening very strange, but it left the back and front of the gown plain, and when she swung the little mirror on the dressing-table backwards and forwards she was amazed at what it revealed. She moved the lamp to get a better view and couldn't believe that this dress had so transformed her. She took a comb through her hair, softening it above the ears, bringing a quiff down on to her brow and, finally, pinning the bun at the back lower down on her neck. This done, she looked at her hands. They were red, the nails were broken. Then her gaze travelled to her feet. She was wearing house slippers, but there was a small heel on them. Anyway, the dress covered them almost to the toes. It dipped slightly at the back and trailed on the floor, which indicated that his mother had been an inch or so taller than herself.

Now she was ready to go. She picked up the lamp, but with one hand on the door handle she gripped it and closed her eyes tightly, and the words that came into her mind were, Goodbye Tol . . .

He was sitting in a chair to the side of the fire when she entered the drawing-room, and he stood up immediately but did not move towards her. His mouth slightly open, he gazed at her as she walked slowly up the room. She had put the lamp on the table before he moved and, now taking her hand, he courteously led her to the seat at the other side of the fireplace. But still he didn't speak. Then he turned from her and, going to a side table, he lifted a bottle and poured two glasses of wine, and as he handed one to her he said, 'The last of the cellar, but none of it before has been drunk on such an occasion and to such a beautiful woman.'

She was hot from her brow to her feet. When he held up his glass, she did likewise and sipped at the wine. It tasted like whisky, only better. Now he was seated opposite to her, but on the edge of his chair, and, leaning towards her, he said, 'I think this is the strangest night of my life, Riah. You are my mother sitting there as she once sat, but you are many things besides. There are so many different ways of loving, different kinds of love. Do you know that, Riah?'

She found no need to answer and he went on, 'I have only ever loved one woman and that was my mother. But it wouldn't be hard, I think, to love you. Why are we made like this, Riah? So complex that we are given the faculty to love yet we are afraid of exercising it, and we dissipate it in other ways that very rarely bring us joy. We didn't ask to be made as we are. Do you understand me, Riah?'

She did and she didn't; and she again had the feeling he wasn't needing an answer, he just wanted to talk; and so once more she sipped from her glass, and he went on, 'I can't imagine what my life was like before you and the children came into it. I look back to those long years spent with Fanny shuffling here and there, garrulous, slovenly, yet, in a way, a friend . . . well, the only one I had. And then one night she comes and tells me she is leaving. It seemed the end of life, my way of life. When she told me there was a woman and four children to take her place, I fought her. I thought, Oh no. It was as if the gods were laughing at me and throwing me back into my early years when I longed for children, and longed to be a father figure, but without having to resort to a woman to bear them. But what I dreaded turned out to be a wonderful experience. You have given me life again. Do you know that, Riah? With your generous warm heart and your understanding, you have given me life again, and a family.'

He lay back in the chair now and sat looking at her, until all of a sudden he rose to his feet and came towards her. Taking her hand, he brought it to his lips; then drawing her gently upwards, he said, 'Thank you, Riah. Thank you. You and your family will always be my concern, especially David. You understand that? I do so want David to be as a son. I want to see him become someone.' He smiled gently as he added, 'I'm talking like a father who has failed in life and longs to see his son achieve his ambitions . . . Now go to your bed, Riah. Go to your bed.'

The last was a whisper and, like someone in a dream, she picked up the lamp, then turned from him and walked with slow step out of the room, across the hall, and, skirting the kitchen, she took the side door into the east wing and to her room.

Once inside, the lamp almost fell to the floor as she put it on the corner of the dressing-table. Quickly righting it, she sat down on the stool. She had thought it would take place in his bedroom, but he had said, 'Go to your bed.' And he knew where her bedroom was, for he had one day made a tour of this end of the house and had seen where the children slept and she too.

The unfastening of the dress took longer than the fastening. Her fingers, she told herself, were all thumbs. But when at last it dropped to the floor, she picked it gently up and hung it in the wardrobe, and just before she closed the door she stroked its soft texture with the back of her hand.

She usually slept in her chemise with her nightdress over it for warmth, but tonight she took off the chemise; and she did not put on her calico nightdress, but a long bodice petticoat that she had made out of the lining from one of the dresses he had given her for the children. One last thing she did before getting into bed was to leave the door slightly ajar.

And now she was lying waiting, the lamp turned low on the bedside table, her hair in two plaits lying on top of the counterpane, her hands joined tightly under her breasts; and her body, she knew, was ready . . .

The travelling clock which she had taken from another bedroom told her that it was half an hour since she had got into bed. Well, she told herself, perhaps he was shy. Hadn't he said he had never loved any woman but his mother. Yes, but that didn't mean he hadn't had one. Good Lord! Young men of his standing went in for that kind of thing in a big way. Perhaps he was having a bath. Of course, he wasn't! he wouldn't bath in cold water and Davey and Johnny always carried the hot water up for his bath . . .

When the clock said she had been lying for a full hour and ten minutes, she slowly swung her legs out of the bed and sat on the edge of it. What did it mean? Was he getting drunk before he came? That was another silly thought. That wine, he had said, was the last in the cellar, but he meant in the bottle and tomorrow, if he bought that pony for Davey, he wouldn't be able to afford any wine at all. What was keeping him?

When the clock said ten past eleven she lay down again. There was now threading the urges in her body a feeling of humiliation. What, she asked herself, was he playing at? Two hours now she had been lying here. What did he mean? Getting her all worked up like this, and then not coming. Go to your bed, he had said. That was plain enough, wasn't it? And the look on his face. There had been love there, or some kind of feeling anyway. But what was that he had said about wanting children but without having to go to a woman . . . Oh that was just his complicated way of talking.

She didn't know what time it was when she turned her face into the pillow to smother her sobbing, but when she woke up she was amazed to find the lamp on the last flicker; it had burned down to the wick.

She stumbled out of bed and, her eyes squinting at the clock on the little mantelpiece, she saw to her amazement it stood at a quarter to five.

Why? Why?

* * *

'You got a headache, Ma?'

'What?' Riah turned from the stove with the porridge pan in her hand, and looking at Biddy, she said again, 'What?'

'I said, you got a headache, Ma?'

'Yes, a bit of one.'

'You didn't sleep?'

'No. No, I didn't sleep very well.'

'I wish I didn't sleep so much; it's a waste of time.'

'Eat your porridge.'

'I could sleep all day.' No one commented on Johnny's remark, but Riah looked at the two younger children who were sleepy-eyed and she said sharply, 'Get on with your breakfast, it's nearly seven o'clock.' Then she looked at Davey. His plate was clean and he asked brightly, 'Can I have another, Ma?'

Once more she brought the porridge pan to the table, thinking as she did so that she knew what had sharpened her son's appetite: the prospect of the pony was oozing out all over him like happy vapour, because today the master was going into Newcastle to collect his allowance and bring back the promised pony. But if the master's promises to her son were anything like the promises to herself, she would have a surly and disappointed boy on her hands tonight. But no, he would bring back the pony all right because he wouldn't want to lose favour in the children's eyes, especially Davey's, for he was obviously very taken with the boy.

But how was she going to face him this morning? Had he been laughing at her? Having her on? Getting her all dressed up just for his amusement? She couldn't think so, for he wasn't an unkind man. But what kind of a man was he to leave her lying there like that for hours waiting? . . . Oh, she didn't know. She only knew that she was shaking inside at the thought of coming face to face with him.

But she needn't have worried. An hour later when she took his breakfast into the morning-room he was dressed and ready for his trip into Newcastle, and he greeted her brightly, so brightly that, after placing the tea-tray on the table to his side, she remained leaning forward as she looked at his face because she was amazed to see that he looked happy.

'It's a lovely morning, Riah, don't you think?'

She didn't answer him, and he stopped in the act of unfolding his napkin and his eyes narrowed as he asked, 'You're not well?'

'I'm . . . I'm all right, sir. I've just got a bit of a headache.'

'Oh, then you must get outside and walk. You're too much in the house, you know Riah. Anyway, here I am all ready to gallop into town to buy a horse.' He actually laughed out loud, then added, 'Well, a small horse, a pony. I'm as excited as David is at the prospect of that animal joining the household. Do you know that, Riah?'

'Yes, sir.'

He now picked up his knife and fork but did not use them on the plate of bacon in front of him, but standing the cutlery on its end, he stared down at the table and more to himself than to her said, 'It signifies so much this day: a new lease of life, and . . . and you have given it to me, Riah. You have in a way given me a son.' He turned his face towards her now, and for a moment she thought, He's not right in the head. Given him a son, indeed! Davey was no more his son today than he was yesterday. And look at him, all smiles, after last night working me up like that, then leaving me high and dry.

'Tell David I want to see him before I go off. Will you?'

'Yes. Aye, yes.'

In the hall she stood for a moment thinking, he's gone a bit funny. It sounded different last night when he talked of them all as his family, but not now when he was singling out Davey as his son. She wasn't going to like this; she knew she wasn't. Davey was hers; she was father and mother to him, and that's how she wanted things to remain. And anyway, he was deluding himself if he thought he was going to make a scholar out of Davey . . . Now if it had been Biddy.

She knew that Davey had started to scythe the bottom field and she could have sent Biddy for him but she went to the garden herself, down by the long hedge to where he had just started at the top corner and she called to him, 'Davey! Davey!' And he laid down the scythe and ran towards her.

'Yes, Ma?'

'The . . . the master wants to see you before he goes into town.'

She watched his face light up, but without a word he ran from her and up the garden towards the house.

She had been in the kitchen a few minutes when he came into it, his face still beaming.

''Twas about the pony, Ma. He . . . he asked me what colour I preferred. Fancy. Eeh!' He shook his head. 'I can't believe it. And I will try. I've told him. I'll do everything he says.' And he made a face now as he added, 'I'll even take note of bright Biddy. I asked him how he was gona get it back, and he said he'd get Robbie Howel, the carrier, to trot it alongside his horse, and I'd have to be at the crossroads around three and pick it up, I mean lead him back, because he himself won't be back till nearly four on the coach. Oh, Ma, I'm excited. An' Ma . . .'

'Yes, Davey?' Her face was straight and her voice flat.

'He's kind, isn't he? the master, kind. If only' – he grimaced now – 'he didn't want to stick so much into me head.'

As she watched him run from the kitchen she felt slightly sick, but she couldn't tell why. She should be happy for her son because she had never before seen him so bright, and because of the pony he would try to work hard at his lessons, she knew that. But why wasn't she happy? Was it because there was still the great want in her body and that she couldn't understand the business of last night? She didn't know.

At half past one Davey was sluicing himself under the pump and when, later, he came into the kitchen, his hair plastered down, Biddy, entering the room from the far door, called to him, 'What you getting ready so soon for?'

'Well, it will take nearly half an hour to get to the crossroads.'

'Well' – she looked at the clock – 'you'll still have nearly an hour to wait.'

She had a duster in one hand; holding one end of it, she kept pulling it through the half closed fist of her other hand as she said, 'I wonder what it will be like, the colour and that? You told him brown, didn't you?'

'Well, I said it really didn't matter, but I liked brown.'

'What are you going to call it?'

'I don't know. I'll have to see if it's a he or a she,' at which they both burst out laughing. Then coming quickly round the table, he looked appealingly into her face as he said, 'You'll help me, Biddy, won't you? I mean with the learnin'. It's those myth things I can't remember, the names like. I'm not good at remembering names, well, not made-up names like that, that don't sound like any we've heard afore. You know what I mean?'

She nodded at him, her eyes shining as she leant towards him and whispered, 'After we go upstairs afore me ma comes up, she's nearly an hour down here or more, and I never can get straight to sleep so I'll come into your room and learn you . . . teach you.' She had stretched the last two words, and now their foreheads touched for a second and again they were laughing.

She watched him run to the corner of the mantelpiece and take down the comb and pull it through his hair. He had lovely hair. He looked lovely altogether, did Davey. She always liked looking at him, even if at times she didn't like his ways. He had a face like some of the figures in the books in the little room off the library. There were special books in there that held paintings. She often glimpsed through them when dusting. She always took a long time to dust that room. She brought her elbows tight into her sides at the thought that she wished she could be like the master and sit reading all day.

'Where's Ma?' He was still combing his hair.

'She's up in the attic, sorting things out. The master says she can have some of the underwear from the trunks. Oh, it's lovely stuff, Davey. I could have stayed up there all day going through the boxes, but she wouldn't let me.' She paused now and, her face becoming thoughtful, she added, 'Ma's not herself the day. Is she worried about something, do you know, Davey?'

He shook his head, saying, 'No, not that I would know of anyway. She seemed the same to me, except she said she had a headache.'

Biddy turned from him, muttering, ''Tisn't only a headache, she's had headaches afore. It's funny like . . . Where you going?'

'To say goodbye; tell her I'm goin'.'

When Davey reached the attic, he saw his mother kneeling on the floor in front of a trunk with a number of garments scattered around her. He walked cautiously down the middle of the room – he didn't know why he didn't like this part of the house – and when she turned and looked up at him he said, 'I'm just off, Ma.'

'Is it that time?' She rose to her feet.

'Well, I'm a bit early.' He smiled at her, and she put her hands on his head, saying, 'Your hair's wet.'

'Aye.' He grinned sheepishly at her now as he made one of his rare jokes: 'I felt I wanted to be spruced so when me pony saw me he would know . . . I was a good little lad.'

She smiled at him now but she didn't laugh. A good little lad, he said. He didn't consider himself a lad; he was coming up twelve and could be taken for fourteen any day. He was tall and straight and so good to look upon. Often, when looking at him, she wondered how she had come to give birth to such a precious thing as this son. She loved all her children, oh yes, she would defend openly to her last breath that she loved them equally, all the while knowing in her heart that this one she held very special. She put her arms out now and pulled him to her and held him tightly for a moment. The unexpected embrace left them both embarrassed, and when he stepped back from her, his eyelids were blinking rapidly.

They weren't a demonstrative family; it was unusual for them to hug each other. And so, remembering the conversation he'd had a few minutes earlier with Biddy, he asked tentatively, 'You . . . you all right, Ma?'

'Oh, yes, yes.'

'You're not bad or anything?'

'Bad?' She now gave a short laugh as she said, 'Have you even known me to be bad? Bad tempered, yes.' She pulled a face at him, and at this he shook his head and said, 'No, Ma, you're never bad tempered. Cross a little at times' – he smiled – 'but never bad tempered.'

'Go on, get yourself off,' she said, only to halt him as he turned and cause him to laugh outright now as she said, 'See if you can pick up a sword and some armour on the way, and you can come back into the yard like one of them knights you've been readin' about of late.'

'Oh aye, ma, that'd be the thing. An' it would please the master. By, that would.'

Listening to him clattering down the stairs, she thought, That pony's going to alter his life.

It was turned half-past four when Davey came back. They were all in the kitchen: Johnny, Maggie, Biddy, and Riah. The children were excited, and she'd just cut them shives of bread to be eaten before going along the road to meet their brother. But unexpectedly the kitchen door opened and there he stood, his shoulders stooped, his face blank, his lips pressed tight.

No one spoke as he came up to the table, and it was at his mother he looked as he said, 'It wasn't there. Mr Howel laughed.'

'Laughed?' The word was just a whisper from Riah, and Davey nodded as he said, 'Aye, he laughed and said, "Shanks's pony is all you'll get out of Mr Percival Miller."' He paused; then his lips trembled as he added. 'He said if he knew anything the day, the master wouldn't even be able to use Shanks's pony, it would be Tol Briston's cart as usual.'

Slowly Riah walked round the table, but when she went to put her hand on her son's shoulder he shrugged himself away and, his voice almost falsetto, he cried, 'I'll get changed an' about me work. An' that's all I'm gona do. Do you hear, Ma? That's all I'm gona do, me work. He knows what he can do with his learnin'. And I'll tell him that. Aye, I will. That's all he thinks about, learning. Well, to hell with his learnin', an' him. An' him.'

And he dashed from the room, leaving them all looking at each other for some seconds, until Biddy muttered, 'There must be a reason, Ma.' Then the girl almost jumped back in surprise as her mother turned, bawling at her, 'Yes! there must be a reason and we all know the reason, an' it'll come rollin' in that door in a very short time. Get back to your work, the lot of you. I'll deal with this. Yes, by God! I'll deal with this. Go on!' She scattered them with a wave of her arm. And when she had the kitchen to herself, she stood beating her fist rhythmically on the chopping board, oblivious of the cut vegetables jumping like puppets on to the table and then on to the floor, and all the while her head jerked rapidly as if with a tick as she repeated Biddy's words, 'There must be a reason. There must be a reason.' And she stared towards the door as if awaiting the entry of a drunken husband.

It was almost an hour later when Percival Miller entered the house. He stood in the hall, his head lowered for some moments before looking first one way and then the other, and finally up the stairs;

then he turned and went into the drawing-room and there he pulled on the bell-rope hanging down by the side of the fireplace.

He must have waited a full three minutes before Riah put in an appearance. She opened the door slowly and she entered the room slowly, her step flat and firm, only to be brought to a halt as she looked to where he was standing solid and sober, his face wearing an expression she hadn't seen on it before.

Slowly he approached her, stopping an arm's length from her and saying, 'Where is he?'

Her reply was soft as she said, 'Scything in the field, sir.'

'Oh, Riah.' He half turned from her; then once again looking into her face he said, 'I had to force myself to come home.'

'What happened, sir?'

'It's a long story, you wouldn't understand. I don't know whether I understand it myself or not. I only know that I was informed by my solicitors that a good half of the shares that provide me with my allowance, as pitiable as it is, have declined sharply in value. Whereas I usually get between twenty-four and twenty-six pounds a quarter, I was given only twelve today, and that to last for three months; and what then?' He spread out his hands, then doubled them into fists before beating them together and adding, 'What could I do? I . . . I did not stop at my usual inn because I knew how the boy would be feeling. How did he take it?'

She swallowed deeply and the concern was in her voice as she said, 'Badly, I'm afraid, sir. But oh, I'm glad there was a reason, a good reason. Biddy said there would be.'

'Huh!' There was a sarcastic note in his voice as he said, 'I must thank Biddy for having faith in me, while you thought, and doubtless David did too, that I would come rolling back or prostrate on the cart.'

'Well, sir . . .'

'Oh, I know, I know.' He swung round, his hand flapping now. 'David hasn't got his pony. But we all stand to lose; I don't know how I'm going to go on.'

It came to her as she watched him pacing up and down at the far end of the room that he was still capable of earning money by his brains, and she dared to voice this. 'Have you ever thought about tutoring, like, young gentlemen, sir?' she said.

He became still in his pacing, his back to her, and it was several seconds before he swung round and faced her, saying slowly now, 'Yes, Riah, I have often thought of tutoring young gentlemen. Oh yes, yes. I have often thought about that, but I have refrained from taking the matter further. You understand?'

No, she didn't, so she remained silent. 'I must go and explain to the boy,' he said.

'Should I go and fetch him, sir?'

'No, no; I'd rather do it on my own.'

He had taken off his overcoat and his hat in the hall, and she now watched him pulling at his cravat as he went towards the front door. When she herself reached the door she saw him crossing the gravelled drive to where the path led into the shrubbery, his step now almost on the point of a run. And as she watched him she recalled Davey's attitude of a short while ago, and this caused her to hurry through the kitchen, then across the yard and into the garden. There her step slowed, and she was halted by Johnny who was humping a basketful of weeds when he called, 'You looking for Maggie, Ma? She's down by the greenhouse.'

'No, no, I'm going to see Davey.'

'He's in a bad temper, Ma, slashing at the grass like nobody's business. He chased me, he did.'

'Go and empty your basket,' she said.

She had reached the high yew hedge when she heard the master's voice, it was coming from the other side of the hedge and she was stopped by the note of pleading in it as he was saying, 'David, David, try to understand. It didn't lie with me, it wasn't my fault. Oh, David . . .'

'*Don't! Don't!*'

Riah's face suddenly stretched and then when Davey's voice came again, louder now, crying, 'Stop it! Stop it! Leave go of me. Leave off!' her feet didn't seem to touch the ground as she started to race along by the hedge. But almost simultaneously with her son yelling, 'Stop it, man. Leave go. Stop it!' an agonized scream brought her to a shuddering halt.

Her shoulders hunched almost up to her ears, she didn't move until she heard the words, 'Oh my God! My God!' She didn't know who had uttered them, but once more she was running, and when she rounded the hedge she stopped in horrified amazement at the sight before her. There, standing with the scythe still in his hand, was her son, and lying on the ground, with blood gushing from his forearm and his hip, lay the master. She watched Davey fling the scythe from him before dashing to her.

Gripping hold of her dress, he cried, 'Ma! Ma! I didn't mean it; I just tried to stop him. He would keep holding me. He would keep holding me. Oh, Ma. Ma.'

'Oh, Almighty God!' It came as a soft groan from her mouth.

The man on the ground was writhing in agony. His hands were now dripping with blood where he was trying to stop the flow from his arm, but for the life of her she seemed unable to move towards him, until Davey, clinging to her, cried, 'What'll I do, Ma? What'll I do?'

What would he do? She stared at him, and she almost screamed aloud herself as she saw him hanging from a gibbet; for if that man on the ground died, that's what would happen to her son. Gripping him by the shoulder, she cried at him, 'Go and get Tol. Find him! Find him!' But as Davey made to dart from her she brought him to a jerking standstill again and under her breath she whispered, 'Don't tell him you did it. Tell him . . . tell him, the master's happened an accident. Just tell him that.'

When she released her hold on the boy he didn't now dart away but stumbled like a youth who had taken his first long swill of ale. And now she moved towards her master who was lying on his side gasping, and he turned his head up to her and in a weak voice said, 'Fetch . . . fetch the doctor.' But not until his head fell limply to the side was she galvanized into life. Flying now from the field, she screamed. 'Johnny! Johnny! Johnny! You, Maggie!'

It was Maggie who came in sight first and she bawled at her, 'Run to the house. Tell Biddy to bring sheets. The master's had an accident. Quick! Quick!'

After staring at her mother a second or two, Maggie turned and flew up the garden; and as she did so, Johnny passed her carrying his empty basket, and when Riah yelled at him, 'Here! Here!' he too came running to her.

Grabbing the basket from him, she yelled, 'You can run, can't you? You can run?'

'Aye, Ma. Aye, Ma. I can run. I'm a good runner.'

'Well, run to the village, to the parson, and ask him to send somebody on a horse for the doctor.'

Johnny turned from her, about to run, then stopped and said, 'I've got to tell the doctor . . . I mean, tell the parson to tell the doctor? Is our Davey bad?'

'No. Tell them it's the master. He's had an accident. He's badly cut.'

'What with, Ma?'

'*Will you go?*'

He went, running as only the young can run. And now she herself turned and ran back round the edge of the hedge and into the field.

Her master was just as she had left him, only the dried grass round about his hip was now soaked with blood. Kneeling by his side, she reluctantly put her fingers into the blood covered slit in his coat and shirt and tugged at them, then gasped as she saw the size of the wound, and all the while she was muttering, 'Oh, my God! Oh, my God!'

Gripping his arm between her hands now, she tried to press the ends of the wound together in order to stop the flow of blood, but to no avail. In desperation she stood up and screamed, 'Biddy! Biddy!' And as if in answer to her cry, Biddy and Maggie came stumbling round the hedge both carrying sheets. Running towards them, she pulled the top sheep from Biddy's arms and began tearing at it frantically, crying as she did so, 'Tear them up! Tear them up in strips!'

When she had finished winding the roughly torn strips of the linen round his arm, she pulled his now unconscious body on to his side, and she herself almost fainted as she saw the size of the gash in his trousers and his small clothes. Again her hands delved into the blood-soaked material and wrenched it apart. Then, rapidly folding a large piece of sheeting, she put it over where she thought the wound was, before strapping it up again with the long strips the girls were handing to her.

'What happened, Ma?'

'Be quiet! Be quiet!' She pushed Biddy aside.

'Where's our Davey, Ma?' There was a trembling note in Biddy's voice and her mother who was about to tell her again to shut up simply muttered, 'Gone for Tol.'

'Oh, Tol. Aye, Tol'll know what to do. Oh Ma, all the blood.'

'Shut up! girl. Shut up!' But then her tone changing, she said, 'He's . . . he's comin' round.'

Percival Miller emitted a long deep groan. When he opened his eyes and saw Riah looking down at him, he murmured, 'Oh Riah. Riah.'

Once he had spoken she felt anger rising in her, and she wanted to yell at him, 'You've brought this on yourself, wanting to play the father, because you're incapable of being a father.' Yes. Aye, that was it, he was one of them who couldn't take a woman. My God! Why hadn't it struck her before. What had he tried to do to Davey to make the lad react like he had done? *Hold* him, Davey had said; but after all, that didn't warrant him almost killing the man; it was the disappointment over the pony that had put the lad in a rage. And yes, he had been in a rage. She had never seen him like that before. But oh God! What was to be the outcome of it? Once again she was seeing her son hanging on a gibbet, for who would believe that these wounds were accidental. The justice had just to question a boy like Davey and the truth would be blurted out. He couldn't talk falsehoods, could Davey. Biddy, yes; Biddy could sell her soul in a like situation, or if it was to save someone's skin. But Davey wasn't made in the same mould; he would have neither the determination nor the ability to face up to authority.

'Riah.'

She looked down into the grey face and the dark eyes that seemed to have sunk deeper into their sockets and she said slowly, 'Help is coming.'

'Riah.' His good arm came out towards her but she shrank from it, and from the look in her eyes he closed his own.

The blood had stopped oozing through the linen on his arm, but it continued to spread over the pads and the bandage on his thigh and she became sick at the sight of it.

Tol didn't arrived by way of the hedge; from the main road, he had cut across the fields which were part of the Gullmingtons' estate and jumped the fence, and so he came into the field by the top way. Standing by her side and looking down at the prostrate figure, who once again seemed to have lost consciousness, he said, 'My God? How did this happen? I couldn't get anything out of Davey.'

'It . . . it was an accident.'

'Have you sent for the doctor?'

'Yes, Johnny went.'

'Johnny?' He turned and looked at her.

'I sent him to the parsonage and told him to tell Parson; he'd ride for him. Where's Davey, Tol?'

'I don't know. He wouldn't come back with me; the boy's frightened. What really did happen?'

She shook her head. 'I'll . . . I'll explain later. We've got to get him into the house.'

'Yes, yes' – his tone was urgent – 'we should put him on a door.'

'A door?' She shook her head. 'We haven't a door.'

'There's a big wheelbarrow, Tol.'

He turned and looked down on Biddy, saying, 'Aye. Aye. Where is it?'

She ran from him, and he, at a run, followed her. A couple of minutes later he was back pushing the barrow. It was grimy but dry, and Riah, after flinging the last sheet over it, stood at one side of the master while Tol stood at the other, and she followed his direction when he said, 'Grip my hand under his shoulder blades, and the same under his thighs.' Then he called, 'Keep the barrow steady, Biddy.'

Once they had laid the blood-soaked man in the barrow, Tol commanded, 'Support his leg, Riah. Keep it straight. And you, Biddy, keep his arm on his chest.' And when they had obeyed him he bent and gripped the handles and, like this, he pulled the barrow backwards out of the stubbly field until he got to the garden path, and then he went forward to the house.

At the front door he said, 'You'll have to help me carry him in. Do you think you can manage it?'

Riah made no answer; but bending, she did as before and joined her hands to his. And when they had stumbled into the hall, he said, 'Where now? We can't get him upstairs,' and she gasped, 'The drawing-room, the drawing-room couch.'

After they had laid him on the couch, Tol looked at his hands and coat; then glancing at Riah, he murmured, 'I . . . I don't think it will be any use cleaning up until the doctor gets here. He's bound to want help.'

She did not confirm this and he, looking at her closely, said, 'You're all in. Sit yourself down. Biddy, can you make your ma a cup of tea?'

For answer Biddy scrambled from the room, taking Maggie with her.

In the kitchen, Biddy thrust the kettle into the heart of the fire, and as she did so, Maggie said, 'Will he die, Biddy?' And Biddy glanced at her, saying, 'I hope not, Maggie, 'cos if he does, we will an' all.'

'We'll die?' There was a frightened note in the child's voice, and Biddy answered, 'Not like that, not graveyard dying; only we'll have to leave here.'

'Oh, I wouldn't like that, Biddy. I like it here.'

'You're not the only one. Fetch the cups.'

'Biddy' – Maggie had run to the window – ''tis a trap coming into the yard.'

Looking out of the window, Biddy saw the end of the trap disappearing on to the drive and she said, ''Twill be the doctor. Ma won't want tea now.'

They had carried the kitchen table into the drawing-room; Tol, Riah, and the doctor had managed it between them. Parson Weeks hadn't offered his assistance; his thoughts were on less mundane things as he sat by the side of this learned gentleman, as he had always thought of Percival Miller.

They stretched the injured man out on the table and Doctor Pritchard made no comment until he had unwrapped the rough-sheeting bandages and pad from Percival Miller's thigh, and then he exclaimed, 'Good gracious! Good gracious! How did he come by this?' Then he leant over the patient and in a high voice as if Percival was deaf, he cried, 'How did you come by this?'

Percival Miller simply stared straight back at him, but did not attempt to reply; and the doctor turned to Riah, saying, 'Have you any spirits in the house?'

'No, sir.'

'No? Well, that's strange, no spirits in this house.' Again he looked down at the patient and, his voice still high, he said, 'This is not going to be pleasant; you'll have to hang on. Some extent of stitching to be done here, mostly on your hip, and I can't tell about the tendons. Just have to sew you up and trust to luck.' He now turned and looked towards Tol, saying, 'You hang on to that arm, will you? I'll start on the other one. And Parson, can you hold his legs?'

'Oh, oh, I don't think I'd be any use at that.'

'Hell's flames, man! all you've got to do is to grip his ankles. Oh, away . . . Woman!' He beckoned to Riah now. 'Press down on his legs, will you? Just to save him rolling off the table.'

As Riah made to grip her master's ankles, Tol said quietly, 'Here, you hang on to his arm. I'll see to those.' And when they exchanged places, the doctor said, 'His arm will be more trouble than his legs in a minute. But have it your own way. Well, let's get at it.'

As Tol watched the needle being jabbed into the flesh and listened to the groans and saw the agonizing pain on Mr Miller's face, he thought to himself, a horse doctor would do it kinder.

The arm sewn up and bandaged, the doctor prepared to start on the hip. He soaked some padding into a liquid and almost dangled it before the patient's face as he called down to him, 'This is going to bite a bit. Get set.'

When the soaked padding hit the raw flesh, Percival let out a cry almost resembling that of a vixen in the night, and then he closed his eyes and lapsed into unconsciousness, and at this the doctor cried, 'That's good. That's good. Now we can get on with it.' And he probed for quite some time before he stuck the needle in one side of the open wound and pulled it up through the other with as much gentleness, Tol again thought, as his sister used on a bodkin when progging old rags through hessian to make a mat.

At last the operating finished and Riah, almost on the point of collapsing herself, brought a bowl of clean water and a towel for the doctor to wash his hands. When this was done, he turned to her and in a quiet aside, he said, 'You're sure there's no spirits in the house . . . no wine or anything?'

'Yes, sir; I'm sure.'

'I understood from the boy that he had just come back from the city.' He jerked his head towards the table and the prone figure.

'That was right, sir' – Riah's tone was stiff – 'but he brought no wine or spirits with him; nor yet had he taken any.'

The doctor looked hard at the woman before him; then he said, 'Indeed! Indeed!' before turning to the parson, standing now with his eyes cast downward, and saying, 'Well, I'm ready, if you are.' He then looked towards Tol who was gathering up the bloodstained strips of linen from the floor and added, 'You staying the night here?'

Tol hesitated, and then said, 'I suppose someone should in case he moves. But sir, don't you think he would be better moved on to a bed of some sort?'

'No, I don't; the less he is moved, the less likelihood of his bleeding again. He's lost all he can I should say. I'll be back in the morning.'

Without further words he went out, the parson going hurriedly after him.

No sooner had they left the room than Riah, going to Tol, said, 'They can't find him. They've been lookin' for him. He's not in the garden anywhere.'

As if he were patting her Tol put his hand out towards her and said quietly, 'Don't worry. I've got an idea where he'll be. Likely in my outhouse. Anyway, I'll slip back there now before it gets too dark, and I'll bring him over. Never fear. In the meantime, rest yourself; you look all in.'

She nodded but made no reply; but after he had left the room she sat down in the chair near the fire and turned her head away from the table and the death-like figure lying there. Her mind was full of recrimination. He had wanted to play the father; and look where it had got him; look where it had got all of them. He had changed their lives when he had given them shelter, but now he had changed them again, for whether he lived or died this place, she told herself, could afford them no more shelter. Only the fact that he was utterly helpless prevented her from going upstairs and bundling their things together and taking them on the road once more.

At this point her thinking was stopped by a question. Would Tol let them take to the road again, or would he offer them shelter? But were he to do that, could she take it, knowing that she would have to share it with his sister? She didn't know. She only knew she was so tired, so wrought up and so frightened at the consequences that might fall on Davey. And besides this, she was ashamed, ashamed that she had waited for a man to come to her last night, when there hadn't been a man to come to her.

It was more than an hour and a half later when Tol returned; but without Davey. And when she gasped, 'You haven't found him?' he put in quietly, 'It's all right. It's all right. He's safe enough.'

'Where is he?'

'In my cottage.'

'Why didn't he come with you?'

At this he looked towards the still figure on the table and said slowly, 'He won't come back here any more, Riah. He swears on that. He told me he did it, but why, he didn't say. Perhaps you'll tell me.'

Her hand was tight on her throat and she swallowed deeply a number of times before she said, 'The master had promised him a pony. Then he . . . he didn't get it, and Davey was upset.'

'Good God! he didn't do that just because he was upset over a pony?'

'Well, I . . . I don't know. The master must have got hold of him. Tried to hold him, Davey said. He's sort of become possessive like of him.'

Tol stared at her for a long moment before he said, 'Oh.' Then after a pause, he added, 'Nevertheless, he shouldn't have struck out like that. No, no.'

'What'll happen to him? He must come back.'

'He won't; no, he won't come back. But don't worry; he can stay with me for as long as he likes. And . . . and I've had an idea. Up at the house, they're wantin' a young stable lad; they've taken on another three horses and the work's heavy. The youngsters are riding now. I could get him set on there, I'm pretty sure. And from what I gather he seems crazy to work with horses.'

'Yes, yes' – she nodded her head slowly – 'he's crazy to work with horses. Oh yes' – she repeated her words – 'he's crazy to work with horses.' Then bowing her head, she burst into body-shaking sobs, and when she felt his arms about her, she leant against him, muttering, 'Oh, Tol. Oh, Tol. What's to become of us?'

He said nothing, just looked over her head as he stroked her hair with one hand while pressing her tightly to him with the other.

When her crying eased, he led her to the couch that had been pushed on one side, and having pressed her down on to it, he sat beside her and, taking her hands, he whispered, 'Don't worry about that.' Then looking towards the table, he said, 'He didn't give the lad away. He must care about him. About all of you, particularly you. I was getting the idea he might be more than fond of you . . .'

At this her manner changed and, leaning towards him and her voice a low hiss now, she brought a look of surprise to his face as she said, 'Well, your idea is as far out as the moon from the earth, see, because he's no man, he's not natural. That's why he liked Davey. Said he wanted to be a father to him. Father, huh! He wants bairns but can't take a woman.' As if she knew she'd gone too far she clapped her hand over her mouth and bowed her head; but in a moment he brought it upwards again as he said, 'It comes as no real news to me, Riah; I guessed there must be something like that for a man like him to hide himself away an' to be so against bairns, then take yours as he did. I'm sorry for him, Riah.'

'*What!*'

'Oh yes' – he nodded slowly at her – 'I can say that again, I'm sorry for him. I think he's been putting up a fight for many a long day, but when somebody as bonny lookin' as Davey was thrust afore his eyes, it was too much for him. There are men like him; it isn't unknown. No, no, it isn't unknown. There's one in the village now. Lived with his mother for years, then got friendly with another fellow from Gateshead. 'Twas then Parson Weeks wouldn't let him in the church.'

She stared at him now in hostility as she said, 'You talk as if you were on their side.'

He smiled softly at her now as he said, 'You've told me you've had eight bairns, yet you're a very innocent woman, Riah. You don't know much about life, do you, an' what goes on, although you were brought up in the town. People get the impression that we're all numskulls, we in the country. My! My! The gentry live in the country, you know, half the year, and if you knew what went on in some of these big houses round about, it would raise your scalp. He's' – he nodded his head again towards the table – 'an innocent compared with some men. Well, the boss, Mr Anthony, he may not be like his father or his grandfather but he has a good try at times. But his grandfather who died some twenty years ago, and I remember seeing him, he was frisky to the end, but in his heyday, he never allowed one of his men to be married unless he first tried the bride. Oh . . . oh, don't look so shocked, Riah. Mr Anthony's father died in the hunting field one morning after carousing all night with a bevy of ladies he and his pals had brought from the town. His wife, madam, is still alive and kickin', she's coming up eighty. She lives in the west wing and still rules the roost. Oh' – he smiled quietly – 'there's a lot of things happen in the country, Riah. Havin' said that, I know this business had come as a shock to you and I don't know what the outcome of it's gona be. But whatever it is, my dear' – he stroked her hand now between his – 'don't worry. Things will pan out. They always do if you wait long enough, things pan out. Now look, go and see the bairns off to bed then settle yourself down for the night. I'll be all right.'

'No' – she shook her head – 'I'll take me turn.'

'Nonsense. I'm a light sleeper. I'll sleep on here' – he patted the couch – 'and I'm only a hand width away from him, and if he stirs I'll hear him.'

'You sure?'

'I'm sure.' He rose to his feet, pulling her upwards, but he did not attempt to kiss her, and at this particular moment it didn't seem to matter because, in a way now, she felt safe. When she left here she knew where they would go, Annie Briston or no Annie Briston.

9

They had brought a single bed down into the drawing-room and Percival Miller had been lying on it for three weeks; and today, on Doctor Pritchard's suggestion, he had attempted, for the first time, to walk, with disastrous results, for he fell on to his side and had to be helped by the doctor back on to the bed. But the doctor's voice was cheerful and reassuring as he did so: 'Oh, that's usual, don't worry,' he said, 'I'll send you a crutch along. That'll help you in the meantime. But the wound has healed marvellously. A good job done, although I say it myself.'

'I can't bend my hip, not even when I'm lying here.' The words were full of bitterness, and the doctor replied, 'That's natural too. Even if you hadn't had such an injury, lying on your back all this time would stiffen your limbs. Make yourself move about in the bed, that'll help. Anyway, it's up to you now.'

'What is up to me? Whether I walk or not?'

'Yes, yes, just that, whether you walk or not. But there's nothing to stop you if you persevere. The sinews weren't cut, for which you can be thankful. It's as well you were such a ham-fist at scything, for if you had swung it with any force it would likely have gone right through you. So you've got that to be thankful for. Well now, I must be off. By the way' – he put his hand into his breast pocket and pulled out a folded sheet of paper – 'that's my bill. I'll leave it there.' He laid it on a side table, then added, 'I'll collect it next time I come, which should be towards the end of the week. Now keep trying, that's a good fellow, keep trying. Good day.'

During all this Riah had been standing some distance away from the bed, and now Percival turned his face towards her, crying, 'Did you ever hear the like?'

'Yes,' she said, 'and he's right.'

'What do you mean, he's right?'

'You've got to make an effort . . . you'll just have to make an effort.'

'Just have to?'

'Yes, I said, just have to, because you're soon to be on your own, I'm goin'.'

She watched him press himself upwards with his good arm, then half lean out of the bed; and, his face screwed up as if in inquiry, he said, 'What did you say?'

'You heard what I said, sir. I'm goin'. Me and the bairns, we're goin'.'

'You mean, you're walking out and leaving me here helpless like this?'

'You can get Fanny back, or someone from the village. There are two girls down there back from place I've heard.'

She watched him flop back on to the pillows, but his head was still turned towards her as he said, 'You would leave me at the mercy of old Fanny, or some half-wit of a girl from the village? You would do that?'

'Yes, I would.'

'Why?'

'Oh!' She tossed her head. 'Do you need to ask? You know why, because I cannot bear to be near you. Have I to say it? You're not natural, you're . . . you're dirty.' Following the last word her lips had puckered, but now they sprang apart and she actually jumped as he flung his good leg over the side of the bed and, bringing himself upright, he screamed at her, 'Don't you dare apply that word to me, woman! Do you hear? Never! Never say such a thing again. What I felt for your son was good. I would never have hurt him.'

Her courage coming back, she now yelled, 'I've only your word for that.'

He looked from side to side as if he wanted to get his hand on something to throw at her; then of a sudden his body went limp, his shoulders slumped, his head drooped on to his chest; and he stayed like that for some moments before he said, 'Woman . . . woman, I'll never be able to make you understand, or anyone else for that matter. I was deluded into thinking that you did. I loved the boy. I still do, in spite of what he did to me. I loved him as I might have done a son.'

He now slowly raised his head upwards and his voice took on the same tone that it did when he was talking to the children: 'There are all kinds of love, Riah,' he said. 'Whoever gave us our beings . . . our feelings, didn't cut us all to the same pattern; here and there he diverged. In the main it was directed that a man should simply love a woman, but then something was left out of a few of us, or, as I like to think, added to our mentality; and we could not only love a woman, but love our own kind. As I think I've already told you, I've never loved any woman other than my mother, but at times I've thought I could love you, Riah. Yes, yes, I've said this before, so don't look like that. But again my pattern was cut differently. My love has never flown to a man in all his gross coarseness, but to the being he was in all purity before his maleness swamped all sensitivity in him. I have always loved beauty in whatever form it takes.' He paused, then shook his head slowly as he said, 'You do not understand, do you?'

No, she didn't understand. Yet she was wild at herself that some part of her was now feeling sorry for him and was thinking, if only he wasn't what he was, because she had liked him so much and had been willing to like him more.

If he had come to her that night she wore the black velvet gown, this awful business might never have happened, everything would have been changed, been normal like. But as he had said, he wasn't that kind of man.

A thought stabbed her like a sharp knife now: That's what he had given her the gown for, sort of payment for Davey. *My God! Yes, yes*, when she came to think of it. He had imagined she had understood the whole situation and he had paid her for her son with his mother's black velvet gown. He may not, as he'd said, have harmed him, but he had in a way meant to take him over, not only with all this education, but as a parent, and eventually she, being a comparatively ignorant woman, would have been completely ousted from her son's life. She seemed to rear up as she said, 'Well, understanding or no understanding, it's as I said, we're goin'.'

'*No, you're not, Riah.*' His voice had changed, the patient schoolmaster tone was replaced by a slow definite firm statement.

'You can't stop me.'

'Oh, yes I can.' He now hitched himself to an easier position on the side of the bed before he spoke again, and he continued in the same tone as he went on, 'You attempt to leave me and I'll immediately inform the justices that your son attacked me, and you know what the result of that would be.'

Yes, yes, she knew what the result of that would be only too well, but she thrust the thought aside as she cried back at him, 'If you did that he has only to say that he was defending himself, and there's good, honest, God-fearing men among the justices.'

'There may be, but it would be his word against mine and defending himself against what? I had promised to buy him a pony and because of my reduced circumstances was unable to fulfil my promise. My solicitor will bear this out. Also, there is no smirch against my name: I am known as a scholastic recluse and come of a very good family, what you, Riah, would call a God-fearing family. More so, I left no trace of my weakness in Oxford.' His voice changed a little now and became more grim as he said, 'I fought my weakness there. As the Bible would put it, I flew temptation, and therefore, I do not consider myself unclean or dirty as you suggest.'

He now attempted to stand upright, then hopped on one foot and eased himself back into bed while she stood staring fixedly at him, her hands clenched in front of her waist, her lips pressed tight. When he had settled against the pillows he let out a long slow breath before he said, 'Your boy has been with Tol, so Tol told me, and has started this week at The Heights. It's a good beginning; he wanted horses, he'll have his fill of them up there. But how long he remains there rests entirely with you, Riah.'

She seemed to have to drag the words up from her stomach and her voice cracked as she said, 'If, as you say, you cared so much for him, you . . . you couldn't do anything to hurt him, not like . . . well . . .'

'Not like having him transported or sent to the House of Correction?' He was looking towards her now, and he said, 'Oh, yes, I could . . . and I would go to any lengths in order to keep you here . . . and the children . . . Oh! Oh!' – he lifted his hand – 'You needn't worry about them being contaminated, my eyes don't see them, my feelings are not touched by them at all. The two youngers ones I see as grubby little urchins, even when they are clean. As for Biddy, I sometimes think it's a pity she wasn't born male, because what good is the knowledge that she soaks up like a sponge going to be to her?

If she marries one of her own kind she'll despise him and there's no hope of her ever marrying her mental equal. But whether I continue to coach her or not, she will learn for herself. She has the grounding on which to build and she is of the type that will use it. I don't envy her her life. So you need not worry about the other three sparrows, Riah. But return to David's future. It all depends upon you, because should you leave me and go to Tol, and it is to him you would go, because he feels for you, I've known this for some time, then I will do exactly as I say. I swear to you, Riah, on your God, I will do exactly as I say . . .'

She didn't know how she reached the kitchen and when she got there she didn't know for how long she sat staring into the fire, nor how many times her mind had repeated, Yes, he would, he'd do it. She could still see the look in his eyes as she'd backed from him and fled from the room.

What kind of a man was he anyway? She didn't see him as an ordinary human being, but part pitiable creature, someone who needed comfort, mothering, loving, and part devil, cold calculating. The opposing natures couldn't fit any other person she had met in her life before. They were two extremes, but they fitted him all right. And so she was stuck here. No Tol, no security . . . no love, no easing of the want in her that could go on for years. She had lost her son. Yes, she knew she had lost him as sure as . . . as if he had been transported, because each time they had met since that fateful day he seemed to be more distant. And the night before he had gone to take up his new post he had said to her, 'You're not gona stay with him, are you, Ma?' And she had said, 'No. As soon as he can walk I'm coming down here to Tol's.' Then not knowing how to put her next words to him, she had begun, 'There's . . . there's something that you must . . . well, you must do, you must be careful of . . . you mustn't ever give a hint that . . . well, the master . . . you know what I mean, that the master liked you, because if you did people would put two and two together and come up with the wrong thing. And . . . and if his name was smirched he'd likely . . . well – ' She did not know what made her say the next words, but she said them, 'he'd likely turn on you, just to protect himself and his name and you could be up before the justice.'

Davey had hung his head as he muttered, 'I know, Ma. I known. And there's another thing. I'm sorry I did it. But he wanted to fondle me like. I don't suppose I'd've minded if I'd got the pony, but I was so disappointed. And anyway, I thought he was drunk . . .'

She had stared at him in amazement as her mind repeated his words, I don't suppose I'd've minded if I'd got the pony. She hadn't heard wrong, that's what he had said; in plain words he would have accepted his master's attitude towards him, as long as he gave him what he wanted. It came to her that she didn't know what went on in her son's head, but she refused to dwell on it, except to allow herself to think, He doesn't know what he's saying.

She was brought out of her reverie by the far door in the kitchen opening, and Biddy came running towards her, crying, 'Master's on the floor in the drawing-room an' he can't get up. I was passing and I peeped in the door. He . . . he was thumping the floor with his fist.'

Riah had risen to her feet, and now she turned her head away from her daughter's penetrating stare, closed her eyes tightly for a moment, then hurried up the room, across the hall and into the drawing-room, but once inside the door she paused a moment and looked to where Percival was thrusting out his good arm in an effort to reach the end of the couch, but when his hand slid down its silk-padded side she saw his head bow almost to his knees.

It was when Biddy's voice, almost in a whimper came from behind her, saying, 'Aren't you going to help him, Ma?' that she spun round and, gripping her by the shoulders, thrust her out of the room, then banged the door behind her without saying a word.

Slowly now she went forward and stood by his side, and as if she was chastising an errant child, she said, 'What's all this, then? Making a big effort?'

He looked up at her and said, 'Just that. But on this occasion I don't want your help, I can manage.'

She made no reply to this but, bending down, she cupped her hand under his good arm and in no gentle fashion she hauled him upwards, and when he toppled and fell against her, she was forced to put her arm around him and guide him, hopping, on to the couch, where he sat for a moment, his body sagged, a picture of utter dejection. But when he straightened himself up and laid his head back, his voice did not represent the picture given off by his body because his tone was curt now as he said, 'Sit down, Riah.'

'I have no time for sittin', sir.'

'Well, stand if you will, but the situation must be made plain. Whether you like it or not, and apparently you don't, you are to continue looking after me and this house, and when later on I gain my full strength and I'm able to hobble, I shall take up the tuition of the children . . . Don't say it, woman.' He thrust out his hand, his fingers spread wide. 'Again whether you like it or not, your children will be given an education not only for their own good, but to give me some kind of an aim, to help me go on living for the time that I might have left to me. And you will consider this in part payment for your services for, from now on, if my finances remain as they are, there will have to be, what is called, a tightening of belts all round. There may be times when you may not get your wage, this will be the quarter day when I decide to indulge my other weakness which, by the way, I am missing sorely at the present moment. Well, having made this statement, I want to say this.' He paused here and, his tone changing, he went on, 'If we have to share this roof, Riah, don't show me your enmity as you have done these past days. You're such a kindly person at heart. I have longed for a sympathetic word from you. Do you know that? Well, you might never find it in your heart to give me one, but at least let us be civil to each other.'

Riah now sat down on the end of the large wing-chair that was set at right angles to the couch, and she brought her fingers tightly across her mouth to stop the flow of tears that threatened to engulf her, and after a moment she said, 'How can you act like this one minute, sir, while just a while ago you threatened to send my boy before the justices, knowing full well the consequences of that?'

'I cannot expect you to understand the complexities of human nature . . . my human nature, Riah, but I would only go to those lengths if you deserted me, because then I would have nothing, nothing at all. You came into my life, as I've said, under protest; your children were thrust upon me; but now they are here and you're here, I cannot bear to think of the days, and perhaps the years ahead, without your presence, and theirs. In fact, I know that I couldn't face the future as I lived it before you came. I might as well tell you, more than once I have questioned my feelings for you. It isn't only the comfort you have brought me, the change you have made in the house; it isn't only that you have revived my interest in teaching; it is something that, even I who have always prided myself on being able to explain anything away through my reasoning cannot do so in your case.'

When the silence fell between them and she found she could not break it, not even by rising from the chair, she was grateful when his voice came at her as a mutter now, 'Would you like to make me a cup of tea, Riah? Please. Very strong.'

She rose and as she went to pass him he put out his hand and caught hers. The contact made her want to jerk her flesh from his, but she left it within his weak grasp, and she was forced to look down on his face as he said, again in the kindly helpless way she had come to know so well, 'I was going to bring you a present of some coffee back that day. I thought I'd give you a treat. Now I have to ask you if we have enough tea to even last the month out?'

While drawing her hand from his now she said, 'It'll do.'

As she walked down the room she found that her legs were shaking, and so, after closing the drawing-room door behind her, she did not walk across the hall but she stood to the side and leant her back against the panelling, and muttered, 'Dear, dear God. What's going to be the end of it?'

She didn't see Tol for three days. He hadn't called in when he left the milk in the yard in the morning, and so she guessed that his sister had returned. Of course, he hadn't expected her to stay away as long as she had done, but he'd had word from his elder sister through the stage coachman and she had wanted to know if he would mind if Annie stayed with her for a while. He had smiled broadly as he said, 'I penned a note back, printed like you showed me. It took me some time but I did it and said, no, she could stay as long as she liked.'

That was a week ago.

It was Tol, too, who had told her about the girls in the village who were looking for a place in service, and she did not ask herself why he was concerning himself with her affairs, for she knew he was trying to pave the way for her leaving when the time was ripe.

Well, the time was ripe, but there'd be no harvest of it; yet she still asked herself why he hadn't put in an appearance . . .

Then there he was, striding across the yard, Johnny hanging on one hand and Maggie on the other. As he came through the kitchen door he pushed them off, saying 'Shoo!' And they ran back into the yard, imitating the cackle of chickens.

'Hello, there,' he said.

'Hello, Tol . . . You all right?'

'Couldn't be better.'

She looked into his face and saw that he was very pleased with himself and she smiled slowly and said, 'Something good happened?'

'I'll say. Look. From our Mary. She must have got someone to pen it.'

He now pulled from his pocket the crumpled envelope and, taking out a single sheet of paper, he handed it to her, and she read the few scrawling words,

Dear Tol,

I hope you don't mind but Annie wants to stay with me for a time. She is company and has taken to the town life and is very cheerful for me. I hope you don't mind.

Your loving sister,

Mary.

She raised her eyes to his and he said, 'Our Annie cheerful for anybody. Can you believe it? And she's taken to the town life. I'd like to bet she's got some fellow in her eye. She was disappointed in love, you know; that's what made her bitter. Well, well.' His smile widened and, catching hold of her hands, he said, 'The road's clear, Riah. You see, the road's clear.'

'Sit down, Tol.' He still held her hand as he said, 'What's the matter? Something more happened?'

She tugged her hands from his and said again, 'Sit down, Tol.' And when he sat down she went round the table and sat opposite him; then looking straight into his face, she said, 'I . . . I know what you want to say, Tol. But it can't be.'

'What do you mean, it can't be? You know how I feel about you, and . . . and I think I know how you feel about me. Am I right?'

She bowed her head, then said, 'Aye, yes, you're right. But still' – her head jerked up again – 'it can't be.'

'Why? What's to stop us?' He turned his face now towards the end of the room and said, 'It'll be all right, Riah. Either of those lasses from the village will be glad to come for a couple of bob a week. He could have them both for what he's paying you. And you could slip back and see they didn't shirk.'

'Tol – ' Her voice was little above a whisper now as she went on, 'I can't leave here. I can't leave him. For as long as he's here, I'll have to stay.'

When his chair had scraped back on the stone floor she looked up at him. He was standing now, bending across the table towards her, asking, 'What is it? What's happened? He can't hold you. He's got nothin' on you.'

'Oh, yes he has, Tol. He's got Davey on me. He threatened, and he means every word of it, that if I leave him he'll take the matter to the justices. He's got proof of attack, hasn't he?'

'No. No.' Tol's voice was high now. 'He told me he had been swinging the scythe himself.'

'Was the doctor there when he told you?'

'No.'

'Then it's only his word against yours, like it is against Davey's. And what chance has either of you against, as he himself said, a gentleman who is known to be a schol . . . astic re . . . cluse.' She stumbled over the words, then repeated them, 'Scholastic recluse, and whose family was highly thought of in these parts.'

'Highly thought of, be damned! His mother had religion on the brain, and his father . . . From what Fanny's old man says, they hardly spoke to each other in years, him at one side of the house, her at t'other. His side was where you and the bairns are now. They were odd, the lot of them. There's other things that people remember an' all about them, when they lived up in The Heights.'

Her face stretched now as she said, 'They lived up in The Heights? His family?'

'Yes, yes. This was just a sort of cottage at one time, a kind of dower-house. Of course it's some years back, near a hundred I should say, but nevertheless that's where they came from. And all the land around here was theirs, at least until they sold out to the Gullmingtons round sixty years ago.'

'That seems to make it worse.'

'How do you make that out?'

'Well, he is gentry. No matter how queer his family have been, he's gentry. And what chance would my word, or my lad's, or even yours, have against him?'

Tol gripped the edge of the table with his fists and ground his teeth together for a moment before he said, 'Aye, you're right in a way, but there's one thing, they'll want to know why he's kept quiet so long.'

'Oh' – she jerked her chin – 'he'll get over that, he could say that he was suffering from shock or some such, his memory had gone. Oh, he could say anything and he'd be believed.'

He narrowed his eyes at her now and, his voice thick, he said, 'And you're willin' to let it go at that and stay on here? . . . Riah – ' He leant across to grip her hand, but she moved away shaking her head, and now he barked. 'Woman! I want to marry you. I've waited long enough. I don't know how I've managed. You're ready for it as much as meself. Don't let's beat about the bush, we're both grown-up beings and we want each other. Riah.' His voice sank now. 'God! woman, you know how I feel. And it isn't only that, it's . . . I like the bairns, and we could be happy in the cottage. I'd build you on a kitchen. And the roof space would take a bed for the lasses. Riah, I've got it all worked out.'

'Tol!' The tone in which she said his name carried such finality that he straightened up and stood with his eyes closed for a minute while his head bowed towards his chest; and after a pause, she went on, 'He knows about us, and he's not for it.'

'Not for it be damned!' He was rearing upwards now, his face red, his whole attitude showing such anger as she had never imagined him capable of. His name she had imagined at first had stood for tolerance; but she learnt it wasn't short for anything, he had been christened after his father and he had been a Tol, as his father before him, and both men had tended the toll gates, and their christian name had become lost in their craft.

'I'll go in to him.'

She sprang round the table, her arms spread wide blocking his way up the room, and she cried at him, 'No! no! It would be useless, and I can't stand much more.'

The raw anger was still in his face as he ground out now, 'Neither can I, Riah. And if this is your last word and you're givin' in to him, then hear mine. I'm not gona wait for you until he pegs out or softens. I'm a man and I have me needs, an' I need you, but if I can't get you, then I'll have to find somebody to take your place. *Do you understand me?*'

She swallowed deeply in her throat before she said, 'Yes, Tol, I understand you, and I wish you luck in your choice. Perhaps it's for the best after all, because although, as you said, my need might be as great as yours, I'd want to be picked for something else besides. Good night to you, Tol.'

She watched his Adam's apple jerk up and down, and then his

mouth open and close a number of times as if ramming back the words that were bent on spewing out, before he turned from her and marched out of the room.

After a moment she herself moved. She went slowly through the passage, and into the east wing, across the small hall and up the stairs and along the corridor into her own room. Still with the same slow steps she crossed to the wardrobe and, opening the door, she took down the black velvet gown and, gripping the front by the shoulders, she wrenched her arms apart, so ripping the garment down to the waist. Then gripping the pleated band, she again flung her arms wide. But her efforts now did not succeed in splitting the skirt, and so, flinging the gown to the floor, she stood on one side of it and, bending down, she wrenched at the material until of a sudden the buckram waistband gave way and with a soft swishing sound the front of the skirt split down to its hem. Not satisfied with this, she followed the same procedure with the back of the gown: first the bodice, then the skirt. When she was finished the sweat was running freely down her face, but there was no water coming from her eyes. This done, she kicked the torn remnants into a bundle and, stooping, she gathered them up, and retraced her steps, but quickly now, back to the kitchen.

Biddy was in the room and she gaped at her mother making towards the fire, saying, 'What you doing, Ma? What you doing?'

Riah didn't answer her for a moment but she took the poker and pushed the red cinders to one side, then she flung the first piece of the gown on to the blazing embers. That done, she turned and looked at her daughter, saying now, 'You ask what I'm doing, Biddy? I'm burnin' me folly. Remember that. Keep this picture in your mind until you're grown up and remember that your mother one night burned pieces of a velvet gown in the kitchen fire.'

'Oh, Ma. Ma.' The tears sprang from the child's eyes and she muttered, 'That was the gown the master gave you, and . . . and you said you'd put it on sometime and let me see you. Ma, what's the matter with you?'

Not until the last piece of velvet was on the fire and the room was filling with smoke and the smell of the burning material was making them sneeze did Riah answer her daughter's question; and then, as if it had just been asked of her, she replied, 'I'm coming to me senses, lass. I'm coming to me senses.' . . .

Later that night when she took the tray of soup into her master, he said, 'I smelt burning, Riah.' And she answered briefly, 'You would.'

He looked at her slightly perplexed and asked quietly, 'What were you burning?' And she said, 'Just your mother's gown.'

She looked at him long enough to see his expression change from surprise to pain, and she was going out of the door when she heard him murmur, 'Oh, Riah. Riah.' And the sadness with which he uttered her name sounded like the cry of a night bird that she often heard coming from the wood. It held a lost sound. The bird's cry had always affected her, sometimes causing her to get out of bed and close the window, for there were some sounds that carried messages that the understanding couldn't grasp.

PART TWO

The Time Between

1

London, February 7th, O.S. 1749

Dear Boy,

You are now come to an age capable of reflection, and I hope you will do, what however few people at your age do, exert it, for your own sake, in the search of truth and sound knowledge. I will confess (for I am not unwilling to discover my secrets to you) that it is not many years since I have presumed to reflect for myself. Till sixteen or seventeen I had no reflection; and for many years after that, I made no use of what I had. I adopted the notions of the books I read, or the company I kept, without examining whether they are just or not; and I rather chose to run the risk of easy error, than to take time and trouble of investigating truth. Thus, partly from laziness, partly from dissipation, and partly from the *mauvaise honte* of rejecting fashionable notions, I was (as I since found) hurried away by prejudices, instead of being guided by reason; and quietly cherished error, instead of seeking for truth. But since I have taken the trouble of reasoning for myself, and have had the courage to own that I do so, you cannot imagine how much my notions of things are altered, and in how different a light I now see them, from that in which I formally viewed them through the deceitful medium of prejudice or authority. Nay, I may possibly still retain many errors, which, from long habit, have perhaps grown into real opinions; for it is very difficult to distinguish habits, early acquired and long entertained, from the result of our reason and reflection.

My first prejudice (for I do not mention the prejudices of boys and women, such as hobgoblins, ghosts, dreams, spilling salt, et cetera) was my classical enthusiasm, which I received from the books I read, and the masters who explained them to me. I was convinced there had been no common sense nor common honesty in the world for these last fifteen hundred years; but that they were totally extinguished with the ancient Greek and Roman governments. Homer and Virgil could have no faults, because they were ancient; Milton and Tasso could have no merit, because they were modern. And I could almost have said, with regard to the ancients, what Cicero, very absurdly and unbecomingly for a philosopher, says with regard to Plato, *Cum quo errare malim quam cum aliis recte sentire.*

The ruler slapped the table. The man with the lined face and white hair hanging over his ears leant towards the tall young girl sitting to his right hand side and slowly he said, 'At last! That's better. But your French accent remains atrocious, Biddy.' And he deviated again. 'You have learned that often "a" is pronounced "ah" when you're speaking in your own tongue, even if your brother hasn't.' He looked now to where twelve-year-old Johnny was staring at him wide-eyed. 'Both he and Maggie' – his eyes now turned on to the eleven-year-old girl whose green eyes were laughing at him – 'who will still say bass . . . kit to the end of her days. Well, there might be an excuse for them, but there is none for you.' He had again turned his attention to Biddy, and she, looking at him calmly, said, 'I can speak it as good as many of the young ladies about, I bet.'

'Say that again.'

'What?'

Now his voice rose and he cried at her, 'Say that again.'

'I can speak it as *good* as many of the young ladies about, I bet. Oh' – she lifted her head – 'I can speak it as *well* as any of the young ladies . . .' She was stopped from continuing by his finger pointing at her as he cried, 'You can omit the last two words. Sometimes I think I am wasting my time with you and that I have been wasting it over the past years.'

'Yes, sometimes I think you have, and, as you say, still are.'

'Miss, have I to remind you again about forgetting yourself?'

'Well, you will keep on.'

She smiled a small secret smile as she watched him close his eyes and bow his head, and she knew him well enough to know that he wasn't vexed with her but was really amused at the exchange. Words from the colloquial part of her mind would daily fight with the world of words her master would insist on instilling into her, and he enjoyed a see-saw with her. And she enjoyed it too. The two hours had grown into three, and she looked forward to them; as she also did to her homework at night, although she knew that this annoyed her mother who would have her sewing and patching or mat-making.

She particularly liked the present phase in her learning. She felt pride in herself that she had reached a good way into the second volume of *Lord Chesterfield's Letters To His Son*, because what that man said was sensible, although it had taken quite some time to get used to the print because all the "s"s looked like "f"s; and she knew she had learned more through reading these letters than she had done through Voltaire, although she liked Voltaire. But he seemed a bit airy-fairy. This man Chesterfield was more down to earth. Still, she knew she didn't hold with lots of things he said for he thought women never grew up, not really, they were always children at heart, just made to prattle, they couldn't reason or be sensible. Well, she didn't agree with that, but she had to admit he was right in lots of other things. And he was funny at times, especially the bit he wrote to his son about picking his nose. She had laughed about that.

She used to read bits out to her ma at night, but not so much of late, for, for no reason whatever, her ma would stop her in the middle of a letter and say, 'That's enough.' And only last week her ma had said to her, 'I think you're getting beyond yourself with this learning.'

She had looked puzzled and said, 'Why! Ma, I thought you liked me learning.' But her ma had come back at her, saying, 'What'll be the end of it? It'll just divide you from the other two, and me an' all.'

'Oh, Ma, don't be silly,' she had said; 'as if anything could do that. It's only a kind of game, Ma, me learning. I find it easy, and . . . and I like it, I mean reading and such.'

'You speak differently already.'

'Oh, no, I don't, Ma,' she had protested loudly.

'Yes, you do,' her mother said. 'You mightn't notice it but I do.'

She didn't mean to speak differently, but he – her eyes flicked towards him – was always on about her sounding her 'g's at the end of words and turning her 'a's into 'ah's when speaking and opening her mouth instead of speaking all words through the front of her mouth.

'Pay attention, you're dreaming again. Continue.'

She took up the book and went on.

> 'Whereas now, without any extraordinary effort of genius, I have discovered, that nature was the same three thousand years ago, as it is at present; that men were but men then as well as now; that modes and customs vary often, but that human nature is always the same. And I can no more suppose, that men were better, braver or wiser, fifteen hundred or two thousand years ago, than I can suppose that the animals or vegetables were better then, than they are now. I dare to assert too, in defiance of the favourers of the ancients, that Homer's Hero, Achilles, was both a brute and a scoundrel, and consequently an improper character for the Hero of an Epic Poem; he had so little regard for his country, that he would not act in defence of it, because he had quarrelled with Agamemnon . . .'

She stopped here and half rose from her chair and, looking towards her master, she said, 'What is it? Have you got that pain again, sir?'

Percival was sitting back in the chair now, his eyes closed, one forearm held tightly under his ribs, and without speaking he turned his head and nodded towards the shelf of the large breakfront bookcase that stood against one wall and on which was a small opaque-coloured glass bottle. As she grabbed it up, she called to Maggie, 'Run into the drawing-room and bring the carafe.' Then looking at Johnny who was standing by the table now, she added quietly, 'Go and tell Ma.'

A minute or so later when Riah entered the room, she saw that Biddy was holding the glass of water to his mouth, and she went quickly up to her and said, 'How many did you give him?'

'Just one, Ma.'

'Give me the bottle here.'

Biddy handed her the bottle and Riah shook out another pill and put it to his blue lips, and after he had swallowed it she spoke without looking at Biddy again, saying, 'Go and turn the bed down and bring a hot shelf from the oven, and take them with you.'

After a moment when the pain eased, Percival opened his eyes and looked up at her and, a half-smile on his lips, he muttered, 'That was short and anything but sweet. Could I lie down, do you think?'

'Yes, come along.' She helped him up from his chair and from the room and into the drawing-room where he had been sleeping for the past four years because Doctor Pritchard had done such a good job on his leg that he had little movement from the hip; nor could he straighten out his left arm, and the flexibility of his fingers in that hand had become restricted.

Like a wife who might be attending to her husband, she helped him off with his outer things, but when it came to his small clothes, she slipped his nightshirt over his head and, like a modest and virtuous woman might have done, he drew his short clothes down from his legs under the cover of the gown. Then sitting on the edge of the bed, he eased himself into it. When he lay back on the pillows he closed his eyes for a moment before saying, 'It would happen today when I have callers coming.'

It was the day when the clerk to his solicitors brought his allowance, which had fortunately resumed its previous standard two years ago and so enabled him to have his little luxury of wine and tobacco and she to have more provisions for the table.

The clerk was a talkative man and from him she had learned that the master's allowance would die with him and go into a religious trust. This was a stipulation his mother had made in her will, but she had been unable to do anything about the house because that had been the property of his father and was without mortgage for neither Mr Miller nor his father had been allowed to raise a mortgage on it, a stipulation made by Mr Percival's grandfather. And the clerk had informed her further that even if it had been open to mortgage Mr Percival would have been no better off, worse in fact; for his father would undoubtedly have mortgaged the place up to the hilt, and the interest would have had to be found.

For relatives, she understood, he had two cousins: one lived in Somerset, and the other was in America. The one abroad was a man in his seventies and the one in England was a spinster lady of uncertain age. That was how the clerk had put it.

When Riah tried to think back over the past four years her memory became blurred. Everything was clear up till then, she could have practically told herself every thought that had been in her head, even to the night when Tol had gone from the kitchen and out of her life and she had burnt the black velvet gown. But from then, for months ahead, the vision of her days was blurred.

She couldn't recall when her attitude towards her master had softened and they had begun to talk, she in monosyllables at first, just listening to him; then glimpsing faintly an understanding of this odd man. Nor could she tell the exact time when pity took over. They said that pity was akin to love, but her pity hadn't reached that stage and never would, but it had picked up a deep kindliness towards him and concern for him. And so life, on the surface, went forward on an even keel, except that there was another current flowing rapidly in the depths below, and over the years it had aimed to wash Tol out of her mind, but without complete success.

It was only six months after their parting that she heard he was to be married to a girl from the village, and she twelve years younger than him. She was one of the two that he had suggested should take up a position in this house. Yet the marriage didn't come off. What happened, she didn't know. It wasn't because of Annie. She hadn't returned, having surprised everybody, even her sister Mary, by getting herself married, and to a man with his own business, that of a pork butcher. She had certainly gone up in the world. Tol had gone to the wedding. All this she had gathered from Fanny whom she saw at rare intervals. But she had never as much clapped eyes on Tol for over two years now, for he had stopped leaving the milk, having one morning told Johnny that in future he must go and collect it from the farm. The farm lay almost two miles away and so she arranged that the boy go only every other day. But in the real bad weather she went herself and was glad of the walk and also to exchange a word with Mrs Pratt, the farmer's wife.

There had been times of late when she hungered for company. She had the children . . . and him, but there was a great gulf between the talk that she exchanged with the children and that which she exchanged with him; it was something in the middle that she was missing, and she knew what it was, the conversation that would flow between her and an ordinary man or woman.

She felt vexed at times that she couldn't talk with Biddy as with somebody ordinary. Biddy was her daughter and fast growing into a young woman. She was fourteen, coming up fifteen, but was developing quickly and was tall for her age. She was thin but she was strong with it. But Biddy's conversation always tended towards things that she was learning and the repeating of things he had said. She had been thinking more and more of late that this standard of education wasn't a good thing for her daughter, in fact, she had become worried over it. Here was the girl spending the main part of her days now outside digging, weeding, and planting, because since Davey had left the work had been too much for Johnny, and she had trained Maggie into the housework, and so Biddy had taken over the garden. But that wasn't as spruce as it should be. Well, it couldn't be, could it, with him taking up three hours of her time in the morning, and also that of the younger ones. And it was in the morning that you got the best work out of people, because as the day waned so did her strength and inclination. She knew it from how she felt herself.

When he had lengthened the two hours of tutoring to three, she had pointed this out to him, and he had laughed at her, saying, 'You're quite right. But what applies to the body applies to the mind also.' And on that day he had said to her, 'I have often wondered why I was born at all; yet lately I seem to have had the answer. I was sent to bring enlightenment to the daughter of one Riah Millican. Yet at the same time I ask, why had she to be born a daughter? For what will she be able to do with a brain like hers. Yet she might suddenly up and blossom into some great personage.'

And to this she had replied, 'Oh, don't talk nonsense.' Such was the feeling between them that she could say that to him without him taking offence as he would have done before the change had come about.

She did not think it strange that he never mentioned Davey's name to her. His going from the house was like a death that neither of them wanted to recall. But she did recall that if she had cried at all during those first months after the accident, it was for loss of her son.

Davey had a half-day's leave once a fortnight. It began on a Sunday at two o'clock and ended at seven in the summer and lasted from twelve to five in the winter. And on his first two leaves she had gone to Tol's to see him; but under the changed circumstances she couldn't go there again. Then when she could bear his loss no more, she sent Biddy down to tell him to come up through the back way and she would meet him on the west side of the house.

At the first meeting she had put her arms around her son and held him close, and he had laid his head on her breast and clung to her. But it hadn't happened after that; in fact, they barely touched hands. If the weather was fine they walked in the fields. If it was raining or storming they went into the small barn at the end of the courtyard; and there Biddy would bring them a pot of tea and some scones.

At first it was only when she mentioned his work did his face ever show any sign of liveliness. There were eight hunters and four hacks in the stables and five dogs running around. He spoke with awe of Mr Mottram who was the coachman and Mr Lowther who was the groom, and the four stable boys under them, two apparently young men.

But as time went on his tongue loosened and he talked of the household. There were so many in it he couldn't begin to count them. When asked what the mistress was like he replied he had never seen her; and that was after he had been there ten months. He had seen the master and the young sirs and sometimes the daughters of the house when they went out riding, but their horses were seen to by the two older stable boys; the younger ones seemed to do nothing but muck out. Yet this was all her son appeared to want to do.

In the changed appearance of her family since the accident the change in her son was the most noticeable. He was nearing sixteen now and he was no longer slight but had thickened out; he had seemed to grow broader instead of taller; his hair was still silver fair, but his features had altered; his skin, from having a fine delicate softness about it, had reddened. But the most striking difference, in her eyes, was his features. He no longer appeared beautiful. Sometimes as she sat in the barn staring at him she thought she only imagined this yet she knew that it was no imagination, and at such times she was made to wonder what the master would think of the boy now for there was no resemblance between the one who had attacked him with a scythe and this thickset youth who was no longer beautiful. But she could find no name in her mind with which to describe how her soon looked, except perhaps, blunt. His cheeks seemed to have fattened out; his face had taken on a squareness. Perhaps this was how his grandfather, the Swede had looked. Perhaps all Swedes were beautiful when they were young. But he was still young, merely a boy. Yet no, his voice had broken and was that of a man. His talk, too, was that of the stable. Oh, if only . . . Again her mind was exchanging him with Biddy, because if he'd had her brain he would have been able to put it to some use, whereas, as far as she could make out, it was going to cripple her daughter.

'Sit down, Riah.'

It wasn't an unusual request. She pulled up a chair to the bedside and sat down, and he lay looking at her for a few moments before he said, 'I'll slip away one of these days. You know that, don't you? Like that.' He snapped his fingers. 'Here one minute, gone the next.'

'Don't talk silly.'

'And don't you talk silly.' His voice had an edge to it now. 'You know as well as I do what's going to happen, and I want to talk to you about it. What are you going to do when I'm gone?'

'What I did afore, take to the road and find another job.'

'How much money have you got saved?'

'Oh! Oh!'

He smiled weakly at her. 'You never spend anything. You haven't bought a new stitch for the children or yourself, except boots, in years now. In the main you've had your four shillings a week, apart from the time when it was reduced to two, so you must have a little pile.'

Yes, she had a little pile. She had save forty pounds of her wages; then added to that there had been the shilling a week for the first two years from Davey. He had brought the sums intact to her each half-year; but in the meantime she had given him tuppence on each of his Sunday visits. But in the third year his wage had gone up by another shilling a week and so his pocket money had risen fourpence. The fourth year it had remained the same, but next year he would get a sixpence rise. Altogether she had had thirteen pounds from him. In all she had over seventy pounds including the money that Seth had hidden in the fireplace. So she was well set. But he, lying there, didn't know anything about that first nest-egg, and so she said to him, 'I've around fifty pounds.'

'Fifty pounds. My! My! That's good. Well, Riah, I'm afraid that you're going to need it, because when I die your life is going to change somewhat.'

'I know that; and you needn't worry, I'm prepared.'

'You are?'

'Yes. So don't lie there frettin' about that.'

'I do fret about that. I fret about you. Do you believe me?'

She didn't answer and he said, 'There is a subject that has long been taboo between us, Riah, but I must bring it to the fore again, because I know my time is running out.'

'*Please.* Please, don't. There're two questions to be answered there, and I say no to both of them. You can live a long time yet if you take care and take your pills when you should, regular like. As for the other, it's buried.'

'It may be for you, Riah, but it's never been that way for me; so I have nobody to exhume. It is here with me all the time.'

She got to her feet, thrusting the chair back as she exclaimed, 'Now I told you.'

'Riah, sit down, please.'

Such was the note of pleading in his voice that after a moment's hesitation she sat down again. He remained lying still with his eyes closed as he said, 'I want to ask one last request of you; and it is a last request, I'll never ask anything of you again. I want to see David, just once more.'

'*No. No.*'

'Don't say it like that, Riah.' He still had his eyes closed, but now his fingers began to pick at the thread-worn silk of the padded eiderdown and he went on, 'I don't mean you to bring him here, not inside. I . . . I just want to glimpse him from the window.'

She bowed her head and rested her hand on the edge of the bed before she said, 'I've got to tell you, he . . . he doesn't look like he used to.'

'No?' He opened his eyes and turned his head towards her.

'No. He's changed.'

'In what way?'

'I . . . I can't explain it. Yes, I can. He's not . . . well, beautiful any more, not like he used to be as a boy. You would only be disappointed.'

'Never.'

'I say you would, because . . .'

When she didn't go on he said, 'Well?'

'Because I myself am disappointed.'

'In what way?'

'In different ways. He's changed. He's no longer the Davey that I knew, he's rougher.'

'Well, of course he would be, working with four stable hands: their minds must become like the backside of their horses, unpleasant.'

'He's not like that. He's not unpleasant, just . . . just different.'

'As you say, just different. Nevertheless, I would like you to arrange this one thing for me.'

'I . . . I can't.' She was on her feet again.

'Why? You see him on his leave days. You have your meeting in the stable.'

'How did you know that?' She paused. 'Our Biddy . . . she had no right. I'll . . .'

'You'll do nothing of the sort, Riah, unless you want to distress me, for Biddy, besides having a brain, has a heart. Oh, if I'd only more time to see the finished Biddy. I'm telling you this, Riah, Biddy has more understanding than you. She is but a girl, a child in years, but her mind is away, away above yours and all your class.'

Her lips trembled as she looked at this man. He could still be viciously hurtful, could this man. Her and all her class. It made her feel like scum, and she said so: 'You talk as if we were scum.'

'That wasn't my intention, but because your kind have been deprived of education your minds have not learned how to function, how to reason. Only when people can do this can they understand fully the pain that they are not suffering, the hardships that they are not enduring and the quirks of nature that, thankfully, they are not burdened with. People of lesser minds, through their ignorance, condemn. If your daughter ever condemns anybody it won't be through ignorance or superstition.' He lifted his head upwards now, saying, 'If I'm not mistaken, that's the front door bell. It will be my visitors.'

Hurriedly and gladly, she turned from him and when she opened the front door it was to admit three gentlemen: the usual clerk, and two other men. The third man was differently dressed and it was apparent from the start that he was also a superior of the other two, for there was a cutting edge to his voice as he said, 'I'm Mr Butler, of Butler and Morgan. Please announce me to your master.'

She took his hat and coat while the other two men divested themselves of theirs; then going to the drawing-room door, she opened it and without any announcement she allowed them in; then closed the door after them.

It had been usual for her, when admitting the clerk, to say, 'Mr Tate, sir, to see you.' But that man had, as she put it to herself, got her goat. What, she wondered when she went back to the kitchen, was this all about? He had no money to leave, nor anything else that she knew of: the house and furniture would be claimed by the cousins. She pictured the spinster lady storming into the house and finding fault with everything. As she set the tray for refreshments she thought to herself, I'll make it me business to go into the town next week and see what kind of jobs go on market day. It was no use her going to the parson to ask him if he knew of any such position that would fill her needs, because since the rift with Tol there had been no lift for the children to church on a Sunday, and in the winter they had often returned frozen and wet to the skin. And so she had dared to keep them away from church. And strangely, this stand of hers had pleased the master, but had, for a time, caused a rift between him and the parson, for he refused to use his authority to force her to send the children to church and Bible school in the afternoon whatever the weather.

The solicitor and his clerks did not stay long, not more than half an hour, and when in the hall they stood ready for departure Mr Butler looked at her through narrowed eyes and, shaking his head, he said, 'Dear, dear.' She did not know what to make of this; but then as he went out of the front door she thought she had the explanation when he turned to her and said, 'When it happens, send immediately for the doctor, and then he will get word to me.'

She watched them mount the shabby looking coach, and after they had disappeared down the drive she went indoors and stood looking towards the drawing-room. Was it really as bad as all that? She would put the question to the doctor when he next came . . .

The following day when Doctor Pritchard called, she did put the question to him as she was seeing him out of the front door. 'Is he in danger of going?' she asked. And looking at her straight in the face, he replied, 'Any minutes, and has been over the past two years. That being so, he could go on for another two, if you tend him as you're doing. Keep worry from him, and – who knows? – he might see you out.' He smiled, a brown-tooth smile.

She had never liked the doctor: his teeth were decayed, his cravat and coat were always snuff-matted, and at times he smelt strongly of spirits. And it was said that he wouldn't be paid in either pig meat or fowl by the common people; if they hadn't a sixpence they got short shrift.

It was a fortnight later on a Sunday afternoon. The October sun was thin; the air too was thin and sharp. There was no wind, a stillness everywhere. It was, as Biddy put it to herself, a real Sunday. Sundays she always considered were funny days: you hadn't to work on a Sunday; you hadn't to read anything but the Bible on a Sunday, although she did; you had to go to church on a Sunday, which she didn't; it was an extra kind of sin for a man to get drunk on a Sunday, yet, and this was an odd thing, it was no sin for couples to roll in the grass, or to cuddle and kiss behind the hedges on a Sunday. Funny that. She would have thought there would be more sinning in that than getting drunk, or reading other than the Bible.

The master had laughed when she voiced her opinion on this matter. She liked to make him laugh. She wished she could make him happy. He had never been happy since the accident, not really, and that was all through their Davey, because, as far as she understood it, the master wanted to act like a dad and make a fuss of him and he didn't like it. She had tried to talk about it to her ma, but her ma had shut her up quick. It was as if she had sworn or used bad words or something, the way she had gone for her that time.

She had never been fond of her brother, and with the years she had grown less fond. But the master had told her himself this morning that there was only one thing he wanted and that was to glimpse their Davey again. And he'd asked her help. She didn't know what she should do. Herself, she couldn't see any harm in it; but why he should want to see their Davey the Lord only knew.

She couldn't understand their mother's attitude towards the master, not really, because he was a kind man. He'd been kind to all of them. She should say he had. Look how he had taught them, particularly her. She couldn't imagine what she would have been like if he hadn't taken time to teach her . . . all empty inside, because her mind would have had nothing to work on, whereas now, she felt learned, and she considered she knew things that nobody else did. Not that she'd brag about them, but she felt sure there was not a girl in the village or in the city itself of her own age who could rattle off things like she did, so therefore she was very grateful to the master. And yes, she would, she would do as he asked. When her mother went to meet their Davey today, she would get the master through the kitchen and along the corridor and to the window at the far end that looked on to the stables and the little barn.

And so she told him.

'Thank you, Biddy,' he said. 'About what time does he arrive?'

'Round half-past two.'

He smiled wanly at her as he mimicked, 'Round half-past two.' He had stressed the round. And she answered his smile with a wider one as she, aiming to imitate his voice in return, said, 'About har . . . f-par . . . st two.'

'You're a good girl, Biddy. What a pity I shall not be here to see the flowering of you.'

'Oh, you could be here a long time, sir, if you took care.'

'What did I tell you about speaking the truth?'

Her lids fluttered and she looked downwards as she said, 'You've also pointed out that diplomacy is made up of white lies and that it's often kinder to use it.'

'Yes, yes indeed, that's true. Do you know something, Biddy?'

'No, sir.'

'I think that you will be the only one who will really miss me when I'm gone.'

'Oh, no,' she was quick to retort now; 'we'll all miss you, sir. We'll all miss you, me ma and all of us.'

'*Me ma.*' He shook his head; then smiling he said, 'I doubt, Biddy, whether *me ma* . . . will.'

'Oh, yes, she will, sir. She's always telling us not to worry you, and to do what we're told, and how lucky we are to have been taught by you.'

'She has?'

'Yes, she has.'

'Well, I am pleased to hear that. Yes, yes, indeed I am.' He paused for a long moment while looking at her; then he said, 'Has your mother talked to you about David and me?'

Her eyelids fluttered again and she said, 'No, no; not much.'

'Have you ever felt afraid of me, Biddy?'

Her eyes sprang wide and her voice registered a higher note as she answered, 'Afraid of you, sir? No, never. I couldn't imagine anybody being afraid of you . . . well, I mean, not when they got to know you.' Her smile was soft as she went on, 'I've never been afraid of you, not even when you used to bellow at me because of my 'a's and 's's and colloquial sayings.'

She felt happy when she saw his body shake slightly as if he was laughing inwardly, and she knew he was laughing when he said, 'Remember the day when you cheeked me because I was reprimanding you all for saying "us this and us that", and you stood up and said, "Well, usses is fed up to the teeth"?'

Her laughter filled the room: she screwed up her eyes and, her arms hugging her waist, she rocked herself for a moment, then said, 'Eeh! yes.' And he mocked her again, saying, '*Eeh! yes.* Well that's an improvement. At one time you would have said, Eeh! aye.'

She became silent, and he too, and they looked at each other; then on an impulse she bent towards him and, putting her hands round his shoulders, she kissed him on the cheek before turning and scampering from the room.

He lay motionless for a full minute; then slowly he turned his head on the pillow and for the first time since he had stood by his mother's grave did he allow tears to roll down his face.

It was with difficulty she had got him through the kitchen and into the passage. He seemed to have no strength in his legs, not even in his good one, and she put her arm round his waist and said, 'Lean on me. It isn't far now and I've put a chair there.'

The passage led into the small hall before going on again to the end of the house. It was narrow and they could hardly walk abreast. There was a small sitting-room went off it and she said, 'There's a couch in there. Wouldn't you like to lie down and I'll tell you when . . . ?'

'No, no. I'll go to the chair.' He nodded to where the chair was set sideways to the wall and opposite the end window, and when she had him seated he closed his eyes, and it seemed for a moment that he was unable to get his breath.

She looked at him in concern. His face had changed colour: it looked grey and seemed to accentuate the whiteness of the hair about his ears. She placed her hand on the back of his head where his hair was straggling over the collar of his dressing-gown and she thought, I'll clip that when I get him back to bed. It looks raggledy. I wonder me ma hasn't done it before now. And at the thought of her mother she felt a little tremor, not of fear, but of apprehension go through her. What if she should find out? Anyway, she'd have him back in the room and tucked up before she returned from setting Davey on his way again.

'They wouldn't have come, would they?' he said softly.

'No, no; the door's open; she usually closes it, me ma.'

'Then what happens?'

'Well' – she paused – 'after a bit she comes over and gets a tray of tea and things.'

'How long does he usually stay?'

'Oh, not very long. If the weather's fine, they dander . . . I mean they walk round the fields, but sometimes he doesn't stay long; that's when he wants to go into the town. But if it's like the day, chilly, he stays longer in the barn. Oh!' – she put her hand on his shoulder – 'here they come.'

He leant slightly forward, saying, 'Where?'

'Oh, you'll see them in a minute, they're coming through the passage. I wouldn't get too near the window in case me ma turns . . .'

He took no heed of this, but, his face almost touching the pane, he waited. Presently, there came into his view a tallish woman and a youth walking by her side. At the sight of him, he felt a stab of pain go through his heart, but it was not caused by the disease from which he was suffering, nor was it connected with the love he had once had, and still felt he had, for the boy David, but the figure he was looking at now was that of no boy. He could not imagine that that bulky form had ever been slim. True, the figure might be exaggerated by the corduroy jacket, but there was no covering except the cap to exaggerate the head which seemed to be so much larger than he remembered it.

The pair was half across the yard and as yet he had only seen the profile of the youth. Then the head was turned in the direction of the house, and now he saw the face in full view and the sight sharpened the pain in his breast, and his head made almost imperceivable movements as if keeping time to the monsyllables *no! no!* that his brain was repeating. As he gazed at this once beautiful boy, who had rapidly been enveloped by rough young manhood, disappearing into the barn he did not see Riah turn, as if drawn by some force, and look across the yard and directly to the window. But Biddy saw her and almost roughly she jerked her master back into his seat. Yet she wasn't greatly perturbed that her ma had espied them for she knew the master wasn't long for the top, and surely she wouldn't begrudge him this; although again, for the life of her, she told herself, she couldn't see what attraction Davey had ever held for a man like the master.

'Come on,' she said gently. 'Come on.'

When he didn't move, she bent towards him and looked in his face. His eyes were closed, and she shook his shoulder gently, saying, 'Master, come on. Come on; you've got to get back to bed or me ma'll be on us.' She put both her hands under his oxters now and helped him to rise; then slowly led him back to the kitchen. But there he had to sit down a moment to gain enough strength for the journey to the drawing-room.

It was five minutes later when she had him settled in the bed, and she put her fingers to his brow and stroked his hair back as she looked at his closed eyes, saying anxiously, 'You feeling worse?'

'No.' He opened his eyes and looked at her as he added, 'It would be impossible, Biddy, to feel worse.'

There was something in his look that pierced her. It went right down through her ribs into her stomach and seemed to twist her guts.

This was the description she gave herself when in after years she tried to describe the weird pain it caused in her. At the moment the pain was such that she had the desire to throw herself alongside him on the bed and cuddle him, stroke his white weary face and tell him that she loved him, and that no matter what had happened that day between him and Davey, although she didn't know the rights of it she didn't blame him because nothing he could do would be bad.

'Don't, don't, my dear Biddy,' he said. 'Please don't cry.' He put out his hand and gently brought his fingers over both her cheeks as he said, 'I am grateful to you for your tears, always remember that; and also, my dear Biddy, remember that love has as many facets as a bursting star. Will you remember that? Love has as many facets as a bursting star.'

She gulped audibly in her throat, then said, 'Yes, I'll remember that: love has as many facets as a bursting star.' Then in a practical way she said, 'Lie you still and I'll make you a pot of tea.'

When the breath caught in his throat his hand delayed her; then after a moment he said, 'Before you go, hand me my writing board and the ink.'

After she had placed the board across his knees and the ink on the side table, she hastily left the room, and in the hall she took up the bottom of her pinny and dried her eyes. She was still rubbing at her face when she entered the kitchen but she stopped dead inside the door for there was her mother about to lift the tray to take to the barn. But she too had stopped, and what she said was, 'By! madam, I'll deal with you later.' And on that she picked up the tray and went out . . .

It was about an hour and a half later when they met again, and whereas previously Biddy had known that her mother was mad at her for what she had done, she had imagined in the time between she would have cooled down a bit; but she saw now to her surprise that her mother was in a real temper. 'I could knock your head off your body this very minute. That's what I could do,' she said. 'You think you know everything, don't you, you with your learnin'?'

'Ma, he just wanted to see . . .'

'I know who he just wanted to see. And he shouldn't have seen him. You're an interfering little busybody.' Riah now gripped Biddy's shoulders and attempted to shake them, but Biddy, her face flushing red, dragged herself away from her mother's grip and yelled back at her, 'I wanted to show him a little kindness and a little gratitude, 'cos you don't. And he's dying and he's lonely, and all he wanted to do was to have a look at our Davey for the last time. But God knows why, because he's nothing to look at, he's nothing but a big gormless lout.'

The blow across her face sent her reeling. She stumbled backwards, lost her balance and fell, her head coming in contact with the end of the settle, and she lay huddled for a moment not knowing where she was, only that her mother's hands were on her, pulling her upwards, and that her voice was rattling in her ears but not with remorse, for she was saying, 'You've been asking for that for a long time; you're getting too big for your boots. And you say anything like that again about our Davey . . .'

It seemed that her brother's name cleared Biddy's head for, blinking rapidly against the sting of tears raining from her eyes and her breath coming in gasps, she once again pulled herself from her mother's hold and, going round to the other side of the table she leant on it and, as if in the last few moments she had grown up into a woman, she gazed at her mother before saying thickly, 'Don't . . . don't you ever hit me again, Ma, for doing nothing wrong, for if you do I'll . . . yes I will, I'll hit you back, because I'm not going to be treated like the others, like numskulls knocked about, so don't start that on me. You haven't up till now, so don't start. As for our Davey, I'll say it again, and you can do what you like, throw me out, but he is, he is a big lout, brainless. Always was and always will be. Your lovely son, you've always loved him better than any of us, and I've known it. Johnny or Maggie don't know it yet, but they soon will, 'cos you only live for the odd Sunday. There . . . there I'm telling you.'

Standing with her back to the fire, Riah wasn't aware of the heat fanning her hips, for she was feeling dead cold inside. This girl, this . . . What was she? She was no longer a girl, she had just upbraided her as a woman might. But this child, for she was still her child, was her daughter and when all was said and done she was very proud of her. And oh god, she was right, she hadn't loved her or any of them like she had loved her first-born. And she was right, too, about the change in her son. But he was not a lout. No, she wouldn't have that. He was not a lout. He could read and write and count; he was strong and healthy and holding down a good job, one he would rise in; he was no lout. She could put a future name to her son, he'd be a good working man, but she couldn't put a name to her daughter. Her eyes narrowed as she looked at her. One side of her face was scarlet, the other a deep creamy white. She was beautiful now, as Davey had been beautiful, but would she change too? Yet if she did, she would still have that mind of hers, that character that had made her take a stand and say what she had done. Was there any girl of fourteen alive who would dare to say she would strike her mother back if she raised her hand to her? What she should do now was go round that table and wipe the floor with her. That's what her own mother would have done to her. But then, she had never been like Biddy, and she doubted if her own mother would have attempted to flail her; with her tongue yes, but not with her hands. She turned from her and took up her usual stance when in despair; she leant her forearm on the high mantelpiece and dropped her head on to it.

The silence began to ring loudly in Biddy's ears as she stared at her mother through her misted eyes, and she was asking herself now how she had dared to say all that. She wasn't regretting what she had said about their Davey, oh no, but that she had dared to say she would hit her mother. What had come over her? Is this what learning did for you? If it was, did she wish she had never been taught anything? No, no. Her fist beat a silent tattoo on the table and again she said to herself, Oh no.

The silence was broken by Maggie coming running into the kitchen, crying, 'Ma! what do you think? There's been a coach hold-up.'

Slowly Riah turned from the fireplace and she stroked her throat twice with her finger and thumb before she said, 'Where did you hear that?'

'Sammy Piggott from the village. He was out walking with his big sister and they stopped me and Johnny and they told us; the highwayman took the ladies' necklaces and rings.'

When her mother made no comment on this, but walked to the cupboard and began to take plates down from the shelf, the girl looked at Biddy, saying brightly now, 'When I grow up I'm going to have a necklace. I'm going to save up and get one from the tinker. He has lovely necklaces. Would you like a necklace, Biddy?'

Biddy patted her sister's head twice, then turned about and went out of the room; and Maggie, going up to her mother, said, 'Ma, has out Biddy got the toothache? Her face is all red.' And Riah answered, 'Yes, yes, she has the toothache,' adding to herself, And I've got the heartache. One as painful as his. And I wish I could die of it an' all and be finished with all this.

2

Percival died six days later at eight o'clock on the Saturday morning.

'It's a strange time to die,' said Doctor Pritchard, 'eight o'clock on a Saturday morning. They usually go around three in the morning, for the body is low at that time; or on towards midnight. But eight o'clock is a very odd time.' He hadn't had anyone that he could remember dying at eight o'clock in the morning.

His attitude to the death shocked Riah. It was as if he were talking about an ordinary happening, like the coach arriving on time, or them being snowed up at Christmas.

Inside, she felt greatly upset, much more so than she had imagined she would be when he went. She had taken his breakfast in. She had made the porridge thin, almost like gruel, so it would slip down, as he hadn't been eating at all these last few days. But he hadn't touched any breakfast. With a weak wave of his hand he had pushed the tray away, directing that she put it on one side; and then he had pointed to the chair. After she had sat down by the bed he had said to her, 'It's going to be a fine day, Riah.' And she had answered, 'Yes, the air's nippy, but the sun's comin' up.' And then he had said, 'You'll have to make your mind up about something very shortly, Riah. I don't know how you'll do it. I . . . I know how I'd want you to do it, but then I am making no more requests.' She had looked at him blankly as she had said, 'I don't quite follow you.'

'No,' he had said, 'but you soon will. And yet I doubt if you'll understand me any more then, likely less. Yes, likely less.' And then his voice halting, he had said, 'Be kind to Biddy. She needs you, at . . . at least now. If you let her go she'll never come back. You . . . you made a mistake when you struck her.'

Her eyes had widened at this. He must have noticed the mark on Biddy's face, yet he had never spoken of it, at least not to her, and she wondered if Biddy had told him. But no, the girl was not like that, she wasn't one to beg sympathy, to create trouble.

He had then gasped for breath before he had managed to say, 'If things had been different, we would have been different, you and I, Riah. Anyway, that is in the past and something that could never have happened because we weren't different. Or perhaps we were different, I cannot make out at this stage. Anyway I am not going to say I am sorry that I have, in a way, chained you to me over these past years. You think you have missed out a lot not having had Tol. Well, there's a large question there. There's one thing certain: in your sacrifice you can feel a certain satisfaction that you have given your other three children a new start in life, for no one of them will lose out by what he has learned during these past years.' Then he had closed his eyes tightly before saying, 'I am very tired, Riah; the pain has been with me all night, not sharp, sort of damped down, just waiting to escape.'

'Will you take some more pills?' she had said.

'No, thank you, Riah. I am past pills now.' Then he had said, 'Can I see Biddy for a moment?'

'Yes, yes.' She had risen quickly and hurried from the room, but went no further from the hall, calling, 'Biddy! You, Biddy!'

When Biddy came running her mother had pointed towards the door and she went into the room and stood by the bed and there he had taken her hand and, looking at her, had smiled faintly as he said, 'I don't know where I'm going, Biddy, as I don't believe in Heaven or Hell, but my spirit must find a place somewhere. Wherever it goes,

I would ask the gods to let it watch over you, and to let me continue to indulge in the sin of pride in having stirred your mind to reason and awareness. Promise me something, Biddy, promise me that you will never stop reading; if it is only for five minutes a day you will read. It will prepare you. For what, I don't know. A governess perhaps or a mistress. Oh yes! you would make a delightful mistress, Biddy. However, learn . . . remember the lines of wisdom you were taught: you can only learn by recognizing your . . . ignorance.' As his voice trailed away she had done what she had done once before, she had bent over him and kissed him; and had then run choking from the room. And Riah had resumed her seat; and she too was unable to speak; and when, twenty minutes later, the chiming clock struck eight, he had given a little start. It was, she thought, as if he had jumped off a step, and then he lay still. She had bowed her head and wept as she hadn't done in many a long day, even as she thought, my God, he would have educated her up to nothing else but some man's mistress.

Strangely, the funeral was well attended. There was even a representative from The Heights. Mr Gullmington was away but his eldest son Stephen followed the hearse in his carriage. Also, the lady's maid had come, but she didn't follow the hearse, because women never did; but she had looked at him before he was screwed down; then she had left, and she hadn't spoken a word.

Several men from the village came too; and the solicitor and his clerks; and the doctor, and two strange gentlemen who had come all the way from Oxford and who had stayed overnight in Newcastle. One was a learned man with Professor to his name. They were both men in their sixties.

After the funeral she had laid some refreshments and ale in the kitchen for the pallbearers and the men from the village, and better class meats in the dining-room for the solicitor, the doctor, and the parson. Mr Stephen Gullmington had not returned to the house; neither had the two gentlemen from Oxford. There had been another man attended the funeral but had not returned to the house. This was Tol.

The doctor and the parson both stayed to hear the reading of the will. This was done in the library. Riah had expected the spinster cousin to arrive for the funeral, but the solicitor had told her the lady was indisposed and of such an age that it was impossible for her to travel. However, he had added, what remained was of no concern to her.

This had indicated to Riah that the property and household goods would therefore go to the cousin in America. Anyway, she would soon know, for here she was sitting facing the three men. The solicitor opened the parchment.

'This won't take long,' he said; then very slowly he began to read the formal opening as in all wills. Riah listened to his voice droning: 'I Percival Ringmore Miller of Moor House in the County of Durham do hereby . . .'

She felt tired. She wondered why she was sitting here. She wished he would get on with it because she had such a lot to do. Most of their things were packed yesterday and she had to go into Gateshead Fell first thing in the morning to see the farmer and his wife. The farmer had half promised her a cottage when he learned she had three lively workers, but it would all depend upon how his wife took to her. One part of her was thanking God they would have a place to go to, another was asking Him why He had to separate her from her son, and seemingly finally this time, for with the miles that would now be between them there was little hope of them seeing each other, except at rare intervals.

'I leave the freehold property of Moor House together with its three acres of land and all contents of the house in trust with my solicitor to Maria Millican until either (1) she remarries or (2) she dies. The property will then pass absolutely to Bridget Millican, the eldest daughter of Maria Millican. On relinquishing the trust through marriage Maria Millican must no longer reside in or on the property.'

Here the solicitor paused and glanced up at the stupefied face of Riah before going on:

'I am sorry I am unable to leave money with which to maintain the property, but Maria Millican, being an enterprising woman, will no doubt find a way to meet the small expense that it entails. Lastly, no mortgage may be taken out on the property during the continuation of the trust and while Maria Millican remains in residence there.

'Signed this day, the twenty-sixth of October,
eighteen hundred and thirty seven.
Percival Ringmore Miller.'

The three men now stared at Riah, but she had eyes only for the solicitor, and he, who was very rarely surprised by anything he experienced in the legal profession, was almost stunned when the fortunate woman sprang up from her chair and, glaring at him, cried, 'Even in death he would prevent me leaving here and marrying. It isn't fair.'

'Woman' – he himself was on his feet – 'don't you realize that you are the most fortunate of human beings at this moment. You have been left this splendid house which is not in any way encumbered, and the like of which, if you lived a thousand years, you in your position could never hope to own. But now you can enjoy it and its beautiful furniture and you grumble at the conditions your late master has laid down. Well, all I can say is, he must have had very good reasons for the provisions he made.'

'Yes, yes, indeed.' The parson was nodding at her; but the doctor said nothing, he only held his head on one side while he gazed at her, his lips pursed, and it was he now who spoke to her, saying, 'Did he prevent you from marrying before, Riah?'

'Yes, he did.'

'How? You are a free woman.'

'You don't understand.'

'No, I don't. Nor do these gentlemen either.' He looked first at the solicitor and then at the parson. 'We would like an explanation.'

Now she surprised them by barking at them, 'You can like all you can, but you won't get one, not from me. It was a private matter. And – ' she now poked her head towards the parson, sitting with a most shocked expression, as she cried, 'I wasn't his mistress . . . never!'

'I am very glad to hear it,' said the parson, now rising; and the doctor put in, 'And surprised.'

'Yes, I thought you would be.' She bounced her head furiously at him. She had never liked him.

'Don't you realize your good fortune, Mrs Millican?' the solicitor broke in, his voice quiet and serious. And it seemed that all the fight began to seep out of her, and she passed her lips tightly one over the other and licked round them with her tongue before she said, 'In a way it's surprising, sir, but the price I've got to pay for it is equally surprising.'

'Well, as I have learned, everything in life must be paid for. In one way or another it has its price, perhaps not immediately on the nail, but somewhere along life's road it exacts its toll. Now I must take my leave.' He turned to the doctor, saying, 'I'd like a word with you, and you, Parson.' And at that, they all walked out of the room after inclining their heads towards her. And there she was, left in this room which was lined from floor to ceiling with books. And as she slowly gazed around it, it dawned upon her that they were all hers now, all these books, everything in this room, everything in this house, and the two sections on both sides of it, and for the first time the enormity of the gift came as a shock to her and she flopped down on a chair and, her head bent, she asked herself why she had gone off the handle like that. It had been unseemly, to say the least. And in front of the doctor. She had no feeling for either the solicitor or the parson, but she disliked the doctor, because he sensed too much. She had always had the feeling he had his own ideas about the master's accident, especially after he had tried to quiz her about Davey's going to The Heights. It was as if he already knew the reason. Yet how could he because Davey had kept his mouth shut. She was sure of that; he had been too afraid of his own skin. Oh, why was she thinking like that about Davey? She was getting as bad as Biddy. *Biddy*. This place would be hers if she herself went into a marriage. But that would never happen because who would she marry? Tol? No, not Tol now. Yet, who knew, that might come about now that she was free. *Free*, did she say? She was more firmly tied than ever.

Why had he done it, making her pay for his own disability? It was vindictive. He need not have bothered to leave her anything and she could have walked out and made a life for herself. She supposed she could still do it. But if she did that, she knew that Biddy would stay behind. Oh yes, Biddy would stay in this house, simply because he had wished it. And yet how would she manage to keep it going? She would have much less chance than herself. Now that was a problem.

She stood up and walked slowly into the hall. She had things to think about. Of course she could live for a time on what she had saved, but it wouldn't last forever. The only way she could keep things going would be if the others went out to work: Biddy, and Maggie when she was a year or so older, and that together with what she got from Davey would enable her to manage. That would leave only Johnny here, but between them they could see to the place both inside and out, for there would be no nursing to do and no fancy meals to make.

Now she must go and tell the others . . . But not all. That bit about Biddy coming into the place if she herself should leave could wait because the girl had enough big ideas in her head, without imagining when she would one day be mistress of this house.

The children reacted joyfully to the news, Johnny and Maggie jabbering their delight; only Biddy remained silent, but the glow on her face told Riah she was not really overcome with the news, and was likely thinking what a splendid man the master had been. And this made her want to show him up in a different light. 'I haven't got this house without paying for it,' she said.

'Paying for it, Ma?' piped in Maggie. And she nodded towards her as she answered, 'Yes, my dear, paying for it. The price is that I haven't got to marry, ever, if I want to stay here and make a home for you.'

'Were you thinking about marrying, Ma?' The quiet question came from Biddy, and Riah almost barked at her, 'Yes, I was, my girl. Yes! I was.'

'But Tol's got a woman, Ma.'

Her young son was sitting next to her on the form as he spoke and she sprung up so quickly that it tipped, causing him almost to slide off the end of it, and she cried at him, 'Who said anything about Tol Briston? There are more fish in the sea than have ever been caught.'

She turned quickly from the table. What on earth was the matter with her? Why was she acting like this? She had never been like this with her children. Oh, if she only had a friend, someone she could go to. Some adult.

She thought of her family in Shields and shook her head. Oh, no, not them. Any anyway, if they knew of her good fortune they would be round like locusts thinking she had come into money, and seeing the size of this place, they wouldn't be past wanting to share it. Well, would that be a bad thing, because she was going to have a lonely life of it if she was left here solely with Johnny. She shook her head at herself. She would have to think of something, do something.

'Did he leave you any money, Ma?'

'Again it was Biddy speaking, and Riah turned on her and, more quietly now, she said, 'No, he had no money to leave; his allowance goes into some kind of charity. It's up to us, if we want to stay here, to work for the place, and so you, Biddy, and you, Maggie, when you're a bit older, will have to go into service of some sort.'

'Service, Ma?' Maggie screwed up her eyes at her mother. 'What can I do in service?'

'You can be trained like your brother Davey but in the pantries or kitchen in a big house, unless, of course, you'd like to go and work in the blacking factory or foundry and such.'

The girl was puzzled by her mother's tone and she drew her hand over her dark hair, saying, 'I wouldn't like to go into a blacking factory, Ma.'

'You'll go where you're sent.'

'What about me, Ma?'

She looked at Johnny, then said quietly, 'There's the garden to see to; I need a man here of some sort.' She forced a smile to her face to emphasize the compliment but, the boy's face sullen, he said, 'I'd rather go out, Ma.'

'You'll go where you're sent an' all, and do what you're told without any backchat. And that goes for you too.' And she inclined her head now towards Biddy who was looking up at her in a quietly penetrating way. And it was as if in this moment her daughter had become her enemy, whereas she should be finding her a comfort and able to talk to her because Biddy was sensible and older than her years. She knew she couldn't because there stood between them the man who had trained her to think and who, in the same way, had put a lock and chain on her own life. Whatever pity she'd had for him was now swamped under a feeling of resentment, that touched on her daughter too, and she thought, She's got to get into service, and soon, for as long as she's in the house, he's here, and I can't bear it. Books, books, books, I'd like to burn the lot. People are right, the gentry are right, the working class shouldn't be allowed to handle them, they're disturbers, trouble makers. Why had she to go and marry a man who could write his name? . . . It had all stemmed from that.

3

'Davey said they were wantin' a laundry hand up at the house and I told him to ask for a place for you, and he's done it.'

'*In a laundry, Ma?* But I don't know anything about laundries.'

'Well, you'll soon find out. You'll be trained.'

'I don't think I'll like that, Ma.'

'It isn't what you like, it's what you've got to do.'

'I don't think the master would have been pleased.'

'Shut up! girl.'

'I won't shut up, Ma. I don't want to go into a laundry. I could go to a nursery and teach children their letters and . . .'

'And who's gona take you on in a nursery around here, a girl of fifteen, no training behind her? What are you going to do? Go up to the lady of the house and say, Can I tutor your children, ma'am? Because I've been learnin' for the past five years. You should consider yourself damn lucky you've been kept at home this long. You've let that learnin' go to your head, girl, and the quicker you forget it the better.'

'I'll not forget it, Ma, and . . . and I'll make use of it. Yes, I will.'

'Tell me, where?'

'Ma.' Biddy's lips trembled and there were tears in her voice as she said, 'I don't want to go into a laundry, not up at the big house. I won't know what to do.'

'Riah's voice came soft now as she replied, 'It'll be all right. They'll show you. Everybody's got to start and it's the only post that's open, and you'll get a shilling a week for the first year and everything found, and it's a nice uniform, Davey said, and the same time off as him, and he'll be there to keep an eye on you.'

Now the atmosphere changed at lightning speed as Biddy cried, 'I don't want our Davey to keep an eye on me; he can't keep an eye on himself. Him! gormless.'

'*Now* girl, I'm warning you. You know what happened when you attacked your brother afore with your tongue.'

'Yes, I know, Ma. But don't let it happen again, 'cos I told you then, and I tell you now, don't let it happen again.'

'Oh, my God!' Riah turned away. 'To think it should have come to this, to be threatened by my own flesh and blood.'

'I'm not threatening you, Ma, I'm only telling you I won't be hit.

I can't stand being hit. It . . . it does something to me, I . . . I want to strike out. It was the same when we were playing and Davey used to punch me, I always punched him back. I . . . I can't stand being pushed about.'

'Well, let me tell you, girl' – Riah was facing her again – 'you'll be pushed about afore you get very far through this life. I'm warnin' you. Now get yourself upstairs and get your things together, for the morrow mornin' I'm taking you up to The Heights.'

'*The morrow, Ma?*'

'Yes, the morrow.'

As Riah marched out of the library Biddy put her fingers on her eyeballs and pressed them tightly, telling herself that she mustn't cry; she had been crying a lot since the master had gone. The next moment she looked about her quite wildly. His papers, all his writings, what would happen to them? Would her mother put them in the fire? It was just possible she would.

She had started sorting his papers from the drawers in the library a couple of days ago. He had been writing a history all about the philosophers. He had talked to her about it. The very last time, a few weeks before he died, he had told her about Rousseau, who wasn't for Voltaire and his philosophy, and how he had been a man who had the courage of his own convictions, although he was born poor, and lost his mother and father, and wasn't recognized in his own time, not until after he was dead, and then he was made into a great man whom others took a pattern from, both poets and philosophers. The master had said they would later start to read his book called *Confessions*, for it was very enlightening. She had been looking forward to this because she wondered if she was going to like the writings of a man who didn't like Voltaire; and she had spoken of this to the master but he had assured her and she remembered she had laughed at him. Why, she didn't know, for he had said nothing that could have evoked laughter. But it was like that: she often laughed at him for no reason, and he seemed to like it, not like Lord Chesterfield, who seemed dead set against laughter, describing it only as the outlet of fools.

She hadn't known he wrote poetry too.

'Eeh! If her mother came across some of his writings she would surely burn them, especially that one about their Davey. She would get that and keep it; perhaps she would take it away with her. Nobody would know. He must have written it that Sunday when she had brought him back to bed and he asked for his writing materials.

She had brought all his papers from the two bureaux in the drawing-room. The bed was no longer there and the room was much as it had been before it became a bedroom.

Kneeling down on the floor, she sorted among the papers she had arranged in piles until she came to the one she was looking for; then sitting back, her legs curled under her, she read it again.

So does the eye mislead the brain;
So does insanity its power gain;
So does the heart dictate the urge;
So does desire all reason purge;
So does man look upon his kind,
And with love drives out of mind his mind.
So did I see David as a boy
And today what four years did destroy,
And as my tears make a pool
I will by dying drown a fool.

She gulped in her throat; then moved her head from side to side before slowly folding the piece of paper and pushing it down the front of her print dress.

Hastily now, she gathered all the papers together until there were six piles, and having tied them up she pushed them well back into the bottom of the cupboard that ran under the bookshelves.

Next, she made a choice of four books which she meant to take with her. One was by Sir Richard Steele and Joseph Addison. They were all essays and very interesting. The master had been particularly fond of this book. The second was the first volume of *Lord Chesterfield's Letters To His Son*. The third was Voltaire's *Candide*. And the fourth book, seeming thought-years removed from the others, was *A Book Of Fables And Fairy Tales*.

She was about to leave the library with the four books held close to her breast when she stopped and looked back down along the room towards the table where she had sat, she felt, for as long as she could remember. And five years was a long time to remember.

She had promised herself one day to reckon up the hours she had spent in learning. If only they'd had another year together, she knew she would have become fluent with her Latin and French. Nevertheless, he had recently praised her progress. Oh, she missed him. Her eyes ranged about the room. Every part of it held his presence; yet he was gone; but where? He had said there was no Heaven or Hell and no Purgatory, the place where Catholics believed they were sent to before they were sorted out. Then where was he? He had once said to her that when you died you went back into a power, and if you could believe this then you would return again, be born again.

The day before he died he had said something very strange to her. She had thought about it last night in bed and it had frightened her a little. What he had said was, 'If you are ever faced with a great obstacle, or decision, Biddy, ask me what to do.' Well, how could she ask him if he was dead? It had made her feel creepy.

She looked towards his chair and whispered softly, 'Goodbye, Master, and thank you. Your work won't go to waste, it won't. I won't let it. No matter what happens, I won't let it.'

PART THREE

The Laundry

1

They started off from the house just as it was getting light. When she kissed Johnny and Maggie, Biddy had only just prevented herself from joining them in a bout of weeping.

She carried in her hand just a bundle of underclothes for she had been told that was all that would be necessary; but nevertheless the bundle was heavy, for in the middle of the garments she had placed the four books. Her mother had gone for her, crying at her, 'When do you think you'll have time to read that stuff?' And she had answered pertly, 'I suppose they'll let you breathe some time in the day.'

It was two miles to The Heights, that's if you took the byroads, it was much longer by the coach road. She had on her Sunday frock and her best hat, coat and boots. She looked, she told herself, as if she were going some place special; but where was she going? Into a laundry. She had no idea of the work it would entail, only that it would be hard and that it was the commonest employment a girl could be put to in a house of the gentry.

As they walked her mother talked spasmodically, telling her how she must behave; also, that everything at first would be very strange.

Biddy was paying little attention to the advice because she had a lump in her throat and all she wanted to do was cry. Most of the time she walked with her eyes cast down, partly in misery and partly to avoid the potholes over which there were thin films of ice for she knew that if she stepped into one and messed up her boots her mother would rave at her. She didn't know what had happened to her mother lately. She could remember the time when they had laughed together. But that time seemed far back now.

On the sound of cart wheels crunching on the rough road, she lifted her head and saw coming towards her a familiar horse and cart. Glancing at her mother, she knew that she had already seen its driver and his companion.

When they stood to the side of the road to let the cart pass Tol drew the horse to a standstill and, looking down at them, he said, 'Well, hello there. You're out early.'

As Riah answered briefly, 'Yes, yes, we are,' she looked past him to the young woman sitting at his side; but he made no effort to introduce his companion, only said, 'Where are you off to then?'

Biddy lowered her head as she heard her mother reply tartly, 'Well, I thought you would have known. News flies around here quicker than birds.'

There was a pause before Tol replied, 'Well, it appears I don't know everything, only that you've had a bit of luck, Riah. And I was glad to hear it, very glad.'

'Thank you.' Her tone was sharp.

'Well, what's this I don't know?'

'I'm taking her to your place, The Heights. She's startin' in the laundry.'

Biddy's head came up now at the sound of Tol's voice that was bordering on a bark as he cried, 'The laundry? She's startin' in the laundry? Biddy? No, you can't put her to that, Riah. And up there; it's slavery.'

'She's got to earn her livin' and she has to start somewhere, and it's the only vacancy.'

'Vacancy, be damned!' There was silence now before, his voice less sharp, he said, 'I can't understand you, Riah. Never could and never will. Gee-up! there.' He took his whip and flicked the horse, and this alone told Biddy that he was very angry.

They had walked some yards before Riah burst out, 'He should mind his own damned business. What is it to him where I put you.'

'He knows it isn't right, Ma.'

They both stopped and faced each other, and Biddy dared to go on, her voice breaking as she said, 'Only the scum go into laundries. I've heard you say that yourself.'

'That was outside laundries, washhouses. This is different. This is a family, where you'll be in uniform. And what does he know about it anyway? He didn't come after the master died, did he?'

So that was it. She still hankered after him. But he had his woman, and she looked nice. That had incensed her ma. Here her mind jumped off at a tangent as she thought, I'm thinking like the master, using words in me mind like incensed.

'Him preaching to me what I should do when his whoring is the talk of the place.'

Whoring. She had never heard her mother use that word before. It was a bad word. But the young woman hadn't looked bad, she had looked pleasant. She wondered why Tol didn't marry her. What did whoring really mean? She'd have to look that up. She should have brought the dictionary with her. Yes, that's the book she should have brought with her. She would get it next time when she got her leave.

The thought of leave brought her mind back to what lay before her and she tried to visualize not only the laundry, but the house and the people in it. She had no idea what to expect. Faintly she recalled the church service when gentry filed into their special seats that were set in a kind of gallery to the right of the pulpit. But they had been dim distant figures. She had seen the rows of servants who sat in the pews at the back, and one thing she remembered about them was that they were nearly all dressed alike. One of the village girls told her that her mother supplied the hot bricks for the gentry's feet, and that at one time they used to have a stove in the gallery, but the smoke from it made them cough, so now they only had hot bricks in velvet covers.

They had reached the main gates, and as if their coming had been announced the lodge-keeper Bert Johnson was throwing open the gates, and so Riah, going up to him, said, 'We are making for the house, we've got to meet the housekeeper at half-past nine.'

'Get out of the way! Go on! outside.' As he flung his arm wide they retreated hastily backwards. And now he cried at them, 'Get out of sight!'

'Out of sight? Why?'

'Why?' He now came towards them, his face thrust out. 'The coach is coming down the drive, that's why. It's the mistress. Move yourself!'

They backed into the main road and stood by the hedge, and presently there came through the gates a coach and pair. The coachman sat stiffly on his box. He wore a high hat, a dark brown overcoat, and he wielded a long whip.

As the carriage turned into the road both Riah and Biddy caught a glimpse of the brim of a hat at one window and the face of a young person at the other.

During the passing of the vehicle the lodge-keeper had stood as if to attention, and now, as he closed the gates, Riah approached him, saying, 'Well, is it all right for us to go through now?'

'No, it isn't. Not this way. Along there.' He thumbed in the direction from which they had come. 'There's a little gate; it leads around the outside of the grounds, take that. You'll come into the yard by it.'

So saying, he turned his back on them and went into the stonebuilt lodge that stood to the side of the drive.

Riah glared after him for a few seconds before she turned away, saying as she did so, 'Come on.'

They found the gate and started to walk between two high hedges, the path being wide enough to allow them to walk abreast; but it could not have taken a vehicle. It seemed to wind endlessly on and on. And then it rose steeply and they were brought to a halt by the sight of the house in the distance. A tree had been cut down here and part of the hedge taken away with it, and there, over a prim patchwork of lawns, beds, and paths bordered by hedges, Biddy first saw The Heights. It looked gigantic, like a whole street that had been lifted from a town, and not just one street, but three piled on top of one another. The early morning sun was warming its frontage which from this distance seemed to be hovering in the air. She made out a myriad of windows and the tops of two archways. She couldn't see the bays.

For a space they were both awed into silence; then simultaneously they walked on together, and the path, still going upwards, began to twist and turn as if it was straining away from the house. Then suddenly they walked out of the dim border of trees and into bright light, and there before them was a high stone wall and in the middle of it, a wooden door.

Having passed through this the whole aspect changed and for a moment Riah thought that she was back in the pit row, for there to the left of her was mound after mound of ashes, and the smell that assailed her nose told her that they were near a cesspool. They rounded a clump of bushes and there it was.

Their noses wrinkling, they crossed a small bridge over a tiny runlet of water and, leading from the bridge, were three pathways. One, they saw, led to a gate in a field, but the other two were hedge-bordered, and, more to herself than to Biddy, Riah said, 'What now?' And Biddy put in, 'The left one, Ma' – she pointed – ''cos the house lies t'other way.'

Without making any comment they took the left-hand path, and they walked almost a hundred yards before they knew they had arrived, because here the pathway widened considerably into a broad ash-strewn space. Beyond was an arch, and through it they glimpsed a yard.

Once in the yard, they both stood looking about them in amazement, because the yard was as long, if not longer, than the pit row and down one side of it were horse boxes; and there were the horses with their heads bobbing over the half-doors. Connected with the stables was a series of buildings and at the end, towering above them, was a big barn.

For the first time that morning her mother spoke pleasantly, and under her breath she said, 'I may see Davey,' she said quietly.

'What do you want?'

They both swung round to see a man in leather breeches and a leather jerkin looking at them.

'We've . . . I've got to see the housekeeper.'

'Oh aye. Well, go along there' – he pointed to the end of the yard – 'through that next arch and you'll come to the back of the house. You don't want the first door you come to but the second.'

'Thank you.' She had to put her hand on Biddy's shoulder to turn her around. She couldn't fathom the look on her daughter's face: it wasn't fear, because she didn't think the girl knew what fear was, yet . . . yet there was some kind of apprehension in her expression.

When they had passed through the second archway and entered

another yard, which she saw at once was bordered completely to the left of them by the side of the house, she pulled Biddy to a momentary stop, hissing at her now, 'Mind your manners when you go in there, and talk natural. Do you hear me? Talk natural. None of your fancy stuff, draggin' your words out, else I can see you'll be in trouble from the start.'

Biddy shrugged herself from her mother's hold and walked a step ahead of her towards the second door, and there, after a moment's hesitation, Riah knocked upon it.

It was opened almost immediately by a boy of about nine years old, and he looked at them brightly, saying, 'Aye?'

'I've come to see the housekeeper.'

'Oh.' He looked behind him, then pulled open the door, saying, 'You should have gone in by the passage.' He jerked his head to the side.

'We were told to come to this door.'

He stood back and they entered a square room, two walls of which had long slat tables attached to them with racks above and below. One table was crowded with lamps, the other was covered with boots and shoes of every description. The boy now left the room through a doorless aperture, and they heard him say, 'Kathy, go and tell cook to send word to Mrs Fulton that there's a wife here to see her and a lass along of her.'

When the boy came back into the room, he looked at Biddy who was staring at the shelves and, his voice as bright as his face, he pointed to the boot rack, saying, 'The first lot's gone up an hour since. These are the spares.' Then jerking his thumb towards the other long shelf he said, 'I've trimmed fifteen of them already this morning.'

Both Biddy and Riah shook their heads; then Riah said gently, 'You've been very busy.'

'Aye, we're always busy.'

Riah now looked at her daughter as much to say: There you are. This young lad must have been up all hours to get this work done and he looks happy enough. So what have you got to turn your nose up at, miss?

Biddy now saw a girl a little younger than herself standing in the opening. She stared at them both for a moment before she said, 'You've got to come this way.' Her voice was broad, her face was round, and her cheeks red. She was wearing a starched cap that covered her ears. She had on a blue print dress, the sleeves rolled up above the elbow and the rest almost enveloped in a coarse hessian overall. As they followed her through the next room Biddy saw the reason for the coarse apron, for the three tables were covered with pans, all fire-smoked, soot-bottomed iron pans, and at the end of one of the tables was a thing that looked like a square bath on stone stilts, and it was full of black scum-filled water.

They were in the next room now, which Biddy described to herself instantly as a huge scullery. A girl was at a stone sink washing dishes, and Biddy had never imagined there were so many dishes in the world as what she saw on those tables. Here, too, there were dirty pans, but these were copper ones.

And now they were in the kitchen, and this was the biggest surprise of all, both to Riah and Biddy. The kitchen in Moor House wasn't small, it was bigger than the living-room had been in the pit row, but this kitchen was almost as large as the entire middle floor of Moor House.

Biddy too, was overwhelmed, not only at the size of the place, but at the contents. One end of the long table had different iron gadgets screwed to it, part of one wall was hung with shining copper pans. Next to them was a row of brass-pronged forks, and the ovens appeared enormous. There was one each side of a large open fire, above which an enormous iron spit dangled; and there was a smaller fire with a round oven above that.

There were three people in the kitchen. The elderly, short fat woman, who was standing at one side of the long table, had a very pleasant face and her manner matched it. 'She'll see you presently,' she said; then she added, 'You're Davey's mother, aren't you?'

'Yes. Yes, I am.'

'And this is your lass?'

'Yes,' Riah nodded now towards Biddy and the fat woman smiled at Biddy as she said brightly, 'Oh, you'll fall into it. They all do. Takes time but they all do.'

The second woman looked about thirty. She stood at the end of the table pushing handfuls of nuts into an iron cup, before turning a handle. From the effort she was using it appeared pretty hard work. There was also a girl of about sixteen, peeling vegetables at a shallow trough sink. They all wore the same kind of uniform: a blue striped cotton dress with white apron. Only their caps were different. And Biddy had already taken in the fact that these must denote their rank in the household.

There appeared now, at the far end of the room, another servant. This one was in a grey dress and her cap was different again; also the broad apron straps were edged with a small frill. She beckoned to them; and now Riah, nodding towards the cook, as if in farewell, pressed Biddy before her towards the housemaid. This woman was tall. She looked a solid woman, almost, as Biddy thought, as old as her mother. She didn't speak but held the door open for them, and they passed through and into a broad passage, off which a number of rooms led. It was on the last door at the end of the corridor that the maid knocked, and when she was bidden to enter she pressed the door open and allowed them to pass in.

As Biddy passed her she turned her head and looked up at the woman and, the impish side of her forcing its way through her misery, she remarked to herself, This is one occasion when the master would have said I could use a colloquial expression such as, 'Cat got your tongue?'

But when she stood side by side with her mother looking at the small figure sitting behind the oak desk, the impish smile vanished. The woman was about fifty years old, she guessed. She had dark hair and her features were prim, indicated mostly by her mouth, which was full lipped and which Biddy was quick to notice kept pursing itself as if she was sucking a sweet. When she spoke her voice matched the rest of her. 'So this is the girl?' she said.

'Yes, ma'am.'

'How old is she, did you say?'

'Fifteen last December, ma'am.'

'And am I to understand this is her first time in service?'

'Yes, ma'am.'

'Tut! Tut! She doesn't look very strong. She's very thin.'

'She's quite strong, ma'am. She's been used to garden work for some years now.'

'Garden work?' The neatly combed head with the goffered cap perched dead in the middle of it and from which two starched streamers fell down just behind the ears, seemed to lift slightly with surprise. 'She doesn't look strong enough for garden work. Do you mean potato picking and such like?'

'No, ma'am. Real garden work, growin' vegetables and tendin' fruit bushes and diggin' and the like.'

'Oh, well.' The cap gave another little jump which seemed to bring the housekeeper up from her chair, and to Biddy's surprise, she saw that she was no bigger than herself. She came round the desk now and, addressing Biddy solely, she said, 'You'll get a shilling a week. You arise at five in the morning. You finish at six in the evening. At eight o'clock you have twenty minutes for breakfast. At twelve you will stop for dinner and see to the cleaning of your room which you will share with another maid. You will attend church with the rest of the staff every Sunday, and every other Sunday you have leave time from two o'clock in the afternoon until seven in the evening in the summer, and from one o'clock till six in the winter. You will be allowed one candle a fortnight. Your room companion is allotted the same, so you have a candle a week. When you are working in the laundry you will come under Mrs Fitzsimmons, at other times you will be answerable to me. You address me as Mrs Fulton. At no time are you to go round to the front, back, or west side of the house. Should you at any time encounter any of the family, you will do your best to make yourself scarce. You understand?' She paused as if for breath.

Biddy made no answer, simply stared wide-eyed straight into the face of this little woman, seemingly fascinated by the constant pursing of her lips when she wasn't speaking. But now she had started again.

'You do not speak unless you are first spoken to, except with those on your own level, who are the three laundry maids and the lower kitchen staff. Do you understand what I'm saying, girl?' She cast her eyes towards Riah, and the look said, Is your daughter stupid? Then her cap jumped even higher as the new member of her staff spoke for the first time, saying, 'I understand you perfectly, Mrs Fulton.'

The housekeeper was so surprised at the tone that her lips stopped their pursing and spread themselves wide. Again she was looking at Riah, whose face was scarlet now. But when Riah offered her no explanation, the lips dropped together again and gave an extra purse before she said, 'Say goodbye to your mother.'

They looked at each other and in this moment Biddy wanted to throw herself into her mother's arms and cry, 'Oh, Ma, take me back. I'll do anything, if you'll take me back.' But the look on her mother's face silenced such a request and when she said, 'Goodbye now, and behave yourself mind. Behave yourself,' she felt she was being abandoned. Biddy watched the door close on her mother; then looked back at the little woman, as she thought of her; and the little woman looked at her.

Behave yourself. So we have a joker here, have we? were the little woman's words to herself. Well, I have a way of sorting jokers out . . . I understand you perfectly, Mrs Fulton . . . So part of her joking was to ape her betters, was it? Forward young brat! And not yet been sent out to work, and she on fifteen. Well, she'll soon learn to know her place here, and the hard way or else.

'Now, Miss Bridget' – the tone was heavy with sarcasm – 'Should I hear you aimin', however badly, to imitate your betters, then you will learn what it is to go without meals for a day, and also to lose your leave time for a month. An' these are only two of the minor ways you can be made to recognize your place in this establishment. Do you understand me?'

'Yes.'

'*Yes what?*' The small body bristled.

'Mrs Fulton.'

'Yes, Mrs Fulton. And never forget it. Now we will see to havin' you properly dressed. Follow me.'

Biddy picked up her bundle and followed the housekeeper, through corridors, and through a maze of doors until she felt she must have come to the end of the house, the working part of it at any rate. In a long narrow room that had a peculiar smell, which she likened at first to moleskin, then to calico, she saw three women. They had all been seated, but they rose immediately on the housekeeper's entrance, and she, addressing the eldest woman, said, 'This here is the new laundry maid. You know what she requires. See to it. And when you're finished, Julie here – ' she turned to the youngest of the three, adding, 'can take her and show her her room. She's sharing with Jean Bitton. Then to the laundry. I will, by then, have advised Mrs Fitzsimmons of her comin'.' And with one hard look at Biddy she marched from the room. And no sooner had the door closed on her than the head seamstress, turning to the woman next to her, muttered, 'We're in a tear this morning, aren't we?'

'Are we ever anything else? Hello there. What's your name?'

This woman was now addressing Biddy, and she said, 'Bridget Millican.'

'You Irish?'

Biddy hesitated a moment before she answered, 'Not that I know of.' And at this two of the women started to laugh.

'Well, come on.' The head seamstress took up a tape measure and began to take Biddy's measurements, saying as she did so, 'They won't be new stuff, just alterations from the last one. Poor thing. But her clothes have been washed, so you won't catch anything.'

Catch anything? What had the girl had? Whatever she'd had she must have died of it.

'Where you from?' It was the woman the housekeeper had addressed as Julie who asked this question, and Biddy replied, 'Moor House.'

The three women looked at each other; then Julie repeated, 'Moor House? That's over the church way, isn't it?'

'Well, we're about a mile from the church, yon side.'

'Moor House,' the second woman repeated now; then looking at the others, she said, 'That's where the hermit man used to live. Well, I mean the one who spent all his time with books, so I heard. Is that the same place?'

'Yes.' Biddy nodded at them.

'But' – the seamstress was now leaning towards her – 'wasn't there something about him leaving the house to the housekeeper?'

'Yes. That's my mother.'

Again they exchanged glances. Then it was Julie who made a statement: 'And you're gona work in . . . in the laundry?' she said. It was as if she was baffled by the situation, and Biddy answered her frankly, saying, 'Yes, because he didn't leave any money.'

They all stood staring at her for a moment, until the head seamstress exclaimed, 'Well, let's get on with it.'

The measurements taken, Julie now led Biddy from the sewing-room. But she didn't take her back towards the kitchen quarters; she led the way still further into the house along more passages, up more stairs, and then lastly to the garrets. And there Biddy saw what was to be her room. It was hardly larger than the store cupboard at the house. The two beds were merely wooden-based pallets with the bedclothes folded at the foot. There was a table with a jug and basin on it, and, except for some nails in the back of the door, nowhere to hang clothes.

''Taint madam's bou . . . doir,' Julie said. 'Worst of the lot. But there . . . Well, put your bundle down an' come on.'

After retracing their steps for some way they entered a yard by a side door, and there at the other side was a long low brick building. It was situated at the end of a number of outhouses. Biddy was quick to notice that this yard wasn't attached to the stable yard.

They were halfway across the yard when Julie paused for a moment and looking down on Biddy, she said, 'You're going to find it hard in there, lass, mind. I better warn you, Jinny Fizsimmons is a real slave-driver. But I'll give you a tip. You stand up to her. And Sally Finch an' all, she's the first scrubber. You'll find Florrie McNulty, she's the assistant, she's all right. And so is Jean Bitton. She's the staff scrubber. But in any case, you're gona have your work cut out. And that's not just a sayin', it's a fact. You know' – she shook her head – 'I can't understand your mother puttin' you into a situation like this after . . . well, you being brought up in that house. You see, we've heard about him, the owner, through Mary Watts. Well, you wouldn't know this, but she's the first housemaid, and she's on speakin' terms with Miss Hobson, she's madam's lady's maid. You see, they've both been in service here over thirty years, so you see what I mean about speakin' terms like. An' Mary knows that Miss Hobson used to visit the owner of that house now and again because at one time she had worked there, Miss Hobson I mean. Do you follow me?' She smiled now, and Biddy said, 'Yes, yes, I follow you.' And then Julie ended, 'Well, I'm only explaining that's how we know. I understand he was a very clever man.'

'Yes, he was.'

'Did . . . did he ever talk to you?'

Biddy opened her eyes in surprise. 'Talk to me? He . . . he taught us, all of us.'

'Oh aye, yes' – Julie nodded now – 'of course, your brother's in the stables. 'Tis said he can read an' write. Can you read an' write?'

'Yes, I can read and write.'

'My, my. Well' – she now bent towards Biddy, saying softly, 'I wouldn't let on to anybody about that if I was you, 'cos it might get up to Mr Froggett. He's the butler, and he's been here a long time an' all, an' he's got the master's ear, an' the master doesn't hold with readin' an' writin'. I know that much. I bet he doesn't know that your brother can do it or he wouldn't reign long. You see, the gentry' – she jerked her thumb upwards now – 'they look upon things like that as an aggravation. It makes people unsettled. And they're right, you know, in a way . . . Well, come on, else we'll starve to death out here.'And she laughed; but Biddy didn't laugh.

They entered the laundry by way of a heavy door giving no hint of what was beyond it; but having passed through it she was immediately enveloped by the smell of washing. It was so strong that it stung her nostrils. She had a sensitive nose, and now she sneezed in the steaming atmosphere of soap-suds, hot irons and the peculiar stench that arises from water on hot ash.

Through the mist she made out four pairs of eyes directed towards her. The first pair were small and round, set in a large red face on top of a bulky body. This she guessed must be Mrs Fitzsimmons.

The woman was standing behind a table in the process of ironing some flimsy material; when she put her hand under it, it seemed to float away from her. The second pair of eyes were like slits in the thin face of a woman slightly younger. She was ironing aprons. The third pair were inserted in a round fat face above a plump body. The girl was standing in front of a bench that had a trough at the side, and she had been in the process of scrubbing some garment. She looked about sixteen or seventeen, and her face was running with sweat. The fourth pair of eyes just seemed to peep at her before vanishing.

The head laundress left her table and walked slowly towards a glowing round iron stove that was set on some stone slabs at the end of the room. The five platforms round it for different sized irons gave it the appearance of a pyramid. Biddy watched the woman put her iron into a space, then pick up another, turn it towards her face and spit on it before walking back to the table, where she rubbed it on what looked like a greasy looking pad before placing it on an iron slab; and then she emitted the word, 'Well?'

'This is the new girl, Mrs Fitzsimmons. Mrs Fulton gave orders to bring her over. She's not properly uniformed yet, but she will be the morrow.'

The big woman left her table now and stood in front of them, and concentrating her gaze down on Biddy, she said, 'What's your name?'

'Bridget Millican.'

'Bridget Millican. Well, forget it as long as you're inside here; you'll be Number Four from now on. Understand?'

Biddy made no reply to this, and the woman barked at her, 'I was talking to ya!' And at this Biddy remarked sharply, 'Yes, I understand.' Again her tone had changed, but unconsciously this time, and the woman stared at her for a moment before glancing at the seamstress as if for explanation. Then she turned and called to the small girl, shouting, 'You! Three.' And when the small girl came running, she said, 'Show her the ropes.' At this Julie turned away and the small girl held her hand out in a beckoning motion towards Biddy.

The head laundress returned to her table and for a moment there was only the sound of the banging of the flat irons interspersed with the grating sound of the scrubbing brush.

The room was a long one, running lengthwise each side of the main door; but at one side it took on an 'L' shape and the young girl led Biddy round into this section, which was a separate washhouse and, like the rest of the laundry, stone floored; and there she turned to Biddy and whispered, 'I'll show you everythin'. Don't worry; I'll show you everythin'.'

Biddy nodded to her and waited, and the girl said, 'Me name's Jean Bitton. Because you've come I've been moved up; I'm a staff scrubber now. You'll be doing what I used to do, so I'll show you.' Her head was nodding again and she was smiling widely; then putting her face close to Biddy's, she said, 'Don't worry. You get used to it.'

She would never get used to it. For the first time she could remember she felt afraid, not so much of the people but of the work. It was all so strange. Whereas, she told herself, she could learn from books like lightning, she felt she'd never learn the things she had to do in this place.

'Look, first thing in the morning, you see to the stove. It's kept on all the time: you bank it up at night, but you've got to fill up first thing in the morning. It needs four buckets. Those are the buckets.' She pointed to two large wooden buckets standing against a door which she now opened and, motioning with her head towards some doors at the far end of a yard, she said, 'Them's the coalhouses and the netties.' She closed the door again and then went on, 'Well, your next job is here.' She now led her to two large low tubs and, pointing down to them, she said, 'You put the roughs in there to soak overnight and you wring them out first thing in the mornin' through the mangle. The water gets freezin' this time of the year, but you get used to it.' She was nodding brightly all the time she was talking.

The mangle was the only recognizable piece of equipment in this whole place. It was like the one they had back home. She thought of the house she had left only a few hours ago as home, and always would. And on the thought it came to her again that the master would have been upset, very upset, had he known what work she was about to take on.

'And these' – the young girl was now pointing to a great pile of working trousers – 'them moleskins and corduroy breeches,' she said, 'are from the stables. It's trouser week for them in the stables. These are mostly the lads' stuff. They get mucky, very mucky, and you've nearly always got to scrub the bottoms after soaking afore they go into the hot wash. Never boil.' This last was accompanied by a vigorous shake of her head and she repeated, 'Oh, never boil them. But these boil,' she said, pointing to another heap. These were shirts, all blue striped.

She was moving on again, and now she was looking into one of three bins. 'These,' she said, 'are the rough coloureds, petticoats and that, from the sewing-room, the kitchen staff, and ours in here; except Mrs Fitzsimmons, she has hers done with the middle staff lot, like the cook and the housemaids an' such.' She now peered into Biddy's face and added, 'You look flummoxed.'

Biddy nodded as she repeated, 'Aye, I am a bit. Yes, I am a bit.'

'Oh, you'll soon come to it. Now this – ' she pointed to a large poss tub already half full of hot water and clothes, and she laughed as she said, 'You've seen one of them afore I bet.'

'Yes, yes, I have.'

'But I bet you haven't seen this kind of mangle.' And she now took Biddy's arm and pulled her towards a box that looked like three big coffins placed together. It was six feet long and about four and a half feet wide and under the two top boxes were two rollers, and as if the great cumbersome thing was the young girl's own invention, she said proudly, 'This is the presser. It's as good as an iron for some things, like the trousers and the rough shirts and things like that. Put them through when they're just off dry and they come out fine. Look.' She now gripped a big handle attached to a wheel all of eighteen inches across, and it took all her strength to turn it, smiling broadly as she did so; and when she stopped she said, 'You'll soon get the hang of it.'

To this Biddy answered in a voice little above a whisper, 'I don't think I ever shall.'

'Oh, you will' – the smile left the girl's face – 'you'll have to. An' you'll get out at times durin' the day an' all. I'll be goin' along of you, takin' the baskets back and collectin' the dirties.' At this Biddy pricked up her ears and said, 'We take the washing back? Will we take it to the stables?'

'Eeh! no.' The girl pushed her. 'They're all left in the sortin' room over in the house an' the staff take it from there. Fancy you askin' that.' And she pushed her again.

Her face straight, Biddy said, 'Me brother's in the stables.'

'Is he?' There was awe in the girl's voice. 'What's he like?'

'He's fair, very fair.'

'Oh, that one. Oh, aye, I've glimpsed him.'

'Glimpsed him? How long have you been here?'

The girl now bowed her head and said, 'Oh, six years coming on.'

'*Six years?* Well, our Davey's been here over four.'

'Oh aye. Yes, that could be.' The girl was nodding at her solemnly now. 'But you see we're not allowed to mix. In church we can see who's new an' that, and at half-year pay-day an' Christmas when they have the staff get-together. But then, up till last year, you see, I had to just look on.'

'Why?'

'Well' – her head dropped again – 'I'm from the house, the poorhouse.'

'Oh.'

The brown eyes were looking into hers now as she said, 'An' there's two lads in the stables. They came at the same time as me. But, you see, we're not allowed privileges like the others.'

'But why?'

'Well, 'cos we're taken out of charity, see.'

The statement was made without bitterness. 'And these are good jobs. I've been very lucky; so are the lads; 'cos they could have been sent for sweeps, an' I could have been put into a factory, and some of them are worse than the House of Correction they say. Oh, I'm very lucky. And you' – she now caught hold of Biddy's hand – 'you'll get to like it. And the food's fine. An' you get your uniform and a present at Christmas an' leave every fortnight. But – ' The brightness left her face as she added now, 'we can't go anywhere on our leave, the lads and me, unless . . . well, unless we're invited, you know like somebody takes us.'

Terrible. Terrible. Terrible.

The word was yelling in Biddy's mind. Eeh! when she looked back she'd had the life of a lady and she hadn't known it.

'What do you two think you're up to? I thought you were told to show her the ropes.'

The young girl almost left the ground, so quickly did she spring round, crying now, 'I . . . I have. I . . . I am, Mrs Fitzsimmons, and she's taken it all in. She'll be all right. I have. I'll start her on.'

'You do, an' quick, an' get back to that poss tub or I'll know the reason why.'

Biddy made another mistake, she turned and looked fully at the woman; and now the bawl of the voice almost lifted her, too, from the ground as the laundress screamed, 'Get your head down over that tub afore I duck you in it!' And as Biddy now turned towards the tub of wet clothes the voice came at her, yelling, 'An' roll your sleeves up first, you idiot.'

It was with great difficulty that she stopped herself from obeying the flash of anger that spiralled up through her body carrying with it such words as Don't you call me an idiot. I'm no idiot. If there's an idiot round here I'm looking at her.

Eeh! she would never be able to stand this. She'd run away. But if she did, what then? She could only run back home, and there'd be another mouth to feed and no shilling a week coming in. And if her mother wanted to stay in the house, then they'd all have to work.

As she plunged her arms up to the elbows into the ice cold water and dragged out of it a heavy garment, there now rose in her a feeling of resentment that overshadowed that which she had for the laundress, and this feeling was against her mother.

2

For the first week, as she told herself, she didn't know where she was. The work in the laundry didn't seem to get easier with the days, but harder; and Mrs Fitzsimmons piled more and more work on her. She had been used to grubbing in the ground in the cold weather, she was no stranger to back-breaking work such as digging, but this, having to skitter from one job to another under the yelled orders of the laundress, had become a torture to her. For the first three nights she had cried herself to sleep. Her fingers were numb with wringing out heavy working clothes in cold water; her shoulders ached with possing and scrubbing; her nose wrinkled in distaste when she even thought of the garments she'd had to scrub. When, at night, she had muttered to Jean Bitton, 'They must all be filthy,' Jean had said, 'They're no different, Biddy, from the house clothes and those of the gentry. Eeh! you wouldn't believe. I've seen some of them, an' they're changed every day you know.'

'Every day?' She had widened her tear-dimmed eyes at this new friend and Jean had nodded vigorously as she whispered, 'Oh, yes. The mistress and old madam change every day. And the master and Mr Stephen, they can go through three shirts a day sometimes. Then there's Mr Laurence. But you don't have much from him as he only comes home for the holidays. But from the two young rascals, Mr Paul and Miss Lucy, you can have three changes a day for them, especially if they're going visiting. And Miss May's as bad. But of course, she's a young lady.'

It was only at the end of the first week that Biddy began to work out in her mind the household staff. She had learned that there were eight in the master's family, one of whom was old madam, who had all the west wing to herself and who very rarely appeared with the rest of the family. She had learned that the butler was one Thomas Froggett. He was fiftyish, thin, and had a wily look; he wore fancy clothes and had garters at the top of his stockings. And the first footman was James Simpson. He was younger, but taller and fatter. The second footman was one John Thompson. He was younger still, a small man and looked ordinary. Then there was somebody called Mr Buckley. He was the valet. But up till now she hadn't seen one of these men, and she had merely glimpsed the first and second housemaids, Mary Watts and June Cordell. They were grown women, as were the first and second chambermaids. The first chambermaid's name was Peggy Tile. She was older than the previous two, well into her forties. But the second chambermaid was younger. Her name was Chrissy Moore. She had merely glimpsed people as she and the laundry staff filed into the servants' hall to have their one sit-down meal of the day. This was at half past six after the rest of the staff had eaten. They were accompanied by the lower kitchen staff. The cook, as did the head seamstress, ate with the upper household staff; the valet and the housekeeper and the governess ate in the latter's sitting-room.

It astounded her that it took twenty-one indoor staff to look after eight people, seven if you didn't count the one who was away most of the time. Then, as she reckoned from Jean's talk, there were thirteen outdoor staff, which included the laundry and the lodge-keeper and his wife. But this wasn't taking into account the home farm and the blacksmith and the three wall men. These, she understood, were a separate unit altogether and miles away at the other end of the estate.

What she had come to fully understand in this short time was that the laundry staff were the lowest in the hierarchy, and she herself was the lowest in that section; also that, in each section in the household there was someone who considered himself or herself superior to the rest. It even happened at the last table, as their meal was called, when Anna Smith, the assistant cook, took the head of it and directed when they could start to eat and when they were finished. She also dictated the time when talking was permissible.

The whole system was so bewildering that Biddy constantly told herself that she would never get used to it. Nor did she want to get used to it. Time and again during the last few days she had been for walking out, just like that. She had imagined herself walking up to the laundress and saying, 'Well now, Mrs Fitzsimmons, you big loud-mouthed individual, there's the washing and if you want it done, get at it!' She was continually forming such cutting sentences in her mind and imagining the ensuing look of utter amazement on the laundress's face.

Looking back over the week, Biddy could see that the laundress's manner towards her had from the first been rough, but on the second day after the housekeeper had made her daily inspection, the woman's attitude towards her had worsened. It was as if she had been told to find fault with everything she did.

It was on the third day she had said to Jean, 'Do you think I could slip along to the stables to see our Davey during the dinner break?' This was a meal of cheese and bread and ale brought to them at twelve o'clock, and they were given forty-five minutes in which to eat it, clean their room, and attend to the wants of nature. It was during this latter period that Biddy thought she would have time to dash around to the stables, but Jean was horrified at the suggestion and warned her that if Mr Mottram or Mr Lowther or the bigger stable boys saw her they would split on her, because one of the lads had been dismissed for keeping company in secret with a girl in the kitchen. They had both been sent packing.

So it wasn't until Sunday when she was being packed into the back of a cart lined with wooden forms that she saw Davey. He was walking with two other young men towards the wagon that was the third in the procession and he turned and smiled at her, and it was a nice smile, a warming smile, and she answered it and nodded at him before she was pushed up into the cart and along the form.

She glimpsed him again as they filed into church, the male staff at one side, the females at the other. Not all the staff were present, but what there were made a good third of the congregation.

She was in the very back row seated between Jean Bitton and Julie Fenmore, and when, after some ten minutes, there was a stir at the front of the church towards the altar, it was Julie who, with her hand over her mouth, whispered, 'The family's in.'

Up till then she hadn't seen any member of the family. She had no idea what they were like and so, letting her imagination run riot, she saw them sitting in their gallery, stately superior, on a par with the gods and goddesses she had read so much about over the past years.

She was bored with the service. She had nothing to read. During the sermon Parson Weeks's voice almost sent her to sleep. She told herself she'd ask her mother for her father's Bible when next she went home. But taking in the rows of still figures, hands joined on laps, she wondered if it would be a wise thing to do, especially as reading was frowned upon.

The day was bright and frosty and as the cart travelled back along the road the girls chatted to each other; but she sat quiet, looking out through the wooden slats that boarded the sides, and again she was crying inside, If only I could go home.

Once they were down from the cart Jean explained the procedure: they were to go to their room and change into their working clothes, then have their bite, which was their midday meal, after which they'd collect the dirty laundry and sort it all up, soak it ready for the early start in the morning.

She had never worked so much on a Sunday even when they hadn't gone to church; her mother had considered it a day of rest. In the summer they had all gone down to the river and had games in the field. The tears came to her eyes when she thought of the wonderful life she had had in that house. She hadn't been aware of it at the time, she had taken it for granted, thinking it would go on forever. If only the master had lived, he would never have let her work in a laundry.

It was as they were later sorting the clothes that Jean said. 'Would you read me a story the night, Biddy?'

'Yes. Oh yes.' She was flattered at the request and she added, 'I'd love to. What d'you like?'

'Oh, I don't know, anything; I just like to listen to people reading, like the parson this morning, about the comin' of the Lord an' things.'

'Well, I haven't a Bible with me, but I'll bring it next time I go home. There're some lovely Bible stories. There are others though that are not so nice; they're all about killings and things. But I've got a book of tales with me, and I'll read you one of those.'

'Oh, ta. Look.' Jean leant towards her and in a conspiratorial whisper said, 'We'll snuff the candle an' get undressed in the dark, an' that'll save it a bit, so you can read more.'

'That's a good idea. Yes, we'll do that.'

For the first time since coming into this strange world she felt the return of her old excited self. Somebody was interested in reading. Perhaps she might even be interested in learning to write. Now it was her turn to whisper, 'Would you like to write your name, Jean?'

'Me, write me name? Me own name?'

'Yes, yes.'

'Oh, aye, that would be wonderful. Eeh! nobody can write their name here. Well, I expect the butler an' the housekeeper can likely. Oh aye, they'll likely be able to write their own names. And people like the lady's maid. An' of course Miss Collins, the governess. Oh, but fancy me being able to write me name.' She now stopped her work and, gripping Biddy's cold wet hands, she said, 'Eeh! I am glad you come, Biddy. Eeh! I am. I've never had a friend afore.'

Biddy was both touched and flattered at this demonstration and, her thoughts jumping ahead, she said to herself, And I'll not only teach her to write her name, I'll teach her to read an' all, and anybody else that wants to. Aye, I will. And that'll show Mrs Fitzsimmons, because she doesn't know 'B' from a bull's foot. As the master might have said, she is proficient in ignorance.

At this she began to laugh as she told herself that was a fancy bit of thinking. And Jean, looking at her, laughed too as she asked, 'What you laughing at, Biddy?'

Lifting up a long white lawn nightdress by the arms, Biddy danced it up and down over the tub of cold water as she said, 'I just thought of something funny.'

'What kind of funny? Tell me.'

What good would it be repeating a saying of the master's to Jean, and so, swinging the nightdress widely from one side to the other in the water, she said, 'I was imaginin' this was Mrs Fitzsimmons and I was dooking her.'

At this Jean put her head back and let out a high scream of a laugh in which Biddy now joined her; then their laughter was cut off and they clutched at each other in fright as a tap came on a window some distance down the room. Slowly they turned their heads towards it;

then Biddy, springing away from Jean, ran to the window and, pushing it up, she said, 'Oh, hello, Davey. Hello.'

'Hello, Biddy.' He put out his hand and touched hers, then said, 'How's it goin'?'

It was some seconds before she answered, 'Not very well. I don't like it.'

'I didn't think you would. But you get used to these things. Give youself time. I'm . . . I'm just on me way home. I'll tell me ma I saw you.'

'Ta . . . thanks, Davey. Oh, It's nice seeing you.' Had she ever called him loutish? At this moment, to her he looked as he had done years ago, beautiful. 'How did you get round here?' she asked.

'Oh, there's ways and means, an' I've got a couple of lookouts.' He nodded to both sides of him.

'You won't get wrong?'

'No, no.' He shook his head. 'Anyway, you're me sister, and I'm surely allowed to see me sister.' His eyes moved from her now to the girl standing some way behind her, and Biddy turned and said, 'This is my friend Jean. We sleep together. She's been very good to me.'

He inclined his head towards Jean and said, 'Hello, Jean.'

Jean made a muttering sound that could have been anything; then Davey said, 'I'll have to be off. I'll see you now and again; an' I'll tell me ma you're all right.' He was already moving from the window when she said, 'Davey.'

'Aye?'

'I wish I was coming with you. Do . . . do you think you could ask me ma to . . . well, take me back?'

After a long pause he said, 'You know the situation as well as I do: she wants to stay on there, and she's got to be kept.'

'Aye, yes.' She nodded at him. 'All right.' Then smiling, she added, 'By, I'm glad to see you, Davey.'

'And me you.' He backed from her now, then turned and disappeared into the shrubbery behind the coalhouses.

When she closed the window and looked at Jean, she noted that her friend's face was scarlet, and rather inanely she said, 'That was our Davey.'

'Yes.' Jean nodded at her now and, her voice small, she said, 'He's lovely. His hair's like those angels you see in the church painted on the windows.'

Yes, she supposed he did look like that to other people, even though his face had changed. He had certainly looked like an angel four years ago. That's how the master must have seen him, like an angel, someone to adore. Of a sudden she felt sad. The laughter had gone from the washhouse. It was full of soiled clothes, dirty clothes, filthy clothes; and it came to her that it was because of that angel that had just disappeared into the shrubbery she was having to work among it all, because if he had never struck the master with the scythe, it was doubtful if the master's heart would have given out as soon as it did. Yet, could she blame Davey? Because it hadn't started with him, nor with her mother taking up the post at Moor House, it had started right back in the pit village when her da had died of cholera in that terrible year. Where then did blame start? The master could have answered it, at least explained if there was an answer to it at all.

That was another thing she was going to miss, was missing already, someone to talk to, discuss things with, explain things; someone to put her on the right path of thinking. But that would never happen now, for never again would she meet anyone like the master. From now on she'd have to think for herself. And she would do. Oh aye, she would do. As the master said, every available minute she got to herself, she must read. She wasn't going to grow up and be like this lot here. Oh, she liked Jean, and she would help her all she could, because she wasn't dull; but as for the rest, they were a lot of numskulls. Yes, yes, they were. But she would show them. And she surprised Jean by taking up a poss-stick and thumping a tub of linen into a soggy mass; then even more, by now drying her hands on her coarse apron and exclaiming loudly, 'It's Sunday. We shouldn't be working on a Sunday. Come on over here in the corner and I'll tell you a story.'

'But what if . . . ?'

'We'll hear the latch lift. Come on, I'll tell you a story.'

That story was the beginning of a chain of events of which even Biddy's fertile mind could not present her with the ultimate picture.

During the following week, Biddy not only told Jean a story but she read her a story. She also taught her to write the first three letters of the alphabet; and she promised her that before Christmas she'd be writing her name and spelling cat and dog.

On the Sunday morning, the day of her leave, she counted the minutes during the service and after it, and up till one o'clock, when she was free to start on her journey home. But before she could leave the house she had to go to the housekeeper's room for Mrs Fulton to look her over. Fault was found with her attire, from her hat to her boots. Her hat, Mrs Fulton said, should not be worn on the back of her head but well over her brow. As for her coat, it was creased. If it had been hung up it wouldn't have been like that. With regard to her boots, they lacked shine. She had, Mrs Fulton said, a good mind to make her go back to her room and polish them, but as this was her first Sunday on leave, she would overlook her slovenly attire. And she finished by saying, 'You may go.'

Biddy had all the trouble in the world to stop herself saying, 'It's clarty outside, the roads'll be muddy, I could be up to me ankles in no time.' Only the effect of that response on the housekeeper stopped her, for she knew the woman was quite capable of cancelling her whole leave. So once she had escaped through the back door and had walked sedately across the yard, as soon as she entered the long hedged path that bordered the grounds, she grabbed up her skirts and took to her heels and raced as if the devil were after her.

The coach road, as she had surmised, was very muddy, and in her running she had to skip and jump over the potholes; and she reckoned she had run almost half the distance to home when she had to stop and gasp for breath. She rested for a moment with her back against a tree at the side of the road before hurrying off again, not running now, yet not merely walking; her step was a trip as if she were about to go into a dance. And all the way along this road, on this Sunday, she hadn't seen a living soul until she came to the old turnpike, and there she saw Tol. He wasn't driving the wood cart today but walking and crossing from one side of the road to the other when she espied him and she cried, 'Tol! Tol!'

He turned round and waited until she came breathlessly up to him, and, his face bright, he exclaimed, 'Well! Well! Where are you running to with your face like a beetroot?'

'Home.'

'Of course, home.' He nodded at her. 'Your first leave day?'

'Yes.'

'Do you like it?'

The smile slid from her face and her mouth assumed a pout before she said, 'No, Tol, I don't like it. I hate it.'

'Aye' – his voice was soft – 'I thought you would. I get word of your doings now and again through the lads in the stables. I bet you were pleased to see Davey that day.'

'You know about that?'

'Oh, I know lots of things.' He turned his head to the side while keeping his eyes on her. And now she smiled at him, saying, 'You always did.'

'What time have you got to be back? Sixish, isn't it?' he said.

'Yes.'

'Well, I tell you what. I'll meet you here with my . . . what do you think?'

'The cart.' She had poked her head up towards him. And now he shook his, saying, 'No, not the old cart. Madam – ' he assumed a pose before going on, 'I have acquired a trap.'

'You haven't, Tol! A trap?'

'Aye. I just got it last week. There was a sale at Brampton Hall, Fellburn way. I went over with the groom. He was looking out for harness and there was this old trap. Hadn't a lick of paint on it for years and spokes missing. And a little old pony. He looked on his last legs. But you should see them both now. Anyway, I'll be off duty around three the day and, madam' – he again assumed a pose – 'I will await you on this very spot.'

'Oh, Tol.' She had a desire to throw her arms round him. She had the added desire to beg him now: 'Come on back home with me.' But all she did was press her face against his arm while he held her to his side for a moment before, without another word, she ran off, asking herself as she did so, why in real happy moments she should want to cry . . .

Riah was waiting for her on the road outside the gate, and they both put their arms around each other and held tightly together, Riah knowing that she had missed the company of her daughter more than she would admit even to herself, and Biddy's feelings telling her that she loved her mother and she always would.

Johnny and Maggie came running across the yard and there followed more hugging and questions came at her from all sides: Did she like it up there? How long had she to work? What did she have to eat? Had she a nice bedroom? And she answered all their questions, not all truthfully, because she couldn't say to her mother as she had done to Tol that she hated the place; at least, not yet, not in front of the other two, because that would have spoiled the merry atmosphere. And it was merry . . . and yet sad, and the sadness was emphasized when she entered the library. And she was near to tears again as her fingers gently stroked the table where she had sat each morning in the week, year after year, as she sometimes imagined, since she was born, because she could not recall life before she had come under the master's teaching.

Over a tea of bread and jam and scones and apple pie, she had to describe to the two youngsters the duties of the different members of the staff. But when she was asked about the house and its occupants, she had to admit she hadn't seen any of them, which even surprised Riah, for she said, 'You've never clapped eyes on the master or mistress yet?'

'No, Ma; and I don't suppose I will, not till half-pay day, and then Christmas. Jean, she's my friend that I told you about, has been there for years, and she only ever sees the mistress when she hands her her present at Christmas.'

'You get a present?' Maggie was looking at her starry-eyed, and when Biddy nodded, saying, 'Everybody gets one,' both children shook their heads in wonder.

It wasn't until it was almost time to leave that Biddy was alone with her mother, and Riah then, straight-faced, asked, 'How's it really going?'

And Biddy answered truthfuly. 'I don't like it, Ma,' she said. 'The work's awful, but . . . but I could put up with that. It's the laundress.

She's a nasty woman and she doesn't like me. And the housekeeper doesn't like me.'

'You're imagining things'

'Oh, no I'm not, Ma. But of the two, Mrs Fitzsimmons is the worse, 'cos I'm with her all day. Still' – her face took on a little lightness – 'you know what I'm doing, ma? I'm teaching Jean her letters and how to do her name and . . .'

'Now, now, lass. Now look. I'd be careful along those lines. Now I warned you about that.' Riah was wagging her finger in Biddy's face. 'They don't like it, not only gentry, but servants in such houses. You see, when people rise in that kind of service they get ideas about themselves. An' it's got nothing to do with reading and writing, it's the difference – ' Her voice trailed away now because she found that she hadn't the words to explain thoughts in her mind with regard to underlings who had risen in a household and were still unable to read or write their own name. But deep within her she had the explanation, for although she herself could read and write there were times when this young daughter of hers, who could rattle off quotations and talk like the master had done, aroused in her a feeling of inferiority, which, in its turn, bred animosity.

But Biddy reassured her now, saying, 'It won't cause any trouble, Ma. And Jean won't let on. Ma . . . Ma, would you mind if I bring her home on me next leave? She can never go out anywhere on her leave 'cos she has nobody belonging to her. She was from the poorhouse.'

'Oh, poor bairn. Yes, yes, of course, you may bring her.'

'Oh, thanks, Ma . . . Ma – ' She turned from Riah now and walked down the drawing-room and into the hall. Still with her back towards her mother, she said, 'I saw Tol when I was coming. He was by himself, Ma.' She didn't point out that Tol had a Sunday duty to do, too. 'And Ma, he . . . he asked after you.'

'Did he?'

'Aye,' she lied glibly. 'He said to give you his regards . . . You know what he's got, Ma?'

'No.'

They were in the kitchen now, 'He's got a trap, Ma, and a pony.'

'Very nice for him.'

'And he's going to meet me and take me back on it.'

'Well, well, now, aren't you lucky?' They were standing in front of the fire and facing each other, and Riah said, 'In that case, it's time you were going. Get your things on.'

'Ma . . .'

'Get your things on, Biddy.'

Biddy got her things on.

The light was fast going as they crossed the drive and Biddy drew them to a halt as she turned and looked along the length of the house and quietly she said, 'I love this house, Ma. I hope you never have to leave it.'

Riah turned abruptly away and walked down the drive, her mind again in a turmoil. Why hadn't she told her daughter that if she died tomorrow the house would be hers, not Davey's, him being the eldest? And too, what was more significant still, if she was to marry she would have to leave, and then again the house would be Biddy's. Why hadn't she told her? Again her mind would not give her the truthful answer which would have been that buried deep within her was a live resentment against the man who had, first, taken her son from her, at least he had caused her son to leave this house, and then her daughter, by first educating her above her station, then by making her the real benefactor of his twisted generosity. And he had left herself what? A home that was hers as long as she remained a prisoner in it, with no company, no man to hold her. And oh God, how she longed to be held. At times she thought, to hell with the house, she'd go down to the cottage in the dip and offer herself to Tol, even as his next woman. And that, her mind had told her, could be a solution: she could be his woman and still have this house. So what was stopping her? What?

3

It was about one o'clock on Christmas Day that Mrs Diana Gullmington leant forward, peered between the light of the small candelabra set at each corner of the dressing-table, and gently moved her fingers through her soft sparse white hair; then looking at the reflection of a woman that topped hers in the mirror, she said, 'I look quite bright this morning, don't you think, Hobson?'

'Yes, madam. Extremely bright.'

'I always do in cold weather. Suits me, cold weather. The boys broke me into it years ago, rolling me in the snow. Give me me hair.'

When Jessie Hobson placed the wig carefully on her mistress's head the reflection in the mirror became transformed: the nut-brown hair piled high seemed to lift the sagging wrinkled skin upwards over the fine bones of the broad face and to take at least ten years off the eighty-two and bring the face more into keeping with the voice.

Once more the old lady looked at the face above hers saying, 'Another Christmas ding-dong, Hobson. I didn't think to see it.'

'You'll see many more, madam.'

'Oh, don't take that note, Hobson. You know, you make me flaming mad when you feel you've got to say the right thing. And how many times have I told you that over the past years? Look, turn me round to the window; I expect the horde is about to arrive at any minute now.'

Jessie Hobson turned the chair that was set on wheels and pushed it towards the long window; and there she pulled the velvet drapes still further back, saying as she did so, 'It's starting to snow, madam.'

'Yes, yes, I can see that. Pity it didn't come down in the night and block the road and they would have had to walk.' She turned her head and there was an impish grin on her face as she looked at her maid, and Jessie Hobson, suppressing a smile, said, 'Oh, madam.'

'Well, all that damn ceremony. It makes me blood boil, not only today but every Sunday. And that woman has as much Christianity in her as a boa constrictor. What was she wearing this morning?'

'Mrs Gullmington was wearing a blue velvet outfit, madam.'

'Blue velvet. That must be new.'

Now the old lady turned and looked at the woman who had been her maid and confidante for more than thirty years and she said, 'You've heard this question before, Hobson, and you can't answer it I know, but I still ask it, and of myself: why had my son, a fellow like he was that could have got any woman from any county in this country, to go and pick a little dark mean-eyed sanctimonious shrew like that? I never liked little women you know, Hobson.'

'I'm a little woman, madam.'

'Oh, Hobson' – a thin blue-veined hand flapped towards the maid – 'you know what I mean. There are little women and little women and this one is as narrow in her mind as in her body. And what would she have been if she hadn't married my Anthony, eh? Tell me that. An old maid likely, in a manor, in a very minor manor, in the backwoods of Northumberland. Why – ' The face was screwed up now and again she repeated, 'Why on earth had he to take her? Now if it had been her cousin Emily, Laurence's mother, I could have understood it, because, as you remember, she was a bit of a beauty. Did Laurence go with them today, do you know?'

'I espied him on the drive talking to Miss May earlier on.'

'You mean you espied him on the drive being talked at by Miss May. She's brazen is May. Holy like her mother, but brazen.'

They both laughed softly together now and the old lady exclaimed, 'Ah, here they come, the chariots.' Then she leant forward to watch the two coaches and three open carts drive past the west wing, which was her private portion of the house, towards the front entrance where the two coaches stopped, while the three carts continued on to the stable yard. Grunting in her throat, she said, 'Now for the pantomime. Get me ready, Hobson. Give me the lot today, tiara an' all. That's the only vanity I have left, to outshine that little shrew.'

When Jessie Hobson went to get the jewel box from the Chinese bureau that stood at the end of the room, her mistress called to her, 'You're walking worse today, Hobson. Are your feet worse?'

It wasn't until Jessie Hobson returned with the box and placed it on the dressing-table that she replied, quietly, 'They've been hurting a lot of late, madam.'

'Why didn't you say, woman?'

Jessie smiled to herself. This dominant woman who could be kind and thoughtful in so many ways, could at the same time be as blind as a bat when to open her eyes would lessen her own comfort.

'You should soak them in brine.'

'I did so, madam.'

'I'll get Pritchard to look at them again.'

'It would be no use, madam, he said he can't do anything. It's the insteps you know, they've dropped.'

'My insteps never dropped.'

Jessie again smiled to herself. No, her insteps had never dropped because she had never to stand for hour after hour attending to someone's wants; nor had she had to be continually taking messages to one of the family and in doing so had to traverse a gallery before entering the main house, then along another gallery and down a great curving staircase. And this could happen ten times a day, and had done for years past, until three years ago when they had acquired a house boy, whose job now was to run errands to other parts of the house . . .

It was about twenty minutes later that Mrs Gullmington again looked in the mirror and, ridiculing herself, said, 'Ridiculous! I look as if I'm dressed up for a ball. Nevertheless, that's how it's going to be. I'm ready.'

On this Jessie Hobson went to the door and gave directions to the small green-liveried boy standing there. Then leaving the door open, she went behind her mistress's chair and pushed it along the broad corridor, to the first gallery that opened out into quite a large hall, from which stairs led downwards; but she passed these, then through a pair of grey-painted communicating doors, held open now by two footmen, and along the second gallery and towards the head of the main staircase. Here, the two footmen took their positions at each side of the chair and, lifting it, walked crabwise down the winding staircase to the hall below.

The men having set the chair down, Jessie Hobson once more took up her position behind it. But she did not immediately push it forward because her mistress was surveying the double line of servants arrayed across the hall. They stretched from the green-baized doors leading into the kitchen quarters, to within a yard of the drawing-room, and as she surveyed them the female knees bobbed and the men touched their forelocks.

The double doors of the drawing-room had been pushed wide and there, in the middle of the room, facing the fireplace, but set well back, was the Christmas tree. And standing to one side of it was the old lady's son, Anthony, a man of about forty-eight, tall, heavily built, with fair hair and blue eyes. And to his side sat his wife Grace. She was older than him by two years. She was small, she had dark hair and grey eyes which were set deep in a round face that at one time could perhaps have been termed pretty.

Standing next to his father was Stephen Gullmington. He was twenty-two years old and in appearance very like his father, but he differed strongly in character. Next to him was his sister May. She was nineteen years old. She was tall, fair and thin, being quite unlike her mother in looks. Her face wore a bored haughty expression.

At the other side of the tree was an empty chair and next to it the young man who was known as Laurence Gullmington and whom most people took to be the brother of Stephen and May and the two youngest children. But he was the son of Grace Gullmington's cousin, and the reason why he had been brought up in this house and to believe for years that he was a Gullmington was entirely the work of the woman he called grandmama. He was of medium height, thin, and of a dark complexion, with deep brown eyes, a straight nose and a wide mouth.

Next to him stood Paul Gullmington. He was sixteen years old and had red hair. Why this should be, the whole family questioned. No Gullmington had ever had red hair; only Grace Gullmington's narrow-minded attitude to all things, and people, saved her from suspicion in this matter.

His sister was the last in line. She was fifteen. Her name was Lucy. In looks she was like her mother might have been at her age. Being the last child, she had been spoiled and pampered.

They and the various guests all watched the old lady being pushed gently towards the empty chair; and now her son and first grandson stepped forward and assisted her to her feet, where she stood for a moment shaking down her voluminous skirts. Then swivelling slowly round, she was assisted into the great black oak carved chair, the arms of which ended in dragon's heads. Her thin bony bejewelled fingers covered these heads as she looked slowly about her.

Then she spoke. Coming straight to the point, she looked at her son and said, 'This year we'll make a change. We'll delay the wine and chat and not keep them standing out there waiting. It's more sensible, because they have the meal to see to, and we can be enjoying our exchanges while they get on with it. Should have done this years ago.'

She now brought her eyes round to her daughter-in-law whose face had become so tight that her cheek-bones were showing white, but

Diana Gullmington smiled at her as if the shrew, as she always thought of her, was conceding her proposal cheerfully.

And now she lifted her hand and pointed towards the double doors as she looked at her son, and Anthony Gullmington, without glancing towards his wife, went to the fireplace and pulled on the bell-rope summoning the staff to its presentation ceremony.

The first one to enter the room was Anthony Gullmington's valet. He walked slowly across the open space towards the family, bowed to the old lady, then stepped towards Grace Gullmington, and after receiving his present he inclined his head towards her, saying, 'Thank you, ma'am,' then took six steps backwards before turning and leaving the room. He was followed by Miss Nichols, Grace Gullmington's maid. Then came Miss Collins the governess; Mrs Fulton the housekeeper; Thomas Froggett the butler; James Simpson the first footman. These were the cream of the staff, and had not headed the queue outside but had awaited their call in a side room.

They were followed by John Thompson the second footman; Kate Pillett the cook; Mary Watts the first housemaid; June Cordell the second housemaid; Peggy Tile the first chambermaid; and Chrissy Moore the second chambermaid; and Mrs Morrison the head seamstress.

There followed a break in the proceedings and an arrangement of the presents before the sewing-room maids came in. First, Mary Carson; then Julie Fenmore. Then came the kitchen maids; Anna Smith the assistant cook; Daisy Blunt the vegetable maid; Polly Neill the scullery maid; and Kathy Ward the second scullery maid. Tagged on to these two were Billy Kelly the pantry boy, and Harry West the boot and lamp boy.

There was another pause before the appearance of the outdoor staff, when Bill Mottram, the coachman, stumped slowly in. On his departure there was a giggle from the young daughter of the house because he always had difficulty in walking backwards. She seemed to have been waiting for this. Peter Lowther, the groom, followed. Then came the five stable boys, Ben Fuller; Rob Stornaway; Micky Taggart; Tot Felton; and David Millican. This boy too, like his outside master, seemed to have trouble in walking backwards. And again the young daughter of the house giggled audibly before being silenced by a look from her grandmother.

The lodge-keeper and his wife followed.

In the order of position, the farmer and his wife and the farm hands and the blacksmith should have been squeezed in somewhere along the line, but it was the custom for their presents to be taken to them by the young members of the family first thing on Christmas morning.

So it showed in what low esteem the laundry staff was held when they came last in the long procession. Mrs Fitzsimmons, walking with mincing steps, assumed a dignity that bordered on the comic. Florrie McNulty came next. This thirty-four years old woman, one could see, was deeply impressed at the honour that was bestowed on her for she not only bent her knee, but almost touched the ground with it. Sally Finch aimed to follow suit; then came Jean Bitton, nervous, eyes cast downward as befitted a creature from the workhouse. Last of all, came the new hand Biddy Millican.

Although Biddy was tired of standing and tired of listening to the whispered Oohs and Ahs of the present gatherers, her mind was bemused by the beauty around her. For the first time she was seeing the interior of the house, and its magnificence amazed her. The hall, with its marble statuary, its beautiful carpets, the dazzling colours of the pictures lining the open gallery above the staircase, brought to life the palaces the gods had dwelt in in the stories that the master had sometimes read aloud to them. By the time she reached the drawing-room door she was quite unconscious of the bustle about her, the to-and-froing of the servants, the whispered directions, so much so that, standing on the threshold awaiting her turn to enter, which Jean's passing her on coming out would signal, she had to be nudged forward into the galaxy of beauty.

Slowly she walked up the space towards the great lighted Christmas tree, and unlike Jean's and those of many of the others, her eyes were not downcast, nor her head held on a downward tilt, as she had been bidden, but it was back gazing at the angel at the top of the tree. She managed to bring her gaze downwards before she approached the half circle of people seemingly awaiting her. She took them in with one sweep of her eyes. She knew she had to approach the lady seated to the left of the Christmas tree with the gentleman standing next to her – they were her master and mistress whom she was seeing for the first time – but her sweeping glance returned to the old lady seated in the big black wooden chair. Her attention was drawn to her because she seemed to be sparkling all over: her hair was covered with jewels, as were her chest and her hands; she looked like a queen.

She was aware of a noise being made in someone's throat. She came to a halt opposite the mistress of the house and when she was handed a small parcel she dipped her knee and inclined her head and said in a clear voice, 'Thank you very much, ma'am.' She thought it was better to add the 'very much', nobody told her not to.

Instead of walking backwards for six steps, she again glanced along the family row and she smiled at them. Then, with great dignity and as if she was acting in a play, she took three steps backwards, paused and let her smile cover them again, before turning and walking from the room, not with eyes front, but with head moving from side to side, even dropping backwards as she took in the colours of the ceiling.

But no sooner had she reached the hall, and the doors were closed behind her than she was almost lifted from the floor by the first footman who gripped her by the collar of her dress and whispered fiercely, 'Little smarty, aren't you? *Get!*' And at that he almost pushed her on to her face.

When she regained her balance, she turned round, her mouth open and about to tell him what she thought, but there, also staring at her, was the magnificently dressed butler.

Mary Watts, the first housemaid, came at her now, saying, 'Get yourself away, girl. You're a ruction raiser, if ever there was one, grinning like an idiot at the family. We'll hear more of this.'

She could have heard more of this if she had been in the drawing-room at that moment, for Lucy was doing an imitation of the laundry maid. Curtseying now to her mother, she said, 'Thank you, *very much*, ma'am.' Then she did the backward walk and was about to flounce round to conclude her pantomime when she was brought to an abrupt halt by her grandmother saying, 'Girl! Behave yourself. Stop acting like a little slut. If the servants don't know their manners, they have little chance of learning from you . . . Well now.' She looked around her family, then with her usual forthright approach, she went on, 'Come on, let me have that drink, and then to the presents. Yours are scattered around there.' She pointed to the tables at the far end of the room. 'Hobson has marked them plainly. No mix-up this year.'

As each of them put a present on her knee, he or she bent forward and kissed her cheek. Even her daughter-in-law did this, saying as she did so, 'I had it especially made for you, Mother-in-law.'

'Well, what is it?' As the stiff old fingers fumbled at the parcel, Laurence Gullmington assisted them to reveal a very fine cashmere shawl and when it was held up for her inspection he said, 'It's beautiful, Grandmama.' And she nodded and said, 'Yes, it is. Thank you, Grace. Very kind. Very kind. Now what have you got me, Anthony?'

Her son brought his present to her and hovering over her, he said with a laugh, 'Well, Mama, mine's a very small present, but knowing you haven't much jewellery, I thought I'd get you these.' When the box was opened to disclose a pair of jewelled ear-rings her eyes gleamed and she said, 'Nice, nice. Thank you, Anthony.' She lifted her face for his kiss.

And so the present giving went on, and two hours later a dinner followed. Then they all had a rest while the staff enjoyed their Christmas meal in the servants' hall, for once in the year sitting down all together, but at four separate tables, the diners at the bottom table waiting on their superiors.

But the dinner was only the beginning of the staff festivities for, after clearing away, the tables and chairs were pushed back as were also two partitions that divided the room from that part which was used for sorting dried goods. Once a year this was cleared to make space for the party.

It was a custom to invite the master and mistress and household to join the party, but it had never been known for the mistress to accept the invitation. The master had sometimes popped in for five minutes or so, but the duty, and it was considered a duty, fell to the eldest son and any other member of the family who would like to join him. But even these did not stay long, knowing that their presence acted as a restraint on the hilarity.

It was said, among the staff, that before the old master died when madam had ruled here, which in reality she did to this very day, she and the master had come in to the party and hadn't been above joining the dancing. But that had all stopped twelve years ago after the old master had died and Mr Anthony had brought his wife and family here, as was his right . . .

It was half past eight when the party began. Sally Finch, Jean and Biddy were sitting on a wooden form near the dividing doors. They were all agog with excitement. Jean was describing how the party had been set off last year, and the year before, and likely would be tonight: James Simpson, the first footman, could play the fiddle and Peter Lowther, the groom, could do wonders with the flute, and they generally played the Sir Roger De Coverley. But just the older ones danced that; it would be the young ones' turn when the games started.

It was as Jean predicted: the party got going with the Sir Roger De Coverley, danced only by the upper hierarchy of the staff. And now the first game was about to start, a game which embraced everybody: a large circle was formed, with one player being delegated to run round the outside and to tap a member of the circle on the shoulder, this one to chase the first player, trying to catch him before reaching the open space. If he couldn't, then he had to do some kind of forfeit before he could take his turn tapping someone else on the shoulder. It was at this point that the door opened and some of the family entered.

Leaving the ring, Thomas Froggett went hastily towards them and conducted them to seats that had been set apart at the end of the room. The visiting party consisted of Mr Stephen, Mr Laurence, young Master Paul, and Miss Lucy. Miss May, like her mother, never put in an appearance on these occasions.

Once the guests were seated, the game started in earnest. There was no feeling of restraint among the staff, this was their night. Shoulders were tapped and the runners encouraged by shouts for one of them to fill the gap. Then the cry would go up: 'Song, dance, or rhyme?' Nearly always the choice was dance, because it was the easiest.

When one of the stable boys tapped Jean, she was so surprised to be chosen that for a moment she didn't run and there were cries of, 'Go on! Go on!'

She, too, chose to dance, and when her feet tried to imitate a clog dance, she nearly fell over, causing great laughter around the ring. Now it was her turn to choose, and she tapped Davey on the shoulder and he beat her to the gap; but they closed it to him and opened it further along and pulled Jean in. And so he had to choose.

He stood for a moment, his eyelids blinking, his fair skin red, while Biddy willed him to do something good. Recite, she said to herself. Recite. Recite, man. He had learned a lot of rhymes and poetry during his lessons. But he too chose to dance, and he was pushed into the middle of the ring, only to surprise them all and make Biddy feel proud of him as, imitating a gentleman, he placed his left hand on his hip, extended his right hand to the side, his fingers spread, and then proceeded to lead an invisible partner forward in a dance, bringing forth shouts and clapping from the others.

Biddy swelled with pride at her brother's achievement. She realized from where he had taken the dance steps. There was a big book in the library with drawings showing ladies and gentlemen dancing, and he had mimicked them.

When he tapped her on the shoulder she went off like a hare, but he beat her to the gap and there she was, pushed into the centre of the ring with the cries coming at her: 'Song, dance, or rhyme?' And she had no hesitation in saying, 'Rhyme.' And she heard some voices repeating, 'Rhyme.'

Part of her mind was in a high state of turmoil, another part was quite calm, for she imagined the master to be standing near the gentry and he was looking at her and she knew she must do him proud. Some of the last poetry he had made her read had been from the poet called Shelley. So she stood straight, her head up as he had taught her, her mouth set with her tongue tucked behind her lower teeth, and as he had taught her to read so she spoke:

'I fear thy kisses, gentle maiden,
Thou needest not fear mine;
My spirit is too deeply laden
Ever to burthen thine.'

She paused here for a moment, her eyes looking straight ahead; then went on,

'I fear thy mien, thy tones, thy motion,
Thou needest not fear mine;
Innocent is the heart's devotion
With which I worship thine.'

There wasn't a movement in the room. If she had blasphemed, spewed out obscene words, she could not have stunned the majority of the audience more than she had done. After a moment there was a smothered giggle here and there from the younger ones, but all the adults in the room fixed her with their eyes, and the brightness that had shone from her face as she recited faded away as she looked back at them. Her head turned slowly. What was the matter with them? It was a lovely poem. She didn't understand it all but she liked it, the sound of it, the feel of the words, and the master had said it was a thing of beauty. Then into the stillness came the sound of a single clap, a hard definite clap, and all the eyes were turned on to the visitors and to Mr Laurence, then to Mr Stephen, who had joined him. The two younger ones were not clapping; but now, as if given a lead, here and there a servant, thinking best to take a cue, joined his hands together and clapped. But they were mostly male hands that did the clapping, except those of Jean and the seamstress, Mrs Morrison, and Julie Fenmore, her second assistant.

Biddy had no need to be told that by reciting the beautiful poem she had stored up trouble for herself, and that in a way she had brought the game to an end, for now the housekeeper had motioned to the butler who motioned to his second-in-command, and the music struck up again.

As Biddy moved down the room to join Jean in the corner, she had to pass the visitors, and it was as she did so a hand came out and touched the sleeve of her dress, drawing her to a halt, and she turned and faced the two gentlemen of the house. It was the one she now understood to be Mr Laurence who spoke to her. 'You recited that very nicely,' he said.

'Thank you, sir.' Her voice was a mere whisper.

'Who taught you to read?'

'The master, sir. I mean Mr Miller from Moor House.'

'Oh.' He nodded at her, then cast his glance at Stephen, and Stephen, bending down, asked her kindly now, 'And what else did he teach you?'

'Oh, lots of things, sir.'

'Lots of things?'

'Yes.' She nodded at him.

'Such as what?' It was Mr Laurence speaking to her again, and from where he sat her eyes were on a level with his and she looked straight into them as she said, 'Reading and writing. But I could do that afore I went there. Then Latin and some French.' She watched the eyes narrow as they continued to stare at her and she knew that the young man was finding it hard to believe her. She didn't like being thought a liar by anybody, and so her tone lost its quiet, even subservient note and took on an edge as she said, ''Tis the truth, sir. He taught me for five years, and my brothers and sister. My brother is over there' – she turned and pointed now – 'the fair one.'

The two men continued to look at her in a dumbfounded way, as did the younger boy and girl, but the expression on their faces represented in this moment exactly that which would have been on their mother's face had she listened to such audacity coming out of a servant's mouth, and not an ordinary servant either, but a creature who was the lowest of the low in the household. As if of one mind, the brother and sister were about to rise and walk away when Laurence's voice stilled them. He hadn't turned towards them, nor yet seemed to be aware that they were about to leave, but he said quietly, 'Stay where you are; you might learn some more for your good.'

Now looking over Biddy's head, he noticed that although some of them were dancing while others sat around the walls, nevertheless all were aware that this child was being taken notice of.

He had alway considered there were too many servants in this house and that there was a form of snobbery among them that outdid even that of their superiors. He hadn't taken much notice of such things until he had gone to Oxford two years ago, but in that city, at least within the confines of the university, one naturally had servants, and some of them were servile individuals. Yet he doubted if their attitude to each other would be the same as that of the servants in this household, and in others round about at which he stayed, and he doubted very much if his father, unlike Lord Chesterfield, would remember any servant in his will, nor say of them: 'They are my equals in nature and only my inferiors in fortune.' And he was sure in his mind that Chesterfield must have been thinking of someone with an intelligence such as this child here possessed when he wrote those words, for was she not surprising, quoting Shelley and saying that she could read Latin and French. It was utterly unbelievable. But he hoped, for her own sake, that this news didn't reach Mama, a title he had always given to Grace Gullmington, although they were but second cousins, for of all minds in the household he knew that his adopted mama possessed the narrowest. So he would have to see that these two rips by his side kept their mouths shut. Stephen was speaking to the child again, saying, 'Let us hear another rhyme.'

Stephen was a good fellow, one of the best. He couldn't have loved Stephen more if he had been his brother, and they were as close as brothers, yet he knew that what Stephen knew about poetry or literature of any kind was minimal. Now had it been horses. Well, that would have been different. Like his father, if it had been possible he would have eaten and slept on his horse. But here he was, unthinking as usual of the consequences of anything he might say or do, urging the child to repeat her performance and by doing so picking her out from the rest of the company. Yet he had himself to blame for that; it had been an irresistible urge that had prompted him to put out his hand and draw her attention.

His voice quiet, while his elbow gently nudged Stephen, he said, 'I think the young miss would like to join the party. You must remember we are just onlookers.'

'Oh, yes, yes, all right. Away with you!' And Stephen made an exaggerated gesture of shooing her off.

She turned from him without further words and went and joined Jean, who was sitting open-mouthed and wide-eyed in the corner near the dividing doors. But when Biddy took her seat beside her neither of them spoke; they watched the visitors rise now and, attended by the housekeeper and the butler, move down the room towards the far door, Miss Lucy muttering, 'Oh, aren't I a clever girl . . . They'll skin her for that.'

In the hall Laurence caught hold of Lucy's shoulder and as he did so he also laid a hand on Paul's arm and, drawing them together, he bent his head down towards them, saying, 'Stephen and I here' – he glanced at the taller young man who was standing grinning now – 'we think it best if you don't mention this episode to Mama or Papa.'

The girl and boy stared back at Laurence; then the boy said surlily. 'Papa doesn't hold with the lower classes learning.'

'Now who told you that?' Stephen gripped his younger brother by the shoulder and walked him across the hall, saying, 'Papa's go-ahead, he wouldn't mind.'

'I think he would. Paul's right.'

Stephen now turned and looked at Laurence and his eyebrows went up as he said, 'You really think he would, Laurence?'

'Yes, yes, I think he would.'

'Oh well, yes, I suppose you're right.'

They had reached the drawing-room door when Laurence spoke once more to Paul and Lucy. In a quiet slow tone he said, 'Mama would be greatly disturbed if she knew of two people who take jaunts on a Sunday and upset the stable lads and the laundry girls; especially would she be annoyed with you, Lucy.'

The brother and sister exchanged glances; then Paul, his tone sulky, said, 'We've got the gist, but why should you worry about what happens to a laundry skivvy?'

'Perhaps just because she is a laundry skivvy, and the lowest of all of them back there.' He jerked his head towards the servants' hall. 'And they can be even more deadly and spiteful than you two when they get going.' He now grinned, and they grinned back at him; then Lucy, putting her head on one side, said quietly, 'You would split on us wouldn't you, Laurence, if we disclosed that that person could read and write?' And he nodded solemnly at her, saying, 'Yes, without a moment's hesitation.'

Then both Laurence and Stephen, and even Paul, were surprised at the girl's next words for, her lip curling, she said, 'It only goes to prove that you are not our real brother.' And on this she flounced from the door and made for the stairs, leaving the three males looking after her.

It was Stephen who, disturbed now out of his usual tolerant and slightly absent-minded manner said 'I'm sorry, Laurence. That's unpardonable, really unpardonable. Why, you're more than one of us than . . . than' – he pointed to his younger brother – 'than Paul there. I'll go up there this minute and shake her guts up, see if I don't.' But as he made to dive off Laurence caught hold of his arm, laughing now and saying, 'No, no, don't be silly, Stephen. Let it pass. I know Lucy. She'll be all over me in the morning.'

Stephen puffed and blew for a moment, but only for a moment for he was quite willing to let it pass; he hated disturbances of any kind. Yet he was certain of one thing, his feeling for Laurence was that of a brother, a beloved brother at that.

He turned now and said to Laurence, who was moving away, 'Where are you off to? Aren't you going to join Father for a drink?'

'I'll be with you shortly.' Laurence called back; 'I'm going to say good night to Grandmama before she settles down.'

'Oh, right. Tell her I'll be up in the morning. Doesn't want too much company at one go. Been a long day for her.' . . .

When Laurence entered the old lady's room, she was propped up in bed, and all except her head and neck seemed to be swallowed in the huge four-poster bed. He did not take a chair at the bedside but hoisted himself up on to the coverlet, cupping one knee in his joined hands. There he sat looking at the wizened face under the pink silk ruffled cap for a moment before he said, 'Another one over.'

'What are they doing down there now?'

'I'm not quite sure except that Mama and Papa and May are in the drawing-room, and Stephen and Paul have just joined them.'

'Did you look in on the party?'

'Oh, yes, yes.' His face twisted into a tight smile as he added, 'And some party it was tonight.'

'What happened? You look as if you'd enjoyed it. Don't tell me you danced with Collins or Nichols, or Mrs Amy Fulton, she of no body and less brain.'

'No.' He shook his head. 'Something much more exciting than that.'

'What could be more exciting that that?' Her lips screwed themselves into a smile, and he said, 'I know one thing, you would have enjoyed it if you had been down there and witnessed what I did.

'Well, what did you witness?' Her voice rose. 'Go on, tell me.'

'Well, I won't be able to give you any real impression of the incident, and I'm sure you won't believe what I'm going to tell you. First of all, let me ask you a question. How do you view your laundry maids? Because they still are *your* laundry maids, the two older ones are anyway. I remember them from I was a boy. But there are three younger ones now, and the youngest of the lot . . . oh, she can't be more than fourteen I think . . . and yet I don't know, there's a kind of age in her eyes . . . Can you recall the present giving?'

'Can I recall the present giving?' Her nose twitched. 'What do you think I am, a bundle of old bones in her dotage? Of course, I can recall the present giving. What about it?'

'Well' – he laughed – 'the very last one to come in was this young girl. She added a couple of extra words to her thanks, then her departure was slow as she viewed the room.'

'Yes, yes.' The old head nodded. 'Yes, I remember the child. And I knew what would happen to her when she once got through those doors and was collared by Mrs Fulton, likely got her ears boxed.'

'Well, that was she. She had to do a forfeit in a round game and she stood up there in the front of the whole lot of them and she quoted a verse from Shelley.'

'Shelley? Who's he?'

'Oh, he's a poet. He died some time ago. His work is quite controversial at the moment.'

'And she was *quoting* him, that girl?'

'Yes, and beautifully.'

'How did that come about, a laundry maid quoting a poet?'

'Well, from what I can gather she came under the patronage of the late owner of Moor House, you remember, Mr Miller.'

'Percy Miller? Oh, yes, yes. Hobson's hero.'

'What?' He leant towards her and she repeated, softly 'Hobson's hero.' She nodded towards the end of the room where Jessie Hobson was putting clothes back into the wardrobe. 'She used to work for the Millers, and apparently was in at that fellow's birth. Visited him until he died . . . Didn't you, Hobson?' Her voice now rose and Jessie Hobson turned round and said quietly, 'Yes, that's so, madam.'

'You heard what was being said then?'

'Yes, I overheard, madam.'

'Well, what do you know about this girl?'

'She's the daughter of the housekeeper who has four children, and Mr Miller taught them for so many hours a day, so I understand.'

The old lady now looked with widened eyes at Laurence as she said, 'Did you hear that? God in heaven, what'll be happening next? And she's in this household?'

'Yes, she's in this household. Well, in the laundry.'

The muscles of the old face moved, making a pattern like water flowing over ridged sand, and then the bedclothes began to jerk up and down as the old lady's whole body shook with her mirth. And when she spluttered she grabbed at a lace-edged handkerchief lying on the silk coverlet and dabbed her mouth and then her eyes before she said, 'Imagine what will happen when Lady Grace gets wind of this, a little scholar in her laundry. Not that she would recognize one laundry maid from another if they were pushed under her nose.'

'That's not all,' Laurence was now joining in her glee and he leant a hand on each side of her shaking body as he went on, 'She says she can speak French and knows Latin into the bargain.'

The old lady's laughter ceased and she said quietly now, 'You're joking?'

'No, Grandmama, truly I'm not joking.'

'Then all I can say, 'tis a great pity for the creature, for where does she think that will get her, only into serious trouble, as her head will be telling her she's too clever to use her hands. I've never gone along with any ideas of your father's, you know that' – she too alluded to her son being Laurence's father – 'but I've always been with him in this business against the education of the lower classes, because where is it going to get them? Nowhere, except where they are at present, serving in one way or another and, in the main, yes, happy.' She inclined her head in a deep obeisance now, giving her words authority as she repeated, 'In the main, yes happy, because they are satisfied with their lot; but teach them to hold a pen and to read from a page, then you are dropping seeds of discontent into their otherwise contented lives. What is more, you know my ideas on God and His supposed directions for the human family. There are many things on which I disagree with Him. One such as you know is the superiority of man, which is rubbish. But with regards to His placing of human beings in certain positions, whereby a servant is subject to his master and in return the master has a duty to his servant inasmuch as he should see that he is fed and clothed in return for his labour, I'm in wholehearted accordance. So with regard to this little genius in our midst I would say that it's a pity she is here. No good will come of it for the child, for as you only too well know once the mind begins to work it gropes at reason, and reasoning has no place in the life of a servant. You would agree with me, would you?'

'No, Grandmama, no, I wouldn't.'

'You wouldn't?' The head came up abruptly from the pillow and the lace frills fell aside, exposing the bony shoulders, and again she said, 'You wouldn't?'

And once more he replied, 'No, I wouldn't. I'm for people using their minds, and whether we like it or not, more and more are doing it. There are great stirrings in the world outside our little domain, Grandmama. You wouldn't believe. Here' – he swept his arm wide as if taking in the whole domain – 'in these two thousand acres is a world behind the times. Outside there are great rumblings below, and there are eruptions bursting to the surface here and there in strikes and murders. You did hear about the gibbeting at Jarrow, didn't you, of the miner who killed the deputy? And that's not all. They are bringing soldiers into towns to quell riots, and the navy into ports to guard the merchants ships. And as for reading and writing, men are defying their masters here and there and doing just that.'

'*Nonsense. Nonsense.*'

'No, Grandmama, it isn't nonsense, it's common sense. It's got to come sometime.'

'What has got to come sometime, equality?'

'Well, since you've said it, perhaps.'

'Oh, *go away. Go away.*' She slumped down into the bed again. 'Jack will be equal to his master when Christ makes a second coming and as, to my mind, He hasn't made the first yet, there's your answer. Go away; you tire me.'

'I don't tire you.' He was leaning over her again. 'I annoy you by stimulating your mind. You know I do. I set you thinking. You said yourself, remember, I'm the only one in this establishment who can set you thinking. And ten to one this time next year you'll be using my tactics on someone else.'

She didn't come back at him with, 'Never! Never!' but surprisingly and in a small voice, she said, 'I may not be here this time next year, Laurence. Sometimes I know I won't be here; other times I'm frightened that I won't be here. Death is a very frightening thing, Laurence, and I'm not prepared for it, I'm still too much alive up here.' She now pointed to her frilled cap. 'And as my mind tells me that there's no heaven and no hell, only a great nothingness, I'm afraid to go into it.' Her hands now clutched at Laurence's, and he brought them together and stroked them as he said softly, 'There may not be a heaven or hell, Grandmama, but there is surely a something. There is no great void, no great nothingness; that thing that's alive up there' – he nodded towards her head – 'will go on.'

'How do you know?' Her voice was a mere whisper now and that of an old woman, and as quietly he answered back, 'I do know. I feel it, and I'm not the only one. There's new thought running through the world. The old ideas are dying; people are laughing at penance and purgatory. There are men who are performing miracles as Christ did, just by touch, and they are not charlatans, no more than He was. All right, all right' – he shook the hands he was holding – 'He may not have been God, or the Son of God, but He was a great man with a great mind, and a greater spirit. So just think on that. Just think that that great mind of yours cannot die. Your body, yes, it will rot, but nothing can destroy thought. It cannot be touched, or seen, or held, yet it tells us everything . . . Go to sleep now, dear, and remember once more thing: I need you, if it is only to argue with.'

He bent now and kissed her wrinkled cheek; then he slid from the bed and walked out of the bedroom and into the dressing-room, where Jessie Hobson was arranging a complete change of her mistress's underwear for the morrow, and, stopping by her side, he said, 'She'll sleep now, Jessie.'

The woman turned to him and, her face solemn, she said, 'You always do her good, Master Laurence, and she's always better when you're at home, but she's very fractious at other times.'

'Yes, I know.' He patted her arm. 'She's not easy . . . You look tired.'

'I am a bit, Master Laurence.'

'You should have help.'

'I've put that to madam, but she won't hear of it.'

He was on the point of wishing her good night when he turned and looked at her and said, 'This child in the laundry, what do you know of her other than what you've said?'

'Only that she's very bright an' that Mr Miller thought highly of her. I'm sure he'd be disturbed if he knew that her mother had sent her into a laundry.'

'Why did she?'

'Oh, well, as far as I can gather, from what little I know, she hasn't any money, and although Mr Miller left her the house . . .'

'He left her the house?'

'Oh, yes, sir, he left her the house, but no money to keep it up, and so she put the girl out to work, as her brother has been for the past few years. I think she hopes that she and her other children will be able to survive in that way, although I can't say how long she'll last with the small wage they both get. Oh, I'm sorry, sir. I know it's enough, because of their uniform and . . .'

'It's all right, it's all right, Jessie. I know what you mean . . . Life's an odd mixture, isn't it?'

She paused before nodding and saying, 'It is. It is, Master Laurence.'

'Good night, Jessie.'

'Good night, Master Laurence.' And watching him leave the room, she thought, He's nice, but he's strange. Fancy talking like that about God. It's a wonder he wasn't afraid. And for a moment she felt afraid for him, because she had seen what happened to people who questioned the Divinity of the Creator.

In the far, far end of the house, in the last room that was ten feet by eight and at this minute deathly cold, Biddy too was thinking that life was very strange, so strange that it was making her cry. She was sitting on the edge of the pallet bed hugging her knees as she stared into the black darkness. Her outdoor coat was draped round her shoulders over her nightgown, and her day clothes were laid over the foot of the bed for extra warmth.

Jean had been asleep this past hour, tired with the excitement of the day and the joy of possessing a pair of mittens given her by her mistress, and a blue hair-ribbon which she had received from Biddy herself.

Biddy too had received a pair of mittens, but she thought nothing of them, she had knitted better ones herself. The whole day had held little joy for her except that she had been amazed at the beauty of the house. As for the party, she would know the result of that tomorrow morning, because after it had broken up the housekeeper had waylaid her and commanded, 'Come to my office at nine o'clock in the morning.' And then as she had passed the butler and the footman, they had looked down on her as if she was some strange creature, and the butler said, 'My, my! it's comin' to something, it is that.'

Oh, she wished she could go home . . . Yet, there had been one bright spot in the day. The two young masters had spoken to her so nicely, and the one called Mr Laurence reminded her in some way of her old master, and he seemed to know about poetry. She thought she could like him, but not the two younger ones. She knew spite when she saw it in people's eyes and the young miss had really turned her nose up at her, as had her brother.

There were a lot of strange people in this house. She had felt lonely at times for people back in Moor House, but here there were too many people, and all of them, it seemed, at one another's throats by what she could make out from the bits of gossip she overheard. So she supposed she wasn't the only one that was going through it.

Oh, she wished she was home. If she did something awful she would be sent home. But then what would her mother say? Perhaps not very much, but she would think all the more, losing two pounds twelve shillings a year, and having to feed her. But surely there were other jobs she could get. But what kind of jobs? What was she fitted for? All she could do was housework, or digging, weeding, and planting, and now, of course, laundry work. Oh, that place. She ground her teeth, then flounced round and into the bed and pulled the covers over her head. If she ever got sent away from this place it would be for going for that Mrs Fitzsimmons.

But the following morning at nine o'clock as she stood before Mrs Fulton's desk in her box-like office, the housekeeper almost took the laundress's place in Biddy's mind as a means of being dismissed, for she kept ranting on at her, as if last night she had committed a crime in saying her poetry. Dirty, she called it. A young girl like her reciting about kissing. And now she seemed to be almost frothing at the mouth as she said, 'And you had the affrontery to stop and speak to the young masters.'

'I didn't. One of them pulled me to . . .'

'Don't you dare answer me back! Don't you dare speak until I give you permission. All you had to do was to dip your knee and listen, then walk away.'

'I'm not dumb.'

'How dare you!' This last was a bellow that brought the woman to her feet, crying, 'If it wasn't that Finch has gone sick with stuffing herself, leaving Mrs Fitzsimmons short-handed, I would send you packin' this very minute.'

Biddy watched the housekeeper's chest move up and down. It reminded her of the bellows back home in the kitchen. And now after one long breath the housekeeper said, 'I have asked you before, I'll ask you again, what did the young master say to you?'

When this question had been put to her before she had answered nonchalantly, 'He just talked,' fearing that if she had repeated what he had said it would have aroused the woman's wrath. But now, throwing caution to the wind, she put it in a nutshell by saying in no small voice, 'He asked me how I'd become educated.'

It wouldn't have surprised Biddy if the housekeeper had collapsed on the floor that moment; but what she did do was turn her head to the side and then move it in a half circle while her eyes appeared to follow an imaginary object. But when once more they were glaring at Biddy she became speechless for a moment; then, her words struggling out of her small puckered lips, she said, 'Girl, you have no place in this household, and I'm going to make it my business to see you leave it at the earliest possible time. Do you understand me?'

Biddy's whole body was trembling, part with injustice and part was a dry sobbing that was racking her chest. When now the housekeeper's arm was thrust out and her finger pointed, like a stick of lead, towards the door, Biddy turned and stumbled out. No sooner had she reached the passage than the tears forced themselves over the lump in her throat and flowed down her face, and blindly now she continued down the passage instead of taking a turning that would lead to the yard door, and so entered the kitchen, and for a moment she quelled the laughter round the table where Kate Pillett was enjoying a joke with Mr Laurence.

Laurence had always been a favourite of the cook's since he was a small boy and when he was at home it wasn't unusual to find him sitting on the edge of the table munching one of her pies.

Anna Smith had her head back laughing loudly, as had Daisy Blunt who was peeling vegetables at the sink, but Daisy kept her back turned which proved she was concentrating on her work and not taking advantage of the young master's visits.

The laughter ceased and they all looked at the girl hurrying down the room and rubbing one cheek after the other with the back of her hand. And she paused for a moment near the table and looked at the cook before running out of the kitchen and into the boot room and so into the yard. She had appeared oblivious that one of the young masters was in the kitchen and she had passed him without dipping her knee.

Laurence now looked enquiringly towards the boot room and then at the cook, and she answered his look by saying, 'Oh, she's been getting it in the neck from Mrs Fulton. It's about last night, sir.'

'What did she do last night?'

'Oh, well.' The cook now rolled out some very thin pastry before she said, 'She made a bit of a show of herself saying those rhymes like that, though meself, I thought it was funny. But coming from such a youngster, well . . . anyway, she's not the type that will reign long here. Mrs Fulton was only looking for an excuse to get rid of her, and this'll be it. Anyway, laundry maids are ten a penny. Would you like another pie, sir?'

'No thanks, cook. No thanks.' He smiled at her now, adding, 'As usual they spoil my appetite for my meal.'

'Go on with you, sir. If I remember rightly, you used to be able to eat six at one go and come back for more.'

'I was filling out then. I've got to think of my digestion these days. But thank you; as usual your pastry is excellent.'

Again the cook said, 'Oh, go away with you, sir.' Then both she and her assistant dipped a knee as he nodded to them before making his way up the kitchen.

Once he had gained the house he stood for a moment considering. It was no business of his, and yet in a way it was. He had stopped the child and talked to her and therefore he knew he had put her in a position of envy, and the little lady Fulton was showing her powers. He paused a moment, then with a quick right about turn he went once more behind the screen, through the green-baized door and into the corridor. And there he knocked on the housekeeper's door, and when he was told to enter the woman was so surprised she popped up from her seat, saying brightly, 'Well, Mr Laurence, what can I do for you?'

'I've come after a position.'

'Oh, Mr Laurence, you're always a tease.' Her voice and manner were coy, and he smiled at her as he said, 'Well, Mrs Fulton, what I've really come about is to apologize.'

'Apologize, sir? What on earth have you got to apologize for?'

'Well, it's about that incident last night, Mrs Fulton. You know, that child.' He paused as if it was difficult to remember the incident, then went on, 'I think now I was very remiss in talking to her. Looking back on it, it seemed as if I was singling her out, and it was never my intention to do so. But at the same time she seems a very bright little girl. Don't you think so, Mrs Fulton?'

'Well, sir, I . . . I find her . . . well, rather forward.' The coyness was slipping now.

'Yes, yes, I . . . I agree with you, but . . . but merely in a scholastic way, which is very unusual I suppose in the position she holds. But perhaps you'll take her under your wing, you're so used to seeing to young girls like her. And – ' He smiled broadly now, even laughed a little as he added, 'I was telling madam about the incident last night and she was most interested in the fact that a child like her should be quoting Shelley . . . you know, Shelley the poet.'

'Er, oh yes, yes, sir.' The tone was flat now.

'Well, I thought I would just apologize for what was really my fault and for what, on her part, might have appeared unseemly behaviour. But I knew you would understand. You must make allowances for me: it was Christmas Day and I'd imbibed a great deal of wine. Well, they are waiting for me in the stables and I must go and shake up an appetite.' He smiled again at her, adding now, 'You have put on a splendid table for us these last few days, Mrs Fulton. It's a credit to you. Goodbye.'

'Goodbye, sir.'

In the main hall once more he stopped, closed his eyes for a second and said to himself, How could you? Talk about being smarmy. Then chuckling inside, he answered himself, saying, All in the furtherance of education. Isn't that what I aim to do? As he hurried now towards the front door he cast his eyes around him as he answered his own question by saying, Yes, but not here or in these parts. By God no. Oxford or no place.

4

Laurence Gullmington would have been both interested and amused if he had witnessed the course education was taking in the very end room of the north wing of The Heights most nights of the week when four heads were bent over a solitary candle.

It happened that Florrie McNulty had learned of Biddy and Jean's midnight vigil, not only of learning letters but of story reading. She had risen one night from her bed next door and come into the little room to tell them to stop talking, as she couldn't get to sleep for the muttering. Florrie McNulty was thirty-four years old and when she saw what the fifteen-year-old Jean had already learned from the newcomer, she was both amazed and intrigued, and in a hesitant way had asked Biddy if she would teach her to write her name. Of course Biddy was only too pleased to have another pupil, but there was a snag. Florrie shared a room with Sally Finch and Sally Finch always sucked up to Mrs Fitzsimmons, and what the three of them were sure of was Mrs Fitzsimmons would never submit herself to being taught anything by Number Four, or the runabout, as Biddy was known. And, as Biddy pointed out, Sally would go and split on them, but Florrie McNulty said, Oh no, she wouldn't, because she had something on Sally that would keep her mouth shut, and even persuade her to join the classes.

So it was that they now had two whole candles a week . . . and not only two, for part of Florrie's position in the laundry was being in charge of the candles there, and she was able to save all the butts. What was more, Florrie had the knack of making candles from the melted wax and string.

The lessons had begun in the New Year, and by Easter three laundry maids could not only write their names, but many single syllable words and almost as many two-syllable words. Moreover, Jean and Florrie McNulty could count up to fifty, and Sally Finch to twelve. Sally Finch did not grasp things as easily as the others, yet because she was learning she had, in a way, become a different kind of person.

They all knew at times that Mrs Fitzsimmons was puzzled by their attitudes towards each other: there was no bickering among them, and when they could, without making it too obvious, they would help each other. The laundress wasn't used to a happy atmosphere. She was a bully by nature and she thrived on discord, but her shouting and yelling seemed to be having little effect on her staff these days, and when she came to think about it, it was all since that smarty miss had come into the laundry. There was something about that one that she didn't trust. And it was said in the house that Mrs Fulton had been on the point of packing her off but had been warned not to from above. Now why was that? Something about old madam having an interest in the girl. Yet to her knowledge, old madam had never sent for her, nor clapped eyes on her, except at Christmas, when, once again, she had made a show of herself.

Every leave day now Biddy took Jean home with her and they would bring back a different book with them. Biddy had taken her little stock of books back home because during one of her weekly examinations of the rooms, Mrs Fulton had seen Biddy's books on the window sill, and having picked up one after the other as if she was able to read them, she had informed Biddy to get that rubbish out of her room or else it would find itself in the fire.

There was a plentiful supply of paper and pencils in the library at Moor House, but she only took a few sheets back with her, and each girl hid her work under her mattress.

Jean being with her on her visits home meant that Biddy had little private talk with her mother, but even so she sensed that she was very lonely, and at times she would say to her, 'I saw Tol, and he was by himself.' And only last week she dared to say, 'Ma, you know something?' And when her mother had said, 'What?' she had added, 'Tol hasn't got a woman now. He's living by himself.' And her mother's stiff reaction was, 'How do you know that? Did he tell you?' to which she had answered, 'No, not really, but I know it's true. It came in a roundabout way. It appears that the mistress got wind of it and he was warned, so the story goes, because the mistress is very pious.'

It was at this stage that her mother almost turned on her, saying, 'And he put up with it, sent her packing? He's gutless. That's what he is, gutless. What business is it of theirs up there what a man does after his working hours? They want to look to their own men if I'm to believe all that Fanny says. Pious indeed!'

Biddy had returned to the house thinking that at times she couldn't understand her mother. She knew for a fact that she wasn't for Tol having a woman, and yet she was blaming him for giving her the push. There were lots of things that she couldn't really get to the bottom of. She had learned a lot about life from her reading, yet it seemed a different kind of life to that which went on under her nose. Real life wasn't so nice or so easy, nor yet, at times, so terrifying as the life she had soaked up from her books, but she knew that the book life was the life the master had led, and it was something apart.

But you couldn't live apart in the house, nor could you be unaware of the intrigues that went on, not only whispered but things seen with her own eyes, like what she had come across up the woodland path between James Simpson the first footman and Mary Watts the first housemaid. She was walking up the pathway on the soft snow and they hadn't heard her, and there they were, standing by the tree in the deep twilight, locked so tightly together as if they were fighting. It must have been Mary Watts's leave day, because she had her hat and coat on. But the footman was still in his bright uniform. He was very bossy, was the footman, and you had always to give him his place and say Mr Simpson to him. As for Mary Watts, she was haughty, almost as haughty as Miss May. And yet they had been doing that. Life was very strange.

But Easter was coming and her mother was making her a new frock from some beautiful material out of the attic trunks. What was pleasing her more than anything was, their Davey seemed to be taking a liking for Jean, and Jean was over the moon. He'd often come to the laundry window on a Sunday and talk to Jean as much as he did to her. He had changed, had their Davey, not only in his looks but in his ways. He hadn't been very ready with his tongue when he was at home, but now he was, and he made jokes. Only one thing he wasn't happy about, that she was teaching the others to read and write. He had warned her, saying, 'That could get you into trouble. Deep trouble. They're funny about that here. For meself, I never let on I can write, I sign me name by a cross.' And she had turned on him and exclaimed, 'Oh! our Davey, after all the learning you got.' And to this he had answered, 'Well, that doesn't stand you in any stead in a house like this. Do your work, know your place, eat your grub, and be thankful. That's what I say, and you'll be wise if you follow the same line.'

She would never follow the same line, for she knew there was something inside her that would urge her to protest, no matter what the consequences. At times she wished she didn't feel like this, and once or twice she'd had to curb the feeling, as when the young master and mistress were out for a game and would come rampaging through the laundry kicking at the bundles of washing and grabbing up ladlesful of dirty frothy water and throwing it over the girls, the while Mrs Fitzsimmons laughed her head off at what she called their pranks.

Today was her and Jean's Sunday on. Mrs Fitzsimmons, Florrie, and Sally, were all on leave. It was a beautiful bright day, and near four o'clock in the afternoon, and they had just finished putting the staff underwear into a sawn-off tub of cold water and the men's underwear into a similar tub standing nearby.

Drying her arms on a piece of coarse sacking, Jean said, 'Doesn't look as if Davey's gona make it the day, does it, Biddy? Perhaps they've made him change his day again 'cos the masters are joining the riders.'

'Oh, there's plenty of time yet, up till six o'clock.'

'Yes, but he's nearly always here afore now.'

Biddy turned to her companion, 'Well, if he doesn't come,' she said, laughing, 'I'll march straight along into the stables and say to Mr Mottram, 'Where's me brother? Why hasn't he come along to see us this afternoon? Now answer me. Quick. Come on now. I'm not having him sent to that Lord Milton's place with the horses, they can find their own way.'

She was mimicking Mrs Fulton, and as Jean doubled up with laughter there came a sharp tap on the window.

Both girls ran to it. Thrusting it open, they looked bright-eyed at Davey. But Davey wasn't smiling today. 'I can't stop,' he said immediately; 'I've just come to warn you to look out, Miss Lucy and Paul are on the rampage, carrying on like two kids. They've been in the harness room and messed things up, dabbed things with blacking. Mr Lowther's furious. He told Mr Paul that he would see the master. And Mr Paul called him a stupid old pig. I think you'd better scoot across to the house as soon as possible.'

'We can't do that, Davey; we're here till six and there's quite a bit more to do. If we went across there afore that time and ran into Mrs Fulton, that would be worse than meeting up with Mr Paul and Miss Lucy.' She smiled now, and he replied, 'I don't know so much.' Then looking at Jean, he paused before saying softly, 'Hello, there.' And she replied as softly, 'Hello, Davey.'

'Well, I'd better be goin'.' He nodded from one to the other and then slid out of sight. And the girls closed the window and walked back to the middle of the room where Jean asked, 'What'll we do if they come in here and start playing up?'

'Well' – Biddy wagged her head – 'if they mess up the sorting like they usually do, I'm going to leave it like that until the morrow morning, and if Mrs Fitzsimmons says anything I'll tell her that the young master and mistress were in here working yesterday and this is the result.'

'You won't.'

'Oh, yes I will.'

And from the look on Biddy's face and the sound of her voice Jean knew that this mentor of hers would do exactly as she said. Her admiration for Biddy was boundless. She had never met anyone so brave and so clever. Each day she told herself that she loved her.

It was almost an hour later when the girls let the big woodenslatted drying-horse down from the ceiling. It was a heavy cumbersome affair, especially when as now the five rails were laden with the rough ironing, which had been done last thing the previous night, and consisted of all manner of towels.

Biddy had just secured the rope around the iron staple in the wall when the laundry door burst open and in marched Paul Gullmington and his sister Lucy. They were both in riding-habit, each carrying a small whip, and as if they were still on their horses they galloped down the length of the long room making whooping noises, until they came to a standstill opposite the two girls.

'Well now! Well now! What have we here? Two foxes?' Paul looked at his sister. His eyes were bright, his mouth wide with laughter. Her eyes too were bright, but her mouth wasn't wide with laughter, she was concentrating her gaze on the skivvy whom Laurence had favoured on Christmas night, and whose face over the past weeks had intruded into her vision more than once, as would have done any face that Laurence favoured. Laurence was her favourite and, she had imagined, she had always been his. She had decided that she would marry Laurence when she grew up, that's if May didn't get him beforehand, because he wasn't her brother. Yet this skivvy here had dared to hold his attention.

'What do we do with foxes?' She looked at her brother, and he replied, 'Chase. Chase! And now they both started to do a standing gallop, smacking their sides with their whips, and at this Jean turned and ran.

They did not, however, pursue her but cried at Biddy, 'Run! fox. Run!'

When, ashen-faced, she remained standing still, the boy grabbed her by the shoulder and pushed her forward; and when she stumbled he pushed her again.

Jean was now standing at the far end of the wash-house pressed tight against the wall, and Biddy was being pushed towards it when suddenly she turned round and faced her tormentors, crying at them, 'Stop it! both of you. You're acting like idiots.'

They stopped abruptly, and their expressions changing, they glanced at each other and the boy said, 'She called us idiots.'

'Well, she would she's very learned. She can write her name and speak French and Latin. Didn't you know?' And she now went into French, saying, 'Que je suis une fille habile.' And now he, throwing his head back and looking upwards to the ceiling and lifting his hand high in blessing, exclaimed loudly, 'Gloria in excelsis Deo.'

The charade might have ended here if Biddy had been able to stay her tongue, but her face scarlet with temper, she cried at them, 'And both your accents are provincial.'

This is what the master had continually said to her over the years: 'Don't talk like a provincial. This is not patois; you are speaking the French language as you would your north-country English.'

The effect of her words on the two young people opposite her was to take the grins from their faces. The very fact that this lackey could use the word provincial, and was applying it to them, enraged them both.

What followed happened so quickly that it brought screams from both Jean and Biddy, for when Lucy Gullmington's whip came across Biddy's ear and the side of her face, the echo of it hadn't died away when she felt herself thrust backwards; and then she was toppling, and for a moment she lay stunned, oblivious of the cold water soaking her clothes, for her head had come in contact with one side of the tub and the backs of her knees with the other. But the ice-cold water did one thing for her, it revived her anger to such an extent that she struggled to rise; but did so only with the help of Jean's hands. Then she was standing dripping in front of her tormentors and as quick as her young mistress had attacked her she reciprocated, for she almost sprang on her now and, twisting her around, she thrust her against the other tub of men's underwear and into it. It was all done so quickly that the boy had no power to prevent it happening.

The strange thing about it was that Lucy Gullmington didn't scream; but the sounds she was making were like throttled groans, and when her brother pulled her out, her riding-habit smeared with the scum from the dirty water, she stood shivering, for the water had penetrated to her skin. Then thrusting her brother's protective hands from her, she growled, 'Get her!' before her eyes, darting from one end of the laundry to the other, came to rest on the lowered drying-horse.

Biddy was now struggling with the young master, wreathing and twisting in an effort to get free from his arms which were tight around her. But she was no match for him. Between her gasping she was aware of two voices, Miss Lucy's giving orders and Jean's crying, 'Oh, don't! Please! don't. Don't!'

She knew a moment of terror when, lying flat on the stone floor now, the young master sitting on her legs while pinning her arms together, she saw the girl sweep the linen from the two lower rails; but her mind still didn't tell her what was in store for her, not even when she heard linen being ripped. Then her arms were dragged above her head and her wrist tied together so tightly that she cried; and her ankles, too, were tied, but not close together.

She screamed out, 'Jean! Jean!' but heard only the young master's voice growling. 'You make a move and you'll be next.'

When they hoisted her to her feet she would have fallen had she not been held up roughly by the back of the collar of her dress. The next thing she was aware of was the creaking of the pulley that lifted the drying-horse; then the girl's voice said, 'Just there.' Now she was being dragged under the bottom rail of the horse and her joined hands were tied to it with strips of linen. But still she couldn't imagine the ultimate until she felt her arms were being wrenched from their sockets and only her toes were touching the ground. Her screams deafened her; then they jerked the pulley rope and she stopped. In the strange silence that enveloped her she looked down at the two faces staring up at her and she imagined she was looking at devils and the last thought she was conscious of was that they had done this before, they knew exactly how to do it, and they were crucifying her like Jesus on the Cross.

So intent had the two young fiends been about their business that they hadn't noticed that Jean had escaped by the back door and into the yard; and now she was flying helter-skelter towards the stables, crying, 'Oh dear God! Oh dear God! Oh dear God!' as she went.

So intent was she in her rushing and so blinded with her own tears that she bumped into two men. One of them had to put his hand out to save her from falling backwards. And now she was looking up into the faces of Mr Stephen and Mr Laurence. They were both in their riding-habits, and she cried at them, 'They've got her strung up. Please come. Come on. Please, come. They've got her strung up.'

'What are you talking about, girl?' Stephen shook her shoulder, and she gulped and the saliva ran out of her mouth before she could say, 'In the wash-house. Master Paul and Miss Lucy, they've strung her up.'

The two young men turned and looked at each other and it was Laurence, his face twisting, who said, 'Strung who up?'

'Biddy. They've strung her up . . . on the drying-horse.'

Again the men looked at each other. Then turning, they ran together down the stable yard, round the corner of the coach house, and into the laundry yard. But when they entered the laundry they both came to a dead halt at the sight of their brother and sister standing below a girl who was hanging by her arms from the bottom of the drying-horse.

It seemed that Stephen took only two strides before he reached them, and what he did was instantaneous. With doubled fist he felled Paul to the ground, then with open hand he brought it hard across Lucy's face, causing her to cry out and to stagger back into Laurence's arms. But Laurence thrust her aside as if his hands had been stung, and then reached up to take the weight of the limp figure in his arms as Stephen lowered the drying-horse and then untied the knotted linen. When he pulled it away from the rail, so Biddy's dead-weight limp body slumped through Laurence's arms to the floor.

As the two young men stared apprehensively down on her Stephen said, 'Oh, my God, no! Try her heart.'

Laurence put his hand inside the collar of her dress. At first he could feel no beat until his fingers moved; and then he nodded and, looking at Jean, who was kneeling on the floor opposite him, he commanded, 'Go and get the housekeeper, quickly.' Then he looked to where Stephen was standing over his younger brother, growling now, 'By God, I'll take it out of your skin for this, young 'un. And wait till I tell our father. If you want to sport, sport with those that can strike back.'

Paul was holding his jaw and he looked defiantly at his brother as he said, 'She pushed Lucy into a butt.'

'There must have been a reason for it. There's a reason why you two are in here. What brought you? As for you – ' He turned and looked to where Lucy was standing staring towards Laurence as he knelt on the ground by the side of the hated girl, and he said, 'This will put the final stamp on it, miss. Mama won't be able to save you now. You had a warning last time: one more escapade and it's away to school with you, where they might knock some manners into you. But as regards manners' – he was glaring at Paul now – 'school doesn't seem to have done much for you. For two pins I've a mind to kick your bare arse till you can't sit on it.'

'Look here.' Laurence was beckoning to Stephen now and gently he turned Biddy's face to the side to show a red weal rising from the middle of her ear down to the side of her chin. 'What does that signify?' he asked, and Stephen, now glaring at his sister, was almost made speechless when Lucy, staring back at him, said, 'And I'll do it again.'

'By God, you will, miss!' He strode to her now and, swivelling her around as if she were a bundle of straw, he almost lifted her from her feet as he hopped her up the laundry and thrust her out of the door. But when Paul made to follow her, he said, 'You stay where you are, laddie. There'll be work for you to do if I know anything.'

Mrs Fulton came hurrying into the laundry, only to stop and look aghast for a moment at the scene before her. Then, as she stood above Biddy's prostrate form, she muttered, 'That girl again. She's always in trouble.'

'And whose fault is that?'

The little prim face became tight as she said, 'No one's but her own, sir, I would say.'

'And would you say there was any reason for her to be strung up to that contraption?' Laurence thrust his arm back. 'What if she had died from shock?'

'Well, it certainly wouldn't have been my fault, sir, as I had no hand in the business.'

No, she was right; she'd had no hand in the business. The hand or hands had come from her betters. He looked at the little woman with dislike as he now said, 'Get someone to carry her to the house and put her to bed, and see that she's attended to.'

As she turned away, Stephen cried, 'No need to get someone, Mrs Fulton, my brother here will be only too pleased to carry his victim to the house. Won't you, Paul?'

'I'll do no such thing.'

'You won't? But, by God you will!' The heavy boot caught the young fellow in the buttocks and nearly lifted him from the ground, and his face red with anger, he cried, 'How many more of those will I have to give you before you do what I tell you? Pick her up.'

'I could never carry her; she's too heavy.'

'She wasn't all that heavy when you strung her up, was she? Now get at it, or do you want another?'

The boy's teeth were clenched, his face almost as red as his hair, and as if he were being forced to touch something unclean, he bent and slipped one arm underneath Biddy's thighs and the other under her shoulders. But he could not have got to his feet with her except for Laurence's help. Then he was staggering up the laundry with his burden, and would surely have dropped her had not Laurence taken the girl from him, crying, 'Open the door,' as he did so.

Paul stumbled forward and thrust open the doors and stood aside and watched the man, whom for years he had thought of as his brother and whom he had never liked, stumble out and across the yard under the gaping mouth and wide eyes of a number of the staff, and into the house through the boot room.

Paul now walked out of the laundry and into the house by the main door; then made his way up to his sister's room. He went in without knocking, and as he looked at her he was surprised to see that she was crying. He put an arm around her shoulders and said, 'Don't you worry. We'll get our own back on that creature one way or another. It might take time, but you'll see, we'll do it. You'll do it your way and I'll do it mine. Oh yes, I'll do it mine.'

5

There was a feeling of excitement running through the staff, and none so high as in the laundry, for tomorrow was the thirty-first of July.

The laundry staff had always been aware of their status in the household. No one could get lower than the laundry staff except the cesspool cleaners, but they came from outside and weren't even allowed anywhere near the house. The nearest they got to any of the staff was when they delivered their loads to the farm and this only happened three times a year. So the combined efforts of the laundry staff – with the exception of course of Mrs Fitzsimmons – was to show them.

It just might have been possible that Biddy would have taken notice of Davey's warning with regard to the signing of names had it not been for the incident in the laundry. It had left a deep mark on her that she could have been subjected to such torment through, in the first place, no fault of her own, except for being audacious enough to answer the young master and mistress back, but to be held responsible for what had happened by those in charge, including both the butler and the valet besides the housekeeper, had incensed her.

What had happened, Mrs Fulton had informed her, had happened because she was what she was, a troublemaker, a harbinger of ill fortune. Nothing, Mrs Fulton said, had been the same since she entered the household, for, before that, who would have thought of Mr Laurence and Mr Stephen going for Master Paul and Miss Lucy, especially when, as everybody knew, she doted on Mr Laurence. All right, they had strung the girl up. She hadn't been the first one that had been strung up; and, too, she had got off lightly because she hadn't been flogged. If it had been in the days of the old master she would have been, and she wouldn't have dared open her mouth. Well, Mrs Fulton had informed her, the matter had gone before the master and mistress and they had agreed that she was to have another chance. If it had lain with her, she knew what chance she would have given her. And poor Miss Lucy being sent off to school when everybody knew Miss Lucy hated school. She would hardly attend to Miss Collins's lessons, all she wanted to do was ride. And what was wrong with that for a young lady? As for Master Paul, his allowance had been cut. What did she think about that? Couldn't she see that she was a troublemaker.

Biddy had lain in her bed for three days, and for the first day she had hardly known where she was. Her mind played tricks with her, taking her into the fanciful stories she had read. She had seen herself gambolling through forests, sailing over seas that were beyond imagination, and, strangest of all, being wooed by a prince. She had hung on to that part of her delirium. They had called the doctor into her the second day and he greeted her with, 'Well, well! the lively pupil.' He had examined her and found her unhurt except for the weal down the side of her face, which, he had said would fade with time.

How the news of the incident had spread to her mother, she didn't know, but she came on the third day and said she was going to take her home; and in spite of this being her dearest wish and then her hope, she had refused to go. The reason for her change of mind escaped her at the time, but shortly afterwards she knew that the reason was to do with defiance, for she meant to show them. She meant to show that she was different from the lot of them: she was learned. She was determined not only to read more, but to carry on studying her French and Latin. This she knew might be difficult without guidance, but she was going to try.

But now the excitement that ran through the staff section of the house would reach its highest point tomorrow at the end of the corridor of the north wing, for the four laundry girls were going to sign their names when they received their half-pay.

The procedure of pay-day was similar in a way to that of the present receiving on Christmas morning. The only difference was, they went one after another into the library where, at the head of the long table that ran down the middle of the room, sat the master, while standing to one side of him on this day was his new steward, Mr Daniel Yarrow, and to the other side of him, his butler Thomas Froggett.

As each member of the staff approached his name was called out by the butler and the steward checked it from a long list and stated the amount to be paid; then the master counted it out before handing it to the butler, who handed it to the recipient, then said, 'Sign,' which meant in every case a mere cross.

The head of each department had preceded its underlings; and now at the end of the long list Mrs Jinny Fitzsimmons sidled into the room, subservience oozing out of every pore of her large body. When she received her six pounds ten shillings, she dipped her knee, looked at the master and said, 'Thank you, sir,' to which he did not reply with a movement either of the eye or head, but sighed as he continued to look down on the long list of wages he was being forced to meet.

When the steward now read from the list saying, 'Florrie McNulty, assistant laundress, three pounds nine shillings,' Mr Gullmington counted the money out, handed it to the butler who then, handing it to Florrie, said, 'Sign.'

And Florrie signed. Slowly, in copperplate writing, she wrote, 'Florrie McNulty.'

A cross takes but a second to make, but fourteen copperplate letters took over forty seconds and brought three pairs of male eyes on her. When she had finished she straightened her back, smiled, dipped her knee, and said, 'Thank you, sir,' backed two steps from the table and marched out. And march is the descriptive word.

The three men now looked at each other but said nothing.

Then there entered Sally Finch, and the steward read out, 'Sally Finch, staff scrubber laundress, two pounds twelve shillings.' The master handed the money to the butler and the butler handed it to Sally, saying after a slight hesitation, 'Sign.' He pointed to the paper, and Sally, before signing, looked up at him and smiled. She had only ten letters to her name, but it took her almost as long to sign as it had Florrie.

After she had dipped her knee and said, 'Thank you, sir,' and departed, the master looked at his butler and said, 'What is this, Froggett?' And Froggett, after a slight gulp, said, 'I . . . I wasn't aware that they . . . could write, sir.'

The steward was now saying, 'Jean Bitton, scrubber laundress, one pound sixteen and threepence.'

Jean looked nervous. She was remembering what Davey had said: unlike Biddy and the rest, if she got the push she had nowhere to go, only back to the poorhouse. But nevertheless, she wrote the name that had been given to her when at the age of six months she had been placed in the care of the poorhouse authorities, Jean Bitton.

There was silence among the three men now as they waited for the last laundry assistant to enter, and at least two of them knew who was the instigator of this insurrection. The butler had no doubt whatever in his mind; and the master had heard of the poem reading on Christmas night, but more so, there was in his mind now the incident when this girl entering the room now had so enraged his daughter and son by ridiculing their French pronunciation that they had strung her up, and in doing so had created a division in the family, which was apparent to this very minute.

Anthony George Gullmington considered himself an easy going man. He did not demand much from life, so he told himself: a good table, good wine, his body needs satisfied, but most of all some good horseflesh between his legs. That's all he asked. For the rest, he paid a large staff to see to the running of his house. By God! he did pay too. Look at the money that had passed through his fingers this morning, besides which he had to pay to clothe them from head to foot and allow them to eat their heads off, and drink his wine. Oh yes, he knew what went on all right, he was no fool. But as long as they kept their place he closed his eyes to lots of things. That was the main thing though, they keeping their place. He was not a religious person, not like his wife, at least he was no fanatic, but he did believe that God had ordered a certain way of life for different beings and that way could not be carried out unless the lower classes were kept in their place and accepted their place; and their place was to work with their hands and only to use their heads as much as was necessary to achieve the best results of their labour. So far and no further. But once a man started reading and writing, then you had trouble. He had an example of it among his own. Well, not exactly his own. Stephen was no scholar and Paul was going to follow suit, but Laurence preferred a book to a horse. And that wasn't natural for a gentleman, except he intended to turn into a crank, like that one who had died recently over at Moor House. *Yes. Oh yes.* And this was the result of his crankiness coming towards him now. How old was she? She was tall; she looked sixteen or more, and good-looking. She'd be a beauty in a year or two's time, with a figure to go with it. Well, if she was wise there were uses for that figure. But he doubted if this one would be wise, for she had already got a taste of the power of the pen and she had sent three examples in before her. My God! He felt an anger rising in him. Here was the kind of person who instigated trouble and upheavals. If she had been a man there was no knowing what she would have caused. Anyway, she had already caused enough in this household, but she'd cause no more.

The steward called out, 'Bridget Millican, laundry' – he paused on the next word – 'runabout'. Apparently he had not heard of such a title before. 'One pound six shillings.'

Anthony Gullmington counted the money out, handed it to the butler, and the butler, pushing it across the table to Biddy, pointed to the paper and in a voice that sounded like the knell of doom said, 'Sign.'

Biddy looked from one to the other of the men; then she signed her name. It did not take her many seconds and she did it with a flourish. When she went to dip her knee and say, 'Thank you, sir,' the master looked at her and he said, 'Since when have you been given authority to teach my staff to write?'

The response of Biddy Millican from the pit row might have been, 'What . . . what do you mean, sir?' But Bridget Millican, who had come under Percival Miller's tuition, said, 'I did not think I needed permission, sir; I did it in my spare time.'

'You knew that it was forbidden.'

'No, I did not, sir.'

'Well, miss, let me tell you, it is forbidden. You are here to work. You have been assigned to a certain position. That is all that is required of you. If I wished my staff to be educated, I would give the order for it. Do you understand me?'

'Yes, sir.' The big brown eyes showed no fear of him. There was a strange quietness in their depth that, for a moment, made him want to retaliate, just as his son and daughter had. Who was this girl anyway? What was she? How dare she! What were things coming to! The platitudes raced through his mind. Now turning his glaring gaze on the butler, he said, 'Fetch me the housekeeper.' Then to Biddy, 'As for you, wait outside.'

Biddy might have appeared calm, but it was only on the surface for inside she was trembling, and she felt sick. There was a slight commotion in the hall, a bustling of servants, some of them looking up the stairs. The butler now passed her with the housekeeper and if she had any doubts that her time here was short, their looks confirmed it.

They had no sooner entered the library than the master's voice could be heard bawling at them, and as he preceded them from the room still bawling, two footmen carried Madam Gullmington's chair down the last of the stairs and placed it in the hall.

It was her custom on a fine day to be wheeled around the garden, and this was a fine day, a soft windless day, but the old lady gauged immediately there was a high wind of temper blowing through he house, and as she saw her son approaching her, she stopped him, saying, 'What's all this?'

'What's all this?' he repeated. 'Defied in my own household.' He pointed to where Biddy stood waiting with downcast eyes. 'That individual has been running a tutoring under my very nose, under the nose of this entire staff presumably. Four sluts from the laundry signing their names in full. How many staff have we here, Mama? You tell me. Have any of them been able to read or write? Oh . . . Fulton' – he waved his hand to the side – 'she can write her name and count, and that's about all, because she has to. But for the rest . . .'

'Be quiet.' She was staring fixedly at her son. Then she ordered Jessie Hobson now, 'Take me to the drawing-room,' and Jessie, obeying, pushed the wheelchair into the drawing-room, and as she turned to leave, Grace Gullmington entered.

She was dressed for the carriage in a voluptuous skirted blue taffeta gown over which was a cream lace coat, its skirt kept up balloon-wise by the dress. Her hat was of cream straw. It was a tall hat, its crown bedecked with flowers, its intent to give height to its wearer, but it achieved only the opposite effect. She had the appearance of an overdressed doll. But her voice was by no means doll-like as she demanded, 'What may I ask, is this narration about?'

'You may ask, woman.' Her husband was bawling at her now. 'If you saw to this staff as you should do, the present occurrence would never have happened: nor would that incident three months ago have taken place. You haven't any idea how to bring your family up, madam. If you stopped praying and did a little more saying, this household would run more smoothly. We never had anything like this in Mama's time, did we?'

His face was almost ruby red as he addressed his mother, and her reply was, 'Shut up, Tony, and sit down and calm yourself, and tell me what this is about.'

As if he was still a young boy, her son immediately sat down and after drawing in a number of hissing breaths he said, 'It's that young skit who apparently was given a little knowledge by that mad bloke down at Moor House, and she has passed it on to the rest of the laundry staff, except the top one. They all came in there this morning' – he thumbed towards the fireplace – 'and signed their names, brazen as brass. Rows and rows of crosses, and there were these three scum signing their names. And all through that miss, who also prides herself that she can speak French. Did you ever hear of any such thing?'

'She'll have to go.'

Anthony Gullmington now glared at his wife as he shouted 'Of course she'll have to go. She should have gone long before now.'

Then the attention of both was drawn again towards the old woman in the chair for she had laid her head back against the leather cushion and was staring upwards, her eyes wide in her face that looked like a mask, so thickly was it powdered. And now she began to talk: 'Yes,' she said, 'send her packing. And the others with her if you like. Yes, do that, and it will be all over the county that Gullmington couldn't bear any of his staff to write their names.' Her head came forward now as she went on, 'Not that I'm for the lower classes writing their names or being educted in any way, no, I'm with you there, Tony, but what I'm thinking about is, you've decided that Stephen must try for Parliament next year. Now as far as I can gather from both Laurence and Stephen there are men up there who are making themselves felt calling for certain liberties for the lower classes, and causing contention in the house at the present moment, trying to get bills through to establish schools for the education of the poor in every parish in this country. Now of course they can push all the bills through the Commons that they like, but it's getting them through the Lords. That is the crucial point; and I think there is as much chance of getting education for all the poor through the Lords as that child who has caused a rumpus becoming Queen of England. But that isn't the point' – she now looked at her son – 'the point at the moment is, education for the lower class is a platform from which young men may spring quickly into prominence, young men like Stephen who have never been heard of outside this county.' She drew a long breath before going on, 'Now Tony' – she nodded slowly at her son – 'it is your dearest wish, isn't it, that Stephen will some day take his seat in the House? Well, can you tell me what his policy is going to be? Is he going to shout for the status quo as ninety per cent of the landowners in the country are doing, or join the other ten per cent, some of them, I understand, factory owners in the Midlands who have cut as much as an hour off their employees' day; and moreover, besides their free Sunday they allow them to finish at four o'clock on a Saturday. Eh? Eh?'

'Now all this you should have learned from your son and Laurence over the past weeks, for quite candidly I have become weary of the conversations that have flowed back and forward over my chair, and even over my bed at night, between them. And I can tell you this, and it's not going to please you, particularly you, Grace.' She was looking at her daughter-in-law. 'If anyone should stand for Parliament it should be Laurence, because his cause seems to be, again this controversial word, education, and if Stephen ever does take his seat up there, he'll have Laurence to thank for stuffing some facts into his head and giving him a purpose, because he would never have found it on his own, being too much like his father.' And she riveted her gaze on her son. 'All you have ever thought about, Tony, from the time you could crawl, has been horses. There may have been one or two other things that have alighted on your horizon, but they've taken second and third places. Horses. Horses. Horses. And Stephen is no better. Oh, I'm not saying – she moved her head from side to side – 'I'm not saying that Stephen is not a decent enough fellow. I'm very very fond of Stephen, and I will prove it if he carries out this idea, for to be a member doesn't so much require brains as money; it will take large sums to pave the way and buy him in. And you, Tony, no longer have any large sums to play around with, have you? I could say, you could of course pave his way with the money you spend on horseflesh, but that would be asking too much, wouldn't it?'

'*Oh, Mother.*'

'Don't say, "Oh, Mother," like that to me; you know I am speaking the truth. But let's get back to the point. If you dismiss this girl and the reason for it spreads, Stephen will have to find another crutch on which to help him limp to London, because education was going to be one of the flags he was going to fly to attract the attention of his peers. Of course' – she pursed her wrinkled lips – 'there's always the other side of it, he could take the opposite course and sit unnoticed among the old fogies up there until his beard touches his knees.'

She watched her son now lumber to his feet and heard his teeth grind against each other before he said, 'I'm against it, Mother. You know I'm against that kind of education.'

Her voice was soft as she replied, 'Yes, I know you are, Tony, as I am, and as is Stephen at bottom, but do you know anybody who has ever furthered himself politically by coming out into the open and standing up for what he knows to be right? You tell me of one. Parliament to my mind is a rookery: every one of them cawing, cawing, cawing, in order to stay on their bit of the branch. And they all caw the same tune. If they changed it, the rest of the flock would attack them.' She now turned and with a grin on her face, she nodded at her daughter-in-law, saying, 'A very good simile that. And when I'm on about birds, compare the number of eagles with rooks. They are few and far between, but by God, don't they stand out. And some of them even come to believe in the noises that they're making. Not that I think Stephen has the makings of an eagle, but he could come in under one of their wings, to be noticed. Well, what about it?'

'What do you want me to do?' Her son's voice was quiet now. 'We can't keep that girl on after this. The staff wouldn't tolerate her.'

'Who's master in this house, you, or Fulton and Froggett? Anyway – ' she now bounced her head towards first one then the other, clasped her thin white lace mittened hands together before stating, 'I'll take the girl.'

'*You'll what?*'

'You're not deaf, Tony; you heard what I said. And this business seems to have come about at an opportune time, because Hobson's feet won't carry her much longer, and this girl can be trained to fetch an' carry. And I shall certainly see that she has no opportunity for furthering her education as long as she's in my house. It's a solution, as I see it, that will benefit everyone in the long run. She can come off your wage sheet, I'll see to that; the staff will be glad to get rid of her; and what's more, your name won't be bandied about for dismissing a poor little mite because she could write her own name. I can just see it. I can just see it . . .'

'I don't see this matter your way, Mother-in-law.' Grace Gullmington's voice cut in deceptively quiet. 'No, I don't. I think she should be dismissed, and I'm sure our neighbours and the people who matter will agree with Anthony's' – she inclined her head towards her husband – 'decision. No one could blame him in the least, in fact I'm sure he would be hailed . . .'

'Don't try to be more stupid than God made you, woman.'

The insult brought a scarlet flush to Grace Gullmington's face and a reproving, 'Now, now, Mother,' from Anthony, and she turned on them both, her eyes flashing now. 'You are a pair of nit-wits,' she cried. 'Always have been and always will. And of the two, you are the bigger, madam.' The saliva actually spurted from her lips on the last word. 'And let me remind both of you, I may keep to my own end of this establishment but what should be evident to you is, I still rule it, because if I were to decide to move myself to another estate, and I could do, my legs may be weak but my head is far from it, I take my money with me.' She now let her blazing gaze rest on her son as she ended, 'And how long would you survive on your two thousand a year? This house is yours by inheritance, but it needs one hell of a lot of money to keep it up. You would, I foretell, be living in a dower house within months. So think on it. As for you madam' – once more she was looking at her daughter-in-law – 'don't you dare say to me that you will not have such and such happen here. How you ever came to be mistress of this place will always be a mystery to me. Now if it had been your despised cousin, Laurence's mother, I could have understood it, because besides beauty, she had brains. And that's why you hated her, wasn't it? Why, if it hadn't been for me, you would have rejected her plea for a home for her child. In fact, you did reject it, didn't you? Although she had been deserted and was dying, you hadn't it in your mean little heart to give her succour and . . .'

'Mama! Mama!'

'Don't you mama me. You will not stop my tongue at this stage; this is always something that I've wanted to say. Now ring that bell for Hobson.' She flung her arm out towards the bell-pull hanging by the fireplace. 'And let me say this finally, if I hear one more aggravating word I will do as I threatened a moment earlier. As you both know, Buxley Manor is up for sale and I've always like that establishment. I would be doing Lord Milton a service in buying it, for he has run out of money for his gambling up in London . . .'

The door opened and when the butler appeared, the old lady cried at him one single name, 'Hobson.'

Jessie now came hurrying into the room as quick as her painful feet would allow and as she turned the chair round and went to wheel it into the hall, the old lady cried, 'that girl, the one that has caused the uproar, where is she?'

'In the hall, Madam.'

'Send her up into my house and tell her to stay there. I will see her on my return. *Now.*' She cried the word at the two footmen, and they once again lifted the chair and carried it out through the front door on to the wide drive.

As this was taking place Jessie Hobson hurried across to Biddy where she was standing in the shadow of the stairs, and said to her, 'Go to the west wing, madam's house.'

Biddy was unable to speak for a moment and she gulped and sniffed before she could say, 'I . . . I don't know which way . . . and why?'

'*Never mind why, girl.*' Jessie now turned and, beckoning June Cordell towards her, she said, 'Take this girl up to madam's house. Put her in my sitting-room.' And the woman said, 'Yes, miss;' then beckoning to Biddy, she took her past the foot of the main staircase, across the hall, through a side door, along a passage, and up two flights of narrow stairs, then through another door; and now Biddy found herself in the gallery of the house for the first time. The maid hurried her along it, then pushed open one side of a heavily embossed cream enamel double door, after which she put out her hand and pulled Biddy inside and into the hall that opened out of the west wing gallery. There were a number of doors leading from the hall, also two passages. At the end of one passage the maid thrust open a door and, pointing, she said, 'Stay there.' But instead of turning immediately away and scurrying back as she had scurried here, she looked at Biddy through narrowed eyes, saying, 'Eeh, the things you get up to. It's as they say, there's never been a one like you here afore. Why do you do it?'

She waited for an answer, but Biddy remained silent. She was too bemused to even think of a reply. In the ordinary scheme of things, she should be on her way out with her bundle after that commotion in the drawing-room, for it had just sounded exactly like a row in the pit row on a Saturday night when some of the men had come home rolling drunk. It was impossible to believe that the gentry could raise their voices like that. Young ones, like the two that had attacked her, oh, yes, them, but not when they were grown up and held positions. Why had she been sent up here? Suddenly she sat down on the nearest chair which was a rocking-chair and to the amazement of the housemaid she began rocking herself.

As June Cordell was to say in the staff room later on that day, the sight of the girl sitting there rocking herself and not saying a word, as cool as a cucumber like, gave her quite a turn. She agreed wholeheartedly with the rest of them that there was something odd about her. And fancy finding all that stuff in her mattress, and that book that the housekeeper said was a foreign one, besides the one with poems. And that wasn't all. Look what they had found in the other laundry maids' mattresses, practically the same, except they hadn't any foreign books. It was right, there was something weird about her, and things had never been the same in the house since she came. And remember what the parson had said last week about evil spirits. Well, there was something in that. But then look where she had landed? Up in the choice part of the house. Any one of them would have given their eyeballs to be promoted up there permanent like, because it was a sure thing that Miss Hobson's feet wouldn't hold her up much longer, and now it could be possible that she would train that one to take her place. Eeh! it was incredible.

Everyone around the table agreed that it was incredible.

But this was to be at seven o'clock that evening.

Upstairs, sitting on the rocking-chair, Biddy did not put the word incredible to her situation, for she was unable to think clearly about it all. She did not know what was going to happen to her, nor why she had been sent up here. There was only one thing sure, she would soon find out.

It was over an hour later when she found out. Jessie Hobson, coming into the room, brought her to her feet, and the older woman, wagging a finger at her, said, 'Now Biddy, listen to me. I haven't much time to prime you, all I can say is there's a chance in a lifetime staring you in the face. It's up to you how you behave, whether you get it or not. Do you understand what I'm saying to you?'

'Not . . . not quite.'

Jessie closed her eyes for a moment, then said, 'Well, it's like this. Madam has saved you from being thrown out. Why, I really can't tell you.' Her voice sank. 'She's a contrary character; she could have just done it to spite the mistress, but for what reason doesn't matter. You're up here and your job will be to run, and fetch, and carry. Do all the menial jobs, but at the same time watch me and all the things I have to do for madam; then if you can fit in, who knows, she might take to you or she might not. If she takes to you, she'll give you a rough time; if she doesn't take to you, you won't be here to have a rough time. Now, do you understand me?'

'Yes, Miss Hobson.'

'Well, come along now. But there's one thing I'll tell you before you start: you've got everybody, except' – she pulled a long face now – 'your pupils, agen you, and I'm not only meaning the staff, but them up top an' all. So if you want to remain here, you've got a battle on your hands.'

She didn't want to remain here. But then what was she thinking? One day she could become a lady's maid. The glory of the sudden realization lifted her chin and straightened her shoulders, and now she followed Jessie Hobson out of the room, along the wide corridor, past four doors, then stopped with her before another set of double doors.

Jessie tapped lightly on one door, then pushed it open, at the same time taking Biddy by the hand, and then slowly led her to where the old lady was sitting in a blue velvet-padded chair near the window.

Biddy had never seen the old lady close up before. She looked terribly old to her. She thought she had never seen anybody look as old, not even the very old women in the hamlets, because even if their skin was wrinkled, it still looked like skin, whereas this face was so painted and powdered it looked like one of the china dolls she had seen the one and only time she had visited Gateshead Fell Fair.

'Well! Well! So this is the creator of all the trouble.'

The voice had no connection with the face for it was strong and vibrant.

'So you can read and write, miss. You have also touched on French and Latin, so I understand. Well! Well! How learned you must be.'

Biddy felt her face growing scarlet. She was being made fun of.

'Speak to me in French.'

When Biddy remained silent the voice barked at her, 'Do you hear me, girl? I said, speak to me in French.'

Her mind was going at a gallop trying to form a sentence. Then the words threw themselves at her; they jumped into her mouth and from her lips and she said, 'Bonjour, madame. J'espère que vous êtes en bonne santé.'

'My God!' The old lady was looking up at Jessie Hobson now, and she cried, 'She can! She can do it. And you know what she said to me, Hobson? No, of course you wouldn't. She said – ' She turned her head now towards Biddy and commanded, 'Tell her what you said in English.'

Biddy wetted her lips, swallowed, then said, 'I wouldn't be so bold, Madam.'

'Do you hear that? Do you hear that, Hobson? What are things coming to, eh? A laundry slut, only one above the sewage cleaners in status, speaks to me in French, then disobeys my order.'

Her manner changing, and her rouged and powdered face seeming to crack as it was screwed up and thrust towards Biddy, she cried, 'Well, let that be the last evidence of your learning I am to hear. Do you understand me? There'll be no more French up here, and no more reading and writing. Speak girl. Do you understand me?'

Yes, Biddy understood all right, but she couldn't answer, or she wouldn't answer, and so Jessie put in hastily, 'I'll see that she doesn't, mad . . .'

'Shut up! Hobson. Let her answer for herself. Do you understand me, girl?'

'Yes, madam. I understand you perfectly.'

The words were spoken in a way that Percival Miller would have approved of, and they caused the old lady to sit back on her chair and to close her eyes for a moment. When she opened them again she stared at the flushed face before her, the brown eyes looking straight into hers, and her voice was deceptively soft as she said, 'You understand me; that's good. But do you mean to obey me?'

A large section of Biddy's mind cried at her: Say yes. Say yes. But when she heard herself say quietly, 'I cannot promise faithfully, madam, to obey you on that point,' some part of her shrank down inside and buried its head, waiting for the onslaught, while she continued to stare into the small faded blue eyes that were glaring into hers. She watched the head turn slowly and look up at her maid, and she listened to her saying, 'We can understand now, can't we, Hobson, why the whole household is up in arms?'

'Yes, madam.' Jessie's voice was small, her face was wearing a pained look, and she cast her eyes towards the girl she hoped would be her charge but whom she could now see haring out the back gates with her bundle.

'Do you think she realizes that she has set this whole household agog today, and, from what I can gather, not only today? Do you think she knows that she's got all the staff against her?'

'Yes, yes, I think she does, madam.'

'You think she does?' The head was turned towards Biddy again, and now the question was put to her: 'Do you know, girl, that you have got all the staff against you? And for whatever time you stay in this house, long or short, their feelings towards you, if I know anything about that class, will remain the same, if not intensify. Do you know that, girl?'

What had she to lose? She was for the road in any case. Yet, of a sudden, she didn't want to be for the road; she somehow felt that she would like to work for this old woman. Why? She didn't know, because she could be a holy terror, she could see that. A small section of her mind asked her how the master would have answered in this case; and then he was in her mind, pushing the words through her throat, into her mouth, and they came out as she said, 'I know fine well, madam, how I am looked upon by the staff, but I would be willing to put up with that if I could be employed in your service, and although I cannot promise you truthfully I shall never read or write again, I can promise that I shall work well for you and give you my loyalty for as long as you need me, that is, if Miss Hobson – ' She now glanced at Jessie Hobson, whose face seemed to have stretched the other way, as she ended, 'if she will guide me to know your wants.'

It was then that the most surprising thing happened, surprising not only to Biddy, or to the lady's maid, but to Diana Gullmington herself, for she put her head back and she laughed. She laughed heartily for the first time for many a long day, for she found that she was being both amused and interested by this creature from below stairs, well below stairs.

When the water from her eyes made rivulets down through the powder and rouge, Jessie grabbed at a fine lawn handkerchief from a box on the table to the side of her and as she handed it to her mistress she smiled at her. 'Take her away and get her decently clothed,' the old lady said.

6

During the time the domestic upheaval was taking place Stephen and Laurence were touring France; May was with a distant cousin enjoying for the first time the London season; Paul was staying with a school-friend in Durham; and Lucy had only on that particular morning taken the coach to Doncaster where she was to spend some weeks of her summer holiday with the family of her father's cousin. She had travelled chaperoned by the family's children's governess who had been sent to escort her. This was the second year she had holidayed with this family; the first time she enjoyed it immensely as there were three sons all older than her, besides two who were younger, and to all she had been able to show off her prowess as a horsewoman.

So it was that only when each of them returned at different times during the next weeks did they learn of the uproar that the laundry maid had caused yet once again; and their reactions were all different.

Stephen had said, 'She isn't up there? Not on your life!' May had said, 'It's disgraceful. How could you allow it, Mama?' And her mama had answered her with one word, 'Grandmama,' which told all. Lucy Gullmington had actually stamped her foot and declared that if she should cross her path, she would slap her face for her, to which Laurence had replied quietly, 'I shouldn't do that if I were you for in some curious way that child has a habit of winning.' To which Lucy had replied, 'Child, indeed! She's no child; if she's a child I'm a child. She's an upstart skivvy, and I'll never be able to understand you taking her part.' And May had put in at this stage, 'He does it just to vex you . . . and me. Don't you, Laurence?' And Laurence had said, 'Don't be ridiculous.'

The only person who didn't make any comment at all was Paul, and Laurence took note of this and didn't like what it signified . . .

He had only been in the house a few hours when he paid a visit to the west wing to be greeted by Diana Gullmington holding her arms out to him and crying whole-heartedly, 'Oh, I am glad to see you back. Do you know I have been very worried, especially when I learned there were summer storms at sea.'

'Oh, Grandmama – ' He kissed her on both cheeks, then took his seat beside her as he said, 'The crossing was the proverbial millpond. Of course it had to be; I ordered the waters to be still. However strong Stephen's stomach is on land, it becomes a weak thing when it is set upon water. He had a fearful time going over.'

'Did you enjoy your trip? Tell me, tell me all about it.'

'Oh, yes, we enjoyed it thoroughly. Paris I found very civilized at the moment.'

'Really!' the old lady cut in now. 'Civilized you say? Which Napoleon is it who's trying to scare the world now? Candidly Laurie' – she put her hand upon his knee – 'I've been worried all the time you and Stephen have been over there. Civilized, you say?'

'Well, in Paris that is, but as one travels through the country there's a great deal of poverty, but it's a different kind of poverty from here.'

'Poverty!' She stressed the word. 'You didn't go to France to seek out poverty.'

'But if it's staring you in the face, Grandmama, you can't help but see it, and smell it.'

'Oh!' She wagged her hand in front of his face and her nose twitched as if she was already experiencing the stink as she said, 'Thank God you're not going in for politics, although at one time I used to think you should, because the trouble with you, unlike Stephen, you would be voicing your own opinions and that would never do in Parliament.'

He wasn't aware of the door opening or that anyone had entered the room until she looked beyond him, saying, 'What is it, girl?' And now he turned in his chair and saw a young person, tall and slim. She was wearing a pale blue cotton dress edged at the neck by a small white collar and white cuffs at her wrists. On her auburn hair was a small cap which in no way covered her head, but was perched like a crown in the centre of it. The face underneath the cap was cream-skinned, the cheeks flushed slightly pink; the eyes were deep brown and long-lashed; the eyebrows followed the bone formation; the mouth was large but well-shaped; the nose was small and the chin firm. The girl was the same, yet not the same as the one he had lifted down from the laundry dryer. That face had appeared like one on the point of death, this face emphasized glowing life. He thought he had never seen a face that expressed life so vividly, yet in what way he found it hard to define, for she wasn't smiling; her expression, he would say, was neutral.

'I have brought your milk, madam.' Biddy set the small tray with a glass of milk on the side table, and the old lady said, 'My goodness, is it time for that again?' Then looking at Laurence, she added, 'That old fool Pritchard has stopped my afternoon wine. He says it's going to my legs. I told him not to be an ass; good wine never drops below the chest.' She gurgled at her own joke; and Laurence joined her, then asked, 'How are they?' And she, looking down at her blue taffeta skirt said, 'Still there I suppose, but sometimes I don't know what use they are. Why should this happen to me? I ask you. I've lived a moderate life; I've never exceeded three glasses at dinner, never; I like my afternoon nip, but what's that, I ask you . . . Girl!' She was now yelling at Biddy, and Biddy half-way to the door turned about, and the old woman, still yelling, cried, 'What have I told you about waiting to be dismissed?'

'I thought madam having company . . .'

'You're not here to think. I've also told you that. Away with you.'

Once the door closed she asked of Laurence, 'What do you make of that, eh? Did you ever see the likes, how she answers back?' Then thrusting her face towards him, and her eyes twinkling and her lips pursed, she said, 'I'll let you into a secret. I enjoy her in a way. You know why?'

'No, Grandmama.'

'She's not afraid of me. Now isn't that strange? She's not afraid of me. Old Hobson was scared out of her wits for the first year or so, and she's been with me now all of thirty years and at times she's still scared. But that one, with her reading and writing which I've forbidden her to continue, she's of a new generation, don't you think?'

'Yes, I do think so, Grandmama.'

She leant back, surveying him through narrowed eyes as she said, 'I suppose you've heard all about the rumpus and the reason why I brought her up here?'

'Yes.' He nodded his head slowly at her. 'I've heard one version of the reason, diplomacy with regards to Stephen and Parliament. But that wasn't the real reason, was it?'

She grinned at him now as she said, 'It's the only satisfaction I get out of life, opposing her. I'm very loyal in my likes and dislikes, Laurence, and I've never forgiven Tony for landing me with a daughter-in-law like her. Why should he pick such a mealy-mouthed, pious piece, I ask you? He was a rake and was off with this hussy and that, and I'd rather have had any one of them any day of the week than that one.' She thumbed towards the bedhead. 'And he became a different character once she got him. He's almost as mealy-mouthed now as she is. Do you know he was the means of two servants being sent packing with their bellies full in his young days? Did you know that?'

He hadn't known that and he didn't smile at the new knowledge.

'Of course he couldn't hold a candle to his father. As for his grandfather, whose exploits Harold regaled me with on our wedding night during the time he had breath – ' she pulled a face now before going on, 'it would appear that if any male servant wished to marry a female one, he had to get his leave, and his price was to test the qualities of the future bride.' She now stopped, her eyes narrowing still further as she said, 'You're not amused, are you, Laurence?'

'No, Grandmama, I can't say I am.'

'You're not against women, are you?' The question was serious and he answered her seriously, 'No, Grandmama, I'm not against them, not at all.'

'How many have you had so far?'

He rose slowly from the bed, saying now, 'That is my business and mine only.'

'Oh' – she flapped her hand at him – 'don't you start being mealy-mouthed, else that'll be the end of me. Go on, get yourself away.'

He didn't obey her, but smiling low, he leant towards her, saying softly, 'You know what you are? You are a wicked old woman.'

She stared back into his face for a moment before replying, 'Wicked I may be, but old I'm not, except from here.' And now she brought her hand across her eyebrows, then added, 'Admitted from here downwards, but above that, I am no more than thirty.'

He laughed out aloud now, saying, 'You're right, perfectly right.'

'Laurence' – her voice was low now – 'have you thought of marrying?'

'Yes. Yes, I've thought of marrying, but that's in the future.'

'Anyone in your eye?'

He cocked his head as if considering, then looking back at her, he said, 'No, no one in particular.'

'Have you ever thought of May?'

The question brought him ramrod straight, and now he drew his chin into his cravat before repeating, 'May! You mean as a wife?'

'Yes, I mean as a wife.'

'Oh, Grandmama, you must be joking. She's . . . she's . . .'

'She's not, she's no blood connection with you whatever. Well, if there is any there it's such a thin line it wouldn't help to make a spider's web.'

'That may be so, but she is my sister in all other ways.'

'She is not your sister in all other ways, and she's got you lined up.'

'Oh, Grandmama' – he gave a slight laugh now – 'this is sheer imagination.'

Her manner changing abruptly, she said, 'don't tell me that I imagine such things. I am versed in the ways of both women and men. I can interpret a look half a mile away, so to speak. May is fond of you, more than fond of you.'

'Well, if that is the case, Grandmama, she's going to be very disappointed, because I don't, and never have, and never will, consider May as anything but a sister.'

'You're a fool then. Next to Stephen, she could be very well off when I go. As for you, do I have to remind you that you haven't got a penny?'

'No, you don't have to remind me, and I am very conscious that I owe my upbringing to you, but as for not having a penny, I understand that I shall come into a little money when I am twenty-five, and in the meantime, if I had to, I could earn my living by teaching. In any case, I mean to teach, and this will bring me in enough to live on.'

'Money when you're twenty-five, and what will that be? a measly three hundred pounds a year. It wouldn't keep you in cigars.'

'Then I won't have to smoke cigars. Goodbye, Grandmama. I'll see you later.' As he turned abruptly from her, she called after him, 'Pighead. Stupid, short-sighted pighead.' And after he had closed the door her voice still came at him.

As he was passing down the hallway Jessie came out of the adjoining room, and he paused for a moment and after exchanging glances with her he shook his head before hurrying along the gallery and to the double doors. As he neared them, one opened and Biddy came through, and she side-stepped quickly and held it back so that he could pass. And he had gone through without a word to her and she was about to close it when, swinging round, he took a step backwards and, stabbing his finger towards her chest, he muttered, 'Don't let her stop you reading. Do you understand? Do it on the quiet, on the sly, but don't stop.'

Her eyes wide, she moved her head once as she said, 'I won't, sir;' then added, 'I haven't.'

'You haven't?'

'No, sir, I haven't, I mean stopped reading.'

He stared at her for a moment longer, his face still expressing his annoyance; then, he gave a shaky laugh before saying, 'Good. Good. Keep it up,' then turned from her.

Jessie was waiting for her at the dressing-room door and immediately she said, 'You shouldn't have told him that. What if he lets it out downstairs?' She pointed towards the carpet, and to this Biddy answered,'He won't.'

'How do you know?'

'I . . . I can't tell, but somehow I don't feel he would give me away.'

'You know, girl,' Jessie said, 'sometimes I think you take too much on yourself, and one of these days it will trip you up. And where will you be then? Flat on your face. Go on' – she gave her a slight push – 'get the bath ready. And I'm warning you, be prepared for squalls because she's got to take it out on somebody, and I know who that'll be tonight.' She nodded and smiled grimly, and Biddy, looking at the kindly woman over her shoulder, said, 'Yes, and I do an' all.'

7

Biddy's leave day had been altered, but Jean would still continue to go to the house. Davey would now accompany her, and this, Biddy guessed, would add to the pleasure of her visit because, as had been evident for a long time, she had definitely cottoned on to Davey. However, Biddy wasn't sure that the feeling was returned in that way by her brother. Somehow you could never be sure how their Davey really felt.

And not only had her leave day changed but she had been deprived of one by way of punishment, and so it was a month before she saw her mother and Johnny and Maggie again.

Riah, of course, had been given all the news from Davey and Jean, but she knew nothing about the workings in the domain in the west wing. And now, sitting on the bank of the stream while the two younger children splashed in the water, Biddy regaled her with the daily routine in Madam's household. And at this point, Riah exclaimed in amazement, 'You've got to bathe her?'

'Aha, every inch of her.' Biddy now spluttered and put her hand over her mouth. 'The first time I helped Miss Hobson I thought I would have died. I did, Ma, I thought I would have died. All the stuff had to be taken off her face with grease.'

'And you had to do that?'

'Well, not for the first week or so, but now I do it.'

'And bathe her?'

'Well, yes, I help. Oh, and Ma, oh' – she closed her eyes and shook her head – 'you wouldn't believe it, because she looks so grand, regal, like an old queen when she's sitting up all dressed, even in bed she looks like that, but in the bath, you know what I likened her to in me own mind? A long piece of wrinkled clay with four sticks attached.'

'Oh, lass.' Riah was now flapping her hand at Biddy while she rocked herself backwards and forwards.

Biddy, in her element now, went on to describe the preparation. 'Imagine that's the bath.' She pointed to two rocks sticking out of the bank. 'Well, at the top end, on the outside of course' – she bobbed her head now – 'there's two hooks and on these goes a special towel, and it covers the whole top of the bath, and madam sits on this, I mean she's lowered on to it so that none of the spelks stick in her.' she swallowed and muttered. 'You know what? The funny thing is the towel keeps floating up between her legs and it's all I can do at times not to burst out laughing. That is until she starts on us if the water's not warm enough, or it's too warm, or the soap slips and we have a job to find it. Eeh! Ma' – her face became serious now – 'I just don't know how Miss Hobson managed on her own. No wonder she can hardly walk on her feet 'cos even with the both of us we're running all day to her bidding . . . madam's bidding, but – ' Her expression changed again and, laughing once more, she said, 'But when we get her out of the bath she has to be powdered all over, you know like you used to put Fuller's Earth all round Maggie. Well, it's just like that except this is very scented powder. Oh, it has a lovely smell. And she has cream put on her face every night, and then last thing a kind of a strap under her chin. I'm not joking, Ma. Listen . . . stop laughing, it's the truth.'

They now fell against each other and during the seconds they remained so, Biddy knew a happiness that she hadn't experienced for some time.

When they were sitting straight again, Riah said thoughtfully, 'You know, when our Davey came back and told me what happened I couldn't believe me ears. I mean, to be lifted out of the laundry and into a position like that. But it was right what our Davey said.'

'What did he say, Ma?'

'Well' – Riah plucked at some blades of grass before going on, 'He said, in a way he wasn't surprised because things always happened to you; you made them happen, and always would.' She smiled now as she added, 'He said he'd never be surprised at anything you did. And he had Jean doubled up in the kitchen when he said, if the King came riding through The Heights and said, "Where is Miss Bridget Millican? I want to take her up to London," he said you wouldn't turn a hair, you'd say, "Thank you very much, sir. Just wait a tick till I get me bundle an' I'll be with you." It isn't often our Davey's funny or cracks a joke, but that Sunday I laughed more than I'd laughed for a long time. Except just now about that bathing business.'

Biddy was looking into the stream to where the children were splashing each other and her voice was quiet and serious sounding now as she said,'He's not right, Ma, I mean about me not turning a hair, because I get very frightened at times. And it's odd, but when I do it makes me do things as if I wasn't frighened. You know what I mean, Ma?' She turned and looked at Riah, and Riah, answering truthfully, said, 'No, not really, lass; I don't think I'll ever know exactly all you mean. But . . . but oh, I'll tell you this, I am glad you're out of the laundry. I did feel guilty for pushing you in there, because I knew you were worth something better than that. But I felt you had to start somewhere, and . . . well, you knew how I was fixed.'

There was silence between them for a moment until Biddy asked tentatively, 'Are you very lonely, Ma?'

'At times. Yes I am at times.'

Impulsively now, Biddy screwed round on the grass and said, 'Why don't you let Tol come and see you again?'

'He has been.'

'He has?' Biddy's voice was high.

But Riah's tone was flat as she answered,'Yes, he has.'

'And . . . everything's going to be all right?'

Riah now began pulling the grass up by handfuls as she said, 'Not as you mean it.'

'Why?'

'Well, it's very . . . well, sort of complicated. I'll . . . I'll tell you the whole of it someday, but . . . well, I can't marry him, or anybody else.'

'He asked you to marry him?'

'Yes, he did.' Riah brought her head forward to emphasize her words.

'But what's stopping you, Ma?'

'A number of things, which would take a lot of explaining. So . . . so don't ask me any more. Don't probe. Everything's all right. I've got a good home, a beautiful home, and I might as well tell you I love the house and I never thought to see the day when I'd own a place like it. *Never. Never.* What's more, you're all set to rise in the world. And that's all I'm gona say for the present, so don't keep on, just let things settle.'

'Will he be coming back, I mean calling . . . Tol?'

'That's up to him.'

'Oh, Ma, why can't you have him? He could do so much here about the place. And it would be lovely, and . . .'

'I'll say two things more and then we won't talk about it for a long, long time. He wouldn't come here, that's one thing. The other thing is, I wouldn't go there, not to his place. Now that's my last word on the subject at present. Come on.' She jumped up from the green. 'Let's go back and get some tea . . . Come on, you two. Stop messing about and come on if you want anything to eat.' She turned away now and walked up the meadow; and Biddy stood looking after her, oblivious of the children sitting now on the bank chatting up at her. She couldn't imagine her mother turning away the love of a man like Tol just because she wanted to live in this big house. Her mother had changed.

For the little while they had been sitting on the bank here and during that moment when they held each other, her mother was the woman she had known during the first months in this place. But during the last few minutes she had reverted back to the other person, still her ma, but not the tender loving creature she seemed to remember from years ago; no, she was someone who was so changed that she was now weighing up the house and its possessions against the love and comfort and companionship of a man, and of such a one as Tol. And the odd thing about it was, she knew her mother loved Tol. Yet, as she had already learned, there were all kinds of love, some outweighing others. And the house had outweighed Tol.

The sun had gone from the afternoon . . .

An hour later she had taken two slim volumes from the library, slim, because she wanted to put them in the pockets of her petticoat, pockets that she had made for this very purpose. Now she was ready to go, and she was giving herself plenty of time because the day was hot and she didn't want to hurry.

They all set her to the gate, but when Riah held her close for a moment the joy of the previous embrace was lacking. Johnny and Maggie insisted on walking a little way along the road with her. Unlike herself and Davey they both seemed to have stood still with the years and she looked upon them as young children, although Johnny was now fourteen and Maggie thirteen. Then Johnny demonstrated his age when, out of earshot of his mother, he said quietly,

'Biddy, do you think you could speak for me to be set on with our Davey?'

Immediately she turned on him, saying angrily now, 'No, I can't. And you're not going there. Who's going to look after the garden here? And Ma's lonely enough without you going. Now get that out of your head. And you don't know what it's like up there. There's no positions like assistant lady's maid down in the stables, I can tell you that; you're knocked from dog to devil. Our Davey had to go through it. It's a wonder he stayed. If he hadn't been mad on horses he wouldn't.'

'I'm fourteen, Biddy.'

'Aye, you might be' – her voice softened now – 'but wait a while.'

'I'm not gona stay here forever.'

'No, I don't suppose you are. But stay put for the time being, and don't upset me ma any more than she's been upset lately.'

'She should have married Tol; he wants her.'

She actually stopped and looked down on her sister now, and Maggie, from the wisdom of her thirteen years, said, 'We're not blind, Biddy. We know what's going on.'

'All right.' She drew in a deep breath, before adding, 'If you know what's going on, then have a little patience and a little thought for Ma. She's not happy at all.'

'Neither are we. We never see anybody from one week's end to the other.'

Biddy stared at Maggie. She was small and slight for her years, but she was pretty. Her eyes were green and her hair was brown and her skin was clear. She understood how she felt about not seeing anyone, because she herself, at times, felt lonely up in the west wing, not that she ever wished herself back in the laundry, but she did wish she could see a few more people, people that she could talk to. The only talking that Miss Hobson did was to instruct her into what a lady's maid did and did not do. She missed the company of Jean at night; she missed the chatter; and so she knew how her sister felt; and her brother also. Her voice much softer now, she said, 'Hang on a little longer. You never know, things might change.'

'Pigs might fly.'

She gently cuffed her brother's ears as she said, 'Go on, Mam's waiting. She'll be wondering what we're talking about. Try to be content. Go on with you.'

'Ta-ra,' they said. And she answered,'Ta-ra.'

As she made her way along the road she felt disturbed, not only about her mother now, but about the two youngsters. Maggie would have to stay put, but Johnny, being a lad and lively, would, if he took it into his head, go off at any time. There were always young lads running away to sea or joining the army.

Having enough time at her disposal, she did not keep to the main road but went out of her way to take the side road leading to the little fall.

The little fall was just what it said, a sheet of water tumbling over rocks not more than eight feet high. At different times during the past summers she had taken Sunday walks here and sat on the bank below the fall. She had never taken the others with her on these walks, it had been too far anyway for the young ones' legs, and Davey, even in those days, saw little beauty in nature, except the sight of horses galloping across fields.

She now took off her hat and short grey coat that her mother had made her to go with her best dress; then taking one of the books from her petticoat pocket, she told herself that she would have five minutes. She hadn't got to be in till seven and she could tell the time from where the sun was. She looked down on the book for a moment before opening it. It was the last one that the master had dealt with. It was a translation from the French and although it was plainly written, there were lots of things she couldn't understand about it but which she wished she could, because one or two phrases had caught her eye and stirred her mind. She told herself she would have to start at the beginning of it again, although the master had taken her almost halfway through it. She flicked at the pages, glancing here and there, reading a line or a sentence, for her mind wasn't really on it; she was disturbed about conditions back home and about feelings that were new and strange and exciting inside herself. She could, in a way, translate these feelings, and in defence of them, she told herself that it wasn't because she hadn't a lad that she was feeling this way, although it would have been nice to have somebody of her own age to talk to, a lad, that is. Yet, where would she find one whom she could talk to about the things that interested her? The lads nearest to her were in the stables, and not one of them could read except Davey, and their Davey was the last person who would talk books.

Would she always be like this, on her own, and end up like Miss Hobson, a spinster lady? Oh no, she wouldn't like to be a spinster lady. She sighed, then looked down at the book and began to read. It was about this rich man in France called Helvétius. She could never pronounce that name right for the master. What she understood about him was that although he was rich, he wanted the poor people to have land and, of all things, to work less hours. He seemed a very good man, as wise as Voltaire. Yet, as the master had pointed out, Voltaire had different ideas altogether from Helvétius.

She became engrossed in her reading. The sun was hot on her neck. She seemed to be back in the library, the table strewn with books and papers, and she could hear his voice crying, 'You are not in England now, you are in France, and Frenchmen don't speak like Englishmen, or women.' She seemed to be in a half-dream world until something intruded into it. She still continued to read, but the words came slow, until they finally stopped. And then she was afraid to turn round, and when she did, she jerked, not only her head but her body, and brought her knees up under her as if about to rise. But when she saw who it was that was standing looking at her, she let out a long slow breath, and when he said, 'I'm sorry if I startled you,' she made no reply.

It was Mr Laurence, and he was leading his horse, and the reason why she hadn't heard him was, they were on the grass and not on the bridle-path. By way of explanation he said, 'My horse has cast a shoe; I was keeping him off the rough road as much as possible. . . . Don't get up. Don't get up.' He put his hand out to stop her, and then when the horse lowered its head and began to munch the grass, he left go of the reins and walked towards her. And he looked down on her for a moment before turning his gaze on to the fall.

'It's a beautiful little spot, isn't it?' he said softly.

'Yes. Yes . . . sir.' She had almost forgotten the 'sir'.

'Do you often come here?'

'Not often now, sir, but when I was at home I used to take the opportunity whenever I could.'

'It's a good place to read.' He nodded down to her book. And now she put her hand on it as if to cover it. Then remembering that he was for her reading, she dropped her hand to the side and said, 'Yes, yes, it is a good place to read, sir.'

'What are you reading?'

She was hesitant in showing him the book, and he said, 'Poems?'

'No, sir, it's French philosophy. Well, I mean, it's translated.'

'French philosophy.' She watched his eyes grow bright; she watched his lips fall together and his head move from side to side; and then he said, 'You know, Biddy. That is your name, isn't it . . . Biddy?'

'Yes, sir.'

'Well, you know, Biddy, you are a remarkable person.'

'I don't feel remarkable, sir, anything but.' She turned her head from him now and looked into the tumbling water before she added in an ordinary tone as if speaking to one of her own kind, 'I only know one thing, wherever I seem to land there's always a disturbance.'

'That's the same name for being remarkable, being a disturber. May I?' He pointed to the bank, and her mouth fell into a slight gape as she stammered, 'Ye . . . yes, sir, yes.' and at that he glanced back at the horse to see if it was still munching, then sat down on the edge of the bank, his legs dangling over it.

Holding out his hand, he indicated that he wanted to see the book, and when she handed it to him he looked at it for a number of minutes before he said, 'Helvétius. My God!' Then as if apologizing, he added,'What I mean is, I've merely touched on this man and his theories. You know – ' he turned and looked fully into her face now as he said, 'you were very fortunte to come under the care of Mr Miller. I didn't know him. I saw him at odd times and I think I spoke to him twice, but now I wish, I wish dearly, that I had been braver and gone to visit him, although, I understand, he didn't welcome visitors.'

'I think he would have welcomed you, sir. He welcomed anyone with an open mind, or, like myself and my brothers and sisters who had minds that needed opening. But I must say' – she pulled a little face at herself now – 'he had to use force at times to get through.' She laughed openly now as she went on, 'He once said that he was competing with a hammer and chisel and that he was losing.'

He laughed with her as he put in, 'Not a bit of it, he was joking. By the way, do you still read Shelley?' There was a twist to the corner of his mouth as he asked the question, and she nodded at him before she answered, 'Yes, sir.' Then the smile going from her own face, she said, 'Shelley wasn't a bad man, was he, sir?'

'Shelley bad? No, of course not. What makes you ask that?'

'Well, it was' – again she stumbled – 'well, the reaction of the staff the night I said his piece of poetry. They said it was – ' She couldn't utter the word dirty, but added, 'Not quite right.'

'What do you yourself think about his poetry?'

'I . . . I think it's beautiful. There are bits that I apply to different things, like the water there,' she pointed to the fall, and he asked, 'What is that?'

'Oh, just a few lines, sir.'

'Go on, tell me. Say them.'

'They will sound silly when I say them, sir. It isn't like reading them.'

'Leave me to be the judge of that. Let me hear them.'

She wetted her lips, wiped the perspiration from each side of her mouth with her middle finger, then said,

> 'My soul is an enchanted boat,
> Which, like a sleeping swan, doth float
> Upon the silver waves of thy sweet singing;
> And thine doth like an angel sit
> Beside the helm conducting it,'

Her head drooped slightly as she finished. There was silence between them until he murmured, 'That was beautifully said. Never be afraid to quote aloud . . . Do you know anything about Shelley?'

'Nothing much, sir.' She was glancing at him now.

'Well, he died just a short while ago. Oh, what would it be? Seventeen years gone, and he was only thirty.'

The master had told her this, but she pretended that it was news to her and said, 'Really! Poor soul.'

No, not poor soul, Biddy, pure soul. Do you know where those lines are from?'

'Well, I know in my mind, sir, but I can never pronounce the name.'

'*Prometheus*. I can hardly get my tongue round it either.'

'Do you like poetry, sir?'

'Some . . . some, not all.'

Again there was silence between them. And now they were looking at each other straight in the eyes when he broke the silence by asking, 'What do you want to do with your life, Biddy?'

'I don't know, sir.'

'Marry? Have children?'

Her gaze slanted downwards before she answered,'Yes, I suppose so, sir. But . . . but there's a problem there.' Again they were silent, until she turned her head and looked at the sun; then, slowly rising to her feet, she said, 'I've got to be on my way, sir, or else I'll be late in.'

He looked up at her but made no attempt to rise, but said, 'Yes. Yes, I understand. And I must apologize for intruding into your solitude.'

'Oh, no sir, no.' Her face was unsmiling as she looked down on him. 'I . . . I never get the chance to talk to anyone like this. And . . . and this is a time I'll always remember.' He didn't move but held her gaze for a moment longer; then he said, 'I also, Biddy. I also shall remember this time.'

'Goodbye, sir.'

'Goodbye, Biddy.'

He watched her walk across the sward to the bridle path. And she knew he was watching her, and not until she was out of his sight did she seem to draw breath. Then she closed her eyes, for she knew in that past short time she had met *the lad*, the only one that would suit her, and that this being so her future was writ in large letters, she would end up like Miss Hobson.

8

It was the first week in December and the day following her birthday that Biddy overheard a conversation that was to affect her future and also explained the real reason why her mother had refused Tol, and the reason gave birth to resentment.

It should happen that madam had caught a chill. Over the past months, she had been attended at odd times by Doctor Pritchard, and on these occasions Miss Hobson had waited on the doctor. But when the doctor arrived this particular morning, Jessie Hobson was downstairs in conference with the housekeeper, and so it was Biddy who showed him into the room; and recognizing her, he said,'Well, well; so this is where you are, girl?' And she had answered simply, 'Yes, Doctor.'

She followed the same procedure as Miss Hobson: she brought in a bowl of warm water and fresh towels; then returned into the adjoining room, which was both closet and linen room. And it was from there that she heard the doctor say, 'Well, well; so you've got the Millican girl at your beck and call now, madam.'

And the reply that came made Biddy close her eyes for a moment as the voice said, 'I don't know about beck and call: servants don't scurry as they used to do in my young days; things have changed out of all recognition; they not only take their time, but they speak before they are spoken to.'

'Oh, well, as you are employing an heiress, in a way that's to be expected. Now let me have a look at your chest.'

'What did you say?'

'I said, let me have a look at your chest.'

'No. About an heiress. What did you mean?'

'Oh, that was an exaggeration, but only in a way. Now breathe in.'

'I'll not breathe in. Take that thing away. What do you mean by an heiress, an exaggeration?'

'Well, it's common knowledge that Miller left the house to his housekeeper or mistress or whatever she was, but on condition that if she remarries she has to move out and it reverts to the girl, lock stock and barrel. In any case it'll come to her when the mother dies, and not to the boy. That was specified.'

'Is this a fact?'

'Of course it's a fact. I was there when the will was read out.'

The result of the imparting of this information had caused Biddy to lean back against the linen rack, her eyes like saucers, her mouth open. Her mother had never told her, had never let on. That's why she wouldn't leave to marry Tol, because if she did the house would come to her. What was more, she had imagined that if her mother were to die the house would pass, naturally, to Davey. The eldest son always got everything. Oh, her ma had been devious. That was the word, devious. She'd rather stay in the house and give up Tol than let her have it. Yet how would she herself have been able to keep up the house? But that wasn't the point. Her mother had kept it from her that the house would be hers one day. And she hadn't given it a thought that the doctor or solicitor would blab.

'*Girl!*' The voice brought her upright and into the bedroom, and there was the old lady looking at her steadily for a moment before saying, 'Show the doctor out.'

She showed the doctor out as far as the double doors, and he said no word to her, nor she to him, he did not even thank her for holding the heavy door open for him.

She had hardly got back into the room before the voice came at her again, 'You, girl!'

When she reached the foot of the bed she said, 'Yes, madam?'

'Why didn't you tell me about this property you're coming into?'

Should she say she didn't know? If she did, this would put her mother in a bad light. What she said was, 'I didn't think it would be of any interest to you, madam. In any case from what I gather it won't be mine for many a long year.'

'Nevertheless, if your mother was to die tomorrow it would be yours, wouldn't it?'

'Yes, madam.'

'And then you'd walk out of here, wouldn't you?'

'That would depend, madam.'

'On what?'

'I'm . . . I'm not quite sure . . . circumstances, money to keep the house up.'

'Yes, yes, a house needs money to survive. But you could sell the house. It would bring a decent sum that place. I remember it well . . . Was your mother his mistress?'

'*No, she was not, madam.*'

'Be careful. Be careful. Don't use that tone to me.'

She cast her eyes downwards and she was aware that her face had turned scarlet, and the voice came at her, saying, 'Don't show any temper here, miss, or you'll soon find out your mistake. Where's Hobson?'

She was about to answer, 'With the housekeeper, madam,' when the door opened and in walked the younger daughter of the house, and the old lady exclaimed in an entirely different tone, 'Ah Lucy, my dear, when did you get in?'

'About half an hour ago, Grandmama.'

The girl came to the bed, leant over and kissed her grandmother; then she straightened up and looked at Biddy, and for a moment Biddy thought she was going to smile at her. She stared at the girl. She had only been away at the boarding school a matter of months, yet she seemed completely changed. She was much taller, and her manner was quieter. She couldn't imagine that this was the same person who had helped to string her up to the clothes horse on that awful Sunday. On her first visit home from the school she had looked surly; now, her expression was different, as was her manner, she had lost her boisterousness. That school was certainly having an effect, and for the better, if she knew anything.

'Well, well, now. Sit down and tell me, tell me all your news. How are things at this school? I hear nothing these days. May gallivanting, Stephen up in London, Laurence in Oxford, Paul in Newcastle. By the way, Laurence should be here tomorrow.'

'I'm afraid he'll not, Grandmama; I've just heard he's changed his plans.'

'What?' The wigged head was lifted from the bed. 'What did you say? Since when?'

'Mother received a letter this morning, so I hear. He's . . . he's going straight on to France to his friend's for the holidays and may not be back.'

'Well, I'll be damned. He can't do that. Do you hear, Lucy? He can't do that.'

'Grandmama – ' Lucy Gullmington took the wrinkled hand and patted it as she said, 'Laurence, fortunately for him, is a free agent, he can do what he likes.'

'What are you talking about, free agent? Doing what he likes. He's to come home for the holidays. You go down and tell your mother to write immediately and say I forbid him to go to France.'

'He's already gone, Grandmama.'

'My God!' The head flopped back on the pillow. Then the eyes were turned on her granddaughter and the voice was quiet now as she said, 'He's gone to France before, but he's always come home first.'

'He likely wants to avoid May, Grandmama.'

'How do you know anything about May?'

'We all know, Grandmama, although I don't think he need worry so much now as I understand she's being escorted by a title.'

'Titles are two a penny and they've got no money . . . And you, girl – ' The old lady suddenly paused for breath as, now pointing towards Biddy, she gabbled, 'get about your business and close your ears to anything you hear in this room – you understand? – or it will be worse for you.'

Biddy retreated to the toilet room and through it into the box-like room that served as her bedroom, and there she sat on the bed for a moment. The news had saddened her: she wouldn't now see Mr Laurence until the Easter vacation. Since that magical afternoon by the fall she had seen him a number of times, but always in the house, and he had spoken to her but once. That was one time when madam had gone for her harshly in his presence; and when afterwards he met her in the corridor he had stopped her and said, 'Don't mind her tongue, it is her only pastime. And you know, I think, in a way, she is rather fond of you. She only bawls at those she's fond of; to the people that she doesn't like, her manner is polite and cool.' He had smiled at her and she had said not a word, but as he turned away she had said to herself, Why couldn't you say something?

She knew that she had been looking forward to his being here for Christmas. She had been reading hard, sometimes well into the night with the aid of candle ends – and there were plenty of them to be had on this floor – and always towards one purpose, to astound him again perhaps with her knowledge. She was once more reading *Candide*. She liked the idea of the innocent man, young yet who had a fund of reason in his head. She loved to follow his adventures through the army, through shipwreck, all in search of a new world. Of course, she realized it was all fairy tale, yet at the same time threaded with common sense. And she longed to discuss it with someone, as Candide himself did, and learn through discussion.

Had she hoped that she might talk with Mr Laurence again? But where could this have taken place? Certainly not inside the house, and apparently not outside either, because she had stopped by the fall on every leave day, even when it was raining and blustery, but no one had even passed by.

When the door burst open and Miss Hobson demanded,'What do you think you're doing girl, sitting there?' she answered, 'I . . . I was feeling a bit sick.' And to this Miss Hobson replied, 'You'll be sicker before the day's out. Madam's in a right tear, and if I know anything, it won't fade with the light. Master Laurence is not coming home for the holidays. I think it's very bad of him. He knows how she looks forward to his company more than that of any of the others. But I know what it is, it's that Miss May. She follows him about like a lapdog, hanging on his arm shamefully, and he's not for her. I know he's not. I've heard him say as much to madam. Madam's for it, left, right, and centre . . . What's the matter with you? You're not sickening for anything are you?' Jessie Hobson leant towards Biddy and Biddy, answering perkily now, said, 'Sickening? Me? Of course not. What would I be sickening for?'

'Well, you look peaky. By the way, what did the doctor say?'

Yes. What did the doctor say? She had forgotten about that. That was another thing. Oh, she was fed up. For two pins she would walk out, go straight home and say to her mother, 'Well now, so this is to be my house when you die, or if you should marry. Why didn't you tell me?' But she couldn't do that . . . she wouldn't let on she knew anything about it. She'd play the same game as her mother, but for different reasons.

She answered Jessie by saying, 'I don't know. He never opened his mouth to me.'

It was a colloquial answer. She would have to watch herself, she was dropping back more and more into them these days. What she should have said was, I don't know. He didn't inform me.

Oh, anyway, what did it matter – learning or anything else? . . . for she was mad, mad, stark staring mad. She must be to harbour the thoughts that came into her head.

Christmas passed and Biddy wasn't sorry, for she felt she was the only one in the house who hadn't in some way enjoyed herself. She hadn't gone to the servants' party. When she had mentioned it to Jessie Hobson, Jessie had said,'You won't be going this year, Biddy; and neither am I. Anyway, I don't have to tell you that there is a feeling against you downstairs, and it isn't because it's you with your funny ways, it would have been against anybody who had risen from a place like the laundry to the top floor.'

To this Biddy had answered, 'It doesn't matter; I don't want to go.'

She had a brief word with Jean. Things were still apparently the same in the laundry. But in spite of this Jean was happy because Davey was continuing to show an interest in her.

She had not even stood in line with the rest of the staff for her Christmas present, because, as Jessie had pointed out to her, hers was a different household. She would get her present from madam.

And she did get a present from madam, and the quality of it had surprised her, and had caused her to express her pleasure quite verbally which had seemed to please the old lady, and for once, she hadn't been barked at for talking. The present was a small silk shoulder shawl, with a yellow pattern on it and hand-worked lace around the edge. Of course, it had been used before, but what did it matter? And she also received six lawn handkerchiefs of good quality; and she knew these hadn't been used before because they hadn't any initial on.

On her leave day before Christmas her mother had said, 'What's wrong with you? There's something on your mind. Is there some trouble up there?' and she had answered, 'Not more than usual.' And Riah had said, 'What do you mean by that?' And she had replied,

'Oh, I always seem to be in hot water. I was having a word with our Davey in the yard before I came away and Mr Froggett, the butler, happened to be passing and said he would report me. I said I was only talking to my brother, and he went for me for daring to answer him back. Who does he think he is anyway?'

The encounter with the butler hadn't really disturbed her because it wasn't the first time that one or other of the upper staff had tried to get at her, but she found this as good an excuse to give to her mother as any other for her attitude, for she had found it impossible to be natural.

Before leaving to return to The Heights she had walked from room to room, and she had looked at the furniture with different eyes. In the drawing-room there were two small writing desks in reddish wood. The master had called them *bonheur-du-jours*. She realized they were beautiful. There were sets of small tables, and chests of drawers inlaid with different woods. And she had thought, If I live long enough, all these will be mine. She hadn't said to herself, when my mother dies, because she didn't want her to die. All she wanted for her was to be happy, and for the old feeling she'd had for her to come back.

But at that moment she couldn't find it in her heart to love her. And she had wondered if their Davey knew about the real circumstances, because if he didn't he would be under the impression that one day it would all be his. And this did seem to be the real state of affairs because he no longer minded coming into the house, which attitude, she thought, didn't say much for his character, after all the fuss he had made and what he had done to the master. She often pondered on that situation, and would ask herself what in the name of goodness would make a man love anybody like their Davey, even when he had been bonny. It was odd, and she had to admit not quite right. Still, she didn't blame the master, she blamed their Davey for being mad about the pony he couldn't have.

Life was strange. She had thought she was very knowledgeable, but the more she read and the more she tried to learn, the more she knew how ignorant she was. And just lately she had read words to this effect that one of the philosophers in Greece had said years and years ago. There were so many things she didn't understand and she kept wishing she had someone to talk to.

9

It had been a bitter winter and now it was a cold Easter. All the family were home for the Easter holidays. There were lots of comings and goings and a great deal of bustle down below. A big party had been held for Miss May's twenty-first birthday, and this had been preceded by a dispute in madam's drawing-room when May declared that she was going to become engaged to Lord Milton's son, and her grandmother had screamed at her, 'He's an imbecile, like his father. There's insanity in the family.'

Then later, madam had gone for Mr Laurence, again calling him pigheaded and a fool.

Mr Laurence hadn't come upstairs for over a week after this, and when he did, he mostly talked politics and about the bills in Parliament. Day after day, they would appear to her to be like two strangers discussing a subject on which they had opposite opinions. It was mostly to do with the contention of how long a child should work in the factories. Some of them it seemed had been known to work eighteen hours at a stretch when the regulated factory hours had been thirteen to fifteen hours a day, but that was all past, madam had defended, while Mr Laurence had said, only in some cases, for children were known to be working from five in the morning till six at night, and dropping on their feet.

Well, she had thought after listening in to this, did he not know that the laundry workers in this very house started at five in the morning and went on till six at night, sometimes seven? Had she not almost dropped on her feet when she had first come here? Funny that people couldn't see what was under their noses. As for the bill he was talking about that had been passed in thirty-one, which prohibited children from doing night work and only thirteen hours a day at most, what about when she and Miss Hobson had to get up and attend to madam in the middle of the night because she wanted a hot drink or her pillow straightening, or some such?

And Mr Laurence had reasoned that the factory owners were taking little heed of the bill, for children were still being exploited. You had to go no further than Newcastle, he said, to see them ragged, verminous, and hungry. As for London, once you passed through some quarters there, you were never the same again, that is, if you possessed a conscience.

And madam had again told him he should go in for Parliament.

During the three weeks of his vacation that he had so far spent at home he had spoken to her no more than the greeting of the day: 'Good morning, Biddy. Good evening, Biddy.' That was all. And she wondered at it. It was as if she had done something wrong. She looked back to the day by the falls. Had she been forward? Yes, perhaps she had. He being a gentleman, he had spoken to her kindly and she had taken advantage.

Well, if that was so, that was so. She must keep her head on her shoulders and think for the future. She wasn't going to stay here forever: another year's training and she would apply for the post of lady's maid somewhere else, and start a new life.

And she was to start a new life in a new post, which, when she looked back on it, came about with a strangeness that was comparable with the mythology the master had made her learn.

It happened in the second week in July. She had taken her half-yearly pay home to her mother and Riah had given her back three shillings; she had also surprised her with a dress and matching coat that she had made out of the still plentiful material from the boxes in the attic. And she had insisted that she put them on and carry her Sunday dress and jacket with her.

She had been delighted with her appearance. Her mother was very good with the needle: her stitches were small and her ruching so fine as to appear to have been done by an expert at such work. She had kissed Riah tenderly and forgotten for the moment the animosity she bore her for withholding what she felt now were her rights in the future.

She had no hopes that Mr Laurence would come riding by and have a word with her for he had been at home over a month now and she'd had two leave days during that period, and on both she had sat by the fall, and no one had disturbed her.

And now here she was sitting on the bank again. She had opened her bundle and spread her Sunday dress on the grass so that her new one would not be marked in any way. She had taken off her hat, and the wind, which was fresh, was lifting her hair from her brow and ears.

Perhaps it was the wind that smothered the sound of the horse's hooves until they were just behind her on the bridle path. And now she swung round, a half-smile of welcome on her face which stayed for only a second before fading at the sight of the horseman. It was Mr Paul.

As she watched him dismount, she got hurriedly to her feet and, picking up her dress, she stuffed it into the bundle.

She had told herself repeatedly during the time she had been at The Heights that she wasn't afraid of any of them; but there was one exception, and she admitted it to herself, she was afraid of young Mr Paul, because since the day he had manhandled her in the laundry he had never once spoken to her or acknowledged her presence when he was visiting his grandmother, even though she was all the while conscious that he was watching her. And strangely, she imagined that each time he returned from boarding school he had aged in years, not in months. Now, as he approached her she seemed to see him as a man, fully grown, not someone around eighteen. She didn't know whether he was coming up to eighteen or past it, she only knew that he didn't at this moment look like a youth.

His voice was civil as he said, 'Hello there.'

It was a second or so before she answered in stiff politeness, 'Good afternoon, Mr Paul.'

He was standing an arm's length from her now, and she noticed that his hair seemed to be the same colour as his polished riding boots. Her eyes had been drawn down to his boots because, as on that memorable Sunday, he was tapping the upper part of his leg with his riding crop.

'I've disturbed you?' he said.

'No, I was just about to go.'

'Sit down,' he said.

'I've told you, Mr Paul, I'm just about to go. I've got to get back.'

'Sit down,' he said. And now his hand came out and pushed her gently, and she stumbled a step backwards to where the gnarled stump of a tree grew out of the bank, and she turned and looked at it, then side-stepped it.

Grabbing her arm, but his voice still quiet, he said, 'Sit down.'

'Leave go of my arm.' Her words were slow and as yet there was no tremble in her voice.

'When I'm ready.'

With a quick wrench she was free; but only for a moment, for now he grabbed her by the shoulders and swung her around and, bringing his boot viciously against the back of her knees, he lifted her feet from the ground, and the next thing she knew she was on her back and clawing at his face until he had spreadeagled her arms and was lying over her. His nose almost pressing hers, he growled at her now, 'I've thought about this for a long, long time, you laundry slut, and I'm going to make you pay for that bloody school I'm now at. I hate it, do you hear? I hate every minute of it, but not as much as I hate you for having me kept there. I'm going to leave some marks on you, miss, that you won't forget in a hurry.' And at this, he brought his face to the side of her and buried his teeth in the lobe of her ear. And when she screamed, he said, 'Shout as much as you like, there's no one comes round this way very often. I've seen to that. I've followed you twice.'

Now he raised himself from her a little and swung her arms upwards until he was gripping both her wrists in one hand; with the other he ripped the buttons from the front of her dress and, thrusting his hand down her bodice, he gripped her breast. Fruitlessly she kicked at his shins, and when she screamed he put his mouth on hers. Now gathering all the strength of which she was capable she managed to bring up her knees, and when she saw his body lift and roll to the side she imagined her effort had accomplished this, but as she lay gasping she saw another figure, and it was bending over him and beating him with a riding crop. It was some seconds before she herself rolled on to her side, and to her amazement she saw that her rescuer was no other than Miss Lucy and that she was laying about her brother as she had once laid about herself.

Managing to stumble to his feet, he cried at her, 'Give over! What the hell do you think you're at?'

'I'll tell you what I'm at, and more, when we get back to the house.'

'Have you gone mad? Do you see who that is?' He was pointing down towards Biddy now. 'Remember what you did to her? She was the means of sending you off and getting my allowance cut.'

'I know what she did, and I know what we did. It was our fault.'

'God Almighty! What's come over you? Is that school a bloody convent you've fallen into? You haven't been the same since you've been there. Mine is hell, but be damned if I would let it change me.'

'No, you won't let it change you; you'll do as father did, and grandfather did, and Stephen is doing.'

Biddy had struggled to her feet and was trying to arrange her clothes, and she watched the brother and sister glaring at each other. He was now dabbing at the blood running down the side of his cheek where her nails had torn the skin away. She watched him turn abruptly and walk to his horse, and the girl follow him, and to her amazement, she listened to her say, 'What . . . what if she'd had a child?' And as he put his foot into the stirrup he said, 'Well, what if she had? It's the lambing season around Easter for her and her type. And anyway, in two months time, I'll be in the army, and she could name one of the stable lads she rolls with.'

As he dug his heels into the horse's flanks she felt a great weakness coming over her – it was the same feeling as the last time he'd had his hands on her – but she didn't want to faint so she sat down abruptly again and bowed her head forward until the mist cleared from her eyes. And when she looked up, there was Miss Lucy standing looking down at her.

'Are you all right?'

'A bit dizzy, miss.'

'I'm sorry.'

She was amazed to hear this, and she didn't answer but kept her eyes on the girl. As her brother had altered, so had she. And she recalled now that during the past two weeks she had been visiting her grandmother almost every day, which was unusual, and most times she had looked at her as if wanting to speak; at least, so she had fancied. But she had told herself to remember what this young lady was really like.

Here she was, though, looking down on her and in a quite kindly fashion. Then she was further surprised when she saw her young mistress lower herself on to the grass, pick up a tiny pebble and throw it gently into the water. And she couldn't quite believe her ears when the young girl said, 'Do you mind if I talk to you?'

'No, miss, not if you wish to.'

Lucy Gullmington now turned fully round and looked at Biddy as she said slowly, 'You are very intelligent. I disliked you for it; in fact, hated you at one time for it. You know much more than I do; apart from Grandmama and Laurence, I think you know much more than anyone else in the house, high or low.'

'No, miss,' Biddy shook her head; 'I don't really. I'm very ignorant. I read a lot, or when I can, and this tells me how ignorant I am. When I first came to the house, I . . . I thought I knew everything, because of what the master . . . Mr Miller had taught me, but I know it was just surface stuff. And he knew it, he told me so.'

'Biddy. May I call you, Biddy?'

Biddy shook her head. She couldn't understand the attitude of this young lady. What was more, her head was splitting, her breast was paining, and her ear was bleeding.

'You . . . you can call me what you like, miss.'

'Oh' – the girl now gave an impatient shake of her head – 'don't be humble, it isn't in your nature. You're not like that with Grandmama, and if you can stand up to her you can stand up to anybody.'

At another time Biddy would have smiled at this, but what she did was to hold her head to one side and put her handkerchief to her ear; and when she took it away and looked at the bloodstain, Lucy said, 'He did that, he bit you?'

'Yes.'

'He's a cruel swine. All men are cruel.'

Biddy's eyes stretched slightly. There was something here she couldn't understand. And she was further puzzled; in fact, she was absolutely amazed when Miss Lucy's hand came on hers and in a low voice she said, 'I . . . I wonder if you would be my friend. I . . . I have no one I can turn to.'

A thought passing through Biddy's mind like a streak of lightning cleared it for a moment, but she repudiated the words it printed, saying, No, impossible. Nevertheless, she looked at the girl and said, 'Are you in trouble, miss?'

Lucy's head was drooped now. There was no resemblance between this girl and the proud, haughty, bossy, even cruel young miss seen by all the staff as well as herself.

She listened now to a muttered voice saying, 'When I saw Paul attacking you like that, it brought back . . . it reminded me – ' She lifted her head now and ended,'You see, I knew how you felt, because I . . . I have experience of a similar situation.'

'No! miss.'

'Yes.'

'You mean, miss?'

'Yes, yes, I think so.'

'*Oh, my God, miss.*'

'That's what I said when I knew. Oh, my God, I said. And I have kept begging Him not to make it so, but He hasn't listened.'

'You . . . you were attacked, miss?'

Lucy now turned her head away, saying, 'No, I wasn't attacked. Well, not really. I . . . I was teasing. I . . . I didn't realize what the outcome would be. I was in love, at least that's what I thought. Then from teasing and playing . . . well, something happened. I didn't want it to happen, I think I was as frightened as you were, but it happened, and then happened again.'

'Can . . . can you not be married, miss?'

The head moved slowly. 'He is married and has children. He . . . he was the father of my friend.' She turned quickly now, her hand over her mouth, and saying, 'But, you'll never repeat that. Promise me you'll never repeat that.'

'I don't need to promise, miss, you needn't worry. But . . . but what are you going to do?'

'I don't know. I only know I had to tell someone. You see, back there' – her head nodded in the direction of the house – 'the men can do what they like. They can have their mistresses, they can go whoring as often as they like, and not a word said against them, but the womenfolk, they must be like the hymn, as pure as the driven snow. No word of scandal must touch a Gullmington woman. I know now what May has been going through, because she wanted Laurence and Laurence didn't want her in any way. And so, she's going to marry this stupid man because she can't wait any longer. We are made in a dreadful way, don't you think, Biddy?'

Biddy thought for a moment and then she nodded her head slowly in agreement. 'Yes, I think we are made in a dreadful way,' she said. 'It's worse because we mustn't speak of it, mustn't show our feelings.'

And then there were the feelings of the moment with which she had to contend, and these were making her feel sick, and her ear was paining, so were her arms.

'What am I to do, Biddy?'

'You must tell madam.'

'I've thought of that, but I haven't the courage.'

'Well, she's the only one in your family that I think could stand it, I mean, the shock.'

'I've . . . I've thought of running away, but I could only run to friends, and all they would do would be to bring me back home. They would be very kind and thoughtful but they'd be shocked too.'

'Are you going back to school?'

'*No. No, never.*'

'Well, then, you've only got just over a fortnight, haven't you? You'll have to do something, miss.'

'Yes, yes, I'll have to do something. But I don't seem to be able to think.'

'How far have you gone, miss?'

'It is past the second month. I . . . I didn't know what was happening at first. I was very ignorant about such things. Mother is not the kind of person you can talk to, at least about private matters, except to say . . .' She now looked upwards to the sky and her voice was bitter as she ended,'Purity . . . keep oneself pure. I should have asked her how one went about it, shouldn't I?'

Biddy got to her feet now, saying,'I have to get back. My time's almost up. Will I walk with you, miss?' while at the same time hoping the young mistress would say no, for she wanted to run back to the house and get cleaned up and see to her ear, and perhaps lie in the bed and cry about her lovely dress being spoiled and the fright she had got and . . . oh, everything.

Lucy was on her feet too now and she said, 'My horse is just round the bushes there. Yes, please walk with me.'

Along the road they remained silent for quite some way and only the clop-clop of the horse's hooves and the wind swaying the trees that bordered the road disturbed Biddy's thoughts. It was Lucy who broke the silence between them when she said, 'Grandmama has taken to you.'

And Biddy was bold enough to answer, 'So I've been told before, but she has a very funny way of showing it.'

'You know what she told me about you?'

'No, miss.'

'She said she had told you to stop reading but that she knew you still kept it up.'

'She told you that?' Biddy smiled a little, and Lucy answered, 'Yes; and that was only last week. Now if it had been last year she had told me that I would have wanted to scratch your eyes out. Isn't it strange how one can change?' She turned and looked fully at Biddy again and now she said, 'Could you, do you think . . . could you break it to her in some way? Pave the way for me? I'm so afraid that if I tell her, she'll have one of her screaming fits. And not only Hobson would hear her, but any of the maids who happened to be passing. But . . . but if you could do it last thing at night when . . . when Hobson is in bed and everything is quiet. . . . Would you?'

For a moment there flashed into Biddy's mind a picture of the reception the breaking of this news would receive; but then perhaps not last thing at night when the old lady would be lying down and vulnerable without her wig, her teeth, and her face devoid of all plaster, for from experience she knew that, in this state, the old lady was always more amenable; still demanding, but her demands couched in quieter terms, more as requests. Yet she was surprised when she heard herself say, 'yes, all right, I'll try.'

'Oh, thank you, thank you. You see, she's . . . well, she's had experience with this kind of thing before, when my father misbehaved and there were results, if not on the doorstep, pretty near it. And then she had a dreadful time with my grandfather, so I've gathered from servants' chatter and such.'

The way she had said servants' chatter made Biddy, for a moment, imagine she herself had been excluded from that category; but then she was brought back to reality when they neared the gates and Lucy, pulling the horse to a stop, said, 'We cannot go any further together, but I will come up in the morning, early. Perhaps you will meet me, say around nine o'clock in the gallery, and . . .and let me know what has transpired. Will you do that?'

'Yes, miss. Yes, I'll do that.'

'Thank you. Thank you very much.'

'Goodbye, miss.'

'Goodbye, Biddy.'

As if she was emerging from a dream, she walked slowly up the long narrow path that skirted the grounds. Had all this happened to her since she had left home not an hour and a half gone, attacked by that devil? And what would he have done if Miss Lucy hadn't come on the scene? . . . Miss Lucy. Eeh! dear God, what a predicament to be in. And it could have happened to her. Yes, it could, because she couldn't have fought him off much longer.

She made her way quietly through the side door, keeping the edge of her loose coat pulled together over the now buttonless bodice of her new frock and she had also tugged her hat to one side in order to cover her ear. But she met no one until, at the foot of the stairs that gave on to the gallery, she came face to face with Mrs Fulton. The housekeeper, deliberately blocking her way, looked her up and down before she said scornfully, 'My, my! we are dressed to kill aren't we? You certainly didn't go out wearing those clothes, did you, Miss Millican?'

'No, I didn't, Mrs Fulton. I acquired them when I reached home.'

'Oh, you did, you did. And you have taken to wearing your hat on the side, I see. Straighten it!'

'I like it on the side, Mrs Fulton.'

'I said, straighten it, girl!' The small face showed fury as her hand came out to push the hat straight on Biddy's head. And Biddy, lifting her hand to prevent her, let go of her coat and it fell open to disclose the ripped bodice, which in turn showed the top of her petticoat.

The housekeeper's face stretched as if it was being pulled from all sides and she emitted the word, '*Well!*' and it said everything. And Biddy, now almost slapping the hand from her head, repeated, 'Yes, well, Mrs Fulton. I was attacked on my way here. I must tell you about it sometime when I have nothing better to do.' And on this she actually thrust the older woman to the side. And when no protest was flung at her for this daring action, she knew that her torn and bedraggled appearance had, for the moment, raised such a question mark in the housekeeper's mind that she had become speechless.

Upstairs, she was greeted by Jessie saying, 'thank God you've come. I'm nearly mad with toothache and madam is in one of her moods, nothing can please her, and she's asked for you twice. She said you were late, but you're not. What's the matter?'

It had taken some seconds for Jessie to realize something was not quite right with her assistant, and when Biddy pulled open her coat, then lifted the hair from her ear and stood silent, Jessie said, 'My God! What happened to you, girl?' and Biddy replied simply, 'Mr Paul. He attacked me.'

'No!'

'Aye, yes. *Oh, yes.*'

'Did he . . .?'

'No, but it wasn't his fault that he didn't; Miss Lucy came along and beat him off.'

'*Miss Lucy*, beat him off?' For a moment Jessie forgot her toothache and her face screwed up in amazement as she repeated, 'Beat her brother off?'

'Yes, yes, she did.'

'Well, well. But I must say, there's a change in that girl since she was sent away to school. She's much better mannered, lost all her devilment. They must have knocked it out of her there.'

'Yes, I think they have. Now . . . now I'll go and change.' She was about to turn away, then stopped and said, 'Me mother made me this dress and coat. It . . . it was lovely when I left the house.'

'Oh, what a shame, lass. But it's still lovely. We'll fix the front. . . . But Master Paul. Eeh! If the master . . . No. But if Mr Stephen or Mr Laurence knew about it, by! my, they would skin him alive.'

'Yet, from what I understand they are not above doing such things themselves, only in . . . well, a more licensed way.' There was a touch of tartness in her tone now, and Jessie replied, 'Aye, well, that's the way of all gentlemen. But I can tell you, they wouldn't stand for what's been done to you, an' by one of their family.' Then shaking her head, she added sadly, 'It's funny, girl, how things always seem to happen to you. I've never known anyone like you for creating . . .' Instead of trouble, she added 'things. And I wouldn't say you were to blame all the time. It's just that, somehow – ' She shrugged her shoulders,then cupped her cheeks with her hand and grimaced as pain stabbed at her again before adding, 'Go on, get changed and go into her, because I'm not going to be long out of me bed.'

'Take some laudanum; it might ease it and put you to sleep.'

'Yes, yes, I will. I thought of that last night, but was afraid I wouldn't waken when she shouted. I seem to forget at times that you're here and capable. It's surprising how she's taken to you and lets you talk. She never did it with me. She still doesn't. Go on. Go on now.'

Biddy went, but she was slow to change into her uniform because she was experiencing reaction to the struggle she'd had earlier on. And as she sat on the side of her bed, she thought, I'll have to try to get me mind clear and think what I'm going to say, and how I'm gona say it. And I'll have to keep awake until Miss Hobson's asleep. And on this thought she felt guilty, because she knew that Jessie was a person who knew how to keep her tongue still; she must be because who else in the house besides herself knew that at intervals Mr Mottram the coachman came up to madam to report on her son and his doings in Newcastle. Madam had brought Mr Mottram with her when she first came into this family, and it was well known in the house that he was madam's man, but what was not equally known was that he was madam's spy and had been for years, so she understood.

This was a queer household. Nothing she had read, she told herself, could hold a candle to it for its goings on. And now, she herself this night was to create more goings on, and she was afraid of the outcome.

Twice she had to get out of bed and sit on the edge of it to prevent herself falling into a deep sleep.

At nine o'clock they had settled madam for the night and the old lady had been impatient with Miss Hobson because she complained of her toothache. 'Go down to the stables, woman,' she had said, 'and they'll put a bit of wire around it and one good tug and you'll have no more aches and pains. Have them all out. That's the best way. I did. Do as I bid you and I'll have a set made for you. Oh, go to bed, woman!' she had cried at last. And Jessie had gone to bed, after taking a dose of laudanum. It was some time, however, before her snores told Biddy that she was well away, yet it was still not ten o'clock and there would be movement in the house down below – the gentlemen played billiards at night, or cards and it was sometimes near twelve o'clock before they settled into bed. She doubted if she could keep awake till then.

At one point she put on a dressing-gown that had been passed on to her from Jessie, and, creeping into the hallway, went along the gallery towards the folding doors. The last window in the gallery overlooked part of the front of the house and when she saw there was no reflection from the lamps outside the front door, she knew that the servants had retired. The butler and the valet might still be up; they couldn't go to bed until the last member of the household was in his room, but she doubted if there was any chance of anyone coming to this end of the house now, and so she crept back and entered the dressing-room, where she stood for a long moment with eyes closed before she gently opened the door and entered madam's bedroom.

Through the light from the turned down lamp on the bedside table, she was surprised to see the old lady, not only awake, but sitting propped up in bed. When she had last left her she had been tucked down into her pillows. But Biddy was quick to note that the pillows were rearranged, which proved that madam wasn't as helpless as she sometimes made out to be.

'Girl, what is it?' The voice came to her soft, as it usually did in the night.

Slowly Biddy approached the bed, and she drew in a long and deep breath as she stood looking into the wizened face before she said, 'Madam, may I talk to you?'

'Talk to me, girl, at this time of night?'

'It's very important, madam.'

'What's important about you that won't wait until the morning?'

'I don't wish to talk about myself. It's about . . . about one of the household . . . the family. I . . . I have been asked . . . I mean – '

The thin body moved in the bed and Biddy for a moment imagined she could hear the aged skin crackling.

'What you getting at, girl?'

'It's . . . it's about Miss Lucy, madam.'

'Miss Lucy? What about Miss Lucy?'

'I . . . I have something to tell you.'

'About Miss Lucy?'

'Yes, madam.'

'Carrying tales?' The voice had lost its softness.

And Biddy's tone also changed when she answered, 'No, madam, I'm not carrying tales. I never carry tales. Miss Lucy asked me to . . . well, the fact is, madam' – she now nodded her head – 'she's frightened, terrified to tell you herself.'

She watched the old lady press herself back into her pillows and move her head slowly from side to side as if to get a better view of her, and when she said, 'Go on,' Biddy said, 'I don't know how to tell you, madam, because it's going to be a bit of a shock.'

'Girl, I'm used to shocks. My life has been made up of shocks. What is it you have to tell me that Miss Lucy is afraid to tell me herself?'

Again Biddy gulped, but she didn't take her eyes off the old lady, and her hands wavered in front of her as if ready to throttle any yell she might give, for from experience she knew that madam's voice had a great carrying quality.

'She . . . she's going to have a baby, madam.'

The body seemed to be possessed of a new life, a young life, for when madam sat suddenly bolt upright in the bed, Biddy's hands actually did go out. But they only touched her shoulders and she was appealing to her now, 'Madam. Madam. Don't say anything. Don't shout.'

Her hands were shrugged away and the voice hissed at her, 'Who's going to shout? What do you mean, girl, shout? And don't stand there. Bring a chair and sit down.'

Biddy brought a chair and sat down, and the old lady now commanded her, 'Talk.'

'Well, Madam, I happened to come across Miss Lucy when I was returning from my leave. I was sitting by the river. Miss . . . Miss Lucy seemed distressed. She . . . she seemed changed, different, and then she told me.'

The small mouth was puckered until the lips parted and demanded, 'Why you?'

Yes, why her?

She said, 'She hadn't anyone else, madam. I mean, she was afraid to tell the master and mistress.'

'Damn well she might be afraid to tell them. Yes, damn well she might be. My God in heaven! For this to happen and at this time. Her mother would go mad.' Then characteristically she added, 'Not that that would matter very much. All right. All right, girl, she was frightened to tell them. But why couldn't she come to me herself?'

'Because, madam, she thought that you would go for her as . . . as you sometimes . . .'

'Yes? Go on, go on. Don't stop now.'

'Well, as you sometimes do in the daytime.' Biddy's head was nodding defiantly now, while part of her stood aside amazed to witness this happening. 'And she was afraid that some member of the household would hear.'

'And so she asked you to do her dirty work?'

'No, it's not dirty work. She's very much afraid. And . . . and you're always quieter at night and . . .'

She closed her eyes tightly and there was a silence between them now. Then the old woman's voice low and with a tremble in it, she said, 'Go on, girl, tell me what you know. Who is responsible? Some weak-kneed, fumbling schoolboy?'

'It . . . I think it is the father of her friend.'

'What!' The body was brought from the pillows again. 'Her friend? That must be the one she has spoken of. He's a teacher in the school, and if I'm not mistaken, has a large family; well, four or five, or something like that. God in heaven! God in heaven!' Her hands were clasped now and she was beating them on her chest as she cried, 'He'll pay for this. He'll certainly pay for this.'

'Madam.'

'Yes, girl?' She was giving Biddy her attention again.

'If . . . if you do that, I mean, accuse him, the . . . the whole thing will be made public, and then . . . well, she might as well have gone and told her mother in the first place. I think she imagines you will come up with . . . well, what I mean is' – her head was moving again from side to side – 'some sort of scheme to . . . to prevent it being made public.'

'What does she mean, some kind of scheme? You can't prevent the birth of a child. You can't cover up the birth of a child. Oh my God!' Now she had her hand on top of her nightcap and as she screwed it round on her head the wisps of white hair fell across her brow and she muttered to herself, 'I've got to think, and think hard.' And turning her eyes on Biddy, she added, 'If this came to light it would clamp the lid on so many things: my daughter-in-law's standing in the county, and the fact that her uncle is to be made bishop. My God!' She rocked her head on the pillow. 'I can see the effect it would have on her. It would even turn her guts white. Then there is Stephen, and Parliament. And we mustn't forget May who is about to marry that idiot out of pique, or perhaps the allure of one day being called Lady So-and-So. Life has its compensations. Oh yes, but what compensation is it going to have for that stupid little young idiot? When did this happen? How long has she carried?'

'Over two months, I think, madam.'

'Oh my God! I've got to think. I've got to think.' She was muttering to herself now, and when Biddy moved uneasily in the chair, for she was feeling weary and far from her healthy self at the moment, the old lady said, 'Fetch a blanket. I . . . I want you to stay with me. I want to think, and we must talk. I've got to reach a solution before the morning when that stupid girl comes hoping I'll have a miracle ready for her. Well, she'll find out I can't perform miracles.'

She was still muttering to herself while Biddy went into the dressing-room and returned with a blanket.

Sitting down to the side of the bed again, Biddy draped the blanket round her knees and her waist while she half turned to face the old lady who, looking at her pointedly now, said, 'She's got to get away from here. That's evident. That's the first thing. But *where? Where?*

Friends are out. If you want a secret spread from here to Land's End, tell it to a friend. I have kept my own counsel all my life, that's why my head is clear today . . . Don't fall asleep, girl. We've got to think.'

'Yes, madam.'

'Are you warm enough? It gets very cold in the night, even in the summer.'

For a moment the thoughtfulness caught Biddy off her guard and she could make no reply till the voice, muffled but still harsh, came at her, saying, 'Well, are you?'

'Yes, madam. Thank you, madam.'

'Well now, sit back. Think what you would do in her place, and don't be afraid to tell me what you think. They always say two heads are better than one. Now if this was happening to you, what would you do?'

What would she do if this was happening to her? Go home to her mother and be rated for a fool, then have the child and live under the stigma for the rest of her life, and alone, for no man would take her after that. Take her to use her, yes, but not marry her. But it wouldn't happen to her. It wouldn't happen to her. For she'd never marry. Never marry. Never marry. To the chant in her head sleep overcame her . . .

She awoke feeling that her whole body had become permanently twisted; her cheek was pressed against the wooden edge of the chair, one hand was on the bed and the other was clutching the blanket up to her neck. Slowly she blinked and tried to rise quickly as she realized that she had fallen asleep, but the effort brought a groan from her and the voice to her side said, 'It's all right, girl. Take it slowly.'

She took it slowly, and when she was sitting up straight she blinked and murmured, 'I'm sorry, madam. I . . . I didn't mean to fall asleep.'

'Nor did I, girl. Nor did I, but we both couldn't keep awake all night. However, it's now five o'clock.'

'Five o'clock!' Biddy went to rise, but the cramp in her legs caused her face to screw up with pain and she repeated again, 'Five o'clock! I've . . . I've been asleep all night, madam?'

'Yes, you've been asleep all night, girl.'

'Have you slept, madam?'

'On and off. On and off. Now I would like a cup of tea. The house will be astir in a little while and then I want you to go and get into your clothes as quickly as possible.'

Biddy made the cup of tea for the old lady, watched her drink it, poured her out another, then retired to the little kitchen and drank two cups herself before going to her room to get dressed.

When she again returned to the bedroom the first thing madam said to her was, 'Well, have you any ideas in your head, girl, concerning this matter?'

'Only one, madam.'

'Then let me hear it.'

'It's . . . It's just occurred to me that wherever Miss Lucy went in England, there might be somebody who knew of her. It's amazing how things pass around. So if . . . well, I thought, if she could go abroad for . . . like a long holiday . . .'

'Huh!' It sounded like a stifled laugh, but the countenance remained grim as she said, 'Under other circumstances you would have likely made something of yourself, girl, because that is the idea that has struck me too, abroad, but not for a long holiday. Young girls like Miss Lucy don't go for extended holidays. For whatever length she's got to be abroad there's got to be a purpose in it, and I've thought of the purpose. But I must have help, and the only one who can help in this case is Laurence. He will take her across to France to school. She will purportedly stay with friends of his. He's got very good friends in France, so he tells me, and they have young daughters and sons. She can supposedly board with them while going to school, but she's got to have a maid, and that maid will be you.'

'*Me, madam?*' Now Biddy thrust her hand over her mouth because the exclamation could have been heard down the corridor, and at this the old lady cried, 'Who's bawling their head off now? Yes, you girl. You, I understand, have bragged about your ability to speak French. Well, this will be an opportunity to learn how the French speak French. And don't tell me, you can't go, because I'm going to tell you something: you, my dear girl, are at the bottom of this trouble.'

Biddy put her hand flat on her chest and was for saying again, 'Me, madam?' But the 'Me!' she brought out was in the nature of a squeak, and madam replied quickly, 'Yes, you. If it hadn't been for that affray in the laundry, Lucy would never have been sent to that school. Her mother was against it.' Madam did not add at this point that she herself was for Lucy's departure from under the wing of an inadequate governess and her psalm-singing mother.

'Now, don't stand there gaping, girl; I want you to go downstairs and see one of the men. Froggett is a lazy beggar, he will not be up yet, but Thompson will likely be about. Tell him to go and wake Mr Laurence and inform him that I wish to see him as soon as possible, and that means before breakfast. Make that point clear.'

'Yes, madam.' Biddy went out of the room and had reached the communicating doors without realizing she had moved a step: there was a feeling as if she was walking on air; for a moment she had forgotten about Miss Lucy's predicament, she could only think, I'm going to France. I'm going to France. And to this she added, Oh, Mr Miller. For it was as if he was standing by her side saying,'Now, what did I tell you.'

It was John Thompson she saw when she descended the main staircase. This man had been more kindly disposed towards her than any of the other male staff. And now he greeted her quietly, saying, 'What is it, lass? I've never seen you down here afore at this time, or at any other time for that matter, not in this part of the house.' He smiled, and she said, 'I've got a message from madam. She wishes you to wake Mr Laurence and tell him she wants to see him immediately . . . before breakfast.'

He leant his face towards her, saying, 'Something up?'

'No.' She shook her head; then again, on a higher note, 'No, except' – she made herself smile now – 'she's had a sleepless night and she wants to take it out on somebody. Miss Hobson and me are not enough.'

He laughed now, saying, 'By, she's a tartar. But we still know who rules the roost, don't we?' He pulled a face at her and she answered, 'Yes, we still know who rules the roost. Will you give the message, Mr Thompson?'

'Yes, I will, lass. Here, just a minute.' He touched her arm as she turned away, and now he looked from his right to his left before quietly saying, 'I'm glad you bested them,' and he jerked his head towards the servants corridor. 'By! you did that, especially Ma Fulton. Keep at it, lass.'

'Thank you, Mr Thompson. I'll try.' With quiet dignity she turned about and went up the main staircase knowing that he was watching her. As she made her way back to the west wing, she thought, Wait till the news breaks and they know I'm accompanying Miss Lucy abroad. It'll burn some of them up. And for a moment she felt a wave of satisfaction pass over her.

What she did next was to go into Jessie Hobson's room. Jessie was still sound asleep, and so she left her, but she thought as she did so, She's got to know. Yet why should she? Miss Lucy could really be going to school in France, finishing, they called it, like when the young men went away on world tours to finish. But finish what? She didn't know, she only knew one thing, that poor Miss Hobson was going to find things hard having to run, fetch and carry all on her own again. But likely she would get help; there were plenty downstairs who would jump into the position, given the chance . . .

It was not more than fifteen minutes later when she saw Mr Laurence coming towards her from the gallery. She could see that he had donned his trousers, but was still wearing his bedroom slippers and a brown corded dressing-gown. She also noticed that he must have sluiced his face, likely to waken himself up, because the front of his hair was wet.

He asked of her immediately, 'What is it? Is there something wrong?' And she answered hesitantly, 'Yes, in a way, sir. Yes.'

'She's ill?'

'No. Nothing like that, sir, but she'll . . . madam will tell you. Would . . . would you like a cup of tea, sir?'

He had moved from her towards the bedroom door, but turned his head and said, 'Yes. Yes, I would, Biddy. That would be nice.' Then he went into the room.

She did not hurry with the tea-making; she wanted to give madam time to tell him all she knew and what she intended to do about it.

When she eventually tapped on the door while balancing a small silver tray on one hand and entered the room, she was surprised by the lack of discussion taking place. Mr Laurence was sitting in the chair she had vacated earlier, madam was propped up in bed, and they were both looking towards her.

She put the tray on a small table and placed it at his side, and he looked at her and muttered, 'Thank you,' the while he continued to stare at her.

Now madam spoke to her, saying, 'Mr Laurence agrees with what I told you earlier. But the matter must be dealt with slowly. He will go across to France with you both and see you settled in with the family.'

'No, Grandmama.' He was looking at her. 'I told you, it can't be with that family. They have too many connections in London, and . . .'

'All right. All right. It's all right.' She had closed her eyes tightly and her bony hand was flapping in a protesting movement as she said, 'Yes, yes, you've told me. But I still think it's a pity. They'll need supervision, both of them.'

'Well, I'll see that they get that, Grandmama. But the centre of Paris is no place to settle them. Anyway, I'll think of something.'

'You do that. You do that. And' – her face brightened a little – 'you could put it to them that you are going across to France to settle the matter. What I mean is, to make arrangements for her supposed school et cetera. And . . . and I think it would be a good idea if you did go across beforehand, and make sure of their apartments. Then take them over just before you return to Oxford. What do you say?'

Biddy watched him nip on his lower lip. She watched his eyelids blink. Then he almost jumped, as she did, when madam barked with her usual daytime voice, 'It's got to look natural.' And she lay back and put her hand to her head as she muttered,'Why should I have this at my time of life? It isn't right.' Now she was glaring at him. 'It isn't, is it, Laurence?'

'No, Grandmama.'

'But you can see the result of what exposure would mean? She would be ruined for life, the stupid little fool. But what will be much more important to her mother and father is that they would never be able to live this down.'

'Don't worry.' He put his hand soothingly on hers and patted it and said again, 'Don't worry. I'll see to things.'

She looked at him, her expression showing pain now as she said, 'Don't worry. You say, don't worry. My worry's only starting. I'll be worrying about her all the time she's over there, and having her child in a strange country when the experiencing of such an event should occur with her family about her. And to think' – she poked her face up now from the pillow – 'it'll be their first grandchild. Oh, it isn't to be tolerated. Don't worry you say. Then there's those Frenchmen. I know what they are like . . .'

'Biddy here, will be with her, and' – he turned and looked at Biddy – 'I think she'll be able to manage most Frenchmen. What do you say, Biddy?'

Biddy stared back at him. Only yesterday she hadn't been able to manage a young Englishman. What she said was, 'Shall I pour your tea, sir?' And he answered,'Yes, please.'

She poured out the tea and was about to turn away and leave the room when madam's voice checked her, saying, 'And I'll be losing her an' all, and Hobson is dying on her feet.'

'You'll have to have someone else to take her place, Grandmama.'

'Who? One of the dudheads from downstairs?'

Biddy had reached the door when madam's voice halted her yet again, saying, 'A moment, girl.' When she turned and looked across the room towards her, the old lady exclaimed, 'You have a sister, haven't you? How old is she?'

'Fourteen, madam.'

'Fourteen. Is she bright?'

'She's as I was at her age. She can read and write.'

'Never mind about reading and writing, is she bright in other ways?'

'Yes, madam. But . . . but she helps my mother.'

'From what I understand of your mother's situation, she's in need of money. You will go home presently and tell her that your sister will take your place for the next few months and she will be paid well. She will begin on three shillings a week and I shall see it is paid to her every fortnight. As for you, while you are acting as companion, five shillings per week will be paid to your mother for you.'

'Thank you madam.' A minute later, standing in the kitchen, she repeated, 'Five shillings a week and three shillings a week, and everything found for Maggie, and in her own case, the means of travelling to a new world. It didn't seem real. Nothing seemed real.

She was standing at the small sink looking out through the window beyond that gave a view of the side gardens when the door opened and she turned expecting to see Miss Hobson. But it was Laurence who stood there, and he didn't speak until he had crossed the small room and stood by her side. Then looking down into her face, he said softly, 'When . . . when is the child expected?'

'I'm not sure, sir.'

'It is very sad, very sad, and, if I may say so, strange that she should confide in you.'

'I thought so too, sir, yet . . . yet she seems changed.'

'Yes, I had noticed that, particularly these last few weeks. She must have been very worried.'

'She was, sir. She is.'

'They say good comes out of evil. I would have dismissed that until this moment, because I think this is a wonderful opportunity for you. There's nothing expands the mind like travel, and you were interested in French, weren't you?'

'Yes, sir. But I must say that I would rather not have had my education extended at such a cost to Miss Lucy.'

He didn't answer for a moment, and then he said softly, 'No. No, you are right, Biddy, the cost is high. Yet I must tell you that once you have been abroad, you'll never feel the same again; I doubt if you will be content to take up this kind of duty.' His hand made a wavering motion which took in not only the room but the whole house. 'And as I see it, there'll be no reason why you should, because I should think you would be qualified to teach. There is a movement ahead to provide schools for poor children, but apart from that, you could go as governess. Would you like that?'

'I would, sir, very much.' He was looking into her face now and she into his and her eyes became misted and for a moment she imagined his face moved closer to hers; but the mist cleared and he was standing exactly as he had been before, only now his hand came up and rested gently against her cheek, and it was with the greatest of efforts that she stopped her own fingers from covering his. Then his voice little above a whisper, he said, 'You are a remarkable girl, Biddy.'

His fingers left her face. He looked at her a moment longer, then he went out. And she turned and leant against the sink and her hands gripped its stone edge until her nails hurt.

10

The commotion in the house was worse, Jessie said, than when Mr Riddle brought his small tribe of chimney-sweeping boys.

The family always went away in September so that the servants could deal with the soot that even the best of Mr Riddle's team brought down in scuttlefuls. The only one who seemed to enjoy the invasion by the tiny boys, aged from seven to ten, was madam. Often she would be wheeled to the gallery window to watch their scurrying backwards and forwards across the yard with the bags of soot. And once, it was said, she had gone into the laundry yard to watch them being washed after they had finished their week's work. It was known that Mr Riddle's boys liked coming to The Heights, for they were always fed well, and each had a sixpenny piece given to him before he left. It was also known that the same boys never came more than twice: they had either died or grown too big for the chimneys.

So the sweep week, as it was known, was a week of commotion. As were the following three in getting the place shipshape again to receive the family back. Yet this didn't happen until September. But here they were only part way through July and the whole house in a buzz, all because Miss Lucy had absolutely refused to go back to her own school and madam had decided that she should be finished off in France. And so she was going to stay with Master Laurence's friends and be educated with the young members of the family.

But what was causing the biggest verbal commotion downstairs was the fact that madam had insisted that *that one*, that laundry slut, should accompany Miss Lucy as maid. Did you ever in all your life hear of anything like it?

When it first came to Mrs Fulton's ears, they said she had almost collapsed, and she had asked for an audience, not with the mistress, but with madam, because she was only too well aware who ruled the house, and she felt that madam should know that the girl she was having trained as a lady's maid was of questionable character. And she had explained the proof she had of this.

No one knew what madam had said to her, except that she had been told to come back within the hour.

The result of Mrs Fulton's visit was that madam asked Biddy the meaning of her torn clothes, and Biddy unhesitatingly answered, 'I was attacked by Mr Paul, madam, and Miss Lucy beat him off. It was following this she gave me her confidence because she saw I could have been placed in a similar predicament to herself.'

No one knew what madam had said to Mrs Fulton on her second visit, only that that lady descended to her own quarters with a very white face and had not been approachable for some time . . .

Riah had taken Biddy's news in dumb silence. She had always known that this child of hers was different and that one day she would achieve something. Yet still, she couldn't believe that she was going across the sea to that place where they had revolutions and people's heads were chopped off. In the ordinary way it was a place where only the gentry were able to go but her daughter was going; true, as maid to a young lady, but nevertheless she was going. And what was more, she was losing her other daughter, at least for the time being, she was told.

At first she had protested at Maggie's going to the house, but Maggie had cried and begged to be given the chance. And, as she pointed out, there was the three shillings a week and not having her to feed or clothe.

Biddy had told her she was to get five shillings a week. It was all too good to be true, or would have been if she herself was happy, for now she'd be left alone in this house with only Johnny, and he so restless that she wouldn't be surprised to find him gone one morning.

And so came the morning of departure. The luggage was packed in the coach that was to take them to where the boat sailed for France. Biddy's mind was in such a whirl that at times, even up till an hour ago, she had closed her eyes tightly and asked herself if she was awake and not dreaming.

She kissed Maggie goodbye and, looking down at her she said, 'Do everything you're told, and don't be afraid of madam. She shouts a lot, as you've heard, but you'll get used to her.'

Then in Jessie's sitting-room, when she held out her hand to the old woman, Jessie had put her arms around her and kissed her, and there were tears in her eyes as she said, 'Take care of yourself, lass.' And leaning close to Biddy she had whispered under her breath, 'I don't know what it's really all about but I'm no fool. Anyway, take care of her, because you've got a head on your shoulders. Goodbye, lass, and God go with you.'

Her own eyes were wet when she went into the bedroom and stood before the figure in the chair sitting near the window.

Madam stared at her; then extending her hand, she clutched at Biddy's, saying, 'Take care of her now, and when it is born bring her back. Laurence will see about an adoption. I'm relying on you to see that all goes smoothly. Do you understand me?'

'Yes, madam.'

'You won't lose by this, girl, I promise you.'

'I want nothing more, madam.'

'A girl in your position will always need more if she means to rise to the top of her station. Goodbye now. Keep me informed.'

'I will, madam.' She bent her knee and turned and walked hurriedly out of the room.

On this occasion she did not go down the back stairs. The coach was waiting at the front door, and she walked with straight back and head up towards the communicating doors, then on to the long gallery where she surprised a number of the servants standing at the windows. But they all turned from watching Mr Laurence helping Miss Lucy up into the carriage to look at the Millican chit walking towards the main staircase as if, as they said later, she owned the place. But she wouldn't have dared to do that if the family had been at home. It was a pity they had to leave for London yesterday to attend Miss May's engagement party. And it was also a pity that Miss Lucy wasn't going along with them. There had been ructions between the master and mistress because old madam had got this idea into her head about her granddaughter's education. But they all knew who would win; like in every other way of life, it was the one who held the purse-strings that called the tune. But oh, the mistress had been upset. She had even called in Parson Weeks to speak to madam. But what had happened there nobody knew except that the poor man came downstairs with a face like a beetroot.

When Biddy reached the foot of the stairs Thomas Froggett turned from the front doors and, his mouth agape, he watched her walk towards him, then pass him without a glance in his direction, and the sound he made was something between a hiss and a choking cough.

The two footmen were standing near the carriage, and John Thompson would have helped her into it, but Mr Laurence, his hand on her elbow, assisted her up the steps; then he himself followed. James Simpson closed the door. Bill Mottram on the box shouted, 'Gee up! there.' And then they were off, leaving behind a mostly indignant and wondering staff.

Even Davey, who had watched the performance from a stable door while standing the chaff of the other boys about his sister rising in the world, felt indignant that their Biddy was once again doing something that brought her to the fore and made her more disliked than she already was.

In the carriage, Lucy sat in silence beside Laurence, with Biddy sitting opposite to them until the coach was passing through the gates when she looked out of the window to where the lodge-keeper was raising his hat to her, and she said, 'I don't care if I never ride through these gates again.' And Laurence, catching hold of her hand, said, 'Oh, now, now, Lucy, don't say that.' And she turned her gaze on him as she said, quietly, 'It's true, Laurence.' Then looking at

Biddy, she asked her, 'Would you like to stop and say goodbye to your mother?' And Biddy answered, 'Yes, if you don't mind, miss, I would.'

'It's been arranged already. Mottram knows when to stop.' Laurence smiled from one to the other.

'You know, you're like Grandmama, Laurence, you think of everything.'

He answered her jokingly, saying, 'I'm not like Grandmama, Lucy; I could never get up to her pitch if I tried. Moreover, her cosmetics wouldn't suit my complexion.'

While Lucy smiled faintly at this, Biddy thought, He is like her. She's not his grandmother, but he is like her.

When the coach stopped, Biddy alighted, saying, 'I won't be more than a minute or so.' And Laurence answered, 'You needn't hurry, we've got time and to spare.'

Riah was waiting for her at the front door and she went straight into her arms, muttering, 'Don't cry, Ma. Don't cry, Ma.'

'I feel awful, lass.'

'Yes, I know. You're bound to. You'll be lonely.'

'Oh' – Riah shook her wet face – 'it isn't that. I've got to tell you, an' I've left it to the last minute. I should have told you long afore. It's about this.' She raised her eyes and her hand, indicating the house. 'You see, the master didn't leave it to me, not really. He said, I could stay here, in his will, as long as I didn't get married. But somehow he felt that I would, and anyway, whether I married or died, the house was to be yours, and I've kept it back from you for various reasons.'

'It's all right, Ma.' Biddy's face too was streaming now. 'It's all right. I know. I know.'

Riah rubbed the tears from her eyes with the back of her hand as she exclaimed, 'You know? How do you know? I mean . . .'

'Oh, it doesn't matter. I've known for a long time. And, Ma, I hope I never come into it until I'm a very old woman.' She smiled now through her tears.

'Aw, lass, lass.' Again they were holding each other close; then Biddy muttered, 'I've got to go; they're waiting.'

'I can't believe it. I can't believe it. All this happening. You goin' to France, of all places in the world. And he learned you the language. It's strange. It's strange.'

'Yes, it is, Ma . . . Are you coming to the gate?'

'No, lass, no. I . . . I'd only make a fool of meself. And look at me, in me house things, I'm not much to be proud of. Go on.'

'I'll always be proud of you, Ma.' Their hands held tightly for a minute, then their fingers drew apart, and Biddy turned and ran down the drive.

She was nearing the gate when through her blurred vision she saw beyond the back of the coach a well-known figure crossing the field at the other side of the road, and when she reached Laurence, who was holding the door open for her now, she looked at him and, a plea in her voice, she said, 'Could . . . is there . . . I mean, is there a minute to spare? There's a friend of mine.' She pointed. 'I'd like to say goodbye to him.'

Laurence glanced at his watch. 'It's all right,' he said. 'Yes, barring accidents' – he smiled – 'we'll be in Newcastle in good time.'

'Thank you.' Her glance darted from him to the figure sitting inside the coach before she turned away and hurried to the drystone wall bordering the field.

When Tol caught hold of her hands across the wall, he muttered thickly, 'All set then, lass?'

'Yes, Tol.'

'Good luck, then.' He nodded at her; then his voice dropping, he added, 'Don't worry about things at this end.'

'Me ma's lonely. She's lost. We've all gone now except Johnny, and I'm worried about him an' all. I feel he could scoot at any time. He's restless.'

'Don't you worry your head, I'll have a talk with him. And . . . and I'm going to see your ma.'

'When?'

'When you get yourself away off the road and on your journey and I can get past you.' His joking reply filled her throat and she leant impulsively forward and kissed him.

Lucy had been watching the meeting from her side of the coach, and now she turned and, looking to where Laurence was standing once again glancing at his watch, she said, 'It's odd how she can create love and hate, isn't it?' And he replied, 'Yes, as you say, Lucy, it's odd.'

The next minute he had his hand on Biddy's elbow and was helping her up into the coach. Then with a word to Mottram, he climbed after her and banged the door, and as it closed they all knew, in different ways, that a period of their lives had ended and what lay before them were many difficult problems.

Tol watched the coach until it had rolled out of sight, then slowly he went up the drive and knocked on the kitchen door. Receiving no reply, he entered the room and found it empty. He now knocked on the communicating hall door before passing through, but he could see no sign of Riah. He crossed the hall and gently pushed open the drawing-room door; and there she was sitting huddled on the couch. She was sobbing so deeply that she wasn't aware of his presence until his hand came on her shoulder, and she started with a cry that ended in a gasp. Then she straightened up and lay against the back of the couch, her face awash with tears and her breath coming in gasps.

Taking a seat beside her, he took hold of her hand, saying, 'Come on now. Come on. It isn't as bad as that. She's taking a chance in a lifetime. She'll be somebody in the end, will Biddy. She's somebody now; in fact, she always has been. But you'll be proud of her, you'll see.'

'Tol.' Her voice was small.

'Yes?'

'They've' – she gulped in her throat – 'all gone, except Johnny, and . . . and he's threatening to run off. They've all left me.'

'But they're all alive, and doing well. You should be proud of them.'

She lifted the bottom of her apron and rubbed it round her face, then muttered,'Yes, yes, I suppose I should, but I can feel nothing except' – she swallowed again – 'lost. It was . . . it is as if I'd never borne them. I'm lost.' She turned her face fully to him now and muttered, 'I'm lost, Tol.'

'Well – ' his voice came low and deep as he said, 'there's a remedy for that, you know, Riah, any day of the week, or any minute of the day. And I'll say this, I'm not asking you to marry me now. If you want to stay in this house, I can understand that, but there was nothing in the will to say you couldn't love me, and me you. Now was there?'

He watched her screw up her eyes tightly; he watched fresh tears stream from beneath the closed lids; he watched her head droop on to her chest; and then he put his arms about her and drew her gently to him and, stroking her hair, he murmured, 'You need me, Riah. You can't go on fighting it off forever, and I need you. Oh, how I need you, because I've loved you from that first time I saw you standing with the bairns in the yard of Rowan Cottage.'

He brought her face round to his now and his eyes held hers for a moment before he kissed her. Then he said, 'For well or ill, Riah, that's a seal as good as any marriage certificate to me. Come on, now, cheer up; everything's going to be bright from now on. And look' – he shook her gently by the shoulders – 'I want a cup of tea made afore I get back to me work. I'm a working man you know, and – ' the smile left his face and, his voice quiet and low, he ended, 'and like a working man I'll come home to you tonight.' And at this she closed her eyes and fell against him.

The following day was Sunday, and Davey paid his usual visit accompanied by Jean.

Both of them regaled her with the talk that was going on up in The Heights. And Davey said that it was a good job Maggie was safe in madam's part of the house because such was the feeling, he understood, in the servants' hall that they might have pulled her hair out. They thought it was most unfair that not one of them from the house had been given the chance to assist Miss Hobson.

It was while Jean was helping Johnny to pick fruit from the orchard that Riah had Davey to herself. And although he wasn't of a perceptive nature he couldn't help but notice that there was a change in his mother; and he said so immediately, 'You look bright,' he said, 'as if our Biddy had come home instead of gone off.' And then he added, 'How did you leave her anyway yesterday?'

'Oh, we were . . . well, a bit upset, me more than her I think, because . . . well, I had to explain something to her that I should have done a long time ago after the master died. It's about this house.'

'What explaining had you to do to her? It's yours.'

'No, not really.'

'*What!*' He had been sitting at one side of the kitchen table and he half rose now, and again he said, 'What? . . . But he left it to you.'

'Just on conditions.'

'What conditions?'

'Well, that I didn't get married again. If I did, well – ' She paused now and he waited, and then she said, 'If I did I'd have to move out and the house would go to Biddy.'

'*To our Biddy?*' His big face was screwed up. 'But it can't. Look, Ma, I'm your son and the eldest. What you own should come to me.'

'Not in this case.'

His mouth opened and closed twice before he said,'What . . . what if you died?'

'It goes straight to her.'

'No, be damned!' He was on his feet now, and she too, and she yelled at him, 'Yes, yes, be damned, Davey. And what are you making such a fuss about anyway? It's only recently you've come back to the house; you wouldn't come near it for years.'

'No, not as long as he was in it.'

'But it is still his house, and you're in it.'

'It isn't his house, he's dead.'

'He may be but his influence is still here, and you must be thick-skinned if you can't feel it.'

'Feel his influence? He's a spiteful bugger, that's what he is, or was. God!' He flung himself round, punching one fist into his other palm as he said, 'I had it all fixed in me mind. I was going to leave up there now that you've got more money from our Biddy and Maggie, and I could turn this into a home garden, like vegetables and fruit to sell to the market. Some people make a mint taking fresh stuff into the market at the week-ends. I had it all worked out.'

'Well, you can damn well get it unworked out. The place'll never be yours.'

'It's not right, after what he did to me.'

She turned now, her face scarlet, her voice ringing: 'He did nothing to you, it's what you did to him,' she said; 'you crippled him and brought on his end quicker than it should have been. He did nothing to you.'

'He tried.'

'He did not.'

He had his hands flat on the table now leaning towards her as he yelled back at her, 'He had a damn good try.'

'He didn't. He didn't. Not the way you put it. His mistake was in caring for you. Aye. Aye, he loved you and he mentioned the word and I didn't understand it at the time no more than you did, but I know now he would never have harmed you, not in the way you're making out.'

'He's harmed me now all right, hasn't he? Spitting at me from the grave 'cos I would have none of him.'

'You can think what you like, but I know one thing, he would have always seen to Biddy in some way or other, because he admired her having a mind of her own and a brain.'

'Brain be damned! All she is is brazen. And I'll tell you something about her that you don't know, she's been up to tricks on her own, because it's going round the place that she came back from her leave all bedraggled and the front of her dress open down to the waist, and her hat on one side as if she was drunk. And she cheeked the housekeeper when she wanted to know how she got like that. You didn't know that, did you?'

No, she didn't know that. She remembered now that Biddy had had a cut on her ear. She'd said she had tripped against some wire. But Biddy wouldn't be up to anything like that; she had more sense.

'That's surprised you, hasn't it, about your brainy miss?'

'Well, all I can say to that, Davey, is whatever happened wasn't of her doing. Somebody likely tried it on; and they would get as much as they sent if I know her.'

'Yes, she's such a clever bugger, isn't she?'

'Don't you use that language here.'

'Oh, shut up!' As he turned from her she screamed back at him, 'And don't you tell me to shut up. By God! it's coming to something.'

'Aye, it is.' He had rounded on her once again. 'And when we're talking plain, I'm going to tell you this. I'm not tipping up anything more: it's everybody for themselves; I can see that.'

'Very well. You're entitled to keep what you earn. Thank God now I've no need of it. All I can hope is when you and Jean marry and start a family . . .'

'Who said anything about marrying Jean?' His face was stretched.

'Well, aren't you? You're courting her.'

'I'm damn well not, nor ever had any intention.'

'Then why do you bring her here on a Sunday?'

'I don't bring her, she walks along of me. Remember, it was your wonderful daughter that brought her.'

'But . . . but the lass understands . . .'

'That's her mistake then, isn't it?'

'She's a nice lass. A good lass.' Riah's voice showed her bewilderment, and he said, 'Yes, she might be, on top, but where did she come from? She's from the poorhouse; nobody knows about her people. I wouldn't be marrying anybody like that.'

Riah's voice was scarcely audible now, but there was a hiss in it as she said, 'Then you better make it plain to her, hadn't you?'

'I've nothing to make plain. If she's got those ideas, it's her fault. And if there's any explaining to do, I'll leave it to you, because I'm off back now, and I don't care if I never come back home again.'

As he made for the door, she called, 'Davey!' And when he turned towards her, she said, 'Those are my sentiments an' all. I don't care either.'

He stared at her, his eyes widening slightly; then he went out and banged the door behind him.

The world had gone topsy-turvy. Yesterday morning she had been in despair with the thought of the loneliness that stretched ahead, then last night she had experienced loving like she had never imagined it, for it had never happened that way with Seth. She had woken this morning and held the pillow to her that had cradled Tol's head until the early hours of the morning, and when she had got up, it was as if the years had rolled off her and she was a young girl again, and this was her first love. And it was her first love. Yes, her first real love. And all morning she had floated around the house, her feet not seeming to touch the ground. Then she had baked and made a fine tea for Davey and Jean coming. And Davey and Jean had come, and Davey had gone, and she couldn't recognize the nature of him. From where had he inherited such traits? Not from her. And oh no, not from Seth, because Seth had been a good honest man. But why was she searching for a match to his nature, because she could now hear her own mother speaking through him. He had the looks of his grandfather but the complete nature of his grandmother. Although she hadn't recognized it then, she realized it now it had shown on the day he took the pip because the master had been unable to buy him the pony. Everything was all right as long as it went his way, but if it didn't then there were sparks flying. That had been her mother's way too.

Well, Biddy was gone across the seas. Maggie was in service. They had both gone from her, but she hadn't lost them. And she hadn't lost Johnny as yet. But she knew that irrevocably she had lost her eldest.

Why was it that happiness was always bought through a heavy price?

PART FOUR

The Outcome

1

Madame Arnaud's house was situated outside the small village some distance south of Paris. It had once been a farmhouse and consisted of eight rooms all on the same floor. Madame Arnaud was living on a small pension and was pleased to let part of her house to supplement her income. What had been the farmyard proper now formed a terrace, on to which her visitors could walk from their sitting-room, which was very pleasant in the summer but which formed a wind tunnel in the winter.

Her present guests had been with her for some months now. They were Madame Lucille Millican and her sister-in-law, Mademoiselle Bridget Millican. Madame Lucille was a young widow, a tragic case really, so the villagers understood. She had married beneath her and the young husband had died, but her family would still not forgive her mistake. That was the English, they knew nothing about love.

But apparently there remained one member of her family who still had a heart and understanding, for her brother came out at intervals from England to see her. And, as Madame Arnaud had told the butcher, he was expected this very day and she hoped there had been saved the plumpest goose for her. And the butcher assured her that she would have the plumpest. And the grocer assured her that the sweetmeats and the crystallized fruits that she had ordered were all ready to be sent to the house.

The whole village knew how generous Madame Millican's brother was: his purse flowed with francs, and he was such a nice gentleman, everyone was out to please him.

A little whisper had stirred through the village that perhaps Madame Millican was not quite a widow and her brother not quite a brother; but be that as it may, that was the way of the world and nobody was going to question it, not here in France. Of course, if such was the case, it would explain why the young person was having her baby in France instead of England, because the English were such hypocrites: a man could be found in his short clothes and a woman in her shift and yet they would both deny knowledge of each other; they were in that state merely to discuss the English weather, which, like their lying, was unbelievable. . .

Back in the farmhouse, sitting at either side of a roaring fire, the two girls were knitting. Biddy had taught Lucy how to knit, and in return Lucy had taught Biddy embroidery. Over the months they had read together, studied French and tested it on madame and the villagers, whose French apparently wasn't Parisian French but a patois, and caused both parties some fun during the exchanges.

Altogether the days passed pleasantly, at least for Biddy, but for Lucy there were periods when she went into a depression so deep that Biddy became worried. It was at these times she talked herself silly, as she put it. She told Lucy about her early life in the pit village, about the master, and went as far in an attempt to stir her interest as to relate his liking for Davey, and the result of it. This last instance had the desired effect and brought the question from Lucy, 'He actually cut him down with the scythe?'

But today Lucy was bright because Laurence was coming. Her hands stopped plying the needles, she rested the shawl she was knitting on the mound of her stomach and she looked into the fire as she said, 'I wonder what the reaction will be to my not going home for the holidays? Do you think they will believe that I've been invited by the family to join them for Christmas in their country house?'

'Oh, yes, yes. Mr Laurence could explain that away.'

Biddy felt a quickening beneath her ribs now as Lucy, looking at her said, 'You know that Laurence is of no blood relation to the family, except very distantly, being the son of Mama's second cousin?'

'Yes. Yes, I understood something like that.'

'May was in love with him you know. She was quite brazen about it. I used to hate her because of that I mean, being in love with him, because I loved him too.' She paused now and, her eyes tight on Biddy, she said, 'I still do. Yet there was a time when I imagined I was in love with – ' After a quick shake of her head she added, 'It's dreadful to be of our age, isn't it? All your values are mixed up: you don't know what you want, but yet you do; your body burns for what you want while you tell yourself it's a sin. I was brought up on sin. Until I was eight I never saw my mother more than five minutes a day, and then there would be days, weeks even, when I didn't see her at all, when she would be on holiday and I was left with Miss Collins, who had been instructed to instruct us, both Paul and me, in all the things that came under the heading of sin, and this included asking for second helpings . . . greed, bathing oneself without a cover on the bath . . . impurity, letting one's mind drift at night . . . bad thoughts. On, on, and on.'

'Really?'

'Yes, really. Did you have anything like that to put up with?'

'No, never. The only thing I can remember is dropping to sleep while my father read from the Bible. After a twelve-hour day at the farm I wasn't very interested in what Moses had to say, although I sometimes got my fingers rapped to make me pay attention.' She smiled now, and Lucy said, 'Do you know, you were lucky. Servants and such always envy those above them, and they imagine they know all that goes on in the household. They don't, at least not in the minds of their masters . . . Biddy.'

'Yes, miss?'

'Nothing much escapes you, does it?'

'Oh, I wouldn't say that, miss.'

'Oh, don't be coy.'

'I'm not.' The protest was made as if to an equal. 'Only your saying that nothing much escapes me makes me feel that I'm sort of nosey and I'm not.'

'I wasn't meaning it that way. But as Grandmama would say, you've got a head on your shoulders. And now I'm going to ask you something. Do you think Laurence likes me . . . I mean, still likes me, in spite of this?' She patted her stomach.

It was a moment before Biddy could answer, 'I . . . I'm sure he does, miss. He's always liked you.'

'What I'm getting at Biddy is, do you think he more than likes me? Do you think he would marry me?'

Biddy put down her knitting and, leaning over, she picked up the poker and pushed a gnarled root into place in the open grate, and now she muttered,'I . . . I couldn't say that, miss. I've got no idea.'

'You could proble and . . . and ask him . . . I mean, not outright, but just gauge his feelings.'

'No, no, I couldn't, miss.' She was standing now looking down on Lucy and she repeated, 'No, I couldn't do that. It isn't my place.'

'Oh, don't keep on about place, Biddy.' Lucy tossed her head impatiently. 'We've been thrown together for months. There's no position between us now, and never could be again. I . . . I've been turned into a woman before my time, and somehow you were already a woman, in your mind anyway.' She paused, then asked, 'Why won't you do this for me?'

'Because I couldn't.'

'You talk to him. You talk to him a lot and he to you. On his last visit you walked miles with him, alone. You must know how to bring a conversation round to any subject you like.'

'That is a personal subject, miss; there should be ways and means of you tackling it yourself.'

'Like this?' Lucy again patted her stomach but harder now. 'I'm . . . I'm thinking about when it's all over. I'll . . . I'll need someone. I don't feel I can carry on alone, not even with you, although you've been marvellous.' She now put her hand gently on Biddy's arm as she added, 'I don't dare to think what would have happened to me if

I hadn't come across you that Sunday. Oh, yes I do.' Now she was nodding her head. 'If I'd told Mother I would have been packed off somewhere, into a convent likely. Look Biddy, please. You . . . you needn't put it bluntly. Well I know you wouldn't, but just . . . well, sound him. Will you? Please. Because I . . . I need him. I can't go back home again. Not to that kind of life. I'd die, or do something.'

'You won't die, or do something.' Biddy's voice was harsh now. 'You'll have a baby to see to, and love . . .'

'*I won't. I won't.*'

Biddy was thrust aside now as Lucy pulled herself to her feet and, seeming to forget that she had dismissed the difference in their positions just a moment earlier, she cried at her, 'I've told you before. I'm not keeping the child. You with your plebeian outlook. Use your head, how can I? Even if I wanted to. And I don't want to; all I want to do is get rid of it.' She now brought her two hands over the sides of her stomach as if she was actually throwing the child from her, and Biddy, also forgetting her position for the moment, said, 'All right. All right. I know what you've said before, but I put it to you, you needn't cast it off altogether. You can have it fostered and go and see it from time to time.'

'*Shut up! Shut up.* I want none of it. Do you hear? I want none of it. Oh, my God.' She turned away, her hands now holding her head, crying, 'I might as well have stayed back home.'

In the small hallway Madame Arnaud listened to the raised voices coming from her guests' apartments. She couldn't understand a word of English, but a verbal battle is understandable in any language. So when she answered the knock on the door and saw the gentleman standing there, she exclaimed, 'Ah Monsieur. Monsieur. Welcome. Welcome. You are just in time to stop the altercation.' And pointing towards the far door, she added, 'When the weather is bad, tempers are short. No one quarrels in the summer.'

As she helped him off with his overcoat he listened to the exchange of voices, both high and angry, and he thought, Oh, dear me, dear me. What now?

But before he opened the door the voices had ceased and when he stood in the doorway and looked at them both staring at him, he said, 'Well, well! No welcome?'

Then Lucy ran towards him, and he took her in his arms and kissed her; and she kissed him, and she leant her head on his shoulder until he gently pressed her aside and walked to where Biddy was standing in front of the fire. Holding out his hands, he took hers and pressed them warmly while looking into her face and saying, 'Hello, there.' And she answered, 'Hello.' She omitted the Mr Laurence, but said, 'We didn't expect you until this evening.'

'I got an earlier coach and I walked from the village. Well now, what have you girls been up to?' He turned and held out an arm to

Lucy. And she came to him and, again leaning her head on his shoulder, she looked towards Biddy as she said, 'We've been quarrelling, and it's over you. She said you weren't at all good-looking and your French left a lot to be desired.'

He was looking at Biddy now – her face had turned scarlet, her mouth was open – and he said softly, 'Well, she was right in both cases.' And when Biddy said, 'Oh, miss,' he didn't need confirmation that the quarrel had been of a more serious nature. As for Biddy, she left the room saying, 'I must see madame about the meal.'

She did not, however, go to madame's quarters but went along the narrow corridor and into her own bedroom, and there, standing with her hands pressed tight together, she muttered to herself, 'Equality.' The last little scene recalled shades of the girl who had taken the whip across her face on that particular Sunday.

For the first time in all the months she had been here, she wished she were home because what lay before her was two weeks of his presence in the house; and what was more, she had, in some way, to find out how deep were his affections towards Lucy.

And she was to find out on New Year's morning, 1841.

2

The holiday had not been without its gaiety. They had all walked together and laughed together; they had played cards; they had even sung together old Christmas songs accompanied by madame on her spinet. And then had come New Year's Eve.

Lucy had not been feeling well for some days, and on New Year's Eve she had kept to her bed. The doctor from the next village had been called in and he said it was but a slight malaise. This often happened in the eighth month, all she had to do was rest. So when the church bells chimed from the village, Biddy, Laurence, and Madame Arnaud, stood round Lucy's bed and drank her health.

After Madame Arnaud left the three of them sat and chatted for a time until Laurence took his leave after kissing Lucy and saying, 'It's going to be a good New Year, Lucy. Just you wait and see.' Then he said good night to Biddy and went out.

Biddy now set about settling Lucy for the night and when she had finished Lucy took her hand and asked softly, 'Have you talked to him?'

'No . . . no, not yet.'

'You will do? Because he goes back the day after tomorrow.'

'The opportunity hasn't arisen,' Biddy said.

'You've had him on your own most of today. Why . . . why didn't you speak then?'

'It's a very difficult subject to raise.'

'It shouldn't be for you, Biddy, your wits are sharp. Try. I must know before he goes back.'

'I'll try. Good night.'

'Good night, Biddy. And a happy New Year.'

'And the same to you, miss. Yes, the same to you.'

To her surprise Laurence was waiting for her in the hall and he beckoned her silently towards the sitting-room door. Once inside the room he took her hand and drew her to where the lamp, by the side of the fireplace, was still burning, and standing square in front of her, he put his hands on her shoulders and said, 'A happy New Year, Biddy.'

She was trembling from head to foot, and the words stuck in her throat before she could say, 'And . . . and to you, sir.'

'Don't call me sir any more, Biddy. Do you hear?'

She remained quiet.

'My name is Laurie. And . . . and you know what I'm going to say, don't you?' She made a slight movement with her head, and he shook her now, saying, 'Biddy Millican of the straightforward tongue, don't lie.'

'I'm not . . . I'm not lying.'

His face became straight and he said, 'No, you're not lying. You have never guessed then how I really feel about you?'

Again she made a small movement with her head before muttering, 'No, only the other way about.'

'The other way about?' His voice was a mere whisper, and she repeated in no louder a tone, 'The other way about.'

'Oh, Biddy.' He went to pull her into an embrace, but she stiffened and said, 'Mr Laurence.'

And at this he put in, 'I've told you, no more Mr Laurence.'

'It'll have to be.'

'Why?'

'You know as well as I do. This . . . this isn't right; it can lead nowhere. And you've just suggested I talk straight. Well' – she gulped in her throat – 'I'll do it now. I . . . well, no matter what I feel, I want no hole and corner affair; I don't want to end up, in fact I won't end up like Miss Lucy. So there.'

His hands dropped from her shoulders, his head bowed; then he said, 'You think my intention is to use you in that way?'

She dared to answer, 'What other way is there between us two?'

'The proper way.' His chin jerked upwards. 'I love you, Biddy. Do you understand that?' Again he was holding her by her forearms and his grip was tight. 'I think I've loved you from the moment I saw you and heard you pouring Shelley into the deaf ears of that thick-headed crowd. Yes, right from that very moment. Don't you know why I haven't stayed at home for the holidays lately as long as I usually did? Because then I would think, as you are thinking now, this cannot be, this cannot come about. Now I know it can, and it will, even if it means our emigrating, going to another country. I needn't ask you if you would be afraid to share poverty with me, because you know what that's like. I don't. You'll have to teach me how to handle it, because I'll have to earn my own living from now on by teaching. That's the only thing I can do. I . . . I love you, Biddy. I . . . I cannot get you out of my mind. When you are in a room, I cannot take my eyes off you. I became more attentive to Grandmama because I knew I would see you.'

She brought out now on a shuddering breath the word, 'Madam!'

'Oh . . . madam. Oh yes, she'll yell her head off. But after all, what can she do? What can any of them do? I don't belong to them, although I must admit I owe them a great deal. Well, at least, I owe Grandmama, because if it had rested with the woman I call mama, and even her husband, I might have been a workhouse brat. My mother was of good family, poor, but with a name. And then there is this disease that mama suffers from, religion and prejudice. My father, I understand, was a very ordinary man, and a bit of a scoundrel. He abandoned my mother just before I was born. That's how I landed up at The Heights. I understand he died abroad when I was six years old, here in France as a matter of fact. I know nothing of his people; and my grandparents, too, are dead. They left me a small sum but I don't come into that until I am twenty-five. So, may I ask if you will starve with me, Biddy, until that time?'

'*Oh! Oh!*' It was as if the exclamations were easing a pain; and then she fell against him and put her arms about him, and he pressed her to him as if he would never let her go.

When their lips parted, their faces flushed, they looked into each other's eyes and smiled, and he whispered, 'Oh, Biddy, Biddy. Oh, my dear. You know you are the most wonderful person I have ever met in my life. Yes, yes, you are,' he emphasized, pressing her hard to him with each of the last four words as if to stifle any protest from her. And now her head drooping, she muttered his name for the first time, 'Laurie,' she said, and to this he said, 'Yes, my dear one?' And she answered, 'I feel like a traitor.'

He pressed her slightly from him and, peering into her face, he said, 'A traitor. You? Why?'

'Lucy.'

'What about Lucy?'

She turned her eyes to the side and gazed down into the embers of the dying fire before she said, 'She's . . . she's in love with you. She . . . she wants to marry you. She hopes that you will feel the same.'

'Lucy?' The incredulity came over in his voice. '*She what?*'

'She's in earnest, so very much in earnest. And . . . and she needs some one.'

'Oh, nonsense, nonsense. This is because of her condition. Now, if it had been' – he pulled a slight face – 'if it had been May, I . . . I could have believed it, but not Lucy.'

'Yes, yes, Laurie. She is banking on it.'

'Then she'll just have to unbank.'

He now took her hand and pulled her down on to the couch beside him, and becoming serious again, he said, 'It's preposterous. I've never acted other than as a brother towards her.'

'Yes, but she knows you're not her brother.'

'You mean to say, knowing her condition and after being with that man who is already the father of children, she would expect me to . . .? Oh, my goodness me. Never! Never!'

For a moment she thought, Men . . . their outlook; even if he had been in love with Lucy, as things were he wouldn't have considered marrying her. She dared to say, 'What if it had happened to me?'

'Happened to you? It wouldn't have.'

'It could have, if she hadn't intervened when I was attacked.'

'But that would have been different, that was against your will. By what I can gather, this was of her own doing. She wasn't raped, she flirted with a middle-aged man. And young girls seem to have an attraction for middle-aged men. Undoubtedly they don't need much encouragement, but nevertheless, what was needed she supplied. The case is different altogether.'

'But you are so caring of her.'

'Yes, yes, I am, because no one else in the family would be, except Grandmama. If the matter had rested with her I am sure she would have commanded Lucy to have the child there. But she knew the result of such an action on every member of the family. What I've done, I've done in part for Grandmama. She's an old dragon, yes, admittedly, but I'm very fond of her. And, you know, there's one thing in our future favour' . . . he drew her into his arms again – 'she's very fond of you.'

'Yes,' she said, 'as a servant.'

'Well, perhaps,' he admitted now; 'but, she'll change her tune.'

'Knowing madam, she never will.'

'Well, that will be a pity, because nothing, Biddy, do you hear me? nothing is going to come between you and me, ever.'

'Oh, Laurie. Laurie.' As she leant her head against him he said, 'How old are you, really?'

'Eighteen just gone.'

'Nearly too old for marriage,' he said, and they both started to laugh. Then his voice becoming serious, he said, 'What are you going to tell her?'

'Nothing. Oh' – the word was high – 'oh, nothing yet, not until the baby is born, because she has bouts of depression now . . .'

'But you must, you must give her some inkling that my affections are placed elsewhere. You mustn't let her go on hoping.'

'Please. Please, Laurie, let us do nothing until the baby comes and she is back home. She's determined to have nothing to do with the child.'

'Well, I can understand that.'

'I can't.'

He touched her cheek gently as she went on, 'I'll be thinking about it all the time, being brought up in some small foreign home when its rightful place is back in England in that house, having all the attention in the world.'

'Well, that can never be. You know that. Just imagine the shock of her landing back there with a baby in her arms, even if she wanted to.'

She looked at him steadily for a moment. 'That shock wouldn't be half as great as the shock of Mr Laurence announcing the fact that he wishes to marry Biddy Millican, who once slaved in the laundry and was considered the lowest of the low,' she said.

He pursed his lips and smiled now and, taking her face between his two hands, he said, 'And who has more brains in her little finger than the rest of that community put together? And who among them can converse, not just talk but converse? Biddy Millican. And it is she I mean to marry, even if the shock paralyzes all at The Heights.'

'And it might do just that, and also close the gates on you forever.'

'No, that won't happen, not as long as Grandmama is ruling that roost. No, I'm not afraid of that, for I don't think there is anything I could do that would turn her against me. Perhaps that sounds conceited, but there it is. I pride myself I know her inside out.'

Biddy could make no reply to this, because she couldn't see madam through his eyes, and there was a section of her mind that was worried, not for herself, but for him.

And all she could say to herself, and in her old idiom, was, 'Oh, dear God, let things pan out.'

3

Lucy's baby was born on a Wednesday in the third week of January, 1841. It was a very bad delivery, her labour having lasted over a period of three days. It was a girl child, and after it was washed it looked so beautiful that Biddy cried over it.

There was a great deal of bustle in the house. A midwife and Madame Arnaud had delivered the baby and now both were anxious as to the condition of the mother for after some hours the afterbirth had not appeared.

The doctor had been long in coming as the roads were in a bad state, and when he saw the condition of the young mother, he shook his head and tut-tutted and gave her a strong dose of laudanum as well as a concoction from a green bottle before proceeding to perform a minor operation on her.

When she screamed, Madame and Biddy held her down. And Biddy seemed to go on holding her for the next twenty-four hours, because every time she neared the bed Lucy would put her arms out and beg, 'Hold me, Biddy. Hold me.'

A fortnight ago she had sent a letter to Laurence in Oxford. It wasn't only a love letter, it was also telling of her concern for Lucy's condition. Now, three days after the baby's birth she wrote again and sent the letter by special coach to Dieppe, hoping that it would catch the mail-boat and then the train, and reach him within two to three days There were no words of love in this last letter, only the fact that the doctor had his grave doubts that Lucy would survive, and would he please come at once.

Two days later, around five o'clock in the morning, Lucy died, her head resting on Biddy's arm. Time and again she had asked, 'Will Laurie come?' And Biddy had assured her, 'Yes, yes. He should be here any time now,' knowing that the letter would probably not yet have reached him.

Repeatedly she had tried to get Lucy to look at her child, hoping that it might, in some strange way, give her an incentive to live. But she had always refused; she even became agitated when the baby was mentioned.

Biddy could not believe that the young girl was dead until Madame Arnaud lifted the head from her arm. She had become so stiff she found it impossible to move for a moment or so; then when realization dawned on her she cried aloud, reverting to her old vocabulary, saying, 'Eeh, no! No! Eeh no!'

''Tis God's will.' Madame covered the still white face with the sheet and led Biddy from the room.

The unreality of the situation stayed with her for the next five days, when the doctor said that the body must be buried; it would no longer be safe to leave it exposed.

Almost at her wits' end now, Biddy didn't know what to do. By this time, either she should have had a letter or Laurie himself should have appeared, because on the morning Lucy died she had sent word straightaway to him, telling him the news, and that he must inform her parents.

She had just enough money to pay for the funeral expenses and the extra meals that madame provided for the mourners who consisted of most of the villagers. The coffin had been borne on a cart to the little graveyard that was sheltered by a wood. The only flowers on it were some bunches of snowdrops and aconites. And as she stood at the graveside and watched the earth being shovelled on to the plain wooden box, she kept telling herself that this wasn't happening. It was a dream. All these past months had been a dream. Laurie was part of the dream too, and all these strange people were part of the dream. The only thing that was certain was the baby lying in the farmhouse in its little crib. And she had to keep her thoughts on it because it was the only evidence she had of reality.

Having had no reply from Laurence to her two letters, the dread increased that something had happened to him. If that were so, what would happen to her and the child? Nobody was going to take the baby unless they were paid for it. But the very thought of passing it over into strange hands was now almost unbearable. From the first moment she had held it it had bred in her a love, a new love, and when she put the pap bags to its mouth and watched it sucking while it gripped her finger with one of its tiny hands, she told herself it would be impossible to part with it, unless it was into very good hands. And the only hands she could think of were those of its own people back in England, in The Heights. It should go back there no matter what. Its mother was no longer here to bear the disgrace, so surely they would find it in their hearts now to forgive her and care for her child . . .

The following day she was proved wrong, for not only did Laurie arrive, but also Anthony Gullmington and Stephen. It should happen that the two letters had definitely been delivered to Laurie's quarters in the university but he had taken leave to go to London to attend a course of lectures. When he returned and found both letters he went straight back to The Heights and presented his adoptive father, mother, and brother with the facts, and had been amazed when

Anthony Gullington had at first refused point-blank to make the journey: 'She's dead? Then she's dead,' he had said.

It was only when Laurence had pointed out to him that the child still survived and that if nothing was done Miss Biddy Millican would undoubtedly bring it back and present the family with it that he was persuaded to come.

Yet, Anthony Gullmington had put it to Laurence that, seeing he had managed the whole affair so far, he could see to the rest of it. But Laurence would have none of this. His daughter, he reminded Gullmington, was dead, and in a foreign country. They could and would presumably say that she had died of a fever. And so what would people think if he didn't have her body brought back?

Madam had seen the sense of this and she had made her wishes known to her son, and so here they all were entering the sitting-room of the farmhouse and looking towards Biddy. That was, until Laurence, going quickly to her side and taking her hand, said, 'Oh, my dear, when did it happen? And how?'

She looked from him to the two tall men gazing at her, no doubt amazed at Laurence's attitude towards her and she said, 'Will you, please, be seated.'

They stared at her for a moment longer before, together, they both sat side by side on the couch.

But when she said, 'Can I get you some refreshment?' Anthony Gullmington growled, '*No! girl*. We don't want any refreshment.' And Laurence put in quietly, 'We had a meal in the hotel back in Paris. Tell us what happened.'

And in a few words she told them; then added,'I had no instructions and the doctor said she must be buried. So two days ago they buried her in the cemetery' – she pointed towards the window – 'a little beyond the village.' Then she added,'The child is very healthy, sir, and . . .'

'I don't want to hear anything about the child.'

'She's your granddaughter, sir.'

'Don't you dare take that tone with me. Remember your position.'

'I do remember my position, sir, and I am not in your employ.'

'*What*.' He was about to rise when Stephen put his hand firmly on his father's arm, saying placatingly now, 'What she means, Father, is that Grandmama employs her.'

'I know what she damn well means, and she's insolent.'

'I have no intention of being insolent, sir. I'm only stating a fact. And I can add to it by saying that I have stayed with your daughter these many months and cared for her, and I care for her child and wish to see the best done for it.'

'God Almighty!' He turned and glared at Laurence now. 'Who does this one think she is?'

'Well' – Laurence put his head back on his shoulders for a moment

– 'this is not the time or the place to tell you, but since you ask, she is someone who has become very dear to me.'

'*Good God! Good God Almighty! What is this?* Have you lost your senses, man? This . . . this slut who has caused more . . .'

Both Biddy and Laurence spoke together, Biddy's voice almost as loud as his as she cried, 'Don't you call me a slut! I'm no slut,' and Laurence saying, 'If she is a slut then she is the least of the sluts in your household, sir, for in intellilgence she is above any of your offspring.'

Father and son now looked at each other, not believing what they were hearing; then together they both rose to their feet, and it was Stephen who said, in a quieter tone but with a stiffness to it now, 'We could talk about this, Laurie.'

'There is nothing to talk about regarding my affairs.'

'I forbid you the house as long as you continue to associate with this . . .'

'That will certainly be no hardship to me. But forget about me for a moment. What you have come here to discuss is what is to be done with your . . . your granddaughter.'

'She is not *my granddaughter*. I have *no granddaughter*.'

'When the child is deposited on your front doorstep, as is the rule I think in such cases, then you will have some explaining to do.'

'You wouldn't dare! Neither of you would dare.'

'Father.' Stephen was speaking again and the mind of the future member of Parliament was evidently getting to work because what he said was, 'There is a way out. We could take the responsibility of the child, Father, and have her fostered. There are plenty of places in this country.'

'Oh no, you don't.' Laurence's voice was quiet as he broke in. 'I know what you would do, both of you, you would dump her, and in the lowest possible place. If she is to be fostered it is to be in England and with suitable foster parents.'

Anthony Gullmington's eyes narrowed to slits now as, looking from Laurence to Biddy, he said, 'You have both emphasized that she is my granddaughter, then as such I have claim to her, and I can do what I like with her.'

'Not if I know it. You . . . you attempt to place her anywhere without my knowledge and, to put it plainly, I shall cry this affair from the house tops of every one of your friends in Durham and Northumberland.'

'My God!' The words came deep, yet on a whisper. 'I just cannot believe it. After all the care and consideration you have been shown in my house over the years, you turn like a viper on me in this my hour of need.'

'*Your* hour of need! Your daughter had an hour of need but she was so afraid of your hypocrisy and that of my so-called mama, that she begged a servant, as Biddy here once was, to break the news to Grandmama, because she was terrified to do it herself.'

Looking at her late master, Biddy imagined for a moment that he was going to have a seizure. Then he growled at her, 'Leave us,' and as she went to walk away he spoke to Laurence, saying, 'You too.'

Laurence paused a moment, then followed Biddy. In the hall he took her hand and said, 'Don't worry. Things are bound to come out right.'

They were joined in a moment by Madame Arnaud who asked, 'Would the gentlemen like some refreshment? I have pie and fresh bread, and . . .'

'No, thank you, madame.' Laurence inclined his head towards her. 'We ate back at the hotel.'

She looked at Biddy and said, 'I shall be very sorry to lose you; you have been such good company. And the baby, she is so beautiful. And your visits, sir. Oh, I'll miss your visits.' She paused and turned to look at Anthony Gullmington and Stephen emerge from the room. Then returning her attention to Laurence, she went on, 'Monsieur will be having a stone put up at the head of his daughter's grave? There's a good stone-mason in the next village. Pierre burnt the name in the wooden plaque, and he had difficulty because it was so long, and he's not very good, is Pierre. But Jean Lacousse, he is a good mason. He charges but his work is good. And it would be good to see Madame Millican's name in stone, and it's such a nice name: Lucille Beatrice Millican. The villagers and me, we would look after the grave well . . .'

'What did she say?' Anthony Gullmington was looking at Laurence, and after a moment's hesitation Laurence said, 'She was talking about a headstone.'

'She mentioned a name, Lucille Beatrice . . .'

'Yes.' Laurence inclined his head; then added slowly, 'She was known as Mrs Millican. Biddy was supposed to be her sister-in-law.'

The father and son looked at each other.

'And she was buried under that name?'

'Yes.'

'What about the certificate . . . baptism, the child's?'

'It' – Laurence glanced at Biddy – 'it too bears the name of Millican. She was christened Louise Grace Millican.'

Almost in horror now Biddy watched a slow smile spread over Anthony Gullmington's face. Then he looked at his son. Stephen wasn't smiling, but he was looking at Laurence, and Laurence said, 'That won't get you out of this.'

'No?' Anthony Gullmington pursed his lips for a moment before repeating, 'No? Well, it will go a damn long way, I should say, for who's to prove that a child called Millican was born of my daughter? My daughter died of a fever, as we were to infer. I had that placed in the Newcastle papers before we left.' He now turned to Biddy. 'You have dug your own grave, miss.'

'I have done no such thing, sir. I can prove that I've had no child.'

'And who would believe it? Who will believe you? Mud sticks. Well now, I shall leave you and your charge, and you too, Laurence.' And all sarcasm leaving his voice now and bitterness filling it, he said, 'You ungrateful swine, you!' And with this he marched out.

Stephen did not immediately follow his father, but he stood looking from one to the other; and then he said, 'I'm sorry, Laurie. Believe this, will you? I'm sorry.'

'I believe you, Stephen. But you believe that it was her child, don't you?'

Stephen cast his glance downwards, paused a moment, turned, and then followed his father.

Biddy and Laurence stood looking at each other. The expressions on their faces were similar: they looked like two fighters who had been told they had lost the battle which they felt they had previously won.

4

Riah looked at Tol standing opposite her in the drawing room, and she said, 'First thing in the morning I'm goin' to the Justices. My girl's in that foreign country. She went with their daughter. I want to know what's happened to her. Have you heard nothing more?'

'Nothing, except that Miss Lucy died of a fever. But there is more. Everybody knows it up there, but what it is they can't fathom.'

'Has Mr Laurence not returned either?'

'No. And that's another funny thing. They were supposed to be with his friends, I mean Miss Lucy and Biddy. That . . . that seemed to be the whole idea, that Miss Lucy's education was to be furthered with the young people of the French family.'

'Ma! Ma!' The door burst open, and Johnny stood there, his hand still on the knob as he cried, 'They're comin' up the road. I saw them from the rise.'

'Who is?' They both moved towards him now.

'Our Biddy. And it looks like she's got a man with her.'

'No, no. You must be mistaken. You couldn't make her out in this light.' She glanced towards the window to see that the twilight was deepening into dark, and the boy cried at her, 'It is! It is! She glimpsed me and waved me from the road. They should be at the gate now. Come on! Come on!'

And Riah and Tol went out, running now, out of the front door and on to the drive, to see coming towards them Biddy, who was carrying what looked like a child in her arms, and a man by her side weighed down with two heavy cases.

As Riah went to put her arms about Biddy, crying, 'Oh! lass. Oh! hinny,' she stopped and peered down on what she now saw was indeed a baby, and her mouth remained agape as Biddy said wearily, 'Let's get inside, Ma, we're tired. We had to walk from the crossroads. Oh . . . this is Mr Laurence.'

Riah turned her head to the side and looked at the man who smiled at her and said, 'Good evening, Mrs Millican.'

'Let me have those, sir.' Tol picked up the cases that Laurence had placed on the ground. 'Thanks, Tol,' said Laurence, and they all moved across the drive and through the front door and into the hall; and there, Biddy, handing the baby to her mother, said, 'Hold her a minute till I get my things off.' And Riah taking the child, looked down on it as she thought, Not our Biddy; no, no! Anyway, who to? And thinking thus, bustled them into the drawing-room.

'You have every reason to look amazed, Mrs Millican,' Laurence said. 'But you are no more amazed than both Biddy and I are to find ourselves in our present situation. We . . . we have a lot to tell you, a lot of explaining to do, which will no doubt amaze you further. But' – he smiled warmly at her now – 'would it be possible for Biddy to have a warm drink, and perhaps some milk for the baby? Both suffered on yesterday's boat crossing. Neither of them, I'm afraid, enjoy the sea, and the train and coach journey has been long and arduous. We thought to stay in Newcastle for the night, but there was a coach leaving nearby, so we took the opportunity . . .'

Trying to regain her senses, Riah muttered quickly, 'Oh, yes, yes of course. I'll get you all something, yes. Will you give me a hand, Tol?'

'Aye. Yes, of course, Riah.'

'And you, you come on with you.' Riah caught hold of Johnny's arm and pulled him from his staring, not at Biddy, but at her companion, because he knew who he was, he had seen him out riding with the other masters.

Biddy sat back in the corner of the couch and looked to where the child was lying asleep at the other end. Then her eyes travelled towards Laurence, and she said softly, 'It's going to be difficult to explain things because you know what she thought when she saw me with the child?'

'Yes, I've got a good idea.'

'Well, if she thinks that, others will think the same.'

'Oh, no, they won't.' His voice was firm. 'Not after tomorrow morning when we present the evidence in Grandmama's boudoir.'

'What if she were to deny it?'

He rose now from his seat by the fire and, sitting on the edge of the sofa, he said, 'She couldn't. I have letters from Lucy. Moreover, there's the French doctor and Madame Arnaud. I'd go to the lengths of bringing them across if she tried. Oh, I'm not worried. When we present the child to her it will be a fait accompli. And as her word is law in that household, she'll see that justice is done.'

Once more Biddy didn't answer, but to herself she said, I wonder.

It was close on midnight. A great deal of talking had been done, mostly by Biddy and Laurence.

That Riah had been astounded at the sight of her daughter bringing home a baby was nothing to what she felt when this man, this gentleman, told her he wished to marry her daughter, and went on to say that he had no money, at least not for another year, and even then his income would be small, being merely three hundred pounds a year, which to her sounded like a fortune, but to him hardly represented boot-blacking money.

What he proposed to do, he told her, was to teach; in fact, they would both teach. Their idea was to start a school. Where, they hadn't decided yet, but if he could find rooms in Oxford they would soon get going. 'But Biddy has a house here,' Riah said. 'Yes, when you have no further use for it.' And taking Biddy's hand, Laurence went on, 'And we both hope that that won't be for many, many a long day.' And Biddy nodded her head confirming his statement with a smile on her face.

Riah looked at Tol, and Tol's eyes were speaking plainly to her, and what she said next brought Biddy up from the couch: 'Tol and me are going to be married, and you know the conditions about the house, so there it is. This is yours now and it's big enough for any school.'

Biddy turned her gaze on Laurence, but her face didn't show any enthusiasm as she said, 'But you wouldn't want to stay here, live here, so close to . . . ?'

'Oh, that wouldn't affect me. They have already thrown me off and I them. I . . . I would be delighted at the idea.' Laurence looked round the room, got up and walked across to Riah and, taking her hand, he said, 'Now are you sure of this?' But before she could answer, Tol put in, 'I am, sir, and it should have happened a long, long time ago.'

And so it was settled. The only thing there remained to do was to take the baby to madam, then return here and prepare for a wedding, and start a new and exciting life together.

* * *

They both new it wasn't any use approaching the house by the main gate because, as Riah had said, she had already tried to get in to speak to Mr Gullmington, but the lodge-keeper had his orders and wouldn't let her through the gates.

So after Tol had dropped them from the cart, they took the servants' path, but only after climbing the wall, because the gate here, too, was locked, which it had never been before. Laurence had climbed the dry stone wall to the side, which at this point was five feet high; Biddy handed him the child, then adeptly she climbed it herself, and when they were both standing on the narrow path, they looked at each other and grinned like two errant children before quickly making their way to the house.

They had both agreed to take the side entrance that led to the west wing. And this they did without being observed until they reached the gallery, and there, coming towards them, was the first footman, James Simpson. His walk was stately, his countenance set in the usual unsmiling mould as befitted his station . . . until he saw them. Then his composure was completely shattered, and he stammered,'Sir . . . I think, sir.'

'Get about your business, Simpson.' Laurence's voice was a command and he waved the man to one side. Then taking Biddy's elbow, he led her towards the ornate double doors and through them towards madam's apartments, there to be confronted by Peggy Tile, the first chambermaid, part of whose duty was to see to the cleaning of the kitchen and the staff quarters on this floor. Standing next to her was Maggie, and at the sight of her sister, Maggie cried, 'Eeh! Biddy. Our Biddy!'

When Maggie rushed towards her, Biddy gently pressed her aside with one hand while she cradled the baby with the other, and she said, 'Where is Miss Hobson?'

'She's with madam.'

'Is madam still in bed?'

'Yes. Oh yes. Eeh! Biddy.' Maggie looked towards the baby; then she added, 'Will . . . will I tell madam or Miss . . . ?'

'No, don't bother. We'll announce ourselves.' Biddy glanced quickly at Laurence, and he, stepping forward, thrust open the bedroom door, allowing Biddy to pass, then closed it quickly behind him. And there they both stood for a moment looking to where, devoid now of her nightcap, madam was sitting bolt upright, staring at them as if she didn't believe her eyes.

Laurence led Biddy towards the foot of the bed before speaking, and then he said to the old lady, 'Good morning.' He had not given her his usual title of Grandmama. And he added, 'We are sorry to disturb you at this early hour, but we thought you would be eager to see your great-grandchild.'

They both watched the old face quivering, with what emotion they couldn't tell. When she did speak, it wasn't to them, but without taking her eyes from them she pointed to Jessie Hobson, saying one word, 'Out!' And Jessie shuffled away from the bed after glancing apprehensively at the two figures standing there.

When the communicating door had been closed, and not until then, madam spoke again. 'What do you expect to gain by this, eh?' she demanded.

'Now, now.' Laurence came round the side of the bed and stood looking down at her. 'Don't let us mince words. You sent your granddaughter away because she was going to have a child. Well, she had that child, and she died, and we've brought the child to you, because your son won't recognize she is the daughter of his daughter. Surely – ' he now screwed up his eyes as if to see her better, and paused for a moment before adding, 'it isn't possible that you're going along with him? No, no. You wouldn't, would you? I know it is a bit of a shock, having your plans go awry . . .'

She cut in now, her voice extraordinarily vibrant and bitter as she said, 'My plans going awry, you said? It was to avoid what this person and you here' – she now looked towards Biddy – 'have accomplished that my plan was put into operation in the first place. What does she expect to gain from it? Marriage into the family? Blackmail? Never. Never. Not while I have a breath in me . . . You are a slut, girl . . . a slut.'

'Don't you dare call Biddy a slut! She has served you and yours without thought of herself. And you'd better know right away, Grand – ' he stopped himself from adding the mama and inserted, 'Madam, that I wish to make this girl my wife.'

In the silence that ensued the child coughed, but that was the only sound in the room, and as Laurence looked into the wizened face he knew that this news had come as no surprise to her, she must have already been informed of his intentions in this matter.

When she did speak, her voice was no longer loud, but each word was spat at him as she said, 'You are in a dream, and dreams are made up of irrationalities, and you are bound to wake to reason in a very short time. You have been brought up as a gentleman, and you were originally from good stock, but to demean yourself by marrying – ' she paused now and held her long, veined hand out flat in Biddy's direction, before she went on, '*this*, which perhaps you have not considered will mean associating with her class. If you want her so much, take her as a mistress. I will condone that, but marriage . . . no, never! And don't' – her voice rose again as she stared into his blazing countenance – 'don't speak until I have finished. Now I am going to address her.'

The bloodshot eyes, like pin-points of red fire, concentrated now on Biddy, whose face had lost every vestige of colour and whose lips were pressed tight, but ready to spring apart at any moment, and she waited for what this old tyrant, as she thought of her now, had to say to her. And what madam said was, 'The child, I understand, was christened in your name, also its mother bears your name on her gravestone so the child to all intents and purposes is yours. Now I shall make a bargain with you, miss. I shall settle on you the sum of five hundred pounds, this to be paid immediately. I shall also pay for the child's upbringing with any respectable family you care to leave it with, if you will promise me to have nothing to do with this young man whom, sorrowfully I say now, I have always looked upon as my grandson. Should you not agree to these terms, then I am afraid you will bring disrepute not only on yourself but on him.'

'She will never bring disrepute on me.'

Madam turned her face with its furious expression towards Laurence now, crying, 'No? You marry her; she has a child; who gave her that child? You. Your name would be mud in the county, not because you gave her the child, no, but because you are imbecile enough to act as any local yokel would, and pay for his pleasure. You would be the laughing-stock of the county.'

'You think so?' Laurence's face was also white except where the stubble on his chin stood out like a dark shadow. And in a quiet voice that seemed to enrage the old lady even more, he said, 'I had never imagined you to be naïve . . . wily and machiavellian even, capable of extremely low cunning, but never naïve. Take one thing at a time with regard to your granddaughter. First; why, if she died in France, wasn't her body brought over and placed in the family vault in the churchyard? There'll be questions asked about that, surely. Secondly, the small fact that she didn't return for the holidays. Of course, these are not proof that she bore a child, but what is proof she stated in her own handwriting in the letters she sent to me in Oxford.'

They stared at each other for what seemed an interminable time. When she next spoke her voice was quiet too. 'Do you know I had never imagined anything could happen in life that could make me say that I never want to set eyes on you again. Yes, indeed, you may look sorrowful . . . and I may add, you will never inherit a penny of mine, you have lost yourself a fortune, for the bulk of all I possess was to go to you.'

He put in harshly now, 'Only if I had married May?' And at this she shook her head saying, with a touch of sorrow, 'No, no. I got over that. But now you will be a penniless nothing all your life.'

His face hardening again, he said, 'Not so. My mind will provide my livelihood. I won't need to spend my days like your son and your grandson, wondering what to do to get through them.'

'That may be so, but you'll spend your days being shunned by your own kind.'

She turned her head slowly from him now and looked at Biddy, and, her teeth wobbling in her mouth, she mutered, 'I curse the day, girl, that you came into this room. I go further back to the time when you first came into service here, a washhouse drab, the lowest of the low.'

As Biddy saw Laurence about to protest she put her hand out to him, while hitching the child further up her arm; then looking at her late mistress, she said, 'In position, yes, madam, but mentally, even at that age, I felt superior to any member of your staff. And not only the members of your staff, because your granddaughter, although I came to have an affection for her, had very little intelligence. As for her brother, he had no mind at all, stables would have been a fitting place for him. I won't go on to name the rest of your family, madam, you have your own opinion of them which I have listened to you voicing often, so, as you have saddled me with your great-grandchild, I accept the responsibility. She bears my name, yes, and doubtless, you and your family will do your best to prove by gossip that she is mine. And so she shall be, until she reaches the age of reason, and then I shall tell her who she really is, and where her rightful place is. And her adoptive father' – she turned and looked at Laurence – 'will show her the letters from her mother. Madam, I am sorry for you. Remember that, will you? I am sorry for you.'

On this she turned and walked out of the room. And Laurence paused a moment, and, looking at the figure of the old woman who seemed to have swelled to twice her size with an indignation that prevented her speaking, he said softly, 'I am sorry for you too, Grandmama, but in a different way. The child will be brought up well. I can only promise you this, that we shall wait some time after she reaches her age of reason before we tell her the truth, because rejection at any age is difficult to bear. I can only hope her training will sustain her. Goodbye, Grandmama.'

His jaws were tight when he reached the hallway, there to see Biddy commanding her sister, saying, 'Do as I tell you, get your things, you're coming home.'

The girl looked from Biddy to Jessie, and Jessie said softly, 'It's all right. Get your things.'

When Maggie scurried away, Jessie, staring at the child, said, 'So that was it?' And Biddy answered tersely, 'yes, Miss Hobson, that was it. Miss Lucy was sent away to have her child because the disgrace would have been too much for the family to bear. And now the child is too much for the family to bear. They are going to put the onus on me. But you know and I know whom she belongs to.'

'Aye, lass. I guessed it from the first, and when she didn't come back at Christmas. Yes' – she nodded – 'I know, but you'll be hard put to make them' – she thumbed to the floor – 'believe this, especially with the tale that's going round.'

'What tale?'

Jessie now looked towards Mr Laurence and he said, 'It's no tale, Hobson.'

'I . . . I just heard a whisper, sir . . .'

'Well, the whisper will grow into a shout shortly, and everyone will put two and two together, won't they?'

'Yes, likely, sir. 'Tis the way of the world. I'm sorry, sir.'

'Oh, don't be sorry for us, Hobson at least don't be sorry for me. I might as well tell you, I had no intention of staying here. I had plans to move to Oxford and make that my permanent residence, but now I'll be living practically on the doorstep, and that will be confusion confounded.'

Jessie looked at Biddy, and Biddy said briefly, 'The house is mine. Mother is marrying Mr Briston. We are to set up a school there.'

'Good Go . . .'

She didn't finish "God" but added, 'I . . . I'm sorry.' Then she smiled wanly as she went on, 'You were always a surprise, lass, right from the very beginning. Things always seemed to happen where you were. I think I said that to you once.'

'Yes, you did. Well, here's Maggie; we must be off. And, I'd just like to say, Jessie' – she said the name softly – 'thank you for your training. It'll stand me in good stead in the future.' She leant forward now and kissed the old woman on the cheek; then turned about and walked through the hall towards the double doors, and there Laurence opened them for her and Maggie, and they passed through and on to the gallery where a number of servants were busily doing nothing and stared in silence at the small party making for the door leading to the back stairs. Then as of one accord they gave an audible gasp as they looked towards the far end of the gallery from where their master was striding towards the intruders who had now stopped and were awaiting his approach.

Anthony Gullmington was not alone. His wife was on one side of him, his son on the other, and they were both remonstrating softly with him. When his wife caught hold of his arm he thrust her off, then bawled at the servants, 'Out of the way!' before coming to a halt a few yards from where Laurence, Biddy and Maggie stood, the latter visibly shaking.

It was evident to all that rage was preventing the master of the house from speaking for the moment. When eventually the words came the spittle dripped from his mouth with them.

'How . . . how dare you, sir, enter my house without my permission and . . . and bring that . . . that slut with you! I could have you both horse-whipped and thrown out bodily . . . bodily. I have only to . . . to say the word.'

'Why don't you? Most of the servants are within earshot.'

'You . . . you damned upstart! I'll . . . I'll – ' As he made to spring forward Stephen caught hold of him by both arms, saying, 'Father. Father, enough!'

'Enough, you say. Enough, after all I've done for him? He's an ungrateful swine.'

His countenance showing an almost equal anger, Laurence cried, 'Ungrateful, never! And what I'll have you understand, sir, is, it was in gratitude that I protected your daughter and tried to spare your family the disgrace it wouldn't have been able to bear. Granted it was on the suggestion of madam, but I carried it out. And this' – he pointed to the child that Biddy was pressing tightly to her – 'is the result. She is . . .'

Two things at the moment stopped his flow: the look of entreaty on the face of the woman who had been his adoptive mother, and whom he had never liked, as she implored, 'Please. Please, Laurence;' the other, the blow that caught him on the shoulder and sent him reeling back towards the staircase door.

The blow had been intended for his head, but so quickly had Anthony Gullmington wrenched himself from his son's hold that he himself had over-balanced as his arm had thrust itself out to strike and now he was half crouched against the wall and within an arm's length of Laurence who had righted himself and was standing with clenched fists, but these tightly pressed against his sides.

It was Stephen who spoke now, saying, 'Go, Laurie, please.' And he pulled open the stair door, but Laurence still stood glaring at the man who had now straightened himself up but remained leaning against the wall and returning his look with equal vehemence.

'Come, Laurence.' Biddy spoke the name quietly, yet it would appear she had shouted it for it widened the eyes of the servants and brought a quiver to Grace Gullmington's face.

Slowly Laurence turned about, but he did not precede Biddy to the stairs. Putting his hand on her arm, he pushed her gently forward, and as he passed Stephen he looked him straight in the eyes and felt a pang attack his chest as he found no bitterness in the look that met his, if anything the message they sent to him was one of sorrow and understanding.

When they reached the yard they stopped for a moment, and her voice trembling, Biddy asked, 'Are you hurt?'

'No, no.' He tried to smile at her as he said, 'The answer might have been different if the blow had landed where he had intended it should.'

'Look, there's Jean.' Maggie tugged at Biddy's sleeve, and Biddy looked to where Jean was crossing the yard holding one end of a large linen basket.

Turning towards Laurence, she said, 'Would you mind? I won't be a moment. I might not see her again.' And hurrying now she went to where Jean stood open-mouthed, staring at her, and she drew her to one side, saying hastily, 'There's no time to talk, and I mightn't see you again, but I thought, would you like to come and work for us?'

'What do you mean, Biddy? At the house? Your house?'

'Yes. There won't be much money but it will be better than here. You could come over next leave day and we'll talk about it.'

'Oh, thanks, Biddy. Ta. Is . . . is that the baby?'

'Yes, this is the baby.'

''Tis . . .'tisn't yours?' It was a whisper.

'No, it isn't mine, but nobody will believe it.'

'Oh, Biddy.'

'Never mind. See you soon.'

'Aye, Biddy. Aye. Ta. Thanks.'

Quickly now, she rejoined Laurence and Maggie, but as she made to go towards the side path Laurence took her arm, and none too gently, saying, 'No, not that way. We will go by the main drive.' She stared at him for a moment, then lowered her head over the child and did as he bid without any protest as to the advisability of it.

As they crossed the stable yard, Biddy glanced about her, hoping that she might see Davey, but she seemed to see every stable hand except him. He had likely got word of their presence and was ashamed of the scandal. In a way she felt hurt. But what did it matter? Nothing could add to the hurt she was feeling at this moment. That awful scene Laurence had had to endure, and that old woman up there who had talked to her as if she was something crawling on the ground. Yet she knew that as she listened to her she had seen herself through her eyes as someone of such a low degree that even the thought of marrying Laurence would be presumptuous.

They were walking on the drive in front of the house now. There was no one to be seen, not outside, but both she and Laurence were aware the house was very much alive behind the windows.

It was an amazed lodge-keeper who opened the gates for them but he raised his cap and his voice was very civil as he said, 'Good morning, Mr Laurence.' And Laurence said to him, 'Goodbye, Mr Johnson.'

They walked over a mile before being met by Tol. He was driving the wood cart. It was half filled with logs and Maggie had to climb among them while Biddy and Laurence squeezed on to the driving seat.

Tol, seeing the look on their faces, remarked briefly, 'Had it rough, sir?' And Laurence replied, 'Sort of, Tol.'

There was no further discussion until Tol dropped them at the gate, when Laurence said to him, 'If they find out what you've been doing this morning, you will very likely be out of work.'

'That wouldn't worry me, sir.' Tol smiled at him. 'Anyway, I'm sure you'd set me on. I've always thought that would be good for market produce.' He nodded towards the wall before adding, 'And I'm not the only one who thinks that way.'

'Thank you, Tol, for the ride.' Biddy's voice was low, her face unsmiling, and he replied, 'It's a pleasure, Biddy. It's a pleasure. And may I say this to both of you.' He looked from one to the other. 'I only hope you're as happy, leastwise in the future, as your mother has made me.'

Biddy turned away, almost at a run, hugging the child to her, for there was an emotion rising in her that she had to quell until she got into the house. But when once she reached the kitchen where, on seeing Maggie, her mother exclaimed, 'Why, what are you doing here?' Biddy for answer thrust the child into her arms, saying,'Take her for a minute, and . . . and leave me be, just for a minute of so.' And with this she ran out of the kitchen and across the hall and into the library, and there, flinging herself into the leather chair which had for so long been used by the master, she gave rein to her pent-up feelings.

After a while her crying subsided and she sat quietly looking about her, and she seemed to sense the master's presence near her saying, 'This is where life begins for you. You are still very ignorant, but you will learn as you teach.' That's what he had once said to her: One learns as one teaches. And sometimes one learns that the pupil is more intelligent than the master.

She hadn't heard the door open, nor was she aware of Laurence's entry until he stood in front of her and drew her up into his arms, and there, holding her close, he said softly, 'I'm sorry, my dear, I'm sorry to the heart you've had to suffer all this through no fault of yours. Are you willing to bring her up as our own? You know, I could do as I said, and bring over the doctor and Madame Arnaud and take the matter to court. Letters would prove . . .'

'No, no.' She lifted her head from his shoulder. 'I . . . I want to keep her. Somehow it's strange, but . . . but from the moment she was born I felt . . . I can't understand it.' She blinked the moisture from her eyes and swallowed deeply before going on, 'It was just as if she were mine. To tell you the truth I would have hated to leave her up there. I'm . . . I'm not crying about her, it's the things that madam said to me, of me. They made me wonder what . . . what I'd be doing to you if we marry.'

He held her gently away from him, his chin pulled into his neck, his eyes narrowed, and he repeated, 'If we married? There's no if about it, we are getting married. I love you. When I say, you are the only woman . . . and I mean woman, that I have ever loved or am likely to love, I would add that many in the same position might say the same things to you, knowing that nothing remains stationary in this life, not even emotions, and that some day they would forget these words or, if not forget them, repeat them to someone else. But with me, Biddy, I can swear to you that that will not be so, because as I have already told you, I have known from the very first that you were for me, and I for you, although, truthfully, I tried to evade the question, even for a time thinking as madam does, that the solution would be to take you for my mistress. Yet, I knew that you would never countenance that.' He pulled a slight face at her now before going on 'When I stayed away it was because I imagined any union between us would be impossible to bring about because of the insurmountable problems. But life being what it is, I know now that there is no problem that I wouldn't surmount to get you, to marry you, to make you my wife. And' – his smile widened – 'you are getting no bargain. My worldly possessions, at least for the next year, amount to eighty-seven pounds in the bank, a few sets of gold cufflinks and studs, and two gold watches, while here I am, not only proposing to a most beautiful, highly intelligent young woman, but she is giving me a home, a lovely home in which to start a dream of mine, a school for young men.'

'*No. No.*' He was amazed at the strength of the push that forced him backwards from her as she cried at him now, 'For young men and young women. Definitely, *young women.*'

She watched him close his eyes while his head drooped, and now he muttered, 'Yes, ma'am, young women. They will certainly be admitted to our school.'

'In even numbers, sir.'

'Yes, ma'am.' He was gazing at her, his eyes bright and twinkling. 'In equal numbers.'

'And with equal attention.'

'And with equal attention, ma'am.' His head nodded with each word.

'In all subjects.'

'As you say, ma'am, in all subjects. I agree with everything you say; in fact, I will put it in writing on the day you first sign your name as Mrs Laurence Frederick Carmichael.'

Her eyes sprung wide. 'Is that your name, Carmichael?'

'Yes, that's my real name, Carmichael.'

'Oh, Laurie, Laurie. What a lovely name. Thank you for offering it to me.' Slowly she went into his arms now, adding, 'I will love and honour it and you all my days.'

On a windy day at the end of March they were married in the village church, reluctantly it would seem, by Parson Weeks. The bride's stepfather, Mr Tol Briston gave the bride away. There was one member missing from the family party. Davey had left The Heights the day after Biddy's visit. He had not gone back to the house, but had given Tol a message for his mother, saying he wasn't going to wait to be thrown out, and that, anyway, he had been half promised a job at a farrier's in Gateshead Fell. It transpired that the farrier had a good business and also a daughter of marriageable age whom he met when stabling the coach and horses in the town.

The bride was attended by her sister and her friend Jean. The groom was supported by two friends who had come up from Oxford.

The combined number should have hardly filled the two front pews of the church, yet it was packed to the door, because it wasn't every day that a gentleman from a place like The Heights married a servant, even one with a head on her shoulders, but who had arrived back home from across the seas with a bairn. Now that was a mystery: was it? or wasn't it? Some said it wasn't hers. Then if it wasn't hers, why was he marrying her? There was more than a whisper that it was Miss Lucy Gullmington's. Now that was a thing to say, wasn't it? But then it was a fact that the housekeeper had seen the bride there all rumpled from her rolling in the grass the day the bairn was conceived. All right, it hadn't run nine months, but there were plenty of people alive today who had been born at seven months, weren't there? Anyway, there she was, at the altar, looking as beautiful as any bride who had ever knelt there, and him looking like a dog with two tails. Well, all they could say for sure was, from the looks of them, they'd like to bet that another bairn would join the present one, seven months or nine months, and it likely wouldn't stop there.

And to think all this had come about because Mr Miller had taken her, her brothers and sister, and her mother in off the road not eight years gone. It just showed you that people should be careful before they do a kindness.